Brushstrokes
of a
Gadfly

E.A. Bucchianeri

Batalha Publishers
Maxieira, Portugal

Hardcover, 2011
ISBN 978-989-96844-5-4

© Copyright 2011 E.A. Bucchianeri

This is a work of fiction and any resemblance between the characters in this book and real persons living or dead is unintentional.

All trademarks, company names, registered names, products, characters, mottos, logos, jingles and catchphrases used or cited in this work are the property of their respective owners and have only been mentioned and or used as cultural references to enhance the narrative and in no way were used to disparage or harm the owners and their companies. It is the author's sincerest wish the owners of the cited trademarks, company names, etc. appreciate the success they have achieved in making their products household names and appreciate the free plug.

Library of Congress Subject Headings:

Bucchianeri, E.A.
Brushstrokes of a Gadfly
    1. Artists—New York (State)—New York—Fiction. 2. Art and society—New York (State)—New York—Fiction. 3. Brooklyn (New York, N.Y.)—Fiction. 4. Künstlerroman. 5. Manhattan (New York, N.Y.)—Fiction. 6. Man-woman relationships—New York (State)—New York—Fiction. 7. Millionaires—New York (State)—New York—Fiction. 8. New Jersey—Fiction. 9. New York (N.Y.)—Fiction.

British Library Catalogue Subject Headings

Bucchianeri, E.A.
Brushstrokes of a Gadfly
    1. Art – Fiction. 2. Art, Modern —20th century—New York (State)—New York – Fiction. 3. Art and society—New York (State)—New York—Fiction. 4. Artists — New York (State) — New York – Fiction. 5. Man-woman relationships—New York (State)—New York—Fiction. 6. Painters — Fiction.

Books by the same author:

Non-fiction titles:

A Compendium of Essays:
Purcell, Hogarth and Handel, Beethoven, Liszt, Debussy,
and Andrew Lloyd Webber

Handel's Path to Covent Garden

Faust: My Soul be Damned for the World.   2 Volumes

For my nieces

Gabriella and Josephina,

Make your lives a masterpiece,
you only get one canvas.

Brushstrokes
of a
Gadfly

"Katherine Walsingham ... ."

Katherine's heart skipped a beat when she heard her name echo over the loudspeakers, finally it was her turn to go onstage to receive her degree. At last! Springing from her seat, gingerly sidling past those seated next to her, trying not to crunch anyone's toes, she sprightly made her way up the main isle, ascended the stairs, and walked across the stage to the podium. Shaking the hand of the President and receiving her hard earned credential in the other, she courteously thanked the giver, paused briefly for the cameras with a demure smile, turned and glided past all the robed dignitaries of the college, the Vice President, the Deans, the trustees, professors and distinguished guests. Returning to her place with her fellow graduates, she settled back into her red velvet seat, breathing a sigh of relief: "I survived!"

She turned to look up at her family seated in the balcony, waving the degree she held in her hand with a triumphant smile. Her father proudly beamed down at his daughter, while her mother, returning the wave, blew her a kiss, and Katherine reached up to 'catch' it before sending one back. How proud and happy Pops looks today, she thought. Dressed in a navy suit, his brown hair starting to grey at the temples, and in her estimation, a very handsome and distinguished man. Of course, Mom, in her quiet elegance, perfect as always, her soft blonde hair artfully styled with an ornamental clip, dressed in the deep rose suit they had painstakingly selected at their favourite boutique on Fifth Avenue two weeks earlier while picking out her own graduation ensemble, a sky blue two piece suit trimmed with a beaded collar. "Perfect with your blue eyes," her mother had decided. To Pop's left sat good old Gramps dressed in steel grey, what a contrast with his gleaming white hair. Although not a lip reader, she could just distinguish the words "That's my girl!" aimed at her. Beside her mother sat the hopeful scientific genius of the family, her 'little' brother Steven, or 'Steves' as she always called him, two years her junior, a younger image of Pops with dark brown hair and eyes, looking elegant in his black Armani suit. How it must have pained him to relinquish his favourite blue jeans and polo shirts for the day! Forever the joker, Steves waved back, tilted his head sideways and goofily crossed his eyes. Katherine tried to suppress a grin as she watched her mother turn and quietly chide him to behave. That was Steves, you would never know that he was top of his chemistry class at MIT, a Nobel Laureate in the making, he could manipulate computer language with wizard-like dexterity, and prattle off information and statistics ala Mr. Spock. She quickly flashed him the Vulcan 'live long and prosper' sign, before she turned around to watch the last of the students receive their certificates.

Now, finally a Master graduate of the Belvedere College of Arts and Humanities, a private institution with a thousand or so students, the old childhood sing-song rhyme came to mind: "No more teachers, no more books! No more teachers' dirty looks!" Well, the book part she enjoyed, she was a bookworm after all, an avid information seeker revelling in the world of art and literature. She was tempted to major in English and perhaps take a few courses in journalism, but finally chose the world of sketching pencils, acrylics and oils. She preferred the quiet solitary atmosphere, to create in her own world of paint and colour, the thrill of anticipating how her works would turn out as she eyed the blank sheets of paper or canvas before starting her next masterpiece. How satisfying it was to mess around in paint gear, without having to worry about spills, starch or frills, that was the life! When the work was finished, to see an image that had lain quiescent in her imagination as a lovely dream captured for all posterity on canvas. It was almost too unreal to imagine she had spent half a decade of her life studying at college, it only seemed like yesterday she was a timid freshman awestruck by the venerable ivy-laced establishment with its neo-Gothic campus, gate tower, halls and arches, and now, the moment was fast approaching when the President would finally announce the winner of this year's coveted Sirrac Prize, a competition open to the Master students of Belvedere. She waited with baited breath as Jonathan Xavier received his degree, there were no 'Ys' or 'Zs' on the list of students this year as far as she could remember, so any minute now!

"You may now applaud the new graduates of 1990!" the President announced, a command quickly obeyed as the visitors were only too eager to show their appreciation to their loved ones, for they knew full well the dedication and hard work that went into achieving their degree and to finally arrive at this auspicious day.

"And now, it is my privilege to announce the winner of this year's Sirrac Prize, and those who have received an honourable mention. The lucky student will have their work displayed in the exclusive Sirrac Gallery on Fifth Avenue."

A hushed, but excited murmur was audible from the students, for they knew this was a spectacular break, a springboard that could provide them instant access to the art patrons of New York, perhaps the world. Practically every Sirrac winner they knew or heard about had received new commissions and opportunities to present their future works in other fashionable galleries.

"As you are aware, the theme for this year's contest is 'Mankind and its Achievements'. The choice of medium was left open to the entrants, within reason of course."

Everyone burst into laughter, the story of the *Iron Vesuvius* was a legend at the college. A very ambitious student interested in theatre design chose to construct an elaborate volcano sculpture complete with gas flames for the particular theme that year, 'The Element of Fire', and caused an explosion that nearly cost the college its auditorium.

The Vice President handed a sealed envelop to the President. Silence descended as everyone held their breath and listened to the ripping of the paper, watching his hand extract the card that would reveal who had been granted this prized introduction to the art world. A slight pause, and finally the announcement …

"*A Giant Leap* by Anna Millbank!"

Listening to the rousing applause, Katherine's heart sank, a wrenching reversal of emotion after the adrenaline serge of the day. Totally deflated, "I didn't win," she thought. Disappointment surged through her as she applauded the winning entry. She watched the two professors wheel a platform onstage from the wings upon which stood a sculpture about three feet long and one and a half feet high veiled under a white canvas. The President removed the covering to display this latest *magnum opus* to the audience. Well, Katherine had to admit, it was an interesting piece, if you believed that theory. It featured a three dimensional rendering of the iconic progression of human evolution, a procession of figures from the ape to the primitive Neanderthals until the procession reached the age of modern man, gradually ascending a rocky outcrop to the precipice of a cliff; the final figure, a graceful Grecian youth poised nude on the very edge, his right foot just touching the cliff, his arms outstretched towards the sky prepared to take flight, the image of Mercury without the brimmed hat and winged sandals. The leaping demigod held a small figure of a space shuttle in his right hand. As far as Katherine could tell, the piece was sculptured from a plaster block and then varnished with clear enamel giving it a shiny protective covering. She had to concede the delicate figures were well executed. The President stepped aside as Mr. Joseph Sirrac came forward to read the results and comments of the judges explaining the reason for their choice, a long-winded list of the work's merits, *vis* its graceful style, the originality of the subject, and the optimistic symbolism it represented. The cameras flashed as the artist rose from her seat and walked to the stage to receive the certificate and have her picture taken with Mr. Sirrac, the President and the prize-winning artwork. When Anna had resumed her seat amidst a new peal of cheers and applause, the President waited until the hubbub died down and *A Giant Leap* was awkwardly rolled to the other side of the stage. A fresh round of applause before the President continued, and finally the auditorium grew quiet again as the second envelope was passed.

"Now, it is time for the honourable mentions. This year, the Sirrac judges have chosen two works. The first honourable mention goes to … Dennis Harrington for his oil painting *Electrovision!*"

Again, two professors brought in an easel upon which they placed the canvas, while a larger image was projected on a screen overhead. Is that a painting, or a Techie portrayal of a psychedelic acid trip? Mr. Sirrac proceeded to read the judges' opinions on this entry, lauding its boldness, its modern futuristic style that captured the energy of this new era. Dennis gave a whoop of victory as he bounded up to the front. Although he did not win, an honourable mention from the Sirrac Galley was also a welcome bonus as it was a known fact that art reporters from several of the New York papers attended the graduation ceremonies at Belvedere to catch the first 'scoop' on who had won the contest. Possibly the runners up would be mentioned in the culture and art columns the next day, and perhaps, attract the attention of other galleries. To the plastic art students, this would be akin to receiving an Oscar nomination.

Dennis approached to receive his certificate, Katherine studied the painting, from the orange swirls, red jagged lines and purple blobs, with difficulty, she could detect the outline of a television, a keyboard with a monitor, a cell phone, microchips and wires. Obviously an animated abstract tribute to the dawn of the electronic age of computers, widgets and gizmos. Well, one cannot account for other people's tastes, Katherine mused, but where is the skill? Sure, anyone could slap paint around with a palette knife and call it high art! It is amazing to think that productions like this actually became accepted as high art. At least she could recognise some objects in Dennis' picture.   He might make a name for himself if he continues in this style. Generally, she could not understand the praise lavished on the vast majority of modern art and the astronomical prices that it commanded on the world market. It was all false hype, Katherine had concluded long ago. How could intelligent, well educated people attend abstract art exhibitions and stand around for hours at a time voicing their self-proclaimed sophisticated interpretations of a piece and listen attentively to each other, while blithely sipping champagne and nibbling *hors d'œuvres* or petit fours, when there *was* nothing to interpret? A measly circle here, a paltry line there, a canvas with a dirty smear on it, and they could envision a new world unfolding before them. It was obviously a pandemic case of wilful delusion, the modern art patrons had fallen victim to an overwhelming fear of being excluded from the 'fashionable set'. They had allowed themselves to be persuaded it was the 'in thing' to attend these exhibitions, to be able to say they were there, that they hobnobbed in the most exclusive art circles, proudly affirming they too were cultured and could appreciate the New Age of expression. They lived off each other's hypocrisy, fuelling a worthless market of trash. Now, take the French Impressionists, their work is truly admirable. Renoir, Degas, Manet and Monet, their paintings victoriously stood the test of time. They had perfected the art of capturing the effects of light with their revolutionary natural style, and their unfettered passion for displaying nuances.

"The second honourable mention goes to … Katherine Walsingham for her oil painting, *Le Sacre d'ingéniosité Humaine!*"

At the sound of her name and the round of applause, her mind snapped back from its ruminating reverie. Although she truly had hoped to win, she watched with mixed feelings of exhilaration and apprehension as the professors brought a second easel onstage and revealed her piece to the auditorium. She eyed her creation basking in the golden glow of the spotlights. Judging from the raised eyebrows, the disgruntled wry faces of the professors and the lively murmuring in the auditorium ranging from sounds of amusement to incredulity, it is a wonder they gave it an honourable mention at all, she decided wistfully. What did the judges have to say about her bold allegorical remake of Jacques-Louis David's monolithic mural? Mr. Sirrac read out the comments of the judges, praising the craftsmanship of the composition, yet diplomatically guarding their compliments of her biting allegory, graciously declaring her piece was a reminder that mankind has a great responsibility to use knowledge and discoveries with wisdom and prudence.

Recalling her first inspirations for the Sirrac contest, Katherine realized at that time she had never seriously considered man's achievements in any great depth, taking her modern lifestyle for granted despite the flaws and imperfections that were evident in the world and society around her. Yet, when probing the theme set for the contest that year, she had to admit much of what could have been accomplished for the benefit of mankind had turned sour. The ambitious lust for power and monetary rewards manipulated many good intentions, therefore, man's greatest 'achievements' were often recipes for future disasters. The human race has always fallen short of its high ideals, the weaker element will take what is good and progressive, and for their own selfish purpose, turn it to evil. What a pity, so many opportunities to achieve true greatness were lost, she concluded.

Curiously, an image of David's work came to mind, *Le Sacre de Napoléon*, known to the English-speaking world as *The Coronation of Napoléon*. Set in the cathedral of Notre-Dame, the Emperor magnanimously crowns the kneeling Empress, while Pope Pius VII, seated behind the man of destiny, gives his papal blessing to the proceedings. In the background sits Napoléon's mother, a touching element of artistic licence as she did not attend the ceremony, but Napoléon was pleased when David had thought to include her. What had brought this particular mural to mind? Could it be that book from the Louvre she had been browsing through? Initially, Katherine could not perceive any connection between the triumphant scene and her cynical observations. Was her subconscious prompting an inspiration? Musing on the subject, she thought, didn't Napoléon crown himself? Well wasn't that a bold action!

Intrigued by this arrogant audacity, she decided a trip to the library was in order, and discovered David originally considered painting Napoléon crowning himself, but decided that image may be too egotistical and would display the Emperor in a bad light ...but it's perfect for my theme, Katherine decided. If Hogarth could satirise the men of his day and be recognised as a genius, why can't I? She thought her idea had possibilities, and hoped it would be original. At least she would graduate with a bang! She could visualise the characters in the new roles she would assign them. She would paint Napoléon as an allegory of man's achievements, pompously holding the crown over his head, his royal mantle copiously embroidered with yellow and black radiation symbols to represent the advent of the nuclear age. The Empress, Josephine, shall also be standing erect crowning herself, no humility there! A nice touch representing woman's equality and her supposed new-found freedoms. Women can be educated, vote, have a career, have it all ... but for sure, we lost respect somewhere along the line, and we never achieved true equality, so, leave her where she stands, a few steps below the Emperor. Now, what can we do with Napoléon's mother? Well, isn't pride the mother of all misfortune? Pride, as an allegorical figure, must be young and beautiful, and she shall not have attendants, Pride always stands alone. Let us give her Iccarus' wings to remind us of his fall, and in case this symbolism is lost on the viewer, the words 'Mater Superbia' should be painted on a sash draped across her breast like a badge of honour. The Minister *for* War in the foreground shall be leaning against the miniature replica of a cruise missile, the Arch Chancellor Prince of the Empire, Minister of Justice, shall be sleeping in a chair holding broken scales and a bulging brown envelope. Hmm, the rest of the royal entourage gathered around the central figures should all be decked out in currency symbols, the

Dollar, the British sterling, the Deutschmark, the Franc, the yen, the rouble. Now, who shall deliver the blessing? A pope would never approve this travesty of humanity. Who should replace him in this scene? Of course! The new figure seated behind 'Napoléon' should have a red cloak and doublet embroidered in gold, a black hat with a few cockerel and raven feathers, he must be painted with red skin and use his left hand. With an icy sneer, the Father of Lies gives his approval to this epoch of industrial and technological 'advancement'. Man, crowning himself as the god of this new age. Well, the crucifix will have to be replaced with a detail more suited to this travesty, the Tree of Knowledge would be a nice touch with the crafty serpent hanging from its boughs. The bishops will have to be replaced … ah yes, men in black suits with large briefcases brimming with bureaucracy, and a steel drum to represent our crude dependence on oil and the barons who pump it. Perhaps the royal insignia on that banner in the background to the left should be changed, a skull to symbolise death? Or better still, Gilbert's famous optical illusion with the lady looking in the mirror to show the vanity of it all. I hope David will forgive the liberty I took with his masterpiece, I'll just leave him scratching his head in confusion where he placed himself above Napoléon's mother. It was a pity she would have to be content painting this great satire on a smaller scale than the original, but then again, five hundred square feet of canvas would be a little over the top, and never get finished in time.

Receiving her certificate of merit and posing with Mr. Sirrac, the President and the college dignitaries for the traditional photographs, Katherine could sense the atmosphere had chilled somewhat onstage. The President stood stiff looking down at his shoes, the Vice President and Deans shuffled back and forth on their feet uncomfortably, the professors gritting their teeth in a strained smile. She knew her subject may be considered contentious, but was not quite prepared for this frigid reception. Was it really *that* bad? One would assume they were accustomed to seeing wild, *avant garde* artworks issuing from exuberant paintbrushes by now. Perhaps they had expected me to paint a generic, trite, or optimistic scene. Did they forget they were the ones who taught us that the unexpected and the controversial are remembered, or hailed as milestones in creative expression? Her thoughts turned to the other entrants, and she contrasted the situation. They were uncomfortable with *her* piece, but could approve a statue glorifying the alleged animal origins of humanity, which was still a hypothesis and could never be proved to her satisfaction. The Evolution Theory was certainly a divisive theme, or where could they see the talent in liberal applications of paint encrusted on a canvas like rainbow-hued soap scum?

Returning to her seat, she mused about this disturbing polarity, but not for long, consoled by the thought … it did not matter. From this point on, she could paint what she liked without having to win anyone's approval. It was a rude experience to suffer the critical evaluation of works that she considered good, if not great. Her days of trying to accomplish what the professors expected and the stress of wondering if 'this' or 'that' will receive a good grade were behind her.

After the President delivered his last congratulatory speech to the graduates, he made the announcements explaining where the contestants were to collect their entries, and the exact location of the official photographers in the main campus quadrangle for formal portraits, the ceremony concluded with cheers, laughter and light-hearted babble. Wondering if she should meet her family or collect her piece first, she decided that the middle path was best and motioned them to come down before edging her way up to the stage. She did not get far before her friend, Susanna Cooper, pushed through the milling crowd and eagerly greeted her.

"Well done!" Susanna commented, hugging her tightly, "I'm glad they gave you an honourable mention, your painting should have won."

"Thanks! Never mind, just wait until we get our own gallery started, then we get to pick the contest winners."

Awarded her place at the college through a scholarship, Susanna had arrived from Iowa and matriculated one year after her. They just happened to meet at the library, Susanna was having trouble learning how to use the catalogue computers when Katherine came to the rescue, explaining she had the misfortune to pick a perpetually glitched computer nicknamed 'Blunder Bolts', which nobody bothered to fix. Learning they both majored in art, a lively conversation ensued. They discovered they appreciated the same artistic styles and shared a love of musical theatre, they had much in common, it was not long before they became fast friends. Katherine learned firsthand the difficulties of a scholarship student from Susanna. Although her tuition fees were taken care of, Susanna found it a challenge to earn enough to keep up with the living expenses and the dorm fees of her new elite surroundings with her summer job in her hometown library. Her father was a high school principal, her mother a paralegal in a law office, and while her parents helped as much as possible, it was never enough for they also had twin sons already in college, and a younger daughter with just one year left to finish high school.

In contrast, Katherine hailed from a wealthy family, the Walsingham cosmetic and pharmaceutical empire to be exact, and never had to worry about tuition fees, in fact, money was never an issue for her. Gramps had already presented her and Steves with an enormous trust fund worth several million when they had turned eighteen—"I want to see them enjoy my gift to them while I'm still here and kicking!" he declared to their sceptical parents, further explaining this would be good training and teach them how to manage money — therefore starting a career was not a necessity as she could live very well off the interest she received from her investments.

Despite her independence, she was not a spoiled darling. An issue of an industrious family, she could just picture her father's eyebrows disappearing into his hairline if she aimlessly whiled away her days playing tennis, attending endless lunches at the club, or foolishly shopping and accumulating stupid articles she really did not want or need. In any case, she could not imagine living that lifestyle. Surely, the world had more fulfilling goals to offer than that! Following a period of self-reflection, she knew she needed to channel her energies into something constructive, something *creative*. It was at this time she began to explore various career options that appealed to her. At one point, she toyed with the idea of becoming an architect, but talking it over with Steves, she realized this would be too technical and confining. Just thinking about the advanced mathematics and physics she would have to master was enough discouragement, definitely not a career for someone who hated to balance a chequebook. In the end, it may prove to be a dreary occupation, battling planning commissions, budgets, deadlines, and all the bureaucracy involved. Interior design had come to mind, but then, that would mean pleasing very demanding clients, restricting her own creative ability. She had displayed a unique talent for the plastic arts in high school, so developing her skills became the logical choice, and if all went well, she was fortunate to have the finance necessary to design and open up her own art gallery with the freedom to display her own pieces and the work of artists that she appreciated.

Although Susanna did not discuss her difficulties, Katherine could see that not everyone had the luxury of arranging their life as she could. Pondering on what she could do to help her friend, she stumbled upon a brilliant plan, namely the spacious three bedroom apartment with the veranda over the garage that in times past served as the residence for the chauffeur and his family. As long as she could remember, her grandfather, father and mother had preferred to drive themselves, and therefore the place had been vacant for years until she decided to turn the living room into her private studio away from the main house. The carpet was old and she could work away to her heart's content without occasioning numerous sighs and pleadings from her mother not to spill paint all over the floor. I know the place needs fixing up, but why couldn't Susanna stay there? I hope Pop will think it's a good idea, she could save the money she would normally have to spend on the boarding fees for the Belvedere dorms. Of course, Susanna would have to commute to college everyday, I hope her clunker can hold out, or we could car-pool … . Katherine was excited with this new plan, for this would give them an opportunity to spend more time together working on their projects. Not knowing how her parents would react to this idea, it took her a few days to think it over before she approached them with her proposal during dinner one evening. She was delighted when they agreed that Susanna could stay as long as she wished, but the interior of the apartment was in no fit condition for occupancy—it had been idle for years. Obviously, it would need repairs and a paint job, undoubtedly the kitchen and bathroom were in dire need of improvement. Susanna was the perfect excuse the family needed to refurbish that area of the property they had not used for an age, and it would have become a necessary repair job eventually. Elated with her parents' approval, Katherine explained Susanna may need a reasonable place to live, but was fiercely independent and would not accept her offer if it looked like charity, especially if she thought they had renovated the place on her account. Her father suggested that if Susanna felt she had to contribute, she could pay half the utilities of the apartment, and he hoped she would find this acceptable.

"After we fix it up, just let her know that the place had been neglected for far too long, it had become a convenient storage area until you used the living room for your artwork, and we thought it would be practical to have someone actually living there rather than let it go to wreak and ruin again. Tell her she would be doing us a favour by looking after the place, which is the truth. I am sure she wouldn't object to this arrangement," her father suggested as he sipped his after dinner coffee.

Katherine could not wait to tell Susanna the good news of her parents' 'plan' to restore the old apartment, that they really wished they had a long term occupant to keep an eye on it, and it was perfect for her artwork, if she wouldn't mind moving in and contribute towards the utilities. Under these conditions, Susanna was happy to accept. It took six weeks for the workmen to rip out the old fixtures, replacing them with the latest models, and when the painters and interior decorators had finished the apartment, Susanna moved into the Walsingham Estate, 3 Oak Meadows, Englewood, New Jersey and became an adopted member of the family.

"I am sorry you couldn't attend the graduation ceremony Suzy, but at least you'll have your own next year." Due to the small dimensions of the college theatre cum auditorium, guests of the graduates were restricted to four family members or friends.

"Me too, but at least I'm here for the end. Come on, let's see the degree."

Katherine unrolled her scroll displaying a long declaration in Latin affixed with a red seal proclaiming her a Master of Art.

"Imagine working for years to obtain a piece of paper we can hardly read," Katherine joked.

"And to officially declare you have talent," Suzy returned.

"Amen! Well, let's go up and take one last look at the pariah canvas in all its infamous splendour before I have to take it down, and let this be a warning: beware of what you paint for the Sirrac Prize this coming year."

Suzy chuckled in disbelief, "It really is ridiculous, your painting is brilliant, and the only reason they passed you over, it obviously struck a nerve too close to home."

"Humph! I guess nobody likes to be reminded of the truth, even though the world badly needs it now and then. Isn't it strange how people are selective about the truth they want to see or hear? I mean, an artist or photographer depicts the countless famines in Africa, or the massacre in Tiananmen Square, and they are hailed as heroes for bringing the world's attention to troubled areas, which is fine, but, just try and point out where the true problem lies, destructive egotism, greed, intolerance, human fallibility, and every other fault of mankind, and people bristle," Katherine mused.

"Sure sounds like everyone wants to treat the symptoms, not eradicate the disease, and we end up with more problems," Suzy replied, "Well, if we can't obliterate the disasters of the earth, at least we can expose them through our art, and perhaps get people to think, it's better than doing nothing."

"I agree. Let's always try to paint the truth," Katherine declared, "our art must be made to mean something."

"You bet your sable paintbrushes. I refuse to portray anything else," Suzy concluded. There and then, the girls embarked on a private crusade. Stopping to survey the other entries, they chatted with a group of graduates who had come to the stage for a closer look before Katherine turned to the side door leading backstage.

"Well, I had better go and retrieve the painting, everyone should be down in a minute or two, and then we have the photographs to take care of."

"Do you need some help with it? I think it will fit in my car if I lower the back seat. I can drop it back at the house, I have to go there anyway and finish some packing before I get ready for the dinner tonight. It looks like you might be here for a while depending on how long the photographers take, and you don't need to drag a canvas all afternoon."

"Thanks Suzy, I'd appreciate that. I should be out in a jiffy."

Katherine went through the side door with a small group of crestfallen entrants who had not received an honourable mention, and she tried to graciously accept their best wishes without appearing too cheerful and pouring salt on their wounded feelings. As two volunteer professors returned their works, Katherine was approached and quietly taken aside by a robed figure who had stayed behind to converse with a few dignitaries still milling around in the backstage area.

"I believe congratulations are in order, Miss Walsingham. Well, I can see why you kept your entry a secret and refused any help," chuckled Professor Matthews in his 'Mr. Chips' tone as he pushed his gold-rimmed glasses up the bridge of his nose. "A David cum Hogarth hybrid, with quite an unusual twist. I believe you did not want to go softly into that good night … planned to graduate in a blaze of controversial glory?"

Katherine grinned.

"Thank you, Professor. I wanted my work to say something important, but obviously my statement was judged to be over the top."

No beating about the bush, that was Professor Matthews, her favourite instructor in the Art department. A man in his sixties, grey hair, down to earth, candid with a dash of elegant humour, he was an easy-going teacher and his classes a pure joy to attend. He never made a student feel uncomfortable and incompetent in front of others when they found a point difficult to understand, how to master a certain blending of colours or had trouble portraying the right perspective. If a student displayed a unique style of their own, they were encouraged, or if they needed assistance, he was ever patient, explaining information in ways they could quickly grasp with a joke or an amusing quotation drawn from masters of the past or the ancient classics. His field of study centred on the French painters from the Neoclassical, Romantic and Impressionist schools, Katherine's favourite styles, and therefore she was fortunate when he was assigned to be her supervisor. She was going to miss working with him, and felt guilty for not including him while her entry was a work in progress. Just once, she wanted to try a piece on her own without relying on the expertise of her tutor.

"Yes, I must admit they were my main sources of inspiration. I almost regret I displayed this satirical subject, but at the same time, I'm glad

I did. Somehow, I don't think I could have painted anything else. Once the idea got lodged in my head, it took on a life of it's own, I had to run with it, it wouldn't let go."

"You have great courage. I am pleased you succeeded in offending their sensibilities, an artist should paint from the heart, and not always what people expect. Predictability often leads to the dullest work, in my opinion, and we have been bored stiff long enough I think. If Delacroix was anxious about portraying what people thought, rather than his inspirations and emotions, his *Liberty Leading the People* would have remained obscure in an attic somewhere in France and would not be hanging in the Louvre as a cherished national treasure."

"Well, I wouldn't presume to be ranked with Delacroix," Katherine replied modestly to this lofty statement, "but I appreciate your comment. Hopefully, one day I will."

"If you continue painting in this vein, I believe you will become a Delacroix or a David of the modern day. You don't believe me? Then listen when I tell you I overheard the judges declare they would have chosen you first."

"But, if they thought that, why didn't they?" Katherine stammered, astonished at this unexpected news.

"Because, while your painting is brilliantly executed and technically flawless, it also wounds, for truth is not always beautiful, and they decided to 'chastise' you for their own feelings of discomfort. Remember that despite its iconic imagery and energy, *Liberty Leading the People* was originally decried for its frank portrayal of the 1830 Revolution, that the freedom fighters of the barricades were little more than scavenging bandits, the figure of Liberty looked like a dirty bare-breasted street tramp leading a mob bent on destroying decency and propriety. Nevertheless, in flamboyant brushstrokes, he displayed a sincere, if artful, patriotic message to spectators, and was remembered. Your picture, like Delacroix's, shall not be forgotten by the judges, nor anyone else who sees it, let me assure you."

"I really don't know what to say, except you have confirmed my latest resolution never to paint anything that is not sincere or truthful. But," Katherine continued, musing aloud, "what did they find 'wrong' with my painting, or what excuse could they give to explain their decision?"

"Oh, I believe it was on grounds of, shall we say, too much reliance on David's masterpiece … ?", the Professor replied with amused hesitation.

"In other words, lack of originality," Katherine interpreted, not a little chagrined with this pretext. "Well that's rich, isn't it? Everyone knows there is no such thing as true originality! Everyone is either influenced or inspired by something else ... Anna Millbank's sculpture can't be declared 'unique', everyone can see her idea sprang right out of the first scene of *2001: A Space Odyssey*."

"Indeed! But, do not let this initial outcome of the contest upset you, remember what I said about predictability. Her work is accepted for the moment, for it follows the current scientific *zeitgeist* of the day that has been drummed into the mass psyche by the modern media, and therefore it is what people expect. However, I predict, in a short time it will become no more than an attractive lobby piece for a natural history museum, and eventually passed by simply because of its familiarity. Yours, while it addresses modern issues, blazes its own trail, and progresses beyond the expected and rouses the mind from its complacent torpor rather than confirm it in its set path."

"I will remember what you've said. I guess this is my last lesson at Belvedere," Katherine replied with a smile.

"I suppose so. My last bit of sage wisdom before you venture out into the big wide world. Well, are you all set for your trip to Paris? You were there before as an exchange student at the Sorbonne during your junior year, if I remember right."

"Yes, that was a wonderful time! I'll be home for the summer until about mid September, and then spend the next four months there, this time I'll be staying at a friend's apartment, a friend of my father. I want to study my favourite paintings at leisure, it was difficult to remain disciplined and attend all the lectures required at the Sorbonne rather than spend every day in the museums."

"Not to mention the tourist attractions, the restaurants, coffee and pastry shops, and the shopping areas, I gather?" the Professor finished with a smile.

"That too! Paris is a different world, you have to live there to truly experience it properly. But I do plan to complete some works that have been in the back of my mind for some time, and this vacation period is exactly what I need. Who knows what I can develop with all that freedom and breathing the atmosphere of Paris?"

"Who knows indeed! I am happy for you. Any other future plans?"

"I would love to open a gallery sometime in the future, but I will have to assemble a collection first, and also do some research into the business end of a venture like that. A gallery is a wonderful idea, but I must also think of the practicalities. So far, all I know is that a gallery may be eligible for tax incentives, and that unless a gallery charges artists at least thirty to thirty-five percent commission, it will inevitably go broke, which means pricing is important as works do not sell everyday, unless you have a sought-after artist on show in your establishment. However, all that is in the future, we have to wait and see how my plans work out."

"I am expecting great things from you Katherine, and I will be keeping a watchful eye on you. And remember, stay in touch."

"I will, you can count on that. You will be top of my guest list for the grand opening."

"I shall await your invitation. I must leave you now, duty calls."

Katherine returned to the auditorium with her painting in tow and joined her family who patiently waited in the centre isle for her to emerge from the backstage area.

"Well, well, Kathy. Congratulations on your honourable mention. Now I understand why you did not reveal your painting to us before you entered it for the contest," her father declared with a chuckle, "I detect the activist returning with a vengeance."

He could not forget her early teens, her days of placards and protesting, beginning with 'Save the Wales' to that day she decided that animal testing was beyond the pale and picketed their own cosmetic boutiques in the city, attracting a swarm of reporters in the process. How he had fumed back then when she cost the family business a small fortune! In this unexpected glare of public notoriety, he was eventually compelled to phase out live animal testing in their cosmetic labs and forced to adopt acceptable methods, but could now look back and smile at her heroic campaigns.

"Perhaps you could have been a little more discreet?"

"Harold dear, leave Kathy alone," her mother interjected as she reached forward to tidy a strand of Katherine's brown hair that had come loose. "It is a wonderful painting. A little unusual perhaps, but the colours are beautiful, and it is certainly much better than the ghastly display at the last art exhibition for the Heart Foundation. What a truly tedious event that was."

"At least you didn't paint Adolf Hitler crowning himself, now *that* would have made their day," impish Steves snickered.

"You certainly did surprise them, Katie my girl," Gramps added with a twinkle in his eye, "but I guess we had better get a move on, we have the photographs to do, and my old knee won't brook dallying around for long."

"I'll take that," Suzy said as she carefully took the canvas from Katherine. "The dinner's at seven, right?"

"Yes, at the 'C'est la Vie'."

"All right, see you there."

Leaving the auditorium, Suzy made her way to the parking lot, while the family waited for their turn with the photographers in the quadrangle.

ꞇ❀ꞇ

The 'C'est la Vie' was one of Katherine's favourite French restaurants, a comfortable semi-formal multi-roomed establishment decorated in a *belle époque* Parisian theme with inviting alcoves. Tonight, they would be seated in the main dining room as the party would be too large for one of the more intimate booths. Ever the punctual businessman, Harold Walsingham made sure they arrived in time to greet the guests invited to share this special occasion but were unable to attend the graduation ceremony during the day. While they waited for the rest of their party to arrive, they chatted in the cocktail lounge. His younger brother Timothy, his wife Barbara, and their three children Jon, Stephanie and William, were the first to make their appearance. Timothy was not tall like his brother, and his hair was much lighter, still, the family resemblance was unmistakable. His ever-ready smile lighting up his face, he greeted everyone jovially, looking quite dapper in his navy sports jacket and grey slacks complete with cravat, while tall and slender aunt Barbara looked charming in her red floral patterned skirt and jacket that perfectly showed off her long wavy brown hair and hazel eyes. Jon, blonde and blue-eyed, as always looking well turned out, like Steves, he had a passion for Armani suits when dressing for an occasion. Stephanie, however, was clad under sufferance this night, Katherine noticed. Blonde like her brother, she was elegant in her cream pantsuit, but she preferred casual wear and obviously missed her jeans and tennis shoes. Quiet, brown haired William was looking handsome in his navy suit, always calm, reflective and steady as a rock, formalities and the business of life never seemed to ruffle him an iota.

Aunt Martha arrives in her usual flurry, her mother's older busybody sister, a curly grey haired plump lady of medium build dressed in a beautiful lilac skirt and jacket, with her ever over abundant festoons of gold and gems. A widow of ten years for Uncle Bob had unexpectedly died of a heart attack in Florida while marlin fishing, and having no children of their own, she busied herself with all the activities of the family. Suzy arrived just behind her, dressed in a lovely white and pink silk dress, her medium length light brown hair neatly held back with matching clips. The family lawyer Edmund Kraylor and his wife Sylvia were detained in Washington on business, so they could not be present, however, their six foot one auburn-haired son, Charles, arrived dressed in a sombre black suit and conveyed his parents' apologies to Katherine and her parents. Steves had also brought his latest girlfriend, Jennifer Davis, a flighty red-headed wisp Katherine thought, how long will this one last? When all the greetings and well wishes died down, the party were finally seated and her father proceeded to order the white wine for the appetizer, and the red wine to be served with the main course. Her mother had pre-ordered a special menu for the occasion, a selection of the graduate's favourite dishes.

Katherine looked forward to this evening, she had been completely absorbed getting ready for exams and had missed all the usual family dinners since Easter. Now she had the opportunity to catch up with the family news, alas, there was meddling Aunt Martha to contend with, she had the most annoying habit of asking those trying questions that rubbed everyone the wrong way at the most inopportune moment, usually putting her large foot in her mouth, inquiring about situations and events that they would rather not discuss and preferred to keep private. The customary questioning began as the waiters served the first course.

"It is so nice to meet you, Jennifer. How long have you known our Steven?" she asked as she intently scrutinized the guest.

"Oh, just about three weeks now, we met at an end of term party thrown by some of the students at MIT," Jennifer replied, unaware she was being reeled in by the overcurious Aunt Martha to reveal her personal details. Steves looked a little unnerved, wondering where the conversation would lead and if it would last long.

"Is that so, dear? Do you also attend MIT?"

"No, I am actually studying at Harvard," she replied.

"How interesting! What are you studying, may I ask?"

"Molecular Biology."

Imagine that, Katherine thought, perhaps she's not as flighty as she looks.

"How wonderful," Aunt Martha continued, "well I am glad that our Steven has finally found someone who shares his interests."

Martha, with her well-meaning interrogations, had no idea how tactless she could be at times to the discomfort of those around her. Despite his genius, Steve's wilful inability to remain steady with anyone for long, in addition to his spendthrift recklessness and his love for fast cars, (Porsches to be exact), was a cause of great concern to their parents. Fortunately, he and Jennifer were quickly released from her Inquisition as Aunt Martha selected her next victim for inspection.

"Have you found a serious beau yet, Kathy dear?" Aunt Martha dutifully enquired with that exasperating wheedlesome tone, "I know a lady at my bridge club who has a charming son with a stock brokerage company who would love to meet you...."

Oh, here we go again! Katherine tried to politely evade this prying conversation. When will Aunt Martha learn to keep her nose out of other people's business?

"That sounds very nice, Aunt Martha, I'll have to think about that...."

"Yes, do dear. It's high time you think about settling down with a nice young man and get a family started," she persisted as she peered through her large rainbow rimmed glasses.

Why can't she be quiet for once and enjoy her food? "Er, well, perhaps one day, but right now I plan to concentrate on my artwork."

Truthfully, Katherine had not seriously considered 'settling down' in the traditional sense of marriage, home, two kids and a dog the minute she left college. This was the 90s for heaven's sake! She never agreed with the 'old school' thinking that girls were sent to Ivy League colleges simply to meet some eligible catch. She was enjoying her independence and just beginning to find her feet. Right now, she was quite happy with thoughts of working on her projects and her plans to open a gallery someday soon, and could not imagine being tied down to that lifestyle, at least not yet. She had never really fallen in love with anyone beyond a schoolgirl crush, and therefore the thought of living with someone on that intimate level was an alien concept. Imagine inviting a complete stranger into your life! In fact, she was quite wary of allowing anyone of the opposite gender get too close, for she seemed to attract the strangest individuals who became a regular pain in the neck and made her uncomfortable. There was the 'greasy bean-pole' in high school covered in a minefield of zits, 'Stammer Sam' who followed her everywhere in the halls between classes like a lovesick puppy. When she did meet someone who seemed nice, one had to be careful, she observed many of her peers were dating simply for the sake of dating and having a 'good time', which could only lead to trouble, in Katherine's opinion. Once, she overhead two jocks mouthing off with masculine bravado about their various conquests, and declaring how lucky that son-of-a-gun would be who could 'nab' Katherine Walsingham. So, she with her fortune was an object to be used, not a person to be respected! Although she knew most teenagers at school had only 'one thing on their minds', this public affirmation by those two morons disgusted her. Her ideals of love gleaned from Victorian novels remained behind an invisible blockade from that moment, a wall protecting her from romantic disillusionment. *Anything past friendship, and I'm outta here.* Better to be safe than sorry! Why does Aunt Martha have to keep bringing this up?

Katherine's mother, breaking off a conversation about the latest society gossip with chatterbox Barbara, relaying the details about the Thorntons who may be getting a divorce; "He went off with the receptionist at his shrink's office, you know," graciously came to the rescue as she usually did when Aunt Martha poked too deep into their private affairs.

"Why Martha, Katherine has plenty of time to think about that. Indeed, she will be going to Paris in a few months, and may be opening her own gallery when she returns home."

Whew! Thanks Mom, Katherine thought with a sigh of relief, with Aunt Martha's curiosity peaked over her career plans, she could relax a bit. Perhaps now we can enjoy our dinner.

"Oh yes, Kathy, that's right. You'll be staying at the Kraylors' apartment. Well, won't that be nice? Not far from the Eiffel Tower, I believe," Aunt Martha prompted, turning to Charles for his input.

"Yes, that's right. It has a lovely view of the tower. My parents bought it a few years ago," Charles replied. "They are only too happy to let Kathy stay there. My parents and I will be going for Christmas and the New Year, and then we will all return together mid January."

"Sorry I won't be home for Christmas, but I am curious to see how they celebrate in France," Katherine added. "I came home for the holidays that term I spent there, and missed the experience."

"Well, Kathy, what will you be doing there all those months alone in Paris...?", Aunt Martha asked, suddenly eyeing the two youngsters with interest.

"Mostly loitering in the art museums and admiring the paintings, it's amazing to study the brush strokes of a work. A photograph can never do justice to the actual canvas," Katherine replied, "I may just paint a thing or two myself while I'm there. Can you imagine, they actually let people into the Louvre with their art equipment and allow them to copy the paintings? At least they have security. Wouldn't it be funny if they didn't, and someone switched paintings, passing off their copies as originals and getting away with it?"

"Imagine that," Suzy said, "I am surprised, you would think the museum authorities would be afraid there could be an accident and an original masterpiece become splotched with paint."

That's if they are originals," cousin Jon remarked, "there's a rumour that the paintings in the public areas aren't real, they're locked away for safekeeping."

"If that's true, at least they can't be snatched or destroyed by stray paint splatters," Suzy replied, "but it's disappointing to think the paintings may be fake."

"Well, I hope the Kraylors will not mind any blotches," Steves interjected with a grin, "At least Kats is not interested in that strange medium dignified by the term 'performance art' and won't be throwing pots of paint around their apartment or howling like a baboon."

"I should hope not, Steves! If I ever experiment with that idea, please get me a straitjacket and march me to Belleview. I could officially be declared insane," Katherine replied as everyone laughed. "And please assure your parents, Charlie, that I will be very careful, I'll have plenty of drop sheets on hand so they won't need to fret."

"No worries there, Kathy. By the way, I heard about your painting for the contest, I can't wait to see what you come up with next," Charles replied with a smile.

"Ditto!" Steves added with his usual mischievous grin, "probably something portraying 'Save the Kolas', or 'Help the Hippos'."

"Very funny," Katherine replied with a resigned sigh, quite accustomed to her brother's teasing, "and what are you up to lately, Mr. Brains? Thinking up plans to achieve world domination?"

"Nothing that ambitious, not yet anyway, just a new medication to ease the symptoms of the common cold."

"That is important," Suzy returned, "no one likes to be sick. It's a pity that you can't discover a cure."

"What makes you think I haven't tried?" he mused, suddenly assuming his hard-to-listen-to scientific mode. "The problem lies with the fact a cold is not one malady caused by one virus, but the same or similar symptoms induced by one of a hundred viruses, and then there are several different strains for each virus. In fact, only a few years ago, scientists using X-ray crystallography on one of the common strains found it had a high degree of antigenic variability…"

"I am afraid you've lost me," Aunt Martha interjected.

"Me too," Suzy added.

"Oh, he's always losing us," cousin William confirmed with a chuckle, "anything that comes out of his mouth that's not a joke sounds like brain surgery."

"It means that producing a vaccine is not viable," Steves replied a little frustrated with their lack of comprehension. "So all we can do is treat the symptoms. At least a cold does not last forever, but they are a right inconvenience when you catch one, which reminds me, I should have the formula ready soon, Pops," Steves said as he turned to his father who had finished speaking about the latest stock results with the other men, "but make sure the lab technicians run through and check the patents and all the other usual legalities, I wouldn't want to find that I have come up with something that has already been developed and end up with a lawsuit."

"What! And deprive me of a defence case?" Charles laughed.

"I thought you were concentrating on your exams this spring? Were you working on this when you should have been studying? I thought I told you to wait on this," Harold replied to his precocious son in a satirical tone.

"Now, now, leave the chap alone," Gramps interjected with good humour, "the young man can pass his exams on what flies over his head in the lectures halls. His grades are top notch, so don't complain if he spends his free time with some extra projects."

When the dishes were cleared, a refreshing lemon sorbet was served before the main course arrived, châteaubriand. The evening continued rather pleasantly, for the most part. The men engaged in their usual conversations on business, politics and sports. The women were occupied with the latest bridge tournaments, the upcoming social events, the juiciest gossip. Aunt Martha was only too obliging with her regular topics ranging from the latest styles in summer wear at their favourite shopping haunts to so-and-so's hysterectomy, which perhaps was not the best topic over a medium rare steak, before she turned to Jennifer and attempted to extract more information. Katherine was happy to catch up on the latest news with Steves, her cousins and Charlie as their lives had become extremely busy in their various pursuits. Jon was at Columbia University studying to become a cardiovascular specialist, while Stephanie had decided she would try fashion photography and attended school in Boston, which fascinated Susanna who loved reading the fashion magazines and studying the photographs. William was still in high school but had already decided he would delve into the world of computers, perhaps software programming, much to Steve's approval. Charlie, Katherine's long time friend, was locked in a major case between two recording companies and their songwriters who were disputing copyright issues over the music and lyrics of an album, he did not have the time to visit as often.

"I know you can't discuss particulars, but how is the case coming along?" Katherine asked. "Are you enjoying the legal profession?"

"I knew the practise of law could be a little trying, please forgive the pun," Charlie replied as he sipped his wine, "but I find setting up the circumstances of a case like this for a jury is the most frustrating part. Copyright issues generally boil down to the originality of a piece and who came up with it first, and therefore who should be entitled to ownership.”

“Well, that’s understandable, but what do you have to explain to the jury?”

“The problem is proving whether an infringement of copyright was intentional or not. Many who are selected for jury duty know next to nothing about the basics of music, and you have to place reasonable doubt in their minds concerning the extent of the originality of a song. Of course, stolen lyrics are easy to identify, but melody and rhythms are more difficult to pinpoint.” Charlie had learned how to play the guitar, and had almost succeeded in forming a band in high school, therefore he was familiar with the technicalities of composition.

“I am sorry to say I hold a similar position. I like musicals, and although I had a two-week introduction to the violin when I was six, and joined the high school choir, I never had formal music lessons. How would you begin?” Katherine wondered aloud.

Although this was annoying in court, Charlie found he enjoyed sharing his skill in legal argument with her.

“Try to picture a piano,” he began. “Do you know how to form a scale?”

“Yes, the only one I know is C major, which is all the white notes, beginning from C of course.”

“Well, despite the length of the keyboard, there are only twelve notes available to a composer. Lets take your scale of C major, that is, from middle C to the next C above, the seven white notes, with the five black notes in between. That’s basically what a composer has to work with.”

“Okay, but surely the rest of the board must matter? And what about the other scales?”

“If you play the same seven note scale on any C-note you choose, either below the range mentioned, or above, it is still the same. It just sounds ‘deeper’ in the lower left section, and ‘higher’ as you proceed further to the right. The other scales, or keys, are also the same scale, but higher or lower in pitch. The key of D major, the next note up from C, sounds exactly the same as C major, but higher in tone.” Katherine was looking puzzled until he offered an example. “Just try singing *Happy Birthday* on the same note you start ‘Do, a deer, a female deer,’ and then sing the exact same thing on the note for ‘Re, a drop of golden sun’. Same sounds, but higher in pitch.” Katherine quietly hummed the first line of *Happy Birthday* in the manner he suggested, carefully trying to keep ‘doh’ and ‘re’ separate.

"Well, that's easy to understand. So, you would argue it is probabile that a composer could accidentally write something similar to another composer, as they would have the same twelve notes to work with."

"Brava my dear! I wish I had you on the jury," Charlie beamed. "Then, proving that a song is original is made difficult by the fact most of the songs for decades have followed the popular 'lyric-chorus-lyric-chorus-instrumental improvisation-lyric-chorus' pattern before the song concludes," he continued. "The melody for the lyrics and chorus are rather short, usually four, eight, or perhaps sixteen lines, so it is possible that a songwriter will accidentally compose a song that resembles one already written."

"Yes, I guess it wouldn't be difficult for a songwriter to write something in a style he likes to listen to, and then find his piece sounds close to something already released." Katherine concluded. "Like you say, it comes down to whether or not a piece was plagiarised, bears an unintentional resemblance, or maybe was composed as a tribute piece and mistaken for property theft."

"Exactly! You catch on fast. Maybe you should have gone to law school and joined us at Kraylor and Kraylor?" Charlie laughed.

"No thank you! I don't know if I could live through the stress of court battles. Red paint I can handle, but not red tape," Katherine joked, "but why do you find that explanation so frustrating? With your example, I could see your argument clearly."

"Aha, this is where the detested red tape enters the scene. Even though I could explain the matter clearly, music is my hobby, but for court you need a professional to demonstrate this principle to make your argument convincing. So, I have to call up a well known composer or a licensed music teacher to testify and give them the run-through in court. 'Now Mr. Whatever, could you please explain to the jury how a scale is constructed?', 'Would you agree a composer has only twelve notes to work with?', etcetera, etcetera," Charlie iterated, marking off his questions to the witness on his fingers in a mock exasperated tone.

"I see, and you can't ask the jury if they understand everything and wait for their response like you can right now with me. You have to cross your fingers and hope that your questioning of the witness was sufficient…."

"Bingo! And that does not include the cross examination of your witness by the other side. See the frustration for such a simple argument? Sometimes I wish I was a prosecutor, if I had to try and wrangle some answers from a criminal who was trying to hide evidence, *that* would be a test," Charlie mused.

"Oh, you're a right Sherlock Holmes! Soon, you won't accept anything unless it challenges your intellect."

"Okay, I confess, I read too much Conan Doyle. I must admit though, I did learn a thing or two from Holmes. Speaking of copyright, did you know that song by Phil Collins, *A Groovy Kind of Love*, was heavily borrowed from a piano sonata written by a classical composer named Muzio Clementi who died in the late 1800s?"

"You're joking."

"I jest not. And, that song was written in 1965."

"Well, who would have guessed."

A raspberry sorbet was served before the last course was brought to the table, a chocolate *crème* gateaux prepared by the chef and decorated with an edible portrait of Katherine traced in icing encircled with exquisite red sugary roses, served with French vanilla ice cream, a speciality of the house prepared according to their own secret recipe, and of course, rounded off with French roast coffee. Suzy manned the camera as Katherine tried to cut the first slice, chuckling as she hesitated.

"It's too beautiful to cut! I feel like I'm chopping my nose off, or something," she laughed, not knowing where she should place the knife in the gastronomic artwork.

"We all love you so much, we could eat you up," Steves added from across the table.

"Here, here!" Gramps replied merrily.

Katherine finally made the first cut, and the cake was taken away to be served. Suzy busily clicked away with the camera while the waiter dutifully enquired if they had enjoyed their meal, and Katherine's father answered for everyone; "A suburb dinner, please convey our compliments to the chef."

"Okay Suzy, we don't want you left out! Could you take a few pictures for us?" Katherine asked the waiter, who graciously assented, quickly examining the top of the camera to find the correct button, allowing Suzy time to return to her seat.

"Certanlee Mademoiselle! Okaee, one, two three…zay 'zneeze'!" Everyone smiled at his French accent, while the waiter continued to take additional shots of everyone, "Zhere, 'Cheeze', 'Sneeze', works everee time," the waiter bowed, "Now you weell have photographs with happee faces." Handing the camera back to Suzy, he concluded, "Enjoee your deszert."

"That's a nice young man," Aunt Martha said.

After the dessert plates had been cleared, two waiters approached with a side table piled with beautifully decorated gift boxes covered in bright wrappings and oversized bows, presents for the graduate. Before the big day, her parents wanted to buy her something very special for her graduation, and said that they were thinking of replacing her car, which was now over four years old. Katherine, however, was not like Steves who itched to own the latest models, and was quite happy with her white BMW and its cream leather upholstery. She did not think it was necessary to exchange it yet as it behaved perfectly, and besides, it did not seem practical when she would be away for months in Paris. In the end, her parents agreed they would talk about a new car when she came home in the new year, or perhaps help her with her gallery, whichever she preferred. However, they still wished to mark the occasion with gifts, and so Pops had selected a beautiful rose mahogany art case complete with Victorian brass fixtures for her paint tubes and brushes, which she really loved.

"As you say, they allow artists bring their equipment into the museums, and we couldn't have you take your old contraption out in public, especially to the Louvre," he said with a smile. On her outings, Katherine used an old battered pine wood art case that looked as though it had been dragged through a world war waged with paint-ball artillery. "Perhaps now we can finally have a funeral and bury it?"

"Pops! It's exquisite! Thank you so much! I shall definitely try to be more careful with this one, let's pray I don't drop it." How am I going to keep it clean, she thought!

Her mother's gift was too bulky to bring to the dinner.

"I found delightful matching luggage for your trip, dear. You know those cases with the tapestry designs in the dusty rose colours? They're waiting for you at home," her mother said, "I hope you will like them."

"Of course I will, I can't wait to see them! Thank you, Mom," Katherine replied.

Gramps had found a gorgeous gold brooch at Tiffany's that he knew she would like.

"Gramps! How did you know I like emeralds?"

"Oh, I did a little investigating," he smiled, "nothing escapes your mother you know."

"Thank you! It matches my ring. I didn't have a brooch to go with it."

She was a little apprehensive opening Steve's gift and carefully lifted the lid, she never knew what to expect. One birthday, it was the box-within-a-box-within-a-box trick, or that Christmas when he 'mummified' everyone's gifts with toilet paper before he used wrapping paper. And, she could never forget that Easter he dyed the marshmallows with edible crazy-ink that stained their teeth and they couldn't open their mouths at church. Opening the box, she was surprised to find he had given her a sparkling Waterford crystal atomizer filled with her favourite perfume.

"He told me what he did to your last one," Jennifer explained, "I said it was high time he made amends. I got the perfume."

When they were younger, Steves had experimented with his chemistry set and decided it would be great fun to switch her perfume with a stink bomb, which made her smell like a skunk for the day, and could never be completely washed out of her old atomizer. How she wished she could have lost him somewhere that time! Katherine was beginning to like Jennifer, and hoped Steves would make a go of this relationship, at least for a little longer than the rest. She certainly can bring out the best in him.

"Thank you Steves, thank you Jennifer! How lovely!"

Uncle Tim and Aunt Barbara's gift was a large colour-plate, special edition of Renoir's life and works, a volume that Katherine did not have in her collection, while the cousins selected a large edition of Leonardo da Vinci. Aunt Martha had found a lustrous, perfectly matched double strand of natural shell-pink pearls.

"I could not decide what to get, but when I saw these, I thought how perfect they would be for you. Pink is your colour, Kathy."

That was Aunt Martha, if one could overlook her prying curiosity and meddlesome habits, she had a soft heart, and always available when needed in times of family crises, someone you could turn to for help, and could always be trusted to find that perfect gift.

"I am so overwhelmed with all these beautiful presents," she said as she reached for a gold envelope sent by the Kraylors, a deluxe gift certificate of two tickets to any show of her choice on Broadway. Charlie also brought her a present, a gold charm, a new addition for her bracelet, featuring a palette and brushes with tiny little gemstones for the paint colours. Since he discovered she had a 'thing' for dangly charms, it became a tradition to present a new one for her collection on special occasions. Suzy, in the hunt for something unusual, found a blue satin covered box in Chinatown filled with soft, short-handled wolf-hair brushes that tapered to a long fine point and fit easily into the palm of her hand.

Delighted with all these thoughtful gifts, Katherine thanked everyone once again, and the evening was happily rounded off with petite forest green after diner mints and extra coffee, casual conversations and Steve's side-splitting yarns before it was finally time to call it a night. At the reception area, Charlie turned to Katherine as he helped her carry the gifts.

"Kathy, I'm free this Saturday. Can we get together and do something? We also have that tennis rematch we never got around to."

"That's right. Suzy will be driving back to Iowa on Friday, I think Steves will be busy with Jennifer before she goes back to Massachusetts Saturday afternoon, and I have no plans. Okay, how about … ten Saturday morning, and then we can have lunch afterwards? I warn you, I shall give you no quarter this time," she replied with a smile.

"It's set then."

೦೫ ❀ ೮೦

Charlie arrived a little before the appointed time at Oak Meadows all ready for the morning's tennis battle, with sports bag in tow, he rang the bell and Mrs. Gonzales, the housekeeper, opened the door with her usual greeting.

"Good morning, Mr. Charlie, looking for Miss Kathy? She hasn't come down yet. Mrs. Walsingham is in the breakfast room."

"Thank you, I'll pop in and say hello."

"Shall I bring you some coffee while you wait, or perhaps something else? Juice maybe?"

"Some coffee would hit the spot, if you don't mind. I was up late last night with a demanding client, and could use some fuel before I face the Racket Whiz."

Making his way down the white wainscoted checker-tiled hall, he entered the breakfast room and greeted Mrs. Walsingham seated at her card table by the window playing Patience. She was enjoying her tea and bran muffins topped with marmalade before she went to town for the day.

"Hello Charlie. I see you are here for that rematch."

"It's about time. We've got to break that tied score sometime."

"Kathy should be down shortly, I think she is looking for her visor, it is bright today, isn't it?"

"Sure is. I am glad we are playing this morning, I wouldn't like to be running about in the afternoon if it hits the high temperatures they predict."

"That's sensible.. Would you like a muffin, dear? They were freshly baked this morning."

"Thanks, they look good. I overslept and missed breakfast."

"Charlie, you know you shouldn't, it's the most important meal of the day."

"I know I shouldn't, but there you go … and here's Mrs. Gonzales

35

with her much needed cup of coffee. Thank you," he said as he helped her with the tray.

"Wouldn't you like something more substantial, some eggs and bacon perhaps?"

"No, Mrs. W., the muffin is fine, thanks. By the way, where is the famous painting? I'd love to see what caused all the fuss."

"Well, we have placed it in the library for now. We don't want to upset Kathy, but we really have no idea where to hang it. Shall we say, it is a subject that may be controversial to some. Hard to know how to handle it, actually. Beautiful to look at, but you know our Kathy and her ideas, she tends to get carried away at times."

"Is it *that* provocative? Well, I guess I shall have to take a look at it."

"By all means, Charlie. It's on the table to the left."

Leaving his bag and his half finished muffin and coffee, he headed towards the library across the hall. Locating the picture, he gently picked it up and leaned it against one of the dark wood bookshelves lining the wall, stroking his chin as he studied the unusual scene. I can understand Mrs. W.'s indecision, this certainly would be a conversation piece wherever they hang it!

"Hello, Charlie, Mom said I would find you here. Sorry I took so long, but I couldn't remember where I put my visor."

How charming she looked in her white tennis outfit!

"Good morning Kathy, I had to view the enigmatic wonder."

"What do you think? I might as well hear the critique now, and get it over with," she joked.

"The picture is executed with great skill Kathy, it really is a work of art, the subject is daring, and the lighting, shading, the figures, the brushstrokes, it is splendid..." he declared with approval.

"But...?" she gently prodded, waiting to hear the worst.

"But, it's so ... so, *cynical*, Kathy. It is a very mordant view of life. If you don't mind me asking, what possible experience could make you view the world from this sceptical aspect? I understand your treatment of the theme for the contest, and yes, mankind fails all the time, but I didn't know you were so ... philosophical," he replied, trying not to offend her. On the contrary, she was not offended. She could always share her innermost thoughts with Charlie and she appreciated his opinions. He was not one to indulge in flattery, and his assessments were always sincere.

"You know, the real inspiration was drawn from a sleepover at a friend's house during high school," Katherine began, "you remember Jackie

Silmore, don't you? It was her sixteenth birthday party, actually."

"How did you get from a sleepover to the destruction of the world, Kathy?" he asked, a little bemused by her answer, trying to unravel the correlation between the two situations.

"Well, we all wanted to watch an Indiana Jones movie, and Jackie accidentally picked the wrong tape, a movie she recorded from TV. We watched the first fifteen minutes before everyone started to voice their complaints, and she ejected it, but I saw enough of it to make me curious. It was *Soylent Green*, with Charlton Heston. I had never seen it before, and I wished we had continued watching it. Have you seen it?"

"No, can't say that I have. I've heard of it, a science fiction flick," he deduced.

"It is, and a truly disturbing one at that. I couldn't get the first scenes out of my head that night, and so I crept down the next morning to get a bowl of cereal and watch the movie before anyone woke up. Let me tell you, that film was a revelation. Imagine that we are several decades in the future, and due to our mismanagement of the earth, our social structure and global ecosystem are in a state of chaos. The earth is so polluted that the sky is dark and discoloured, the sun can no longer be seen, and green foliage and trees are nearly extinct. The greenhouse effect has become intolerable and winter never occurs. Farmed food, forget about organic produce, is a luxury as nothing will grow outside a strictly controlled environment. Real food, down to a jar of jelly, is only available to the rich as they are the only ones able to afford it, and armed guards patrol farms walled up like prisons. To keep the impoverished overpopulated masses alive, a company called Soylent distributes these horrible green processed rations Socialist-style, which they claim are made from ocean plankton, supposedly the only wildlife left on earth. To secure the survival of the human race, the government has become Socialist and manages the population according to rank and position, and assigns housing and food accordingly. The homeless have become numberless and literally crowd the streets, sleeping right on top of each other at night on the pavements. The world is depicted as hell on earth."

"That really is a bleak, dystopian picture, but where does Charlton Heston come into all of this?"

"It's been a while since I saw the movie. If I remember correctly, he plays a police officer in New York. Since he is a city official, he is fortunate to have a dilapidated apartment, which he shares with an old man, who I think was supposed to be a professor at one time. Remember that actor who was in those old gangster movies, Edward ... Edward...," Kathy hesitated trying to recall his name.

"You mean Edward G. Robinson?"

"Yes, that's him. He played the old man. Well, one of the wealthy Soylent company directors is found murdered in his penthouse, and Heston is called in to investigate. Instead of showing any interest in the case, he rifles the man's refrigerator, an appliance that is now a luxury, and he steals some of his 'real' food, another luxury, a steak, lettuce and tomatoes I think, and shares them with the old man. In the end, they weep over their dinner, and Robinson wonders how on earth did they allow the world to get this bad. Apparently, he works at the library, and is surrounded by books that record what the planet once looked like."

"Well, that movie would provide food for thought, I can see that," he concurred.

"But wait, that's not the end of it, Charlie. It gets worse. Heston finally works on the investigation and brings home some data he collected so Robinson can look into it for him, company records or scientific information from Soylent that the director was going to make public before he was killed. Well, what the old man discovers shocks him so much that he decides he cannot handle his situation any longer, and he declares he 'wants to go home'. At first, you don't know what he means until you see him arrive at an ominous looking building that looks like a protected research facility. It turns out to be a government operated euthanasia centre. The medical faculty make him comfortable, ask him what music he likes and what his favourite colour is. In his last moments, he is shown a movie on a large screen of how the earth once looked with green hills, animals, forests and blue lakes accompanied by his selected soundtrack, and the room is all lit up in his chosen colour. Heston arrives too late to save his friend, but just in time to see this panoramic film and to hear his last words, urging him to disclose the truth to everyone. In the end, Heston follows his body to find that the cadavers at the facility are collected by dump trucks and then delivered to Soylent—the rations were manufactured from human remains."

"That's gruesome, Kathy. A nightmarish situation. But aren't you taking that story too much to heart? Surely, the planet will never get that bad? You know how they over emphasize things in Hollywood, display everything over the top, and it's bound to sell."

"I know, and there were other details in the movie too upsetting to watch, but I can see it beginning to happen all around us. Can't you see it too, Charlie? I'm still trying to get my head around it all. For instance, the planet is slowly being poisoned, and anything that is organic and naturally grown without the use of modern methods is more expensive than other produce. Who knows what will happen to the food once they succeed in genetically modifying it for the market? Who knows what will happen to everyone after eating it for years? What if we alter the ecosystem and damage it irreparably, wiping out our food supply? No one has looked that far ahead, because no one can foresee the outcome until it actually happens."

"Except, perhaps, for the people who wrote the story for *Soylent Green*," Charlie mused.

"You said it! Haven't you noticed that everyone has a 'We'll-deal-with-it-when-we-get-to-it' attitude? In the end, caution is thrown to the wind. Scientists now do things because they can, and have no concern for the long-term consequences of introducing modified produce. Who knows how much more is actually hidden from the public? Do you think the government tells us everything? Certainly not, in my opinion. It's scary to think that this food crisis is only one of the issues presented in the movie."

"Well, I don't think the human race will ever get to the point of eating itself *en masse*," Charlie replied, "although I can't say anything about the head-hunter countries. Somehow, I can't see us packaged on supermarket shelves in the near future."

"We're closer to it than you think, from what Steves and Jennifer tell me, there is talk of inserting human genes into animals for medical purposes, so that organs for transplants can be taken from animal donors that won't be rejected by human recipients. That sounds like a great philanthropic breakthrough, but there's no mention of what could happen afterwards. People always make mistakes, and you can't be sure that those modified animals won't get mingled with the agricultural system eventually. What if we end up eating meat or drinking milk that contain human genes, and never know it? Every time someone says, 'That will never happen,' it usually does."

Charles felt the coffee and muffin churn in his stomach as she finished this unsettling statement.

"Kathy, you're ruining what little breakfast I got this morning," he replied with a sheepish grin.

"Well, it's your fault you got me started on this subject! I could go on for an hour, but I guess we had better get to the game before we become utterly morose for the day, or it gets too hot. Let's have some fun. Besides, I need the exercise and so do you. I've been sitting at my books or the easel for too long and you spend most of your time sitting behind a desk. This will do us both some good."

"Okay, let me get my bag from the breakfast room, I got new rackets last month, you can try them out if you like."

"Thanks, just for the first set, I wouldn't want to scratch them up before you get to use them. Let's be on our way then."

⊙

The next morning, Katherine was stiff from the previous day's exertion, aching in places that had not registered pain in a long time. Drowsily getting ready and dressing in her Sunday best, she made her way down to the breakfast room. How she would love to sleep in today, but that was not an option. One Sunday morning during their early teens, Katherine and Steven decided to assert their desire for independence and declared with a passive lie-in protest they did not feel like going to church. The protest was quickly halted as their father stood in each doorway and quietly declared in his steeled business tone that made board members quake:

"When you have homes of your own, you may live as you choose, but while you are under my roof, you shall go to church."

They quickly hopped out of bed and never complained again. Unless it was a dire circumstance, their parents never used corporal punishment, one chilly look from their father was enough to inform them when they had crossed that line and were courting a long period of house arrest or the revoking of certain privileges. Respect was demanded and returned when earned.

Making her way downstairs to the breakfast room, she greeted her parents who were relaxing with their Sunday papers and discussing the news of the day.

"Morning, Pops. Morning, Mom."

"Good morning, Kathy," her father replied. "How did the game go yesterday?"

She had gone to bed early the night before and did not see her father who had come home late after a protracted business conference preparing for Wednesday's board meeting.

"Tied again, wouldn't you know it? Charlie won the first set, I won the second, and then it got too hot to play the third, so it stands as before, well, almost. I think I ache more than last time! I'm so out of shape, it's been a while since I played a hard game like that," Katherine said as she sat down gingerly in her customary place across from her mother and helped herself to some coffee, waffles and bacon.

"Maybe you should soak in the hot tub when we come home? You will feel better," her mother suggested.

"That sounds good, I might do that. Let's pray the Reverend won't preach for too long today. My back won't handle it. Hey Pops, can I have the Art and Cultural section?"

"Of course Kathy, here you are."

Her father handed her the desired section already taken out and neatly folded. He had learned long ago if he wished to read his section of the paper in peace, and in one piece, he should remove the sought after sections. Steve's sports and technology sections were also neatly folded and placed to the side.

"Kathy, look and see if anything is mentioned about the Sirrac contest, there wasn't anything in the daily papers the last few days, and this doesn't seem to have anything either," her mother said as she flipped though her paper one last time. "I was sure that someone would write an article about it."

"Perhaps the editors decided it just wasn't newsworthy this year. Or, they're going to wait and write their articles when the winning piece is exhibited at the gallery," Katherine replied as she thumbed through the pages her father had passed to her. She was surprised, however, when she discovered an article in the exhibition reviews. "Sorry, got it, just found something."

"Well, let's hear it. Read it out, dear."

"Oh no, it's by the 'Art Hacker'," Katherine groaned in dismay, "I'll have to wear a paper bag over my head when I go out from now on!"

"Who?"

"Robert Horace, critic *extraordinaire*, better known to dismayed artists far and wide as the 'Art Hacker', or 'Robert the Horrible'," she explained, "he nearly always slashes a piece he reviews, or every exhibition he attends, not that many deserve a good review, but he also discredits really good works. I guess the editor believes bad publicity is a good thing for the art columns."

"Come, come now Kathy, it can't be all that bad," her father said reassuringly.

"Pretty much! Just listen to this; '... *perhaps the one saving grace of the Sirrac contest this year was a piece by Katherine Walsingham entitled, Le Sacre d'ingéniosité Humaine, which was executed with flair and insight* ... .'"

"You see Kathy, dear? He liked your work," her mother interjected.

"But he misunderstood the whole thing! I didn't get to the bad part: '*Miss Walsingham, heiress to the illustrious Walsingham Industries fortune, has dared to present a provocative exposition concerning the corruption of Catholicism during the twentieth century using David's famous painting of Napoleon's coronation. In Walsingham's rendition, the pope officiating at the ceremony has been replaced with the Prince of Darkness giving his blessing to the effects of war, an obvious reference to the Nazi-friendly Pope Pius XII and Adolf Hitler's attempt to crown himself and achieve world domination leading to the disastrous upheaval of World War II and the annihilation of millions...'.* How on earth did that idiot come up with *that* interpretation? He didn't even interview me and ask what it was about!" Katherine replied, completely scandalised by the review. "We may be Episcopalians, but I don't hate the Catholics or the pope, and I don't know anything about Pope Pius XII, except I heard he did help to save many Jews during the holocaust, so this can't be right. My painting was just an allegory for the pride of the human race in general, nothing that specific! They didn't even print a picture of it in the column so people can decide for themselves. This is terrible!"

Her father's abrupt coughing echoed Katherine's horror of the article as he tried to clear his throat from a sip of coffee that went down the wrong way, in addition to her mother's quick intake of breath, her hand placed over her heart.

"Oh Harold, I hope Reverend Dobbson and his wife do not read the art columns, and the ladies at the Bridge Club, what will they say? Oh, Bishop Morrison! You always donate to the Catholic Relief Fund and we always attend the charity dinners, not to mention we have the dinner at the Country Club tonight! I pray he will not credit this report!"

"I certainly hope not, Helen."

"Thank goodness Mrs. Gonzales and Juanita, haven't read the papers yet, for heaven's sake, don't let her take the Art section of the paper! I shall have to go to the kitchen and take her aside, I should explain the situation before they hear any gossip. It would be just awful to lose an excellent housekeeper and good help on false reports of religious intolerance. Oh dear, I don't think life at Oak Meadows will ever be the same after this!"

"My dear, I don't think you understand the full implication of this situation," Mr. Walsingham returned, his eyes pensive. "This affects more than our social life and our domestic felicity. There is the board of directors to consider, Heinrich Merrick and Thomas Riordan are on the board, they're Catholic, and Joseph Zedder who is Jewish. I have no idea what will happen now at the meeting this Wednesday, it may not go well if they believe this article. We could lose some important investors for out latest projects. We must not forget poor Nancy Thornton who is on the board, she introduced us to Bishop Morrison. She may be facing a divorce soon, she is a devout Catholic and adheres to the doctrine she cannot remarry. With the prospect of raising two young children on her own, she will be going through enough without reading this and assuming the worst concerning our opinions of her beliefs. This is a very troublesome situation indeed."

Katherine was feeling utterly miserable at this point.

"But I didn't intend this to happen! How did the 'Art Hacker' come up with Hitler, for goodness sakes! I inserted an allegorical Napoleon!"

"So, someone *did* think it was Hitler," Steves quipped as he came in for breakfast and helped himself to the waffles. "Let me see that article. Hmm, pretty good review, I think."

"Steves! It's not funny! How could you call it a good review? It's horrible!"

"Now, sis, you shouldn't have chosen art for a career if you can't take the criticism, it's part of the territory. Look, if you give a speech to fifty people in a room, they will repeat what they heard, not what you said. Art is in the eye of the beholder, and everyone will have their own interpretation. The review is good from the standpoint you have received some great publicity. Bad publicity is good publicity, after all."

"Everyone is so upset, and I don't want my work misinterpreted to this extent. I may not agree with everything that happens in the world, but I am not an anarchist or a religion-basher! Perhaps I should write a letter to the editor explaining the true symbolism, and make sure from now on I add a commentary to my works somehow … ."

Their mother nodded in agreement with this last suggestion.

"I wouldn't, sis."

"Why not?" the ladies chimed. Steves sighed with impatience.

"Well, you take away the thrill of discovery. If you explain everything for everyone, nobody will want to look further and study the work. It's the unknown that draws people. Remember what you told us about the *Mona Lisa*, if da Vinci revealed why and how he painted it, would they still be gaping at it today, trying to figure it out?"

"No, I suppose not. That really is the ugliest portrait I've seen, the only thing that supposedly makes it famous is the mystery behind it," Katherine admitted as she remembered her trips to the Louvre and how she shook her head at the poor tourists crowding around to see a jaundiced, eyebrow-less lady that reminded her of tight-lipped Washington on the dollar bill. Surely, they could have chosen a better portrait of the First President for their currency?

"Exactly. Take away the ambiguity, and nobody would pay two cents to see it. Let people try to fathom the meaning of something, and the mystery grows. So let certain misunderstandings and misinterpretations run wild, for there will always be those who want to see the work for themselves, and see it exactly as you intended. The more controversial a work is and talked about, the more famous it becomes."

"How will I be able to handle the onslaught until they figure it out?" Katherine mused in dismay.

"Or Walsingham Industries, for that matter," their father replied. "This notoriety may be wonderful for artists, but not for a multi-national corporation, let me assure you. However, I am afraid this cannot be undone, so now it will be a matter of damage control. We have to put our best foot forward and pray no one gives credence to the article."

"Well, the reputation of 'Robert the Horrible' precedes him, so I don't think they will take his interpretation too seriously. Just think, the news is only as good as the next day's paper, people have short memories," Steves reminded them.

"I don't know if I can face everyone at church, and I ache so much anyway … can't I stay home this once, Pops?" Katherine begged. There was also the dinner at the Country Club that night, if only she could run away!

"Certainly not. You brought this situation about and should not expect us to brave it out for you alone. I am afraid you lit the fire, you must now take the heat, not to mention the rest of us."

"At least she didn't join Greenpeace after high school like she wanted to and sail off with the hippies on the *Rainbow Warrior*," Steves declared.

"I should hope not," their father replied, indignant with the idea.

The conversation was interrupted by the sound of a car pulling up outside and the clackity-click of high heels scurrying down the hall.

"Isn't it just dreadful! As I live and breathe! What possessed you to paint such a thing, Kathy? Don't you know how vulgar it is to brandish your religious and political opinions in public?" Aunt Martha exclaimed as she arrived in the breakfast room, breathless, clutching a copy of the paper. "What shall the neighbours think, and the Fitzgeralds next door?"

Oh no, not Aunt Martha now....

"Aunt Martha, I can't believe you think I painted that! I don't know how the 'Art Hacker' came up with his review. He purposely twisted my whole idea," Katherine tried to explain.

"I wouldn't believe everything you read, Aunt Martha, although *I* can see the similarities," impish Steves interjected.

"Oh you would, too," Katherine darted. "Where may I ask, you rogue?"

"Just look at Napoléon and Hitler, they had similar military careers. They both wanted to unify Europe under one dictatorial government, failed at invading Britain, and were frozen in their tracks outside Russia. The only difference between them, Napoléon tried to promote the rights of man for the betterment of mankind, while Hitler wanted to make the perfect race and 'better' mankind through eugenics and genocide. It looks like Robert the Horrible chose this interpretation accordingly," Steves explained.

"Shoot! That wasn't in my head at all," Katherine replied. "I wanted to highlight the atrocity of war in our modern times, but this is ridiculous."

"Perhaps you should have asked for advice before you painted. You have come up with some crazy ideas in the past, but I guess this tops them all. And to make matters worse, I told all our friends about the contest and Kathy's entry! How are we going to face everyone? Katherine, you've dragged the whole family into a catastrophe! When will you ever learn?" Aunt Martha huffed as she reached for the coffee pot.

Her appetite completely ruined, all Katherine could do was dejectedly shuffle the rest of her waffle around the plate with her fork.

"Oh, do be quiet, Martha, we have enough worries without all your interjections and adding fuel to the fire," her sister replied. "Have your coffee and eat, we have to think this over, I don't know how her father and I are going to handle this. I can't imagine the consequences."

"Thundering tarnation! What is all the hullabaloo about? Has the sky collapsed or something? Why hello, Martha, what brings you here for breakfast?" Gramps said as he came in, perplexed with the unexpected visit and the atypical tense atmosphere around the family table.

"Nothing much," Steves replied as he reached for more bacon, "our Kats has made a splash with her colouring and single handedly turned our world upside down."

"A new family crisis? That's normally your area of expertise," Gramps rumbled back with a chuckle. "What could our Kathy possibly have done to throw everyone into such consternation?"

"Read this," Steves said, handing him the detested article.

Gramps took out his spectacles from his inside breast pocket, looking serious for a moment as he read before his eyes lit up with their usual cheerfulness.

"What tripe! Is this the cause of all the fuss? Surely you don't believe it?"

"Of course not, father, but others will. You know how important the upcoming board meeting is, and this negative publicity could affect our business."

"Nonsense, I don't think an article in the Arts section is going to create that much havoc, and, if the stocks do drop, we can buy them back, especially the common stock, we could profit from this," he replied as he sat down and poured some coffee. "Cheer up, Kathy, I've seen worse things happen. This certainly won't create a second Great Depression."

"No, but it could make things uncomfortable. What if we lose some of our investors," his son returned with a preoccupied frown.

"Well, I don't see anything like that happening. People don't give up good investments over one paragraph in a newspaper, particularly if it concerns someone's religious opinions. If we lose some investors, there will be new ones, hopefully individuals who have enough sense not to read that trash and who can appreciate art," he replied with a wink and smile at Katherine, trying to make her feel a little better, which she appreciated.

"Well, Harold, I suppose I had better go and see Mrs. Gonzales and her niece," mother announced as she rose from the table. "I shall have to clear this misunderstanding before we leave, they won't be here when we return as their church service is at twelve o'clock and they have the rest of the day off. I had better prepare them in case they may hear something disagreeable."

Mr. Walsingham looked at his watch.

"You had better hurry, Helen dear. We have fifteen minutes to finish breakfast before we get ready to go."

"I guess I shall tidy myself up, and see you there," Aunt Martha said as she rose from the table and headed to the powder room down the hall.

"Well Kats, I thought that with school out, things would be pretty boring around here, but leave it to you to add some spice to our life," Steves teased.

"And as for you, Steven," their father announced, "there will be no tomfoolery in the labs this summer, too many reports have come to the top floor about your extra projects holding up the equipment and cluttering the work areas. We currently have three medications that will be undergoing stringent testing and it is imperative that they are ready and approved by the FDA early next year. I expect your cooperation in this matter, you will be under strict supervision by the head of the Research Department and Dr. Stirling. You *may* have the use of the equipment for your own research, when and if it can be made available, and on your own time. Do I make myself clear?"

"Yes, Pops," Steven replied with a sigh.

"Come come, all rules, work and no play will make Steves a dull bore," Gramps said as he polished off one last waffle with gusto before it was time to go.

ଓ ✿ ଚ

It was perhaps the most nerve-wracking drive to church Katherine could ever remember. Mom sat in front with Pops, while Gramps sat behind with her and Steves. While the drive itself was pleasant, the atmosphere inside the Lincoln was tense to put mildly. Although Gramps and Steves tried to lighten the mood with their customary jovial humour, it was obvious that the question of how they would be received by the parishioners was foremost in her mind and in the minds of her parents, silent for most of the journey. *Let's hope no one saw the Arts section this morning!*

Arriving at church, the family received the usual greetings from the regular attendees when they wished them a good morning, the Smyths, the Harringtons, the Forsyths before they entered and selected a pew mid-way up the aisle. Aunt Martha, who had arrived before them, gave a quick wave before she returned to her engrossing 'whispersation' with a group of elderly ladies seated a few rows in front, apparently all part of a damage control crusade. When she had finished, Aunt Martha joined the family with her usual air of self-assurance. Katherine had no idea what she told them, and could only hope she had helped and not hindered the situation, but the ladies smiled back at her, so perhaps they didn't read the article after all, or they knew it was a complete misunderstanding. Everything appeared normal, no one seemed to act differently towards them, except perhaps for a few across the isle who raised their eyebrows and scrutinised her a little closer than she liked. *Not so bad. Soon, they will forget about it, and this will all be past history. Perhaps we may survive the day yet!* Cheered by this hopeful sign Katherine finally began to relax and willingly prepared to face a long protracted service this Sunday as the church slowly filled. She had breathed her sigh of relief too soon. At the appointed time, Rev. Dobbson began an insufferable generic sermon on love, neighbourly friendship and respect, with specific emphasis placed on tolerance. *Criminy! Is he looking at me?* Feeling herself turn a discomfiting shade of pink, she slunk slightly in her seat under the Reverend's pastoral gaze much to Steve's amusement, who could hardly restrain himself from laughing out loud, kept only in check by their father's frosty glare. *Were all the parishioners scrutinising them*, she wondered, but too mortified to glance around and see

47

for herself. Every second felt like an oozing, syrupy stream of molasses. When will the prayers be over so we can get out of here? Finally, the service drew to a conclusion with the usual hymn and the worshippers leisurely exited the church. At the door stood Rev. Dobbson with his wife, still dressed in his colourful vestments, ready and waiting to greet his flock as they all departed.

"Good morning! Beautiful sunshine today, isn't it? How is your knee, Gregory, your rheumatism is doing better this week I hope?"

"Much better lately, knock on wood, thank you. Inspiring service as always, Reverend," Gramps offered with a twinkle in his eye, apparently amused by the sermon as much as Steves.

"Thank you! And how are you this week, Harold?"

"I am fine, thank you," he politely replied, he was not in the mood for the expected pleasantries.

"Steven! How is the genius doing at MIT?"

"Just fine. I haven't blown up their research facilities yet," he dutifully reported.

While the men talked, Mrs. Dobbson greeted the ladies.

"How wonderful you look today, Helen," Mrs. Dobbson said, admiring her peach outfit. "Is that a new dress? That shade is beautiful on you."

"Why thank you, Elena. Well, yes and no, I found it in the back of the closet with the ticket still on it from last year. I bought it near the end of last summer, but never had a chance to wear it before the autumn came."

"Ah Martha! Are you finally over your summer cold? They are the hardest to get rid of...."

As the ladies chatted briefly, the Reverend turned to Katherine.

"Good morning my dear. Congratulations on your graduation. Will you be free sometime this week? My wife and I would like to have you over for lunch."

"Er, I suppose I could come on ... Thursday afternoon ...?" she hesitated, not expecting this invitation. I don't believe this. They are planning a thorough preaching session! *Drats!*

"That will be splendid, dear. We'll see you at twelve then."

Finally, they said goodbye, and with much relief, the family could retreat to the car. Aunt Martha decided to remain behind to chat with anyone who would stay long enough to hear all her epistles on the latest doings in the parish.

☙ ❀ ❧

Safely over the first public hurdle, Katherine now had to face that evening's dinner at the Country Club, a benefit for the Wheelchair Association, which she did not look forward to. Arriving at the house, Pops and Gramps decided to go to the club to meet with their fellow golf aficionados and talk tees, greens and fairways, while her mother went to rest in the living room and watch one of her favourite movies, *Gone with the Wind*. Steves barricaded himself in his room working on a new computer program, Katherine hoped he was not trying to hack into any mainframe somewhere. With several hours finally to herself, she took her mother's advice and fixed a light afternoon snack before changing into her swimsuit to soak in the hot tub that had been installed in the conservatory. Slipping into the water, she tried to let the anxiety of the morning dissolve with the swirling currents. Her good humour returned briefly when she recalled that one rare occasion Pops decided to use the tub, and did not know that Steves had added bubble bath to the water, thinking she would be the brunt of his joke. Soap suds floated everywhere, smothering the ferns and drifting atop the large palm tree in the corner. She could not remember how they got all the suds out after that escapade, but the flabbergasted look on their father's face was priceless as he emerged exclaiming oaths and spluttering bubbles, stumbling out of the foam with arms flaying. Steve's car keys were confiscated for a week on that occasion.

This comical moment lingered in her mind until it was gradually overshadowed by the morning's events. Tonight, she would not be sheltered by a church service compelling people to stay in their seats and keep silent. Dinners were all about eating and conversing, conversations meant questions and wearying explanations. While she enjoyed spending social occasions with the family, benefits usually included dancing, and how she *hated* to dance, not the perfect ending to a trying day. She believed one did not have to swirl, skip and bob around to enjoy the music, and she always felt awkward on a dance floor as though she was the latest exhibit in the zoo, and she never understood how others could find it pleasurable. It was a puzzle why most girls were anguished with thoughts of remaining wallflowers and considered it a personal slight, on the contrary, she simply cringed when anyone politely asked her to dance and wouldn't take 'no, thank you' for an answer, assuming she was just shy. "Oh, don't worry if you can't dance, just come out and have some fun". That always made the situation worse, she could dance, but did not find it 'fun', and decorum dictated she could not declare her opinions in this instance without appearing ill mannered and reflecting badly on everyone. In the end, she was emotionally constrained against her will to comply with the request to avoid offending anyone's feelings.

Returning to her room, she decided to lounge around and try to relax with a good book before she had to brave that evening's dreaded event. She selected a novel by Jules Verne she had not read in ages, but found she could not get past the first paragraph. Her thoughts continually returned to her present dilemma, wondering what will be the outcome of this misinterpretation. Will people talk about it? Perhaps they won't. But if they do? Will they listen to me? Will this really affect Pop's board meeting on Wednesday? Perhaps the reaction at the dinner will be an indicator? Maybe they will have forgotten the article by then. If I ever meet Robert the Horrible, I shall verbally throttle him! I simply will not dance tonight, that's flat. Glancing at her bedside clock for the umpteenth time, she concluded this is surely how a condemned man must feel on death row, wishing that every minute ticking towards the inevitable could be halted, only to see the dreaded time approach ever closer with each tick. At least her situation was not that drastic, she was not facing a literal death sentence. Deciding to dress in her most conservative outfit, she hoped it may be possible to avoid drawing attention to herself tonight.... Searching through her closet, she selected a full-length white skirt and a demure dark navy satin beaded top, white medium heeled shoes and a petite white beaded evening purse. Maybe this might help? *Oh, stop borrowing trouble! Chill out!* If you keep this up, you'll need a wheelchair to get there, courtesy of the beneficiaries of the evening, now that would be rather funny, wouldn't it? Steves would enjoy that.

Finally, it was time to get ready. She could hear Pops and Gramps returning from the club and heading straight for the den, animatedly discussing John Murdock's mishap of last week, having lost a ball in the water at the ninth hole together with an exorbitant bet. Her mother had finished watching her movie, and was now on her way to change for the evening, she could also hear the water running, Steves was taking a shower. Dressing in her strategically selected attire, Katherine put on her make-up and styled her hair, clipping it behind with a white satin rose barrette. After putting only the most essential items in her dress purse, as it was too small to fit anything else, there was still time to spare and she wondered what she could do. Perhaps she should check her e-mail? Turning on her computer and waiting for the mystifying programs to boot up, she typed the necessary passwords to connect her online and access her account. Nothing arrived but an e-mail from Steves marked '*You've got to read this*'. Clicking on the mail, her screen went blank for a few moments before a graphic resembling a large sugar cube made of steel plumbing appeared with a scrolling message in electronic green;

> *'Greetings, human. I am Virus of Borg. We have analysed your defensive capabilities as being unable to withstand us. Resistance is futile. There is no escape. The programs on your hard drive shall be assimilated in ten seconds … nine seconds … eight seconds….'*

Watching the menacing countdown and panicking in the process, she hurriedly thumped on the 'Esc' key, tried hitting the reboot command of 'Alt'-'Ctrl'-'Del', and unplugged the telephone wire to discover all *was* futile. To her dismay, the screen went blank while an audio clip played a sizzling laser sound-effect. Not again! This was the fifth time Steves glitched her computer. He was constantly programming viruses just to annoy her. *She didn't need this right now!* Were her files completely wiped out? She did not worry for long, the screen popped back on:

> *'Q to the rescue, frail mortal. Your computer has been returned to its primitive state. Have a nice day.'*

Just great! He wasted his whole afternoon with this nonsense! It was difficult to live with him since the *Next Generation* series had aired. She was about to send him a scathing e-mail, but figured it was too much trouble and she did not want to add more frustration to the night. Closing down her computer, she went downstairs to the den.

"Hi, everyone. How was your afternoon?"

"Hello, Kathy. You look very pretty tonight," her father commented with a smile. "It was quite pleasant, although it was noisy there today with all the ongoing preparations."

"Indeed! It would appear they are expecting more than the usual turnout, judging from all the champagne buckets lined up like soldiers," Gramps added. "Had a hard time making it to the bar for a cup of coffee this afternoon. They should gather in a lot o' loot for the disabled tonight, I'm looking forward to the whole shebang."

"The weather has been so good lately they have erected the pavilion outside on the lawns for the occasion, and the musicians were setting up before we left," her father added.

They seemed in relative good humour, so perhaps those they met brushed the article aside. Maybe there was nothing to worry about, after all.

"I wonder what they will serve tonight?" Katherine mused.

"Oh, I don't know, the kitchen was hopping, you can be sure of that," Gramps replied. "There was enough clattering and clanging to wake the dead. I hope they fix something with a little spice in it tonight." Pops shook his head.

"I wish I could share in your expectations, but not with my ulcer. It just stopped acting up, and I don't want to upset it again."

"Nonsense! Hot chillies are the best thing for you. Why, I followed the doctors' advice for years, eating toast and drinking milk, seizing up in agony before the latest drugs came on the market. Ulcers hate diary products, try chillies, worked for me," Gramps advised. "Try not getting so stressed out all the time, that would help too. Take time to smell the roses more often, will you?"

"Perhaps if I plant them in the office," Pops returned with a smile. "There's always a mountain of work to get through."

"Well, I'll go watch TV and wait," Katherine replied.

"All right, dear. Perhaps we should go and get ready."

Pops and Gramps went upstairs to change into their tuxedos while Katherine sauntered into the living room and turned on the 'idiot box' as Gramps called it, surfing the channels, searching for something of interest. *Sports, sports, sports, commercials, foreign channel, news, commercials, sports, news ... aha, movie channel ... swearing, blood and guts. Yuck. Any good movie anywhere?* She spent more time thumbing through the numbers with the remote than watching a program. Since satellite TV was introduced with all the additional subscription channels, there seemed to be less to watch, or perhaps the wide variety made it more difficult to settle on anything, Katherine could not determine which at that moment. She could put on a video, but there was not enough time to finish a tape. Turning off the TV was not as frustrating as stopping a video mid-way. Aha! A documentary channel. She settled in to watch an engrossing study of the ancient Egyptians while she waited. Unfortunately, she missed most of it, having switched to the program near the conclusion. She was not certain if she would enjoy the next show, the *Life and Philosophy of Socrates and Plato*, but found she was mistaken. Always repelled by the dry word 'philosophy' and assuming it was reserved for the academically adept, she had never read much on the ancient classics apart from Greek and Roman myths, and had no idea how fascinating their life and times actually were. *I wonder if there is anything in our library about them? I'll look into it when we get home,* she decided.

"Is everybody ready?" her mother asked as she entered the room,

"Did anyone see Steven? He said he was coming tonight." Mom looked beautiful in her aquamarine silk dress, with matching evening purse and high-heeled shoes.

"Maybe he's avoiding me," Katherine replied. "He sent me another virus and I thought my hard-drive was fried again. He is so *frustrating*! I didn't hear Pops and Gramps come down yet, but they should be ready soon."

"Watching anything interesting?"

"A documentary about Socrates and Plato, I had no idea how advanced their ideas were back then. Isn't it strange if we look back to other times, like that of ancient Greece, we see these people as primitive? Almost cavemen-like. Of course, the ancient Greeks didn't have all the technology we have now, but their philosophy was intense."

"Their mathematics and building skills were equally remarkable," Steves replied as he entered dressed in his tuxedo. "They had the rudiments of geometry and architecture down to a fine science."

"Oh, I don't want to talk to you," Katherine replied irritated. "Your little stunt today gave me quite a start. I've had just about enough of your game-playing! *Stop* going into my room, and *stop* messing around with my computer!"

"Touchy, touchy, sis."

"Steven, we all have had quite enough of your pranks. I *do* wish you would grow up and act more responsibly," their mother replied with maternal authority, "Kathy has had a trying time, and your idea of amusement only makes it worse. Now, I don't want this to go any further tonight and upset your father, you know he is under enough pressure as it is lately without your stunts disturbing the whole household. Now, be on your best behaviour tonight."

"Geeze, everyone is so uptight around here! No need to go all manic," he replied disgruntled. "I thought an invasion from the Borg might cheer Kats up, she was looking so depressed this morning."

"And do stop calling your sister 'Kats', she is not a feline!"

"Okay, okay, Mom. No more tirades, all right?"

Pops and Gramps came down and they prepared to leave for the Club.

Gramps was right, the Club was expecting more than the usual number of guests, and the chefs could be heard flurrying in the background in their effort to surpass their usual Sunday night menu, judging from the enticing aroma that wafted from the kitchens. Katherine was almost glad she went, it looked as though all would not turn out as horrible as she had expected. Uncle Tim and Aunt Barbara were there already, and so was Aunt Martha. She wished her cousins had come, she did not feel like talking to Steves yet, and Charlie and his parents were absent, but a few of her acquaintances from high school had come with their families. Good! Although they had lost touch, she knew she would not be left adrift in a sea of 'elders' who were more interested in business, economic reports, and who had the latest tummy-tuck. At the same time, she knew she could not escape the preliminary greetings and conversations that always occurred in the main reception areas with a round of cocktails accompanied by live piano music before everyone was seated at their tables. Aunt Martha linked her by the arm and pulled her over to meet a few of her friends, the same ladies she saw at church that morning.

"Kathy! You remember Dorris and Ester? You met them at the Bridge Club luncheon not too long ago."

"Oh, yes, of course. How are you?"

"We are just fine dear," Dorris replied collectively for them, "we read the report in the paper. Wasn't that just dreadful, Ester?"

"Yes, truly terrible. I wouldn't take it too seriously, however. I don't think anyone pays much attention to what that critic says. Don't you remember his opinions on Mount Rushmore, Dorris?"

"No, I can't recall..."

"That it was large-scale environmental vandalism and a crass exemplification of our nation's political hubris," Ester informed her.

"You don't say...! Imagine that! What nerve to debase one of our national monuments! One would wonder what he had to say about the Statue of Liberty. Now, there you are, Kathy. No one will believe him after a statement like that," Aunt Martha concluded smugly.

"No, but I wish he wouldn't write such trash, everyone still reads it. It creates many problems," Katherine replied. "If only people had seen a picture of my painting and could judge for themselves."

"Never mind, dear," Ester responded, "this will all blow over pretty soon. Enjoy the party."

Nodding in agreement, she waited for an opportune moment in the conversation to politely break away and seek out the company of her peers, who were relieved to see her too, wishing they could be anywhere but there. At least they could be consoled that the dinner was for a good cause. After catching up on the latest news, they slowly sauntered over to examine the items donated for the auction to be held later that evening ranging from a three week first-class cruise for two in the Bahamas, first-class vacations in Europe, full year memberships at elite beauty clinics in New York, to crystal sets, and various pieces of collectable porcelain. The famous artist, Alan Hanley, had also donated a sculpture for the event that the committee expected to fetch a tidy sum.

Katherine considered putting a bid on one of the trips to Europe, but her forthcoming trip to Paris and her plans for the future would make further travel impossible for the present. The thought of being poked, lathered, prodded and massaged in a beauty clinic would be repulsive, and she needed another porcelain piece sitting around like the sky needed more stars. Nor did Hanley's piece attract her, a strange sandstone projectile of curves, globules and spirals that only confirmed her aversion to modern art. Auctions for charities were certainly peculiar, she noted. At least anyone who bid for the vacations or the memberships at the beauty spas would have something to enjoy or use after paying triple their value to egotistically display their extravagant generosity to their fellow club members. The other items and *objets d'art*, which no one would dream of buying for themselves, would most likely be doomed to White Elephant Limbo, destined to become temporary adoptions gathering dust in some obscure corner or closet shelf until the next wedding, Christmas, or charitable event. She had a presentiment she would meet several of these articles again in the future. It would be easier to give a donation Katherine thought, but then, absurdity always prevailed.

Time for the guests to be seated in the lavishly decorated banquet room with round tables set for twelve. Katherine wished her cousins could have come for the dinner. If the extended family were there, they could fill a table, except, of course, for the one extra seat, which usually remained empty as 'solitaires' rarely came to these affairs, allowing the family to engage in more personal conversations ranging from personal news to anecdotes and the usual monologues, repetitive reminiscences of times past from the older generation. Tonight, however, there were four seats available, meaning other guests would be seated with them. It was not that she was antisocial, but just this one night, she wished to be spared making a myriad of introductions, annoying small talk and vague generalities. As it happened, Ester and Dorris happily joined their table, and a retired couple, a Mr. and Mrs. Williams who made their fortune on Wall Street and continued to dabble in stocks and bonds. There was the usual round of polite pleasantries with the Williams and the questioning begins. *You just graduated from Belvedere, how wonderful! Congratulations! What was your major? Who is your favourite artist? What are your plans now?* Questions that she was getting tired of answering for they were becoming repetitive. Hearing she entertained plans to open a gallery of her own someday, the conversation took an unexpected turn, which she found to be irritating, but amusing.

"How interesting," Mrs. Williams replied. "I do hope you patronize artists for your gallery who actually paint something worth hanging up, and avoid those extremists who will do anything to make a name for themselves, like Mr. Horace described in his column. Did you read about the Sirrac entries this year? Especially the last one, now that *was* irreligious. Do you know the student who painted that?"

Apparently, Mrs. Williams did not make the connection between the Walsinghams seated at the table and the artist mentioned in the paper, or perhaps she paid no attention to the name that was mentioned. The table went uncomfortably quiet, and Aunt Martha was only too ready to jump in and correct this misunderstanding, but Katherine, now weary of having the column brought up everywhere she went, could not resist the opportunity and beat her to the punch. *It's time to have some fun with this.*

"Oh yes, I know the artist very well, in fact. But Mr. Horace misreported the symbolism of the painting."

"Indeed! I wonder why Robert Horace would lie like that?"

"Oh, he didn't lie, he just interpreted it according to his ideas, without asking the artist. I can confirm that the painting has been misrepresented."

Steves, who was dour after the reprimand he received at home, suddenly perked up and took a roguish interest in the conversation.

"She's telling the truth, Mrs. Williams. I've seen the painting myself. Robert Horace went a little overboard," he replied with a twinkle in his eye. "I've known the artist a long time, and she wouldn't have painted anything like that, at least not on purpose."

"That's true. In fact, I think I shall try and include her future works in my gallery whenever I open it … ."

"That's a good idea, sis. After Robert Horace's article, she will need the patronage."

"Honestly, you two," Aunt Martha interjected, cutting their fun short, "our Katherine painted it."

"I confess. Actually, my work was a general satire on the destructive tendencies of our modern age. It has absolutely nothing to do with the pope or Hitler."

"Well, I am relieved to hear that," Mr. Williams replied approvingly.

Oblivious to Katherine's practical joke and thoroughly pleased to be talking with an artist honourably mentioned by the Sirrac gallery, Mrs. Williams continued;

"Can you describe your painting?"

The ice finally thawing, everyone is getting engaged in the usual dinner chatter, while Katherine launches into a description of her misunderstood masterpiece. I suppose tackling this problem head-on is the best way, she thought. I just hope I won't have to explain this Horace fiasco for the rest of my life.

Unexpectedly the dinner was turning out rather pleasant, even Aunt Martha was on her best behaviour, refraining from publicly listing her various medical complaints and minor ailments that prevented her from selecting certain items from a menu. The food was delectable as always for these grand events, however, with all the dainty *haute cuisine* servings delicately positioned in the centre of enormous platters with a slight suggestion of sauce, in addition to the uninterrupted conversations that ensured no one would be allowed to eat, she knew she would be going home just as hungry as she came and would need sustenance before she went to bed, inevitably a peanut butter and jelly sandwich with a glass of milk. After dessert, the auction began and the White Elephants were auctioned off first before the more enticing vacations and spa memberships were presented, the finale of the auction was, as expected, Hanley's artistic indistinguishable deformity, which sold for an exorbitant sum. There was obviously an enthusiastic admirer in the building Katherine thought, or perhaps it will be presented as a donation to some unsuspecting institute.

The auction concluded and the live music commenced in the pavilion outside, indicating the dance was starting. It was a lavish setting with a burgundy and pale pink striped marquee, the band formally dressed in bow tie and satin lapels, and a bar with a champagne fountain set up with all the usual fanfare for the guests.

"Pops, are we staying much longer?" Katherine asked, hoping they were not heading towards the gleaming dance floor.

"No, dear. Just long enough to mill around and have a brandied coffee in the Captain's Lounge."

Gramps thought it was a capital idea, while Mom and the other ladies preferred to have an after dinner grenadine. Steves, however, decided to meet with the younger crowd who were gathering outside.

"Kathy dear, why don't you go out with Steven to the pavilion?" her mother suggested. "If you would like to dance, we will wait until you are ready to leave."

"That's all right, Mom. I don't feel like dancing, and would prefer to have a Shirley Temple."

Making their way to the Captain's Lounge, they ordered their drinks. While Gramps, her parents and Uncle Tim were detained by a group at the bar who wanted to chitchat, Katherine went with her aunts to stand guard over a couple of tables and chairs before they were all taken. Katherine hardly placed her glass on the coaster before a young man named James, whom she recognised from the tennis courts, approached her politely.

"Katherine, would you like to dance?"

Katherine turned and graciously thanked him, but very politely refused.

"Oh, now Kathy, you should go and dance with your friends, listen to the music, and have a little fun. Don't feel you have to stay with us," Aunt Martha interjected. "You should enjoy your young years while you have them, believe me, they don't last long."

Katherine glanced at James, who had a slightly embarrassed look on his face, for he had no idea at that moment what he should say or do next. Katherine felt uncomfortable, and as usual, capitulated to Aunt Martha's suggestion, feeling obliged to save the moment. The dance floor was already crowded with young and old, resulting with more bumping and jostling than graceful dance manoeuvres, and the band was too loud, causing her to wince every time James led her too close to the bandstand when they could actually move through the seething throng, all the time graciously trying to smile and pretend she was enjoying herself for James' sake. *How I wish everyone would stop trying to decide what is fun for me! When will they get it into their heads that what they consider a pleasure I do not, telling me what I should like, what I should do, and who I should be with. I am so tired of people's false ideas of being helpful!* Aunt Martha would do well to let me decide what I wish to do for myself. Whatever happened to live and let live? When the musical number had finally concluded she graciously thanked James, using her abandoned Shirley Temple and her growing thirst as a pretext to return to the Captain's Lounge, now thoroughly vexed.

"There now," Aunt Martha piped up with an exultant beam on her face, "didn't you enjoy that?"

"No, not really," Katherine replied, finally revealing her irritation, albeit as courteously as possible, "I don't like to dance, but I may still enjoy the music, I can hear it fine from here, and that is close enough, my ears can't tolerate loud noise."

Katherine was not exaggerating her last point, for her ears were sensitive, and it remained an enigma to her why large bands, especially jazz or brass ensembles, insisted on using colossal amplifiers when they were already deafening without them. The worst torment occurred when someone inadvertently disturbed a microphone by brushing against it or playing into it too loud, sending out an electronic tsunami of shrieking sound waves in the process that pierced her inner ear and vibrated against her eardrums with nerve-wrenching velocity.

"Well, I tried," Aunt Martha replied resignedly, she had done her best to ensure her niece was having a good time, before shaking her head and murmuring about the youth of the day to Aunt Barbara, unable to comprehend why they could not enjoy the same pastimes her generation did.

Relieved she had escaped the dance floor, Katherine finished her watered-down Shirley Temple, which by then had diluted with the thawing ice. True to Pop's word, they did not stay too long after their coffee. Steves was also glad to be leaving, finding the last of the evening to be a thorough bore with the antiquated music and all the watchful eyes of the adults upon them, parties at the college Frat houses were certainly more 'bad-ass' fun in his estimation.

Getting ready for bed, her grumbling stomach informed her she had not eaten enough to keep body and soul together, and as she predicted, headed to the kitchen dressed in her comfy robe and slippers, rummaging for the simple ingredients of peanut butter and jelly to make young America's favourite sandwich and poured a glass of milk. She was not down long before she was joined by Gramps in his night attire, who favoured a turkey roll with cranberry jelly, followed shortly thereafter by Pops who hunted through the refrigerator for the roast beef cooked the night before. Mom came to see what the ruckus was, and Steves soon joined the raid. Sometimes, the simple things are more fun and meaningful than all the banquets in the world, Katherine thought as they sat around the kitchen table tucking into their midnight nibbles and sharing their experiences of that evening interspersed with Steve's droll comments before finally turning in for the night.

⁊❀⁊

Katherine rose earlier than usual the next morning before everyone else got up. Monday was housekeeping day, and she wanted to be dressed, fed and out before the team of cleaners from the maintenance company overran the house as though they owned it. Monday truly was a manic day, it was difficult to do anything, either sitting or standing as the uniformed troopers rushed through with their vacuums, dusters and polishers under the vigilance of Mrs. Gonzales and her niece, who made sure they did not break the china, chip the crystal, scrimp on the detergents and waxes, scratch the antique furniture in the parlours, filch the silver, avoid polishing the brasses, or swept anything under the carpets and missed the corners behind the doors. On Monday, everyone felt 'in the way' or underfoot, even their bedrooms were not off limits to the invaders, and the noise and bustle so distracting — it was easier to leave the premises. Pops usually escaped by heading off to work early, Gramps disappeared to the golf club, and Mom vacated to her bridge gathering in town. Now that they were out of college, Steves went to the labs while she could hide away in her studio across the driveway.

This Monday, Katherine did not feel like painting. The disagreeable experience of the Sunday paper still weighed heavily on her mind, not to mention Wednesday's upcoming board meeting and the luncheon at the rectory the following day. Grabbing a bowl of cereal while the espresso machine churned away, and heating up a package of chocolate Pop Tarts in the toaster, utterly disregarding the unhealthy nature of her sugary repast, she considered what she might do for the day. She thought of starting out on her fact-finding mission, that is, scouting the various art museums and galleries for inspiration, but that did not appeal to her. She needed a break from art for a few days, the idea had not completely sunk in yet that she was *free*, those student days attending an educational institution were over, having to worry about fulfilling credit requirements for each semester and stressed out over homework and exams. Entering the art and business world would create its own demands in the future, and she figured she should enjoy some time not directly connected with her chosen career.

Perhaps she could just take it easy and settle down with a book for the day? Her mind thought of the Jules Verne novel she started to read, but then remembered her promise to look into the works of Socrates and Plato. She almost decided this sounded too educational for a day of complete recreation and nearly dropped the idea, but something reminded her not to judge the proverbial cover at least. Finishing her cereal and coffee, and placing her Pop Tarts on a plate, she went to the library only to be confronted by that now infamous painting, which was left exactly as Charlie had positioned it, leaning against one of the mahogany bookshelves next to the marble fireplace facing the doorway. Imagine all the trouble that created, simply because I wanted to depict the sad truth of our modern days, she thought as she placed her plate on the table. Katherine considered throwing the source of her latest troubles on top of the next bonfire the gardeners would light when they disposed of the mountain of leafy refuse Oak Meadows produced each autumn, and yet, she still could not think of how she would have painted *Le Sacre d'ingéniosité Humaine* different if given the opportunity to do it over again. It would be terribly wrong to depict a utopian setting, a monstrous pretence, a visual lie that all was right with the world when obviously it was not, and had not been for a very long time, if ever.

Returning to the project at hand, she walked over to the bookshelves and began to examine the rows of vertical leather-bound spines all neatly aligned like sentinels. There were books of all sizes, descriptions and colours, small pocket editions, slab-sized historical books, poetry, law books, encyclopaedias, medical books, novels, a number of recognised classics, Dickens, Hugo, Goethe, Steinbeck, Hemmingway, but she could not find anything related to her current project other than general chronicles and anthologies of Greek and Roman history and mythology. Perhaps she would do better in a public library that had catalogues rather than this vague browsing? Having reached the lower shelves, she moved her picture aside to examine the last rows and discovered hidden behind her canvas an extensive set of maroon hardback books with gold lettering and scroll decorations, featuring its own index in a separate volume. *At last! Maybe there is something here?* She found that Volume Two of the series contained a selection of Plato's works describing the trial and undeserved execution of Socrates. Taking out the desired volume, she glanced at the elegant cover adorned with a gold escutcheon surrounded by filigree patterns. In the centre of the shield were three open books each displaying a word, VE, RI and TAS. '*I wonder what they mean?*', Katherine thought, until she realized that when combined, they sounded very close to the French word *vérité*. Now that *is* interesting, she concluded.

Taking the book and her plate of goodies over to the window, she settled into one of the oxblood leather wingchairs to finish her breakfast before it went cold. The tome in one hand and balancing her chocolate pastry in the other, with difficulty she opened the first page of the *Apology of Socrates*. The title confused her, for what did *he* have to be sorry about? Recalling the documentary she watched the previous day, his accusers should be making the apologies. Perplexed by this conundrum, she placed the book on the side table and headed for the dictionary to find if the word 'apology' had been used incorrectly. Might as well clear this matter up before I start, can't stand ambiguities! Thumbing through the 'As', she found that the word originated from Greek and actually translated as a speech made in one's own defence. Enlightened by this discovery, she returned to her seat, resuming her balancing act between book and breakfast.

Katherine had no idea that a trial dating well over two thousand years could be engrossing as any courtroom drama, or anything Hollywood could produce. As far as she could discern, Socrates was brought before the judges and citizens of Athens on charges of misleading the youth and teaching them atheism, which obviously was a horrific crime against the State, and merited him the death penalty according to the documentary on television. Socrates began his defence by declaring his innocence, that his accusers had dragged him to the court with their malicious lies, further adding while he was over seventy years, this was his first appearance in a court of law, requesting they excuse his inexperience with the formalities of oration expected in legal proceedings. That's interesting, Katherine noted. If he truly was a public menace of the first magnitude, surely they would have brought him to court before then? He couldn't have become an atheist overnight. Obviously, something rotten was smelling in Athens. Socrates then declared that the accusations made against him could be classified into two categories; slander spoken against him in times past, and falsehoods now put forward by his latest adversaries. He announced he would tackle the old lies first as they frightened him the most, because they not only poisoned the minds of his present accusers and witnesses when they were yet children, these old accusers were unknown to him, preventing him from currently questioning them and pointing out the error of their accusations. That is a predicament, Katherine mused, to be dogged by lies and malicious accusations your whole life, and not be able to challenge or refute them, causing the next generations to perpetually condemn you without due process. That would be a living death!

Socrates began by reviewing the one charge that his enemies continually accused him of, that he was an evil-doer who dared to seek knowledge about the hidden workings of the earth and the heavens, and taught the 'worst' doctrines and not the 'better' ones to the youth of Athens. Katherine puzzled over this statement, until she deduced he was accused of contradicting the ancient beliefs relating Creation as understood by the Greeks at that time, the 'better' teachings, replacing them with a new doctrine that discredited their deities, which they considered the 'worst' doctrines. *Now that's a switch!* Those who do believe that a Divine Being created the universe are open to ridicule today, Katherine wryly noted. Socrates declared he had nothing to do with this alleged intellectual probing into the workings of nature, and had witnesses present in court ready to vouch for him.

The next accusation Socrates tackled; that he considered and professed himself to be a wise teacher and charged for his services. Socrates denied this puerile report, declaring he was not a teacher, nor was he paid, further demonstrating the stupidity of this falsehood with an example that questioned why he should be singled out for this 'offence', when others, who claimed to be teachers and received payment, were not apprehended by the authorities. They also requested very little in return for their services and extensive expertise since they alleged to be knowledgeable in divine matters of virtue and ethics, and in the philosophical and political fields, knowledge that Socrates claimed he did not possess. Well, he was right, surely they would expect a teacher to be paid, Katherine thought. However, his claim that he was not a teacher, nor a wise man, struck her as peculiar. Why did he say this? To this day, he is recognised to be one of the most influential philosophers in Western civilisation. She continued reading.

Socrates finally addressed the cause for all these accusations, that he had made many enemies who were determined to destroy him. The oldest motive in the world, Katherine reflected, nothing has changed in over two thousand years. That is disturbing. Why men hated him was indeed curious. Socrates admitted he inadvertently made adversaries when he endeavoured to refute the reputation of his alleged wisdom, further declaring he *did* possess a certain wisdom that could be attained by any man, yet lacked complete superhuman wisdom. That's a bit confusing, Katherine observed, and hoped Socrates would clarify his point.

According to the *Apology*, his troubles began when an impetuous friend went to the famous shrine of the sun god Apollo at Delphi and inquisitively asked the pythian oracle to reveal if there was anyone wiser than Socrates and was informed there was no one wiser than he. When he heard this report from the prophetic shrine, Socrates was confused for he did not believe he possessed this great wisdom the god had declared, and yet, he was convinced the god would not lie, therefore, he decided to travel and question individuals from every stratum of society to find someone wiser than he. Katherine brushed some crumbs from the side of her mouth. He wanted to prove the oracle wrong … wouldn't that be trying to call Apollo a liar? She knew that Apollo did not exist, but Athenians believed in the power of that famous oracle. She was curious to find out the results of his travels.

The first person he talked to was credited with wisdom, and a politician to boot. Katherine found this first examination amusing, for Socrates declared the man was not as wise as others thought, "I am better off then he is—for he knows nothing, and thinks that he knows. I neither know nor think that I know." Socrates deduced he had the advantage in this instance when compared with the politician, and trying to demonstrate his error and enlighten him, had made an enemy. No wonder Katherine thought, a man doesn't like to have his ego popped, especially when he prides himself on his sagacity, and then to be proved wrong by a man who claims he doesn't know anything. I wish I knew the questions he posed to *him.*

Socrates then examined a philosopher who had a reputation for wisdom, but was also found wanting, with the result he acquired another adversary. He questioned the poets, the artisans, everyone he met, but found similar results, and each time gained new enemies. Socrates then realized the oracle had spoken the truth, but not in the context people assumed, for he continually admitted he had no wisdom. He finally concluded that the true 'wisdom' he possessed was the knowledge that only gods were wise, leading him to interpret the oracle's statement accordingly. He could not find anyone wiser than himself because they all prided themselves on their knowledge and placed themselves higher than the gods. Socrates declared the god had used his travels and questioning to display that mankind's wisdom was worth little or nothing. So, that's what he meant when he said he had the wisdom that man could acquire! From that time onward, Socrates believed it was his sacred duty to spread the truth of this oracle, and his devotion to Apollo caused him to endure great poverty, to travel the country and demonstrate to people the true value of their pretended wisdom when only the gods were wise.

Now that was deep. Katherine thought about this for a moment, and could appreciate the logic of this argument. Could mankind declare it was truly wise? Did man know everything on earth, or would he ever? Certainly not! The more one learns, the more one realizes there is still much to discover, she concluded. How often she browsed through the library at the collge and mused it would take more than a hundred lifetimes to read every book there, indeed, the world was filled with books she would never see. With the little knowledge mankind does possess, we certainly do make a mess of things. Socrates was giving everyone lessons in humility, and no one wants to be humbled when they think they are correct. They may also have been jealous and covetous, misunderstanding his use of the word 'wisdom', thinking he was bragging that he possessed the *intellectual* skill he found wanting in *them.* He wounded their pride and they wished to be rid of him, levelling countless accusations against him.

Socrates then addressed the new allegations brought against him by three accusers led by a certain man named Meletus. He began by debunking the claim he was an evildoer who corrupted the morals of the youth by showing that Meletus had no real interest in this issue, proving the charge had been trumped up against him and questioned Meletus on this point. Since he seemed concerned with the ethical improvement of their young citizens, who did *he* believe was able to fulfil this important duty? Meletus was struck silent, not expecting the question, and did not reply. Socrates prodded Meletus further, and received the answer that the laws of the state improved them, which did not answer his question as he asked for an individual who could fulfil this task. Aha! He's evading the issue, Katherine noted, besides, laws by themselves can't 'improve' anyone. Socrates continued his examination, if that is your answer, who then has knowledge of the laws? Meletus declared the judges present know them. Do the judges then instruct and improve the young? Meletus replied that they do, but then, Socrates dropped the million-dollar question — *all* of the judges, or just a few? Meletus replied that all of them did. Well, that *would* be a miracle, Katherine wryly noted, recalling all the scandals she heard on the news concerning the judicial system of modern times. Socrates honed in on this absurdity. There must be a myriad of improvers! What of the audience present, and the Senators and the ecclesiasts, do they all improve the youth? They all improve them, Meletus dumbly answered. I am the only corrupter? That is what I affirm, was the lame reply. Socrates then drove his point home. Would you say the same about horses, for another example? Can one person only do them infinite harm, while the rest of the world can accomplish everything for their good? Rather the opposite is the case, a few have the skill to train and handle a horse without injuring it, while everyone else in the wide world may harm it. "Happy indeed would be the condition of youth if they had one corrupter only, and all the rest of the world were their improvers." Why, Socrates is beating them down with pure logic. Good for him! He certainly made this Meletus creep look ridiculous.

Katherine was about to find out how Socrates, using his deductive reasoning *ala* Sherlock, set out to discredit the charge that he intentionally planned to destroy the youth of Athens, when she heard steps descending the stairs and proceeding to the kitchen. Picking up her empty plate and leaving the book in her seat, she went to see who had come down. She found Gramps neatly dressed in casual shirt and slacks, preparing a bowl of corn flakes and a cup of cappuccino, and obviously not looking forward to his banal breakfast.

"What? No eggs and bacon for you today? No pancakes soaked in butter and maple syrup?"

"Hello, Katie. Nope, I'm afraid not. I nearly forgot about my doctor's appointment this morning, I'd better abstain from the cholesterol bombs."

"You never told us. Obviously you were planning not to go, and then thought better of it," Katherine replied with a chuckle.

Gramps detested going for his medical check-ups, nor could she blame him with the poking, prodding, needles and the dreaded diet sheets, *thou shalt not eat this, thou shalt not eat that....* "I've got to die of something someday," he always declared, "and a good meal seems the happiest way to go."

"So, you've caught me! Okay, you know how I hate physicals."

"You know, Gramps, one bowl of cereal will not make up for all the previous days of gastronomic delights," she replied, "you cannot fool the doctors or science."

"Nor the scales," he returned with an amused 'Hurmph!'. "I know the Doc will only be too eager to tell me I've not reached my target weight loss. More exercise. Less food. Less *good* tasting food."

"I guess Garfield the cat was right," Katherine thought out loud.

"About what, Katie?"

"That a diet was nothing but 'die' with a 'T' stuck on the end."

"Funny, but true. He may have something there," Gramps noted as he chopped at his cereal with the spoon, sinking it into the frigid milk. "So, made any plans for the day?"

"I was thinking maybe a dose of 'R and R', I'm not in the mood for painting, or traipsing around the art museums just yet. I won't be doing anything special today, do you want me to drive you to the clinic? He might give you a shot and you could be left woozy for the day, or something like that."

"No, that's okay, pet. I don't think I'm in for any jabs. You enjoy your free time."

"That's okay. Look, I found an interesting book in the library and planned to bury my nose in it, I could bring it with me and read it while I wait for you."

"Well, if you really want to, I wouldn't say 'no' to the comfort of your company."

"That's settled then. When's the appointment?"

"Eight thirty, I avoid making afternoon appointments. Dr. Hendricks is always late after lunch, or he decides not to come back for the day, the fairways are more inviting than looking at tonsils and waxy ears, no doubt. Better to catch him on the hop in the morning."

"Okay, that doesn't give us too much time. I'll go get my purse and book."

As she left the kitchen, the grandfather clock in the front hall began to chime the half hour, seven thirty to be exact. Mrs. Gonzales and her niece promptly appeared, entering the kitchen from the housekeeper's apartment, ready to cook breakfast for those who wanted it, and tackle the maintenance invaders when they arrived at nine.

"Good morning Miss Kathy," Mrs. Gonzales said as she came through the door. "Aren't you having any breakfast?"

"Hello, Mrs. Gonzales, good morning, Juanita. Yes, I mean, I've already had mine, and so has Gramps." Katherine then took her aside, lowering her voice and casting a quick glance over in his direction, hoping he would not overhear her as he glumly crunched his flakes. "He's trying to be good today, so please help him to keep his resolution, don't let him break down and raid the frying pan."

"Oh, so it's a doctor-day, is it?" she smiled.

"Yes, I am afraid so. I'm driving him over, so I have to get ready. I think I can hear Pops and Mom stirring, they should be down soon, I have no idea about Steves."

"How was the dinner last night?" Juanita was dying to know.

"Oh, it was so-so, and we all came home famished as usual. I'm sorry about all the dirty dishes we left for you this morning, we were so tired last night, we just dumped them in the sink. I promise I'll make it up to you, I'll do the dishes tonight."

"Don't worry about that, Miss Kathy. By the way, did anyone mention the painting last night?"

"They sure did, but thankfully it wasn't as bad as I expected. You know, I am sorry that Horace the Horrible wrote what he did, I didn't intend an interpretation like that ... ."

"Of course you didn't, I've seen the painting. It's very good, I'm sure he was jealous he couldn't paint it himself. Don't worry, news like that will not be remembered for long, it is only as good as the next day's newspaper."

"I guess you're right. That reminds me, the painting is still in the library. Could you make sure the cleaners don't punch a hole in it or anything? I won't have time to take it out to the studio before I leave with Gramps."

"I'll watch them," Juanita replied.

"Thanks! I'd better go, I'll see you later."

"All right, see you later."

Katherine quickly went upstairs to her room, grabbed her purse and ran down to the library for her book. She joined Gramps in the kitchen, still eyeing the carton of eggs and the package of bacon Mrs. Gonzales laid out on the counter.

"Oh no you don't, Gramps!"

"No, what?" Steves replied as he entered behind her, stifling a yawn.

"No greasy stuff, we're heading to the clinic this morning," Gramps grumbled.

"Well, that sounds better than my job today, staring at bacteria and fungi in Petri dishes," Steves replied.

"Not if you're the one getting peered at," Gramps returned. "Well, I guess we should get going."

As Katherine and Gramps were leaving the kitchen, they met her parents coming down the stairs.

"Good morning, where are you off to?" Pops inquired.

"'Morning, I'm off for my regular physical at the clinic, Katie is driving me over. Now don't look so worried, it's just the usual old stuff, I didn't want to bother anyone with talk of pills and ills," Gramps replied, noticing the concerned look on their faces.

"Good morning, I don't know how long we'll be, or if we'll do anything later. Must stay out of the way today, you know."

"All right, Kathy dear. Drive carefully now," her mother advised.

"I will. See you later."

They decided to take Katherine's car, and she turned on the heat as the morning was still chilly. It was nice to be able to chat and spend time alone with Gramps. He took her book down from the dashboard, put on his spectacles, and browsed through the cream-coloured pages.

"Hmm, so this will keep you occupied while I'm under medical scrutiny. Well, well! I haven't looked at this in years," he said, pausing at a page and laughing quietly to himself. "There's quick thinking for you."

"What is?" Katherine was curious to know.

"Listen to this; *When a youth was giving himself airs in the Theatre and saying, I am wise, for I have conversed with many wise men, Epicteus replied, I too have conversed with many rich men, yet I am not rich!*"

"That's funny, but true. He means talk is cheap, right Gramps? Who is this Epicetus?" Katherine enquired, "I've only just started the first part of the book on Socrates."

"Ah, good old Socrates, now *there* was a great mind for you. Epicteus was another Greek philosopher. I didn't know you were interested in philosophy, Katie."

"I didn't either until I saw a documentary yesterday. You know, from what I've read so far, it seems to me that Socrates got into trouble simply because he tried to get people to think. It would appear no one wanted to face reality back then, and it seems people haven't changed much in the last two millennia, I'm beginning to understand why my painting was misconstrued. Perhaps I should just stick to painting lush fields teeming with buttercups and daisies, it might be a lot safer," she mused aloud.

"What, and follow the path of least resistance?" Gramps retorted. "You have a keen sense of integrity, and you wouldn't be able to keep that hackneyed style of art up for long, stifling your originality. Sure, you could sell many pretty pictures, but that's not like you, Katie. Anyone could do that, paint images of pipe dreams seen through rose-rimmed glasses. They've even got machines nowadays that spit those works out for the mass market."

"That's true," she conceded, "but look at the trouble my first newsworthy picture has caused. I wonder if I can go through that over and over again, I mean, people constantly misreading what I depict."

"Hmm, I have an answer for you there, or rather, Socrates does if I recall the *Crito* correctly, let me see... ."

"*The Crito*? I didn't come to it yet. What's that?"

"Socrates' last private conversation with his friend, Crito. It occurred while he awaited the day of his execution."

"That must have been a heavy conversation," she replied.

"It is profound, but wait until you get to the *Phædo*, his death-bed disputation. Ah, just what I was looking for...yep, fits the bill here. Crito visits Socrates and entreats him to escape, but he refuses. Crito then worries about his own reputation, if he doesn't help his friend to flee, many people would think he cared more for his money and refused to pay a bribe to aid Socrates' escape, not to mention Crito was also using a little emotional blackmail to encourage him to take his advice. Socrates replied he should not let thoughts like this upset him and that he should not worry about the judgements of the populace, for a few good people would see the matter clearly and their opinions were the ones worth any consideration."

"What you are saying is, if I know I'm right, I should not worry about what people think."

"Correct! There will be those who understand your work, so don't worry. Just paint the truth."

Just then, they pulled up outside the clinic. Although she was not the one with the appointment, her stomach flipped as they stepped into the reception area. She immediately sympathised with poor Gramps, it did not matter how elaborate the medical office was decorated, the tables laden with the latest periodicals and reading lamps, comfy armchairs, floral arrangements and aquariums, there was always that faint antiseptic smell and therapeutic atmosphere that suggested images of lab coats, tongue depressors, stethoscopes, needles and nervousness, not to mention the general apprehension of the patients seated in the waiting room.

The receptionist at the clinic was not a welcoming sight, a grim-faced buxom woman with black hair pulled back into a bun so tight it appeared she just had her eyes done at the cosmetic branch of their establishment. Perhaps she was best suited for this job Katherine thought, considering all the disgruntled patients she had to deal with when appointments were unavoidably delayed or cancelled without warning.

"Good morning, Mildred. I'm here for my eight-thirty appointment with Dr. Hendricks."

"Hello, Mr. Walsingham," she replied, looking through her computer files, hardly cracking a smile, "Dr. Hendricks should be here soon. You'll need to fill out these forms while you wait," she declared as she handed him a clipboard with the necessary documents. "Please, take a seat."

They settled into a set of armchairs in a corner and made themselves generally comfortable. While Gramps took out his spectacles and began to fill in numerous little boxes, Katherine glanced around the room and surveyed her surroundings. At that early hour, the office was not too busy, a few people with an obvious case of the flu had come to obtain prescriptions for antibiotics. She cringed inside as she heard the odd cough, snort and splutter, and wished that the windows were open to allow fresh air into the room. Instead, the ventilation system was working full speed ahead recycling the contaminated air already there. In conditions like this, one could go home with a few more ailments than they bargained for.

Katherine tried to ignore the situation and picked up a copy of the latest fashion magazine lying on the table beside her. Looking through the pictures, she could not help but conclude these periodicals were a waste of time. Why on earth would Stephanie choose fashion photography for a career? The photographers are working overtime to justify their jobs, she thought. Who could keep up with the so-called fashions these magazines continued to churn out? In any case, she did not see many items she would dare wear in public, the clothes were too revealing or were positively cheap in appearance and did not reflect their boutique price tags. The models were disturbing to look at, for it seemed these days they were half-starved, brash and brazen faced, with their hair frizzed in a style that suggested they had stuck their fingers in an electrical socket, or went to the other extreme, greased down with a gallon of oil. They were modelling see-through garments minus their brassieres, and cheesecake lingerie shots or bikini beachwear, posing in the most undignified positions, looking more like prostitutes than models. The catwalks had become nothing more than glorified pole dancing exhibitions, minus the pole, disguised by the elitist flag of 'The Fashion World', making it acceptable in society, and they accept this travesty as a glamorous career for the modern woman. Katherine decided it was best to return to Socrates and his trial, curious to see how he would disprove the evil reputation they had pinned on him.

Socrates continued by asking his accuser to confirm a logical deduction. Will not good citizens do good for their neighbours while the bad do evil to them? Meletus agreed with this statement, allowing Socrates to proceed. Now, is there anyone who would not prefer to be benefited by living with good people? Do people like to be injured? Meletus agreed that people would avoid all injury. Socrates then posed the important question; now that you accuse me of destroying the morals of the youth, do you say my actions are intentional, or unintentional? Meletus declared they were intentional, an answer that Socrates disproved with his logic. For example, if I must share a dwelling with a man, and I intentionally do him evil, would he not be inclined to return the evil? I would be in danger of receiving some form of reprisal from him if I intentionally committed any wrong, and yet, you say that people would avoid receiving an injury. Either I have not committed evil and I am innocent, or my actions were unintentional, and that is an issue that should not have been brought before this assembly, as our laws do not recognise unintended offences. You would have done better to take me aside privately and admonish me for my error, and I would have stopped the errors I committed unintentionally, but you have brought me to a place of punishment, not instruction. This simple reasoning fascinated Katherine, Meletus had no interest in the welfare of the youth, no concern for his fellow citizens, he simply conjured a pretext to humiliate and punish Socrates before the Athenians.

Katherine was about to continue when the door opened and Dr. Hendricks rushed in and headed for his office.

"Finally," Gramps complained under his breath, it was now eight forty-five, and he appreciated punctuality. Shortly, Mildred called out names and conducted the patients into the various examination rooms.

"This shouldn't take too long, Katie."

"All right, see you soon."

Now Meletus, you accuse me of teaching the youths to disbelieve in the deities acknowledged by the State, and teaching the existence of other deities and spiritual agencies. This is how I corrupt their morals, is this your accusation? This makes no sense, Meletus! How can I teach about the existence of any god, while you claim I am an atheist? Of what do you charge me? That I teach about diverse gods, or that I am a complete atheist? Meletus argued the latter, declaring that Socrates did not believe in the deities of the sun or moon, but taught that the sun was made from stone, and the moon from earth. He intimates that Socrates does not believe in Apollo or Artemis, Katherine thought. How interesting, this doctrine stating the sun and moon were made from physical matter sounded very scientific. Were they already speculating on the true nature of the cosmos back then? Socrates replied that Meletus was confusing him with the philosopher, Anaxagoras, who already proposed these theories, and whose unorthodox doctrines were freely available in writings and in the theatre, and yet people were not condemned for studying them.

Socrates continued with an unusual proposition. Can a man believe in horsemanship, but not in the existence of horses, or, in flute playing but not flute players? No, that would be absurd, Katherine mused. Meletus said it was impossible. If that is the case, can a man believe in spiritual and divine agencies, whether or not they are from the recognised pantheon, and not believe in spirits or demigods in some form? No, of course not, but this is the contradicting riddle you present, Meletus, that I believe in spiritual agencies, implying I believe in spirits and demigods, and yet you insist I don't believe in the gods. If I believe in demigods, I must also believe in their parents, who must also be gods. It is no different than saying I believe in mules, but not in their progenitors, horses and asses. From an Athenian point of view, that would sound true Katherine thought, amused by his example.

Katherine was about to continue when the door opened and a young woman entered with two little boys, who were obviously her sons. While she went to the front desk, the children, who looked between the ages of five and six, headed immediately to the other corner of the reception room, the designated play area, complete with multi-coloured miniature tables and chairs piled high with books and various toys. The quiet room was now echoing motor imitations as the boys ran the toy trucks around the floor, 'Brrroom, Brroom!' Their mother sat on a sofa not far from the play corner, keeping on eye on her boisterous youngsters in case they annoyed or pestered the other patients.

My dear Athenians, I know that I have made many enemies, and this will inevitably bring my destruction, for the envy and slander of the world have been the death of many good men, and I will not be the last. You may ask me why I would continue to follow a path that I knew would make many enemies and may deprive me of my life, but you do not think soundly. A man should not consider the odds of living or dying, but that he should always consider whether he is doing right or wrong. Why should I then do evil, abandoning my mission given by the oracle for fear of death? That would be desertion, for where a man is placed by his commander there he should remain in the hour of danger, like a solider who has received orders from his general. Should he flee from the front lines? If I forsake the god for fear of death, I deserve to be brought here on charges of atheism and having pretence in wisdom, for the fear of death is indeed a pretended wisdom, thinking that death is the worst evil. No one knows if death is either the greatest evil or the greatest good. I do know that disobedience to one's better, whether God or man, is an evil and a dishonourable thing, and I would fear to commit this evil more than fearing death. I love you, men of Athens, but I shall obey God rather than you, and while I live, I shall not cease to teach. The State of Athens is like a magnificent steed that lumbers along due to its immense size and needs to be roused to action—I am the gadfly sent by the god to awaken the State, always questioning, examining, persuading and reproaching its citizens. You may ask why I do this in private, and not take a public office and advise the State, believe me when I tell you, a man cannot correct the wrongs of the State by entering politics without placing his life in peril, a man must remain a private citizen if he wishes to live for a while and fight for what is right. Socrates proceeded to relate his experiences in this matter when he was a Senator, and how he had riled the authorities on several occasions when he was the only member of the senate who opposed the illegalities committed by the State.

Katherine stopped reading for a moment to consider this disturbing point. Was the world always that corrupt? People were continually saying that 'things were better back then', but were they really, she wondered. Was a career in politics that dangerous? For whom and why? The first example that struck her right away was America's sixteenth president, 'Honest Abe', who reportedly never told a lie. Every child in grade school learned about Lincoln, at least the generalities of his biography, that he came from a poor farming family and for the most part self-educated, splitting rails at one time to earn his living. With honest hard work and determination, he achieved greatness. However, it was much later that everyone learned the tale of his mysterious dream. He was in the White House, and the sound of weeping filled the air. Searching the rooms for the source of this lamentation, he discovered a funeral wake was taking place. Curious, he drew close to the coffin and looked inside, to find that he was the deceased laid out in state. Disturbed by this dream, he searched his Bible for an answer, and read, "Does not interpretation belong to God?" At that point, the Civil War was raging, but rather than fear death, it apparently drove him onward to work all the harder in his endeavours to abolish slavery in the Union, convinced all men were created equal. The existence of slavery in the land of the free was an outrage. For his unshaken principles and his efforts to regain the rebellious southern states, Wilkes-Booth, a frenzied supporter of the South, shot him on a Good Friday. Now, this is one obvious example of the age-old clash between virtue and politics. If Lincoln was murdered for this reason, I wonder what truly caused Kennedy's assassination, Katherine mused. To this day, it is considered a mystery that has never been fully explained to anyone's satisfaction.

Rereading that particular page of the *Apology*, one remark stood out as peculiar, Socrates declared that he refrained from entering politics after listening to the warnings of an oracle that accompanied him from the time he was a child, an oracle that came to him as a voice, warning him in advance to consider the consequence of his actions, yet never commanding him, a revelation that he continually disclosed during his life, which the Athenians could never understand.

Katherine paused for a moment, reflecting upon Socrates' mysterious oracle, watching the two boys on the floor circling around the coffee table, 'berrroom-ing' their trucks along the carpet. They quickly tired of this activity and returned to the corner to survey the contents of the toy trunk. The younger boy found a bucket of building blocks and happily set out to build the highest skyscraper in the world. The older brother considered this block-building boring and found some wooden jigsaw puzzles instead. However, he quickly tired of fitting the brightly coloured pieces into the frames and tried to interest his little brother in the trucks again, it was no fun running around in circles by himself. The little one was still happy with his tower no matter how many times it fell down, he continued to rebuild, experimenting with the wooden arches, cylinders, squares and cones. Big brother, disgruntled that his whining suggestions were ignored, was not content to let his sibling alone with his grand endeavour and found new entertainment by knocking the budding metropolis over with mischievous glee when it reached a certain height.

"Stop it, Jimmy!", the little boy exclaimed in frustration as he watched his blocks scatter over and over with a muffled clatter on the carpet, "Stop it!"

Looking over, Mother issued a word of warning to the offender.

"Don't tease your little brother, Jimmy. That's not a nice thing to do. Now, be quiet and behave both of you, or you will have to come and sit quietly."

Jimmy continued to push the issue, threatening to knock the tower over, keeping one eye on Mom. Josh's little eyes began to well up and his lower lip trembled into a pout. Katherine expected him to burst into tears or to snitch, but that meant he would have to stop playing too if he called Mother's attention and she lowered the boom. Katherine wondered how this issue would resolve itself. Big brother knew Josh wanted to play as much as he did and could not resist muttering a taunt under his breath.

"You gonna cry now, Josh? You're a little cry-baby! Go on ... cry!"

The eyes of the little construction man suddenly grew aloof. "I'm no cry-baby. You won't let me build my skyscraper, I'll do something else then!" he retorted with a huff.

"Watcha gonna do, then?" Jimmy goaded, confident of his self-appointed dominance of the play corner. Josh went over to the children's books lined up on a shelf, picked one out, and ran over to their mother.

"Mommy, will you read me a story?"

"Of course, dear," she replied as she put down her magazine while Josh happily settled into the couch beside her. Jimmy looked crestfallen, having won all the delights of the play corner, a *niche* filled with colourful plastic delights, now realized this was a hollow victory for he had no one to share in the spoils. There sits a fine example Katherine mused, the power of that higher authority and the warnings of the inner oracle, but there too lies the deafness of those who refuse to listen to them.

She was about to return to her book, but glancing at the clock on the wall, she noticed it was getting close to ten o'clock. Getting up and walking to the front desk, she asked Mildred if everything was all right with her grandfather.

"He's fine, don't worry. He's getting the full program this time, blood tests and glucose analysis, heart rate monitoring, the usual battery. He'll be out soon, just takes a little longer, that's all."

Returning to her seat, she resumed reading, the best way to block out images of syringes. No wonder he wanted to avoid this appointment. Socrates continued his defence, declaring he never sought disciples, or those willing to pay tuition, but allowed all to listen to his words, rich and poor alike, while he continued in pursuit of his own mission. You may question why many people enjoy conversing with me, but in truth, they are just amused hearing the pretenders to wisdom cross-examined. Furthermore, if it be true that I corrupted the morals of the youth, then surely those who have now advanced in years and understanding could discern if I committed an evil against them in the past and would testify against me. I see many sitting in the assembly, and yet Meletus does not bring them forward to question them. In fact, the men I have mentioned are ready to come to my defence for they know I speak the truth.

Socrates continued his speech, declaring he would not, like others before him, drag his young family into the court to plead for his life with tears and supplications, hoping by this strategy to obtain an acquittal. Now that people insist that he is wise, he ought not to debase himself before the court, especially at his venerable age. Often he had seen distinguished men suddenly cower and weep before the tribunal, making spectacles of themselves and the court, behaving as though death was the ultimate catastrophe, and the court, by pardoning them, were granting them immortality. He has a point Katherine thought, they would only be delaying the inevitable, life is, and death comes to all. Socrates refused to lower his dignity and beg for his life, perhaps Meletus and his enemies expected him to break down. She looked over at little Josh, who had also refused to erupt into a tantrum, relinquishing his fun-time in the play area for something far better, the attention of his mother.

The gap in the next part of the text obviously marked the pronouncement of guilty as charged by the court. From the context, it would appear the accused had the right to plead his case for a particular punishment, the same right afforded the prosecutor. Socrates did not bat an eye when Meletus declared the penalty should be death. In contrast, Socrates proposed everyone should be rewarded according to his works. If another man had renounced everything, family, wealth and possessions to devote all his energies to instruct the citizens of Athens during his life, surely, the very least he could expect would be a state pension. However, he would not presume to declare his own penalty, for he was convinced he had not committed any intentional crime deserving of one. He would not declare exile upon himself, for if the Athenians refused to listen to his words, would any another city permit him to remain? He could not be silent, for talking to men about virtue was the greatest good, and that a life unexamined was not worth living. Socrates expected no worse than to pay a fine, but in the end, received the death penalty. Upon hearing his sentence, he uttered a warning; before long, the Athenians would become known for their evil judgements, adding that a heavy punishment awaited them. You tried to escape the divine accuser and avoid giving an account of your lives by disposing of *me*, but now the opposite shall befall you, as no one can escape the accuser. I go to die, while you shall live under the ignominy of injustice and villainy. In the end, Socrates concluded that accepting death was a great benefit, he would be delivered from those who administered justice according to the world, while he joined the true judges and sons of God. His inner oracle did not warn him to avoid the court, confirming that this judgement of death pronounced upon him was indeed a blessing. He could not think of a more blessed circumstance than to converse with those who had gone before him, in a place that was happier than the world, where all had reached immortality. "The hour of departure has arrived, and we go our ways—I to die, and you to live. Which is better, God only knows." Katherine could not help but think upon the similarities of a trial that occurred four hundred years later initiated by a trusted disciple who betrayed his Master, turning Him over to his enemies for thirty pieces of silver, and sealed it with a kiss.

I guess this is what Gramps means by everyone choosing the path of least resistance, it is much easier to do what the world expects, take the easy way out and don't make waves if you want to get ahead in this world, she thought. Isn't that what Professor Matthew's said Anna Millbank did with her sculpture for the Sirrac contest? Design a piece that was controversial, but in a manner the world expected, in order to win? Is this what Robert Horace does to make a name for himself and achieve success, no matter how despicable the method, even if it means tearing artists' work and their reputation to shreds? We are all taught the importance of integrity, but the world does not wag that way today. Is it possible to be honest and truthful, or will we be condemned for trying? Worse yet, how many no longer care, or go beyond that point and crush their inner oracles, stopping at nothing to achieve what they want at the expense of everyone and everything around them? This is heavy stuff. This will take a quiet time to ponder and mull over. What possessed me to start reading Socrates when I had enough on my plate already?

At last, Gramps emerged from the examination room while the mother and her two boys were called in.

"Glad that's finally over! I was right, first thing was my weight, must get more exercise and watch my diet," he grumbled as they left the office and made their way to the car. "The results from the other tests will be in later this week. He'll probably tell me my cholesterol levels are off the chart."

"Why don't you use the exercise bike in your room more often, instead of using it as a clothes hanger?" Katherine queried. "That contraption was invented for a reason you know."

"Aw, that thing is so boring, Katie. It doesn't go anywhere, and if I must exert myself, I should have something constructive to do at least."

"I think Sherlock Holmes said something similar during one of his adventures, about not wasting one's energy unless you're doing something worth the effort," Katherine replied with a smile.

"He really was a genius."

"Well, where should we go next? I think it's too early to head back home, the maintenance crew usually don't leave until five, so the fort will remain invaded for awhile. Perhaps we should go to the Club, we might meet Mom there. We can have an early lunch, my treat."

"Now you're talking!" Gramps replied beaming.

"And it's the salad bar for you today," she chided.

"That's big talk coming from the Pop Tart addict."

"Okay, I'll share your punishment and eat rabbit food too. Misery loves company, right?"

C3 ✤ 80

Next morning, after her usual caffeine jolt, carbohydrate and sugar rations, Katherine remained uncharacteristically lethargic when she thought of painting. "What is this, 'Painter's Block'?", irritated by her lack of motivation. No, it must be the thought of the board meeting tomorrow and the lunch at the rectory hanging over me, she concluded. Just the idea of picking up a paintbrush reminded her of the whole Robert Horace fiasco. She thought of the previous day's experience and sighed in relief she would not have to face a doctor's reception room again for a while. Hmm, I could channel my restlessness, think of another problem to be solved, a diversion tactic. They say if you concentrate on something else, the solution to your first problem comes more easily to mind. As she looked at her chocolate tart, Gramp's lack of exercise struck her as a good constructive project to begin with. Sure, he could live off carrots and celery, but if he did not find some entertaining way to exercise, he would never burn off the excess weight. Everything edible except for water has calories, even cows get fat on grass. He can't play golf like he used to she recalled, not with his arthritis, and the work-out bike might be too much on his knee, and it is a real bore, he's right about that. Maybe we could interest him in taking walks, but he would have to be away from the club, everyone wants to have a drink or a chat with him while he is there, so he could never walk more than a few feet in the grounds before he got halted in his tracks. He could walk around the neighbourhood, but I know him, he would consider that an aimless occupation, walking in circles with no particular place to go. Wait a minute, not if he *had* to walk around …well I can't send him out on errands, that's stupid. But, what if he had a dog…? He likes dogs, he always talks about the golden retriever he had as a boy, Dexter. Gosh, maybe *that's* the answer … I'll get him a dog! It's been a long time since we've had a pet

78

around here!

Excited with this new plan of action, she ran to the mahogany hallstand in the front hallway and took out the telephone book. She knew she could get Gramps the pick of the purebreds from the kennels, but she could never forget the time Steves horrified her with tales of the city pounds, explaining the gory details of the fate that awaited those unfortunate inmates who did not find a home within a certain length of time, and now if she found Gramps a companion, she could not pass up this opportunity to rescue a canine from animal death row. After finding the address for the pound, she looked up the location of the closest pet shop, she would need to buy food, a collar, leash, and a doggie bed. What should she do first? She decided to get the equipment and then drive to the pound, she did not think it would be a good idea to find a dog and then leave it alone in the car while she did the shopping. She ran to her room, grabbed her purse and bumped into Steves as she came down the hall.

"Hi Kats, off to the galleries?"

"No, not today. I'm getting a surprise for Gramps."

"A surprise? It's not his birthday. Can you let me in on it?" he asked, raising an eyebrow with undisguised curiosity.

"Nope. All I can tell you, it should help him with his exercise routine. You'll find out when you come home from the labs tonight. If anybody asks where I am, can you tell them I've gone into town to do some shopping?"

"Sure, no problem. What are you planning to get, a personal gym-set? He'll just hang his stuff on it," Steves laughed.

"No something better, I'm not telling you any more than that," she said as she dashed down the stairs and headed out the front door.

Pamela's Pet Emporium was a heart-warming environment with its cages brimming with fuzzy mewing kittens, yipping puppies, jabbering multicoloured parrots and languidly swimming fish. First, she selected the collar, an eye-catching one in red leather, Gramp's favourite colour, before she choose a sturdy leash, the latest 'expando' model. There were many dog beds to pick from in all sizes, including real wickerwork basket-beds, but she thought these were too hard and poky underneath, even with the padding inside. She planned to get an adult dog, so the largest size was in order, and decided on one of the plastic ones with an elite overstuffed doggie bedding made in Scotch plaid fit for the king of pooches. Then there was the food to think about, and she had forgotten about the dog bowels and chew toys. There was a *chic* set of stainless steel food and water bowels she just had to get, and she wasn't sure what to buy in the line of playthings, so she picked out several rawhide bones, a few squeaky balls and other chewable wheezy goodies. Of course, the dog would be hairy and needed a brush or two, and perhaps a stock of dog shampoo. She was about to select a canine brand when she noticed bottles of *No Tears* doggy shampoo on the shelves. Hey, that's a good idea! The proprietor must be a dog-lover she thought, if the stuff gets in their eyes, at least you know it won't hurt them. Chuffed with her purchases, it was now time to select the canine.

Katherine frowned when she drove up outside the city pound. Built and maintained by public funding, there were no architectural frills to be found here. The building was a mere cement rectangle with windows, a bleak bunker-like construction built for the sole purpose to temporarily shelter strays and unwanted animals. With the main compound surrounded by rows of dog-runs fenced with the typical chain-link mesh, it certainly looked like a pet penitentiary. There were all types of dogs confined in them, pacing up and down, barking madly or sleeping on the ground. She entered the reception area and approached the front desk. Hearing the bell jingle on the main door, a brown-haired man with a moustache greeted her without looking up from his newspaper.

"Hi there. Are you bringing one in?"

"Ah, bringing what in?"

"A new inmate."

"Oh, no! I'm thinking of adopting."

The man looked up, quite relived to hear this piece of good news.

"I'm glad you've said that, we're overcrowded as it is. What are you looking for, cat or dog?"

"A dog, an adult golden retriever if you have one."

The man twisted his moustache as he thought for a moment.

"Hmm, don't think we have a retriever. They're kinda popular, usually the first to find a home. Are you sure you want a purebred? It's a lot easier to pick a mutt, we've got plenty of them."

"Well, I don't know. I'd like a friendly dog, anyway."

"Come on in and look around."

Showing her through a door, he brought her to the canine section of the compound. There were so many, yapping terriers, howling hounds, strange fur ball mutt breeds, the choice was endless. Walking down one corridor of dog-runs, she spotted an enclosure that contained a litter of sleeping puppies that looked like Labradors, two were black, while the other two were creamy gold. They are good people dogs too, I think.

"They came in two days ago," the man informed her. "I'm not sure they're purebreds. The people that brought them in didn't have the time to find them homes."

While she had come looking for an adult dog, these chaps were simply adorable, and she could not find it in her heart to pass them by. How she wished she could save all of them! Perhaps she could talk Charlie into adopting a pup too? Maybe that would be pushing it. She could only pick one, so she began by narrowing her choices, Gramps would probably prefer a golden pooch like his Dexter, so now it was down to two. She had a hard time deciding, curled up into little balls, they were positively cute with their black-button noses.

"Psssppp, pssssp!" she whispered, trying to wake them from their nap. One lifted his head, cocked an ear, and opened a curious brown eye, looking in her direction to see who had made the noise. "Hello there! Come here, come, here!" she called, putting her fingers through the chain-link. The little fellow did not need a second invitation, clumsily getting to his feet, he bounded to the fence and licked her fingers, wagging his tail and putting up his front paws through the chain-link. "You're a frisky one, aren't you? Would you like to come home with me?"

"Brwow, brwow!" he barked, lifting his little snozzle into the air before returning to the all-important puppy business of licking fingers and wagging his tail.

"I guess that settles it. I'll take this one, please."

Sitting with the wriggling puppy in the car, she realized things were not going exactly according to plan. She had bought adult dog food, a hefty collar, and a doggie bed big enough to fit a moose. I'll have to go back and exchange the food for Puppy Chow, but he can grow into everything else, she decided. Starting the car, it was near impossible driving with the frolicsome pup, he refused to remain in the back seat for long or to lie still and insisted on sitting in her lap, jumping up every minute or two and setting his little paws on her chest, licking her face and ears. She slowed the car down to a snail's pace. I don't know how I can see where I'm going! If a cop spots these antics, I'm as good as dead! It was a miracle she arrived back at Pamela's Pet Emporium in one piece. With the puppy under one arm, she struggled with the bulky bags of food, but the clerk was kind enough to help her out with her exchanged goods. Before she got back in the car, she took one of the new squeaky toys out of the trunk and hoped the little fur ball would find playing with that more amusing than licking her to death while she drove home. It worked, for a moment or two, sitting in the front passenger seat, he happily chewed away on a plastic shoe, but quickly jumped back into her lap smearing her face with puppy dribble. Well, he's a people-dog, that's for sure. Gramps is just going to love him, if only he would let me drive home!

While Katherine tackled Gramp's exercise problem, back at Oak Meadows her mother and Mrs. Gonzales were discussing the new culinary arrangements in the kitchen.

"Well, here are the diet sheets that Dr. Hendricks gave him yesterday, Mrs. Gonzales. According to this pyramid, he must avoid cookies and desserts, or have very small amounts. No more of your homemade cheesecakes for him, I'm afraid. Fats will have to be reduced, which means no more fried breakfasts," Helen said as they studied the four food groups chart on the island counter-top. "This is going to be difficult, he needs to cut back on red meat and eat more chicken, turkey and fish."

"Yes, Mrs. W., and he needs to eat plenty of salads and fruit, he'll be like a bear, but he'll just have to suffer through it," Mrs. Gonzales replied.

"This will put a terrible strain on you, cooking for him separately, and it would not be fair to him either, watching us eat everything that is forbidden to him. Perhaps it would be easier if you cook the same fare for everyone. Besides, we should all eat a healthier diet. Somehow, I have a feeling we may be eating out more often if this is the case."

"All right, but I can't keep my eye on the kitchen every minute, I can't order him to stay on his diet, you know. If you all stick to his diet, and he cheats, it wouldn't be right."

"I suppose we shall have to help him along," Helen replied. "We could lock all the sweet and fatty articles away in the walk-in pantry. You would be in charge of the key, and could select a hiding place for it somewhere in the kitchen, so if anyone wants anything, except him of course, they know where to find it."

"Very well Mrs. W., that sounds like a good plan, but I can't chain up the refrigerator either."

"No, of course not, let me see. We could get a small refrigerator for the pantry, you can put the eggs, sausages and bacon in there. The desserts too, your cheesecakes, the ice creams, whipped cream, things like that. I'm sorry that this will place extra work on you Mrs. Gonzales, rearranging the kitchen."

"Don't worry about it, Mrs. W., this should work, and it's no trouble really. I can stock the kitchen shelves with healthy things for him. He'll need bran, oatmeal, and other high-fibre cereals for breakfast. I'll make sure the main refrigerator will have nothing but skimmed milk, fresh fruit, low-fat yoghurts and veggie sticks, the usual diet fare."

"I'm glad that's settled, I'll leave it to you to choose an appropriate refrigerator unit for the pantry, I'm sure Mr. Jeffery would be happy to take you to get all the necessary items. He may be finished mowing the front lawns by lunch-time, you could ask him then."

"All right Mrs. W., I'll try and rearrange my afternoon to do the shopping and organize the pantry. I'll have them deliver the refrigerator as soon as possible."

"Thank you for being so accommodating Mrs. Gonzales, I truly don't know what I would do without you! Of course, we can watch him while he eats at home, but we'll have no control over him when he eats out. He may even bribe the chef at the Club. At least we may have cut the problem in half."

The two ladies had just solved this dietary complication when Katherine awkwardly bumbled through the back door of the kitchen, proudly bearing the king-sized bed with the pup swimming around in an ocean of navy plaid.

"Look what I found! Isn't he just *adorable?*"

"Katherine! Where on earth did you find *that?*" her mother replied, startled by this unexpected delivery.

"At the pound, the puppy I mean, not the bed. I got him for Gramps."

"Whatever for? Does your grandfather know about this? Did you ask him if it was all right?"

"No, it's a surprise!"

"You seem to be full of surprises lately, young lady!"

"Listen, Mom, I thought if he had a dog to walk, he would finally get the exercise he needs. He doesn't like doing anything unless it's constructive, so he says."

Katherine was about to put the bed down on the floor when Mrs. Gonzales held up her hand.

"Oh, no you don't, Miss Kathy. I will not tolerate dogs or cats in my kitchen."

"You know very well, Katherine, the kitchen wing is Mrs. Gonzales' domain, and she has the last word on everything in this area," her mother interjected.

"Thank you, Mrs. W.," Mrs. Gonzales stoutly replied, folding her arms defiantly over her middle.

"Katherine, you should have checked with us before you did something like this," her mother continued, "I don't know *what* your father will think, or if Gramps will like your idea of an exercise program. Oh dear, and from the *pound*, of all places! Who knows what company that puppy was keeping, I hope he is not infested with fleas!" Mrs. Gonzales' dark brown eyes widened in horror at this suggestion. "What if your grandfather decides he can't take care of him? There's no place for him in the house, with potty training and the various puppy duties that are required! Good heavens, Katherine, what are we going to do? And *you* have landed this responsibility on us while *you* have plans to leave for Paris? Katherine! Will you ever stop to think before you jump into making decisions that concern the whole family without asking our opinion?" Katherine froze where she stood, holding the basket with the hyperactive puppy that was whining with frustration and doing his utmost to jump out. Mom's right, I didn't think of that!

"Katherine, do you suppose they would take him back?"

"Mom, to the pound? I don't think so, I've just rescued him from the death chamber!"

"Well, he cannot stay near the kitchen, and we cannot have him in the house, not in his untrained condition, that much is certain."

"Look, maybe I can set him up in the apartment, or even the garage, he just needs a place to sleep at night, and I know Suzy wouldn't mind watching him, she loves animals. I'll just have to figure out a way to coral him until he's house trained."

"Oh dear, and I thought we were all through with your aquariums, the ant farms, the turtles, the guinea-pigs, and those horrible white rats your brother brought home," her mother replied in consternation. "Take him over to the apartment for now, we'll think about what we're going to do later. You'll have to watch him and make sure he doesn't have an accident on the carpet."

"Brwow! Brwow!" the little fellow barked.

Just great, this is going over like a lead balloon, Katherine thought as she turned towards the back door. She did not get far as Steves unexpectedly came in from the main hall.

"What's up? Everyone holding court in the kitchen? Damn! So *this* was your master plan! Now that was a good idea, sis," he burst out with enthusiasm, as he went over to inspect the new arrival.

"Steven! Watch your language! You know we don't appreciate bad language in this house," their mother replied indignantly. "We didn't expect you home this early. Did you know anything about this?"

"Sorry, Mom. Just slipped. I left some of my lab calculations here, so I figured since I had to come back and get them, might as well come home for an early lunch," he explained as he lifted the roly-poly pup out of the bed to take a good look at him, "and no, she didn't say a word, just that she was shopping for something to help Gramps with his exercise. I figured she was going to get him a real bike and tie a pole on the handlebars with a hot dog dangling from the end for motivation, but she has surpassed my expectations. Where did you get this little tyke?"

"At the pound, I wanted to get a golden retriever, like Gramp's Dexter, but found this itty bitty fellow instead."

The pup wagged his tail madly and began to smother Steve's ear with a profusion of puppy kisses.

"He's a blast! Did you name him yet?"

"No, I think Gramps should have that honour."

"Master Steven, be careful, he could have a disease, not to mention fleas," Mrs. Gonzales warned.

"Yes, make sure you both wash your hands!" their mother protested.

"Relax, Mom, we have antiseptic soap strong enough to skin the hide off a rhino. Where were you going with him, sis?"

"Out to the apartment, he's not allowed in the house, especially the kitchen. He's not house trained."

"Don't worry, I can help with the training. If they piddle where they shouldn't, they say you're supposed to bang the floor with a paper until Spot gets the idea."

Their mother grimaced, imagining the stench and the yellow puppy stains all over their carpets.

"Brwow!"

"Now Steven, you know you will be leaving for MIT this fall, and Katherine will be leaving for Paris in a matter of weeks, who will take care of it then, may I ask?"

"I told Mom he just needs a place to sleep at night, and Suzy could watch him," Katherine explained.

"I know she likes dogs, but she's not here right now, one of us will have to sleep over there I guess, maybe take turns," Steves suggested.

"But we can't watch him every minute of the night, we'd pass out from lack of sleep," Katherine replied. "Wait a minute! What if we got our old playpen out of the attic? We could line the thing with newspapers, he certainly can't escape from that. We could keep any midnight accidents confined to that area at least."

"There's an idea, good thinking, sis. I suppose he hasn't had his shots yet, we'll have to take him to the vet."

"Oh, I forgot about that, too. The poor thing, imagine jabbing him with needles!"

"Better a poke here or there than a case of rabies, let me tell you."

"Do you think Gramps will like him, Steves?"

"Of course he will. He'll have to wait until he gets a little bigger before he can take him for walks though. Sure, he'd be mad if he didn't have a soft spot for him. Come on, let's get the playpen."

"All right, but I'll have to hang onto him, Steves. I can't leave him alone in the yard, he's small enough to get out the front gate, and who knows what he would get in to in the garage until we puppy-proof it. The apartment is off limits, except under supervision. How are we going to manage this?"

"With difficulty, that's obvious. Hmm, this is going to be interesting," Steves decided, checking his watch. "Okay, you hold Spot while I run the dog bed over to the apartment, and then we'll head to the attic. We've got to do this in a hurry, I have to eat and get back to the labs soon."

"Brwow! Brwow!"

With the bed out of the way, they rummaged through the catch-all section of the house and located the folded infant confinement contraption, heaving it gingerly down the narrow attic stairs and into the upstairs hall with the wriggling puppy in tow.

"Okay, I can carry it from here Kats, it's not heavy, just awkward. While I bring this to the apartment, you can hang on to Spot and get the newspapers. Man, I'm getting my exercise today," he laughed.

Her brother headed out the front door and Katherine went to the breakfast room to gather up the morning papers with her free arm. The copy of last Sunday's arts section was still to be found amidst the bundles of daily reading materials. Well, well! Looks like I've found the perfect practical use for your column at last, Mr. Horace. That's all it's good for, anyway. I'll be glad to set this feisty fellow down, he sure is a handful.

Once they had set up the pen lined with newspapers and added the toys, Spot was finally placed inside. Suddenly, Steves declared;

"You know sis, this isn't a sure thing yet. All it will take is one 'no', and he's headed back to doggie Sing Sing."

"Oh, no! What are we going to do? Right now I wish I had decided to paint for the day."

"Don't freak out yet. Well, he looks irresistible for one thing, but he could smell better. Let's give him a quick bath and a blow-dry. Looks like no lunch for me today."

Katherine went to the car and unloaded the dog supplies while Steves filled the guest bath.

"Careful! Not too hot or too deep, we don't want to burn or drown him. Here's the shampoo. I'll go get the pup."

Katherine once more held the squirming puppy in her arms and lowered him into the tub.

"Brwow, Brwow!"

Steves took off his watch and rolled up his sleeves.

"Hey, don't drink that! At least I didn't add the soap yet. He's thirsty Kats, it's probably been ages since he's been fed too. Oh, no…"

"What?"

"He just did a 'number one' in the tub. Great! Must be all the water. Now we'll have to empty this, rinse it out, and fill it up again. I suppose it's a wonder we haven't had an accident until now."

Katherine held the puppy in the air dripping into the bathtub while Steves manned the drain and handled the faucets.

"Well, he didn't do anything in the pen yet. Golly, maybe I'd better check my car, he didn't stay long in the back seat, but probably had enough time to do something unmentionable. Just wonderful, that's all I need."

"Okay, we're all ready again. Crikey, he likes this, Kats! Except I'm getting wetter than he is. Hey, Spot, I've had my shower today."

When he had him thoroughly scrubbed, Steves pulled a towel off the rack and began to rub him dry. Katherine ran across to the main house to get her hairdryer and to look through her stash of old hair ribbons. Finding the desired objects, she hurried back to the puppy drying at hand. The *No Tears* shampoo worked wonders, the little fur coat felt like silk, gleamed in the light, and smelled like a spring bouquet. For the finishing touch, Katherine took the red satin hair ribbon she found and tied a large bow around his neck.

"Looking so irresistible, how could anyone think of sending you back to the pound?"

Apparently, Spot did not care to appear adorable and pawed at the unfamiliar red object, whining his disapproval.

"Well sis, that's all I can do for now, I'll have to grab something to eat and rush back. They need the calculations I finished last night," Steves said as he rolled down his sleeves and put on his watch.

"Okay, I'll tidy up here, I'd better wash the tub with disinfectant in case a human wants to use it. I guess I'll have to wait with the little fellow until Gramps arrives home. We'll see you later."

"I wish I could see the look on his face, but since you found our furry friend, that joy is all yours. Bye, Kats."

Steves left in a hurry and she went to the kitchen area, filled out a bowel of water and opened a can of Puppy Chow, which Spot lapped up hungrily. Poor thing, we should have fed him first, he's starving! Well, this should fill him up for now. After the pup was finished, she placed him in the dog bed and lifted it into the playpen. Worn out from the excitement of the day and his little belly full, he curled into a ball and fell into a deep asleep. Peace at last! Now it was time to tackle the repugnant jobs. Katherine donned the rubber gloves and washed out the tub, and then went to check the back seat and carpets of her car. To her dismay, there was an unmistakable pong and a dark splodge on the floor behind the driver's seat. Just great! If it wasn't for bad luck, I wouldn't have any at all. Maybe I could stick diapers on him?

She finally cleaned the doggie mess and sprayed the inside of her car with liberal amounts of air freshener, she scrubbed her hands thoroughly once more and went to the main house to grab a quick bite to eat before heading back to the apartment to baby-sit. She had just settled into the couch to watch TV for a short while when the telephone rang.

"Hello?"

"Hi Kathy, it's Charlie."

"Hi Charlie. What's up? Did you win your case yet?"

"No, not yet, but it looks good. It might wrap up later this week. I know this is short notice, how would you like to go out to dinner tonight? Everyone at the office is recommending a new Italian restaurant that just opened, and I thought we could check it out."

"Oh, I'd love to Charlie, but I've got my hands full at the moment … I'm afraid I've jumped into it again…" she replied glumly.

"Not another painting dilemma?" he asked with concern.

"No, well, I went out to the pound today and got Gramps a puppy. I took Gramps to the clinic yesterday and he was told to exercise more, so I thought a dog would be a great excuse for him to get out and walk."

Expecting more bad news from the tone of her voice, Charlie laughed at this unexpected confession.

"A puppy? Did Mr. G.W. see him yet?"

"No, it's supposed to be a surprise, he should be home from the Club soon."

"I bet it will! I guess Fido isn't housebroken, the cause of your woe, right?"

"Exactly, Mom had a fit, and Mrs. Gonzales won't let him near the kitchen. The house is off limits until he is trained, that's if we get to keep him. Steves helped me give him a bath and set him up in the apartment in our old playpen. Pops hasn't heard about it yet either, at least, I don't think so. The stupid thing is I didn't think anyone might say 'no', and I forgot I won't be here much longer, and Steves is returning to MIT. I know Suzy will love the pup and would watch him at night, but how I'm going to mange this with all our different schedules, I don't know. It's a dilemma!"

"Well, it never rains but it pours. Kathy, a puppy is quite a handful, I guess dinner is out then."

"No it isn't. Why don't you come over here? You know Mrs. Gonzales usually prepares veal on Tuesdays, you would be more than welcome."

"Okay, I'll be there."

"Besides, you've got to see the puppy, he's real cute."

"Is it a mutt?"

"A golden Labrador, I think, but no one's sure."

"I can't wait, see you later, Kathy."

"Okay, bye Charlie."

As she hung up the receiver, she heard the familiar sound of Gramp's Cadillac coming up the driveway. Well, here we go. Gingerly tiptoeing around the pen and exiting the apartment, she went to the front of the garage and waited for him to park the car.

"Hi Gramps. I got something for you today that should help with your exercise."

"Oh? I hope it's not an aerobics tape," he replied with a smile, "I can't keep up with those young whippersnappers and their fancy moves."

"No, nothing like that, you'd stick it on a shelf as a new dust catcher."

"Too true, my dear."

"Come on, it's in the apartment," she replied, tugging him by the arm.

"Hmm, what could you possibly have hidden in there I wonder?" he mused aloud as they went up the stairs to the veranda. Leading him inside, she put her finger over her lips and then pointed towards the pen in the living area.

"Ta, da!" she whispered with a smile.

"Good gracious! Wherever did you find that?"

"At the pound, isn't he cute? You can take him for walks, a dog has to be walked at least twice a day you know."

Gramps looked down with a sceptical eye at the sleeping puppy.

"I'm not sure about this. Does you mother know?"

Katherine was slightly deflated with this dubious reception.

"Unfortunately, yes. No in the kitchen, no in the house, and I was so happy with my idea. You do like him, don't you Gramps?"

The little fellow began to stir, and looked up, two little black eyes and a little black nose, his pink tongue hanging out from a sea of champagne fuzz, and the red bow, who could resist him? Gramps rumbled a deep chuckle, for he always had a soft spot for man's best friend.

"I'd be a heartless old coot if I didn't. Well, well! Let's take a look at you, little fella." As Gramps lifted him out, the pup eagerly wriggled in mid air before Gramps held him close to receive his fair share of slobbery greetings, "You're a spunky little tyke, aren't you? I suppose he'll have to stay, can't send him back to be exterminated now, can we? Does he have a name yet?"

"No, I thought you should name him, I got him for you. Better pick one out fast though, Steves keeps calling him 'Spot', and before that sticks, I think he should have something more original."

"Hmm, original, eh? How about 'Trouble'? Every time he comes running we could always say, 'Here comes Trouble!'"

"Oh Gramps, now you're being silly, I can see where Steves gets his sense of humour."

"All right, what do you think about ... 'Jasper'? Short, sensible, but with a touch of sophistication. No doggie clichés like 'Rex' or 'Rover'."

"Well, if you like it, Gramps. He does look like a 'Jasper', doesn't he? Yeah, that seems to suit him. Jasper... it sure is a lot better than 'Spot'."

"If we can't house break him, it may go back to that," Gramps chuckled as he put the puppy back into the pen, "Okay, Jasper it is, then. I'll try and convince your parents, we can sort something out with the training and all that, pups don't stay little forever, you know."

"Too true, it shouldn't be that difficult. Well, we'll leave Jasper in the pen for now, I'll try and puppy-proof the apartment, he'll need to run around in here sometime. He can't stay cooped up in that thing every minute."

Jasper yipped his approval with this decision, jumping madly in an effort to escape his cell.

"All right, Katie. I'll head over to the house. I could use a nap."

"Okay Gramps, I'll see you at dinner then. Dinner! That reminds me, Charlie called, and I invited him over, I'll have to buzz Mrs. Gonzales."

"The more the merrier."

Gramps went out the door, and Katherine buzzed the intercom to the main house.

"Mrs. Gonzales?" A few minutes passed before a reply came from the speaker.

"Mrs. G. here! Is that you, Miss Kathy?"

"Yes, I hope you don't mind, I've invited Charlie over for dinner. That won't be too much trouble, will it?"

"Not at all, Miss Kathy."

"Thank you, Mrs. Gonzales, you're simply super!"

With the arrangements for dinner accomplished, Katherine looked around to survey the apartment, and how to puppy proof it. She would have to pick up her paint tubes for one thing, then store the easels away in the closet, and put all the canvases up higher, just in case her paint equipment became the new chew-toys, or mistaken for trees and fire hydrants. Close all the doors to the other rooms, keep him in one area, for the time being she decided. What about the kitchen? That seems safe enough. I don't think Jasper can get into the cupboards. I'm exhausted, imagine all this work when you add one, small, two-pound puppy to the household!

Due to all the flurry of this extra activity, Katherine had lost track of the time. Glancing at the wall clock, she was aghast to see how quickly the hours had flown, it was a quarter past seven, and dinner would be served at eight. Looking down at her dishevelled clothes, it was obvious she needed to do something about her appearance. I'll have just enough time for a quick shower and change, too bad I won't have time to wash my hair. If I leave bowls of food and water in the pen, Jasper should be all right for now. Luckily, he had nodded off to sleep and she could escape without occasioning a barrage of heartbreaking whines and yips.

Hurrying through the front door, an unexpected aroma greeted her. Is that fish I smell? That's odd, it's Tuesday. Could Mrs. Gonzales be making clam chowder? Oh, who knows. I have to get dressed before Charlie arrives, and I'd better be downstairs when Pop gets home, I'll have to break the news to him about Jasper if Steves hasn't already.

It just took half an hour for her to get washed and changed. Gramps woke up from his nap and headed to the den to read his newspaper until dinner. Helen had finished the book she was reading that afternoon and went to the kitchen to check on Mrs. Gonzales. Five to eight, Katherine heard Pop's car pull up the drive, announcing his arrival. Well, best get this over with, she thought. Harold came through the door with his leather briefcase in hand, weary from a hard day at the office and his battle with a heavy stream of traffic leaving the city. Maybe this is not a good time, she thought.

"Hi Pops. Was it a tough day?"

"Hello, Kathy. No more than usual. Just the expected hassle in going through humdrum reports and preparing the presentation for the board meeting tomorrow." Oh, this really is not the best time to drop the bombshell, she thought. "How was your day, dear?" Oops, I guess I will have to now.

"Umm, it was okay, Pops. Did Steves say anything to you when he came back from lunch?" she probed, wondering if she would be spared breaking the news.

"No, he didn't call me or send anything up to the office. Why? Did something go wrong in the labs today?" he queried, expecting a scientific catastrophe.

"Oh, no! Nothing like that! It's just ... I've got some news, I ..." Katherine hesitated for a moment.

"Well, make it quick, dear. I have to get ready for dinner, you know."

"IwenttothepoundandgotGrampsapuppy!" she anxiously blurted in a rush.

"Say that again? You ...?"

Katherine took a deep breath and let it out.

"I went and found a cute puppy for Gramps, his name is Jasper. I thought Gramps could take him out for walks."

There was a slight pause as Pops mulled over this information.

"I see. Well, I don't think that is a major crisis. Did your grandfather approve of this?"

"It was a surprise, but Gramps didn't say 'no'. Mom and Mrs. Gonzales do not want Jasper in the kitchen, or the rest of house, so I've got him in the apartment for now. Steves helped me give Jasper a bath and everything, I'm surprised he didn't tell you."

"Perhaps he wished to keep it a surprise for me too," Pops said with a smile. "Never mind, your grandfather and I will discuss this with your mother and see what we can arrange. Where is she, by the way?"

"Here I am," Helen replied as she came down the hall from the kitchen, giving him a quick peck on the cheek. "Dinner will be ready in a few minutes. Why, Harold dear, you look positively worn-out tonight."

"I am, but it's nothing that a good night's sleep won't cure. Steven should be home in a few minutes, I saw his car behind mine, he must have worked late tonight, he obviously was held up at lunch for some reason," Pops said, giving Katherine a quick, humorous glance.

"Did our Kathy give you the latest news?"

"Yes, she did, a puppy by the name of Jasper has taken up lodgings in the apartment," he replied.

"As if there wasn't enough to handle."

"Now Helen, dear, worse things have happened. Come to think of it, this might be a good idea for Dad.   Look, we can discuss this during dinner, I have to get ready." As he turned towards the stairs, a car pulled up the driveway. "That must be Steven now."

"Or it could be Charlie," Katherine said as she opened the front door to look outside, "I invited him over for dinner."

"That's nice dear," her father replied, "I'll go put this away and get washed up."

Katherine and her mother stayed to greet Charlie at the door bearing two bottles of cabernet sauvignon.

"Good evening, ladies."

"Hi Charlie, sorry I messed up your dinner idea."

"Hey, you didn't mess anything up, Kathy. I hope I'm not too late, Mrs. W., I was unavoidably held up on the phone."

"Not at all, dinner will be served in a minute or two. Charlie, you didn't have to bring anything," Helen protested as he gallantly handed her the bottles.

"I know, but this is a really good wine, you must try it."

"Come on in, I'll bring you over to see Jasper after we eat," Katherine said, "Pops will be down in a moment, and Gramps is in the den. Can I get you something to drink before we sit to the table?"

"No, I'm all right Kathy. So, his name is Jasper, huh? How did Mr. G.W. like his surprise?"

"Well, he didn't jump over the moon, but he became a right marshmallow at the sight of him."

Helen looked to heaven and shook her head.

"You and your animals! What will you and your brother think up next? I'll check on Mrs. Gonzales and see if she is nearly ready."

"All right, Mom. We might as well go to the dining room, Mrs. Gonzales gets into a tizzy when we let her food go cold."

Gramps had the same idea and met them as he came out of the den.

"Hullo there, Charlie. So you've heard the latest, I reckon."

"Hi, Mr. G.W., yes, and the 'latest' answers to the name Jasper. So, has the jury come in with the final verdict?"

"Well, Pops doesn't seem too pushed out of shape with the idea, and Mom seems almost resigned right now…" Katherine mused aloud.

"Hurmph! I suppose the jury is still out, but the verdict might go favourably," Gramps joked. "Let's sit down, I'm famished. Something smells good, clam chowder, do you think?"

"I thought so, maybe it's a 'surf and turf' feast tonight," Katherine replied.

Everyone except for Steves sat to the table, Pops at the head with Mom to his right, while Gramps liked sitting at the other end. Charlie chose the chair next to Katherine, leaving the seat next to Mom free for Steves who arrived just as Mrs. Gonzales was going back and forth from the kitchen bringing in the hot covered dishes, and Juanita placed the salads of endive and cherry tomatoes on the table.

"Sorry, I'm late, I tried my usual shortcut, but couldn't avoid the traffic," he explained as he sat down. "Hi, Charlie. Nice to see you. What's for dinner? I'm so hungry I could eat a bus."

Mrs. Gonzales lifted the covers off their plates, one by one.

"Enjoy your dinner," she said before returning to the kitchen.

Everyone looked and surveyed their plates, no one expected *fish* for dinner, except Mrs. W., a slender poached salmon steak drizzled with a thin lemon dill sauce, served with steamed string beans and three boiled new potatoes, more like pebbles, no bigger than marbles.

"Harold, dear, will you say the blessing?" Helen prompted.

He dutifully said the grace before meals with as much dignity as he could muster. As soon as he was finished, Steves piped up as he examined their repast.

"Well, that explains the fish smell! Did Mrs. Gonzales have a senior moment, or what?"

"Steven! Be quiet! Do you want Mrs. Gonzales to hear you? She has been a treasure in this house for the past seven years, and she is in the prime of life, I'll have you know!"

Harold smiled at his wife, knowing to what lengths she was willing to go to keep Mrs. Gonzales, remembering the hard time they had trying to find a housekeeper after eight months of having no housekeeper at all.

"Yeah, but *fish*? What gives?"

"Mrs. Gonzales and I have agreed that your grandfather needs to adhere to his diet, and it would be simpler if we all followed it. Besides, it's healthier for us too." Gramps lifted an eyebrow and poked his dinner with his fork.

"Oh Mom, I told Charlie we would be having veal tonight," Katherine said, mortified with the humble fishy supper that was served instead of the promised spread, gone were her visions of scrumptious breaded veal chops served with Duchess potatoes. Charlie could hardly keep a straight face.

"That's all right, Kathy. I like salmon," he diplomatically replied.

"Anyone for pizza?" Steves quipped.

"Not a bad idea," Gramps grumbled.

"Now, stop it you two. Mrs. Gonzales has gone to a lot of trouble, and it is excellent food. The diet sheets call for more fish and white meat, and less red meat," Mom informed them.

"Yes, but why couldn't we have lobster or shrimp?" Katherine queried, as she looked at her plate.

"Because sis, they're full of triglycerides, or in layman's terms, fats, particularly the saturated fats, or cholesterol," Steves explained. "Shell fish and calamari, too. Salmon is much better, it contains an important source of Omega oils that helps to counteract the dangerous form of cholesterol that builds up in the body. There are studies also being carried out on how it may help prevent arthritis."

"Well, thanks for turning our dinner into a science lesson. So, clams are also a no-no? That means clam chowder hits the dust too?"

"I'm afraid so, sis. Good chowder has lots of butter and cream. Whole milk equals animal fats, and therefore cholesterol."

"Well, hang the cholesterol, I'll take you up on your pizza offer and add a steak house," Gramps interjected.

"Come now, it's not that bad," Pops replied as he ate his unexpected diet dinner with resignation. He was too tired to protest against anything edible that was placed in front of him.

"I hope dessert will be better," Gramps replied.

"It won't take us too long to find out," Steves added, eyeing the portions, "Looks like Jasper won't be getting any scraps from *this* table."

Charlie was finding it more difficult to keep that straight face.

After the plates were cleared, dessert turned out to be honeydew melon wedges served with a bittersweet strawberry sauce. Katherine had a feeling there would be another midnight raid on the kitchen in a matter of hours, and so did everyone else.

As promised, Katherine took Charlie to meet Jasper when dinner was over. The minute Jasper saw them, he wagged his tail and barked his excitement, he wanted out. By now, he was not looking as pristine as before, his bow had nearly come undone, he had sent his food rolling around the pen, and was wet from slopping around in his water bowel.

"Oh, he looked better a few hours ago, so much for the bath," Katherine sighed, "he's made a real mess in there."

With an irrepressible grin, Charlie reached in to pick up the prisoner.

"Hello, squirt! Kathy's right, you have made a pigsty of your pen," he joked as he lifted Jasper up and scratched his ear.

"He's wet Charlie, let me get a towel before you get sopping too," Katherine said as she ran to the bathroom.

"Okay. Listen, do you have any more newspapers? Let's get him set up for the night," he called after her.

"I do, but you don't have to worry about that," she called back, "Jasper's going to be my responsibility now for awhile, it was my idea after all." She hurried back and dried Jasper off … again.

"It's no problem, Kathy. He's a real sport this one," Charlie replied as he tried to hold the wriggly fellow still for her. Charlie loved dogs, he once had a Weimaraner named Duke that followed him to school everyday and devotedly sat outside waiting for him to come out. Unfortunately, a car that was travelling over the speed limit hit old faithful Duke.

"Well, there are three more where this one came from," she hinted with a smile.

"It's too bad I can't have any pets right now, I am just too busy at work," he replied, which was true. However, he could never bring himself to find another 'best friend' after Duke was killed. When Jasper was all dried off, Charlie set him down on the floor. "We'll let him run around while we clear up this mess."

Katherine began rolling up the soggy newspapers, while Charlie went to the kitchen for the garbage pail and the paper towels to dry the pen. Jasper rummaged around the room, sniffing out his new surroundings, poking his head into every nook and cranny before returning to the humans to give them more slobbery affection.

"You're going to have your hands full with this one. Jasper will need a licence in case he escapes, you know puppies have a tendency to wander off if left outside, and perhaps a flea collar would not be a bad idea."

"I forgot about the licence! It seems all I thought of was the puppy today, and forgot everything else that comes with it."

"Talk about tunnel vision when you have a goal in mind," Charlie laughed.

"Or a really bad case of short-sightedness," she returned, "I'll have to take him to get his shots too, but fleas? I don't see how Jasper could have fleas, we did give him a bath."

"They stick worse than burrs, so chemicals are your only resource."

"How can you tell if he's got them?"

"Let me take a look."

Katherine picked the rambler up and handed him to Charlie as he sat down in one of the armchairs and turned on the reading lamp. Katherine held Jasper still as best she could while Charlie gingerly lifted the golden fur little by little from the neck down, gently searching through the soft fuzz, feeling around with the tips of his fingers.

"You can't see them right away, they hide down near the skin and cover up under the downy fur. You can feel a small lump, or you might see them, they're about as big as a gnat, but hard. Whoops! There's one," he said as he lifted another centimetre of puppy hair.

Katherine peered closely, a tiny oval dark speck was lodged head-down into the skin, as soon as Charlie picked at it, the intruder rapidly dislodged and scurried through the fur in the blink of an eye. Charlie tried to get ahead of it, lifting the hair where the bloodsucker disappeared, but once discovered, it scooted through the tangle of fuzz and out of sight in a flash.

"I didn't know they could be so hard to catch," Katherine said as she watched Charlie hunt his quarry for a minute.

"They move like greased lightning, they're flat, and so they can swim through the hair like a fish." He just then pulled out a pinch of fur, eliciting a yip from Jasper. Tangled in the fuzz was the minuscule parasite, which Charlie quickly disposed of, running to the toilet and flushing the vermin away. "They jump like crazy," he continued when he returned, "and multiply like cockroaches too, so you don't want them getting out in the house. Where you see one, there are probably twenty more."

Katherine felt an irresistible urge to scratch her scalp and then her arms.

"Uck! That gives me goose bumps!"

Finally, Charlie gave up the hunt and placed Jasper back on the floor, dispatching fleas was not his idea of a romantic evening, unless you happened to be a twisted exterminator, he thought.

"When you get the flea collar, or whatever bug killer you want to use, make sure he's outside when you put it on, and keep him out for the day."

"Okay, but I better not tell Mom, she will go ape! I'll have to watch Jasper in the back yard where she can't see. Perhaps I could get him used to the leash."

"Good idea, she might send him back if he's infested. Oops! No you don't Jasper," Charlie said as he quickly jumped out of the chair and scooped up the squatting canine. Whether it was from fright or late timing they could not tell, but Jasper simply could not hold it before Charlie dashed to the door, duly spritzing his suit to Katherine's mortification.

"Well, so much for the first lesson in house breaking," Charlie said as he gently put Jasper back in the pen with a sheepish smile bordering on amusement.   The last hope of salvaging a romantic evening had now dissipated as Katherine handed him the towel they used shortly before, wide-eyed and embarrassed beyond words, stammering profuse apologies for Jasper's accident.

"Oh Charlie, I'm so sorry! I'll pay the cleaning bill for your suit, this is just terrible, I feel awful!"

"Now don't get all upset Kathy, it's my fault I tried to do the one hundred meter dash with him," he replied as he mopped away, now finding the whole proceedings of the night an occasion to laugh. "Oh well, I guess I'd better go home now and get out of this."

"I suppose so, Charlie. I really am sorry, about everything! The dinner was disappointing, not what I expected, and now this...."

"Oh, don't worry about it, Kathy. I was happy to come over, however, it turned out to be a night we'll find hard to forget," he said with a Stevenish grin as he prepared to leave.

♥

Katherine woke the next morning early, she wended her way to the kitchen, rubbing the sleep from her eyes. She was quite famished, in all the hubbub of the previous evening, she quite forgot her planned kitchen raid the night before, and went directly to bed. Time to grab a quick breakfast and check on Jasper before everyone wakes up, she thought. She decided not to sleep over in the apartment as Steves suggested, hoping a nightlight would suffice, but was concerned how Jasper accepted his first night alone in a new house. Firing up the espresso machine, she opened the cupboard that held her favourite chocolaty collation only to discover boxes of raspy wheat flakes, bran 'twig' cereal, pasty coloured oatmeal, stocky granola bars, and packages of rye crackers that could serve as makeshift emery boards. Opening the bread drawer, she found a new stash of brown loaves instead of the cherished fluffy white variety, and parcels of puffed-rice 'Styrofoam' slices. Uh oh, Gramp's diet has extended to the breakfast foods already. Surely, Mrs. Gonzales didn't throw everything else out? Delving through the rest of the drawers, she discovered the cookies and other sugary snacks had also disappeared into thin air, in their wake were repulsive changelings ... sugar-free nibbles masquerading as delectable treats. Finally, she thought to look in the pantry, to find the door hermetically sealed.

Resigned that she must share Gramp's dietary fate, she poured out a bowel of wheat flakes with a sigh. To top the morning off, the sugar was also gone, replaced with a jar of artificial sweetener that fizzed when she

98

poured the milk on her cereal. She sat at the breakfast table by the bay window as Gramps made his way in, muttering under his breath.

"Don't know why I bother to look for anything, it's all gerbil food …."

"Morning, Gramps."

"Oh, hullo Katie, didn't see you there. Did you take a look in the cupboards? Nothing but sawdust, we're out of eggs and bacon, and the pantry is locked! I came down for a midnight snack last night, and all I could find worth eating was a granola bar," he grumbled.

Katherine held up her bowel of wood chips.

"I guess I've joined the club. Come on, grab something and sit with me, misery loves company you know."

Mumbling away, he finally made a cup of caffeine-free coffee and snatched a couple of bananas from the fruit bowel on the counter.

"Looks like they've finally made a monkey out of me," he chuckled.

"Perhaps you had better lose the weight as fast as you can before we all starve to death."

"Well, that won't take too long … ."

"To lose the weight?"

"No, before we all starve to death," he replied as he patted his rotund stomach, "Even with a diet, I'd need a blowtorch to burn this fat off in a hurry. The older you get, the harder it is to get rid of it."

"That's where Jasper comes in, the walks will do you good."

"I suppose so," he replied as he sipped his coffee.

"I have to go check on him after breakfast. You won't believe what happened last night," she continued, retelling the latest incidents that occurred with Jasper in minute details, the messy pen, the flea chase, and of course, the grand finale, "Gramps, it was so embarrassing, Charlie's suit was simply drenched."

Imagining Charlie stiffly holding the puppy while caught in that predicament, he nearly burst out laughing, but forced himself to look sympathetic for Katherine's sake, who he knew was humiliated beyond words.

"There, there now. It's not the end of the world, accidents do happen. At least you now know not to try and run with Jasper if he's ready to do something, just put him back on the paper in the pen, and praise him when he doodles on it, and reprimand him when accidents occur."

"But how do we progress to the great outdoors?"

"Well, when he gets the idea to use the paper, put a sheet of paper outside, and start making new associations, 'paper equals outside', and then you can try to wean him off the paper altogether."

"Okay, Gramps. That sounds like a plan, but how I will get any work done or get ready for my trip is beyond me. Oh, well, I'm sure I'll figure something out. I have to run and get him a flea collar, and perhaps make an appointment with the vet, and sign up for a dog licence. Oh, I haven't called Suzy yet! She's probably wondered what's happened to me, I said I'd call a few days after she arrived home."

"Looks like you've got a busy day ahead of you."

Although she planned to head out early, Katherine decided to stay and wait for everyone before she left to do her puppy errands. In a few minutes, the rest of the family came down just as Mrs. Gonzales and Juanita emerged from their apartment to fix breakfast, which wasn't worth writing home about Steves noted, freshly squeezed orange juice, diet yoghurt, brown toast with diet margarine, and a bowel of fresh fruit salad and oatmeal.

"This is cruelty beyond measure," Steves quipped as he dabbed at his gruel with a spoon, "someone call Amnesty International!"

Pops suppressed a smile while he opened his yoghurt.

"Now Steven, stop your complaining and eat your breakfast, it's good for you," their mother replied as she ate her fruit salad.

Discussing their plans for the day, Helen was off to her Wednesday bridge club meeting, Steves would be writing up reports on the various lab tests completed of late, and Gramps planned to meet with a group of train aficionados who had booked a group tour to see a visiting exhibition on the history of Victorian steam engines after the board meeting. Katherine relayed her plans to make an appointment at the vet's office for Jasper and to find out about a dog license, carefully keeping his flea infestation a classified topic with her mother present, while Pops just had the board meeting for the day, after which he had nothing specifically on his agenda, he might come home early for a change. Until Gramps and Pops had brought up the subject, Katherine had completely forgotten about the board meeting, her plan to concentrate on Gramp's woes to block out her own troubles had worked, and her stomach lurched with the thought of Gramps and Pops facing disgruntled board members, wondering if they still remembered the Sunday paper, and there was the lunch at the rectory tomorrow! What a mess!

With breakfast over, everyone went to their respective occupations for the day, and passing the library, she collected her painting and headed straight to the apartment. She quickly hid the painting in the hall closet with the others, "Out of sight, out of mind," she thought as Jasper greeted her with a profusion of barks and whines, he obviously hated being left alone. She fed him in the kitchen and cleaned up the soggy newspapers, laying a fresh supply in the pen. Might as well let him run around for a while, she thought, poor little tyke, locked up all night, and there's plenty of time to do the shopping and fussing later. Perhaps it was time to look over her unfinished canvases? She was about to return to the closet where she had stashed them out of harm's way when she spied Jasper preparing to do his business, and she quickly put him back in the pen on the paper. At least she got to him in time! Praising him up a storm, she took him out again and changed the papers … again. She then realized that she might not get him to the temporary puppy latrine every time, so she decided to lay convenient 'paper stations' in selected locations. Training puppies must be a danger to the environment, she mused, Jasper will have used half the Amazon rainforest before I can get him to go outside!

She finally rummaged in the closet and took out three unfinished canvases, inventive works with a Victorian theme. Rather than paint existing city and rustic village scenes that anyone could do, and did, she delved into the depths of her imagination and experimented with fabricating fantastic buildings featuring unusual architectural designs of her own, and horse-drawn carriages with figures dressed in styles dating from the 1800s. Well, in her expert opinion, the pictures were unfinished. In the spirit of Monet and his celebrated Rouen cathedral series, she painted the same imaginary city at three different times of the day, morning, noon and evening, but unlike Monet, who worked in rapid-fire mode, painting his subjects directly from life at breakneck speed while the sunlight was perfect, Katherine was drawing her subject from the recesses of her imagination, taking care to achieve the effects she desired. It was always difficult knowing when to stop, just one more brushstroke, and the highlighting would be faultless, no, perhaps one dash more, maybe a touch or two here and there she mused. She set up the third canvas of the series, the scene basking in the brilliant glow of the setting sun. Surveying the canvas, I think it needs a few more flecks of vermilion and orange to bring out the rich colours of the evening. Not wanting to bother changing in and out of paint clothes today, she donned a large smock before setting up her equipment. Squirting the necessary colours on her palette, she selected her brush and mixed the bright blobs in different quantities until she achieved the desired hue, adding the required touches to her picture with care and deliberation, pausing after each stroke to examine the effect of her application.

Sighing, she realized time had come to call a halt to her continuous daubing on these three canvases, perhaps now is as good a time as any, she decided. She would never have a collection completed if she painted at this rate. One could be become too much of a perfectionist, destroying months of work with a few strokes while attempting to satisfy an obsessive compulsion to ornament and embellish. She must not forget the importance of understated elegance. Nevertheless, it was difficult to declare a work finished once and for all. Considerable time and care had been lavished on each piece, and for some inexplicable reason, to 'finish' was similar to saying 'goodbye', it was like a separation, a parting of the ways, and she did not like having to say farewell.

It was time to move on. While it was important to learn from the masters and appreciate their styles, she knew she had to develop her own style. Looking at her cityscapes, imaginative though they may be, they were still indebted to the Impressionist Monet. Her entry for the Sirrac contest may be striking, but it was a reinvention of David's work after all. Perhaps her sources of inspiration were far too obvious. When people viewed her work, she wanted them to think Walsingham, not Manet, Ingres, or Degas. She needed to be original, to create works that challenged the intellect, offend the expectations of the world, make it sit up and take notice, or slap it in the face, whichever came first. How she would achieve this, she did not know, to begin a new painting was difficult enough, waiting for that serendipitous moment of inspiration that would spur her into a flurry of excitement and eagerness for action, to launch a revolutionary movement in the world of art would require considerable effort, possibly years of painstaking development.

Come to think of it, perhaps 'painstaking' was an apropos description at this time she thought, considering she had already tried her hand at shaking up the world, and look what happened when it decided to return the favour with only one miserable newspaper article! Steves did have a point, she would have to develop a thick skin if she wanted a career in art because it would be out of character for her to take the easy road as Gramps remarked. What was it he said about painting fields of flowers? That anyone could paint pipe dreams seen through rose-rimmed glasses? Hmm, that's what people expect, just like Professor Matthews explained, prosaic scenes of floral Elysium. I must progress beyond the expected, and display the unanticipated ... but that landed me in my present dilemma! Oh, I am sick and tired of running this around in my head! So, let's have it out once and for all ... are you humiliated enough to give up painting entirely? Of course not, she answered herself. Abandon painting? Unthinkable! Then, why is this a big deal? This detachment does not develop overnight, it requires a succession of whiplashes and an eon of weathering. That's the problem, she mused, arguing the various points back and forth like an intellectual tennis match. I can barely tolerate a paper cut, and must be prepared for a succession of hard knocks, at least from an artistic standpoint. So, is it the criticism you cannot tolerate? Constructive criticism is one thing, it's the unjust denigration I can't accept. But why do you listen to it? You don't believe it? No, of course not. Then, why does it bother you? I hate to see my work deliberately misunderstood. Everyone will have their own thoughts and opinions, no one will look at a work of art and interpret it in the same way. Who would write, draw or design anything if they allowed these qualms to take hold? Why let an unfounded fear keep you from your work? That's true, however, my work no longer affects just me, but everyone around me. I never realized one painting could cause such a series of aftershocks. Perhaps I *am* making too big a deal out of this, everything has worked out so far. I guess I'm anxious about Pops and Gramps, and the reactions of the board members, I mustn't let it get to me.

Katherine did not have time to muse any longer as Jasper began playing tug-o-war with the end of her smock, pulling her thoughts away from her one-to-one argument.

"Hello, Jasper. Are you telling me I should get off my duff and get your stuff?"

As though he had understood her whimsical rhyme, he stopped yanking on her hem, flopped with a slight 'whump' and began scratching behind his ear before nibbling with frustration near his hindquarters.

"I see there should be no delay. All right, I guess it's time for a quick trip to the 'Pet Emporium' and debug you."

Placing Jasper back in the pen, Katherine quickly pulled off her smock and hung it in the closet, tidied her clothes, and covered her drying canvas with a white sheet to prevent dust and small insects from sticking to the work. There was nothing more gruesome than to see a fly stuck on a painting, struggling to get away, trapped like so many unfortunate prehistoric victims of the Rancho Le Brae tar pits. Since she had used most of the paint she had prepared, cleaning her palette was relatively simple, a quick wipe with white spirits with a thorough rinsing of hot water, and she was ready for the next session. One quick peep in the mirror, and off we go. Many times she had unsuspectingly ventured out of her studio with a rainbow smudge or two on her face, having involuntarily rubbed her nose or cheek with paint-bedecked fingers. Picking up her purse, she was about to leave when the electronic *bzzzzzttt* of the intercom stopped her in her tracks.

"Miss Kathy?"

"I'm here, Mrs. G," she replied. "What's up?"

"You just received a call from someone at the Sirrac Gallery."

"What? The Sirrac Gallery? Are you sure?"

"Positive Miss Kathy! They wanted to talk to you, but I know how you hate to be disturbed when you are working, so I did the usual, asked for their number and told them you would return their call. Was that all right? Maybe I should have made an exception and put the call through?"

"No, that's okay, Mrs. G. This gives me time to let this sink in. Wow! Did they say what they wanted to talk about?"

"Only that they wished to discuss the painting you entered for their contest. Will I give you their number now, or do you want to wait until later?"

"Gosh, might as well give it to me now, let me get a pen and a piece of paper, okay, fire away." She quickly wrote down the necessary information, wondering what this could mean. "Got it. Thanks, Mrs. G., I'll see what this is all about this afternoon."

"I hope it is good news."

"I hope so too. I'll see you later, I have to pop into town for a few things right now. I'll be back for lunch."

"Okay, Miss Kathy, see you then."

Releasing the intercom button, she glanced at the number before she put the paper away in her purse and made her way down to the garage. *That's odd! I wonder why they are calling me about the contest? Perhaps they have disqualified the other works for some reason and have promoted my painting? Now, that's a little egotistical, isn't it? Don't get ahead of yourself. Perhaps Robert the Horrible's article has something to do with it, maybe he has also caused them problems and it's *my* painting they wish to disqualify! They're obviously regretting they gave it an honourable mention after all. Imagine the first public recognition of my work, and it could be revoked. Just my luck!* Well, I'll worry about that when I come home, I have a flea infestation to deal with at the moment, she thought as she drove down the driveway.

It did not take long to buy the armaments she needed, a few flea collars and some cans of pet insecticide. Parking in the driveway, she decided to spray the inside of her car with the odd smelling concoction before turning her attentions to the carpets and sofa in the apartment. *Wonderful, the place smells just like the chemical labs, imagine Steves putting up with this reek all day. Jasper, now sound asleep, was oblivious to the consternation his army of uninvited guests had occasioned. Sleep well, my little friend,* Katherine thought as she washed her hands after her fumigation, you're next after lunch when I can take you and your bed outside.

Closing the door quietly, she went over to the house for lunch where she found Mrs. Gonzales making a racket in the pantry.

"Are you okay in there?" Katherine queried, wondering what on earth she could be up to. There stood Mrs. G. equipped with a large pair of pliers, wrestling with a stubborn shelf-bracket.

"Just fine," she replied through gritted teeth as she banged upon the unyielding metal bit, "I want to move this shelf up, but *this* stupid thing won't budge."

"It likes its old home and doesn't want to move. Here, try some olive oil in the groove, it might loosen it up."

Katherine ripped off a paper towel and daubed the offending metal arm. With a few wriggles, the bracket lifted up without further ado.

"Well, what do you know? Thanks Miss Kathy, I've been at that for a good ten minutes. I am trying to make room for the new refrigerator."

"New refrigerator?"

"To keep all the non-dietary articles away from your grandfather."

"Oh dear, he's not going to like this one bit, that's for sure." Katherine looked around, "Aha! So this is where all the good grub went, there's my Pop Tarts, and the cookies. Are these things off limits to us too?"

"Of course not, dear. Didn't I tell you? The key to the pantry is behind the ivy plant on the shelf over the sink, if you want anything, just help yourself, but don't tell Mr. G.W., he's the only one barred from the pantry."

"*Now* I find out. Does Steves know about the key?"

"Didn't have to tell him, he knows how to pick the lock. I can see he found the brownies sometime last night," Mrs. Gonzales said as she looked into the extra bread box she reserved for the baked goods.

"Figures, and he wouldn't get me a nibble while he was at it," Katherine sarcastically replied as she helped Mrs. Gonzales lift the shelf to its new position. "He must have had a nice laugh letting me think I would be forever reduced to fibre flakes for breakfast."

"Thank you, Miss Kathy, I can arrange the rest myself. Can I fix you anything?"

"No thanks, I'll make a quick ham and cheese sandwich," she replied as she reached for a loaf of white bread and some brownies from the breadbox. She had a second round of flea spraying to see to, an important telephone call to make, and she rarely stopped for an elaborate lunch, she would only feel like falling asleep afterwards. She quickly had her sandwich with a glass of ice tea, munching on her brownies as she headed back to the apartment to tackle Jasper, who was now wide-awake yapping for his liberty.   Taking him outside, she yoked him with the flea collar and tied him to a tree with the expando-leash, covering his eyes, she sprayed him from snout to tail.

"There you go. Job done. I suppose I should return that call now, no you stay here, Jasper. Look, nice green grass." Jasper did not care about the grass, and tried to follow her up the steps to the veranda, barking his indignation and whining with anxiety as he was stopped in his tracks by the leash. "Oh, for Pete's sake! Look, you have to stay out here for a while, you're in quarantine. A few hours in the yard won't hurt you." Trying to ignore his heart-rending yelps, she went back to fetch his bed and dosed it outside with the spray, returning once more to the apartment to clean out the pen. Time to see what the Sirrac Gallery had to say about her painting.

Rummaging through her purse for that crucial slip of paper, her stomach gave a slight lurch as she cleared her throat and dialled the number. For some strange reason, she felt as though she was suffering from a case of stage jitters. After a few ring tones, her call was answered by whom she assumed was the receptionist.

"Good afternoon, Sirrac Gallery. How may I help you?"

"Hello, my name is Katherine Walsingham. May I speak to Mr. Kevin Alcott please?"

"Certainly, wait one moment, I'll put your call through."

"Thank you."

Katherine was put on hold, and obliged to listen to a lilting melody played by a classical string quartet. Letting her thoughts drift off with the music, she was startled on hearing a voice suddenly say;

"Hello, Miss Walsingham?"

"Yes?"

How she disliked being left on hold, she always felt like a sleepwalker rudely shocked out of their midnight stroll, and hoped she did not sound like a complete idiot as she snapped back to attention out of her semi-somnambulistic daydreaming.

"Good afternoon, I believe you called earlier today about the painting I entered for the Belvedere contest."

"Yes, the painting with Napoléon, is that correct? A client asked us to enquire if it was for sale."

"For sale?"

Katherine's thoughts spun for a moment, she certainly wasn't expecting *this* piece of news.

"Yes, have you considered selling it?"

"Not at present, actually. ..." her voice trailed off. Katherine could not believe what she was hearing. Imagine! Here I was thinking of burning it in the garden bonfire only a few days ago.

"Our client, who wishes to remain anonymous, has offered twenty-five thousand for your consideration. You understand, we would deduct our usual commission from the purchase price."

"Of course." Well, it was their contest, she probably would not have thought up the subject *Le Sacre d'ingéniosité Humaine* at all were it not for the theme chosen that year, and this unknown buyer was *their* client. "What is your regular commission, may I ask?"

"Forty-seven percent."

That sounded a little exorbitant, she did not realize galleries charged that much, according to what she had heard. Gallery managers had to eat and pay their bills like everyone else, but did that mean fleecing the artists who made the work in the first place? Naturally, exclusive establishments on Fifth Avenue could demand whatever they saw fit, the prestige associated with the location was enough to draw those customers willing and able to pay the excessive prices, she did have to keep that in mind. At least forty-seven percent did not sound as grasping as fifty did, however, it was droll that the gallery managers refrained from snatching the latter percentage as though giving that extra three percent to the artist was a great act of magnanimity.

"I see, well, I will need some time to think this over. I made no decision yet."

"Of course, please call me back when you've made a decision."

"I will, thank you, Mr. Alcott."

"My pleasure, Miss Walsingham. Have a nice afternoon."

"Thank you, you too. Goodbye."

Katherine replaced the receiver, exhilarated, but dumbfounded by this unexpected brief telephone exchange. Who could possibly want to buy her painting? Did someone see it on graduation day, or did the competition organizers show the entries to their clientèle while they were being judged? Perhaps she should have enquired while she had the chance, but it all happened too fast. Possibly, they would not divulge any information as the client wished to remain anonymous. In any case, it was good news for a change! She could hardly believe her good luck, that someone was willing to pay twenty-five thousand for an unknown artist's work, a newly graduated student at that. Should she sell it? She did not need the money, but to sell her first notable piece *via* the Sirrac Gallery was without doubt a *coup d'art*. Smiling to herself, she savoured this triumph, and decision or no decision, she could not wait to break these glad tidings to the family, perhaps it might offset whatever Pops and Gramps had to suffer from the board members. Going over to the closet where she had quickly stashed her canvases out of Jasper's way, she took down the painting and set it up on an easel, surveying it with a kind benevolent once more. Well, take *that*, Robert Horace! Someone appreciates it, *and* is willing to pay for it.

Musing over the telephone call, she realized that it was very quiet outside. Looking out the window, she noticed Jasper had wound part of his leash around the tree, with the rest tangled about his midsection and legs. I had better rescue him, she thought as she went outside.

"How did you get yourself in this state, you silly pup?" she muttered as she unravelled him before picking him up and walking around the tree, unwinding the rest of the leash. "All heart, and no brains I guess. Come on, let's see if you can take a walk with this thing."

Jasper seemed to like this idea of a promenade having discovered the delights of frolicking in the grass, but he had no concept of a straight line, continually bounding off in all directions, wrapping her legs with the leash and tripping her up as she tried to give him his first tour around the grounds. Eventually he discovered an old tennis ball near the court and laid down to gnaw on his weather-beaten treasure. Making the most of this moment, she stretched out on a nearby lounge to mull over the event of that afternoon.

Exciting though the prospect of selling her painting was, she felt conflicting emotions, something that bordered on sadness, but not quite, it was a feeling she could not easily identify. If she thought finishing a painting was hard now, the likely prospect of seeing one drift out of her possession was certainly more difficult. She wondered if other artists felt the same, if they mused about their works once they were released into the world, thinking about where they could be, if they were cherished, if the same owner still had them, perhaps the buyer had donated or sold them to someone else. Were they in someone's home? Would they become famous and placed in a museum? Would they meet an untimely fate, to be destroyed in a fire, or perchance stolen by some thief, to be hidden away for years until they are rediscovered? How hard it is to let go of something like this, she thought. At the same time, she knew these melancholic reveries were illogical and impractical. Few artists in history had the luxury to worry about the destiny of their works, forced to sell their art, having to eke out a living. She did not have to contend with that hardship, but hoarding her work for her own pleasure like the proverbial wizened miser who gawked at his lump of gold in the hole was downright idiotic. How ridiculous she would be, surrounding herself with piles of canvases, hiding them away from the public. Perhaps she could open a private art museum? Somehow, that did not sound as dynamic as running a gallery, besides, filling a museum with her own works might be considered a little too pompous. There would also be no way of knowing how her paintings would fare the test of time if she set them up on a pedestal herself. After all, self-praise is no praise. In the end, she reasoned, saying goodbye to her colourful children may be an unavoidable fact of life, pleasant or unpleasant though it may be. But, should she sell *this* particular work? That was the question.

Katherine meditated on this important decision until she heard Pop's car pull up the driveway.

"Come on, Jasper. He's home early, I hope everything turned out okay."

Already bored with the tennis ball, Jasper was eager to be on the move and bounded along behind her as she returned to the garage. She waited outside until Pops had parked the car. When he emerged with briefcase in tow, he looked more relaxed than he had been in days.

"Hi Pops. Where's Gramps?"

"Hello, Kathy. Don't you remember? He headed off to that train exhibition after the meeting."

"I remember now. Well, how did it go today?"

"Better than I expected, I'll tell you all about it when I change into something more comfortable," he replied as he loosened his tie. "I see you have been kept busy," he continued as he looked down at the boisterous ball of golden fluff.

"Oh, you haven't seen him yet! Pops, meet Jasper," she replied as she picked him up. "Careful though, I've sprayed him for fleas. But don't tell Mom! She doesn't know about his hidden cargo, he should be all clear pretty soon."

Harold smiled as he tried to rub Jasper's ear, but ended up with slobbery fingers instead.

"Don't worry, Jasper's stowaways won't be mentioned. Anything for peace, right? I reckon we have a new addition to the family. How is the training going?"

Katherine decided to skip Jasper's encounter with Charlie, one embarrassing retelling of the incident to Gramps was enough for now, and proceeded with her latest success.

"So far, the mess is kept to one area in the pen, and this morning I got him to the paper in time. How long it will be before he goes outside is anyone's guess."

"Well, he shouldn't be too hard to train. Anything else happen today?"

Katherine ticked off the day's events on her fingers in the order they occurred.

"I finished up the last touches on my remaining cityscape, I'll bring them all over to show everyone when it dries … Mrs. G. has ordered a new refrigerator for the pantry, I don't know when it is to be delivered, I forgot to ask … and I've got good news to tell, but I'll wait until I hear your news first. I'll put Jasper back in his pen, he's had a nice outing, and meet you back in the main house when you've changed."

"All right, dear. Bye, Jasper."

Katherine took her charge back to the apartment and placed him once more in solitary confinement. Poor thing, it's too quiet for him when left on his own, she thought, and brought out the radio from the kitchen, setting the dial to an easy-listening station before going over to the house. Leaving the apartment she noticed a delivery truck had pulled up outside, Mrs. Gonzales appeared immediately and directed the men to the kitchen at the back of the house. They had arrived just in time Katherine noted, the new fridge will be set up before Gramps returns from his steam-engine tour. There won't be anything decent left to eat in the other one, he's going to have a fit. It will be hard not to give in and keep the pantry key a secret. Katherine went to the kitchen, poured herself another glass of ice tea and went to the den to wait for Pops, she was bursting to hear his news, and to tell hers. Just then, he came down, dressed casually and in slippers, making a quick visit to the kitchen as evidenced by the cold beer can and large glass he brought with him.

"Well now, it's nice to be home early for a change," he sighed as he snapped open the can and poured his well-deserved libation before stretching out in his favourite recliner. "Tell me, what is the good news?"

"You first, Pops. I've been on pins and needles since that confounded article was printed."

"All right, to tell the truth and make a long story short, most of the board members did not read or hear about the article at all, and the few who did, knew it was all stuff and nonsense. So, no major catastrophe, no unexpected demise of Walsingham Industries," her father replied with a slight smile as he took one long sip of his beer, watching the relief wash over her face from the corner of his eye.

No point retelling the details that would only upset or embarrass her, like the apology he made to those who might have read the article before the meeting commenced, and the various reactions from the confused, the sympathetic and the slightly amused as an explanation was offered, to discover, as his father had predicted, that little or no notice was paid to the 'Art Hacker Affair'. After the board had concluded their business for the day, Nancy Thornton and another friend and member, Tom Conrad, approached him to give a reassuring pep talk.

"Harold, don't give it another thought," Nancy began, "I read the article and know for certain your Katherine could never have painted anything like that. Robert Horace is infamous for his 'butcher reviews' and few actually believe the trash he prints."

"So I've been told," Harold replied before taking the time to clear the matter and explain the actual meaning of the controversial allegorical painting. "It's amazing all the unexpected events parents are confronted with," he concluded, "I wish Kathy had been a little more circumspect with her subject, but once she gets an idea, she fails to consider the consequences."

"Like every kid," Tom continued, "they all jump into things without looking ahead. Harold, you are truly lucky to have Katherine and Steven, just look at what happened to us with our Jason."

"Yes, that's true," Nancy nodded sympathetically, "you've been truly blessed."

"I know," Harold replied, "I shouldn't complain. How is Jason?"

"Well, he is doing much better, he hasn't stopped attending the meetings since he came out of rehab," Tom continued. "I hope we can begin to put the last six years of hell behind us, and what a hell it was. We never knew where he was day or night, what crack-house he was passed out in, dreading every phone call, expecting it to be the police or the hospital telling us the worst. His mother will never be the same from all the worry and stress. I thank my lucky stars our other two did not get mixed up with the same crowd."

"It's difficult being a parent," Nancy affirmed, "there are so many destructive allurements out there today that our generation never had to deal with."

"Too true," Harold replied.

Despite all the ups and the downs, from the strange misadventures during their childhood years, like Katherine's scribbles all over the walls and company documents, and Steven's experiments with the microwave and a combination of metal cooking utensils, to their teenage years and beyond, in the end, they were remarkably level-headed considering their privileged upbringing and the spending money his father's trust funds had provided. Steven may like his fast cars and the frat house parties, but he never actually goes too far, and putting all joking aside, will knuckle-down when he is needed.   Katherine is always moderate, completely goal and family orientated. Neither had taken up smoking, and the thought of drugs was out of the question — Katherine was not stupid, and Steven was far above *that* sort of experimentation despite his curiosity, he got his 'highs' through his scientific work and computer programming, thank heavens. Harold dreaded to think what might have happened if the opposite were the case, considering he had whole labs and distribution warehouses chocker-blocked with all the equipment and substances needed to satisfy a drug user's wildest psychedelic dreams. Yes, Harold felt truly blessed.

"Okay, I've told you mine, now you tell me yours," he continued, taking another sip.

"You'll never guess, I was just about to get Jasper's spray when the Sirrac Gallery called."

"Really? Did it have something to do with the article?"

"I don't know, I didn't think to ask, I was a bit flabbergasted."

"How so?"

"Some anonymous buyer wants my painting, and they've offered twenty-five thousand for it."

"Well, that *is* good news. You now have your first artwork sold. That is something to celebrate."

"But now, I actually don't know if I want to part with it," she finally admitted.

"Oh? Why not? Isn't that why you entered the contest in the first place? To have it displayed in the gallery for prospective buyers to view? If a buyer came while it was in their showroom, surely they would expect you to agree to the sale."

"Hmm, I see what you mean, but the circumstances are different. It didn't actually win, it was never placed in their exhibition, I don't think I am obliged to sell it now. Besides, I was more interested in the publicity from the contest, and it is my first artwork to receive a prestigious notable mention, and some infamy in the press to boot. I just might keep it for sentiment's sake, in fact, come to think of it, I can picture my Napoléon in all his radioactive glory hanging up in the foyer of my future gallery … ." she replied with a thoughtful, introspective expression.

"Well, it's your call, Kathy. I would sleep on it first, don't be too hasty in making a decision."

"I will, sleep on it, that is. I can't wait to see everyone's reaction when I tell them tonight, a nice change from last Sunday."

"It is indeed. I am very happy for you, Kathy. So, what do you plan to do next? Is there a new budding masterpiece in the works?"

"Not quite yet, I am waiting for an inspiration to hit me. I'm divided between two styles, to tell the truth. I want to paint beautiful scenes that people would love to hang on their walls but I don't want to stick to the pure pictorial, or decorative, if you know what I mean. I also want my pictures to say something important too, like the one I entered for the contest. It's hard to know which direction to take."

"That's no big dilemma," her father sagely replied. "You don't *have* to adhere to one style and forsake the other, you can do both, paint in one style when you feel so inclined, and then work on your 'symbolic controversies' when an inspiration strikes you. In time, you may learn to combine the two, and develop your style accordingly. Any time I hear about an artist and their works they are described according to 'periods', like Picasso's 'blue' phase, and so on. Frankly, you would be an absolute bore if you dogmatically chose one style and refused to evolve. Think of the poor art critics and historians in the future whom you would deprive of a living. You would give them nothing to study or write about."

Katherine laughed at his light-hearted conclusion, he was right after all. Why not work in a myriad of styles and stop fussing? Perhaps she was concentrating so intensely on the importance of developing her own style, she could not see the forest for the trees.

"Thanks for the advice, Pops. I guess I had better follow it and stop yakking, I think I sense an inspiration coming...."

"Well, hop to it my dear, far be it from me to hold up the whispering of your artistic genius."

"I'm off, see you at dinner."

Katherine returned to the apartment and brought out a new canvas that was stored in one of the spare bedrooms. Jasper was asleep, good, she could work out her latest idea in peace. Pop's conversation on working in distinctive styles or combining them set her mind on the rudimentary importance of contrast. Time to get back to the basics. What grabs a viewer's attention, a harmonious blending of white and creams, or the classic starkness of black and white? Taking this one step further, if there was a message she wished to portray in her works, would it not be more effective if she could contrast her subject matter? How could she achieve this? She thought about Gramp's comment that anyone could paint beautiful flowers, but what if she contrasted this idyllic image with some hard unpleasant fact that nobody was willing to face? Now that would be interesting, she thought. Maybe her other painting was still too closely interwoven with her present thoughts, but she could not shake the radiation symbols from her mind. Of course! Mankind, in its expedient efforts to save the planet, adopted one of the most absurd 'solutions', nuclear power. Yes, it may be the cleanest form of fuel, emitting only steam from the generators, but what about the by-products like the spent fuel rods, not to mention the prospect of another Chernobyl. Could anyone really guarantee that an accident like that will never happen again? One major radiation spill, and the surrounding countryside is poisoned for well over a thousand years, a catastrophe that would be far worse than the present smog caused by carbon emissions, a pollution that *can* be cleaned up. The human race, the eternal child, is playing with the power of the sun like a book of matches. With these thoughts, she imagined a field of flowers, but in the midst of this scene, she could also envision the so-called answer to the world's pollution problem, a nuclear power plant with its distinctive pottery-pot towers. However, the image was not stark enough, she decided. What if the field of daisies and buttercups was also a cemetery? An eerie reminder that while we may be saving the flowers of the world at present, we are also digging our graves. It cannot be just any cemetery, she would have to do some research and find out what the grave markings looked like in the Ukraine and Belarus.

Excited with her idea of contrast, she mused about other applications of this concept. She thought of other world issues that bothered her, like the poverty and underdevelopment of the third world, while other nations lived in superabundance. By now, with all our modern technology, there should be no poverty left on earth. Although she was fascinated with the latest exploration in outer space, she could not see the sense in burning up billions of dollars to bring back a few lumps of rock or a picture or two when so many went hungry and homeless. If the world had its priorities set right, poverty and disease should be eradicated first before man turns its attention to the stars, she decided. Right then, she could imagine a picture of hungry African children standing outside their little mud hut, their stomachs distended from the effects of malnutrition. Now for the allegorical punch, one of the children holds up a postcard sent to them by the developed world, a picture of an astronaut on the moon waving into the camera: 'To the Third World – Wish You Were Here!' Katherine wondered what Robert Horace would say about paintings like these.

She started to sketch her first idea, rarely making preliminary drawings on paper, preferring to capture the initial momentum of her inspiration directly on the canvas. Completely engrossed in her work, the afternoon flew, and before she realized, it was dinnertime. Judging from the latest kitchen arrangements and last night's menu, her expectations for dinner were set low, therefore, she was not overly disappointed when Mrs. Gonzales brought out grilled chicken and steamed rice and broccoli served with another salad.   Her thoughts turned to the pantry and its hidden delights, while Steves could hardly refrain from laughing at Gramp's disgruntled look.

As usual, everyone shared their experiences of the day. Pops began by announcing that Katherine's painting had no negative effects on the board, and his new proposal had been accepted without much opposition.

"I told you Katie, there was nothing to worry about!" Gramps interjected.

For almost a year, several members complained that the profit margins of the company had not increased according to their expectations, and pressed that a motion be passed to develop a line of contraceptive pharmaceuticals. Like his father, a staunch conservative, Harold would never consider overturning one of the core principles of his family's business for the sake of vulgar profit. Walsingham Industries would never stoop to produce products of that nature. With his father and brother behind him, they held the majority vote, and therefore was confident that these motions would never be passed. However, his own brother finally admitted, to the dismay of him and his father, that he was persuaded they were doing little to bring the company into line with modern trends and that 'reproductive health' was worth considering. Harold knew who was pushing his brother along these lines, Mr. Morgan, the most liberal member on the board who was more interested in profitable progress, not ethics. If Timothy did the unthinkable and voted against them, they would lose the voting majority and the other liberals could press the company in a diabolical direction. It was at times like these Harold regretted that their company went public in order to raise funds for their research and development, but now the damage is done. Until now he was able to keep abreast of the situation, stressing upon the conservative members of the board that Walsingham Industries had always been recognised as an ethical institution, anything that deviated from this ideal was bound to devastate the reputation of the company. He also reminded them that birth control drugs were not 'contraceptive' at all times, that is, conception prevention as the word implied, but that 'the pill' with its contragestive properties was in reality an abortive. Women were still conceiving unaware of the fact.   His father always continued to back him with his own arguments *vis* he did not approve of any medication or treatment that manipulated the natural hormonal cycle.

"You may think my rationale simple-minded without all the scientific jargon to back it right now, but if you push the body beyond its limits, or force it to go against nature, you can expect it to revolt," his father declared, "and that usually means cancer. Of all the diseases and illness, cancer is nothing but an internal rebellion."

Morgan condescendingly requested Walsingham senior to explain his point for the elucidation of the board. Gregory obliged him.

"What is cancer? Cells that refuse to stop multiplying or think they have a better idea and want to make organs and other things in the wrong places, invading healthy tissue. You've seen the slides from our medical research library showing ovarian tumours growing hair, teeth and bone. Cancer cells are not team players, they're rogue rebels, and where the body is concerned, unity is paramount for survival. Illnesses and parasites are foreign invaders that can be dealt with. Genetic disorders are a shame, but their presence doesn't necessarily mean the body *purposely* works against itself, but with cancer, it's pure cellular disobedience that doesn't give two figs for the body that supports it but thinks only of itself. Mark my words, one day the medical journals shall publicize findings that the contraceptive revolution and this new fangled HRT treatment may increase the risk of breast and cervical cancer, and God knows what other side effects will crop up. For almost a century this company has saved lives and eased pain, and I'm not going to approve of any treatment that could bring about any Luciferic plague."

Usually Timothy would not disregard their father's viewpoints, but this time, he did not look fully persuaded and seemed to waver. How could Tim be swayed by the argument of the 'population explosion' and 'free choice'? Perhaps Morgan had finally won him over by the false theory that the human being doesn't exist until arms and legs appear? If Tim broke ranks, it would only take a few votes, and the Walsingham ideal of preserving life and honestly promoting good health from a moral aspect could become the ideal of the past. Rather than give in to the liberals on the board, Harold knew he had to introduce some other avenue for profit, money could always influence a decision, even the liberals knew they also had to keep the preferential stock holders happy. He began researching the rising popularity for alternative and natural medicine, concluding that natural remedies would obviously appeal to the ecology-conscious market. In addition, there were many natural properties that could be used in their cosmetics branch, they could introduce a whole new line of products, in particular, a brand harnessing the anti-ageing properties of antioxidants Tim liked that proposal, why wouldn't he? He was in charge of the cosmetic end of the company after all. To Harold's relief, Tim and the other members of the board, with the exception of Morgan, accepted his proposal.

"Don't worry, your brother always sees sense eventually," Helen consoled the men, "Tim wouldn't do anything to purposely undermine the family business."

Helen offered an account of her day, reporting who turned up at the Club, the latest gossip, and all the charity events they were planning for the fall, or hosted by the other clubs. Gramps, after grumbling about that 'idiot Morgan' trying to come between him and the members of his family, he pushed aside the affair with a wave of his hand. No point upsetting his ulcers or making everyone miserable at home with talk of business that was settled for the present. He changed the subject and described the model steam engine exhibit he attended after the gruelling board meeting, recalling all the toy engines he used to play with as a boy. Katherine finally relayed her good news to the family and listened attentively to everyone's advice, ranging from Pop and Gramp's counsel to take her time, to Mom's elation and Steve's logical head-spinning disputation arguing both sides of the issue and whether she should sell or not sell, eventually concluding it was up to her in the end. Steves had only a humdrum account to give about his day of filing reports, conveniently withholding the fact he played one of the oldest medicinal pranks on Dr. Stirling, slipping him a harmless concoction, methylene blue, that would turn his urine the same colour for the day. The laboratory was positively tedious of late, he needed a laugh, and in any case, that joke was so common among medical staff he knew it would never be reported upstairs.

"And Steves, please do not blend any more Romulan Ale while in the labs, agreed?" Pops calmly requested with a twinkle in his eye.

Steves spluttered for a moment, clearing his throat from the piece of chicken that almost went down the wrong way before breaking out into a sheepish grin.

"Sure, Pops."

Helen looked up with a concerned expression,

"Ale? What nonsense is this, Steven?"

Katherine, who could not see the connection with their father's sentence, offered the most obvious explanation;

"Don't worry, Mom. The stuff doesn't exist, it's a blue coloured drink they made up for the Star Trek series, and is supposed to be banned by the Starfleet Federation. Obviously, Steves must have been experimenting again when he shouldn't have."

Finally understanding his son's cryptic line, Gramps burst out laughing. How often he had been the brunt of the same practical joke.

"What a rouge you are, Steves!"

Mrs. Gonzales arrived with what they assumed to be one of her delectable cheesecakes for dessert, but to Gramp's dismay, gourmet beauty was also skin deep. The ingredients used were either fat or calorie reduced versions, thus the confection was a shadow in comparison to her former baked glories. Instead of the fork-bending, stick-to-the-ribs cheese filling they were accustomed to, the cake was a mass of whipped fluff that quickly dissolved in the mouth.

"Oh well, don't look so glum, Gramps. At least it's better than having no dessert at all," Katherine noted, trying to sound positive.

"Well, we're not far from it, sis," Steves replied, "this dessert could almost be marked absent."

Later when dinner was over, Katherine finally made that long delayed call to Suzy and was glad to hear she had arrived at home safe and sound without any hiccups or breakdowns along the way. Her family was doing well, and she had started her customary summer job in the local library. She was particularly appalled at the number books that had been damaged or not returned that winter, some had the pictures cut out, others had dog-ears, some sported florescent highlight marks, coffee rings, and a few had food smashed between the pages. For the past few days, she was assigned the task of printing out overdue book notifications, and stuffing them into envelops to be mailed out to the offending culprits.

"You won't believe this, one looked as though someone used their peanut butter sandwich for a bookmarker. Some people should not be allowed any books," she concluded in disgust, "not to mention public books, they don't care if someone wants to read them later, or think about the cost of supplying new copies. What a waste."

The book-lovers verbally flayed the destructive disregard of the ignorant book-trashers, and then Katherine relayed her news, the Robert Horace fiasco and the following consternation, Gramp's diet and the resulting change in eating habits at Oak Meadows, and finally Jasper's arrival to the household. She did not want to mention the offer made by the Sirrac Gallery yet, somehow, it seemed inconsiderate to discuss the possibility of refusing this amazing opportunity to a friend who was finding it a financial struggle to get through art school. At least she could talk about Jasper, and Suzy was delighted with this news.

"Of course I'd just love to look after him while you're gone. I think getting him was a great idea for Mr. G.W., but I won't be there all the time during the week, not with lectures and everything when the semester gets into full swing, Jasper may not be fully trained by the time you leave, and he can't be left in the pen, he might get too big by then. It's early days yet, and until we see how things go, he can't be left outside on his own."

"That's true, oh dear, this is a mess."

"Hey, don't fret, you could consider setting up weekly boarding arrangements at a local kennel, just for the time you're in Paris. I could drop him off for the day, and pick him up later. You know, they might also offer training services, depending on the kennel. It might be worth looking into."

"Wow, there's an idea. Thanks, you're marvellous, Suzy. That's a simple solution, I don't know why I didn't think of it."

There, another load off her mind, it was true, a problem shared is a problem halved. All she had left to face was the lunch at the rectory tomorrow, and the worst would finally be over, at least for the time being. She guessed that depended on when her latest ideas would be painted and introduced to the public.

ଓଃ ❀ ଓ

The next day Katherine rose earlier than usual, the thought of the preaching that lay ahead kept her tossing and turning. Resigned to her inability to sleep in that morning, she went ahead and dressed in the appropriate attire for a semi-formal luncheon. How she would love to don her work clothes today, but she would have to wait until the afternoon. She thought of using the smock again, but she knew that she could not set her mind or hands to work in earnest, afraid that a rebellious blob of paint would stain her clothes, she had already risked it yesterday, and would not tempt fate twice. Going downstairs, she went to the pantry and grabbed a packet of her favourite breakfast, carefully returning the key to its hidden location. No sounds of stirring from anyone else yet, so rather than make a racket with the espresso machine, she settled for a cup of lukewarm instant coffee, whisking the kettle off the stove before it could whistle too loud. With breakfast over, she quietly went to the apartment to perform the necessary puppy duties, looking wistfully at the outline she sketched the day before. She hoped the Reverend's sermon would not last too long at lunch, how could she shorten the obvious well-meaning advice? Well, isn't one picture worth a thousand words? I'll just bring it along, let them see it for themselves. Immediately, she took the painting off the easel where she had positioned it the day before, wrapped it in a sheet and placed it on the back seat of her car. Talk about a ghost appearing at a feast, she mused. I don't think they'll be expecting this.

Returning inside, she found she needed the smock after all, Jasper was insistent on receiving cuddles, and she did not want to be covered with golden fluff before she arrived for her appointment. How she wanted to mess with her paints and forget about going to the rectory. It reminded her of those Christmas mornings when she and Steves had no sooner opened all the goodies Santa had brought when it was time to get dressed and go to church. It was the most frustrating thing to begin playing with all the shiny new toys, only to set them back down, to get trussed up in their new Christmas outfits, and to sit for a very, very long time while the Reverend droned on and on before they could return home to Toyland. Somehow, the situation would not have seemed so intolerable if they had not unwrapped everything beforehand. She could still see Steves when he was five, logically deducing that if Santa could fly around in a magic sleigh and fit through every chimney in the world, that he could very easily bring all their toys to the house while they were at church. Only a couple of years older, and still believing in the red-velvet wonder-worker, his argument made perfect sense to her.

Strange how thoughts tend to meander she observed as she recalled the day she discovered the truth about the mysterious toy deliveries and how deflated she was beyond all belief, for this not only meant Santa Clause was a fake, but the Easter Bunny and the Tooth Fairy were also non-existent. Steves, who had suspected the truth before she did courtesy of the blabbermouths at school, was not as devastated, he understood it was all a trick and got over it faster. For her, it was a different matter, in one fell swoop, all the magic and the 'entrancing' aspects of the two most important holidays of the year were obliterated. As long as she believed, her faith remained unshaken in all things fantastic, it became a matter of pride to remain steadfast amidst the growing number of sceptics in school each year. So much was made of the mysterious presents and chocolates that would arrive if they were good, and the expectation to receive these gifts was so great, that in the mind of a child, they overshadowed the original reason for the holidays. What made matters worse, all the gown-ups around them shared in the joke and went to great lengths to maintain the charade until the day of truth dawned. "It's all a lie," her little mind screamed, "and they thought it was great fun to lie, and yet punish *us* if we tell fibs." What a bunch of cheats, why should we believe anything they tell us now?

As they went to the Christmas service that morning, the questions continued. Why should we believe anything? Angels and saints, salvation and resurrection after death? It all sounds as fantastic as Santa Claus.

Looking around, she noted how attentive all the parishioners were. Perhaps all the grown-ups are duped too? If so, why make all this religious stuff up? Hmm, the Reverend makes a lot a money, come to think of it, she thought as the collection basket made its rounds. She pondered on this soul-searching dilemma during the service, and came to a number of conclusions. No, surely they could tell what was real and what was fake if they knew that Santa Claus didn't exist, except for the story of Saint Nicholas. The world was a big mystery, but somebody must have made it, there must be a God somewhere. She had to admit there were many things grown-ups couldn't explain so they called them miracles. Miracles don't happen on their own. What did the Bible say? If you don't believe Me, then believe the miracles? So there must be something to all this religious stuff after all. However, she remained suspicious about what is true and what is false after the grown-ups turned the story of a real saint into a fairytale and passed it off as truth. When she was older, Katherine firmly decided that if she ever had children, she would not abolish moderate gift giving, but neither would she introduce the customary delusion of Santa Claus during Christmas, a practise that only fuelled the materialism that blighted the holyday and distorted children's view of reality. How can Christians teach their children the importance of Christmas when the Christ Child and His humble arrival in a freezing cave no longer seemed the focal point, replaced by a jolly magic-man who brought a bunch of colourful goodies, even though they needed batteries and broke after a few short months? Pondering upon this old crisis of faith, she sensed another inspiration forming for her next picture ... amazing, three inspirations in less than two days? A whole collection was practically introducing itself already. I suppose I shouldn't be too pushed out of shape, considering this dratted lunch has actually given me a few good ideas.

Rather than sit idle all morning, she leashed Jasper to take him for a walk around the main house. Stopping outside the kitchen window, she noticed a flurry of activity, it was Mrs. Gonzales busy fixing a healthy breakfast for the reluctant dieters. Katherine waved in the window and continued her walk, or her 'trip-up' session, since Jasper did not know whether he was coming or going half the time. When she figured they had enough playing 'dance around the maypole', she brought him back to the apartment, took off the smock and returned to the house. By then, everyone had come down for breakfast, such as it was.

"Why Kathy, you look lovely," her mother remarked, "of course, you have the luncheon today, I almost forgot."

The Reverend and his wife were admired, among the adults that is, for their devotion to the younger members of their parish, insisting on becoming involved whenever a moral issue was at hand that had an important bearing on their Christian upbringing. The most common instance occurred whenever the local stores reported cases of shoplifting from the candy shelves. The Reverend would duly request that every child remain after service, to whom he gave a thorough preaching on the Seventh Commandment. If a certain youth was suspected, he or she would receive a private chat at the rectory, witnessed by the parents, a dreaded affair. Then there were other times when certain delicate matters had to be addressed, which were too important to be left in the hands of the secular authorities. So when the time was deemed appropriate, the Reverend and his wife, with the consent of the parents, made it a point to have every teenager dropped off at the rectory to discuss the facts of life from a Christian perspective.

"You have my deepest sympathies," Steves added in a mournful tone.

"Thank you, Steves, they are much appreciated."

"Just grin and bear it, Katie," Gramps replied with a chuckle, "try and concentrate on having a nice lunch, I don't think he will launch into his speech until sometime near the end, and then it will all be over."

"I hope you're right," Katherine sighed as she finished her espresso.

She had several hours to wait, so decided to run by her favourite art supply store and stock up on canvases and paints before she bought gifts for the host and hostess. At last, the moment had arrived to face the music, or the lunch, as was the case, and she drove to the rectory, a quaint colonial style red brick house with white trim and shutters, complete with manicured lawns and hedges surrounded by a white picket fence. Katherine made her way up the brick-cobbled path and rang the bell.

"Hello, Katherine. Do come in, I'm delighted you're here," Elena Dobbson said as she let her in. "You didn't have to bring anything, but they are simply gorgeous."

Katherine had bought a bouquet of pink roses, Mrs. Dobbson's favourite flowers.

"I've brought some goodies too," she said, handing her two shiny boxes, one filled with an assortment of hand-made chocolates, the other with gourmet caramel fudge, the Reverend's favourite.

"Thank you so much, my dear. My, how lovely you look. Have you lost some weight?"

"How nice of you to say, Mrs. Dobbson. I don't think so," Katherine replied as she thought of the rationing program at home. "Gramps has just been put on a diet, and we are all following it to make it easier for him, but it's too soon to tell yet."

"Is that so? Now that is a helpful thing to do."

"Don't think too highly of us," Katherine laughed, "we know where the forbidden food is hidden away and sneak some when he isn't around."

"Speaking of food, I do hope you like prawns, I've fixed us a prawn and avocado salad with Marie dressing."

Although they had a housekeeper, Mrs. Dobbson preferred to do her own cooking and enjoyed experimenting with recipes.

"Yes, I do. Do you need any help?" Katherine asked as they made their way to the kitchen.

"No, I'm fine, everything is ready. You can keep me company while we wait for the Reverend, he is busy with someone on the phone. Probably a parishioner complaining about the choice of hymns for last Sunday's service. Can I offer you something to drink? Ice tea, soda?"

"An ice tea would be nice, thank you."

Gramps was right, when the Reverend appeared and lunch began, he did not bombard her with his sermon, and the afternoon passed with pleasant small talk and chit chat about anything and everything ranging from her family and her current plans now that she had finished college, to the latest activities in the parish and the world at large. However, the sermon could not be avoided, and right on cue, he began as the dessert dishes were cleared and the coffee was served, leading up to the matter at hand by first discussing the art world before broaching the matter of the latest articles he had read.

"I saw the article in the art section in last Sunday's paper," he declared in a calm, pastoral tone as he stirred his coffee, carefully selecting his words, "I must admit, Kathy, I feel obligated to remind you about our Christian charity towards our Catholic brethren, we must not judge too harshly, even though they may have gone astray a few times through history."

"Yes, my dear," Mrs. Dobbson continued, "we must keep ever before us a kind charity and non-judgemental attitude towards our fellow Christians…"

"Reverend, Mrs. Dobbson, can you wait a minute?" Katherine interrupted as politely as possible, "I brought the painting to show you and give you an opportunity to judge for yourself. I left it in the car, I'll go get it, if that's all right."

"Oh? Really?" the Reverend replied, surprised by this development, an unexpected display of action from his usually impassive audience among the youth. Mrs. Dobbson was delighted with the notion.

"Why yes, by all means, let's see it."

Katherine brought in the shrouded picture and unveiled it.

"Oh my, Katherine," Mrs. Dobbson declared after a few moments of study. "The subject is a bit daring, but I don't see anything that could have elicited that provocative review. The colours and the figures are so vibrant! Your family must be so proud of your accomplishments."

"Well, I haven't accomplished much yet, this is only my … début piece, so to speak."

"Come now, you're too modest. It's not everyone who receives an honourable mention from the Sirrac Gallery."

"No, and this has actually been a very successful début, really. Someone has already made an offer to buy it."

"You don't say? How exciting. Will you sell it?"

"I think I've decided to keep it," she replied, making a mental note to call the gallery that afternoon to announce her decision, "I've grown quite attached to it."

"You know, Kathy, I always wanted to paint myself, but they assured me at school I had no talent in art. That's a gift God only gives to the chosen few, I'm afraid."

"I believe," Katherine replied, "anyone can learn to draw and paint, if they have the proper tuition. I myself needed help, and there were many hits and misses, it didn't all come naturally to me. Besides, you don't need to go to school to paint for enjoyment. Much of it you learn as you experiment."

While they discussed the technicalities of drawing, the Reverend continued to study the painting, eventually asking Katherine to explain the figures to see if he had correctly interpreted the allegory of the piece.

"Now, let's see, this group represents corrupt executives, right? Hmm, and this fellow looks like Justice has fallen asleep. The devil is a rather dramatic touch, but I see you are trying to say that the world is going to hell on roller-skates … no beating around the bush, eh?" he concluded with a chuckle. "Well now Kathy, I truly don't get the same interpretation as Mr. Horace, I fully appreciate your concept of how mankind is going wayward. It's truly admirable of you to try and point out the mistakes of mankind for the welfare of humanity, but we must be careful, not everyone will view this painting with an open mind, there will always be those who wish to see the world the way they want to, and we all run the risk of being misunderstood."

"I know, there is nothing one can do about it either," she replied. "I can't let the thought of that stop me from painting. Everyone keeps reminding me, I can't let the fear of what other people think affect my work.”

“No of course not,” the Reverend agreed as he finished his coffee. “If the Pharisees had the audacity to accuse the Son of God of blasphemy, we cannot expect anything better. So, there will always be the proverbially blind who will try and interpret your work according to their impaired viewpoint.”

“I suppose so.”

At long last, the dreaded homily was over and the conversation returned to general pleasantries before it was time for her to leave.

“Thank you for inviting me to lunch, it was delicious.”

“You’re welcome. Thank you for your lovely gifts, and letting us see your painting,” Mrs. Dobbson replied as they showed her to the door. “Of course we’ll be sure to see you at the service next Sunday, and please give our kindest regards to your family, dear.”

“I will,” she replied with a smile as she carried her painting back to the car, very much relieved the luncheon had not turned out to be the didactic ordeal she expected.

⊰❀⊱

Life at Oak Meadows experienced a relatively calm period after the turbulence of Katherine’s graduation week and her painting début. On the spur of the moment, Aunt Martha had decided to take an old friend up on an invitation to visit her in Connecticut for a few weeks, giving them all a respite from her well-meaning matriarchal probing. Pops, as regulated as a sergeant-major, dutifully showed up to work and took care of business as usual, but refused to let it take him over these days, coming home early when it was possible. Gramps looked forward to his afternoons at the Club for one obvious reason, he could eat what he liked, and with the generous tips he gave, he knew he could count on the staff to keep his little secret, although his clandestine cholesterol indulgence sessions were not any great secret. Helen returned quite content to her bridge club meetings and afternoon get-togethers with the ladies of society, while Steves was well-behaved and settled down to work, he refrained from pulling his usual practical jokes and satisfied his urge for impishness by amusing everyone with his engaging sarcastic wit. In fact, his mind was elsewhere, and the quick weekend trips he took to Boston signalled Jennifer was the main interest, thinking up pranks to play on the family took second place. Katherine remained immersed in her art, busily capturing for posterity her latest ‘symbolic controversies’ as her father aptly described them. Until they

125

were finished, she kept them a close secret, leaving everyone to wonder, not without some trepidation, what could possibly keep her so engrossed.

One of the few interruptions she allowed was Jasper, who had gained several pounds and had outgrown his pen. Playful and vivacious, he was working his way into everyone's heart, except for the gardeners. When it was decided he was big enough to be out in the garden on his own, he started burying his bones and other toys in the soft flower beds, ripping up the delicate blossoms edging the borders. Dog repellent was immediately added to the list of garden supplies. Luckily, Jasper was a fast learner when it came to house training, and soon he was allowed to come into the main house when it was affirmed he was free from his uninvited guests, although the kitchen continued to remain off limits, Mrs. Gonzales trained him so well that he refused to enter the kitchen in the apartment, much to Katherine's chagrin as she now had to give him his food and water in the carpeted area of the studio, keeping her forever tied to the chore of laying down newspapers.

Charlie's phone calls and occasional visits were also welcome disruptions from her work. He could not visit as often as he would have liked. After winning the big copyright dispute, he was acquiring a reputation in the legal profession, and clients of the firm requested he personally take their case. One night, he was simply ecstatic with the news that his father had decided to assign him one of the coveted spacious corner offices, and he called her immediately to relay his good fortune. Delighted, she wanted to present him with a special gift for the new executive area, particularly as he insisted on remaining gallant and refused to send her the cleaning bill for his ruined suit. Similar to his custom of giving her gold charms for her bracelet, she learned he loved collecting unusual office puzzles and novelties, and therefore she kept her eye open for amusing items for his birthday and Christmas. One year it was the silver sphere pendulum clackers that knocked back and forth by the force of gravity, another time she found an exquisite leather bound table-top race track executive gizmo that worked by hand-crank action allowing little silver horses whir around a green felt field. Then there were the wooden 3-D interlocking and disentanglement puzzles that needed certain pieces to be removed or refitted without touching or moving other bits, and of course, the little silver Rubik's cube with the semi-precious stones for the colours, one of her favourites. It reminded her of the time when she received a Rubik's cube for her sixth birthday, she could not figure out how to put all the colours back once she mixed up the square and resorted to the next best solution, taking off all the stickers and re-sticking them back in order.

Somehow for this occasion, one of her customary novelty gifts did not seem appropriate and she wanted to give him something special, eventually deciding that painting him a picture was the best idea. What would she paint? She did not know what colour scheme he would choose for his décor, so decided a landscape would be the least likely to clash, and therefore tried to think of a scene he would appreciate. Eventually, she recalled his favourite 'one-of-these-days' dreams featuring a little secluded getaway house by the ocean somewhere around Cape Cod. Setting her cynical canvases aside for the moment, she imagined Charlie's dream spot and set to work, painting his often-talked-about cottage on a peaceful sandy stretch of beach off in the distance with a majestic yacht clipping through the foamy waves in the foreground. As soon as it was dry, using a hairdryer to speed up the process, she had it framed, wrapped it in gift paper and tied it with a large bow. She presented it to him one Saturday afternoon when he could make time for the next tennis re-match, and he was deeply moved by her thoughtful choice of subject. It was the first thing he put up in the office, saying it would be his great motivator, a constant reminder of the goals and dreams he hoped to achieve.

Now it was time to resume her vibrant sarcasms, and settling down to work, she was interrupted by a second call from the Sirrac Gallery. The same anonymous client was still interested in her Napoléonic wonder and was now offering fifty thousand. At this point the gallery realized their client was serious about acquiring this artwork, and declared if they played their cards right, they could negotiate for an even higher price. Although she was excited with this unexpected news, she was curious to know why the customer was so insistent. Did they show they painting to anyone during the contest while it was under the scrutiny of the judges? No, it was not. Unless this client was at the graduation ceremony, she could not understand why they would want a painting they had never seen, and was told they had probably read the article by Robert Horace. Suspecting the social standing and influence of their clientèle, it would not be impossible for this mysterious John Doe to enquire of the paper if any photographers had taken a picture that was not included in the article. Elation immediately changed to scepticism, somehow she felt uncomfortable with this conversation and became suspicious. She decided to stick with her decision not to sell. Whoever this client was, they obviously believed Mr. Horace and wanted her picture based on his twisted misrepresentation of her allegory. Steves had already demonstrated to her that it was not difficult to see the warped scenario offered by the 'Art Hacker' if one looked hard enough. Obviously, this client had some dastardly intentions concerning her painting, but she did not have the foggiest notion what it could be. Was it some Neo-Nazi or Arian Brotherhood cult who wished to purchase it? Perhaps someone who wanted to harm her family's company and their reputation? She could not be sure, so kept this telephone call to herself, no need to worry everyone with these thoughts of doom and gloom if she was not going to sell it anyway. For a few days, however, her resolve to paint challenging subjects was shaken as her old doubts resurfaced. Was she prudent to continue similar controversial subjects? She wrestled with this issue before finally setting it aside, reminding herself that she could not control how people thought, and therefore was determined not to let them deter her from continuing her work.

Before Katherine knew it, the weeks had slipped by into August, and soon it became time to prepare for her trip to Europe. Her mother would not dream of sending her off to Paris without new outfits and accessories, and so a few days of shopping were in order. Imagine shopping for Paris fashions in New York! By then, Aunt Martha had returned, and simply had to tag along during the shopping spree, offering her opinionated and not-always-asked-for advice when it came to the final selection of the perfect styles and colours. Katherine also had to think about which of her favourite art supplies she needed to pack, since she could not bring her whole studio with her, and staying in someone else's home, she would have to think of neat, compact travel. There were also other practicalities to consider, Jasper in particular. Gramps decided now that Katherine would be gone for a few months, it was high time he assumed his share of minding the rascal, and so for the two weeks previous to her departure, she taught him the feeding program and relinquished the leash with a warning Jasper had not yet mastered the art of trotting along in a straight line. Remembering Suzy's advice, she suggested Jasper could use a few obedience classes, but Gramps was sure that he would eventually grow out of his boisterous spunk, he was still a young whippersnapper after all. With that decided, Gramps began to take Jasper for his daily jaunts around the neighbourhood.

On the fourth day, however, they were gone longer than usual. Gramps always brought Jasper back by three thirty or four o'clock, but not today. Katherine did not think his tardiness could be due to anything out of the ordinary and assumed he must have bumped into an old acquaintance who wanted to chat. She had decided to spend the day tidying up the apartment before Suzy came back for the beginning of term, and continued her reorganization of the art supplies, leaving her notes informing her where to find everything, when at a quarter to five she was startled by the buzzer of the intercom system, not the soft 'bzzzt' of the internal line, but the loud 'brrrippp' indicating someone was at the main gate, followed by the anxious voice of their neighbour from down the road.

"Hello? Anyone home?"

"Is that you, Mr. Fitzgerald?"

"Kathy? Am I glad someone is home! Now, I don't want to alarm you, but your grandfather has had an accident … can I come in?"

"What? Oh, yes, of course!"

Katherine quickly buzzed the gate open and anxiously waited in the driveway as Mr. Fitzgerald drove up, bringing Jasper in the back seat of his car, minus Gramps. Mrs. Gonzales, who could not get to the intercom first as she was in the pantry, had overheard everything and rushed out to meet them while Mr. Fitzgerald let Jasper out, handing Katherine the leash.

"Mr. Fitzgerald, what happened? Where is Gramps?"

"Is Mr. G.W. all right?"

"Now, try and be calm," Mr. Fitzgerald began, "I was coming home from work when I found him on the sidewalk, Jasper here wrapped the leash around his legs before wrapping himself around a tree. Gregory was in a lot of pain, and I thought it best not to move him, so I called the ambulance and waited until it arrived."

"Oh no! Will he be all aright? This is terrible," Katherine excalimed as Mrs. Gonzales gasped, her hands flying up to her mouth.

"I overheard the paramedics say he may have fractured his hip, they are taking him to the general hospital."

"Thank you for your help, Mr. Fitzgerald. He was late coming home, but I didn't think … I must call my parents and let them know what's happened."

"Of course, you do that, and please let me know if you need anything," Mr. Fitzgerald replied as he got back into his car.

"I will, thank you," she replied before he drove off.

"Miss Kathy, is there anything I can do right now?" Mrs. Gonzales anxiously enquired.

"I don't know, let me call my parents and see what we should do," she replied as she let Jasper off and ran back to the apartment where the nearest telephone was available. She called her father's office first, trying not to sound panic-stricken, barely keeping her voice level.

"Mrs. Davidson, it's Katherine … could you put me through to my father please? It's an emergency … ."

"Of course, wait one moment." He answered a few seconds later.

"Hi, Kathy, what's the matter?"

"Oh Pops, Gramps is on his way to the general hospital."

"What? Kathy, what happened?"

"He took Jasper for a walk and tripped over the leash, Mr. Fitzgerald found him lying on the sidewalk and called the ambulance, he was just here to bring Jasper home and explained what happened. Mr. Fitzgerald said he may have fractured his hip."

"Kathy, calm down, where's your mother?"

"She hasn't come home yet from the Club, you're the first I've called … ."

"All right, now listen … you call her next and tell her what's happened, while I call your Uncle Tim. Steven and I will go directly to the general hospital, and we'll all meet there. Okay? Now don't panic, everything will be all right."

"Okay, Pops. See you there."

Following his instructions, she called the Club and relayed the message to her mother. Like her father, her mother remained composed.

"Kathy, Aunt Martha and I will go directly to the hospital and meet your father. Listen, this is what I want you to do. Your grandfather will need an overnight bag packed for him, you know, pyjamas, his robe, a few days supply of everything, soap, toothbrush, toothpaste, his razor, things like that. Ask Mrs. Gonzales to help you, she knows which drawers to look in, and tell her not to worry about fixing any dinner, we will have to wing it tonight. Can you remember all this?"

"Yes, Mom, I'll bring the bag and meet you at the hospital."

"All right, we'll see you there."

Katherine wondered how her parents could remain so clear-headed under stress and pressure, always knowing what to do in times of crises. No doubt, it was their difference in age and life-experience. She ran over to the main house and enlisted Mrs. Gonzales' help as instructed to search through her grandfather's wardrobe and pack his bag, laying everything out on the bed first and making sure they did not forget anything. She zipped the case as fast as her uncharacteristically fumbly fingers would allow and ran down the stairs. Opening the front door, she was about to sprint to the car when the telephone rang. It was Charlie, and she quickly informed him of the latest tragedy. Anxious to be of help, he offered his assistance.

"Is there anything I can do for you right now?"

"Oh, Charlie, that is so kind of you to ask, but I can't think of anything off hand…."

"Well, be sure and let me know, won't you?"

"You know I will. I've got to run, Gramps needs his bag …."

"Yes, I'd better let you go, I'll call later to find out how your

Gramps is doing, if that's okay …"

"Of course it is, Charlie, or I'll call you, whichever way it turns out."

"Okay."

Arriving at the general hospital, Katherine drove around for what seemed like an eternity as she searched for a parking space, and was tempted to use one of the places reserved for the medical staff or the disabled. Finally, a car pulled out and she could park. She hurried to the reception area where she found Steves waiting.

"Everyone else is upstairs, room A 512," he explained as he took the case and motioned the way to the elevators, "they've taken him for more x-rays, and he should be back pretty soon."

If she disliked doctor's offices for their clinical atmosphere, hospitals decidedly had the most demoralizing environment. The first item that terrorized the senses was the overpowering sterile antiseptic smell that clung to the nostrils like some dreaded nightmare. Then the eyes are assaulted by the bleak uniformity of the extensive vinyl-lined halls painted in insipid colours with their endless series of doors, all illuminated in blinding white florescent lighting. Adding to the growing sense of interior horror were the various contraptions that loitered in the passageways until summoned, wheelchairs, gurneys, tall intravenous pouch-racks on wheels, a heart monitor or two. Then comes the cacophonous soundtrack to accompany the bustling spectacle of medical staff, public calls over the loudspeakers for doctor so-and-so to go to room B 213 or to O.R. 4, the occasional rings at the nurses' stations summoning them for assistance, the creepy burbling from rooms with patients wearing oxygen masks, the high-pitched electronic *bip, bip, bip* from medical machines of all descriptions. To add insult to this psychological injury, one avoided touching any surface for fear of contracting a virus, and as if that were not enough, the sense of taste was not spared, beginning with the black instant sludge spewed out by the coin-operated coffee machines, to the pitiful rations doled out to the patients, not to mention the mushy, colourless overcooked curiosities served to everyone in the cafeterias.

Overshadowing the sensory barrage was the ambience exuding from the very nature of these buildings, vast sickness-stations laying bare the physical frailty and misery of the human condition, edifices that had now metastasised into malignant breeding grounds of soulless pride, egotism, indifference. While there were exceptions, it was almost impossible to know who to trust. Seldom did anyone enter the medical profession nowadays mindful of the reality that tending to the sick was a vocation, restoring health and giving relief an act of mercy. Lucrative careers with substantial rewards were now the priority, the costs of health-care continuing to soar beyond the average person's means. Life, the gift of existence, was no longer considered sacred from the Alpha to the Omega, now there were silent, self-appointed arbitrators of life and death who judged existence by its quality and usefulness to society, and ministered to patients accordingly.

Within a few minutes, Katherine and Steven met the family on the fifth floor in a waiting area not far from the room assigned to Gramps. Pops and Uncle Tim were standing in one corner and in sober tones discussed how fast they could move Gramps to the private hospital, while Mom and Aunt Martha were worrying how serious the fracture was and wondering when the doctors would come and disclose any information to them. Katherine made her apologies for taking so long, she could not find parking. It seemed an age and a half before anyone came to see them, and preoccupied with their private thoughts, few words were spoken. They watched each minute on the clock, paced around the room before sitting back down, feeding coins into the vending machines for coffee, thumbing through the magazines or reading the informative medical posters on the walls to keep busy.

"Mr. Walsingham?" a doctor inquired matter-of-factly as he entered the waiting area, carrying a clipboard.

"Yes?" Harold and Timothy both replied as they quickly approached to hear the latest developments. "We're brothers," Harold explained to the doctor, who was not certain whom he should address first.

"I see. I'm Dr. Anderson, I've received several opinions from my colleagues concerning your father's x-rays."

"How bad is it?" Harold replied.

"Well, the fracture is serious, your father needs a hip replacement. We understand your desire to have him transferred to a private hospital, but it would be inadvisable under the circumstances."

"Of course, we understand."

"Are those the x-rays?" Steves asked as he peered at the clipboard.

"Why yes," Dr. Anderson replied, "you may take a look if you like."

Steves took the blue-hued transparent sheets and held them up to the light.

"Ai! That looks nasty," he commented with a slight grimace.

"Are you a medical student?"

"No, but close enough, chemistry in fact, I study medical books in my spare time."

"We have scheduled the operation for tomorrow morning and made him as comfortable as possible for the night," he continued, "we don't expect any complications, hip replacements are usually routine, and his own doctor, Dr. Hendricks, has been contacted and will participate in the procedure, so please rest assured your father will receive the very best of care."

"Thank you, Dr. Anderson," Timothy replied. "How long is the recovery period after this kind of surgery?"

"Oh, recovery is usually not that long. He will be sore for a week or so, but the sooner he can get up and moving, the better. Of course, the physiotherapists will monitor his exercise program, but I'd say he could go home within a week or so."

"Thank you, doctor. May we see him?" Harold replied.

"Yes, of course. By all means. If you'll excuse me, I must go now and make my rounds."

"Certainly, thank you again doctor."

Before the family went to see Gramps, the gravity of the situation was discussed in a quiet corner when the doctor had left.

"Harold," Helen began, "you know he can't be left here on his own, someone will have to stay at all times to monitor him."

"Yes, I know. I would have preferred if we could have transferred him to the private hospital, but obviously it's best not to move him for the present."

"We'll have to manage the best way we can," Tim continued.

"I'm glad we were able to straighten out his insurance status at least, imagine listing him as a Medicare-only patient — at his age," Helen declared, not without a measure of alarm.

"Okay, this is what we shall do, Katherine and Steven will take turns sitting with him during the day, the rest of us will take turns with the night shifts. I'll stay with him tonight," Harold proposed.

"I'll start tomorrow," Steves offered.

"No, I should start tomorrow," Katherine protested, "it's my fault he broke his hip in the first place!"

"Now, Kathy, why would you say a thing like that?" her mother enquired, "of course it isn't."

"Yes it is! If I didn't get Jasper, Gramps would be all right!"

"Come now, you didn't know this was going to happen. It is a simple accident, don't blame yourself. Besides, it's best that Steven takes the first day shift in any case, your grandfather will be out of surgery, and we need your brother to inquire into everything that is administered since he is familiar with medications."

"All right, Pops."

Aunt Martha was not convinced of the necessity for this extraordinary guard duty.

"Really! I don't see what all the fuss is about. Gregory is in good hands, I'm sure."

"Martha, I know you think we're taking things to the extreme, but don't forget what happened to father. He had no sooner arrived at the hospital for a simple examination, and unexplainably died less than an hour later. You can't tell me he died of natural causes."

Katherine was just old enough to remember when her maternal grandfather had passed away. Suffering from a touch of Alzheimer's, he had slipped in the shower and bumped his head, and while there was no major cut or bruise, the family brought him to the hospital, just in case. How he hated hospitals, and was not in the best of moods when he was checked in for the night, vociferating his disapproval. The doctors on duty told them that they would give him something to calm him down, suggesting to the family that they go ahead and have dinner, and by the time they returned, he would be settled in his room. When they arrived back approximately an hour later, the doctor met them at the door with the news he had just 'slipped away'. Since her father and Steves also took this matter seriously, not to mention the myriad of other anecdotes they heard from acquaintances about family members who mysteriously grew ill in hospitals for no reason before they unexplainably expired, Katherine concluded there could not be smoke without fire smouldering in the medical world. *The world may not look like* Soylent Green, *but have we reached that point already?*

"Come," Helen continued, "we don't need an argument right now. Let's go see him before he gets too tired."

A private room was not available, and so Gramps was sharing with another gentleman who had his hip replaced that day and was fast asleep. The family were glad to see Gramps was not laying completely flat to avoid the threat of pneumonia, one of the dangers arising from the stuffy, over heated environment. If he did catch a virus, or his lungs began to fill up with fluid, raised at a comfortable angle, especially while asleep, would give him a fighting chance. Considering the other sleeping patient, everyone spoke *sotto voce*.

"Hullo," Gramps whispered as they lined up around his bed, "I gather they've told you about the surgery."

"Yes, it looks like you're going to be here a few days," Harold replied quietly, "but as soon as we can, we'll have you back home. We'll get you a private nurse, and whatever you need."

"Are you in any pain?" Helen asked.

"No, as a matter of fact. They've given me some strong stuff, I feel rather loopy...."

Steves began to unpack the case and took out one of the pyjama tops.

"Someone came prepared."

"I had Kathy pack a bag for you," Helen explained.

"Mrs. Gonzales helped me," Katherine continued, "Gramps, are you sure you're all right?"

"My head is a little off in the clouds, but I'm fine."

"At least you'll be happy to know Dad, you are probably stoned on one of our brands," Tim continued with a smile. "This is one of the hospitals we supply."

"That's something! No quarter to our competition!"

"Well Gramps, let's get you out of that pathetic excuse for a covering into something more respectable," Steves said as he eyed the scanty gown provided by the hospital. "With the hip, we can't do anything about the bottom end, but the top of you will be decent at least."

"Now, be careful, Steven," Aunt Martha warned, "don't jiggle him around."

"How are you going to put it on over that?" Katherine asked, pointing to the intravenous unit attached to Gramp's right hand.

"Elementary, my dear," Steves replied. "I shall demonstrate. Here, hold this," he said as he unhooked the pouch from its stand and placed it in Gramp's right hand, gently putting his arm into the pyjama sleeve, pouch and all, then pulled the clear tubing through.

"Hey, that's pretty good, David Copperfield. But you forgot to get me out of this chequerboard dress first," Gramps replied as he tugged at his public clothing.

"Come, let's give the men some privacy while Steven straightens your grandfather out," Helen replied as she closed the curtain around the bed.

The ladies waited in the hall and Katherine figured it was a good time to find a phone and call Charlie about the latest developments.

"Hey Charlie, it's Kathy. Gramps is scheduled for surgery tomorrow, a hip replacement ... in the morning, early I think. ... No, I don't know when they will allow visitors, probably not the first day, but don't hold me to that, everything is up in the air. Pops is staying tonight to watch him, Steves will be with him tomorrow. I'll be staying here the day after. It looks like he will be home in a week or so ... No, I can't think of anything, honestly. ... I will, ...okay ... okay, talk to you later, bye Charlie."

Katherine hung up the receiver and joined her mother and Aunt Martha.

"I called Charlie, he says 'Hi' and hopes everything is okay with Gramps, and if we need anything to let him or his parents know."

"That's thoughtful of him," Helen replied as they went back into the room.

Gramps did look more comfortable in his burgundy pyjama top. The other patient was still fast asleep, apparently, the anaesthetic had not completely worn off, and the family continued to speak as softly as they could. They stayed until visiting hours were over, and since Harold needed something to eat before he assumed his post for the night, they all decided to find the cafeteria.

"Ick, look at this Steves," Katherine said as she motioned towards one of the dishes for his inspection, "the label says it's rigatoni in a tomato *ragu*, but I've never seen tomato sauce *that* colour before. It's like someone dumped a bottle of orange finger-paint into it."

"Eww! I could have used it for one of my science projects during grade school, that's for sure. Look over there, that fried fish looks like it's been curled up gasping for days. This is a hospital for crying out loud. Whatever happened to 'you are what you eat'?"

"I guess that's just it, we are in the perfect place if we get food poisoning or botulism. I'm sure they have a whole wing set aside for casualties from the cafeteria," she joked back.

"I'd take Mrs. G.'s diet menu any day to this."

"Okay you two," Uncle Tim replied, "just pick something out before you turn us all off our food."

"Believe me, you don't need us to do that," Steves replied, "just look around."

Eventually they found a table and ate sombrely as they discussed the guard shifts. Tim would gladly do some of the night watches, but then someone needed to carry on the company business as Harold pointed out. Tim decided he could do double-duty at the office and give his brother time off, allowing him to continue the night relays. Helen wanted to take one of the nights, but Harold turned down her suggestion. He did not want her tired out, and if he had the days free, he could get enough rest. In any case, they needed to hire a nurse and possibly make different sleeping arrangements for Gramps on the ground floor, which she, and Aunt Martha, were only too happy to organize. Steves, as previously agreed, would start the first day, while Katherine would come in on the second. They finished their meal and went home, with the exception of Harold who returned to the patient's room and sat down in the chair next to the bed, settling in for the night despite the nurse who pointed out it was past visiting hours. Although reluctant to fabricate a pretext, it was often easier to do so, explaining that if they wished to keep their patient calm before his surgery, a family member would need to be present at all times.

"My father suffers from certain phobias, you understand."

Harold was handed a blanket and pillow and made comfortable for the night.

At home, everyone was finding it difficult to sleep, watching the clock and wondering how long the operation would take, if it would be successful and if he would come home soon. Steven headed into the hospital at cockcrow and waited all morning with his father to see Gramps come out of recovery. Dr. Hendricks was the first to see them and reported the operation was successful, and while they had him on the table, they decided to drain the fluid off his arthritic knee. Before the doctor left, Steves rakishly wondered aloud if the anaesthesiologist gave him thiopentone, sodium pentothal, before giving him the inhalation anaesthetic.

"Imagine, you doctors get all the fun listening to everyone's deepest, darkest confessions as they come 'round."

"Well, your grandfather was quite well behaved, so your trade secrets are still safe," Dr. Hendricks replied with a diplomatic smile, "although he did mumble several times, insisting that we give him Walsingham pharmaceutical products only."

"Ah yes, no quarter to the competition," Harold replied with amusement in his voice.

"Is he staying on his diet?"

"The same as the rest of us, eating healthy when he's at home, cheating when no one is looking I'm afraid."

Dr. Hendricks had to admit it was better than nothing, at least he was having his largest calorie intake mid-day at the Club and was not going to bed on a heavy dinner, allowing him to use up most of the energy. However, it was the cholesterol they had to watch, and advised they try to persuade him to eat more mono and polyunsaturated fats. They promised to try. Before he left, Dr. Hendricks gave them a list of private nurses he recommended.

At last, Gramps was wheeled in, groggy and half awake from the anaesthetic.

"How are you feeling, Dad?"

"Huh? Oh, hullo. Everything is way off in the distance. Is this what a 'trip' feels like?"

"I don't know Gramps, Woodstock was before my time," Steves replied.

"Now Dad, don't be giving him any ideas. Any nausea?"

"No, just very tired," and with that, he fell asleep.

"Okay Pops, you go home and get some rest, it's my turn to man the fort," Steves declared. "Looks like he's going to be out for a while. I'll let you know if he feels up to seeing visitors later tonight, and if they are allowed, you know everyone will want to see him."

"All right, son. Call if there is any change. I'll see you later."

Back at the house, Harold immediately fell into bed after telling everyone the latest news and giving the list of nurses to Helen and Aunt Martha. They were already busy compiling several numbers recommended by their insurance company, but decided to use Dr. Hendricks' list instead. Mrs. Gonzales, who tended to create extra work in times of anxiety just to keep busy, and with no dinner to prepare for the family the night before, over-baked a profusion of edibles. The pantry abounded with blueberry muffins, cupcakes, brownies, and a real honest-to-goodness raspberry *cheese*cake.

While everyone else had something practical to do, or invented tasks to keep occupied, Katherine felt at a loss. How could she return to her painting as if nothing had happened? Her heart was not in it, and there was nothing she could think of that would help Gramps or the family, not until she could assume her post at the hospital. Then, when she did have something to do, it reminded her of the awful accident. There was Jasper to feed and take for his walk, and the barrage of telephone calls to answer from well-meaning friends who had heard the news and called to find out if Gramps was all right. Katherine had shut off the cell phones and routed the incoming calls to the apartment so her father could get some sleep, and her heart sank every time she recounted the incident to those who wanted to hear the gory details. She knew her father was right, how could she see this coming? Yet, she still felt that heavy weight of guilt and continued to hold herself responsible. If she had only stopped to think before leaping, perhaps Gramps would not need to have part of his body sawed off and replaced with an alien metal object. The thought made her shudder. Why couldn't I have left things alone, she complained. She could not help wondering if the family felt the same way and held her responsible for Gramp's accident, despite what they said to make her feel better. With these disturbing reflections lodged like bugs in the brain, to even consider making the last-minute preparations for her trip was out of the question. Although it looked like he would be released from the hospital within a matter of days, it did not seem right to plan a wonderful vacation as if nothing had happened while he was convalescing and learning how to walk all over again. Imagine, from now on, he probably won't be able to walk without the help of a cane.

Steves called later in the day with the good news Gramps was recovering from the anaesthetic, although he was sore from the surgery. He seemed to be in good spirits and was determined to get out of there as soon as possible. These tidings did not help to raise Katherine from her doldrums, and while she said she was fine and tried to put on a brave face, it was plain to see that something was bothering her. The problem was laid bare when her mother suggested she begin packing some of her cases, and Katherine finally admitted she was not going to Paris. She could not go merrily off with all that had happened and leave everyone else to grapple with Gramp's recovery. Her mother and Aunt Martha tried to talk some sense into her, it would upset him if she did not go, but it was useless. It was not mentioned over dinner, but when Helen could have a private word with Harold before he went to the hospital, she told him about Katherine's latest decision. Thinking the matter through, he knew that badgering her would do no good, she would have to hear it from Gramps himself.

"What's this, Katie?" he rumbled when she arrived at the hospital the next morning. "Cancelling your trip over an old fool like me? Who warned me Jasper would be a handful, eh? And who ignored that piece of advice? Yours truly, so don't go knocking yourself over the head for my mistake," he said with a 'hrumph!' "Don't you give up your trip on my account and my stubborn stupidity, so let that be an end to it. You go to Paris, wave 'hullo' to the Eiffel Tower and eat a genuine French croissant for me. Okay?"

She did not feel happy about going, but how could she argue and upset Gramps in his current predicament? So there, the matter was settled.

 C3 ❀ ೞ

A little over a week, Gramps arrived home, welcomed by a profusion of visitors, get-well cards and gifts. The den had been rearranged with a hospital bed and a private nurse was hired for as long as he needed her. He was determined to put a stop to all this fuss—he would get rid of her soon enough. While everyone resumed their normal schedules after the hectic upheaval, Gramps continued to regain his strength and Katherine was busy packing. She also arranged for Jasper to board during the day at a kennel offering obedience skills as Suzy suggested, he definitely needed some lessons before Gramps would walk him again.

The Kraylors came for dinner a few days before Katherine's flight to Paris. They had a set of keys and a list ready for her detailing how to turn on the heating, the gas, and work the other appliances in their apartment, that is if she did not want their housekeeper full time whom they paid to come in twice a week to maintain the apartment while they were not there. A list of the local shopping areas to buy groceries was also prepared. Charlie gave her a present of a guidebook with all the latest information to help her plot her way through the quarters of Paris.

Then came the expected parental warnings, do not stay out late at night, her mother stressed, especially the Montmartre quarter, her father continued. Aunt Martha, who was also present at the dinner, was typically inquisitive as to know why that area in particular.

"To be frank, Martha, it may be the artists' haven and attracts tourists during the day, and I know Kathy has friends living there, but just on the other side of the hill is the red light and night club district," Harold declared before turning to Katherine, "while we don't want to restrict your freedom, at the same time I hope you can appreciate why we do not want you out there alone."

"Now Harold, our Kathy is quite sensible, and can take care of herself," Aunt Martha returned.

"Oh, is it that bad? Please listen to your father Kathy, don't go roaming that area by yourself! You may visit your friends, but please leave early," Helen exclaimed.

The Kraylors tried to calm her, and reassured her that their apartment at least was safe and in an excellent neighbourhood.

"Of course it is," Helen replied, "but just hearing about this other district does nothing for my nerves. I dread to think what could happen to her, wandering around a place like that."

"Look everyone, I promise to be careful. The precautionary measures we take in New York apply to any city, right?"

That was all Katherine needed, for Mom to have a panic attack, but she knew her father was correct. The area, with the notorious Moulin Rouge, had a liberal, sordid bohemian reputation all the way back to the days of Toulouse Lautrec when the can-can was considered a danger to public morality. Her first inkling that the area had retained its ill repute was on one occasion when she and her friends, whom she met during her school trip, were heading out to dinner at one of the famous bistros in the Saint-Germain-des-Prés and found that the Metro carriages were escorted by the gendarmes armed to the hilt until they left Montmartre. Unnerved by this experience, she did not think she would have trouble adhering to his good advice.

"Come now, let's not fuss over imagined disasters," Gramps interjected, "Kathy has not even left yet, and I am sure she won't get into trouble while she's there."

"Unless she feels inclined to join a student protest ala *Les Misérables* and help erect a barricade or two," Steves jovially declared.

"Very funny, Mr. Worse-Case-Scenario."

At last, the day of her departure arrived. Although everything was planned well in advance, it was one of those awkward mornings, the more she hurried, the less she accomplished. Fidgety with excitement, she could not get things right. Buttons would not button, mascara got smeared all over her eyelids, and, she could have *sworn* she put her tickets and passport in that certain pocket of her purse yesterday. Eventually Pops and Steves packed the car and they were off to JFK, just in the nick of time. Everyone wanted to wish her a *bon voyage* before she boarded, and not wanting to prolong the goodbyes, she gave the troop a quick hug, promising as she walked to the departure gate to call the minute she arrived at the apartment.

It was exciting to be off on a journey she had looked forward to for months. Oddly, the billowing diesel fumes of the airport did not smell like suffocating effluence, it assumed a peculiar pungent scent that morning, like the beginning of a new adventure, if an adventure could exude a fragrance. It did not strike her that she was finally on her way until she settled into her seat on her Air France flight and heard the captain greeting the passengers, welcoming them aboard in English and French. Picking up the latest in-flight magazine and reading the bilingual articles extolling the latest fashions and the trendiest places to visit in Paris, already she could feel the novel ambience of another culture envelop her. Although it had been some time since she spoke French, the sight and sound of the language was like the voice of an old cherished friend who had returned after a long separation. It would take some practise to become as fluent as she was in the past, there was something to be said for the old phrase 'use it or lose it', and she was prepared to have a few headaches for the first couple of weeks. Until French expressions are familiar again, she would inevitably be translating everything in and out of English before she could read, speak or write anything without annoying mental blocks or speech impediments.

As always, the flight was long and relatively uneventful. There was the expected entertainment, the latest Hollywood blockbuster, and the few books she brought onboard helped to pass the time. The well-dressed gentleman sitting next to her in the aisle seat was busy with his papers and reports, obviously heading across the Atlantic for a meeting somewhere in the world, and therefore left her in peace, with the exception of the usual pleasantries of 'hello', 'excuse me', or 'thank you'. On her student exchange voyage a few years previously, she was seated next to an excessively curious buxom lady who did not know when to quit, yakking away to her like she was an intimate confidante, or peering over her shoulder as she endeavoured to read her book, with hardly a respite. After that trip, she was almost grateful for Aunt Martha's tame inquisitions. At least her neighbour on this trip was polite and remained intent upon his own business.

The plane touched down at Charles de Gaulle, in the afternoon according to New York time, but it was well into the evening in Paris, the change of time zone lurching her interior clock into a strange chronological wormhole. She was still ready and eager to be on the go while the Parisians were at the end of their day. Finding a taxi, she felt like a child pressing her nose to the window of a candy store as she watched the changing vista pass by while the twilight descended and the capital became bathed in a translucent misty lavender glow.

Entering the city from that airport was truly unique. Charles de Gaulle, built nineteen miles north of the bustling metropolis, ensured that the final point of destination was veiled from the eyes of the traveller as they descended. No doubt, the officials scrupulously planned the airport's location to prevent the incessant air traffic and roaring engines from visibly or audibly polluting the ambience of their beloved capital, and apparently, they succeeded. If one flew over during the summer months, the visitor would be visibly presented with beautifully managed quilt-like fields of alternating gold and green appearing as though they were tilled and clipped with the mathematical precision of a slide rule. The countryside was dotted with quaint villages and towns that were obviously under meticulous planning control. When the aircraft began to descend, this prevailing sense of exactitude and order made the visitor long for an aerial view of the capital city and its famous wonders, hoping they could see as many landmarks as they could before they touched ground, as was the usual case with other major international airports, but from this point of entry, one was denied a glimpse of the city below. Green fields, villages, more fields, the ground grew closer and closer, a runway appeared, a slight bump or two was felt as the craft landed, and they were surrounded by the steel and glass buildings of the airport. Slightly disappointed with this mysterious game of hide-and-seek, the voyager must continue on and collect their baggage, consoled by the reflection that they will see the metropolis as they make their way into town. For those travelling by road, the concrete motorway with its blue road signs, the underpasses and the typical traffic-logged hubbub of industrial areas were the first landmarks to greet the eye, without a doubt, it was a disheartening first impression. Then, the real introduction began. Quietly, and almost imperceptibly, the modern confusion of steel and asphalt was effaced little by little as the exquisite timelessness of Parisian heritage architecture was gradually unveiled. Popping up like mushrooms were cream sandstone edifices filigreed with curled, swirling carvings, gently sloping mansard roofs, elegant ironwork lanterns and wood doors that charmed the eye, until finally, the traveller was completely submerged in the glory of the Second Empire ala Baron Haussmann's master plan of city design, the iconic grand mansions, tree-lined boulevards and avenues, the quaint gardens, the majestic churches with their towers and spires, the shops and cafés with their colourful awnings, all crowded and nestled together like jewels encrusted on a gold setting.

The Kraylor's apartment was situated in the exclusive west-end *haute bourgeoisie* neighbourhood of the Chaillot Quarter, an area on the right bank of the Seine. In addition to the opulent dwellings, there were many embassies, a number of company headquarters, elegant restaurants, cafés, and of course, the tourist attractions. The famed Neo-Classical Palais de Chaillot built on the Place du Trocadéro dominated the area, and the myriad of museums with diverse exhibits ranged from the history of human evolution, to the art of wine making, the adventures of maritime history, the film industry, and the counterfeiter's trade, from *objects d'art* to clothing design and modern art. There was much to discover in this one quarter of Paris, and Katherine hoped to explore the area thoroughly if the artistic attractions of the city did not absorb all her time and attention.

Obviously, sightseeing would not be an option at this hour, the museums would be closed, and she might as well get unpacked and settle in. The apartment was certainly exquisite with its high corniced ceilings and crystal chandeliers, the large double French windows and their long velvet or brocade draperies, the gilded mirrors, the oil paintings, and the carefully chosen furniture combining the antique and the latest Belle Époque reproductions perfectly interspersed with the modern comfort of large overstuffed sofas and chairs, everything pointed to the expertise of an interior designer. In addition to the large formal parlour, there was a sitting room, four spacious bedrooms *en suite*, a dining room, den cum office, and a large kitchen with a breakfast area, walk-in pantry and a utility room.

Walking around the apartment, an unexplainable feeling of emptiness gradually enveloped her, a heavy stillness she had never experienced before slowly wrapped itself around where she stood, the silence seemed to be almost audible. She paused and slowly realized that for the first time in her life, she was truly alone.

Now, this won't do, I'm getting morbid. I must get busy, I have unpacking to take care of. No more of this nonsense! Put on some music … . She remembered seeing an entertainment console in the den, and opting for an instrumental arrangement, the soft melodic strains of the orchestra wafted comfortingly through the apartment. *Now, that's better!*

The Kraylors had chosen the rose guest room for Katherine's use, third on the left down the hall, which she observed had been prepared for her arrival, a bowel of fresh damask roses had been placed on the dressing table. It was a beautiful room, with an inviting warm glow, she felt right at home as she unpacked and hung up her wardrobe, hoping the creases would drop out overnight. Organizing her bits and pieces, she realized there was one slight hitch — where would it be safe to paint in this apartment? It will be difficult to find a space where she can mix colours and paint freely, and not be anxious about the usual accidents. Of course, the utility room would be the best place, but it lacked adequate lighting. The kitchen was bright with more space to work in, and the tiled floor covered with drop sheets, to be on the safe side, would be the best option she concluded. No need to worry about it for the present as she planned to spend the first month revisiting the art museums, on this trip she would have ample time to fully appreciate the work of the masters and their craft, then she could begin to paint her *own* path to glory.

However, before she could put any of these plans into action, the mundane necessities of the moment were pulling her back to the humdrum of reality. Better check the refrigerator, it's getting late, the shops will be closing, and while she planned to go to a restaurant the first night, she may need supplies for breakfast. Scouting the contents of the pantry, to her surprise, she found the refrigerator stocked with the essential items, cartons of milk, fruit juice, eggs, blocks of butter, cheese and ham, while the main cupboard next to the refrigerator contained fresh bread rolls, cereal, and coffee. On the counter she found a note from Lucille, the housekeeper:

> *"Dear Mademoiselle, Monsieur Charlie requested I*
> *pick up a few supplies for the kitchen. I hope everything*
> *is to your satisfaction. I will be here on Tuesdays and*
> *Fridays, please let me know if you have any special*
> *instructions, my telephone number is below, Lucille."*

Now that was thoughtful of you Charlie, Katherine mused. That reminds me, I had better call everyone, they must be wondering if I have arrived yet.

She called home first to find her mother had not gone to the Club that day, she had waited for her call. Helen was pleased to hear her trip had gone well and she had arrived without a hitch. Her mother chatted for a while, she missed her already, reissuing her warnings about Montmartre and to be careful in the city before she handed the telephone to Gramps who reassured her not to worry about them and to have a good time.

"Remember you promised me a painting of the Eiffel Tower …" .

"Oh Gramps, I can see the Eiffel Tower from the salon in the apartment, and it's all illuminated in a misty glow, we have a slight fog this evening. It's simply beautiful, I'll try and capture this image, there's a certain mystique about it tonight. I'll talk to you later Gramps, and give my love to Mom again. I have to call Pops at the office next, and then the Kraylors. I must thank Charlie especially who arranged everything for my arrival, with roses no less. Bye Gramps, tell Steves I'll give him a buzz later at home. Can't bother him while he's in the labs you know. Love you, Gramps. Bye for now."

The unpacking finished and the expected phone calls accomplished, it was time to think about dinner, she was beginning to feel a little peckish. Some restaurants would be closing at ten, no time to take a shower if she wanted to find somewhere to eat. Consulting her guidebook, she scanned the recommended restaurants in the area. She turned the page and was surprised to find an eating establishment in the Rue Vital lightly circled in pencil with a note in the margin, '*Nice place, pleasant owner, great food, open late, just the ticket for your first night. Try their chocolate cake. Charlie.*' Well, if Charlie recommended it, it's bound to be good, he knows all the best restaurants wherever he goes.

⊰ ❈ ⊱

The next morning, she woke up early and dressed with as much speed as she could muster. How exciting, her first free day in this artist metropolis with so much to see, and the Louvre must be first on her list. Recalling her trips to the Louvre on her previous visit, she remembered the long lines of tourists that mobbed this vast treasure-trove, and presuming the museum had reopened to the public, she hoped to avoid the expected traffic jam at the entrance. There had been plans as far back as '81 to renovate the main entrance to accommodate the millions of visitors that queued for blocks to get tickets. Plans had been in the works to eventually turn the entire north wing into exhibition space that currently housed the Finance Ministry. Arriving by Metro, she could see that the first phase of the project had now been accomplished, but it looked so out of place, this great glass pyramid sitting up in the middle of the classical stone courtyard of the former palace like a poky vitreous wart, she did not approve of it one iota. Although the original buildings showed through the glass structure and sunlight could filter down into the new subterranean entrance, the angular shape was completely alien to the graceful architecture of the Cour de Napoléon. Katherine was not the only one who was disgruntled, there were several tour groups already in line waiting for the doors to open, and she overheard the same disapproval voiced aloud:

"Who on earth decided to put that monstrosity there? It's an eye-sore!", "So out of place!", "Why won't people leave well-enough alone?"

The sight of this modern glass and steel Giza forcefully married to the elegant palace gave her an eerie feeling, and somehow, although she could not understand why, she felt an inexplicable negative premonition, no good would come of this.

Reaching the main lobby area, she wended her way through the corridors to the galleries where the paintings were exhibited, and once again felt awed by the sheer size of this labyrinthine edifice. It would take a lifetime to fully appreciate all that the Lourve had to offer. Katherine smiled as she recalled the last time she hurried through these hallowed halls. With all the class assignments she was expected to accomplish, it left precious little time to see all the famous sites that Paris boasted. Frustrated that her visits had to be limited, and not wanting to miss anything, she marched double-time up and down the endless corridors on her last day, turning her head left and right as she rushed past the paintings, sculptures, the archaeological exhibits, speed-walking around the famous moats of the original palace in the cellars, running back up to the main galleries, stopping for only a brief moment if a particular item caught her attention, casting glances of admiration around the old nineteenth-century exhibition rooms with their ornate ceilings that were an art form unto themselves. Imagine all these countless beautiful paintings, and what a pity that only a handful seemed to capture the attention of the art historians. How she wished a full commentary could be posted with each artwork, explaining all the hidden mysteries that researchers had uncovered, particularly the tantalizing details rejected by the artists and covered up with layers of paint, which could now be seen with x-ray machines. Sadly, it was only when she returned home and poured over her art books or watched documentaries that she learned about the laborious creation process of the masterpieces she had seen up close.

On this trip, she resolved to take all the time she needed and not rush through the galleries like a miniature tornado. She had three months before the Kraylors arrived, and was bound and determined to savour every moment of this artistic pilgrimage. She decided before she started her round of all the galleries, she would make a reverential visit to the original masterpiece by David of Napoléon's coronation, and silently apologize to him for her less than perfect modernistic remake. How wonderful to see this painting again! Although Professor Matthews had praised her attention to detail, she knew she could never measure up to David's faultless brushstrokes. How could so many of the critics believe this was not one of his best works? The lighting and shading he achieved for the interior of his Notre Dame was extraordinarily natural, his figures were full of life, and in a mysterious way, engaged the spectator in the actual proceedings. The vibrant colours and the various materials of their regal ensembles were truly sublime. She marvelled on how he attained this degree of perfection, the very textures were so perfect that one could almost feel the plushness of the crimson velvets, the embossed surfaces of the rich, multi-coloured brocades, the soft fur of the ermine-lined mantles, and hear the rustle of the silks and satins. The pearls of particular note, had a flawless lustre and moonlight sheen that very few artists achieve. Imagine, here it hangs in open view, with only a slender rope separating me from the canvas, she thought. How surprisingly easy it is to forget this is a painting, the temptation to reach forward and gently touch the rich garments was overwhelming. Its sheer size, the height and breadth of the canvas, added to this optical illusion of reality. It was obvious to Katherine that David not only used monolithic dimensions to suggest the grandeur of the occasion, but also to pull the spectator into that moment, as if they were hiding behind a pillar in the aisle of the cathedral. His skill in portraying dimension and depth was so successful, it was difficult to resist the urge to walk directly into the painting. He had a wonderful sense of perspective considering the size of the canvas and the venue in which the coronation occurred, however, David did enlist the services of a set-designer from the Opera to help with the scale of his mighty endeavour, if she remembered correctly. You'll never persuade me this is a copy and not the original.

After she examined the painting up close for some time, inspecting every detail, she sat on one of the benches in the middle of the room to gaze and admire it from a distance.

"Katherine, what a surprise! You're here already!" a familiar voice with a thick French accent whispered from behind.

Startled by this unexpected greeting, Katherine turned; of course, it was Martin, one of her friends from the Montmartre whom she met during her student exchange term. She tried to hide her agitation to this rude interruption of her reverie.

"Martin! It's so good to see you again," Well, I'm not lying about that, anyway…. "Is Justine with you?"

"No, she's at work today, but I have a day off, and I need to do some sketches for my next project. We received your letter, but you didn't mention the exact day of your arrival. When did you get here?"

"Just last night, when I wrote to you, I didn't have my tickets yet, so I couldn't give you the date, but you certainly found me in record time, I was going to call you in a couple of days…"

She knew it was not a very courteous thing to do, but she had purposely sent her letter with an ambiguous timeframe. As long as she could remember, she had been restricted to time schedules of one form or another to the point even the mundane and trivial expectations had become morally abrasive. These few months would perhaps be the only time she would be truly free, without having to worry about appointments and obligations, jostling between things she would like to do with what she had to do, or have to report where she would be going for the day, nor set an exact time when she would be home in the evening. Not that she had planned to run amok, it was simply liberating to think that if she did not feel inclined to inspect the commercial galleries for business ideas, she could sit all day in a café and read a book if she felt so inclined, or burn the midnight oil on a painting project should the Muses inspire her. She had hoped to enjoy this sensation for a week at least before she called them, knowing she would not be free from well-meaning interruptions when the word got out she had arrived.

"How have you been?"

"Oh, we're managing, as always," Martin replied.

She was not sure, but she thought she heard a faint tone of melancholic detachment in his voice. Katherine felt a twinge of guilt for her agitation and her self-indulgent craving to jealously safeguard her time. Martin seemed all right, but they had obviously hit a rough patch she realized, now having graduated from art college and probably wondering where they were heading next, considering how insecure an artist's life could be if they failed to find avenues to promote their works.

"I don't want to hold you up now, can we get together for a cup of coffee or lunch later? I do want to hear all the news."

"Of course," he replied, with a smile. "Shall we meet in our favourite café here for lunch, let's say ... twelve? I don't have many sketches to do, and I should be finished by then," glancing at his watch. "That gives us an hour and a half."

"What?" She glanced at her watch. "Oh my, look at the time, I didn't realize I had been sitting here that long. It seemed like only a few minutes."

"You are obsessed with that painting," Martin pronounced as though he were a doctor announcing his diagnosis.

"I guess I am, it's simply magnificent. Although it has made the history books, I feel it deserves more attention than it usually gets. Just look at it! I know David planned every detail with meticulous precision, but it's not ... stilted, like his painting the *Oath of the Horatii*, the three soldiers all stand frozen in time as if staring at the head of Medusa. The coronation is so vibrant, you can become mesmerized by it."

"Like I said, obsessed," Martin laughed. "Speaking of David, you must tell me more about the Sirrac contest in all its colourful details, but unfortunately, I have to go or I'll never get these sketches done. See you at twelve."

"All right, see you then." She watched Martin as he walked through the gallery until he disappeared from sight. Well, so much for her first free day, she was already tied to the mechanical tic-tic-tic of a clock. Oh, never mind, it was good to see Martin again, she would not let the unanticipated timing of this meeting ruffle her. She was going to get together with them anyway, so why not now rather than later? Their first encounter was also unexpected she recalled, this was becoming a tradition.

She was in the Opéra Metro station one afternoon when they first met. Katherine was on her way back to class after lunch, and she stopped to listen to one of the street buskers perform, on a 'cello of all things. While there were always the expected piano accordion players belting out *La vie en rose* for the tourists, she was continually surprised by the number of talented musicians and the myriad of instruments they played below the streets of Paris as regular performances, their instrument cases always open for a donation or two. Obviously, several were students from the *conservatoires*, others were there simply for the pleasure and the applause of a metropolitan audience. Several sold recordings as they played, perhaps they hoped to be discovered by some great recording studio or impresario. She had to admit the acoustics were phenomenal as she listened to the classical melody echo hauntingly around the tiled underground stations, drifting through the tenebrous tunnels while waiting for the next train.

She listened to the 'cellist, oblivious to the teenager who walked up behind her, and in a flash, grabbed her purse and sprinted up the nearest stairway.

"My purse! He's got my purse!" she screamed in English, while the 'cellist dropped his bow in surprise and yelled for help.

Thankfully, the would-be thief never made it past the first five steps as a young couple were heading down at that same moment. The tall young man reacted instantly, snatching the stolen purse from the criminal's hand while punching him back down onto the platform. The thug quickly rose to his feet and fled in the other direction before the stranger could lay hands on him.

"Well! I guess that's enough *Swan Lake* for one day," the 'cellist declared as he quickly set his 'cello back in its case. "Are you okay?"

Katherine nodded in the affirmative, although her knees were beginning to buckle.

"Yes … I think so."

The young couple came up and handed her bag back.

"Are you sure?" the hero asked, "I don't think so, you need to sit down for a minute."

"Yes, you must be in shock," the young girl said as she took Katherine's arm, "Come, you need some tea. English tea with sugar, I think that's the perfect remedy."

The trio decided that she also needed fresh air, and so the Café de la Paix became the latest shock treatment clinic for purse-snatching victims.

Although they refused at first, Katherine insisted that they have something with her, it was the least she could do for all their help. After they ordered a round of coffee, she sipped her suggested cure-all and realized she had seen the couple around the art college, but had not met them formally. The 'cellist, whose name was Maurice Clermont, remarked it was lucky that the incident occurred while they were coming to meet him, and so had the pleasure to formally introduce them, Martin Dubois and Justine Ambroise.

Martin, who had penetrating hazel eyes and light brown hair, was a serious character, but not morose, neatly groomed and precise in everything he did, exuding an aura of eccentric distinction. He had a wonderful sense of humour with a quiet cynical twist, he never took the world at face value. His father owned a stock brokerage firm and expected him to take over the business at one point, but was resigned to the possibility he may choose to become a lawyer or doctor, never expecting his son to turn his back on these respectable options and the comfortable lifestyle he was accustomed to for the life of an artisan. Martin realized the family business was not for him, he had seen too many people stake all their fortunes on the up and down slide of a graph, and would have nothing to do with glorified gambling. The practise of law did not necessarily mean the practise of justice, and he simply did not have a strong stomach for medicine. Consequently, his father acted as though he had disowned him until he came to his senses and learned that living on the meagre means of an artist was not the idealistic life he imagined. Martin dug in his heels nevertheless and managed to scrape through art college, compliments of a scholarship and a sympathetic uncle who helped to cover part of his living expenses. To earn a little extra, he found a part-time job in one of the famous Montmartre cafés and sold paintings of the usual attractions of Paris to the tourists near the Place du Tertre or along the banks of the Seine.

Justine with her petite five-foot one figure, blue eyes and a fair complexion all ringed in soft blonde curls, was an endearing sprite. Infatuated with a romantic notion of the bohemian life of an artist, she flamboyantly wore stylised gypsy skirts flowing to the ankle and elegantly patterned tops with long sleeves. Her one weakness, indulging in regular hunting expeditions through the markets and the *chic* second hand shops specialising in unusual shoes, hats, beaded handbags and other rare accessories not appreciated by their former owners. She came from a quiet village not far from the little town of St. Brieuc where her parents ran a small bakery. She dreamed of a career in the art world of Paris, and longed for that day to start college and head to where the city lights beckoned. At least her parents did not object to her choice of subject, allowing her to make up her own mind. She returned home for the summers to help in the family bakery and found a job during the weekends while at college working in one of the museum gift shops. Martin and Justine started dating in their second year of art school, and for the obvious plus financial reasons they decided to move in to Martin's little garret apartment.

Quiet, black-haired, brown-eyed Maurice was in medical school. This surprised Katherine who was convinced his true calling was music. His father and grandfather were doctors, so medicine was the logical choice for him, a practical career, and he wanted to help people. He explained to Katherine his first love was music and he would continue lessons, but as a hobby. After all, he explained, doctors were always in demand and it could turn out after studying music for years in a *conservatoire*, he would discover in the end he could not make the grade and fail to obtain employment with a professional orchestra. The stress put on student musicians robbed them of their natural love of the music, and he did not want that to happen to him. Why not practise his music and play in the Metro for fun on his free days? He found it truly enjoyable to get together with Martin and Justine, and serenade them as they painted, or go out with them to the bistros and at times play with the other musicians.

Life was certainly not dull when Martin, Justine and Maurice became her friends, Katherine never knew what to expect. They insisted on being her guide, showing her the sights of Paris, and she would never forget the day they arranged to give her the Grand Tour of the artist Mecca of Montmartre. Just as the four sightseers entered the little cable-car *funiculaire* that transported visitors up and down the steep climb to the famous Sacré-Coeur basilica with its distinctive egg-shaped domes, Martin and Justine began a heated debate on which of the masters had accomplished the most for art. Reaching the top of the hill, Katherine stood up and prepared to get out when she noticed that the two debaters were not budging an inch … and refused to leave until they settled the matter. She was about to sit back down until Maurice shook his head and rolled his eyes with a sigh;

"Come on, looks like I'll be the tour guide today."

"You're not going to wait for them?" she asked.

"No," he said with a smile, "Trust me. You'll see."

They exited the car and walked around the basilica, then visited the various art galleries until Katherine finally insisted they had better check on them. She could not believe it, there they were, still in the car disputing, travelling up and down the hill until the conductor finally asked if they planed to disembark sometime that year. Katherine noted neither had won the debate, and wondered aloud if they would have stayed on the contraption all night if permitted.

"Probably!" Maurice replied, "once they get started on something, they won't stop until a conclusion is reached."

On another occasion, they arranged to meet at one of the Metro stations. Katherine did not consider this unusual as they often agreed to meet up with Maurice after one of his subterranean performances. Arriving on time, she found him playing, but did not see Martin and Justine anywhere. Rather than disturb Maurice in the midst of the *Sleeping Beauty* waltz, she tried to occupy her time reading the large posters and Metro maps, stopping to look over at a couple of mime performers at the other end of the platform gathering a small crowd every time the train stopped, hoping she did not look out of place since she was not getting on any of the carriages. She heard her named called out, but she could not see them. Perhaps she was on the wrong platform? No, they were definitely not on the other side….there! Someone called her again. Finally, she saw one of the mimes break down and laugh, followed by Maurice. Just for the sheer hilarity of it, he had dared Martin and Justine to try their fortune at putting on a street performance for an afternoon, and they never refused a challenge if the gauntlet was thrown down. Dressed as robots covered from head to toe in gold lamé and sparkle greasepaint, Katherine had to admit they were remarkably good, she did not recognize them at all, and they had managed to rake in almost forty dollars in francs.

There were days Martin and Justine ran her around to all the museums, or the unusual backstreet bookshops in odd nooks of the city when they discovered she loved to read. In addition to the second hand boutiques, Justine wanted to show her all the markets in Paris. Katherine's favourite was the Marché aux Oiseaux, the colourful outdoor bird market on Sunday mornings in the Ile de la Cité filled with exotic parrots of every squawk and hue. In the afternoons when school work could no longer be avoided, it was fun to join the three of them in Martin's compact apartment overlooking the sloping mansard rooftops for their study and painting sessions accompanied by Maurice's music, the nights rounded off with Justine's simple, but excellent home cooking, onion soup, her specialty, served with cheese and ham quiche and crusty bread. The four friends would talk and laugh into the wee hours of the morning, bombarding her with questions about her American culture, listening to old recordings of popular French singers playing in the background. Those were certainly her most cherished memories of Paris.

Katherine continued to survey her favourite painting for a few more minutes before she meandered around the galleries, stopping every now and then to watch some art students copying the priceless originals. She eventually came across Martin who was busy sketching a forlorn figure from the foreground of the eerie *Raft of the Medusa* by Géricault, a young man lying prostrate with head bowed low, his arm hanging limp from the wreckage. She wondered why he would concentrate on this painting depicting a handful of dead and dying sailors who had managed to survive a shipwreck on a makeshift raft, the murky waves surging upwards and threatening to swamp them, the turbulent scene overhung with sable clouds illuminated by a disquieting sulphuric glow. A sail is visible in the distance, but the ship, a mere dot on the horizon, appears too far away to see the struggling castaways, hope turns to agonizing despair, realizing they may be passed by. This image, as always, disturbingly surreal and apocalyptic. When she saw this original for the first time, she felt an inexplicable urge to run away, she could not explain why the painting had this effect on her. Perhaps it was its larger-than-life size, it was only a few feet short of the dimensions David used for his Napoléonic canvas, the waves seemed ready to crash down on the gazing spectator along with the unfortunate victims clinging to the raft. No, it was more than that. When she eventually discovered the history of the painting, the full horror of the subject impressed upon her an ineffaceable grotesque foreboding.

It was clear from the outset, this young painter sought a spectacular and striking subject that would seal his reputation as a great artist. Obsessed with the latest political scandal of his day, Géricault decided to capture the controversial tragedy for posterity. It was a bold decision. Painters at that time concentrated on depicting past history with the exception of portraits or special commissions to commemorate an event, few had attempted to paint current news issues that grabbed the attention of the public. The populace had grown dissatisfied with the newly restored monarchy following Napoléon's exile, and the scandal in question only exacerbated the negative public opinion of the new regime. It began when the British had surrendered the colony of Senegal to France. The French King appointed a royalist as captain of the frigate *Méduse* with the mission to join a convoy and sail to Africa to accept the British surrender. Attempting to make good time on the journey, the captain decided to overtake the other three ships, but mistakenly veered nearly one-hundred miles off course, and ran aground on a sand bank sixty miles from the coast of modern-day Mauritania. The ship carried over four hundred passengers, unfortunately they had room in the small lifeboats for only two hundred and fifty. The captain ordered a raft to be built for the remaining passengers and declared they would tow them. The order was hastily carried out, and the remainder of the passengers, one-hundred and forty seven to be exact, piled onto the rickety half-submerged, makeshift vessel.

Then the horrors began. The lifeboats towed the raft with great difficulty for a few miles, and they decided to set the raft adrift with only one bag of biscuit ration, two casks of water, and a few casks of wine for its passengers. The little food they had was exhausted on the first day and panic overwhelmed them. Fighting broke out, the water barrels were lost overboard, only the wine was left. Drifting for days on the great saltwater desert of the Atlantic, their hunger and thirst became unbearable, mutineers were slaughtered, the weakest succumbed to the strongest, cannibalism became their only means of survival. Those who were not killed or thrown overboard in the brawls became half-mad from drinking seawater, dying of starvation and dehydration, or threw themselves into the sea in despair. When the *Argus* from the convoy finally rescued the survivors nearly two weeks later, their number had dwindled to a mere fifteen souls. When the captain was rescued, he made no mention of the raft he had set adrift, therefore no effort was made to search for those survivors, the *Argus* found them by mere chance. The horrific tale outraged the public and they raised a hue and cry, turning their anger upon the grossly incompetent captain who had not commanded a ship in twenty years, and upon the King who obviously assigned him this position due to his royalist political persuasion, not for his seamanship.

If the story of the *Méduse* and its hapless victims was not disturbing enough, Géricault went overboard in his fixated endeavour to capture it on canvas to perfection. Moving his studio across the street from a hospital, he walked the wards observing the faces of the sick and terminally ill to find the exact visage of hopelessness. He frequented the morgue and peered at the cadavers to discern the proper colours of dead flesh. Not satisfied with this preliminary work, he brought severed limbs back to his studio to study the effects of decomposition at leisure, he once borrowed a severed head from an insane asylum and stored it on the roof when not required for study. Irritated by the least distraction or noise, he became oblivious to the world as he worked, barricading himself in his studio until this monolith of human misery was completed. No wonder Katherine considered running away from it, the painting exuded disease, death and decay.

Somehow, she felt uneasy with Martin's apparent preoccupation with this work. His downbeat mood earlier still bothered her and it seemed like the lifeless bodies slumped across the foreground threatened to draw him into their number. Walking up to him, she took a closer look at his sketches. She knew the identity of the figure, it was Delacroix, who had posed for one of Géricault's shipwreck victims.

"Hi," she whispered, "I thought you believed copying from the masters was pointless. You were always fired up by the artists who explored new avenues of stylistic expression. Have you recanted your principles?"

"No, not completely," he replied with a smile as he continued sketching, "I just thought for once it would be amusing to experiment with a pasticcio painting by including in one work all the 'anonymous' portraits of famous people who posed for iconic paintings. It should be interesting to see the muddle of different styles and periods melded into one picture."

"Like a collage, that sounds fun actually," she admitted.

"Let's face it, I'm sick and tired of painting the Arc de Triomphe for the tourists. I need to do something different."

"I can imagine, that must get rather boring."

"You have no idea. Well, I'm finished here," he concluded as he closed his sketchbook and began packing away his supplies, "time for lunch, better go before all the tables are gone."

Looking over the menu, she was surprised how quickly she could fall back into their old school day routine. The four students had set down a rule to go Dutch and avoid a fracas about the tab, a rule that allowed them to choose whatever they wanted, she tried not to make them feel uncomfortable with their tight budgets and ate accordingly.

It was wonderful to talk with Martin again. He was very interested in her latest adventure, the Sirrac contest. However, she also felt guilty about telling him her decision not to sell the canvas in question and concentrated on the article instead. Martin nodded his head thoughtfully.

"I heard about him, the Hacker. His infamy has reached us over here. That review is just shameful," he declared, "but it is publicity. Have you had any negative reactions to it?"

"No, thank heavens. Nothing more than the usual round of explanations when people ask about it."

"That's to be expected. I hope the Hacker hasn't turned people off anyway. Any buyers yet?" he asked as he ate his Croque-Monsieur.

Katherine could not conceal that part of her news any longer, it was good to talk this over with someone.

"Yes, but I don't like how the offers were made," she admitted, explaining the exorbitant figures and her suspicions about this mysterious client, explaining how they may have acquired their information about the painting. Martin's eyebrows furrowed as she laid out her misgivings.

"Yes, I agree with you. I would give my front teeth for a sale like that, but I think you're right, follow your instincts. Why offer those prices to a mere graduate? They obviously know about your family circumstances, and tried to offer you something that you could not refuse. Another student starting out would have grabbed a few hundred dollars, but you are not in the same situation. I can't imagine very many clients at the Sirrac Gallery interested in a graduate's work anyway. It's odd, and if they believe the article as you suspect, they want the picture for questionable purposes, that's obvious. I think you're right about not selling, it sounds fishy to me, as they say in English."

"I'm glad you think so, it just didn't seem right. But that's enough about my fiascos. How have you been, and how is Justine and Maurice?"

Martin began by telling her that he and his father were still not on speaking terms, he had refused to come to his graduation, but his uncle continued to check and see how he was doing every now and then. That's why he's feeling down, Katherine thought. I can't imagine Pops doing that to us, sure he gets mad at times, but he has always been supportive about our plans. Poor Martin. He was trying to put on a brave face, she saw that now, she could still sense that same vague feeling of quiet, pained detachment. He continued with his general news, Maurice was busy at the hospital now that he had finished medical school and did not visit as often due to his hectic schedule, which was understandable. He also had to curtail his Metro solos, but when he could come over to see them, he brought his 'cello. Martin then laughed a little, divulging the latest news that Maurice had a crush on one of the nurses, and was trying to pluck up the courage to ask her out, without success up to now. When he tried to talk about Justine, he hesitated.

"Is everything all right?" she asked with concern.

He quietly set his coffee down, searching for the right words.

"Kathy, I'd like to say she's fine and pretend everything is as before, but I can't lie," he finally stated, "you'll probably find out everything eventually ..."

"Oh, Martin, don't tell me you two are breaking up?"

"No, at least not yet. I hope not."

"Is it cold feet? Marriage is a big step, that feeling is normal, so everyone tells me," Katherine replied, trying to offer some helpful advice. They had been planning to get married for the last two years, but decided not to make any definite arrangements until they were more secure, perhaps after they got that illusive 'big break' they hoped would come their way.

"It's more complicated than that," he admitted, "I don't know how to say this, even though I am involved, it really is Justine's private matter and she's asked me not to talk about it to anyone. I can't say too much unless it's all right with her, which makes this difficult to explain."

"It's not my business, but is she seeing someone else?"

"Oh no, it's not like that either. I guess it's easier if I just say she hasn't been herself lately, in fact, she's been very depressed these last few months, and I think it may get out of control. She missed many days at work, but thankfully, she was granted sick leave and has not lost her job ... yet. She went back to work today, and I'm so glad she finally felt like going out. She has lost her interest in painting, and when she does find the energy to work, her pictures are very dark, I don't know how many tubes of black and purple she's gone through these last months."

"Depressed? That doesn't sound like Justine, we could always trust her to find the silver lining in a hurricane. Has she gone for help?"

"Yes, she's been to a counsellor, but it seems not to have made a difference. I wish she would just talk to me. She seems so distant, I'm afraid I won't be able to reach her ...."

"Oh, how terrible! What could have happened? Could it be bi-polar disorder?"

"Not really, and I can't tell you the reason, Justine would be very upset if I did. Like I said, it's up to her when she's ready to talk. If she found out I told you, it might devastate her."

Katherine was lost for words. She had no idea they were in this predicament.

"Martin, I wish I could help. Is there anything I can do?"

"To be honest, I was really glad when we received your letter, I thought your visit would pull her out of this black hole she seems to be falling into, perhaps she might be able to talk to you eventually if she can't talk to me right now."

Katherine really felt like an ogre for not telling them when she was arriving.

"Of course, do you want me to stop by tonight?"

"Perhaps tomorrow, let me tell her you're here first. But please don't let her know I told you how bad things have been."

"All right, I'll just pretend you told me she hasn't been feeling well for awhile. That wouldn't be lying. Tomorrow afternoon then?"

"Yes, we can have an early supper, that would be perfect. I'm sorry to drop all this on you the first day …."

"Oh, don't give it another thought. Like you said, I would have noticed if Justine, of all people, was depressed. I'm glad you told me, perhaps I can help."

"I sincerely hope so."

 CB ❁ BO

Katherine was certainly not prepared for this distressing news. They seemed to be such a happy couple, and she could not imagine what had come between them to where Justine was isolating herself and Martin was at his wit's end. She had promised not to pry, so dwelling on this at length in an attempt to guess the nature of their dilemma would not help, she would have to wait until Justine would be willing to share whatever was troubling her.

She arrived at their apartment in the late afternoon the next day and rang the bell. It was so odd to be back here after all this time, and yet it felt like only yesterday. The main entrance buzzed open and in she went, listening to the sounds of a 'cello echo through the upper halls as she ascended the familiar narrow twisting stairs to the top floor. Martin opened

158

the door before she had a chance to knock.

"Hi! It's so good to see you again," he said jovially as Maurice launched into his special rendition of the *Star Spangled Banner* in honour of the occasion. "Enter, oh, you didn't have to do that," Martin continued.

Katherine had brought a few bottles of wine and a fresh chocolate strawberry cream gateaux.

"It looked so pretty, I couldn't pass it up, so let's not argue. I know everyone here has a sweet tooth. Hi Maurice, *Doctor* Maurice now! What a lovely welcome, I thought you would be busy at the hospital."

"Not today, but I'm still on call and may be beeped at any moment, so please forgive me if I have to rush away," he replied as he cut the performance short with a colourful cadenza before going to meet her. "It's been a while, how have you been?"

"Pretty good, it feels so strange to be finished with college. My whole life to this point has been figuring out how to finish schoolwork on time and survive all the exams. All that is over now, time to move on into uncharted waters. My, someone has been busy."

Katherine looked around the sitting room, the walls were covered with different sized canvasses at various levels of completion, most of them featured the Arc de Triomphe with a few other famous Parisian attractions nestled in between. Martin had developed a one-man assembly line, working out the details of one group of paintings while the backgrounds of another set were drying.

"You see what I mean," he said with a smile.

"No wonder you needed a change. If it's not a secret, I can't wait to see your pasticcio idea. Where's Justine?"

"She just woke up from her nap, she's getting ready and should be out soon. I'll bring these into the kitchen and see if supper is ready," Martin casually replied as he took the cake box and bottles, but his voice betrayed his worry.

Things look bad, Katherine thought, Justine was not in the habit of lying down during the daytime, and she usually did most of the cooking. If she was not hunting through the markets for the next bargain of a lifetime, she was always working on a new masterpiece or fussing in the kitchen trying out the latest recipe she had discovered. Katherine realized it was going to be hard pretending everything was still the same without betraying she knew otherwise, despite her ignorance of the details.

They headed into the small kitchen cum dining space, Katherine helped Maurice to finish setting the wobbly fold-up table while Martin prepared to serve their favourite meal, just like old times. The aroma issuing from the oven was delightful, which actually bothered her. Martin had never been handy in the kitchen before and tended to let everything brown too much if he did not outright turn good food into charcoal. Judging from the golden colour of the quiche and the perfectly roasted cheese topping on the soup as he took the bowels out of the oven, Katherine could see he had a lot of practise lately. He disliked cooking, and obviously had perfected this skill out of necessity. How long has this been going on, she wondered.

"Justine, Kathy's here, and supper is ready," he called towards the bedrooms.

A faint creak of a doorknob could be heard in the background.

"Hello Kathy, I'm so glad you've come."

Katherine was shocked when she turned around, she could hardly recognize Justine. The bubbly music in her voice was gone, she had grown incredibly thin and looked very pale, her eyes tired and shadowed, her appearance betraying the anxieties that Martin promised not to mention. Katherine put on a brave face like everyone else, hoping her initial reaction did not show.

"Justine, it's good to see you again. I hope you are feeling better, Martin told me you have not been feeling well for awhile…"

"Oh … yes, I'm much better lately. How was your trip?"

Katherine knew Justine was trying to hide the truth, but she carried on the conversation, telling them about her uneventful journey and her surprise to have bumped into Martin during her first day in Paris. She drifted into other topics, telling them about the family news, the latest escapades with Jasper, and Gramp's accident, but he was now recovering nicely. Maurice was curious about the hip operation, while Martin wondered how her plans for the gallery were coming along. Katherine admitted it was early days yet, but hoped to get it open within a year or two, perhaps sooner, she was not sure yet. She promised Martin and Justine that their artworks would be exhibited at her grand opening. Martin said that would give him enough time to assemble a collection, he had been preoccupied selling souvenir paintings to the tourists and was eager to begin working on serious original creations. He looked forward to this project, and hoped he and Justine could save enough to come to New York and attend the opening. Maurice announced if they were going, he would not be left behind, he could always put in for vacation time, decision made. He would not miss their big début in America for the world.

Excited with these plans, Martin and Maurice wondered if she had decided upon the layout of her gallery, and offered some helpful advice after they finished their dinner and began serving the dessert. They pointed out that she was in a fortunate set of financial circumstances, she need not start out small as with most ventures, and could begin on a 'medium' scale by including a café cum restaurant, and perhaps a small gift shop. Katherine admitted she was thinking along those lines, she knew not many people could afford to invest in art, but nevertheless loved the artistic scene and would enjoy spending time looking around the gallery, stopping for lunch, perhaps buy a colourful print or two in the shop. If she could attract more people, it would keep the place active and welcoming, judging from her own experience, over-quiet galleries without any 'buzz' put her off making regular visits. In any case, a restaurant and shop might help to cover the costs of running the gallery when pieces were not selling. They agreed, but ever practical Maurice reminded her that she could not serve two masters, a bustling gallery like that would take some time to manage and she would be divided, torn between the business end and trying to continue with her own art. He suggested she think about hiring a manager and perhaps investigate the complexities of leasing out the restaurant and gift area, which could supply a steady income without having to absorb all her attention. She could arrange a studio in a backroom area for herself, and would be on hand if needed. Martin had a few ideas of his own; to include ample packaging space in her work area for receiving and shipping items, and don't forget to have a large loading entrance. She laughed as she imagined several UPS men bumbling through a small door with a large awkward crate, a large back door would definitely be a necessity. They offered some great suggestions, which she appreciated immensely.

However, she was troubled by Justine's lack of active input during their conversation, only nodding at a statement, or adding a simple "That sounds like a good idea," to their proposals. She really had become detached Katherine thought to herself. It was completely uncharacteristic for Justine not to become totally engaged in a discussion, particularly when it involved art. It seemed she had drifted a thousand miles away. The Justine she knew, and the quiet anxious person sitting beside her at the table, were two completely different people. Katherine tried to continue as before, playing the chitchat masquerade and hiding her worry as best she could.

After they finished their dessert and cleaned up the kitchen, Martin showed her his sketches for the pasticcio while Maurice topped up their coffee cups. Martin had only begun to work out his ideas, but she could envision the result he was aiming for, a bizarre montage of portraits and famous poses lifted from the different masterpieces, from the slumping Delacroix, to an impressionistic Oscar Wilde that Toulouse-Lautrec painted in some of his larger works. Of course, Martin had to include some famous self-portraits, like Vincent van Gogh with his bandaged ear, Michelangelo's face hidden on St. Bartholomew's skin in the *Last Judgement* from the Sistine Chapel, and Raphael disputing with the geographers in his *School of Athens*. It would be interesting to see how all the diverse periods and styles would blend into one work. It had the possibility of becoming an iconic print she noticed, and he agreed. Maurice added that prints were another possibility, which gave Katherine an idea. She could sell posters and limited edition lithographs of the works featured in her gallery, and in return for the exclusive rights to print and sell them, she would give all the artists a percentage of the sales. Martin said that sounded like an excellent plan, if the artists will let you get away with it. On the other hand, she and her affiliated artists could still make a profit long after the original artworks had sold. Maurice cautioned her that if she went ahead with that idea, to make a thorough investigation into the legalities of copyright. Again, they offered such excellent advice, and she could give Charlie, the copyright expert, some extra business too.

Reminded of Charlie, Katherine told them she could not wait until they would finally get to meet him. They were aware she was staying at his family's residence, and wondered how she fared in that large apartment by herself. She admitted that while it was luxurious, it was not like staying in the bustling student accommodations at the university during her last trip, the first night was rather lonely but she would get over it, there was always her artwork and the TV to keep her busy. Martin suggested if she needed human company, she was free to come and go as she liked, bring her paint gear too, just like the old days. No ceremony! She expressed her appreciation for the open invitation. Martin and Maurice turned to Justine, hoping this arrangement would cheer her up, expecting to see a display of effervescent enthusiasm over Kathy's visits, even for a second. Although she did not refuse, telling Katherine she was always welcome, Justine was completely passive and atypically inert, it was apparent she had lost all interest in living. Getting up from the table she asked to be excused, explaining she still felt exhausted, and retired for the evening. It was barely eight-thirty. Justine had always been a night owl, she hated going to bed early. Martin was not exaggerating that things between them had deteriorated, it was obvious it would take more than a visit or two to help her. Perhaps she needed more time.

As soon as Justine left the kitchen, Martin quickly put his finger to his lips, a sign pleading with Katherine not to speak out loud about the current situation, the walls were notoriously thin, and he did not want

Justine to hear them discussing any particulars that could upset her. Fortunately, Maurice's pager went off, a providential distraction.

"Looks like duty calls," Katherine said with a smile.

"Yes, I must dash off. It's wonderful to have you back, we'll get together when we can arrange it."

"Of course we will, it's nice to see you again too. But don't let me hold you up, I don't want to get you into any trouble at the ER."

"All right, good night, Kathy," he replied as he grabbed his jacket, heading for the door and running down the stairs.

"You know, I should be getting back too," Katherine noted as she looked towards the window, "I said I wouldn't venture out in the city after dark, and I don't like travelling on the Metro at this time, it's a little unnerving."

"I agree, I had better accompany you," Martin suggested.

"Oh no, I'll be all right. No point in you leaving home to take me home, but I thank you for offering."

"Nonsense, I'd be happy to. I'll be over and back in just half an hour, and besides, it's not a good idea for you to travel this particular Metro line alone."

Remembering how they first met, she accepted his offer. Lightning can strike twice, and she did not want to face another purse-snatcher, or worse.

Walking to the Metro station, Martin admitted he needed to talk, and accompanying her home provided the perfect opportunity.

"You can see that things are different," he began as they boarded the carriage.

"Martin, I really don't know what to say. Justine is not herself at all," Katherine replied, "I know you promised not to mention anything, but I don't see how I can help if I'm left in the dark. Does Maurice know all the details?"

"No, he thinks it's depression, just like you did, which is not far from the truth, but that's not the whole story. He's prescribed some anti-depressants, but she refuses to take them. She doesn't think they help, and prefers to sleep her life away instead. Maurice believes she's using sleep as a form of escapism, but can't figure out the reason for it, which again, leads him to conclude it's some form of depression."

"Martin, I am so sorry! I don't know what the answer is, it's obvious if all she wants to do is sleep, she's not ready for visitors, and I might end up being more of an irritation to her than a help. Are her parents aware of her condition?"

"No, and she can't face them right now. Perhaps Justine is not ready to talk, but I can't stay silent any longer, I'll go insane!"

"All right, we'll be at my place in a few minutes," she replied, not a little alarmed by the desperation in his voice, "we'll have some privacy there."

As they travelled the rest of the way in silence, she wondered what could have happened to cause this distress, something that Justine did not want anyone else to know about. Maybe she was diagnosed with a serious illness, and can't face the outcome. It might explain why Martin was the only one to know. Cancer? No, I don't think so, Maurice is a doctor, I can't see why she wouldn't discuss it with him, at least to ask for a second opinion or for additional medical advice, he was a close friend after all. Could it be AIDS? That would certainly be difficult to talk about, but Martin doesn't suspect her of cheating on him …oh no, perhaps she has a drug problem and shared an infected needle … she could have passed it on to Martin not knowing she was HIV positive at the time, he did say he was involved in some way … perhaps that's it, but I really shouldn't speculate and jump to the wrong conclusion, better wait and let him explain.

Arriving at the apartment and hanging up his jacket, she asked if he would like coffee.

"If this is a night for confessions, I think I might need something a little stronger…" he said, settling for a brandied coffee while she made a cup of tea.

Making their way into the sitting room, they sat across from each other on the large sofas. Martin stirred his cup and pensively took a sip as he tried to figure out where to start, while Kathy set her tea down on the side table, patiently waiting for him to begin.

"Well, it's no secret Justine and I are more than room mates," he said after taking a deep breath, "and you know we had plans to marry when we are more secure. However, something happened we hadn't planned for. This last December we were invited to a Christmas party and had a little too much to drink, which can happen on such occasions. While under the influence, we didn't bother taking the usual precautions. Justine found out in March she was pregnant."

"Pregnant! Oh Martin … ."

No wonder they were in a terrible state. It was obvious her parents did not know, he had explained Justine could not bear to face them yet. Since Martin was practically cut off from his family, they were probably unaware of his predicament. She felt relieved it was not the tragedies she thought about that evening. Then, she realized that Justine did not look like she was expecting.

"Did she lose the baby?"

"Worse … she had an abortion."

Katherine was struck speechless, that idea never entered her head. She could feel her heart drop into the pit of her stomach. She had no idea what to do or to say next, this was the first time she faced this issue head on. She opposed abortion and knew she could never consider such a thing, but neither had she expected to confront this issue at any time. Although she was fully aware *it* was happening, *it* was 'something' that other people did *out there*, a distant transgression she did not think would ever personally affect *her*. Suddenly, things looked very different: how on earth could she help them when the decision was already made and now hopelessly irreversible?

"I'm not accusing anyone, but did you both decide to do this?"

"We weren't ready for children, not until we were married anyway, you understand. We were worried how we could bring a child up properly in our current circumstances. However, I told her that while it would be difficult, we would find a way to manage with a baby. Okay, so things may not be as perfect as we originally planned, and we could go ahead and get married, besides, we did have the second bedroom, our place may not be a mansion, but we could make the necessary changes to our apartment. I told Justine she could give up work and stay home with the baby if she wished, and she could still continue her artwork."

"But she wasn't happy with this arrangement …"

"She still felt guilty I would have to find a full-time job to support the three of us, which meant losing most of the time I would have for my art. She knew something would have to give, and said she could not bear the thought I would be sacrificing everything I worked for. I told her stuff and nonsense, I would crawl back to my father and join the firm like he wanted if it came to that, but she wouldn't hear of it."

"What about adoption?"

"I suggested that too, and she did think about it for a few weeks, but eventually concluded she could never give the baby up if she went full term, and was convinced she was just not ready for children yet. I asked her to think about it some more and not rush into anything, I would support any decision she made. That was a horrible mistake … it was the most terrible experience waiting in the clinic … I should have demanded that she keep the baby! I can't stop blaming myself, I could have stopped her! I mean, let's face it, in a few weeks, I could have had a son, or a little girl, and now I will never know!"

Katherine had no idea what to say after this profound declaration of blame and guilt. He took another deep breath before continuing.

"I know Justine is thinking the same thing. She has become more withdrawn these last few days, I even found her reading the horoscopes for Libra. She never used to look at those things before, she always said they were for idiots who couldn't plan their own life and had to be told what to do."

Katherine mulled this over, taking a slow sip of her tea before replying.

"You both need help, Martin. I'm surprised you didn't tell Maurice first, especially as you know him longer than me. No wonder you're at your wit's end, keeping this bottled up for months. I wish I knew what I can do to help."

"Just being able to talk about it is a relief, Kathy. I couldn't tell Maurice because of my promise to Justine, but I had to let it out, and talking with you seemed easier."

She had no idea why he felt he could disclose all of this to her, perhaps he did not want to hear Maurice's clinical comfort, expecting him to declare that there was nothing to feel guilty about, it was only a cluster of cells and not a person, yet. It was plain Martin and Justine knew otherwise, they allowed themselves to be persuaded by their circumstances at the time but could no longer live with the scientific charade afterwards. It was for this reason they both felt wretched, they knew they terminated a human being, whether there was only one cell or a billion.

"At least you're able to talk about it, Martin," Katherine concluded.

"If only Justine could do the same thing, she might come through this black bout of depression," Martin stated before finishing his coffee.

"But she can't be forced, not with this sensitive issue. If she feels I'm prying, she'll just shut me out. For now, I'll pretend you haven't told me anything. To be honest, it's going to take more than a few visits, even if she does decide to talk," Katherine advised.

"I know. But now that I've told you everything, you will continue to come and see us, won't you?" he asked with hesitation, not knowing if this dark secret would sunder their friendship.

Katherine could hear the shame in his voice, and her heart went out to them. She knew what they did was wrong, but they needed healing, not punishment. She never faced such a decision, and only now was beginning to see the psychological burden that abortion caused for the parents. Who was she to add to that burden? Let us not play the righteous man who saw a boy drowning in a river and yelled at him for jumping into deep water without lifting a finger to pull him out.

"Of course I will," Katherine reassured him, "just don't expect too much for the present, she needs some time. Right now, the best thing for me to do is wait, I won't drop by for a few days, perhaps sometime next week. I'll bring my paint stuff, it's quiet work, I won't bother her outright if I'm busy with something, she'll get used to having me around again, like the old days."

"Good idea, she has Saturdays and Sundays free. I really appreciate you letting me unload our problems. You didn't need to hear this right now, not on your vacation."

"What are friends for? Before I forget, let me give you my phone number here in case you need anything or just want to talk," Katherine said as she went for the notebook in her purse. Ripping a sheet out, she quickly jotted down the number.

"Thank you, I suppose I should head back, it's getting late."

"Of course, let me get your jacket. I'll see you on Saturday."

୧❀୨

Katherine never imagined an unfortunate tragedy like this would greet her on her first few days in Paris, it was too overwhelming to take in all at once. What a change from the boisterous four-some they were! Some invisible fiend of doom that could not be banished had overshadowed their artistic clique. No wonder she felt Martin was slowly being swallowed up by the raft of the Medusa, he was drowning in a sea of hopelessness. He had reached out to her, calling for help as though she was that sail that unexpectedly appeared on the horizon. *He's clutching at straws if he thinks I have an answer! This is way beyond me!* Yet, she could not be so heartless as to drop the towline like that miserable lot who abandoned their fellows to the mercy of the pitiless sea. *All I can do is be there for them, and it feels like so little … so little.*

She avoided returning to the Louvre that week, she needed some breathing space to let the initial shock of this sad state of affairs wear off, and heading back there right now would only remind her of it. The Musée d'Orsay was the next place on her list of must-see galleries, and she spent the week studying the brushstrokes of the Impressionist works, admiring the museum's Palais Garnier display and wandering through the collections of Art Nouveau furniture. However, no matter how she tried to block her friends' terrible predicament from her mind, even for a brief period, it would continually resurface. She had promised Martin to bring her paint supplies on her next visit, and therefore thinking about setting to work was one instance that brought it all back. Sometimes the artwork she was viewing became a grim reminder. The most poignant image was Regnault's grisly painting of an execution set in the fantastic Alhambra Palace in Granada. It was odd that the scene in the painting reminded her of *grenade* ... pomegranate in French, the fruit of the underworld according to Greek myth. A Moorish king stands over the decapitated body of some unidentified enemy, he cleans his sword with the hem of his robe as he watches the blood of his foe spilling down the white marble steps towards the severed head. She found herself wondering if the baby had been terminated by induced miscarriage or by vacuuming it up, literally ripping it out. The thought made her shudder. Her knowledge of such procedures was very general, but she knew enough to understand this was something that should not be legalized. *Better not dwell on this now, or I'll never be able to pretend everything's normal when I'm with them.*

Later that week Katherine stopped at her favourite art supply store and bought a new canvas, in addition to replenishing her stock of paint tubes. She promised Gramps a picture of the Eiffel Tower, which seemed like the best subject to start with since she had left her other works at home until she returned. Although she was not in the habit of working from preliminary sketches, Martin's apartment did not have a view of the ironwork structure, so she would need a picture to work from while she was there. She bought a few postcards to send back home and decided to select her favourite postcard with the best view as her model, perhaps that was the way to go. The chosen card featured one of the famous Notre Dame gargoyles grimacing in the foreground with the tower rising in the distance. Gramps always thought the gargoyles were amusing oddballs, she could put both Parisian themes in the one picture, he definitely would enjoy that. She also picked out some exquisite floral stationary complete with embossed envelopes, rather than simply call everyone back home once a week, she planned to write them a letter or two to send with the postcards. Her mother loved writing and receiving letters, and Katherine knew she would appreciate a note or two, time permitting. Despite the rapid advance in telecommunications, there was always something exciting about finding a handwritten message in the mailbox, especially one that had come from a far away place complete with unusual postage marks and exotic international stamps.

Saturday finally came and she arrived as promised that afternoon. Martin was out selling his souvenir paintings and probably would not be back until that evening. Justine had managed to put up a pretence of wanting to paint, perhaps to keep up appearances Katherine thought, it was plain Justine was not in the mood. She was spending more time concentrating on blending the right colours than actually applying them on the canvas, when before she performed with brushstroke speed like Renoir combined with Delacoix's 'trowel and mortar' technique of layering paint. The most disturbing change was her current partiality for jet black, deep purple and midnight blue as Martin pointed out. Justine had always loved the warm spectrum, firebird reds, sunflower yellows, and lustrous ambers highlighted with vibrant greens for contrast. She silently daubed away at her shadowy abstract swirls while Katherine carried on with her project as though nothing was amiss. The afternoon slipped into evening and the light was fading, still Justine remained aberrantly quiet, with nothing much to say beyond the generic pleasantries. *Well, it would be too soon yet, anyway ... .* Martin came home with good news, he had sold a number of his paintings, they would get to see part of the wallpaper again for a time. Katherine had a feeling earlier that day Justine would not want to go out to dinner, so she had picked up some groceries on her way, four large steaks (just in case Maurice dropped by), and the usual salad and vegetable accompaniments. Stopping at the bakery to pick up the bread, she was tempted by an apple tort, a nice way to top their feast. After they had eaten and cleared up the dishes, Justine turned in early just as before, no evening conversations or debating sessions like their student days. Perhaps another time. Katherine thought it best she also call it a night, Martin could use a rest.

Now that one week had passed, she decided to gradually increase her visits in an effort to close the gap Justine created. When Katherine was visiting as a student, they insisted she keep her equipment at their place knowing how difficult it was to continually unpack and set up, especially when a work was in progress. She knew where they hid the key in the outside hallway and gave her *carte blanche* to come and go as she liked. On this trip, she planned not to bother them with her painting projects knowing they were no longer in college and were busy with work, but now her picture for Gramps would give her a serendipitous pretext to check on Justine with Martin's full approval, and she hoped there would be some improvement in her condition before she returned to the States. She spent the mornings playing tourist, and at least four or five afternoons working at their apartment. Before she realized, September had slipped into mid October, and still there was no sign of Justine coming out of her depression, no willingness to talk, no desire to venture out besides having to go to work. She was suffering terribly, and Katherine was at a loss. However, she continued to paint with her, and was surprised one day to find Justine had decided to open a tube of yellow, carefully brushing a pair of golden scales over the brooding ethereal whirlwinds she had applied. The blackness was still in the background, but at least there was some light! Is this a ray of sunshine glimmering through the darkness? Is she finally coming out from the deep into the light of day? Katherine did not pass any remark, perhaps she needs to paint it out of her system.

The days progressed and she was alarmed to find what she assumed to be a symbol of hope gradually develop into one of despair. The scales, which tipped to the right, now featured a crimson stream flowing to the bottom of the canvas. A few days later, there was a new addition, a series of bright orange flames leaping up to meet the vermilion flow. Katherine instinctively knew what it symbolised, death, judgement … damnation. If that were not enough, Martin's painting began to worry her too. During his days off, he continued to work at his montage, but had changed his original design, becoming preoccupied with only three of the myriad of famous portraits he had sketched, the bandaged van Gogh, which dominated the left side of his canvas, while St. Bartholomew stood upon the dying Delacroix, overwhelming the right. Like Justine's work, his picture was also one of self-accusation and chastisement, but visible only to the discerning eye. The van Gogh portrait was perhaps the easiest to decipher, everyone was familiar with the tale, how he cut off part of his ear after a violent fight with his friend, the painter Gauguin, whom he threatened with a razor. He obviously blamed himself for the incident, consequently he inflicted an appalling self-punishment with the same weapon for destroying their friendship. The combination of the other two figures was slightly more involved. From her art history reading, Katherine understood Bartholomew was invoked as the patron saint of those who grappled with sins of the flesh, he had been flayed alive with a knife. In the original fresco at the Sistine Chapel, the saint dangles his skin above the reprobates dragged off to hell in the lower right foreground, the association was not hard to figure out. There was one unusual detail, Michelangelo's elongated likeness artfully hidden in the contours of the saint's skin looked eerily like a self-portrait of her friend. The last figure was the most challenging aspect of Martin's tragic allegory. *Why* is the apostle standing on Delacroix? Is it the death of the Romantic Era? No, too vague and historical for something this personal. The end of idealistic notions of romance? Then, Delacroix's name struck her as the final part of the puzzle: de-la-croix … of the cross … a cross that was too heavy to bear, it was crushing him … crushing them both. Martin and Justine needed to find help soon before their desperation spiralled out of control.

ଔ ❀ ଓ

Katherine continued her visits, however, in the growing tension of their unfortunate dilemma, she began to feel a restless irritability about her own canvas, a fidgety dissatisfaction that puzzled her. She was painting someone else's photograph after all, and she had vowed she did not want to end up a copycat. It was essential to get out and see the location if she wanted to call the painting her own, the last time she had been in Paris, she never visited the towers of Notre Dame, it was always too late when she arrived, or she was too busy with other things when they were opened to the public. At last, she gave up trying and decided to call it quits. She had not made any plans to visit it again this trip, and now, the urge to make her way over to the ancient cathedral was strong, it was as though some inaudible summons was calling her. Following her strange impulse, she put a new roll of film in her camera, packed up her art case and organized her sketchbooks for some real fieldwork at last. She hoped the towers would be unlocked this time, especially after toting her art material all the way.

Arriving early on a Thursday morning, she found they would not be open until an hour later. Resigned to a long wait, she decided she might as well make a tour of the venerable building, it certainly was awe-inspiring. She first wended her way around the exterior, admiring the graceful flying buttresses that bore the brunt of the gravity of the soaring stone walls, an architectural breakthrough that allowed the builders to add more windows without causing the entire structure to collapse. She returned to the front façade and gazed upon the carvings depicting the life of Mary and the Last Judgement. Overhead, the rascally gargoyles could be seen peering down from their perches way up in the towers. Imagine, with only wooden pulleys and a few crude tools, they managed to build all this over seven hundred years ago. There were also several panels of the original stained glass in the rose windows dating from the 1300s, how they survived the ravages of the Revolutions and wars was a real miracle. Of course, the building did suffer massive scars from those periods when the angry Parisian mobs hacked many of the carvings, but in the 1800s everything had been restored to its previous magnificence. Katherine could not help but consider that in this day and age, spoiled with all the new methods of building and the array of hydraulic equipment available, was actually proving to be one of the most backward and 'disposable' of them all in many ways. I doubt our concrete and glass monstrosities will survive fifty years, she mused. Besides, who would want to restore them when they became too worn and haggard

171

looking? They certainly are not architectural beauties. Surrounded by numerous ancient buildings in this one city, not counting the rest of France, she could appreciate why many historic sites in America did not easily impress Europeans unless it they were at least three hundred years old, landmarks that were definitely rare or practically non-existent at this point in their young nation.

Entering the main portals, she tagged along with a tour group making the usual rounds and listened to the commentary about the various works of religious art, from the colourful carved choir stalls and chancel screen, to the various statues and the 'May' paintings by Le Brun that adorned the side chapels. The most interesting nook was the cathedral treasury where priceless manuscripts and rare gold reliquaries are housed. From the tour guide she learned that these treasures are actually the property of the state and from early times it was customary for the kings of France to seize upon the gifts donated to the cathedral as their own, rendering the golden statues and reliquaries for coinage when the royal pockets went threadbare. How many priceless works of medieval art had disappeared into the smelting pots from greed? Happily, the last raid on the cathedral was in the 1800s and the current items were considered a national treasure. When the tour was finished, she amused herself with her favourite investigative hunt, to find the exact spot in the nave where David intended the spectator to observe Napoléon's coronation, determining how accurate he was with perspective or if he had aggrandized the setting on his canvas for effect, a common trick she discovered the masters constantly employed. She often observed that people were depicted slightly smaller in historical locations to make the buildings seem larger or sometimes more grandiose than they actually were, a detail she only discovered when she visited a number of the places in question. Artistic beauty has its illusions and special effects to amaze she noted.

At last, the entrance to the towers opened and up the countless stone steps she filed with the rest of the tourists. Halfway up Katherine began to feel shortness of breath, although she was not overweight, she was in no shape for this medieval exercise routine and longed for an elevator. Finally reaching the top, the 'Quasimodo Workout' was rewarded with the spectacular view. It was a beautiful fall day, the sun bathing the city below in golden morning light. The Belle Époque skyline had miraculously been left unscathed by the modern development of monolithic steel and glass skyscrapers. The iron latticework of the Eiffel Tower was so graceful, it stood out like a distinguished sentinel keeping watch in the distance. Turning her attention back to the cathedral and walking around the stone balcony, she studied the floral ornamental crockets budding from the spires and the ghoulish chimeras making faces at the people below. Some of the imps were quite comical. There was a quirky Rumpelstiltskin dwarf with a Smurf-style hat, a droopy Dumbo-like figure, and a shell-shocked what-ever-it-was childishly sticking out its tongue. Others were obviously borrowed from classical mythology, a griffin and a manticore leered from one balcony, while other figures were plain demonic with their goat heads and bat wings. They certainly were a bunch of oddities, Gramps was right about that.

Now that she had observed the famous vista, she knew what was wrong with her picture, it was set during the daytime for one thing and she had promised to depict the tower in all its nocturnal glory, swathed in a glowing mist. There were also more interesting grotesques to choose from rather than stick to the statue on the postcard. Besides, there was no law stating she had to paint what was actually there. Since all the figures were basically protruding from the balconies, it would be an easy matter to switch them around while using the same background ... if the masters could resort to a little artistic illusion at times, why couldn't she? It meant she would have to start all over, but the painting would certainly be more spectacular. She could see it now, the tower gleaming in the horizon in that misty glow she saw the first night she arrived, with the moon illuminating the gargoyles with silver light from behind. Making one last round of the galleries, she inspected the gruesome denizens of the bell towers, making charcoal sketches of the various grotesques in addition to taking several photographs before she made her final decision.

Continuing her work, she was reminded why she hated sketching or painting in public. Although it was refreshing to be out in the open, it was difficult to concentrate with the crowd circling and jabbering, having grown accustomed to peace and quiet while she worked. Several curious bystanders looked over her shoulder to see what she was doing, one insufferable know-it-all who fancied she was an expert had the nerve to 'whisper' audibly to her companion she was adding too much shading to the gargoyle. I know what I'm doing, stupid twerp, she thought in vexation while trying to ignore the remarks, of *course* there's too much shading, if it's for a nocturnal scene! Moving on to the next group of monsters she began outlining a ferocious character and was struck by a particular feature she had not noticed before. The griffin-like creature was gnawing on some strange morsel it held in its claws, an oblong form that looked very familiar. Pausing for a moment, she realized it was a human, the beast was devouring some unfortunate man who had fallen into its clutches. That's odd, she thought to herself, I thought the gargoyles and grotesques were symbolic guardians to frighten evil spirits away. Observing the man-eater closely, she realized this figure represented evil, not protection. If the gargoyles were supposed to guard the church, weren't they to protect those who came to church too? This one did not conform to the supposed norm. She then realized how brainless that old myth sounded: how can evil spirits that made war on heaven be frightened by a piece of stone? Whoever came up with that concept was certainly abusing the intelligence of those who put them there. She had only recently discovered the ancient Greeks were serious philosophers and scientists in their own right, and the so-called Dark Ages had its share of great theologians, mystics and scholars. Just looking at the architectural design of the cathedral told her they certainly were not ignorant hackwork builders. Katherine began to ponder this unexpected revelation. If this grotesque depicts evil, then they *all* must represent evil. Why on earth would they stick devils all over a church, she wondered. There had to be some hidden meaning attached to them, they were not merely a decoration, that's for sure.

After a few moments, she discovered another clue to the puzzle. But of course, you dimwit, she chided herself. Hadn't she learned in their classes on medieval art history that nearly all artistic endeavours in the Church at that time were intended to inspire devotion or to instruct the illiterate about the faith? Gothic cathedrals with their statues, stained glass windows and elaborately carved porticoes were, to all intents and purposes, gigantic three-dimensional Biblical illustrations in stone. The statues and exterior portals were originally painted in bright colours, unfortunately the painted surfaces were damaged by weathering until eventually no one bothered to paint the churches, leaving them in the stony state. However, she could not figure out why the demonic grotesques and gargoyles could be intended as devotional pieces, leaving her with the conclusion they were carved for spiritual instruction. Katherine wondered how successful this type of tutoring was back then since coming to any understanding about the carvings, for someone who *was* literate, still involved a lot of speculation. Then, the thought struck her: what if their meaning was common knowledge back then? One had to know the answer first to appreciate the question. *That's it!* Many of the carvings were reminders, not really instruction pieces. The illiterate would have learned from the preachers, and unless you knew your Bible stories, you would never be able to recognise the carvings and scenes on the doors in the first place. However, this did not explain why these evil little beasties were dotted all over a place of worship. Perhaps I'm not getting the full picture, she thought, they're not simply on the church, they're *outside* the church. Although not an expert in the mystic books of the Bible, she could faintly remember several Sunday readings from the Apocalypse that foretold hardened sinners would not be allowed to enter the Heavenly Jerusalem at the end of time. Paying more attention to the stony man-eater, she realized this demon must represent the sins of the flesh, its human prey looked extraordinarily like the elongated skin of the apostle Bartholomew, the image that Martin had borrowed to express his own guilt. The theme of damnation brought up the disturbing similarities with his and Justine's artworks, if only she knew what to do for them!

"The gates of Hell are terrible to behold, are they not?"

"Excuse me?"

Katherine was startled out of her meditative rambling by the unexpected voice, and turned to see who had spoken. A priest dressed in a black jacket and long cassock stood beside her, arms folded, carefully eyeing the gruesome statue as though he were nonchalantly critiquing a picture at a gallery and proffering an opinion, but his comment addressed her most private thoughts. *How did he know what I was thinking? Must be a coincidence ….*

"The Gates of Hell," the tall, thin figure continued, "you see the sinner he is swallowing? In the Medieval and Renaissance periods, Hell was often depicted as a monster swallowing up lost souls and referred to as the 'insatiable gullet'. You will see the similarity in the Latin word *gurgulio* … ."

"Of course! That's how they became known as gargoyles," Katherine continued, surprised by this unexpected but fascinating conversation. "But these ones aren't technically gargoyles, they don't spout water."

"No, that's true, but the symbolism behind them is the same," the priest continued, "but forgive me, I haven't introduced myself. I'm Father Reinold."

"Pleased to meet you, Father. I'm Katherine … oh, I'm sorry!"

She had offered her hand, but withdrew it quickly with a sheepish smile when she saw how black it had become from her charcoal sketching.

"No need to apologize, I must say, these are excellent sketches."

"Thank you, I'm working on a painting for my grandfather. Are you visiting too?"

"Yes for a few weeks, then it's off to Rome for a few more weeks before I head back to New York."

"Oh, we're close neighbours then," Katherine replied, "I'm from New Jersey."

"Are you interested in the history of the gargoyles?"

"Well, I took a course in medieval art history for some extra credits, you can't help being curious about them."

"Indeed, they are a good source of meditation."

"I thought that might be it," she replied, "but I don't know how it works. I mean, they are difficult to decipher if you don't know what to look for."

"But the answer is very simple when you know it is in front of you. The riddle to the gargoyles is unlocked when you realize the key is the scriptures and basic Christian symbolism. You have already reached the first step by the discovery they are outside the church, the Eternal House of God …."

She nodded her head, but then realized she had not revealed her discovery to him. How did he know that? A lucky guess?

"There are some excellent examples of 'reprobate' carvings on certain pre-Gothic Romanesque churches, with people and not monsters displaying the sins leading to damnation," he calmly continued, "there are also 'reprobate' statues at the monastery of Batalha in Portugal, for another example. They are weeping, gnashing their teeth and rending their clothes in despair."

"Do the other monsters here have a significant meaning?" Katherine enquired.

"Absolutely. Would you like me to explain them to you?"

"Yes, if you don't mind."

Putting away her sketches and cleaning her grubby hands with handiwipes, she once again went around the towers, this time accompanied by her unexpected guide, amazed by the wealth of information he had to offer. The Classical figures she saw represented the pagan Greek and Roman gods, while the pachyderm was a representation of the Hindu god, Ganesha. In other words, desertion of the true faith incurred damnation. The Greek and Roman grotesques were also reminders to scholars not to become too enamoured with classical myth and thereby lose the faith, while Ganesha, the Hindu patron of scribes and merchants, was another reminder to avoid the sins of academic conceit, greed, avarice and profit acquired by unjust trading. She also learned dwarf-like figures that pulled their beards symbolised strife and violence, if they stuck their tongues out or were holding their mouths open with their hands, they represented liars, gluttons, and those who bore false witness. 'Tongue-stickers' could also represent avarice and lust simultaneously as those who hungered for wealth usually acquired it, often dishonestly, and could afford to indulge their weaknesses of the flesh. Monkey gargoyles could also have the same meaning.

Fr. Reinold then smiled when he returned to the dwarf figure, commenting that some of the grotesques were used for political criticism and the sculptor must have been a supporter of the monarchy when he carved this statue. He explained the little dwarf was wearing a Phrygian cap, a symbol of democracy that was used by the revolutionaries. This did not make sense, for the cathedral was built long before the revolutions, until she was disappointed to learn the gargoyles perched on the balconies were not originals but additions dating from the mid 1800s. He understood her disappointment, remarking that it would have been better if during the restoration they had built the sections that were never finished, namely the two spires that were to top the main bell towers in front, rather than concentrate on adding statues that were not part of the original plans. However, he consoled her with the knowledge that the medieval symbolism remained the same for these recent additions. The allegorical statues were mostly beasts, which displayed man's continual shortcomings in desiring to follow his fallen animalistic nature rather than rise in spirituality. He then pointed out one unusual example from the original medieval carvings she had not observed closely, many of the floral crocket buds sprouting from the towers below the balconies resembled whole branches growing out of a snarling animal.   If the spectator looked at the crocket base first and followed the pattern upwards, the beast turned into a graceful plant, but if observed downwards, the artwork told a different story, spiritual beauty transformed into hellish grotesquery.

"Goodness! All that symbolism from these few statues," Katherine exclaimed. "Do the ones that spout water have a meaning too?"

"Yes. Notice how the demonic spouts are performing a useful task in directing water off the roof. While the real demons chose evil, God has the power to turn their malice into good, thereby making them vessels of His grace, which is symbolised by the water they spout."

"How simple, I wonder why they are up near the roof though," she mused aloud. "I thought demons were supposed to be under the earth."

"The idea of Hell is actually confused by people. While Hell is symbolically under the earth, it is everywhere at the same time, for the demons carry their torments with them. When they were cast out of heaven, they were made exiles on the earth, and they continue to inhabit all the elements, especially the upper atmosphere. That's why St. Paul describes them as the 'powers and principalities in the high places'. Nevertheless, they will all be imprisoned in a specific place of torment at the end of time when the new heaven and the new earth will appear."

"That is a little heavy for me, but it makes sense," Katherine replied. "Thank you for taking the time to explain everything, I think I've learned more today than in my whole art history classes combined. I wish I had known all of this when writing my essays."

"Are you still attending art school?"

"No, I graduated earlier this summer. I'm here on a long break and won't go back home until this coming January."

"Are you visiting Paris alone?" he asked.

"Well, I'm staying at a friend's apartment, it belongs to his parents. They'll be over in December, but I'm not really on my own, I do have other friends here in Paris. They've just graduated too."

However, just mentioning them made her heart sink. Her understanding of their artwork, now combined with the explanations about the symbolic carvings, made her feeling of helplessness in their regard all the more poignant.

"But this visit is not going as planned," he observed.

How did he come to that conclusion? Am I that transparent? She could not understand why, but she felt it was all right to confide in him. How come I feel comfortable with this perfect stranger?

"To be honest, two of my friends are going through a difficult time, and I don't know how to help them. They've made a terrible decision, and are trying to find some way to live with the consequences. We met at art school several years ago when I came here as an exchange student. Lately, their artwork is beginning to worry me, it's all about judgement and damnation, like all the gargoyles here. I'm particularly worried about my friend, Justine. She has become deeply depressed and is shutting everyone out. I think it's time that they seek help somewhere, but …"

"This is something that involves the conscience, which is beyond the help of a secular counsellor, and you do not know how to suggest it to either of them."

"Exactly, not without looking like I'm prying, and Justine doesn't know I'm aware of the details. She refuses to talk to anyone and just wants to hide away."

"When a tremendous sense of guilt oppresses the soul, that is a natural reaction, but very dangerous. She cannot forgive herself for the unfortunate choice she made, and believes no one else will either, including God."

"I don't know why she would believe that, I mean, I know they both are Catholics. Can't they just go to confession where they are literally told they are forgiven?"

"When you feel you are not deserving of mercy, it is difficult to comprehend how willingly God is ready to forgive, making it equally difficult to ask for mercy. Of course, confessing the darkest secrets of your innermost soul to a complete stranger is always a humbling experience if not downright humiliating. However, it draws great graces upon the soul. Your friend, Justine, in particular, needs a little encouragement to show her the path to take. Do you have any paper with violets on them by any chance?"

Katherine was puzzled by his unusual question that did not seem to have anything to do with the problem at hand.

"Violets?"

"Yes, and a pen if you have one, a little message might help her."

"Oh, I see. Come to think of it, I have a package of note cards here in my case, and I know there's a pen or two rattling around in the bottom somewhere, here we go."

She opened the assorted cards and searched through them for the desired flower. Perhaps there was some Catholic symbolism behind that too?

"I have one."

She handed him the card with the pen, and offered her sketchbook as a support.

"Thank you, this will do nicely."

He leaned on the balcony and swiftly wrote the message while Katherine tidied her case from her rummaging. Sealing the envelope, he handed it to her.

"This should help. I also have something else," he continued, reaching into his pocket and carefully taking out a string of pearly beads with a golden crucifix and a little silver medallion attached to the end. It was a rosary. "Tell her to be more careful with it in the future. This important lifeline will pull her away from the gates of Hell," he declared as he placed it in her hand. "It was providential that we met today, Katherine, a day of healing."

"Really?" she replied, now thoroughly puzzled by the whole proceedings.

"Yes, it is the feast day of St. Luke, the physician and evangelist who wrote the Gospel that provides the most details about the Virgin Mary. You did not decide to come to her cathedral today, you were called."

"I don't know what to say, I'm … I'm not a Catholic," she replied, a little bewildered by this statement.

"That does not matter, as long as one answers the call and follows wherever it may lead. Now, I'm afraid I can't stay any longer, I have another appointment to see to."

"I understand, Father, and thank you for everything."

"You're welcome, God Bless," he replied before heading towards the stairs, pausing to add one last comment;

"And remember, there is no such thing as a coincidence and there are no accidents in God's creation."

Watching him as he left, Katherine did not know what to think about this unusual encounter. She carefully placed the note and the rosary in her case, wondering what he meant by 'be more careful with it in the future'? Perhaps he assumed Justine no longer practised that particular devotion. No, it had to be more than just an assumption, he seemed to be aware of many things, which she could not figure out. How did he seem to know so much? It was too bizarre to contemplate. Then she wondered how something so simple as a note could help Justine. Is that all it would take to bring her out of this vortex of despair? She would have to wait until Justine came home that evening to find out.

Finished with her study of the carvings, Katherine stopped for lunch and bought a new canvas before heading to their apartment. Might as well spend the afternoon on Gramp's picture she thought, and the sooner the better. It was difficult to concentrate while waiting for Justine to arrive, but at last, she heard someone coming up the old stairway followed by the metallic click of a key in the lock. Katherine put her brush down and went to meet her.

"Hi, Justine. How was your day?"

"Hello, Kathy. It was all right. Not as busy in the gift shop now that summer is over. Don't let me disturb you," Justine replied as she hung up her jacket and put her handbag away.

"Not at all, I need a break. Will I make us some coffee?"

"That would be nice, it would perk me up, I'm rather tired ... oh, you've changed your picture."

"Yes," Katherine replied from the kitchen as she prepared the pot. "I wasn't satisfied with the first layout, so I went to Notre Dame today to see the gargoyles for myself and the visit gave me an idea on how to improve it."

"That's good," Justine replied.

"But you won't believe what happened while I was there," Katherine continued, "I met a priest from New York who knew everything about the gargoyles and he told me what they represented. I liked what he said about the water-spouts in particular."

"Oh? What did he say?"

"It's a bit involved, but basically they are reminders that God knows how to turn evil into good."

"Really?" Justine raised an eyebrow, sceptical with this statement.

"The odd thing is, he gave me a note and a rosary for you, they're in my case, I'll go get them."

Katherine retrieved the items and handed them to her. Justine's eyes widened with undisguised surprise as she stared at the objects in her hands, the rosary in particular.

"Kathy! Where did you get this?"

"Like I said, a priest gave them to me. When he gave me the rosary, he told me you were to be more careful with it in the future. Is there something wrong?"

Justine went slightly paler than she was already and stared at the rosary a few more moments before stammering;

"But how did he get this? That's impossible!"

"What do you mean?"

"I know these beads! They belonged to my grandmother, she gave them to me when I was a little girl just before she died. You see the little medal hanging with the crucifix? She got that on a pilgrimage to Lourdes, I'd recognise these beads anywhere!"

"But how would he have … ?"

"That's it! I lost them years ago! How did he find them?"

"I don't know, he didn't tell me."

Justine feverishly opened the note and read the contents:

"*It is time to talk, no use crying over spilt milk* … my grandmother used that expression all the time! I could always talk to her when something went wrong … look here, there's an address included."

"Maybe you are supposed to go there," Katherine suggested. "Hey, it's not far from my place. If you don't mind me asking, do the violets mean anything to you?"

"My grandmother's name was Violette. Kathy, you must tell me everything!"

It was so wonderful to see this sudden change in Justine that Katherine did not mind the constant retelling of her unusual morning repeatedly while carefully keeping her knowledge of Justine's personal details secret, admitting she only expressed her concern about her latest battle with depression. She was also requested to provide a thorough description of the extraordinary messenger. Besides his simple black jacket and cassock, he was tall, dark, and was somewhere in his late thirties or early forties, she could not be sure. The one characteristic that was unusual, his penetrating sea blue eyes seemed to see right through you, down to your very depths, and yet, it was a strange comforting feeling, that you could be yourself because he knew you somehow, even though you had never met him before in your life. Katherine racked her brain, could she have seen him around town back home at one time, considering he was from New York? No, she could not recall his face. Justine, or any of her family members as far as she knew, were not acquainted with any priest from America, which only deepened the mystery.

"Is there anything else? Did he say more?"

"Umm … oh yes. That the rosary was a line that would help pull you away from the gates of Hell."

Justine pursed her lips slightly as she thought upon this reply, gently fingering the beads before she spoke.

"Grandmamma said I should never neglect to say the rosary everyday, it would give me strength in times of trouble, and it's been ages since I've prayed, let alone go to church … if I had done what she asked, I would not be where I am now!"

With that, she burst into tears. Katherine retrieved the box of tissues from the bathroom.

"Do you want to talk about it?" she asked as she sat back down.

"I've done something terrible!" Justine began, revealing her private suffering, which Martin had already disclosed, concluding with the sobering realization, "I stopped a baby from coming into the world who was already here and had a right to live like everyone else! That baby can never come back. I don't know how people can say there will always be other children, no baby is the same, they can't be replaced! Why do they always say, 'mother-to-be' or 'expectant mother'?" Justine continued amidst her sobs, "you're a mother from the first moment before the baby is ever born … what a mother I turned out to be!"

"Justine, don't. You're only tormenting yourself. From what I've seen today, God and your grandmother wouldn't want you to do that," Katherine replied.

"Then what do I do? Where do I go from here?"

"Well, you could go to the address in the note for a start, and take one step at a time after that."

"Kathy, you must think me a real monster after hearing all this … ." Justine continued, afraid how her friend would view her from this point onward.

"Now, I don't see any fangs or horns sprouting out of your head,"

Katherine replied, putting a brave face on a bad situation. Fr. Reinold mentioned how humiliating it was for most people to confess, and she could understand it now, worrying about how people regard you was indeed a torment. She was still her friend, after all, and must try to help her through this if she could.

"To be honest, I don't agree with the choice you made, but I don't see why this should come between us. In fact, I am very glad you told me, you are not yourself lately, and you needed to talk to someone and find someway to get through it before … well, let's just say your painting was very ominous."

"I just couldn't talk, it felt better to paint it, but after a while, that didn't help much, it just brought it all back again."

"Martin's work is also worrying me," Katherine added, "from the figures he's painting, I can tell he is blaming himself for the whole thing."

"But it was my decision, why should he blame himself? It's my fault, and I'm surprised he would ever want to speak to me again let alone look at me. I don't think he will ever forgive me for what I've done to his child!"

"Martin's not like that, it's obvious he's worried sick about you."

"I don't know, it's been so difficult facing him everyday, I don't know how we can stay together after this. I … oh, I hear him coming up the stairs."

Justine quickly wiped her eyes and blew her nose.

"Look, don't think drastic thoughts right now," Katherine replied in double tempo, picking up the speed of the conversation. "Like I said, take one step at a time. I'd go to the place listed in the note first, see what that's all about."

"Oh yes, will you come with me? I don't want to go alone."

"Of course. The note doesn't list any specific time though."

"Well, I'm free Saturdays and Sundays …."

"Okay, why don't you stop by my place Saturday morning? We'll walk over there together."

"All right, but can you keep this to yourself, until we see what happens?"

"Okay. Shhh, here he comes now."

"I'd better go and tidy up before he sees me in this state," Justine replied as she jumped up and headed to the bedroom, wiping the smeared mascara from her eyes.

Gee, how did I end up being the secret keeper, Katherine thought. This is getting difficult!

Martin came through the doorway dragging his art equipment and several canvases, not many tourists today, so naturally, there were less pictures sold. Katherine helped to hang them back up on the walls. How she wished she could tell him there and then about the unusual happenings of the day, and that Justine had finally talked to her! She kept the conversation as general as possible, telling him about her introduction to Fr. Reinold and his vast knowledge on the subject of gargoyles. When Justine eventually came back, she still clutched the beads in her hand and continued to finger them. Although she remained quiet through supper that evening and went to bed early as before, Martin sensed a change had taken place somehow. As usual when Katherine stayed after dark, Martin escorted her back home eager to discuss this slight sign of improvement.

"There's something different about Justine tonight," he declared as he rubbed his chin, "I can't put my finger on it. She didn't seem to be as anxious, and I think I saw her smiling to herself occasionally when she thought I wasn't looking. I got the idea she wanted to share something, but couldn't bring herself to do it. Kathy, did anything happen today that I should know about?"

She could not hide everything from him, and admitted that Justine had finally opened up to her.

"Thank heavens," Martin exclaimed.

You have no idea, Katherine thought to herself, recalling her strange morning.

"If you don't want to go into details, I understand, but can you tell me *anything* at all?" Martin pleaded.

"She told me the situation pretty much as you explained it to me, and I think you should know she doesn't hold you responsible at all, she said in the end it was her decision, and she's finding it difficult to forgive herself. I've just learned if she feels that way, she also believes everyone else will be unforgiving too, especially you. She admitted it was difficult to face you," Katherine disclosed.

"Is that why she can't look me in the face anymore? It's like she expects me to slap her, or something," Martin replied. "How I wish things could go back to the way they were! She skirts around me like a whipped dog that expects nothing better."

"She is desperate to find forgiveness. You said it was okay for her to have the baby, and now she realizes that she not only aborted her baby, but yours too. What a tremendous guilt to carry! Since she believes everyone around her is unforgiving, perhaps it would help if you reassure her about your feelings."

"Of course I wish she hadn't jumped so fast into making this decision by herself, but I have never said anything to make her feel guilty."

"She needs to hear it, Martin. She needs to know you forgive her, and you need to forgive yourself, too."

"Justine I can forgive, I just wish I knew how to forgive myself. I thought I was doing the right thing in supporting her decision, but what you *think* is right isn't the same as *knowing* what is right. It's too late now, this is something we shall have to live with for the rest of our lives."

"Well, I told Justine to take one step at a time," Katherine replied, "and you should too."

"I wish I knew how to do that," he sighed. "At least Justine has taken the first step. Do you think it would be a good idea if I talk with her tomorrow?"

"No, it's too soon yet, give her a few more days," she answered while concluding to herself, *let's wait and see what happens on Saturday.*

CB ❀ BO

Saturday morning turned out to be cold, grey and miserably wet as intermittent showers drenched the city. Katherine waited for the doorbell, not sure if Justine would come to this mystery meeting, particularly since she was so withdrawn, but she arrived as promised, not a little bedraggled from the weather. They had a quick cup of coffee, hoping the rain would stop before they walked over to the address provided in the note. Finally, there was a break in the clouds, allowing them to venture out before another downpour. Katherine did not know what to expect, she hoped she was not walking Justine, or herself for that matter, into an unsavoury situation.

Arriving at the building, it turned out to be another block of elite apartments like many in the area. She searched the portico of the main entrance for a brass plaque or some indication of a psychiatrist's clinic. Perhaps the priest was recommending something of this nature. On second thought, this did not make much sense since he agreed with her Justine could not be helped by a therapist. Well, let's approach the concierge and see what happens, Katherine decided. They introduced themselves, and he informed them the apartment was on the first floor, pointing to the elevator, they decided to take the stairs. They rang the doorbell and to their surprise, it was answered by none other than Fr. Reinold.

"Good morning, ladies," he replied, "I'm glad to see you."

"Hello, Father. What a surprise to meet you again. This is my friend Justine. I hope you don't mind, she asked me to come with her,"

185

Katherine replied as she shook hands.

"You're welcome, Katherine. Hello Justine, I'm very glad you came."

"Hello," Justine smiled shyly as she shook his hand, quietly studying the enigmatic figure dressed in black.

"Come on in, your timing is providential."

"Oh, why is that?" Katherine asked.

"My brother likes to collect art, he buys and sells every now and again, and a new delivery has just been dropped off, which I think you might enjoy."

Leading them in to the sitting room, he uncovered a painting set upon an exhibition easel.

"No *way*," Katherine uttered in surprise.

"Oh my," Justine exclaimed. "Is that what I think it is?"

"Beautiful, isn't? God certainly gave Vermeer an extraordinary talent."

"Goodness, it is beautiful," Justine replied as she stepped closer to examine the treasure for a moment. Like many of Vermeer's paintings, it featured a young girl, here, his subject is reading a letter by a window.

Katherine glanced around at the other works of art adorning the room, there were several Classical antiquities, various oil paintings and framed sketches, some modern, some older, but definitely all originals.

"Is that a Monet?" indicating towards a canvas on the wall closest to them.

"Yes, and the sketch in the frame next to it is a Rembrandt."

"That picture over there looks like Seurat's style," Justine exclaimed.

"I think that one was painted by one of his associates," Fr. Reinold continued, "Signac, I think, but I'm not one-hundred percent sure. You would have to ask my brother about that."

"It's like a museum," Katherine replied, "I'd be afraid to touch anything. This urn here does not look like a reproduction."

"No, you are correct. It was unearthed in Macedonia and has been dated around 150 BC."

Katherine clutched her purse, that was all she needed right now, to have the shoulder strap slip and send a rare archaeological artefact crashing to the floor.

"I'd be afraid to walk through here," she noted, "we have antiques at home, but nothing from ancient Greece. I can just imagine your brother's insurance bill."

Fr. Reinold smiled.

"Come, would you like something to drink? Coffee, tea? Perhaps a soda?"

They decided on coffee and chatted pleasantly about the various paintings in the room. They suspected his brother must be wealthy if he could dabble in the fine arts as a hobby, until Father explained to them their family were owners of a large international shipping enterprise. Katherine did not want to be rude, but was curious to find out why he decided on the priesthood, and he explained to her as best he could the nature of a vocation, that it was a spiritual call from God that is not easy to ignore.

"Oh, is it like the 'call' you talked about the other day at the cathedral?" Katherine asked.

"Yes, something similar. Of course, God will never take your free will away, you can choose to follow the summons or not."

"However, like you said, it is difficult to ignore. But how do you know for sure it is really a vocation?"

"Well, you aren't made a priest or religious right away, you have several years of prayer and reflection as a seminarian or a novice and postulant to help you discern if this is the path God has laid out for you. If a vocation is there, you and also your superiors will know."

"Even if you know you have one, it still must have been a difficult thing to do," Katherine remarked. "I mean, in my church, our pastors can marry and have what everyone calls a normal life."

"Yes, there are sacrifices, but when someone becomes a priest or religious, they give up one good for a greater good. I may not have an earthly family, but I do have a bride and many spiritual children. In any case, every path in life has its crosses," Father replied.

Katherine pondered upon this answer while Justine took the rosary out of her pocket.

"Father, I want to thank you for finding this. Where did you discover it?"

"Your grandmother gave it to me," he replied.

"Goodness, how can that be? I lost it sometime after she died."

"I know, she told me," he continued.

The story that followed amazed Katherine, she had never heard a tale like this before. Father related one night not too long ago, he was busy in the den writing letters when a lady entered the room, without opening the door, and sat down before him at the desk. He described her as having silver grey hair and sparkling blue eyes. She was dressed in a floral patterned blue dress, a little hat with a blue rose and held a beaded handbag. The lady also wore a pair of gold spectacles hanging on the end of her nose. Justine gasped, he had described her grandmother's favourite dress and handbag to perfection. After asking the lady how he could help her, she requested one Mass to be said for the repose of her soul, which would grant her release. After he had written her name in his Mass book, she opened her handbag and laid the rosary on the desk, explaining what happened to it, and to see that it was returned to her granddaughter and to convey a short message … .

"Not to cry over spilt milk," Justine added.

"Exactly," Fr. Reinold replied. "She told me I would meet your friend and give it to her, who would see that it was returned safely, and that I would know the person when I saw her."

"Meaning me," Katherine replied astounded.

"Yes. I was inspired to visit Notre Dame that day instead of going to Rue du Bac as I normally would do, and you know the rest."

"I don't understand this at all," Katherine interjected.

"I do! Grandmamma was allowed to come for help. She always had a particular devotion to the Holy Souls."

"It was due to her exceptional charity towards them she was allowed to ask for help and send you a message," Father affirmed.

"I heard stories like this, but it all seemed too fantastic. I must admit the rosary beads is certainly proof that you haven't invented a fable. But why didn't Grandmamma send you to me directly?" Justine wondered.

"Would you have been receptive to a strange priest arriving unexpectedly on your doorstep?"

"No, I suppose not."

"You see? Your grandmother sent someone you are comfortable with."

"I don't mean to interrupt, but I'm still confused," Katherine interjected. This is just plain creepy she thought, they're talking as though priests see the dead in their offices every day of the week! "I mean, how can Justine's deceased grandmother appear? I don't know too much about 'Holy Souls'."

"They are the poor suffering inmates of Purgatory," he explained.

Katherine had heard of that place before, that strange twilight zone between Heaven and Hell where people not good enough for Heaven, yet not worthy of Hell, were sent to be purified.

"I know a little about that place, but didn't know they could come and ask for help."

"Usually, they are not, but on rare occasions they are allowed to. Special cases are granted permission by God."

"Is it really a place of torment like they say? It sounds too much like Hell, I can't see how God would want us to suffer like that if we aren't deserving of Hell."

"At least you believe in a Hell," Father replied. "You are correct in saying God does not desire our suffering, but sometimes it's the only way to purify a sin-besmirched soul. Gold is purified by fire. We believe not all torments in Purgatory are the same, they differ depending on the sin."

"I thought God forgives everyone if they are sorry," Katherine mused aloud.

"Oh yes, of course, but there is a price attached to evil that must be paid. Let's say you broke some object belonging to someone and they forgive you, but you still have to pay for the damage. You can pay right away, or wait until later."

"I assume the 'later' is Purgatory," Katherine finished.

"Yes. It is much better to work off your Purgatory here on earth through prayer, sacrifice and making restitution."

At this turn in the conversation, Justine became slightly downcast. Katherine understood: how could anyone make amends to God when their guilt seemed as immovable as Mount Everest? Father also seemed to notice her pensive musing.

"Do not worry, nothing is impossible to God. I think we should consider your grandmother's message now."

"Not to cry over spilt milk?" Justine asked.

"Yes, but also the first part — it's time to talk." Justine, knowing what was coming, looked as though she had received a death sentence. "Come now, the thought is worse than actually doing it, you'll feel much better afterward," he continued brightly as he rose from the couch and opened a door, which obviously looked like an office. "You don't mind waiting a little bit, Katherine?" he enquired.

"No, not at all," she replied as Justine timidly got to her feet, unable to say 'no' to the looming confession at hand, and entered the office with Fr. Reinold, closing the door behind her with a soft *click*.

While her friend was making her peace with heaven, Katherine admired the treasures positioned around the sitting room once more as she grappled with the incredible story she had just heard. There was a satirical etching by Goya, a small Roman statue, a Renoir pastoral beside a grotesque Salvador Dali and an exotic Egyptian Canopic jar. She could not believe that anyone would leave such items sitting around as though they were of no consequence. She thought these priceless items should be placed under glass at least. Returning to the Grecian urn to study the graceful dancing maidens painted in black over the orange pottery, she heard the main door open down the hall and the sound of footsteps approaching.

"Oh, hello, I didn't know my brother was expecting visitors, at least not today. Vous parlais anglais?"

Looking up, she knew she had seen this man before, but could not quite place him. Well dressed and brandishing a leather briefcase, he was tall and dark like his sibling she noticed, but with soft brown eyes, and was a few years younger as far as she could tell. Obviously, he did not mind her unexpected presence, or her close proximity to his valuable collection for that matter.

"Yes, he invited us to come, he's speaking with my friend in there," Katherine replied as she indicated towards the office door.

"Ah, you're American! That's good, I'm tired of speaking French, I'm not very good at it, and it gives me a headache. You know, that's just like him," the gentleman sighed as he laid his briefcase on a nearby chair, "always working, even on his vacation. We were supposed to go for lunch together, but now I guess I'll just have to wait for him to get finished. Better put on a fresh pot, we might be here for awhile. But please forgive me, I'm Gerard, but you can call me Gerry," he said as he reached out his hand.

"I'm Katherine, but everyone usually calls me Kathy. So this is your collection?" she asked as they shook hands.

"Yes, my expensive folly I'm afraid, but at least I make it pay for itself. Ah! The Vermeer has arrived safely, I have a prospective buyer for it in the States."

"You mean you're not going to keep it?"

"No, I wish I could, I only helped to secure the sale for a friend this time. Do you like art?"

The question was answered in the affirmative, leading to an interesting conversation as she explained she was a newly fledged artist recently graduated from Belvedere. He took her into the dining room and showed her other fascinating miniature canvases from the Dutch school, and a collection of rare coins and medallions on display in a locked case. Katherine asked why he was not afraid to leave all his valuables sitting out, and he explained they were to be enjoyed, not tiptoed around. At least he did have insurance. The coins had to be locked away of course, they would be a temptation for the housekeeping staff who came to take care of the apartment every few days, but everything else would be too easy to trace. Besides, there were ways to secure certain items, the Grecian urn was filled with bags of fine sand, making it too heavy to knock over accidentally. She was surprised by this simple solution, she never would have thought of that herself. Her attention was then drawn to the Canopic jar, stating surely he did not fill *that* with sand? No, that one had its original contents, or what was left of them, and opening it would perhaps not be a good idea he replied with a wry smile. Returning to the sitting room, he asked about her plans now that she had graduated and was interested on hearing her ideas about opening a gallery.

"You'll be taking a risk by supporting new and unknown artists," he commented as he took the coffee tray into the kitchen. "That's why I chose to stay in the auctioneering end of things. If you must do business in art, at least the old masters already have a set market."

"I know, but a restaurant and shop might defray the costs of a gallery," she replied as she followed him. "Can I help with the coffee?"

"No, that's okay, just make yourself comfortable while I try to remember how this thing works," placing the tray down on the counter and fiddling with the knobs of the commercial-sized coffee machine. "These contraptions are getting more complicated every year."

"Be careful with that one, it's the steam jet," she warned as she sat down by the breakfast counter.

"Whoa! Thank you. So tell me," he continued while grinding some fresh grounds and steaming a jug of hot latte. "Have you thought about a location yet?"

"No, I'm still trying to piece my own collection together."

"Hmm, it's going to be difficult to juggle both aspects. The idealism of art and the daily grind of business do not mix, if you're an artist, that is. One will continually pull you away from the other."

"My friends warned me that might happen."

"My advice would be to make sure you always set time aside to do your artwork, then run your gallery, but don't let the gallery run you." As he poured them a fresh cup, he asked, "why do I get the feeling we've met before?"

"I don't know, I was thinking the same thing."

After several moments, he snapped his fingers with a smile.

"Of course! The flight! We should recognise each other after sitting several hours together."

"Oh! How silly of me not to remember, it really is a small world," Katherine replied.

"Do you mind me asking where you are staying in Paris?"

"No, I'm practically around the corner. I'm staying at a friend's place, it belongs to his parents. They will be here in December and then I will be going back with them in January.”

“Around the corner, perhaps I know them.”

“The Kraylors, they’re from New York too.”

“You’re kidding! Not the same Kraylors of the distinguished Kraylor and Kraylor law firm by any chance?”

“Yes, you know them then.”

“I’ve had the pleasure, they helped get us through a rather tedious tangle of corporate bureaucracy with the city and dockyard authorities not too long ago.”

“Wait a minute, your firm isn’t Reinold Enterprise International?”

“My father’s, but yes, it is. How did you know?”

“Charlie mentioned the case, oh no particulars of course.”

“Their son, if I remember. He’s your friend?”

“Yes, before he graduated from law school, he was sent out with all the research teams for experience. He said he spent much time at city hall and the law library over that particular case.”

“Well, it was a rather complicated business. Have you known him long?”

“We’ve practically grown up together, same schools and everything, except for Belvedere of course.”

“So, how did you meet Pete? Or perhaps it was your friend in the office who met him?”

“Pete? Oh, you mean your brother. We met at Notre Dame the other day. He knows a lot about the carvings there, he could teach our art historians a thing or two. Speaking of which, I’m sorry to hold you up … .”

“Not at all. Forgive me, but I didn’t catch your last name.”

“Oh! Everyone seems to be going on a first-name basis lately. It’s Walsingham.”

“Not the same Walsingham … ?”

“Yes, of Walsingham Industries, makers and providers of fine cosmetics and pharmaceutical products since 1906,” she replied with a smile, rattling off Gramp’s old company blurb that was deeply engrained in her family since childhood.

“I’ll be darned! I should have connected the dots sooner,” he said as he set his cup down. “A Belvedere art graduate named ‘Katherine’ staying with the Kraylors … my sister, Charlotte, knows all the gossip in the city, but I usually don’t pay too much attention to the socialite chatter, unless I can tell which way the art trends may veer. Tell me, what’s the truth behind the Art Hacker’s article? I’d be interested to know.”

“Oh, *that.* It’s following me like a bad penny wherever I go,” she groaned in mock dismay followed by a laugh. After she explained the allegory of her painting, she realized the article had nothing to do with the Kraylors, and asked exactly what gossip his sister had heard.

"Nothing excerpt you make a charming couple, I mean, sweethearts since childhood, all the ladies are simply infatuated with the idea. Lotte thinks it's absolutely romantic."

"Now, let me set you straight," Katherine replied, surprised by this revelation, "We're just good friends. He's like an older brother and member of the family, that's all. I can't imagine how things can get blown out of all proportion."

"Seriously? You're just friends?"

"Of course," she affirmed, finishing her coffee and wincing at the thought of Charlie as her romantic beau. Were they really the gossip of the city? Like her host, she too never bothered much with the whisperings that seemed to intrigue everyone else. The life of an artist was a solitary job to a certain extent, and in any case, she was completely happy in her own comfortable niche surrounded by her family and a select number of trusted friends. How long had that gossip been going around, she wondered. She did not appreciate that she or Charlie were the latest sources of New York's idle amusement, perhaps this is what it's like to be targeted by the tabloids.

"I'm sorry if I spoke out of turn."

"Oh no, it's just ... odd to hear this chatter. At least it's not anything like Robert Horace's critique."

They were interrupted by the sound of the office door opening in the sitting room.

"Ah, he comes forth at last. About time too, I'm famished."

Leaving the kitchen, Gerard jovially declared, "hey Pete, have you declared a universal fast or what? It's not Lent yet."

"Very amusing, Gerry. If you are implying I forgot our lunch, I haven't." he returned with a smile. "I see you've met Katherine, let me introduce you to her friend, Justine. Meet my brother, Gerard."

Justine shyly said 'hello' and shook hands. Katherine tried to read her expression, she could not tell if she was relieved as Father promised, perhaps it was too soon to tell. In fact, she still looked surprised, as though he had handed her another item belonging to her deceased relative's cherished possessions. She probably needed some space for reflection, and it was a good time to say their goodbyes.

"Well, I suppose we should be off, we've taken up enough of your time today," Katherine replied. "Thank you for the coffee and showing us your art collection."

"You're welcome," Gerard replied.

Although they were hungry by now after their unusual morning, Justine declined Katherine's offer to take them out, saying she would be happier to go directly home, and asked if she wouldn't mind having lunch with her there. Katherine could not help but wonder about her meeting with Father, hoping he had set her on some path to recovery, but remained hesitant to ask anything, knowing one should not delve into the private matter of a confession session.

"Did … everything go okay?" she finally enquired as they sat down to a simple lunch of sandwiches and fries. Justine paused to think for a moment.

"It was different from the usual confession," she admitted. "That priest is … *different*."

"I'll say," Katherine replied, "I hope he's not a confidence trickster, like those fortune tellers who find out all your private details to earn your trust. How else could he have described your grandmother perfectly?"

"No, it wasn't like that. The rosary beads are definite proof, I lost them on a school trip to Germany, in fact, he knew I lost them on the train. I didn't find out until we arrived at the hostel, and I never said anything, there was no point causing a fuss. Unless his story is true, I don't know how he could find out about it, and it is highly unlikely that a perfect stranger knew where to return them."

"It's odd how he seemed to know certain things, almost like he could read thoughts."

"No, not thoughts, *souls*! He knew everything before I began, I'm sure of it."

"How do you know?"

"Well, after I told him everything, he said perhaps it was time for a clean slate and a new beginning, in other words, a general confession. I certainly wasn't prepared for that! This was a first for me, but he promised to help me through, and he did. I mean, if I forgot something, he gently reminded me, and prompted me into remembering many things from the past."

"Is confession always like that?"

"Not really, but I heard Grandmamma talk about certain priests who had a special gift of discernment, and maybe this priest is one of them. I can't say we Catholics understand everything, much of our religion is based on faith."

"Do you feel better now?"

"I suppose I do, a little bit. I don't know what to feel yet. Come to think of it, he was right. The thought of confessing is worse than going ahead with it. In a way, it was almost too … *easy!* I keep thinking I should be struck with a lightening bolt for what I did."

"I don't think God just waits around the corner to thump us on the head all the time, we do enough of that ourselves," Katherine replied.

"The thing is, Father wants to talk to Martin too, but I don't know how to suggest this to him."

Katherine understood her reticence, receiving forgiveness from God was one thing, but to hope for it from everyone else was another matter. Justine was convinced Martin still blamed her, so how could she approach him?

"Justine, why don't you just ask him how he feels and finally get it out into the open? The silence between you is doing more damage than if you talked about it.   Think of it like your confession today, the thought of it sounds worse than actually doing it."

Justine sighed and nodded her head.

"That may be a good idea, I'll try," she replied.

Finishing their lunch, they chatted about the other unexpected surprise of visiting a miniature Louvre before Katherine decided to leave. Her painting for Gramps could wait a day or two, and Justine needed some space after the day's events, especially if she was going to try and pluck up the courage to talk with Martin that night or perhaps the next.

ርଷ ❀ ଇ૭

After these last few weeks of tension, Katherine needed a distraction and decided to do a little gift shopping for everyone back home. She would have to begin early if she wanted everything wrapped and shipped in time for Christmas, not to mention she had a few letters to catch up on. It was fun searching through her guidebook, looking for the perfect places to shop, taking the Metro and popping up all over the city on her treasure hunt. Gift buying was becoming more challenging each year. How do you shop for people who literally had everything? This year, she also had to restrict her buying to non-breakable items.

On the fourth afternoon of her shopping spree, she arrived home to the sound of the phone ringing. Fumbling for the key, she ran through the door and dropped her packages on the sofa. It was Martin wanting to relay good news. Justine seemed more like her old self the last few days, she did not seem depressed, and even went to church last Sunday. She had never bothered to do *that* before. To top it all off, she finally broke down and

195

talked with him at length last night. He admitted Katherine had been correct, when he reassured Justine he was not angry or laid the blame on her, she seemed more like the old Justine. Of course, things may never be as they once were, they had suffered a lot. He was happy she was venturing out of the apartment and communicating with him again.

"She had a lot to tell me," he continued, "and I don't know what to make of it."

Katherine enquired if it had anything to do with Fr. Reinold. Martin said yes, and Justine asked if he would go and meet with Fr. Reinold before he left for Rome. He had misgivings, but Katherine reassured him the story was true, and he would not regret meeting him. Martin concluded that if a rendezvous with the man in the moon would make Justine happy, he would take next Saturday off and go along with her, but he was not about to make a confession any time soon. He was not overly religious, convinced the Church was too authoritarian, and he would not be lured back to the fold like some gullible fish.

The next Saturday, Katherine arrived at their apartment in the afternoon to finish her painting. No one home yet, hmm, perhaps they had some errands to run. Daubing away at her canvas, she finally heard them coming up the stairs. When she looked at Martin's stunned face, she knew his resolve had crumbled away, Fr. Reinold had caught him hook, line and sinker. He certainly had a way with him, and an unexplainable gift for healing souls, Katherine no longer doubted that. Busily filling the pastry dish and making a pot of coffee, they recounted their meeting. Similar to Justine's experience, Martin could not say 'no' when ushered towards the office, and found he was confessing everything since his childhood, remembering incidents he had long forgotten. When it was all over, Father talked with them at length about their plans to be married, and offered very helpful guidance. He told them this tragedy had taught them the true value of the married state, it was a partnership built on love, self-giving, trust and sacrifice. Katherine wondered how their recent crisis could do that, and Justine explained they had learned a hard lesson by their errors that led to the abortion and the pain of guilt that followed. Living together first without making a firm lifelong commitment through matrimony, and taking all the usual modern day 'precautions', they were living a life of false love on many levels. Father explained that while they were not open to the reception of life or would only accept it in the future on their terms, they were not completing the act of self-giving love that would bear lasting fruit, but only using each other, which culminated in a sterile gratification of the senses. Then, when blessed with life, there was no foundation set, because everything was based on a temporary platform, and panic ensued. Not prepared for the sacrifice involved with bringing a life into the world and afraid to see their plans eschewed, the drastic choice was made, which rocked that temporary foundation further. As the gravity of their decision began to sink in, their trust in each other was put to the test and Justine could no longer communicate with him. Her fear was causing a separation, a lesson they needed to take to heart, for all marriages are held together by communication as well as love. Justine admitted this made sense.

Katherine thought this was heavy until Martin declared she had not heard all of it yet. Now that they were planning on getting married, Father asked them what they thought marriage was really all about. They agreed with him it was a lifelong commitment between husband and wife, but when asked to what end or to what purpose, they were stomped for an answer. Father continued by explaining marriage was ordained to maintain the continuation of the human race according to God's words "be fruitful and multiply", but not in an aimless fashion, God not only wants multiplication, but fruitfulness, quality as well as quantity.

"Satan subtracts and divides, God adds and multiples," Father had declared.

They wondered what that meant until he said earth was a temporary home, and our main object is to reach our eternal home. Unless a family directs all its energies towards heaven, it is spiritually barren. Father then discussed the issue from another perspective, marriage was also intended as a support for the couple, for God saw it was not good that man should live alone, He intended a loving unity from the beginning, and not just for earthly matters, but for the spiritual life as well. We are to wish the highest good for our spouse, and enable them to reach that good by shouldering our spiritual burdens and bearing with each other's faults, to remove them if possible. Justine wondered what that highest good was, and Father simply said, God and Heaven. Unless we wish our loved ones and children that highest good and enable them to attain it, our love is lacking. It is natural to wish for all the material goodness for our families, but without God, everything else loses its value or becomes empty. Katherine pondered on this advice, and admitted she had to agree. While she sympathised with them in receiving the 'Reverend Dobbson treatment', at the same time, she could tell Fr. Reinold was not patronizing as the Reverend could be on occasions. On the contrary, Father was simply ... *enlightening*. He dished out his golden nuggets of wisdom freely and in a manner that the value of his words was truly appreciated rather than simply tolerated.

She would have liked to hear more of what he said, but Justine looked at the clock, muttering bashfully under her breath she may as well get a move on before it was time for dinner, and asked Katherine if she wouldn't mind helping her to tidy up the other bedroom, which was currently being used as a canvas drying station. Judging from their self-conscious expressions, she understood there would be new living arrangements, at least until after they were married. She had to admire their new resolve, it would not be easy, but she could sense their determination to make things right with each other. Clearing off the bed and putting the room in order, the ladies continued to discuss everything that had happened. It certainly had turned out to be the most unusual couple of weeks. They finished their task just as Maurice bounded up the stairs to announce his good news, he finally asked Therese the new nurse for a date, and she accepted. Martin declared it was about time! Maurice's main love in life had always been his 'cello, he had little experience in going out on dates, accounting for his past apprehensions. Katherine noted with amusement that Therese was probably waiting all this time for him to ask her. Maurice then declared as it was supper time, it was his turn to cook, until Justine noticed there was nothing in the cupboards and suggested they go to a bistro. He raised a surprised eyebrow, but praised her capital idea. It had been ages since they all went out together, and pleased with the obvious change in Martin and Justine, he wondered what could have brought this about.

CB❀BO

Katherine had not realized how fast time was flying. In a few days it would be November and she had not accomplished half of her plans. She had expected to be exhausted by now from visiting every known museum in Paris, and hauling home bags of film to develop, loads of finished sketches and paintings, not to mention mountains of notebooks filled with new and innovative ideas for her gallery. So far, she had visited only a few museums, her one painting for Gramps was still in the 'finishing touches' stage, and she had not set foot in any of the commercial galleries. She would have to step up her efforts before the Kraylors arrived in December and her free time would be curtailed. She had no idea if they planned to do anything special when they arrived, so she would have to leave her schedule open to a point. There may be days when Charlie might like to tag along with her, but that was it, the whole idea of 'tag along'. It would be difficult concentrating on her market research if she was continually worrying if he was bored with the whole proceedings and felt obliged to cut her work

198

short.   For the present, she decided she had better start her investigations now and simply forget about doing any more paintings until she returned home. She also had all those gifts to wrap and get ready for shipping mid-month if they were to arrive for Christmas. Time was running short and she was beginning to feel a little overwhelmed by all that was still left undone.

Katherine was very sorry to limit her visits to the 'Montmartre Club' as they had dubbed their little gatherings, and was grateful for their understanding, reporting her findings when she had the odd hour to stop by. She made her way to the established art hubs the first two weeks of November before checking out the rising stars of the gallery world in the Marais and Bastille districts. She liked the idea one gallery adopted of keeping an area reserved for a permanent collection that was not for sale, a quasi-museum commercial effect. If the owner could afford to keep a valuable collection on display, they could attract a ready stream of visitors. That was worth thinking about, she had never contemplated collecting paintings herself and always concentrated on painting her own. It would be a wonderful thing to share an art collection with the public she noted, perhaps she could expand to include exhibition rooms after she was firmly established and could afford the luxury of non-profit floor space. Although she had a generous trust fund, she was not brainless. There was no point sinking everything into the gallery, it was going to be a business after all and must be able to support itself. That was just plain common sense. However, she disliked the idea of becoming completely mercenary, it marred the idealistic aspect of art. As so often pointed out to her, it was difficult to balance the two, the practical necessities of a bread-and-butter business and the impractical passion of imaginative creativity. If only she could add more of the human element to the whole gallery-cum-business idea, that would certainly be interesting. Perhaps later expansions could also include a community area where general art classes could be offered to the public? Perhaps a few art appreciation seminars as well? There was also the possibility of school trips to encourage children to become more engaged in the art world. That would be fun to arrange! She resented how the various arts and humanities programs at schools were the first to be axed whenever a budget crisis loomed. Her gallery was blossoming into a whole cultural centre for the community. However, that was far in the future, Katherine discovered it was easier to plan big than start out small. Baby steps, she tried to remind herself, you can't do everything right away.

Her plans could only go so far until she selected the actual premises. One thing she noticed, Europeans were not overly concerned where any particular business was located, for instance, if it was on the ground floor or not, provided there was a well-marked access. If they wanted to shop, they would climb stairs, go into basements, hunt out quaint little arcades in out-of-the-way places, it did not matter. Americans, however, were generally spoiled. Unless businesses were placed on main thoroughfares, preferably with ample parking space, and accessed from the street level, few people would bother entering. Escalators and elevators are a must, large department stores could not survive without them. Of course, if a shop had more than two floors, the necessity of machinated conveyance was a universal understanding, but in America, convenience was the catchword, eliminate anything and everything that would cause unnecessary effort or exertion! She would have to find somewhere that met these criteria for the American market; ground floor entrance, parking, something near a major shopping or cultural area if possible. This would take a lot of space, Americans loved their amble elbow room and wide open skies, which meant she may have to sacrifice the ideal of a quaint artistic-looking environment for something that bordered on the large and modern, which would compromise several of her ideas for an old world décor. Building a premises would probably be out of the question, and she did not like the idea of renting or leasing where she would be tied to a contract. It would make more cost-effective sense to buy or convert something already built, restricting her to what was available on the market. She would have to wait until she actually saw the place to get the feel for it, to know exactly how to arrange and decorate the interior, and to determine if all her ideas were feasible, the restaurant and gift shop, the possible expansion to include exhibition and cultural spaces. Last but not least, there was the competition —how to find your own niche in a city that boasted some of the finest art galleries in the world? Would her gallery prove successful or go belly-up within a few months? This called for marketing plans and strategies ... Katherine grimaced at the thought, it sounded like warfare. Are all businesses like that? Is it not enough to earn a living, and live and let live anymore? No wonder Pops and Gramps had ulcers. Yes, setting aside time for her art would definitely be a 'must' on her daily agenda if that were the case, or the dog-eat-dog nature of the outside world would drive her to distraction. In the end, after all her running around, she realized it would be necessary to wait until she saw what was available back home before she could literally plan anything. The next logical step would be to research the technicalities of opening a café or restaurant in conjunction with the gallery, not to mention the other corporate red tape tied to the management of a business, which would also have to wait until she returned home. No point doing any more gallery hunting Katherine decided, time to enjoy what is left of your vacation and check out a few more museums you missed. The medieval art and tapestry collections at the Musée National du Moyen Age-Thermes de Cluny might be interesting to see, the name was certainly imposing. She also wanted to visit several of the churches and historic landmarks that she previously missed.

The first week of December had passed before Lucille approached Katherine to inquire if the Kraylors had communicated any instructions regarding their arrival. Katherine wondered what Lucille meant until she explained this would be their first Christmas at the apartment, and she did not know if they wished to have decorations, or what specialty food items they would like to have on hand, she only had a general knowledge of American holiday traditions. It struck Katherine that unless Lucille had reminded her, she was letting time flit away and did not stop to think how close Christmas was looming. She had finished her Christmas shopping early, and therefore missed most of the usual signs that reminded everyone. At the end of November they were already lighting the famous street lights around Paris, but in general, the build-up towards the holiday in France was not as commercially high-pitched as in America. Of course, it did not help staying indoors most of the time at the museums and returning home before dark.

"Oh Lucille, I'm so busy sight-seeing, I nearly forgot the time of year," she laughed. "In America, they start bombarding you with reminders as early as October. Sometimes September! The businesses try and get everyone out shopping as early as possible."

"I heard," Lucille replied. "Here, we give gifts too, but everything is around the meaning of the holiday. The Christmas nativity scene is more important than the tree, and it is a time to enjoy the company of family and friends, with plenty of good food of course."

"Well, I must admit everyone loves the tree over in the States, but family and the food is important too, so we share that tradition."

Katherine admitted she had not spoken about Christmas plans with the Kraylors via her weekly phone calls, maybe they decided not to make a fuss and put anyone out for only a few weeks. However, this gave Katherine an idea, they could surprise them when they came by having the place all prepared for a French Christmas. That would be a fun thing to do, and a nice way of saying 'thank you' for letting her stay. Katherine inquired how the French celebrated the holidays and Lucille eagerly shared stories how as children they would place their shoes by the fire for Père Noel to fill with nuts and candies. The main feast, called Reveillon, usually occurs before midnight Mass on Christmas Eve and begins with a starter of oysters, salmon, or other seafood, followed by *foie gras*, then the main course of turkey or roast goose with a rich chestnut stuffing, followed by another course of a fresh salad and a selection of cheeses, and finished with a Yule log cake for dessert, this meal is accompanied by copious amounts of champagne and wine. For the New Year, a special cake is baked called the Galette des Rois, Cake of the Kings, to celebrate the arrival of the wise men from the east, a treat usually served with tea or coffee. All these festivities carried out with due pomp and ceremony. There were other symbolic traditions too, like the Yule log fire, if the log burned all though Christmas night, the New Year promised to be a happy one. The superstitious would sometimes pour a measure of wine or oil on the log first to ensure a good harvest, or throw a bit of salt on it to scare witches away.

Lucille also warned her about acts of courtesy that were expected, for one instance, to wish everyone New Year greetings, and that meant practically *everyone*, or they would feel snubbed. Even in the workplace, a morning or two must be set aside when the vacation period is over to extend New Year wishes to all your colleagues, a custom that extended until the end of January. When the local postman, fireman and garbage collectors come knocking and ask if you wish to buy a calendar for the year, do not refuse. The sale of the calendars is their gratuity for all their efforts during the year without having to indelicately ask for one up front. To refuse would be to inform them they have performed a bad job all year. This was a new piece of information and Katherine was very grateful for this advice, better watch my p's and q's she thought, she certainly did not want to offend anyone!

After discussing the various traditions with Lucille, it was decided maybe a compromise was in order. Since they were Protestant and not Catholic, they would most likely go to the Christmas Day service, which meant they could still eat that sumptuous Revillion fare at the customary hour Christmas Eve. A turkey dinner was the same for both countries, so no major change there, although she was not sure if the Kraylors would like to begin their feast with oysters on the half-shell and decided American fare might work better for certain courses. She also had decorations to think about, the Kraylors did not have any for their vacation apartment. A nativity scene was a lovely idea, and she could envision all the paintings, guilt mirrors and the white marble fireplace festooned with dark green pine, holly and ivy sprigs that would compliment the old-world charm of the surroundings. She must not forget the centrepiece for the table, candles positioned around the main living area would add an atmospheric touch, and of course, they would need the perfect Christmas music. Perhaps Justine could point out the best markets to hunt down holiday recordings.

Last but not least, what to do about the Christmas tree? Should she choose a live one and have a royal mess at the end of the season when the needles began to fall, or choose a plastic one? She ticked off the pros and cons, she was not partial to the idea of cutting down a living tree, but was unsure if the Kraylors would want an artificial one, it would take up precious storage space. She finally settled on a traditional live tree, berating herself for having to renege on her environmentalist principles. She would have to work fast, now was the time to order the cake at the bakery and begin packing the larder before all the best delectables were picked over, she could then think about the decorations, which would take time to arrange on top of it all. Scanning her notes, Katherine calculated the preparation involved, and to make things more complicated, she had barely two weeks to accomplish everything before the Kraylors arrived. Now she understood why her mother and Mrs. Gonzales seemed to transform into military commanders when the holiday season approached. Preparing for Christmas was a complicated business.

Martin and Justine were only too happy to help her on their free days and afternoons. Martin arranged for the Yule log for the fire, the tree and the extra pine boughs to be delivered, and Justine showed her around all the festive Christmas market booths and the famous specialty food shops in the Madeleine and Opéra quarters, helping her to pick out the best turkey and the usual accompaniments, before taking her to find Christmas decorations. She very much appreciated their help and hoped she was not imposing on their own preparations, and Justine explained they would be celebrating the holidays with her family, a perfect time to break the news about their wedding plans, so they had very little to do before they left. With the shopping done and the larder stocked with all manner of sweet and savoury delights, Katherine worked on the decorations with Lucille, transforming the already beautiful apartment into a Christmas wonderland. She hoped the Kraylors would be pleasantly surprised.

They arrived on the evening of the twenty-first, and indeed, did not expect the festive welcome that greeted them.

"Surprise!" Katherine declared as she opened the door. "Merry Christmas everyone!"

A large bedecked wreath with colourful red bows and golden baubles decorated the front door, while cinnamon-scented candles with their flickering flames gave a merry glow inside accompanied by the lilting voice of Crosby and his 'White Christmas' carol. Bouquets of red roses covered the side tables, and the mirrors and paintings were simply handsome with their verdant pine, holly and red berry garlands. The pungent fragrance from the greens wafted around, blending with the perfume of the cinnamon candles and the floral displays. A fire blazed invitingly on the hearth, the pastoral nativity scene adorned the mantelpiece amidst the greenery, while in the sitting room the tree sat in all its twinkling glory, decorated simply but elegantly with white lights, golden garlands, red bows, colourful ornaments, all crowned with a magnificent angel holding a banner declaring *Gloria in excelsis Deo.*

"Katherine, it's so good to see you! Did you do all this?" Mrs. Kraylor asked as she gave Katherine a hug, amazed by the festive transformation.

"Well, I didn't do everything, I had a lot of help from Lucille and my friends," Katherine admitted, "we did the shopping too. I hope we picked out the right items."

"Everything is absolutely beautiful dear," Mrs Kraylor beamed as she looked around admiring the roses and greenery, "we didn't make plans, it seemed too much trouble for only a few weeks. We thought we could book a Christmas dinner somewhere, but this is simply wonderful."

"Oh, I'm so glad you like it. Hello Mr. Kraylor. Did you have a nice trip?"

"Can't complain, the flight came in on time and all our luggage arrived in one piece. My, the place looks festive, doesn't it?" he commented as he managed the suitcases, chuffed with the holiday atmosphere.

"Hi Kathy, I've missed you. Wow, you really made yourself quite at home," Charlie noticed with a big smile as he dropped his carry bag and gave her a bear hug.

"Charlie, it's been so long, I'm happy to see you. I hope everyone doesn't mind, but I took the liberty of booking a table for us at the restaurant around the corner. I wasn't sure about dinner plans, and with the run-up to Christmas, it was safer to secure a reservation."

"How splendid," Mrs. Kraylor declared. "That certainly was thoughtful of you, Kathy. We'll go unpack and rest a little bit before we go out."

Katherine was dying to hear all the news from back home, although she called every week, she did not want to stay on for long and run up any bills, and it was difficult to think of everything to discuss over the phone when talking-time was an issue. For some reason, she did not find writing letters any easier, it just took too long, and she often succumbed to the temptation to generalise. The men were the first to have everything unpacked and organized. Mr. Kraylor, who detested flying, sat in his armchair with a glass of bourbon and soda to help him relax, carefully taking out his pipe and tobacco pouch from his jacket pocket. Charlie decided on a Coke, it was still the afternoon according to their internal clock, and he was not ready to down a heavy libation, too early for that. Katherine could not stop herself from barraging them with questions.

"How are Mom and Pops? Is Gramps okay? How's the hip? Steves hasn't hacked into the FBI mainframe or anything like that? How are Mrs. Gonzales and Juanita? Is Suzy able to manage Jasper with college and all? Jasper's not creating havoc, is he?"

Charlie and his father relayed their reports from across the pond, her parents were doing fine, her father hoped she was enjoying her trip, and her mother looked forward to her phone call every week, constantly worrying on how she was getting along. She loved the letters, and would Katherine please write her a few more? Gramps was improving in leaps and bounds, he could now manage the stairs and was taking Jasper out for his daily walks having graduated from obedience school. Gramps was still bribing the Club for some decent lunches, but everyone still adhered to the diet fare when at home. Since she left, her parents confessed the house seemed too quiet after Steves had returned to college, and no, he had not hatched anything overly crazy to the best of their knowledge. He was too busy lately scouting the auto magazines and showrooms, deliberating on the colour and interior of the new Porsche, perhaps a silver grey one this year, and surprise, surprise, he was still going steady with Jennifer. Suzy sends her regards and a message to relay from Professor Matthews, he thanked her for the letters and hoped she was having a splendid vacation. Charlie also had good news to tell, he negotiated another settlement without having to go to court just before they left. Katherine congratulated him, a great reason to celebrate, and was just about to tell them her news when Mrs. Kraylor entered the room, her unpacking completed. While she did not want to interrupt, she hinted it was time they get ready and head over to the restaurant.

During dinner, Katherine relayed the results of her museum visits and fact-finding missions, her observations, as well as her disappointments.

"Imagine, only one picture finished in all this time," she replied, not a little chagrined.

Charlie tried to console her.

"Come now, Kathy, don't be too hard on yourself. There is much to see and do in Paris, you're only human you know. Besides, with all your plans, how often will you be able to come back?"

"That's true, dear," Mrs. Kraylor added, "might was well enjoy the scenery, and worry about work when you return home."

Mr. Kraylor was interested in her business ideas, and agreed the

American market was different.

"Have you thought about a warehouse conversion? Think of the space you would have, not to mention all the various urban renewal schemes offering grants and the tax incentives. It would be perfect for your concept of an inner-city cultural centre."

"That's an option," Katherine mused, "I should look into that, thank you, Mr. Kraylor. Hopefully there may be something available in an appropriate location."

Charlie offered his help, he would be happy to look into the legalities of a warehouse conversion.

"I know some people who have warehouses, we'll see if they are in a good area and are willing to sell a property that might fit the bill," Charlie added, "we wouldn't want you stuck in some old rundown industrial zone, not at all suitable for the arts."

⅓❀⅔

Katherine's assumptions were correct, her free time was curtailed when the Kraylors arrived as they had plans to enjoy the festive Parisian Christmas attractions. On the following evening, they booked to see an opera at the new modern opera house constructed over the site of the infamous Bastille. On the next night, they went on a promenade down the large boulevards and the Champs-Elysées admiring the fabulous holiday light displays. When they did not plan everything as a group, Charlie wanted to take Katherine to different sections of the city she had not seen, the Château de Malmaison, Napoléon's out of town retreat that became Josephine's main residence after their divorce was one daytime destination. The following day, he proposed an unusual visit, the Père Lachaise cemetery where many famous people were interred. Katherine thought this was a little morbid, but decided to humour Charlie. She had to admit, the cemetery was not as creepy as she expected, it was quite elegant and well worth the visit searching out the tombs of Molière, Oscar Wilde, Chopin, Gericault of the *Raft of Medusa* fame, Marcel Proust and other celebrities. They were not the only visitors, although it was out of season, several tourists came to pay their respects to a favourite artist, musician, writer or actor who had influenced them.   Jim Morrison of 'The Doors' still continued to draw a crowd of Rock and 'Goth' admirers, including those who were too young to have attended any of his concerts. When it was time for a break, Charlie always knew where the best cafés and quaint places for lunch were located, he had learned the rule to avoid the main tourist thoroughfares.

Christmas Eve, naturally, was not a day for sightseeing as Mrs. Kraylor began preparing their holiday feast early with Katherine's help. Before the kitchen went into full swing, Mrs. Kraylor slipped several packages under the tree next to the gifts Katherine had bought for them.

"You don't think your family would leave you without Christmas gifts now?" she replied with a smile, "they wanted it to be a surprise."

With the cooking going full steam ahead, the men were duly barred from the kitchen precincts to keep them well out from underfoot. Tempted by the first whiff of the roasting turkey and curious to see the cause of all the laughing and clattering, Charlie would poke his head around the door every now and again, or Mr. Kraylor would pretend he was looking for some important article, which *could* be in the storage cupboard in the pantry ... . Finally, Mrs. Kraylor ordered them to go find something constructive to do, read a paper, watch TV, go take a walk, do *whatever*, but stop pestering us while we are trying to prepare. Fed up with sitting around, they decided to take her advice and go for a walk, no point upsetting the women. It was late afternoon when they returned with an unexpected announcement, they had an extra guest coming for dinner.

"You don't mind, do you, honey?" Mr. Kraylor asked semi-rhetorically as he briefly popped his head through the kitchen door.

"Oh? Well, we have enough food to feed an army. Who is it by the way?"

"Mr. Reinold's son, oh you know. Remember that big case about the docklands? Anyway, we bumped into each other at the corner. Said he was on alone over here for Christmas and would head back to New York before New Year's day. Couldn't let him spend the night alone like a bunch of Scrooges now, could we?"

"No I suppose not," Mrs. Kraylor replied aloud, before muttering to Katherine and looking up to heaven after he retreated to the sitting room, "I was hoping we could spend one Christmas without having to invite the clients. Lawyers and politicians always end up taking their work home. It's something you just have to get used to, I hope you don't mind?"

"Not at all," Katherine replied, "it really is a small world, you know I've already met Mr. Reinold, and his elder brother. My friend, Justine, needed to talk with Fr. Reinold and asked me to come along, and he was there too."

"Really? Now that's interesting, you didn't tell us about that," Mrs. Kraylor remarked as she whipped the cream.

"There's been so much to talk about, and I just didn't think it was important," Katherine explained, peeling the sweet potatoes and popping them into a bowel. "He has a wonderful art collection stashed over in his apartment, I still can't get over he had a real Vermeer delivered the day we visited."

"So his brother was visiting him then?"

"Yes, but he had to go to Rome before he returned to New York."

"Hmm, really sad how that all went," Mrs. Kraylor commented, "I heard their father was grooming him to take over the business, but suddenly he tossed it all aside and decided to become a priest. He was practically disowned, but the rest of the family still keep in contact. Now the younger brother will be managing everything, or so I've heard. What a pity, he had everything going for him."

"Well, I guess he heard a call he just couldn't refuse," Katherine replied. "Perhaps the world of business did not appeal to him. It's a shame his father disowned him though, I think he found what truly makes him fulfilled. You would think a parent would be happy their child discovers their niche. For instance, my friend Martin is in the same situation, his father refused to speak to him when he decided on art for a career and waits for the day he will 'come to his senses'. What a waste! Those years they could have had together will never come back."

Finishing the food preparations, all they had to do was set the table, dress for dinner, and await the arrival of the guest. The doorbell rang half an hour before it was time to be seated.

"He's punctual, thank goodness for that," Mrs. Kraylor quietly remarked as she went to answer the door. "Hello, you must be Mr. Reinold, do come in."

"Please, call me Gerry. I hope you do not mind me dropping in on your Christmas dinner."

Elegantly dressed, he entered bearing a few bottles of Don Perignon and a Christmas basket of authentic Russian beluga caviar.

"Not at all. You know my husband of course, this is Charles, our son, and I hear you have already met our guest, Katherine. Here, let me take your coat, oh my, you didn't have to bring anything," Mrs. Kraylor said as she received his gifts, allowing him to shake hands with everyone.

"You are so welcome, this is a time for sharing," he replied. "Hello Charles, I'm glad to see you again."

"Please, no formalities. Everyone calls me Charlie."

"All right. Hello Katherine, it's a pleasure … ."

"Likewise, this is an unexpected surprise, but please, call me Kathy."

The men settled in with a round of cocktails while the two ladies returned to the kitchen to take care of the last minute details, inviting everyone to be seated in the dining room when all was ready. Although the evening passed pleasantly, Katherine felt something was lacking, and then realized she was feeling a little homesick. While it was simply wonderful to be in Paris for the holidays with the Kraylors, it was not like sitting at her own family table. Her heart gave a slight twinge as she watched Mr. Kraylor carve the turkey, she was used to her father or uncle doing that honour year after year, and it was odd to see someone else performing the task. It was also a little nerve-wracking trying to help Mrs. Kraylor in the kitchen as she was unfamiliar with her method of doing things, and while she put on a brave face, she felt like a complete bumbler, and to top it all, everyone had become terribly stiff and starchy all of a sudden, perhaps it was for the benefit of their guest. How she missed Gramp's jolly round of toasts and Steve's amusing quips, she was beginning to appreciate his roguish renditions of all their favourite Christmas carols now that he was not there to sing them, nor would she object to a little gossip from Aunt Martha, come to think of it. I wonder how all the cousins are doing, she mused. Perhaps it would be best if she did not dwell on all that, she did not want to turn the evening into a complete downer. At least there was Charlie, he could always lighten any heavy mood, she just wondered why he was acting a little nervous all afternoon. Maybe he disliked sitting around with nothing to do, he always had to stay active or go someplace, maybe he did not feel like doing anything without her while she offered to do kitchen duty and was stuck cooking for the day.

The dinner was excellent and the evening was entertaining with the polite conversations that flitted from subject to subject, their impressions of Paris at that time of year, the hassles and rewards of business, the woes of the current recession, the latest developments in art, the recent smash hits and flops on Broadway, the ins and outs of politics, the Iraqi invasion of Kuwait that August, the latest dealings and rumours circulating New York, all spiced with the usual pleasantries and amusing comments, anything and everything. After dessert, and not a *few* glasses of champagne, Mrs. Kraylor announced it was time to open the gifts, explaining it was their custom to unwrap them on Christmas Eve, so she invited everyone to take their champagne glasses and retire to the living room.

"I am sorry, Gerry," Mrs. Kraylor declared as she read the tags and handed the brightly bedecked packages to the intended recipients, "if we had known sooner … ."

"Please, no apologies," he replied, "my presence was unexpected. You go right ahead, don't let me interrupt the family traditions."

The Kraylors were delighted with Katherine's presents, and she was grateful they thought to haul gifts from the States for her. The mood was certainly festive now as the gifts began to crowd the coffee table and the shiny wrappers littered the sofas and floor. Just when she thought the gift-giving had ended, Mrs. Kraylor addressed Charlie from across the room.

"Why Charlie, you haven't given Kathy your gift yet."

Charlie looked a little uncomfortable, replying quietly, "I … would rather give it to her tomorrow, if that's all right."

"Now, Charlie. Don't tell me you didn't get her anything."

"Yes I did, but…"

"Come, come, Sylvia, he can give it to her when he wants to," Mr Kraylor interjected, casting a knowing glance at Charlie.

"Fiddlesticks, dear! Now is the perfect time," she continued, "it's almost Christmas Day, in a few hours anyway, and after all the trouble Kathy took to see we had such a lovely holiday … ."

Charlie slowly fumbled around in his pocket and took out a little black velvet jewellery box, painfully embarrassed with the situation. He had given her many like it before, her gold bracelet was now getting rather heavy with charms, she would have to get a new one pretty soon. Yet, why was he so embarrassed? Perhaps his parents had expected him to be slightly more original this year, but he simply could not break with their little custom that had become a comfortable routine and was dreading a sermon in front of her. Obviously, the situation was made more difficult for him with their guest present. She tried to ease the situation.

"Oh, thank you Charlie. But I'll be happy to wait until tomorrow if that's what you'd like."

"Don't be silly, Kathy dear! Go ahead, open it up," Mrs. Kraylor interjected, with another sip of champagne.

Well, I tried.

Reaching across the coffee table and taking the little box as prompted, she opened the lid, and could now share completely in his mortification. The object glimmering in the candlelight before her was not the gold charm she expected, it was a lot more than she expected, a sparkling three carat diamond ring flanked by two gorgeous emeralds that in all probability cost him the entire commission he earned from his recent case. She was correct, his parents *did* expect him to be original this year.

"Oh, Charlie…!"

"I'm so happy for you both," Mrs. Kraylor exclaimed, enraptured with the scintillating jewels, "it's absolutely beautiful, I had no idea you had such fine taste!"

"It's about time, son," Mr. Kraylor laughed.

"Now, there is so much to think about! Charlie, that old bachelor's pad of yours simply will not do now. What about moving somewhere closer uptown?" his mother suggested.

While the proud parents were blissfully imagining their son's future, moving them into a Manhattan apartment and planning how many children they would have, Katherine was stunned into silence. She had no idea Charlie felt this way about her, if there were any 'signals' like everyone talked about, she was clueless on how to read them, he was not in the habit of displaying his emotions and always kept a respectful distance. Perhaps that's why he was an excellent lawyer. They had never even kissed! According to romance in general, everyone was supposed to do that on their dates out at one time or another. But then again, she should have known. He never went out on dates, and how many times did he take her out alone for quiet dinners in romantic places? How many times had he confided to her almost everything he enjoyed, or things that bothered him, a confidence that she believed was only extended in friendship? On the contrary, his feelings had developed further, while hers had remained the same.

Stupid, stupid, stupid!

Everyone else saw what was coming next, the marriage proposal. The socialites in the Big Apple were anticipating an engagement, everyone … except her. Were her parents aware of his intentions too? This state of affairs would not be so humiliating if Gerry was not present, he was the only one who knew her true sentiments, and was inadvertently made a witness to this unexpected fiasco. To make matters worse, Charlie's parents were acting as if everything was already signed and sealed. How on earth could she tell them she had not even thought about marriage?

Charlie noticed Katherine was not displaying the signs of elation he had been hoping for and feared something was amiss.

Damn, damn, damn!

He *knew* he should have waited, this was not the right time to pop the question, and now Kathy was strapped on the hot seat by his parents and with a complete stranger present. Perhaps he had better come to the rescue before his eager mother planned the date and scared her away entirely.

"Mom, stop making a fuss, I don't expect an answer right now. Kathy needs some time to think it over, I'm sure."

"I … I don't know what to say," Katherine stammered.

"Please say you'll think it over?" Charlie asked quietly.

"Al…all right," she replied simply, hitting the emotional 'pause' button on her current predicament, anything so they could move on. Please, *please* let's discuss something else! Avoid a scene at all costs!

Mrs. Kraylor finally got the message, things were not going according to plan. The jovial mood was quickly sinking into uncomfortable nervousness, they too had assumed Katherine's answer would be 'yes' and had not the foggiest notion she might think otherwise. Mrs. Kraylor quickly changed the conversation, time for damage control.

"Oh, yes, of course, there's no rush," she interjected in a chirpy voice, "think it over dear. Why, you already have a busy time ahead of you with your gallery project. I think we've had enough champagne. Anyone for coffee?"

With this banal statement introduced after all the dramatic flurry, Gerry decided to take this as an opportune cue for retreat, no coffee for him thank you, it was time for him to leave, it was getting rather late. Everyone thanked him for coming and politely saw him to the door.

Embarrassing as it was to have Gerry present, it was more uncomfortable in the company of the Kraylors when he had departed. How could she continue to face them during the remainder of their vacation as though nothing had happened? Charlie looked like a dejected puppy as he poked at the smouldering fire, attempting to appear occupied with something. Mr. Kraylor tried to block out the poignant silence by reading his paper on the latest squabbles at the UN over the deterioration of Yugoslavia and the Iraqi menace, and Mrs. Kraylor hardly said a word while Kathy helped her to clear the table. Nevertheless, Katherine was thankful for the relative quiet, she needed to think, the unexpected incident continued to swirl in her mind as she tried to unravel all that had occurred. No wonder his parents were so pleased to offer her their apartment and invited her to stay with them for Christmas, they obviously had an ulterior motive, playing the game of matchmaker. She felt horribly manipulated. No doubt, they considered her a fine catch for their son.

She was not angry with Charlie, she knew him too well. She now understood why he nearly burned himself out at the family firm when he left college. He was trying to prove himself, to establish a career and show that he was able to make it on his own and demonstrate he was worthy of her. No wonder he was so proud of his recent successes and eager to give her daily reports, he probably concluded he had attained enough security to finally approach her with his proposal. She felt so terrible, she did not want to hurt Charlie for the world, but how could she convey to him her feelings were not the same as his? She dreaded the time of reckoning when she would have to confess how she actually felt, but she could not string him along with false hopes and indefinite 'maybes'. Under these circumstances, would their friendship survive this recent development? This thought hurt the most. How could they continue to be friends when she was unable to give him that one 'yes' he wanted to hear? Every time she saw him from now on, he would be a reminder of this night. No, things would never be the same.

She was relieved when she could politely retreat to the solitude of her bedroom shortly after the table was cleared, it was good to finally be alone. Unfortunately, the ostrich solution was only temporary, she would have to pull her head out of the proverbial sand the following morning, and the next morning, and the next morning after that until they returned to the States. How she wished her mother was there so she could talk it over!

It certainly was difficult to put on a diplomatic face the next day and try to enjoy Christmas, the tension from the night before continued to linger like an oppressive fog. Finally, she decided she needed some air, a walk along the Seine might do some good and clear her head before they went to the Christmas Day service. As she went to take her coat out of the hall closest, Charlie asked if he could accompany her. She knew what this meant, he needed to talk with her alone, and while she dreaded to hear what he had to say, she could not say 'no', everything would have to be discussed in the open before long anyway.

They walked for a considerable distance taking in the brisk winter air without speaking a word, simply holding this quiet time with each other before the dreaded words became audible. They eventually stopped at the Pont de l'Alma to admire the river view and watch the barges and boats float past. Beautiful though the scenery was with the magnificent Grand Palais and the ornate Pont Alexandre III in the distance, everything seemed to be shrouded in a sombre grey mantle of *tristesse*. At last, Charlie broke the silence.

"I'm sorry about last night, Kathy. I hadn't planned to propose to you like that," he began, "I was hoping would could be alone, but things didn't turn out the way I expected. I had no intention of putting you under any pressure."

"It wasn't your fault … I was a little … surprised."

"You love Paris so much, I thought it was the perfect place to finally ask the important question. I can understand if you want to wait, if you're not ready to settle down yet, if it's still too soon."

"Charlie, I don't know how to say this … it's a little more than … too soon." His heart froze, he was dreading this might be the case. The concern and hurt showed in his eyes.

"Kathy, what are you saying?"

"Oh, Charlie, call me blind if you like, I had no idea you felt this way before last night."

Dang! Why was it so difficult to look into his eyes?

He took a deep breath before tentatively asking;

"You mean, all this time, there has never been ... anything ... between us?"

"I wouldn't say that," she replied slowly, wondering how to explain the nature of her feelings until the words slipped out in a rush, "it's just that marrying you would be like marrying Steves!"

He pursed his lips for a moment.

"But Kathy, the love is there, it's just ... misplaced, don't you think?"

Katherine now took a deep breath before continuing.

"Charlie, we've practically grown up together, you're part of my family, like an elder brother. I don't know if I can go past that."

He wistfully took her hands in his.

"Are you sure you are not mistaken? Don't let how close we've become cloud your judgement. Perhaps you are waiting for some romantic notion of being swept off your feet, I believe true love is not fuelled by fickle chemistry or fiery passion. It's a mutual desire to grow together, the development of a deep bond stronger than any capricious emotion. I'm not saying there shouldn't be any emotions, but ... maybe I'm not explaining myself."

"You are saying I'm confusing this feeling with sisterly affection," she added.

Could that be true?

"Yes, Kathy. We've become so close, we know each other as well as our own family. We've always been able to talk about anything, we've shared all our happy times and sorrows, isn't the foundation set? Could we ever find anyone else who would care about us as much as we already care for each other?"

There was a long pause before she replied.

"Oh Charlie, I ... I can't deny I care for you deeply, but I don't think I can give you the 'yes' you're asking for. I mean, I can't make any promises ... ."

"Is there any hope for us?" he asked looking so sad. "It's just friends then?"

"I'm so sorry."

Charlie nodded his head in resignation, no point discussing the matter further. They silently made their way back to the apartment. As they walked along, she thought about the ring nestled in its little velvet box on the dressing table.

"Charlie, about the ring … ."

"I want you to keep it, Kathy. I don't want it back."

"But, I can't keep something like that! It must have cost you a small fortune."

"Yes you can. I got it for you, and for you only. If you can't see a future for us together, I still don't want the ring back. No arguments, please. Besides, I would be a cad to take back your Christmas present."

He was trying to make her feel better, but nothing could cheer her up after this. She was certain of it now, things would never be the same again.

og ❀ go

Her vacation was certainly not going as planned. While she had accomplished very little these past few months, Katherine imagined the holidays would be enjoyable at least, and now everything felt infected with an undercurrent of tension as she and her hosts pretended things were the same as before and tried to carry on as normal. How she wanted to call home, but the thought of maintaining the façade with her family was too stressful knowing she could not talk with them in detail with the Kraylors there. Her mother would immediately sense something was wrong and would press her for an answer, and she did not want to blurb everything out with others present. For some reason, the Kraylors were not interested in leaving the apartment that often, and it was no use trying to call from a public phone on one of her museum outings, Charlie continued to accompany her wherever she went. Perhaps he did not like her going out in a foreign city alone, or he dreaded to be separated from her, fearful the fiasco of his proposal would drive a permanent wedge between them. She prayed he was not entertaining those false hopes she was trying to save him from, waiting for the day he would see that glistening ring on her finger. That alone would drive in the wedge. It would be better if he took it back, the little black velvet box continued to stare her down from the dressing table until she quickly slipped it into the drawer and hid it under one of her sweaters. The sight of it made her feel terribly guilty for some reason, as though she had made a selfish decision in refusing. Why should she feel at fault? She could not see how it would have worked if she looked on Charlie as a sibling, and she was determined not to be emotionally pressured into making a serious commitment like that under these circumstances.

Maybe writing a letter to her mother was the next best thing, it would do her good to pen down what had happened. They could pick up the threads and discuss the whole thing thoroughly when she returned home. She took out her stationary and started to convey, as best she could, what had happened and her utter confusion. While it seemed a pity to mar her floral greeting card with her melancholic apprehensions, it was cathartic to see them laid out in ink, making the surreal nature of the situation appear more tangible and less difficult to assess. However, this correspondence therapy was an imperfect solution, she would have to wait until she heard her mother's advice, and manage as best she could in the meantime.

For the present, since Charlie insisted on following her around, she decided to keep their days occupied in the museums, better to direct their thoughts and conversations away from the personal sphere and onto something more general like the exhibitions. This tactic did nothing for her nerves, however. While they discussed the fabulous brushstrokes of a painting or marvelled at magnificent medieval treasuries, she was constantly harangued by the thought Charlie wanted more from their close relationship, to bring it to the next level, while she could only see a ceiling. Was she wrong about her feelings like he suggested? She did not think so. Would he be satisfied with friendship? The disparity between their expectations was taking its toll, she was mentally worn out. How could they continue like this? Oh Charlie, why couldn't you have left things the way they were? She could not wait for New Year's to be over, Martin and Justine would be back, and perhaps she could talk to them, if she could get them alone, that is. She had promised to bring Charlie over to meet them, and so would have to continue the pretence that everything was all right. So what, she finally chided herself. It would be a comfort to see some friendly faces, it was uncomfortable being with Charlie's parents after Christmas Eve, she did not know what they were thinking, or how they were taking the present development. She counted the minutes, waiting for the day she could go up to the old hangout on Montmartre. Never before had the beginning of a New Year seemed so fraught with emotional tension.

At last, the third of January seemed like the right time to go see Martin and Justine, not too soon after they returned on New Year's Day to be a nuisance, or too late to be accused of being too busy for them. Calling ahead to make sure it was not a bad time, they were delighted that they would finally meet Charlie whom they had heard so much about. Katherine silently wished it was under better circumstances, but life had a way of throwing unexpected surprises. They showed up for dinner with a few bottles of wine and a cake for dessert, and were greeted by a truly appetising aroma, Justine decided to prepare a special French home cooked meal in honour of the new guest from America, a hearty beef bourguignon. Unfortunately, Maurice was called away on duty at the hospital again, and would have to take a rain check.   Martin and Justine certainly seemed happier, Katherine noticed.   After they exhausted the general areas of discussion, asking Charlie how he liked Paris at this time of year, his thoughts and opinions on the recent events in the news, what it was like to work in an American law practise, and so on, they relayed their own happy news.   Justine's parents simply adored Martin, and being the perfect gentleman, he seemed to hit it off with them from the very first, their announcement of marriage was expected and greeted with profuse congratulations. Justine and Martin had not agreed on the date yet, perhaps sometime during this summer or the next. Katherine was so glad they had come through the worst of the crisis.

However, the talk of marriage was difficult to listen to, especially with Charlie present. She wondered if their personal problems showed as they once did with Martin and Justine? Whether they could tell or not, she knew they liked him and had immediately accepted him into their little bohemian circle. After dinner, Martin cracked out the old French Edith Piaf records, time for one of their musical *soirées*, their wacky discussions and peals of laughter amidst the clutter of easels and drying canvases, just like the old days. Charlie certainly seemed amused with the proceedings and joined in the fun of the moment, singing along to *La vie en rose* and the few songs he recognised. They had such a pleasurable evening, it was difficult to call it a night. Martin and Justine extended an invitation for another get-together on Saturday, their day off, which was accepted.

They arrived early the next Saturday afternoon, and to Katherine's delight, the melodic strains of a 'cello resounded through the hallway.

"Oh good! Maurice is here today, I was hoping you would get to meet him before we returned home. The artistic clique is not complete unless all are here."

"You mean that's not a recording?" Charlie asked in disbelief, "Julliard would love to nab him. I can't believe he gave up the chance to become a professional 'cellist to rummage around in someone's chest cavity."

When they had introduced Maurice to Charlie, it was suggested they all go out to their favourite café on the Place du Tertre and watch the other artists for a change. Enjoyable as their rendezvous was, Katherine feared she would not have some time alone with them to talk privately. While the men were engaged in an animated discussion about the differences of American and European football, and whether or not war with Iraq was eminent, Justine remarked,

"I'm so glad we could all get together and meet Charlie before you returned to America."

"I am too," Katherine replied.

"When are you actually leaving? I was hoping we could have a 'women's day out' before you go."

Yes, Justine was almost back to her old self if she thought about shopping, Katherine thought.

"Well, we don't leave until the eleventh, but we do have to pack, and I offered to help clean up the apartment before we left. I did help to wreck it after all. The Christmas tree is in a sorry state now, it's dropping bows and pine-needles all over the place."

"So that's the rest of this coming week out of the picture. That means we will only have tomorrow. I know we're not supposed to shop on a Sunday, but there's no harm in looking, is there?"

"I guess not. Okay, the day is set. Shall we hit the malls in the morning, or the afternoon?"

"Oh as soon as possible!"

"Morning it is then."

It was getting late and time to get back to the apartment. Everyone said their goodbyes since this was the last night the group would have an opportunity to be together. Martin and Justine promised to have a plethora of paintings ready for her new gallery, and Katherine promised to get it opened as soon possible so they could all be together again. Partings were always difficult. She was glad she would see Justine one last time at least.

Ϗ✾ʀ

As it was their last day together this trip, Justine decided they should visit the Galeries Lafayette located in the heart of the Opéra quarter, a glorious multi-storied *chic* department store completed near the end of the Belle Époque years. Although Katherine had been there many times before, she never tired of browsing through the magnificent store. Its original interior complete with a stunning multi-coloured stained glass dome and grand central staircase were left exactly as the day it was built, she loved visiting buildings like this, they evoked the ambience of a great period of the city, the time when Renoir painted his first Impressionist work, the opening of the first Metro station, the construction of the Eiffel Tower, the invention of the movie camera by the Lumière brothers, the development of Art Nouveau, the opening of the Moulin Rouge, many of the events that shaped the romantic idealism and iconography of Paris all occurred within this epoch.

After they browsed through the various sections whiling away the morning, with Katherine wondering how she would broach the topic of Charlie's unexpected proposal, Justine suddenly gasped.

"I forgot about going to church! Imagine, here I was worrying about shopping on a Sunday, and forgot about going to Mass, especially on the Epiphany! I'm just not used to going on a regular basis yet. If I miss Mass without a good reason, I have to confess it."

"Well, I don't want you to get into trouble. Is there somewhere close you can go?"

"Yes, the Madeleine, if we hurry, we just might make it on time."

"But I'm not a Catholic…"

"So what? I'm not leaving you alone on our last day together. You can still attend the service, you just can't go to communion. We can come back to the Galeries for lunch and finish our poking around. Hurry up now!"

With that, Justine grabbed her by the hand and they started running for the Metro. It was difficult to say 'no' to Justine when she got an idea into her head, and in this case, was literally dragging her along. How forgetful was Justine actually, Katherine was slightly suspicious. This was an odd twist to the day she did not expect, but then, that was just like Martin, Justine and Maurice, they liked springing surprises. On this occasion, she had a feeling Justine wanted her to attend a Catholic mass, but was afraid to ask her outright in case she received a refusal on grounds of her Episcopalian beliefs and thought up a plan to get her there by hook or by crook. After their unusual episode with Fr. Reinold, was she trying to extend the religious experience and make her a convert? Katherine was not sure how her family would take it if they knew she ran to attend the service of another denomination, she was grateful the Catholics were Christian at least! In any case, she was curious to see their ceremonies.

Arriving at the church, they ran up the never-ending front steps towards the main entrance. Katherine had only a fleeting moment to admire the façade of the gigantic Neo-Roman building as they raced through the monolithic row of Corinthian columns that supported the portico and sculptured frieze. Finding a couple of empty wooden chairs in one of the back rows, most French churches did not have pews, they sat down and tried to catch their breath. They made it just in time with only a few minutes to spare. She had visited the venerable edifice before. After the Battle of Jena, Napoléon commissioned the imposing classical-style plans as an eternal Temple of Glory in tribute to his Grand Army. These plans were eventually waylaid with his defeat and subsequent exile, and it was undecided whether the monument should become the new parliament building or a bank, but was finally consecrated as a church in honour of St. Mary Magdalene forty years later. During the day, the place was usually left dark and dismal, only an electric bulb or two and the flickering flames of the candles lit by the faithful near the side altars dispelled the heavy gloom for the meandering tourists. Today for the Sunday service, the interior was bathed with light radiating from the white glass globes of the gilt chandeliers, revealing the magnificent gilt and marble décor. She could now admire the beautiful sculptures, a depiction of Christ's baptism was masterfully executed, and the high altar with angels bringing Mary Magdalene to Heaven was certainly eye-catching.

Lost in her examination of the building, she was startled when the organ echoed loudly around the building and the choir began to sing. The congregation rose from theirs seats and she followed suit, looking nervously at Justine.

"Don't worry," she whispered, "just do what I do, and you'll be all right."

With this reassurance, Katherine watched as the service commenced. My, there was an orchestra! She was attending a full sung Mass for the first time, it was a wonderful experience, she had only heard classical recordings of masses before, but had never heard one performed during worship. Rev. Dobbson's little volunteer choir paled in comparison.

"This is really beautiful," she whispered over to Justine.

"It is, isn't it? The Madeleine is famous for its music."

She now understood why Justine wanted to bring and she was glad to be there, it helped her to forget for an hour the tensions of the past Christmas. Following along with Justine's movements, standing, sitting, saying 'amen' at the appropriate times, she found to her surprise, the mass was not all that different from the Anglican service, obviously this was one of the modifications the Church had brought about not long before she was born. The prayers were recited in French and easy for her to follow. It was a pity there was such a division between Protestants and Catholics, not much of a difference according to her first impressions. After the Gospel reading, the priest came forward to the lectern to give his homily on the great faith of the three wise kings of the east, and upon seeing the star rise, they followed it to adore the newborn King of the Jews no matter what the cost or the hardship. This was not any ordinary king, and they knew it, or they would have come to pay homage to Herod when he ascended the throne, or paid tribute to Caesar, who at the time was the mighty ruler of the unconquerable Roman Empire. These kingdoms were finite, while the star announced the birth of the Eternal King promised by the one true God of Israel to mankind, and despite their differences in religion, the wise men knew where to find the Eternal Truth, leaving all behind to find the Christ sent to bring salvation to earth. For some odd reason, this simple description about the three kings reminded Katherine of Socrates, who finally came to believe the prophecy declaring him one of the wisest men with his conclusion that only the gods, or God in the Christian interpretation, was wise. In the end, he gave up his life to defend the truth he discovered. The three kings were considered wise because they recognised the oracle of the star God sent to them and followed it on faith, while Herod, or even the priests of Jerusalem for that matter, did not recognise its significance. Instead, Herod feared the dissolution of his earthly reign and tried to destroy the Eternal King. What a pathetic decision, she noted. Why did the allure of finite worldly power always manage to blind everyone?

Katherine continued to follow along as the service continued, and eventually it was time for the congregation to receive communion while the orchestra and choir sang Frank's *Panis Anglicus*. She dutifully followed Justine's instructions to stay in her place, she did not want to give offence. Watching her friend get in line in the nave with the others, she wondered why Protestants could not receive communion too since they were Christian after all, or why Catholics were instructed to abstain from receiving in Protestant churches when they attended on rare occasions like weddings or funerals. There was some fundamental split in their beliefs at this point, she wished she could figure out exactly what and why. Thinking back to her first meeting with Fr. Reinold and his explanation of the gargoyles, she noted their basic Christian morality and ethics were not different for she agreed with all his explanations. Okay, so that bizarre incident about Justine's grandmother was beyond her comprehension, but the carvings on Notre Dame she could relate to. An observation then struck her: when the medieval gargoyles and grotesques were invented, *there were no divisions between the Churches*. The Anglican or Episcopalian Churches did not exist.

This was a point worth mulling over. While many in her parish insisted they were still part of the universal Catholic church but were 'reformed', Katherine could not see this supposed unity, the Roman

Catholics definitely did not see them as part of *their* unity. There was a visible parting of the ways at some point in history, and she wondered how she could get to the root of the issue. An idea then came to her, she liked working things out with simple analogies. Perhaps that's why she liked Socrates' no-nonsense method of deductive reasoning. If a tree was known by its fruit as Christ said, than the fruit also bears witness to the tree it was generated from. Just by looking at an apple, everyone knows it came from an apple tree. Good trees bear good fruit, and pure fruit comes from a long line of pure trees. Since Christ established a church, then logically that church should be able to trace its lineage back to Him. Katherine pondered on the hundreds of Christian denominations that the world boasted. Hmm, Christ said he would build His Church ... not *churches* ... he specifically mentioned *one* church ... . The Roman Catholics claimed a direct line of descent via their popes back to Peter, and hence, directly back to Christ Himself. Contemplating the history of the Anglican church, she had to admit its origins were not as splendid. King Henry the VIII wanted a divorce, and was refused by the pope. He was granted papal permission to marry his dead brother's wife, but when she could not bear him an heir, he pushed for an annulment to declare the union null and void, allowing him to remarry. In this case, there were no actual grounds for an annulment. A childless marriage did not indicate that it was invalid. On the other hand, if the queen did not want children, or refused to bring them up in a Christian manner, perhaps the request for an annulment might have been granted. Instead, Henry split from Rome and declared himself head of the Church in England, which later morphed into its own denomination despite the Anglican claim it was still 'Catholic' in essence. To put it bluntly, he sounded like a spoiled brat throwing a tantrum because he could not have his own way and decided he would do things as he saw fit, with bitter consequences. Katherine could not help but think this obsession with producing an heir for the throne to secure the Tudor line bore a striking resemblance to Herod who feared for his earthly kingdom. Of course, Henry's bloody succession of wives was a cause for suspicion too, and she found herself questioning his motives. The disobedience and lust of a king was certainly not a glorious beginning for any church.

With a sinking feeling, she realized she was reaching a conclusion she did not want to face, a conclusion that was opening a whole can of worms she could not deal with right now—*her church did not begin with Christ.* If it did not begin with Him, could it be called part of His Church? If it was not, what did that make her a part of? The paroxysm of an overly indulged king? *Here you go again, borrowing more trouble!* Don't you have enough to handle with Charlie and his parents right now? If my parents knew what I am thinking today, not to mention Reverend Dobbson, they would all have a stroke!

The Mass concluded to the harmonious strains of heavenly music. Justine and Katherine waited for the congregation to leave.

"I hope you didn't mind the long service," Justine whispered. "It's a feast day today, so it was a little more festive than other Sundays."

"Not at all, this was my first time at a Catholic service. To be honest, it's very much like our own, nearly word for word, in fact."

"Really? No wonder Grandmamma used to complain about how they changed it," Justine chuckled quietly. "She did not approve of all the changes brought about by Vatican II."

"That's the council that modernised your religion, right?"

"Yes. Some still believe we have become too modern, but actually, our faith itself has not changed. Well, looks like we can go now," Justine said as she turned around, "I can't stand it when the crowds push out the door."

As the interior of the church returned to a state of quiet cavernous tranquillity, Katherine's stomach gave a large rumble.

"Perhaps we should go eat lunch, I'm famished," Katherine replied with a suppressed laugh. She was glad *that* did not happen in the midst of the service!

Returning to the Galeries, they made their way to the café area on the top floor. The view over the rooftop of the Palais Garnier was a grand setting for lunch. It was a pity she had to bring up uncomfortable topics on her last day with Justine and confide Charlie's recent marriage proposal that had sent all their festivities askew, but she desperately wanted to hear her opinions, or any advice she had to give.

"Justine, you know I'm so glad we have this opportunity to be alone," Katherine began.

"Me too," Justine replied, "we just had to have a day away from the men."

"You don't know the half of it," Katherine continued. "I need to talk, and you're the only one I can turn to."

"Hmm, I thought something might be wrong, you didn't seem like yourself the other night. Well, here I am, tell me your troubles."

"It's about Charlie…. "

After she relayed the disastrous events of Christmas Eve in minute detail, Justine sat back in her chair.

"Oh my! That is a predicament! You poor thing …and you've had to stay with him and his parents after all that too. No wonder you looked out of sorts."

"It was so embarrassing! To make matters worse, he won't take the ring back. I don't want to lead him on, but I don't want to add insult to injury. It's easy to hurt him. I really don't know what to do."

"Well, if you want to send a definite message, you will have to return the ring, there's no way to avoid hurting someone at sometime or another."

"But I don't want to destroy the friendship we've had since childhood. I'm afraid this is going to be an 'all or nothing' situation, isn't it?" Katherine replied in dismay.

"Hmm, he could have a point about misplaced feelings."

"How can I be sure? I mean, how do you know when you're really in love?"

Justine thought for a moment before she answered.

"It's not easy to put into words, it's something that goes far beyond mutual attraction. I think the first signs are you can't wait to see him, even a quick 'hello' when passing will keep you going for the rest of the day. You can't wait to hear his voice, you keep an ear strained for the first ring of the telephone, and when it does, your heart gives a little flip hoping that it's him. You find yourself thinking about him all the time and musing 'I wonder what he's doing right now?' and 'Is he thinking about me?', little things like that."

"Are you sure that's not just a crush?" Katherine asked quizzically.

"Well, it begins like a crush, so the initial feelings are similar, but you know things are really getting serious when you start scribbling on a piece of note paper and find yourself adding his last name to yours to see how it would look, asking if you could ever get used to it! But seriously, when you finally start thinking about what it would be like to make a real commitment, to actually live and start a family with him, and find you like the idea, it's a sure thing. That brings us to the ultimate test, when you are just waiting to hear him propose."

"I guess that settles it in my case," Katherine concluded, "I certainly didn't go through that list of wishful thinking, and didn't expect him to pop the big question."

"Well, make sure you're not in the earlier stages," Justine added, "just because Charlie was the only one ready for the proposal doesn't mean you aren't somewhere along the line. Maybe you have to wait for your feelings to catch up?"

"No, I'm pretty sure. I don't hang around waiting for him to call, and while I like being with Charlie, it's not like I pine away waiting for his next visit."

"Hmm, you'll have to fall in love at least once in your life, or Paris has failed to rub off on you," Justine replied with an impish pout.

"Some day maybe, but this isn't it I'm afraid," Katherine concluded.

Justine sat back in her chair, pausing for moment.

"You know, there just might be another way to fix things, if you can't say 'yes' to the proposal, but don't want to lose his friendship … ."

"Come on, I'm all ears. What do you have in mind?"

"Help him to fall in love with someone else, that should do the trick."

"I'm afraid that might be mission impossible," Katherine replied, shaking her head, "You didn't see the size of the ring, he's really serious. How could I accomplish that anyway? I'm not a matchmaker."

"Well, I don't know, it just seemed like the best solution."

"I appreciate the advice, if only it could be that easy … ."

They finished their lunch and continued their browsing through the Galeries before walking up and down *les grandes boulevards* amidst the city's bustle and stopping for coffee, chatting until the twilight descended. They reluctantly had to call it a day and concluded their farewells with a big hug before separating at the Metro station.

"Give my love to Martin and Maurice. The next time we meet will be in New York," Katherine declared.

"I can't wait," Justine replied, "have a safe journey home and keep in touch."

CS ❀ ∞

Her last few days in Paris passed in a blur, she lost all track of time. It was a pity she had to spend her last week cleaning, but no good deed goes unpunished. Her glorious winter wonderland was looking like a bad dream and she could not in good conscience leave it to the Kraylors or Lucille to clean up the mess. The holly and garlands were littering the floor with their shrivelled berries, and the wilting tree was too pitiable a sight to behold. The once apple-red roses were now drooping pathetically and had transformed into a dull reddish-black, while the water in the vases had turned an unusual shade of green and exuded a pungent swamp gas odour. The fireplace was an ashen, sooty mess that needed to be shovelled out, and if that was not bad enough, the tape player decided to chew up the holiday recordings into a mangled mass of black ribbons. In a strange way, it poignantly mirrored the disquieting conclusion to her dream holiday. The men helped with the bulky items, dragging the dying tree and bags of drying garlands to the bins, and cleaning out the fireplace, while the ladies concentrated on the vacuuming, dusting, and wrapping up the nativity scene, the remaining candles, baubles and velvet bows for storage. The work did not take long with everyone pitching in, but then they had their own packing to see to during the last couple of days. There was also a few last minute errands she had to accomplish, like wrapping up Gramp's picture. She definitely was going to need a day to sleep. As much as she loved Paris, Katherine was glad to be going home. There is no fireside like your own fireside.

Their morning flight to JFK was relatively uneventful. Katherine was relieved to have a separate seat away from the Kraylors, she had booked her ticket after they had made their flight reservations allowing her to co-ordinate the journey home with them, and therefore was not assigned a seat in close proximity. She looked out onto the runway as the aircraft left the ground, watching a few drops of water stream across the window. It was not long before they were swallowed up in a grey wintry mist, soon they would break through the clouds and be bathed in glorious sunlight. She could now relax with a book and block out all the anxiety of the past week and a half. Yes, it was good to be heading back to the old home turf, things might not seem as bad when in familiar, secure surroundings.

The flight landed in the morning hours, and just like Charles de Gaul, the airport was bustling with holiday travellers late for their flights or scrambling to make their connections back home. She could not wait to exit the arrivals door. As she eagerly anticipated, Pops had taken the morning off to pick her up with Mom beside him waving enthusiastically to catch her attention in all the commotion, and of course, Gramps had joined them to welcome the wanderer home. Steves was back at college, she would have to call him later, and she could not wait to see Suzy and catch up on all the art-school gossip, it had been over a quarter of a year since she last saw everyone, half a year in Suzy's case. Impulsively she abandoned her luggage cart to give everyone a double kiss to the cheek with her usual big hug, the French form of greeting had almost become second nature after her prolonged stay. It was so good to see them!

"How I missed you," she exclaimed.

"Well, how is our artist after the European Tour?" Pops asked, amused with her adopted French custom, not knowing which way to turn and ended up bumping cheeks instead. "Just brimming with new ideas I assume?"

"Oh, lots of ideas, I just don't know how practical or feasible they are yet. Just wait until I take out my notebooks and get all the film developed."

"We missed you too dear! Where are the Kraylors?" her mother asked, looking towards the arrivals doorway.

"They're waiting for one of their suitcases. I told them I would go on ahead to see if you had come and then wait for them out here."

They exchanged a split-second knowing glance. Yes, Mom did get my letter, I wonder what she thinks? What would she do in this situation? Judging from Pop and Gramp's jovial humour, they were not in the loop yet, Mom was keeping it strictly between them for the present.

"Tired of the Louvre yet?" Gramps wittily enquired.

"Not by a long shot," she replied, noticing the cane he prudently kept by his side. It was an elegant, shiny black ebony rod with an intricately embossed gold handle. As guilty as she felt over the accident with Jasper, Gramps looked quite the distinguished gentleman with his new ambulation accessory. "Hey, swift stick, Gramps."

"You like it? The guys at the Club got together and sprung for it as a get-well present. They couldn't see me stuck with some medical cattle-prod, and found this in an antique shop."

"That was thoughtful, I guess, if you don't mind receiving a cane as a gift."

"Honestly," Pops remarked, "I don't know whether they were trying to be funny, or were offering it in all seriousness. The shop owner told them it belonged to a well-to-do undertaker in the 1800s. It's quite the statement-making article though, isn't it?"

"Undertaker? It's fit for the opera, Pops. Speaking of the Louvre, I hope you like your picture, Gramps," she replied, pointing to a flat cardboard box perched precariously on top of her suitcases. "Some nice people at the local post office helped me wrap it up for travel."

"That's my girl. Always keeps her promises."

"I'm glad the luggage handlers didn't thump a crate or suitcase on in it. Oh, I have another surprise for you. I think we can forget doctor's orders today, let's hope they didn't get squished," she continued, pulling out a brown butter-stained paper bag from her hand luggage. He opened the unexpected parcel.

"Croissants! Real ones from France! You're a pet."

"Oh, Kathy," her mother *tsked* semi-disapprovingly with a little smile.

"I think he deserves a reprieve today, Mom. Look Gramps, there are some chocolate ones hiding in the bottom. I got them this morning, I hope they're still fresh."

"Don't worry, they'll taste good any way I can get them," Gramps assured her.

"I also got some dark chocolates for you Pops, and Mom, I found a box of those little marzipan fruits you like. I figured I dragged home enough Eiffel towers and other touristy souvenirs on my last trip."

"Oh, you didn't have to bring anything, Kathy dear," her mother replied, "especially after sending all those lovely gifts for Christmas. Here come the Kraylors. Over here!" she called.

Charlie and his father wheeled their cumbersome carts towards them followed by his mother. They looked cheerful, at least they appeared to look cheerful as they came to greet her parents, but it was difficult to read the actual mood of their little homecoming gathering.

"Hello Harold," Mr. Kraylor declared as he shook her father's hand.

"Welcome home, I hope everyone had a pleasant holiday," he cordially replied.

"Positively splendid," Mrs. Kraylor affirmed, "you should have seen how Kathy decorated the apartment for our arrival, it was absolutely beautiful."

"Unfortunately, live Christmas greenery is a frightful mess to clean up, I'm afraid I added some extra work on everyone when the holidays were over," she replied.

"I hope she was not too much trouble," Mom said.

Was she probing the situation? Making small talk or both?

"Nonsense! No trouble at all, only took a day or two to clear up with everyone pitching in, it was fun while it lasted," Mrs. Kraylor replied. Yeah, it was fun while it lasted. "We were very happy to have Kathy." Even after Christmas Eve? Katherine could not help but notice how quiet Charlie was.

"Thank you for letting me stay," she replied, her stomach tightening into a knot as she played along with the pleasantries. "I had a wonderful time."

While she did not want to be an ingrate, at this point, she was not completely appreciative of their offer now that it was obvious they had ulterior motives concerning her and Charlie. She had learned one important lesson, beware of favours and gifts offered from beyond the family circle, they could have a weighty string or two attached. She was resolved to be more careful in the future. This diplomatic act was driving her round the bend, how did politicians live everyday with the charade of people pleasing?

Maybe they loved living off their nerves like a seasoned poker-player addicted to the adrenaline of bluffing and wondering how long they can get away with it. Bluffing, such a nice term for deception, perhaps that is why there was an old saying that the devil would never refuse a game of cards, if she remembered her readings from Edgar Allen Poe correctly. Hmm, *bluff*, interesting word, also a cliff or precipice, lying always leads to a fall, the term was apropos then…. *Snap out of it!* Strange how quickly the mind wanders on to other topics to block unpleasant situations. She hoped they would not stand chatting for too long, things were uncomfortable enough already.

At last, Pops hinted it was time to go, expressing his concern over the traffic. As everyone said their goodbyes, the one awkward moment that Katherine was dreading to face had now arrived: how to say goodbye to Charlie. Knowing his feelings for her, she could not say 'Bye, call me later' or 'I'll see you soon,' as she always did as a friend, now the situation was far more delicate. Right now, she needed some time and space to think everything out. How do you say 'goodbye' at this point without making it sound like they would never see each other again? She did not want their friendship to end, but she did not know how to part without displaying that everything between them was different. Maybe she should let him say it first. The knot in her stomach grew tighter.

"Well …" he began.

"Well," she repeated, parrot fashion, hunting around in her mind for something intelligent and appropriate to say.

"Well, I guess I'll call you later …," he tentatively probed.

"Er…okay, then."

Stupid, stupid, stupid!

ෆ❀ෂ

It *was* good to be back home. Being away for so long, Oak Meadows felt new, and yet warmly familiar and satisfyingly comfortable. As they could get out of the car, Jasper bounded out from the back garden to greet them. Katherine was amazed at how large he had grown, she wondered if he would recognise her after all this time. Need she ask? She was greeted with a profusion of barks, hand-licking and tail-wagging. Entering the main house, Gramps gave Katherine a little demonstration of Jasper's newly acquired tricks, showing him roll over, play dead, 'heel', 'come' and 'fetch'. The obedience lessons had certainly paid off, but looking at Gramps with his cane, she thought it was a cruel irony that Jasper was now so handsomely trained after the accident. She was beginning to understand the wisdom of the old *clichés*, in this instance, the barn door was closed after the horse had bolted. She wondered why Mrs. Gonzales and Juanita did not meet them at the front steps, especially as they loved homecomings, but soon discovered the reason for their absence. They had their hands full accomplishing culinary wonders preparing a special lunch for the traveller. In the happy spirit of the occasion, Mrs. Gonzales let Gramps join in the cholesterol revelry much to his delight, not aware he had polished off a couple of croissants on the drive home. Jasper however, still mindful of Mrs. Gonzales' reprimands, obediently stayed out in the hallway, barely sliding his nose across the threshold to sniff the delightful aromas wafting their way towards him.

As the family tucked in to the culinary surprise, Katherine could not wait any longer and handed Gramps the parcelled canvas. Mrs. Gonzales went to get the scissors and then everyone crowded around as he carefully cut the cardboard box and unwrapped the masterpiece.

"Well, look at that," he declared with a beaming smile, "you put the gargoyles in too, what a nifty idea."

"I thought you might like that."

"It's a beauty, Katie."

"Certainly is," Pops agreed.

"How lovely, we should have it framed right away," Mom announced.

Katherine was delighted, she would have had it framed in Paris, but she wanted Gramps to pick out the frame he liked. Mom suggested she and Gramps could go on Monday to have it done and make a day of it while the cleaners bombarded the house. Katherine thought that was a great plan, she could also get her film developed while they were in town. Between courses, she excused herself to rummage through her suitcases looking for the goodies she had brought for everyone, and get her notebooks to share her gallery ideas and get their opinions. They agreed with many of her findings, particularly the concept of incorporating a community art program in the future. Her ideas on a coffee shop and small gift shop also gained her an applause for her good business sense, in time, and if it became feasible, she planned one area for a permanent art museum. Gramps was all for her warehouse conversion idea and stroked his chin as he pondered upon this prospect, while Pops commented on how well she had thought out the intricacies of the business end, even at this general stage. It was comforting to hear their approval and receive their enthusiastic encouragement.

With lunch over, Pops helped her upstairs with her suitcases before heading back to work while Gramps announced it was time for his constitutional with Jasper. Now that the men were out of the house, and Mrs. Gonzales and Juanita were kept busy in the kitchen, Mom suggested they take the opportunity to unpack her cases and stow them away. In other words, go upstairs while they had some privacy and talk over the urgent matter expressed in her letter.

"Kathy, I am so sorry you had to face all that on your own. Learning to handle these unexpected occasions is part of growing up. I admit, your father and I thought you and Charlie were perfect for each other. Are you absolutely positive about your feelings for him?" she asked as they unzipped and sorted the contents.

"I'm quite sure," Katherine replied, shaking out a skirt that was pitifully crushed by the interior luggage strap. "How could I be so stupid not to see how he felt? It's embarrassing when you think about it. There he was, planning on marriage, and all I thought about was a tennis match here or there, perhaps a trip to the movies every now and again as a friend. I mean, I felt no romantic attachment at all, and things are really uncomfortable now that I know how he feels."

"You did tell him how *you* felt?"

"Yes, at least we were honest with each other."

"It's sad things have worked out this way. You two have always been so close and seemed to share everything, it's one of the reasons I thought you would be happy together someday. So many marriages fall apart because couples fail to communicate."

"But the thought of marriage had not occurred to me, so where do we go from here? Like I wrote in my letter, he refused to take the ring back using the excuse it was my Christmas present, that makes it a sticky situation, and he is so easily hurt."

"May I see it, dear?"

"Of course, but I warn you, you may need your sunglasses," she replied with a note of wry humour to lighten the mood. She searched through her handbag where she had packed her jewellery and removed the little black box. Big troubles come in small packages, she thought.

"Oh my, it *is* stunning," her mother replied, sitting down on the edge of the bed, "I may just need those sunglasses, and here I was thinking you were exaggerating. Did you try it on?"

"What? Are you serious? I can barely look at the box. It reminds me of how things will never be the same again."

"Oh, do go on dear, just this once."

Katherine reluctantly sat down beside her and took the ring out of its velvet cushion. She slowly slipped it on her finger, a perfect fit. They gazed at it in silence for a few minutes, Katherine turning her hand slightly to the left and the right, the diamond sparkled miniature rainbows and the emeralds flashed with a blue-green fire. She slipped it off and returned it to its casing, closing the lid with a muffled *snick*.

"Hmm. Well, there's no easy solution to this turn of events," her mother agreed, "I understand you wish to return the ring, and that would be the correct thing to do, but if he insists you keep it, you'll have to wait awhile and see what happens."

"But, I feel so ... so ... *mercenary* doing that! I can just imagine what his parents are thinking."

"Remember, we explained to you many times, you can't help what people think, and if Charlie would be happier knowing you had it, it's his decision. This is another instance where you may have to humour him, for the present."

"Other than humouring him, keep it for what? I certainly can't wear the thing, it's a shame it will end up hidden in the back of my jewellery box."

"Well, if this is what he wants, what else can you do for now?"

"Yeah, I guess you're right. I just hope he does not misinterpret this and keep hoping I will give in and accept it eventually as an engagement ring. Like most men, he may take my 'no' as a 'maybe'."

"Since you were honest and told him your true feelings, it will be his fault if he allows false hope to linger. Look at it this way, if he truly loves you, he will respect your decision and not pressure you into something more than the friendship you have offered."

Katherine truly hoped that would be the case, but she could not deny a strange feeling of separation had invaded their time together. If facing difficulties like this on a daily basis was part of 'growing up', she wished she knew how to turn towards the second star on the right, and head straight on 'til morning.

After they had accomplished the unpacking and the suitcases deposited in the attic, Mom went downstairs while Katherine decided on a shower, hanging around airports and sitting for long stretches on aeroplanes always made her feel grungy. The hot shower did nothing to revive her, feeling the proverbial jet lag starting to set in, she succumbed to the inviting coverlets and fluffy pillows on her bed, just a quick nap and I'll feel better.

When she woke up, she found her surroundings enveloped in darkness, she could barely make out the wisp of light filtering through the window shades. Just for a brief moment, the darkness induced a feeling like

'Traveller's Disorientation'. Where am I? She fumbled towards the side table until her hand found the small digital clock, which had been accidentally turned the wrong way around during her unpacking. The familiar glowing numbers jolted her memory, *my* room … back home…oh, thank goodness! The electronic digits informed her she had slept until ten o'clock, well, nine to be correct, spring ahead, fall back, right? Her clock had not yet been changed to reflect standard time. Katherine could hear faint sounds coming from the dining room, judging from the hour, she had missed dinner, everyone must be finishing up by now. Obviously, they decided not to bother her and let her sleep. Turning on her bedside lamp, she got up and stretched before reaching for her robe, and sliding her feet into her slippers. She brushed her hair in a hurry, she did not want to miss all the conversation.

Tripping lightly down the stairs, nearly losing one of her slippers in the process, Katherine rushed into the dining room.

"Sorry everyone, I konked out."

"Well, well! Looks like Sleepy Head made it just in time," Gramps beamed, "couldn't miss dessert, huh kiddo?"

"You must have been tired, and it's sure great to have you home. We all missed you terribly," Suzy joined in.

"Didn't intend to sleep that long," Katherine replied, "it's so good to see you all."

"I thought it best not to wake you, dear," Mom explained, "you were looking rather tired."

"Thanks Mom, I guess I needed it. What's for dinner, I mean, what *was* for dinner?"

"Diet fare, what else?" Gramps replied, rolling his eyes with a bemused grin, "we're already back on sufferance rations."

"At least you didn't miss much, Kathy," Pops added.

"Oh Harold, be quiet," her Mom replied with a *tsk tsk* in her voice.

Katherine did not feel very hungry after her nap, but to please her mother, she picked at a plate of grilled chicken, catching up on all the family news while they ate dessert. Although they had tried to keep up their general good humour, complete with their teasing over the calorie famished fare, she noticed Pops and Gramps seemed a little more, what was it? Introspective? When the subject returned to her extended vacation, only Suzy brought up the uncomfortable topic of staying at the Kraylor's apartment with her innocent questions on everything about her trip, not in the loop of the current state of affairs, and Charlie. Mom obviously had a quiet word with Pops, who undoubtedly passed it on to Gramps, but they had not said anything to their adopted guest yet, leaving those details up to her. Katherine skirted the sad experiences and the disastrous ending to her trip, recounting the pleasant aspects that Suzy expected to hear. Eventually, she was able to move the conversation towards Suzy's time at college. Her friend, however, became confused with the sudden change of subject, am I missing something she thought? Were we not all waiting to hear the big announcement? If Suzy had guessed Charlie's intentions and expected to hear news of an engagement, Katherine realized she must have been dumb not to see what was coming. Imagine, even Suzy guessed what Charlie planned, and I hadn't a clue! *Idiot!* Well, I'm not up to explaining things to her right now, I'll handle that tomorrow or the day after when I've settled back into the familiar cosy rhythm of Oak Meadows, she decided.

∛❀√

The next morning Katherine strolled over to the apartment without having any particular plans for the day. An extra day of rest after her emotional ordeal, not to mention the trip, was not a bad idea, but moping around battling with the vivid memories of the humiliating Christmas fiasco and poor Charlie, morosely speculating about the gossip that would eventually circulate beyond earshot, was not a pleasant thought. Better stay busy with something practical, try to stay positive with a constructive project. Might as well *do* something while I fret everything out rather than aimlessly wringing my hands with all my woes, she decided. She remembered the contentious sketches on canvas that she had left unfinished. Apart from her gallery research, there was only one painting for Gramps to show for all those months away and she was restless to get back to serious brush work. Katherine entered the 'Studio' to find Suzy just settling down on the sitting room floor in front of the coffee table to begin drafting her latest assignment, a cost analysis report for an imaginary exhibition. Suzy had decided earlier that year, with the permission of her tutors, to opt out of her applied Master's program with its emphasis on drawing and painting for a graduate degree in arts administration. Katherine hauled an unfinished canvas from the closet and set it up on the easel.

"Good morning, how's everything going today?"

" 'Morning, Kathy, a bit scattered to say the least. I'm just catching up on a project I should have started earlier this week. Coffee is still hot if you want a cup."

"Thanks, but I've already had my fill. I guess it's time to get busy."

"I hope you don't mind, but I couldn't help myself and took a peek

234

at your new creation," Suzy admitted as she stopped to sharpen her pencil. "To be honest, I don't get it. I mean, the sketch is a little weird. Is a nuclear power plant to become the new image of high art?"

The puzzled look on her face made Katherine laugh.

"Wait until you see what I'm going to do with it! I haven't filled in all the details yet, I guess in this crude cartoon state it must look rather funny. I'm developing a thematic concept with the idea of visual contrast. I don't know how it will work out, but it should be interesting," Katherine explained as she stood back to eye the stark lines outlining the menacing electricity provider.

"Okay, now you've really got me curious, but I'll wait and see how the image develops. If I can understand it, then we can definitely say your experiment is a success. Darn, wish I didn't have this bookwork to do, I'd love to be painting, but a deadline is a deadline, and this bogus exhibition report has to be plotted on paper by Monday." Suzy's frustration showed as she briskly flipped her notebook open and began to jot down several figures related to the cost of hiring caterers to supply the expected champagne and petite appetisers. "Maybe if I stay with it this afternoon, I might be able to paint later tonight."

Katherine sympathized with her, what could be more unbearable for a person with an artistic temperament than having to repress the ardent impulse to create when called to obey the inexorable summons of duty, to carry out the repetitive routines of daily life, or be forced to deal with the unexpected furores that appeared from nowhere with guns blazing like an enemy ambush. Assignments had to be handled, but this piece of homework was no doubt a repugnant chore for Suzy. Although no words were spoken explaining her change of course, no words were needed. Katherine could easily guess it was not for love of the business-orientated subject, the reason was survival. The insecurity of wondering how she could live between collections, praying they would sell and worrying if she would make it at all, despite the promise of a showing in the new gallery when it eventually opened, was obviously too much of a strain. Settling for a regular job with a secure paycheque was an understandable concession for any artist. There were no guarantees of success. In all, Suzy had abandoned her dream and resolved to find an art-related day job. She could continue her painting as a sideline, when and if time permitted. How many talented and gifted people had to compromise their abilities and stifle their creativity? After all, they have to live. The world would never know, and it was the world's loss, and all because that was the way the world worked. Katherine knew she was blessed she could escape the burdens of financial constraints suffered by many young artists. It used to be enjoyable painting together, but today she felt somewhat guilty as she sketched with Suzy, how sad it was to see her friend compromise for security. It reminded her of a scene she once saw in a movie featuring a restaurant with an insatiable gourmand seated at table feasting while callously ignoring a hungry beggar standing outside with his mouth watering at the sight of the platters laden with bounty.

"Is it a tough report?"

"Not really, I just have to plan this event within a set budget, and I'm at a loss to know how to arrange for caterers. I know how to budget, but organizing anything past a plain balloon and ice-cream cake party is beyond me," Suzy admitted as she furiously rubbed out one row of numbers, "I'm basically making it up as I go."

"Uh oh, I wouldn't go down that road," Katherine warned with a light-hearted hesitation in her voice, "I have a feeling Professor Get-Your-Details-Right will see through that immediately."

Professor Adams, who taught the Arts Administration course and several of the arts history lectures at Belvedere, was a stickler for impeccable research and fact checking. He had a terrifying photographic memory indelibly seared with almost all the information contained in the art books of the college library and could spot a plagiarised line in their essays within a New York heartbeat. Additional information offered from footnotes gave the industrious student extra credit points, and everyone had learned to peruse his published works if they desired to pass his courses. Why he chose art for a career instead of mathematics or quantum physics was an inexplicable mystery.

"You're right. This is hopeless! How am I ever going to do a report that will earn *his* inspector's seal of approval?"

"Well, just think big and slightly more formal. What if this was a real exhibition? What would you do?"

"According to the assignment sheet, we have to plan for about fifty to eighty people. I'd have to call up places and get estimates, I guess."

"Hmm, this may not be as difficult as you think. Mom does this kind of thing all the time for her get-togethers, it shouldn't take too long to get the information."

Katherine put down her pencil and retrieved the phone book from the kitchen.

"We're not really going to hire caterers! How can we call up companies and not offer them a real job?" Suzy replied horrified at the idea. "Wouldn't that be a terrible thing to do? We would be wasting their time."

"Professor Details will be far more upset if you waste his, that's for sure," Katherine returned as she flipped through the Yellow Pages. "Looks like it's time to take a leaf out of Steve's book—no guts, no glory. Besides, they won't know the difference, just don't say the event is a fake. People ask for estimates about everything all the time, from baking to plumbing."

"You don't think we'll upset anyone?"

"It's not like we're Bart Simpson pestering Moe on the phone. It could be what Professor Adams had in mind, to get some actual experience in obtaining estimates. Aha!" she concluded, landing her finger on the C's. "Here we go. Okay, Suzy, get your notebook ready."

The startled look on Suzy's face promptly changed to amusement as Katherine called the first number at hand, introduced herself, and began asking the pertinent questions in relation to their services. Did they cater for small gatherings, cocktail parties and public exhibitions, a list of their regular menus, if they also supplied drinks and the waiters that would be needed. Suzy's pencil raced as she jotted down the details. She soon got into the swing of it, calling one caterer after another, gathering the information needed, including the cost of ice sculptures. The winged pegasus *did* sound absolutely fabulous.

"Why would you want that?" Katherine laughed as Suzy hung up the receiver. "This is supposed to be a small gallery exhibition, not a gala at the Met."

"Since I've kinda got the hang of it now, I'm not leaving any stone unturned. The Professor of Particulars is not going to be satisfied with the name of one affordable caterer, he's going to look for the process of elimination too."

"Right, good thinking. Why not give him a list of everything from the humble canapé to the finest ice sculptures your budget will allow? This should get you an A plus, or he's an implacable idiot."

"This is great, I'll have this assignment done by lunchtime. Thanks, Kathy."

"Sure, you're welcome."

"Hey, do you think Charlie will come by today?"

Katherine's stomach lurched. Those few hours sketching and gathering estimates had mercifully blocked out the persistent feelings of discomfort that plagued her, and now that one word, the simple mention of his name, made them all roll back with an appalling intensity. It was an experience that was becoming too familiar lately. Was this how an ulcer started?

"No, I don't think so," she replied, attempting to sound casual as she pencilled in the perspective lines for the gravestones to ornament the grounds of her allegorical Chernobyl. It was hard enough to concentrate knowing he would call eventually. She dreaded to hear his voice, unsure of what to expect, what to say. Perhaps he won't call? Was he still upset with her? The anxiety generated by this ambiguity was terrible.

"How stupid of me. You two have only just come home from your trip, it's probably too early for him to pop by yet."

"Probably."

Katherine continued sketching. This was getting tiring, all this pretending. Things just weren't the same anymore, *accept it!*

"I was expecting you to tell me all your news. You've been rather quiet, I thought you'd be all happy and excited when you came home."

"News? Not that I can think of off hand … ."

"Okay, if you're keeping secrets, I guess I understand," Suzy replied with resignation.

"I'm not sure what you mean. I really don't have anything special to relate."

"Oh, come on!" she teased, "don't pull my leg. Spending the holidays together in Paris? How romantic can you get? It would be the perfect setting. Besides, he seemed over the moon before he left with his folks," her voice then trailed off with her thoughts, "oh my, perhaps I was wrong … oh, I'm sorry to have brought it up, Kathy. I could have been mistaken … ."

Katherine sighed, it was time to face the music once and for all.

"No, you weren't mistaken, he did propose, if that's the big secret everyone seems to know about."

"But isn't that just wonderful?"

"I was completely taken by surprise," Katherine returned as she shook her head. "Indeed, Christmas turned out melodramatic to say the least. I never suspected what he had in mind, I was literally the last one to find out, can you believe it?"

Why did everyone automatically assume she would say 'yes'? Once more, she was obliged to relay the particulars of that awful evening and the ensuing aftermath, but at least it was out in the open, well almost. There was Steves to tell, she had no idea how he would react, and then there was Aunt Martha! By now, she probably had drafted a list of all the suitable venues to be considered for the rehearsal dinner, the reception, and the honeymoon destination, not to mention the first baby shower. Who can we count on to meddle in the planning of every important family occasion, Aunt Martha of course. This was just too surreal.

"Gosh, I guess we got it all wrong," Suzy mused. "Are you sure you've made the right decision? You both seemed so happy together."

"I'm pretty sure, I never thought of Charlie as anything but a very close friend, and I don't think my feelings for him can ever go deeper than that."

"Charlie must be devastated, this will not be easy for him to get over, but I know he will understand and respect your decision."

"I know, Suzy, and that's the really hard part. I wouldn't hurt him for the world, and now it can't be avoided."

"You both need some time to let things blow over and settle down, and then see what happens."

"It's just so … *hard!*" Katherine concluded, finding no adequate word to sum up the emotional complexity of her decision.

"Don't worry, I'm sure everything will work out. Come on, you need to clear your head, think of something positive," Suzy suggested, closing her notebook and making her way to the kitchen, Katherine followed. "A fresh pot of coffee might be in order, besides, it's close to lunchtime and we both could do with a break."

"I guess you're right, I'll worry about it tomorrow. I have so many things on my mind."

"That's the spirit. Have you thought about a location for the gallery yet? The ideas you shared with us last night are very impressive, sounds like you've done your homework."

"Actually, I *have* thought about a couple of spots. Since I'm considering the warehouse conversion plan, the SoHo district is the place to investigate, or perhaps Chelsea, I hear galleries are starting to move there."

"Cool!" Susanna enthusiastically replied, "a real upmarket address for a gallery."

"Sounds right, one problem, there may not be a warehouse left for remodelling, no bargains on offer," Katherine mused as she rummaged through the refrigerator in the hunt for sandwich ingredients, "developers have moved in big time, and it's not going to be cheap to buy there now. How about ham and cheese?"

"Okay, but I'm outta mayo, and I've only got hot-dog buns. Why not buy someplace already fixed up? Like the commercial premises on a ground floor?"

"No problem, I'll run over to the main house and get some mayo and bread. I could actually, browse around real estate agents and see what's on offer … hmm. It would be a start. Yeah, SoHo or Chelsea, they're certainly the ideal spots."

"Hey, you expecting company today?"

"No, *I'm* not," Katherine looked out the kitchen window to see Jasper racing down the driveway barking at a strange grey car at the gates. "Could be someone looking for Gramps, or Mrs. G. is having something delivered. Hang on, how do they know the security code?" The large gates swung open, and a curious metallic vehicle cruised up to the house.

"That's odd, I feel I've seen that car before," Suzy thought aloud.

"Oh my gosh! It's Steves!" Katherine burst out with delight. "What's he doing home now?"

The friends scrambled down the apartment steps to the driveway. The car door lifted majestically in the air like a wing, revealing a chuffed Steven eager to show off his new acquisition in all its brushed stainless steel glory.

"Hi Kats! Hi Suz! So, what do ya think? Isn't she a be-*yout*?"

Katherine burst out laughing, "Hey, it's an alien! Shoot it!"

"All hail McFly!" Suzy joined in.

"Ha, ha very funny you two," Steves replied, amused by the reception. "Hey Jasper, yuck, stop slobbering on me."

"I heard you were going to buy a silver Porshe, but a DeLorean!"

"Oh, I got the Porshe," Steves declared with a flourish, "didn't you see it in the garage? Hey, I've been waiting for this prize for yonkers. I had a few classic car dealers keep an eye open, and at the first hint an '81 DMC-12 was available for sale, I told them to nab it," he explained.

"Cool!" Suzy replied.

"Isn't it? I was thinking of getting personalized plates. '*mytime*' sounds pretty good, or maybe '*timeless*', it might fit if I drop an 's', or lose the first 'e' and change the 'i' for a 'y'."

"But what are you doing home?" Katherine asked, "you should be at college, Mom and Pops are going to go ape."

"Relax, I took an early flight this morning and will fly back tomorrow night. Things are only getting back into the swing of things after the holidays, and I don't have to be at college on the weekends. Besides, can't I surprise my big sister with a visit?" he rakishly concluded as she gave him a hug.

"Somehow, I think your new car has more to do with your unexpected presence than my return home, but I am glad to see you. Come on, we were just about to get some lunch. Perhaps we can try out your new zoom buggy afterwards."

"Sure thing. Too bad it doesn't have a flux capacitor, it would be fun to tour a few centuries while we were at it and be back in time for dinner."

Unfortunately, the promised ride had to be postponed as another car pulled up, it was Aunt Martha who had come just in time for lunch to quiz Katherine on her trip to Paris, she had been starved for gossip. While Mrs. Gonzales quickly prepared something more substantial than their customary sandwiches, Katherine finally broke the news.

"Oh Kathy, I'm devastated! We were all looking forward to a big wedding! How could you possibly turn down *Charlie?*" Aunt Martha lamented. "Be careful you don't end up an old maid."

"Well, that's that. I guess no free legal advice for us after all," Steves added.

"Must you turn everything into a joke?" Aunt Martha retorted.

"Hey, losing free legal advice is no joke, considering the fees attorneys fleece us with these days," he replied in a rascally tone. Steves loved to wind up Aunt Martha at every possible opportunity, the effect was quite comical as she grew more flustered with his devil-may-care flippancy.

"I'll have you know, this is a serious matter, young man!"

"It certainly is, a lawyer in the family would have been a great asset."

"Oh, you're incorrigible!"

"Well, I just can't help it."

"I'm sorry to have disappointed you all," Katherine interjected, "but it just wouldn't have worked."

"Listen sis, you don't have to explain, it's your life and your decision," Steves consoled, putting all joking aside. "Don't let anyone pressure you into something you're not ready for."

"I agree," Suzy added, "perhaps it's too soon."

"Besides," Steves continued, "I don't know why everyone expected to hear wedding bells at this point when you've been talking about setting up a gallery for ages. Obviously your plans were taking you elsewhere."

Steves was correct, she had not yet launched her career and already people were expecting her to 'settle down'. What an odd perception people entertained for women, she thought. Why did she have to marry to be regarded as 'settled'? Didn't a career require a sound sense of duty and emotional stability? Just because her interest lay in art did not mean she was a ditzy flake, at least she hoped not, and running a gallery would certainly demand that she be a 'settled' individual. Steves, who had heard enough sermons on taking his responsibilities seriously, seemed to understand, and for once, she was thankful for his input despite his tendency to make light of everything. At least he prevented Aunt Martha from prying deeper into a sensitive issue, but now he became the target.

"And who brought you home from Boston this weekend, young man? Don't tell me you have a new girlfriend with a flashy sports car? I saw it parked in the driveway, I wondered who it could be."

"You've got that right, and her name is DeLorean … ."

"What makes you think you can advise your sister when you can't stick to anyone yourself, leading a wanton lifestyle. And that nice girl Jennifer I met at Katherine's graduation, whatever must she think of you, not to mention us?"

Katherine burst out laughing, Suzy tried not to react, the conversation was becoming more bizarre by the minute. Poor Aunt Martha. Thankfully, Helen just arrived home from her bridge club meeting.

"Hello everyone. Steven! What are you doing home?"

"Hi Mom, just making a surprise visit."

"I can see that, dear. I hope that's all it is. You haven't been suspended have you?"

"Gee, it's nice to see you too," he replied with a sigh.

"Helen, what do you think of Steve's new girlfriend?" Aunt Martha queried, the usual greetings suspended as she probed the depths of this new piece of information, calculating the smirch her nephew had managed to inflict upon their honour, again.

"A new girlfriend? You must be mistaken, Steves hasn't mentioned anything to me."

"I heard it from him myself, her name is Delores," Aunt Martha asserted.

"*DeLorean*," Steves calmly corrected her.

"Delores, Delorean, whatever," she sniffed, "it's such a pity, I so liked that Jennifer."

Katherine and Suzy broke into peals of laughter.

"Delorean? For heaven's sake Steven, stop teasing your aunt. Martha, when are you going to wise up, you know what he's like. He really tests our patience at times. Honestly, I don't know who in the family he takes after."

"Great, thanks Mom, I'm just chopped liver around here," he interjected, rolling his eyes.

"Whatever has he been talking about then?" Martha said, looking perplexed.

"Goodness Martha, he's talking about a *car*, obviously the one parked outside. By the way, will you be staying for dinner dear? That reminds me, I must go and see Mrs. Gonzales." One problem now eliminated, it was time to tackle more important business at hand.

Steve's unexpected stopover certainly helped to make the weekend more enjoyable. The mood in the house brightened for that brief period the family could be together, although Harold did not appreciate the spendthrift ways of his son, hoping his recent transaction of the DeLorean in the midst of a recession was not indicative of his acumen in business. Buying this expensive vehicle in addition to the new Porsche was in Harold's view over the top, especially a ten-year-old stainless-steel rarity made by a company that went bust in a few short years. How could he waste his time and maintain a car that was now defunct? While a frustrated Steven tried to explain it was a modern-day collector's piece and well worth the money and attention, Gramps came to the rescue.

"Leave him be, son. It's only an extra car, it won't break the bank. He'll figure it out eventually, that's what the trust fund is all about. Overall, he seems to be handling things better than I expected."

In fact, unknown to the family, Steves *had* figured out a thing or two, investing in the stock market. In junior high he started small with his weekly allowance, dabbling in the penny shares before progressing to the big guy's turf. In those early apprenticeship years he had quickly grasped the basics and what to watch out for, speculate a little, but don't get bitten by that speculation bug. He played it safe, secure stocks with steady growth for the long haul, not much gambling for him. He opted for the prudent strategy of the waiting game, now using most of the interest from his trust fund to pick up stocks issued by secure companies when the price was right, or once in a while taking a chance on getting in on the ground level of a promising new market. What a stroke of luck, picking up those MS shares in the early days! Later he planned to continue building up his stocks using the profits earned just from the dividends and let his interest accumulate again. He had a gut feeling cell phones were going to rocket skywards in the not too distant future, not to mention the Internet now that the World Wide Web had been introduced, the possibilities for mail-order marketing alone would be endless. Gramps was right, one extra car in the garage and a few extra flights home were no reason to file for Chapter 11.

Despite Pop's ruffled feathers, Katherine could not help but enjoy Steve's new toy. It was fun to cruise the highway with him after Sunday service despite the gloomy winter weather, cracking jokes about avoiding all bazooka-wielding terrorists and to stick to the legal speed limits lest they be tempted to punch it into 'time travel mode' at eighty-eight miles per hour. The reception from their fellow motorists was also entertaining, some drivers took a double-take as they passed, while children in back seats pressed their noses to the windows pointing or waving energetically at them.

There was one tense moment when a motorcycle cop cruised up beside them while they were in a double lane and motioned at Steves who promptly rolled down his window. Were they being pulled over?

"Hey kid, you wouldn't mind driving into the next season and find out if the Yankees are ever going to shape up?"

"Sorry officer, no can do, I'm fresh out of plutonium," Steves laughed.

The cop smiled, gave a quick salute, and turning on the sirens went in pursuit of a driver who was not paying attention to their speedometer. That was the first time she ever saw a patrol officer in a good mood. What a pity Steves had to return to college so soon, now life would slip back into the usual mundane routine. Although she looked forward to spending Monday morning out with Gramps, their planned trip to the framers seemed to pale in comparison with a joy ride in the DeLorean.

೫❀೪

She was surprised when Gramps offered to drive the following day. Since his retirement he left that chore to the 'whippersnappers' whenever possible, and considering his hip, she had automatically expected to be the designated driver. Obviously, he had important business to take care of as he announced he had a stop to make before they went to the framers and hoped she would not mind a drive into the city. Dressed in a crisp business jacket and slacks, no doubt he was going to drop by the company offices, just to keep them on their toes, he continued to hold a significant portion of Walsingham stocks. Retirement was all well and good, but who really retires? Good thing she dressed in something appropriate for the city, we can surprise Pops, it had been ages since she was in Manhattan, perhaps if he was free, they could take him out to lunch. However, the executive offices were not on Gramp's agenda today she noticed. *Drat*, we must be heading to the plant in Williamsburg, she disliked the chemical labs, the odour always seemed to linger long after she left. Whoops, wrong again she thought as they turned for the Manhattan instead of the Williamsburg Bridge. After crossing the East River they drove into an area she was not familiar with and pulled up outside a commercial building, an old Victorian-style industrial edifice that had been converted into a textile unit, a cotton T-shirt and undergarment factory with an outlet store on the ground floor.

"So, what do you think?" he enquired as they stood in front.

She eyed the gawky mannequins modelling the gamut of articles produced by the establishment in a variety of colours, patterns and poses,

244

the large plate glass windows emblazoned with large glaring 'Sale' signs.

"Umm … that's interesting… ."

Katherine was not sure what to say, Gramps had a quirky sense of humour similar to Steves and she suspected he was throwing her a trick question. This could be an oddball shopping trip, maybe he actually lost a few pounds and his unmentionables had to be replaced. She knew he liked to find bargains, but if he needed new underwear, did they have to drive all the way to the outskirts of Brooklyn to buy it on sale? What a strange occasion to get all dressed up for.

"So, is that it? Just 'interesting'?" he returned with a 'hrumph'.

"I can't see you wearing this stuff, but that doesn't look too bad," she replied, indicating a mannequin sporting a T-shirt with matching boxers covered with yellow smiley faces. If he was playing a joke on her, at least she could try to join in the fun.

"What?" He started to laugh. "I think you've just made my day. You think we drove this far just to buy my skivvies? I wasn't talking about the merchandise, think big," he hinted, still chuckling.

She paused for a few moments.

"You mean the shop?" she queried.

"You're getting warmer, kiddo."

It then sunk in, he meant the building.

"Hey, this isn't one of the old warehouses you fixed up all those years ago?"

"Sure is."

So they were looking in on some property, she did not know Gramp's held on to anything in this neck of the woods. She was young at the time Walsingham Industries went into a major expansion program and was only vaguely aware of the details, usually the men in the family kept track of these things. The firm moved out of their old factories and distribution warehouses for larger modern plants in Williamsburg and several international zones like Mexico and Jakarta where production costs were cheaper. Most of the older properties were sold off, but Gramps was a sentimental 'old coot' despite his better business judgement, some of these relics dated from his grand father and father's time, and he could not let them all go, turning a few sites into apartment buildings when the opportunity arose, leasing others out to smaller industries as in the case of this undergarment factory they were now observing.

"Too bad it turned out this recession hit them hard," Gramps began to explain, "they relied too much on credit to run their business, and since several of the orders they received have been cancelled, they can't pay off their debts and are now forced to declare bankruptcy. To make a long story short, they won't be renewing their lease."

"That means you'll be stuck with an empty building bringing nothing in but costing you taxes and a load of other things, right?"

"Yes, it's one of the headaches of owning property. I'm too old to worry about such nonsense now, and your father and uncle are too busy with the company to bother about my little projects. They are tied up enough as it is, and I don't plan on looking for another tenant."

"You're thinking of selling this place then," she deduced.

"Actually, I'm going to give it away."

"What? Are you *nuts*? Why would you do something like that?" she replied, disbelief ringing in her voice. "You're obviously having a senior moment. The property must be worth a lot of money."

"You really think so, Katie? That's a pity, means I'll have to make you pay for it then," he teased with a twinkle in his eye.

The light dawned—Gramps was offering her the entire edifice for her future gallery. She was thunderstruck, and it obviously showed in her expression as he replied with a belly laugh.

"By Jove, I believe she finally got it! Well, *now* what do you think of the place? All joking aside, I would never expect my granddaughter to pay for any of the family property. Of course, I realize you may have another location in mind, but I'd be delighted to say it's all yours if you want it, my dear. Naturally we would have to see to the paperwork and all that annoying tripe to make it official … ."

"Gramps, I don't know what to say! I'm overwhelmed by your generosity, but I just can't accept a whole building like this for nothing! It wouldn't be right … ."

"Stuff and nonsense," he insisted.

"No, I'm serious Gramps, you've got to let me pay, maybe you could give me a discount."

"Now Katie, no arguments. Look at it this way, if you accept my offer, I may not be doing you a favour, the whole place needs to be refitted and brought up to code again, which will be enough of a headache, so you're going to need your dough to fix it up and deck it out properly. Besides, how can I charge family for this real estate? I'll have you know this is where all our fortunes began."

"You're kidding."

"Nope, this is the original building, the first foothold of our pharmaceutical empire, although technically speaking it didn't start out that way," he declared, putting an arm around her shoulder as they continued to view the building, considering its future prospects.

"I can't believe you want to give it to me," she replied, giving him a big hug. "How can I ever thank you?"

"Don't worry, I'll think of something, and you're welcome. Come on, let's get a cup of coffee and we'll talk it over before we go to the framers. Maybe we can drag your father away from the office later and grab a bite to eat somewhere."

"Okay," she replied as they turned and walked towards the car, "but it's my treat today, although that seems such a poor exchange for a present of this magnitude."

"Never you mind, pet. Just imagine," he chuckled, "one day you'll be able to tell your grandchildren you got the cornerstone of the family business for the price of a lunch."

"Now you're being silly, Gramps."

Over steaming cups of cappuccino the origin of Walsingham Industries was finally revealed, not that she was completely ignorant of the history having heard it umpteen times before, it was only now she truly began to appreciate the finer details that as a child she used to let slide from her memory when those old tales repeated by the elders did not seem that important. She found herself hanging on Gramp's words, more attentive this time around.

The family enterprise commenced as a humble cardboard and paper factory nestled amidst other factories and foundries manufacturing machinery, roasting coffee, refining sugar, bottling varnish, cobbling shoes, weaving Brillo pads and a multitude of other household or industrial goods. The story went that her great grandfather had fallen seriously ill, and receiving no relief from the concoctions prescribed by an incompetent doctor, swore he would never again place his faith in the medical profession, or, risk falling into the hands of another quack whose sole interest was in turning a profit on people's ignorance and trust. Knowledge was power, and he literally took to heart the old proverb, physician heal thyself. What the malady was no one could remember, or the nature of the dubious cure for that matter, but grave enough to cause great grandfather to enter medical school on a part time basis solely for his personal enlightenment regarding that mysterious world of compounds and potions. Considering he never intended to practise as a physician, his sheer determination, or perhaps his alarming brush with death, had sparked a driving obsession to master the art of healing, a compulsion that enabled him to complete his studies while continuing to run a demanding manufacturing business. He became fascinated with the discoveries made by Pasteur in the field of fermentation and the new science of microbiology, the French chemist's recent development of a rabies vaccine was considered a miracle. Without Pasteur's findings on the unseen organic intruders that caused infection, Dr. Lister would never have made his breakthroughs in antisepsis. To this day, the library at Oak Meadows could testify to great grandfather's academic zeal, certain shelves groaned under the weight of the medical books he had collected, old and new. It was obvious he had achieved his goal, although death itself was inevitable, never again would his health be left to the mercy of a quack.

A friend he met at the school encouraged his zealous interest beyond a mere scholarly pastime, channelling his energies in a more productive direction. This friend pointed out the travesty of a highly educated man not putting his vast knowledge into practise, he was wrapping the knowledge he acquired in the proverbial handkerchief and doing nothing with it. How could he abandon it all? The illness that nearly killed him and changed the direction of his life was no doubt Providential, he was duty-bound to serve mankind and help others. This pronouncement struck him deeply, an acquaintance merely enjoys your company, a fair-weather companion flatters when all is well, a true friend has your best interests at heart and the pluck to tell you what you need to hear. Yes, he was correct. It was one thing to improve the intellect and acquire knowledge for pleasure, it was an entirely different matter to obtain medical credentials and accomplish nothing with them. Certainly, he could do more with his life than produce packing material, and with so many illnesses around, he could not stand idly by. He may not be inclined towards general practise as a doctor, but given half a chance he could do wonders in the world of pharmaceuticals. He experimented with various combinations of traditional drugs and medicinal herbs on the top floor of the factory after company hours, prescribing his medicines to family members and a close circle of friends in the beginning. The positive results of his remedies spread and in time, he became renowned for his painkillers, cough elixirs and indigestion powders. They may not have been the latest miracle vaccines, but it was a start, and when he realized the potential his packaging plant presented for his remedial creations, the sky was the limit.

Of course, this was probably a romantic retelling of the story, gradually ascending to the realm of idealism as it was handed down. Looking back, it was more than likely great grandfather had planned to expand the business from the onset, deciding it was high time to seek new horizons. The family company was suffering from the heated rivalry with another factory that had quickly dominated the area. The competitor, a certain Mr. Gair, had a fortunate mishap when filling an order for seed bags, the mechanical paper-creaser slipped during production, simultaneously folding and slicing the wrapper with the result the faulty bag became the prototype for the pre-cut cardboard box. Gair's empire quickly grew with his new discovery that revolutionized the packing industry, his name becoming synonymous with the area as he expanded throughout the district. How could great grandfather compete with that? Produce another product, that was the answer, but what to produce was the next problem. He tried to think of a new cardboard creation that could outdo Gair's invention, but was getting nowhere until he realized he had to think inside the box for once, he could produce something to fill his packages and sell this new merchandise at reasonable prices since he could wrap and print for less, thus eliminating a middleman operation in the process. Conceivably this was the reason he entered medical school, to acquire expertise in the field of medicinal ingredients and the qualifications to work with them. However, no one could dismiss the patriarch's philanthropic motives regarding his medical research considering his descendants continued to uphold the conservative principles of his business contrary to the liberal trends of the world. Perhaps there was an element of truth to both renditions of their family corporate history, with the passage of time, it was now hard to tell.

Gramps was definitely making his offer a little difficult to turn down. How could she, the third generation, say 'no thanks', refusing to accept a building that literally was the bedrock of all their family's industry? He knew she was the right person to hand it on to for a number of reasons. First and foremost, he wanted to make her the first offer since she was the eldest grandchild. He also knew that like him, she would want this venerable old edifice kept within the family for she was the sentimental one where hearth and home were concerned. He had come to accept that no matter who inherited the business, the heart of the manufacturing and executive branches of the company were now planted firmly elsewhere. Furthermore, his other grandchildren had chosen careers where they would have little need of this particular piece of property, while she on the other hand had expressed the possibility of investing in conversion space. Who else in the family but Kathy would be interested or had the time to maintain the old place? She treasured the historical links handed down from the olden days, everything was working out perfectly in his view.

Katherine did not want to disappoint Gramps, but there were other details to consider before she could formally accept his generous gift. Just because it was prime real estate for a renovation project did not mean it was gallery material. As with all businesses, location was everything, but in the visual world of art, image and first impressions were of equal, if not paramount, importance. In this particular case, there was a double dilemma. No longer was the neighbourhood called Gairsville in honour of the rival cardboard company, or Fulton Landing after the local pier, or Rapaile after the family who originally owned the land, or Olympia or Walentasville. A relatively new custom of referring to their districts by their acronyms had become trendy, and unlike other neighbourhoods whose shortened appellations had a stylish ring like 'SoHo' for South Houston or 'TriBeCa' for Triangle Below Canal Street, this district, known as Down Under the Manhattan Bridge Overpass, was stuck with the unfortunate contraction— Dumbo. She hoped it was not a sign of snobbery, but she had set her heart on SoHo or Chelsea in Manhattan and could not imagine a business card bearing the elegant title 'Walsingham Gallery' toting 'Dumbo Brooklyn 11201' in the address line. The name was catchy to be sure, but for all the wrong reasons. For one thing, customers might find it hard to take a location or business seriously that made them think of flying baby elephants, clowns and circus tents.

Gramps had to agree that the address was humorous to say the least, but may not be the mark of Cain she feared it to be. In contrast to the other city acronyms that had been assigned by developers, this district was named by a group of artists and locals determined to discourage contractors from overrunning the area and rendering it unaffordable. A construction company was trying to take credit for the name, but the locals were stoutly defending the title as their own invention. Katherine wondered where Gramps was leading with this piece of information, she was not ignorant of the 'gentrification cycle' of the city. It was common knowledge that whenever the urban bohemians discovered cheap lofts in abandoned warehouses to live and work in, the developers usually followed when the next generation of creative geniuses had succeeded in stamping an area as a fashionable 'art district'. The old warehouses that were too costly to convert were doomed to destruction to make room for new apartment blocks and industrial units with inflated prices, forcing the artist-tenants out of the community to cheaper pastures. She could understand their point of view, but in this case, the artists had not only discouraged developers by branding the area with a daft title, they risked dissuading prospective gallery owners from considering the area who might actually promote their work.

Gramps had to argue the contrary, she was not viewing things in their proper perspective, the local grievance with developers had designated this area as an artistic zone, it was the publicity of a lifetime. He was sure there was a lot of history attached to the place that he was not aware of, but they could find out. As it turned out, one of the waitresses was only too happy to fill in some details. Thomas Paine once lived on the corner of Sands and Fulton, and the French diplomat Talleyrand also lived here at one time. Of course, they must not forget the old Fulton Ferry crossing was immortalized by Whitman in his poetic epic of America, *Leaves of Grass*, not to mention the first edition was printed in Fulton Street. In fact, Katherine had overlooked that piece of literary trivia. A customer at the next table overhearing their conversation asked to be excused for eavesdropping and offered his two-cents worth. There were already excellent artistic establishments and attractions located here, the Brooklyn Arts Council, the first co-operative for women artists at the AIR Gallery, and the St. Ann's Warehouse theatrical enterprise. Don't forget Bargemusic on the old ferry landing, the waitress interjected, that was a real gem, an old coffee barge completely restored and used as a venue for classical chamber music concerts.

There are other advantages to this location Gramps continued, it was not yet registered as a historic district. How long that was going to last he could not be sure, so now was the time to make an overhaul of the building before the regulators tightened all the legalities. It would be difficult to alter even the interior if it was earmarked for preservation, which could happen, the original factory was built in the late 1880s after all. The man at the next table seemed delighted with that piece of news, it was one of the old wooden beam factories then, which pre-dated the reinforced concrete and steel buildings constructed at the turn of the century. He hoped she would consider the area and help to preserve a piece of their local history, too many sites in the city were falling to the ravages of progress. If more people would come and restore the area, it would be well on the way to becoming a designated historic district. Gramps was delighted with the encouragement the locals gave her and declared those other snappy addresses may be fine and dandy, but nobody could forget Dumbo, it was down to earth and made people smile. Everyone had grown quite attached to the name, even strangers in New York knew exactly what part of the city everyone was referring to. What a real interesting challenge, to 'be' in on the ground floor of something and start out in an area that was just coming into its own.

Wow, she had to think on that for a moment, Gramps had struck a profound chord. He was right, she really wanted to 'be' part of something great, and not jump on someone else's bandwagon after they got the ball rolling. Gramps was giving her the opportunity to get in just at the right time and play an active part in a great urban transformation, to watch a neglected neighbourhood grow into a new cultural Mecca. Here, she could actually become a pioneer of sorts, a new enterprise where her great grandfather started all those years ago. The idea was beginning to be exciting. After they finished their coffee, she asked Gramps to drive her around once more, she was sorry they did not stay longer and take a closer look at the building earlier. The area did have an attractive character of its own, not quite the glassy manicured look of Manhattan, nor the old brownstone hue of Brooklyn, yet it did have an old world ambience with its antique factories surrounded by streets lined with vanishing train tracks set in quaint Belgian block cobblestones half-patched with asphalt. In certain streets, there were unique vistas of the Brooklyn Bridge tower on one end, and the Manhattan Bridge tower on the other. Many photographers flocked to the neighbourhood over the years, taking panoramic shots of the iconic suspension crossings and the soaring scrapers of downtown Manhattan. The area had a unique potential to become the next cultural icon of New York.

Bumping over the rickety cobbles and splashing through patched potholes, they pulled up outside the underwear factory a second time. Gramps suggested they could make a tour of the place, but Katherine declined for the present, taking a look at the exterior would be enough for now, she did not want to march around as the next prospective owner while all the workers inside were in trepidation over the inevitable loss of their jobs. There would be time enough when the lease ran out in a couple of months. In any case, the size of the brick building nearly took her breath away. It comprised five formidable stories situated on a corner that seemed to run forever down the side street, its rows of sashed windows with their brick arches virtually disappearing into the horizon. Walking down to the end to scout the dimensions, she discovered a semi-abandoned weed-ridden lot attached to the back of the property with an additional building, a sizeable old boiler house that once powered the turn-of-the-century machines. Well, at least she had a parking lot, that was one bonus, what to do with the boiler extension was another issue she would have to solve later. She studied the front and side once again, almost becoming mesmerized with the rows of dusty windows looking out upon the streets below like glazed uniform eyes. The front definitely needed a face-lift, the security shutters with their battered metallic boxes protruding over the display windows like bulbous eye-lids denigrated the look for one thing, while everything else appeared so long, tall and … red. Apart from the curved brick semicircles over these lifeless apertures, the old fashioned cornices lining the third story and roofline plus the round arches of the loading doors out back, the building had little going for it in the way of artistic features that would say to the passer-by, '*chic* gallery here', and, the rusty coloured bricks were looking tired from the city pollution. The fading mural ad dating from yesteryears painted down the side now rendered almost illegible by weathering did not help matters. She definitely had her work cut out if she intended to make the place look like something special—and this was only the exterior. The interior was another thing, but already she could tell the floor space was monolithic.

Gramps eventually talked her into browsing through the shop to get a feel for the place at least. The décor was as she expected for a factory outlet that had not been upgraded in decades. The walls that were painted white once upon a time had acquired a sad, smoky yellow patina, the only splashes of colour came from the merchandise displayed on battered old metal wall brackets and clothes racks. The ceiling was pathetic, she always loathed suspended grid panelling, and the hanging rectangular florescent light fixtures dangling from steel chains were simply too miserable to look at. All of this would have to go. She could only imagine what the factory setting behind the outlet looked like. To adapt the inside of this old workhorse and make it comfortable, appealing ... beautiful, without stripping it of the character it possessed, wherever that was, what would it take? She had many other things to consider, like the property tax ... and the insurance! Good grief, if it had a wooden structure like that man said, the fire insurance would be astronomical! Gee, what if rot had set in somewhere? New plumbing, fire sprinklers, electrical upgrade ... Gramps knew what he was talking about, this restoration project could actually deplete her trust fund, mortgages may be unavoidable if she wanted to hold on to some capital. At the end of it all, she would have to stock a gazillion paintings to fill the huge space plus sell an equal amount to keep it solvent, and to top all that, she had barely started to piece together a collection of her own. The handful of canvases in the closet at home now seemed like a raindrop in the ocean. She hoped Martin and Justine were feverishly painting like Trojans. The final blow came with the thought of the current recession, art sales usually dwindled in times of economic downturns. Would anyone come to browse let alone buy anything? Perhaps this was all happening at the wrong time. Her initial exhilaration began to settle into a heavy paralysing fear matching the leaden January sky as she realized the colossal task she would be assuming. It was one thing to plan a gallery on paper and imagine how the décor should look, it was another matter to face the sticks and stones of that dream and to reckon the costs before that vision could even approach the threshold of reality. Was she getting in over her head?

Having finished their tour, they made their way to the framers and

Katherine silently mulled over a thousand details as Gramps viewed the wide selection of samples.

"You've gone very quiet all of a sudden, young lady," he remarked, taking a scalloped frame joint off the wall and holding it to the corner of the painting.

"Sorry Gramps, there's so much to think about. I hope I'm not biting off more than I can chew. It's a lot bigger than I planned, and there's a lot of work to be done."

"Hmm, can't argue with you there. At least the roof is in good shape, just had it done a couple of years ago, so that's one thing taken care of. Everything else will have to be checked. There are some things that will have to be upgraded all at once, like the exterior to make it attractive, I saw how you eyed the place," he noted with a touch of humour, "then there are a number of inside jobs like the wiring, plumbing, fire sprinklers, modernise the heating and air conditioning, and replace the commercial elevator, that could be getting a little worse for wear by now, but you can work on the rest later. Don't try and do everything all at once."

"Like, decorate a couple of floors and expand later when I can," she thought aloud.

"Yes, something on that order. It will also give you a project to look forward to without loading yourself with debt. Take your time, don't try to renovate the building all at once, space yourself. Hey, what do you think of this one?"

"Um, I like the curly q's, but definitely too shiny."

This was one issue she was particular about, it was an odd thing, but after all that work, a picture could be enhanced or ruined depending on the frame.

"To be honest, it looks a bit modern."

"Hmm, you're right, this one over here might do the trick," he declared as he held up an antique reproduction with stylised acanthus festoons and volutes. "Ah yes, I like this one, suits the subject."

"I agree, it looks similar to those I saw in the art museums in Paris," she added.

"It was painted there after all, I think we have a winner then. Let's get this one and head off before it gets too late to pull your father away from the office, or we won't get a table."

Today Harold did not put up much of a fuss about joining them for lunch, it was a long time since his father had come to town, especially with Katherine present, he sensed something special was afoot. They went to their regular business-lunch haunt that had become an institution itself, the

21 Club. Gramps loved the place with its curious history and memorabilia collection, and although she had not been there often, Katherine had to admit it had a unique atmosphere, even if it did feel like an exclusive men's club catering to the 'big boys' of the city. Outside the guests were greeted by a strange combination of elegance and comedy, elegant black wrought iron railings and lamp posts, footmen in top hats, and a host of colourful vintage jockey statues presented to the establishment over the years by members of the equestrian set. The interior was equally bizarre with its mixture of stylish rooms in European décor or dark wood panelled walls set in contrast to the famous Bar Room with its red chequered table cloths and masses of period toys plus other Americana curiosities that were donated by various patrons, that for obvious reason, were suspended from the ceiling. Amidst the sports trophies and corporate logos, one item received particular veneration from the staff and regular patrons, a model of torpedo boat PT 109 presented by President Kennedy. The most curious of all the rooms was the cellar that they cleverly altered to conceal their sizable stash of alcohol during the Prohibition era, the Club originated as a speakeasy after all.

The Walsinghams contributed their fair share of collectables over the years from old medicine bottles to antique apothecary jars and packets of modern cough lozenges, all bearing witness to the evolution of their corporate insignias dating from the horse and buggy days to the advent of computers and jets. Celebrities from every walk of life patronized this establishment at one time or another, presidents, politicians, famous movies stars, directors, actors, authors, writers and artists, big business tycoons and Wall Street wizards, the very tables becoming synonymous with the distinguished individuals who frequented them. The place was brimming with amusing stories, Groucho Marx once ordered a single bean and then sent it back declaring it was undercooked. Colonel Sanders had the audacity to send out for his own Kentucky fried chicken and had it delivered to his table. Gramps liked the area that held the famous 'Bogie Corner' named after Humphrey Bogart, and was glad table thirty-two was available. In any case, they were always seated at the best spots as regulars were treated like royalty, their family had become a institution there as well. Big deals were signed and sealed on these tables over the years, including many decisions concerning their own family business. They were pleasantly surprised when Uncle Tim arrived as they were handed their menus, he was in the neighbourhood and decided to join them, after all, the office always knew where to find them.

"I'm glad you're here to get the news firsthand," Gramps declared,

"I've just offered Kathy the old place in Dumbo for her gallery."

"Really? That's something to celebrate," Uncle Tim replied, "that's great, I'm happy for you Kathy."

"You know Dad, I had forgotten about that place," Harold replied, "I thought you sold it ages ago when we expanded, it's an excellent idea if the area is suitable. Well Kathy, this is good news. Have you accepted it?"

"I haven't said 'no' yet," she replied, the myriad of challenges attached to the project continued to swirl in her heard, "there's so much to think about."

"I admit the place will be a handful," Uncle Tim agreed, "but it is a great opportunity. You know, it would be a shame if we let it go to an outsider, we should keep it in the family as long as we can."

"Yes, it would actually," her father agreed.

"I hope the family agrees with my decision," Gramps interjected, "I did think of all the kids, but Kathy is the only one with career plans that fit the building."

"You're right Pops, I'm pretty sure my kids wouldn't hang on to it, they'd fix it all right, but sell it off to the highest bidder," Uncle Tim admitted, "they've got their own agendas and probably wouldn't want to be bothered. Come to think of it, the place is perfect for an art gallery."

It was a relief to get her uncle's approval. Katherine did not want to be accused of being the favourite in the family or cause a feud between the cousins over a piece of property, that possibility had dawned on her. She wondered what Steves would think, she did not want anything to come between them, no matter how many times she threatened to throttle him for his stupid pranks.

"Do you think Steves will be okay with this, Pops?"

"I don't see why not," Harold noted, "Steven will probably come home to work in the company and take over the labs one day. He'll have too much on his plate to worry about a building across town. I'm sure he'll be happy for you."

"Then I guess Gramps has made me an offer I can't refuse," she replied, her heart pounding as she heard the words out loud. What was she saying? He only made the offer this morning, this is all happening too fast!

"It's settled then!" Gramps exclaimed, "waiter, a bottle of champagne, it's time to celebrate."

"Very good, sir."

"Champagne? Dad, we've got to go back to work," Uncle Tim protested.

"Don't listen to him. Bring on the steak and French fries, and top that off with Death by Chocolate and a double dollop of French ice cream," he continued before turning to everyone at the table, "and not a word of this to Helen or Mrs. Gonzales, I'm not celebrating on a diet."

"Do you ever plan to stick to it?" Harold calmly wondered while Uncle Tim suppressed a laugh.

It was strangely thrilling, Katherine felt as though she had been invited to join some secret inner sanctum as she savoured her first official business lunch in their company. She listened to their warnings about the pitfalls to avoid during the refurbishing process and locked within her memory bank all the advice they had to offer. When the check finally came Pops and Uncle Tim could not understand why she insisted on picking up the tab, but Gramps explained, "That's the deal." It was the most bizarre deal that had happened within those walls for a long time, the cornerstone of the multinational Walsingham empire was exchanged not for a few million but for a lunch at the 21 Club. Katherine was excited, speechless, ecstatic, sailing over the rainbow … and downright scared half to death.

ᘒ ❀ ᘔ

Everything seemed to turn upside down from that moment. In fact, the whole world seemed ready to explode the next day as the rumours of a possible war with Iraq had become a reality. The government quickly made preparations to launch Operation Desert Storm and liberate an occupied Kuwait with its hoard of black liquid currency that helped fuel the world economy. For weeks prior to the event, the news blared with special reports on this new threat to world peace and waxed thick with debate programs discussing the upcoming costs to the taxpayer, not to mention the repercussions of this latest confrontation.

The palpable apprehension in the world at large did not help to calm her jittery nerves, the word 'war' spread through the air like a malignant plaque, what strange timing! Business had its own battles and grim missions that had to be faced. Similar to the military, she now had costs to consider, but unlike the government, she could not rely on the taxpayers to cough up if she inadvertently got into financial difficulties. No wonder her stomach was knotting since lunch the day before, she was stepping out on a ledge and risking everything on an idea that could turn into a horrific failure. It was too late to back out now, all she could do was forge ahead. Her gallery *had to make it*, by the time it was ready for the grand opening, her trust fund would be a mere shadow of its former glory, if it still existed at all. Gramps wasted no time when it came to business and made arrangements for them to go into town that morning. Of all things, it was a Tuesday she wryly noted, Mardi in French, the day named after Mars the god of war. What was she told about coincidence?

The first formality was the transfer of deeds, not that this was unexpected, but there was an additional facet complicating the matter. All the legal requirements of the family were executed by Kraylor and Kraylor, and if one of the seniors did not handle the current transaction, she would finally have to face Charlie for the first time since they returned from Paris. The day would definitely be a strain to say the least, he had not called over the weekend as he promised, which was not like him. On the other hand, she was relieved, not knowing how they would overcome this hurdle and keep their friendship intact. Eventually they would have to span the invisible chasm that had abruptly opened between them or the breech would become irreparable, it was unfortunate they would have to meet within the diplomatic confines of a formal legal appointment.

It turned out as she suspected, Charlie was assigned the task, another surreal incident to add to her growing list. The secretary promptly showed them in.

"Hello Charlie, haven't seen you in awhile. How are you?" Gramps asked, launching straight into the pleasantries before getting down to business. His question was a matter of courtesy, but certainly more poignant than on other occasions, Katherine wondered how Charlie would react.

"Hi Mr. G.W., not too bad. Hello Kathy, it's good to see you both. So what's this I hear about a transfer of real estate?" Charlie asked, obviously deflecting his own discomfort by tackling the matter at hand, it was one diplomatic way of breaking the ice. At least Charlie looked interested and did not seem upset, he could deduce what the property was destined for and wanted to hear all the details.

While he motioned for them to sit at a separate and more comfortable seating area away from the main desk, Gramps obliged him with the same explanation he gave yesterday, it was too much work to maintain the old place for a man of his age and it was time to hand it on to a younger generation, telling him the history of the factory, allowing Katherine a few moments to take a quick glance or two around the new corner office. She had not seen the décor as she rarely bothered Charlie at work other than an occasional telephone call. The two interior walls facing the panoramic view of the city were papered in a soft royal blue and wainscoted with dark oak, blending the old with the new. The theme was carried through with period-style ceiling panels reproduced in a golden oak tone. His executive desk, a fabulous piece of workmanship, was positioned in the corner by the large windows, while decorative tables and stylish brass reading lamps with golden coloured shades were placed about the room, the floor was carpeted in a plush royal blue weave with round gold medallions in the pattern. The large honey-coloured leather sofa and matching armchairs in which they were now seated were comfortable and fit in perfectly with the surroundings. The combination of the various woods and the blues with creams and golden tones was simply luxuriant. She complimented him on his exquisite taste during a break in the conversation.

"I love how you've decorated your office, Charlie. It's really beautiful."

The words were out before she realized it, the inspiration for his colour scheme was drawn from the painting she had given him. The large seascape in its antique frame and illuminated from above by an elegant gallery lamp, held pride of place on the main wall, the blues of the sky and ocean combined with the golden sunshine and the oak trim of the crisp white yacht perfectly fit suited the graceful surroundings.

"Oh that's right, you haven't seen my new office until now." His eyes seemed to brighten for a moment, "Do you really like it?"

"Yes, very impressive. I bet your clients love to do business here, it's almost too comfortable for a work environment."

She did not quite know what to say, this one room revealed how much he truly cared for her. The entire room revolved around that one painting, even the odd puzzles, novelties and office curiosities she had given him over the years lay arranged on his desk and tables like so many priceless relics or precious collector's pieces.

"Yes, quite comfy," Gramps agreed as he settled back into the sofa, "wouldn't mind working here myself, if I hadn't retired."

"I'm sorry, would you like some coffee or tea?" Charlie offered. "I made the firm spring for a new machine, our brew has improved immensely since your last visit."

"Coffee sounds good to me," Gramps replied. Katherine nodded her head in agreement. Charlie paged the secretary for the desire coffee and some Danish pastry. Getting back to business he made the comment,

"So, the place is in Dumbo."

Was he trying to keep a straight face? Apparently, he could see the funny side picturing the *chic* gallery she had envisioned with that acronym for an address. Gramp's reaction to the suggestion of Danishes was also comical, morning pastries were another weakness. Sadly, joking with Charlie seemed difficult now, it was like giving him permission to assume things were back to normal. Thank heavens she had business to discuss, it made their first meeting a lot easier and kept things at a discreet distance.

"Yes, and it's really big too. Unfortunately, it's going to need a lot of improvements to transform it into a gallery."

"Well, I'm happy for you, Kathy. You've dreamed about this for ages, and it's finally becoming a reality."

"All thanks to Gramps, I didn't expect to be starting out this soon, or on such a large scale to tell the truth."

"Best to jump right in," Gramps noted, "all you young ones need is a push in the right direction to get you going. You'll be glad I did, Katie, no point planning and daydreaming, and doing nothing about it."

"Well, I guess we should not delay the wheels of artistic progress," Charlie replied, trying to make pleasant conversation. Since this would only be a transfer of deeds, explaining the legalities did not take long, in fact, Charlie said he could drop the papers by the house to be signed within a matter of days if that was all right with them, filing them would be no trouble. She wondered why they had to come by his office for so little at this stage if Charlie could take care of most of the formalities and deliver everything to them. Gramps could be crafty when he had more than one agenda in mind, he was not above resorting to ulterior motives when the occasion demanded it. Perhaps he was trying to get them back on speaking terms under neutral circumstances.

Katherine was not far wrong, Gramps, like everyone else, was disappointed how events had transpired in Paris. Similar to stepping out on a new business venture, young ones often needed a nudge in other areas too. He heartily approved of Charlie, he was a decent young man, one of the few if not the only suitable match he could imagine for his Katie. Quite the gentleman as a matter of fact, the Kraylors had to be commended for his upbringing. If she only knew that before Charlie joined her in Europe, he had made a special appointment with Harold and formally sought his permission before he made his proposal. Yes, she would be safe with Charlie, he would never purposely do anything to hurt her. Although she was not naïve, she still had a lot to learn about the ways of the world, sheltered by a caring family and the cushioned circumstances of her privileged upbringing. Entering the world of business, she would begin to see the fangs that life concealed from the inexperienced, especially a woman trying to make it on her own. During the difficult times that lay ahead, she would need someone to talk to, and as everyone knew, she could always share everything with Charlie. In time, she might be able to picture a future together with him. Although he appeared to be all concerned about business, Gramps too had noticed how Katherine's gift had influenced the surroundings, and hoped she would see in it a sign of how perfect they were for each other. He had the best intentions, but had no idea that the carefully arranged environment was actually working against his hopes.

Katherine's reaction was quite the opposite, it only confirmed her fears Charlie may continue to expect more from their friendship, sinking the invisible wedge lodged between them even deeper. The longer she stayed in his presence, the more she felt obliged to distance herself physically as well as emotionally in an attempt to spare him from entertaining any false hopes. How she wished she could return that wretched ring, but that would be impossible without cutting him to the very core. For now, it was best to maintain the status quo and keep things on an even keel. It was a relief that they did not stay long once the business arrangements were concluded, allowing her to retreat to the quiet world of paintwork and planning. She was getting overwhelmed by all the details she had to consider, and it was difficult knowing where to start.

Obviously, it would be necessary to consult with experts on the restoration, but until she could see the floor space available, she could not tell if the ideas she already had for a gallery would work. There was no point sketching interior designs until the building was vacated and cleared of the underwear. For the present, she had better produce some work and take each day as it comes. What else can I do? Nevertheless, she could not set the project completely aside as the ageing and banal façade of the exterior beleaguered her mind. When she was not concentrating on something that required a considerable amount of attentive energy, her thoughts irrevocably turned to the 'outside problem', working out a hundred and one ways to spruce up the massive lump of bricks and assuage the optical assault waged by the repetitive ranks of sashed windows. All that red, she needed to add some colour, green and white preferably, maybe she could add shutters, no…that would only make the windows worse. Great, that's all she needed, to make the place look like a chequerboard straight out of Salvadore Dali's nastiest nightmare. Well, large forest green awnings on the front windows wouldn't be a bad start, maybe green and white stripes, nah, better go with one colour, green is good. Yeah, a turn-of-the-century look, that would be the right thing to do. Still have to figure out about the side, should she place awnings all along the ground floor to match the front? She didn't want to overdo it, maybe she could paint the archways above the windows a different colour? Hmm, then it could use some plants or trees to give it a little life, break up the hard look of the pavement, perhaps she could plant manicured bushes in Greek or Roman urns by the front door and between every second window. It was hard trying to picture the effect. If she was not playing around with these images, she was thinking of those practical jobs that had to be done first before these concepts could be put into effect, the back lot would have to be paved for one thing, the bricks power hosed and repointed, and that dated aluminium front door made in the 70s had to go. Of course, these were only minor issues, the thought of the inevitable accumulation of costs and the work involved would then set her artistic musings aside, her nerves became taut with apprehension.

She found it difficult to concentrate or even to eat as the worries began to weigh her down, shuffling food around her plate, feeling instantly full after the first two mouthfuls. She knew she was allowing stress to take over when she could no longer face her Pop Tarts in the morning. To make matters worse, she felt strangely alone in the midst of company. Despite all the encouragement she received from the family, she could not discuss her concerns with them. She definitely could not talk to Charlie, and she was certain Suzy would not be able to understand the difficulties she was facing. In any case, everyone was busy with their own projects, and at the end of the day, she had to accept the reality that they could only help her so far, it was up to her to see this project through and to live with the consequences, be they good or bad. These anxieties began to take their toll, everything around her seemed so frivolous now, like the light hearted conversations at dinner and Mom's bridge club meetings. Reading books and keeping up with the latest television drama now became a terrible waste of time. Who cared who ran off with who, or whether so-and-so got axed off the show and would be absent the next season? The only relief she found for the moment was in her paintwork and sketching, as long as she was physically occupied with tangible tasks, it gave her the reassuring illusion she was handling everything pretty good.

Sometimes, it was a challenge living with her delusion of confidence. Katherine became increasingly aware of the limited nature of time, the minutes, hours and days seemed to rush past her, and there was too much pulling her attention in all directions. She played with a few drawings of the building to try out the new ideas she pondered on so that she was not completely unprepared when the building became available, but then felt terribly guilty she was not finishing the canvases she started ages ago, let alone try to find the time to investigate new themes for other works. However, when she did return to her burgeoning masterpieces, she felt a surge of panic, oil paintings took so long to dry in between the different stages, it seems as though they would never be finished. In the end, she wondered if what she was doing was practical and worth the time and stress.

Would people want artwork with the stark realities of life she depicted? Could she afford to paint art that may not have a ready market or concede to the temptation to paint scenes that she knew would sell? The intrusion of the mercenary rigours of the world upon her hours of creativity was downright distasteful. Under these circumstances, could she still remain true to her ideals? Her decorating plans gave her that space to take a deep breath, but guilt set in again when she glanced at the works lined up against the walls waiting to be finished. The race was on, she had to assemble a decent collection for the grand opening, whenever that would be, or what was the point in owning a gallery? She would just be another art dealer trading other people's work. *Snap out if it!* You love your work, painting is important! Look at all the people who have been influenced by art! Just forget the business end when you're painting, she reminded herself. No wonder everyone advised to set a special time aside for her artwork, concentrating full time on the practical necessities and the monetary concerns would eventually drive her to distraction.

Like clockwork, Charlie arrived with the paperwork as promised, although his presence at the house now felt … strange. Of course, he was welcome for dinner, but Katherine continued to feel awkward in his company and remained quiet during the proceedings. When they had signed the papers making her the official owner of the property, and the day's formalities had transformed her conceptual fears into certified realities, the thought of dinner was not appealing. She had the niggling suspicion her family silently sympathised with Charlie, making her loss of appetite more acute. The conversation at the table and the banter back and forth sounded so frivolous, she hoped the dinner would end soon and Charlie would go home. She needed to work and renew that illusion of assurance everything would sort itself out. Before he left, he asked if she was free that weekend to try the new Italian restaurant he missed taking her to last summer, the day of Jasper's rescue from the pound. She politely declined, using the work that had fallen behind as her excuse. At least she was telling him the truth, but that was not her sole reason; anything bordering on the romantic must be discouraged, lunches would be better sometime in the future letting him down slowly, but it was still too soon.

Gradually, she developed a routine over the weeks that followed waiting for the factory to be vacated. She worked on her paintings by day, and made endless lists of 'must think about' and 'have to do' for the gallery in the evenings. She finally dropped her rolls of film off to be developed, she had forgotten all about them that day she went to the framers with Gramps. She did not feel the need to rush that errand, it was difficult enough to do anything that reminded her of Paris, but she had to see if the galleries she visited would inspire her somehow. Unfortunately, many of the ideas she gathered would not work in the old Americana factory setting. Perhaps the city views might give her some ideas for a painting, but that was uncomfortable too, memories of her visit to that romantic city became blighted with feelings of disquiet. It was one of those mysteries of life where an enjoyable and memorable experience would, at one point or another, have a sorrow or a disappointment unexpectedly juxtaposed, forever marring that happy occasion. Charlie called occasionally on the phone, but Katherine maintained a subtle distance, keeping their conversations light and more general than in the past. She decided it was best to keep busy on the weekends and remain generally unavailable. In any case, how could she allow herself to be distracted right now with so many worries and uncertainties in her life to deal with?

È✿ಂ

Finally I'm achieving something, Katherine concluded as her first three experiments with artistic contrast came to the point she could at long last declare them finished. Maybe it paid to be a workaholic at times. Except for Suzy who watched her work on them, she did not show these oddities to the family until they were completed, she wanted to get their first impressions and hear their criticism, hopefully it would be constructive. They were big, they were colourful, they were … not what anyone expected, except the one with the nuclear power plant. After the Chernobyl disaster they had grown accustomed to her 'No Nukes' protest rallies at college. Her efforts also extended to the Radiac center, and no one could blame her for marching off with her placards in that case. Who in their right mind wanted a storage facility for radioactive medical waste in Brooklyn? Her second canvas, the pictorial condemnation of the billions poured into moonwalks while the destitute peoples of planet Earth starved received a few raised eyebrows, but they could understand her point and commented on her novel approach to the subject. However, the last painting met with mixed reviews. After the initial shock, Gramps had to stifle a bemused chuckle, Pop's eyebrows disappeared altogether, while all her mother had to say was,
"Isn't that a little irreverent, dear?"
It was the first time she dared to approach a religious issue, or rather, the absurd and deceptive traditions that people introduced to religious celebrations all in the name of having a good time. The painting featured a Nativity scene the like of which they had never laid eyes on

264

before. The stable, executed in a lavish Baroque style, was the only traditional element, gone were Joseph, Mary and the Christ child. In their place stood jolly images of Santa and Mrs. Claus in their red velvet outfits and fuzzy white trim, the manger filled with toys of all descriptions. Cute little elves masqueraded as the shepherds and wise men, while reindeer had assumed the roles of the ox and donkey. The final touch was a string of Christmas lights strung around the roof of the stable.

"I'm not making fun of Christmas," Katherine tried to explain, "I'm just trying to show how our culture has become ridiculous and irreverent."

"Don't you think you may be adding to the problem?" her father asked, a little nonplussed with the concept.

"I don't think so, satire is supposed to make people take stock of a situation. Let's face it, kids tend to associate Christmas with Santa and what they're going to find under the tree, everything else pales in comparison. Celebrating a historical religious event with magic fairy-fables stirred in the mix and pretending all of it is true just doesn't seem right, it's like we're telling kids it's okay to lose touch with reality. I've just put it in a picture to show what's happening and maybe get people to think. I mean, look at how people complain that the meaning of Christmas has become an afterthought in the midst of all the festivities, and yet no one really does anything about it. The holidays pass and all is forgotten until the following year, but no one can escape the blunt truth in a full colour picture."

"It looks like Norman Rockwell hallucinated or something," Gramps replied, "but I'll take your word for it."

It was probably a good thing Steves was not home, he would have a field day with this reaction and his comments would certainly not have helped matters. Maybe she should paint little farmyards and ranch houses, trying to be original did not seem to be working out very well.

There was one result she had not expected, a growing sense of dissatisfaction with the painting featuring the power plant. She could not put her finger on it, maybe asking them again what they thought would shed some light on the problem.

"About the first one, any additional observations?"

"Umm, definitely Chernobyl, the Russian letters on the grave markers display that," her father noticed.

"Yes, but it's not a sad graveyard," her mother continued, "the bright sunlight with the daisies, poppies and buttercups soften the industrial harshness of the plant. That's a nice touch."

"Yeah, it means we shouldn't lose hope no matter how bad things look," Gramps concluded, "one must always find the positive side to everything if you want to stay sane in this life."

Well, Katherine could not argue with this last remark, she had not considered that aspect before. He was right, there was always room for optimism.

However, these latest comments also proved that her initial concept using eye-catching contrasts was not very effective. The prettiness of the cemetery flowers was intended to symbolise the mixed up priorities of environmentalists in trying to keep the planet clean regardless of the means, brushing aside the constant threat of nuclear catastrophes. Just look at Three Mile Island! Okay she agreed with Gramp's observation about hope, but something was definitely missing in this painting. What was wrong? Everyone liked how she represented the Chernobyl incident. Of course! No wonder she was not content with this simple interpretation, anyone could paint a work commemorating that recent disaster to highlight the dangers of relying on nuclear power. Her idea went further than that, but apparently, no one could see it. It was more than just about nuclear plants, it was about mankind's audacity in playing god with the higher elements of nature. Oh foolish man, it is better to burn fossil fuels than to deceive yourself, you are not in absolute control of the sun or the atom's power. She thought the bright noonday sunlight might provide a clue to this reflection on nuclear physics, but Mom was right, it made everything look *too* happy and cheerful.

Time to go back to the drawing board she thought as she walked with her canvases to the apartment. How to depict the rashness of human nature without changing the whole thing, that was the question. She had put so much time into this one piece already, it would be a shame if she had to start from scratch. Maybe she was being too critical and should leave the painting as it was? She did not have the time to mess around, not with the huge projects she would soon be facing. No, you can't leave it slide, that definitely would be taking the easy way out. I could do something symbolic maybe, paint an Icarus figure in the sky, it would immediately solve my dilemma, but borrowing from Greek myth would not make the image unique. She had already used that concept for her parody on Napoléon's coronation. It was time to try something new, but what? It would have to be good and powerful, she refused to settle for the mediocre or second best.

She looked long and hard at the power plant, carefully observing the details of the towers and various structures that reached to the sky, hoping for some inspiration to dawn. At last, it occurred to her that part of the answer was staring her in the face, the towers *were* an Icarus-figure. According to biblical history, the first time the human race challenged the powers of heaven it designed a mighty tower for the purpose. Babel! It was an interesting concept, but how on earth could that theme be worked into this image? She could make the association after a lot of thought, but as her picture currently stood, there was nothing intentionally placed in the work to help other spectators connect the modern power plant with Nimrod's monolithic ziggurat of ancient history. There might have to be some additions, but then she did not want to completely eradicate her reference to Chernobyl either, a pictorial allusion to one millennia might cancel out the other. Time to visit the public library for some assistance, she might figure out what to do if she saw how other artists worked with a Babylonian theme.

The project did not turn out as easy as she imagined, it was one thing to find art books about individual artists or artistic periods, it was another trying to find one exploring a specific subject like the tower of Babel. It was a pity she was not familiar with those artists who painted Biblical works, that would have saved her precious time. She spent hours browsing through books, including a few historical tomes on ancient Mesopotamia. One picture continued to turn up in several publications, a Renaissance interpretation by Pieter Bruegel dated 1563 depicting the tower's construction. His skill in illustrating the many chambers within the spiralling structure clustered like so many cells in a honeycomb was fascinating, but other than that, the various renditions of the tower she managed to find did not offer any solution on how to proceed with her idea. Most of the paintings portrayed one of four events; the construction, the completed building, the destruction of the edifice, and the scattering of the races. How to incorporate any of these themes into her allegorical Chernobyl remained a mystery. Hmm, maybe not, the element of destruction was already suggested with the headstones, but she still needed a reference to Babel's demise to convey her theme of human arrogance.

Katherine continued browsing through the numerous volumes on the shelves, and as often as not with these research excursions, became side-tracked by the artwork that she happened upon. This time it was a picture of a well-dressed businessman in a bowler hat with a green apple for a face printed on the front cover of a book that lay on one of the reading tables, the life and times of the Belgian surrealist René Magritte. This bizarre image was strangely engaging. She was not familiar with his style as she had concentrated on the earlier periods of French art, but judging from the illustrations, she was almost sure he worked on achieving the same effect of contrasts she was currently attempting. She scanned his biography in the first three chapters, and it would appear he endeavoured to use 'magic realism' by placing average objects in unexpected combinations or unusual contexts to give new meaning to familiar things. Supposedly, these combinations and images were unrelated and not intended to be symbolic, or associated with the subconscious as with other surrealist's works, and yet he declared his pictures displayed the inexplicable nature of dreams. Katherine wondered how this could be since nothing could be more symbolic or more closely related to the subconscious than dreams, and did not understand why an artist would spend so much time painting random objects that he said had no allegorical purpose, unless it was a practical design for a roll of decorative wallpaper. His vague and paradoxical description of his style was perhaps his attempt to avoid all those incommodious questions probing into the personal significance of his paintings. Intrigued by this curious artist, she decided to check out the book, his works were definitely worth examining.

☙❀❧

Spring arrived and the factory was empty at long last. Gramps decided to accompany her on the first viewing of the premises, solemnly handing her the keys as they stood outside the shop.

"Here you go, kiddo. It's all yours."

It was a momentous occasion hearing the lock click open and stepping over the threshold, although there were no fanfares or a ticker-tape parade, it felt as if her existence had tilted on its axis. A new phase in her life was just beginning, she was now entering the art world as a fledgling entrepreneur. Passing through the shop to the industrial section, she was amazed at the space she had to work with. In addition to the high ceiling, the floor stretched practically unhindered to the back, save for the false wall segregating the shop at the front end and the large worktables left behind by the undergarment company at the other. The upper levels were also littered with worktables, a few old commercial sewing machines had been abandoned. The offices were on the top floor, most of them sectioned off in an open-space arrangement with prefabricated cubicles for desk areas. Gramps was happy with the overall condition, no major damage was visible to the structure or walls, and the floors were in good condition despite the heavy machinery installed there over the years. The recent repairs to the roof were holding out to his satisfaction, there were no signs of dampness or leaks running down the walls or marking the ceilings.

Katherine could finally see what needed to be done rather than imagining umpteen hurdles that may not exist at all. To a certain extent, the entire building was left in its original condition. The three external redbrick walls had not been plastered over, only the interior wall, while all the floors were a stained pinewood save for the concrete ground floor. The large wooden beams were also intact, including the old wide staircase with its iron railings ascending from the centre of the interior wall to the right, and the turn-of-the-century iron radiators, somewhat rusting, were still there notwithstanding they had not been used for years. Bearing in mind it had been a factory, the old place did have a certain charm about it. It was a pity that the high ceilings were scarred with the large massive air vents and ducts for the modern heating and cooling system, not to mention the endless criss-crossing wires powering the old fire alarms, the intercom connections and telephone hook ups, various sewing machines, and other industrial equipment that once buzzed with activity. The rows of suspended florescent lights flickering and humming over the former work areas were eyesores she would have to eradicate. The large commercial elevator with its steel shutters for doors situated in the back right corner was spacious, it was a shame it looked so outdated and tended to jolt around a bit, stopping at each floor with a loud whine and a large grinding *whump*. The bathrooms were located next to the elevator, and considering their age also knowing how dilapidated public facilities could become after years of use combined with the reluctance to keep them absolutely sanitary, Katherine was almost afraid to inspect this area. Her fears were realized ... Gramps may have upgraded the place at one time, but at this point, who could tell.

"No respect," he grumbled as they surveyed the damage, "wasn't like this when I last inspected the place."

Faucets dripped and pipes hissed, rust stains streaked the porcelain fixtures, while chipped or missing tiles left gaping holes on the walls like missing teeth. The rusting, cracked mirrors defied all reflection, and it would be difficult to know what colour they used to paint out the windows to deter any peeping Toms. The stalls were a wobbling disaster complete with broken locks, the finish worn off in areas and covered with such indecent graffiti that it made her blush in Gramp's presence. He too was not pleased with the obscenity defiling the family property, his disgruntled 'thunder'n tarnations' echoing off the ceramic lined walls. The large toilet bowels were crowned with black industrial ∩-shaped seats or none at all, and of course, more whuzzing and cracking florescent lights, the decayed setting enveloped in an incredible reek ineffectually masked with cheap air freshener and the stale odour of generic chlorine cleansers. Next to the bathrooms, a steel door, stark and battered over the years, closed a corridor out to the old boiler house that now contained the furnace systems, old and new, and the large dented hot water tank. The back house also had its own loading entrance opening out onto the parking lot.

Yes, the place would need some work, but it had great possibilities, including the bathrooms. She went over the whole area from top to bottom once more, this time taking numerous photographs and making extra notes. The upper levels could easily be adapted for exhibitions, but the ground floor, the most important of all, would pose a problem. After all, the entrance made the first good or bad impression on visitors, and she had to get it right, namely where to situate an industrial kitchen to accommodate the café without upsetting the rest of her plans for the entry way and the gift shop. The visually ideal place for the café would be in the front at one of the large windows and the gift shop on the other side, the front door leading to a welcoming and spacious reception area that invited the art lover inside. However, if she placed the café where she wanted it, the kitchen would have to be somewhere close by, which meant the exhaust fans and related outlets would have to be vented out the side of the building near the front, turning the exterior into an unsightly steaming mess. The side street was a main thoroughfare and as visually important as the main entrance, it was not some byway she could hide with a large gate. Then, if she blocked out a room for the kitchen on the side, she would lose valuable floor space, the building was long and rectangular, she did not want it to appear more narrow than it was, creating an optical illusion that would be made worse by the gift shop if it was situated on the other side, her main entrance would become an uninviting bottleneck. To top that aesthetically challenged scenario, she would have deliveries for the eating establishment wheeled in and out to the kitchen right through the main gallery rather than simply dropped off in a storage facility away from the public area.   In light of all these considerations, she may have to situate the café near the back where all the exhausts could be vented into the parking lot and goods delivered discreetly, but then, how could she attract pedestrians who simply wanted to stop for a morning coffee and pastry? Tucked away inside, people might think the café was only for the gallery patrons or those interested in looking around. The gift area might have to be situated closer to the back as well, which could also deter casual shoppers from entering similar to the café. The staircase area might get a little crowded. Obviously, everything had to be relocated.

Katherine paced the floor, sectioning out the different areas in her mind and standing back trying to imagine the effect.

"Something the matter?" Gramps inquired.

"Kind of, I'm stuck about the café and how to arrange everything around it," she explained, pointing out the areas and demonstrating the problems she could visualise. He thought for a moment, rubbing his chin.

"You know, the front windows are not original, this was all just factory space. You could do what I did when I added the shop, you might be able to break a second entrance through the side and add more display windows. I think the structure could hold that. It would shift the focus of your main entrance away from the narrow section to the wider part of the building and prevent a bottleneck between your café and shop. You'd also have several entry points to bring people in, and the code requires more exits in case of fire these days."

Katherine's eyes brightened. Gee, why didn't she think of that? She had concentrated so diligently on the existing rectangular features that she had psychologically bound herself to their limits rather than thinking outside the narrow elongated structure. His solution was perfect, a new main entrance at the long side would permit her to have plenty of room for a beautiful open-plan reception desk and exhibition area, the iron staircase would be facing the visitor beckoning them to explore the upper galleries. The café could be placed at a convenient spot on the left of the new side entrance near the large window for light, and still be close to a suitable place for the kitchen right next to the loading doors and parking lot. The gift shop could be situated on the right of the original entrance with the other display windows to attract prospective shoppers and draw them further into the gallery, not to mention the café for a bite to eat. There was also an added advantage, with a set of large awnings over the new side doorway and windows on the exterior, the ground floor would no longer look like a chequerboard strip.

"Hey, what a great idea! Thanks Gramps, you're a genius."

"We aim to please," he smiled.

Before they left, Katherine went over to inspect a few cartons abandoned under the stairs by the previous tenant and opening up the top box, she burst out laughing.

"I guess you get a smiley T-shirt after all," she said as she took a men's double extra large off the top and held it up, "this should do the trick."

"Only if you take one too," he conceded, "just don't expect me to wear the shorts."

Their tour completed, they stopped by the main offices in the city to pick up an important item, the blueprints of the building. This time they did not have lunch with Pops but drove straight over to the country club after they said a quick 'hello' to everyone and retrieved the large roll of schematics. Gramps had arranged for them to meet with one of his old friends, the contractor who carried out the original refurbishment on the old place, Mr. Francis Harding. Although Mr. Harding had long relinquished the business to the next generation similar to Gramps, he was very happy to look over the blueprints and make some preliminary suggestions. Katherine had already met Mr. Harding on many occasions at the club, short and thin with a bushy moustache, a calm individual who always seemed to have a smile for everyone. He had made his fortune on large development and refurbishment projects, and could now sit back and relax after battling with the construction business for years, retirement seemed to fit him well. She was glad this first business encounter with a developer would be conducted with someone she already knew and who possessed a cheerful personality. Moreover, he was someone that Gramps trusted, nevertheless, he was not familiar with the family members who now ran the company and advised her to seek other estimates.

Mr. Harding was very obliging, listening attentively to her ideas while they ate, after which they proceeded to the billiard room where they could roll out the massive plans on an unoccupied table.

"Ah yes, I remember when we worked on this," Mr. Harding recalled as he examined the intricate lines and symbols printed across the broadsheets while simultaneously plonking a few pool balls on the corners when they threatened to roll up. Now she understood why Gramps did not show the plans to her immediately, she might have panicked at the sight. The weeks of waiting had helped her to grow accustomed to the huge task of refurbishing ahead, now she could examine the blueprints with less apprehension and become familiar with the geometrical diagrams.

Mr. Harding traced a finger along the line marking the wall on the side and agreed opening a second entrance was a good proposal. Of course, she might require planning permission to alter the exterior for the exhausts and new entryway, but as the building was not yet marked for historical preservation, plus the proposed changes were minimal and would help to enhance its appearance without detracting from its architectural features, she should have little problem acquiring the necessary authorisation. This was one good piece of news. He then advised her to consider the inside design thoroughly and make as many detailed sketches as possible to show how she wanted the place to look so the architectural plans could be drawn. Despite all these variables to keep in mind from plug sockets to ceiling heights, at least she was aware of the next steps that must be taken in the process.

Time had come to inform the Montmartre Club about her good news, plans were really starting to move ahead. Although she had called her friends in Paris and wrote a letter or two, she had not told them all the details about acquiring a property for the gallery other than she had a place in mind. She had been reluctant to say too much, because for some reason, plans had a way of becoming jinxed if disclosed before they were put into action, and she did not want to raise their hopes should something unforeseen cause it all to fall apart. Now she felt confident that everything was well on track and decided she had better find the time to give them a call. Justine's voice was positive and cheerful over the telephone, plans for the wedding were set for June of the following year at Montmartre, not in the huge basilica of Sacre Coure, that was too grand, they would be quite content with a small ceremony at the St. Jean l'Evangélist, and as soon as the invitations were printed, she was getting the first one. They were also accumulating a nice collection and hoped they would find an appreciative clientèle for the gallery as well as their own art. Katherine was so happy for them, she hoped the grand opening would be a success for them all. Hanging up the receiver, she headed off into the city, no time to sit around, others were counting on her gallery too.

03 ❀ 80

Katherine spent much of her time for the next couple of weeks at the future gallery, sketching floor layouts and decorative ideas. When not at the property, she visited interior design shops to browse through books of wallpaper and drapery samples, plus chandelier lamp shops and lighting establishments scouting out every form of track lighting available. She investigated homebuilding and hardware suppliers to examine objects from doorknobs and light-switch guards to polished countertops, flooring and ceiling panels. Naturally, this busy schedule kept her out of the house for considerable stretches. It was a relief to be gathering practical information and getting familiar with the material that was available. However, these excursions into the ornamental side of decorating quickly displayed her expensive tastes. She would have to budget her resources wisely if she expected to decorate the place in a manner befitting a fashionable art establishment.

When Charlie called on the phone, he was beginning to sense a distance growing between them. Occasionally he stopped by the house, but she was either away on her design expeditions or too preoccupied with work. He tried inviting her out to dinner many times, but she declined and changed the invitations to lunch appointments, keeping their conversations strictly to business and generalities. What had gone wrong? He could not

273

help but wonder if he sounded that matter-of-fact when discussing his promotion and the latest cases with her, perhaps that is why their relationship did not blossom as he had hoped. She was concerned for his career, yes, but perhaps he had spoiled everything by giving her space to finish college and grow up, keeping his true feelings hidden while maintaining their close friendship. Well, let's face it, I'm in denial. One way or another, I have to accept the fact she's not prepared for any commitment past that of sisterly affection. I didn't see that coming, better learn to live with it.

Acceptance was not an easy thing to master when denial continued to linger. He decided to drop by one Saturday afternoon, hoping Katherine could spare some time and take a few hours off with him. She had been tied up for weeks, oblivious to everything going on around her, he wondered if she even knew Easter had come and gone. He knocked on the apartment door.

"Hi Charlie, come on in, you've just missed Kathy, she's got a meeting with the architect and engineer today. Can I get you something to drink?"

"No, that's all right, Suzy. I hope I haven't disturbed you."

He should be getting used to this by now. When would he learn to stop setting himself up for disappointments?

"You're not, I've just finished my painting and was about to take a break. I've got some fresh coffee brewing and a plate of Mrs. Gonzales' brownies."

"All right, that sounds good."

He did not want to be rude.

"Gosh, let me get out of this first, I must look a fright," she replied as she tugged off the old smock, shyly smiling with embarrassment while quickly rolling up the paint-encrusted garment and ushering him in to the sitting room.

"No you're fine, don't fuss. What are you working on, if you don't mind me asking?"

"Oh, not at all, it's my entry for the Sirrac contest. Although I changed my course, the contest is still open to the graduate students of Belvedere. I thought I'd give it a shot."

Charlie inspected the tall drying canvas. It was an arresting representation of a river and a waterfall, or to be more precise, a flowing river in several waterfalls descending in one linear path giving the spectator the impression of standing directly in front of a staircase, the last cascade engulfing the foreground and apparently flowing to the edge of the border.

It was a beautiful Edenesque setting with luscious trees and a blue sky dotted with fluffy cotton-ball clouds overhead, yet, something seemed strangely upside down or rather sideways as the trees and rocks along the cliff were not depicted from the vertical side but from above. He was not wrong, the painting was a partial illusion, the viewer seemed to hover in mid air over the first gigantic cascade, watching the large torrent descend from the foreground and up into the horizon line, the river becoming smaller with each descent until it empties into a clear rippling lake reflecting the summer sky above.

"Wow, that's amazing, I don't know whether I'm standing in front of it or soaring above it. The water powerfully tugs at you and pulls you in."

"Thanks, that was the general idea. Have you ever noticed if you look over the side of a bridge for too long, the running water seems to draw you to itself? Oh, I don't mean you intend to jump or anything, but the flow of a river is strangely mesmerising. I wanted to capture that feeling if I could."

"Yeah, I've felt that, I can't look over the side of a bridge without getting a bit queasy, and I'm not ordinarily bothered about heights. What's the theme this year?"

"The Power of Water."

"The stuff they come up with!" Charlie noted, shaking his head. "'The Element of Fire', 'The Struggle for This', 'The Triumph of That', they try to sound so high-brow it comes across a little affected. Too bad they don't leave the theme open and let you paint what you want, but I think you got their title nailed."

Suzy laughed, it was true, the titles were becoming more insufferably academic each year.

"Their main aim is to challenge us and see what we can produce from their stilted ideas," she replied as she poured the coffee. "I must admit last year's theme was more interesting, trying to think up something original with water is off-putting. Everyone else is probably going to do a variation on tidal waves, Noah's Ark or hurricane Hugo."

"Yours is certainly different, calm, but powerful."

"I hope so, there are so many talented students at Belvedere, let's pray the judges are kind and that Horace the Horrible doesn't show up this year."

Charlie sat down on one of the stools at the breakfast counter.

"I nearly forgot about him, but I wouldn't worry, even he would find it difficult to find something disparaging to say about your painting."

"You really think so?"

"Absolutely," Charlie assured.

Suzy could use a little encouragement he thought, her work was just as good as Kathy's, but she obviously lacked confidence in her talent.

"You'll definitely get an honourable mention at least."

"That would be nice, talk about making graduation day complete."

"Oh yes, graduation, your family will be coming, I assume?"

"Yes, my parents will be taking a few days off and my sister is coming with them. I wish I could invite all the Ws to the ceremony, they've been so kind to me these past few years, but with the seating restrictions, it makes it impossible. I can only invite Kathy, everyone else will have to wait for the get-together afterwards."

If Kathy can find the time, Charlie thought. *No, don't be so harsh, it's just the way things have turned out.* He tried to keep the conversation upbeat.

"Don't let it bother you, they'll understand, you're not the only student they know who's graduated from Belvedere," he noted. He tried to be humorous, but his voice sounded too wistful, he did not want his feelings to show.

"Yeah, that's true," Suzy replied. Despite his attempts to keep a stiff upper lip, she knew he was finding Kathy's uncharacteristic detachment difficult to cope with. "I hope she'll be able to come, we probably should consider it a great privilege if we see her at all before the refurbishment is finished," she tried to joke before continuing, "she's been so busy of late with the new gallery. It's a wonderful opportunity having a whole building handed to you like that, but I feel anxious for her, it's a huge responsibility. Frankly, I wouldn't want that mountain landed on top of me, I don't think I could handle it."

"That's right, she does have a lot on her plate," he reflected as he finished the brownie, wiping his hands with his napkin. Suzy had read his mind, Kathy never seemed to be around lately, but her friend was right, she could get worked up about the smallest thing, and now she had real worries to keep her occupied. "She definitely has her work cut out for her, fixing up an old building is no joke, especially a commercial building."

"More coffee?"

"All right, just half a cup."

Charlie was glad he stayed awhile, it was a relief to have someone to talk to at this point and he had missed visiting Oak Meadows. An hour soon passed as he talked about his upcoming summer trip to Cape Cod with his parents, and she told him about rural life in Iowa including her uneventful summer job in the local library back home. Suzy did have a calming effect, maybe it was the result of growing up in a small town atmosphere or the quiet solitary life associated with artists, her relaxed personality was evident in her painting. His thoughts were interrupted as his stomach rumbled, one brownie did not make a substantial lunch, the embarrassing gurgles reminded him about the time. Although he had hoped Kathy would have lunch with him, there was no point letting a reservation go to waste. Suzy seemed alone and abandoned these last few months too, an afternoon away from the apartment would do her good.

"It's almost lunchtime, would you like to go out and grab a bite to eat? I have a table booked and we could just make it," he declared, looking at his watch, "I'm sorry it's such a rush, but we got busy talking."

Would you like to go out?

Suzy could not believe she had heard those words. How long she had waited to be noticed! Her heart almost stopped, or it was beating too fast, hard to tell. She wanted to grab the moment, but wait, remember it was Kathy he came to invite. Would she be okay with this? Suzy was not sure if her friend had misread her feelings about Charlie, it would be a horrible thing if she came between them.

"I don't know, Charlie," she hesitated.

"Come on, it's a nice place, you might like it."

That's what I'm afraid of, she thought to herself, I *would* like to go out with you, but would it be right?

"Are you sure, Charlie?"

"Sure, we won't be gone long, you can get back to your work afterwards."

Hmm, maybe just this one time, he's only trying to be nice anyway, it's nothing special. How could she say 'no'? Charlie had a lot of disappointments lately.

"Oh, okay, but only if we go Dutch."

She certainly appreciated his offer, but she was not an opportunist either. She was aware of his weakness for fine dining and she did not want him to go to that expense if he was just trying to be kind to her. So what? She could live without that new jacket she was saving for, it was worth it just to have a lunch alone with him.

"Now, no fuss, it's nothing over the top, I promise."

"Please, I insist, or I won't go."

"Okay," he sighed, "no argument," but thought to himself this situation will require gentle diplomacy, he never handled going Dutch before. His 'Old School' upbringing would not permit a woman to put her hand in her pocket for his invitations.

☙❀❧

Katherine got back from the city several hours later somewhat drained after her meeting with the architect, explaining in minute detail the plans she envisioned with the aid of her various drawings and notes. Now it was up to him to draft the professional plans and she hoped he had grasped what she aimed to achieve. Despite her tiredness, she felt good knowing the initial work was underway, that something was being accomplished. All she could do now is wait for the results and continue with her painting. Grabbing a sandwich from the kitchen in the main house, she decided to relax and put her feet up before tackling the unresolved problem with her nuclear satire, she knew she would not be able to concentrate on any new works until that was fixed. Oddly enough, solutions always presented themselves when she was not struggling to find them, inspirations seemed to fly further away when the mind tried to seize upon them like a roving conqueror. She was so tense lately and desperate to move ahead with her work that she was probably striving against the intellectual current, she needed some time out, and television was always good for that.

Searching the channels she eventually settled on a documentary, it was much better than watching daytime programming that consisted mostly of brain-numbing melodrama. She needed to relax, but there was a cut-off point in any form of passivity she was willing to indulge in. Those soap operas could really rot your brain with all that sensational drivel, not to mention those live tabloidian talk shows with enraged husbands slinging abuse along with a few chairs at their wives' secret beaus who dared to appear on the program, the incessant censorship bleeps were enough to land one in solitary confinement at Bellevue. The government should make the stations flash health warnings from the surgeon general along with the censorship notifications before each program she concluded. "Warning: extended viewing of this program may lead to hearing loss, dementia, paranoia, panic attacks or manic episodes. If one or more of these symptoms occur, please contact your local doctor immediately." Documentaries on the other hand were a lifesaver, or rather, a safeguard for the intelligence. They were one of the few media sources where scientists and historians released their years of research to the public in an interesting and understandable way that made their data applicable to the working world. People resented being lectured at, or forced to take notes and read books from prescribed reading lists, but nearly everyone loved to watch

278

documentaries that shared the same information, even if in a general format. It was a pity the school system did not observe this phenomena and improve their teaching methods accordingly. At least the math teachers could be spared the torture of indifferent and unresponsive students. Except for the practical basics of addition, subtraction, multiplication, division, geometry and measurements, everything else seemed an insufferable waste of time to a classroom of thirty boisterous kids. How often they would bombard their teacher with the pertinent questions, 'Why do we have to learn this? What do we need it for? Will we ever use it?' only to be told, 'It's something you have to learn … get over it,' without giving any valid reason to keep the interest of the enquiring student fired up with enthusiasm. Nearly everyone she knew hated going to school, but when cable and satellite TV appeared, they were all proud to boast they were the proud recipients of the National Geographic and Discovery channels.

The program Katherine happened to find on this occasion explored the importance of astronomy in the construction of the great buildings and mysterious sites of the ancient world. She liked to gaze at the stars on the rare occasions they were not drowned out by the glaring city lights, searching for the constellations she knew like the Big and Little Dippers, or the hunter Orion, this show should be interesting she concluded, settling back into the corner of the sofa. She listened to the discussion on how the ancients discovered the importance of star positions to navigate their journeys, and how the Celts and Druids calculated the longest and shortest days of the year with their extraordinary stone circles. She was amused by the story recounting the discovery of the ancient Megalithic tomb of Newgrange. The elaborate passage tomb had been buried under hundreds of years of accumulated soil, but the local townspeople knew that if the mound was excavated, a ray of sunlight would penetrate directly into the burial chamber on the shortest day of the year. The learned academics and archaeologists laughed at the people until the site was excavated in modern times to find that their centuries-old story passed down from one generation to the next proved correct. The most fascinating example of an equinox calculation was the cleverly devised shadow illusion of the plumed serpent descending into the earth at the Kukulkan Pyramid of Chickén Itza. Then there were other discoveries she had not heard about, scientists had studied various star positions dating thousands of years ago and discovered that certain sites were in alignment with major constellations. The giant animal pictures drawn in the sands by the Nazca people of Peru were one example, the Egyptian pyramids were another as the monuments at Giza were positioned to line up with Orion's belt.

When the program came to an end, the wheels of her imagination continued to turn, the combination of the constellations, ancient chronology and lofty constructions, where had she seen this before? She remembered the Gothic carvings of Notre Dame and went for the photographs she had developed, yes, there they were, signs of the Zodiac and carvings of other constellations encircled the building, there was Pieces, she could just make it out. Obviously, they were not carved to represent fortune-telling symbols, but to mark different months and seasons of the year, she had seen the same effect used in the brightly coloured pictures of medieval manuscripts like the *Très Riches Heures*. Perhaps the signs on Notre Dame marked a special alignment to certain patterns in the sky that held religious significance for the Christians of that time, she wished she knew.

Placing her photos back in their packet, she went over to the apartment. If the ancient Egyptians and Medieval cathedral builders could figure out how to construct those grand monuments, surely she could find a way to fix her painting. She continued to stare at the sunny canvas for a few moments and was struck with a brilliant idea. What would happen if I get rid of the sunlight, oh my! Would it work? She flipped through the library book she had borrowed, they're in here somewhere, aha, the *Empire of Light* series. Magritte had experimented painting day and night simultaneously in the early fifties, the resulting pictures were eerily reflective and melancholic. The first image showed a quiet country house situated by a still lake enveloped in darkness, the scene illuminated by a single lamppost, the skyline broken by the sable shape of a solitary tree. The second picture featured an extension of the theme with a deserted cobblestone street dimly lit by a similar lamppost and the muted lights from the house windows, the street overshadowed by dark bushy trees painted in midnight hues. However, the sky in both nocturnal pictures was eccentrically offset with the noonday light in bright turquoise and ornamented with puffy clouds. The concept was perfect, just what she needed, a reversal of the surrealist Magritte! She could keep her sunlit flower-covered graveyard with its tinge of hope and paint out the sky using a sombre nocturnal shade, an excellent contrast, but that was not the final touch. The documentary had revealed to her that an important event in history could be commemorated using the stars. Now all she had to do was find out the exact date Babylon's mighty tower was razed to the ground.

Unfortunately, their Bible was not much help, the event recorded in Genesis did not give a reference in time other than a list of the generations that came after Noah, there was no day, date, or year, a star calculation would not be possible without these three elements. She might pin down a biblical year if she was patient enough to work out the tangle of who-begot-who from the time of Adam, but that might require substantial knowledge of ancient methods in keeping track of generations. She would also have to calculate the exact latitude and longitude of ancient Babylon as the sky changed aspect depending on the position of the stargazer at any given point on the globe. Her so-called perfect solution was opening a fresh can of worms she had not expected, she was opening a lot of those lately, but it was impossible for her to let go of a project once she started. 'Encyclopaedia Stevecanica' may have the answers, she wondered if he retained any of his interest in astronomy. It was Saturday, he would not be at a lecture anywhere and might be home, perhaps she could give him a buzz.

She dialled his number, eventually she was greeted by his infuriating answering machine, she never knew what he would put on that contraption. This time his recorded message was accompanied by the theme music from the *Next Generation, "Greetings, you have reached the President of the Starfleet Federation. I regret to inform you I am busy solving the problems of the universe and cannot attend your call, the Klingons are getting restless again. After the tone please leave your name and number and I shall send a communication through as soon as possible."*

"Hello Mr. President, it's Kathy, pick … up … the…phone … I know you're there … ." she droned, trying to get his attention. She did not have to wait long.

"Hi Kathy, it's Fred, your brother's not here, he's with his tutor right now working out a snag with his thesis, can I take a message?"

Oh well, Steve's room mate was just as brainy, his major was nuclear physics, maybe he could help. How ironic!

"Hey Fred, nice to talk to you again, I need some help with an astronomical calculation and was hoping Steves could give me the answer. Sorry to pester you, but you wouldn't happen to know anything about astronomy, would you?"

"I know a little, shoot away," Fred replied.

"Well it's an archaeoastronomy problem I need solved to continue an art project," she clarified.

"That's sounds fascinating, I hope I can help."

"I'm working with a Tower of Babel theme and need to know the exact time it was destroyed so I can look up the star charts when that event occurred. You see, I want to paint them into my skyline."

"I get it, but you may have a problem figuring that out, to get the position over the site, you not only need the geographical co-ordinates of latitude and longitude for Babel, you also have to figure out the exact hour and minute of the day in addition to the year. No one has discovered that as far as I'm aware, but you may pin down a biblical estimate for the year, you know, an Anno Mundi calculation determining the creation of the world. I haven't gone into that area, I leave that to the theologians who insist the Earth is approximately six thousand years old."

"At least it's something to go on," she replied a little disappointed having already figured out this may be the case. "Thanks Fred, say 'hi' to Steves for me."

"No problem, bye Kathy."

Great, she was back at square one. Was there anyone she knew who could work out the chronological complexities of ancient history? Of course, Professor Matthews, he might know something, and I haven't contacted him in ages, it would be the right time to call him too.

"Hello?"

"Hi Professor, it's Kathy, I hope I'm not disturbing you."

"Well, if it's not the student who painted a thousand truths and burnt the topless towers of Belvedere," he replied with a touch of amusement in his voice. "No you're not disturbing me, you've called at a good time. I'm taking a break from correcting some essays, the Freshmen this year still cannot tell the difference between Manet and Monet. By the way, thank you for sending all those cards from Paris, I enjoyed receiving them. How are you keeping?"

"It's funny you should mention towers," she replied, "but first let me say I'm sorry I haven't been in touch, so much has happened since I came home from my trip."

She told him the good news about her promising establishment beginning to take shape in Dumbo, and proceeded to describe her latest painting idea, hoping he could shed light on Babel's demise.

"If it was a question about the Fall of Troy, or the Peloponnesian and Punic Wars, I might be able to help you, but unfortunately the tribulations of ancient Mesopotamia are beyond my scope of expertise," he replied with regret. "However, I have a friend who works at the Wagner College planetarium, he could map out the sky and perhaps make a few photos or printouts for you to work from, if you can discover the exact information. Perhaps you should talk to a biblical scholar or a theologian, they might have the answers you seek."

"Thank you for the advice, I hope I can work something out,"

"Best of luck, let me know if you find those co-ordinates, I'll pass them on to the planetarium."

"Okay, will do, Professor. Thanks again."

"My pleasure, I can't wait to see this new astro-piece of yours."

"Oh, you should see the other two I've painted!" she laughed.

"If they're anything like the eye-opener you presented for the Sirrac contest, I can't wait," he chuckled.

"Like I promised, you're at the top of my invitation list for the grand opening. Well, I guess I'd better let you go, I don' want to hold you up."

"Good bye, Kathy. Remember, if this idea doesn't work out, don't forget you can always find a solution, don't let one hiccup frustrate you and impede your creativity."

"I'll remember that, goodbye Professor."

It was true, sometimes solutions did come when you least expected them. Perhaps she had not found the exact information she was seeking, but a second step she had not yet considered was solved, namely where she would obtain precise diagrams of the sky for that specific date. It was a stroke of luck Professor Matthews thought of that, now all she needed was the precise time.

Hmm, scripture scholars, theologians, Anni Mondos, whatever, the only person she knew who had studied theology was Reverend Dobbson, he might know, but she dreaded having to ask him, his Sunday school lessons were an absolute bore. How could she forget that tedious ordeal? Just great, she knew what would happen, all she needed was a piece of information, but the minute she asked, the Reverend was bound to get sidetracked in the spirit of some biblical brainwave and prattle on about the moral behind the passage, he just loved to preach. Was she prepared to suffer all for the sake of art? Maybe you had to suffer to be beautiful, but she was not yet convinced affliction was an absolute necessity for creativity and was determined not to repeat the scriptural tedium of those Sunday afternoons. Might as well head back to the library, time to return the book on Magritte anyway.

Hold on, she did know another expert in scripture, remembering that most unusual encounter at Notre Dame. He knew so much about the gargoyle carvings, possibly he understood those star signs sculptured on the cathedral too and could help her with the stellar confusion of Babel. Did Justine keep his brother's address? Perhaps if she wrote him a letter, it might reach him somehow? Maybe this was not a good idea, they met a long time ago and for such a brief period, would it be right to bother him unexpectedly for just a painting? Oh, why not, if he thinks it's a nuisance, he can just ignore my letter, no big deal. I'll go ahead and call Justine, I hope she kept the address he gave her. Gee, what a bug I'm becoming.

Intrigued by Katherine's astral-plan, Justine was glad she could be of assistance, as it happened, she did have the priest's address, his American return address in fact. She wanted to write a thank you to him for the spiritual guidance he had given her and Martin that summer, but as he was no longer in Paris her letter was forwarded to him.

"He said we could write anytime we had a question or needed advice in the future, he has been really good to stay in touch with us," Justine replied, "yes, I'm sure he would be willing to share any information that would help with your painting."

Katherine thanked her, what a stroke of luck, she would not have to wait as long for her letter to reach him, maybe this was meant to be, she could have it ready for the morning, however, as she replaced the receiver the telephone rang.

"Hey Kats, it's me. I just got your message, Fred filled me in on your latest quest. I can't figure out the calculations you want, not without the day and year, but I looked up the co-ordinates for the archaeological site of Babylon, it's a start. You know, you should really use the Internet more often. Got a piece of paper?"

"Yeah, right here. Oh, you're the techno expert, you know I'm hopeless searching for things with the computer, I end up with junky sites offering nothing but basic factoids. Thanks for looking it up for me though, any information would be a help."

"No sweat, copy this."

"Great! Before you hang up, how are you doing? Fred told me you've had a snafu with your thesis, is everything okay?"

She heard a disgruntled sigh over the line.

"Fred may be the next nuclear Einstein of our time, but he could really learn to keep his mouth shut," he grumbled, before continuing, "my thesis is fine actually, it's my tutor that's holding things up, he misread some of my calculations and hauled me in for a protracted do-nothing session … again."

Maybe it was not the best thing to ask about Katherine noted with a silent grimace, once Steves received an opening to rant about his pet grievances or the world's stupidity, nothing could stop him.

"These so-called tutorials just waste time when I could be accomplishing some real work," he complained. "Every time I write a footnote, he wants to see it, the work is going so slow you think he was writing the thing with me as the ghost writer. If he realized I've had the whole thing written two months ago, he'd have a fit."

"You've written it already? Gee, do you want to leave Boston that bad? I thought you enjoyed the place," she replied not comprehending his frustration.

"Oh, Boston's great, I'm getting bored stiff with college, I'm itching to move on to something serious. I mean we should be busy trying to find a cure for Alzheimer's disease or something. You know, I've learned more in the family business growing up under the lab counters observing first hand how the scientists and technicians operate than a school environment can ever pass on. Not to blow my own horn, but I've gained enough experience to work in the labs right now if it wasn't for the fact the world demands that we have that scrap of paper to prove our qualifications."

"Now don't be ridiculous, can you imagine what would happen if there were no systems dispensing official qualifications other than blowing a lot of hot air? Complete and total Pandemonium, it would be a rouge's world," she concluded.

"We're almost there already anyway, the politicians are doing a good job," he wryly replied.

"You know what I mean," she sighed, "you can't just skip into the labs without going to college, even if you are a medical wizard. Remember, our great grandfather had to finish medical school before he started the company."

"I know," he conceded, "I understand the need for these documents, you can't have quacks and con-artists setting up offices pretending they're surgeons or engineers, but it's simply infuriating to think that without an official approval of some college, my knowledge and practical experience here in the firm count for next to nothing."

"Gramps and Pops know differently," she consoled.

"Yeah, but the government doesn't. At least I'm registered on the books as an intern simply gathering experience and Dr. Stirling oversees all my regular work. I know Pops would like to move me up the ranks, but without a degree imagine what would happen if the shareholders discovered that one of the head research scientists in the company had no qualification to determine the most important details, like the correct dosage of a medication or the nature of possible side effects. Just watch our shareholdings plummet, not to mention the feeding-frenzy of the press. Pops would come down with a legion of ulcers, even Gramps would blow a gasket."

"You're right, it is a Catch-22 situation, I'm sorry you're having such a hard time of it. Try not to let it upset you, suffer through the next year, and it will all be over soon."

After he had halved his problem by sharing it, Katherine finally had a chance to ask how Jennifer was doing.

"I think I've met my match," he laughed, "an only girl in a family with four brothers, she knows how to handle us guys."

"I don't get you."

"On April Fools I put baby powder in the nozzle of her hairdryer, *poof*! You should have seen the look on her face, but she got back at me by varnishing my soap bar."

"What?"

Katherine had been the brunt of the baby powder trick once before, but she had never heard of varnished soap. Did Jennifer stick coloured dye in it? How she would have loved to see him all streaked like an Indian in war paint for the day!

"She took a fresh bar of soap and polished it with clear varnish and put it in my shower when it hardened. Geez, I nearly scrubbed myself raw trying to get some lather until I figured out what had happened."

Katherine laughed now too, it was not the old dye trick, but just as funny. Sweet revenge for all those years of gags she did not have the courage or the heart to pull on him despite her anger.

"Serves you right you annoying goofball. How do you like a taste of your own medicine?"

"Please, spare me the puns," he groaned, "listen, I've gotta run, say 'hi' to the folks for me."

"All right, bye Steves."

April Fools, she nearly forgot. Since he went to college, they did not suffer from his pranks as they did when he was younger. In those childish days, everyone he knew had wrung a promise from him to curtail his more outlandish practical pranks to that one day if he could, and he was true to his word, for three hundred and fifty days out of the year at least. However, on that one day they would know for certain something would happen, they kept their eyes peeled and were cautious about everything they touched, sat on, opened or put in their mouths. Aunt Martha stayed well away from the house, and even Mrs. Gonzales did not escape some of his pranks. However, when their father's ire deterred him from inventing pranks at home without danger to life and limb, or worse yet, house detention, the attendees and employees of the high school became the main targets, usually if some benefit could be derived from the stunt. The worst trick he ever managed to pull off was when he poured a laxative into the teacher's communal coffee pot bubbling away in the staff room, the students all had an unexpected holiday the next day when half the teachers never showed up.   Katherine was the only one who knew her brother was the culprit, the secrets siblings had to keep! Nowadays, he would play a trick or two, but they were becoming less frequent.

Perhaps college work was getting to him, he was chaffing at the bit over his thesis, at least talking to her got it off his chest. He had a point, if they were in the Middle Ages she mused, working in the firm under the watchful guidance of the other scientists would have been an apprenticeship, in seven years, he would be put through some strange initiation, accepted into an apothecary guild and be allowed to practise his trade. Experience and skill were all that were required, whatever happened to the beautiful simplicity of that system? Or, perhaps it was not yet eradicated, just made terribly difficult by a bunch of nincompoops these days. Thinking of ancient times, she returned to the subject at hand, now that she had the location of Babylon pinned down, it was time to write that letter to the priest she met. Perhaps it was too much to expect an answer about a trifling matter of a painting from someone she hardly knew, but it could not hurt to try.

03 ❀ 80

Many days passed and the end of April approached. She wondered if she should consult with an interior designer for some ideas, but then she knew what she wanted, and it would be an added expense, so she continued browsing through the building suppliers and home improvement stores gathering estimates and looking for the best prices. An interior designer would only be a nuisance anyway, trying to stamp their ideas on *her* gallery, she was an artist and should decorate according to her own tastes. If only Aunt Martha could understand that, she loved to bombard her with a thousand and one suggestions whenever they met.

In the evenings, she tried to work on ideas for new paintings. Unfortunately, she did not feel particularly inspired to portray additional flaming controversies, an attack of 'Painter's Block' had unexpectedly reared its ugly head from the deep. Of all times when she was under pressure to build up a collection! It was the strangest affliction to suffer, for when her creative blocks were not caused by a lack of ideas, the opposite was the case, they were induced by an over abundance of workable images that caused her mind to draw a blank as though a clump of paint had congealed in her mind causing an artistic stroke. On other occasions, the dreaded paralysis was brought on by sheer lack of enthusiasm for the subject matter, the daily news could provide enough material to work from, but she was now feeling a little depressed depicting the woes of the world not to mention a tad concerned about becoming too predictable, how to ensure her work remained original knowing there was no such thing as true originality was always a worry. In the end she decided to experiment with geometrical abstractions, not the mindless splattering reminiscent of certain painters who thought spilling paint trails on bed sheets was art, but rather a carefully crafted blending of three-dimensional shapes in a myriad of shades that still made people want to stop and gaze for a moment despite the lack of anything remotely traditional or classical in the figures. To paint abstractions was better than not painting at all, and there was something satisfying in yielding to that primal urge to use nothing but colours and bizarre shapes. She was beginning to appreciate a few of the Surrealists and their forays into the subconscious, to create for the sake of creating as long as the pictures were interesting enough to look at. Perhaps she could experiment with optical illusions like her friend and see where that would lead.

Suzy however was busy accumulating research material and writing a draft for her arts administration dissertation that would contribute to her overall grade. Some evenings she was not at home, perhaps she was at the library Katherine thought, other nights she was very studious, keeping her nose to the grindstone leaving little if any time for conversation. Wow, Professor Get-Your-Details-Right must be pushing all the students extraordinarily hard this year, Suzy is looking positively stressed-out. Come to think about it, she was now beginning to notice Charlie was not calling as often as he used to, in fact, she could not remember the last time he did. Uncomfortable as she was with the deterioration in their friendship, she was also relieved to a point, and at the same time, made her feel terrible.

Finally on a quiet weekday she thought it was safe now to pick up the phone and see how he was doing, enough time had passed. Yeah, this afternoon would be a good time after she got some work done, she did not have any running around planned. She was about to prepare her palette when the mail van pulled up, might as well see what arrived before I get stuck into something. She was happy to find the priest had replied to her letter, she did not expect a response:

Dear Miss Walsingham,

Yes, I remember our meeting, I hope you are doing well. I apologize for not answering your letter sooner, but now that I have put pen to paper I hope my information may be of assistance, your project sounds very interesting. Unfortunately, I cannot help you with the significance of the constellations on Notre Dame, that is one area of the carvings I've had no time to study, perhaps one day in the future an opportunity may present itself. Concerning the correct dating for the Anno Mundi, my preferred choice for the calculation is printed in the Douay-Rheims version of the Bible, if you are interested, this edition also calculates the years for events in the Old and New Testaments. I wish I could look up the year of Babel's confusion, but as it happens, I have loaned out my copy I do not have it at hand. If I recall, the estimated year was around 2100 or 2200 BC, but you may have to verify this. However, this is only one approximation, the fathers of the Church have differed in the calculations, and there are other calendars you may want to consider for the Anno Mundi, such as the Eastern Byzantine calendar or the Hebrew calendar, there are many variances, it depends on which chronological tradition you intend to incorporate into your painting. As for a specific date and time, I cannot help you there, those details remain a mystery. I understand the lack of these essentials places you back in the same position as before, therefore another reason for my delay in writing was to think of an alternative suggestion—don't abandon your Babylonian theme, but do keep in mind the modern event you wish to satirise, continue to blend the ancient with the new. Like the gargoyles, the answer is already before you, you just have not seen it yet. Forgive me for answering your riddle with another riddle, but you will enjoy discovering the solution more than if I simply revealed it to you. Of course, if you have any other questions, or find you are completely at a loss with the enigma of Babel, I will be happy to help. Please feel free to write anytime.

God Bless,
Yours Sincerely,
Fr. Peter Reinold

Riddles? This did sound interesting. Katherine liked to solve puzzles, or at least attempt to solve them. He was right about one thing, if there were many calendars to choose from, how could she pick a year let alone try and find the right date and time? She would need a universally accepted calendar for her one theme to be understood and appreciated by all. In any case, she decided to begin with the bible he recommended, if only to rule out her original idea before she tried to figure out his unusual clue of separating the forest from the trees. Perhaps she could figure it out before the architect returned the plans and it was time to send out for estimates on the reconstruction. She worked on her abstract canvas for awhile trying to understand how she could find a precise star date by blending the old with the new before remembering she had resolved to call Charlie. As it turned out, she had just missed him by a few minutes, he had already gone out for lunch, the secretary did not know when he would be back. Well, she could always try again later.

C3 ❀ 80

The months flew and summer was drawing near, meaning she had events to look forward to, namely Steven would soon be back home to lighten the mood and Suzy would be graduating. Since the middle of winter, everything had been all work and no play that these few happy distractions would do everyone some good. It would be nice to see Suzy's parents again, Katherine occasionally talked with them on the phone if they happened to call while Suzy was out, they always sounded so pleasant. Suzy continued to appear under serious strain however, she was not as talkative and seemed fretful. Katherine assumed it was the pressure of exams and the worry of facing the real world once she held that degree in her hands, wondering where her path might lead now that her student days were ending. She had to agree that despite the general dislike for school, there was a sense of security in knowing that a large period of your life was predetermined to a certain extent within the structured environment of the educational system. For so many years you knew what you had to do, namely turn in your homework, study for an hour or two, and then pass all the required tests to proceed to the next year, hopefully you might retain something from all the subjects inflicted upon you according to the required curriculum and could actually use a smidgeon of that information someday. Third level education was a grand progression, you could finally choose your field of interest, but on the day of graduation, all those former periods of certainty were over.

Katherine was partially correct, this matter did begin to weigh on Suzy, but there were other anxieties burdening her of which she was unaware. In the midst of Katherine's hectic schedule and prolonged absences from the house due to the gallery project, Suzy and Charlie had more opportunities to become better acquainted. Charlie needed someone to talk to and was not that pushed out of shape as before when Katherine was too busy and Suzy answered the telephone instead. They talked for long periods, she was very happy to listen. He had arranged lunch on other occasions, and she could not find the will power to turn him down. She tried to reassure herself they would only be friends, nothing would or could

290

ever come of this, a handsome guy like him from a prosperous family could not possibly find *her* interesting. In any case, a few lunches and a dinner out here and there did not mean anything, especially as she continued to insist they go Dutch, much to his chagrin. Yet, if they were only friends, why was she afraid to tell Kathy they had gone out together and kept silent on the subject? Why did she have such devilish temptations not to tell her Charlie called when she was away on business? No, she was fooling herself, she did want their acquaintance to grow into something more serious and was afraid of what Kathy might think, she was still convinced her friend had not rejected all notions of romantic feelings towards him. Eventually Kathy would hear about their harmless get-togethers, then she would have to explain and admit her own feelings. This was a difficult prospect to face for Suzy who already felt guilty for having feelings for him, behind her friend's back, let alone disclosing her deeper emotions. With her graduation coming closer every day, her unease grew as she desperately wanted to invite Charlie to her reception afterwards but was not sure if that would be proper under the circumstances. She would hate to leave him out because of this nagging scruple since the Ws would be there too, he had been really kind to her these last few months, yet she remained so uncertain! Indecision was certainly a psychological plague.

Suzy finally decided she had better broach the topic before it was too late to invite him. In any case, it was a sure way to test the waters as her friend's reaction to her inviting Charlie would certainly reveal how she truly felt. What she really wanted was a sign, a good omen sent from above that the way was clear, she was tired of trying to hide everything. If the worst should happen, she solemnly resolved to stay in the background, she was not the type to play the bitter rival and declare with the bravado of Shakespeare that all was fair in love and war, especially after all Kathy and her family had done for her. She let it drop one morning during a casual conversation before they went their separate ways for the day.

"Kathy, since practically everyone I know here is invited to my graduation dinner, I was thinking of inviting Charlie too, you don't mind do you?"

Katherine was surprised, but what had she to say about the matter?

"Really? That's nice of you to think of him, Suzy. It's your party, you know. You don't need my permission to ask whom you like."

"You truly don't mind?"

"No, not at all."

Although they did not say much before heading out the door, Suzy was relieved this one dilemma was settled. In fact, she was afraid to elaborate on the subject in case her worse fears were realized. As long as Kathy seemed okay with this, all would be well. That must be the sign! She could hope anyway.

Katherine on the other hand was a little curious, why did she want to invite Charlie? Suzy didn't do that for her bachelor's graduation. It's none of my business really she thought, but still considered it a little unusual and wondered how she was going to manage that day, even after all that time she still found it difficult to act casually around Charlie. She had a sneaking suspicion Suzy was actually trying to bring them back together, but no, she wouldn't do that, not after telling her there was nothing serious between them and never could be. Charlie had read too much into their friendship, she was positive she had been completely clear on this point with Suzy. She was just being nice to him, it was kind of her to consider inviting him, Katherine concluded. Maybe she felt bad she didn't the last time. So what if he's there too? The dinner party will be relatively large so everything will be kept on a more formal basis, don't worry about it, she reassured herself.

È✺ۃ

The chilly weather that spring finally gave way to sunny days, it was now mid-June. Steven arrived home, and after a few leisurely rest days went straight to work in the labs without much ado. He was no longer interested in turning their world upside down for amusement, although he did continue to tell the odd yarn or two. To everyone's relief, it was as though some invisible switch went off in his psyche deadening his inclination to indulge in practical gags.   Only later did he finally reveal to them Jennifer had broken up with him a week before, although he did not divulge the reason. Maybe he realized his jokes could wear too thin, Katherine thought, everyone had their breaking point, especially Jennifer who had to contend with four prank-loving brothers, she did not need to date a buffoon as well! Aunt Martha had suspected as much and was determined to lecture her nephew with several reiterations of 'I told you so' on this point, she had really liked Jennifer. Poor Steves, maybe when things cooled down over the summer, he might be able to patch things up with her. Had he finally learned his lesson?

Suzy's parents and sister Grace arrived not long after Steven, and as on her last graduation, the family invited them to stay at Oak Meadows, no point wasting money on a hotel when they could be with their daughter. Not wanting to put anyone to extra trouble or be underfoot, Mr. and Mrs.

292

Cooper declined the use of a guestroom in the main house and were happy to lodge with Suzy in the apartment. After the usual greetings, and their profusion of gratitude for having been so kind to Suzy, they excused themselves and set about unpacking. They tended to be a very quiet couple Katherine noted, and her sister was definitely shy. Obviously they were still a little self-conscious meeting with the Ws in person, the media reports of the company and all the socialite gossip read so grandiose and uppity in the various papers that they may have thought the same applied to the family. This was not the first time Katherine noticed a similar reaction from others, she was not sure what the 'average' person expected of them. Come to think of it, maybe it was hard for the general public to believe that they did not have a fleet of private limousines or an army of butlers and footmen at every door crowned with powdered wigs and bowing endlessly to them as they passed. Yes, believe or not, the Ws preferred to fly commercially, the company jet was used only for important business, emergencies and the odd special occasion, not for frivolous hopping about. Pops was not in opposition to leisure activities but was definite in his conviction that the possession of wealth did not warrant abuse of the privileges they enjoyed. Katherine hoped the ice between them and their guests would thaw once again, although Pops and Mom were always polite and engaging in conversation, she could always count on Gramps and Steves who were usually good at warming the atmosphere with their sense of humour.

It felt so odd attending Suzy's graduation two days later now that she was no longer a student at Belvedere herself, watching the proceedings from the balcony as an invited guest. How long it seemed since she had walked up the aisle and was handed a similar-looking roll, so much had happened within that year! The gallery would be ready in a few months if everything went according to schedule, the first three floors anyway, and then she could keep that promise in deciding whose art would grace the walls of her establishment. She especially looked forward to the results of the Sirrac contest, not only for Suzy's sake, the judges' final choices would give her an indication where creativity was heading and what to expect when it came time to discover and promote the next generation of promising artists.

This year, it was decided that the awards ceremony be conducted in reverse order so that the honourable mentions would be disclosed first. The auditorium went silent as the envelopes were brought to the President, an honourable mention was nothing to sneeze at, she knew from experience. Her thoughts began to meander, I wonder if that anonymous buyer is still interested in my Napoléon. Should the costs of remodelling her place in

Dumbo continue to skyrocket, it would be a serious temptation not to give in and sell the one showpiece she planned to keep, especially as it might help with the expensive elevator she had set her eye on, it really was something else, the kind that the five star hotels used with the polished floor, wood panelling with gold tinted mirror inserts, elegant brass railings, piped music, and of course, all those burnished buttons. If all goes according to schedule it should be installed within the week, she hoped the workmen would be careful and not break the mirrors, that's all she needed right now before the doors even opened, to have the place jinxed for the next seven years.

Her rambling thoughts were interrupted by the proceedings, the first honourable mention went to a three-dimensional curiosity constructed of welded metallic bits and pieces entitled *Water Rush*. A pile of glorified scrap metal was promptly wheeled on-stage, however, it turned out to be more than a sculpture. While the President of the college read out the judges' comments on the piece, one of the assistant professors hit a switch hidden out of view that turned on an electric pump concealed inside, water began to trickle down various grooves and fissures. It was just a fountain, big deal, she thought, so much for originality. At least Suzy made the effort to think up something distinctive despite the insipid theme that year. It would be a shame if she didn't win or receive a mention, it wouldn't be worth painting anymore. Why struggle trying to create unique masterpieces if this watery contraption was considered worthy of a commendation? The local garden centre had better merchandise to offer.

Without warning, *Water Rush* began to drip ... drip ... drip ... onto the stage as the President continued his speech. The professors and dignitaries sat motionless, growing stiff as they tried to pretend nothing was wrong. Those closest to the statue slowly moved their feet aside or under their seats as far as possible, quietly avoiding the growing puddle inching its way towards them, doing their best to avoid making a scene. Soon it became necessary to tuck up the edges of their flowing robes until at last a number of them were forced to stand up from their seats and step aside, trying not to slip. The auditorium hummed with suppressed amusement as the graduates watched the impromptu pantomime unfold before them. The janitorial crew made their entrance and mopped up as best they could while the dignitaries tried to pull themselves together, the watery piece was quickly rolled off to the side. Finally, as the student went up to take the customary photographs with the President, he looked mortified that his *magnum opus* should behave so badly on its first public outing. How embarrassing! The next time he made a metallic sculpture, he definitely would be more careful with the welding.

The second honourable mention went to a painting called *Ride the Storm* depicting a cityscape battered by a fierce hurricane, a blatant homage to J.M.W. Turner and his wild blurry canvasses, and finally, the winner was announced.

"*River of the Mind* by Susanna Cooper!"

"Hey! Well done Suzy!" Katherine called out while her family clapped and waved. What a wonderful break for her friend, her first major work would be shown in the Sirrac Gallery on Fifth Avenue. What a début! After that, would Suzy want to have her pieces shown in humble old Dumbo? Oh well. If anyone deserved a break it was Suzy, she had struggled to keep up with the elite at Belvedere and felt compelled to abandon her master's degree in painting due to practical necessity. Now she had won one of the most prestigious prizes the school offered, that should give her the encouragement not to toss in her brushes and palette just yet.

The award was handed out, the applause died away, and the ceremony was closed allowing everyone to converse freely and disperse for the class photographs or to reclaim their artworks with the exception of the winning piece that would be taken directly to the gallery.

"Congratulations Suzy!" her parents said, giving her a hug.

"You did it! Good for you!" Katherine cheered, "I'm so happy for you!"

"Well, it's hard to get that excited," she said bashfully, "the competition was not hard to beat this year."

"Oh, don't be so modest," Katherine replied, "it's a great painting."

"When will they show it?" Grace was dying to know.

"I think within a few days, they have an exhibition lined up and plan to include it. Mom, Dad, do you think you'll be able to stay for that?"

"I think we can take an extra few days off, can't we Caroline?" Mr. Cooper affirmed with a smile.

"Sure honey, we wouldn't miss it for the world. I'll call the office. I hope your parents won't mind if we stay a little longer, Kathy," Mrs. Cooper added.

"Of course they wouldn't mind, you're welcome to stay as long as you like. It's not every day someone wins the Sirrac contest you know," Kathy replied.

"I suppose we should go for the photographs," Mr. Cooper suggested.

"That's a good idea, you have to get a head start or you'll be waiting in line for ages," Katherine noted, "I'll see you later. I'm just going to say 'hi' to Professor Matthews before he leaves."

"All right, Kathy, see you later," Suzy called after her.

Katherine quickly went backstage and caught the professor's attention, he was a little preoccupied with his wet robe, taking it off, wringing the ends out a bit and giving it a good shake.

"Hi, Professor, looks like you got caught in the flood."

"Hello Kathy," he replied, swinging the bedraggled robe over the crook of his arm with a dry smile before straightening his bow tie and pushing his glasses up the bridge of his nose, "it should have been expected, whenever the elements are included in the contest themes, we narrowly escape a disaster."

"Trial by water and fire. Let's hope earthquakes or meteor showers aren't chosen for next year," she replied.

"Indeed, should that happen, I might take a leaf out of the students' books for once and be conveniently sick for the day. Speaking of upheavals, how is Babel progressing?"

"Well, I did as you suggested and got in touch with a priest I met, but he just gave me another riddle to solve, and I'm stuck on it."

"Oh?"

"Yeah, he said it was impossible to find an exact day and time for the event, but he wouldn't tell me the solution he came up with. He also said I would enjoy the answer more if I discovered it myself, but I wish he had just given me the answer, I'd have the painting done by now and could move on to other works."

The professor rubbed his chin.

"No, he was wise in not telling you."

"How come?" Katherine asked. She had expected him to commiserate with her on this point.

"Speed is not always a constituent to great work, the process of creation should be given time and thought. Even God, who could create the whole universe in an instant, chose to take His time and carried out His designs in successive stages," he declared with a half humorous, half knowing expression before continuing, "the priest also withheld the answer for the same reason, everyone tells you to look a word up in the dictionary when you ask for the spelling, the effort compels you to remember it. If he gave you the answer, the work could not really be called your own now, could it?"

He was correct, if she did not make that final effort, someone else's idea would have provided the masterstroke to her work, it could not be considered entirely hers. Her signature in the corner of the canvas would be a partial hypocrisy.

"I guess you're right. He did give me a clue, but I can't quite figure it out, he said to continue blending the old with the new, but I was doing that to begin with so I don't see how that is much help. He said I could write to him again for the answer if I got stuck, but after what you just said, perhaps it's better if I don't."

"I think I know what his solution is, if I may give you another hint: what does modern history have that ancient history lacks? Combine the result, and you will have your answer."

Katherine looked confused.

"Media coverage? News reports? Electricity?"

"You're getting closer with the first two," he smiled, "just think about it some more, it'll come to you."

"If you say so, Professor."

.ɓ

Suzy was nervous from excitement eagerly anticipating the exhibition at the Sirrac Gallery, she had no idea what to wear and for the next few days continually asked everyone's advice. When she had finally selected her outfit, Katherine gladly offered her a few matching accessories to go with it. She was so happy, Katherine hoped that the evening would pass without a hitch. Having attended a few charity art exhibitions with her mother and Aunt Martha, plus other ladies from the country club, Katherine knew that these functions could be enjoyable if the atmosphere was just right, or they could veer completely in the opposite direction and flounder within the doldrums of stiff formality and yawn-inducing conversations, from her experience, the latter scenario was almost always the case.

Suzy handed her invitation to the doorkeeper, and Katherine took a quick glance through the entrance. She held her breath for a moment, oh dear, it was exactly as she feared, stiff and starchy with guests in evening jackets and formal dresses gingerly milling around sipping wine or nibbling petite titbits served by the dutiful caterers on silver salvers, everyone quietly engaging in small, meaningless chitchat, hesitant to raise their voices above a bare murmur as casual 'elevator' music played over the sound system. The formal atmosphere was intensified with the minimalist décor, black polished floors, stark white walls, strange halogen spot lamps suspended from steel wires from the high ceilings, with the usual track lighting illuminating the latest artwork on display, a little stark to put it mildly. Suzy could invite up to four guests, and judging from her initial inspection of the place, Katherine suspected that their little group would end up huddled together for the night, trying to look interested when the artwork could no longer hold their attention, unless they bravely asserted themselves and made a few introductions, seeing she did not recognise any of the other guests. This would be difficult considering the Coopers were a little intimidated with the formal atmosphere and the prospect of rubbing shoulders with the 'upper crust'.

The first thing on their agenda was to look for Suzy's painting and they hesitantly made their way through the gathering, stopping to inspect one of the exhibition pieces in an attempt to blend in with the other art admirers. This particular gallery was noted for its support of controversial styles and modernist mediums, Katherine did not take long to arrive at the conclusion the works presented that evening were atrocious, the canvases were mere colour washes with a streak here and there, a neo-lunacy somewhere between Colour Field painting and Lyrical Abstraction. Hardly any shape or feature were discernible, while the three-dimensional sculptured pieces were a conglomeration of nondescript blobs. At least the Cubists and Dadists took the trouble to depict figures, this was pure … finger painting. Except for Suzy's work, Katherine could not find one art piece she remotely liked. If asked to provide a critique on the other items on display, she knew she would be at a loss for words other than 'my trash can has more style tossed in it on any given day', but would not dare state her opinion out loud. Did anyone else see this, or was she the only petulant stickler for tradition?

All five in their little group stood gazing at Suzy's painting, it was amusing to eavesdrop on the other guests' commentaries as they quietly sipped their wine, apparently, her picture was garnering approval from the art lovers that night who were fast growing tired of the formless splotches of colour. Listening to the positive comments, Katherine wondered if Robert Horace was invited to the event and voiced her thought aloud to the others. They scanned the crowd hoping to see if they could guess who he might be, or indeed, if he was there. Judging from the grating sound of his name, Hor-ace … Hor … ace, not to mention his acidic reviews, he must be an old bald codger furrowed with a hundred wrinkles and wearing a perpetual Scrooge-like scowl on his face Katherine surmised. She looked for anyone with the misfortune to have this depressing physiognomy, but there were few present who could be singled out as likely suspects. After awhile, the Horace-hunting fun wore thin, and the people-watching grew a little monotonous.

"Is this it?" Grace finally had the courage to whisper to Katherine, "I mean, we just stand around, and just … gawk at each other?"

"Well, you're supposed to gawk at the art too," she whispered back, "I know, that doesn't take too long when there's not much to see."

It was as she predicted, their little group were becoming a petite clutch of bored exhibition attendees. Was there anyone she knew to whom she could introduce them? Exhibitions were all about hobnobbing, and they had better get started if they hoped to enjoy the evening. If they could only break the introduction barrier, that might do the trick. How she disliked the idea, it always seemed so impolite to introduce yourself, and the small talk necessary to get the ball rolling was never a pleasant experience for her, but someone had to do it. Katherine was spared the trouble of opening a conversation with a complete stranger when she espied a rather confident looking man peering over the heads of the guests, he was obviously searching for someone, and looking in their direction, he headed straight for them.

"Good evening, have I the pleasure of welcoming Miss Susanna Cooper?" he gallantly enquired, holding out his hand to Katherine. "Let me introduce myself, I'm Kevin Alcott, curator of the Sirrac Gallery. What a pleasure it is for us to introduce your art to the world."

Katherine was slightly embarrassed about the mix-up.

"Ah, I'm not Susanna, I'm her friend," she explained.

"Oh *do* forgive me," he replied as he turned in Suzy's direction, "Then I presume, *you* must be Miss Cooper."

Suzy smiled shyly and nodded as she shook his hand before introducing her parents, her sister, and then Katherine. The look of surprise tinged with admiration flooded his face at the mention of Katherine's name.

"Oh Miss Walsingham, do forgive my *faux pas*, I haven't had the pleasure of meeting you until now. How wonderful of you to attend our exhibition this evening, and are you all enjoying our petite affair?"

"Oh yes," Suzy fibbed, "It is an ... interesting collection."

They all nodded their heads and added similar pleasantries, including Katherine to her chagrin. She could not help wryly smiling to herself, what else could they say? '*It's horrible, boring, everything is way overpriced and not what we expected?*' Everyone was definitely thinking it. This certainly was an awkward moment, a little insincere diplomacy now and then never hurt, did it? *Drat!*

"I'm delighted to hear it," he replied, not batting an eye. "I wanted to greet you and fill you in on the proceedings of this evening's program. In a few moments I will be requesting the artists present to introduce themselves and say a few words about their work to our guests," Suzy looked petrified with this unexpected development. "Oh, nothing to worry about, tell them how you became inspired, and thank them profusely for attending, and how happy you are to become acquainted with everyone," he explained, before turning back to Katherine.

"Miss Walsingham, forgive me if I appear forward, but I must know, are you still in possession of your painting, *Napoléon*? I am absolutely positive that the prospective buyer is still interested in acquiring that particular piece."

How embarrassing! Katherine hoped Suzy was too panicked with her speech-making to pay much attention to this conversation, she had not told her all the details about the extravagant offer she received last year and her decision to refuse it at the time. It never failed; whenever she tried to keep a secret, someone or something managed to bring it out into the open at the worst possible time. Blast Murphy's Law! If she ever met this Murphy, she would give him a piece of her mind along with Robert the Horrible. She cringed as she tried to think sharp on how to avoid prolonging this scene and not reveal too many details to Mr. Alcott as Suzy stood close by.

"Er, yes, I still have it. I've decided to keep it actually," she replied hesitantly. No, she was tempted to sell it, but she could not divulge that to him right there, he could bring up the whole issue of price haggling and the astronomical fee she was offered when Suzy's painting had a mere five thousand attached to it, forty-seven per cent of which would be lopped off and given straight to the Gallery's coffers if it happened to sell.

"Oh how disappointing, but if that's your decision .... Do tell me, are you currently assembling a collection? It would be my greatest pleasure to arrange an exhibition of your work and a great honour for the Sirrac Gallery to introduce you to the art world."

I'll bet, she thought, at your commission rates, you'd try and flog off anything, forget about selling beautiful art. In fact, they already had, judging from the showing that evening. However, this was an excellent piece of news, not that she would give her collection to *them*, but it was an indication there could be a demand for her artwork. Why else would he make this offer? Fantastic! Her gallery just might prove to be a success, maybe she could keep her Napoléon after all. She could not give him any definite details on her growing collection as it was destined for her own establishment. That would be rather tactless, revealing she was going to be a new competitor within a matter of months, the evening would definitely have ice thrown on it after that. She might be accused of casing the place, plotting schemes to shanghai their artists and steal their customers.

"Thank you, Mr. Alcott, I appreciate the offer, but I don't have a collection at present," she replied without further comment, it was best to say as little as possible on the subject.

"Of course, but you do know how to get in touch with me, you have our number?"

"Yes, thank you."

"I will await your call then," he concluded before addressing the group, "if you would all please excuse me now, there are more guests arriving, and I must attend to them... ."

"Of course," Mr. Cooper replied politely, allowing Mr. Alcott to withdraw.

Thankfully, Suzy did not hear everything, she was so worried about what kind of impromptu speech she could think up to entertain that sea of faces that she resembled a deer caught in headlights.

"Ohm'gosh! Ohm'gosh! What am I going to say? I've never done anything like this before! I'm going to sound so stupid," she whispered breathlessly to her parents. "How I wish I had joined the debate club in school, I would be able to get up in front of all these people now without feeling so squeamish."

"Now calm down, honey," Mrs. Cooper soothed, "they don't expect an elaborate proclamation, just a few words on how you got your idea."

"That's right," her father affirmed, "don't panic."

"Breathe in, that's it," her sister reminded her, "deep breaths now, don't hyperventilate!"

"Just think of the Oscars," Katherine suggested, "that should do the trick, thank the Gallery for their award, how wonderful it all is, talk about your picture, and thank you ... thank you, blah, blah, blah, that should be easy enough."

"Oscars ... right," she murmured to herself, "just think about the Oscars, right, okay, I'll try."

While Suzy prepared for her upcoming ordeal, Katherine turned to see who had commanded Mr. Alcott's attention since he did not greet many other guests at the entrance, including the winner of their own art contest. It was a distinguished looking couple, the lady entered first, followed by whom Katherine assumed to be her date or husband. She did not recognise the former, but the latter she knew immediately—it was Mr. Gerard Reinold, Fr. Reinold's younger brother. She turned as quickly as possible while taking a sip of wine, pretending she had not observed his entrance and hoped he had not seen her. What a night! Of all the people she knew whom she could introduce to the Coopers, it would be the one individual who witnessed Charlie's awkward proposal to her. The prospect of meeting him again after that experience when he was the only person who was aware she had no intention of accepting Charlie's proposal … oh how mortifying! He was the last one she expected to show up at the Sirrac Gallery, it would appear he was not a collector of modern art judging from the collection he had stashed in Paris. Should she take evasive measures and avoid bumping into him for the evening, try somehow to get lost in the milling crowd? That would be near impossible, he was bound to see her eventually, and she could not spend the night hiding out in the powder room.

She slowly sipped her wine as she helped Suzy discreetly practise her speech, trying not to notice him or draw attention to herself. Eventually, it became difficult to ignore the effect his arrival was having on the formal gathering, a noticeable thaw began to permeate the room as she overheard the lively greetings exchanged. He appeared to know many people there, striking up animated conversations with everyone he met. Obviously, he attended many exhibitions at this gallery. Huh, imagine that, maybe he did dabble in modern art, she knew better than to judge a book by its cover. Although it was not polite, Katherine tried to listen in on his comments as he and his companion made their way around the room, wondering if he truly liked the absurdity paraded as art or if he bought the stuff merely for investment purposes, but the growing hubbub of the conversations made eavesdropping near impossible. Certainly, his tour around the gallery would inevitably lead him to their corner of the room, and she braced herself for the encounter that could not be avoided.

"This is unusual," the lady commented as they drew closer to examine Suzy's work, "it stands out from the rest, it's the contest winner from Belvedere too," she continued, reading the description label.

"Yes, it is different," he agreed, "an optical illusion, and a picturesque one at that."

"*River of the Mind*, this *is* a nice piece, and they only have five thousand marked on it," the lady noted rather surprised, "they're not asking much for it, are they?"

"I suspect that Kevin is hoping to … well, hello there," he trailed off in mid-sentence, finally noticing Katherine as he stood back to admire the painting, "we meet again."

Katherine politely shook hands.

"Hello, how are you?"

"Never better," he replied, before continuing, "let me introduce you to my sister, Charlotte. Lottie, this is Katherine Walsingham."

"Hello, it's a pleasure to meet you, just call me Lottie like everyone else."

"Okay, you can call me Kathy."

"Are you 'in' to modern art?" Mr. Reinold asked.

"Well, to be honest, I'm not an avid admirer." Katherine could not lie again that evening, playing diplomatic dodgems with Mr. Alcott was enough. "My friend won the competition this year and I was invited as a guest. Forgive me for being inquisitive, I didn't know *you* liked modern art, one would never tell from your collection in Paris."

He laughed.

"It depends on the art, sometimes I find a piece I like, mostly I buy just to invest in new talent that may hit it big. You never know what may become the latest 'school' to collect."

Aha, she thought so. He then drew a little closer with a knowing smile;

"To be honest, I really can't stand a lot of the nonsense Kevin tries to peddle off on me, but *this*," and he indicated to Suzy's picture, "I *do* like."

"Oh, I'm forgetting my manners, let me introduce you."

Katherine expected the Coopers to say a polite 'hello' and bashfully clam up, but Mr. Reinold had a way of making everyone feel at ease.

"Call me Gerry, please," he insisted, and they seemed happy to meet a few engaging people at last.

"Have you met the other artists here tonight?" he enquired, "we came to see good old Yoris and his latest collection, but his work is rather disappointing this time around."

"Perhaps he is suffering one of his 'grey periods'," Charlotte interjected.

"You know Yoris Stansislov?" Suzy asked impressed with their connections in the art world.

"Yes, our father has been a patron for several years now. The sculptor John Fielding is here too. Don't tell me you haven't been introduced to anyone?" Charlotte asked incredulously.

"No, actually," Katherine replied, "only Mr. Alcott who came over to inform us Suzy was expected to give a short speech and introduce her work."

"Typical," Gerard wryly noted, "he tries to catch everyone on the hop. Listen, don't worry Suzy, take it from me, these people are easy to please, keep it simple and you'll do fine."

"Okay, keep it simple, and think of the Oscars," she repeated nodding her head.

Their conversation was interrupted by the sound of a spoon striking a glass. *Ting, ting, ting, ting, ting.* The music was turned down and the room grew silent.

"Good evening ladies and gentlemen, I'm delighted you could honour us with your presence for this exciting exhibition," Mr. Alcott declared, bowing to his audience with a flourish when he had everyone's attention. "I regret to inform you that Mr. Sirrac is unable to attend this evening as he is away in Berlin on business, therefore the duty of Master of Ceremonies has fallen to me...."

"Oh, that's why we haven't seen Stefan tonight," Charlotte whispered over to her brother.

"I *thought* I heard he was flying to Europe to sign on a new *wunderkind* painter," he quietly replied, "he kept it quiet, that's for sure."

"Obviously, he didn't want anyone else to beat him to it."

Mr. Alcott continued;

"As you all know, we are privileged to have the artists Yoris Stansislov and John Fielding showing this evening, and it is my pleasure to introduce this year's winner of the Belvedere Contest, Susanna Cooper, a very promising young artist. Customary to our showings at the Sirrac Gallery, I would now like to request the creators of these masterpieces to say a few words to all you beautiful people gathered here this evening. Mr. Stansislov, would you do us the honour of addressing your guests?"

Dressed in the 'typical' dishevelled artist garb, wrinkled jacket and shirt, no tie of course, Yoris made his way to the platform, and standing next to Mr. Alcott, in hesitant English launched into a poetic elegy about his days growing up under Communism, the bleakness of his childhood and the general hardships of life in what used to be called the Soviet Block.

"That's getting a little old now, isn't it?" Charlotte whispered to her brother. "Can't he find a happy subject to paint?"

"Hey, they all love that old 'how bad it was under Stalin' spiel, it makes for great inspiration," he returned, "artists live on misery I'll have you know, that never goes out of fashion."

Grace suppressed a chuckle.

Yoris eventually finished his woe-begotten speech and the guests applauded politely. Fielding's turn came next, and walked smartly up to the platform, confidently dressed all in black complete with a three-quarter length fitted evening jacket, his appearance was not wrinkled, but he had the tendency to tousle his long blonde hair, which was meant to be held back in a ponytail, giving him that frizzed look of a character straight out of the movie *Amadeus.* He placed his hand on his breast, and looking up to the ceiling as though he were gazing at some heavenly image, he cleared his throat and in a solemn tone began with the words:

> *"Moon dribbling honey upon lips of lunatics*
> *Orchards and country town tonight grow greedy*
> *Stars resemble bees*
> *Of a luminous liquid that drips from trellises*
> *Each honey beam oozes from heaven*
> *Taking its own sweet time."*

"Good evening, ladies and gentlemen, I submit this poem to you as my inspiration for my latest collection."

Without offering any further comment, he made a polite bow to the guests and stepped down from the platform.

"I wonder what that was all about?" Mrs. Cooper enquired before the applause died away.

"Oh, Fielding sculpts images and shapes suggested to him by certain poems and short stories he reads," Charlotte explained, "*we* may not see any connection, but *he* seems to be happy with the result."

The Coopers and Katherine suppressed a smile, only Suzy was too nervous to react knowing her turn was next. The clapping ceased and Mr. Alcott summoned her forward.

"Good luck!" Katherine whispered. Poor thing, she still had a startled expression on her face.

"Hello … it's … a pleasure to be here with you this evening," she hesitantly began. *So far, so good*, Katherine thought, at least she didn't freeze up with all those spotlights on her. "The theme selected for the Belvedere Contest this year is *The Power of Water*", Suzy continued, "we can appreciate the ferocity of a storm, the pounding of waves on a seashore or the roar of a cascade, but water also has a mesmerising power to attract like the gentle flow of a stream. My inspiration was relatively simple, I wanted to capture humanity's fascination with this element in a double-image depicting the captivating pull of a river, the crashing fury of a waterfall and the calm reflection of a peaceful, crystal-clear lake. I want to thank the Sirrac Gallery for their contest and the amazing opportunity it presents to young artists graduating from Belvedere, and I am so surprised and happy to win the contest this year. Thank you very much," and smiling timidly, she left the platform.

"Well done, Suzy," Mr. Cooper said still applauding as she approached.

"I'm so proud of you," Mrs. Cooper beamed.

"Me too," Grace added.

"That wasn't so bad now, was it?" Katherine observed.

"That was perfect," Mr. Reinold smiled for he could see how nervous she had been. Charlotte nodded in agreement.

"Thanks, I'm so glad that's over," Suzy sighed with relief, "my knees are still shaking a bit."

"We had better find something to revive you," Gerard offered, looking for the waiters who had disappeared while the speeches were being made.

"No, that's all right, I don't need anything, really," she replied.

The music was turned back on and the room began to buzz with activity, the mood was definitely more animated. A few people detached themselves from their current *cliques* and came to meet Suzy now that they were aware she was the winning artist. Gerard and Charlotte were happy to introduce the Coopers and Katherine to everyone seeing Mr. Alcott had failed to fulfil that courtesy at the beginning of the evening. In the midst of one of the conversations, Gerard noticed one senior couple looking over Suzy's painting with great admiration. Momentarily, the lady clasped her hands with an expression of glee as the gentleman searched his inside pocket for something as he made his way over to Mr. Alcott, and with a smile and a nod he said;

"I would very much like to buy that painting for my wife."

Gerard straightened up with interest, and walking across to where they stood, smiled at Vincent, the man with the chequebook in his hand, and turning to Kevin said;

"I am also interested in buying that piece, I'm offering six thousand for it."

The room filled with various reactions from exclamations of surprise to excited murmuring.

"Now Gerry, that's not fair," Vincent joked back, "do you wish to deprive my wife of her anniversary present?"

"I apologize, but yes, unless you can beat my offer," Gerard shrewdly replied.

"All right, sixty-five hundred," Vincent conceded.

"Seven thousand," Gerry returned.

The murmuring grew a decibel.

"Attention! Attention everyone! It's seems we have an impromptu auction taking place!" Mr. Alcott announced in somewhat of a flurry, clasping his hands in undisguised delight. "Goodness gracious, this hasn't happened before at a showing! The bid stands at seven thousand for Miss

Susanna Copper's painting, *River of the Mind.* I say, everybody, attention!"

Vincent with a grunt turned to Mr. Alcott;

"Oh well, eight thousand then."

Calmly and with quiet determination Gerard turned and said;

"Fifteen thousand."

There was a gasp and then a quiet hush, and after a moment's silence, Vincent declared;

"If you want it that bad, it's yours."

"Sorry old chap, my sister wanted it for her birthday, better luck next time. No hard feelings I hope."

"You win tonight, I'll get you next time," and with that, he turned on his heels and walked back to his wife.

The stilted atmosphere of the evening vanished as the excited murmuring of the guests crescendoed to an electrical buzz while Gerard wrote out a cheque and made arrangements for the painting to be delivered the next day. Mr. Alcott, all a flutter, came breathlessly to give the good news to Suzy as if she had not heard one syllable of the unexpected proceedings.

"Upon my stars! This is just too marvellous for words!" Mr. Alcott gasped, clasping and rubbing his hands with excitement, "your painting has just fetched fifteen thousand, at an impromptu auction no less, that's a first for the Sirrac Gallery! I must congratulate you, it is *such* a pity Mr. Sirrac was not here to see this!" and with that, he shook hands with her before hurrying back to conclude the sale with Mr. Reinold. The guests began to crowd around and congratulate the Coopers.

"Oh my, I think I have to sit down," Suzy declared, as she sought out a bench not far away. Katherine sat with her while the family and Lottie continued to chitchat with the guests, giving Suzy some space to recover from the shock. She turned and whispered;

"Kathy, fifteen thousand, I never expected anything like this to happen. Oh do you realize what this means to me? Imagine fifteen thousand, oh, not quite, less the commission, but it gives me room to breathe, now I will be able to put new tires on my car, I couldn't say anything to my parents, I've cost them enough already. Oh, I just don't believe it, Kathy! Is this truly happening?"

"You bet it is, just relax, take a few deep breaths, and you'll get through this okay. I am so happy for you Suzy!"

Katherine had no idea how tight things had become for her friend in the last few months, how selfish she had been lately, so busy with her own project in Dumbo that she did not pay much attention to what was happening around her and just dismissed Suzy's anxieties as exam pressures. How could she be so heartless? Stupid idiot! Katherine was truly happy, tonight was definitely a fantastic surprise, to think Mr. Reinold would offer that much for her work as a beginner, maybe he was not such a bad guy after all. Katherine felt sheepish for letting resentment towards him take hold, it wasn't his fault her friendship with Charlie was somewhat estranged at present. He too was an unsuspecting victim of Christmas Past, invited to a cheerful holiday dinner only to become a witness to that melodramatic fiasco. On further reflection, now that she met Charlotte in person, she could not stay vexed with her either. Lottie seemed to be a very quiet and gracious individual with a quaint sense of humour, and she had a feeling Lotite was someone she could grow to like if she had the chance to get to know her better. It was a pity they had gotten off on a wrong foot before they ever met, she did not seem the type that would purposely set out to spread gossip. How on earth could they believe the idle notions spread abroad about her and Charlie? Well, Gerry did admit in so many words that his sister had a romantic streak. Okay, so what if Lottie liked to read the society papers once in awhile, but she should know by now not to pay attention to the gossip that appears in print, especially false stories relating amorous attractions. Come to think of it, she should have known they intended no harm, look how helpful their elder brother was to her friends in Paris last summer, not to mention how gracious he was to answer her letter and offer assistance for something as trifling as a painting. She should remember not to jump to conclusions.

Katherine and Suzy rejoined the group, Gerard followed shortly after.

"Now that we have made our appearance for the evening," he announced, turning to Mr. Cooper, "Lottie and I have reservations for dinner, and we would be honoured if you and your family, and of course Katherine, would join us, that is, if Susanna feels she has fulfilled her obligations to the gallery."

"Why, we thank you for your offer, but we couldn't possibly impose upon you," Mr. Cooper began.

"Oh, especially after paying that enormous sum for my painting," Suzy added, "you've spent enough already, it just wouldn't be right."

"Stuff and nonsense," he replied, "for all you know, your painting may be worth a hundred times that in the future and make my sister the envy of the art world. It would be our pleasure to have you join us for dinner, the perfect finale to a successful evening."

Suzy smiled bashfully to this unexpected compliment. Charlotte nodded in agreement.

"Yes, do join us, it's time to have some fun, with Stefan absent, it was stuffy enough until you saved the evening, Gerry."

The Coopers and Katherine looked at each other, waiting for Suzy's cue, this was her big night, and the decision should be hers.

"Thank you, I *suppose* we can leave now, there's nothing else I have to do here I guess …." She did not wish to be rude and thought best to accept their offer.

"That's settled then, let's make our excuses to Kevin and we'll be on way," Gerard concluded.

Mr. Alcott, still not recovered from the excitement of the auction, was now startled to see them preparing to leave and quickly made his way to the main entrance.

"I hope you are not thinking of leaving us so soon?" he enquired somewhat distressed.

"I'm afraid we must, Kevin, we have reservations for supper and we'll have to take our leave of you," Gerard explained, "it has been a most enjoyable evening."

"Oh, I am glad to hear that, I hope we shall see you again soon, please give my kindest regards to your parents."

"Of course," Charlotte affirmed.

"It's been a pleasure to meet you all," Mr. Alcott reiterated, turning to Katherine and the Coopers.

"Thank you," Mr. Cooper returned.

"We had a wonderful time," Mrs. Cooper added.

Mr. Alcott watched reflectively as the party left, but recovered his vibrancy as he turned to attend to the other guests. It was a most fortune night, there could be another auction, one can always hope.

03 ❀ 80

Katherine was up first the next morning despite their late night supper. She did not get much sleep, she had a lot on her mind these past weeks that she wanted to discuss with Suzy and hoped to have a long chat with her before she went back to Iowa with her parents, she had not found find the right time with all the graduation preparations and the excitement of the Sirrac contest. She was sorry she had left things slide as this was their last morning together and the Coopers may become too preoccupied with packing for the trip home to allow an opportunity for a personal chat. Still dressed in her sleeping attire, dressing gown and slippers, Katherine quietly made her way to the apartment, bracing herself against the chilly morning air as she hurried across the driveway. Suzy would be disgruntled with this early intrusion, she did not do mornings well, but this was something that could not be handled over the phone. She gently knocked on her bedroom door.

"You're up awfully early," Suzy sleepily noted, pulling on her fuzzy pink robe and fumbling for her bunny slippers.

"Sorry to wake you, but I wanted to have a talk before you went home to Iowa, and we might not have a chance later. We can make some coffee over in the main house, you don't mind, do you?"

"Nah," Susanna yawned, "I hope we don't wake up everyone."

"Don't worry, they're used to me puttering around in the wee hours by now, they won't take any notice if we whisper."

The coffee machine churned away as they discussed the events of the previous night over a plate of doughnuts raided from the pantry. Suzy could not believe what that had happened, first winning the contest, and then Mr. Reinold stealing the show with a dramatic auction before whisking them all off to a fancy dinner, they were bound to become the talk of the town. Still basking in the afterglow of that grand adventure, Suzy wanted to hear again how Katherine met him in Paris, that whole episode sounded so unusual. Katherine did her best to oblige without revealing Martin and Justine's private affairs since it was through them she met the Reinold brothers. Suzy was all ears about Gerard's amazing collection in Paris, in a vacation property no less! If that was the case, what pieces could he possibly have adorning the walls of his Manhattan apartment overlooking Central Park? How thrilling it all seemed, they were at liberty to address everyone at the Sirrac Gallery on a first-name basis, and their parents were well-known collectors, perhaps they might consider opening their own museums someday, not to mention setting up a charitable foundation or two for the arts, it was not unheard of, just look at the Guggenheim dynasty.

"Guggenheim wanna-be's?" Katherine quietly laughed, "anything is possible, so they say."

When they had thoroughly reviewed their impressions of Gerard, they turned their attentions to Charlotte, admitting they liked her well enough, imagine, she was reading Greek and the ancient classics at Harvard although she was taking a year off at present. Wow, imagine learning to study Socrates and Plato in the original language, that had to be interesting, texts invariably lost their true significance in translations.

"You've read Socrates?" Suzy asked with surprise, "that sounds a little boring."

"Actually, Greek philosophy is quite fascinating once you get into it," Katherine affirmed. Suzy said she would take her word for it.

Exhausting the topic of the previous night, Suzy wanted to know what was so important that Katherine had them up at the crack of dawn. Through all of Katherine's comings, goings, and upheavals, she felt she had neglected Suzy these past few months, which was not intentional. It was time to clue Suzy in on the Grand Plan and disclose the proposal she wanted her to consider over the summer while she was back in Iowa.

Katherine began by admitting she had her doubts that Suzy had made the right decision in changing her course to Arts Administration, but now her experience would be a great advantage. During the reconstruction of the old factory, Katherine became painfully aware of how completely ignorant she was with the running of a gallery, not to mention how much time it would take from her artwork should she try to manage the place by herself on a full time basis. However, if Suzy would agree to help run the place with her, working together as a team, they could take turns watching the floor, allowing each other plenty of free time to continue with their artwork. Katherine had plans to leave most of the top floor free as a studio, it had plenty of light and room to work in. If anything should happen in the gallery, they would be on hand to deal with whatever might come up. There would also be ample time for all those other little necessities, like running for doctor appointments, dentists, whatever errands they had to do, in effect, Suzy would have a full salary on a part time basis, if she would not mind contributing just twenty-five percent of future sales of her artwork to the costs and maintenance of the business. She was welcome to stay at the apartment at Oak Meadows as long as she liked, no need to move out right away just because college was over, and now she might actually have the sitting room to herself. With their painting studio relocated to the gallery in Dumbo, they could lock up their artwork for the night, no point taking their work home with them, they needed to get a life at some point Katherine noted. For instance, starting out with a new business, they might have to stay open six days a week, they *had* to turn the key on their stresses at the end of the day, or they wouldn't be doing themselves any favours or the gallery if they crashed from psychological burnout. Besides, painting at night was never a good idea, electric light was simply not conducive to blending the perfect colours for an oil painting. There were so many aspects to consider, Katherine hoped she articulated her points clearly and did not forget anything or sound too confusing.

"Well, there's my proposal … that's if you still want to exhibit at my gallery now that you've become a hit at the Sirrac…," Katherine tentatively noted, "this is just an idea I wanted to run past you."

"Of *course* I'm still going to give you an exclusive on my artwork! Don't be silly!" Suzy replied. "You know I wouldn't run out on you now that the gallery is almost ready, but only twenty-five percent as the commission fee, free time for my artwork, *and* a salary? I don't know what to say, it sounds too good to be true!"

"Naturally, I can't offer a *huge* salary right now, it will take time to grow the business, it's a new venture, we need to attract other artists and build up a clientèle, but since we've graduated Belvedere with a bang, you in your way, and I in mine, we may have already obliterated the problem of attaining some notoriety."

Suzy laughed.

"*That's* for sure, Kathy. Oh, I really don't think I need any time to arrive at a decision. Wow, this is so exciting! I've never had so much good news hit me at once! Wait 'till the folks hear about this!"

"Well, please sleep on it anyway when you go home. I don't want to put any pressure on you, or make you feel you *have* to accept."

"*What* pressure?" Suzy laughed. "In fact, your offer will take a load off. Who else is going to give a graduate like me a regular salary with practically free use of an artist's studio, or charge that amount of commission for my paintings? I'm grateful I have a place to come back to and not have to worry about packing up or go apartment-hunting now that I'm sorta settled here. You *know* I'd be real stupid not to accept."

Katherine was delighted, since Suzy seemed eager to start right away, there were many things that needed to be discussed, for one thing … Suzy's old jalopy. Katherine was positive the old clunker would never make another trip to Iowa, and it was not a good idea for Suzy to throw away her first artistic earnings on that old oil burner. Each summer Katherine dreaded to think of her heading out on the highways all by herself, imagining her stuck in some back road in the middle of nowhere surrounded by endless grasslands, fields of wheat or corn until news came that she had arrived unharmed. Why not trade in her clunker for a new car now that she had a job prospect waiting for her? Couldn't she go home with her parents in their car and just wait until she came back? It seemed silly to fork out good money on new tires or a tune-up for that matter, that miserable clunker was belching its swan-song. Suzy's eyes lit up, she had not even considered a new car, she had been nickel and dime-ing her old rattletrap for years it had become second nature to resuscitate the thing whenever the cash became available. There was a slight hitch, how could she come back if she left her old monster at Oak Meadows? A one-way plane ticket was just as expensive as a tune up, and if she was moving to New Jersey, there was a load of old stuff to clear out at home, flying would be out of the question with the weight restrictions. Thinking about it for a moment, the idea came to them as they exclaimed simultaneously:

"U-Haul!"

Perfect! Great for dragging a load with you for a one-way trip Katherine noted, she could hire the vehicle for a few extra weeks after Suzy used it until she figured out the logistics of purchasing a company van for transporting artworks or resorting solely to shipping companies. Ugh, imagine driving around in an old orange and black rent-a-contraption, not very stylish, she had pictured a beautiful white van with her colourful Walsingham logo designed by her emblazoned on the sides, but until that day, she would have to use something without spending too much until things fell into place, right now everything seemed so touch-and-go.

Talking about art deliveries, Suzy wondered if Katherine was already on the lookout for artists to showcase, if the grand opening was scheduled for the end of September, she should start the process of requesting portfolios and setting up interviews right away if she did not have a list of people to contact personally. That was true, there was considerable wall space to fill, regardless of their own collections, not to mention her friends' work in Paris, they would barely make a dent in that vast area, and she was only opening two thirds of the place for starters! It was imperative she informed her chosen artists well in advance so they too had time to prepare and have collections ready. Suzy suggested contacting a few art schools until Katherine observed in dismay it was already too late, all the students would be gone for the summer. Oh, why did she not think of that sooner? Not to worry, Suzy interjected, they could try running a few ads in the art sections, and we'll have artists crawling out of the woodwork.

"Are you kidding?"

Katherine laughed until her sides ached, they would have every would-be-artist from nine to ninety slapping paint on canvases lined up for blocks around Dumbo to peddle their wares. Drawing a line or two and colouring it in does not an artist make, and not everyone was fortunate to be a Grandma Moses. They both cracked up at the image this suggestion conjured up. Maybe they should go back to the first idea, Katherine concluded it was safer to contact the professors in the art schools as they could pass on interview invitations to master students they recommended, if their pupils were interested, they would certainly show up. Upcoming artists were always hoping to be spotted by galleries, that was the one immutable reality of the art world she could count on. Suzy promised to return to New Jersey earlier than planned to help with the interview process, they would need to make their selections by August to allow one month to set up for the exhibition, mail out invitations for the first private showing, including press releases to the critics and reviewers, they had to be invited if they hoped to gain a little publicity and a free write-up in the papers.

"All right, but if Robert Horace thinks he's getting an invitation, he can forget it," Katherine declared.

"Oh, speaking about him, you wouldn't mind sending on any reviews that might be printed about last night?" Suzy asked, "I won't be here to see the papers."

"Sure, no problem."

They heard movements in Mrs. Gonzales' apartment and footsteps on the stairs. Finishing their coffee, Gramps came through the door, and spying the plate of doughnuts, he lit up with his good fortune and quickly grabbed a few.

"Aw, Gramps, you know you shouldn't do that," Katherine protested.

"Finders keepers, never look a gift horse in the mouth," he mumbled as he chomped on his forbidden fruits. With a resigned sigh, Katherine suggested they had better get dressed, there was a busy day ahead of them.

03 ❀ 80

July arrived, it was down to the wire and panic threatened to rear its ugly head. That was the problem with setting a deadline Katherine observed, the workers hired by the contractor may not meet it, especially if things continued to go askew. Only a day or so ago, the engineer finally decided to check out the old turn of the century fire escape. Katherine wondered what all the hollering was about until she went out the back door and looked up to see him hanging on a bar attached to the wall with his feet skidding around on the old iron platform, tilting at a precarious angle after it had jiggled free from its anchors. What idiot walks out on a potential death trap before taking a closer look or giving the thing a good shake? She yelled at the decorators for help and they managed, with difficulty, to haul him back in. She did not wait around after that and hustled for insurance right away while the contractor hired a few good iron welders. She was glad most of the major remodelling was finished, she was getting tired of having the workmen in their saggy pants and overloaded tool belts wolf-whistling at her from the scaffolding like a bunch of monkeys or calling out "Yo, mama!" when she came to check their progress.

Unexpectedly, the local hysterical, or to be more precise, the *historical* society, made its presence known. One day she was surprised when a smartly dressed man asked to see the new owner and on discovering it was her, politely handed her a petition signed by all those concerned requesting in the spirit of historical preservation that she refrain from washing off the large faded advertisement painted on the side of the building. When he left, she looked at the large envelope in her hand and could not help but laugh, how often she had sent out petitions crusading for various causes and now she had become a recipient! Well, their request was nothing outlandish, she went outside to observe their local treasure in its fading green and white lettering of yesteryear; *"Walsingham Pharmaceuticals, makers of fine and agreeable pills, elixirs, powders and clysters for all your health requirements."* Although it was an old Walsingham ad, she could not leave it in its dilapidated condition, maybe she could have the thing painted exactly as it was in the old days when Great Gramps ran the place, complete with the picture of an antique pestle and mortar. At least the sign had an old fashioned charm, and Gramps Junior would certainly appreciate the fact it was not power-hosed into oblivion. Even though it was a pharmaceutical sign, Katherine was happy to restore it until she looked up the last product of the ad in the dictionary, imagine painting *that* back in! No wonder Gramps changed their company slogan. Maybe saving the article in its original form was not the brightest idea in the world, no one would know if the premises was a gallery or a pharmacy, they might have people dropping in and asking to have their prescriptions filled. Time for a compromise here, she could salvage the original word, 'Walsingham', but using the same antique lettering change the rest to, '*Gallery, Provider of Fine Artwork since 1991*'. Technically, the sign was the billboard for the factory, not an ad, so she could change it to something that suited the new establishment while honouring the old.

Getting the larger problems of the renovation sorted out and the local history buffs appeased to a point, she was down to handling the most annoying details, like the decorators using the wrong paint colours after she had assigned custom blended shades for each of the partition walls, or scuffing the new wainscoting in the smaller exhibition areas, at other times, knocking off a few of the track lights with their ladders, not to mention giving the larger chandeliers a bash or two. Her heart went crossways every time she heard a crash resounding from somewhere in the building, or a mighty thumping that had her imagining scenes of costly destruction wreaked upon work already accomplished by the renovators, she was only a hair's breadth away from suffering a stroke.

Happily, it was not all a hard slog as the family were eager to contribute towards her new endeavour. Mom and Pops had not forgotten the promised graduation present, but instead of a new car, decided to purchase a suitable mercantile van for all her moving needs complete with her Walsingham Gallery logo. Helen in particular was not about to have a "U-Haul" parked outside the premises after all the work and expense Katherine had lavished on it. Aunt Martha had to agree: what would people think? Gramps simply loved the new elevator Katherine had selected and decided to pay for the elegant machine despite her protests he had already given her too much.

"No 'buts' now Katie, just give me a decent lunch at your new coffee shop when it's open."

Steves did not intend to be left out, the budding Wall Street tycoon was not a miser at heart, and he insisted on providing the latest security and CCTV systems. Uncle Tim, Aunt Barbara and the cousins wanted to know what they could contribute as she had so much accomplished at this stage, but insisted they would not be excluded. At last, she gave in and suggested they could help with the hi-tech climate control system that monitored humidity levels and the temperature to protect the artwork on display, which turned out to be far more expensive than she anticipated. Katherine was overwhelmed by the generosity and the enthusiasm shown by the family. How could she *possibly* fail with all this good will showered on her? Aunt Martha, not to be outdone by anyone, had a surprise in store for the prospective permanent collection:

"Well, I was going to leave you Uncle Bob's five paintings in my will, but you might as well have them now while I'm alive, and I'd like to see my name on the wall of the gallery as a contributor. I have my heart set on a shiny brass plaque, if that's all right with you."

How could she refuse? Uncle Bob had managed to obtain two Henry Matisse paintings, a charcoal sketch by Chagall, and miracle of miracles, a backstage scene by Degas plus an early rugged Van Gogh depicting the sombre life of the Belgian peasantry. Although she had not planned to acquire pieces for her permanent exhibition space at this early point, it looked like the matter was taken out of her hands, she was off and running. Wow, these works were bound to attract the art enthusiasts to the gallery, but another thought struck her: how could she possibly afford to add comparable artworks to this remarkable donation? Would her budget stretch to acquire extra pieces to fill the large space? However, this was a great start, maybe she could interest some of their friends to loan their private collections for showing until such time as she could build her own.

When it did not seem possible that anything could beat Aunt Martha's donation, her parents made an announcement one Sunday before anyone else came down for breakfast.

"Kathy dear, your father and I would like to contribute towards your gallery."

"But, you just got me the van..." Katherine replied, a little confused.

"Well yes," Harold began, "but that was really your graduation present, nothing special or lasting that was a significant contribution towards your new enterprise."

"It is though!" Katherine protested. "The van will be a great help, and it's a great piece of free mobile advertising."

"I know dear," her mother replied, "but we want to be part of your artistic endeavour. Using your graduation present is not all that different from giving a child born on Christmas only one gift."

"Since your grandfather has provided the most important element, the building itself, we thought as your parents we had better donate something comparable," her father interjected with a smile, "we thought about the few paintings we owned to add to your permanent exhibition space, but as we never collected anything like your uncle that would be of the calibre suitable for a noteworthy gallery, we decided to donate a cash amount that you can use at Sotheby's to buy paintings you consider worthy to exhibit."

"Are you serious, Pops? I can't accept that!"

"Oh, yes you can, dear. It would make your father and I very happy," her mother replied.

Katherine gave them a big hug, this was all too much to take in. How could she ever repay or thank them? Imagine! An art spree at Sotheby's!

෴

Thank heavens she could escape to her painting after each day's eclectic whirlwind of hard knocks, excitement and surprises. It was soothing to brush away the tumult by working on her strangely calming abstract scenes. Her nuclear power plant and the Babylonian enigma continued to bother her however as she tried to fathom the clues Fr. Reinold and the professor had given her. *Blend the old and new...something that modern history had that ancient history lacked* ... it was obviously one of those situations when the answer was so simple she would feel like kicking herself once she discovered it. Although she understood why they did not provide the solution to her problem immediately, she had no time to sit around and wait for it to dawn upon her, she had to have the painting finished before the grand opening, and the days were slipping away too fast for her liking. She had so many things to accomplish, invitations to think about, press releases to send to the art columnists not to mention artists to contract, a deadline that would have to be met ... *tick* ... *toc...tick... toc.* She could literally hear time passing her by. While all these details swirled in her mind, the pieces of the puzzle finally came together. Thanks to the newspapers and TV reports of today, modern history had a system of record keeping with accurate dates, days, hours, minutes, the few details she was searching for to calculate the stars. All she had to do was figure out down to the second when the Chernobyl catastrophe occurred, but use that information to plot the star chart over the site of ancient Babylon and add it to her skyline, the double link to the old and the new would be accomplished.

It *was* simple! She really did feel like an idiot for not solving it sooner, but there was no time to waste on self-reproaches. She scoured the encyclopaedias and microfilm reels at the public library looking for that vital piece of information. At last, she found it: Chernobyl blew during the early hours on April 26, exactly at 1:23 AM Moscow time. All that fuss for something as easy as one, two, three. Now, all she needed was to find the hour difference for Iraq. Were they one or two hours ahead of Moscow? She was not sure, Steves had all the international time zones down pat in that photographic memory of his, she decided to bug him on the phone.

"Hey Kats, whazzup?"

"I figured my painting out, but I need a little help with something. How far ahead is Iraq from Moscow, hours I mean. One or two?"

"Depends on the date," Steves replied.

"April 26."

"April, oh, Iraq is in the same time zone as Moscow then."

"Really?"

"Yes, really."

"Thanks Steves, you've saved my bacon."

"No sweat. Listen I gotta go, we're in the midst of some clinical trials here."

"Whoops! Sorry to catch you at a bad time."

"No problem, see you later tonight. Any idea what's for dinner?"

"Umm, I don't know, I don't ask anymore ... ." Katherine noted wryly.

"Uh, huh. I think it's time for the drive-through contingency plan, I'll sneak some burgers into the apartment and we'll have a little party before the main course at the house, how does that grab you?"

Katherine laughed.

"Okay, and pick me up a large strawberry milkshake while you're there,"

"Of course, and super-size fries."

"Great! See you later."

Now it was time to call Professor Matthews and give him the proper co-ordinates for the planetarium, but she had one more thing to decide before she bothered her former tutor, namely, when she should set a date for interviews with the graduates of Belvedere, and if he knew of worthy applicants for the gallery. Well, time to set things in cement so to speak, perhaps mid-August, yeah, the sixteenth, no the seventeenth, it would fall on a Saturday she noted while checking the calendar, that would be all right, she could notify the other art colleges now that she had that settled. Dialling the professor, she had reached his answering machine but he quickly picked up the receiver when he heard the first part of her message.

"Ah, hello. So you figured out the riddle of the stars, I'll pass on your information, I don't know how long it will take to print out the charts, I hope within a couple of weeks."

"That's okay, just as long as it's before September if that's possible, I need to finish my poor neglected *magnum opus*."

"How is the construction in Dumbo progressing?"

"Almost finished, which is another reason I'm contacting you: I need a few good artists, I was hoping you could pass on the word to any of the graduates who might be interested in having their works included in a showing. Interviews will be held at the gallery on the seventeenth of August, from ten AM until twelve, and from two PM until six. You have the address already I think."

"Yes, I have it, all right," he said slowly, obviously jotting the information down. "May I pass this on to my colleagues? They may have suitable applicants."

"Of course, please do, I need to discover new artists that have some decent pieces to fill my walls. I can't have a gallery without any art to showcase."

"That would certainly be a new record for Minimalism. The interviews are open to *all* art graduates?"

"Oh yes."

"Any specific restrictions we need to be aware of?"

"Umm, well, I'm more interested in paintings, but sculptures will be considered too, just as long as the artwork doesn't explode fireballs, spout water, or pitch stuff at the prospective customers, it should be all right, but if at all possible, please, nothing too … too …”

“Nouveau Futuristic?”

“Yeah,” she laughed, “you know what I mean. If anyone can’t attend, they can send in their portfolios before the seventeenth with their contact information. Oh, before I forget, my commission rate for the present is set at thirty-five percent, just in case anyone asks.”

“All right, I’ll be sure to pass the word.”

“Thanks, I really appreciate it, bye Professor.”

She took a deep breath as she put the receiver down, another ball was set rolling, and until she had those star-charts, her power plant would have to wait. Maybe it was time to start transferring the studio out of the garage apartment and over to the top floor in Dumbo, Suzy would need more room when she came back in a few weeks, and Katherine decided the sooner she got used to working in her new studio and going to the gallery each day, the better. How long she had waited to have a *professional* work area with adequate sunlight, proper workbenches, architectural desks that adjusted to comfortable angles, roll-able tables and carts with a plethora of brush-holders set for convenient reaching, and of course, industrial-sized sinks and storage spaces. Suzy will not believe the set-up she had installed complete with special wall cabinets for the smocks and work-clothes, the paints, the brushes, and the new canvases. There were plenty of easels for multi-tasking, they could paint several pictures at once and allow for the different drying stages. Katherine had even thought to install plenty of bug zappers to ensure no insect got stuck in the paint, however, it was always best to play it safe and use cover sheets, there was plenty of storage space for them too. No longer the necessity to shove things in the spare bedrooms or be forced to tip-toe around canvases due to lack of elbow room, and, no more getting pelted on the head with their finished works as they tumbled out of the hall closet, Suzy could actually use the area now to hang up her jackets and coats. What bliss! Now that they had a dream studio, she prayed the Law of Irony would not jinx their future work. When she did not have the proper space and had to make-do, everything turned out better than expected, the limitations she had to tolerate mysteriously brought out the ‘genius touch’. Now that her work environment was more than she could ever hope for, would her paintings measure up, or would they lack that ‘awesome’ quality and fizzle into boring mediocrity? Better not tempt Fate and dwell on that, or it just might turn out that way.

Clearing the apartment did not take long with the new van, everything could be moved in one trip. She had taken to driving the snazzy vehicle almost full time, it was a great opportunity to gain publicity, and she used any excuse to park it in the most conspicuous places. It seemed to be working. The day the telephones were installed they received a number of calls asking all kinds of questions about opening hours, and if they painted portraits ... Katherine had not thought of *that.* Did they have a listing of artists currently showing at the gallery? Were they seeking any new artists? The word was spreading, she could not wait until the grand opening and finally present the new Walsingham Gallery to the public. Now that all her plans were starting to snowball, Pops decided to send in reinforcements, namely, calling in the PR team at the firm to help prepare the press releases, that was a welcome relief, Katherine had no idea how to deal with journalists or the media. Suzy arrived a couple of days before the interviews were to take place. She jumped right in to help at the gallery, she could worry about her own sorting out at the apartment later and decided to stash everything in the bedrooms as usual until things calmed down.

"Wow! I can't believe how *gorgeous* the whole place looks," Suzy exclaimed.

"Wait until you see upstairs, this is just the ground floor you know," Katherine laughed as she gave her the grand tour of the gallery, watching Suzy marvel at the decorative details, the glistening terrazzo floor, the burnished Victorian-style ceiling panels reflecting the warm glow from the reproduction brass and crystal chandeliers, not to mention the large semi-circular reception desk with its golden marble polished top and dark mahogany facing that Katherine had positioned in front of the private office constructed under the iron staircase against the internal wall ensuring that it commanded a perfect view of the ground floor. The restaurant area was partitioned off to the left of the new side entrance with a three-foot convex mahogany panelled wall capped with a two-foot high, thick bottle-glass screen trimmed with brass holders to allow the patrons privacy as they dined. Inside, the dining space featured deep forest green leather booths under the windows, thick bottle-green glass set in curling wrought iron for the tables, and plenty of comfortable leather chairs that all blended beautifully with the terrazzo finish and the freshly painted iron staircase in the gallery area complete with its new brass railing. The gift corner to the right of the old entrance, glassed off with a rectangular partition, also had plenty of custom-made mahogany display cabinets and stands with soft lighting, all that was needed was a budding entrepreneur to lease it to. The front corner of the building between the two main entrances was reserved for exhibition space.

This one corner had been a particular challenge to arrange as

Katherine wanted to retain her concept of an open plan for the ground floor, but that would have entailed compromising precious wall space necessary for exhibiting paintings. At this point, any additional partitions set into the floor would only box the place in and wreck her terrazzo, movable easels would not work as people could easily knock them over and cause havoc. Finally, a solution came to her when she recalled the old wooden chalkboard on wheels that Professor Matthews constantly employed, he disliked the new whiteboards the college had installed, the markers always dried out no matter how carefully he put the lids back on. What if the display partitions were not too large and could be rolled around like the old chalkboard? They would not seem as rigid or confining … imagine adjusting the floor space according to their needs at any given moment, manoeuvring artworks closer to the windows or under the lights if people wanted a better view.

"Oh, these *are* nifty," Suzy declared as she tried rolling one around. "They look like giant double-sided pictures on wheels."

Well that's the idea, Katherine had several partitions custom-made at different heights and lengths, but nothing too unwieldy, covered with period-piece silk-sheen wallpaper, each framed around the sides and edges in large mahogany borders featuring carved scrolls and volutes specially designed for gigantic paintings found in castles and manor houses, the final touch, large matching double mahogany wheels for stability as well as mobility.

"You know," Suzy continued, "it's amazing, everything is so new and shiny, and yet you've managed to keep the old-world ambiance, it's simply fantastic."

"Thanks, like I said, just wait until you see the rest of it," Katherine replied as they made their way towards the elevator, "of course, there are a few more details to finish, like the large potted ferns for instance, we'll dot them around to give the place some life, break up all the hard surfaces. They should arrive tomorrow."

"Plants, yeah, that would be good," Suzy agreed, admiring the glistening elevator.

"Then the theatre ropes for the permanent collection should be arriving any day."

"Theatre ropes?"

"Oh you know, barriers to keep people from getting too close to the paintings, plus I still have to order some of the seating arrangements, you know visitors will get tired standing around, or they'll want to sit and study something that catches their interest. Most galleries provide seating."

"Antique benches perhaps?" Suzy suggested.

"Come to think of it, I had pictured Roman benches in leather, but not in green," Katherine noted as she pushed the button for the second floor, "we need a different colour for the other floors, maybe a deep oxblood for the second floor, the kind you see in old English libraries, and a cream or a golden tone for the third floor."

"That *would* be nice … oh, wow …."

The old-fashioned theme had been continued on the second floor with the burnished ceiling panels and chandeliers, but instead of terrazzo, the factory wood floor was sanded, refinished in a dark stain, buffed to a high-gloss and carpeted with elegant runner-rugs in the main walkways. Wainscoted partition walls silk-panelled in royal reds, blues, greens evoking the exhibition rooms of the Louvre had been permanently set in, sectioning off exhibition spaces and roomy walkways, but they did not reach the ceiling, allowing the sunlight to filter overhead through the whole floor giving a sense of space. Katherine also had the walls constructed at various heights that allowed them to peak over each other and reveal the different coloured panels, exciting curiosity to see what was displayed on the other side. There were also unexpected doors and passageways cut through at strategic points lending the impression of an elegant Victorian maze to draw the visitor in and invite them to explore every room and corner. The third floor was arranged in a similar maze-like design, but with white wainscoting and calmer colours painted on the upper sections of the partitions, off whites, creams, champagnes, and pale golds. Katherine explained some artworks may scream with the stronger colours downstairs, not to mention the old-style patterns in the silk panelling, and would be better suited to this muted setting.

"However, until such time as I can remodel the forth floor for the permanent exhibition space, this area will have to do for now."

"It's gorgeous! But it's going to take a lot of paintings to fill this area."

"I know, and I'm waiting for the opportunity to attend one of Sotheby's auctions, I hope they offer something of interest before our grand opening. In any case, let's hope the interviews go well."

"Just imagine having the opportunity to acquire art at Sotheby's," Suzy sighed.

"Yes, Mom and Pops insisted, but I have mixed feelings about accepting another large donation from the family, I'm a little uncomfortable about all they've done for me, to tell truth."

"I can understand that, but remember Kathy, the value is still there and will most likely increase, at any event, this donation will remain with the family permanently. Think of this as your chance to augment the family heirlooms." Suzy always had a level head.

Katherine took her to see the fourth floor, the last section of the building still in its semi-original condition before they went to view the studio.

"You mean we get to work in *here*," Suzy exclaimed, "I don't believe it, this is a painter's paradise, and all the light!" Katherine smiled, she just knew Suzy would get a bang out of their deluxe studio. "I had no idea your project was this large, you've certainly worked hard, that's obvious, I don't know how you pulled it all together!"

"It wasn't just me, I could never have accomplished all this on my own. Gramps came to the rescue, he's been around a while you know and has seen a thing or two, so he set me on the right path. He got me a first-class contractor and an excellent architect, plus he kept his eye on everything. You won't believe it, he arrived daily with Jasper in tow, those two have become inseparable, he even sleeps in Gramp's bedroom now. Come to think of it, this project has given Gramps a whole new lease on life, he felt useful again in his role as volunteer inspector, without him, it certainly would never have been finished on time. His help was invaluable. Just wait until the restaurant opens, we can expect to see him and Jasper drop by any time."

"He must have kept everyone on their toes," Suzy laughed before commenting, "on top of all the work, I can't imagine what it must have cost."

"Oh don't talk!" Katherine replied shaking her head. "As you see, I'll have to wait until I can afford to finish the fourth floor. If the family hadn't chipped in with their contributions, I would have needed to take out a loan to augment our working capital, but as it stands, we'll be able to manage until we get on our feet."

She proceeded to explain that for now, they would work with a skeleton crew until things smoothed out, for instance, they may need an extra reception assistant, and depending how the first couple of weeks go, they would hire additional help, which she hoped would not become necessary for the present, for the most expensive element would be hiring the security personnel. The insurance company had suggested she follow the recommendations of the company who installed her hi-tech alarm system, they would send her bonded men experienced in securing a gallery. So far, the bare minimum of personal the company deemed acceptable for a gallery with famous works on display was six officers in total. The logistics of the operation were confusing to say the least. They had it worked out she would only need one officer on during the day, but a rotation of two night watchmen to cover the graveyard shifts, in short, she needed one team of officers to cover the five day work week, plus a second for the extra two days. At least the company that set up her system offered this additional security personnel service, for a fee of course, but boy, was it going to be pricey! Katherine admitted they would have to wing it, this was a whole new experience.

"We'll just have to hope for the best and learn as we go."

Suzy suggested they had better start looking for help right away, they would need staff on duty to watch the artwork once it began arriving, especially Aunt Martha's priceless donation, not to mention looking for someone to whom she could lease the restaurant and gift area, they would require time to set up their business too before the grand opening.

"True," Katherine replied, "I wouldn't like to see the gift corner empty that day, and if we use the restaurant to do the catering for our functions, we would definitely need that area up and ready to run. Okay, I'll call the employment agency the firm uses, they'll recommend qualified people I'm sure, but how I'm going to decide on someone suitable for the restaurant, that's going to be a tall order, maybe I should have started sooner."

"Don't worry, I'm sure the right person is there waiting for an opportunity like this, they don't come along everyday, that's for certain."

"Gosh, I nearly forgot about the maintenance, it should be a simple matter to hire the company used by Walsingham Industries, that would be safe as they're a bonded company."

"Right, we just need to start dialling some numbers and get the word out."

03 ❀ 80

The following day before the garden centre delivered the ferns, Katherine showed Suzy the nuts and bolts of the premises located in the main office under the stairs, namely, the master light switches, the climate control knobs and thermometer readings, the intercom and piped music system, the security buttons and camera switches, the keys to the different locks—plus the special key to the elevator allowing her access to the fifth floor—their studio would be absolutely private. Katherine had thought to construct a special partition and door around the staircase on that floor to ensure no one could sneak up and mess around with their dream work area.

Eventually, they might hold art classes there, but under their close supervision. This area would be just for the two of them.

After Suzy received her set of keys, she wondered how well prepared Katherine was for the interviews tomorrow. Did she expect many to show up, and if so, how were they going to handle the steady stream of arrivals and departures? Katherine had not thought about it in too much detail, she did not expect *that* many to appear. Suzy warned her to be prepared for a stampede in any case, it may prove difficult with only the two of them to manage the operation. Maybe they could devise a 'take a number' system? No, they should be able to register the names as they arrive, they could always close the doors if things got out of control. Hey, where should they hold the actual interviews? They had no idea how big the portfolios were going to be, some of the artists may bring actual canvases instead of sample photographs for larger pieces. Katherine would have to set up a desk somewhere upstairs in a private section to conduct the interviews away from the others. Everything might be overheard if she held them on the second floor, perhaps the third floor might be the best option as their sacrosanct studio space was off limits for now, while the fourth floor was too cavernous and factory-like, a rather intimidating atmosphere for a nervous interviewee.

The third floor it was then, *dang*, now they had to move suitable furniture to equip the place. The desk in the office was too big and would be hard to manage, they would never get it through the office door and around the reception area without scratching or damaging something, so they struggled to lift one of the heavy wrought iron glass-topped tables from the restaurant into the elevator, hitting their shins unmercifully against the curly-q table legs as they wobbled along. Katherine could only imagine the big ugly bruises that would grace those sore spots next morning. Gee, later she might have to hire a few men for hauling things around or to help them manoeuvre ungainly pieces, especially if they decided to exhibit large sculptures, Katherine observed. After they rubbed off their unsightly fingerprints from the table, they retrieved a few leather roll-chairs from the main reception desk and transported them to the designated interview spot. Everything seemed set up to the best they could manage for now, they would have to handle any unforeseen circumstances that might pop up tomorrow.

ଓଃ❀ ଅ

The excitement and tension mixed with the feverish activities ensured that Katherine and Suzy had a restless night. When they met next morning for coffee in the kitchen of the main house, they looked a little worse for the wear, and Katherine hoped they could keep up this momentum without crashing before the grand opening. It was an early start and they headed straight to Dumbo to face their first official day at work in the new gallery. Until the applicants were due to arrive, they rearranged the ferns and roly-poly partitions for maximum artistic effect, adjusted the lighting *via* the master dimmer switches, selected easy listening music to play over the sound system, and did everything they could to set a relaxed but professional mood for the day. Just then, the telephone rang: it was the engineer, he was coming by that afternoon with the inspectors, and no, he could not come at another time, it was take it or leave it, lady!

"Just great! Not today, not with all the interviews," Katherine grimaced, she felt a headache coming on.

"Well, you don't need to personally show them around do you? They should be able to find they way through the place, we can still manage on our own," Suzy tried to reason.

"It's not just that," Katherine tried to explain, "you saw the mess that the construction teams and decorators left piled up in the parking lot, and it was looking so nice after the paving company had finished it." She took out a little notebook and pencil from her pocket and looked over the lists she had jotted. "The garbage company said they'd drop another commercial dumpster by today, but they haven't arrived yet, and we can't leave the back as it is, the inspectors can't okay a building with all that cardboard stacked by the loading door. Talk about bad first impressions!"

She had images of the inspector taking his first step out on the iron fire escape, and hoped the welders finished the job right, she could not afford a repeat performance of the wobbling escapade.

"Don't worry, when the dumpster comes, we'll just work fast and throw everything in to it during our lunch break," Suzy noted. "You did set a lunch hour."

"Sure, I just hope the dumpster comes, we can't do anything until then," putting her notebook back in her pocket. "I'm sorry, it looks like we're going to miss lunch."

"That's okay, I could do with losing a pound or two. Well, I'll go take a look and see what we can do for now," with that, Suzy left to tackle the parking area.

Returning to the main office to test the security cameras one more time, Katherine was surprised to hear a light knocking on the side entrance, it was too early for anyone to show up ... well! There stood Professor Matthews waving to her through the glass. She hurried to open the doors.

"What a nice surprise, what brings you to our neck of the woods?"

"Oh, I thought I'd drop by," he replied with an expression of undisguised pleasure as he admired the elegant surroundings, "and to think I was expecting a modest boutique gallery, you've started out in grand style as always I must admit."

Katherine smiled.

"You can thank my Grampa for donating the family building to a worthy cause, but please come in, you're most welcome, let me conduct you on a Grand Tour. Suzy's in the parking lot, she should be back shortly. I don't think I've told you, but she's going to help me manage the place."

As he entered, she saw he had brought with him a large black portfolio case.

"Why Professor, you're not thinking of applying, are you?"

"You did say *all* graduates were welcome, no restrictions. I just assumed this generous liberality also extended to age and experience," he astutely replied, pushing his sliding glasses up to their proper position.

"Oh, of course. Well, you've certainly arrived in time, that's for sure."

Katherine showed the Professor around, and then proceeded with the business at hand, settling into one of the comfy booths in the restaurant area, no need to be too formal. She did not have to look at his portfolio to make a decision, she had seen only a few of his paintings while in college, but they were, in modern terms, to die for. In any case, she delved through samples and photographs of his latest collection. They were absolutely beautiful, he always preferred the crisp classical methods of the French painters like David and Ingres with a touch of Delacroix's wild sense of movement, but employed these styles with a modern touch depicting classic scenes of Americana: landscapes of New England in the Spring and Fall, a day out at Yankee Stadium, winter in Central Park, street scenes of Manhattan to name a few. He tried his hand with various historical pieces, recreating scenes from World War II battles in France, also capturing a protest rally and a modern political campaign on canvas. His style was admirable, it was as though someone from the 1800s had painted these scenes from modern life, they were not trite or folksy, but true works of art.

"I'm surprised you didn't give them to one of the Manhattan or Chelsea galleries, or that a museum hasn't picked them up, they are really beautiful."

"Thank you, my dear. Am I accepted then?" he queried with a smile.

"Do you have to ask?" she returned with a raised eyebrow. "You know, this feels so strange, here I am, yea-ing or nay-ing your masterpieces, when looking at them I feel I should be back under your tutelage, there is still so much I could learn from you."

"I'm flattered," he replied, "naturally, as a professor I have to keep my hand in and practise, or I'd be a fraud teaching others, however, I've never had time apart from the summer breaks to really concentrate on my craft, but as I'll be retiring next year, there will be ample opportunities to work."

"You're retiring? Oh, I didn't know, I guess congratulations are in order."

"I hope so, you see, my wife Esther decided to retire early from her position as head librarian at the college six months ago and she's finding it difficult, she misses the activity, you understand. She continues to drop by the library three days a week to ensure the place is running smoothly despite her absence, she finally had them throw out Old Blunder Bolts and get a new computer."

Katherine chuckled, she had not met Mrs. Matthews personally, but she vaguely remembered a smartly dressed lady with short grey hair and glasses sprightly delegating orders to some of the shelving staff.

"Despite the well-earned rest, I know I'll miss teaching at Belvedere," the Professor continued, "it's good to know I can count on my painting to keep me active."

"Well, we will always have space for your collections here. To be honest, I really don't know what to charge for these," she replied, looking over the photographs once more, "you've certainly worked hard on this collection, and I don't want to short-change you. Listen, the best thing is to just write a list of what you hope to make on each painting, I'll leave the pricing up to you. When we can fit it in, Suzy and I will drive by with the van and pick them up."

"All right, I'll have them ready in a few days and give you a call. Oh, I nearly forgot, here are the star charts you requested, they weren't sure which type of graph you required, equatorial or azimutal grids, or the directions you were interested in for that matter, so the planetarium printed up a whole series," he explained, unzipping a special side-compartment in the portfolio and taking out the desired charts.

"Wow! These are great! How much are they?"

"No charge, they owed me one for a presentation I prepared on classical astronomy depicted in ancient epics when their guest speaker fell sick, I just called in the favour."

"Thank you, Professor, these will help a lot. Now I owe *you* one."

At that moment, Suzy returned from the parking lot looking somewhat dishevelled.

"You're right Kathy, I've tried to stack the junk out back a little better, but it's still a ...oh, hello Professor, what a surprise."

"Hey, Suzy, meet our first applicant!" Katherine laughed. "Come and sit down for a minute, we have the first collection set. I hope the rest of the day goes as smoothly as this, all considered."

"Wow, these are really gorgeous," Suzy commented as she leafed through his work.

"Is it just the two of you?" the Professor asked.

"Yeah, for now, this is all new to us, so we're just playing it by ear," Katherine admitted.

"I have to say you and Susanna do look a little exhausted, and looking around it's plain to see why. If I could be of any help, I could man the reception desk or keep everything rolling for you, I didn't have anything else planned for today. School just got started and things have not reached their usual hectic pitch."

"Oh would you be willing to do that? I wouldn't want to take up your free day...."

"Nonsense, I'd be delighted Katherine."

"That would be a help, we planned to hire some assistants before the place is up and running, but we didn't think we would need anybody just for the interviews."

"Assistants?" The Professor looked thoughtful for a moment.

"Yes, you know, a receptionist who can give tours and help with the general management, and we'll need to find a driver to help with the van and move the heavy equipment around here, maybe someone part time for the moment, a student who could use the extra cash, we really don't know what we need yet."

"I'm sure there are plenty of interested students, I'll put a notice up on the board next to my door. About a receptionist, it's too late to ask for today's agenda, but would you mind if I run the idea by Esther? She was thinking of returning to work at the library, to be back amongst people again and be busy, but let's face it, the students were getting a bit too much for her at her age. This would be ideal, I wonder if she would be interested? I know she would be of enormous help to you, and she loves art."

What an idea! Remembering the no-nonsense code enforced at the library, and she and Suzy were in complete agreement, the place was bound to run like clockwork with the former head librarian of Belvedere at the helm.

"Why of course, please, suggest it to her."

They heard a faint knocking at the side door and Suzy went to see who the next early arrival could be. Jasper came running through and began licking Katherine's fingers.

"Hey, I'm happy to see you too, but do you have to slobber on me every time?"

"Here boy, be good now," Gramps called as he entered the restaurant area. Jasper immediately obeyed, wagging his tail as he stood guard next to him. "I see we have company before the rush," Gramps noticed, "I've brought a surprise visitor with me too."

"Yeah, looks like we've got a small party here," Steves announced, his arrival completely unexpected.

"Steves! What are you doing here?" Katherine exclaimed, giving him a big hug.

"Well, college only just started, nothing major is happening, so I thought I'd take the weekend off and fly over to see if I could help."

"Oh, let me introduce you both to Professor Matthews: Professor, this is my grandfather, and my brother, Steven"

"It's a pleasure to meet you," the Professor greeted, rising from the booth and shaking hands.

"Likewise, we've heard so much about you," Gramps replied.

"Don't worry, all good reports," Steves added.

"The Professor is going to be one of our artists," Katherine announced, "plus he's offered to help for the day."

"That's mighty kind of you," Gramps noted, "as we've come over with the same idea in mind seeing you're hard pushed for time to get this finished, what can we do to pitch in? I came to take you all out to lunch, I thought that's how I could do my bit."

"But Mr. G.W.," Suzy jumped in, "we won't have time today, not when all the applicants arrive, and we have the inspectors coming to give the building the once-over this afternoon, the engineer just called Kathy to let her know, it's hectic, you get the picture."

"Oh not to worry," Gramps calmly replied, "I'll arrange for a take-out lunch that you can eat if and when you get the time. Can't have you running on empty stomachs all day. Any requests?"

"No, just surprise us, I know you'll pick something too good to pass up," Katherine replied.

"Well, that's Gramp's task assigned, and here I am. Name your job, I'm your slave for the day," Steves piped up.

"Really?" Katherine queried with a mischievous note in her voice, "you have no idea how long I've waited for you to say that." He simply laughed.

"That's great of you Steves, I couldn't do anything with the parking lot, and the new dumpster hasn't arrived yet. I tried to tidy things a bit, but it still looks pretty bad if the inspectors show up," Suzy explained, hoping he could help.

"Ladies, leave it to me," he gallantly replied with a wave of his hand. "By the way, are you expecting more deliveries today? I hear a truck pulling into the parking lot, it's making quite a racket."

"You're right," Katherine confirmed as she looked out the side entrance, "it must be the dumpster, UPS or deliveries don't come on Saturdays. Oh Steves, if you could make the parking lot presentable, I'll be forever in your debt."

"Ha! I *definitely* want that in writing," he joked back.

"Steves, if you don't mind, I'll leave Jasper with you, I'll go and arrange for some decent grub to be delivered, or perhaps I'll bring it myself," Gramps announced, wistfully looking around at the unmanned restaurant and over at the empty kitchen. It seemed a heinous sin to have such a marvellous gastronomic establishment left desolate of culinary activity, even at this early stage.

"Okay, come on Jasper, time to work."

Dutifully, Jasper followed Steves out back while Gramps left on his foraging expedition in search of the perfect gourmet picnic.

"What would we do without all this help?" Suzy mused aloud. "You had no idea what you were getting into, Kathy, and it's a good thing, or we couldn't hack it if we knew what was ahead of us everyday. All I can say is hang in there, we will survive."

"With everyone getting busy with their designated activities," the Professor observed, looking over the rim of his glasses, "the time has come to take my post, especially as I see we have our first applicants at the front door ..."

Katherine and Suzy looked over to check the first arrivals, sure enough, there they were, a small group of hopefuls carrying various portfolio and tubular poster cases peering through the glass.

"Do you have a clipboard handy, ladies? Our work begins."

Katherine was grateful for the Professor's assistance, his presence on the main floor was so reassuring and allowed Suzy to join her upstairs. She had never held interviews before and it seemed like a woeful responsibility to carry out single-handed, it was good to have someone beside her with whom she could share her opinions. Only then did it fully strike her that she had the power to make someone very happy that day by her acceptance, or possibly crush them by her rejection. She could not let sympathy influence her decisions and accept *everyone*, could she? No, she not only had to pick good art, but art that would reflect well on the gallery. Image would have to be first and foremost. But then, what if the styles she liked did not *sell*? Well, let's wait and see what is presented, and how the first few months will go. The interviewees may have thought they were nervous, if only they knew the trepidation she was feeling as each one arrived through the elevator door.

In some cases, the decision making was relatively easy, the artwork was stunning and the calibre of work was truly surprising. Bright still lifes, city scenes, land and seascapes, a few examples of the Gothic touch with medieval cathedrals, old monasteries and castle ruins, these were bound to attract. One artist had travelled with his father to an archaeological dig on an expedition down the Nile and captured the famous ruins of Egypt in lustrous water colours, another had travelled to Cancun and using the photographs he had taken, painted various scenes of that tropical paradise. There was one series that truly captured her attention, the river people of the Ganges—this artist had depicted the colourful life of India in the *batik* medium, a specialized form of image-production using a laborious process involving cloth, dyes and melted wax. In fact, this artist had two collections to offer, the second was the boat people of Indonesia, also created in *batik*. The colours of this collection were vibrant and full of life, she had not expected to see collections like these. There were also a few surreal canvasses and some examples of Pop art offered for their consideration, but nothing too disturbing or outlandish that merited a rejection, several pieces were quite captivating, and, there was a market for this style after all. However, they were truly appalled by some of the portfolios, she couldn't help but wonder if the artists were trying to insult them or were they genuinely serious about these ... creations. She expected the modernist, off-beat brigade to make an appearance, toting their lifeless blobs of nondescript trash in sculpture as well as pictorial form, no big deal, it was easy to say 'don't call us, we'll call you', but the others? Good grief! She and Suzy nearly blushed Ferrari red when presented with a couple of portfolios bulging with nudes, the erotic variety suitable only to hang in bordellos. Maybe other galleries would stoop to that level, but not here, thank you.

All considered, by the end of the day, they had to admit, everything had gone very well despite the interruption occasioned by the engineer conducting the two inspectors through the gallery. They had accepted the work of ten artists, eleven including Professor Matthews, and were quite pleased not to mention relieved that the interviews had gone off without a hitch. Steves had cleared the back lot in plenty of time and kept the Professor company, he enjoyed the whole affair. Gramps came through like a champion with his picnic that afternoon, having requested the head chef at the 'C'est la Vie' to prepare a special take-away lunch: watercress salad served with asparagus and stuffed quail eggs, smoked salmon and shrimp croissant sandwiches, petite-fours and French pastries, all neatly individually boxed inside a deluxe gold container for each person complete with a royal blue bow. To top it off, he had three bottles of white wine, plus a coffee container ready to plug in with little creamers and sugars on the side, silver ware, coffee cups, serviettes, all packed in a laundry basket. He was so proud of his contribution, but reminded Katie and Suzy they would have to return the basket with all the equipment when they finished their program. Professor Matthews told the new art entrepreneurs how much he enjoyed his day, particularly the lunch with Gramps.

"Can you believe he's supposed to be on a low cholesterol diet? If only the family knew how he cheats, and he uses us as an excuse at every opportunity," Katherine replied.

The day went so fast, it was already seven o'clock, so the Professor decided it was time to go home to Esther, he had forgotten to call and inform her he would be helping out at the gallery for the day,

"Oh dear, it simply slipped my mind, I'd better start for home, she has no idea where I am. Thank you Mr. Walsingham for the wonderful lunch and the excellent wine, went to my head a little bit."

"You're more than welcome," Gramps jovially replied, he appreciated a man who enjoyed his vitals, "great food and great conversation, we'll have to get together and do this more often."

Katherine thanked her former tutor Profusely for all his help.

"Having you here, Professor, made everything go smoothly, please let me know how Mrs. Matthews feels about a position with us here at the gallery. That would be just perfect for us, I hope she says 'yes'."

"Jasper took care of his business," Steves informed the group as he came through the back door. "Is everyone getting ready to leave? Oh, I didn't know it was that late already, I was really enjoying the whole proceedings."

Katherine and Suzy locked up after the Professor left, checking all the doors and turning on the security system for the night. As Steves was lifting out the laundry basket for them to the van, a brilliant idea struck him.

"You know, we don't *have* to go home for dinner ..." he whispered to Katherine, shaking the basket a little, hoping she might get the hint without Gramps becoming suspicious, he had cheated too much already that day.

"Oh, ah ... I think we forgot to close the window on the top floor. Sorry Suzy, we need to do one more check-over... ."

"Okay, whatever, we certainly can't leave the place open."

"Save yourselves the trouble," Gramps replied, "I'll go around to the lot, see if it's closed ... ." *Drat*, they hoped he would just start home without them, that did not work. Perhaps no one would notice if the girls did not show for dinner, but with Steves missing too, Gramps would guess what they were up to, and they could not leave him out like that. Katherine unlocked the doors and called home from the reception desk, sorry, we won't be back in time for dinner, we'll have to go out. Boy, Gramps was making off like a bandit today, imagine, another dinner at the 'C'est la Vie', even Jasper would be in dog-heaven, they would have to send a steak out to him in the van.

"Hey Gramps, since we have to return the basket, we might as well have dinner there if we can get a table, it'll be too late to get home on time," Steves informed him as he put Jasper in the back of the van, "he'll have to stay in here for dinner, can't have him locked up in a car. Kathy has already called home to let them know not to expect us."

"What a good idea, I'm tired of Mrs. Gonzales' dried out grilled breasts of chicken and her anaemic snapper, and I just know she's going to have those long steamed green beans with almonds laid out like a bunch of stiffs on the side. She means well, but who wants to live if you have to do it in misery? I already get the aroma of 'C'est la Vie' ... ."

Katherine felt guilty as she pictured her parents dining on rabbit rations while the rest of them were having a night on the town, she hoped she called in time for Mrs. Gonzales to change the courses, well, if not, her mother always watching her diet, would appreciate the meagre fare, but poor Pops ...?

"Yes, it's a great idea Gramps, please don't go overboard tonight, you will try to be good, won't you? Don't rule out the chicken dishes anyway if you can help it."

"Sorry, can't make any promises there, pet, definitely not with Parisian cuisine on the menu."

Just as she feared, Gramps went for the 'whole shebang' as he usually phrased it, baked French onion soup with a mountain of toasted cheese on top for the starter, he ordered chicken as requested for the second course, unfortunately, to her dismay, it was cooked in a rich buttery cream and wine sauce, plus he could not pass up anything that would round off a suburb meal, often it was something thick and gooey with a good dose of chocolate and fluffy Chantilly. Well, she did understand that one weakness and joined the culprit in polishing off a slice of hot fudge pie. Gramps sent his compliments to the chef, "… and please tell him thanks again for putting that fancy picnic together for me this afternoon," with a slight wink, an odd gesture that puzzled Katherine. Within a few moments, the head chef personally came out to render his thanks just as they were finishing their coffee.

"I'm glad you found everything to your satisfaction, including the lunch," he began. They all voiced their compliments, especially Gramps, however, the chef did not return to his post in the kitchen right away, but began a quiet unexpected conversation, carefully glancing around to ensure he could not be overheard by the surrounding tables.

"Sir, did I hear correctly this afternoon that your granddaughter had a restaurant that she wished to lease?"

"You did indeed," Gramps beamed, "it's a fine place, but you'll have to talk to her about the details," nodding to Katherine. "Kathy, meet chef Andre Garneau."

She was slightly startled with this unusual development.

"Er, yes I do have a place actually… ."

"Ah, you're Katherine, I'm glad to meet you." They shook hands. "Forgive me for approaching you at your table," the chef apologized, "for over a year now I've been thinking of starting out with a place of my own, and I would like to see what you have on offer if I may. Unfortunately I can't discuss anything further right now during working hours … would it be possible to arrange a meeting?"

"Umm, oh, well, what about Monday morning? Is nine all right with you? Here, let me give you my card." She rummaged around in her purse for the desired object.

"Thank you, yes, nine is perfect. Well, I shall not disturb you any further, good evening."

Sly old Gramps, he went on a recruitment mission without telling her, and succeeded in piquing the interest of her favourite chef.

"Gramps, how did you manage *that*?" she asked, still in a state of astonishment.

"Oh, I just dropped the hint today, wondered if he knew of anyone that was interested, you know, try and get the gears moving for you, but I didn't think he *personally* would answer the call."

He looked positively chuffed with this unexpected good news.

Things *were* happening fast, imagine, the head chef of 'C'est La Vie' was interested in the restaurant. Suzy could not believe their good luck, she wanted to be there that Monday just to see how things went, but as she could not find half her belongings after the hectic move back from Iowa, she needed some time to sort herself out and requested a day or two off.

Andre arrived promptly at the designated time, she almost failed to recognise him. When they last met on Saturday, he was all bundled up in his white chef's jacket, neck kerchief, long apron and tall cylindrical hat, it was difficult to discern his features, plus the muted restaurant lighting did not help to make a reliable first impression. Now dressed in a shirt and slacks minus the kerchief and hat, she saw he had deep dark eyes and black hair. In fact, he was not as old as she first assumed, must be the uniform that adds the years. Although he toted his CV, she did not need it, she had been to the restaurant often enough to be convinced he was thoroughly qualified. She was also well aware he commanded a large patronage, for sure his regular customers would remain with him, no worries, the gallery restaurant was sure to be a success, but not to be rude by appearing disinterested in his accomplishments, they took a seat in one of the booths while she looked over his résumé.

"Wow, you've studied everywhere," she noted, scanning the impressive list of Parisian and Canadian culinary schools, she was sure Julia Child had attended a few of them. The list of awards he earned was incredible, truly amazing what can be accomplished if you set your mind to it.

"Yes, as you know, my specialty is traditional French also the new variations of *haute cuisine*, and of course, pastry, my favourite, but I also have experience in American and Canadian fare. However, 'C'est la Vie' is strictly French and won't let me experiment or dabble too much with the expected courses."

"This looks fantastic, and frankly I'd love to try your other specialties," *Gramps would too*, she thought to herself.

"I've been at my current place of employment for almost ten years, I've managed to put enough aside to run a nice place of my own, but I never expected anything quite so beautiful, and … *new*."

"Come, I'll show you around the kitchen, the architect did the planning, and since my contractor was a specialist in building restaurants, he advised on the equipment."

Monsieur Garneau was thoroughly impressed with the premises, masterfully arranged, plenty of work and storage space, walk-in freezer and a walk-in pantry, tip-top equipment , nothing was short-changed.

"Of course, there aren't any pots, pans, dishes or cutlery, I hadn't thought about it yet, in fact I didn't know if the chef or lessee would choose their own equipment."

"Oh, that's fine," he replied, "I have pots and pans, and I would appreciate picking out my own cutlery and dishes for the dining room, this is perfect."

Between them, they decided on the initial opening hours, as she was not prepared for late nights at this stage, coffee, pastries and lunch between the hours of ten and five would be fine for now. He could manage with two waiters or waitresses, one helper in the kitchen, a bus boy and a dish washer, for the present. If at any time they decided to extend the hours and stay open for dinner, then naturally a full staff would be in order. Andre thought, with these beautiful tables, a semi-formal setting of linen place mats and linen serviettes would be ideal. Later if she wished the hours to be extended to dining in the evening, then a complete formal setting would be a matter of course, with full linens, candles, the works. He was so pleased with the restaurant area, the rent seemed to be the last thing on his mind, finally, she brought up the topic.

"I know we're not in Manhattan, but honestly, this is a little more reasonable than I expected, particularly for a top-rate place like this," he declared.

"Maybe if I was already firmly established and knew what my average customer turn-out to the gallery would be, I could charge more, but since you're just starting out too, and you will be furnishing the restaurant with the remainder of the essentials like the china, cutlery, glasses and linens, it will give you breathing space, not to mention a chance for me to figure everything out. We'll just have to wait and see how it goes. If I do eventually raise the rate, I promise it won't be a cut-throat increase."

"Sounds very fair, oh, have you named the restaurant yet?"

"No, actually, but you can name it if you like, something that fits the gallery setting and has a bit of flair if possible."

"Okay."

Katherine nearly forgot, how long would it take to set up? The grand opening would be the last weekend of September, and she had expected the restaurant to handle all the catering for their gala events, that would be the only nighttime gastronomic activities for now. Well, he would need to give four weeks notice to the 'C'est la Vie', if he prepared during the mornings, he just might make her deadline in time, the place was finished in the most essential areas, there was not a lot left for him to do, just get used to the new kitchen. It looked like the deal was sealed.

Now that the formalities were out of the way, Katherine wished she had a cup of coffee to offer him, but as that was not possible for the present, offered him a tour of the gallery instead. Meandering through the maze-like walkways of the second and third floors, through their casual conversation he disclosed that he was French Canadian, although his résumé already hinted this information. So, you speak French, great! She now had someone with whom she could practise speaking her adopted language on a regular basis, the French expressions were different on this side of the ocean, much like the variance between American and British English, but who cared? The conversation switched to French, she got back into the swing of it quickly. He loved the layout and the décor, very *chic*, old French but with a modern twist, sections reminded him of the Louvre. Well, that was the idea, she loved visiting that temple of art, even if the size was rather intimidating. He agreed, so much to see there, it was difficult to tear himself away when he had to attend classes or practise his recipes while at the culinary-school. "I find a kindred spirit at last," she noted, explaining she had been an exchange student in Paris and knew how he felt. She complimented him on his cuisine, and recalled the exquisite graduation cake he had prepared for her. Oh, he remembered *that* one, it was fun working on it, he did not get many requests with edible artwork in the frostings. He then revealed that while he had learned much through the cooking schools, the real source of his expertise was his grandmother from Burgundy, there were quite a few recipes and tricks of the old country passed down from one generation to the next that the schools never knew about. Aha! So *that* was the secret to his success … grandparents seemed to be the bedrock of everything. Katherine told him the history of the old factory building, how Gramps simply gave it to her, facilitated the restoration, and now, helped to find the perfect chef. Andre thought that was amusing, would her grandfather let her run the place when it came down to it?

"No worries," she laughed, I'm afraid Gramps will be too busy sampling the delights of the restaurant when it opens to notice anything happening in the gallery."

The conversation rambled on to comical topics while they made their way downstairs. Considering her love of French food, did she ever muster the courage to try a plate of *escargot*? Uck! She winced at the thought and confessed she was not brave enough to put one of those things in her mouth. How could anyone *think* of eating those big, slimy, gross-looking creepy-crawlies? He laughed.

"They're quite good actually, taste just like clams with loads of garlic, butter and parsley. They're from the same family, molluscs, so it's no big surprise," he explained.

Still wondering how anyone could think of eating those strange things, Andre surmised it was probably down to what a nation had been forced to experience, in this case, maybe famine, the people ate whatever was available and made it taste good, eventually it became a delicacy.

"That would explain the frog legs then," she noted, she hadn't tried them either, people said they tasted like chicken, but she decided to leave it as hearsay and not chalk it up to experience.

"Come to think of it, no wonder they served so many potatoes in Ireland," he mused aloud, "it had to be that notorious famine"

He had heard about the famous spiced beef of Cork and wanting to sample it, visited the Emerald Isle for a week. Almost everywhere he ate, they served from two to three different kinds of potatoes at meals, usually a trinity of mashed, fried and crumbed croquettes at one sitting.

"How odd," Katherine replied, "starved for their staple food, they were now making sure they had a decent serving of it."

"Yes, maybe necessity had a lot to do with a nation's traditional dishes."

At this point, he dared her to try his *escargot* when the restaurant was open, she would be glad she did. Darn! She could never refuse a dare, ick … she hoped he would forget his challenge in the midst of the fuss getting his business up and running. By this time, they were back in the main lobby and noticed someone had been waiting by the front door.

"Can't be a customer," Andre joked, "there aren't any paintings for sale yet."

Katherine had not expected this visitor, it was Gerard Reinold.

"Hello! This is a surprise," Katherine said as she let him in, "gosh, I hope you weren't waiting too long."

"That's all right, I was in the neighbourhood and thought I'd drop by," he replied, glancing around, "well, frankly, I wasn't sure what to expect when you explained it was a factory conversion, but very impressive. You've managed to spruce up old Dumbo, I must say."

"Oh, thank you, do come in, I'm just finishing business with Monsieur Garneau, so if you don't mind waiting a few minutes, I'll be right with you."

"No rush, take your time."

Gerard took a closer look around and examined the rolling partitions while she wrapped up the minutiae of the deal, which only took a moment or two. It was a good thing her friend came Andre noted, he had lost track of time, better get going to prepare for the lunch hour, the *sous-chefs* need a watchful eye over them, they tend to slack off.

"When the cat's away, huh?" she smiled.

"You've said it.   Well, it was a pleasure doing business with you," he concluded as they shook hands.

"Likewise, I'll leave a copy of the lease at the desk, it's really straightforward, there shouldn't be any difficulties. I can give you your set of keys when it's all official, but if you need to come in before then, I'll be here every morning."

"Okay, see you then, I don't want to hold you up further, I may stop by Wednesday, if that's okay."

"Sure no problem."

Andre left by the side entrance as Suzy came around the corner.

"I thought you needed time to get settled," Katherine said, holding the door for her.

"Honestly, I don't know what I was fussing about, it never takes as long as you think it will, and I'm bursting to know if Monsieur Garneau is going to lease the restaurant. Just had to get here!"

"I'll tell you in a minute, Gerard also dropped by, and he's wandering around in here someplace, I had to leave him to finish up the business with Andre."

"Oohheww, first name basis already, huh? I guess he took it then."

"It looks like it, but keep your fingers crossed that it goes well, he still has to put his name on the dotted line. Anyway, Gramps is definitely going to be in his element."

Gerard approached during a break in their conversation.

"Well, forgive me for eavesdropping on you, ladies, but who has been creating all the furore just now?"

"Oh, that would be Andre Garneau, the head chef at the 'C'est la Vie'," Katherine explained.

"Yes, Garneau, I've heard of him, been at that restaurant a few times, good food, Lottie likes going there," Gerard commented.

"Well, he's interested in starting his own place, so it looks like we've just nabbed the best French chef in town," Katherine was pleased to announce.

"That's quite a feather in your cap," he noted, "you can expect Lottie to be here often, of course, she'll love the gallery too, she admires everything with a classical touch."

"How is your sister?" Katherine asked.

"I do hope she still likes her birthday present, and you haven't regretted spending that much for my work," Suzy added.

"Oh she's just fine, she simply adores your painting. She has recently redecorated her sitting room and it's the crowning glory. Besides, Vincent wasn't getting it at any price," he concluded with a note of finality.

Wow, Katherine knew Suzy's painting was good, but never thought it would occasion competitiveness with collectors. She wondered what would happen when her own collection was publicly unveiled.

"Well, I'm glad she likes it," Suzy replied.

"Yes, she can't wait until you open and see what else will be on offer."

Katherine had to stifle a smile as his comment matched her own comical musings.

"Would you like to see the upper floors?" she offered. "No paintings yet, but that will soon be corrected. We'll be picking up the first of the collections within in few days."

"I'd love to."

"If you don't need me," Suzy added, "I guess I'll head up to the studio, if that's all right, I've got a few new ideas I want to work on."

"Sure, Suzy, no problem. No deliveries are expected today."

Touring the second and third floors, Gerard admired the attention paid to detail and had to admit he was impressed.

"I knew you wouldn't head down the modernistic road like the Sirrac, but I did not expect anything this spacious or elaborate. Those rolling walls were an inventive touch, and your use of colour is a refreshing change from all that starkness you see in other places, it certainly will display the artwork to its best advantage. I predict the gallery will be an unparalleled success."

"Thank you, that's very kind of you to say so. I didn't want the place to look like a 'hands-off' museum, most galleries tend to give you that feeling. How can anyone purchase artwork when they're afraid to really browse around and enjoy it? I know galleries *are* exhibition spaces, but they don't have to feel like a … a hospital ward."

"Precisely, like I said, art was not meant to be top-toed around."

"Well, I understand that a little better now. However, I will have a permanent exhibition space on the fourth floor, but the third will have to do for the present."

Katherine explained how Aunt Martha had unexpectedly given her collection a head start, naming the paintings she would soon be receiving. Gerard's interest was hooked, you mean an early Van Gogh and a Degas, not to mention Chegal and Matisse?

"Oh, I can't wait to see *those*. You are fortunate to have an aunt willing to part with them."

"It's not like they're going half way around the world, she knows where to find them, plus she gets a nice brass plaque into the bargain."

Gerard laughed, he had heard about Aunt Martha.

"Nothing like a permanent loan, huh?"

"Well, Mom and Pops decided not to let Aunt Martha steal the show, they have given me a 'grant' for an auction at Sotheby's, but I haven't gotten around to that yet. It is a bit over the top, you know."

"Let me give you some advice: don't buy simply for the sake of filling a wall. Wait until you hear of something that you truly want to acquire. You don't have to rush into anything, after all, your art sales is what you should be concentrating on."

Of course, she knew she did not have to run to the auctions immediately, but Aunt Martha's donation had put her in a dilemma. Now she needed to fill the rest of the permanent exhibition space for the grand opening as the third floor would look rather bare with only a handful of artworks, after all, they could not be put on display amongst the artwork for sale. Already Gramp's friends from the Club had offered some pieces as temporary loans, she wasn't sure what they were willing to lend her, but was not about to look a gift horse in the mouth. She was going to pick them up on Thursday, while one piece was going to be delivered on Friday.

"Just one?" Gerard asked, a little amused. "That will hardly make a dent here."

"Well, it's a sculpture, perhaps it's big enough to make up for a collection of paintings," Katherine replied, she didn't want to accuse anyone of being stingy.

"Not likely, some collectors are the possessive type, museums and galleries have a hard time persuading people to loan items from their private collections."

"I can understand that, people don't know what might happen to them along the way. What makes the temporary loans difficult is that I can only have them on display for a few months at the most, I don't want the donors thinking I'm not going to return them."

"Right, and if you intend to wait until you find something at Sotheby's, quick replacements will not be possible, especially at this early stage."

"Yeah," Katherine nodded, "we're talking about serious collection-building, it's not like running to a store and finding a vase or two to fill an empty space among the knick-knacks.”

“Maybe it depends on where you shop, I know a dealer who specializes in Ming and Han Dynasty vases,” he laughed. “Tell you what, I’ve got a few pieces that might help fill the gaps, I’d be happy to contribute towards the temporary loans, and you don’t have to worry about returning them any time soon, my place is getting cluttered enough as it is.”

“Oh, would you consider doing that?”

“Of course, I loan to museums all the time.”

“I really don’t know what to say, you’re very generous.”

“Don’t mention it. Are there any particular artists you had in mind? I might have a few.”

Katherine was stunned, he was talking about famous paintings as though she were borrowing a few books from his library or a fistful of CDs.

“Er…I guess I hadn’t thought about it yet.”

She wasn’t sure what she wanted to collect when the time came, it also depended on what she found in the auctions and if the prices were manageable.

“Okay, I’ll surprise you.”

“You already have,” she laughed.

“I shall astonish you then, a few ‘golden oldies’ should do. How about a Holbein, a Rubens, Watteau? Oh, I won’t forget the other French favourites, I’ve got a Delacroix sketchbook along with a finished painting, a couple of Monets, Pissarro if you like, and some Sisleys, poor guy was always overshadowed by the other Impressionists, which is a shame really. Hmm, I might be able to talk Lottie into lending something, perhaps her Rembrandt, the Ingres too, but she might have something else,” he concluded as he rubbed his chin.

“Oh my! This is all just too much,” Katherine gasped.

“There, you’re astonished; mission accomplished,” he smiled, “I could have it all dropped off by the end of next week if you like.”

“Er yes, of course. Please let me assure you they will be guarded carefully, I’m waiting for the security company to send the security detail over, however, if they don’t come by this week, at least this place is wired so thoroughly that if you sneeze or even look crossways at something, the alarms go off lickety-split.” Thank heavens Steves knew his electronic equipment. “Every wall has a trip-wire system embedded within, if a would-be thief tries to lift a painting off its hangings, expect to find them minus their eardrums.”

“I trust you,” he laughed, “besides, I’ve everything insured as loan pieces, no worries.” He checked his watch. “It’s well past lunchtime, you must be famished. Would you like to go out with me for a bite to eat?"

Oh no, she hated to turn him down, especially after his spectacular offer, but she still had some running to do, the benches were a problem, and she would have to skip lunch. Perhaps he would not mind taking a rain check? Of course, he understood. Could he give her a call or maybe drop by in the meantime? Sure, no problem. Before he left, she had a question she wanted to ask if he did not mind: by any chance, was he the art collector who wanted to purchase her Napoléon piece? No, it wasn't him, had to be someone else he declared, but if she already had anonymous admirers calling the Sirrac, he could not wait to see what she painted for *her* gallery. She locked the doors after he left, so much for trying to solve *that* mystery.

Katherine thought she better check on Suzy busy working in the studio, maybe she would come help her pick out the benches. Suzy had just finished her sketches and was glad to take a break. They combed the furniture stores and warehouses, only stopping for a moment to grab a sandwich at a coffee shop, discussing the latest contribution to the temporary loans. Suzy could not believe it; Gerard had practically saved the day, again. Katherine would not have to worry about finding other loans for a long time, that was simply fabulous. They wanted to sit and savour the moment, imagining what paintings he was possibly offering, if Lottie would actually loan a Rembrandt … at last, they had to get back to business. Within a few hours, they managed to find a number of suitable seating arrangements, the only problem; there were not many items for sale in the showrooms, and they happened to cast their eyes on seats made in Europe, but if they wanted more, they would have to order them, a matter of six to eight weeks waiting period. Just great. Well, they must take what was on offer and wait for the rest, even if they arrived after September. It was a good thing Katherine did not plan to order exact matching benches but a mixture of antique and classical styles to offset the uniformity, for now she was obliged to extend her choice of furniture to elongated chaise lounges and chairs. Maybe that was meant to be, too many benches was also a bit monotonous no matter how they differed in style, the additional lounges were elegant, and the chairs would help neutralise the angular starkness of the corners in the exhibition spaces.

What a relief, another job taken care of, but of course, another round of deliveries to expect. A few more hours before it was time to stop for the day and head home, perhaps she could join Suzy in some quality paint time now that she had selected the star chart she wanted to use. Oh, I almost forgot, one last thing to do, call Charlie and ask him to have the lease ready to pick up in the morning. Thankfully, it was another business call, nothing that would last too long, a few minutes at the most, plus she had to be at work, there would be no time for things to get uncomfortable. His secretary answered the phone, Charlie was at a meeting, but she would pass on the message. Katherine had just settled in and started to paint out the bright sky over the nuclear plant in midnight blue when the telephone rang, sure enough, it was Charlie, he was coming out of the boardroom when she hung up.

"That was fast," he noted with astonishment. "How did you find someone so soon?"

"That was Gramp's doing" she replied, "leave it to him to find a good cook in a shot."

Charlie chuckled.

"Top rate chef then. Anyone we know?"

"You bet, just wait for it … Andre Garneau."

"*You're kidding.*"

"Nope, Monsieur Garneau of the 'C'est La Vie' is going to lease the restaurant at the Walsingham Gallery."

"Well, stop the presses," Charlie replied, "this is good news, you'll have every food critic there, which will draw the art critics."

"I know, isn't it a blast?"

Oh dear, Katherine had missed talking with Charlie, but she could not let things run away like this, *pull yourself together.*

"Umm, well, I said to Monsieur Garneau I would have a copy of the lease ready by Wednesday morning, is that all right?"

"Sure, we have discussed the particulars already, and it's all cut and dry. You can drop by tomorrow on your way in. If I'm busy somewhere, Marcy will have it ready for you. By the way, I haven't had a chance to call, how's Suzy? How are you two holding up?"

He sounded really concerned, he needn't worry, they were handling everything so far.

"She's fine, we're just taking one step at a time," Katherine sighed, "we have a lot of deliveries coming in this week, and the week after that, it's going to be quite a rush, but so far, nothing we can't deal with."

"Good to hear, well, I won't hold you up."

"All right, see you later."

He seemed relieved with her answer, nevertheless she had the impression he was not being completely open but decided to leave whatever was bothering him and not push the issue. That was strange, or was it? He always tended to worry about her too much. Well, he has no need to be a fusspot, things are going just swimmingly, for the present anyway.

Katherine returned to work and tried to concentrate as she applied the corrective touches to her canvas, but she could not help multi-tasking while she brushed, thinking about the various jobs that lay ahead. There would be so many deliveries arriving, art to pick up, people to hire ... before she knew it the alarm clock she had set beeped intermittently, causing them to jump. Six already? Gosh, it was like obeying the summons and dismissals of a school bell all over again. Despite her frustration in having to quit for the day, Katherine was glad she thought of bringing the clock, they could become so wrapped up in painting and forget to factor in the time for the long commute home. Capping their paint tubes, cleaning the brushes, covering the canvases, and closing the gallery for the night, Katherine finally noticed how quiet Suzy was, more so than usual. In fact, she had not said a word since they came back from the furniture stores, even to talk about Gerard's generous offer. Never mind, she must be exhausted from running around with her the last couple of days, especially after that long drive from Iowa. *Gee, give her a break why don't you.* You would be crashing too after all that. She needs some quiet time, she hasn't had a chance to settle in with all the activity around here, Katherine thought as they climbed into the van, I'll just keep my mouth shut, she needs some space. They were buckling their seatbelts when Suzy unexpectedly broke the silence.

"Kathy, I have something to tell you, and I don't think it can wait any longer," she said as she looked down and fidgeted with the belt straps, not quite knowing where to begin. Whoa, that did sound serious, something *was* troubling her then, best not to make her nervous, give her a chance to gather her thoughts.

"Er, okay. What's on your mind?"

A long pause followed. Was she in trouble of some kind? Katherine wasn't sure what to expect.

"Umm, I don't know how to say this, you're probably going to be very upset and..." she hesitated.

"Now what could I possibly get upset about? Well, if the artists pull out, Aunt Martha wants to take her pictures back, the temporary loans fizzle away, and Monsieur Garneau gets a better offer somewhere, all the day before we open, maybe," Katherine joked, trying to offset the growing tension. "Come on, talk to me. What's got you so worried?" Suzy took a deep breath.

"It's about Charlie," she began, "I ... well ... how do I say this? He's ...,"

"Been preoccupied with us," Katherine jumped in, assuming the course her conversation was taking. Suzy was startled until she continued,

"I know, he's a born worrier. I told him we're going to be fine, the first days here are going to be rough, but we're not doing too bad I think."

Suzy just looked down at her feet. *So that's it*, Katherine thought, Suzy has sensed Charlie's concern, I don't know why that would bother her though.

"It's not just that, it's a bit more than that," Suzy eventually replied, now fiddling with her purse strap. She was interrupted as a yellow cab haphazardly cut them off, causing Katherine to honk the horn and issue an impassioned speech berating the DMV for giving that guy his licence before lamenting the insanity of New York drivers in general.

"You know, he could kill someone someday! God help the passengers he picks up! Sorry, you were saying, Suzy? It's hard to hear over all this traffic, and the horns and the sirens ... ."

"I ... I ... I'm falling for Charlie!" she blurted out, the shock of the near fender-bender had flustered her into making a sudden confession, all tact and diplomacy had flown out the window.

"What?" Katherine nearly hit the brakes. "Did I hear you right? ... *You're falling for Charlie?*"

Somehow she had a feeling she looked just like Pops whenever his eyebrows were raised, a quick glance in the rear-view mirror told her she was not far off the mark.

"Ye ... yes!" Suzy gasped, ready to burst into tears. "You don't hate me, do you?"

"Hate you? What would give you a silly idea like *that?*"

This was all completely out of the blue.

"I know you say there's nothing really between you and Charlie, but I thought maybe you weren't sure of your feelings ... I didn't want to come between you if that was the case," Suzy replied, finding a tissue and wiping her eyes, half laughing, half ready to cry from an ambivalent jumble of shock and welcome relief.

"Listen, I wasn't making up stories when I said I could only think of him as a big brother and close friend."

"Oh! I'm not saying you were, just ... uncertain. I dunno ..."

"Well, don't worry about it, you know for sure now, but *do* tell me, how did this all come about?"

"Well, since you both came back from Paris, you've been terribly busy, he missed talking with someone, eventually he dropped by and we had a chat, and then one thing led to another, oh, all completely innocent. We went to lunch, then a few more lunches, a dinner out before I went home ... he called a few times over the summer ... but it wasn't just this past summer, I've always liked him, had a crush since the first time we met, but I thought you two were an item, I … ."

"Oh, I wished you had believed me," Katherine replied, "you could have gotten this all off your chest sooner. You have no idea how happy I am for you!"

"Really?" Suzy sniffed, wiping her nose.

"Yes, really. I know Charlie has been a little lonely lately, but since I did not want to give him any false hopes, I must confess I *did* allow work wedge a certain distance between us, which was easy to accomplish with everything I had to face. If only I knew, I could have saved myself the whole charade. I just wanted to remain his close friend, and now that there is a possibility things might work out for you, it will be easier to keep it that way without having to hide or avoid him. I hope you don't think I'm prying, but do you know how *he* feels about all of this?"

"Well, I don't know if he is in the same place I am, maybe he just needs someone to talk to. I'll be honest, I know his feelings for you run deep, he has known you far longer than me, they'll always be there, I'm not stupid, but if there's any hope for us … perhaps he can learn to love someone else, I'd be so happy," Suzy declared.

"Oh, I couldn't wish for anything better, and I *know* he would be happy with you, he just needs to move on."

It all made sense, no wonder he asked how Suzy was, they had grown closer in the midst of her busyness with the gallery. It was so clear now, that explained why Suzy was so stressed and quiet before her graduation, it was not just the exams and college pressure, she felt guilty thinking she was interloping between her and Charlie and did not know what to do or say. Judging from Charlie's strange hesitation during their phone conversation, he must be feeling guilty too, wondering if she knew he was getting close to Suzy and worried she might resent it. The poor things! If only they knew what a relief this was for her. Justine was right, the best solution would be to find someone else for him, but she never thought the answer lived right next door.

⊶❀⊷

The seating arrangements started to arrive in dribs and drabs the following morning and the next, Katherine thought they could manage with what they purchased until the remainder of the orders from Europe arrived, but the floor space was so large it seemed to swallow up the chairs and lounges as they positioned them in the various walkways and corners. Well, it would have to do for now, can't expect to have everything perfect. We're inviting a lot of people for the opening, no one will notice with the crowd, at least she could hope so. In the meantime, Andre came to drop off the lease and helped them move a few of the heavy objects around, sharing his suggestions for the name of the restaurant with Katherine as they rolled the latest delivery of chaise lounges into the elevator. There was not much he could do until this was decided, he could not print business cards or order monogrammed linen place settings and china, even the elegant menu covers with tasselled brocade features would have to wait. There was a problem though, several of the names he had thought about were already taken or were too difficult for English speakers to pronounce. Finally, Katherine thought it best to keep it simple:

"What about 'Chez Garneau'? You always wanted your own place, why not stamp your name on it?"

That was a winner, he looked like the Cheshire Cat as he left to tackle the lunch hour that day.

Now that the chairs were all in place, Katherine and Suzy were about to head up to the studio when a call came through, the security agency had finally selected a team of suitable officers for the gallery.

"That's great! Could you send them over this afternoon to discuss the details and get the particulars sorted out? We need them to start tomorrow as the permanent collections and temporary loans would be arriving."

Whew! That was close! She did not like the idea of having a fortune of paintings not properly secured, especially the loans. The windows, doors and walls were all wired, but unless these collections were under the care of a watchful guard at all times, Katherine knew she could become a nervous wreck with the responsibility. If they were her own paintings, it would not be so bad, but those belonging to others? Hmm, this all seemed a good idea when she first thought of it… no point worrying about it now, at least the security team was almost in place.

Just as they thought they could go upstairs, another interruption arrived, this time it was a delivery man knocking at the side entrance. Katherine motioned him to go around to the back door, another few chairs perhaps, no can't be that, she was certain they had all arrived, and it definitely wasn't any of the European shipments. This new arrival was unexpected, a square wooden crate that looked as if it weighed a ton. On second thought, she had better have it delivered in the lobby just in case it was too heavy to shift from the boiler house. Oh, it's got to be the sculpture sent to us on loan.

"It's come early than we expected. It wasn't supposed to be here until Friday," she noted, scratching her head.

"Listen lady, I just drive the truck and deliver the goods, it's not my fault if it arrived early."

Katherine sighed as she signed the forms and then turned to look at the crate. Suzy tried to see if there was some easy way to open it, nope, the lid was nailed tighter than a drum. Gee, this was not going very well, Katherine had set up for *packing* artwork once it sold, but not for *unpacking* it. They quickly drove to the nearest hardware store to pick up an array of crowbars. After a prolonged struggle, they finally lifted the lid, parted the mound of wood shavings and peered inside:

"Oh no!" Katherine gasped, "I had a feeling I would meet you again somewhere, but not under *my* roof!" She then fell into peals of laughter.

"What's so funny?" Suzy had to wait until Katherine could catch her breath.

"It's the Hanley sculpture!" and with that, she burst out laughing again to the point of tears. Suzy looked at the strange sandstone coloured form peaking up through the shavings like some featherless hatchling in a nest, she was not sure what was so funny, but the mood was contagious, she caught a case of the giggles.

"Kathy, there's a note here."

Katherine wiped the tears from her eyes before she could read what it said:

"It says to '*please accept this contribution as a permanent donation*' … I never thought *I'd* end up as the unsuspecting establishment!"

She could not read any further and started laughing again, hanging over the crate. At last, she had enough breath to let Suzy in on the joke, telling her about the charity auction for the Wheelchair Association, how this malformation was one of the raffle donations, wondering who on earth would bid for such nonsense … where would it end up? Now she knew. Suzy looked down at the foundling dropped on their doorstep in a hurry, she could not stop laughing either.

"Look on the bright side," Suzy wheezed, "we have a dead corner over there in front, it just might fill it."

"Yeah, I wonder if the donor wants a brass plaque too."

"You know, Hanley is making quite a name for himself, or so I've heard, and in time he may become famous, and *then* the laugh will be on us!"

Suzy did have a point; maybe this could become one of their star attractions and end up the centrepiece of the ground floor. Stranger things have happened. Katherine then straightened up:

"Oh no, I wonder what Gramps is up to, I haven't seen him and Jasper around here in a couple of days, come to think of it. He must be out soliciting everyone for donations, it would be just my luck to end up with every white elephant from New Jersey to Manhattan and beyond! I'll have to have a word with him …."

"Oh, you can't say a thing!" Suzy piped up. "His heart is in the right place, and whatever you say, would upset him. You know he's been so good, and all the help he's given, you can't take the wind out of his sails now. We'll wing this one like everything else, come what may. If we have to, we can hide some of the undesirables behind the rolly-polies …"

"Yeah, don't forget behind the bathroom doors."

They nearly suffocated laughing.

"Wait, we just can't let it sit on the floor. What will we do?"

"Well," Suzy observed, "we have to get a pedestal, and I don't know where we will find something sturdy enough, we definitely can't use your average plant stand."

"I wonder where they get pedestals? Oh, I have an idea … a tombstone carver. Do you think that's where they buy them?"

"How should I know? We'll just wing it."

"Okay let's look up a tombstone maker in the Yellow Pages and see what we can find."

As they were on their way to the reception desk, they saw a lady dressed in a crisp skirt and jacket tapping on the side door. Katherine recognised her right away, it was Mrs. Matthews. Wonderful! She unlocked the door and let her in.

"Hello Mrs. Matthews, I'm Katherine, it's nice to see you. We haven't met, but I saw you a few times in the library."

"Oh, of course, it's a pleasure to meet you finally. My husband told me so much about you, you were one of his star pupils."

Katherine wondered if she was blushing, maybe her cheeks were just hot from all that laughing.

"Do come in, please excuse the mess, we're just unpacking one of the displays."

Mrs. Matthews lifted her glasses and looked into the crate for a moment as they walked towards the reception desk, she did not seem too impressed with the orphan. Katherine struggled to retain her composure.

"It's a donation for the permanent exhibition space," she explained, "we really had no choice in the matter."

"Ah, I see," Mrs. Matthews nodded, placing her glasses back on the edge of her nose. Katherine introduced her to Suzy still thumbing through the phone book, she thought she should try looking under 'F' for funeral parlours, just in case.

"Don't forget 'M' for morticians," Katherine added.

"Oh, did someone pass away?" Mrs. Matthews enquired with concern. Suzy burst out laughing.

"Not exactly, we're trying to find a place that sells stone pedestals to place *that* thing on," Katherine clarified, pointing to the crate, "a tombstone carver was our first idea, they might have something like a polished piece of granite or marble, maybe in a Romanesque style."

"You've got your thinking caps on, girls," Mrs. Matthews declared, relieved she had not arrived in the midst of funeral arrangements. "It's good to see ingenuity is not completely dead these days. Well, to business, I understand you need an assistant."

"Yes, that's correct, someone who can handle the reception desk, give tours, help customers with the paintings, talk a little about the artists and explain the meaning of their work when possible, perhaps keep track of purchases, I suppose it won't be all that different from being a curator at a public museum, only most of the artwork is for sale. To be truthful, I don't know what the assistant's duties will entail as this is a new venture, at least I can tell you I don't expect a rude or demanding clientèle, people are usually well behaved in galleries."

"I'm sure it would be a very pleasant work environment, my dear, and I think I could handle the position. It will be good to get out of the house and see people again. I have some experience as an accountant, I did not start out as head librarian, I can offer my expertise with the bookkeeping if needs be."

"Wow, you're hired!" Katherine smiled. "Of course, I can't offer a huge salary at this stage, Mrs. Matthews."

"Please, call me Esther. Oh, don't worry about that, while I appreciate any extra income, I'm more interested in the activity. After stacking all those art books for years, it's nice to get out and see the art world for a change. When would you like me to start?"

"Well, tomorrow morning, if that would be okay with you."

"All right, tomorrow it is."

The morning went well Katherine had to admit. She and Suzy finally had an hour or two alone to paint before the security men arrived, a small host of vetted ex police and military officers with either an Irish or Italian background, it was like hiring her own private army. It did not take long to fill them in on their duties, showing them where to find the security panels and operate the cameras before giving them a tour of the floors and indicating where all the trip-wire features were installed. Now all they needed was the artwork.

Thank heavens they finally had staff on the floor, Esther was there right on time the next day allowing Katherine and Suzy the freedom to drive around and collect the rest of the temporary loans. However, before they could head out the door, Aunt Martha gave them a call. She was not about to be seconded by any of Gramp's idiot associates and declared they should pick up her donation immediately before any of the others arrived. Besides, hers was the best offer of the lot in her opinion. Katherine hoped Mom did not tell her about the unexpected arrival of the Hanley waif! She would never live that down! Dutifully, they did as Aunt Martha commanded, making her house the first stop of the day.

Lost in thought, Katherine and Suzy admired the exquisite treasures after the security guard helped to set them in place. Truly beautiful, amazing iconic gems Katherine never expected to own as she always assumed Aunt Martha would eventually leave these canvases to the Metropolitan. Unfortunately, there was little time to daydream as the other exhibits needed to be picked up, there would be time for admiration later.

Katherine was surprised at the number of artworks offered on loan, there were thirty seven paintings and sketches wrapped in everything from sheets to cardboard, a few special metal travel cases, and of course, a wooden crate or two, good thing they got the crowbars. It took several days to unpack them all. There was an eclectic jumble to be sure, some were contemporary American artists she was not familiar with but whose work had become well known, others were easier to recognise, works from the Hudson River School, and yes, there were two Andy Warhols, hmm, that's not a Whistler sketch, is it? Yep, says so on the list, and ...*gasp* ... they let her walk out of their house with a Picasso! Gee, they must really trust Gramps, and me for that matter. Katherine's knees wobbled as she thought of the fortune sitting around them on the floor or leaning against the walls. She finally felt relieved when each picture was wired into place, also a sense of excitement as these famous works slowly broke the monotony of the large exhibition space. Yes, the silk-panelling was colourful, but the gallery came to life with the new arrivals.

The works for sale began to file in sooner than expected. The first surprise was a micro-collection of acrylics Suzy had managed to paint during her vacation, a series of country scenes honouring classic Main Street America using her quiet hometown with its old town hall, red brick general store and lazy summer streetscapes for her models. Katherine was delighted, she did not expect her to have anything prepared, not with all the packing she had to do, and how did she find the time to have them framed before returning to New Jersey? Just perfect! She needed a few medium-sized works for the rolly-polies, the sunny scenes brightened up the main entrance.

If only the other works now arriving were as simple to handle, some pieces came without frames, which she had to set aside for a trip to the local framers, an added expense to factor into the commission. Of course, most of the artists were just starting out and could not afford these finishing touches, but that left her to cover the cost for now. Thank heavens the framers were happy to agree on a bulk-order discount for all her framing needs, a good deal for the artists too. In Martin and Justine's case, she did not mind framing their works, she advised they let her do that job as it might be cheaper on her side of the Atlantic, plus eliminate extra weight from the shipping costs, which she also agreed to absorb until their works sold. She was excited when their delivery finally arrived, between them they had compiled a considerable collection, which was no small feat since it was only a matter of months since she last saw them. There were paintings from their college years, and the 'Canvases of Despair' as she dubbed Justine's images of the flaming scales and Martin's dying Delacroix, but they also sent several new canvases they completed after her visit. Katherine was relieved to find they were much more positive, abstract, yes, but definitely bright and cheerful. It looked like they were going to be just fine. Opening the last box from their shipment, Katherine laughed, Martin had thrown in a few of his little Parisian gems, this time more carefully executed than the rapid-fire productions he usually peddled to the tourists.

She called them that night to tell them the collection had arrived safely, only to meet her first major disappointment: they would not be able to make it for the grand opening, they had the expense of their wedding to consider.   Katherine had mixed emotions, how sad that they would miss their first public showing, but of course their wedding must take precedence, and she felt very happy for them. She could hear the disappointment in their voices, they wanted to be there and support her new endeavour. Katherine crumbled inside, she wanted to offer them the plane tickets and lodgings at Oak Meadows right away if it would help, but then she realized they would want to pay her back for the travel expenses and would not accept if she refused. In the end, it would prove to be an extra sum swiped from their commission at a time when they could least afford it. It would be selfish to put pressure on them. However, if the show went well, they would have enough money to come to New York for their honeymoon, and perhaps bring a few more paintings with them for the gallery. Katherine was delighted, she had every intention of going to the wedding, and now they would be travelling back with her. Imagine that! I get to crash their honeymoon. They thought that was funny, next June it is then.

Her disappointment would have to wait, another truck had just pulled up outside, this time from Reinold International Shipping Enterprises.

"Where do you want this shipment, ma'am?"

Good grief, *how* many items are on the list? There were more than she expected, Suzy watched dumbfounded as the movers filed in and out, taking each custom-made metallic travelling case off the truck and stacking them in the lobby under Esther's watchful eye.

"Please sign here, oh yeah, I've got a note for you too, thank you, ma'am."

After the men had left, Katherine opened the official-looking envelope with the Reinold corporate logo. Amazed with the whole proceedings, Suzy simply bounced on her toes with excitement; she could hardly wait to find out what it said:

Dear Katherine,

I apologize for not delivering my contribution to your gallery at the designated time. I expected several pieces to be returned from other exhibitions within the same week and decided to include them in your consignment. I hope they meet with your approval.

Yours Sincerely,

Gerard

Katherine looked over the list, wow, not only were the paintings he mentioned included, there was a considerable selection of medieval art; triptychs, an altar panel, pages from illuminated manuscripts, one whole illuminated volume, two hand stitched tapestries, these were priceless! They should be in the Louvre or the Cluny, and yet here they were in her own gallery, piled over the lobby floor like your everyday bric-a-brac. Suzy was so excited she wanted to open them up right away, but when Esther heard the words 'medieval manuscripts' her curatorial skills came to the fore and she immediately stepped in to prevent any accident or catastrophe. If the illuminated pages were not set in special frames, they would need to use gloves when handled to stop any oil transferring onto the ancient velum. It would not be a bad idea to use gloves with the Delacroix notebook too, she pointed out. They carefully opened the cases: no need to worry, all items were properly set in protective frames. Esther also reminded them to put up signs forbidding cameras in the permanent gallery and take as few photographs as possible of the works for sale as the flashing would damage the artwork, they would have to dim the lights over the manuscripts in particular, to ensure the vibrant colours would not fade. Good thinking Esther, they had nearly forgotten all of that in the midst of the excitement, what would they do without her?

Time was in short supply and they would need to get everything in place and prepare the catalogues for the guests at the grand opening complete with a short biography of the artists to compliment the photos showing a sample of their works. Esther was an enormous help keeping them all organized and prodding them to accomplish their tasks. She made a file for each artist and compiled all the relevant material for the catalogue project as the pieces were set on display. Katherine employed cousin Stephanie as the official photographer of the gallery, family had to stick together. Stephie also knew a professional printer who could do excellent colour magazine-style catalogues in time for the opening, so Katherine assigned her the job of designing the layout for the printed material. Stephie had a flair for graphic design and she could be trusted to produce a first-class publication.

The gallery was not the only area taking shape, with the name of the restaurant decided upon, Andre came in every morning to oversee his deliveries as they arrived; business cards and community silverware one day, linens the next, glasses and condiment servers on another, the luxury menu covers, the stylish monogrammed chinaware with the slender gold ring around the edges, silver table-top buffet food warmers for the catered events, there always seemed to be a mountain of boxes and crates to open these days.

One morning Katherine's attention was drawn to the empty gift area, only a couple of weeks to go, and still no takers for the space. Maybe she could fill it with something until a renter came forward, *anything* to fill the emptiness in that corner. She was glad Martin had sent a few of his smaller pictures of Paris, she could place them on the shelves, but there was still so much space to fill, and Suzy's latest paintings were several inches too tall, that wouldn't work. She could wheel a roly-poly or two behind the glass and just close the door to the gift area, customers could always ask to see the works on them if they wanted to. However, it would be terrible if that section had to be cordoned off during the gala, a bleak area of empty shelving and gift displays would continue to stare from behind the impromptu window arrangement. What a pity the other artists were not 'in' to small paintings, she could have filled the shelves with little works for the present, but of course, it was easier and more profitable to paint large works, the smaller the canvas, the less she could charge and the less they would earn. It became an issue of quantity over quality. She was tempted to sketch a few items to fill the gap, but in the end knew she could not offer an assembly line product to her customers! She wanted to present artistic creations she could be proud of. Whatever she did, be it traditional, surreal, or plain outlandish, she had to do it well with plenty of time and effort put into it, no short cuts. This was becoming a real headache. Darn, even if someone did take the space now, they would never get their inventory stocked in time, not if it took weeks to ship in like her benches. Wait a minute, I *do* have something to put in there … .

Suzy found her rummaging through a stack of boxes in the corner of the boiler house.

"What have you got in there?"

"T-Shirts!" she called out with glee. "Lots and lots of T-shirts!"

Suzy opened one of the boxes.

"You've got a lot of boxer shorts too," she noted. "What do you want them for? Dusters?"

"For the gift corner," Katherine explained, "that space is very dead, and until we lease it out, these will fill it and brighten it up a bit. The gift shop will probably sell T-shirts, hats and stuff anyway, not too sure about the shorts, but for now, what else can we do?"

"I suppose that's a good idea, they do look colourful, don't they?" Suzy commented, holding up a black shirt with *New York, New York* printed in bold rainbow letters across the chest.

"Wait until you see the smiley faces."

They foraged through the other boxes to find designs in all colours and sizes. There were quite a few printed for the tourist trade, graphics of the 'Big Apple', the Statue of Liberty, the Brooklyn Bridge, and a pink elephant design with 'I love Dumbo' printed underneath. Suzy cracked up with the tops that said, 'My parents went to New York and all they got me was this lousy T-shirt'. The boxer shorts matched the designs on the T-shirts: now the big decision, should they go on display too?

"Hey Kathy, should we dress up those two mannequins in the corner?"

"What? I thought Steves threw them into the dumpster. Oh no, not *them*! One of them is missing an arm, the other has no nose. Did you ever see anything so *pathetic*? People will think we raided the morgue."

The mannequin suggestion was just too funny to keep a straight face. Katherine had visions of the grand opening, everyone dressed to the nines in formal attire, with *this* motley crew over in the corner dressed in their newfound wardrobe.

"I think we'll just fold the stuff and put it on the shelves for now," she said as she looked over at the two moribund figures leaning against each other. "It might be time to lay them to rest in the dumpster, obviously they've passed their prime."

⊰❀⊱

"Now girls, it's only a few days before the opening, don't you think it's time to go shopping for your outfits?"

"Oh dear, we don't have time for that Aunt Martha, there's too much to do, and besides, I've got so many clothes I never wear, I don't think I need to add to my collection," Katherine explained. She did not like to burst Aunt Martha's balloon, a shopping trip to find the latest fashion ensemble before any grand occasion had become a tradition, but this time it did not seem that important. Suzy did not think it necessary either, not when she had worn her graduation outfit only once. Although Helen had also looked forward to a day out, she appreciated their practical decision.

"Quite right girls," she nodded while finishing her herbal tea after dinner. "Come to think of it, I have suitable items to wear with their price tags still hanging. Martha, surely you don't need another outfit just for this occasion?"

"Oh what a disaster that will be if the invited guests have seen you in those outfits before! Have you lost all sense of propriety? Surely we must keep up appearances, it's expected in our position," Aunt Martha replied with all the dignity she could muster. "Just look at your hair girls, you're so unkempt lately, and your broken nails! Certainly, a once-over at the salon would not go astray. Oh dear, whatever will people think or say?"

The men, who usually remained silent during Martha's constant nit picking and the ladies' frivolous excuses for their shopping sprees, dared to add their opinions on the subject.

"Now Martha, the girls are overwhelmed with all the work they have

359

to do, and they have accomplished a miracle," Harold replied, "this is no time to berate them about incidentals. You know they show up perfect for every occasion, and you have no need to worry that they will embarrass you."

"True," Gramps added, "the girls will turn out models of convention for the occasion, and can you imagine Helen ever looking ruffled? Give yourself a break Martha, and enjoy the whole occasion without worrying all the time. The girls need a day's rest before the big event more than anything else, they've got the right idea."

Katherine did admit she had let her hair grow too long to manage, and her nails had seen better days before opening all those crates. Time to pay attention to their grooming, she and Suzy needed a little pampering. The shopping trip abandoned, Aunt Martha had to be content with a trip to the salon for all the ladies and oversee their makeover, not to mention catching up on the local gossip with the beauticians, trust them to know everything going on in town. Gramps had his own plans for that day:

"Take a day off, go relax and spruce yourselves up a bit," he declared, "I'll keep an eye on the place for you, I'd like to see how the security guys are getting on, can't be too careful you know."

Katherine smiled, she had a hunch the first person he would 'check up on' was Andre and the new menu, but she decided to keep quiet.

The day before the opening was settled upon for their official primping session, with Aunt Martha's approval. Katherine tried to relax as Gramps suggested, but it was difficult under the circumstances, she was already a bundle of nerves from excitement and anticipation, and now to face a day at the salon … oh joy. She could never figure out what was so important about a trip to the beauticians, it rarely felt like a luxury to her. Try relaxing while reclining in a sink with your neck stuck in an uncomfortable porcelain notch while someone tugged at your head, followed by the whine of commercial hair dryers in your ears. Ah yes, and the chemical smell of perm lotion permeating the air like a noxious volcanic plume, truly a calming environment. She was willing to suffer this for one day, at least it was another job taken care of; nails repaired, hair trimmed and curled, she was presentable again.

Katherine decided not to take the whole day off and dropped by to close up the gallery.

"Hullo Katie, you look wonderful," Gramps commented.

"Oh, your curls are beautiful," Esther remarked, "but what are you doing here? I thought you were taking a beauty break."

"Thanks for the compliments. Well, I couldn't stay away, tomorrow is the big night you know, I wanted to see if there was anything left to do."

Esther gave her a progress report: while Andre had set up the restaurant floor into a buffet area complete with champagne fountain, she had finished setting up the payroll system on the computers and had the art catalogues all ready and waiting to hand out to the guests tomorrow evening. Gramps approved of the guard on duty, seemed quite capable of handling the place, had to hand it to Steves for finding this security company for her.

"I see you found a use for the T-shirts too," he added, nodding towards the gift area. Katherine laughed.

"Well, I couldn't throw them out, they do help fill a corner. I don't expect to sell any, but who knows?"

"Very sensible," Esther agreed.

"I just don't know how we'll keep an eye over there with everyone busy here in the gallery," Katherine mused.

"Well I could look after that, perhaps I could model one of your fine cotton ensembles while I'm at it, how about the 'Big Apple'?" he suggested with a twinkle in his eye.

"Don't even *think* about it Gramps!" she gasped. "Don't go silly on me now!" Oh, he wouldn't dare show up on her big night in a T-shirt and boxers. The mannequins would be better than that!

"I'm just joking, pet," he laughed. "Can you picture your Aunt Martha's face if I turned up looking like that?"

"You *are* as bad as Steves," she replied just before the telephone rang.

"It's for you," Esther informed her, "it's a Fr. Reinold."

Oh, I do hope he's coming, after all his help with my painting.

"Hello Katherine, I hope I'm not calling at a bad time."

"No, you called just in time, we were about to close for the night."

"I wanted to thank you for inviting me to your opening tomorrow, and if you like, I would be happy bless your gallery while I'm there."

Katherine did not know what to say, it would be rude to refuse, there was one slight hitch … .

"Oh, thank you Father, but I must tell you, Reverend Dobbson offered to give his blessing, and he and his wife will be arriving early tomorrow. Er … if you would like to come early too, we can arrange everything then … ."

"Of course, I'd be delighted. I'll see you tomorrow."

Katherine hung up the receiver. Oh dear, I hope they get along.

"What was that all about?" Gramps asked.

"Fr. Reinold wants to bless the gallery too, I couldn't refuse his offer. Looks like I'm getting showered with blessings. What could I do?"

"Nothing for you to worry about," Gramps confirmed, "the Reverend constantly preaches on the importance of Christian unity, let them figure it out when they get here. What can you do when everyone wants to bless the place at the same time?"

⁂€

At long last, the day of the grand opening dawned. There were so many last minute details to handle, she hoped she and Suzy could keep up the momentum. The floral arrangements would be arriving and had to be set in position, and the jazz trio she hired would need a space made ready for them and time to set up. She was glad Charlie suggested live music to set the mood, playing the sound system would not seem appropriate for a big event like this. With all the activity beforehand, she and Suzy would have to bring their outfits to the gallery and change there later, they could not possibly work all day dressed up in their finery.

Better set up for the musicians first, there was plenty of room by the side entrance across from the restaurant. It took only ten minutes to manoeuvre the rolly-polies into position. The florists made their deliveries that afternoon, Mom and Pops sent a beautiful floral display for the reception desk, the other pre-ordered arrangements were mostly for the refreshment tables. At this stage, everything looked all set for the event, Katherine wondered why she and Suzy bothered to come in so early. Never mind, just being there reassured her that everything would go according to plan rather than sitting at home fretting she may have forgotten something.

Hidden in the kitchen, Andre worked feverishly with his *sous-chefs* preparing the gourmet finger-foods and desserts. They were so beautiful, edible artworks with colourful glazes, trays and trays of mouth-watering delicacies she wanted to try right away, the miniature pastry swans filled with creamed crab and shrimp looked so tempting. Katherine liked his buffet idea, the whole area now decorated with beautiful flower displays set amidst the silver food warmers, serving platters, champagne fountain and coffee area. However, there was a space left in the centre of the main buffet table, something was missing. Andre brought Katherine out back to the freezer and asked her to peek inside where she found an ice sculpture of a 'W'. Oh, what a wonderful idea! I hadn't thought about that!

Finally, it was time to get dressed and be prepared for the family and the first guests to arrive. Everything looked perfect, Suzy checked the lights and dimmer switches while Katherine surveyed the security systems and tidied the catalogues one last time. Gramps was the first to appear with Jasper trotting along beside him all decked out in a formal collar and black dickey-bow. Katherine and Suzy laughed.

"Hey Gramps, were did you find Jasper's outfit?"

"I got it today at the Pet Emporium when we went for his usual grooming session, had to dress him up for the occasion don't you know. Can't let Martha complain we aren't keeping up appearances."

Jasper turned his head in the direction of the restaurant and sniffed the air.

"Good idea boy, but we have to wait, it's not time yet," Gramps replied.

"Esther and the Professor should be here by now," Katherine noted, looking at her watch, "she said they would come early, not to mention the family wanted to be here for the blessings, I wonder what's delaying them?"

"Traffic perhaps," Suzy suggested, "it's Friday you know, everyone rushes home early, wait a minute, someone's coming now."

It was Mom and Pops, Katherine could not wait to see their expressions, apart from the construction plans and sundry photographs, they had not seen the final transformation of the former factory.

"Well, we made it," her father announced. "My, so this is what you did with the old place, I hardly recognise it, I'm very impressed."

"Oh, it's just gorgeous! It's more beautiful than I imagined," Mom added, "it feels more like a palace than a gallery."

"You really like it?" Katherine asked.

"Of course, dear," Pops nodded, "you've put a lot of work into your venture, and it certainly shows."

"Just wait until you see the rest, but I want to make sure we're all here first."

Aunt Martha made her appearance just then, she looked positively excited despite the delays that normally would leave her palpitating with exasperation.

"What dreadful traffic, bumper to bumper! Hello everyone! Kathy, this is wonderful! I can't wait to see where your Uncle Bob's paintings are hanging."

Katherine did not have time to reply, the guests began to arrive in a continuous stream. Esther and the Professor came through the side entrance, followed by Uncle Tim and Aunt Barbara, the musicians began warming up as Katherine made the introductions. The Reverend and his wife were the next to appear on the scene, oh good, she could let them know about the impromptu ecumenical service just in time. Stephie came flying through the back door clutching her camera with William following behind, making profuse apologies and hoping she had not missed anything, especially as she was the gallery's official photographer. Jon would not be able to make it, but hoped to call later that evening to congratulate her William explained, a little disappointed his brother would not be there. Katherine understood, with college taking precedence now, the cousins hardly got together anymore. Hopefully Steves might show up later if all went well, he had to attend a meeting with his tutor that could not be moved to another time, therefore he booked the first flight he could get afterwards. How he was going to get dressed and rush down from Oak Meadows to Dumbo and not miss everything was beyond her, but leave it to him to figure something out. Fr. Reinold came in and apologized for his late arrival, the traffic was unavoidable. Katherine introduced him to everyone and told him not to worry, he made it, that was the important thing. The group chatted for a moment before the Reverend turned to Fr. Reinold:

"Shall we say the blessing then before the official reception starts?"

"Yes, by all means. Please, after you."

Gramps motioned the musicians to stop jazzing for a moment while the Reverend asked them all to begin with the Lord's Prayer after which he prayed for God's grace and blessings upon the new gallery. Father then took a small prayer book out of his pocket and a little silver container. Opening the book to the desired page, he said a blessing for a new business before unscrewing the silver lid and sprinkling holy water in the sign of the cross. "Amen," he concluded, placing the lid back on. Gramps waved the musicians back into action.

"Thank you for the blessings," Katherine replied, quite relieved at how simple it was. "Let me give everyone a tour before it gets too busy. I told the artists to be here on time to greet the guests as they came in, but who knows, they might *all* be late with the traffic."

"If you don't mind, I think I'll stay down here," Gramps declared, "need to rest my knee a bit."

What a fib, Katherine thought, hopeless, in front of the pastors too! She knew exactly what he had in mind; try to talk Andre into letting him sample the buffet while they were upstairs. She was tempted herself earlier, how can anyone ignore that aroma wafting from the restaurant?

"Esther, Suzy," she whispered before following everyone to the elevator, "try and keep him away from the goodies until we come back down, you know what he's like."

"You're asking us to stop a locomotive with our bare hands," Esther whispered back, "but we can try."

"Oh never mind," she replied with a sigh, "we've got enough to do tonight without babysitting his cholesterol count." Well, just leave him at it, this is a special occasion after all, and as he said, who can have a ball on a diet?

"Whoops, we forgot to pass out the catalogues," Suzy observed, handing Katherine an armful.

"Gee, and I spent all day organizing them."

Katherine hurried to the elevator and passed everyone a copy as they ascended to the next floor. Stephie did an excellent job and deserved her share of the praise.

"So *this* was your secret project for Kathy," Aunt Barbara noted, obviously Stephie wanted to surprise them on the gala night.

"Yep, did all the photos, arranged the layout, picked the colour scheme, everything to match the feel of the gallery of course," Stephie replied, "it was a lot of fun to work on."

"This is really well done, good work Stephie. I'm going to have everyone sign it," Uncle Tim announced as he flipped through the first pages.

"Autographs! I never thought of that," Katherine admitted as they exited the elevator, "nearly all the artists will be here tonight, it's the perfect time. Okay everyone, this is the second floor, feel free to explore."

She was so proud as the family 'oh'd' and 'aw'd' at the dramatic change. The surroundings glowed in the soft golden lighting as the twilight settled in. Pops was certainly cheerful, commenting on the colourful ambiance and reminiscing as the others walked around to see the paintings.

"Tim, can you credit that this is the same old place?"

Uncle Tim laughed.

"Hardly, the change is incredible. Maybe our kids had the right idea all along Har, your Kathy with her art, my Stephie with her photography … we've been so caught up in business, pills and beauty creams we haven't taken time to enjoy the lighter side of life."

"It's not all light," Katherine had to admit, "most of the artists on show tonight are struggling to make ends meet and are hoping this night goes well, me too for that matter, I've sunk so much in at this point."

"Looking at this vibrant marvel," her father replied, "I don't think you'll have anything to worry about."

"Right, your gallery will be the hit of the season, I'm sure of it,"

Uncle Tim agreed before continuing, "okay, which ones are yours? I can't wait to see the latest masterpieces."

Katherine indicated to one of the walls displaying her fantasy cityscape sequence.

"That's the first set, the others are around the corner. Since these are more in the Impressionist vein while the others are surreal or abstract, I didn't want to mix the different styles."

"Wow, you painted those?" Uncle Tim said with amazement. "What an unusual city, and the colours, they're something else."

"Wait until you see the rest," Pops chuckled.

Katherine was used to her family's reactions by now, she expected mixed responses ranging from praise to perplexity, but she had forgotten about the other guests invited that evening and *their* possible reaction until she rounded the corner to see the Reverend and Father Reinold standing with their arms crossed contemplating her satirical nativity scene.

Uh oh.

"Ah, there you are Kathy," the Reverend called out. "I must say, your choice of subject for this one has me a little concerned … ."

Oh great, I'm going to catch it now! She could hear the conversation as she approached.

"I don't think blasphemy was intended," Fr. Reinold consoled, "just … exuberant sarcasm. The title *Noël Fatal* is self-explanatory, and quite frank actually."

"Yes, yes, I can see her point, at least I hope so, but *Fatal Christmas?* I pray this is not an indication of any Puritanical sentiment. The young always hop to extremes these days … surely Kathy my dear, you don't believe we should suppress Christmas celebrations?"

"Oh of course not! That's not what I meant, it's a message of moderation, you know, that we give more consideration to the nature of the festivities," she tried to explain.

"I see," Reverend Dobbson replied, stroking his chin as he took a second look at the oddity.

"I don't disagree with you Kathy," Fr. Reinold sighed as he shook his head, "but it's so blatantly graphic."

"I'm afraid our Kathy can be a little impulsive at times," the Reverend replied apologetically.

"Not to worry, even the Apostles could be impetuous," Fr. Reinold reminded him before moving on to the next picture. "Ah, we now progress to Babylon I presume."

"Babylon? That does not sound very progressive," the Reverend commented, "hmm, *Bricks for Stone, Slime for Mortar*, very interesting … a power plant, a graveyard, night and day undefined, but I don't quite see the connection to Nimrod's city other than the materials in the title."

"The answer lies in the stars," Father hinted, smiling at Katherine.

Standing back to admire it, Katherine was rather proud of this paradoxical canvas, the blending of diurnal-nocturnal opposites was visually striking. She set the vanishing point on the left of the horizon, and with unyielding straight lines, fanned the sunlit graves dotted with meadow flowers towards the right foreground, but the polarity was truly brought out with the north star positioned in the upper right-hand corner of the sky encompassed by a purple sphere sending sweeping equatorial circles and arcs over the nuclear plant to the ground in the opposite direction like the rays of a ghostly midnight sun.

"It certainly is an unusual concept," the Reverend agreed, "but what do the stars tell us?"

"Hmm, my astronomy is a bit rusty, but let's see … correct me if I'm wrong Katherine, that's an equatorial grid, yes? Polaris … ursa major … the night sky is facing north west, but judging from the elevation of the north star, the viewer is looking at the landscape from a position set close to the south, definitely not as far as the equator or the north star would appear closer to the earth with the longitude lines running relatively parallel with the horizon line. My guess for the position is somewhere off the lower edge of Europe."

"You're doing fine so far," Katherine confirmed.

"Okay, the daytime scene is different however, the graves are facing towards the left, so I assume the left is *east* since graves traditionally face the rising sun, therefore left is east, right is west … we must be simultaneously facing due south as well."

Katherine had not considered the direction of the *daytime* scene, she hoped this unforeseen element had not stymied her nocturnal symbolism.

"How interesting," Reverend Dobbson commented, "a clash of north and south, that usually means trouble, storms and twisters from an elemental standpoint, wars and revolutions from a historical and a poetical perspective."

"Wow, to be honest, I had not thought about all of that, but it's not beyond the bounds of my theme, the concept of danger and unpredictability," Katherine declared.

"True," Fr. Reinold agreed, "in fact the Reverend's observation is quite apropos to your subject. If I may return to the cardinal points, I see your graves are fanning towards the southwest." He followed the grassy rows with a motion of his hand. "Yes, that would be southwest, no doubt the graveyard of your nuclear plant points us in that direction, while the star chart tells us our global position when we get there."

"Very good." Katherine was impressed.

"Don't tell me the mysterious southern site is ancient Babylon?" The Reverend asked with enthusiasm, now the puzzle was beginning to unravel.

"Yes, but I suspect the stars mark the time Chernobyl blew, right?" Father smiled. "A blending of the old and the new?"

"Precisely!" Katherine beamed.

"It makes sense now," the Reverend noted, "mankind playing God with modern technology like the builders of old with their tower. Hmm, a picture of slime and bricks indeed; inferior finite materials prone to the ravages of Time and the decrees of Justice."

"Yes, and don't forget the only time we have an authentic combination of day and night is during a solar eclipse," Father reminded him.

"Of course, an omen of destruction or fell foreboding to the ancients who could read the signs of the sky."

"It's interesting the direction you focused upon is northwest, it's sometimes considered the 'darkest' point in the sky, how apropos indeed," Father Reinold concluded half to her and half to himself with a contemplative expression.

Goodness, the other two works in this series were a potential worry, but Katherine had no idea *this* painting could spark an in-depth theological cum philosophical debate. At least the two pastors seemed to be getting along very well. Pops and Uncle Tim, who had finished admiring her abstracts, came to see the 'Surreal Three Collection' depicting her grievances with the modern world and to overhear the lively discussion.

Her Uncle looked closer at the famished African children and the allegorical 'wish-you-were-here' postcard sent by the developed world before reading the title—*The Poor Relations*.

"Oh boy, move over Napoléon," Uncle Tim joked, "there are some new controversies in town. Why couldn't you just paint the Rodney King débâcle like everyone else?"

"Too popular, not original enough," she replied, not knowing whether to laugh or to give him a disapproving frown for his teasing.

"I did warn you," Pops replied rather stoically to his brother.

By this time, the Professor, who had joined the group, stood thoughtfully examining his star pupil's latest contributions to the art world.

"Truly remarkable," he commented, "I must say this is your best work yet. The compositions … the themes … and the power plant, if I'm not mistaken, a leaf borrowed from Magritte."

"What was that about originality, Kathy?" Uncle Tim laughed.

"Oh these are original," the Professor continued, "quite unique, but definitely in the same vein as Magritte's experimentation."

Katherine wanted to hear more, but the intellectual discussion was cut short by Suzy's voice over the sound system;

"*Kathy, the artists and guests are starting to arrive, we need you at the front desk.*"

"Looks like duty calls, oh dear, I'm sorry I won't be able to show you the third floor now." She was a little disappointed.

"Don't worry, I'm sure we can find our way around," Pops reassured her, "you must attend to your guests."

"If you would please excuse me, I should go too," the Professor nodded, "as one of the artists on show tonight, it's best to meet everyone as they come in."

"Of course, don't let us hold up the works," Uncle Tim replied.

At least she had a few minutes alone to talk with the Professor as they went downstairs before it became too busy.

"So, you really like my latest paintings?"

"Yes, very arresting. You certainly have a unique talent for experimenting with different styles and periods according to your subject."

"But despite what you said back there, they're not *really* original, are they?"

"As a wise old king once proclaimed," the Professor observed, taking off his glasses and polishing them with a handkerchief, " 'there is nothing new under the sun, nor can any man say, *Behold, this is new*'."

"Sounds like a riddle," Katherine mused.

"An eternal riddle," he replied, putting his glasses back on, "as you once noticed, there is no such thing as *absolute* originality, to which I replied a great work is an *unexpected* work. Your sources of inspiration may be unmistakable, but it's your unique *interpretations* developed from your own experiences and insight that makes the images innovative and fresh."

"Yes, I agree, but are they inventive enough to start a new school or movement?"

"Only time will tell," he smiled, "perhaps you should publish a bold aesthetic manifesto lauding the ideals immortalized in your pictures, that should give the historians and critics a head start."

"I need a catchy name first, some strange 'ism' no one has thought up yet," she laughed, "just as long as it doesn't have 'neo' stuck in front of it."

Their conversation would have to continue later, it was time to greet her guests. Several of the artists and their families had already arrived, followed by her family's circle of associates such as Pop and Gramp's friends from the Club, then other members from the Walsingham Industries board, a number of Aunt Martha's friends too, the Kraylors, followed by a few art critics hand-picked from the less hostile art review columns … members of the senior faculty of Belvedere … nearly everyone connected with Mom's bridge club … there were so many names to check off the list and catalogues to hand out, she hoped they could keep track of everyone. Pops and Uncle Tim were right, the place looked like it was gong to be a hit. She was congratulated so many times, she felt like a parrot repeating 'thank you very much, I'm so glad you could come,' like a broken record. The atmosphere started to buzz with excitement, animated conversations resounded, several couples danced to the favourite jazz tunes played by the trio while others milled around with their champagne and finger foods, admiring the art and discussing the latest trends with the artists or engaging in conversation with the other guests. Gramps, who was supposed to help out with the T-shirts and keep his eyes off the smorgasbord, continued to sneak out plates of titbits to Jasper exiled from the restaurant area. In the midst of the activity, Suzy called Katherine over to take a glance at the security monitor for the third floor:

"Quick, you've got to see this," she chuckled.

There was Aunt Martha showing off her donation to Dorris and Ester, her friends from church, with poor Stephie commandeered into taking photographs of her posing in front of the brass plaque.

She could not enjoy the scene for long as Esther came to inform her that a few of the critics were requesting an interview. That prospect was a little intimidating; she knew this was coming, here we go, just like a speech, think 'Oscars' if you get into difficulties. It was not as uncomfortable as she imagined, not at first. They wanted to know the history of the building, what her family thought of her new venture, the ideals she intended to promote in her gallery, why she chose to exhibit these particular collections on display, questions that naturally led to her own artwork. Was she willing to divulge the sources of her inspiration? How in her words would she describe her style? The last question was not easy to answer; how could she express the fruits of her creative inclinations with mere words? She took a deep breath and launched out into the deep:

"How would I describe my style … to be honest, it's experimental at this stage. I paint what I feel like painting at the time, be it fantastic, moody, or satirical. Unfortunately, my works may be misinterpreted, but I cannot help what others see."

"Miss Walsingham, would you say your activist principles have played a major role in the creation of several of your works on display tonight?" one reporter queried into his pocket recorder before pointing it at her to capture her reply.

"Oh, of course, I felt an impulse to depict issues in our modern culture that I believe call for closer examination."

"Then you object to modern technology and the progress we have made in this century?" he continued.

"Certainly not, but I do think mankind should look before it leaps … ," she began, but was promptly cut off before she could explain her viewpoint further.

"It is your opinion then, we don't do enough for the third world?"

Katherine did not like the sound of that: where was he going with this?

"Not when we burn a fortune up in the atmosphere that could help to eliminate extreme poverty. There are so many problems to solve on this planet first before we begin to trash other worlds."

"But what about the advances in the sciences that the space program has brought about? Surely this can help us to aid the less fortunate?"

"Yes, but it's an afterthought, those technological advances weren't primarily made *to* help the third world now, were they?"

This interview session was developing into an acerbic disputation, and the succession of barbed questions misrepresenting her artistic symbolism combined with the see-sawing of the mini-recorder between them began to exasperate her.

"Then we in the developed world are inconsiderate and wasteful … ."

"We can be, yes… ."

"But wouldn't you say that nuclear energy, one of your prominent themes, is *not* wasteful? Surely as an animal rights activist and environmentalist you do not object to clean, cost-effective sources of energy?"

"I dispute the point that nuclear energy is 'clean' and 'cost-effective'. As I recall, when we first harnessed nuclear power it was to drop an atom bomb on a civilian population, not to save the environment. However, you must admit, the victors are never tried for war crimes."

Before any more questions could be thrown at her, Esther came to say she was needed for a moment. *Just in the nick of time, this could have turned really nasty* Katherine thought, she rarely backed down once someone thrust her on her soapbox. The timely interruption was cousin Jon, he finally had a moment to call and offer his congratulations. She had a quick chat on his latest news, then everyone in the family wanted to talk with him, giving her the chance to enquire into the identity of that insufferable idiot brandishing the mini-recorder who had slipped somewhere out of sight.

"Don't you know?" one of the reporters replied while nonchalantly sipping his wine.

"No, I didn't recognise him. I thought he was with you. Who is he?"

"Why, that's Robert Horace, we all assumed he was invited."

"Are you *nuts?*" she blurted out completely taken aback.

What nerve! The Art Hacker dared to crash her opening! Goodness! What did she say in the heat of the moment? Oh, how she wanted to give him a piece of her mind! She looked through the crowd to find the wispy blond haired, blur-eyed weasel, but her efforts were hampered by everyone pulling her aside to compliment her on the wonderful party and introduce their spouse or a family member to her. By the time she could break free, it was too late, he had vanished into thin air now that his dastardly reconnaissance mission was accomplished. She had to find Suzy or Esther quick to tell them what had happened, but they were busy upstairs with a number of the guests interested in purchasing pieces on display. Charlie noticed her searching feverishly through the crowd and came over to inquire the reason for her distress.

"You won't believe it! Robert Horace came uninvited and took over the interview I was giving to the art columnists! I said quite a few things that he will no doubt twist out of context to suit his own distorted opinions! This is terrible!"

"Tell me what he looks like, I'll find him and kick him out on his ear," Charlie declared with quiet vehemence.

"I think he's gone already, I dread what I'm going to find in the papers this weekend," she groaned. She had no time to dwell on this unfortunate turn of events as Steves made his way through the crowd to give her a hug.

"Excuse me, hello … hello, excuse me, hi Mr. and Mrs. Forsyth … yes nice to see you too … coming through. Hey, I made it!" he beamed. "Wow, this is a lively gathering I must say, I hope I didn't miss anything."

"You have no idea," Charlie replied as Katherine greeted Steves, surprised to see him all dressed in a dinner suit.

"Look at you! How did you get here so fast? With the flight and everything, I didn't think you would be ready and down here until it was almost over."

"Simple, I just went to my tutorial in my dinner jacket and headed straight to the airport afterwards. You should have seen the professor's face, he must have thought I dressed for the occasion. I may be a little rumpled, but not as bad as I expected."

"That was quick thinking. Come on, lets go find the folks, they're around here somewhere, they were worried you might not make it."

Speaking of delayed guests, two people were missing from the throng: Gerard and Charlotte. Where could they be? It would be dreadful if they, of all people, missed the grand opening. Oh, there they are now. Katherine excused herself to welcome the latecomers.

"Hello Katherine, I'm sorry we're late," Gerard apologized as he shook hands.

"I hope you will forgive us," Charlotte added.

"Of course, I'm so glad you could make it," Katherine replied. "Please come this way, let me introduce you to everyone." Observing their arrival, Fr. Reinold excused himself from the group he was currently conversing with to join his siblings.

"Well Gerry, I can forgive you for being fashionably late as always," he joked with a smile as he gave them both a hearty embrace, "but must you hold up Lottie to make your grand entrance?"

Gerard simply laughed.

"Oh Pete, it's so good to see you, it's been awhile since we all got together," Charlotte replied, hugging her elder brother as if he had just returned for temporary leave after a protracted tour of duty in some brutal trench-war. "You're doing okay, aren't you?"

"Of course, never better," he replied with a smile, "you mustn't worry."

Katherine did not want to be rude, but she could not help overhearing their emotional exchange as she waited to show them around. Of course, it was only natural that his parish duties kept him very busy. In her own congregation, the Reverend and his wife were very active, it was amazing how they could keep going. Maybe Father was not in good health and Charlotte was concerned he may not have the stamina for the work demanded of him.

"How is the new appointment working out?" Gerard asked with a roguish note in his voice.

"So far so good," Father replied.

"New appointment, that sounds interesting," Katherine said, trying to make pleasant conversation.

"Oh, didn't our Pete tell you? He's been appointed one of the diocesan exorcists," Charlotte informed her, "I hope you will keep him in your prayers."

"Er, of course." Katherine was a little surprised with the news. He was now an exorcist? That was just ... *cool!* "Seriously?" she queried with interest, she could not help it, there were so many questions she wanted to ask. "Forgive me for being curious, I've never met an *exorcist* before. Is it anything like the movie? Can things like that really happen?"

"Only in the most exceptional cases, which thankfully, I have not come across yet," he replied.

She wanted to ask more, but it would have to wait until later. The atmosphere calmed down as Suzy switched on the sound system while the musicians went to take a well deserved break, making it a little easier for Katherine to perform her duties as hostess as she looked for her family members and introduced them to the newcomers. After meeting practically everyone and making pleasant conversation, Gerard and Charlotte insisting everyone call them by their nicknames, decided to make a tour of the gallery before trying the refreshments.

"Speaking of refreshments, I should go and see how Andre is doing," Katherine said as they headed for the stairs. She was relieved to see he had everything under control, there was no shortage of delectable titbits as trays continually issued from the kitchen.

"If you want to keep people happy, just keep the food and entertainment rolling," he whispered to her while setting out another round of pastries. "You know, you haven't eaten all day, you shouldn't be running on empty, grab something now while you have a minute."

"They're tempting, but I can't eat, I'm too keyed-up right now, maybe after it's all over, we can have a nice picnic then," she suggested, "you've enough here to feed an army."

"Oh, just try one, here," he coaxed, holding up a tray of miniature pastry boats filled with caviar.

"Okay, just one."

'One' quickly turned into a small plateful of nibbles, she did not realize how hungry she was. Gramps came over with a few of his chums to survey the new platters of goodies and to gab with her for a moment.

"So Kathy, that's the fellow who eclipsed our loans," Mr. Jacobs laughed as he refilled his plate, obviously referring to Gerry, "his medieval collection alone makes our few pictures look like postage stamps."

"Speak for yourself old chap," Mr. Netherfield retorted with a smile, "my Picasso is just as impressive and commands equal attention."

"Ah yes, but yours is not placed on the ground floor with a brass plaque like mine," Mr. Sanderson noted with a hint of satisfaction.

"No quarrels now, gentlemen," Katherine chuckled, "all contributions are gratefully received, the exhibition would not be the same without your notable collections," she confirmed, turning to include them all.

After awhile, Gerry and Lottie returned to the main gathering downstairs and admired the art displayed on the rolly-polies. By this time, the musicians had returned to their post, causing the conversational atmosphere to pick up into a lively beat once more.

"Kathy, I just love your gallery," Lotte declared as Katherine came over to see how they were enjoying the evening, "it is so much … fun! It's definitely more vibrant than the Sirrac."

Although she knew Lottie spoke the truth, Katherine was bashful with the compliment.

"Oh, it must be the festive atmosphere, I won't have a grand opening every night."

"I'm serious Kathy, I really mean it. It's not just the party. The surroundings are really beautiful, the setting reminds me of the Louvre. You know, you could hold art competitions, better ones than the Sirrac," Lottie continued. "Wouldn't that be exciting?"

"I suppose so, I hadn't really thought of that," Katherine confessed.

"Now that *is* a capital idea," Gerry replied, "it would be great publicity, giving the Sirrac a run for its money, not to mention adding some spice to the art culture around here."

The mention of 'publicity' and 'spice' suddenly brought to mind her disastrous introduction to the Art Attacker.

"I think I'm going to have plenty of that already," Katherine sighed shaking her head, relating to them how Horace the Horrible managed to crash her party. Lottie was indignant with such bold audacity, how dare he! Gerry simply laughed,

"Don't worry, better to be talked about than ignored, that would be the tragedy of the evening. Art usually thrives on scandal."

"Yeah, but *I* don't", she replied with consternation.

"It's only a column, it will be read in ten minutes and passed over for the next juicy gossip."

"A tornado is short-lived too," Katherine returned, "considering how nasty he was before with only one of my paintings, and now with an entire gallery for his subject, I don't think the Attacker's critique will be anything less than caustic this time around."

Their conversation was interrupted by Lottie who noticed the 'orphan' in the corner.

"A Hanley sculpture! How wonderful! How much is it?"

Katherine did not know if she could keep a straight face. Lottie liked to collect Hanley? Of all the pieces she had in the gallery, she could not sell the waif no matter how much she wanted to, not with Mr. Sanderson so proud of his donation. Katherine was obliged to inform her it was not for sale but part of the permanent collection, it was given to her by one of Gramp's friends. Lottie was a little crestfallen, but she understood. Never mind, there were other pieces there that she liked, the New England scenes by her professor were beautiful, the *batiks* were quite unusual, and decided she would take one or two from each series. Gerry had his eye on the Professor's painting of Yankee Stadium, a number of the Egyptian scenes, and he seemed to like the disturbing pastiche by Martin, and Justine's ominous scales, so decided to place a reserve on all of them before returning to the throng to engage in conversation.

Uncle Tim was eager to speak with him for a moment.

"Does your shipping company have operations in Indonesia?"

"Of course, Jakarta is one of our main hubs in Asia," Gerry informed him. Pops came over to join the group. Katherine sighed, she knew Uncle Tim was thinking of reorganizing the importing and exporting operations in their international locations, and decided to leave the men talk business. Networking could not be avoided on these occasions, but did she *have* to join in on a conference meeting in her artistic environment? Already she heard Charlie complain about all the free advice expected from him that night, no matter how well off they are, people always want something for nothing, but his answer was the usual, "Come see me at the office." All these parties play the same old song. Helen interrupted just then:

"Harold, let's go and get some food and a glass of champagne, I'm feeling a little famished. We have been so busy meeting and greeting we didn't get to try the restaurant yet."

"You and Martha go ahead dear, I don't feel like eating anything just now, I have a touch of heart burn, must be something I ate for lunch, or it could be my ulcer acting up again."

Helen looked at him with concern.

"Are you sure you're all right? Did you bring your medication? I'll get you a glass of water if you need it. Martha, go get him a glass of water."

"Oh now don't fuss ladies, maybe I'll sit somewhere quiet for awhile. Okay, I'll have that glass of water, if it's indigestion, that should fix it."

Katherine suggested he sit in the office while he waited for the medication to work, which usually didn't take long. The ladies went to sample the buffet while Uncle Tim and Gerry continued to talk about shipping lanes. Gramps came over to hear the latest dealings and to ensure Tim was not forgetting any points.

"I'll tell you what, I'll have a portfolio ready with all our port fees and other expenses within a few days, you can see if any of our services fit the bill," Gerry offered, "depending on the size and frequency of the shipments, I just might be able to cut you a discount rate."

"All right, sounds good to me," Uncle Tim concluded.

At that moment, Stephie came over to take a few extra photos. Gramps suggested it was time for her to take five, she had worked continuously all evening, surely she needed a break and get something to eat? With that, he steered her in the direction of the restaurant. Getting to the doorway and seeing Helen and Martha already there, he decided it would be better to take the bench behind the fern, he wanted a quiet moment alone with her, and would she please bring him a plate of nibbles too?

"Get a tray from Andre, and a couple of glasses of champagne while you're at it," he requested.

"Oh Grandpa, are you allowed to have that kind of food?" Stephie enquired with her hand on her hip.

"I've hardly had anything all day, whatever I can get now wouldn't do me any harm," he replied, "just run along dear, don't argue with your poor old Grandpa, and leave your Aunt Helen and Aunt Martha to enjoy their food, they told me they're famished, and don't forget Jasper, no fishy items for him. Hurry back now, there's a good girl, I have something I want to discuss with you."

There was nothing for Stephie to do but hop to it, bring back the requested items and settle next to him on the bench to hear the news.

"Okay, what's on your mind, Grandpa?"

"I was just wondering," he began as he gave Jasper his plate, "with your photography and all, have you thought about setting up your own studio?"

"Well sure, Grandpa, when I'm finished at college, naturally. What photographer doesn't think about it?"

"Humph, I thought so," he replied while munching on a puffy lobster-filled *vol-a-vent*. "Now that Kathy's all sorted, I thought it was your turn. I've got just the perfect place, oh, nothing quite as big as this, you don't need all this space. In any case, with a studio it's the location that's important. How does Manhattan grab you?"

"Are you serious?" Stephie asked wide-eyed.

"Of course I am. You know that office space that's leased out at the moment? That should do the trick."

"Gee Grandpa, I don't know what to say. That place is enormous, I can't just take it from you …"

"Come now, I expect you to pay me the same as Kathy did, just give me a lunch or dinner at the 21Club, and we'll call it even."

While Gramps was concluding his latest business deal, Katherine had been cornered by Aunt Martha's friends, Dorris and Ester, who wanted to gossip about anything and everything. She finally excused herself to check up on Pops, but on the way, Gerry stopped her and asked if she would give him the pleasure of a dance. Darn! She thought no one would bother her with such a request, not with all the activity. Of all people, how could she refuse Gerry? *Well here goes*, she thought while accompanying him to the area that had become the designated dance floor.

"Now Kathy finally looks like she's enjoying herself," Aunt Martha stated with delight to her sister, "it's about time she got out and danced a bit."

Katherine, however, hoped the trio would play a quick tune this time and be done with it, but as it turned out, he was an excellent dancer and she had to put a little effort into it, people were beginning to clear the area and stop to admire them.

"You're a natural," Gerry declared after Katherine made a stylish turn.

"Not really, it must be all those classes I was marched to every Saturday," she replied.

"I assume you got the piano treatment too," he laughed.

"No, the violin actually, but I sounded so much like a screeching poltergeist Pops begged Mom to stop sending me to the lessons," she confessed.

"We had an old nun at school who called us 'dunces' and 'blockheads' every time we hit a wrong note. I never could master the piano, just waited to hear the criticism every minute I sat in front of it. Pete hung in there a little longer, I think he can still play a tune or two," he reflected.

"I don't know how anyone can learn under those circumstances, that's just, cruel."

"Oh, she was just a crabby old lady who didn't know how to handle kids. Thank God they weren't all like her. We had a young novice in the convent who loved baseball, she was a blast. You should have seen her running between the bases with her veil flying."

Before she knew it, the number had come to an end and they were politely applauded. Katherine wanted to evaporate as her cheeks became beet-red. Nuts! How embarrassing. The idea of slipping away was not possible when someone yelled out,

"Speech! Speech!"

*Oh no…*she was hoping to avoid that woeful necessity of speech-making. With all that good food and company to keep everyone happy, couldn't they just enjoy the night without expecting her to make an idiot of herself? She was an artist, not bloom'n Shakespeare. At least she was not completely unprepared, she had a few things ready to say just in case, but as other voices jovially repeated the call, "Speech! Speech!", the words just faded away in her growing anxiety. *Oh, better face the music, send in the clown, think of the Oscars* … thank goodness everyone is in a good mood after all the wine and champagne. She looked for a vantage point to address the party and decided on the first steps of the stairs, motioning Suzy to pass the microphone when she reached the front desk. Applause erupted and then gradually died away as she stood above the gathering with the amplifying apparatus in hand. Stephie snapped a few photos to record the grand occasion.

"Hello everyone, I am so happy you all could be here tonight, thank you so much for coming and helping to make this celebration truly special. I hope you are enjoying the party," she began.

Many guests cheered and clapped in the affirmative, *so far so good* Katherine thought.

"No one likes a long speech, but there are so many here tonight I wish to thank for making this evening possible, first and foremost, my grandfather, who literally gave me the heart of the family business to see my dream come true."

Familiar with the history of the old factory, the crowd laughed and applauded Gramps who seemed chuffed with this acknowledgement.

"Of course, I wish to thank my parents," she continued, "my brother, Stephen over there, Uncle Tim, Aunt Barbara, and my cousins for contributing towards the refurbishment project, I was truly overwhelmed by their generosity."

More applause.

"Naturally, you cannot have a gallery without artwork, so let's give a big round of applause to the artists on show this evening.”

A hearty ovation resounded.

“Now I wish to thank everyone who contributed a donation to my exhibition gallery, my Aunt Martha in particular for her fabulous collection, and last but not least, those who loaned their priceless collections, Mr. Jacobs, Mr. Netherfield, Mr. Sanderson, who also donated the Hanley sculpture, and of course, Mr. Gerard Reinold and his sister, Charlotte Reinold, for their magnificent contributions.”

Polite clapping continued between each of her acknowledgements.

“Now a special thank you to my friend and colleague, Susanna Cooper, and to Mrs. Esther Matthews, whose hard work and invaluable assistance helped to make this evening a success, and to my cousin Stephanie for the wonderful catalogue she prepared for this show, and her continuous work all evening photographing the event. Of course, let us not forget Chef Garneau for his gastronomic marvels, and your impromptu dancing displays how much you are enjoying the *Hazy Crazy Trio* tonight, let’s give them all a round of applause. Thank you all for making this evening one to remember. By now you must have enough speeches for one night, time to get back to the festivities.”

There was one last enthusiastic ovation before the musicians started up into fill swing once more. Katherine was relieved she could finally step down. *Whew*, another milestone accomplished. Now that the formalities expected of her were over, maybe she could begin to relax a little.

“Lovely speech, dear,” her mother said, “I’m so sorry your father missed it.”

“Yes, where is he?” Aunt Martha queried as she looked around, a little indignant he should be absent during this important event. “I thought his medication would have worked by now.”

“Oh dear, I was about to see how he was doing when I got distracted,” Katherine replied. Despite Aunt Martha’s edginess, she was correct, he should have come out of the office by this time. Must be a bad ulcer attack Katherine concluded, poor Pops, he never gets to enjoy himself, this always happens when he should be having a good time.

She was about to make her way to the office when the Reverend and his wife stopped her for a moment.

“Lovely speech my dear, I must say we’ve really enjoyed the evening, but unfortunately we’ll have to make our goodbyes now,” he announced.

“Oh do you have to leave already?” Katherine asked.

“I know it’s early yet, but we have a busy day tomorrow preparing for the youth group, not to mention choir practise and the service for

Sunday," Elena explained.

"Friday is like a school night for us," the Reverend smiled.

"I understand, I'm so glad you could come."

"This has been so exciting, we've never been invited to a gallery opening before, mostly bake sales, the Christmas parties, the dedication of the new church hall, but nothing quite like this, I truly had a wonderful time," Elena said, before congratulating her on her new collection, "I can see the message you are trying to get across, if only more people would be as brave."

There, Katherine thought, people *will* 'get the picture'!

"Well, we must be off, thank you again, Kathy. We'll see you on Sunday," the Reverend replied. She thanked them again and showed them to the door. Time to go now and check on Pops before any more interruptions.

"Suzy, did you see Pops come out yet?"

"Oh, I didn't notice, I was busy with someone in the T-shirt corner."

Katherine went behind the reception desk and knocked on the door.

"Hey Pops, are you all right? Are you still in there?" No answer.

"Maybe he's in the bathroom," Suzy suggested.

Katherine opened the door and saw him slumped over the desk, holding his chest.

"Pops! What's the matter?" she cried, running to his side. She could see he was breathing with great difficulty. "Someone call 9-1-1!" she yelled out. Esther rushed into the office, quickly closed the door and called the emergency services from there while Suzy ran for Gramps and Uncle Tim. Tim and Steves were first on the scene.

"Har! Are you all right? What's wrong?" Uncle Tim said as he put his arm over his shoulder. Harold opened his eyes slowly.

"It's my chest …." he whispered with great effort, "I can't breathe … my arm …."

"Okay, help is on the way, hang in there, try and take slow deep breaths, cough if you can."

Harold tried to follow his brother's advice, but could only look at him with a dazed, almost fearful expression. Katherine, in shock, could hardly register what was happening. Unable to react, she could only watch on in dismay as her uncle and brother tried to keep him focused. Gramps poked his head through the door to see what had caused the panic.

"Suzy said Harold has had some kind of attack … *thundering tarnations!* What's happening?"

"It's not a bleeding ulcer, he hasn't spit up anything. It looks like his heart," Steves informed him while attempting to stay calm, "he keeps saying his arm hurts. It can't be a heart attack, or he'd be unconscious right now."

"The paramedics have been called and should be here any minute," Uncle Tim added.

"Harold!" Helen cried out as she, Martha and Barbara tried to come in, but Gramps closed the door and barred the way to prevent them from seeing the distressing scene.

"No you can't go in there, there's nothing you can do. Give them some space, he's going to be all right Helen," he quietly but firmly insisted, trying not to display his own anxiety. By this time, a few of the guests had noticed the commotion and began to whisper to each other, probing to find out what happened.

"Did someone have too much champagne?", "I think someone's collapsed….", "You really think so?", "I don't know.", "Who is it?", "It's someone in the family … no couldn't be.", "Did I hear 'heart attack'?"

The lively atmosphere of the party plummeted once the ambulance arrived, sirens blaring. The glaring lights of the emergency vehicle blazed through the windows, sending blue-red rays careening around the walls like some freakish carnival ride while the paramedics rushed their equipment through on a gurney, parting the astonished guests who stood around staring with morbid curiosity. Faltering for only a few minutes, the musicians decided it was best to keep the spirit of the party going, continuing with the next number, the show must go on, but their light-hearted jazz performance in the midst of the sudden catastrophe only added a macabre touch to the distressing panorama as her father was wheeled away with Uncle Tim following close behind.

"Only one family member in the ambulance, please."

Semi-oblivious to the guests crowding around trying to offer support, there was a sudden rush as the family made arrangements to get to the hospital. Gramps and Steves were already on their way to the parking lot, while Helen, Aunt Barbara and Aunt Martha discussed if they should take one car or drive separately. It was quickly decided that Helen and Martha should go together while Aunt Barbara brought Stephie and William with her. Charlie offered to drive Katherine who was still in a state of confusion as to what would be proper for her to do under these circumstances. As hostess, she felt guilty leaving her guests, but could not bear to be the only one in the family stuck at the gallery while her father was fighting for his life in an emergency room. Her mother and aunts agreed she should come, while Suzy, Esther and the Professor told her not to worry, they could close up the place with the help of the security guards, leave everything to us. Gerry and Lottie came forward to offer their assistance, now that they had met everyone, they should be able to keep the guests occupied since there was only an hour or so left. Fr. Reinold approached and tried to reassure her:

"I'll stay here with Gerry and Lottie. Don't worry, he will come through this and will be home within a day or two."

Katherine thanked them all profusely before making her way towards the back door with Charlie.

The hospital where the ambulance was taking him was not far away, but the journey there seemed like an eternity. In the car, Katherine was too worried to speak. Charlie tried to reassure her that all would be fine, but he knew better than to force a conversation under the circumstances, trying to keep her distracted would only add to her stress. There are times when one can only suffer in silence.

At last, they arrived at the emergency entrance and joined everyone in the waiting area. Katherine dreaded the thought of them all standing around there anxiously waiting for news as night approached. She had never been to an emergency room before, she had only visited someone in hospital after they were admitted. Her imagination was conjuring the worst scenarios. It could be she watched too many television dramas, but it seemed this was the one time when victims from violent incidents tended to arrive: horrific car accidents, domestic abuse cases, junkies who overdosed, gunshot fatalities from a robbery gone wrong or perhaps a gang-related drive-by shooting, broken humanity inevitably ended up in hospitals during the dark hours, at least on the small screen. While she and Charlie pensively waited, pacing around the seating arrangements, her mother, pale with shock, sat down with her aunts who tried to comfort her. Gramps decided to keep the grandkids company, motioning them all to take a seat beside him, while Katherine went to call Mrs. Gonzales and tell her what had happened, they would not be home early that night. Uncle Tim was detained at the emergency reception desk taking care of the official red tape, filling in forms, acquainting the doctors with a short medical history, their insurance coverage and the name of their private doctor. Finished with the tedious admittance routine, he came in to pace the floor with Charlie.

Every minute felt like an hour as they watched the clock. Eventually, they began to frequent the vending machines for the sepia coloured sap flogged as coffee, anything was palatable as long as it helped to keep them going. Once in a while, someone would pop their head into the room, causing them all to look over in expectation only to see another unfortunate visitor trying to find their relatives who too had come to this place in the wake of a tragedy. Other times it was a doctor searching for family members of a patient, but not for them.

"Excuse me, are you the family of Mr. Harold Walsingham?"

At last, an officious doctor with a clipboard arrived to deliver the diagnosis; in layman's terms, Harold had suffered an angina attack, but they had it under control. It was a good thing they caught it in time, it could have developed into cardiac arrest. Everyone breathed a sigh of relief, at least it was not as bad as they feared, but that was not the end of the news. The narrowed artery would need correction. Not familiar with the particulars of angina, Katherine did not like the sound of that, however, Gramps, Uncle Tim and Steves seemed to know what the doctor was talking about and asked the relevant questions. Would he need angioplasty, or would his condition necessitate a by-pass? The doctor believed that a by-pass was not necessary and recommended angioplasty, of course, they could consult with their own doctors for a second opinion. They would keep him over night for observation and transfer him in the morning to their private hospital.

"May we see him now?" Helen asked anxiously.

"Of course," the doctor replied, "only for a few minutes, and two at a time, please. He needs to stay rested, too many visitors will exhaust him."

Helen and Gramps went in first, leaving the younger generation to discuss the diagnosis with Uncle Tim and the aunts.

"I never would have expected *Pops* to have heart trouble," Steves remarked, "Gramps seemed the obvious candidate."

"I wonder if his work load is getting to be too much for him, maybe the stress has something to do with it," Aunt Barbara mused aloud.

"Oh no! I hope the grand opening didn't stress him out," Katherine gasped.

"No, don't blame yourself Kathy, this isn't something that develops overnight," Uncle Tim reassured her, "this has been building up for a time."

"Yeah," Steves added, "stress may trigger the angina, but any exertion may also spark an attack, even something simple like walking a few steps can do it."

"I don't get it, what's the difference between angina and a heart attack?" William asked.

Steves switched into 'scientific mode', explaining a heart attack is caused when the coronary arteries get blocked by a blood clot, angina is when fats build up in the arteries and restrict blood flow. Angina may feel like cardiac arrest, but the victim remains conscious and the heart may not suffer any lasting damage.

"Well, that's good to know," Aunt Martha piped, "but why would a by-pass be suggested if there's no damage?"

"Because the arteries are still clogged and could be a potential risk for a heart attack," Steves continued, "but his heart would have to be in really serious condition to have a by-pass. I'm glad angioplasty may work."

He then launched into a description of the procedure, explaining how Pops would first need an angiogram to detect the affected area, namely, injecting a special dye via a catheter into the coronary artery that would allow the doctors take detailed x-rays of the heart veins. The doctors may decide to do the angioplasty right there and then since he would be in the cardio catheterisation lab. This would entail inserting a special catheter with a tiny balloon on the tip that would inflate in the affected area, flattening the arterial plaque to allow the blood flow. They may insert a stent, a metal mesh to keep the artery open. He would need to take blood-thinning drugs after that.

"The good thing is he will hardly feel a thing, they won't even have to knock him out for the procedure. He'll be home by tomorrow night, although he will have to take it easy for the first week or two, no heavy lifting or exercise." Steves concluded.

Katherine felt relieved, it sounded like he was going to be fine. Gramps and Helen came back to allow Uncle Tim and Aunt Barbara visit with Harold for a few minutes before Aunt Martha and Katherine's turn came. Although everything sounded routine, it was difficult to see Pops laid out in a hospital bed with an I.V. attached to him, especially when he was the one always in control and on top of things. This sudden attack brought home the sobering awareness of life and death: no one was invincible. The unseen blade of mortality would inevitably scythe even her parents who had always been there from before she could remember. The question of *when* and *how* could no longer be ignored or consigned to some far off period in the unforeseeable future. The answer would forever be *anytime, anywhere*.

"How are you feeling, Harold? Does your chest still hurt?" Aunt Martha queried, fussing like an old mother hen.

"No, I'm fine right now. Good thing you came when you did Kathy, I was hoping the pain would pass, but I should have called for help."

"Stubborn as always," Aunt Martha protested with a worried grimace.

"I suppose so, however, I'm sorry for giving you such a scare and ruining your opening," he apologized, turning to Katherine.

"Nonsense Pops!" she replied, giving his hand a reassuring squeeze.

"You didn't ruin it, it was rather successful I must say, a number of paintings have either sold or been placed on reserve. Besides, you can't control a medical emergency."

"No, but this is something that could have been prevented. I wouldn't mind that much if it wasn't for the irony of it all: while your grandfather has been cheating right, left and centre, I stuck to his diet," he confessed with a grin.

Katherine could not help but smile. Who knew better than she did how he constantly cheated? They talked for a few moments before returning to the waiting room to allow Steves and Stephie make their quick visit, while William and Charlie went in next. While the last visitors were in the emergency ward, Uncle Tim and Helen were deciding what to do: Tim offered to stay the night with his brother, but Helen argued against it saying he would be too exhausted, and someone had to be at the firm tomorrow. She thought it best if she remained with him, and everyone else could visit the next day after he was transferred. Katherine wondered how or if she could be there, now that she had the gallery to manage.

"Leave it to us, sis," Steves consoled her, "I'd stay with Mom, but they'd never allow two people stay overnight."

"That's all right dear, you can pick me up in the morning when they transfer your father."

"Are you sure you want to be here alone?" Uncle Tim asked.

"Yes, I'll be fine, go home with Barbara and get some rest," she assured them.

"I can be at the other hospital tomorrow," Gramps suggested, "the procedure is relatively simple, he'll be out in a few hours, I'll drive him home."

Since everything seemed under control and Pops was not in immediate danger, Katherine decided she had better go back to the gallery. Charlie offered to drive her and anyone else who needed to pick up their cars. Stephie and William decided to hitch a ride with them, while Steves said he would travel with Gramps. Aunt Martha had taken her own car, so she might as well head home from there. Katherine agreed to drive Pop's car back to Oak Meadows after she checked on the gallery, Suzy was quite capable of handling the van.

"My, what a scare he gave us," Aunt Martha admitted, breathing out a sigh of relief as everyone made their way to the exit, "I honestly thought he was having a heart attack."

Katherine was about to reply he did not set out purposely to upset anyone when they were met by Gramps and Steves, who had tried that particular exit and were making a hasty retreat.

"I wouldn't go that way, a few reporters caught wind of what happened and are trying to accost anyone for an interview. Security had to be called to keep them out," Gramps warned with a disgruntled 'hrumph!'.

"Geeze, I forgot the press might get a hold of this, I'm going to have to prepare something," Uncle Tim grumbled, "but not tonight, they'll have to wait until tomorrow, I'm not up to it right now."

"Oh no, I forgot I had critics there tonight," Katherine replied, putting her hand to her forehead, "they probably followed us here, or maybe called their colleagues at the papers. What a pain!"

"Don't worry, they would have found out anyway," Gramps consoled.

"We'll have to give them the slip," Steves suggested, "let's try another door."

"Someone has to pacify them for now," Uncle Tim sighed, "I'll go tell them to expect a statement tomorrow while everyone heads to another exit."

"If they see us escape and follow us, just say you have no comment, Kathy, and lock them out of the gallery," Charlie advised, "let your uncle handle the press in the morning."

"Okay, I'll just ignore them."

"All right you guys, get away if you can, I'll keep them at bay ... here goes," Uncle Tim declared as he and Aunt Barbara went towards the emergency exit where the security guards were trying to keep the doors clear, everyone else went down the corridor in the opposite direction. So far, so good; they made it to their cars while Uncle Tim kept the reporters busy.

That was one of the drawbacks of being a member of a prominent family; nothing they did or said was sacred, the least variation in their health or social life was newsworthy material. Every success or misfortune of the CEO or the company, be it large or small, was factored into the indexes used to evaluate the Walsingham stocks. Her mother could never credit that vast fortunes weighed in the balance of such silly notions and just shook her head at the insanity of the market.

"Honestly, if your father sneezes, he could send Wall Street into a tizzy," she once joked.

They had learned to put up with reporters, the ladies usually had the more frivolous society columns to contend with, and that too was an unavoidable nuisance.

The drive back was relatively uneventful; at least no reporters spotted them. Katherine wondered how everyone managed while the family were at the hospital, she could not worry about that in the midst of the confusion. Perhaps the gallery was closed by now … no, the place was still lit up. Although several of the guests had left early, knowing when it was time to make a discreet exit, there were quite a number of stragglers still hanging on, milking every drop of the party atmosphere, and the champagne, for all its worth. Katherine decided to leave everyone go home, so they said their farewells in the parking lot, it was getting rather late. Charlie decided to stick around and see that everyone was all right.

"We didn't think you could come back, I guess this means your Dad is doing better," Suzy said.

"He's going to be okay, it was an angina attack, he'll be home by tomorrow," Katherine explained.

"Thank goodness for that," Esther said, putting her hand over her heart. "Well, not much happened after you left, a few guests decided to leave early, but the party just went on for everyone else."

"I must say the Reinolds were a great help keeping everyone entertained," the Professor added.

"Maybe too much of a help," Katherine laughed, "the party should be over by now."

"I know, the jazz band packed up and left already, I thought everyone would get the hint," Suzy added.

"Maybe it's time to start switching off a few lights," Esther suggested.

That seemed to do the trick, they could hear people moving around and making their way downstairs, while everyone on the ground floor wished them a good night before heading to the doors. The artists, who had remained, thanked her again for giving them this wonderful opportunity before saying their goodbyes. The Reinolds were the last to come downstairs.

"I think that's everyone," Gerry announced.

"Kathy, you're back," Lottie declared, rapidly tripping down the steps. "How is your father? Is everything okay?"

"He's going to be fine, it's angina, nothing he can't handle."

"That is good news," Father Reinold acknowledged, "we did our best at this end."

"Thank you, I really appreciate all you're help. I'm sorry you were all put to work."

"Nonsense," Gerry replied, "we're glad we could be of assistance."

Andre, who was busy in the kitchen sorting out the trays of leftover finger foods, came out to hear how things went at the hospital, he was relieved that Mr. W. was out of danger.

"What a shock this must have been for you Kathy, and on top of it all, you still haven't eaten anything substantial. I'll tell you what, I can clear a table and have an informal dinner whipped up for everyone in no time, I have all the food in for tomorrow's lunch shift."

They all declined his kind offer, it was a long day, and he had worked so hard preparing the buffet.

"You have all this food to put away too," Kathy said, "it would be too much work."

"Then what about that late picnic you suggested earlier? Like you said, I've got enough here to feed a regiment."

"Gee, I didn't think it would be this late, I'm more tired than hungry to tell the truth."

"Okay, we'll compromise," he said as he shrugged his shoulders with a smile, "I can't let this food go to waste, give me a few minutes everyone, I'll be right back." Going through the trays and picking out a selection of nibbles, he put together a fancy to-go carton for everyone to take with them, and a few extra boxes for Kathy's family back home.

"Thanks Andre, I can't tell you how much I appreciate the effort you put in for tonight, you definitely went above and beyond the call of duty."

"We aim to please," he replied modestly. "I don't like to rush off, but I've got to finish the kitchen for tomorrow, I expect a busy day ahead of us."

"Yeah, I suppose we had better start shutting down here too."

The Reinolds decided it was time to leave and thanked her for inviting them. Charlie also said his goodbyes, had to be up bright and early for a meeting. In fact, so did Katherine, she had to be there before seven to let the cleaning crew in, the place needed a pick-me-up after the reception, there were crumbs and drips spilled everywhere, right on the terrazzo. All right, it was not easy eating flaky pastry while standing around, but did people have to be so messy? The two waiters, who kept the tables filled and tidied the whole evening, were occupied searching for plates and glasses abandoned on the benches or up the steps. She had the foresight to put up signs forbidding people to bring refreshments into the main exhibition space upstairs, but did not expect them to litter the place with their tableware when they read the interdict. Couldn't they at least bring their dishes back to the restaurant area?

Suzy, Esther and the Professor chatted with Katherine while they cleaned up the reception desk and helped to bring some of the dishes back to

Andre.

"You won't believe it, we've sold quite a few of the T-shirts this evening," Suzy announced. Katherine went to look at the gift corner and saw some of the stacks had indeed diminished.

"You sold some of the boxer shorts too? Who would have thought anyone would be interested? I'm glad we put them out," Katherine laughed, it felt good to have something to smile about after the panic that evening.

"The smiley faces were one of the best sellers," Esther added in her usual matter-of-fact tone.

"Hey, at least we know there's a demand for the stuff, I can advise whoever leases the corner to put in plenty of T-shirts and souvenirs."

"Oh, I forgot to tell you, there was a bit of a flurry in the midst of our sales, we never thought of setting up a cash register for the shirts, so I had to raid everyone for change," Suzy admitted. "We owe Esther and the Professor forty I think, they were kind to donate to the cause, and Andre's register was not free from the pilfering, he said we could pay him back in the morning."

"Change! What a dope I am! Thank you Esther, thanks Professor, I don't know how we'd manage without your help, and who would have thought they would sell? I only stuck them out there for a little colour, the corner looked so dead," Katherine replied, rummaging through her purse for her wallet.

"Don't worry about it, you can pay us later," Professor Matthews replied.

"Nope, must pay it now before I forget, one must never put off their debts," she smiled. "I won't have enough for Andre now, he'll have to wait 'till tomorrow like he suggested. Well, I guess we should call it a night. I'm sure everyone's exhausted."

At last, they could head home, she could not wait to get out of her formal clothes and slip into something more comfortable. Poor Pops, he was stuck in hospital gear, and Mom was still in her cocktail dress too, it would not be an easy night for them she mused as she drove home. Steves must have got the same idea, she met him coming out the front door with a night case after she parked the car.

"Hey Kats, I'm going to the hospital, I threw some things together for Pops, I'll be back later."

"Good thinking. Should we get a change of clothes for Mom too?"

"I don't know, do you think she'd want to get into another dress?"

"To sit up in all night? Hmm, you're right, maybe we could pack her a nightgown and robe."

"Well, we'll have to decide soon, Kats."

"Gee, I'm not quite sure what to do ... okay, I'll get her a pair of slippers anyway, those high-heels must be killing her by now, and perhaps her make-up bag, she'll want to tidy herself before you pick her up in the morning."

Katherine ran upstairs, had the items ready in a few moments and returned to the driveway.

"Before you go, can you tell me what's going on the kitchen? Mrs. Gonzales is making an awful racket."

"Oh, you know how she is; since she heard the news about Pops, she's mopped the floor twice, cleaned the stovetop, and was rattling things in the pantry the last time I saw her, anything practical to keep her mind occupied. I've got to go, I'll be back soon," with that, he took off down the driveway.

Aw, what is she doing? Pop's is going to be fine, I'll have to stop her before she wears herself out, Katherine thought. She found her as Steves had described, busy washing the shelves and rearranging the bottles and cans, mumbling in Spanish under her breath what sounded like prayers judging from '*Dios mio*' and '*pobre Señor Walseengham*'.

"Mrs. Gonzales, I think you need a break, come have a cup of something with me," she suggested, "Pops is all right, no major surgery is required, he'll be home by tomorrow afternoon."

She was happy to see Katherine and was eager to hear all the news, sending up a few "Gracias a Dios!" while they made some herbal tea and sampled Andre's to-go package. When she finally convinced Mrs. Gonzales that all was well and had related every detail about the grand opening, she went to check on Gramps who was now in his robe, watching the late news in the den with Jasper sitting beside him.

"Hi Gramps."

"Hello Katie, come on in and sit with us for a bit."

"I would, but I'm exhausted, I think I'll just head up to bed."

"All right, see you in the morning. It's been a long day."

ଔ❀ଓ

Katherine felt like she had just fallen asleep when the alarm clock began its insufferable bleeping. Five already? I'm so groggy, she thought, it will be a miracle if I can keep my eyes open today. She felt better after a hot shower and a steaming cup of extra strong coffee, time to hit the road, despite getting up early, she was running behind. The very idea she would be late for her first day in business helped to dispel the last traces of drowsiness, it would be a race to get to the gallery on time. As it turned out, she arrived at ten past seven, she could see the cleaning company's truck parked outside … *oh dear.*

"Sorry I'm late," she called out while fumbling for the keys to the back entrance, "I don't know what held me up, I usually do mornings better than this."

"No problem, we just arrived five minutes ago," one guy called back as he opened the cargo doors of the truck and began offloading their equipment.

"I'm sorry, I have to warn you, the ground floor is a disaster after last night's reception," she informed them.

"Don't worry, lady, we've got it all under control."

She had to admit they were efficient workers as she watched them fly around with the vacuums and polishers, the place would be spic and span in no time. One of the guys chatted as he buffed the reception desk with a special cloth for marble before taking out a clean cloth for the handrail up the stairs.

"I wish I could paint like that," he said nodding to one of the rolly-polies. "Is that price for real? Will people really pay that much? For a car, I can understand, but for a picture?" He looked over at one of Professor Matthew's paintings priced at three thousand.

"Yeah it's for real," she smiled, "and that's actually a reasonable amount. If the artist is well known and there's a demand for their work, collectors consider the paintings are worth the price."

"Man, now I *know* I shoulda stuck with art," he replied.

"Why not try painting as a hobby?"

"Maybe, I dunno. You gotta have real talent to paint like that," he replied, nodding once more at the displays, "and I don't think anythin' I could paint would have luck gettin' inta a gallery like this."

"How do you know? Have you ever tried drawing?"

"A few sketches 'n stuff at school, but we really didn't have no decent lessons, more of an arts n' crafts kinda thing. I don't do so bad with spray cans though, even if I say so m'self," he admitted as he polished the brass rail.

"You mean street art?" she asked. "Like … artful graffiti?"

"Yeah, somethin' like that," he smiled, "I do some real funky murals, but no gangbanger stuff, I don't do that hate hash no more."

"I'll tell you what, if you bring in a couple of samples some day, maybe a few sketches, I'll take a look at them."

"Well, I kinda just spray right on th' wall ..."

"Hmm, okay. What about a large canvas then? Do one for me and I'll put it up, we'll see what happens, just as long as there's no profanity or obscenity, if you don't mind."

"Nah, doesn't bother me, I don't do that no how. I'm more inta public messages, social injustice, that kinda thing."

"My kind of art," she smiled.

"Ya think I could get that much for it?" he said pointing towards the Professor's painting once more.

"Maybe, if it's good enough, you just might, minus the gallery commission of course. However, if you want my advice, paint for the love of it first, work on a subject that's important to you or on an image that means a lot. You are sure to do your best work then."

"Hmm, I hear ya," he agreed, "well, there's no harm in try'n I suppose. Thanks, miss, I'll try 'n work somethin' up for ya."

"That's the spirit. Hey forgive me for being rude, but I forgot to ask, what's your name?"

"Derrick, Derrick Smith."

"I'm pleased to meet you, Derrick."

"Nice to meet ya too, Miss Walsin'ham," he replied, rubbing his hand on his sleeve before shaking hands with her, "I kinda guessed who you were. Well, I should get go'in or I'll be in hot water," he said, indicating with his thumb towards the stairs, obviously where his boss was working, she could hear the vacuums running around the carpets on the second floor.

"Okay, don't let me get you into trouble."

Katherine hoped she did the right thing to encourage him. She had seen excellent murals in a fantastic graffiti style dotted around the city, they could be quite dazzling, in fact, they were artworks in their own right, but she had no idea what he was going to bring in. Oh well, no risk, no gain, at least he doesn't 'do' obscenities, she thought. Who knows, she may have discovered the next Picasso.

At that moment, Andre rushed through the door, he too was running late.

"Lord, look at the time, if I don't hop to it, I'll never be ready for the early lunch bunch," he puffed half to himself, "good thing I stayed until three this morning preparing."

He did not look like he was in a great mood, she had heard about the proverbial short tempered chefs who were always constrained for time, and wondered if it was safe to greet him, he definitely did not look like a morning person today.

"Hi Andre," she said tentatively, "I'm sorry I don't have your change yet."

His expression softened as he returned the greeting.

"Good morning, Kathy. Don't worry about it, I think I have enough to get us through over here, you can pay me back later."

"Well, I have some cash left in my purse, not much though, the Matthews got paid first," she laughed, "it's something anyway."

"No, you might need it, honest, I can wait."

"Okay, no arguments. You know, I can't wait to try one of your lunch dishes, I'm starving, I was running behind too and didn't get any breakfast," she confessed.

"That's the most important meal of the day, but I should talk, I only have coffee in the mornings. Listen, I have a box of chocolate-cream croissants in the fridge out back, I'll heat up a plateful with a cappuccino for you. It's not the healthiest breakfast in the world, but that should tide you over until lunchtime."

"Thanks Andre, where would I be without you?"

Katherine watched the security monitors as she munched her unexpected treat and sipped her coffee, observing the cleaners busy with their chores, stopping now and again to admire the artwork. Everything seemed uneventful after the reception last night. Of course, the gallery was not open yet, things might be different when people came to browse and eat at the restaurant. Katherine yawned, she hoped the caffeine would kick in soon. She needed to stay focused, something not easy to do, especially when her thoughts continually returned to her father's attack. Perhaps she was in some mild state of shock that had not completely registered yet: how could she ever forget the sight of him slumped over the desk and the panic she felt not knowing what was wrong? She hoped Pops was doing all right now, maybe Steves had already picked Mom up and had some news to report. Eight is probably too early, but might as well call and see what's happening. Mrs. Gonzales answered the phone and paged Steves via the house intercom. Her brother gave her an update: Pops was doing fine, he was stable all night and had a good rest.

"I've just arrived home with Mom and I'm ready to take Gramps to the private hospital."

Since the angioplasty was scheduled for early that morning, Pops might be home that afternoon. Katherine was thankful and relieved to hear the news, maybe now, she could concentrate on the gallery. She still had some time before Suzy and Esther would show up. Should she paint for a while up in the studio? The front doors were locked, the guard was there on patrol, she did not have to stay at the desk, but since she had not come up with a new inspiration to work on, she had a feeling she would only end up staring at a blank canvas. There was the possibility of experimenting further on her geometrical abstractions, but that plan sounded a little tedious, *I'm just plain tired today.* Might as well look at the business end of things she finally decided, it would be a good idea to see how the first night went.

She studied the list of paintings that were sold or placed on reserve. *Not too bad,* she thought, more than I expected. However, she had to be realistic, most of the people invited last night were close friends and acquaintances, they could have been trying to do her a kindness with their purchases. The real test would come with the general art collectors and if they liked what she had on display. In any case, looking at the list and the reasonable prices combined with the commission rate she was charging, she already had a hunch she would need a larger turnover in sales than she first anticipated if she hoped to stay solvent let alone make a profit. She would have to exhibit more artworks—that was obvious. Thank goodness finding space was not a major problem; she had plenty of walls in her floor design, she could easily add more pictures than she had now, perhaps double the amount if she positioned them closer together, triple the amount when the permanent exhibition could be moved to the fourth floor. Organized clutter could be attractive in its own way, something on the order of the old Parisian Salon of the nineteenth century, that would be interesting. Of course, she would need artists working to ensure other collections would be ready to fill the empty spaces as pieces were sold. Katherine thought for a moment. How *did* galleries scout for new talent? That was the question. Mr. Sirrac went all the way to Germany to secure one up-and-coming artist, while she was going to need a small army. Turning to the art colleges helped this one time, but she would have to consider other options. Would she end up running monthly ads in the papers for 'open interview days' after all? No, they would be overrun with amateurs, there had to be a better solution. She needed to attract more professional artists whose work was sought after, or at least, discover more promising talent. This was something she would have to talk over with Suzy, of course, Professor Matthews and Esther might have some suggestions too.

Nine o'clock finally rolled around, the security guards changed shifts as the cleaning crew packed up, next came the *sous-chefs* for the restaurant. She was so glad when Suzy showed up, she was getting bored watching everyone rushing around, doing their own thing. Suzy had a stack of newspapers draped over her arm.

"Good morning Kathy, as you see, I got your note and the keys.

Thanks for letting me drive your car.”

“You’re welcome, you had to get here somehow after I took the van,” she laughed. “One of these days we’ll have to find the time to shop for your own car.”

“Okay, maybe next week. Any news about Mr. W?” Suzy asked, she too was anxious after witnessing last night’s emergency.

“Pops will be fine, Steves just told me everything. He’ll be home this afternoon after they do the angio-something-or-other, I can never remember the names.”

“I’m so glad to hear that, I really thought he was having a heart attack.”

“Me too, I don’t think we’ll mind the low cholesterol diets anymore,” Katherine replied.

“You said it. Anyway, I stopped at a kiosk and got all the morning papers, well, the ones with the art critics you invited last night ... and the one you didn’t,” Suzy added with a wry smile.

“Good thinking, I didn’t have time to worry about that, the cleaners were waiting when I got here. Speaking about cleaners, I’ve got some news, hold on a sec,” Katherine said as she got another plate of croissants and a cappuccino for Suzy before telling her about the spray-can artist she accidentally discovered.

“He admitted he was basically self-taught. I said I’d give him a chance, let’s hope I didn’t do something we’ll regret later,” Katherine said, half-laughing.

“Street art? I never thought about that,” Suzy mused as she sipped at the hot beverage, “I wonder if there’s a market for that kind of stuff on canvas. I’ve seen some pretty cool murals around town to tell the truth. Hmm, Derrick Smith, the name’s not familiar ... Smith, Derrick, Smith ... d ... s ...DS...of course! Don’t tell me you’ve discovered the mysterious DS?” Suzy finally exclaimed after her verbal rambling.

“Who?”

“Oh you know! Those murals with the ‘DS’ initials? He’s got a cult following already, but nobody knows anything about him.”

“Good grief, I’ve seen a couple of those,” Katherine replied, a little shocked. “Do you really think I just nabbed the same DS?”

“I guess we’ll find out,” Suzy replied, “that really would be something. Oh, the reviews!”

In the excitement of this latest revelation, they had nearly forgotten to read the critiques.

“Well, here goes,” Katherine said as she took a deep breath, picking up one of the papers and thumbing through the cultural columns for the first reviews, or in other words, the first impressions. She was relieved to see most of the critics actually gave her a decent write-up and included a few colour photographs of the event. The reports nearly all sounded alike: mentioning a few details about the emerging interest in the Dumbo area and explaining the history of the Walsingham building, they praised the old European-style restoration, and gave a list of the artists on display, including a critique of her owns works. 'Bold', 'daring', and 'controversial' seemed to be the catchwords when describing her style. All in all, it sounded pretty good, she could not ask for better publicity. Andre's buffet got a fabulous plug into the bargain. However, three critics went ahead and quoted her notorious sentence on the dubious history of nuclear power, and her father's angina attack was reported like one of the main events of the evening. Perhaps it was expecting too much, but she hoped they would diplomatically leave those items out. Darn it, they *would* have to put a damper on the good parts of their reviews. Katherine groaned when she read them, and they had not yet come to Horace's column.

"Kathy, someone's knocking on the door, I think it's Gerry," Suzy said, quickly getting up from her chair. "Oh, it's five to ten, time to open up. I'll go let him in."

"Good morning ladies, I see we're all ready for the business day," he cheerfully greeted.

"Hi Gerry, we were just reading the first reviews," Suzy informed him.

"Hello, have a pastry and a cappuccino with us, they're pretty good," Katherine offered.

"Thank you, I would, but I can't stay long, I must get to work. I just dropped by to pay for the paintings, Lottie's too."

"Okay, but there's no rush," Katherine replied.

"I know, but these are your first sales, and one shouldn't delay a payment. Is a cheque all right with you?"

"Of course. Do you want them delivered right away?" Katherine asked. "To be honest, I'm grateful for the sales, at the same time I was hoping the pictures would last longer than one night ... I still have to find more artists, you know what I mean ...."

"I understand," he smiled, "we don't need them right away, you can let them hang for a while. Anyway, let's have it, how are the reviews?"

"So far, so good. They're even better than I expected, one guy gave us a full page with pictures and everything," Katherine replied, "of course he's one of the critics I invited."

"There's one left we haven't read yet," Suzy added, lifting an eyebrow.   "Saved the worst for last, I see," he laughed, "you might as well know what everyone else will be reading and get it over with."

Katherine heaved a sigh as she reached for the newspaper.

"Well, it's not as long as I thought it would be, but the title is not encouraging, that's for sure … *Delirium Hits Dumbo Art Scene* by Robert Horace. What a jerk! Get a load of this: '*The Walsingham name, distinctly associated with medicine for as long as we can remember, is now also the name of the newest gallery in Dumbo, which happens to be a conversion of the original Walsingham pill-producing factory. 'New' gallery did I say? Don't get your hopes up, you won't find anything too new or modern here, more like a reinvention of the old potion-plant into a hypermarket for art that is veritably a laudanum-induced daydream of Parisian days gone by. The owner, none other than Katherine Walsingham, the same Belevdere graduate who's work made a controversial appearance in the Sirrac contest last year in the honourable mentions category, continues to look back to the past in her choice of décor and style of painting. Walsingham prefers to use methods already well established by the masters to express what can only be described as appalling anti-American and anti-technological sentiments … .*

"Oh my, this isn't good," Suzy groaned. Katherine continued:

"*Lacking artistic flair, Walsingham reverted to the Impressionist and Surrealist periods to make a quick mark on the art world, so obviously has nothing new to offer. In fact, considering how she mimics styles ad infinitum to try to put her sensationalist themes across, we see what could be rightfully called 'continuism' reflecting the continuance of someone else's techniques. Of course, her collection was not the only one on display, many of the gallery's offerings hail from the Belvedere Art College, including the works of Professor Cecil Matthews and this year's Sirrac Contest winner, Susanna Cooper, suggesting a touch of favouritism at play. The surprise of the evening was the display of loans and permanent donations from private collectors in the quasi-museum section, works by Matisse, Picasso, Chagall and Warhol, were among the mix, a nice consolation in the midst of the medieval antiquities. Perhaps the most astounding revelation, Miss Walsingham managed to persuade one of Manhattan's finest French chefs, Andre Garneau, to run her adjoining restaurant in the heart of downmarket Dumbo, depriving the 'C'est la Vie' of its long-time celebrated chef. At least the buffet and the champagne served at the reception was worth the trip across town.*'

"Where does he get off?" Katherine complained, "he hardly said anything about the other artists, and he certainly didn't seem impressed with your loan, Gerry, I'm sorry about that."

"Well, medieval art is not appreciated by everyone," he politely conceded.

"You know, Andre was lucky he got a half-way favourable sentence, although he attacked his intelligence for setting up here. Horace seemed to aim all his poisoned darts at me. *'Anti-American sentiments'?* That's rich, especially after his description of Mount Rushmore. Is his column libellous? Do you think I can take him to court?"

Gerry chuckled at her questions.

"Only if you are prepared for a lengthy and costly legal battle to prove your case. I'm sorry to say you can't force him to make a retraction either. He basically printed his interpretation of your style, and his opinion about your work cannot be held libellous. I notice he didn't actually quote you, so he was covering his bases. He would have to print some malicious lie that would be damaging to your character to bring him to court."

"But he *did* print a malicious lie! I didn't express anti-American sentiments *ever!*" she blurted in frustration.

"Just what *did* you say?" he asked, leaning on the desk with an air of amused curiosity.

"Oh, he provoked me with those needling questions! He got me so flustered I could spit fire!" she replied as she settled back into the chair, folding her arms. Suzy picked up one of the newspapers that printed the quote and read aloud:

"*When asked why she did not approve of nuclear energy, Miss Walsingham replied ...*" Katherine groaned when she heard her biting observations read aloud once more.

"Whew! There's no beating about the bush with you, is there?" Gerry replied. "With that weighty prose, you should be a playwright. I'm surprised Horace let you off the hook that lightly."

"I suppose so. I just hope people won't boycott the gallery when they read his review on my statement taken out of context, and he didn't quote it."

"Don't worry, just forget about it if you can. He always finds something negative to say about everybody. Remember how he described my painting for the Sirrac contest? *'A watery deluge of insipid illusion'*," Suzy reminded her. "I don't think he used English correctly, isn't a deluge already 'watery'?"

"Yeah, he was just trying to be smart-alecky. I'm sorry I went ahead and sent you his column," Katherine apologized.

"That's okay, I asked you to send me all the reviews."

"My piece of advice to you Kathy, listen to your friend, Suzy," Gerry replied, "don't let it get to you. People may just flock here to see what the furore is all about. Like I said, art thrives on scandal."

"I don't think I can or will," Katherine sighed. "Thank God Pops won't get to read the morning papers before his operation, he nearly blew a gasket after the last critique written by that idiot."

"Oh forgive me, I haven't asked about your father. By 'operation' I assume the angioplasty…"

"Yes, he's okay though, he'll be home today."

"I'm glad to hear it. Sorry ladies, I have to leave you, I must be off. However, Lottie said she might stop by today to try the new restaurant."

"Oh, that's nice, we'll look forward to seeing her," Katherine replied.

"Have a good day, ladies."

"Okay, bye Gerry."

Esther arrived for work a few minutes past ten o'clock. Katherine was glad to see her, she wanted to be at the hospital with Pops, but did not wish to leave Suzy alone on their first day. She promised to be back as soon as possible, maybe before lunch. Esther told her to run off and not to worry, they could handle everything while she was gone. Katherine grabbed her purse and hurried to the back parking lot. It was a long drive to where Pops was transferred, the traffic was awful. Using her car for this journey, she could not see how far the congestion extended and began to miss the height advantage of the van; it was amazing how quickly one could become accustomed to new things. It did not seem as frustrating when she could see the problems in front of her rather than feel boxed in by them and not knowing what lay ahead.

By the time she arrived, the procedure was nearly over. Gramps was waiting in the room reading a newspaper while Steves went to call home and relay the latest updates to Mrs. Gonzales, who would in turn pass it on to Mom when she woke up after her nap. Gramps was a little disgruntled to see his son's attack reported, but at least the media did not harp upon it at length.

"No respect," he grumbled under his breath, "can't leave anyone or anything alone."

"Well, reporters have to make a living too," Katherine replied, surprising him with her unexpected entrance.

"Katie! What are you doing here? I thought you would be busy at the gallery," he said, removing his glasses.

"Oh, Esther and Suzy can handle the place this morning, I just had to be here and make sure Pops will be all right.”

“Everything is going okay, grab a chair, he’ll be out in a few minutes and very glad to see you.”

“So, how bad is the damage this time?” she asked, indicating to the pile of newspapers, “to be honest, I haven’t checked the other sections yet.”

“It could be worse,” Gramps replied, “Timothy has not made a statement yet, I suppose that will come out in the evening editions when he knows how Harold’s procedure turns out. Our shares dipped a little when the market opened, but they should rally later. Of course, it may have nothing to do with Harold, the markets are erratic and fickle lately, but enough about the company, how are *you* doing? I hope you got a load of good reviews, I was about to read them next.”

Katherine sighed.

“I can’t complain, they were good overall, except for one. I’ll give you three guesses who wrote it…”

“The gatecrasher! Hrumph! What has he printed now?” Gramps wondered as he put his glasses back on his nose and searched through the papers for Horace’s column, “nothing more about Hitler I hope… .”

“Umm, no, but almost as bad,” she hesitantly replied, shuffling her feet a little, dreading to see his reaction. Gramps furrowed his eyebrows as he read the article before slapping the paper on his knee with another ‘Hrumph!’

“That young pup has one big chip on his shoulder,” he concluded, “if anything, *he’s* the one who has an anti-establishment issue, and just where did he dig up this ‘anti-American’ tripe?”

Katherine explained how the Art Attacker irritated her with his interrogations until finally she let him have it with a verbal bombshell. Gramps just looked at her for a few moments and then broke out in a big grin that grew into a hearty laugh.

“By gum, Katie, you’re just like your grandmother, she was not afraid to tell anyone what she thought, even if the truth was difficult to swallow at times. Nobody could get away with anything, including me. I wish you had the chance to know her better, you were so little when she passed away.”

“You’re not mad I said that?” she asked.

“Why? Should I be?”

“Well, everyone got so upset after the Attacker’s last review, and I *did* say in so many words our country was guilty of a war crime …” she continued.

“Socrates has rubbed off on you all right,” he chuckled, “it seems you have become the gadfly of the nation. Our government has done some despicable things, there's no denying. It's not unpatriotic to denounce an injustice committed on our behalf, perhaps it's the most patriotic thing we can do. Don't lose heart, just keep on stinging them with your paintings. It will certainly keep things interesting."

Wise old Gramps, he always could find some way to cheer her up.

"Hey, you made it after all," Steves said as he came through the door. "I thought the gallery would hold you up."

"Nope, couldn't stay away. How is he? What's happening? Did you get any news while you were out there?" Katherine asked in a rush.

"Yeah, I did, in fact they're wheeling him down the hall right now, I just came in to tell Gramps. Everything went A-okay, no adverse reaction to the dyes or anything, it all went as expected." Katherine jumped up to look out the door.

"Here he comes."

"That's marvellous," Gramps said as he reached for his cane.

Pops looked pretty good, even dressed in hospital garb and pushed around in a wheelchair. Steves got his robe ready for him.

"Hello Kathy, I didn't expect to see you here."

"Of course I had to come and see how everything went. How do you feel now?"

"A lot better than last night," he smiled as he stood up from the chair and put on his robe. "I have an odd sensation in my chest right now, but that could be from all the dyes they injected, it should go away shortly. I'll be on blood-thinners for some time, and no exertion for at least a week, can't even drive the car."

"That's what I'm here for," Steves piped up, "the chauffeur is at your service."

"The good news, I can get dressed and go home right away."

"Wow, that's great Pops," Katherine said as she gingerly gave him a hug.

The doctor popped in for a few moments with words of advice: if he felt any persistent pain in his chest, to call his doctor immediately. In very rare cases, the metal stent could move and cause some blockage in the heart resulting with another angina attack, or cardiac arrest, however, he did not think that would happen as his procedure was a success.

"The nurse will be coming soon to wheel you downstairs, I'll leave you now to get dressed," he concluded as he exited the room.

"Gee, thanks for bursting our balloon," Steves replied dryly under his breath.

Katherine agreed: that was annoying. Just when everything seemed okay, some practical killjoy always had to remind them to be wary of problems that may never occur at all. It was like reading the side-affect warnings in the fine print of prescription medication, the cure was potentially worse than the disease.

"Oh, he was just doing his job," Gramps reminded them, "come on, we'll let your father get dressed. Take your time, Harold, don't rush anything."

Despite Gramps advice, they did not have to wait for long, Pops was ready in a few minutes and glad to be leaving. It was good to see him out of his hospital garb, he looked like his old self and ready to tackle the world, except the nurse insisted on wheeling him to the front door of the hospital to his chagrin. Now there was nothing more she could do, Gramps and Steves would drive him home, she might as well head back to the gallery. She promised to try and make it home early.

Katherine was surprised when she returned and found the parking lot full, thank goodness she had reserved an area for the van. There was quite a crowd browsing the gallery and eating in the restaurant, the first day was turning out better than she hoped. Suzy was relieved to see her arrive.

"Kathy, this all just happened within half an hour or so, we were just sitting around hoping it would pick up and then 'woosh'!" Suzy reported. "How's Mr. W. doing?"

"Everything went okay, he's on his way home for a week of R and R. I guess Uncle Tim will be handling the firm for now."

"I'm so glad to hear that," Esther replied, "I have some news: we've got an art class booked for a field trip to see the exhibition next Friday, they called just after you left, and there are two artists waiting to see you, they're over there," Esther continued, nodding to a couple of young men with portfolios sitting in the waiting area outside the restaurant. Perhaps they were local artists who had not heard about the interviews.

"Well, that is good news," Katherine noted, "we're going to need a lot more artists than we have on show right now, at least the artists are coming to *us*."

Katherine interviewed them in the office one at a time. The first portfolio displayed a partiality for apocalyptic variations of Surrealism; the works were colourful, not obscene, and definitely an interesting concept. How could she turn them down? Unfortunately, the next interview was not a success, she could not accept the second artist whose interest in 'artistic' nudity was too graphic for her taste. She was sorry to disappoint him, but there were many other galleries that would welcome his style. He stormed out of the office very angry, knocking a few of the browsing visitors aside and muttering some unpleasant remarks with a few expletives included —'that b—h', 'free country' and 'censorship cr-p'. A startled hush settled as everyone watched this abusive scene, staring at the enraged artist as he flung the side door open and marched down the sidewalk. The witnesses murmured amongst themselves as they continued with their browsing.

"Would you listen to *that*! What is the world coming to?" Esther declared. "What happened in there?"

"Oh, I just refused his collection. He should have known just by looking at the calibre of art we show here."

"That bad, huh?" Suzy commented, afraid to imagine what he had painted.

"I can't describe it, let's just say I'm not running an X-rated establishment. Although I'm not enamoured with the Renaissance fad for classical nudity, it's a lot better than the outright porn that is passed off as art these days. What nerve!"

Hearing the commotion, Andre came out of the kitchen from the back entrance to see what had happened.

"Are you all right? What was that all about?"

"Don't worry, the drama is over. I just enraged a demented artist," she explained, "I refused to display his work here, it was revolting to say the least."

After he made sure she was okay he went back to his post, the place was packed for the first day and he could not leave the kitchen for long. It seemed as though everyone in the city had found out where his new restaurant was located and was curious to try it. The waiting area was already filling with expectant diners looking through the menu placed on display.

To be honest, she was not completely over that little episode and decided to sit in the office for a few minutes to cool off. Sure this was Brooklyn, but she had never been called a b—h in public and certainly did not expect anything like that to happen in a professional establishment, especially in her own gallery on the first day of business. Perhaps he deserved to be rejected after all she thought, obviously with such an ignorant attitude, he will never get ahead, in places that matter. Censorship, darn right I'd censor his work, it's appalling, she mused to herself. There has to be a cut-off somewhere between the freedom of expression and a graphically explicit free-for-all. She wondered if Socrates mulled over that dispute out at one time or another, it would be interesting to find out. However, it looked like she would have little time for reading now with a business to run. It was amazing all the activities she was able to fit in amidst the bustle of a demanding college schedule, it seemed time in the business world was more restrictive, there was always something that had to be taken care of. For one thing, she wanted to call Martin and Justine to let them know how the grand opening went, and to give them the good news that Gerry had bought nearly half of their paintings. That would help dispel the nasty incident she experienced.

Checking her watch, she figured now might be a good time to call, unfortunately, Justine was not home. Maybe she was out shopping, of course, she was in the midst of planning a wedding. She could try calling again later. Katherine sat for a moment watching the security monitors and observing the reactions of the visitors. Some simply walked around, passing from painting to painting, others stood for a moment to read the accompanying title cards and study the artwork. Certain people seemed to loiter in front of her allegorical works for quite some time, obviously trying to correlate her bizarre images with their unusual titles. Martin and Justine's symbolic 'Canvases of Despair' seemed to attract people too. Gramps is right, perhaps figurative works *do* keep things interesting. Well, if she was now dubbed the unofficial 'gadfly of the nation', she had a good idea where to start biting next. Rather than just take the verbal abuse she received a short time ago, she could turn that incident into a productive experience. An idea for a new series of paintings came to mind: would it be possible to create a pictorial exploration into the true meaning of freedom and how that ideal has constantly been misapplied to justify the most atrocious acts? Anything is possible, but could she do it? The thought of this new artistic crusade was invigorating. Too bad she could not work out this concept right away, Suzy and Esther needed some help to watch the floors, she did not expect this many people the first day. Obviously, the press releases and advertising were paying off, the reviews could not be having this effect already, or maybe they were, it was hard to tell.

Katherine decided to make the rounds of the second and the permanent exhibition floors and see if anyone wanted to know more about the artwork on display and answer any questions they may have. So far, people seemed happy wandering around on their own reading the title cards and listening to the light music playing over the sound system. The atmosphere of the gallery was quite relaxing she thought to herself as she moseyed through the walkways at a leisurely pace. She admired Gerry's medieval collection once again, stopping to study each of the illuminated manuscripts with their flamboyant lettering and brightly coloured pictures. Things were certainly different back then. In an era before the printing press was invented, it would be reasonable to assume they would have spent less time and effort on these handwritten documents, preferring to make copies as fast as possible, but no, every letter was painstakingly inscribed, each page took months of dedicated work, a book would take years to complete.   Now that timesaving and cost-cutting technology had been invented, everything is ironically reduced to a stark minimum she mused, aesthetic beauty is now rendered obsolete in favour of a soulless utilitarian practicality, ornamentation was almost eradicated from society today. Looking at the manuscripts, she admired the vibrant borders and how they wrapped around the texts, turning the written word into a beautiful work of art. It would be fun to try something like that, perhaps not exactly the same as a book, but a similar two-dimensional piece with a combination of images and words. Why not? It might be the perfect method for her new inspiration—if she were to try and devise a Socratic disputation on the abuse of freedom, she just might be able to include it in her next allegorical collection. Well, this project will take much contemplation, after all, she was not a philosopher, and writing out a Platonic dialogue will be reaching pretty high. Me and my big ideas, she taunted herself, who's the aspiring Icarus now?

Katherine returned to the ground floor after making one last tour while assessing the intricacies of composing an imaginary discourse with one of the world's greatest thinkers. She found Suzy occupied in the T-shirt corner tidying the cotton wares. Esther told her they had sold quite a few of them, if things kept up like this, they might have to order more from somewhere to keep the space filled until a renter showed up. The funny part was she and Suzy did not think to have shopping bags printed, so they were forced to 'borrow' Andres fancy take-out bags with 'Chez Garneau' printed on the sides. Poor Andre Katherine thought, she not only owed him change, put some bags too. Imagine, when the building was a T-shirt factory, it folded up, and now it looked like they would not be able to keep the shelves stocked! At least she knew a gift shop might do well.

Despite all the people, there was not a lot for her and Suzy to do when they were not packing a T-shirt to go, the visitors were content to browse by themselves, and Esther was occupied updating the computer files. Katherine suggested to Suzy that after her lunch, she might as well go paint something rather than dawdle around.

"Are you sure, Kathy? Don't you want to go work in the studio first?"

"Well, I'm mulling over a new idea, I don't have anything substantial yet, so you go ahead."

"Okay, but I don't think I should leave you when it's this busy just in case they all decide they want a personal tour guide."

"Don't worry, they look quite happy wandering around. Honestly, I wasn't expecting the gallery to be this laid back, Andre is the only one under pressure the way he's hopping around the kitchen filling orders."

Suzy had to admit she was right, apart from the restaurant and the gift corner, the place *was* almost taking care of itself.

"Thanks Kathy, there are a few sketches I wanted to finish." Before she had a chance to pick up the sandwich she ordered to bring upstairs, the telephone rang. "Kathy, it's Gerry, he wants to speak to you."

"Really?"

That's odd, he dropped by early this morning, she hoped he was not calling to say he had changed his mind about purchasing the paintings. Suzy waited a moment, a little curious about the unexpected phone call.

"No, it's not a bad time, that's the restaurant. … Sure, ask away. … You mean this coming Friday? Well, I don't know if I can … ."

There was a long pause. Suzy filled in the blanks and could easily guess the outcome, he just asked her out.

"Oh don't turn him down! Say yes!" she whispered excitedly while Katherine quickly clapped her hand over the mouthpiece and tried to 'shush' her, mortified he might hear the commotion at her end of the line. "You *can't* turn him down now," Suzy quickly continued, ignoring Katherine's frantic attempts to hush her, "you've been doing that for weeks. He's been so kind, and besides, what excuse can you give this time?"

Drat, Suzy was right. She *did* say she would have a lunch or dinner with him at some time or another, but the preparations for the grand opening had put paid to that. Now that everything was starting to settle down, a little sooner than she expected, there was no way she could wriggle out of her promise.

"Well, okay then … ." Suzy nearly bounced on her toes with glee. "Shall we meet somewhere first or …well, it's a long drive to my place and then back to town … well, okay, if you don't mind … five thirty? Hmm, it's a bit early, but I suppose I can find *someone* to close up the place for me," Katherine simultaneously hinted to Suzy who nodded in agreement. "All right, my place is at 3 Oak Meadows Englewood. Do you need directions? You might get lost … oh okay, I'll see you then, talk to you later." She hung up the receiver and tried to process what just happened. "What did I do? This is nuts, I don't want to get involved with anyone right now," she said half to herself.

"Good grief Kathy, chill out, it's only a dinner," Suzy commented, rolling her eyes.

"Dinner and a show, actually. He had tickets for *Miss Saigon* and wanted to know if I'd like to go with him."

"Wow, that *is* serious," Suzy half teased. "Besides, I hear it's really good. You haven't been to a musical in ages, you should be pleased, this is something to look forward to."

"I know, especially as I wanted to see it when it opened, but never got around to it. Even so, I don't want this to turn into a date or anything," Katherine reflected.

"Gosh, don't you want to meet 'Mr. Right' someday?" Suzy queried, "you'll never find him if you don't try and be sociable once and a while."

"You think I'm antisocial?" Katherine replied a little amused.

"That's not what I meant, just … don't let your career plans become an invisible fortress around you. I know you're happy with your work and everything, but are you sure that's all you want? Don't you want *more*? I know I do, yes, I want a career, but I also want a family of my own. We don't have to choose one over the other anymore, Women's Lib managed to do something for us after all," she concluded with a comical shrug.

"I know, but I guess I've never given it much thought," Katherine admitted, "the idea of it feels so … strange and unfamiliar, like I'm about to walk on water."

"Well, you've got to have confidence, you shouldn't let the fear of the unknown keep you from stepping out of the boat and living life. Even if you never find 'Mr. Right', making new friends is always a good thing. Strangers never become friends until you get to know them better, and that won't happen until you start spending some time together. One evening out won't kill you, and Gerry seems like a really nice guy."

"Yeah, I guess you're right. He is nice, I'm just not used to going out with anyone really."

"There's no mystery to it: you talk with each other, enjoy a dinner, watch the show, just let things go with the flow. In the event you actually have a good time, he just might ask you out again to repeat the experience, no big deal. Well, there you have it, that's my 'Agony Aunt' advice for the day. I better eat this before it curls up at the corners," she finished, nodding down to the sandwich.

"Oh, sorry to hold you up, you must be famished. We'll see you later."

"Okay, it shouldn't take me long to finish my sketches."

Katherine watched her walk towards the elevator before settling back in the chair to think things through. Suzy seemed so sure of what she wanted in life. How did she know? Is it one of those 'things to do' that women keep on some invisible checklist in their mind, just waiting to be marked off as 'mission accomplished' like everything else? So far, her own aspirations had not extended past the excitement of establishing a career. Would she ever feel like Suzy and want 'more'? Naturally, she wondered what it would be like to be swept off her feet, but romance did not seem to be a big priority right now. Should it though? *Just, how do you know?* Katherine was not sure how to analyse these intangible affairs of the heart when she had not experienced them yet. No time to think about it now as customers started approaching her with T-shirts they wanted to buy, it looked like her meditation moment was over. Never mind, she thought to herself, she should not take things so seriously, she could give herself a headache.   Suzy was right, take it easy, Friday night out should be something to look forward to.

03 ❀ 80

Katherine did not know why she should feel so indecisive, this was not like her. Everything she tried on just did not seem right, an outfit either felt too informal for the theatre or not formal enough, while others looked strangely *passé*, or the colour was too flamboyant and did not look appropriate. Is that a little too much? Umm, this makes me look fat…what possessed me to buy it? Darn, she never had this much trouble getting ready for a show before, of course, she had rarely gone out with anyone else but Charlie, the whole idea was so … different. After another thorough search through the closet, she finally settled on the semi-formal and comfortably demure outfit she wore for the Wheelchair benefit, classy but not over the top, best to keep things on an even keel. Now she had to hurry to make herself presentable, she still had her hair and make-up to do, and all that foraging left her little time to waste. Hopefully, Gerry might be fashionably late and buy her some extra minutes. She barely finished clipping her hair up when Katherine heard the buzzer for the main entrance resound downstairs, Mrs. Gonzales answered the summons and opened the gate for their visitor. *Oh no, he's a bit early! Quick, hurry up!* In her haste, she tipped half her bottle of foundation into the sink and knocked her tray of eye pencils to the floor. Just great, that was all she needed. Well there's no time to clean it up now, just fix yourself. A minute later, she heard Mrs. Gonzales answering the door and conduct Gerry to the parlour to wait while she notified the family. It sounds like Mom was going out to greet him, if she keeps him busy, I might have those few minutes after all. She could hear their polite conversation as she came down the stairs.

"Oh, here she comes."

"I'm sorry to keep you waiting," Katherine apologized as she entered the room.

"Please, no apologies," he replied, standing up to greet her, "I did arrive earlier than I said. I must say, you look lovely this evening."

Katherine always felt awkward when she received compliments, particularly when they were undeserved, after all, it was a mad dash to get ready. She did not quite know what to say except, "Umm, thank you." At any rate, it was a relief she had decided on semi-formal, he too had chosen the middle path and came dressed in a dinner jacket.

"Kathy, look at these, aren't they just beautiful?" her mother asked, drawing her attention to the bouquet she was holding.

"Oh they are, but goodness, Gerry, you didn't have to go to all this trouble."

He had not only brought flowers for her mother, but a corsage and a box of specialty Belgian confectionery. There was also a curious wooden box with brass latches tucked under his arm, obviously a gift for her father.

"I wasn't sure if you would like orchids or chocolates, so I decided to get both," he explained as he handed the corsage to her first.

"Thank you, it was very thoughtful of you," she replied, admiring the exotic flowers before slipping them on her wrist, "they're simply gorgeous, and chocolates too," she continued, taking off the gift paper, "you have just discovered my weakness. Come, you must try one with me," she insisted, holding the box out to them.

"You go ahead, I got them for you."

"I agree the chocolates look divine, Kathy, but don't ruin your dinner," her mother chided as she watched her sample a coconut cream bonbon. Gerry simply laughed. Hearing the conversation from the den, Harold guessed Katherine had finally come down and came out to wish them a nice evening before they left.

"Hello Gerard," he said as they shook hands.

"Please, call me Gerry. I have something for you, I hope you like cognac, this particular bottle is from a special reserve I picked up on my last trip to Paris," he explained as he handed him the small wooden case.

"Thank you, I don't know if I'm allowed spirits yet," he said as he opened the box and admired the antique style bottle, "but I shall save it for a special occasion. So, I hear you're taking our Kathy to see the new musical."

"Yeah, heard great things about *Miss Saigon*, but it seems we have all been so busy lately, just couldn't get the time to see it, and I know Kathy has been too preoccupied getting her new gallery off the ground, a night out with some good music might be the ticket."

"Kathy always enjoyed musicals, she hasn't been to one in a long time," Mom admitted, "I can't count the times she went to *Les Mis* and that Phantom show."

"Aha, I think I have discovered another weakness," Gerry noted, "I'm a bit of a Sondheim fan myself. Well, I suppose we should go, or we won't fit dinner in," he concluded, checking his watch.

"Yes of course. Have a good time," Harold said as they went to the front door.

"Thanks Pops, see you later."

Gerry held the passenger door of the sleek ebony-black Jaguar open for her. Katherine thought she saw Suzy peeking out the apartment window, ducking her head before they drove off.

Now that she was on her own with Gerry, she felt unusually shy and awkward, not sure what to say or how to begin a conversation. How much easier it is to converse on a business level. From her brother she had learned men usually end up talking about gadgets and machines, so that might be a good starting point.

"I like your car," she began, "it's really nice."

Darn, that sounded stupid for some reason.

"You like it? Got her a few months ago. Would you like to hear some music? I'm not sure what you're 'in' to, there are a few CDs in the arm rest if you want to look through them."

"Hmm, *Agamemnon by Aeschylus*," Katherine read from one of the cases, '*The Libation Bearers…*"

"What? Not again! Lottie is always leaving her Greek audio books behind when she borrows the car, talk about tedious listening. Let's see what's in here…well, it's either a feast or a famine," he concluded, pulling out a compilation of recent Broadway hits, "I hope you won't be 'musicaled' to death after tonight."

Katherine laughed.

"No, that's fine, a musical feast it is. So you like Sondheim."

"Mostly his *West Side Story*, I really don't have one 'all time' favourite composer, I just like certain shows. For instance, I like *Sweeny Todd*, a bit gruesome, but interesting. I can't understand how Sondheim could go from that to *Into the Woods*, it's funny and entertaining all right, but that's about it."

"Oh, I know what you mean, *Into the Woods* lacks a certain …

depth. I can't believe it got the award for Best Score at the Tonys when *Phantom* clearly deserved it, especially after winning most of the other awards, including Best Musical of the Year."

"Well, the judges were giving Webber a slap on the wrist that time," Gerry said with a knowing air, "awards sometimes go to those who tow the line, and not always for merit. "

"Well, that's not fair. Is it because he's British?"

"Partly, the Actors' Equity union is constantly objecting to foreign composers importing original cast members from other countries to open Broadway premières, they claim it's prejudicial to American artists. However, Webber wrote the role of Christine for Brightman, and certain people have taken a dislike to her, calling her a Jezebel because he left his wife for her. If you remember, she wasn't nominated for a Tony while practically everyone else in the show got one."

"That's just stupid, the judges are supposed to consider the quality of the productions and the talent of the performers, not the personal lives of the people involved."

"I know, but that's how it is sometimes. Speaking of prejudicial criticisms, I know I shouldn't drag up business, but how are you coping after the Art Attacker's review?"

"Well, I'm happy to say the gallery has done very well the first week," she smiled, "you were prophetic, so much for Horace and his sarcasm, he may have done me a favour. My 'Motley Three' sold Monday afternoon. A few more art critics showed up too and gave some fabulous reviews on the other artists."

"You see? What did I tell you? He has put you and your new enterprise on the path to fame and glory," Gerry replied with a nod, "that is good news, we have something to celebrate tonight."

"I don't know about fame and glory," she replied modestly, "it's early days yet."

"All great milestones in the art world begin sometime, why not now? You may be one of the lucky few who become renowned before they're old and wrinkled." Katherine laughed. "Come to think of it, something told me I should have snapped them up," he said half amused, half dissatisfied with himself, "*never delay what you can do that day*, I should follow my own advice."

"Well, if it's any consolation, I've got ideas for another controversial series, not exactly on the same visual order, but just as philosophical."

"Oh? Now that sounds interesting."

Before she knew it, they had arrived at the restaurant and the *maitre d's* was escorting them to their table, a very elegant setting if one was attracted to that refined masculine starkness. Tables graced with white roses and candles on scarlet linen, polished black granite floor, panelled walls of gleaming black granite and white marble illuminated with teardrop chandeliers whose glistening lights reflected around the room, intermingling with the city lights from the panoramic glass wall that overlooked the urban skyline.

Katherine realized her gallery and art projects had monopolised the conversation during the drive and decided to ask how he became interested in art before they looked over their menus. Gerry explained his father started collecting when he figured it would be a good long-term investment and simply passed the interest on. As far as he knew, his father simply 'jumped in' and learned by experience, but he on the other hand took a few courses in art history while studying business at Harvard. Unfortunately, he never delved into the practical side, there were so many other things to do.

"So collecting has become a passion," Katherine concluded. "Your brother likes art too, and astronomy, without him, I may never have figured out the dilemma of my stellar chart."

"Oh, that sounds like Pete all right," Gerry nodded, "he studies everything he can lay his hands on, astronomy, mystic revelations, he's quite the scholar. In fact, he might be able to help you sketch out your Platonic dialogues."

Katherine felt it would be an imposition to bother his brother again, she explained he had already helped her with her last collection, she might end up becoming a nuisance.

"Well, he just might be too busy chasing ghouls somewhere," Gerry reflected in a cynical tone, "maybe Lottie could help then, she prefers drama, but she has read the major philosophical tracts as far as I know."

Gerry added that Lottie went to study art first but became fascinated with ancient literature when she sat in on a few of the lectures and decided to change her major. Katherine asked how Lottie was: as it happens, one of her friends had talked her into attending a special series of seminars at the Sorbonne, so she was preparing to leave for Paris within a few days. Katherine could not help but admit she was a bit envious, however, she was planning to be there next year for Martin and Justine's wedding, so that was something to look forward to, if she would be able to get away now that she had the gallery.

"In that case, you would be more than welcome to stay at the apartment," Gerry offered, "I don't use it as often as I should, plus Pete and Lottie seldom have the time to stay in Paris these days."

Katherine thanked him for his kindness, but she could not accept and politely declined his offer.

"Very well, if you change your mind, just let me know."

So far so good, Katherine thought, at least they had some interests in common. It was difficult to tell if she was broaching topics that were considered too personal when making polite conversation, especially as they had only recently become acquainted. Speaking about his apartment, she thought about the miniature treasure trove he had accumulated there and wanted to ask a few more questions about it, that should be okay to talk about. She thought about the ancient Macedonian vase and wondered if it was difficult to collect antiquities like that?

"Well, there is a mountain of red tape to go through when exporting antiquities," he explained, "but it can be done. Like everything else, it all depends on who you know."

Since she seemed interested in Greek philosophy, was she considering collecting antiquities? Oh no, she was still getting used to the idea of having an opportunity to shop at Sotheby's for paintings, the thought of picking up priceless archaeological finds was a little overwhelming. She simply liked the delicate figures painted on the sides of his vase, it reminded her of the Portland vase in the British Museum.

"It's amazing how sophisticated ancient Grecian and Roman art is", she commented.

"Have you been to the British Museum?"

"No, I only saw pictures in my art books," she explained, "in fact, I've never been to London."

"You'll have to fly over some day," he suggested, "you would definitely like the art museums and the West End."

"Well, it would be difficult to plan a vacation now," she noted.

"Ah yes, with a new business, you will be tied up for awhile," he agreed.

By now, the waiter was approaching to take their order, but Katherine still had not decided what to choose, it all looked good. Gerry recommended the Chateaubriand, it was excellent here, so was the Chef's Salad if she wanted a starter. Okay, that sounded great. Gerry went ahead and ordered the wine.

"Now, where were we," he rhetorically asked.

"The busy-ness of business," Katherine answered with a smile, "you are fortunate to have a shipping company, I have a feeling it gives you opportunities to travel a lot." Gerry laughed.

"Sometimes the merchandise we ship for our customers travels more than I do, but it's not difficult to delegate the workload every now and then and take time off, and then there are the business trips."

"Of all the places you've visited, which is your favourite?"

"Hmm let's see," he paused to think for a moment, "I must say I've never forgotten my first trip to Rome, that would probably be my choice."

"Italy, now that is a country I would love to visit," Katherine mused for a moment, "the birthplace of the Renaissance, Donatello, Raphael, Michelangelo … just think of all the masters that sprang up in that era, one day I would love to see the Sistine Chapel, what an experience that must be."

"Imagine lying on your back almost four years just to paint a ceiling," Gerry laughed, "you must hand it to Michelangelo, he certainly was dedicated to his art."

"I don't know if anyone today would be willing to go through what he did, they say he became a hunchback after he finished those frescoes, and then he got landed with the commission for the *Last Judgement* on the main wall."

They touched on many subjects during dinner, he told her stories about the other cities in Italy he had visited and the unusual sights he came across. For one thing, she had never heard about the 'talking statues' of Florence, a group of outdoor sculptures that were used as remonstration points since the Renaissance. In that era, public protests criticising the government were not tolerated and so the people designated a statue in the main square on which to hang up posters with manifestos or sarcastic doggerel verses to voice their complaints. Eventually, the political platform of one *clique* had become associated with the first statue, so a rival party designated their own statue to voice their concerns and 'dispute' with the other faction. Soon various groups claimed several other outdoor artworks, the political exchange grew and a novel tradition was born.

"Today, people mostly use the statues to display their graffiti rather than make public statements, but the scribbling still continues," he explained.

"Imagine," she laughed, "a bulletin board that has been in use for over five hundred years."

Katherine wished she had fascinating things to share like that, her travels had not extended past Paris, and since he was already very familiar with that city, she wondered if her conversation was sinking to the interest level of the daily weather report. However, Gerry had a knack of keeping the conversation rolling, he always came up with an interesting point that led to another subject. He then stopped and checked his watch, they had been so busy talking over their coffee they had nearly forgotten the time.

"We'd better make tracks, or we'll miss the opening curtain."

ⓒ❀ⓑ

"Well, how did it go?" Suzy asked the following morning as Katherine turned on the coffee machine. "Did you have a good time?"

Nuts, she should have known that the well-meaning interrogation could not be avoided. She thought about it for a moment, yeah, she did enjoy the evening out, even if she preferred *Les Mis* to *Miss Saigon*. Suzy was a little amused, she was not asking about the show as much as how she liked the company.

"Come on, what happened?"

Suzy was not satisfied until she had vivid descriptions of the restaurant, the food, and of course, how they got on together. On reflection, Katherine had to admit she had more fun than she expected, Gerry had so many things to talk about, he has travelled to almost all the major cities in Europe and seen so many different cultures and customs, she wondered if there was any place left on the map that he had not been to at one time or another. On the other hand, the few things she could discuss was Belvedere, her own experiences of Paris, and the few pastimes she engaged in, or used to when she had time, such as tennis and reading. Gosh, even her brainy brother seemed more interesting to talk about. She felt like a stay-at-home-stick-in-the-mud in comparison, it was a wonder Gerry did not find her boring. Suzy told her not to be silly, she always came up with interesting ideas.

"Just look at your paintings, I doubt if anyone would ever accuse you of being dull."

Since they were on the subject of enjoying an evening out, Katherine asked how she and Charlie were doing. Suzy announced;

"We're going out tonight to try a new Japanese restaurant. I'll have to bring something to change into at the gallery."

Raw fish? Bleh! Katherine grimaced, the thought nearly ruined her morning cup of java. Why did Charlie suggest *that*? As far as she knew about sushi bars, the portions were minuscule too; they would leave the place hungry. Suzy laughed, she was not exactly thrilled either, but he promised to take them out to anywhere she suggested next time, she had never been to a German restaurant.

"It can't hurt to try raw fish once, right?"

"Um, I think I'll skip some experiences," Katherine replied shaking

416

her head, smoked salmon was as far as she was willing to go in the department of semi-uncooked fish ingredients.

Although she had forever relinquished all ideas of eating sushi, Katherine came face to face with one squelchy delicacy that day when lunchtime came around—Andre had not forgotten his dare and personally served her a plate of *escargot* right at the reception desk dressed in his chef's regalia. To her mortification, he was not budging either until she ate one, and she could not leave him standing there, his place was starting to fill up with diners, they certainly would want their orders filled. Some of the visitors were starting to eye them with curiosity. She was cornered now. *When will I ever learn to refuse a dare?* Suzy and Esther stared at the upturned shells the size of golf balls, their contents swimming in a garlic and parsley sauce.

"I don't know about you," Suzy piped up, "but I don't mind the sushi dinner now."

The look on Katherine's face was priceless as she reluctantly reached for the tongs to grasp the shells and the long tapered fork used to extract the meat. How Suzy wished she had her camera! Katherine mustered all her resilience, eww…don't think about it! Expecting the texture to be nothing more than gloop, she popped one in her mouth and tried to swallow it fast, but was pleasantly surprised by the buttery morsel …I t *did* taste like a clam.

"Mmm, that's not too bad," she admitted, picking up another shell with the tongs, making sure she did not lose one drop of the sauce. "They're *better* than clams."

"You've *got* to be kidding me," Suzy replied in disbelief.

"No seriously, you should try one."

"Umm…that's okay, no thank you dear," Esther replied.

Andre laughed and headed back to the kitchen, at least he had made one new *escargot* convert.

Katherine was just about to tuck in to her third tit-bit when an unexpected floral delivery arrived. What was this? She was not expecting a new arrangement for the reception desk until Monday.

"Hi, I have a delivery for a Miss Katherine Walsingham?"

"That would be me," Katherine replied, dropping her fork and tongs to receive the large multi coloured bouquet. The deliveryman tried to ignore the strange morsels on the plate as he took care of business.

"Sign here please, thank you."

"Wow, they're gorgeous," Suzy exclaimed after he left, "quick, what does the card say?"

"*Dear Kathy, I enjoyed our evening out, I hope you did too.*

Gerry."

"Short and sweet, but hard to beat," Esther noted.

"I have to give him a call now, gee he didn't have to send flowers."

"Well, while you do that, I'll go find something in the studio to put these in," Suzy offered.

"Okay, thanks," Katherine replied as she went into the office.

She did not want to bother Gerry at work, but that was the only number she had to reach him. She waited while his secretary put her call through.

"Hello Kathy, I hope the flowers arrived."

"Oh yes, they're beautiful, thank you. I just wanted to say I enjoyed last night, I had a good time."

"Me too, we'll have to do that again sometime."

"Er, okay," she replied.

"Or maybe something different, perhaps not so late at night. You must be exhausted."

"No, I'm fine," she assured him, "we really didn't stay out *that* late."

"I know of a daytime event that you just might like: there will be a rare book convention all this week starting this coming Monday, the last day will be next Sunday. I know it's your only day off right now, I thought you might enjoy a lunch out and a leisurely browse around the book stalls, you never know what treasures may be on offer."

Hmm, that sounded rather interesting, she had never been to a book convention before.

"Okay, that might be fun."

"Great. Will I pick you up at your place then, let's say, eleven thirty?"

Hmm, Katherine had to think about her schedule, she should be back from Sunday service by then, as long as the Reverend did not have a lengthy sermon prepared and they do not get held up by anyone at the church doors wanting to gab afterwards. Just in case, she had better warn him she could be a few minutes late.

"It will be cutting it tight, my Pop is a stickler when it comes to attending church, and no skipping is allowed except for emergencies. The service is usually over by eleven, but I could be late."

"I see, I don't want to put you under any pressure. We can meet up somewhere. How about the restaurant? I'll make a reservation for twelve thirty, that should give you plenty of time."

"That sounds fine." He then gave her the address.

"Okay, see you next Sunday."

They said their goodbyes and hung up. Huh, rare books, did he collect those too? How interesting, well, this was something to look forward to.

Suzy was heading off for lunch and she was just about to finish her *escargot*, now cold and congealed in the dish, when she spied Aunt Martha heading straight for her from the main entrance.

"Hello everyone," she greeted in her usual high spirits, "I just finished my shopping and thought I'd stop by to offer my services. My, there are quite a few people browsing today. Good!"

"Oh?" Katherine replied, wondering what this was all about.

"I heard about the art class that came yesterday, and thought since there's nothing I *have* to do most days, I'd be more than willing to help with the tours when you, Esther and Suzy get overwhelmed. I do happen to know a little about art too," she affirmed.

"Martha, how wonderful of you to offer your assistance," Esther replied before Katherine could say anything to dissuade her, "I'm sure you would be an immense help."

Oh no, Katherine knew what that meant—they would spend their whole tour in front of her donation with little attention given to anything else on display. Oh what the heck, if it would make her happy and keep the peace.

"By the way, your mother told me about last night. How absolutely marvellous! *Do* give us all the news, I want to hear all the details."

Okay, there had to be *some* limits in keeping Aunt Martha happy, dragging up her personal life seemed one of them, but it was 'mission impossible' when it came to avoiding her nosy inquisitions.

"It wasn't all *that* special, just a dinner and show," she replied, "I hardly know him really, there's nothing serious going on."

"Well *someone* made an impression last night," Esther drolly noted, indicating the bouquet.

"My, did Gerry send you those? They're simply gorgeous," Aunt Martha commented, skipping behind the desk and stealing a quick peek at the card.

"Quite the proper young gentleman," Esther added.

"Yes, does everything correct that one, picked her up at her home and greeted her parents with *such* thoughtful gifts, dropped her off at a reasonable time, you seldom see that nowadays," Aunt Martha declared as she sniffed one of the soft pink roses. Katherine thought it better to keep quiet about next Sunday for now, you could never tell what Aunt Martha might make of it, a proposal … who knows?

"And, what is *that* you're putting in your mouth? Good lord, they're snails!" Aunt Martha exclaimed with a shudder, "you've let this fascination with French culture go to your head completely, haven't you?"

"You can blame Andre for the snails, he dared me. They're not that bad, of course they're better hot, I let them go cold."

Just then, Gramps and Jasper came through the side entrance.

"Hullo Katie, I see we have a gathering. What brings you in today, Martha?" he asked.

"To see Kathy of course. I came to offer my help if and when she needs it."

By now, however, his attention was drawn to the plate on the reception desk.

"Hey, *escargot*! Is Andre serving that now? About time, here, let me try one," he said as he commandeered the shell tongs. "Cold, but not bad. I've got to order me a hot plate of those."

"I think they look revolting," Aunt Martha huffed.

"To each his own. Come on Martha, join me for lunch, you too Esther, it should be close to your break time by now, the more the merrier. You don't have to order the snails you know." Despite his odd tastes in food, Martha thought this was one of the best suggestions he had come up with, she would enjoy a lunch with her friend, Esther. Esther asked Katherine if it would be all right.

"No problem, you go ahead, this place is basically taking care of itself. Just send me over a plate of chicken, a salad, and a glass of Seven Up while you're over there, Andre knows the dish I like. I'll eat my lunch at the main desk while I sketch out my next project."

Katherine shook her head as they went into the restaurant. Pretty much as she predicted, Gramps was showing up for lunch on a regular basis. Already he had a favourite table reserved for him as an honoured patron, while Jasper had a special bowel waiting by the back door in the service hallway that was routinely filled with all his favourite gourmet scraps the moment he arrived. She had just settled in to the chair and was playing around with a theoretical disputation for her next masterpiece when the Professor came through the main entrance.

"Hello Kathy, where is my better half? I thought I'd take her out to lunch today."

"Hi Professor, you're too late, Gramps and Aunt Martha nabbed her first, they're in the restaurant."

"*Tsk tsk*, and they left you out here all by yourself," he chuckled.

"Well, someone has to be on the job. Anyway, this isn't exactly slavery," she replied as a waiter dropped off her lunch on a silver tray adorned with one of the petite floral table arrangements. "Go ahead and join them, I know Gramps would be delighted. Suzy will be back shortly, I'll be just fine." The Professor decided to settle behind the desk in one of the chairs for the time being.

"Well, in that case, I'll keep you company until Suzy gets back, I can join the trio in the restaurant later."

"Okay, can I order you something from the restaurant?"

"Not right now, thank you."

Katherine was glad he stopped by, she had his cheque ready for the paintings that sold from his collection and was going to give it to Esther later that day, but now she could hand it to him personally. The paintings would be delivered to their new owners on Monday.

"My problem now is to find suitable artists to fill the holes while you work on new paintings," Katherine admitted, "I wasn't prepared for a rapid rotation of displays, but it looks like that is the only way this place is going to work, in other words, no waiting around for artists to make one large collection at a time like other galleries, I'll have to find people who wouldn't mind sending individual works the moment they're finished."

"I would be happy to work under that arrangement," he replied as he tilted back in the chair, "I don't stay focused on a single theme for a series that often anymore, and besides, I think your 'rapid rotation' is a good idea. It will give artists a chance to earn on a regular basis rather than waiting long stretches before they see a dime. That would be one attraction. On the other hand, you will not have many opportunities for holding gala receptions, not with single paintings, that might be a deterrent to your artists that want a little publicity. However, keeping the gallery in the black and out of the red is the main thing."

"Hmm, but how do I find new artists? Gallery owners don't like their 'discoveries' hopping between places, they lose their exclusivity, and few artists are willing to switch venues in case they are blackballed and find they are unable to exhibit anywhere."

The Professor suggested she go ahead and risk holding an interview session open to the public to supply the shortfall, it might be messy, but she could weed out the amateurs from the professionals. Then, she could take the time to search overseas for popular foreign artists who had not yet made their American début and catch some 'exclusives'.

"Don't forget to keep an eye out for the winners of various art competitions," he advised, "and attend the various art conventions, that is where the rising stars are spotted."

What a great plan, why didn't she think of that? There was so much to learn.

"At present, I have one picture finished and currently at the framers," he announced, "it was not included with the others because it was still in the drying process, it should be ready by Tuesday, I'll bring it in that afternoon."

"Wow, that would be a help, I could call the other artists and see if they too have a few odd pictures they didn't include for the opening, in any case, I have to notify them of the 'rapid rotation' system."

"I am curious, do *you* have any pictures waiting in the wings?" he asked with a chuckle.

Katherine explained her new idea of composing Socratic dialogues in the style of Plato and superimposing them upon an allegorical image representing the theme of each disputation.

"By Jove, that is an impressive concept," he admitted. "How are you doing so far?"

"I have definitely bitten off more than I can chew this time," she confessed with a sheepish grin. "Can you imagine *me* trying to write a dialogue on that level? I was completely blown away by the *Apology* and *Crito*. I'll never be able to reason out issues like Socrates could."

"Even a Herculean journey begins with the first step, and you're starting at the right place my dear."

"Oh, how?"

"By admitting your limitations just like Socrates with his humble assertion he knew nothing and knew that he knew nothing."

"Okay," she hesitantly replied, "where do we go from there?"

"Try using his methods," the Professor suggested, "start out with a 'sound principle', like an observation that is an undeniable fact, and use that to compare or contrast points in your argument to see if they are logical and may help you arrive at a definitive conclusion on your topic."

"Some accepted 'truths' are in reality fallacies," she noted, "I could end up meandering down a thorny road, even Socrates came up with a few conclusions I would not consider correct or accurate."

"That is true," the Professor agreed, "but that is the exciting part of the challenge, to use your reasoning to try and find the truth and keep 'meandering' until you do."

"Hmm, I would like to bounce some ideas around with you, judging from the texts I read, Socrates worked out the validity of his observations by sharing them with others and examining their responses."

"Ah, an intellectual banter! I'm all for a little academic argument now and then, this should be interesting … let's see," he said rubbing his chin, "your initial topic was the ideal of Freedom and the abuse of it. In other words, does 'freedom' mean we are allowed to do *anything* we want, or should we be allowed to? We can start our examination with that question."

"Hmm, that is a tricky one, technically we are free to do anything we want, but not everything is allowed, so at the same time we are *not* free to do everything."

"Then we can agree the *application* of a true and just 'freedom' has limitations," the Professor replied.

"Yes, I suppose so," she nodded.

"What kind of limitations?"

"Umm, laws preventing us from doing any harm to ourselves and to others, for example. We shouldn't go out and shoot someone just because we dislike the shirt they are wearing," Katherine reflected. The Professor laughed at her analogy. "However," she continued, "we still have the ability to react on that negative thought and pull a revolver on the poor guy. So, we have the freedom to act upon our likes and dislikes, but in this case, it would be a crime and a great injustice deserving of punishment."

"Splendid reasoning. Then the correct idea of freedom rests upon the pursuit of what is good and the avoidance of evil, while the *misuse* or abuse of freedom is the pursuit of evil and therefore is a great evil in itself."

"I think we can agree on that," she smiled as she grabbed her notebook, "excuse me, Professor, let me jot this all down before I forget it, this is great stuff." After she had rapidly inscribed their philosophical debate, she raised the logical question:

"If we agree that true freedom is acting upon what is right and good, while the abuse of freedom is evil, why do so many people insist they are doing nothing wrong and they are correctly exercising their rights when they do something that's inappropriate? For instance, let's take the artist I refused the other day, he didn't see anything depraved with the obscenity he painted and declared he was exercising his freedom of expression. He declared, in very impolite terms I might add, that I was wrong to be selective."

"Hmm," the Professor replied, leaning forward for a moment, "let's think this one through. If freedom of action can be misused, can freedom of expression, be it verbal or visual, also be misused?"

"Certainly, one conclusion follows the other," Katherine's pencil raced across the page, "this means there should also be proper limitations to freedom of expression if it is to be practised correctly, causing no harm to anyone else."

"It follows then that these limitations associated with or placed upon the pursuit of true freedom are a good thing, and are not evil."

"Oh, the argument so far seems to prove that," she agreed, "we can't make up lies about people for example, that would be spreading slander and ultimately destroy their reputation."

"All right, let's continue with an observation: recall the explosive reaction you caused by refusing that distasteful collection. You were reminding him of these necessary limitations for the practice of true freedom, but he refused to see them as something good, only a negative hindrance. Obviously, your angry artist was not convinced he was misusing his freedom of expression and unaware he was actually committing evil."

"In other words, he was not aware true freedom requires these limits, and in disregarding them, was in reality abusing his right of free expression. But how do we convince people like him that his pictures are just … *wrong?*" she mused, tapping her pencil.

"Ah! Spoken like a true Socrates," the Professor beamed, pushing his glasses up from the edge of his nose.

"Could you please explain?"

"Socrates believed that men would not willingly do evil if they could be convinced that their misguided ideas were wrong. In the case of our argument, we would have to show Mr. Angry why his images are not acceptable and need limitations imposed upon them."

"You would think it would be obvious," Katherine replied, looking up to heaven.

"Indeed, but for some people it is not, or rather, they prefer to deceive themselves."

"We would have to go into a debate on ethics and morals to figure the rest of this one out," Katherine concluded.

"It's not that difficult when we have already reached the conclusion that to do harm to yourself or to someone else is one way to abuse freedom, which is an evil act in itself. So, the next step is to determine if his nude images are harmful to himself or someone else."

"Well, they're certainly indecent," Katherine observed, "I don't want them hanging on *my* walls. However, this conclusion only displays how he insulted my sensibilities, but may not ultimately convince him why painting pornography is evil."

"That's one aspect to consider, he would be definitely committing an error by knowingly painting images that would offend people, but can 'adult material' like that actually be harmful and declared an evil?"

"Oh my, we're getting off my original topic now," she laughed, "I was just trying to find out where freedom begins and ends, and somehow we've ended up discussing the 'X-rated' industry!"

"Yes, we have rambled a bit," he conceded, "but at least it extends our observation to include certain rights associated with freedom of the press, or rather, the misuse of them."

"Hmm, okay, let's see if we can untangle this one," she said, pausing for a moment. "We know that these images are disrespectful, downright smutty in fact."

"Your observation implies that when the body is not displayed in a noble light, you are made to feel a certain disgust and contempt for the subject matter," he replied.

"I guess you could say that," she nodded.

"All right, since true freedom should inspire us to seek and act upon what is good and noble, and the abuse of freedom implies the promotion of evil, anything that incites feelings of disrespect and contempt towards our own humanity must be a great evil. We may conclude when true freedom is correctly exercised or abused, we shall know by the effects that are produced, after all, by their fruits you shall know them. I'm afraid the adult industry and the growing lack of censorship has done nothing to uphold the dignity of humanity, rather it has planted it firmly in the gutter."

"Wow, that's true," Katherine agreed, "there is great harm done when these images are constantly presented as 'natural' and therefore something we should not be ashamed of. We are literally blitzed with awful images in the media today. Everyone is now conditioned and are blinded to the evil this material promotes, namely conditioning us to completely disrespect ourselves and others."

"Too true," the Professor added, "and since art is considered a noble field, art should be used to promote all that is good and noble, and in a noble fashion."

"I couldn't agree more," Katherine nodded, "the problem is, people mix up what are 'good' limitations and consider them *hindrances* to their freedom, they do not see them as necessary guidelines in becoming truly free."

"Then we return to the Socratic ideal of trying to convince mankind of its blindness."

"Oh golly, that is a tough one," she replied, sitting back in her chair, "like I said, people tend to shrug off pornography as 'natural' and therefore acceptable."

"Hmm, like I said, people also prefer to deceive themselves. If there is such a thing as true freedom and an abuse of freedom, abuse that in turn equals a form of slavery, then everything, even acts of nature, can be used correctly or utterly abused. May we do whatever we want with our bodies, or are there good limitations that should be imposed if we are to act with true freedom and not become slaves to our passions?”

“Yes, of course. We can be angry, but not kill someone, so we must limit our emotions. We can eat everything we like, but should we? We’ll get fat and kill ourselves off if we don’t learn to eat with moderation!” she laughed.

“So every action must have its good limitations if we are to be truly free.”

“That makes sense, but what if people still refuse to see this conclusion?”

“*’Ah, if thine eye be evil, how great must the darkness be,*’” he enigmatically replied, “If they adhere to their blindness, there’s nothing you can do but hope they learn from their mistakes.”

“Obviously,” she continued, “you cannot force them to do what is right against their free will, at the same time, if we know that certain people are more inclined to misuse their freedom, it is our duty to try and stop them, for one example, that’s why good laws that protect citizens must have police to uphold them.”

“Yes, that is true.”

“But haven’t we arrived at a contradiction?” she asked in a puzzled tone. “We know it is good to have limitations for true freedom to exist, but now we discover it is *not* good to enforce them at all times, we end up *abusing* people’s freedom and free will. If there are ‘good’ limitations, can there be ‘bad’ limitations?”

“My, we’re full of ethical conundrums today!” the Professor laughed, “Never mind, we shall try and unravel this one too if we can.”

At that moment, Suzy came through the side entrance with a boutique bag hanging on her arm.

“Hi Professor, I’m sorry I’m a bit late, um, where’s Esther?”

“She joined Gramps and Aunt Martha for lunch,” Katherine replied. “What have you got in there?”

“Oh, this is what held me up, I thought I’d treat myself to the dress I saw two weeks ago and wear it tonight, but if I thought you were going to be here all alone, I wouldn’t have gone shopping,” she said apologetically.

“Hey, good for you, I’m glad you got the dress. Don’t worry, everything is under control, and besides, the Professor and I have had a real humdinger of a debate.”

"Quite!" he replied with a chuckle.

Before he could say another word, the 'trio' came out to the reception desk.

"Why, it's Professor Matthews," Gramps declared, "we had no idea you were out here. Why didn't you come in and join us for lunch?"

"I had every intention to do just that, but as it happened, an engrossing philosophical disputation with Kathy had me a little preoccupied," he explained with a grin. Esther shook her head.

"That's just like him," she sighed, "always forgetting to eat when some absorbing project or study commands his attention."

"Kathy, you left your food go cold again," Aunt Martha chided. Katherine looked down at her plate; she had completely forgotten about the chicken, which was now drying out around the edges, the sauce thickening from the prolonged exposure to the air. The salad was not looking any better.

"Like teacher, like pupil," Gramps observed with a chuckle.

"I'll show you my dress later, you should really eat that before it completely curls up," Suzy said as she tucked her bag under the desk and resumed her station with Esther.

"You should eat something too, dear," Esther said to the Professor, "before art and philosophy starve you entirely. Just look at you, thin as a rake," she *tsked*.

"I hear and obey," he replied, looking over the rim of his glasses with an amused expression.

"I'll join you," Katherine said, "I can just take this with me and eat it in the restaurant."

"Splendid! We can continue our stimulating discussion."

"Now Kathy, please do me a favour and make sure he actually orders something," Esther added. Katherine laughed.

"Okay, I promise."

"You know, I could do with another coffee," Gramps mused, "I think I'll join you." Aunt Martha decided to stay with Esther and chat a while longer, so the Master, the student … and Gramps … made their way to the restaurant to occupy their designated 'Head Table' again. Andre peaked into the dining room, and observing her tray with the food untouched, came out to see if anything was wrong with her dish while the waiter took the Professor and Gramp's order.

"No, it's fine. I just started gabbing and never got around to it. I'll just eat it as it is," she explained.

"Like that? Unthinkable! I'll get you a fresh plate," he insisted, whisking the tray from her before she had a chance to stop him. Andre could be very temperamental when it came to his culinary creations, food is not simply organic fuel to keep body and soul together, it is a perishable art that must be savoured at the peak of perfection. At least she tried not to waste her lunch, Jasper was making out like a bandit today.

"So, you and Kathy have been discussing philosophy, eh?" Gramps declared.

"Yes, we were practising a Socratic debate for a series of paintings she has envisioned, an intriguing concept I must say," the Professor replied. Katherine described the initial images and the overall effect she had in mind.

"That does sound interesting," Gramps agreed.

"I have one problem," she noted, "I'm going to have a tough time fitting book-worthy disputations on the limited space of a canvas, just look at my notebook after our discussion! I may end up painting out my pictures with a wash of letters. Never mind, I should be able to figure something out," she mused.

"Well, if it can be thought, it can be done, a problem can be overcome," the Professor sagely observed.

"A new challenge keeps the brain kicking and the heart ticking," Gramps added, "at any rate, I would be interested to know what you have selected as your first topic."

Katherine thumbed through her notes, giving an overview of their debate on the nature and practise of freedom as they waited for their order to arrive, ending with "... which leads us to the question if 'good' limitations should be enforced, are there such things as 'bad' limitations."

"I can name one 'bad' limitation," Gramps offered while sipping his coffee, "... diets."

"You're being silly again, we're trying to be serious here," Katherine replied, shaking her head. The Professor looked amused.

"Never mind Kathy, this is an opportunity to test your reasoning skills and dispute his example."

"Well, that's easy. Diets are a 'good' limitation, especially if they have been suggested by a doctor who is aware of your overall health and medical record," she replied, with a little emphasis to give him the hint, "according to our argument, if 'true' freedom means avoiding harmful things and doing what is right, taking care of our health is a good thing, including diets recommended by a doctor."

"Hrumph," he replied, amused by her answer, "we're really on a thinking streak today. Okay, since we are having a little 'smarty party', what do you say to the fact I have the freedom *not* to follow a diet if I so choose?

You did say 'suggested' and 'recommended'," he added with a twinkle in his eye.

"Touché, the Professor observed, chuckling at how the debate had developed, "you *did* use those words, Kathy." She thought for a moment.

"Hmm, even if a doctor orders you to follow certain directions, you can still disregard them," she conceded, "and no one can tie you up and force you to do anything, that would be taking away your ability to choose, that would be another form of slavery. There really is no complete freedom without the freedom of choice," she concluded.

"In that case," the Professor interjected, "since the diet is a 'good' limitation, and while we would hope the patient would follow it, to prevent him from making the choice *not* to adhere to this regime is a 'bad' limitation."

"Of course," Katherine replied, "that makes sense. Freedom requires the ability to choose, even if the person decides to do the wrong thing, or it's not freedom but oppression and tyranny."

"If that's the case, waiter, please bring me another piece of cake," Gramps said as lunch was brought to their table, "I'm all for fighting tyranny and oppression."

"Oh Gramps!" Katherine laughed. "You are still practising your freedom incorrectly according to our argument, you wouldn't be truly 'free', not in an ideal sense anyway."

"I dunno, this sure looks ideal to me," Gramps replied as he observed the waiter approaching with the slice of cake.

"All right, what have we observed so far?" the Professor enquired, stifling a chuckle. "Can we summarise our points?"

"For freedom to exist, there must be 'good' limitations imposed upon our actions, but we must have freedom of choice," Katherine began, "nor can we have 'bad' limitations impinging our right to choose in case we find ourselves under some form of slavery or oppression."

"So moderation must be factored into the equation," the Professor observed.

"I guess so," she replied. "We cannot have unrestricted freedom, that would be ignoring the 'good' limitations, some order must be imposed, nor can we have tyranny ruling our every move, leeway must be allowed."

"Then, certain 'enforcers' and 'guides' must exist to help us find this middle path of moderation between the two extremes," the Professor continued.

"Hmm, yes, you could say that. The police force I mentioned earlier would be an example of 'enforcers', maybe the doctor and his diet can represent a 'guide'. This means if a person does not know how to use their freedom correctly and in the 'ideal' sense as we discussed, their ability to make free choices that are good depends on guidance and enforcement to a certain extent."

"Ah, now we approach the importance of making *informed decisions*," the Professor added. "To practise true freedom, namely, to pursue and act upon what is good and avoid deliberately harming others, we have to know the difference between good and evil."

"That's true," Katherine reflected, "basically, we have to teach or convince ourselves and others when certain actions or ideas are good or evil, but then, we return to our problem of trying to convince people certain decisions are wrong, even when they believe their choices are correct. Oh dear, we could ramble on like this for ages," she laughed, "good thing lunch is here and I can't take notes, my book was filling up already."

"Well, just keep rambling," Gramps prodded, "listening to your little Platonic Academy is rather amusing I must say."

"Let's see if we can make it clear with another analogy. Suppose you have a teenager who has just received their driver's licence. He or she has been taught all the rules of the road by the 'guides' and 'enforcers', such as parents, their driver's ed instructor, perhaps the police if they visit the high school promoting a 'Safety First' program. Our teenager knows how to read the speed limits and is aware of the reason why they exist, concisely, for his or her safety and that of the other drivers on the road."

"Okay, I'm with you so far," Katherine replied.

"However, our young driver not only knows the rules of the road, but is aware of the *consequences* when he or she breaks them, namely tickets for speeding, and in the worse case scenario, a car accident that may result in their or another person's death."

"Of course, like you said, by their fruits you shall know them. Hmm, reward and punishment ... you would think, considering all the possible consequences of an action this would deter people from making the wrong decisions and do what is right," she mused aloud.

"Well, let us consider why our teenager might decide to ignore all the good information they have received."

"In breaking the speed limits? That's just it, 'limits', some people don't want limits, they simply want to drive fast."

"There we have Mistake Number One: the insistence on seeing the 'good limitations' imposed on our freedom as something negative to the detriment of everyone else on the road rather than accepting them as something necessary and good. Of course, our teenager can drive at any speed they like, but will eventually be forced to face the consequences of their actions. Can you name another reason why they would ignore the good information they have received about the rules of the road?"

"Umm, the idea that the rules don't apply to them," she proposed.

"Aha, Mistake Number Two: acting as though the rules and laws of society do not apply to *them*. What is good for one is good for all, especially when a law is good and not evil. By disregarding the law, that teenager cannot be called a model citizen, and in the end will eventually face the consequences allotted to reprehensible citizens. Can you think of any more reasons?"

"Let's see, the last thing I can think of is to ignore the consequences altogether, tuning them out so to speak," she ventured.

"Yes, now we have Mistake Number Three, and it is a common one: the assumption that the consequences will never happen to *you*, but then the law of averages must be considered. Chances are they will. One can take risks once too often. Of course, we arrive at another question: why do you think our young driver would choose to ignore the consequences?"

"You know, this reminds me of when your father read your brother the Riot Act before he got his first car," Gramps laughed.

"Don't I know it! He could have wallpapered his room with all the speeding tickets he collected," Katherine replied, "it's a wonder he didn't lose his license."

"Well, we have another example to draw from," the Professor noted. "Why do you think he chose to ignore the consequences of hazardous driving?"

"Now poor Steves is under our philosophical microscope," she said with a smile, "I don't know his reasons for being reckless at the time, but I can guess. I suppose he … oh golly! Look at the time!" she declared, eyeing her watch, "I can't be sitting here discussing the ethical enigmas of the universe all day, I've got a gallery to run. I suppose the responsibilities in owning a business haven't fully sunk in yet."

"Now Katie, you have to make a little time for yourself too," Gramps added, "You're working six days a week."

"We've only been open one week Gramps," she wryly noted.

"Never mind that," he continued with a wave of his hand, "I know this place is big, but don't let it take you over. Besides, you *are* working right now, aren't you? Didn't you want to thrash out a philosophical debate for your next set of paintings? You can't sell what you don't paint." She laughed.

"That's pushing it, and I'm slacking off too much already, I left early yesterday, remember?"

"That's one of the perks of owning the business," Gramps replied, "come on now and let's thrash out this debate some more."

Katherine would have loved to oblige, she was enjoying their little disputation as much as he, however, before she could probe the reasons for her brother's driving foibles and if they were related or unrelated to the ideals associated with freedom, Suzy came over to their table.

"I'm sorry to bother everyone, but we have a fussy customer who insists on speaking with Kathy personally," she explained.

"Er, okay. At least I finished lunch. I guess duty calls, please excuse me."

"Of course dear, the debate can wait," the Professor replied.

"We can resume when you come back for your coffee," Gramps declared.

"Okay, on a level of one to ten, how fussy is our customer?" Katherine enquired under her breath as they left the restaurant area. "I mean, is she 'fussy' fussy, or 'I'm-going-to-give-you-a-piece-of-my-mind' fussy? After the Art Attacker's glowing comments, I have to be prepared."

"I think she's between a three and a five, 'fussy' fussy and just plain demanding," Suzy concluded, "she wants to see the owner and no one else."

"All right, I'll take it from here," Katherine replied.

The demanding customer was a spry little lady who weighed about ninety pounds with short dark hair and wore a navy blue skirt and jacket with a gold and diamond brooch pinned on her lapel. She also clutched a silver-handled cane. Katherine towered over her as she shook hands and introduced herself.

"So you're Miss Walsingham," she stated mater-of-factly while giving her the once over, "and I am Mrs. Georgina Hunt. I wanted to meet you. I saw your new gallery mentioned in the papers and I was thinking of adding fresh talent to my art collection. If you must know, I read what Robert the Horrible had to say and thought there must be something good here if he was up to his old malarkey, just had to come see what rocked his boat for myself."

"I don't think anything can win his admiration," Katherine smiled.

"Well deary, pay no attention to him," Mrs. Hunt replied as she looked around with satisfaction, "I like the place, very cheerful, plenty of colour, don't know how he could find fault, probably wished he owned it. Now, to the artwork, I would like some recommendations if you don't mind."

"All right," Katherine began. "So I have an idea what to suggest, are there any particular styles or a specific subject you prefer to collect?"

"No, if I like a picture, I just take it," she replied, "it can be about anything, as long as it's not something racy that I'd be ashamed to hang in my parlour."

"Okay. I must say you've come to the right place, I make a point of not patronizing obscene art."

"Glad to hear it deary, you've just got your second 'A plus' in my book."

"Thank you," Katherine replied, this new encounter was amusing to say the least. "Have you looked around to see what catches your fancy?"

"Nope, can't deary, my hips hurt, arthritis don't you know. Have you a chair handy I can sit on?" Suzy jumped to attention and rolled one of the leather desk chairs around. "Ah, that's better. Now, what can you show me?"

"Well, I suppose the best place to start is by looking through our catalogue," Katherine suggested, "all our current artists are listed alphabetically, there are a few samples of their work shown under their biographies … ."

Mrs. Hunt flipped through the pages and eyed the portrait photos.

"I like the look of him … no… no … don't like him … hmm, she's got possibilities … her too … nope, don't like that one … oh, he looks like a genius all right … and there you are deary, yes, definitely creative … ."

Suzy did her best to keep a straight face. After she had thoroughly examined the physiognomy of the artists from cover to cover, Mrs. Hunt wanted to see a few samples from the *batik* collection.

"Do you collect *batiks* too?" Katherine politely asked.

"Nope, I've heard about it, but never collected that style before, don't even know what it is really, something on the order of a fancy 'tie-dye' my grandkids were raving about a few years ago, but I do like the colours in this photograph."

Mrs. Hunt made Katherine explain the intricate process of *batik* dying until she understood it thoroughly.

"You mean, if he wants blue for the river that's shown here, he has to pour hot wax on everything that's *not* going to be blue,"

"That's right, so when he dips it in the blue dye, only the unwaxed part turns blue."

"Then he boils the cloth to get rid of the wax, and then he waxes it all over again, this time covering over the blue on the cloth, if he wants to do green for the trees let's say."

"Yes, that's how it works."

"What's the point? It's easier to paint a picture isn't it?" Mrs. Hunt observed.

"Not really, painting has it's own difficulties and requires patience too. I suppose it's a matter of style connected with the medium, the repeated waxing and boiling process produces a unique effect with the dyes on the cloth," Katherine replied, "the picture literally seeps into the material. Sometimes the colours blend together depending how the wax was poured, even if the artist made a copy, no two *batiks* are the same."

"Oh now that does sound interesting, who figured out how to do that anyway?"

"I think the technique originated in Indonesia," Katherine replied, Suzy nodded her head confirming her information.

"My, my! An Eastern exotic! I'd like to see one, bring me this one shown here."

Uh oh, Mrs. Hunt may not be able to get around herself, but did she really expect them to unhitch the artworks from the walls and bring them to the first floor? *One by one?* Obviously, she did.

"Okay…but this may take more than a few minutes," Katherine tried to explain. "Every picture is wired to the security system with a direct link to the security company. We have to disarm each wall and unhook every picture with the security guard's assistance so we don't set the alarms off and have a platoon of guards show up."

"That's all right deary, I have plenty of time, I can wait."

Katherine looked over in amused disbelief at Esther and Suzy.

"I'll get the keys and call Patrick upstairs to let him know," said Esther as she went into the office, Katherine was not sure how to read the look on her face.

"Thank you Esther. I'll be back as soon as I can Mrs. Hunt … ."

"Before you go, do you have something to drink? I'm a little parched to tell the truth."

"Oh! Let me get you something from the restaurant. Tea, coffee, cappuccino, maybe something cold? I'm sure Andre can offer you anything you like."

"Why, an herbal tea would be just fine, you can pick one out for me, deary."

"Please, call me Kathy."

After she had ordered Mrs. Hunt a fruit infused tea, she went upstairs to retrieve the requested picture.

"My, it's big isn't it?" Mrs. Hunt noted when Katherine held it up, eventually leaning it against the reception desk. "Oh now that's different, I like the temple in the background, look at those colours! Do you have more like that that aren't in your catalogue, Kathy deary?"

"Oh yes, of course, the artist made two series, the Ganges and a river scene of Indonesia."

"Okay, I want to see which ones I like best. Let's line them up."

She wants all of them brought down?

"I'll call Patrick again," Esther declared, looking up to heaven.

"Okay, and tell him to leave the system on the second floor turned off," Katherine added.

"Will do."

Mrs. Hunt certainly kept them hopping for the afternoon. When she had seen all the *batiks* not already sold, she went through the artists whose creative countenances had merited her approval, one by one. Mrs. Hunt pivoted around in the chair and surveyed each picture when a suitable propping space had been found, it was not long before she was swivelling in a sea of colour. Pictures were leaning everywhere, against the desk, on a few of the chairs, Suzy finally retrieved the battery of easels from the studio to prevent the masterpieces from sliding down and clattering on the terrazzo. At least the rolly-polies were a help, Katherine and Suzy could manoeuvre them when Mrs. Hunt requested any picture that was set on them, however, the place was now looking a little chaotic with half the gallery and the rollies hodgepodged around the main floor, compelling the other visitors to zigzag their way to the stairs and elevator. It became more confused when the visitors, after wandering around the upper floor admiring half-empty walls, realized that they had already passed the items that were supposed to be on display and came back down in groups to survey the growing clutter.

"All right. Who painted this one again?" Mrs. Hunt demanded, pointing to a vibrant surreal canvas with her cane, completely oblivious to the other customers trying to admire the paintings. Katherine turned the pages of the catalogue and handed it back to her.

"And this one?" This time the cane pointed to one of the Professor's cityscapes. Katherine thumbed through the catalogue.

"Hmm, and this Miss Cooper, it says she won the Sirrac contest this year," Mrs Hunt noted as she flipped back to the first part. "Which ones are hers again?"

"Oh, these are mine," Suzy replied, swinging a few of the rollies around once more.

"Yours?! Yes, it *is* you! Why didn't you speak up sooner?" Mrs Hunt exclaimed, "I love to meet the artists when I can." Suzy shook hands with the feisty art aficionado. "I wish I was there for the exhibition this year," Mrs. Hunt continued, "I missed it, had other business to attend to at the time. Has your picture sold yet? I might go over and take a look at it sometime."

"Oh, it sold that very night I'm afraid," Suzy replied.

"Well, that's the way the cookie crumbles," Mrs Hunt replied, "at least I know where to find you now."

"Would you like to meet another artist? The Professor is over in the restaurant," Katherine replied, "let me introduce you to his wife, Esther. She has just retired from Belvedere as head librarian, and we're so lucky to have her with us, she's a real treasure here."

"My, my! You are a close knit bunch, aren't you?" Mrs. Hunt commented as Esther shook hands with her.

"Yes, we're the Belvedere Bunch all right," Esther added. Katherine and Suzy laughed.

"Well, I like your husband's work, I can see why they have him at Belvedere, best art school around," Mrs. Hunt replied, "I definitely want those two New York scenes over there, and three of his New England pieces, they will be just perfect for my summer home."

"He will be please to hear it," Esther replied, "you know, Belvedere won't have him for much longer, he will be retiring soon, which means he will have more time for his painting."

"Splendid! I hope to see more of his canvases, Kathy deary."

"As far as I know, he's offered the Walsingham Gallery an exclusive," Katherine replied with a smile.

"That's good to know. Now, what about you? Which ones are yours again?" Mrs. Hunt asked. Katherine indicated her Nouveau-Impressionist fantasyscape series and her surreal geometrical collection.

"They're nice, I don't know what Horace had against them. Where are the ones shown here in the catalogue?"

"Well, they're the paintings Horace had a gripe with, actually those three have sold already," Katherine explained.

"Oh well, the early bird gets the worm. What about this big red one here?" Mrs Hunt enquired as she poked at the photograph of the controversial coronation scene.

"I'm afraid that one's not for sale, I'm a little sentimental in this instance, it received an honourable mention at the Sirrac Contest last year and had the dubious honour of landing me with my first critique from Robert the Ripper, however, it's on exhibition in the permanent gallery."

"You don't say," Mrs. Hunt replied, "now that is something I've got to see. Goodness me, I nearly forgot you have a permanent gallery here too," she said half to herself as she turned to the last pages of the catalogue showing a few samples from the exhibition. While she intently studied the pictures, Esther took Katherine aside for a moment.

"I'm so glad your aunt left before Mrs. Hunt arrived, their personalities would certainly have clashed, she would never approve of Mrs. Hunt's impromptu art show, that's for sure. By the way, is Cecil still with your grandfather in the restaurant, Kathy? Imagine, he came to bring me out to lunch, and he's forgotten about me all afternoon, again." Katherine tried not to laugh.

"You can blame me and my Socratic debates this time, but is the Professor always like that?"

"Oh typical, he lives in a world of his own, the earth doesn't seem to exist for him at times," Esther replied shaking her head, "leave it all to when he finds someone who will join him on his cloud. I hope the two of them are not upsetting Andre by taking up the table all this time, he's such an accommodating young man."

Suzy decided to run upstairs and see if she could find more easels, leaving Katherine and Esther behind the desk. With everyone so busy, nobody noticed Jasper as he came from the back hallway to look for his master. Knowing the restaurant was a no-go area, he sauntered around the paintings, wagging his tail, hoping someone would be willing to give him a little attention. Mrs. Hunt, thoroughly engrossed with the catalogue, did not see him approach. His presence was finally announced when he placed his furry muzzle on her lap, hoping to earn a few rubs behind the ear.

"Hound! Hound! Get that hound away from me! Shoo! Shoo, hound!" she shrieked while simultaneously flinging her hands up, sending the catalogue flying through the air and her cane clattering to the floor. The visitors looked around in alarm not knowing what had caused the furore. Startled by the commotion, Katherine immediately went to retrieve the confused pooch who had retreated a few paces by now and sat down in front of her still wagging his tail, wide-eyed, observing the human's strange behaviour.

"Don't worry! That's Jasper, he won't hurt you. He's friendly. He's my grandfather's dog," Katherine hurriedly tried to explain as she called him over, "Jasper, good boy, come here, leave Mrs. Hunt alone."

"Oh .. oh... the hound won't jump up on me?" she gasped as she watched the unexpected intruder obey Katherine and retreat behind the desk.

"No, he won't. He's very well trained, I'm so sorry he frightened you," Katherine apologized, "he likes being around people, and we've all been ignoring him today."

"Oh…oh…I suppose that hound's all right," she puffed, "I should apologize too, my late husband always kept a couple of wolfhounds around the house, scared me half to death! Hated those things! I just detested those hounds!"

"They sound like they were a couple of Bigfoots, or Bigfeet," Katherine replied as she retrieved Mrs. Hunt's cane and handed it back, not knowing quite what to say. "Didn't you let him know how much they upset you?"

"He insisted on keeping them, said they were part of his heritage," Mrs. Hunt continued, "you can't come between a man and his dogs."

At that moment, Gramps and the Professor came out to see what had caused the ruckus to find they had to weave their way through a maze of paintings.

"Thunderin' tarnations! What's going on here?"

"Don't worry Gramps, Jasper startled one of our visitors," Katherine explained. "Mrs. Hunt, this is my grandfather, and this is Professor Matthews."

While they all shook hands and made polite conversation, Jasper poked his nose around the desk and decided it was safe to come out. Mrs. Hunt eyed him warily as he sat next to his master; the golden furred brute seemed safe enough, although she kept her cane firmly planted between her and the 'hound'. Katherine did not have a chance to join their conversation as Suzy came from the elevator laden with the additional easels. Katherine excused herself for a moment.

"What happened? I could hear yelling," Suzy said as Katherine came over to help, "I thought someone was dying, or we were being robbed, perhaps both!"

Katherine shook her head as she explained the latest upheaval while assembling the easels and placing the paintings. Katherine was not allowed to help for long as Gramps called her over.

"You know, I think it's safe to head back and see how your father is doing, I'm sure I've been out from underfoot long enough, your mother and Mrs. Gonzales must be tired fussing over him by now."

"It's been such a pleasure meeting you," Mrs. Hunt affirmed, "perhaps we may see each other again."

"Oh I'm around here most days, it would be a pleasure. Well, goodbye everyone, see you on Monday," Gramps replied before heading to the door. Katherine decided to accompany him. "You've got your hands full there, she's a right pistol that one!" he chuckled under his breath, "I had heard about Mrs. Hunt and thought people were exaggerating, but they weren't kidding … Calamity Jane would be easier to do business with.   I sure hope she takes a few paintings after putting you girls through your paces."

"Don't worry Gramps, we'll survive. It won't take us that long to put the place back together," she assured him.

"If you say so," he smiled, "come on Jasper, time to go home."

Jasper, who was still sitting close to Mrs. Hunt wagging his tail, obediently got up and followed Gramps out the door. Katherine smiled at the irony of it all, the 'people pooch' seemed to have taken a liking to the feisty old lady, even after she screeched at him like a distraught peacock.

"Kathy deary," Mrs. Hunt called, "I'm so happy to have met the Professor, he says I really should take a look upstairs and see the other works, even if they are sold. In fact, I do want to see your permanent exhibition too.   Are the other floors big?   I can't walk for very long." Katherine hurried back to attend to her fussy visitor.

"Well, they're big enough.   I'll tell you what, I can roll this chair around with us, if you need to sit, it will be ready and waiting."

"Now that's thoughtful of you," Mrs. Hunt observed.

"Um, what shall we do with all of these in the meantime?" Suzy asked Katherine, indicating towards the recumbent pictures. Mrs. Hunt had an answer ready:

"Oh, just leave them there Suzy deary, I want to take one last look at them when we come back down."

"Well, come Cecil, make yourself useful and help us put the last of these up on the easels," Esther ordered, "the cleaning crew will be here shortly, and we can't have the merchandise sitting all over the floor."

"I hear and obey," the Professor replied, looking over the rim of his glasses.

It was a slow trek to the elevator, poor Mrs. Hunt really did have a hip problem. At last, Katherine suggested she sit on the chair and tuck her feet up, it was easier rolling her around than having her painfully shuffle through the extensive exhibition spaces. Katherine was glad most of the pieces were downstairs, meaning there was less for her to see: at this point, it was getting close to closing time, the cleaning crew would be arriving as Esther had dutifully reminded them, all the pictures had to be set back in place, Suzy needed time to get ready before Charlie came to pick her up— and Mrs Hunt still had not made her final decision on which paintings to take. At least Mrs Hunt was as rapid in her viewing as she was with her catalogue browsing, she had Katherine stop for a few seconds before each painting before moving on to the next. How the meticulous lady could appreciate art like that was beyond her, but to each his own Katherine decided. They made one brief stop as she suddenly remembered Joseph was waiting for her.

"Joseph?"

"Yes, my chauffeur, he's out in the parking lot with the limousine. Would you be a dear and tell him to come in to the restaurant and get a bite to eat?"

"Oh, the restaurant isn't open for dinner, not yet anyway, but I'm sure Andre will whip up something for him, let me call the main desk." Katherine hurried to the nearest intercom phone and notified Suzy of the latest development. What can we expect next?

"*You're kidding me*," Suzy said over the private line, "you mean she left the poor guy sitting out there all this time? I'll go get him," she sighed before hanging up.

At last, they had toured the permanent gallery and were on their way to the elevator.

"Well, thank you Kathy deary, I enjoyed my tour, you've got yourself quite a collection here."

"I wish it was all mine, but most are on loan. It's a pity that in a few months I'll have to return quite a number of pieces," Katherine explained, "that Picasso was actually starting to grow on me too, I don't know why."

"Maybe because it's unique, even if it is a bit crazy. You know, if the truth must be told, I've got a few pieces I'm getting tired of, time to clear the decks. You can have them on loan when you send the other exhibits back, how does that sound?"

"That's very generous of you," Katherine replied, "are you sure?"

"Course I'm sure, you've got a nice set-up, and I can't abide gappy walls, besides, I can't let Gerry have all the fun around here," Mrs Hunt concluded with a nod. Katherine laughed.

"You know Gerry then?"

"Sure do, know the whole family for years."

"Well, I've only recently met Pete, Gerry and Lottie," Katherine admitted. Mrs. Hunt was only too happy to fill her in on the gossip.

"I met them through my husband actually, he had business dealings with their company. As it turned out, their father, Richard, started collecting art, and I got to know them better. Strange how things turn out, the eldest son seemed the perfect candidate to take over the business, but he decided on a religious life, don't know what got into his head, and he one of the most eligible bachelors with a brilliant future ahead of him. Caused quite an uproar in the family, particularly with his father, so now the reins will eventually fall to Gerry," Mrs. Hunt declared matter-of-factly, "of course, he had his own share in the business already, but sure had a lot of unexpected responsibilities dropped on him after that, seeing Pete was being groomed to take over."

"I can imagine," Katherine noted, she didn't know what to say, unaware of the intricacies of shipping, exporting and importing.

"Then Lottie had her fair share of misfortune. She met this really nice fellow during their first year in college, I think he was an engineering student. Two weeks after their engagement they discovered he had an inoperable brain tumour and he rapidly went downhill, I think he just lived a few short months, terribly tragedy that was."

"Poor Lottie!" Katherine exclaimed. "How can she be so cheerful? I would never have guessed."

"I know, poor creature, she wanted to have a house full of children too. Well, she certainly knows how to put on a brave face, she may be crumbling inside, but still fusses about everyone else and tries to keep the family happy, doesn't want them worrying or adding additional stress. Come Kathy deary, let's see the next painting."

That probably explained why Lottie was taking a year off from college, and also why the three of them seemed very close, Pete and Gerry were watching out for her, trying to cheer her up any way they could Katherine thought to herself as she rolled Mrs. Hunt to the last piece.

"Good heavens, Kathy deary, I do tend to prattle on at times, don't let her know I told you, or she'd be mortified," Mrs. Hunt added, now that she had spilled the beans, "she doesn't want people feeling sorry for her."

"No, I won't say a word, but how sad. I hope she will meet someone someday, she deserves a little happiness like everyone else."

"That may take awhile, she stays to herself these days, won't go out you know. The brothers persuade her now and then to try enjoying the art scene, renew her interest in life," Mrs. Hunt added.

"Well, I guess it's hard to put your life back on track after a tragedy like that," Katherine nodded.

"Hmm, that's a dark one," Mrs. Hunt commented, looking at the Van Gogh.

"Oh, he was pretty dour in those days during his early years in Belgium," Katherine informed her.

"And what about you?" Mrs. Hunt asked unexpectedly, quickly moving on to the next subject as rapidly as her art-viewing, "do you have a boyfriend?"

"No, not yet, I've been busy. I mean I have *friends* ... ."

"Come Kathy deary, I can't believe that a beautiful young lady like you doesn't have a knight in shining armour. Besides, nothing escapes an old-timer like me, I saw the bouquet sitting behind the desk, and it wasn't matching any of the other fancy arrangements you have here either." Katherine wondered if she was blushing.

"Oh ... that's nothing special," she replied, trying to divert Mrs. Hunt's attention from her personal life, silently praying Mrs. Hunt wouldn't ask who it was from, or all of Manhattan would be jumping to the wrong conclusions by tomorrow night. It really was nothing *serious*, just a 'thank-you' arrangement.

"I suppose you have the right idea, best not to rush into anything, got to watch out for those gold diggers don't you know, even at my age, they'll try anything."

"Umm, that was the last piece in the exhibit," Katherine was relieved to announce.

"Already? My how time flies, I enjoyed that. Let's go back downstairs, I have to see the others again, time to make up my mind."

Katherine wheeled her customer to the elevator. In fact, it was quite dark now. While Mrs. Hunt swivelled around and scanned the clutter of pictures, Katherine hooshed Suzy towards the elevator, time she went and changed, Charlie would be along any minute to pick her up.

"Are you sure? You're going to need help restoring order to the place," Suzy whispered.

"Don't worry, Patrick will help I'm sure."

While Mrs. Hunt was a trigger-happy viewer, she became a shot of molasses when it came to purchasing. Katherine shook her head as she tidied up behind the desk. Obviously, Mrs. Hunt paid no attention to business hours. The chauffeur sat in the restaurant waiting area, trying to look patient as his fussy boss eyed each artwork and flipped through the catalogue now crimped at the edges from constant thumbing. Katherine hoped Andre was able to feed the poor man before he closed the restaurant up for the night. Since it was ten minutes past closing time, Suzy had let Esther go home with the Professor while she waited for them to return to the lobby area. The art collector was so intent on her browsing she did not seem to notice how quiet the place had become. Katherine tried to stifle a yawn before she was struck with a distressing thought: after all their heaving and hauling that afternoon, it was not beyond this peppery lady to abruptly change her mind, declare she was just browsing after all and that she did not want to purchase anything, that really would take the cake.

"Kathy deary, could you possibly rustle up another pot of that delicious tea?"

"Well, the restaurant's closed now, but I'm sure I could fix it myself," she began. Finally, Mrs. Hunt took notice of the hour and her 'treacle trickle' method of deliberation mercifully morphed into quicksilver speed.

"Oh, look at the time! Dear me! Never mind, forget the tea. I'd better make this snappy: Ill take this one … this … that, and yes, I like those two over there, oh, and better throw in that one there by the stairs, I'll be kicking myself tomorrow if I don't get it too. I suppose that'll do for now."

"All right. Is there any specific time you would like them delivered?" Katherine enquired, relieved the whole day's running was not in vain.

"Not really, I thought maybe I could come by tomorrow and pick them up myself, got plenty of room in the limo. Isn't that right Joseph?"

"Yes, plenty of room ma'am."

"I'm sorry, we're closed on Sundays, but we'll have them packaged and waiting for you Monday."

"That's just splendid, Kathy deary."

Katherine hoped she did not want to take them right away, now she really needed to find new artists and fast.

The sale was interrupted as Charlie knocked at the side entrance all dressed for dinner.

"Hi Charlie, Suzy's upstairs changing, she should be down in a jiffy."

He looked around in amusement at the colourful clutter.

"Are you redecorating so soon?" he chuckled as he manoeuvred around the misplaced artworks.

"Not exactly," she half whispered under her breath, "we had an unconventional private viewing as you can see."

Although she was relieved he and Suzy had gotten together, it was a little awkward nevertheless, especially when Mrs. Hunt noticed his arrival.

"Well, who do we have here? I see knights do exist," she called out.

"Nights?" Charlie queried Katherine through his teeth. Katherine quickly introduced him to Mrs. Hunt and clarified he had come to take *Suzy* out for a night on the town. Yeesh, and she thought Aunt Martha had mastered the art of indiscretion. Suzy finally came down, she looked lovely in her new aquamarine dress.

"I suppose we should be heading home," Mrs. Hunt announced, "I hope you young ones enjoy your evening."

"Thank you Mrs. Hunt," Suzy replied.

"We shall see you on Monday then," Katherine added as she and Joseph helped Mrs. Hunt to the door.

"Of course. And do *you* have any plans? Looks like your friend is having all the fun."

"Actually, I'm looking forward to having a quiet evening in tonight. Goodnight Mrs. Hunt."

"Goodnight, Kathy deary, see you soon."

At last, Katherine could finally lock the doors and call it a day.

"Gosh, Kathy, I feel guilty leaving this mess for you to handle," Suzy said apologetically as she looked around at the sea of canvases and easels.

"I could pitch in too," Charlie added, "it wouldn't take long with all of us helping, we have some time yet."

"Oh don't you two worry about anything, go and enjoy your sushi, hanging a few pictures is nothing after an afternoon with Mrs. Hunt," Katherine tried to assure them. However, Suzy and Charlie refused to walk out until they did something. In the end, Charlie was delegated the task of folding and returning the cumbersome load of easels to the studio while Suzy helped Katherine return the artwork upstairs. One more trip to the elevator, and it was soon accomplished.

"Honestly, no one ever warned us we'd have days like this," Katherine declared as Patrick the guard wired the last picture in to place.

"At least we know the next one will fall on a Monday," Suzy added.

"O happy day, I can't wait."

೮⊛ನಿ

"I believe condolences are in order, only two weeks into business, and already you've weathered your first bout of 'Hurricane Hunt'," Gerry laughed.

"Is she always like that?" Katherine wondered as the waitress brought their lunch to the table. "I couldn't get over it, when she came on Monday, she insisted on having her pictures unwrapped so she could have another look at them, then of course we had to repack them afterwards. Thank heavens she didn't have us unhook the exhibits all over again."

"Yes, that's her way. She's an enthusiastic patron of the arts, but at the same time, galleries dread to see her come through their door. Kevin keeps a bottle of Valium within reach for whenever she shows up to terrorize the Sirrac."

444

"Oh no!" she laughed, "I hope it won't get that bad for us."

"Just grin and bear it, your gallery is just the latest novelty, so expect to see her at least once every two weeks until it wears off and she finds someone else to spend quality time with."

"Quality time? Why? Doesn't she have any family?"

"She has two kids, but her eldest went off to start his own software company in Silicon Valley, and her daughter married a big financier in Denver, so she sees very little of them, she is pretty much left on her own, except for the odd vacation and holiday gathering," he explained.

"That's terrible," Katherine reflected, "so she just wants someone to fuss over her. Gee, I feel like a troll now, losing patience with her I mean, and she was so kind to offer art on loan from her collection too."

She also felt a little guilty losing her cool with Aunt Martha after hearing about Mrs. Hunt. It was a growing epidemic in these modern times, elderly people with no one close left, either widowed with no children, or children who had 'moved on' who made little time for the 'old folks'. Mrs. Hunt's solution was to adopt the art scene and have everyone hop to attention in order to feel important and to have people around her. It was no different than all those hale and hearty hypochondriacs who held up the emergency rooms or pestered their doctors and had to be placated with placebos. Sometimes it was good to be alone, but there was a huge difference between 'being alone' and feeling 'lonely'. Katherine had never really thought about the true desolation *loneliness* could prove for some people. At least Aunt Martha had her family, she noted. Katherine resolved to try and be a little more understanding with the older generation, they had their problems too.

"Well, you must have made an impression, she usually doesn't offer loans. In any case, don't be so hard on yourself," Gerry replied, "she can be overwhelming at times. I think even our Pete came close to cracking once, he wouldn't say anything of course, but if *he* can come close to the breaking point, you get the picture. Enough about Mrs Hunt, you know what to expect when she arrives, I hope the rest of your week was not as chaotic."

Happily, it turned out pretty good. Several of the artists were quite willing to work with her on sending in single pictures at a time, so she already had a few pieces at the framers and could replace a number of the gaps as soon as the new arrivals were ready. Katherine couldn't help but reveal she was also waiting for a mural-sized canvas from a street artist who happened to be working with the janitorial company she had hired. Gerry was amused by this turn of events.

"*You* patronizing graffiti? From Watteau to wall art, now that is a journey I never thought you would travel."

"Don't poke fun," she *tsked* back, "I'm not *that* snobby about modern art, and there are people who show an interest in this form of expression."

"For your sake I hope it'll *sell*, but I can't say anything, it's your gamble," he laughed.

"Now look who's being snobby," she teased, "at least street art is better than some of the other scrawls passed off as God's gift to the world. Besides, this guy may be famous already, in fact, you may have seen a few of his works, that is if he happens to be the anonymous 'D.S.' like Suzy seems to think, he does have the same initials."

"I can't say that I've seen any of these murals you mention, but I will certainly drop by and critique the new display when it arrives."

She could detect a slight note of amused sarcasm in his voice.

"You don't think I've discovered a real artist, do you?" she queried.

"It's not that, I just can't imagine spray can paint in 'bicycle red' and 'front gate black' hitting it big," he continued, sipping his white wine.

"So, you think I've goofed this time," she added, raising an eyebrow.

"Granted a gallery owner hopes to find the undiscovered Donatello of the modern age … let's just say in your eagerness to promote new talent you may have detoured too far from the cultivated path."

"Oh, how so?"

"I don't want to offend, but somehow, showing graffiti in your Louvre-like setting is not much different than … if the Art Council decided to open a tattoo parlour at the Metropolitan."

At first, she felt a tad indignant with his bizarre analogy, but after a quick moment of reflection, she relented a little, it *was* rather funny. She tried not to laugh. Somehow, she did not think she had descended *that* far, or had she? Surely all good art, be it from the brushes of a traditionally trained art college major or a can-wielding natural, had the right to a showing in her gallery.

"Okay, okay, let's put your doubts and my confidence to the test: let's make a bet," she announced.

"Hmm, this sounds interesting, I'm all ears. What do you have in mind?"

"If his mural fails to attract a buyer in … one month let's say, you get to … hmm, I dunno … ."

"Make the loser, that would be you, pay a forfeit or complete a dare," he suggested.

"And if the mural sells?"

"Then you get to demand the dare," he finished.

"All righty then, this should be fun, as long it isn't anything we wouldn't want the world to know about." A safety-clause was always a good idea.

"Fair enough," he replied, "you're on."

Now it was up to Derrick. She silently prayed he would do her proud and paint a wonderful sought-after rarity, or God knows what kind of antics she would be performing as payment in dare-tribute to the conquering art critic. Come to think of it, she would have to plan something too, she did expect to win after all. Hmm, maybe Steves might have a few suggestions.

"You know, we've talked about my business so much, you haven't had a chance to put a word in about your week."

"Not much to say, not as colourful as running a gallery, government hassle, shipping lanes, getting shipments to their destination in one piece, trying to find underwriters to secure it all, nothing you would find very interesting I'm sure."

Whoops, perhaps I should not have touched upon that area, she reflected. Mrs. Hunt *did* say he had everything dropped upon him unexpectedly and perhaps was feeling the strain, maybe he wanted to do something different with his life and got stuck with work he loathed.

"It seems very involved, 'Hurricane Hunt' sounds like a breeze after the list you just mentioned, but no more about business. Tell me, what I can expect to see at this book convention of yours?"

"What? And spoil the suspense?"

"Gosh, it's just a hall with tables full of books, isn't it?"

Assuming he was taking her to something on the order of an average swap-a-book meet that would occur at high-school, she was surprised to find rows and rows of professional commercial stalls and elegantly outfitted store-like units occupied by official book sellers and rare manuscript dealers. There were quite a number of people browsing around, she noticed certain visitors had brought in some books to be appraised, wondering if that old dusty volume they discovered in the attic was in fact an original edition, or if that musty copy they bought a few years ago had finally increased in value.

"Wow, this place is great! If I hadn't chosen art, I'd love to run something like this," Katherine exclaimed as she looked through one set of shelves managed by a dealer specialising in nineteenth-century books.

"Found something interesting?" Gerry asked, noticing the petite tomes she gazed upon with special reverence.

"Look, *Sense and Sensibility* 'By a Lady', the date is 1811, and an

1813 publication date of *Pride and Prejudice*? These two are first editions! Oh my, and look at these books over here, the authors are Currer Bell and Ellis Bell…"

"Ah, a Brontë admirer too," he noted.

"Well, I appreciate the rarity of seeing the first editions, but the Brontë's stories are a little dark for my liking, yet strangely compelling nevertheless. After *Wuthering Heights*, I couldn't help but wonder what kind of black vortex those girls grew up in to have them invent such depressing characters."

"While art thrives on the blazing colours of scandal, literature blossoms on the dark soil of tragedy," Gerry affirmed.

"Not all," she declared, turning to view a rainbow-hued store-like front displaying early editions of children's literature, "some memorable books have a happy ending, aww, I remember that," she said, pointing to *Charlotte's Web*. "Got an 'A' on my book report too," she laughed before espying another childhood classic, "look, there's an early print of *Charlie and the Chocolate Factory*, I'll never forget the report Steves turned in for that—'A Dispute on Why Wonka's Factory would never Survive in the Real Business World'—and he was only in fourth grade."

"That's intense."

"A real Mr. Brain," she affirmed, "he did make some good points though, like how the Everlasting Gobstoppers would no longer bring in substantial profits after everyone had bought one, that Willie Wonka had refused to apply ethics in the workplace by using his visitors as human test subjects, not to mention the illegalities in hiring all foreign labour with the Oompa-Loompas effectually circumventing the unions."

"He certainly took his homework seriously didn't he? Hmm, book reports, those were the days," Gerry mused as he picked up an old edition of the *Adventures of Huckleberry Finn*, "*Tom Sawyer, James and the Giant Peach*, one of the few enjoyable assignments we had at school, other than P.E. of course."

"Any favourites from your book report list?"

"We were usually delegated books to read, I suppose they were afraid we might choose material not 'educational' or would try and write a report on a comic book. Some stories stood out among the rest though, like *The Call of the Wild*."

"Oh, I know what you mean, we got landed with a few books I wouldn't have picked myself, but have stuck with me, like the *Slave Dancer*, that was really sad."

"See? Tragedy prevails," he chuckled. "I didn't read that one."

"Well, it's about this poor boy that lives with his mother who tries to make money as a seamstress," Katherine began, "she can't afford to take a moment off and has to work through the night. However, they run out of candles, so she sends him out to buy some more and he is kidnapped by a bunch of sailors who force him to work as a cabin boy on their slave ship. One of his tasks is playing his flute when the crew exercise the slaves on deck, hence the name of the book. Basically, it's a narrative about the horrors of the slave trade and what happened to the 'cargo' on board, the conditions the slaves endured were truly terrible, and that was *before* they were forced into a life sentence of hard labour when they reached land. God, I don't know how our country could have allowed that," she mused, "what a large blot on our constitution if you ask me. It stomachs me to think even Washington owned slaves."

Gerry quickly lost interest in the children's book display.

"Come on, there's a particular booth I want to show you."

"Oh … okay."

He led her through the walkways until he found the desired booth, a stylish store-front panelled in dark old-world oak tones. He courteously opened the door to let her enter first. Inside were elegantly carved wooden shelves and cases with special glass enclosures and climate control settings, all softly lit with a golden light. She felt like she had stepped into a lost library hidden deep within some ancient castle, but with all the modern technological upgrades. Katherine took a closer look at the contents, venerable-looking volumes were carefully lined up on the glass-sealed shelves, other hand scribed manuscripts were tastefully displayed open face on stands in curious looking cabinets with legs tapered into claw features. Katherine was held spellbound by the bright blues and reds of a carpet page illuminating a medieval gospel, eventually tearing herself away to look at another stunning page of an ancient song book filled with modal musical notation, probably a hymnal, she could make out a prayer judging from 'Jesu'. Displayed next to it was another book with music, this time the illustration featured a musical instrument, the outline drawn with colourful musical notation and the words to a love song, she was able to make out some words in medieval French from the ornamented calligraphy. Single sheets of velum were also available, odd leaves that had become separated from their original volume at one time or another, pieces from old almanacs, official chronicles, gospels and meditation books. She could easily guess this is where he acquired the manuscripts currently loaned to her exhibition.

"This is truly remarkable. How on earth do they get hold of something like this?" she asked, admiring the delicate foliage traced in another carpet page from a gospel manuscript. "I would have thought all the national libraries would have first dibs on material this precious."

"Usually they acquire their texts from old estates that go up for auction, private collections that have never been open to the public. The libraries do manage to acquire a number of pieces, but their budgets can only extend so far. Look over there, they have a nice selection of incunabula," he said as he indicated to one of the cases at the other end of the showroom.

"Incu...? I'm not sure what that is," she shyly admitted.

"Sorry, I'm becoming too technical. They're books from the first printing presses, generally before 1500."

While looking through the glass, a gentleman with silver hair, smartly dressed in a crisp suit, entered from a door almost hidden in the back wall.

"It's good to see you again, Gerry. Browsing today?" he enquired in a notable British accent.

"Hello Jeremy," they shook hands, "yes, just looking for now. Anything new I haven't seen?"

"Yes indeed, you might be pleased to hear we've just acquired a couple of Caxtons, complete editions I might add," the gentleman replied, turning to the case they were looking at, unlocking it with a key and taking out the volumes.

"Now that is something," Gerry noted with interest, taking a closer look at the time-weathered pages before realizing he had not yet introduced Katherine. "Jeremy, you've distracted me with your treasures, let me introduce you to Katherine Walsingham." They politely shook hands.

"I'm very pleased to meet you," Jeremy replied.

"Katherine here has just opened an art gallery. The Flemish manuscripts you sold me are currently on loan in her permanent exhibition space, I thought she might like to see other pieces in your collection."

"Ah, now those were fine specimens. Do you collect as well?" he politely asked.

"Well, not exactly, not *yet*," she tried to explain, "actually, I'm a newcomer to collecting rare items, I'm afraid I don't know much about old books like this," she continued, looking down at the texts he had retrieved.

"These certainly would be one magnificent way to start; Caxton is a rare find, he was the first to print books in English," Jeremy informed her.

"Wow, that's fascinating ... but I really like the illuminated manuscripts," she confessed.

"In that case, feel free to look around."

While Gerry examined the Caxtons, Katherine quietly went from bookshelf to cabinet, eventually stopping to inspect a special frame displaying four illustrations featuring unicorns. The pictures were not as intricate as the gospel carpet pages, but they possessed a distinctive charm, it was fascinating to see unicorns drawn in authentic medieval styles. It brought back those wonderful times when she believed these fantastic animals existed and had papered her wall with numerous posters of them, plus a Pegasus or two for good measure. After giving instructions to have one of the volumes delivered, Gerry came over to see the illustrations that were absorbing her attention, Jeremy followed.

"This is a favourite with the ladies, here we have a few leaves taken from several early fourteenth-century bestiaries," Jeremy declared, "the previous owner was interested in unicorns, hence the singular accumulation of these four pieces."

Two of the images featured the animals seated in stylised poses framed in bright foliage, while the third showed a young noblewoman with a unicorn resting its head on her lap.

"I like that one," Katherine said, "just for curiosity's sake, how much is it?"

"The four sell for fifteen thousand US dollars. I'm sorry, we're not splitting this collection," Jeremy said apologetically, "I'm afraid the whole set must go together."

"That's a pity, I wouldn't mind the other two, but the last one on the bottom is disturbing, I don't care for it at all."

Well versed in unicorn lore, she knew only a maiden could attract these pure animals, but in some instances the damsels were used as bait to lure the creature to its doom by some adventurous 'hero' as the last picture graphically displayed: a maiden looks on helplessly as a knight stabs the unicorn through the heart to claim its prized alicorn believed to be a powerful remedy counteracting the most deadly poisons.

"Be a sport and make an exception, just this once," Gerry light-heartedly coaxed.

"I'm sorry, that's the way it is, it wouldn't be right to break the set," Jeremy said, raising his hands.

"Now don't pressure him, I don't think I could stretch that far right now anyway, even for one of them," she replied, "my gallery is in the early days to consider major additions like this."

"What about that art grant your parent's promised? Wouldn't they be willing to set some of if aside for other items you like?"

"It's tempting, but I would hate to ask them, it just wouldn't seem right, it's like exchanging a birthday present or telling my parents I'd rather have something else."

"Fair enough, perhaps another time," Gerry replied. "You know, there are other collectables you can acquire, they also have more reasonably priced items, like letters and private documents belonging to celebrities. Jeremy secured the Delacroix sketchbook for me too."

"Really? Do you have more like that?" Katherine asked Jeremy.

"Unfortunately, we have no documents by famous artists at present," Jeremy said apologetically, "however, we do have a number of composers in stock, a few letters written by Gounod for one example," he continued, opening a drawer under one of the sealed bookshelves and taking out a Victorian style portfolio casing in the shape of a book with an oxblood morocco binding. Inside were a bundle of notes, letters and a few envelopes with the antique postage stamps still attached. Katherine looked a little closer at the yellowing letter paper, examining the neat handwriting traced in what looked like early fountain pen ink. Judging from the content of one page, it was a thank you letter for a score he received from a certain music student.

"This is a real time capsule, I'm afraid I would need something more in keeping with an art gallery, but thank you for showing it to us," she replied.

"I quite understand, you're very welcome," Jeremy nodded as he closed the lid, returning the deluxe box to its drawer.

"I suppose that will be all this time around," Gerry concluded, "and you *will* let me know if you ever secure a Gutenberg Bible? A complete vellum edition mind you, no 'Noble fragments'," he warned with humour.

"Of course, you shall be the first to know," Jeremy assured him.

They said their goodbyes to the dealer and quietly resumed their browsing through the stalls of the large convention floor. Katherine was lost in thought, Gerry certainly knew a lot about books. Although she was what she called a 'literature buff', she had never stepped into the world of a serious collector. It was an interesting experience, there was nothing like feeling the thrill and novelty in seeing or doing something for the first time. Did he really want a Gutenberg Bible? While she wasn't familiar with the minutiae of inculab … incalobe … whatever the term was, she knew a copy of *that* wouldn't be cheap since it was the first book ever printed. At least her history classes were good for something. She wondered if she was catching the collecting 'bug' too after noticing a few tomes on a shelf that looked very much like the old medical volumes tucked away in their library at home dating from Great Gramp's days. Out of curiosity, she picked up a copy of an anatomy book and gingerly looked for a price, only a mere eighty bucks for a book printed at the turn of the century. Oh come on, it had to be worth more than *that*. Did books have to be more than five hundred years old before they were considered valuable? What about the information printed in them? Knowledge was power, or so the saying went. Gerry inquired if she was interested in medicine, and she explained the reason for her curiosity.

"Yes, or sort of. When I was little, I wanted to become a nurse. I think the petite curly hat was the main draw, but medicine was immediately crossed off my list: although I love the valiant concept of saving lives, I can't stand the sight of blood or needles." Gerry laughed. "However," she continued, "I was just curious to see what something like this would be worth to tell the truth. We have an old copy like this at home, it came in handy for biology class. I'm surprised it's not worth more considering its age. My artwork sells for much more than that, and it's brand new."

Gerry inspected the title page and imprint information.

"Well, age is not everything with a book. The physical value basically depends on the edition and condition, whether it's rare or not, plus how many copies are still in existence, if that information happens to be available. Hmm, *Gray's Anatomy*, I don't know much about medical texts, but this title is a classic. I see this is one of the later American editions, not as valuable as the first 1858 British edition, if I have my years correct."

One of the unit attendants approached to ascertain if they needed any assistance, and hopefully make a sale.

"I'm sorry, I couldn't help but overhear your conversation," the brown-haired man apologized, "but you are correct. 1858 is the year of the first British edition."

"If you could secure a first edition in good condition, what would it cost, approximately?" Gerry asked. Katherine listened with interest.

"Approximately? If we could find one in good condition, several thousand would not be unheard of, perhaps three, maybe up to seven, there are various factors involved in the pricing," the attendant explained.

"Thank you, we'll think about it," Gerry replied, gently nudging Katherine under the arm, obviously a signal it was time to move beyond his range of hearing and sales pitch.

"Here let me give you our card," the man insisted, "we can secure other books you may be interested in."

"Thank you, we'll keep that in mind," he said as he slipped the card inside his breast pocket.

They casually continued on their way through the convention floor.

"Well, you now have an idea what it would be worth. Do you know when your book was printed?" Gerry asked when they had reached a safe distance.

"This is exciting," Katherine quietly noted, trying to contain her exuberance with this new discovery, "it's definitely a British print, I'm sure of it. I can just remember the bibliography I wrote for the science essays I told you about."

"Maybe the second British edition from 1860, but if it's the first... you might want to take a look at it when you get a chance. Remember 1858, not 1860. It's a good thing you didn't say anything out loud until we had some notion of the going rate. I know that fellow back there, takes advantage of the uninitiated," Gerry disclosed, "he would have tried to talk you into bringing it in, hoping you couldn't tell a first edition rarity from a pulp fiction paperback, see if you unwittingly laid before him a collector's piece, then try to get it for a fraction of its value, maybe five or six hundred to make it seem like he was giving you a great deal. Naturally, he would sell it later for a prince's ransom."

"I guess there are scams in every trade," she reflected, "I probably would have fallen for that one."

"If you ever wanted to dabble in serious book trading like this, I suggest you stick with Jeremy. While he mostly deals with early items, he's not above handling later books. He would ensure you get what it's worth."

"How does he make his living?" Katherine wondered, "commission rates, like a gallery?"

"Sometimes, or he'll hold on to certain items until they increase in value. Patience is required if you speculate in books, artwork too for that matter. I'm sure he had those Caxtons a few years longer then he was willing to let on," Gerry laughed, "but at least he makes his profit without overtly swindling anyone."

"Thanks for the advice, but the family library is not mine to sell, even if it was, I wouldn't part with Great Gramp's collection for the world. Nevertheless, it *is* rather thrilling to think we have a rare book like that at home. Who would have guessed? Gramps is going to get a kick out of this when I tell him."

They were about to inspect another storefront when a voice suddenly announced over the sound system the convention centre would be closing in twenty minutes.

"Look at the time, we've wandered around for ages," Katherine said as she checked her watch, "I wish we could stay a little longer, this was fun."

"We do have twenty more minutes, let's make one last dash before they boot us out," he suggested.

"That reminds me of the day I raced through the Louvre trying to get in as much as I could, you can't enjoy art or books in a hurry," she laughed.

"How about another bite to eat then? Since I've taken your whole day, it would be terrible to send you home starving."

"Oh, I couldn't impose."

"It's no imposition, please, I insist."

"Well, okay, but it's my turn to pick up the tab."

"I wouldn't hear of it, I invited you out today, my treat," he declared.

"Uh uh," she declined, shaking her head, "that would be three meals in a row, it has to be my turn sometime."

"Save us from independent women!" he laughed, "I couldn't let you do that."

"Goodness, let's call a truce, shall we? We'll go Dutch, that settles it," she announced resolutely.

"This is all new to me, I don't know how to handle this, my date insists on paying for her fare? I can't agree to that truce," he admitted, looking a little perplexed with the situation.

"Hey, it's the 90s, it's not such a big deal," she replied, not knowing how to get beyond this unexpected impasse without awkwardly refusing altogether and heading straight home.

"I never let a lady put her hand in her purse," he replied with a debonair persistence, "call me old fashioned, but that's how it's got to be."

Gosh, he was stubborn. At last, Katherine shrugged her shoulders, what the heck? She would never make it back home in time for dinner anyway, and he was trying to do the gentlemanly thing, might as well make an evening of it. There was only one problem … .

"I don't think I'm dressed to go out to dinner, that was something I hadn't expected."

"Don't worry, you look great."

"I don't feel right about this, but okay, you win. I can't stay out late tonight, mind you, it's a work night, got to be up bright and early," she reminded him.

"Same for me, I know a quaint bistro with good food, nothing too fancy, but prompt service. We'll be home before dawn, I promise," he joked.

"Okay, I'd better call home at let them know. Do you see a phone anywhere?" she asked, scanning the walls and the corners for the public booths.

"Here, use my cell phone," he offered, taking the apparatus from his inside pocket, switching it back on and handing it to her, "save yourself the steps."

"Thank you. I should get one, but they are so cumbersome," she explained while waiting for her call to go through, "even with the new designs, they still weigh like small bricks."

"That will change in a few years, I'm sure," Gerry replied, "technology is advancing every day."

After notifying the family of her change in plans, they decided to take his car and pick hers up later when they were finished, the area was secure enough.

Katherine did not feel like eating anything too heavy, she still felt satisfied after their lunch and was content with a shrimp and crab salad with a glass of white wine. Gerry ordered a medium rare steak with all the trimmings and red wine. She then realized she wasn't sure what to discuss next, it was easy talking about literature and texts while they were at the convention, but now it was just the two of them again. Getting to know someone better was a delicate business, every question she wanted to ask seemed too personal, every comment she felt like offering had to be guarded, afraid she might offend or go beyond some invisible boundary that he did not wish her to cross. She felt a sense of uncertainty slowly welling up within, how ordinary and uninteresting she was in comparison. Maybe it's best if I leave the conversation up to him, he's probably bored talking about books by now.   He seemed quiet, so rather than sit there looking stupid, she had better say something.

"Do you really plan to buy a Gutenberg?" she asked. She was curious about this anyway.

"Oh that," he chuckled, "it's an old in-joke between Jeremy and I, it would be like asking him to secure the Holy Grail. Of course I would love to have even a tip of a page. There are only forty-seven or so known copies out of a total of one hundred and eighty, but some are more rare than others. For instance, forty-five of the whole series were printed on vellum, but only four complete copies are now in existence. There are incomplete vellums out there of course, but discovering a fifth complete book would be a dealer's dream, a new page in the annuals of incunabula. The last complete Gutenberg to go up on auction was in '78, so the chances of another intact text becoming available are pretty slim, even a 'Noble Fragment' is difficult to come by, loose leaves have not been sold since the 1920s, except for that auction in '87 when a Volume One sold for five and a half million. When you take all of this into account, the cost of a complete edition would be prohibitive at this date. Add a few more years from now when one might be found, and you're talking about five to nine million for a paper edition, a vellum copy would be much more than that."

"This is a serious business," she reflected, "I thought collecting was supposed to be fun."

"It is, in it's own way. With rare items, it's like an archaeologist finding the remnants of a lost civilisation or forgotten treasure hoard, it's all about the thrill of discovery."

"Fortune and glory, a real Indiana Jones, librarian style," she laughed. "You know, you could just visit the New York Public library, they have one there. I saw it on display once during a school trip."

"Ah, that one: paper edition, missing only one page so its still incomplete, what a shame. Bell donated several sections when he sold the Noble Fragments, so it was in worse condition before the 1920s. It would be something to have one of those, practically all editions and leaves of the Gutenberg are owned by national or university libraries, a private collector would love to get his hands on a fragment like that now."

"What are these 'Noble Fragments'? I've never heard of them before."

"They were the bright idea of a dealer named Wells who decided to break up a copy he acquired and sell it piecemeal."

"That's a terrible idea!" she exclaimed, "I can't bear to dog-ear a paperback, while others deliberately split up antique manuscripts as if they were coupons in the daily papers. Why would he do something like that? That's just ... I don't have words for it." He smiled at her analogy.

"I know how you feel. Believe it or not, Wells actually thought he was doing bibliophiles a favour. The copy he acquired was missing a substantial number of pages and several of the illustrations were already cut out at some point, so he decided since it was in a poor shape to begin with, he would make the remaining sections available for libraries that would not have an opportunity to acquire an existing edition. He issued the detached pieces with an essay by a well-known author and book collector of the time entitled *A Noble Fragment Being a Leaf of the Gutenberg Bible*, so the name stuck."

"I guess he had a point, but still, he shouldn't have dismembered a Gutenberg no matter what condition it was in, it's nothing short of sacrilege. What a pity all those illuminated manuscripts are detached too," Katherine reflected, thinking back to the convention.

"Well, it's not all deliberate, a lot has to do with time and circumstances, maybe the original owners were not as careful with them and books fell apart from either general wear and tear or ill use, it does happen."

"I suppose so," she conceded.

"Then, there are numerous new copies of all the old literature, for instance, we have a hundred different versions of the Bible still in print, so older manuscripts are prized more for their artistry and rarity rather than the actual texts, although some historians would beg to differ, but they are researchers, not collectors."

"So, the value depends on who is doing the collecting," she concluded.

"I guess it comes down to that," he agreed.

"If you don't mind me asking, what got you started with books? Is it a family tradition, like your art collection?"

"Sort of, we all like to read, and the appreciation of art usually progresses to literature and *vice versa*."

"Too true," Katherine admitted, "the arts are difficult to separate, it's hard not to like something from every field, even if you have a preference for one over another. I wouldn't have thought about collecting books though."

"Well, the concept of owning first editions always intrigued me, but my interest began around the time I discovered a first French edition by Victor Hugo in a second-hand shop during my freshman year at college, I didn't know it at the time, in my ignorance of French and collecting books in general, I nearly fell for a similar trick I warned you about, good thing I never intended to sell it."

"What an awful trick to try and pull. Which of Hugo's books is it?"

"*Notre Dame de Paris*," he said, settling back in his chair.

"You're kidding," she exclaimed wide-eyed, nearly tipping over her water glass,
"I love that book! You have a first edition of the *Hunchback of Notre Dame*?" That was something else, one of Hugo's most famous novels, and to be almost diddled on it too.

"Yes, although I had to read the story from an English translation. It was Hugo's comments on books that I found intriguing: *'The great work of humanity will no longer be constructed, it will be printed.'* While he may have inspired others to restore the old cathedrals, I turned to the early products of the press."

"You know, it was a good thing you decided to keep it," Katherine replied, "can you tell me what happened?"

"The dealer I took it to made out it was a less valuable issue that was not in good condition and tried to buy it for a fraction of what it was worth. It wasn't until a year later that I found out I had narrowly escaped being hoodwinked when a similar copy of the same book went on auction and sold for a pretty penny. Still, it's not the money end that bothers me, it's the thought of being outsmarted simply for not knowing the ropes."

"But wouldn't it have been easy to check out the first year of printing?"

"Sure, but it was the manner in which it was originally issued that created the opportunity for the scam. I wasn't familiar with the various terms associated with its printing, like I said, my French is not that good. The first edition was also divided into four issues. In other words, the first eleven hundred copies were grouped into four issues of two hundred and seventy five. The publishers purposely confused the matter in order to make it look like copies were selling out faster than they actually were and help fuel a demand for the book by describing these groups as 'first' impression, 'second' impression, etcetera. My copy is a 'quatrieme' issue, not as pricey as a 'premiere' issue, but it is still a first edition and quite valuable. The unscrupulous dealer was hoping I'd take him at his word and assume it was a fourth *edition* just printed from the same press in the same year, which I did of course until the auction I mentioned."

"That's rotten. Why can't people just try and be honest anymore?"

"It is a bleak fact of life, but crime does pay for some people, and strategic *coups* equal success, it just depends on the crime and the loopholes they can jump through or make for themselves," he declared.

"That's depressing," she noted.

"It's the truth. I'll give you an example, even if it is from a fictional source. Have you seen *Gone with the Wind*?"

"Who hasn't? That's a classic. Mom watches it all the time."

"Well, just think of the schemes Scarlett comes up with to survive, and yet she scrapes through, eventually making out better than everyone else she knows when the war is over. Rhett is another example. You remember the scene when Scarlett dances in her widow's weeds at the fundraiser ball?"

"Yeah, hard to forget actually."

"Then you recall when Rhett was saluted with a standing ovation: what was it for? Braving the Northern foe as a blockade runner to get valuable shipments through to the South, yet, while basking in the glow of a hero's welcome, he unashamedly admits to Scarlett his sole reason for undertaking the dangerous mission was to make a tidy profit with hard-to-get goods raised well over the usual market prices."

"At least he had the decency to admit he wasn't a gentleman,"

Katherine noted, "hmm, I wonder, does crime and conceit really pay in the end? That would be a good argument for my next Socratic painting," she mused.

"Oh yes, tell me, how are your new paintings progressing?"

"Still in the planning stages to tell the truth. Allegorical works are not as easy to do, not like a landscape for example. If I had stuck to something simple," she laughed, "I'd be painting loads of trees and hills right now, but when each image has a specific meaning, putting them in the wrong place or using the wrong colour could spell disaster, so I've discovered from my first experiments."

"Sure, every angle has to be thought out, and still mistakes can be made, or other significances could be construed that you never intended," he agreed, "still, you can't help it sometimes, interpretation is in the eye of the beholder."

The conversation continued on to general topics in which they both had an interest while their plates were cleared and coffee ordered, Gerry offering more of his travel memories when topics on art and literature had finally worn thin. She wished she had an equal amount of comparable stories to share, her few stints at summer camp didn't seem to count when compared with his trek through the Himalayan foothills in Nepal.

"Did you ever get to the top?" she joked.

"No, the lowlands were enough for me, the change of altitude is a killer when you're not used to it, and besides, I did want to come home in one piece," he replied with a wry smile. "Do you know how many return maimed from frostbite after their attempts to scale Everest? Not to mention all the other hazards, hurricane-force winds, hypothermia, rapid ice breaks, avalanches, hidden crevasses … and for what? To plant a flag on top and say you've been there, a sentence or two in a history book, to gain their five minutes of glory on National Geographic."

"I suppose it's like owning a first edition, to say you're the first one to do something that no one else or few others have ever accomplished," she reflected.

"Ah, I should talk, I stand corrected by the philosopher," he joked.

"Oh, don't get me wrong, I know what you are trying to say, I always give Steves a bad time about astronauts risking their lives, sitting on a potential bomb just to bring a few moon rocks back to earth, but the challenges, rarity and danger of adventures like that are powerful magnets for some people. Let's face it, not everyone gets to experience a space walk or see the world from the top of Everest."

"Too true, well, let's toast the bravery of those intrepid adventurers and their illusive 'first edition'," he suggested with a touch of humour, raising his cup.

"With coffee? Okay, whatever," Katherine chuckled as she reached for hers, inadvertently knocking the spoon off the saucer. Gerry looked at the miniature mixing utensil for a split second with an amused expression. "A penalty for them," he remarked.

"Huh?"

"Oh, I'm sorry, it's a childish quirk I've never been able to shake. I shouldn't have said it."

"Why not?" she asked, "are you superstitious? Is dropping a spoon bad luck or something?"

"It depends on what direction it's pointing in," he mysteriously added with a smile before continuing, "when we were kids, Pete, Lottie and I were always daring each other with a variant of 'forfeits' called 'spin the spoon' but any eating implement would do, Lottie started it. It eventually became a joke when we'd drop a fork or knife at meals. We'd crack up thinking about all the dares we made each other do during past games, of course, no one knew our private joke and thought we were mad."

"You mean something like 'truth or dare'? I haven't played that in a long time." She didn't think he would ever get himself entangled in a game like that, but it *was* addictive, a compromising icebreaker featuring all the strategy of Poker, minus the cards, mixed with a dash of danger from Russian Roulette, without the revolver. "Let me guess, whoever the spoon turns to has to answer a question or perform the dare suggested by everyone else, and if the dare is refused, they must perform the penalty."

"You got it, but if it doesn't point to anyone in particular, everyone gets to ask each other a 'yes' or 'no' question, which has to be answered truthfully. If everyone else thinks you're lying, you have to perform the penalty, no 'buts', even if you *are* telling the truth. You have to cross your fingers and hope the other players are honest enough not to call you a liar."

"Huh, this sounds interesting," she noted, "I hadn't played it that way before."

"Would you like to give it a go?" he enquired with a rakish gleam in his eye, "I promise not to inflict anything too outlandish, there's only so much we can do in public, but the spoon has dropped, there's no turning back."

"You know, trying to come up with a penalty was always a tough one," she noted, "I could never think of anything worse than an embarrassing dare, yet nothing that would cost life, limb or reputation."

"I'll tell you what happened to us once, we finally picked taking the garbage out as the ultimate penalty. Sure we had help at home, but our parents insisted on us having chores to teach us responsibility. No one wanted to do that job, we always tried to pass it off to each other by begging, bribery or blackmail.”

“I don’t blame you,” she laughed, “sounds familiar.”

“Well, I got stuck coming up with a new dare for Pete, so I dared him to take out the trash, it ended the game sooner than expected, but it was a win-win situation: he couldn’t back out, and Lottie and I didn’t have to do it.”

“That’s awful,” Katherine laughed, shaking her head, “but ingenious I must admit.” No one would ever dare dishonour the unspoken ‘Code of Completion’, it was no different from breaking a legally binding contract: enter the game at your own risk, player beware.

“Okay, we need a penalty,” Gerry said as he rubbed his chin before looking around the bistro for mischievous inspiration.

“Nothing too embarrassing, you promised,” she reminded him.

“I’ve got it: whoever refuses has to ask that waiter over there to do a tap dance … and a bonus to the player if he actually does it.”

“Oh my gosh,” Katherine shyly grinned, looking over at the waiter that was singled out before quickly putting her head down, “I guess that would count as a good penalty.”

“Since the spoon fell my way, I’m the first victim,” Gerry declared, “name your question or dare.”

“That wouldn’t be fair, we didn’t actually spin it, let’s start this right,” she insisted, reaching for a clean bread plate from an extra table setting and placing the spoon on top, giving it a gentle twist while trying not to make too much of a clatter. “I hope the table is level, or it’ll keep stopping in the same direction.” The spoon ceased its gyrations and pointed towards her right. “I guess it’s a ‘yes’ and ‘no’ round, we can’t ‘truth’ or ‘dare’ the people next to us,” she laughed.

“Shall we give it a try?” he asked with amusement, rising from his seat as if he intended to intrude upon the diners at the neighbouring table.

“Oh no you don’t!” she giggled, bashfully looking away from the unsuspecting people caught up in their roguish amusement.

“Just kidding. Okay, you ask first.”

Katherine thought for a moment, it would be rude or maybe too nosy to delve into anything too personal for the first round. Better keep it simple, she thought, but what to ask?

“Take your time,” he laughed.

“Wait a minute, I’ll think of something…oh *now* I can’t,” she declared, looking at her watch, "speaking of time, it's getting rather late, I've got to be getting home." He also looked at his watch.

"Well, I did promise, but we were only just getting started, you should be made to pay the penalty for pulling out and not asking the question."

"Hey, you're getting off lightly! Oh all right, umm …you like Jaguar cars, yes or no?" she finally asked, thinking about heading home didn't give her any better inspiration than that.

"Thank you for the tame question," he smiled, "for the record, yes I do, but you should be made to pay the penalty anyway for giving such an obvious question."

Well she had done it now, he was right, the whole idea was to get the other player to open up and confess all their foibles, their likes and dislikes, her question was rather lame. She would have to do the right thing and take her penalty.

"This is embarrassing, but you're going to hold me to it now, aren't you?"

"Uh huh. Waiter?" he called, making a quick motion. Katherine watched as he brought the bill over.

"I hope you enjoyed your dinner," he dutifully enquired.

"Yes, very well indeed. If you don't mind, my friend has a question to ask…"

"Certainly," he replied, turning to Katherine.

"Umm, this is probably going to sound very strange," she began, casting Gerry a glance betraying a little mortification and amusement, "but … do you know how to tap dance?"

"I … never learned how to dance," the puzzled man answered, "will that be all?"

"Um, yes thank you," she replied. They watched him depart with the cheque.

"You couldn't do it," Gerry noted smugly, crossing his arms.

"There was no need to ask him since he doesn't know how to dance," she reasoned.

"Nice try, but it won't work, you still have to ask him."

"I beg to differ, you can't ask someone to do something they don't know how to do. When you think about it, the penalty has been compromised."

"Oh really?" Garry laughed, leaning on the table. "The whole idea of the penalty is to do the specific task assigned, and you haven't done it yet, but look, you have another chance," he noted as the waiter came to return the change. Katherine couldn't bring herself to ask the embarrassing question, silly as it was. Gerry thanked the waiter one last time before rising from the table and helping her with her coat. "Penalty still unpaid," he teased as they went to the parking lot.

"I couldn't ask him anyway, so it's no penalty," she returned, "he *wouldn't* do anything he *couldn't* do, so it's compromised, I tell you."

They bantered good-naturedly on the impasse they reached as he drove her back to her car.

"All right, I shall let you get away with it this once, my pretty," he conceded as he held open her car door, "but mark this well, I shall give no quarter with the results of your street mural."

The mural! Oh dear, Derrick had better paint something spectacular, she thought, or I'm in for it.

"It might sell within the month, so that goes for you too," she remembered.

"Fair enough, give me a call when it arrives. I've got to see what has us both on the wire."

"Will do. Thank you for the lovely day, it was really interesting. I had a good time."

"Me too, well, we'd better start our engines, or it *will* be dawn before we get home," he concluded, "I'll see you later. Drive safely," he called after her, watching her buckle up and drive off before getting back into his car.

Gramps had already gone to bed when she arrived, but Mom and Pops had stayed up watching TV.

"Did you have a nice time?" her mother asked.

"I did actually, I didn't expect to stay out for dinner, but it would have been impolite to refuse...." she didn't have a chance to tell about her day, ambushed by a large yawn, "excuse me!"

"I guess somebody had better head up to bed," Pops observed.

"You can tell us all about it tomorrow," Mom added.

"All right, I can't wait to tell you about the medieval manuscripts, I wish you could have seen them. Well, good night everyone."

"Pleasant dreams, dear."

Before Katherine was completely overcome with drowsiness, there was something she wanted to check. Crossing the hall to the library, she turned on the nearest lamp, searched for the old anatomy book and opened the imprint page: 1858. *Oh cool*, a first edition nestled quietly at home, hidden in a corner for all these years, Gramps is just going to love this.

It was good to finally lie down after a day of activity. She looked up at the darkened ceiling for a few moments thinking about the rare literary treasures all accumulated in that one convention. He knew where to find the most interesting places, had travelled to many exotic destinations, a real mystery man, come to think of it. She had met him almost a year ago, and still he was like a closed book with an odd loose leaf poking through here and there, barely giving a glimpse of its text. Hmm, I wonder what I can 'dare' him if the mural sells, tattoo parlour my foot, she mused just before falling asleep. Her parents were asking each other their own questions in the den below.

"What do you think, Harold dear?"

"You know how artists are when they get together, Helen, they like to share their interests, they may have been talking shop all day for all we know. Kathy is a woman braving the working world now, she has business associates to socialise with, things to do, people to see...."

"Of course, but when do business associates bring chocolates, corsages, and formal presents to the parents?"

"That's true," he conceded, "well, we've only met him a couple of times, and despite the rumours, so far, I find nothing disagreeable about him."

"The stories about his family could be unfounded. Hmm, they *do* seem to have a lot in common, and he has always been a proper gentleman," Helen noted.

"Kathy's a big girl now, and she really doesn't need our permission to see anyone if she wishes. We've always been able to trust her, we have to trust her judgement for the moment."

"I know, I hope she finds someone who will make her happy, it's hard to see them all grow up so fast."

છ⊛ಬ

Finally getting into the working rhythm of the gallery, it was easy to lose track of the passing seasons were it not for the changing display on the front desk, the little porcelain pumpkin of Halloween poking through the flowery sprays grinning its toothy grin was eventually exchanged for a new decoration, a miniature model turkey with its fanned tail covered in chicken feathers. She couldn't wait for Thanksgiving, Steves would be coming back home, and all the family would be getting together this year at last, including the cousins. Mrs. Hunt came to the gallery at least every other week like clockwork as predicted, requesting each new painting on display be brought down for her inspection, but they were gradually growing used to it by then. The benches had all arrived from Europe in one piece, and there was always people browsing around, things were looking pretty good. Gramps, however, had some distressing news, he didn't know how to approach Katherine about it until she joined him at their table for a coffee break.

"You know Katie, I was wondering, is there something amiss in the kitchen?" he probed, looking a little flustered.

"Amiss? No, everything is going all right as far as I know. Why?"

"Well, I don't like to be the bearer of bad tidings, but since I sort of arranged your eating establishment, I feel I should say something first, before the customers do … ."

"This doesn't sound good … is there a health issue I should know about? Don't tell me you've seen flies swimming in the soup or something," she whispered, glancing around, hoping the diners were not eavesdropping.

"Hrumph! No, no! Nothing like that. It seems that Andre is … well … slipping a bit. There, I said it."

"Oh Gramps, I don't think so, I order lunch here practically everyday, and I've never had a bad experience, except when I let it go cold, but that's my fault. Why would you think his food is not up to par?"

"Well, it's just not tasting like it used to," he said thoughtfully, "can't put my finger on it. Oh, same food all right, but it's … lacking somehow. Could you have a quiet word with him? Find out if he's broken up with a sweetheart or something?"

"Gee, you're asking me to snoop into the man's private life, but I'll try and find out what's wrong, perhaps he's experimenting with his seasonings."

"You're a pet," Gramps smiled.

After dutifully enquiring with Esther and Suzy if they had noticed any change in Andre's cuisine and receiving a negative reply from them, she gathered up the courage to tell Andre Gramps was detecting a slight difference in his favourite dishes.

"Oh *that*, don't worry, he's the only victim," he replied with a humorous nod before showing her his 'experimental seasonings'—sodium reduced salt, imitation butter, low calorie mayonnaise and every other dietary substitute he could find to doctor all the favourite dishes. "I understand he's supposed to be on a diet, so I've tried to keep him on the straight and narrow path. What he doesn't know won't hurt him I figured."

"Andre, you're a champ. The problem now will be keeping him from figuring out your little swap-a-roo in the *roux*."

"He's not the only one under wraps," he continued, "I've had to get some healthy dog chow for Jasper, scraps only once a week, this place is not doing him any good either you know." Come to think of it, Jasper *was* starting to look a little podgy around the middle.

One morning, as she supervised the hanging of a few pieces recently completed by their artists, Katherine began to wonder if Derrick ever planned to bring in his mural. He wasn't always working with the same cleaning crew as the company often changed their employees around, and on the odd occasion she did spot him polishing or vacuuming, he always said: "I'm think'n about it," when asked how the work was progressing. It's a good thing he didn't know about the build-up his promised work was having on them all she thought, reclusive as he is, he may never bring his work in. Suzy and Esther had grown curious when Katherine disclosed the bet she and Gerry had waged, and as it always happens when a little frivolity is let loose, it spread like wildfire. Andre and Gramps had started a pot, five bucks per person for the fun of it, and soon the *sou-chefs*, waiters, the security guards, even Esther, were all betting in how many days it would take to sell, and for the pessimists, how many days over the allotted month just in case it didn't, one winner take all.

"Aw," Esther sighed as she dropped her Abraham Lincoln into the designated coffee can donated from the kitchen, "count me in, I can't be the only party pooper."

"You aren't joining them in this nonsense?" Aunt Martha enquired, not a little surprised to see her usually straight-laced friend waiver from the moral high ground, "Aren't we supposed to be setting the young a good example?"

"Oh come on, live a little," Gramps insisted.

"I'm living quite well, thank you," Aunt Martha retorted.

"Hrumph! Okay, suit yourself, party pooper," he rumbled with a wry smile.

Andre informed Katherine later that day he spied Aunt Martha calling one of the waiters over and slipping something into his hand, which was placed into the can, a bet the mural would sell within the month during the last five days. Katherine couldn't help chuckling when she heard.

At long last, the feverishly awaited delivery arrived: rather than request the gallery pick up his work, Derrick had taken the day off and enlisted the help of two friends dressed in jeans and leather jackets with chains to unload the cargo from an old Chevy pick-up with a Doberman sitting on guard in the back. The delivery looked like a carpet roll, but instead of the usual long tube of wool pile, it was a rolled canvas. The menacing looking mastiff growled when he saw Katherine approach.

"Shut up Slayer, Geeze stupid mutt. Don't worry," Derrick assured her, "he's all bark and no bite, he's a joke, couldn't catch a thief if a prime rib was stuck to his b'hind." Katherine thought it was an exaggeration until she saw the dog cower and back away after the reprimand. Derrick then introduced his companions, "These here are m' pals, Big George and 'Trigger T'." Katherine shook hands. She could plainly see how George got his nickname, but was afraid to speculate on where 'trigger' originated. "I wasn't sure how t'do m' style on yr' artist-type stuff, 'til I found this guy in a real cool art shop," Derrick explained as they brought the delivery into the boiler house. "He didn't have anythin' large enough to work on, but he said I could get canvas by the roll, don't need no pre-stapled stuff ya stick in frames. I didn't know how t'paint on the thing when I unwrapped it all, and my girlfriend said just hang it like a curtain. That gave me an idea, I saw yr' fancy tapestries upstairs, they're just radical bad, real cool. I thought I'd do somethin' like that. So, here y'go. I got the iron rods from 'Trigger T's' scrap yard, that'll b'okay with your walls, won't it? They'll hang alright?"

"Umm, I guess so," Katherine replied, watching them unload the long black metal bars, "modern 'tapestries', that certainly is a novel twist, but … what do you mean by 'they'?"

"Oh," Derrick smiled, "I had two drawn's I wanted to try, couldn't make up m'mind, so I did both. I know ya' said to bring *one*, but ya' can pick what y'like," he suggested, not sure how a double offering would be received.

"Two? That's great. We'll take a look at them," she said, eyeing the contents rolled up tightly around the cardboard tube. "Umm, this is not going to be easy."

"Yeah, they need t' hang, or ya' won't see 'em right," he agreed. Katherine looked around the old boiler place, it had an ironwork gangway circling the upper levels, perhaps they could hang them there. Derrick thoughtfully eyed the old walkway.

"They won't snag on anythin'? The material is not as strong as I woulda liked, not when it's this big," he anxiously warned. He was right, even if they managed to hitch them up, they would have to be taken down and re-hung in the main showroom. All that pulling, folding, rolling and dragging on the delicate paintwork, brush or spray, was not a good idea. The two helpers looked on as the artists tried to figure out the logistics.

"Well, I usually inspect everything before it goes out," Katherine tentatively replied, realizing she might have to make an exception, "just to make sure, there isn't anything objectionable in the subject matter I should know about?"

"Only if ya support apartheid, or have a grudge against street dancers," he replied, a little pushed out of shape that his word would be doubted.

"Oh no, I'm all for civil rights, but I don't know enough about 'street dance'," she admitted.

"I just did a bunch of street dudes doin' the grooves," he tried to explain, "Hip Hop … Bee Bop, old classics from Break Dance, the Moonwalk, ya know, that kinda stuff."

"Why don't we show her?" Big George suggested. Before she knew it, Trigger T and Big George were rapping impromptu while Derrick started up a head spinning and hand standing performance on the concrete floor.

"Well somebody had their breakfast of champions this morning," she laughed after the show, "I didn't know you could do that, Derrick. A man of many talents."

"Thanks," he shrugged, "I'm not as good at it like som' others out there."

"You could have fooled me," she replied, raising an eyebrow. "I certainly feel out of shape just watching you. Well, we'd better see what these paintings are all about, I'm really curious, we'll have to clear two walls though, you don't mind waiting? I'd like you to be here when we place them, just to make sure we've got them hanging correctly."

"Nah, that's fine. If ya' don't mind me suggestin', one'll look good on red, the other on blue, since ya've got such a colourful place an all."

"No problem, how about the inside wall near the stairwell? Since the big facing partition is blue, they'll complement each other."

"That'd be swell," Derrick grinned, "I kinda did them with them two walls in mind."

"Is that so? Okay, I'll go set things in motion," she replied.

"D'ya mind if I show th' guys around?"

"No, go ahead, you don't have to stay back here," Katherine reassured them. She hoped her other clientèle wouldn't be frightened by their 'Hell's Angels' apparel, they were quite friendly really. However, she nearly lost her steady business demeanour when they entered the lobby from the back, Suzy and Esther both leaned over the desk, staring in stunned bewilderment as the three leather-clad homeboys patiently waited for the elevator.

"Who are *they?*" Suzy probed as Katherine approached the desk, "they're not here to extort protection money from you, are they?" Esther offered to contact the security guard upstairs.

"Shh! They're fine. That's Derrick with his friends," Katherine replied, "you'll be pleased to know that they just helped to deliver his mural, or rather, a painted 'tapestry', two of them if you don't mind."

"Well bless my soul, it's about time," Esther noted, "the odds were beginning to include a possible no-show, it's becoming a bookie's haven in the pantry, I'm expecting the Vice Squad to raid us any day now."

Katherine and Suzy began moving the paintings around with the help of the guard, making space on the designated walls while Esther manned the desk in the lobby, taking a quick glance at the security monitors every now and then to see that everything was proceeding smoothly, and to make sure the three ruffians were on their best behaviour. She was surprised to see the three 'hoods' eventually stop their browsing and help the girls move the pictures to their new locations.

"Man, you've got one nice crib here," Big George affirmed.

"Yeah, real smooth," Trigger T added, carefully clutching one of the Professor's paintings.

"Thanks," Katherine smiled, "okay, that's the last one," she declared as the guard took the artwork from Trigger, "time to hang up your masterpieces, Derrick."

The roll and bars were too large for the elevator, so the motley trio brought them up the stairs on their shoulders after which Derrick went to retrieve a duffel bag filled with the remaining equipment, a series of rings and other metallic objects hidden from view. Katherine and Suzy watched as Derrick supervised the unveiling, giving commands to George and Trigger as they rolled the tube along the middle of the large passageway. At first, they couldn't see anything as they unrolled the pictures face down on the floor, but noticed a series of openings like button holes running along the length of the gigantic canvas at measured intervals. Derrick and the guys carefully snapped special brass rings on what Katherine assumed was the top of the first tapestry, after which they inserted one of the black painted rods, the black bar and brass rings proved an elegant combination.

"Okay, let's lift it up," Katherine announced. The guard and Derrick gingerly mounted the two large ladders and hung the picture in place. She couldn't believe the colours, a fantastic rainbow-hued mural of 3D zigzags, waves, abstract shapes and starbursts in the background filled with multi-coloured silhouettes of dancers dressed in the latest street fashions all frozen in time, each positioned in a vigorous pose featuring twirls, handstands, head spins and acrobatic high kicks, and there in the bottom right-hand corner, were the initials 'DS'.

"I *thought* you could be 'D.S.'" Suzy said, "that's amazing! How do you get the paints to blend like that? Looks like an airbrush or something."

"Sometimes I use an airbrush, but ya take the cans like this," he tried to show her, using imaginary canisters, "ya' hold the spray ends close together, and kinda fire them like that, I'd have to show ya sometime though."

"What are the holes in the bottom for?" Katherine asked, nodding to the series of openings along the border of the canvas.

"Oh, I'm not done yet. Give us a sec." Derrick rummaged in the bag and brought out a handfuls of medium-sized S-shaped hooks painted black, which he thread through the gaps. The final touch, a row of polished brass plumb-weights in the shape of an antique toy top or pointed teardrops was hung along the edge.

"When I first hung it up, it looked too, wussy or somthin', just didn't sit straight. So my girlfriend suggested curtain weights to keep it pulled and level, but when I saw these in a hardware store, I had to try 'em out."

"It works perfectly," Katherine agreed, "practical but very artistic, very unique accessories actually. I like the effect, they compliment your brass rings and the dark metal rail."

"Excuse my interruption, but the other tapestry should be put up soon, or it might get trampled on," Suzy noted, watching a group of browsers exit the elevator and look in their direction, eventually wending their way over to see what was happening.

"Right," Derrick replied, quickly jumping into action, snapping on the brass rings and motioning for George and Trigger to get the bar. Katherine was impressed: Derrick had painted an electrifying montage featuring Martin Luther King Junior and Nelsen Mandela on an epic scale surrounded by famous scenes and images related to the struggle for civil rights and the end of segregation, all in a vibrant 'pop-art' style. The iron rail and brass pendant weights just added the finishing touches to the slightly rippled material. The browsers could be heard 'ohhing' and 'awing' off to the side. "Jiminy," Suzy exclaimed, "that's *unbelievable*."

"Is it alright then?" Derrick asked.

"Are you kidding? This is fantastic," Katherine beamed as they stood back to admire the mammoth productions.

"Do you think they'll make somethin' like yr' other pictures here?" Derrick wanted to know.

"It's hard to put a price on them. What did you have in mind? It's your work, I just take the commission for showing it." Katherine explained.

"Gosh, I dunno, about a grand or two maybe, it's not brushwork, nothin' 'art school' ya know," he shrugged.

"Goodness, that's not enough," she *tsked*, shaking her head, "considering their size, plus the creative energy you put into them, not to mention the materials. It couldn't have been easy trying to get the proportions right. So what if they're not 'art school'? Listen, the French painter Lautrec became famous for his posters of dancers, they were so popular people would rip them off the walls and lampposts of Paris in the middle of the night.   Come on, lunch is on me, we have business to discuss."

"We're not really in the right threads for a fancy restaurant," Trigger pointed out.

"You look fine to me, Trigger. Don't worry, as you can see, today is my work day too, so I'm not exactly in my Sunday best at the moment," she assured them, holding out a paint-splattered sleeve, "we can take a table near the back. No one will notice."

While Suzy rejoined Esther at the main desk, Katherine, Derrick and the gang settled into one of the more inconspicuous booths. Derrick didn't mind her talking shop in front of the others, that was fine by him, and wondered if she could suggest a price. In her opinion, they were definitely worth ten thousand each, there were pieces in other galleries selling for far more, in fact, she would go so far as to list his tapestry-murals at fifteen thousand, if she was certain of the demand for them. Derrick nearly choked on an intake of beer while Trigger's jaw dropped.

"Geeze, D.S., and there you were, spraying your stuff on walls all this time, and all for free'," Big George jovially remarked, giving him a big slap on the shoulder, "no more polish'n floors for you, m'man"

"I gotta sell 'em first," he observed, still clearing his throat from rogue bubbles, "starting at ten grand a pop sounds good to me."

"If they sell, I'll certainly have you bring in more artwork, we can try for fifteen then, see how it goes," she added.

"No argument there, fine b' me."

"Great. Now about your biography," she continued, pulling her trusty notebook out of her pocket.

"Why d'ya need that?" he asked, not looking too happy with this turn of events.

"For the customers of course, they like to know a little about the artists on display. Don't you want a little publicity? Since we now rotate paintings rather than show entire collections at once, it's easier to hand people leaflets about our artists rather than try and keep a current collector's catalogue in print. That reminds me, I have to call Stephie to take some pictures for our records.”

"If I’da known that was necessary, I wouldna agreed to bring in anythin’,” he confessed gloomily, shuffling the food on his plate with his fork.

"Er ... well, it’s not *necessary*. You don’t have to give a bio if you don’t want to,” she replied a little puzzled, closing her notebook, “you can remain anonymous, it just might make your work all the more mysterious, come to think of it.”

"If ya don’t mind, I don’t want anyone to find out ya know me ... or that anyone here knows me ...” he continued, searching for the right words.

"I get it, it’s the day job, right? Don’t worry, your secret is safe with us, we won’t tell a soul, I’ll make everyone sign a confidentiality agreement if I have to.”

"That’s one of them court orders that make people keep their lips buttoned, right?” Trigger enquired.

"Oh yeah, I heard about them,” Big George added, “a real ‘no squealer’ decree, all legal like.”

"Something like that,” she smiled, “magicians make their assistants sign them so they don’t spill the beans about their stage secrets. They can get into a lot of trouble if they do, court cases, hefty fines, you name it.”

Derrick still looked a little uncomfortable.

"I trust ya, I don’t need no court order or anythin’ that fancy, it’s just that I wanta stay away from the law for now. I suppose I should tell ya, wouldn’t be right not ta. It’s not really the job, though it wouldn’t be a bad thing if that wasn’t spread around either ... .”

Katherine felt her conscience twitch as she thought about the pot overflowing with fives in the kitchen.

"I’m afraid everyone here knows about your day job, but that’s about it really. I’ll make sure it won’t spill over into our clientèle,” she assured him. “What’s troubling you? Whatever it is, it won’t go beyond this table.”

"Straight out, I got mixed up in some really nasty business a while back, gang stuff, can’t stand it now, but that’s all I knew at the time. It was like the family I didn’t have grow’n up, with parents always gone, or fightn’ when they did come home, the homies made me feel like I belonged somewhere. We stuck up for each other, bashed a few bad-mouthers if they didn’t show us no respect, that sort of thing. Some days it was real cool, hang’n around, cruisin’ our streets, getting high when selling our stuff, sure there were the few stints in jail, it wasn’t pretty, but noth’n major, you were the ‘Man’ if you took your time. All was gold chains and smooth riding until one night when one of the guys, Snake Jake I think it was, just rapped out this thing that stuck in m' head, don't know where he got it, but can't forget it, burned in m' mind like a brand'n iron."

"Can you repeat it?" Katherine asked, slightly awed by the grisly details of a side of life she had never seen up close, stunned by this disturbing revelation.

"Oh sure. It went like this," he replied, breaking out into a rapping rhythm, quietly beating the edge of the table using his fingertips as makeshift drumsticks, '*We real cool, we left school, we lurk late, we strike straight, we sing sin, we thin gin, we jazz June … we die soon.*' Ain't that the truth," he concluded flatly, ceasing his drumming.

"Sure is, man," Trigger agreed.

"Then it stuck real deep when we had the bad times, I mean when it used to get outta hand like when turf wars would break out, I never did no shootin' but saw quite a bit of killin'. One day it just hit me like a silver river from an AK47…if I stayed with them, I'd end up like some of my friends, dead before they had a chance, shot down in some alleyway or club. I'd been seen hang'n with the guys who pulled the guns, so I was just as good a target as any when the paybacks came due."

"So you left them," Katherine concluded, seeing where the story was leading.

"Sure did, wasn't easy though, Big George and Trigger here helped me get cleaned up, find a safe job way across town and a new place to live, couldn't stay in the old hood no more, too dangerous. It ain't easy, but I feel a lot better, an' then I met Sheila, so things are look'n good".

"Uh huh, she's the best thing that happened ta ya.," George agreed before turning to Katherine, "she don't put up with no … ."

"Mind yr' trap, remember what I told ya," Derrick muttered.

"I … er … I was gonna say 'garbage', she don't take any a' that stuff from ya, that's for sure." George continued.

"Yeah," Derrick smiled, "ain't that the truth, but geeze, now my work is up in a *gallery?* I never saw that com'n. … Ya gonna kick me out now, after hearing all of that, I s'ppose," he finished, shuffling his food again. Katherine thought for a moment before looking him square in the eyes.

"Just when you're trying to turn a new leaf? Now that wouldn't be playing fair, would it?   You deserve a break just like everyone else," Katherine replied.

"Really? Ya mean it? Thanks, that sure means a lot, more than ya know," he nodded, brightening up for a moment before growing serious again, "it's just, I don't want anythin' about me spread'n around, I have to keep low, I mean *real* low. It's not a cool thing to break with your home boys," he tried to explain, "ya become a Judas, so no protection from a lotta yr' old mates, in fact, they may want to pop ya off, just n' case ya turn snitch, and the other gangs won't never forget who ya belonged to anyway, so it's just better if I can disappear. Good thing is, they won't find me in a place like this," he grinned.

"What about your initials? DS? Aren't you afraid someone might recognise your art?" Katherine wondered.

"Nah, it's all right, I used to be called 'Dance Dog', so I used to sign w'that, my real letters are new on the street, so they won't figure 'em out, I'm pretty sure. And I don't do none of the gang code no more, my stuff is clean all out, no hidden trouble or 'reverse recordin' crud, nothin' that ties me to the old stuff, I'm playing it cool."

"What do you mean by 'reverse recordings'?"

"Ya know when people say ya can hear weird stuff like 'Lennon's not dead' when you play old vinyls backwards? The gangs have their own code stashed in the graff that no one but them can see. I'll show ya, can I have a bit a'paper?"

"Sure," Katherine replied, tearing a few sheets from her book and slipping the pencil out of the spiral binding. Oh, what the heck, she *was* morbidly curious. Within a few minutes with a variety of squiggles, letters, numbers, ciphers and explanations of the colour codes, she was allowed to peer through the dark veil of the street world and its clandestine activities. One quick design displayed something as simple as where boundaries to their home turf lay to ward off other gangs, another showed when a party was happening at such-and-such a time and place, a letter or two could warn that the cops were patrolling an area more often than usual. Then there were other signs that were more disturbing, where the best 'snow' could be had, where and when pick-ups and cash drop-offs were to take place, and more sinister yet, when war or revenge had been declared on another gang. These symbols could include anything to announcements of who the next target might be, and if they were 'Man' enough, who actually killed who, in other words, trophy signs. One picture was worth a thousand words, or a thousand kilograms of pure 'smack', even a thousand rounds of ammo let loose during a drive-by assault. Just looking at the smattering of graffiti symbols sketched on those few pages denoting turf boundaries and ghetto conquests brought the *cliché* 'urban jungle' into a whole new dimension.

Katherine couldn't help but feel apprehensive, like some wide-eyed newborn gazelle sitting in the midst of these once-upon-a-time street corner cheetahs, and yet, she knew she had nothing to fear. When she thought about it, wild animals did not attack unless they had reason, usually for food or self-defence, even territory patrols were only to secure a safe 'patch' to ensure their survival, it couldn't be that much different for humans. It was rare that anyone became a true cold-blooded killer, and she could sense that these guys weren't *born* bad, just born into bad circumstances. It was easy to be a conscientious citizen if you were raised in a garden of roses, it was a different matter to be brought into the bleak wilderness of deprivation blasted by the pitiless tempests of emotional trauma. Some people have to do whatever it takes to survive, and as Derrick admitted, it was the only life he knew. The important thing was, he *didn't want* to live that lifestyle anymore. Unlike the animals caged in their own natures and consequently, locked in the brutal and inescapable cycle of predator and prey, he *knew* he had options, that there were *choices* to be made, and with a little will power, okay, a *lot* of will power, he could amend his life. He made a break from his old existence, and it looked like he was making a serious effort to maintain the new. Mulling this over, she thought about the new allegorical painting she was planning and flipped her notebook to a fresh page.

"You know, what you escaped from sounds pretty serious," she observed.

"You bet," Derrick agreed.

"Well, I was wondering if you guys could help me out with an idea I have for a new painting, considering what you experienced, if it's not too personal."

"Umm… er, all right," Big G hummed.

"Geeze, you want *us* to help with *your* fancy art?"

"Sure."

Katherine described her new allegorical concepts and the philosophical discussion she was planning to superimpose on to her pictures.

"Sounds like preachn' to me, yr' askin' the wrong guys for help," Trigger noted with amusement.

"It's not a sermon, I'm presenting *discussions*," she corrected, trying not to chuckle, "arguments to try and get to the bottom of things, or at least unveil different points of view."

"Okay, I'm game," Derrick replied.

"Right, my question, does crime actually pay?"

"Sure it does, depends on what you're inta," Big George replied. Derrick and Trigger broke into a hearty laugh.

"I think she wants to know if it's *righteous*, ya know what I'm sayin'? If there's *virtue* in it," Derrick replied between chortles, "brain storm'n stuff, like being a gang banger doesn't 'pay' in the end."

"That's okay," Katherine smiled, "you know, he's made a good point, a counterargument to the old saying. We have to find out which is true, or perhaps which is better than the other."

"Shoot miss, we all know what's *better*," Trigger affirmed, "but try livin' it, that's what hits ya in the gut when you've got your old man or old lady in jail and family countin' on ya, an bills to pay. Some just can't keep do'n the right thing all the time."

"Yeah, it's tough not ta slide," Big G agreed.

"Ya know how much one of my old gang suppliers made?" Derrick asked her. Katherine assumed he was talking drugs, and shook her head. "A good fifteen million a year at least, just grown' or smugglin' dope n' stuff. I'd like to see *him* live off a vacuum cleaner, bussing tables or fry'n fries."

Derrick had struck upon a grim reality; although she had never known the hardships of a paycheque to paycheque existence, she could imagine how tough it must be to stomach the minimum wage mundane after living the life of the rich and infamous.

"I always wondered, if guys like that could figure out all the intricacies of smuggling and running such a difficult operation, why can't they just use their brain power to do something honest? My family comes from a long line of 'drug pushers', and we're legitimate." The guys chuckled.

"Yeah, I s'ppose so, but then, *you* got *connections*," Trigger replied, "old money, family history an' all of that. When ya grow up on the wrong side of the tracks, there ain't much goin' for us, it's all 'bout who ya know."

"Yeah, help don't come like greased lightnin' to the likes of *us*," Trigger admitted, "even if I *liked* school, we can't go to no fancy college, get the degrees or the know-how to go legit' big time like that, an' not everyone gets one of them scholarships."

"That's tough, I admit, but why not just 'surrender the empire' after you made your millions? Of course, I'd wouldn't want another 'pot lord' taking over the role as your local neighbourhood destroyer, but you could make your fortune and then skip," she argued, "why do they keep doing it?"

"Oh, some just like the action, get'n high from beatn' the system, dodge'n the danger, keep'n ahead of the cops an' outguess'n the Feds," Derrick explained, "it's like a drug too, dough's no longer the thing really."

"Gosh, how do they justify starting the whole thing then? How can they sleep at night knowing they're literally peddling chemical death?" They may have wandered from her original topic, but she found this strain of thought interesting nevertheless.

"It's easy ta make it sound right," Derrick admitted, "I should know. Look, they don't tie people up and shove it down their throats or grab 'em and stick 'em with needles to get the hunger go'n. People know they could get hooked if they try it, so basically it's up to them. '*They don't want it, they don't buy it, but if they do, we just supply it*,' that's the think'n."

"When it's put like that, it's no different than a bar selling booze," Big G continued, "ya know ya can get wasted on it, beat up the wife and shout murder at the kids when ya come home, or get yourself smashed in a car wreck, but it's up to each Joe Schmo in the end, the bartender ain't gonna lose much sleep over what the customers do, he can try an' get 'em to go home before they get sloshed, grab the keys to their wheels, but it ain't gonna to do any good in the end, it's only a matter of time before Schmo gets mowed, you know what I'm say'n?"

"I get it, but at least alcohol is a *controlled* substance," Katherine mused, "the damage is contained to a point. Is there any solution to the problem I wonder?"

"They could try n' make it legit', like booze," Derrick shrugged.

"Way ta go man! At least *crime* wouldn't be pay'n", Trigger laughed.

"Whoa, that's going a little *too* far," Katherine observed, "we'd have a nation of tweakers."

"I don't mean the hard stuff, but make grass okay," he continued, "just think about it: when someone tells ya ya can't have it, almost everyone wants ta try it at least once, especially when the law says it's a no go. People don't like be'n told what to do, so I reckon if they thought they could get some whenever they want ..."

"It wouldn't be as appealing," she finished.

"Yeah. What causes a lotta the big gangsta wars is control of the shippin' operations, the smuggling routes, holdin' on to their corner where it's sold. The danger of get'n caught spikes the prices too, so that's how the millions add up. If it was all legit', the same kinda money wouldna be there, you'd have legit' competition, prices fall, and so on. Turf wars would end if legit' shops could open, ya can put in those controls so kids can't get it, and everybody's swing'n."

"I don't know if I agree with you, but it's something to think about," Katherine replied, "still, kids will get into trouble, especially if drugs are made affordable, minors are able to get their hands on liquor despite the controls," she added.

"Yeah, but the problem wouldn't be as bad as it is now," Derrick pointed out, "people rob in order to pay the high prices, at least if the soft stuff was legit', you'd have a lotta crime go away.   Look what happened during them Prohibition days, gave them old gangstas their patch. All I'm say'n is the lawmakers could give it a try, if it don't work, they can change the laws again."

"I don't know, you're asking them to initiate one big controversial experiment," Katherine said, shaking her head.

"Look, the dope ain't go'n away, it's here to stay, they gotta deal with it somehow. Things are getting' pretty raw out there as it is, I reckon if they don't do somethin' soon, we'll have real massacres in the streets, in the grow'n fields, in the smuggling lanes, real Al Capone military style, with AK47s, I see it com'n, I tell ya."

"Gosh, I don't know what to say to that," Katherine admitted, "talk about the breakdown of society." Was it really getting to the point that the only choice left was to choose a lesser evil over a greater one? If she had her way, she would not have evil at all. "Well, it's a good thing you turned your back on all of that."

"Yeah," Derrick nodded, "it really *don't* pay in the end, ya never know when some home boy is gonna pop ya off, and even if noth'n bad like that happens, ya know ya gotta pay *sometime*. I've never yet seen anythin' without a price. I don't know what's gonna happen on th' 'other side' when we get there, if ya know what I'm say'n, me, I don't wanna take no chances with the Big Boss no more. Can't hurt ta believe 'n the 'other side' and do the right thing by it, 'cause if there *is* somethin' there, then yr' all right, and if there *is* nothin' there after that, then it's no loss really, ya did yr best while ya was here to make things run smooth."

"That's an interesting way of putting it," Katherine admitted, "still the temptation is always there to slide down the slippery slope like you said."

"Yeah, it's hard at times, but I got me another good reason to keep go'n the right road," Derrick disclosed, "me and Sheila got a little'un on the way, and I wanna do the right thing, I don't want no kid of mine get stuck in what I got stuck in. If it was jus'm'self, I wouldn't be as mindful, but havin' a kid sure changes how ya see things, ya've got someone else to look out for."

"Well congratulations. When is the baby due?"

"Feb'rary sometime," Derrick announced.

"You just may have a Valentine's Day surprise," Katherine smiled.

"That'd be swell, if it happens," he grinned.

"Listen guys, I hate to run off," she said, noticing the time, "I could sit and chat with you all day, but I've got to let everyone else off for lunch. I hope you enjoyed your meal."

"Oh yeah, some grub you got here, real fine," Big George complimented.

"Yeah, thanks miss, if yr wheels ever needs a new coat or somethin', just let us know, we'll fix it for ya," Trigger added.

"Um, thanks, I'll keep that in mind."

As timing would have it, Gramps entered with Jasper through the service hallway just as the three reformed homies made their way back to the old Chevy. They gave him a polite nod as they continued out the door.

"Hrumph Katie, looks like you had a tough crowd this morning," he commented, leaning on his stick, "everything all right?"

"Yeah sure," she laughed, "that 'tough crowd' was Derrick and a few of his friends, you'll be pleased to know they came to make a very important delivery. Go on up and take a look before you have your lunch, the new pieces are right next to the stairs, you can't miss them."

"'Pieces'? Can't wait to see what *that's* all about, but before I do, did you have that word with Andre yet?" he enquired in a low voice, leaning over the desk counter.

"I did, Gramps. No sob stories or break-ups," she replied.

"Hmm, I hope he's not pulling the old 'cut back' shell and pea game."

"The what?"

"The 'now you see it, now you don't' switch-a-roo, waiting for the place to get popular, then cutting corners and skimping the food once the place has regulars," he reflected, "that won't be good for his business, yours either." Somehow, she couldn't let on that he was the only one playing 'shell-and-pea' at *Chez Garneau.*

"Oh Gramps, how can you suspect the poor man of doing such a thing?" she *tsked,* shaking her head, "Maybe you're just getting ... *too* used to his food."

"How so?"

"Oh, you know ... when you get to like something and eat it everyday, it doesn't quite taste the same, not like when you had it for the first time. You're getting ... browned off, yeah, that's it ... an illusion of the taste buds," she concluded, hoping he wouldn't tumble to the culinary conspiracy.

"I never thought about it like that," he noted, lowering an eyebrow in contemplation while he rubbed his chin, "but you could have something there. I guess I'll try a different dish today, right after I take a look at what you've got upstairs that is," he finished, heading for the elevator. *Whew,* that will keep us safe for a while, she thought. That reminds me, time to give Gerry a call. As it turned out, he was away at a business meeting in Istanbul and wouldn't be back until the following Monday. The secretary asked if she would like to leave him a message.

"Yes please, could you tell Mr. Reinold when he returns that the tattoo parlour is now open and ready for inspection at his convenience."

ೞ❀ೲ

Katherine was downright chuffed that her confidence in Derrick was not misplaced, his work was quite astounding, and the fact he brought in two pieces only fuelled the anticipation. Gramps quickly raised the stakes another five bucks, placing odds that both murals would go within the allotted month, and the bets were on. However, Katherine soon realized the next day things may not swing in her direction, not that the artwork was lacking, but that it had been delivered at an unfortunate time of year, Thanksgiving week. Fewer people were stopping by the gallery than before, everyone was too preoccupied making arrangements for the traditional family get-together to consider investing in art, booking flights to see loved ones far across the country or busily preparing their feasts at home. Then of course, Katherine decided after a few six day work-weeks, a decent break was required, so the gallery would be closed for the full four days on top of it, not just Sunday, now her business week was sliced down the middle. Never mind, she had until Christmas week to win her wager.

In any case, it was good to take a few consecutive days off, not having to get up so early for the long morning commute, and then, there was the family 'shin-dig' as Gramps called it. This year it was Uncle Tim and Aunt Barbara's turn to host the dinner. As usual, Aunt Martha was included, and Katherine was finding it difficult to practise her new resolution of being patient when she continued to chide her during dessert about her generosity in giving everyone at the gallery a full four day holiday. Hearing Aunt Martha jabber on about all the 'wrong' decisions she was making didn't help boost her confidence when her decisions were on 'the wire' as Gerry had phrased it.

"Why, the day after Thanksgiving is the first important shopping day before Christmas! You'll go broke if you continue to run your place like that, you're sending your potential customers to the competition don't you know, and chances are, they won't come back."

"Thanks for reminding me."

When would Aunt Martha learn that being tactful meant giving your point of view without stabbing people with it? Somehow, Katherine didn't think she had that much competition when it came to the art she had on display, there was no comparison with the minimalist mush sold elsewhere and her own elegant offerings, and besides, if people really wanted their wares, they would wait, the gallery wasn't going anywhere. Finally, the coffee was served, and while the 'elders' went to enjoy their aromatic Arabian wine in the sitting room, the 'young ones' went into the den, the guys huddling together to talk sports, cars and computers, leaving Katherine and Stephanie to discuss the creative spheres.

"Pay no attention to Aunt M., we all know the gallery is doing great. You know she just wants to see the murals sell as much as you do."

"Yeah, I know. Anyway, how's the new studio coming?" Katherine enquired.

"It's not," Stephie laughed, "there won't be much to do with the space really, not like all the work with your place, so I'm taking it easy, just waiting until I get my photography credentials. Your commissions are keeping me busy enough as it is."

"Sorry," Katherine sheepishly smiled, "at least you're getting some publicity already. I was just asking because quite a few of my clients like your pictures in the first catalogue and brochures, in fact, I had enquiries on Wednesday about hiring you to do some photo shoots. I took down their information if you're interested."

"Geeze, really? That's great! I do hope it's someone connected with *Vogue*, I'd love to break into one of the fashion magazines. By the way, has 'Mystery Man' been in to see the new wonders yet?"

"No, he's in Istanbul on business, he won't be back until Monday."

"That's a hard rap, who plans an important meeting on Thanksgiving weekend?"

"I don't know, of course, they don't celebrate Thanksgiving over there, he probably got tied up with some important Middle-Eastern big-wig who insisted on seeing him. It's none of my business really."

"Never mind, he'll be back. I wish I could be there to see his reaction, even *I* was worried about you displaying pop art sight-unseen like that, but I'm impressed. How's the 'sports bar' going?"

"Oh don't ask, it's getting out of hand," Katherine laughed, "someone is going to go home with a coffee can full of cash, even Aunt Martha added another five bucks. The problem is, I don't know what to dare Gerry when I win."

"*If* you win," Stephie roguishly added, "don't worry, I'm sure you will. I have a feeling the civil rights mural will go first, 'going political' is always a seller in these kinds of things. Hmm, what to dare him … ."

"I promised nothing dangerous or too kooky that a blackmailer would like to have photos of," Katherine interjected.

"Shoot, I guess making him climb the Empire State Building in a gorilla suit is out."

"You can say that again," Katherine noted, rolling her eyes to heaven, "that would really look good on the front cover of the papers. I can just see the headlines, *Heir to Reinold Enterprises Makes an Ape of Himself*."

"You could take it easy and ask for a nice dinner out somewhere."

"That's not really a 'dare' dare … ."

"Does it have to be? Now, if it were *me*, a nice romantic weekend for two wouldn't go amiss."

"Stephie! What an idea! I hardly know the guy! I hope you don't fall into that loop of one-night stands, that's a loser's game."

"Oh, lighten up Kathy, I'm just kidding around. Thing is, I wonder what he has planned for *you*, that's what I'd like to know."

Katherine thought about it all that weekend. What was *he* planning when she was having a difficult time thinking up some harebrained challenge? Well, she didn't have to come up with anything just yet, she could wait and see how the month panned out.

At first, she was very optimistic, judging from people's reactions on the security monitors, the murals were a hit, it was just … they weren't selling, and the days were slipping by. Oh well, she was waiting for the pot to boil, that's all. Obviously, the anxious excitement was making her too watchful. Calm down, think about your own paintings, you have some work ahead of you, art usually doesn't sell fast anyway, she continued to remind herself. Of course, the 'run' up to Christmas was not helping, there was so much to do and decorating to arrange, time to make the place look festive. Once again, she was faced with a big decision, live or plastic? Katherine was not enthusiastic with the idea of setting up a *live* tree in the lobby, but people expected the best when it came to the artistic side of life.

"Oh Kathy, don't be such a tree-hugger this time, it's simply gorgeous," Suzy said as she watched the team from the professional decorating firm hang the glittering red and gold ornaments on the spiky green boughs.

"I'm sorry, I love the smell of the fresh pine, but I could never understand this whole live tree business," she replied, "how would you like someone to saw you off at the ankles, stick you in a bucket of sand or a metallic stand, cover you in tinsel and say 'how lovely you look' when you're slowly shrivelling up?"

"Look who's a 'bah, humbug'," Esther replied with a smile.

"You're hopeless!" Suzy added, putting her hand on her hip and shaking her head.

"Oh, it's all *nice*, just bizarre. Holidays and how we celebrate them is just one of those 'things' with me, they always seems to bring out the weird quirks in everyone. Thanksgiving is one if not the only sane holiday we have, with everything else, we seem to follow the strangest customs just because it's the time-honoured thing to do."

"I guess that rules out hanging up some mistletoe," Esther noted with a comical nod.

"See what I'm saying?" Katherine laughed. "Kissing a complete stranger simply because you stand under a parasitic plant that grows on oak trees."

"Well, with the pine trees, I don't think plastic is the answer anyway," Suzy reflected, "who knows how much chemical goop gets poured back into the atmosphere when they make one of those? That has to be a lot worse then replenishing the Christmas tree forests, they just don't cut them and leave the land bare, it's a real farming business."

"True … actually, I didn't think of that before," Katherine noted.

Standing admiring the tree, they never noticed Charlie enter the side door.

"Good day ladies, beautiful tree you have there," he declared.

"Hi Charlie, long time no see. Where have you been?" Katherine greeted.

"In court," he smiled. "Where else? Haven't had much time to drop by, thought I'd make a break during a long recess and have lunch here today."

"Great," Suzy replied, "Andre's been trying a few new dishes, he wants us to taste them all before he adds them to the menu."

"And he didn't ask Mr. G.W. to volunteer his services?" Charlie noted in amusement, "your Gramps certainly knows his 'vitals', or so he says."

"Well, let's just say he's no longer in a position to give an accurate opinion on Andre's cuisine. I'll explain later," she chuckled as she reached over the desk for the telephone, "let me answer this first." It turned out Mrs. Hunt was on the line and wanted to hear if any other pieces had arrived. Oh no, this could take awhile, she liked to 'bend her ear' during these friendly telephone chats. Katherine decided to put Mrs. Hunt on hold and resume her call in the office where she could settle in for a protracted 'description' session, Mrs. Hunt liked it when she described vivid word 'paintings' of the new items recently delivered those occasions she decided not to drop by and see for herself.

"Yes, I'm back Mrs. Hunt, yes, we have a new *batik* … no … another river scene, yes…turquoise blue water flowing in the foreground with jade and grass green forests behind, … yes, a jungle scene, plenty of strange vines, the sky can be seen with an unusual shade of royal blue and purple tinged through the wax ripple-work….shots of gold too, perhaps an abstract interpretation of lightning at sunset, it's certainly different … ."

After a few minutes Mrs Hunt moved on to things she had done that week and the people she met, society butterflies, many of whom Katherine had not met and had no idea who they were. Inevitably, her mind began to wander, every now and then she twisted her fingers in the phone wire, doodled waves, endless circles and curly-q's on a piece of paper, or, stared at the browsing visitors on the security monitors in an absent minded fashion, letting the video images and calm 'elevator music' wash over her, putting her into an almost hypnotic state as Mrs. Hunt continued on.

"Yes…Mrs. Hunt, uh huh … oh, you don't say? Really?"

In her lackadaisical condition, she wasn't paying too much attention to the people on the screens, they all usually did the same thing, slowly saunter through the walkways, look at the next picture in their path, advance to see the details or read the title cards, back up a bit to see the painting in its entirety, make a few comments to the person or persons who might be with them, and then leisurely stroll along. Watching this predictable slow flow of humanity did nothing to help keep her alert. However, there was one visitor that seemed to stand out from all the rest, jaunting at a slightly quicker pace, weaving past other browsers who were not moving at the same speed as he, stopping resolutely to look at one of the *batiks* or paintings before moving on. This fellow seemed to be alone, she could see no other person with him. Hmm, new customer? Her alertness was raised a notch. She noticed he dived past certain pictures and singled out others, the new ones that had come in as a matter of fact. She watched as he headed up to the museum section, making a speedier tour than on the commercial show floor, he obviously had seen everything already. She tried to remember if she had spotted him before, he *did* look familiar come to think of it. Hmm, tall and blonde, stylish crème trench coat, she couldn't place him, she had seen too many new people in the last few months since she opened for business, she needed more clues. Never mind, nothing worth fussing over, just a regular visitor. She returned to her doodling, keeping one eye on the monitors and an ear on Mrs. Hunt. Nuts, where had she seen him? It bothered her when she couldn't place a face. He went back down to the second floor and, standing in front of Derrick's mural-tapestries, pulled out a black object from his breast pocket, a notebook? Camera? That woke her up a bit. She appreciated the interest, but shoot, they had signs informing everyone that photographs are not allowed. There were always a few who tried to bend the rules a bit, hiding the flash with their hands, hoping they wouldn't be noticed. However, before she ruptured the calm atmosphere and scare everyone to death with a loud public announcement over the sound system, she had better zoom the video in for a closer look and make sure she wasn't mistaken. Instead of raising the unidentified contraption to his eye … he raised it to his lips. That wasn't a camera.

"I'm sorry Mrs. Hunt, I have to go, we have an emergency on the floor, an unwelcome trespasser, yes … all right, we'll see you next week, I'll certainly hold the *batik* for you, okay, bye for now."

Katherine firmly put the handset down, watching the offending trespasser from the screen as he took vocal notes before she resolutely exited the office.

"Something wrong?" Esther enquired, looking over her glasses as she watched Katherine round the main desk and head toward the stairs, no waiting serenely for the elevator today. He had given her the slip before, he would not pull that off again.

"Yes, as a matter of fact, it seems none other than the infamous Robert Horace has come to pay us a second visit."

She felt her temper boil with each step she took. *Battle time, defend my territory, once and for all.* Coming around the handrail, she briskly walked up to the trenchcoated villain of verbosity as he continued to make God-only-knew-what kind of comments about the new murals into his confounded machine.

" … and we now rise to new heights on the pinions of psychedelic and political mayhem with an array of … ah, here comes our latest mogul of the art world now. Good day, Miss Walsingham. Any comments about your new offerings for our inquisitive readership?" he enquired, pointing the recorder towards her face to capture any inspiring remarks.

"No comments," she coolly replied, snatching the machine from his outstretched hand, and in a blink of an eye, sent the contraption flying in an elegant arc over the handrail and down the stairwell. Horace, not losing his boyish smile, turned his head slightly and listened as the recorder went … *thump …thump … thump, clunk, thump, clunkclunk* before finally breaking apart on the hard terrazzo below, a few startled "Ohs!" and gasps followed the unexpected racket. "... Except that I suggest you follow your recorder and head straight out the front door, your presence is not welcome here. Of course, you can send me the bill for your machine," she finished. Unruffled by this icy yet ferocious encounter, he whipped a spare recorder from another pocket, obviously, this wasn't the first time something like this had happened to him.

"Wow," he smiled, "that throw deserves two points, Michael Jordan, move over! Are you sure your real calling is not ladies pro basketball? Now where were we? Ah yes, any comments about the new works?"

"No!" she retorted, making a grab for the backup machine, aggravated that her demonstrative tirade hadn't phased him one bit.

"Whew! Feisty today, all right, no comment," he continued, quickly slipping the recorder back into his pocket with a smile still on his face. "Honestly, I thought you might have cooled off by now."

Geeze, this angel-faced intruder was annoying! He reminded her of someone, of course ... Tom Hulce in *Amadeus*: for his sake, he had better not laugh like him, or he would be the next thing sailing over the handrail.

"I didn't come to cause any trouble, in fact, I wanted to offer a peace-pipe," he disclosed, thoroughly amused by her reaction. By this time Esther, Suzy and Charlie were charging up the stairs, while the security guard on duty exited the elevator.

"Kathy? What happened?" Suzy anxiously enquired.

"Are you all right?" Charlie added, his brows knit into a concerned frown.

"Good thing no one was going up the stairs, or they would have gotten a bad bump on their noggin," Esther added in an alarmed tone.

"Shall I escort this gentleman out?" the guard asked simultaneously.

"Whoa! I just came to talk," Horace added, throwing up his hands, "but I'll go quietly if you want. No need to call the cavalry."

Katherine sighed, mollified by the realization she could have injured someone, the wind was taken out of her sails. Nuts, it wouldn't hurt to hear what he had to say anyway.

"It's all right everyone, you can all go back to what you were doing, the show's over," she reassured them.

"Are you sure?" Charlie asked.

"Yeah, no problem, let me handle this."

"All right, but if you need us, just give a holler," Esther advised before they hesitantly left her alone with the interloper, looking over their shoulders as they went their different ways, either to the elevator or back down the stairs.

"All right, I'm giving you one minute to light that peace-pipe of yours. You better get puffing," she announced, looking at her watch, "time flies."

"Well, that doesn't give us time for lunch."

"Lunch? And what, pray tell, would give you the idea I would ever consider having lunch with *you*?" she smartly replied.

"Other than to enjoy my fine company … ."

"Huh," she huffed sarcastically.

"… to hear the 'Art Attacker' make a rare apology," he continued, "just a little one mind you, for any offensive comments that were printed … ."

"Well, you don't need to take me to lunch to do that. Apology accepted. Now please … ." He didn't let her finish.

"… and also, to hear an atypical and infrequent disclosure of why Horace is so dastardly with his column at times, that is, if you haven't tumbled to it already."

Hmm, this was interesting.

"I suppose that *would* be worth giving up my lunch hour for you," she conceded warily before sighing in resignation. "All right, I've got to hear this. However, I can't be off the floor for long, so if the house restaurant meets with your approval … ."

"By all means," he gallantly accepted before bowing slightly, "ladies first."

As they came close to the desk, Esther plonked a ritzy *Chez Garneau* take-out bag on the counter.

"I believe this belongs to you, young man."

"Ah, are we having lunch to go?" he asked, with that aggravating smile of his.

"More like trash removal," Esther replied in a deadpan tone. He glanced inside the bag.

"Poor old Dictaphone, it's seen better days, that's for sure. Well, thank you for preparing it for burial in style," he said to Esther before continuing into the restaurant with Katherine. Suzy and Charlie watched incredulously as they took a booth near the back. Katherine waited as he read the menu and the waiter took their order.

"Okay, now that we are having it out, and before you make this rare disclosure of yours, let me give you my opinion first. I don't like your column, your writing is deplorable, your reviews are brash, incorrect, and outright scandalous. How you are able to hold onto your job as art critic and continue to defy all concept of human decency the way you do is beyond me. You should be ashamed for all those nasty things you print.”

“I appreciate your honesty, but now we’re getting somewhere,” he smiled, “in fact, this has a lot to do with what I wanted to say. People like controversy, if that makes them indecent, well, I’m not going to go *that* far, but let’s say ‘honest’ is ‘boring’ in the critiquing racket. No one wants to read a tedious column. People want a little excitement injected into their dreary little lives, I just happen to give it to them.”

“So you do it just to entertain. Making sport of people’s hard work and creativity for the amusement of others is just … not ethical,” she retorted.

“Well, who ever said today’s world is ‘ethical’? Besides, people are curious, they want to see what bug flies up Horace’s nose each week and view the artwork or visit the victimised gallery for themselves. It’s quite good for business. In all, looking around here, I don’t see that the Art Hacker’s column has hurt you one iota, now has it? I hear that my reporting of the Sirrac Contest last year secured some interest in your Napoléon painting, plus, you’ve got quite a clientèle building up for your gallery already, in fact, if I’m not mistaken, Mrs. Hunt came to see you since that little piece hit our paper.”

“News gets around fast,” Katherine replied.

“I’ve got my connections,” he grinned.

“Well, I do understand what you are saying, you look like a nice guy, …”

“Why thank you … .”

“I just wish you would tell the truth and not make up such terrible nonsense.”

“Listen, I am sorry you find my style disturbing, but it does work. However, if you noticed, I *do* have a smidgeon of conscience left, I didn’t print that whopper of a one-liner of yours after all, although I was mightily tempted. It’s not often someone has the guts to criticise our bomb-happy government.”

Katherine rubbed her chin: that’s true, he didn’t print her overheated comment.

“I do thank you for that, but *why* didn’t you? It was hot material.”

“Well, it wouldn’t be right because one, you didn’t know who I was, I did crash your little party, and two, there are some things people can’t release into the public domain,” he continued, “it wouldn’t come across right, unfortunately, the other reporters were there that night and heard what you said, so I couldn’t do anything about that. You know, I had no idea how strong your opinions were," he laughed, "it certainly explains your artwork, that's for sure."

"Like my Gramps says, you've got to stand for something, or you'll fall for anything. However, I noticed you gave Andre and his food a good line, why does he get the praise while my gallery received a right snubbing?"

"It's like I said, some things cannot be printed. A gallery can have a controversial review a mile long, it creates buzz, but one negative word about a restaurant, and the joint becomes an overnight flash in the pan—out of business, period. Horace sets out to lambaste art and cultural events, not destroy livelihoods."

"Huh. Considering all you have said," she reflected, "even if your ire makes for a zesty column, you can't be happy writing like that."

"It's just a job," he replied, "I simply put my mask on everyday and assume a new role, the actor's cloak and garb gets left behind when I'm off the clock. I'll let you in on a little secret," he said, lowering his voice, "few people know this, but you look like an honest lady, so I'm placing my confidence in you not to let the cat out of the bag … my name is *not* Robert Horace."

"Really?"

"Yes, let me finally introduce myself, I'm Christopher Smith. I *think* you can appreciate the reason for the name change."

"Ah, a stirring column must have an equally intriguing name."

"Yes, 'Robert Horace' has a good, gritty ring to it, don't you think?"

"I guess so," she reflected, it certainly fooled her, she always pictured the Art Hacker as some nasty irritable geezer. "If you don't mind me asking, how did you come up with it?"

"Oh, the first part was easy. I had a crotchety grand uncle named Robert who never had a good word to say about anything. If anyone could teach you how to see the dismal and sarcastic side of life, it was him. Everyone called him 'Old Misery', I think he made it a sport to find a smudge of tarnish in every silver cloud. Now, the last part of my new moniker was tough until I researched the names of famous satirists and 'Horace' popped up, the name seemed to fit, so that's how 'Horace the Horrible' came to be. At least Uncle Robert's foul moods have been put to good use, I'm now moaning and groaning my way to the bank."

"That may be, alter ego and all, but if it were me, I don't think I could keep it up, especially if that's not what I truly think about the work I'm criticising."

"You'd be amazed at the stuff you're capable of doing when you have to," he noted, "Horace the Hacker does pay my bills, and at least I live off stirring up some controversy, not harping upon people's tragedies, we have enough reporters in the office doing that. With me, the paper gets its readers, the galleries get publicity that works, and I get a nice big pay check at the end of the week, everybody is happy, well, almost. While they recognise the benefits of bad publicity, many gallery managers still bear a few grudges, but at least it's *Horace*, they're mad at, not Christopher Smith. Having an alter ego is not such a bad thing, it helps keep you sane."

"I suppose when you look at it that way," she reflected, "everyone has to earn a living. Anyway I do want to thank you for not mentioning my father's heart condition in your last review, but like you said, the other reporters were there ... ."

"Yeah, it was a bum rap, but like I said, I try not to harp on other people's tragedies, I've got enough of my own, so I wouldn't like it myself."

"The Golden Rule, huh?" she smiled.

"Something along those lines."

"Still, even with the publicity and all that, you wouldn't like someone to write such things about you, would you? Why not write how you feel? Do you like *any* of the artworks you review?"

"Oh sure, but like I said, 'boring' doesn't pay. The boss likes controversy too." Smith then thought for a moment, before continuing. "I must admit you're right, devising acidic fulminations to the terror of the artistic community is not the most principled of careers. In fact, if my career plans went the way I wanted, Horace would never have seen the light of day. I don't know why I'm telling you this, we've all got our hard knocks to face in life, but now that we are heading in this direction, and since you know *how* Horace came to be, I think I should also tell you *why* ... ."

"Well, you don't have to tell me, if you don't want to."

"No, it's okay. It's not a long story anyway, not that I want sympathy mind you, but just so you know. My parents were killed in a car accident when I was ten, so my grandmother brought me up, she stood by me through all the tough times, you name it. She didn't mind that I choose art for a career, she was very supportive despite all the *clichés* about starving artists."

"You studied art?"

"Sure did, anyway, I couldn't go for the MA like I had planned. You see, Grandma was diagnosed with Alzheimer's during my senior year of high school."

"Gosh, that's terrible," Katherine replied.

"Well, she went downhill pretty fast those few years afterwards, her memory fading in and out at longer intervals. The hardest part was when she could not recognise me most of the time, those periods became more frequent until finally, it became obvious they were here to stay. It's like a living death, the person you knew is no longer there, you mourn for them, and yet, the shell continues to live and breathe. You hope for some glimmer of life, like some miraculous resurrection, but it never happens … the eyes just look at you as if you are some alien from another planet when you try to remind them who you are. I wouldn't wish this on my worst enemy. Anyway, I was not about to send Grandma to an institution, I was bound and determined that she would stay in her own home, so that meant getting private help, which I couldn't afford if I extended my student loans and went on for the MA. Something had to go, and I still had the rest of my loans to pay off …"

"So you had to cut college short, that had to be tough," Katherine reflected.

"I won't lie and say it is easy, but Grandma is certainly worth it, I owe her a lot. Anyway, I needed to get a career started … and fast. My art was out too, couldn't wait for that to take off, building up a collection, hoping to be shown in a gallery one day, well, you know the situation, I don't need to tell *you* that, but what to *do*, that was the question. Art criticism was the next best option, I had the BA after all, so I landed my first job as a freelance art reporter, used my own name, did everything above board, all polite and positive pieces, but they didn't get very far, a few got printed, but I knew that wouldn't work for long, not with the bills I got landed with. Anyone can write glowing comments, there's nothing original about it, nothing catchy."

"Hmm, like you said, 'tedium' will not sell," Katherine nodded.

"Exactly, I had to change persona, become a real first class horse's behind … pardon me, you know what I mean. So there you have it, the low-down, 'indaspicable', no good, flea-bitten varmint was hatched on a night of heavy brain-storming induced by stress, ratcheted into high gear by a looming deadline and fuelled by an obscene amount of caffeine, plus a crate full of Ding Dongs."

"That explains a lot," she laughed. She knew what it was like to pull a few 'all-nighters' when exam pressure wouldn't let her sleep, somehow, that just didn't compare with his experience.

"My first articles got me a full-time job, the readership soared for the art section of the paper and a nice raise came my way, then I got promoted to supervisor of the Art and Cultural section, so there must be something in the saying that 'nice guys finish last'," he concluded.

"Perhaps in this instance, but not in everything, at least I hope not, but why did you want to let me in on all of this? Like you said, this a rare disclosure for Horace to make," she noted.

"I guess it's because I like you and I like your art. You remind me of how I was before all of this happened. It's a relief to see someone can still hang onto their ideals in this city and actually make them work. I just wanted to let you know that it can be real tough out there, grow a thick skin, leave your stresses and stomach-wrenching have-to's at home when you punch out your time card and close these doors every night, and you'll do fine. Oh, and don't pay attention to 'negative' reviews, they *can* produce rewards," he added with a big smile.

"Thanks for the advice. I'm just curious, have there been any ... uh, oh..." she stopped short.

"What's wrong? I don't mind a personal question or two."

"It's not that. You know that 'thick skin' you were just talking about?"

"Yes?"

"Well, you're going to need to grow at least three extra layers in about thirty seconds, my aunt just arrived, and you have no idea how caustic she can get, especially where *you're* concerned," Katherine tried to explain as she watched Aunt Martha enter huffing and puffing through the side door, wrapped up to the gills in her mink coat, her head crowned in a matching mink hat. In a blink of an eye, she found Suzy and Charlie, who then pointed her in the direction of the booth.

"Ah, there you are Kathy. My, it's cold out today, isn't it? Thought I'd take a taxi, too icy on the roads. You don't mind if I join you?" she asked as she skootched her along the booth.

"No, not at all," Katherine replied, there wasn't much she could do. She tried to sit as far away from the dead coat as possible.

"I heard you have a school trip coming in today, and I thought I would lend a hand. And who is this nice young man? Aren't you going to introduce us?" she chirruped.

"Um, Aunt Martha ... this is Mr. ... Robert Horace."

"Please to meet you ma'am," he replied, holding out his hand.

Aunt Martha, jumping up with unabashed indignation from the shock of this unexpected introduction, jolting her furry cap askance and nearly tilting the table in the process, gave him a scathing ocular 'once-over' before staring at him with a wide-eyed glare flashing between antagonism and disbelief.

"Well, I never! How *dare* you show your face here! Do your parents know what you do for a living? I suppose they don't," she huffed.

Katherine felt herself sliding down the booth a tad as she watched the tittering glasses and their sloshing contents settle back into balance. Aunt Martha seemed to revel in making a scene, she wondered if all eyes in the restaurant were on them.

"Oh Aunt Martha, leave the man alone. He came to explain his article, there's no harm done."

"No harm done? I'll say there's harm done! What terrible comments you wrote! How *dare* you attack our Katherine's gallery like that after all the work she has put into it? How can you live with yourself, you horrible article! You should be ashamed of yourself! *And* another thing, are *you* an American citizen?"

"Er, of course, ma'am."

"Well, one would never guess it! Our Katherine is *not* anti-American I'll have you know, and writing the way you did about one of our prized national monuments ... how disgraceful! Mount Rushmore is a shining example of our cultural heritage, how dare you belittle it! And...!"

"I couldn't agree more," he conceded, standing up, wiping the edge of his mouth with his napkin, "that was an ill-conceived article I wrote at the time, it was only after it was printed that I realized my error. I do apologize for having upset you and our fellow citizens' fine sensibilities."

"Er, well, I suppose we all make mistakes," she replied, a little flustered with this gallant admission of culpability, "but you shouldn't continue to write rubbish like that. It's a disgrace I tell you."

"Be that as it may, as I was just explaining to your charming niece, it attracts the public. The true art lover can easily see what a beautiful gallery she has, I just create the curiosity."

"And you know Aunt Martha," Katherine added, "most of the pictures he gave a good review *were* from your own collection ... ."

"Yes, superb Warhols, the Matisse, and that Chagall? Just superb," he complimented, "why, I bet there is a constant stream of people breaking their necks here to see them."

"Well, they *are* the most distinguished pieces in the museum section," Aunt Martha sniffed, "I suppose you had your reasons writing the way you did, but *do* consider changing your ways, young man, before it's too late, you're good looks won't last for long, and no one likes a crab apple, you'll die a grouchy old bachelor, mark my words."

"I'll certainly keep that in mind," he replied with a slight nod.

"Aunt Martha, I must rush off, I have to leave Esther off for lunch, so you won't be left alone anyway," Katherine informed her, scooting out of the booth before she was pinned again.

"That's all right Kathy, you run along now, attend to your business, I'll see you later."

"It's a pity, you don't want dessert then?" Horace ... Smith politely asked Katherine. "At least a cup of coffee?"

"I'm fine, but I won't refuse that cup of coffee, you can join me at the front desk if you like."

"All right, that sounds agreeable," he replied as he took out his wallet and paid for their lunch with Aunt Martha looking on in a state of bewilderment, wondering at the strange inconsistency between the columns she read in the paper and this well-mannered young gentleman standing before her buying lunch for her niece.

"Whew, that was some pasting," Katherine remarked as they headed towards the front desk, "I'm sorry about that episode."

"Don't worry about it, Horace gets it all the time, he can take it," he shrugged with a smile, "I can see speaking candidly is a family trait."

Katherine looked down at the *Chez Garneau* bag in his hand.

"I'm so sorry about that, I don't know what possessed me to grab your tape recorder, I better take a look at the damage I've caused." She peeked inside the bag to find a pile of plastic bits and chips. "Well, look at the bright side, your tape didn't get smashed. Like I said, just send me the bill."

"It's all right, I've got a few more where that came from," he laughed.

"Thank God I didn't kill someone."

"Don't lose sleep over it, who uses the stairs anyway? You know how people love their conveniences, I bet everyone uses the elevator."

"Except when someone has a bee in their bonnet like me. Hi Esther, off you go for lunch, we'll mind the fort," Katherine announced, "Aunt Martha is waiting for you."

"Okay," she replied, warily eyeing the Art Hacker as she passed, leaving the two youngsters to man the leather swivel chairs. Katherine could only guess what she and Aunt Martha were going to chatter about. In a few moments, a waiter brought out their steaming cups of coffee.

"Ah, this is the life," Smith said, as he sipped his beverage, languidly pivoting left and right using his heels, "I wouldn't mind having a gallery like this myself."

"It's a lot of work," she *tsked*, "it's not all fun and games. For starters, you should see the bills for this place."

"Oh I know, but still, it's a nice pipe dream for some of us. Anyway, you were going to ask me something before the melodrama went into full swing.”

“Well, what you said partly answered my question, but I was wondering, are there any lines you regret writing since you’ve donned the double robe of Jekyll and Hyde?”

“So it’s to-the-last-dregs type of confession today, is it?” he laughed, rubbing his forehead for a moment, “okay, no more secrets. Sure, you can really do some stupid things when you first start out. You have to get your fingers burned before you see the limits. My scorching experience came with that ill-devised comment on Mount Rushmore, you have to be careful when you criticise national treasures and people’s political views. You should have seen all the letters that were sent to the editor that week, I still get the odd flare up, as you just saw yourself.”

“Hmm, I suppose we should be grateful to witness Horace’s rare apology then,” Katherine noted.

“Ah, I should make a slight correction, *Horace* never apologizes, but Smith does on occasion,” he smiled.

“So, what does *Smith* think of my Napoléonic wonder, seeing it was hacked to smithereens by your alter ego?” she asked, raising her eyebrows.

“Smith concedes that to be his favourite of all your paintings, although I find the last three you did quite intriguing,” he smiled, “in fact, I wish I could have written the truth about your Napoléon, but it wouldn’t have been a great read, I’m sorry to admit. Horace had to have his say if it was to receive some attention. Honestly, it was difficult trying to find something maniacal to say about it, and in my outrageous efforts I may have dug a little too deep there, I hope I didn’t hit many nerves or draw blood in the process, I’m sorry if I did.”

“We’re full of apologies today, aren’t we?” she laughed, “well, your little rant about Hitler certainly made things interesting for awhile, that’s for sure. You said you studied art, did you ever plan to continue your painting at some stage?”

“I don’t have the time anymore, not with my work at the paper.”

“That’s a shame, especially as we are now showing pictures when they are ready, our artists like this rotation system, they don’t have to wait and build up a collection like you said.”

“It’s a pity it’s too late for me,” Christopher reflected.

“It doesn’t have to be,” Katherine noted, “I’ll tell you what, even if you do one picture a year, you’re welcome to bring it in. Besides, you’ve got quite a readership with your column already, you will have a guaranteed following for your work.”

“Oh ho!” he laughed, “I can’t use my usual alias, that’s part of the problem.   People will expect Horace to paint *his* vision of the perfect example of art, seeing he has slashed so many artists and their style to ribbons with his critiques. Sure, Horace's name is well known and would supply instant customers, but Smith would not like to paint his corrosive ideas, not at all."

"I didn't think of it that way," she reflected, "hmm, that would be something to see, though. What *would* Horace have to paint in order to keep up his grim façade?"

"Well, I haven't given it too much thought, let's see, it wouldn't be that much different than drawing a caricature or political cartoon I suppose … give me a topic or subject, we'll see what ideas he comes up with."

"Hmm … oh, I know. What would Horace do with the Statue of Liberty for instance?" After Mount Rushmore, this should be interesting.

"Whew hew! Political, another national treasure at that, this could be a brutal one. Okay, Horace would have to find something ironic or paradoxical about the object, let me see … *'Keep ancient lands, your storied pomp!' cries she with silent lips. 'Give me your tired, your poor, your huddled masses yearning to breathe free, the wretched refuse of your teeming shore. Send these, the homeless, tempest-tost, to me, I lift my lamp beside the golden door.'* Okay …how about we in the U.S. love to spout freedom, but like to keep a bit of 'storied pomp' of our own, not to mention having no problems shipping desperate people like 'refuse' back to their own countries no different than the garbage barges that float around our harbours here, denying the huddled masses a chance to become residents or citizens. Oh yes, *'give me your homeless'*, a lamp is all she'll give you, a glaring street lamp to light your way to the bridge or overpass you sleep under every night, and these are our *veterans* we're talking about, *citizens* who risked their lives for home, country … and Lady Liberty."

"Gee! And Gramps dubbed *me* the gadfly of the nation. I couldn't hold a candle to you. No pun intended."

"There's more I could rave about, for instance, we love to criticise the 'ancient lands' of Europe for their socialist style systems, taxes may be a crippler, and they may not be efficient, but at least they provide free or very affordable healthcare for their citizens. Look at us, one of the richest nations on earth that has the best of all healthcare, yet only a percentage of our people have access to it, not to mention many of those that *do* can barely pay their medical bills or keep up with the insurance costs. Medicare is a joke: I sure could do with a little extra help if it came my way, I can tell you that, and I'm only one of millions."

"Wow, anything else you would like to add, *Horace?*"

"Well, this could be an urban myth, but I once heard a rumour that the statue was modelled on the designer's mistress. I should look into that sometime, see if there's any truth to it. Wouldn't that take the cake though, to find out that our celebrated symbol of liberty is based on the image of a painted woman?"

"You're awful!" Katherine chuckled, astonished by his audacity.

"Of course, this would make for a pot-boiler of a column, trying to come up with a corresponding image is something else, perhaps writing cataclysmic critiques has finally eclipsed my art," he noted, swivelling in the chair.

"Oh, I don't think so, like you said, it's not something *Smith* would want to paint. If you like, you could invent another *nom de plume*, or rather, a *nom de pinceau*, start afresh, do something nice for a change."

"Hmm, it's worth thinking about. Speaking of good things, where … or *how* did you find those radical murals upstairs? No one knows anything about this 'DS', his pictures appear practically overnight, the artist disappears without a trace, and yet, lo and behold, I find two works of his hanging on your walls as if you knew him all your life. Come on, give us the dirt," he wheedled, "Horace will be nice this time, I promise."

"Oh, that's my little secret," she smiled, "and besides, I don't think Horace can ever play nice."

"Ouch!"

"Honestly, the artist wants to remain anonymous, no name, no details, no info. I hope you can live with that."

"Sure. Just makes it a little more challenging for Horace, that's all. Anyway, how did you secure all those loans from the private collectors? The Reinold Collection is particularly impressive, I've seen a few of those pieces before, they usually make the top municipal museum rounds. Someone has made an impression."

"Oh, I met the Reinold brothers when I was in Paris a year ago, I happened to travel over on the same flight with Gerry, and we crossed paths on a different occasion, it's just one of those 'things-that-happen' without planning it, actually."

"Well, well, speak of Old Nick," Horace wryly noted in an undertone, still lazily swivelling from side to side. Katherine looked over the desk to see Gerry enter the side door wrapped in a black woollen coat and carrying a substantial cardboard box under his arm.

"Well, what have we here? Armistice Day? What brought this about? Good afternoon Kathy, Mr. Horace," Gerry greeted in a tone of surprise as he observed the unanticipated camaraderie between the passionate artist and New York's most read and reviled art critic.

"Good afternoon," Horace greeted politely, still enjoying all the comforts of the swinging chair.

"Um, I guess this must come as a surprise," Katherine agreed as she stood up to return the greeting, "you could say Mr. Horace and I have come to an amicable understanding about his column: you're correct, art needs a little spice every now and then."

"Indeed," Gerry noted.

"How was Istanbul?"

"Oh, just so-so. I am afraid to say I've come to add a sour ingredient to your artistic gathering, as it happens, I must have the Flemish manuscript back, today as a matter of fact."

"Oh, that's a pity, I have a school tour coming by in a few minutes, and it was one of the most popular items with the kiddies."

"I am sorry for this short notice, but I need the manuscript for an important project, however, I passed through Paris on my way back from Turkey and brought a consolation piece to help take its place for now. I do hope you will find it acceptable."

He opened up the box, and after removing all the newspaper wrappings, placed the new surprise on the counter: it was the orange and black pottery amphora she had admired in his apartment.

"Wow! Can I hold it?"

"Sure, just don't pick it up by the handles, they could break."

"It's more than likely," Horace wryly remarked, "it seems you've received a downgrade."

Puzzled by his comment, she followed Horace's gaze and gently turned over the vase to find a 'Made in Taiwan' label stuck to the bottom. Gerry laughed when he saw her elated expression change to one of perplexity.

"I thought you said it was from ancient Macedonia," she exclaimed.

"It is. Don't pay attention to the label," he advised, "I swiped that from a souvenir coffee mug, one sticker, and *voilà*, instant disguise. It was a quick way of getting past customs without all the additional red tape required for bringing in an ancient antiquity. They thought it was a worthless piece of tourist junk from a street market or bazaar, plus I had my Istanbul tickets for additional backup."

Katherine carefully turned the delicate amphora right-side up and gingerly set it back down on the counter.

"That was quick thinking," Horace noted, making one last swivel before standing up, "I guess I should leave you to it. I must head off, more columns to write and artists to rattle, and remember," he said coming close to whisper in her ear, "beware of Greeks bearing gifts. *Ciao*, bella." She laughed, not sure what he meant, old Horace was obviously up to his pranks as usual.

"Whatever, and thank you for lunch."

"What was that all about?" Gerry wondered as they watched the critic depart.

"With him, I don't think anyone can tell," she said, "well, I'm sorry the manuscript has to go so soon, but thank you for bringing this instead, it's beautiful. However, I don't think I'll have a moment's peace while it's on the floor, I'll be terrified someone will knock it over."

"It's insured, so don't worry, besides, you have a few nice display cabinets in your future gift shop that will keep it safe I'm sure, unfortunately, it means you'll have to move one to your museum area."

"Oh, that's a good idea, I don't mind doing that, the guard will help. Whew, I feel a little better now," she said as she continued to study the graceful dancing maidens on the amphora.

"So, where's the tattoo parlour?" he asked, jovially looking around.

"Second floor, next to the stairwell, you're in for a surprise," she smiled.

"Well, I also stopped by to take you out for lunch, but that has already been taken care of," Gerry noted, looking a little pushed out of shape.

"Oh, I had to eat early today anyway, I had to give Suzy and Esther a chance to grab something before the field trip arrives. They should be out in a moment, I'll get the manuscript for you then."

"Plus see the new discovery."

"Of course. I must warn you to be prepared: you are going to lose," she smiled.

"Oh really? These street art pieces must be better than I thought."

At that moment, a stream of thirty animated third graders came in the side door in pairs holding hands accompanied by who obviously were two teachers.

"All right class," one older lady called out, "quiet now, remember what we told you, no loud noises in the gallery, other people are trying to look."

There was an instant hush followed by a bevy of whispering.

"Uh oh, here we go," Katherine sighed, "to your battle stations."

Gerry found the prospect amusing. "They look rather young to be taken to a gallery like this, will they get anything out of it I wonder?" he said under his breath.

"Well, the teachers are trying to instil a little culture into the minds of their pupils," Katherine quietly replied with a shrug, "you have to give them credit for that."

"Yes, but coming here is like giving them caviar and smoked salmon when all they can appreciate right now are burgers and hot dogs."

"Oh hush, we have to *make* it interesting for them," she whispered back before addressing the advancing hoard. "Hello everyone, you must be our school trip. I'm Katherine Walsingham, but you can call me Kathy, it's a lot easier," she smiled.

"Say 'Hello' to Miss Kathy, everyone," the teacher prompted.

"Hel,lo Miss, Ka,thy," the children droned in the expected sing-song mode when greeting someone new, group fashion.

"Are we all ready to see some interesting things today?" Kathy enquired.

"Yeeeeesss!" the kids called out, while a few cheeky voices called out "Noooo!"

"Hey! Who said no?" she smiled. The children laughed. "Well, we're starting out with a nice surprise, so the 'No People' may change their minds. We just received a new delivery," she announced, indicating towards the vase on the counter. "Do you know what this is?"

"Ah, that ain't nothin' special," one boy piped up, "my gran gets loads of that stuff in Mexico." The teachers tried to keep a straight face.

"You've got a tough crowd today," Gerry observed.

"Well, we can see why your sticker worked," she replied in an undertone, before continuing with the first item on the tour. "Well, what would you say if I told you this was not from Mexico, but all the way from Macedonia?"

"Where's that?" a girl called out.

"Ancient Greece, not far Italy all the way across the Atlantic Ocean. And what would you say if I told you this vase is over *two thousand* years old?"

"Wohhhhhhhhh," the group returned in unison.

"It's very special because it lasted all those years without breaking, and pieces like this show us how people used to draw back then. They were pretty good at it, don't you think?"

"Yeeaaahhh," the group commented, looking wide-eyed at her and the vase.

"What's it worth?" Mr. Cheeky in the back of the group wanted to know, maybe to compare prices between Mexico and ancient Macedonia.

"Well, they say it's priceless," Gerry explained, "one-of-a-kind, but if you want a number, a few million might work," he smiled.

"Wohhhhhhhhh," the group called out once more.

"Perhaps it was owned by some king a long time ago, or a beautiful princess, perhaps a powerful chieftain, we don't know for sure," Gerry continued. The children seemed to like this information.

"Like a real king and princess in a real castle?" another little girl was curious to discover.

"Could be," Gerry continued.

"Wow!"

Hearing the excited babbling, Suzy, Charlie, Esther and Aunt Martha exited the restaurant.

"Well, I guess I had better put this away now, you're the first who get to see it out in the open without a display case, so I guess you're very important," Katherine noted, placing the vase back in its box. "Now I want you all to meet Mrs. Esther and Aunt Martha", Katherine announced, "they will take you on your tour upstairs."

"All right children, this way please," Aunt Martha ordered as she and Esther commandeered the group up the stairs.

"I may have to rescue the kids from her later," Katherine whispered, "poor Aunt Martha has no experience in handling children. She orders then around like they're soldiers, she never had any of her own, you understand."

"Hi Gerry," Suzy greeted, "I hope you had a pleasant stay in Turkey. What have you got there?" she asked, peeking inside the box.

"A piece for your exhibit upstairs, actually, a trade for one of the manuscripts, I'm afraid. Why, hello Charlie, long time no see," Gerry said, politely shaking hands.

"Hello, Mr. Reinold. It's an unusual piece," Charlie agreed, looking over the counter,

"Please, call me Gerry."

"All right. Well, I suppose it's time to take my leave of you, I can see you girls have your hands full, and I must head back to court."

"Hope you win your case," Katherine replied.

"Thanks, me too. See you later."

As Charlie left, Katherine decided it would not be a bad idea to lock the vase in the office safe until arrangements could be made for its public exhibition. Suzy was now on hand to hold the fort in the meantime while she took care of business. Katherine invited Gerry to follow her around as she first locked up the priceless artefact before going to the boiler house to retrieve the metal case belonging to the recalled manuscript.

"So, does young Master Kraylor drop by for lunch often?" Gerry wondered now that they were alone.

"Not that often. He's usually held up with legal business. I don't see him that much anymore."

"Oh?"

"No, it seems he's too busy for me lately, which is a good thing," she smiled, "if you must know, it looks like he and Suzy have become an item."

"Really? You don't say, I suppose that lets you off the hook," he replied.

"Oh gosh, I'm so sorry you had to witness that episode last Christmas," she groaned, recalling the disastrous scene with the Kraylors, "I was surprised myself, but everything has sorted itself out now, I hope it works out for the two of them. Ah, here it is," Katherine announced, reading a tag attached to the handle of a deluxe metal case stacked neatly on top of a pile of similar containers, all belonging to his donated collection.

"Here, let me get that," he replied, reaching for the casing, "now, when are you going to satisfy my curiosity and take me to see the new arrival created by your mysterious new discovery?"

"Right now," she replied as they returned to the lobby area and waited for the elevator.

"May I ask have you thought up a 'dare' yet?"

"No, but I will, just you wait, Mister," she laughed. "So tell me, did you do anything interesting while you were away? You probably were homesick, having to go away for Thanksgiving, and all that."

"Well, I did get to see Lottie for a few days, she's still attending those lectures at the Sorbonne you know, she sends her regards."

"Ah, that's nice of her, I hope she's enjoying her 'study-cation'."

"I don't think she's attending *all* the lectures, it's only an excuse for her and her friends to do a little travelling, she needed a break away from here."

"Oops, here we go," Katherine announced as the elevator stopped, "second floor, be prepared to be amazed," she chuckled as she led the way.

"Well, I didn't expect *two*. Okay, not bad ... not bad at all," he commented, looking slowly from left to right, nodding his head as he studied the multi-coloured paintings, "if Warhol could get away with his designs, I *suppose* you have slight a chance," he conceded.

"Thank you," she replied.

"But remember," he continued, "our agreement was it had to sell, so until *one* of these budge, the wager is still on."

"That's sounds reasonable."

"When did they arrive again?"

"Thanksgiving week, Monday, which would make it the … twenty-fifth of November," she noted, calculating out the days in her mind.

"One month, so you have until Christmas Day," he declared.

"Hey, that's not fair! We won't be open on Christmas Day, I have to be given my full month, and I'm giving everyone a few extra days off afterwards too."

"It's not my fault your curtain-murals came in when they did," he laughed, "but okay, until the end of December it is. I should tell you, you're going to have a problem selling them," he roguishly warned.

"Why's that? Pray, enlighten me."

"They're simply too big: the potential collector would need a large space to display them properly, so you're customer base is limited to a corporate art investment for a public lobby somewhere, or perhaps a museum."

"Well … well… you don't know … maybe someone will have a large warehouse apartment," she stammered, flustered at this revelation. *Nuts*, he was right, they *were* rather big for the regular art collector. How was it she was always missing important details like this?

"Now don't worry, you still have a chance," he replied.

"Oh come on, let's get your manuscript."

With that, they returned to the elevator. Katherine was amused to find the school trip on the third floor, still rooted in front of Aunt Martha's donation. The children were obviously bored by this time, one little boy was hopping on one of the benches.

"Young man, please, pay attention now!" Aunt Martha commanded. The energetic hopper was not paying any attention, maybe he had a case of ADHD Katherine figured. One teacher ordered him off the bench, while Esther went with the second teacher to hunt down a couple of wanderers that had separated from the group and were conducting their own tour.

"Aunt Martha, I think they would like to see something else now," Katherine hinted quietly.

"'Bout time," one boy pouted.

"That's just fine by me," Aunt Martha nodded, "they're getting more rambunctious all the time, children were never allowed to behave like that in my day, I must say," she huffed, "will I see you for coffee later, Esther?"

"Of course, Martha dear, see you in a little bit," she said as she shepherded the rovers back into line.

"What have you got in there?" one little girl in pigtails asked Gerry, pointing to the case.

"Nothing yet, but would you all like to see what's going in there?"

"Yeeesss!"

"All right, follow us," Katherine replied as she went to the manuscript, the troupe of children following behind.   On their way, they bumped into the guard on patrol, good, he could follow them too and help unhook the thing.

"It's just an old book," one boy piped up.

"Not any old book, this is over seven hundred years old, way before they invented printing, no computers, no nothing," she explained, "everything was hand-drawn back then, even the letters." To Katherine's surprise, instead of putting it away immediately, Gerry took out his leather gloves, opened the special frame, removed the medieval tome and turned the pages to let the children see the various illuminations.

"Wow, is it a *magic* book?" the little pig-tailed girl asked, amazed by all the vibrant colours.

"Ah, don't listen to her, she's such a *bay-bee*, there's no such thing as *magic*," Mr. Cheeky was proud to observe. The other kids began to snicker.

"I disagree, *all* books have their own special magic, and because this book is *really* special, we have to take very good care of it," Gerry replied with a wink to the little girl, who started to smile again as she watched him place it carefully back in its frame and laying it within the soft foam fittings in the case.

"Yes, and just imagine, you're the last ones who get to see it before it goes back to where it came from," Katherine added, "it's really a special day for you guys, isn't it?"

"Would you like me to continue the tour?" Esther asked.

"Yes please, I'll see you downstairs." Katherine replied.

"All righty, who wants to see some real ancient tapestries? They were in a castle once upon a time you know," Esther informed the troupe who replied with a chorus of "Cool! From a real castle! Wow!" Katherine smiled as she and Gerry went to the elevator.

"That was a nice thing you said back there," Katherine noted, "the poor little thing probably gets teased all the time just because she has an overactive imagination."

"Well, I didn't say anything that didn't have a grain of truth to it," he replied, "I should know, I collect books. Listen, since lunch is out of the question, may I offer you dinner later?"

"Thank you, but after today, I don't think I'm up to anything but a quiet night and a long soak in the hot tub."

"All right, but may I tie up your Saturday night? I have tickets for the opera, *Rigoletto* I think, it's the last performance before they change to the next opera. We could have dinner afterwards. Before you say 'no', the billing says the opera will be produced with the traditional-style sets and costumes, so no 'post-neo-ism' atrocity shall be forced upon you." Katherine smiled.

"Well, I don't know, it's such a hectic time right now," she replied hesitantly.

"I'll tell you what, you don't have to say anything until tomorrow, just give me a call whenever you like, be it yea or nea. How does that sound? Do you have my home number?"

"No, I don't, just the office number."

"After all this time? That's terrible of me," he said as he put the case down for a moment and hunted in his pockets for a pen. Katherine gave him her notebook. "Okay, you have it now," he said while jotting down the figures, "if you don't want to go, I'll understand. It *is* a busy time of year."

"I'll think about it, thank you for the invitation," she replied as the elevator touched ground.

"You're welcome, I guess I shall see you later then, I mean, whatever your decision is," he added, "if the opera is out, we can always go back to lunch plans".

"Oh sure, drop by anytime."

"Goodbye for now," he said, heading towards the side door, "I shall await your call."

"Kathy, how's it going upstairs?" Suzy enquired as Katherine sat down with her.

"Well, the kids are safe from Aunt Martha and Esther has taken over the tour. Gerry has his manuscript, and I've got another decision to make," Katherine sighed.

"Where to put the vase?"

"No, if I should go to the opera on Saturday with him. What do you think, should I?"

"The opera? Wow, that sounds great , but why do you need to ask me? It's your social life, you can make it as energetic or as non-existent as you want it to be. Do you feel like going, or don't you? That's the question. Don't you get bored being stuck at home?"

"Well, I haven't thought about it really. I've had so much to do," Katherine reflected, "it's just that he has asked me out so much already, I don't want to impose, and yet, I can't really say 'no' to him, can I?"

"Who says you're an imposition? He wouldn't ask you to go if you were. Besides, who was the one who said we needed to get a life after we closed the doors on this place every night? You could take your own advice once in a while," Suzy laughed.

"I did say that, didn't I? But the gallery and my art *is* my life. I'm not sure if I need or want anything more than that. My time is limited, and I don't know if I want to overload it with more than I can handle right now."

ᘒ❁ᘔ

"Does this look all right?" Katherine asked her mother while studying the contours of the full-length sapphire blue evening dress in the standing mirror.

"Why it's beautiful, it is very becoming, don't fuss so much. It's been awhile since you bought a new one, I'm so glad you decided to take the day off to get it."

"Well, it *is* the opera. As Aunt Martha keeps reminding me, I can't show the family up and go in some old thing that's been seen there already. Personally, I think that is a little silly, I don't think anyone would remember when I was last at the Met, let alone keep tabs on what I wore, but if it keeps her happy, no big deal, I can get a new dress."

"You know dear, I *do* wish you would borrow one of my furs for once, it is cold out tonight."

"Oh Mom, you know I can't stand the things, cruelty committed in the name of fashion, and besides, someone might spray paint it. I'll wear my black velvet coat, that's dressy enough for this evening."

"All right dear," her mother replied in resignation as Katherine took the coat out of her closet and proceeded to give it a vigorous sprucing with the clothes brush.

"It still manages to attract some fuzz, even with a garment cover," Katherine protested to herself as she tried to hurry the process.

"Here, let me hold it for you, he'll be here any minute. There you go, you're all set. Don't forget to check your bracelet clasp, you nearly lost your diamonds the last time you wore them."

"I know, I'll be careful," she replied, checking her wrist, also taking a moment to ensure her earrings and necklace were fastened and hanging properly. She didn't want to lose them, a beautiful tear-drop set, they were a special Sweet Sixteen present from her parents. At that moment, Jaspar began to bark at the front door.

"Have a good time tonight, dear, but don't stay out late. You've

507

been very busy lately, and you're starting to look a little tired. Are you sure you're taking your vitamins?"

Uh, oh, that didn't sound good. Do I look that washed out? Great, the 'Night of the Living Dead Goes to the Opera', there's a sequel for you. Katherine took another quick peek in the mirror to determine the state of her complexion in case damage control was necessary, perhaps she needed more blush. She seemed to look like her normal self, it must be Mom fussing again.

"Don't worry, I'm taking my vitamins, and it's just the rush of getting started, things are almost on auto pilot at the gallery, I'll even have more time for my painting now."

"That's good to hear. Now hurry up dear, don't keep him waiting, I can hear Mrs. Gonzales at the front door."

"All right Mom, I'll see you later," she replied, giving her mother a quick kiss on the cheek and retrieving her evening purse from the dresser before heading to the stairs.

Coming around the balustrade, she descended the first steps. Gerry turned in her direction as he heard her approach. Gallantly dressed for the formal occasion complete with a long evening frock coat with half cape to the elbow, his hat, gloves and silver-handled umbrella in one hand, in the other he held a bouquet of long-stemmed red roses. She found herself pausing for what seemed like an age before continuing down the stairs. Although his handsome features had not escaped her before, it seemed as if for the first time she noticed how truly distinguished he looked, while he in turn felt the rare yet strangely pleasant sensation of being at a loss for words, struck silent in a moment of admiration as he watched her descend. It was not until she reached the last step that he recovered from this quiet, mesmerising moment.

"You look simply enchanting," he bowed slightly, offering her the roses, "I do believe I am taking a princess to the opera tonight."

"Thank you, oh these are beautiful, " she replied, admiring their red velvet contours and slight shimmering sheen. Mrs. Gonzales offered to put them in a vase.

"Shall we go?"

"Yes, we don't want to be late," Katherine nodded as he helped her with her coat, and opening the door to let her pass through first. Expecting the Jaguar, she was surprised to see a sleek black stretch limousine parked outside the front door.

"Well, we're getting an extra dusting of snow tonight," Gerry remarked as he looked up, taking the umbrella off his arm and opening it up. He then put on his hat and offered her his other arm, she shyly hooked her arm into his. The crisply dressed chauffeur hopped to attention, and taking the umbrella from Gerry, escorted them to the back door of the vehicle.

"Samuel, may I introduce you to Princess Walsingham," Gerry announced with panache. The chauffeur looked a little startled, not knowing if his employer was joking or not and wondering if he should say, "Pleased to meet you, Your Highness".

"Oh don't pay attention to him, he is burying me in flattery tonight," Katherine smiled, immediately putting the poor man at ease.

"Very good, Ma'am."

Katherine thought she could see Suzy peeking out the apartment window and wave slightly to her before they sat inside. Admiring the elegant leather interior, she noticed champagne had been prepared in the mini-bar for their outing to the city.

"My, we're painting the town red tonight, aren't we," Katherine remarked, feeling unusually reserved, yet enjoying this wonderful indulgence.

"Surely you've been in a limo before? I would have thought your family would have a couple of these lying around somewhere," he joked as he popped open the bottle.

"Well, they get taken out of storage when some big meeting is taking place," she laughed, "so all the visiting CEOs get to use them more than us. We don't need them personally. In fact, I think the last time I was in a limo was for my other grandfather's funeral. I can just remember what it looked like."

"I hope I haven't inadvertently triggered any unpleasant memories … ."

"Oh no, that was such a long time ago, and I was very young then, I don't think I knew what was really happening at the time."

"I'm relieved to hear that. You know, why *not* paint the town red tonight? In fact, let's just paint the town. Since you're the artist, pick any colour you like, be daring," he said with a flourish.

"Hmm, yellow I think."

"Yellow? Why yellow?"

"You said to be daring," she laughed.

"So I did, but why yellow?"

"It's one of my favourite colours, it's bright and cheerful. I think it reminds me of Van Gogh's sunflowers, I love those paintings, but that's not to say I don't like red too," she concluded with a smile.

"Then we shall paint the town red and yellow, an interesting combination I must say," he noted with amusement.

"Oh, that is awful," she laughed, "we'll have to stick with one colour."

"Why? All artwork has it's share of contrast," he noted.

"Too true, but what a circus! I was wondering, just where *did* they come up with that expression? Paint the town red … we have the oddest sayings."

"I think it originated when a English lord a little off his rocker used to go out at night creating mischief and mayhem, including painting several buildings red," he explained.

"And I thought it meant someone was just going out to have a good time," she replied with a puzzled expression.

"Depends on what your version of a 'good time' is," Gerry noted with a wry smile.

"Well, I'll paint the town with you, but I'm not becoming a late-blooming delinquent tonight," she said in a resolute tone that was somewhat comical in its finality before continuing, "you know, I meant to ask, what will the opera be about? I don't follow opera like I do musicals."

"Oh, like most operas, it's about love, tragedy and death all set to the most breathtaking music, defying reality and the imagination at the same time."

"Ah, I thought so," she smiled, "well, if I don't understand the story, at least I can listen to the music."

It was a long time since she had attended any event at one of the cultural establishments at the Lincoln Center, by now, the area almost felt new to her. Arriving at the celebrated plaza in the Upper West side of Manhattan and approaching the opera house she found herself studying the modernist triple-cube arrangement of the quarter decorated with a splashing circular fountain, the buildings illuminated with golden hued lights from within, the surroundings lightly veiled in a dreamlike wintry haze after the light powdering of snow. To the right stood the Avery Fisher Hall, a plain white rectangle of travertine with tall narrow rectangular arches that housed the New York Philharmonic orchestra, to the left, a similar box-like structure of rectangular arches dubbed the New York State Theatre, home to the New York City Ballet, and the New York City opera company. In the middle stood the Metropolitan, it's simplistic yet distinctive row of five round arches partitioned from the outside world with expansive glass windows segmented with frames, not unlike Piet Mondrian's simplistic neoplastic squares and rectangles, revealing a complete view of the four-tiered lobby interior flanked on either side by Chagall's surreal multicoloured murals celebrating the sources and triumph of music, singular touches setting the edifice apart from the neighbouring cubes.

Inside, the lobby was as minimally decorated as the exterior, starburst crystal chandeliers, plain white stone, simple lines and unassuming curves with simple brass rods for handrails and balustrades comprised the main staircases, the floors carpeted in a bright royal red. The reddish-hued auditorium, with its stage area shielded by the world's largest gold damask curtain, was an odd rectangular space, while settling into their seats in the first tier to the far right overlooking the orchestra pit, it felt like they were nestling inside a gigantic set of organ pipes or a variation on the ancient Greek syrinx with niches carved out for the exclusive boxes. It was the artist in her, she could not help but study the lines, light and colours of her surroundings, but she also noticed as they entered the opera house and made their way upstairs, a number of people seemed to take notice of them, and continued to do so from their various vantage points around the auditorium. Katherine decided to flip through the pages of the program in an effort to shake off the peculiar feeling of being observed by a hundred eyes.

"You're certainly quiet all of a sudden," Gerry noted.

"I'm sorry," she replied, putting the booklet down, "I feel like I'm out in the middle of a gigantic red ocean with no land in sight, or perhaps a meadow in the height of hunting season," she admitted.

"Well, it's the nature of an opera house, a 'Vanity Fair' if you like, people come to see and be seen. I'm sorry, I should have introduced you to a few people I know here tonight," he said as he politely waved to a group who were in the box opposite them, looking in their direction and simultaneously finding their seats, "it's not as intimidating when you can see a few friendly faces. They're all probably curious to know who this beautiful woman is if they don't know her already. In fact, you must be the envy of the house tonight," he smiled.

"Oh, there's the flattery again. I do see a few people I know, and I'm sure they're just here to see the opera, perhaps it's the large open space, I always feel odd in a theatre."

"Theatres are curious places, magician's trick-boxes where the golden memories of dramatic triumphs linger like nostalgic ghosts, and where the unexplainable, the fantastic, the tragic, the comic and the absurd are routine occurrences on and off the stage. Murders, mayhem, political intrigue, lucrative business, secret assignations, and of course, dinner. Did you know that in Italy during the early days it was the custom to place kitchens near the boxes so their patrons would not miss out on their macaroni suppers while the opera was in progress?”

“No I didn’t,” she laughed quietly, “I know there are dinner theatres, but I can’t imagine something like that happening in an opera house.”

“I suppose you could call it an aristocratic prototype of the TV dinner.”

“Oh stop! You’re terrible, I won’t be able to take the opera seriously if you keep making jokes like that.”

“Well, you are going to be disappointed if you try, the heroine in tonight’s opera sings her dying aria for nearly half an hour, with a dagger stuck straight into her heart no less,” he pointed out with a touch of light sarcasm.

“You *are* awful, thanks for ruining the ending,” she chuckled, “but that *is* opera.”

“Ah, the magic of music, with it, all things are possible.”

She didn’t have time to comment, for the magic was beginning, the lights dimmed and the sombre notes of the overture began to resonate from the depths setting the mood for the tragedy about to unfold in sixteenth-century Mantua. It was a delight to see the opera set in a period setting; in her mind, there was nothing more ridiculous when listening to such beautiful melodies from another era but have the eyes affronted with an incongruous stage design, to have a classical score ingloriously married to the stark bleakness of a modern setting with the singers immodestly clad in tasteless and flimsy costumes that made the benevolent ‘angels’ of the great opera houses of the world wonder where all their donations were disappearing to. However, it was difficult to bask in the traditional scene forever, it must be the curse of every artist, writer and musician to find they can no longer enjoy the thing they once loved after they have become an insider to their craft. Could a magician watch another magician perform knowing the secrets of the trade? Can an artist look at a picture and enjoy it for its own sake without analysing its graphic composition? All her training in art made it impossible for her to admire a canvas without looking for the vanishing point, or determining the brushstroke technique employed, how the colours were blended, or how the artist used a thematic construction of shapes to achieve maximum visual effect. Viewing the scenery and the backdrop, she found herself studying the layout of Renaissance Italy in its chipboard, fibreglass and canvas glory, wondering if she would have used that colour, or if she could have designed that set piece a little better. It was getting harder to enjoy a stage production, the delusion of television making it more difficult to enjoy the illusion of opera.

Yet, there was always a sense of excitement when attending a live show, for that simple reason, it was live. An electric charge generated by human emotion whirred through the air at each scene change or at the appearance of a performer onstage, a lively force that intensified with each round of applause or during an ovation at the conclusion of a famous aria. There was also the anticipation: one could memorize every inflection and note in a favourite recording, but each live performance was an entity unto itself. She could watch the same musical five times over, and yet each interpretation of a line or a situation would be unique, the performers trying out different effects and deliveries, or attempting to bring out a facet of a character in a way they had not been portrayed before. Perhaps she could sense a little of their tension too, playing before a live audience took nerves of steel, and that was when all was well, that did not take into consideration if the actors or singers had to improvise should things happen to go wrong. Notwithstanding all the obvious illusions, it was difficult not to become enveloped in that kaleidoscope world of colour and sound. The stage possessed a certain magic after all, enveloping the audience with its enchantments, drawing them away from the hustle and bustle of the real world as if they were the children of Hamlet following the beguiling music of the Pied Piper to an irresistible wonderland. Every spectator came anticipating a spectacular performance, it was the thrill of the unknown.

Before she knew it, the illusion was dispelled by the intrusion of the intermission. On their way to the refreshment bar Gerry and Katherine politely nodded to people they passed, stopping to chat with a couple they both knew, introducing each other to certain individuals the other had not met before, all polite socialising and hobnobbing.

"How do you like the opera tonight?" "Oh it's a pity the understudy had to be called in." "Do you think this company will tour next year?", the usual operatic pleasantries. When these trifling matters had been dispatched, the chatter proceeded to their daily lives, polite questions asking what they did if they had not met them before.

"Why Katherine has just opened up an art gallery," Gerry told one elderly couple, friends of his family who were the time-honoured members of an elite banking empire.

"Of course, I read about it in the paper," Mr. Rochester noted, "where is it exactly? My wife and I might stop by sometime."

"Oh it's in Brooklyn, Dumbo to be precise," Katherine replied, "I'm sorry, I didn't bring one of my cards with me," she said apologetically. She had not thought about it before; to her, a night out was supposed to mean a night free of the daily grind. This one encounter however taught her she was going to have to get used to the fact that business would always intrude, so be prepared, but at that moment, she was empty-handed, no cards to offer, she felt a little ridiculous.

"Here, I have a few extras," Gerry offered unexpectedly, pulling out his wallet.

"Thank you," Mr. Rochester returned, reading the card.

Now that she had been gallantly rescued from one embarrassing situation, she was now facing another: one of those rare occasions she wished the address on the card was a little more impressive where the word 'gallery' was concerned. To her surprise, Mr. Rochester did not display one of those aggravating smiles that bordered on condescending amusement or pitiful politeness.

"Well, it seems you've got the jump on everyone, with plenty of time to spare," Mr. Rochester observed.

"Oh?"

"Yes, don't say I told you, but the first inklings of turning the area into the next historical and cultural district are gaining momentum, the current renovation of the Brooklyn museum has helped immensely, in a couple of years, they'll have the new gallery section in the west wing opened up."

"I am so glad to hear that," Katherine replied

"Of course, it's early days yet," Mr. Rochester continued, "but before this hits the official channels with the bureaucrats slapping historic building preservation codes everywhere, you can expect some serious investment to be heading your way in the next decade. Dumbo is going to mushroom, apartments, galleries, conversion projects, you name it."

"In fact, there are plans for redeveloping the Fulton dock sections," Gerry added, "it was a good thing we invested in the area before the prices start to skyrocket."

"Yes indeed," Mr. Rochester agreed, "I hope you don't mind the competition when new galleries begin to open up."

"Oh dear, must you gentlemen always talk business?" Mrs. Rochester piped, "I'm sure Miss Walsingham finds this all rather tedious."

"Actually, this is wonderful news," Katherine admitted, relieved her cultural enterprise was now viewed as a pioneer project among the Dumbo renovations. Gramps was right, again. "I hope the area will be developed, it has a character all its own."

"Forgive me for interrupting, but can I get you anything at the bar before the curtain call?" Gerry asked the Rochesters.

"No, we're fine, thank you," he replied.

"I'm still sipping my brandy," his wife added, "no more for me, thank you."

"Kathy, how about you?"

"Well, I *am* a little thirsty," she returned.

"All right then, we mustn't let you return to your seats parched," Mr. Rochester laughed, "it's was a pleasure meeting you, Miss Walsingham."

"So nice to meet you, I hope you have a pleasant evening," Katherine returned before she and Gerry started to make their way to the refreshment area. However, to her chagrin, she noticed Mr. Morgan and his wife sitting in a corner not far from their path. He being a prominent albeit tolerated member on the Walsingham board, it would be impolite not to say hello. Mrs. Morgan was a shy, quiet lady, she didn't know her very well, but Mr. Morgan was another matter although she met him only a few times and was compelled to invite him to her grand opening. She disliked having to shake hands with the man, there was always something leering and sinister about him, his close-set dark beady eyes always darting here and there, seeking to find who would provide the next business opportunity no matter the source.

"Why hello, Katherine, it's not often we see you at the opera," Mr. Morgan greeted, standing up from his seat.

"That's true, but here I am. It was all Mr. Reinold's doing, I do believe you met Mr. Reinold before?"

"Oh yes," Mr. Morgan said as they politely shook hands, Mrs. Morgan remaining in her seat as she also returned the gesture, "we met at the grand opening of your gallery."

"That's correct," Gerry affirmed.

"Um, are you enjoying the opera?" Katherine asked.

"Well, it's not as bad as some productions, I've seen worse," he commented before taking a sip from his cocktail, "so, how are things south east of Manhattan?"

"Very well, thank you," she was not about to give *him* a full progress report on her business, which was really none of his. The problem with having to say a courteous 'hello' was not knowing how to progress beyond that initial greeting and the first round of chit-chat, especially when she disliked the man intensely. Gerry seemed to sense her agitation and quickly jumped in.

"If you would please excuse us, I see a friend of mine whom I promised to introduce Kathy to, and if I'm not mistaken, the curtain call will sound in a minute."

"Of course, don't let us detain you, it was a pleasure seeing you both. Give our regards to the family, Kathy."

Katherine was relieved to turn away from the beady-eyed corporate shark.

"Am I wrong, or did I sense a hint of dislike for that fellow?" Gerry calmly enquired.

"A hint? I'm glad that's all I was showing, I'm grateful for your timely interruption, I didn't know what else I could think of to say to him. I know I shouldn't judge, but I can't stand the idiot."

"Whatever did he do to you?" Gerry noted with curious amusement. For some odd reason, she had an endearing expression whenever she looked flustered.

"Oh, nothing to *me* personally, other than the fact he thinks he can run the family company better than Gramps, Pops and Uncle Tim, but you mess with my family and you mess with me, you know what I mean? Yet it's more than that, he just gives me the creeps, there's something about him that I can't put my finger on."

"Best not to then," Gerry replied, "don't let one idiot spoil your evening. You did your duty and said 'hello' like a trooper. Come, let's get that drink."

"You know, a few appetisers wouldn't go amiss either," she added.

"Good idea, next time we'll have dinner first. That's the problem with planning a late night supper after the opera, not only does the hero or the heroine die singing, but you end up famished after the last notes of the finale."

After the few glasses of champagne during their drive, Katherine decided to play it safe and have a ginger ale, ensuring it was served in a champagne flute, no one would know the difference. It was odd, people who drank socially were usually convinced that everyone else around them could not possibly enjoy themselves unless they had alcohol in their glasses, and were uncomfortable with anyone one who didn't, eventually pressuring the 'Abolitionists' to have a drink on them against their better judgement.

"Are you sure you don't want the real thing?" Gerry enquired under his breath after he ordered his scotch.

"Well, it's safer if I don't drink any more until I have a few nibbles, champagne always goes to my head," she replied as she helped herself to a savoury flaky pastry.

"Wise girl. Where did you learn that trick?"

"At the club with all the ladies and their charity benefits, I can only drink so many glasses of wine and bubbly before I fall asleep in a quiet corner somewhere. You don't want me snoring in the middle of the next act, do you?"

"It would be an interesting addition to the chorus," he smiled before taking a quick look in the direction of the Morgans, who were also eyeing them, "hmm, I'd better introduce you to that friend of mine before 'Mr. Morgue' suspects the extent of our desire to extricate ourselves from his creepy company."

"Yes please," she chuckled, finishing the pastry in delicate haste, "I wouldn't want to show you up as a fibber after your timely rescue."

Gerry offered her his arm and led her in the direction of a distinguished looking-man, tall, middle aged, black haired but starting to grey at the temples. He looked like one of the gentlemen seated across from them in the auditorium.

"Hey Philip, how are you?" Gerry jovially called out.

"I *thought* that was you," the man returned, "I see you've decided on a night of culture. Now don't keep us in suspense any longer, aren't you going to introduce your beautiful companion?"

"Of course, I have the honour of presenting Miss Katherine Walsingham," he began, "Kathy, meet an old friend of mine, Philip Weaver."

"Not *the* Miss Walsingham…?"

"Yes," she sighed with a smile, "from the same purveyors of fine pharmaceutical products since 1906."

"And who now owns the most celebrated art gallery of the city," Gerry added.

"Well, what is a nice young lady like *you* doing with a scoundrel like *this*?" Philip said with a quiet guffaw. Before she could even reflect upon this bizarre comment, the curtain call was announced.

"I suppose we should head along, come Kathy, we don't want to miss the beginning of the next act," Gerry politely nudged, ignoring the ignoble comment. It was simpler to follow his lead and avoid a mini melodrama rather than try to answer this so-called friend. In any case, what *could* she say? Was the guy teasing? Not expecting this unpleasantry, she was caught off guard, powerless to devise any witty statement to parry this cutting remark. If she were Gerry, she would have to think twice before even giving this Philip the title of 'acquaintance'.

"With friends like that, you don't need any enemies. Does he always treat you like that?" she asked under her breath after they withdrew a few paces.

"Philip just has a strange sense of humour. Don't let him bother you. I don't."

"All right, if you say so."

Gerry was right, no point letting another idiot try to ruin their night. If he *was* joking, she disliked his version of comedy; there were few things more humiliating than to be made a source of derisive amusement, or receive a verbal 'dig' under the guise of camaraderie. Perhaps this Philip was dredging up from the murky gutters of Memory Lane some old school day prank that was in very bad taste back then as it was right at that moment. She felt terrible he would make a derogatory remark about Gerry right in front of her, especially as she could not say anything in his defence to lighten the situation. It was odd, although she knew little of his childhood or teenage years other than his tortuous piano lessons, Gerry did not seem the type that was troubled by bullies or hooligans at school, she always assumed he was one of those few lucky ones who were unanimously selected head of the 'Popular Party'. Well, there was always jealousy and competitiveness to deal with too. Yes, that must be it, she concluded. It was a shame that in an effort to spare her from remaining in the company of 'Mr. Morgue' a second longer than she had to, he saved her from the frying pan, but landed straight into the fire. At least Gerry seemed to be taking it pretty well, it was a good thing the curtain call came when it did, allowing them to make a clean getaway from the social throng.

The lights in the auditorium dimmed once more, and the magic of the stage resumed its hypnotic sway, until the understudy arrived on the scene. Disgruntled with the robust soprano, Katherine made herself as comfortable as possible in the theatre seat, sitting back and closing her eyes, preferring to imagine the action as the orchestra played rather than watch the rotund singer below. It was difficult to tell how long she remained in this relaxed position, time seemed to transform into liquid sound as the melodies soared around them. Was it fifteen minutes? Twenty? Did it matter? She then felt a light pressure on her arm, a voice whispered in her ear:

"Are you awake?"

"Yes," she whispered, her eyes still closed.

"Are you positive?"

"Yes."

"No world première of the 'Snoring Chorus'?"

"*No!*"

"Hmm, *I'm* not so sure, it seems the bartender slipped someone some extra bubbly in their ginger ale … ."

"I'm fine," she whispered back, trying not to giggle.

"You look like Sleeping Beauty to me," Gerry continued.

"I'm listening to the music," she explained.

"Between snoozes?"

"No! Let's just say I now know the full meaning of 'when the fat lady sings'."

"I see," he whispered. There was a pause before he continued, "I must agree, she *is* an intimidating sight. You know, if she opens her mouth any wider, she just might hit us with her tonsils."

"Shh!" Katherine quietly protested, putting her hand over her mouth. It was getting harder to stay quiet, it was like trying not to laugh in church.

"Perhaps this is how Jonah felt when he saw the whale."

"Gerry, quiet! You'll get us thrown out," she replied giving him a warning tap across the arm with her program. A few 'shushes' were sent in their direction. Well, no point giving him any more ammunition, she opened her eyes and watched the cast as they performed the last act, down to the heroine's dying breath. She was glad the ovations began, she could feel her stomach singing for its supper.

"I'm sorry you didn't like the opera," he apologized with a smile as they sat in the limousine, "I was hoping you would like to see the new one that will be premièring sometime next week, brand new work too, specially commissioned."

"Oh, don't get me wrong, I enjoyed the opera, the music was wonderful, and I did like the traditional production," Katherine replied, "it's just that … I don't get it at times. The part of Gilda calls for a innocent maiden barely in her teens, and then this … this … *woman* thunders out on to the stage … she could be older than Gilda's mother for all we know … and it's just … unbelievable!" she concluded, throwing up her hands. "It offends my artistic sensibilities." Gerry laughed.

"Well, in case you *do* decide to accompany me to the next opera, it's an *opera buffa*, so you will be permitted to laugh during the performance, just for your information."

"What's it called? I might have seen it advertised."

"*The Ghosts of Versailles*, I don't know how good it will be, it's a continuation of the *Barber of Seville* and the *Marriage of Figaro*."

"It sounds interesting, but I don't know Gerry, I'm afraid to plan anything for the next couple of weeks with Christmas coming."

"Fair enough, you're under no obligations. Just sleep on it … no pun intended. That reminds me," he continued, reaching into the mini bar, "we have a fresh bottle of silly sauce sitting here. Is it safe for you to have another glass?"

Her stomach made an audible percolating sound.

"Probably not until after dinner," she reflected.

"Ah yes, famishing finales," he laughed as he put the bottle back in place.

In a few moments, they arrived at the restaurant. Everything on the menu looked delightful, but she was so hungry, there was no time for ceremony and settled to order the same as Gerry.

"You are an amazing bundle of contradictions," he smiled.

"Me? How so?"

"Well it takes a very determined fifteen year old to wage a placard battle protesting the cruelties of animal testing, against your own family's company no less, and actually make an effective change … yet here you are, preparing to tuck into a medium rare steak with all the trimmings. I always assumed you were a vegetarian."

"You heard about that, did you?" she said, lowering her head, this was a bit embarrassing.

"I saw it, well, more like the other side of the crowd as I was on my way to something important at the time, I can't remember what it was now, but I'll never forget the news clip that night showing the security guards at the front door of the building trying to pull you away from a motley assortment of Greenpeacers. You put up a brave fight."

"Oh nooo," she groaned before laughing, trying to remember what she looked like, she used to experiment with so many different styles at the time. The sequins, the beads, that rainbow coloured beret, that stupid crimper that frizzled the ends of her hair. Worse yet … was she still wearing braces? As to the events of that day, everything happened so fast, it was all a blur, however, she could vividly recall banging one of the guards repeatedly over the head with her animal rights poster and being on the receiving end of the most fuming lecture Pops ever gave in the history of the executive boardroom. "I can't believe you saw that let alone remember it. Not that my priorities have changed, but those were really my gawkish days," she chuckled.

"So you never considered vegetarianism."

"Of *course* I did, but I could never make it past two weeks of cheese and soya bean products, not with everyone all around me eating roast beef or chicken, and don't mention trying to walk past a burger joint, *my* joints went weak with the aroma of whoppers and fries."

"A compromise was in order."

"Not really when you think about it. We're born with a set of canine teeth in front like other meat-eaters, and Steves tells me scientists are looking in to a specific taste area on the human tongue that reacts to meats as well as vegetable protein, so it's *natural* for us to eat meat, it's part of our diet. Food is one thing, what gets me angry is when we're cruel to other creatures for our vanity's sake, kill them for amusement, or hunt them into extinction, *that's* what bothers me. Gosh, don't tell me you *really* saw that news clip?"

"Sure did, but never mind, we all had our share of growing pains, you should see my old school photos, I had to wear corrective glasses for a couple of years, something about split vision."

"You? In glasses? I can't see it."

"God's honest truth," he replied, holding up his hand, Boy Scout fashion.

"You know, I used to dread those yearly photo sessions, they always rushed us through the process and the results remain to prove it."

"They might be good for something someday."

"Like what?"

"Oh, I don't know…blackmail?"

"Mine would certainly be perfect for that," she laughed.

"Come now, you couldn't have looked that bad. You must have been the most popular girl at school."

"Not really," Katherine admitted. "Oh sure, everyone knew my family, I wasn't persecuted like some poor kids by the elitist groupies. I loved to read books, paint and keep my grades up, so I was targeted as a teacher's pet by some classmates, which is almost as bad as being labelled a nerd, and then on the other hand, I was considered too much of a loner by some of the teachers, that had its own set of repercussions."

"Ah, the dreaded traits of the 'solitaire' whom they all assume will grow up to be a psychotic sociopath."

"Exactly," Katherine replied with a determined nod, "at last, someone knows what I'm talking about. Honestly, I don't know what those teachers expected. I was happy with my paints and books, but oh no, some goody two-shoes said it was not healthy for me to spend too much time on my own and I should go 'socialise' with my classmates. Then my parents got the same spiel from the counsellors during the PT meetings, so in order to make everyone happy, I hung out with the so called popular crowd, but I didn't have anything in common with them and just did whatever they did to fit in, and *then*, I got in trouble for staying out late at the mall or something like that, my grades started to suffer, I couldn't keep up with the groupie's frivolous social schedule, it was a vicious circle. So I said to heck with it all and became a solitaire again, I liked getting good grades, those so-called friends were causing nothing but trouble, and the teachers were happy my work had improved. They should have left well enough alone."

"Wow, you're hard to stop once you get wound up. Feel better now?"

"I'm sorry," she replied, shrugging her shoulders slightly, "it's just another one of those things I don't understand: everyone impresses upon you how unique you are, encouraging you to cultivate your individuality while at the same time trying to squish you and everyone else into the same ridiculous mould. It's an artist's right to rebel against the world's stupidity."

"*Viva la revolución*," he replied, holding up his wine glass.

"*Viva*," she replied, clinking his glass with hers, "so, how about you? Any gripes with your school days?"

"No more than the usual issues with authority, arriving late for class or playing hooky altogether, 'forgetting' my algebra homework and trying to come up with a good excuse every time, nothing that two thirds of the student population wasn't doing."

"You know, it was easier just being honest and turning the work in, I could never come up with anything original, the teachers heard it all before. If you said you ran out of paper for instance, they reminded us there had to be *some* around, we could always improvise and chop up a grocery bag."

"It did take some cerebral energies to outsmart the nuns I must admit, they had a sixth sense about these things."

"Fib to teachers is one thing, but to nuns? How *could* you?" Katherine laughed, "I'd be waiting for a bolt of lightning to strike me any minute. Care to reveal one of your dastardly ploys?"

"Oh, there were a few of us who knew no bounds. You can get away with a lot if you weren't scrupulous about forging fake notes asking you to be excused for a late doctor's appointment. It was great for playing hookey too."

"You *didn't... .*"

"I did, but I had to come up with other ideas after the school called home one day to ask how I was faring after my acute case of *bilharziasis*. Good thing Lottie answered the phone before our mother did, it kept me off the hook for awhile."

"Well, that one does sound a little fake," she replied.

"Actually, it's a real disease. That was the problem: it was *too* good. I couldn't keep playing the old flu routine every month, I had to give them something original. Amazing, the words you can find in the dictionary. So, did you ever try to ditch school for a day?”

“No, I thought about it, but always chickened out.”

“Oh come on, no one could be that perfect, you had to have pulled a ‘Ferris Bueller’ at least once. Admit it, and I’ll forgive you for not asking that waiter to do a tap dance in accordance with our dare penalty the other night.”

“You’re still holding that over me?” she laughed.

“Come on, let’s have it,” he wheedled.

“I’m telling the truth, I never ditched school, I’m a bad fibber, no point trying to run anything like that past Inspector Mom.”

“You mean you’ve *never* tried to get out of anything,” he said incredulously, “you can’t be human.”

“Of course I’m human, there are quite a few things I wish I didn’t have to go to at the time, I just couldn’t bring myself to skip certain obligations, not without a good or unavoidable cause.”

“Well, name one. What did you dread attending the most?”

“That’s easy, my formal introduction to society at the débutante ball, I dislike dancing, oh the dress was beautiful, but all the other hype that went with it was just annoying. Mom and Aunt Martha were enjoying the whole affair more than I was. At least I figured out what all those dance lessons were for.”

“I wonder what you plan to do when you decide to get married,” Gerry mused, “have everyone play ‘pin the tail on the donkey’?”

“I’ll cross that bridge if and when I get to it.”

“So, you went along just to please everyone.”

“No actually, as it turned out, we missed the whole thing, I’m actually ashamed to say.”

“Really? What happened?”

“Well, knowing I would never con my way out of the situation, Steves decided to do me a favour without my knowledge and stormed up one of those brainy schemes of his, but like they say, genius can border on madness at times.”

“This I have to hear. What did he do?”

“He prepared some kind of concoction in the lab and dosed our lunch with it the day of the ball. Everyone had to get it so no one would suspect anything, even he became a willing victim for the cause. I don’t know what it was, but all I can say is that no one could leave the house. It was only a few months afterwards he confessed to me what he did, I’ve never been able to tell anyone else. Mom would be devastated if she knew.”

"You mean to tell me your brother gave everyone food poisoning?"

"Nothing that drastic. Um, I don't mean to be indelicate, but let's just say it was not safe to light a match at Oak Meadows that night."

"And I thought I had come up with everything, maybe your brother and I could compare notes sometime," Gerry laughed.

"He certainly came up with some pranks that's for sure, I can't imagine what he got up to when he first went off to college, it's better not knowing. At least he's starting to grow up a bit now."

"Ah college years, those were the days. Pure freedom ... leaving home for the first time…the parties…"

"What about the tutorials, the lectures, the large building with all the books called the 'library'?"

"Is *that* what those were?" Gerry blithely replied. "Seriously, I did knuckle down and make it to graduation. But what about you? I mean getting out and spreading your wings. I don't mean to pry, but didn't you ever feel the urge to actually *leave* for college? You know, find your own place away from home?"

She thought about it for a moment.

"I never really felt *out* of place at home to begin with, so waiting for the day to move out was not a big issue I guess."

"Didn't you ever feel like you needed to get out from all the 'house rules'? As an activist, you felt no teenage rebellion whatsoever on the home front?"

"I *am* human, remember? But honestly, Steves and I weren't loaded with a lot of rules and restrictions, not really, and we were always allowed our space, just as long as we did our best at school, went to service on Sunday and didn't do anything in public that would make the family feel like they had to leave the area in disgrace. Then there was the practicality of it: can't cook, I never progressed past the toaster, the kettle, and the espresso machine. Mrs. Gonzales offered to teach me, just help her out in the kitchen during dinner and watch how it was done, but it was all 'Double-Dutch' to me. Anything past making a sandwich, peeling a potato and boiling a few eggs is like brain surgery. The medical equipment in the labs would probably be easier to figure out than the oven knobs. I mean really, how could an artistic individual stay grounded in the nitty-gritty of how many minutes per pound meat has to stay in the oven when trying to fathom the creative philosophy behind the greatest artistic minds of the world?"

"You could have hired your own housekeeper," he smiled.

"For sure, but there was so much to do, my interests lay elsewhere. Even trying to manage my own place with a housekeeper would be a waste of time, not to mention it seemed ridiculous to move out and buy an apartment or pay rent when the college was not far off to begin with. I don't think my parents minded me staying either, they never pushed us to leave like other families who can't wait for the kids to turn eighteen."

"Well, it's nice to know you're always welcome."

"That's true. I heard quite a few stories from other classmates at college that when they moved out, even though they couldn't wait to get their freedom, it felt like they were no longer a part of their family, their room was given to a younger brother or sister, and they felt they didn't belong anymore, like the family divorced them. That's a terrible thought, and it must have been hard for those kids to feel excluded and maybe unwanted. I think my parents understood that and didn't want us to feel like we were a burden. In fact, Mom went to bits when Steves decided to go to Boston. Just look at us, three generations under the one roof, we're 'old establishment', to the manor born as they say," she laughed.

"Of course, it would have been difficult to try and venture out on your own in the midst of commencing your gallery project," he reflected.

"There was that too," she nodded, "although I can see why people would like to move closer into the city when they can, the commute is a bit of a killer. I'm up and out to work early and I find myself coming home later than I would like, I hardly get to see the family these days unless they drop by the gallery, and yet, if I had my own place, I can't see the sense in being all alone and leaving Mom, Pops and Gramps rattling around in that big house."

"You could try it as an experiment, see what happens. I'm sure everyone will survive the 'empty nest' syndrome. Life is all about experiences."

"I know, it's just that … sometimes I feel like Josephine in *Little Women*, I don't like too many changes all at once, especially when I'm just finding my feet with the gallery, I'm not up to another major change for the moment."

"Like I said, you're a bundle of contradictions, a homebody determined to brave the world as a career-orientated workaholic. Shall ever the twain meet?" he chuckled.

"Hey, moving home is the third biggest shock after a death and a divorce, so they say," she chided.

"My, my, such a gloomy outlook for someone so creative."

"I'm not being gloomy," she returned, "just … practical."

"A 'practical' artist, eh? Who said they couldn't be bothered about oven knobs?"

"Very funny."

"You said it, not me," he laughed. "Well, now that your dream to own a gallery and launch an artistic career has come true, are there any other great yearnings yet to fulfil?"

"Other than visit every art museum in the world, there's nothing else that I can think of," she replied.

"Then I shall propose a new toast: may you live a thousand years."

"I know," she laughed, "it is a rather ambitious dream. I suppose I shall have to stick to a few museums and be happy with that."

"Is that all you want to be happy about?"

"What do you mean?"

"No needs of the heart to be met?"

"Oh, I really haven't thought about it much," she replied, looking down at her plate and shuffling the garnish with her fork.

"Really? It's hard to believe that someone who knows their Jane Austen editions has not even considered the possibilities of dallying in a romance of their own."

"Well, I'm not *completely* without feelings you know," Katherine replied, "it's … not as easy as reading about it in a book. What about you, Mr. Questions? Did you ever meet anyone that knocked you head over heels?"

"Hmm, I don't think the crush on my fourth grade teacher counts, but I did have the steady girlfriend here and there through high school, nothing that lasted for long, the chemistry fizzled fast, especially when we went our separate ways for college. I met a few girls at college too, but same short burst of chemistry, nothing serious ever came of it. Is it safe to return the question now?" he smiled.

"Well, since we've headed down this road, I did have a crush on *one* guy in high school, the captain of the basketball team, but he was going steady with the a cheerleader, and I got over it pretty quick. I mean, artsy scholar meets up with the head jock? It wouldn't have worked," she laughed. "I don't mean to be cruel, but all the other guys ranged between outright nerds or unbelievable jerks."

"I never thought you were the 'Ice Queen' type. A real heartbreaker you must have been, turning everyone down flat. You'd love the opera *Turnadot*," he observed with some humour.

"Oh? What's it about?"

"A beautiful but pitiless Chinese princess seeks revenge on the whole male population in return for an atrocious crime committed against one of her ancestors. The princess gives each of her suitors three impossible riddles to answer if they wish to wed her: if they fail, off with their heads.”

“Good grief, I couldn’t have been that bad, was I … a*m* I?” she reflected aloud.

“I’m sorry, I’m sure you never set out to impale anyone,” he replied apologetically, “it was a bad comparison. It was only high school after all, definitely one of the most bizarre periods in a person’s life. How anyone can come through that time well adjusted on any level is an absolute miracle.”

“Well, maybe I was a bit of an icicle back then,” she sighed, “I never let anyone get that close, like I said, a lot of the high school guys were complete jerks, and I didn’t have anything in common with the others who seemed nice, it just felt … weird. They had no interest in art, just sports. I was so busy with other things, the whole concept of ‘dating’ seemed like a complete waste of time.”

“Forgive me for raking up the past, but you’re honestly telling me you never went out with anyone before?”

“Before Charlie you mean? No.”

“Seriously?”

“Yes. It seemed pointless going out since I didn’t have much in common with most of the guys. Dating is a big decision, and I just didn’t … *feel* anything on that level with anyone to take that step. Come to think of it, all I did was hang around with Charlie, at least, that’s all *I* was doing not knowing how he really felt. I don’t think he really counts as ‘going out’ anyway, it didn’t feel like …reading one of Jane Austen’s novels,” she said searching for the right words, it was awkward trying to plumb this sensitive topic with someone she was just beginning to get better acquainted with. “They say you’re supposed to *know* when it happens, some connection that you never felt before and are positive you won’t ever feel with someone else. The thing is, how do you *know* what it’s supposed to feel like in the first place? It’s like asking someone if they have any questions about a new job: *because* it’s new, they have no idea what to ask, so they’re left just as confused as before.”

“Perhaps you’re *thinking* too much about it, you have to *feel* it, remember?” he smiled.

“I guess so, but how?”

“You like everything to be packaged in neat little boxes, don’t you? You can’t ‘box’ a feeling.”

“I suppose not, I just like to have answers for everything or know what to expect.”

“Maybe that’s the problem: love, like everything else in life, should be a discovery, an adventure, and like most adventures, you don't know you're having one until you're right in the middle of it. If you try to analyse it, you will never find a definite answer. Look at all the poets and philosophers that have been racking their brains for centuries in an attempt to divine the mysteries of the human heart, did they really get anywhere?"

"Maybe because they do think about it too much as you say," she laughed, "but I'll have to look into it. I'm sure Plato wrote about it somewhere."

"You definitely need to get out more often."

She never remembered talking about anything like this with Charlie, at least, not until after he popped the unexpected question, and then afterwards the whole topic was terribly uncomfortable. It was the strangest thing, but after this little *tête-à-tête* with Gerry, she felt better somehow. For one thing, she didn't feel awkward conversing with him now that he had somehow managed to have her open up about things that she felt too self-conscious to let bubble to the surface, even in private with her parents. Their conversation rambled around to different things, and she discovered an assortment of interesting details about him along the way: he liked the colour blue, hated getting in elevators, preferred to remain independent in politics, and was planning to buy a villa near Rome hopefully someday soon. However, just when it seemed like they were really getting started, Gerry requested the tab.

"Well Princess, I think it's time to get you home, I don't want Pappa Bear to get mad at me for keeping you out late on a church night. Come to think about it, it's already very late."

"I didn't realize it was that late, the time passed so quickly," she smiled.

Gerry decided to pop open the last bottle of champagne in the limo, no point letting it go to waste. Katherine still insisted on only half a glass, she didn't want to attend service next morning with a splitting headache, and it would be like the Reverend to suspect she had a slight hangover.

"We're almost there. I thoroughly enjoyed our evening together, and I do hope you'll reconsider and come to see the new opera with me."

"I'll think about it," she mused, "I did have a wonderful time, thank you for everything."

"Before we say goodnight, there's something I ... *feel* ... I must do," he replied in a reflective tone.

"Oh? What would that be?" Perhaps propose another humorous toast with the last of the champagne. Before she could register what was happening, he leaned forward and gave her a kiss, not on the cheek or on her forehead, but softly on the lips. Surprised by this intimate contact, she sat in silent bewilderment, unable to speak or move.

"I had no idea I could have this affect," Gerry quietly remarked after several seconds had passed, half amused and slightly puzzled, "the princess has been cast into a trance! How shall we revive her? I think another kiss is in order."

He gently leaned forward and repeated the gesture, this time letting the moment linger.

She had never felt anything like this before, she was not sure how to react or what to think, what was proper or not, the strangest part, she was unable to resist. When she did feel him draw back, she felt an unexpected sense of … wishing it could have … just … lasted a little longer. That wasn't wrong, was it? After a few more seconds of stunned silence had passed, she finally found the strength to say something.

"My…that was … I …," she mumbled quietly.

"At last, she speaks! Are you … all right?"

"I …'m fine," she replied, unable to meet his eyes or control the blush rising to her cheeks, "I … well, I…" She didn't know what to say, words seemed insignificant after that experience. Thank heavens the partition separating them from the chauffeur was closed.

"You mean … this was your first kiss … *ever?*" he asked gently, his voice reflecting a hint of astonished disbelief. Still unable to raise her eyes, she simply nodded with a timid smile as she fiddled with one of her coat buttons. "I'm sorry, perhaps I should have asked your permission first, I didn't intend to send you into a … catatonic trance," he chuckled quietly. "To think, after all this time, a beautiful woman like you, to never have known what it felt like … . You know, my dear Scarlett, you *need* to be kissed, and often."

Katherine's blush deepened at the suggestion.

"That's not … very original," she replied finally raising her eyes, still finding it difficult to say something halfway coherent let alone intelligent.

"Perhaps not, but it's a great line given to a great man," Gerry smiled. "I may not be Clark Gable, but it would pain me to think that I left you in a state of paralysis, especially on your first kiss," he continued hesitantly, "as they say, third time is a charm, but now I shall ask you. May I … before … we say goodnight?"

Although it was difficult to see in the diffused lighting, she could not take her eyes away from his, they seemed to be gently waiting for her to answer, and somehow, her own must have returned a favourable reply, for he leaned closer, closing the distance between them and completed the proverbial charm. How long it lasted, it was difficult to tell, the moment was almost beyond comprehension. It felt … beautiful, too beautiful to last she thought as the limo pulled up to her front door. When they slowly drew apart, she felt that they were holding hands, she could not look to verify the curiously reassuring pressure, unable to take her eyes from his, semi-veiled in the muted light. How did she fail to notice how captivating his eyes could be, deep, curious and reflective; it was hard not to feel bashful as she noticed he too was quietly exploring the expression in hers. In that brief, fleeting moment, she understood that after tonight they would never see each other in the same way, it was a new, sombre, yet stirring realization.

At that moment, the lights brightened slightly as Samuel opened the door for them, slowly drawing them from the intensity of that enchanted moment without dispelling it entirely. Not knowing what to say, there remained a calm, introspective silence between them as he helped her out and offered her his arm once more.

"I suppose it's time to say goodnight," she remarked quietly as they reached the front door.

"So it is," he said as he took her hands in his. "May I … call you tomorrow? After service of course … ."

"If you like," she smiled.

"Pleasant dreams then. Goodnight."

"Goodnight, thank you … for everything."

A few more seconds passed before he reluctantly released her hands, allowing her to retrieve her key from her purse. Walking back to the car, he turned and waved.

"You know what Samuel?" he rhetorically asked as he watched her step inside and close the door.

"What sir?"

"I must be the luckiest Joe Bloke on earth," Gerry declared before settling back into the seat. He was feeling operatic tonight and could not resist humming a satisfying strain or two from the opera as they drove off.

Katherine too felt an almost uncontrollable urge to sing as she gazed at the bouquet of red roses and locked the door behind her for the night, but thinking better of her musical début lest she disturbed the house, decided to hum quietly to herself instead. However, she noticed someone had stayed up for her as the sounds of the TV drifted down the hall. Tiptoeing to the den, she found Mom and Pops fast asleep on the large overstuffed sofa, they looked so comfortable nestled together in their plush winter dressing robes, it would be a shame to wake them. She quickly wrote them a note saying she had arrived home safely and would tell them all about it in the morning, a censored version of course, she couldn't tell them *everything*; she had no way of knowing how they would take the news she had received her first kiss, three to be precise. Feeling overcome by the first stages of drowsiness, she made her way to the stairs but paused once more to admire the flowers sitting in their crystal vase on the hallstand. They were too beautiful, she couldn't leave them there in the dark hallway for the night; for the first time, she felt the possessive sensation of not wanting the delicate buds handled or admired by anyone else. They would look perfect on her dressing table. While she could hardly fathom what had just happened to her that night, she reached some conclusions before she fell asleep, certain things now made perfect sense; *Moon River* didn't sound so syrupy, mistletoe wasn't such a bad idea, and perhaps dating was not such a frivolous waste of time after all.

When she woke the next morning, she wondered if it had all been a dream until she opened her eyes and saw the bouquet standing on her dressing table exactly where she left it the night before. She smiled to herself as she closed her eyes and snuggled her face into her pillow, enjoying the happiness of her first truly romantic experience. Although he had always struck her as handsome, after last night, she could finally admit to herself how deeply attracted she was to him, having been too mistrustful and even a little fearful to face this unfamiliar feeling. Moreover, the attraction was mutual, or he would never have made the 'first move', the knowledge of which made her feel light-headed in a good way. It was a pity last night ended so soon. However, she could not dwell in this delightful reverie for long as she heard everyone getting ready and about to head downstairs for breakfast. She had better hurry and get dressed, 'Pappa Bear' would not be very happy if she were late.

"Well, here she is," Gramps beamed as she sat at the table, "my, someone looks like they had a good time last night."

"It certainly does," Mom replied, giving a quick glance at Pops as she sipped her coffee. Katherine found it almost impossible not to smile, she was in a very cheerful mood, it was bound to show.

"I did have a good time, I don't know where to start."

"Oh do tell us," Suzy asked, forgetting her pancake. She was obviously a little impatient to hear one snippet of last evening's adventure, adding "he picked her up in a limousine you know, and he cut quite the dashing figure too."

"*Su...zyyy!*" Katherine intoned with a touch of self-conscious embarrassment and amusement.

"I'm glad you had a nice evening. Did you meet anyone at the opera?" Pops asked.

"Yes, as a matter of fact, you won't believe who we bumped into."

The doorbell rang, and before she could continue, they heard the familiar *clickety-clock* of Aunt Martha's heels resounding off the tile floor and growing louder as she made her way to the dining room. *Oh no.*

"Good morning everyone, thought I'd drop by before church. Well Kathy! I heard about your romantic *soiree*," she announced as she made herself comfortable in one of the empty chairs and helped herself to the pancakes, "I'm dying to hear the news! Well, how did it go? I'm all ears."

Gee, how did she find out? Someone at the gallery must have let something slip. Oh well, she was bound to scout out the gossip anyway.

"Gosh, Gerry just took me to the opera, it wasn't anything outlandish," Katherine began, hoping Aunt Martha wouldn't pry too deep and budge her way in on something that was truly … special and private. However, she was saved by the buzzer. "I'll get it Mrs. Gonzales, I'm closer to the door, don't rush," Katherine called out. Buzzing open the main gates, to her surprise, it was a special floral delivery: on a Sunday morning? *Someone* went to a lot of trouble, she could easily guess where this delivery came from.

"Is there a Miss Katherine Walsingham at this address?"

"That would be me."

"Sign here please."

My, he was showering her with flowers these days! When the deliveryman handed her the new bouquet, she was confused at first: he had sent her a curious assortment of red roses and bright yellow sunflowers with stylish sable paint brushes poking through the lustrous decorative ferns. She couldn't understand what this meant until she read the tiny card: "*I enjoyed painting the town with you, let's do it again soon.*"

"Hey Katie, what's going on?" Gramps called out.

"A special delivery," she laughed. Aunt Martha poked her head out the dining room doorway.

"My, what have you got there? Come on now, bring in it, let's see it," she prodded. Katherine obeyed the summons.

"How beautiful," Suzy exclaimed, "I think we know who sent them." "They are lovely," Mom agreed albeit a little mystified, "but roses and … sunflowers?"

"Paintbrushes too," Gramps observed with a touch of amusement.

"If that isn't the oddest thing I ever did see," Aunt Martha added with a puzzled little pout, "young men these days have no idea how to romance a girl. What does the card say?"

"Martha, it's for Kathy's eyes only, that is, if there is a card," Mom *tsked*.

Katherine smiled, she didn't mind reading the greeting aloud. Not only did Gerry have a great sense of humour, but now she was learning how perceptive he was. Somehow he knew this jolly floral display would delicately diffuse any suspicions of what happened, making the previous evening appear like a general night out on the town to everyone else, yet remain special just between them. Maybe the Victorians knew what they were doing with their secret 'language of the flowers' Katherine reflected as she placed the bouquet on the sideboard.

ଓଃ❀ଃ୨

"Earth to Kathy," Suzy laughed one Monday morning as they opened up the gallery and switched on the main lights, "I don't think you've heard a word I said."

"I'm sorry, I don't know where my head is lately," Katherine replied.

"*I* do, you've been like this all last week since Gerry took you out, not to mention you've raced to get to the telephone first every time it rings," adding with a knowing tone, "it's official—you're hooked on him."

"I don't know, it's … still early days yet. I've only gone out with him a few times," Katherine replied awkwardly. Was her growing attraction for him that obvious? She thought about what Justine told her all those months ago, that this was one of the 'First Signs', waiting for the sound of the ring and hoping it would be 'him'. If it was, at last she knew what it felt like, the twinge of disappointment when it was someone else on the other end of the line, or a slight rush of adrenaline when he did call. The odd thing was he didn't have to pronounce anything poetic or earth shattering on every occasion, it was enough to hear him say 'hello', ask how things were doing and enquire if one of the murals had sold yet. Sometimes she just liked to listen to his voice. There was a distinctive timbre to his speech that she found quite fascinating when he inflected his words a certain way, it was a challenge to focus on what he was actually saying when that happened.

"Sometimes a few dates is all it takes," Suzy noted.

"To be honest, I'm new to all of this. I've never had any real boyfriends, not in a serious way," Katherine painfully admitted, "and now I feel like I'm floating in space, no solid ground under my feet, not knowing what I'm really feeling or what direction to take … ."

533

"Just take it one step at a time. Speaking of which, here's your next opportunity," Suzy concluded, looking down and acting busy. Katherine looked over and saw Gerry struggling to enter through the swinging side door with a large flat package in tow, trying his best not to rip its colourful wrappings. Her heart skipped a beat or two, it was a little over a week since she last saw him, but it felt like an age had passed. She hurried to the door and helped him in.

"Hello, Princess. Cold morning, isn't it?" he said while leaning the package against one of the rolly-polies before rubbing his fingers together.

"Good grief, what's all this?" Katherine wondered.

"Why, this is your Christmas present. Can't you tell?"

"I know it's a *present*, but it looks like you've gone to considerable trouble...and I didn't expect any gifts, not after all you've done already... ."

"Nonsense," he beamed. "I've loaned many things to galleries, but it's time you received something special. Is there somewhere you can open this in private?" he asked in an undertone. "I want you to see it first before the rest of the world does."

"A new loan? You didn't have to, I'm quite happy with the Macedonian vase, it's proving quite popular with the visitors."

"This isn't a loan. This is just for you," he replied quietly.

"Oh...are you sure you want me to open it now? Before Christmas?"

"Yes, I want you to enjoy it before you become distracted by the usual holiday madness. Besides, its fun to have one present to open early, don't you think?"

"Speaking of early presents, I have something to show you too, it's up in the studio."

"Well, what are we waiting for? Lead the way."

Arriving at the top floor, Katherine turned on the lights and tried not to smile as she watched him step off the elevator double time despite the bulkiness of his package.

"So this is the secret workshop?" he said as he looked around. "Nice set-up you have here. You've kept the antique ambience too."

"Thanks. It's great isn't it? All Gramp's doing, working with this much space is an absolute dream come true."

"Now that we're here, you share your surprise first."

"Okay ... but I hope you won't be disappointed, it's not finished yet. Unfortunately, I probably won't have it ready in time for Christmas like I wanted, I hope you don't mind," she said as they approached one of the easels.

"No I don't mind. I wonder what you have under there."

He placed his parcel down and stood back a little with his arms folded as she uncovered the canvas. She couldn't help smiling as he raised his eyebrows in surprise, looking first at the picture, then at the photograph taped to the side that she was using as a guide before stepping back to examine the canvas over again.

"I don't believe it … *how* did you get that?"

"I had a little help from Lottie, she sent it to me," Katherine explained. "It is your favourite picture of Rome, isn't it? I hope she didn't send the wrong one, especially now that I've progressed this far."

"No, that's it all right, but I can't believe what you've done with the sky, your sunrise certainly looks more vibrant than the actual photograph."

"It's the oil paint, getting the right blending of colours while keeping the brushstrokes light and airy was tricky. Now that I've got the sunlight just perfect, I'm waiting for that to dry before I paint the actual city."

"You're a definite perfectionist, it's beautiful. I've been meaning to have this photo enlarged, but never got around to it, another one of those projects that gets shoved in the 'I'll do it later' drawer, but this is much better than I had planned. What gave you the notion…?"

"For awhile, I wanted to get you something really nice to say 'thank you', Christmas seemed the perfect time, but after last weekend …well *you* know … going to the shopping mall for your average gift didn't seem good enough, then I had no idea what to get since trying to find something for the man who has everything is mission impossible anyway, plus I wanted to do something really special, and after you told me how much you liked Rome and about the villa you wanted, this came to me. Lottie was happy to lend me one of your pictures, it's too bad I didn't think of it sooner and get started on it a little earlier, I had to wait for the photograph to arrive, and *now* I don't know how unique it will be because I promised Lottie a picture too for all her kindness, so I have to paint the Acropolis next, and of course I don't want to forget your brother either, perhaps there's a sacred picture he'd like a copy of, so you're all getting a similar gift … ."

"Whoa, slow down Miss Locomotive, take a breath," Gerry laughed. "This *is* something special. You go right ahead and paint Lottie and Pete something, when you can of course. I'm honoured you would devote some of your precious creative time for this, I know Lottie and Pete will appreciate it too."

"You really like it?"

"I'll say. I have just the perfect spot for it, whenever you finish it.

Now it's time for your gift."

"It looks so cheerful, it's a shame to tear it. It's so big too, I wonder what it could be… ."

Carefully plucking off the shiny red ribbon and slitting the paper carefully around the top edge, she discovered a professional metallic protective case not unlike the pile stored in the boiler house belonging to certain paintings he had loaned her.

"Wow, this sure is fancy, I don't know when I'll be loaning my own pieces to other galleries, but this will certainly keep them safe when I do," she noted.

"You think this is it?" he laughed.

"Don't tell me there's something *in* there…?" she asked not a little astonished, a case like this could only mean that something extravagant lay inside.

"Well, go on, open it," he prodded, thoroughly enjoying her reaction, "I hope you are surprised." Katherine tore off the rest of the paper, laid the case down and snapped open the catches, taking a quick breath before lifting the lid.

"You didn't," she gasped.

"I did," he smiled.

Inside was not one, but four brightly coloured medieval images set within a single customised frame. She had seen it before: it was the unicorn collection she admired at the antique book show.

"But this is too much," she protested, "I couldn't possibly accept something like this."

"Yes you can."

"No I can't."

"Now let's not argue, I've never had a Christmas present refused, and besides, you *know* you want to keep it," he concluded in a good-natured tone.

"It's just … I don't know what to say," she stammered, it was too much to accept, and yet, it would be more than rude to refuse such a gift.

"You're welcome," he hinted.

"Oh, I *do* thank you … so much," she smiled shyly, "you certainly did surprise me."

"Let's have a better look at it," he suggested, setting up an easel and testing its level of sturdiness, "I too wanted to find you something special, and when I saw how you were drawn to this, the decision was made, an offering truly fit for a princess."

"It's too generous," she said as she placed the frame on the easel and stood back to admire the illuminations, "you know, my present to you doesn't seem so grand now compared to this. It reminds me of when our teachers used to make us do arts and crafts widgets for our parents," she sheepishly reflected.

"Hey, don't knock the sentimental value of those wonky clay ash trays and construction paper greetings cards. Come here you," he chuckled, placing a comforting arm around her shoulders. "Honestly, I love your gift. Considering all the artists I know, you're the first to actually paint a present for me, a picture I really like, too. Not to change the subject, what about this week? You *have* thought about coming to the opera again with me this Thursday, haven't you?"

"Of course. I haven't forgotten," she smiled, after their last outing to the Met, she was unable to think of anything else. " I *suppose* I can fit in another night on the town, but I'll have to check my agenda first," she joked.

"Funny girl. I'm taking that as a 'yes'. As much as I would like to stay with you all day, I must dash off," he regretfully announced.

"Are you sure you can't stay a little longer? Maybe have a cup of coffee and a croissant at least?"

"Sorry princess," he apologized, "the office beckons, no rest for the wicked. However, there *is* something I wouldn't mind having to help keep me going for the day, if it's all right with you."

She was about to ask him what that could be, but his eyes provided the clue to decipher his veiled comment. This time she knew what to expect and timidly met him half way, calmly closing her eyes. After they kissed, he gently enveloped her in his arms and held her close for a moment before whispering in her ear, "this is definitely better than caffeine, don't you think?"

"And croissants," she added, not quite expecting the embrace, her eyes still closed. They had never hugged one another before, not even during a friendly hello or goodbye, yet she found this new experience very agreeable.

"I've got to go," he sighed.

"Me too. I guess it's back to the plough." He offered her his arm and they slowly made their way to the elevator.

"At least we have Thursday night to look forward to."

"That's true. You know, I'm beginning to like going to the opera again," she replied with a smile.

"Me too. I shall call you tomorrow, we can go over our 'agendas' and decide upon a time I may pick you up."

"All right," she laughed.

The elevator touched ground too fast for her liking. After saying a quick goodbye and thanking each other again for the gifts, he gave her a friendly hug before finally making his way out the side entrance.

"I can see he liked your painting," Suzy noted as she sat down beside her at the front desk, "I'm just dying to know, what did he bring?"

"Remember the time he took me to the book fair, and the unicorn manuscripts I told you about? They were in the package … and they aren't a loan."

"No way! Are you kidding? Can I take a look?"

Katherine simply nodded her approval, slowly settling into the chair. She felt like singing again and quietly 'la– lahed' a tune to herself until Suzy returned from the studio.

"That's one heck of a Christmas gift, they're really beautiful."

"I know," Katherine replied a little distracted, she could still feel the comforting pressure of his arms around her, bundled up in his woollen winter coat. Yes, definitely better than coffee and croissants. "He's taking me to the opera again on Thursday."

"Uh huh," Suzy noted, "things *are* getting serious between you two."

"I seem to be in a whole other place when I'm with him, and I'm beginning to like it."

"Well, you finally know what it's like to be 'seeing someone'," Suzy laughed.

"Gosh, isn't it too soon for that? I'm still just getting to know him. How do I know when basic friendship has passed into that 'seeing someone' stage?"

"It depends on the person I guess. Tell you what, I'll run a few hints by you, say 'check' if I'm getting warm. Number one, you like spending time with him."

"Check."

"You definitely would like to get to know him better."

"Check."

"You're not interested in anyone else."

"Check."

"You don't particularly like the idea of *him* spending time with anyone else right now, and I'm referring to any female friends he has."

"That's a hard one, I don't mind him having causal acquaintances, I don't expect him to drop all his friends for instance."

"Not that, I mean … hmm … how do I put this? There are some moments that are special between you that you don't want him repeating with anyone."

Katherine took a minute to reflect, she hadn't experienced the pangs of heart gnawing jealousy, but imagining him with someone else and giving this lady a similar good night kiss like he did with her was not a pleasant thought. That was their 'moment', so was their tender goodbye this morning, gestures that she hoped he would only share with her. Maybe she *was* having serious feelings for him. "Check," she slowly replied, this new realization was something to think about.

"I think that makes it official," Suzy concluded.

"Good morning, girls," Esther greeted as she came through the back door. "What, may I ask, is now official?"

"Umm nothing," Katherine replied, giving a sideways glace to Suzy. This was all too new to share with anyone else just yet.

"Something that has been declared 'official' cannot be 'nothing'," Esther astutely observed, looking over the rim of her glasses, "but of course, if it's a secret, I won't pry. Secrets always 'will out' as they say. So, any news before we get started for today?"

"Gerry just brought in the biggest doozy of a Christmas gift for Kathy," Suzy disclosed, "it's gorgeous."

"Oh? You don't say? Now, that sounds exciting. What is it?" Esther asked.

"Remember the unicorn manuscripts I told you about…?" Katherine hinted.

"My Kathy, that is one generous gift. May I see it?"

"Sure, it's up in the studio."

"You know, we should hang it today, make sure it's secured," Suzy advised.

"Good idea, we should have that job done before we get busy for the day," Esther continued.

Although Katherine wanted to keep it sequestered in the studio all to herself for a little longer, she knew Suzy was right. Esther went to help Katherine as Suzy manned the reception desk. It did not take long before the task was accomplished, they had now become experts at arranging the exhibition spaces and working the alarm mechanism. The four images looked beautiful with the other medieval exhibits. It was difficult for Katherine to stay focused as she admired the colourful set as they now had acquired a pleasant memory that gave her a cosy, cuddly feeling.

"Hmm, that is one serious present," Esther observed. "I said I wouldn't pry, but tell me, are the skies painted with rainbows yet?"

Katherine didn't quite know what she meant until she saw Esther look at her with a knowing expression.

"I guess it really is obvious," she sighed, "okay, I'm very attracted to him, and it looks like we're actually … dating. He asked me to go to the opera again, and I'm really looking forward to it. Suzy says I'm 'hooked', that's what she declared was 'official', but this is all so new and unexpected, I don't know what to feel."

"Just be happy and enjoy it, dating can be lots of fun, within reason."

"Well, it does feel wonderful," Katherine admitted.

"Ah, wait until you hear the blue birds singing," Esther smiled.

Although she would love to have asked Esther how to recognise when and if things became really serious, hearing the huge racket Andre and the crew were making in the kitchen, she realized there was no time to dawdle at that moment, business had to be taken care of. Katherine declared a general 'pow-wow' as she called it and ordered a round of cappuccinos to be brought to the front desk.

The first matter to be discussed was the arrival of new paintings expected that afternoon *vis* the new collection by the young artist whom she had accepted on her first day. It was about time, he had spent so long choosing the frames, she thought they would never arrive.

"This is great, we have twenty new paintings in all, that'll help fill up some space," Katherine noted, "if he had hurried, he might have sold some during the Christmas shopping season."

"You know how artists are, he probably wanted to add more finishing touches before he brought them in," Suzy reflected, "it's hard letting a painting go and wondering if you could have done a little better."

"That's true," she agreed.

"Speaking of new paintings, Cecil has nearly finished another one he was working on, I think you're going to like it," Esther added, "it's a nautical scene, one with the old fashioned tall ships. It probably won't be ready until January though."

"So we have to wait until next year to see it," Katherine laughed, "that's all right. Hmm, tall ships, that will be different, we haven't had many seafaring scenes, I can't wait."

"Speaking of new paintings, how are your pieces coming?" Esther wanted to know.

"Well, they're on hold for awhile, I promised Lottie a picture after I finished with Gerry's, and I said I would do one for their brother too. Gerry said not to rush, but I don't want to delay keeping a promise. How are you doing with yours, Suzy?"

"I'm not painting as many as I thought I would," she sighed, "I just get started where I left off, and it seems it's time to stop again."

"You know girls, you're not going to be able to keep burning the candle at both ends, trying to run this place and find time for your own work. Considering how good things are going, you might want to think about hiring extra help," Esther advised.

"That's a very good idea," Katherine reflected, "even finding someone part time during the week would help. Suzy, mark that on our January 'to do' list."

"All righty, 'hire … help'," she mumbled as she jotted it down in the gallery agenda, "any date we should send a notice to the employment agency?"

"Not yet, keep it open, put it in the general list area, I have to go over the books, plus we have to discuss what would be the best time for us to paint so we can advertise the working hours."

"Okay, open date it is."

"You know, I wish I could find someone willing to take the gift area first," Katherine reflected, "the T-shirts are almost gone, and it's looking pretty bleak over there."

"We may have to close off that area for now," Esther noted, "there's nothing else we can do I'm sorry to say."

"With all the customers coming to *Chez Garneau* and the visitors this place is generating, you would think someone would jump at the chance to open a shop here," Suzy commented.

"Of course, it must be the recession, we're not out of it yet, and few people are going to take the risk starting their own place during times likes this," Katherine replied, "I don't like closing the blinds over there though, so I've got an idea, during lunch I'll pick up some rolls of gift wrap, we can paper the glass and make it look festive at least."

"Won't it look a little garish?" Suzy wondered. "It might clash with your *décor*."

"I'll pick nice paper," Katherine replied, "perhaps people might think it's part of our Christmas decorations. Anyway, if it is garish, it just might attract some attention to that corner, we need it now."

"There you go, when life throws you lemons," Esther began.

"You make lemonade," the two girls concluded.

"Good lord, what is Andre doing over there today?" Katherine wondered aloud, "is he whacking the kitchen to pieces or what? I can hardly hear myself think."

"He could be trying his new steak dish, sounds like they're pounding meat in there," Esther guessed.

"*That's* what's going on," Suzy laughed.

"Gee, and I thought I was all done with the sound of hammers around here," Katherine joked.

"Talking about food, we haven't seen your grandfather for awhile. Is everything all right?" Esther wondered. Katherine laughed, she had a good 'inkling' why Gramps was scarce these days.

"Andre has been slipping him food specially tailored to his cholesterol diet, Gramps doesn't know, but he could be guessing it by now and has decided to go back to the Club for awhile."

"Andre! He didn't," Esther chuckled.

"He sure did, Andre confessed and showed me where all the food substitutes are stashed, I can bring out the fake butter to prove it. Can you imagine a French chef having that in his kitchen?"

"Oh well, at least he tried," Suzy said as she finished her cappuccino.

"So girls, any special plans or 'doings' this Christmas season?" Esther asked.

"Well, I'm going with Charlie to his parents' place for Christmas," Suzy announced.

"That's great," Katherine replied, "things are getting really serious now for you two," she smiled.

"I know, but I have no idea what to bring as a gift, and on top of it, I don't think his mother likes me very much, she's a little frosty."

"Well try not to let her get to you, he is the only son, you know how that goes." Katherine tried to make excuses, but after the way Mrs. Kraylor had pushed Charlie into making his proposal to her when he wasn't ready displayed how much his mother had set her hopes on her to be the lifetime partner for her son, she would not accept anyone else that easily. "If you don't mind, I could make some suggestions."

"Oh yes, please do," Suzy replied, relieved to receive any advice.

"Mr. Kraylor has a thing for those fancy English tobaccos, and Mrs. Kraylor always likes to receive practical holiday gifts she can share, like holiday food baskets."

"Gee, thanks Kathy, that's a great help. I should have guessed about the tobacco, Mr. Kraylor likes that pipe of his."

"Well Esther, what about you? Big plans in the works?"

"Nothing new or different, just the usual dinner with all the trimmings. Our eldest son and his wife are visiting from Connecticut for the holidays, he and his father always look forward to a traditional spread."

"That's wonderful. Sounds like our place this year, Uncle Tim and Aunt Barbara put on Thanksgiving this time, so we do the Christmas end. Then we switch next year, it helps to keep things simple."

"You aren't getting dragged to any office party or charity event this year?" Suzy asked.

"No thank goodness, Mom and Pops said I don't have to go, they said now that I've got my own business it's too much trying to fit everything in. You know," Katherine reflected, "maybe I should have planned something for the gallery, it seems like every business is supposed to have an office party this time of year, but I just feel like I got over organizing the grand opening, and to have another major event on top of it seems like an overkill."

"You're quite right to take it easy this year, and besides, it's a little late now, you can plan something next Yuletide," Esther agreed. "If I were you, I'd try and enjoy your free days with your new beau," she hinted with a smile.

☙❀❧

Getting ready that Thursday evening felt different from the last time she dressed for the Met. Previously, she had simply followed social convention, chose suitable formal attire to be properly clad, hair curled and pinned up nicely, diamonds for accessories and velvet coat for protection against the winter chill, but this night was more than simply having a nice evening out: she was really going *with* someone, actually *seeing someone* as Suzy put it. She was glad she had made the effort the previous week and bought that new blue gown, especially since she discovered his favourite colour. It was a pity about the unspoken dress codes, it *would* be considered rather odd if she went in that again. At least she had other dresses, deciding what to wear during those days of waiting was difficult, but she finally narrowed it down to two. There was the black and white dress, hmm maybe it was too sombre, the deep burgundy red velvet was also nice, winter was the time for darker colours, and it still fit perfectly. It also had a matching winter cape with an elegant hood that draped around the shoulders. Her set of delicate tear-drop rubies would be perfect with this outfit. Decision made. As she clipped up her hair, she wondered if he was going to wear that handsome frock coat again. As she was finishing up and slipping on her satin shoes, there was a knock on her door.

"Come in," she called out.

"You look beautiful," her mother complimented.

543

"Thanks Mom."

"You don't mind if we have a word before you leave?"

Uh oh, was she in trouble or something?

"No, what's on your mind?"

"Well, your father and I couldn't help but notice you're seeing this young gentleman quite a bit lately," she began a little hesitantly, sitting next to her, "of course, you're at the age now to where you don't need a chaperone, but … ."

Perhaps she was worried about her staying out late like the last time.

"If you're worried about me coming home late, we'll try and be more punctual tonight. Really, all we did was talk, and we lost track of the time."

"We trust you dear. To be honest, in these liberal times, you're much more conservative than other girls … women your age," she corrected herself, "this is what I wanted to talk to you about. Is he … respectful towards you? Of course, this is a private matter, but we hope he's not rushing you into anything you are uncomfortable with. The only reason I'm asking is we only met him a few times, we don't know this young man very well."

"Oh, he's very respectful, it hasn't come to anything … like that," Katherine replied, now understanding her mother's concern. Somehow, parents had a hidden radar when it came to new experiences in their children's lives. Should she finally tell her about her first kiss so they did not jump to extreme conclusions? This was a rather delicate situation, she didn't know if it was all right to talk about it with her.

"I'm relieved to hear that," her mother admitted. "You really are attracted to him, aren't you?"

"Um hmm," Katherine nodded with a smile.

"It shows, I've never seen you hum so much. You know dear, you should invite him over for dinner some night."

"Really?"

"Of course! I'm surprised you haven't asked him already. It'll give us a chance to get to know him better, however, you might have to wait until after New Year's, considering all the holiday plans… ."

"Sure thing, okay, I'll invite him."

"When you do, don't forget to ask if he has any favourite dishes, and if he has food allergies, we don't want to ruin his first night here."

"Okay Mom," she smiled.

Katherine had allowed for plenty of time to get ready, so they decided to go downstairs and wait in the front parlour. Dinner plans were foremost in their conversation, although they couldn't decide on any definite details at that point. It was just exciting to talk about inviting him over for the first time. At last, they heard a car pulling into the driveway, Jasper scampered through the front hall barking his usual greeting, Mom following close behind to let in their guest. Opening the door, she discovered a large poinsettia bouquet with legs.

"Merry Christmas," a voice jovially called out from behind the display, "could someone please direct me in? I can't quite see where I'm going."

Helen smiled as she took his arm and directed him to the hallstand. Katherine couldn't stop laughing when see could finally see Gerry after he safely put the flowers down: he was wearing the frock coat she admired, but this time he was sporting a furry Santa Claus hat with a sunflower pinned in front and hooked over his arm, an old fashioned walking cane painted in Christmas candy stripes. Hearing the laughter, Pops and Gramps came out from the den to wish them a pleasant evening before they left, but Gerry was not finished with his deliveries.

"Wait, the sleigh is not quite empty," he said as he skipped out the front door and skidded across the slippery path to the limo, returning with bottles of wine and a large box of holiday chocolates for the family.

"Gosh, you didn't have to go to all this trouble," Katherine replied, trying to catch her breath from laughing.

"Nonsense, it's the time of year to spread good cheer, and I'm not done yet," he added before sliding out the door once more, this time carrying back a dainty corsage box filled with sunflowers. "You look gorgeous tonight," he complimented as he opened the petite carton.

"Thank you, you look very jolly," she replied, slipping the yellow blossoms onto her wrist, she was trying not to laugh again, "I just love your accessories."

"Well, don't keep dallying around here, skedaddle and have some fun," Gramps called out.

"Okay," Katherine smiled, "see you all later."

"I'll try and bring her back early this time," he promised as he shook hands with Pops and Gramps, "although it depends on the opera tonight, I have no idea when it will be over."

"We understand, just bring her home safe and sound," Pops replied.

Gerry offered Katherine his arm and escorted her to the limo, she turned and gave the family a goodbye wave before greeting Samuel and settling inside. On this occasion, she noticed there was a generous tray of *hors d'oeuvres* prepared for their evening commute.

"What's all this?"

"Wait a sec, here you go," he said, giving them each a champagne flute with a Christmas ribbon tied on the stem before reaching into the mini-bar and retrieving a humble bottle of ginger ale, "I'm better prepared this time as you can see," he announced as he poured them a glass of the non-intoxicating bubbly. "Since I said we would have dinner first, I thought we should have our starter now and give us some extra time to enjoy our meal before we have to run for the first curtain."

"Hmm, you have this all planned out, don't you?"

"No famishing finales this time, I have something else too," he continued, reaching into his breast pocket and taking out a slender gift-wrapped box, "open it."

"Another gift? Gerry I ... ."

"Just open it."

At this point, she was mortified with the extent of his generosity until she lifted the lid to find a black satin set of night time eye covers used by those who worried about getting enough beauty sleep. Katherine gave him a questioning look.

"Your shield, for any incoming tonsil torpedoes," he explained, "a good knight must protect his princess from the onslaught of unexpected understudies."

"Very funny, Lancelot," she laughed, folding the blinders and putting them in her purse.

The restaurant that night was packed with diners and the mood felt electric with holiday merriment, it was a miracle Gerry was able to secure a reservation Katherine realized. Just when she thought things couldn't get any funnier, she noticed that when the waiter had taken his coat and 'hat', Gerry had a sprig of festive holly stuck into his front jacket pocket where the handkerchief would normally be artfully folded. Slightly crushed under his coat, the bruised sprig dropped a few leaves every now and then, eventually landing a few berries onto his plate.

"It seemed a good idea at the time," he sighed, plucking the branch from his pocket and finding a new home for it in the table floral decoration before hunting the rogue berries out of the sauce with his fork.

"Be careful, they could be poisonous," she warned, trying not to laugh.

"I guess I wasn't that hungry anyway," he said, leaving the plate aside, "now, where were we?"

"You were saying Lottie will be flying back from Paris tomorrow," Katherine reminded him, "I'm glad she had such a good time, it sounded like it when I called her to borrow your photograph."

"You and Lottie seem to be getting very friendly, even with the Atlantic between you. She never forgets to ask about you."

"I like her very much. She's a kind-hearted person. I probably shouldn't mention this, but I did hear about her tragic loss. Sometimes I can't understand why terrible things happen to such nice people."

"It was certainly a shock for all of us. I hope this trip will do her some good."

"I'm sure it will," Katherine reassured him.

"Well, it will be good to have her home for the holidays."

"How is your brother doing? You know, I haven't seen him since the grand opening."

"I guess Pete's fine, it's difficult for him to keep in touch, he's quite busy. I didn't realize there was such a demand for an exorcist in these modern times. You probably haven't heard, he's just been made a Monsignor too."

"Is that … good?" Katherine asked, she wasn't sure what this new office meant.

"I suppose so, it's more of an honorary title really. I think his superiors wasted their time, Pete doesn't care for such things. He has other big plans in motion, but whether anything will come of them is up to the Church."

"Oh? That sounds fascinating. What are these plans?"

"He's got this idea in his head we need another order, as if we didn't have enough of them already," Gerry said, shaking his head. "Personally, I think he's batty. Even after Vatican II, there's nothing but hassle when something new is proposed, especially what he has planned. He could save himself the trouble and stick to parish duties, he's got enough people lining up at his confessional."

"Gosh, if that's the case, you should be supporting him, not discouraging him," Katherine reproved.

"I know, I must sound pretty bad, he's already had enough of discouragement from our family. I just don't understand why he has to keep making it harder on himself."

"Well, what is this new order he wants to start since it seems to be such a headache? I think the idea is fascinating, and I'm not even Catholic."

"I could have it all wrong, you'd have to ask him about the particulars sometime, but it definitely has to do with exorcism. I think he wants to help start an official association of Ghost Busters or something, there's a group of like-minded clerics who constantly meet up in Rome lately, don't know if anything's going to come of it."

"Sounds a little more serious than 'ghost busting'," she mused.

"I guess so, but hey, this is Christmas, not Halloween. How did we trail off into zombies and ectoplasm?" he laughed.

"I don't know, let's get back to Egg Nog season," she suggested.

"Uck, an image just as gross: who ever thought drinking raw eggs was a way to celebrate?"

"You don't like it then? I can't get enough of it, I think it's the nutmeg."

"The only way I'd get it down is to dose it with a double shot of brandy."

"That would be the end of *my* Christmas celebrations," she laughed, "you might find me snoring under the tree."

"Shall I order you a glass of ginger ale, my dear?"

"No the champagne is fine," she assured him, "as long as I eat something substantial."

"Well, more champagne it is then. Speaking of celebrations," he continued while attempting to catch the attention of the waiter, "do you have any plans for the holidays?"

"Nothing major, dinner at home with the family Christmas Day, that's about it."

"What about New Year's?"

"I think everyone's heading off to the Club as usual, I don't think they like sitting at home for the countdown, although my brother may have something else planned."

"What about you, are you joining them?"

"I don't know yet, my parents have released me from all social obligations this year, so I might just plonk my feet up and watch the mayhem at Times Square from the comfort of our sitting room."

"You staying home all alone on New Year's Eve? Unthinkable. Take my advice and borrow a leaf from your parent's book, the countdown should be shared with someone, or it's just another set of numbers passing you by. I have an idea: since you will be on your own, and I have nothing on my 'agenda'," he said with a smile, "why not have a quiet dinner at my place? I'll have my housekeeper arrange for a catered party for two, no boisterous diners to try and shout over or operas to rush off to, we can watch the fireworks light up the sky from my balcony. Doesn't that sound like a capital plan?"

She paused for a moment. Hmm, that sounded like a truly romantic way to celebrate, she wanted to accept his impromptu dinner party right away, but paused before answering as she thought about her mother's concern that evening. An invitation to a private supper in his apartment was a serious step, and she hoped enjoying a romantic dinner with her was all he expected. He sensed her apprehension and quickly reassured her of his honourable intentions.

"Don't worry, I won't keep you out late, Princess. Lancelot swears to hear and obey the commands of Pappa Bear and always see you return home safe and sound."

"All right then," she smiled.

"Speaking of dinner, perhaps we should finish this one first. The *tiramisu* sounds good to me."

"I think I'll sample their special hot chocolate fudge cake."

Finishing their dessert in a hurry and telling Samuel to push the petal to the metal, they arrived at the Met just in time. Gerry was right Katherine thought while watching the comic antics of the opera characters as they tried to rewrite history and save Queen Antoinette from the guillotine, it would be nice to spend some quiet time together with no other interruptions. She and Gerry would hardly have a conversation started when they had to rush somewhere else, or she had to go home. It was fun spending time together, and they still had much to discover about each other. At least she found out he didn't like Egg Nog, that was something new. They were obviously both glad the intermission came, giving them a chance to chat.

"Whew, thank goodness for that, I needed a break. Well, Princess, would you like something from the bar?"

"No, not really, thank you. I'd like to stay here right now. I think 'Mr. Morgue' is here again, and I don't want to bump into him."

"All right, we shall avoid the maddening crowd. Speaking of which, what do you think of the performance so far?"

"The opera is a bit odd, isn't it?" she laughed, "I can't keep up with the plot and sub-plots."

"It's certainly one of the strangest productions I've seen in a while, but then, it is a new opera," he reflected, "I thought it might be worth seeing since the Met hasn't commissioned anything since the sixties. They were really secretive about this too, no outsiders were allowed in for the rehearsals, so I heard."

"They wanted to keep it a surprise I guess."

"Oh, enough about opera, I wanted to ask you, did you read Horace's column lately?"

"Actually, I haven't. I just thought I'd let him get on with it, no point taking everything he writes to heart.”

“Then you missed what he said about your D.S.’s paintings,” Gerry roguishly replied, “not as bad as other reviews, but a little cutting to say the least.”

“Ah, that explains the influx of visitors,” Katherine reflected, “Horace just did me a favour then. I’ll sell one yet, you just wait and see, mister.”

“Don’t you want to know what he said about them?”

“Not really,” she replied, “not anymore.”

“That’s a switch,” Gerry noted with interest, “just what did you two talk about the day he dropped by? You were ready to skewer him with a palette knife.”

“Well, his tape recorder caught it instead, so I guess my need for vengeance is appeased,” she began, confessing to flinging the harmless machine to its doom.

“I’m sorry I missed the beginning,” he laughed, “that must have been some ‘hello’. Just how did you two manage to make up?”

“It’s kind of confidential, all I can say is he’s not that bad, I understand him now. Like you explained, there’s nothing to his column really, it’s all smoke and mirrors, like the set designs tonight.”

“So you like him after all, do you?”

“I only met him that one time, I don’t think gate crashing my grand opening counts, but I guess he’s all right.”

“Hmph! Will wonders never cease,” Gerry teased, “anyway, have you thought about your dare yet?”

“I’m still thinking ... .”

“What? Such confidence in your artistic discovery, and you haven’t devised a impossible challenge for your intrepid knight,” he grinned.

“Okay Sir Lancelot, since you are so high and mighty, I don’t suppose *you* have a dare all prepared.”

“Maybe,” he answered with an air of mystique.

“You’re just saying that to nettle me,” she teased, “come on, tell me what it is, if you really have one.”

“Uh uh,” he said, shaking his head, “not until we see what happens at the end of the month.”

“Oh, you’re going to be difficult, are you?” she laughed. “At least give me a hint so I can come up with something comparable.”

“No way, my lips are sealed until then,” he insisted.

At that point, their conversation was interrupted by one of Gerry’s business acquaintances and his charming wife who decided to make their way over to their box and say a friendly 'hello' that extended into a long-winded chitchat brimming with small talk pleasantries. At last, Katherine grew a little annoyed when the gentleman finally hinted the reason for his visit, he just wanted to find out if certain shipping arrangements could be made for him regarding his exotic fruit exports. Oh here we go, Katherine thought, business again. Couldn't these people guess there was a reason they stayed in their box and just wait until tomorrow to pester Gerry? She was sure Reinold Enterprises could be found in the Yellow Pages if they didn't have his card already. Her quiet frustration grew when they heard the curtain call. Gerry told 'Mr. Fruits' to call his office and he would sort something out. After shaking hands and saying goodnight, they were finally left in peace, although with hardly a minute left to themselves.

"Sorry about that," he apologized, "now, where were we?"

"Our dares," she reminded him.

"Ah yes. I'm afraid we've hit a dead end there, until next year."

"I suppose so Sir Secret, Master of Suspense," she smiled.

"Funny girl. Listen, before I forget, I have to ask you ... oops, I guess it'll have to wait until the opera's over," he remarked as the lights dimmed.

"Okay, just hold that thought," she replied.

"All right," he smiled.

The opera turned out to be entertaining that night and she didn't have to close her eyes. Some scenes were outright hilarious, she did have a good laugh or two, and she couldn't believe her ears when a band of kazoo players dressed as Arabian musicians arrived on stage to play their part. However, events that night took another unexpected but pleasant turn when she applauded at the end of one act, her program slipped off her lap and landed on the floor between their two seats. They instinctively leaned forward to retrieve the booklet and their hands brushed for a moment. This gentle, unplanned touch in the dimmed light of the theatre vividly brought back all the emotions she felt the other night when he held her hands. She was tempted to repeat the experience, their heads were so close as they leaned forward it would be possible to steal a quick kiss before they settled back in their seats, but she couldn't bring herself to do it in front of all those people, even in the semi-darkness. He too remembered that special moment, for he couldn't take his eyes away from hers in the shadowy light as they slowly sat upright, he politely handing her the program, yet instead of re-establishing the space between them, he extended his right hand towards her, an invitation to prolong their close encounter. She smiled and slowly slipped her left hand in his. Holding hands, it was such a simple gesture, yet in many ways more difficult to initiate than a kiss. As they sat with their fingers gently interlaced, pretending to pay attention to the opera, she could sense some unspoken milestone had been reached. Now that permission to hold hands had been given and accepted, an invisible bridge had been built in those few moments, allowing them to pass beyond the recognition of mutual attraction and explore a new sense of closeness growing between them. They broke contact when obliged to applaud between scenes, but now that the delicate question of sharing their personal space in public had been so beautifully addressed, their hands did not hesitate to meet again when the clapping died away.

The performance drew to a close quicker than they would have liked and they were forced to applaud longer then usual as the house rose to give the singers a thunderous standing ovation. At last, the audience began to slowly filter out and it was time to leave. Gerry helped Katherine with her cape before retrieving his coat, festive Santa hat and cane, then bowed slightly and offered her his arm. Even this gesture was now more intimate as he gently tucked her closer to him than before, feeling her arm so snugly sheltered gave her a satisfying sense of security. They did not say anything for awhile, not even when they sat inside the limo, they simply joined hands as they before. For some inexplicable and yet completely comprehensible reason, they knew that speaking was not terribly important, it was enough to simply 'be' while they interiorly explored what they were feeling. Katherine eventually remembered he wanted to ask her something.

"You wanted to ask me a question earlier."

"Hmm? Oh yes, nothing too exciting, just what you might like for dinner on New Year's Eve. Is there anything special I can have prepared for us?"

"I can't think of anything right now, you can surprise me."

"All right. Anything in particular I should shun like the plague?"

"Well, if you don't mind, nothing with liver please."

"What? No *foie gras* for the Francophile?"

"Uck." The thought made her shudder.

"No *paté* it is then, your wish is my command. Come here you," he laughed, putting his arm around her and holding her close. They sat quietly not saying anything, words would only spoil the moment. She then realized she was resting her head on his shoulder, which gave her a warm, pleasant feeling. "I take it you liked the opera," he finally commented.

"Um hmm, especially our own little opera," she humorously admitted.

"Yes, we do make good music together, don't we?"

"This act is pretty good too," she added.

"Well, I'm sorry it has to come to a close so soon, but you're almost home now," he noticed, "but we have a wonderful finale to look forward to," he reminded her.

She smiled, she wouldn't mind an encore performance of last week. They leaned forward, expecting to blend in perfect harmony when an unanticipated interruption in the form of a furry pom-pom softly bopped them on the nose. Katherine started to laugh as he grabbed his Santa hat and flung it away with a flourish.

"Wearing that seemed such a good idea at the time."

"Shall we try again, Maestro?" she smiled.

"But of course," he replied leaning forward, this time he reached up, gently holding her head in his hands with the end of his palms near her cheeks, the tips of his fingers nestled in her hair. Katherine could almost hear a full string orchestra with this new experience. She half-unconsciously emulated his gesture, feeling his wavy soft hair between her fingers for the first time. How long they remained suspended in that blissful sensation, she didn't know, or when the limo stopped, she couldn't say, but at last they drew back, he with one hand caressing her cheek, she likewise, gently curling a small lock of his hair around her finger, then holding his hand closer to her cheek for a brief second or two before they returned to holding hands.

"Hmm, if the other morning was cappuccino and croissants, I wonder what this was?" he mused.

"Definitely a second helping of hot chocolate fudge cake."

"Good comparison," he chuckled under his breath. "Well, our opera is over, the curtain is drawn, I suppose it's time to say goodnight," he regretfully announced with a sigh, lifting his hand once more and giving her cheek a reflective caress with the back of his finger before he opened the door. "It's a shame I'm going to be tied up until New Year's Eve, I wish I could see you before then, but my agenda is really and truly booked. Perhaps you might call me? Or I'll call you in the meantime?"

"All right. I'll let you know when one of the murals sells," she replied, wrapping her arm in his as he escorted her to the front door.

"Oh ho!" he laughed, "no whispering 'sweet nothings' over the line to each other then?"

"Umm, I suppose we could fit that in," she smiled, "I have to work too you know."

"How tragic, must reality set in so soon?" he joked.

"Well, we are at my front door," she observed, "we must say *au revoir* sometime."

"I guess we won't see each other until New Year's Eve."

"Until New Year's Eve."

"All right then, sleep well, my princess," as he gallantly kissed her hands goodnight.

"Pleasant dreams, Lancelot."

଼ଷ ✾ ଼ଓ

Oak Meadows became a hive of activity leading up to the 'Big Feast'. Mrs. Gonzales and Juanita always had Christmas Day off, so it became a true family affair when the festive dinner was planned and prepared. Aunt Barbara, Aunt Martha, Katherine and Stephanie were drafted for kitchen duty, while the men were told to stay out of the way and go find something to do, usually that meant they ended up lounging around in the den until it was time to eat. The women had everything planned like clockwork, so it was safer to let them at it Gramps figured; in fact, they had practically made a game of the work, assigning tasks as if they were endowed with official tasks of a realm. Helen was 'Queen', it was her kitchen, so the turkey, and supervising the activities of her 'subjects', were her primary concern. Aunt Barbara was Cabinet Minister of Ham, while Aunt Martha, famous for her pumpkin pie, became Duchess of Desserts. Of course, the younger members of the kitchen kingdom did not receive the most glamorous duties and were assigned tasks suited to their various skills. Katherine was delegated the office of Prime Potato Peeler and Head Whip Cream Whippersnapper, while Stephanie was nominated Chief Vegetable Preparer, eventually they were both promoted to Royal Table Setters when their KP work was finished.

"Hey, we should revolt this year," Stephie joked as they set out the silver and crystal, "why do we woman have to do all this while the Lords and Dukes sit around on their patahs?"

"Down with the Bastille," Katherine returned, "but seriously, you know what would happen if we let the men folk help. The kitchen would be in a mess, nothing would get prepared on time, the men would be poking half-raw nibbles out of the pots all day rather than cooking the stuff, plus all the tableware would end up in the wrong place, and our mothers would be having a heart attack. We'd have pandemonium in the palace."

"Wouldn't it be funny if we turned the kitchen over to the men just one year and see what happens?"

"I know I should talk, but we'd probably starve," Katherine laughed.

"So we ladies are the power behind the throne and the keepers of peace in the domestic domain, right?"

"I guess so, not to mention this gives us a chance to catch up on news."

"True come to think of it. So how are things between you and 'Mystery Man'?" Stephie wanted to know.

"Well, let's say things are getting interesting," Katherine smiled, "I think we're officially dating."

"Oh my gosh," Stephie gasped, "stop the presses, my cousin is finally getting a life … pigs are flying and I'm a monkey's uncle."

"Stephie," Katherine *tsked*.

"Looks like I missed quite a bit lately. Well, go on, tell me the news," Stephie cajoled, "you can't drop a bombshell like that and then clam up."

"There's nothing to talk about really, we went to the opera a few times and … now don't make a big deal of this … I'm going to his place for New Year's Eve."

"Wow, you're having that romantic dinner for two after all," Stephie smiled, "well, good for you, Miss Bennet, I'm glad you and Mr. Darcy are hitting it off."

"Oh, Stephie, stop teasing."

"Hey, who's teasing? I'm serious. You're finally getting your nose out of the books and gaining some real experience. So, have you seen him since you went to the opera?"

"No, he was tied up, and so was I. Thing is, we said we would call in the meantime, but I guess he hasn't had the chance, and I've been up to my ears with work."

"Romance blossoms, and then no contact? Hmm, when did you last see each other?"

"A little over a week ago."

"You guys haven't called each other since then?"

"I don't want to bother him at his office, and I don't know when would be a good time to phone him at home, whenever I had a free moment, it was well past any reasonable calling hour. I'd hate to pick a time that would be inappropriate."

"Gee, you spend late nights at the opera together, but don't want to call late. Well, does he have your house number?" Stephie asked.

"I have his, but gosh, I don't think he has mine," Katherine suddenly realized.

"Just great, if that doesn't send a guy mixed signals," Stephie said shaking her head, "you belong in the medieval ages! It's okay for a girl to call a guy these days, got it? Since you have his number first, he's probably waiting for you to call him, and your radio silence is not helping the matter. I really don't think he'd care about the time."

"I'm surprised he didn't ask for it," Katherine remarked.

"Did you ask for his?"

"Well no, he just gave it to me."

"Obviously, he's waiting for you to volunteer your number then. Don't you get it? Asking for someone's number is a bit personal, it's like inviting himself to dinner. Gifts are one thing, phone numbers are another, he's afraid he might come across as pushy and scare you off. You'd better act fast, or he'll thing something is wrong, and don't forget to give him your number."

"I suppose I could do that," Katherine reflected. Why did things like this come so naturally to others and so complicated for her? Sometimes it felt like she was absent the day the Higher Powers of the universe handed out the rulebook on dating. "Now that you've sorted me out, how about you? What about the guy you met last month?"

"O *him*," she said, tossing her head in disgust, "I got rid of him, pronto. What a rat!"

"That was fast. What happened?"

"While he's dating *me*, I walk in on him and his sister's girl friend, and let me tell you what I saw…"

"Stephie, remember it's Christmas, no graphics please on today of all days. I can just imagine."

"Well, you got the picture. Good riddance, *Adiós enemigo*," she finished with a wave of her hand, "creeps are a dime a dozen out there, and if you find a guy that's decent, hang on to him, that's my advice. Anyway, how is Steve and the girlfriend? You know how touchy he is if we ask him outright."

"As far as I know, they're still together, I never thought I'd see him stay with anyone this long," Katherine noted.

"Wow, love really is in the air. She could be the one for him. Do you think he'll pop the question?"

"Gosh Stephie, I haven't a clue. He hasn't settled down yet, hardly marriageable material."

Their conversation came to a halt when Helen came in to see how they were doing, Katherine knew better than to mention 'Steves' and 'marriage' in the same sentence around Mom, she still had to accept they were all growing up.

"My, the table looks beautiful, you did a lovely job. Dinner is on, and it's time the ladies took a well-deserved break."

Katherine and Stephie obeyed the summons and joined the matriarchs for a festive helping of pre-dinner nibbles of all descriptions after they had brought out similar trays of delectables to the 'Lounging Lords' to help tide them over.

"How are they doing in there?" Aunt Barbara asked the girls.

"They're having a blast. Uncle Har just cracked open a bottle of something fancy," Stephie reported, "he gave everyone a taste before lacing the Egg Nog with it."

"It's the bottle of cognac Gerry brought for Pops," Katherine clarified.

"I hope they won't overdo it," Helen worried.

"Oh yes, do tell us more about you and Gerry," Aunt Martha interjected, "I saw he brought in a new medieval artefact to replace the book he took away."

"Really? That's news. What is it?" Aunt Barbara wanted to know.

"It's a series of unicorn manuscripts," Katherine explained.

"Sounds impressive, I'll have to drop by and see it sometime. You know, it's really kind of him to help you out with your exhibition area, Kathy," Aunt Barbara commented.

"Well, it's more than a loan, he gave it to her as a gift," Helen clarified with a knowing tone.

"Oh, you don't say," Aunt Martha said, lifting an eyebrow. "My word, this is wonderful, he really has taken a fancy to you, hasn't he? I do hope this works out this time."

"Give them a chance, they've only just started going out," Helen observed. "The thing is, he's too generous. I don't think you should have accepted it, Kathy."

"I know, but he wouldn't take it back. I can't help it if people go overboard," Katherine replied, "I'm always getting stuck in the most awkward predicaments."

"Hmm, it would have been rude if you refused," Aunt Barbara pointed out.

"True, but from now on, make it clear to him that any gifts in the future are kept within certain bounds," Mom advised, "in fact, I would outright tell him you don't expect anything else after that."

"Gee, I don't expect anything at all," Katherine affirmed, "it's bad enough he won't let us take turns picking up the tab or go Dutch at least."

"Oh, he's a dying breed, definitely old school," Aunt Martha observed, "you know girls, in our day when a man invited a lady out, it was his duty to pay for everything, even to the powder room assistants. A decent man would never think of letting a woman pay for anything."

"Thanks for the history lesson, I'm so glad I'm living now," Stephie piped up, "no one buys *me*. "

"Gosh, I don't want to be bought either," Katherine jumped in, "maybe I should give the manuscripts back, be it rude or not."

"Now you've done it," Aunt Barbara chided Martha before turning to Katherine, "look, he likes you, that's obvious, but knowing you basically can have anything you want has made him go overboard to try and impress you, do something over the top to make you notice him."

"Gosh, he doesn't feel he has to buy all the tea in China to do that," Katherine shyly confessed.

"In your case, yes he does," Stephie laughed.

"My, he *is* a good looking young man, isn't he," Aunt Martha affirmed with a sigh, "makes me wish I was young again."

"Hey, does anyone want to know about *my* love life?" Stephie asked, putting her hands on hips. "In case you're interested, I dumped Mr. Worthless."

"Oh I'm sorry honey," Aunt Barbara apologized. As the women commiserated with her, they heard boisterous laughter coming down the hall.

"Someone had better go check on them, they sound a little tipsy in there," Aunt Martha noted. Katherine hopped up, scouted out the den and delivered her report.

"I can't tell if they've had any more or not, but Gramp's nose is starting to go a little pink."

"Uh oh. Let's hope dinner is ready soon, or they'll all be doing double mileage to the table," Aunt Barbara noted.

"What?" Katherine queried.

"Weaving side to side from too much gaggle juice," Stephie explained. Eventually, dinner was cooked to perfection and conveyed to the sideboard in the dining room and laid out buffet style.

"Quick, call them in before it gets cold," Mom ordered, "or before their legs won't work."

"Oh Aunt Helen, you're so melodramatic, they're fine, a few shots of brandy won't kill them, I'll go announce the summons," Stephie offered.

"All right guys, grub's up," she called, poking her head into the den. As soon as they arrived, the main course were ceremoniously brought out. This year it was Pop's turn to do the honours and carve the bird, while Uncle Tim sliced the ham.

"Turkey for a turkey," Tim noted.

"Just keep hamming it up," Pops smiled.

"If we were having goose, *I'd* be given that to carve," Gramps chortled.

"Be thankful we're not having duck," Steves pointed out, "that's means you'd be a bit daffy."

"That would be for *you* to carve," Uncle Tim laughed.

"They're at it again, Helen," Aunt Barbara sighed. It was the same every year, the old predictable threadbare jokes that still managed to pull a smile or two, of course, the 'gaggle juice' did nothing to temper silliness.

"Hey Dad, what are you doing to the ham?" cousin Jon called out. "They removed the bone, you're hacking the thing to pieces. Uncle Har's doing a better job on the turkey, and he's got all the bones, and limbs to deal with too."

"Don't mind him Dad," William answered, "saw away."

"Double vision as well as double mileage, he can't see where's he's cutting the thing," Stephie joked under her breath to Katherine.

"All right everyone, come and help yourselves," Mom announced. After they had filled their plates and returned to their seats, she enquired who would like to say grace. Steven volunteered.

"Grace," he piped up.

"Steven, be serious," Helen chided.

"I am serious, seriously hungry," he affirmed.

"Perhaps your grandfather should say the blessing," she decided.

"The blessing," Gramps quipped.

"You're as bad as he is," Helen said with a disapproving look.

"What? I'm starving too," Gramps said, comically raising his hands.

"Hi, 'Starving Too', I'm 'Seriously Hungry', nice to meet you," Steves bantered, reaching across the table and shaking hands with Gramps.

"Honestly! After the tit-bits they've managed to pack away all afternoon, you would expect them to stay sober," Aunt Martha sighed rolling her eyes while the younger members at the table began to chuckle.

"All right, I'd better say it, before we have to heat everything up in the microwave," Pops announced. Authority had spoken. Everyone at the table held hands and waited silently for him to begin the prayer.

"It."

"Not you too, Pops," Katherine laughed.

"I think everyone has had enough to drink," Helen announced, "no more wine shall be served until you all eat something."

"We still have to say grace first," Steves reminded her.

"Grace first," Tim replied.

"Okay, that does it," Aunt Barbara declared, grabbing Tim and Helen's hands and launching into the prayer, "Bless us O Lord, and these Thy gifts … ." Everyone quickly followed suit and Christmas dinner could finally commence.

Gerry's cognac certainly helped to get everyone into the festive spirit, Katherine thought. While everyone chatted and bantered with each other, the only thing on her mind, when she was given a chance to think between the conversations, was wondering when she should call him and worrying what to do about the manuscripts. Should she keep them? Should she actually bring up the issue of giving the manuscripts back when she called? Were things developing too fast between them? She really had nothing on which to measure the 'velocity' or 'mileage' of a romantic relationship, perhaps reviewing recent developments might help. Come to think of it, they only met about a year ago, and she didn't see him again until six months had passed, that's a very short time to get to know someone. Then later, since they happened to cross paths at the Sirrac, it was as though he didn't know what he could do for her; the exhibition loans, dinners, the book show, nights to the theatre, bouquets up the ying yang, and now the manuscripts, he was definitely going overboard. Aunt Barbara may have a point: everyone kept remarking she had made an impression upon him, and he was going to great lengths to make sure she was aware of it. Well, it *was* flattering, but maybe now it was time to slow things down a bit.

The next day she decided to call him during the afternoon lull before the family arrived to enjoy the usual Christmas leftovers. At first, she thought he answered the phone until she realized it was his answering machine. Great, she had something serious to discuss, and now all she could do was leave a message; she always felt stupid talking to a machine, it scattered her thoughts.

"Er ... hi, it's me, Kathy. I'm sorry I missed you, this is ... not a good time to call I guess. I'll try again later… ." Before she hung up the receiver, she heard a *click*.

"Hi Kathy, don't hang up."

"Hi, is this a bad time?"

"No, not at all. You just saved me from the banality of daytime TV programming. I've missed you this past week, I wanted to call, but I didn't want to distract you at work."

"Me too, and I only realized yesterday you didn't have my home number, then Christmas didn't seem like a good day to call you. Before I forget, you had better write it down now," she declared, rattling off her number.

"Wait up! Let me get a pen first," he laughed, after a pause, "okay, fire away. So," he continued once he verified her number, "are you enjoying your days off?"

"Oh well, I suppose, I'm just hanging around. You would think I'd be tired of art right now, but I'm itching to pick up a paint brush."

"I know the feeling, just when you look forward to a break, cabin fever strikes and you want to run back to work."

"Well, speaking of art," she began, wondering if she should continue. She would have preferred to talk with him face to face than over the phone, but perhaps it was best to get it out in the open. "Honestly, I'm still flabbergasted over your gift. I hope you don't take this the wrong way, but you've been too generous to begin with, and then to receive something that costly, I'm seriously having second thoughts about keeping it."

"Uh oh, I feel a winter chill descending," he said teasingly, "seriously, I didn't intend to make you feel uncomfortable, please, do accept it. I couldn't help splurging this one time. If it would make you feel better, I shall become an absolute Scrooge from this Christmas onward."

"So you'll change your name to Ebenezer just for me?"

"If that is what your highness wishes, but," he added with mock seriousness, "I reserve the right to send you bouquets, shower you with chocolates, and invite you out to paint the town."

"Now who's a bundle of contradictions? Well, I suppose that would be all right, just as long as you exercise your rights within moderation. You don't have to break the bank."

"Her ladyship has spoken, I hear and obey. So, any news? Are the murals still gracing your walls?"

"Oh, you're not going to let up, are you?" she laughed. "Yes, they are still adorning my establishment, but we have a few more days yet, the bet's still on."

⊰✿⊱

Christmas had fallen that year right in the middle of the week, making it difficult to arrange days off at the gallery. After their two days of holiday R and R, they opened again for two more days, remained closed on Sunday, and then opened again for the last two days of December, with New Year's Eve landing on a Tuesday.

"Today's the last day," Esther reminded them as they enjoyed their mid-morning coffee clutch, "I'll dance the hula if by some stroke of luck one of those tapestries goes before we shut the doors."

"I won't hold you to that," Katherine replied. "It's a pity, they're pretty good, I was sure someone would take them by now."

"Well, you still have today, even if we are going to close early," Suzy consoled her, "just keep your fingers crossed."

"It really is down to the eleventh hour," Katherine said, shaking her head. "Come on, girls let's try and get our minds off it. What is everyone planning tonight?"

Suzy and Charlie were going to try and brave the crowds at Time Square.

"Who knows, you might see us on TV," she laughed.

Esther advised her to bundle up, it looked like they might have snow later. She and the Professor, on the other hand, were going to stay in and have a nice quiet evening by the fire and stay glued to the set.

"We'll keep an eye out for you, be sure to wave at the cameras," she told Suzy.

Katherine said she would probably be doing the same thing as Esther, that is, if she hadn't been invited to a special dinner … .

However, they weren't allowed to take their minds off the murals for long, Gramps and Jasper arrived followed by Aunt Martha, who had decided to make a day of it and wait to see what might happen. The Professor had the same idea and popped by just before lunchtime, joining the 'high rollers' at the head table in the restaurant. Andre had the waiters running up to the front desk on a regular basis asking if there was any progress, and everyone was finding it difficult to stay away from the security monitors, sneaking back into the office at least once to watch the visitors as they passed by the murals on display. After the huge publicity Horace's column had created, it was hard to credit they hadn't been snapped off the walls. Lunchtime rolled around and Katherine stayed behind to watch the main desk while Esther and Suzy joined the gamblers for lunch. She might as well face it, a couple of hours, and it would all be over. Oh well, she knew the mammoth pictures would sell eventually, but perhaps one month was too ambitious for pieces this size. While she and Gerry may now be an 'item', nuts, she was still nettled by the thought of giving him the satisfaction he won their challenge. Shrugging to herself in resignation, Katherine tucked into the plate Andre insisted on sending out to her, but was suddenly startled by a deep voice issuing from a character looming over the desk, nearly causing her to choke.

"Whoa! Somun call da paramedics! You okay, ma good wo-man?" the man asked in a thick, measured Caribbean-like accent.

"Yes," she coughed, "I'm fine, my lunch just took the wrong way south."

As she cleared her throat, she had a moment to observe the eccentric dread-locked 'cool cat' dressed in a long black leather trench coat with a matching leather hat and boots tipped with gold. When he smiled, he flashed a gold tooth, in addition to the plenitude of gold rings and chains weighing him down. He also sported stylish sunglasses, oblivious to the fact winter officially began eleven days ago.

"How may I help you?"

"Is this da place?"

"Depends what you're looking for," Katherine replied.

"I hear that there be som' art by D.S. hang'n in the neigh-bo-hood."

"This is the place then. We have two pieces upstairs on the next floor, right by the stairwell, you can't miss them."

"Thanks, s'ppose I'll jus go mozy on up then," he said spying the elevator, then tipped his hat to her, "much obliged."

"You're welcome."

Katherine returned to her lunch, but had to drop her knife and fork when the 'cool cat' returned from his brief browsing and stood politely at the front desk beaming down at her with a big grin, almost mesmerizing her with his glittering dental accessory.

"Wo-man, yo've got yo'self som real righteous art here, real class," he declared, his speech lilting in a relaxed reggae rhythm.

"Thank you, I'm glad you're pleased," she returned.

"Sorry to break in an yo like this, I jus wan'a know: are dose be-you-ta-ful creations still fo sale?"

"D.S.'s works? Yes, they're still for sale."

"Oh, dis is ma lucky day. I need som large works fo my new club, and dey will do jus fine, that fo sure."

"You want *both* of them?"

"Yeah."

"Well, in that case, you will be the proud owner of D.S.'s first two works on canvas, this is his debut showing in a gallery," Katherine informed him.

"Oh man, this *is* ma lucky day. Imagine the year ending on this righteous happen'n," he mused to himself. "Dat means they are real pieces of art hist-o-ree, right?"

"Yes, you could look at it that way, depending on how famous D.S. becomes."

"I d'hon think dat will take too long," the cool cat smiled, then continued looking a little uncomfortable, "yo see, I only came to look, check out the word on the beat, but they weren't kiddin'. D.S. has work here all right, an now I'm not carryin', no cash, no cheques, an I d'hon wan' any'on else laying their claim."

"That's not a problem," Katherine assured him, "I can place a reserve on them for a space of time."

"Oh, dat be fine," he agreed.

"Okay, may I have your name please?" she asked, grabbing a pencil, nearly breathless with this serendipitous turn of events.

"People call me Jim 'The Breeze'."

"All right Mr. … Breeze," she said, jotting down his moniker. He broke into a peal of musical laughter.

"Wo-man, yo is funny, I give yo dat. Call me Jim. Here, 'till I com back, I s'poose some secur-it-ee is required, dis should do," he said, eagerly pulling off a few diamond rings, a Rolex, and several gold chains, several with a large medallion pendants, and confidently plonking the lot on the desk.

"That's not necessary," she said as she eyed the pile of jewellery.

"Even so, yo keep it 'till I com back," he insisted. "By th' way, will D.S. be do'n more?"

"I believe so, however, I don't know what he plans to paint next."

"Oh, dat be real fine," Jim smiled. "Would yo give me a call when he does? Place another one of those ree-serves on it till I can take a look?" he asked as he gave her his card, "I d'ohn care what he paints, I wan the next one."

"Sure, no problem, he might do more than one though."

"In that case, hold 'em all. Thank yo, kindly. Yo have a Happy New Year now," he said, tipping his hat and giving her a flamboyant nod.

"Many happy returns to you too. I guess we'll see you next year."

His laughter resounded as he exited the side door. As soon as he disappeared from sight, Katherine triumphantly shimmied a victory dance.

"Yes! Yes! Yes! Ha *ha*! Take *that* Mr. 'Tattoo Parlour'! Whoo hoo!"

Curious to find out the cause of the hubbub, there was a quick Exodus from *Chez Garneau* to the front desk.

"Katherine! What on earth has taken hold of you?" Aunt Martha chided.

"A piece of good news, I reckon," Gramps beamed guessing the reason for her jubilant outcry, "well, stop prancing about and let's have it."

"Hey Gramps, were there any odds on selling three or more?" she laughed.

"What!?" Suzy gasped, "you've got to be kidding!"

"My word, I can't believe we just missed the big event," the Professor observed, amused by the whole affair.

"This I've got to hear," Esther said, looking over her glasses and eyeing the pile of expensive trinkets left in pawn, "especially since it looks like I'll be dancing the hula after all."

Katherine was about to tell them the story of the Walsingham Gallery Miracle when Gerry entered through the side door.

"Well well, look who's here," Katherine called out, "you're just in time to hear how, on today of all days, D.S. is a sell-out."

"Oh? When did this happen?" Gerry wondered, a little surprised.

"Hardly ten minutes ago," she laughed, "okay everyone, gather 'round. Once upon a time, there was a jolly man named Jim 'The Breeze'...." When she finished her tale, Gerry folded his arms looking a little bemused, while Gramps jovially rubbed his hands.

"All right, someone hand over the loot, time to count my winnings," he beamed.

"Not so fast," Gerry smiled, "did you bet both of them would sell?"

"Sure did," Gramps said, "I won fair and square."

"Hmm, I'm not so sure," Gerry mischievously returned, looking over at Katherine, his arms still folded, "when you think about it, the penalty has been compromised."

"What?" she retorted, "they're sold, and the next ones too."

"Oh really? *Are* they sold? They're only on reserve, you still own them, and Mr. Breeze hasn't paid for them."

"Aw, that's just moot," Gramps pointed out.

"Yeah Gerry," Katherine chided, "don't be a spoil sport. Besides, he has paid up front, maybe a little unconventional," she said, poking through the shiny chains, "with all this jewellery Breezy Jim left behind for surety, I could open up a pawn shop in the corner now."

"Ah, but what if he doesn't come back? Sure, you get to keep the surety, but you still have the murals that would have to go back on sale, so it's still not signed, sealed and delivered just yet."

"Oh really, Mr. Smarty Pants, even if I agreed with your argument, since they *are* on reserve, I *can't* sell them now, and I still have until closing time this day to fulfil our bet, so since I *can't* sell them, they're technically sold. Put *that* in your pipe and smoke it," she counter argued matter-of-factly.

"I beg to differ, the penalty has been compromised I tell you."

"So you're going to be *that* way, bailing out, are you?" Katherine replied, raising an eyebrow.

"Oh, for Heaven's sake, what's this about?" Aunt Martha piped, growing impatient with the rigmarole. "They're look sold to me. Don't be so captious, young man."

"Oh don't mind him Aunt Martha, Gerry loves to tap dance," Katherine replied.

"Yes indeed," he said with a twinkle in his eye.

"Let us see if we can clear a path through this impasse," the Professor offered.

"Please do," Andre interjected, "it may be quiet today, but I've got to get back to the kitchen."

"Now, if only we had a dictionary," the Professor mused.

"There's one behind the desk," Esther informed them. Katherine had brought one in for working on her philosophical arguments, Esther also found it handy for the crosswords during coffee breaks.

"Splendid, now, let's look up the definitions of 'sell' and 'pawn', or 'surety' if 'pawn' is insufficient, and we'll see which comes closest to our present situation."

"Hmm, not a bad idea," Gramps approved.

"Okay, I'm for it. Winner takes all. Agreed?" Katherine returned, looking over at Gerry.

"Agreed."

"To the first word then," Suzy said, flipping to the 'S's. "Sell: '*to dispose of the ownership of goods, property or rights to another or others in exchange for money*'…do you want me to read the examples too, or just the definitions?" Suzy wanted to know.

"The definitions are fine," the Professor clarified.

"Well, since the ownership is still in question, and you accepted gold not money, you have a problem, Kathy," Gerry laughed.

"Keep reading, Suzy," Katherine directed.

"Okay, next one; '*to effect such a transfer as an agent*', '*to offer for sale*', '*to lead to the sale of*', '*to betray for a reward*', '*to persuade others to accept*', '*to cheat or deceive*', '*to offer something for sale*', '*to find a buyer*', the rest have to do with expressions, so I don't think they count in this instance," Suzy noted.

"Well, I have 'offered for sale', so that's two of the definitions, plus a reserve technically 'leads to a sale', and I have 'found a buyer', so that's four of the definitions in all," Katherine said, smugly folding her arms.

"Okay, on to 'surety' since I'm in the S section," Suzy continued, "'*the condition of being sure*' ..."

"Whoops, no point for you there Gerry, since you say the sale is *not* sure," Katherine smiled.

"Continue please," he returned, nodding to Suzy.

" '*A person who makes himself a guarantor for another's actions*', '*something pledged as security*', then we have, '*to stand surety: to pledge a sum of money for a person's appearance in court or for his payment of a debt.*'"

"Well, m' boy, you have only one point out of four definitions so far," Gramps chuckled.

"Since I'm in a good mood, I'll be nice, and let you have two words," Katherine offered, "go ahead and look up 'pawn', Suzy, and see what we find."

"'Pawn'; '*the state of being pawned*, '*something pawned*', '*to hand over as a pledge or security for a loan of money*'."

"Mr. Breeze didn't hand over his gold for money," Katherine noted.

"If time is money, money must also be time," Gerry reasoned, "and since a reserve *is* a request for additional time before payment is given, I have four points too."

"That's pushing it," Katherine argued.

"You shouldn't have given me the extra word," he laughed.

"It seems we have a tie here," the Professor noted.

"Wait! We can't have that!" Gramps interjected, "what do we do about the loot?"

"Well, nobody saw this coming, that's for sure," Andre noted.

"Oh, this is disappointing," Aunt Martha grumbled, "Gerard, you just ruined all our fun, you're a dead pan."

"I thought you didn't approve of gambling," Katherine *tsked*.

"Well, one ... still likes to see concrete results," she sniffed in reply, before continuing, "there's nothing for it, you'll just have to go find this Mr.

Breeze before midnight and tell him his bullion is just not acceptable. He can give you the cash or a cheque right there and then.”

“Oh Aunt Martha, be reasonable, I can’t do that,” Katherine protested, “I’m running a respectable establishment, I just can’t reject the reserve, and I’m sure not going to start a race up to …wherever… on New Year’s Eve. Hmm, let me see,” she stopped, looking at the card he gave her, “hey, there’s only his name and number; no club title, no address.”

“That sounds a bit shifty to me,” Gramps noted, “how does he expect you to deliver the goods?”

“Maybe his business runs by word of mouth,” Suzy suggested.

“Not to mention on a need-to-know- basis,” Esther added.

“Well, I certainly don’t want my special dinner to go to waste,” Gerry piped up, “so the Cinderella Midnight Marathon is out. Listen, since it looks like a tie, either we can forfeit the dares, or we can end this in sporting fashion by actually having both of us do them, a capital way to end the Old Year I think.”

“No way José, I have no idea what you plan to do to me,” Katherine laughed.

“Or I you,” he returned, “but I’m willing to play dangerously.”

“I got it,” Suzy said, “since it’s fifty-fifty, why not draw lots to see who gets the dare?”

“Suzy! Don’t give him ideas,” Katherine begged, hoping she could escape from the dreaded penalty.

“Hmm, I’ll go for that,” he smiled.

“Oh, okay,” Katherine sighed in resignation, at least it would finally end the matter, once and for all.

“Andre can we borrow another one of your bags?” Suzy asked.

“Sure, help yourself,” he laughed, “well, I hate to miss the fun, but I’ve got to go, you too,” he said to the waiters, who reluctantly followed him. Suzy retrieved the bag from the restaurant, and fishing out a handful of individually wrapped complementary Christmas candy from the glass bowel on the desk, counted out equal amounts of red and green edibles and tossed them into the paper receptacle.

“Now, there are ten red ones, and ten greens, pick a colour.”

“Ladies first,” Gerry offered.

“Okay, green for me,” Katherine called out.

“That leaves red for the gentleman,” Gramps called out.

“Now, the winner will be the colour drawn and they get to give the penalty,” Suzy declared.

“Fair enough,” Gerry agreed. “Who shall do the honours?”

"How about the Professor?" Katherine suggested.

"Thank you," he chuckled, pushing his glasses back up. Suzy shook the bag to ensure all the colours were thoroughly mixed. The Professor reached in, and rummaging around for a second … .

"Well, this places us in an impossible situation," he drolly observed, holding up a shiny yellow and gold wrapped chocolate for all to see. It was one of the complementary candies Andre served with each and every cup of French roast coffee. Everyone burst into laughter.

"Oh, for Heaven's sake!" Aunt Martha said petulantly.

"Hrumph! A maverick munchie," Gramps chortled.

"How did that get in there? Oh Suzy, you didn't check the bag!" Katherine thought her sides were going to split. "Didn't you feel anything rattle around in the bottom?"

"It must have gotten stuck in the paper flap," she protested, "I didn't see anything."

"It seems we're back to a tie then," Esther smiled.

"Oh no we're not," Katherine jumped in, "since yellow is also my colour, I win."

"Oh really," Gerry chuckled, "declaring your own rules now are you?"

"Doesn't everybody eventually?" Esther wryly noted.

"Well, if you get two words, I get two colours," Katherine quipped.

"Tell you what: how about we get rid of the rogue candy and have a second draw instead?" he proposed.

"That sounds fair," the Professor agreed, unwrapping the chocolate and polishing it off. This time he checked the contents of the bag before doing the honours, again. He held his hand in the bag for a few seconds before finally pulling out a green candy. "Fate has spoken."

"I stand before you, humbly admitting defeat," Gerry conceded. "What punishment does her ladyship mete out to the vanquished wretch trembling before her?"

"Her ladyship will take that into consideration," Katherine replied, with a playful aristocratic air.

"Oh come on, we've go to hear the dare," Suzy wheedled.

"I would tell you, but honestly, I still must deliberate further," Katherine continued.

"No dare yet?" he laughed. "Very well, I shall await my doom at your good pleasure," he replied with a bow.

"Okay, now that we have *that* settled, someone go get the loot," Gramps interjected.

"Actually, the penalty is decided, but not the state of the tapestries," the Professor pointed out, "we still haven't determined if they are sold or not."

"Oh Cecil, stop being so precise," Esther *tsked*.

"Goodness, we'll never get to the end of this if something isn't decided soon," Aunt Martha pouted.

"Another five bucks Mr. Breeze will come back the second week of January!" Gramps called out, bringing his cane down with a light-hearted thump.

"Here we go again," Suzy sighed.

"I'll place five for the first week of February," the Professor added.

"Cecil! I'm surprised at you, don't egg him on," Esther reproved.

"Well, at least he's saved you from dancing the hula," Suzy noted.

"That's right," Gramps interjected with a laugh, "come on, everybody, looks like we've got some 'book keeping' to do."

With that, he and the Professor headed back to the restaurant.

"Oh well, might as well finish our lunch, even if it has gone stone cold, that is, if they haven't cleared the table yet," Esther said. "Are you coming, girls?"

"All right," Martha agreed, while Suzy said she would like another cup of coffee since it was still within their lunch hour, leaving Katherine and Gerry time alone at the desk.

"Come on, sit down, tell me your news," Katherine offered.

"All right, oops, I see I've caught you in the middle of your lunch too," he noticed, looking down at her plate, "perhaps I should leave you to it."

"Oh, don't mind that. I'm used to *poulet gelé* by now. Besides, I should leave room for dinner you know. However, did you get anything to eat yet? I'll order you something at the restaurant if you like."

"No, thank you, I'm fine. I was in the neighbourhood and just thought I'd drop by for a few minutes to say 'hello' and see how the last day of our wager was faring, but I certainly got my answer," he smiled, sitting next to her.

"I'll say! What timing. I never guessed they'd sell like this," she replied as she scooped up the pile of costly baubles.

"Let's take a look. Hmm, I'm not so sure about this surety, it could be a knockoff you know," he said, examining the Rolex and raising it to his ear to hear it tick.

"Gerry, don't be so difficult," taking the watch from him.

"Only kidding," he laughed, "no, it's the real deal all right, this man *is* serious about his art collecting. Well, I believe congratulations are in order for formally introducing Mr. D.S. to the art world."

"Thank you," she said, heading to the office, "better lock Mr. Breeze's valuables in the safe. And what have you been up to?"

"Nothing really. I just wanted to see you, news or no news."

"You are going to see me tonight, you know," Katherine pointed out as she went into the office.

"I know. It's just that we haven't been together in almost two weeks, I couldn't bring myself to drive on by without catching a glimpse of your beauty."

"You and your flattery," she chided. "So now that you have basked in my radiance, what's next on your agenda?"

"Funny girl. I suppose I should head home and see how the preparations for our New Year's Eve celebrations are progressing. What time shall I pick you up? Eight?"

"Oh, you don't have to keep picking me up, I can drive to your place this time if you like," she said, closing the office door.

"All right, here's my address," he said, jotting it down on a piece of paper, "it's on the Upper West Side, right over Central Park, you can't miss it. Go ahead and park in the garage for the residents, I'll let them know you're coming."

"Okay, great. Sounds easy enough to find. I shall be there at eight."

"Excellent. Then, my dear, I shall see you later," he replied standing up and gallantly kissing the back of her hand before leaving her to her thoughts. She was glad he stopped by and actually felt an odd twinge of regret as she watched him leave, wishing he could have stayed only a few moments longer. Time seemed to stop after that. She was tempted to join the family gathering at the head table, maybe engage the Professor and Gramps in another one of their philosophical debates, but she had other work to do. In any case, Gerry's picture of Rome would help to keep her busy. Since it was rather quiet, Esther noted she could handle the floor by herself and call on her 'hubby' for backup if needed, so Suzy joined Katherine in the studio for the few hours they had left.

"Gosh, I can't get over what happened today," Suzy said, shaking her head, "who would have thought?"

"That reminds me, I should call Derrick before we go home. He'll be very glad to hear the news. I wonder if he has anything else ready?" Katherine mused as she prepared her palette.

"Well, you could tell him to get started on something if he doesn't."

"True, I hope he can have something prepared before we have to deliver the other two, considering all the space we have to fill. Uh oh … ."

"What's wrong, Kathy?"

"I just realized, the van isn't big enough, we can't have his work sticking out the back with the doors open, we could lose them on the way, or perhaps get pulled over."

"You have a point," Suzy agreed, "maybe we could ask Derrick to arrange the delivery? Have his friends drop them off or something?"

"We could, but if someone recognises him or his friends, he may find himself in a lot of trouble."

"Darn, I didn't think of that.   Gee, maybe we should have gotten a bigger truck.   I guess it's back to U-haul after all," Suzy shrugged. Katherine started to laugh.

"We can't have that, not now anyway. I don't think Mr. Breeze would be impressed, the gallery might come across as a fly-by-night operation."

"It was only a suggestion, but we do need a bigger truck for this job. You know, instead of searching for a new car, perhaps I could get another van, a large one, then we'd have a little extra advertising into the bargain."

"Suzy, I appreciate the offer, but I couldn't let you spend your own money doing that, however, now that we're on the subject, it's high time you get a new set of wheels. I thought you'd have it taken care of months ago."

"I know, but I've been so busy, and I've grown a little attached to your luxury liner to tell the truth."

"Honestly, I practically forgot I had car, I love toodling around in the van, the view is great. You know, I'd be happy to give you my car since you like it so much. It may be six years old now, but hey, the mileage is decent, you can't beat the engine in it and it's certainly a lot safer than yours." Suzy nearly dropped her brush.

"Kathy, I can't take your car, but … would you consider selling it to me?"

"If you're going to put money down on a car, don't you want to get a new one?"

"Sure, but a new BMW in that category is beyond my price range, and in any case, I'd rather have a good second hand car. The main drawback of a new one is the fact that the minute you stick the key in the ignition, the value plummets. With your car, at least I would know for sure it only had one previous owner."

True, Katherine never really had to think about that before.

"I'd sell it to you then, but I really don't want to take your money Suzy, and I can't see how we're going to work this one out because I know you're not going to accept it as a gift."

"That's for sure," Suzy agreed. They were silent for moment, quietly brushing away, trying to come up with a solution. Suzy then had a brainstorm. "I have it!" she exclaimed, holding her brush up in mid-air. "If you won't let me get a second van to help out, and since you insist on giving me your wheels, why not let me pay to have it painted like a company car with the gallery info? Free advertising!"

"It's an idea, but it's supposed to be your personal car. You don't want my stuff plastered all over it, do you?"

"Why not? It helps me too, you know. The more customers we get, the more paintings we get to sell, not to mention I'd be helping to bring in more to cover my salary. Just think of all those long drives to Iowa, the word would spread cross-country."

"Iowa? You still want to drive it? I think you can afford to take a plane now."

"Gosh, I never thought of that," Suzy reflected, "still, a paint job is probably cheaper for me in the long run than buying it, and you'd get extra advertising, it's the only win-win solution I can see without you directly taking my money, or me having to accept the car without making some form of payment."

"I guess it is the only viable option with this conundrum," Katherine replied, plunging her brush into her jar of white spirits and swirling out the excess paint. "Hmm, okay. You have a deal. Now, I won't hold you to the adverts, if you get sick of them, you can paint them out, or whatever."

"Wow, this is fantastic! Thanks Kathy."

"You're welcome. Of course," Katherine continued, "let's make sure we do our homework on this, I'd hate to find out you paid a fortune for paints and decals if the car itself wasn't worth the expense. I think my parents got scalped when they had the van spruced up for me."

"All right, I'll do some research, get some estimates. You know, I wonder if Derrick's friends would give us the low-down on a job like that? They might know where to get the best deals."

"Come to think of it, that's not a bad idea. I'll ask Derrick when I call him. Oh nuts! That brings us back to our original problem: how are we going to move his artwork?"

"Think 'Big Truck', we'll find the answer to this too," Suzy said, returning to her daubing. After several moments of silent, reflective creativity, Katherine suddenly burst out laughing.

"What's so funny?"

"The answer has been staring me in the face," Katherine replied, nodding to Gerry's present in the making. "Big truck? Why not get Reinold Enterprises involved? I can turn his penalty into a favour, it would serve him right to make his company deliver Derrick's mural-tapestries after poking fun and predicting a flop."

"Talk about rubbing it in," Suzy laughed, "but I have to agree, it's the perfect solution."

"Yeah, plus I think Gerry's moving teams are used to hauling his art around, so at least we'd have someone who could handle the tapestries properly," Katherine observed, "gosh this is not a bad idea. Since Mr. Jim the Breeze wants additional pieces, I can hire Gerry's firm to handle the shipping end after these two. We now have a future problem solved before the next pieces are even painted."

"Not to mention, after all Gerry's kindness, it would be good to throw some business his way too," Suzy reflected.

"It would, problem is, he's been too generous lately, and he's probably going to want to offer his services for free even after his penalty. I can't have that either," Katherine noted, "I may have to hire another shipping firm."

"Don't do that, he might take it as a snub if he ever found out. Tell you what, when you ask him if he would be willing to move items for you in the future, tell him it's strictly business. Be ruthless, at least on the exterior, and tell him you expect a no-nonsense discount. Compromise is key here if you want to find some middle ground."

"That makes sense, but I'm getting to know him a little better now, I think he'll insist on doing it for free."

"Tell him you don't want freebies, or the deal's off. It's an understood thing that you can't let feelings interfere in business, and he'll be happy if he thinks he's helping by giving you a cut rate. If not, you can then hire that other firm with a clear conscience."

"Put my foot down, eh? Maybe I should have taken that arts administration course."

"Well, there are some things you can't learn at any university, except for one … the University of Life," Suzy laughed.

"Of course, the only college where everyone is a permanent student," Katherine smiled.

"You said it," Suzy nodded. At that point, the alarm clock went off, it was time to pack up and get ready for an evening of celebration.

"We didn't get much painting in today, but we always have next year," Katherine noted, capping her oil paints and stirring her brushes in the cleaning solution.

"I don't have too much left to do, and this will be finished," Suzy replied, indicating her canvas. Since the Sirrac contest, she liked experimenting with optical illusions, taking everyday objects and arranging them to make hidden pictures. On this piece, however, she had painted the Brooklyn Bridge, but had filled the sky with 'motion teasers', strange multicoloured circles that when combined gave the illusion the whole background was moving.

"That's amazing. I think that one will be a hit," Katherine predicted.

"I hope so, it took too long for those acrylics of midtown America to sell, perhaps they were too ordinary. All things weird seem to have ready buyers. Odd, isn't it?"

" Yes, 'Weirdism' is definitely the cornerstone of many an artist's career."

"How is Rome doing? Looks like you're not too far from completing it."

"Oh you know how it goes, it wasn't built in a day, but a few more should do the trick. I've got to work on the Acropolis next, but like I said, I have next year to do that. Speaking of which, I can't believe you and Charlie are going to brave Time Square tonight. It'll be a madhouse there."

"I know, but I wanted to see what it was like. I'm always home in Iowa for the holidays, so this is the first time I'm really going to experience the city during the festivities."

"I hope you and Charlie have a good time. By the way, you never told me how the other night went. Did you do anything special?" Katherine asked.

"First, we tried this fun Italian bistro where all the waiters sing arias, they were really good too. I don't know why they are waiting on tables when they should be onstage in an opera house. Of course, the food was excellent, but everyone goes for the singing. Then, we went to see a movie, a simple evening out really."

"Sounds like you had a nice time," Katherine replied, "I'm so glad things are working out for you and Charlie."

"I'm beginning to wonder if it is," Suzy admitted, pausing for a moment before covering her canvas, "I mean, we've been together for a few months now, but it feels like we're …idling or something. He doesn't let his feelings show that much, does he?"

"Not really, but I do know he cares for you, he wouldn't be spending this much time with you if he didn't."

"I know, but ... this is embarrassing, I thought he'd at least kiss me goodnight by now, something that would give a hint of what's going on behind that quiet exterior of his, but ... nothing! Is he afraid I might take it the wrong way?"

That was a bombshell of a question Katherine wasn't anticipating. Although she personally had never thought about Charlie in that light, even she had noticed he never tried to kiss her before his proposal. Perhaps Suzy was right, maybe he was trying too hard to be the proper gentleman, apprehensive he might offend or was simply unsure if it was appropriate, he was sending mixed signals without realizing it. Katherine found it hard not to wonder if things might be different now between them if he had taken that simple step. Would her feelings for him have changed? Eventually become what he had hoped for? Even imagining that happening felt odd, as though there was some connection or element missing. No, she was certain her decision would still have been the same, but at least she would have known how he felt much sooner, things would never have ended the way they did.

"Maybe he is. It could be he's not sure about your feelings, or if you're ready for a serious relationship yet. You may have to give him a hint," Katherine suggested.

"Give *him* a hint? How? I'd have to grab him by the shirt and say, 'Kiss me, you hunk.'"

"Suzy! Really! I'd put it a little more delicately than that," Katherine laughed, hanging up her smock, "you don't want to scare him off either. When he drops you off tonight, just say ... 'you may kiss me goodnight'. It's worth a shot."

"Sounds easy enough, even he would that as a green light. Kathy, if you don't mind a personal question, did Charlie ever try to ...?"

"No Suzy, he didn't, that's why if you really want him to know how you feel, you'd better try my suggestion."

"Kathy you don't think if he had, that things ...?"

"No, Suzy. I'm pretty sure I'd feel the same way, so please, stop feeling guilty. Honestly, if I had thought about him like that, I'd have followed my own advise instead of giving it to you right now."

"But you *have* thought about it," Suzy noted.

"I'd be lying if I said I didn't, but I know it wouldn't feel the same as when ..." Katherine suddenly grew quiet.

" 'The same as when' what? So we're making comparisons now. Oh my, Gerry kissed you, didn't he?"

"Um…well … um hmm," she confessed with a slight nod.

"But isn't that wonderful? Don't be shy, give us the news. What was it like? Is he a good kisser?" Suzy wheedled.

"Suzy! If you must know, it's hard to tell, he is my first after all."

"How romantic! Well, did you like it? Stupid me, you must have, you've been floating on clouds for almost a month. I should have guessed."

"Um, let's say it's better than cappuccino, croissants, and hot fudge cake."

"That's an odd description," Suzy laughed.

"I am an artist you know," Katherine replied matter-of-factly, "it's my right to be odd. Hey, look at us dawdling around, we had better get a move on, it's time we close this place up."

While Suzy and Esther closed shop for the night, Katherine called Derrick and gave him an extra reason to celebrate.

"I don't believe it," he exclaimed, giving a 'whoop' into the phone. Katherine held the receiver at a distance until she could hear he had calmed down.

"Well, I still have to wait for the customer to pay for them, but I think he's serious."

"Hmm, what if this guy don't want 'em after all?" Derrick worried.

"The funny thing is, he left a number of valuables for security, so in case this doesn't pan out, I promise you won't go empty handed until they do sell. However, the customer wants more of your works, so I don't think he'll back out. You don't happen to have any other pieces ready?"

"Are you kidd'n? This is great! I couldn't wait to try some new stuff with this canvas, so I've been busy. I've got two more bits done, not as big as the first 'uns, but I can bring 'em around when ya like."

"Wonderful. Maybe on your next day off. We can discuss prices then."

"Sure, no problem. I won't be clean'n yr place this week, but I'm off Friday."

"Great. Perhaps you know the customer, he calls himself Jim 'The Breeze', I hope you aren't offended, but he wants your artwork for his new club."

"Whoa! Not *the* Jim 'the Breeze'?"

"I assume there's only one," Katherine replied.

"Oh man! I sure ain't offended, ya couldn't pay me any bigger compliment than that," Derrick assured her. "He owns the coolest dance clubs, the best of the best go there to hang out and move the moves, and he don't tolerate no stuff on his turf, if ya know what I mean. Never guessed my graff's were gonna hang there," he laughed.

"I'm glad to hear that. Oh before I forget, I wonder if you or your friends could help me, I need some advice on a paint job for a car."

"Sure, what da ya have in mind?"

"Nothing exciting, just the gallery address and logo."

"No problem, that's Trigger's thing, I'll see what he says, have him give ya a call, or somethin'."

"Thanks, I hope I've helped to make your New Year a happy one."

"Yo sure did! Wait 'till I tell Sheila," he laughed, "ya have a good New Year's too."

"And say 'hello' to George and Trigger for me, will you?"

"Sure thing, bye now."

"Bye Derrick, see you on Friday."

Last job of the day done, everyone said their goodbyes and wished each other the umpteenth Happy New Year before going their separate ways. Good thing she decided to close the gallery early to beat the rush hour, she would be home in plenty of time to rest up before she had to get ready. Having over a week to prepare, at least she knew what she would wear this time, the black and white evening dress with her delicate gold necklace and matching earrings, just the right touch. Naturally, she didn't want to arrive an empty-handed guest, and since she was not very good at picking out wines, not to mention was unaware what Gerry would serve for dinner, Andre was only too happy to help her out and personally selected a few bottles of special reserve white and red wines, and Dom Pérignon. That should do the trick she thought, she couldn't carry any more than that anyway, and let's face it, they couldn't imbibe six bottles of booze in one night.

The house was quiet when she arrived, Pops was probably still in the city, she wasn't sure where Mom or Steves were, but she found Gramps snoring loudly in his favourite recliner in the den, muttering something unintelligible about stocks in his sleep. That was a good idea, maybe she could get a quick nap in before she had to get dressed, not to mention try and charge the batteries for a late night out. She slipped out of her clothes and put on a warm fluffy bathrobe, set the alarm and snuggled under the bedcovers. It didn't feel like she had fallen asleep, she remembered just lying there, wondering what his place was like now that she was invited to his private abode, worrying if she would find it, or end up arriving late after getting hopelessly lost and driving aimlessly up and down the west side of

Central Park, and now that she was awake, had simply picked up her thoughts where she last left them while she dressed. Would he like the wine she brought? Would she get lost? Stop fussing she tried to tell herself, he said it was easy to find, don't keep borrowing trouble. Of course, these were only diversionary distractions, she knew the real source of her restive thoughts; this was a little more than an evening to see in the New Year, a private dinner for two in his apartment meant one thing, a romantic opportunity for them to be alone together. She was excited and nervous at the same time, not knowing what to expect or what the evening would reveal.

All dressed and ready to go, she was about to go downstairs but hearing her parents talking, she knocked on their door.

"It's me, just thought you'd like to know I'm heading off."

"Come on in, Kathy dear," her mother called

Katherine loved to see them all decked out, Pops in his ebony tuxedo, Mom in a stunning evening gown, this time she was wearing a forest green satin dress with matching shoes. Mom was busy trying to straighten out Pop's bow tie, he was impeccable about everything, but this was one skill that he had not yet managed to master.

"There you go, dear," she said, giving the bow a friendly pat, "all done."

"What would I ever do without you," he smiled.

"You both look wonderful," Katherine complimented.

"Thank you Kathy, so do you," he mother replied, "now, you will be careful driving in to the city tonight, won't you? You know what it will be like out there."

"I do, madness and mayhem, but I'll watch it," Katherine assured her, giving her a kiss on the cheek, "I've got to go, or I might get stuck in traffic."

"All right," Pops returned, "listen to your mother and be careful."

"I promise," she said as she hurried down the hall. She bumped into Gramps as he came out of his room, also dressed to the nines in his tuxedo, Jasper in his Dickey bow.

"Well, Cinderella is off to the ball! You look lovely, Katie."

"You look dashing tonight, hot-stuff, sorry, no time to chat, must go. Hope you have a good time at the Club."

"Don't worry, I plan to," he smiled, "I just might cut the rug tonight, I feel romance in the air. You never know… ."

"Oh Gramps," she laughed as she tripped lightly down the stairs. He chuckled as he watched her flit away and heard the front door open and close.

"My, our Katie is walking on air lately," he commented to Harold and Helen, "she has feelings for this young fellow, doesn't she?"

"Yes, I believe she does," Pops replied as the three of them descended, "he seems to be an upright individual, I just wish I knew him a little better. Katherine has led such a sheltered life, and although she is wise for someone her age, she still is inexperienced in many things. I don't want to see her get hurt."

"Of course not," Gramps agreed, "none of us do."

"Well, I asked Kathy to invite him over for dinner sometime soon," Helen informed them. "As far as I can tell, Gerry is treating her with respect. He may be a little persistent with his generosity, but hasn't pressured her into anything, at least, that's what she tells me."

"That's good to know," Harold replied, looking a little relieved.

⊰ ❀ ⊱

Gerry was right, it wasn't difficult to find his apartment building. Following his directions, she went to the residents' parking area, hoping the van would fit under the height clearance sign. She felt odd driving her commercial vehicle to a date of all things, but she didn't feel right about using the BMW now that she had promised it to Suzy. Technically it was hers now, Suzy used it more than she did, and besides, any chance for some free publicity with the van could never go amiss.

"Oh, you must be Mr. Reinold's guest," the attendant said, looking at the logo, "at first, I thought it was another art delivery."

"No, just me," she smiled.

"Still, a very pretty picture. Go on in, it's to the left, you'll find an extra space with the apartment number. Elevator is on the other side. Happy New Year, ma'am."

"Thank you. Happy New Year to you too."

She parked next to the familiar Jaguar, retrieved her bags of 'silly sauce' from the back and prayed the bottom wouldn't fall out of them, maybe she did go a little overboard for only two people, especially since she couldn't have more than a couple of glasses of champagne. Stop fussing! Waiting patiently for the elevator to stop on his floor, the doors finally opened onto a private foyer decorated with plush carpets, ornamental oversized porcelain vases, marble topped tables with floral displays,

580

chandeliers surrounded by intricate stucco work, his front door with gleaming brass handles just a few paces away. Gosh, why was she so nervous? They had kissed each other on several occasions; they weren't total strangers anymore, not after that. She rang the doorbell, and waited for a moment.

"Hello gorgeous," Gerry smiled, opening the door, handsomely dressed in a black dinner jacket, "I see you found your way all right. Welcome to my humble abode. Hey, what's all this?"

"Just a little something for dinner," she replied.

"A *little* something?" he laughed.

"Well, I wasn't sure what to get, so there's two of everything, red, white and champagne."

"You didn't have to. Here, let me help you with that," he said as he took the bags and closed the door with an elbow. "The sitting room is straight through there," indicating a large archway with a nod, "go ahead and make yourself comfortable while I bring these into the kitchen, you can put your coat in the closet there, I'll be back in a jiff. Can I get you anything to drink?"

"Um, a ginger ale would be fine."

"All right," he laughed, "we can open one of these at dinner."

Hanging up her coat, she followed his nod, taking a quick look around as she sat down in one of the large sleek-lined sofas across from a blazing fireplace, the mantle decked with flickering candles. Behind the seating area through another archway and up three steps was the dining room, the formal table set with candelabras, a vase of red roses and sunflowers, the end section set for two. Although not decorated in a strictly minimalist sense, everything looked purposely simplified, straight lines, glossy wood floors, monochromatic or two-tone colour schemes, glass-topped tables, the contemporary look softened by a variety of patterned plush rugs, ornate period table lamps and other curiosity pieces like intricate display cabinets, an elegant chest of drawers, a few bookcases with delicate foliage carved on them. The true eye-catchers were the paintings adorning the walls lit by soft wall lightening and the numerous collectables sitting around, statues, strange vases and other unusual ornaments peeking out amidst various photo frames. A classical orchestral recording was playing softly on the stereo system. To the side was a large window leading out to the balcony overlooking the park and the twinkling city skyline beyond. In all, spacious open-plan, luxurious, certainly artistic, but definitely a gentleman's dwelling, there was a certain rigidity in the overall decorating that she couldn't quite describe.

"Ginger ale it is," he said, bringing in a tray and setting it down, "you don't mind if I have my scotch?"

"Oh no, not at all. You have a beautiful apartment," she complimented, she wasn't fibbing, it was an elegant environment.

"Thank you, but most of it is the interior designer's work, my place in Paris turned out a little better, I must admit. With work and all, I just let them get on with it." Ah, maybe that was it she thought, décor applied according to his guidelines, but just shy of the effect he wanted to achieve. It was always that way, better to do things yourself when you can. How can an interior designer actually capture what you want or make your space feel like home?

"Honestly, it really is beautiful."

"Thank you, I'm glad you like it. Let me give you the tour, you can take your glass with you if you like. Since you've seen the sitting room, let's go to the den next."

"Okay, but … can I have a closer look at the paintings in here first?" she timidly asked.

"I thought you would have taken a peek at them by now," he smiled, "go ahead, take your time. Dinner won't be ready for awhile, so they tell me in the kitchen."

"Aha! I thought so," she said as she went to view a seascape, "a Renoir, and a Manet, oh…I'm guessing, but that could be a Rouault. Is that a Goya over there?"

"Yes, a real hodgepodge. Now, try and guess out of these four which one is the fake."

"What do you mean?"

"Sometimes I collect the work from famous forgers who managed to fool the experts in the auction houses. They've created quite a name for themselves with their counterfeits."

"Oh Gerry, I hope you don't loan them out as the real thing now, do you?" Katherine chided. "If I find out you had me hang up some worthless forgery in my exhibition space … well, I don't know what I'd do."

"I would never give you a cheapo repro," he assured her, amused by her astonishment, "come, give a guess."

"Well, it's hard to tell," she admitted, examining each picture, leaning forward to view the brushstrokes and the signatures, "the French ones look pretty real to me. I don't know about the Goya, I'm not very familiar with his style, but the Rouault has to be it. Cubism shouldn't be too difficult to copy, his would probably be the easiest to forge, plus people would be more on the look-out for forged Romantics and Impressionists, so the counterfeiter probably wouldn't take that risk, so I'll guess the Cubist piece is the one."

"Your logic for choosing the Rouault is interesting, but I'm afraid you're wrong. It's the Renoir," he revealed, taking a sip from his scotch.

"What? Now that's embarrassing," she laughed, "I love Renoir's work, you would think *I* could recognise the difference between a counterfeit and the real thing."

"Don't feel bad, like I said, they are masters when it comes to copying."

"This guy is definitely good," she noted, looking closely at the brushstrokes once more, "it's a pity, come to think of it. If they have the skill to do produce this calibre of work, they should paint their own creations."

"They do, but then, it's only a lucky handful that become well-known and make a living on their own merit. It's tempting to hitch your wagon to past artists already worth millions. Forgers who have become infamous after a prison stint can demand several thousands of dollars for their copies."

"I know, but that's certainly a high price to pay to make art profitable."

"True, but in the case of this particular canvas, it was more of an anti-establishment crusade, it's a genuine Keating," Gerry explained. Thomas Keating, Katherine was vaguely aware of him. He was notoriously blatant about his counterfeits, purposely leaving clues in his work to show they were forgeries, either including deliberate anachronisms in his pictures or painting hidden texts on his canvases with white lead paint that could only be seen via x-ray analysis.

"Oh, isn't he the one who wanted to get back at the so-called middle-men dealers and critics who made fortunes off inexperienced collectors and struggling artists?"

"The very same. I've got a few Hory's too, and a fake Vermeer by Han van Meegeren, that poor guy had a sad end."

"I'm not familiar with all the forgers. What happened to him?"

"Well, if I heard the history correctly, during World Word II a Dutch businessman was afraid that the Nazis would buy up or steal all the nation's cultural treasures, so he bought up Meegeren's fakes and sold them instead. However, one of the fakes sold to the Nazis came into the possession of a Dutch official who obviously thought the painting was real and accused Meegeren of selling out to the enemy, an act of treason punishable by death."

"So he was executed?" Katherine asked, wide-eyed, "that's a tough end, even if he was a forger."

"Actually, he wasn't given the death penalty. He admitted to the forgery and was compelled to paint a counterfeit Vermeer in front of the court to prove his claim. He received a one year sentence, but I think he died of a heart attack before he was put in jail."

"No wonder, the stress of it all probably did him in," Katherine said shaking her head. "You know, seeing your other pieces, the real ones, I didn't think you would be interested in the world of fakes. If you don't mind me asking, why collect them?"

"Well, for one thing, they're great conversation pieces, but seriously, it has its practical side. If there are paintings you like owned by museums that will never end up for sale, you can always have a famous counterfeit instead. Any painting is always better than a print."

"I can understand that. Is this your family?" Katherine asked, noticing a portrait photograph standing on the table under the counterfeit Renoir.

"Yes, that's the 'Rogues Gallery'," he smiled, "my father and mother, and us three hoodlums."

"You don't look like hoodlums to me, you guys look so cute," Katherine replied, observing a pre-teen Gerry and his siblings dressed in their best outfits. It was interesting to see a picture of his parents, they were a very distinguished-looking couple. She noticed a strong resemblance between Peter and their father, Gerry and Lottie were closer to their mother with regard to their facial expressions.

"Thank you. Come, le me show you the rest of the casbah."

He took her down the hallway to what she assumed was the den, similarly decorated as the sitting cum dining room, but sporting an elegant pool table with a burgundy felt top and the latest state-of-the-art entertainment centre. However, the artist in her was immediately attracted to the paintings.

"Are all these real?" she asked, admiring a series of what looked like sixteenth-century Dutch school pieces and an honest-to-goodness Holbein.

"These are, but not the co-called 'Vermeer' over there, that's the Meegeren I told you about."

"Wow, he was good, his colouring is just perfect. Gosh, was the painting you had delivered in Paris real?"

"That one was, it's a pity it was for someone else. I wouldn't mind adding it to my stash, speaking of which, the next section of the cottage might be of interest to you," escorting her to the room across the way.

Inside was an odd array of what looked like a giant built-in set of mahogany wardrobes or closets but with a security keypad on the outside. Keying in the code and opening the doors, a long row of vertical sliding panels similar to patio doors was revealed. "Go ahead, pull one out," he offered.

"Here goes; eenie, meeny, miney, mo," Katherine said as she handed him her glass before gently sliding out the fourth panel. "Well, this is clever, it reminds me of my rolly-polyies," she laughed, admiring the exquisite collection hanging on the storable gallery-grade exhibition partition.

"Excellent choice: Rembrandt."

"Now, I assume these are real," she checked with him.

"This cabinet is, old masters to the left, modern pieces on the right, while the other cabinet over there," indicating with a nod, "holds the forgeries."

"This is fantastic, I could spend all night just studying your collection," she replied, although it would definitely take more than one night to appreciate this enviable horde. She then noticed the third cabinet.

"If you don't mind me asking, is that where you keep your book collection?"

"No, they're in my office 'slash' library, *that*," he continued in a mischievous tone, "is my little 'Chamber of Horrors'."

"Uh oh, I dare not guess what may be hidden in there."

"Nothing *too* sinister," he noted, keying open the cabinet, "just artwork painted by temporary and lifetime guests of the Federal government, just commit a few felonies or capital crimes, and *voilà*, into 'Penitentiary Plaza' you go where you may while away what remains of your days creating these," he clarified, pulling out one of the partitions. Katherine gave a sigh of relief, she wasn't sure what she would see, he made it sound like he collected ancient dungeon implements, but they were only paintings.

"Well, this is beautiful," she complimented, nodding to the landscape featuring a plateau somewhere in the Rocky Mountains. "This was painted by a prisoner? Talk about conversation pieces, this certainly gives the term 'con artist' a whole new meaning."

"It does, doesn't it?" he smiled.

"Wait a minute, now I've caught you," she laughed, "you accuse me of trying to open tattoo parlours, and here you have a bevy of con art."

"Touché. I'd love to show you some more, but I believe dinner is just ready to be served," he announced, checking his watch, "we can finish the tour later."

"All right."

Offering her his arm, they returned to the dining area, he politely assisting with her chair.

"I wasn't sure what you would like, so a gourmet 'surf and turf' spread seemed the best solution, I hope you like lobster Thermadore and veal Picatta."

"That sounds delicious," Katherine replied as she straightened her dress and laid her napkin across her lap, "I don't know what to choose."

"Live dangerously, have some of both. Speaking of danger, and while we're still close to the subject of our plebeian art projects, have you decided to pronounce your dare yet after your amazing victory today?" he asked, sitting across from her.

"Oh that. To be honest, I had no idea what torture to put your through, so I hope you don't mind if I ask for a favour instead."

"A favour? Not at all," he replied, straightening up with interest, "what does her ladyship require? Even if you name half my kingdom, you shall have it."

"Nothing that extreme, I just need a larger van to deliver the mural-tapestries when Jim the Breeze eventually pays for them, therefore, I 'dare' you to deliver them for me when the time comes."

Gerry laughed good-naturedly at her proposal.

"What an ingenious penalty my dear, to have the vanquished deliver the goods to the customer who vanquished him. I believe I've met my match in dare and penalty invention. Of course, I'll be happy to deliver them for you, just give me a call, I'll arrange everything personally."

"I'll have to go too, the artist wants to stay anonymous, so I'll have to be there to supervise the hanging."

"That won't be a problem, you can boss the men around, they will be on strict orders to do everything you command."

"That's great. Thank you."

"You're quite welcome," he commented as the caterer opened the wine and served the first course, basil soup specially prepared with *crème fraîche*,

"You know, I'm rather curious: did you have a penalty all ready for me in case you won our bet?"

"Umm, maybe," he confessed.

"Would you be willing to tell me?"

"Well, it was only half thought out, and perhaps a very ... awkward one at that."

"Hmph. Dares are supposed to be embarrassing, remember the waiter and the tap dance penalty," she laughed. "I'd be interested to hear your half-baked idea anyway, I'm not obliged to perform the dare now, so it shouldn't be such a biggie."

"Here goes then; I was going to invite you to meet my parents," he said, taking a sip of wine, waiting for her reaction.

"Oh … I certainly wasn't expecting that, not as a *dare*," she admitted. "Are they cannibals or axe-murderers that I should be afraid of them?" He chuckled with her question.

"Of course not, but the prospect of meeting anyone's parents for the first time can be daunting, since we've only known each other on a personal level for a brief period. I know this is a little below the belt, but I was going to use the dare to secure the acceptance of my invitation. Lottie, and Mrs. Hunt I might add, has told them all about you, and they've been nagging me to introduce you."

"Well, dares are always a little underhanded anyway. Of course I would love to meet them, you don't have to challenge me. Wait a minute, I don't believe it," she suddenly exclaimed, "I would never refuse such an invitation anyway, so we're *both* doing the penalties after all."

"So we are," he chuckled.

"We really did come to a tie, who would have predicted that? Oh, that reminds me, I too have an invitation to give, I've been so distracted lately, I didn't get a chance to tell you. How would you like to join our family for dinner at Oak Meadows?"

"I'd be delighted," he replied, "when did you have in mind?"

"Sometime after the holidays, our free time will be over, so we'll have to check our agendas," she smiled, "maybe next weekend, if that's all right with you."

"Of course. We'll plan on you coming out to our old 'homestead' the following weekend."

"Perfect. I have more time on weekends. Where is your old homestead?"

"Down on Long Island, right by the sea."

"Imagine growing up by the ocean, living close to the beach must have been fun."

"It was, we could sneak out at night and play pirates, challenge each other to duels to the death by moonlight, or burying our treasures, making sure the landlubbers couldn't see where we hid them. Then, the strangest thing happened, I found an old packer's hook washed up by the tide, probably came from an old fishing ship. Well, we played Peter Pan for ages after that. Pete got to be Peter of course, Lottie was Wendy, and you guessed it, I was designated the role of Captain Hook. Those were good times. Of course we all grew up and our interests changed, living far from the city became a real drag then, but we had promised at a certain time, we'd all go back and dig up our hidden wealth from times gone by."

"Aw, that's adorable. So you buried time capsules, it's a nice idea actually. When is the big unearthing to take place?"

"You know, I can't remember," Gerry noted, rubbing his chin, "this pirate is getting forgetful. I think we were supposed to go digging when made it to junior high, but we never got around to it."

"It would be funny to dig it all up now and see what you find."

"That's if the tide hasn't washed it all away. I think I just buried old baseball cards, comic books, some marbles and my lucky rabbit foot."

"The cards and the books might be worth something now," she observed.

"I know. I bet some other kid has found it all while building a sandcastle and has made off with our loot, talk about losing your marbles," he laughed. "Out of curiosity, if you were going to put something in a pirate's treasure chest, what would you choose?"

"Well, at that age, I might have put in some drawings, plus the first blue ribbon I won for a colouring contest, my favourite book at the time, *Black Beauty*, a few short stories I tried to write during creative writing class, which were terrible by the way, and I'd definitely include some family photos."

"So you wanted to be a writer at one time."

"You know how creative people are, we have to try everything until we find our niche. Writing was not it, I always wanted to get to the exciting part and forget about the beginning or end, let alone try to develop a coherent plot."

"The paint brush won then," he smiled.

"That's how it went. Look, it's been snowing," Katherine noticed, turning towards the window.

"So it has, and for some time now too, it's starting to gather in drifts. That's a shame, I was hoping we could see the fireworks from the balcony, but it will be too cold now."

"That's all right, we still might be able to see something from here."

The caterer brought out their main course, or rather, courses, and informed Gerry dessert and coffee was waiting for them on a trolley in the kitchen, he then wished them a good evening with a little bow and quietly withdrew.

"I told them we could manage it from here," Gerry explained, "now it really is a private candle-lit evening for two."

Their conversation rambled on many topics. Katherine discovered he liked the old classic *film noir* genre, she telling him about her favourite books and her observations about certain pieces of art, like the Venus de Milo. How did they know it was Venus? Katherine had her own theory that it could be Hera, Athena, or actually a statue of Diana startled by Actaeon for all they knew, a new point of view Gerry found intriguing. After they had exhausted literature and art, they returned to more personal topics. She in turn finally had the opportunity to satisfy her curiosity in one area: how he came to dislike elevators. It turned out he and his father got stuck between two floors during the blackout of '77.

"Somebody eventually pried the doors open, but after hanging in mid-air for several hours, the thought of being pulled up through the doors mid-floor was just as unnerving," he concluded, "few things bother me, but the possibility that the stupid contraption might move while we were clambering out has given me the creeps ever since."

"That must have been a terrible experience, I can only imagine what that must have felt like."

"Put simply, very claustrophobic. Now that you know the cause for that strange phobia, I'd love to discover what you have against dancing when you yourself can put many a ballroom dancer to shame."

Katherine thought for a moment.

"It's not easy to describe. It's a combination of things. First of all, I don't feel graceful, so if you don't feel it, how can you *be* graceful?"

"Forgive me for interrupting, but that is one phobia I can lay to rest right now, judging from the one dance we had, you have no need to worry on that score," he assured her.

"Well, the thought just makes me feel awkward, especially when you have a roomful of people crowding around you."

"You're too self-conscious, you need to relax, forget about the idiots on the side lines."

"I know I should, but then, it was the whole concept of learning to dance in the first place, it didn't do me any good. I mean, it was like I 'had' to do it, like everything else I had to learn, but if I could discover it for myself, it would probably be more enjoyable."

"Now we're getting to the nub of it," he noted, "excuse me, hold that thought while I serve us our dessert," he interjected, taking their plates and changing the recordings around on the sound system before returning with two servings of hazelnut chocolate tort.

"Good old 'Blue Eyes'," Gerry commented, "he has a song or a verse for practically every experience in life."

"That's true," Katherine smiled.

"You know what jumped into my head the other night when you told me about your culinary skills, or lack thereof?"

"No. I'm all ears."

To her surprise, he broke out into song.

"*What a funny girl you used to be, you always had a thousand things to do, getting all involved with something new, always some new recipe in the kitchen, always looked like World War III, what a funny girl you used to be.*' Forgive me for breaking with etiquette and singing at the table," he smiled.

Katherine didn't care about table etiquette that particular moment, or that his song had clashed a little with the melody then playing. He had a stunning voice: that captivating intonation she loved to listen to when he spoke had suddenly come alive in an unexpected way and seized every iota of her aural concentration. Moved by this new discovery, dessert was forgotten. She wished he had continued, if only for a few more verses. It was strangely overwhelming, as though sound and emotion had vanquished the power of words. It was difficult to speak.

"Where did you learn to sing like that?" she finally asked.

"Blame the nuns. They trained us for the school and church choir, after that, we had the school Christmas performances, the Gilbert and Sullivan operettas, it was one way of keeping us occupied and out of trouble."

Well, bless those nuns, Katherine thought to herself. "You have a wonderful voice," she complimented. Oh Lord, I wish he would sing again!

"Thank you."

"Are there any more verses that jumped into your mind?"

"Actually, right after you surprised me with your picture of Rome and our wonderful 'repast' of coffee and croissants, a swinging little tune hit me:

> '*Down each avenue or via, street or strada,*
> *You can see 'em disappearing two by two,*
> *On an evening in Roma.*
> *Do they take 'em for espresso, yeah, I guess so.*
> *On each lovers arm a girl I wish I knew*
> *On an evening in Roma.*'

"Well it half fits, Rome and the cup of espresso part," he concluded with a smile. Hearing him sing, even 'swing' style, she had to remind herself to breathe again. "Now, before we become completely sidetracked," he continued, "let us address your dislike for dance." How could she engage in any discussions after this? *Please don't stop singing*, her mind silently implored, however, address the situation he did. "The art of dance was forced upon you, and rather than show how enjoyable it could be, became something miserable that had to be tolerated, much like poetry. The most thought-provoking, heart-searching verses are pounded into your head when you are not old enough yet to appreciate their significance, when they can only be fully grasped after understanding is acquired through life's experiences. Dance is the same, it needs to be put into the right context, which, I believe, is right about now," he quietly announced, standing up from the table and offering her his hand. "Would you please do me the honour? There are no prying eyes to stare at you here, it's just us two, no *have to's*, only … *want to's*."

For the first time in her life, she found the invitation to dance irresistible. Slipping her hand into his and placing the other on his shoulder, the world seemed to stop spinning as he led her through gentle turns and circles, conscious only of their own intimate universe held together by the harmonic gravity of melody, rhythm and emotion. Track after track played, their pace quickening with each swing tune, or slowing down to a calm, waltz-like lilt. It felt so different dancing this time, even if there were a thousand people watching, it didn't matter, her thoughts were centred on him alone; feeling the confidence in his steps, reading the expression in his eyes, wondering why such simple things were so fascinating, the curve of his jaw line, the way his hair fell into natural waves, the gentle touch of his hands, the feel of his steady shoulder, and again, the intoxicating resonance of his voice as he sang along with the next easy-paced track:

"Some like a night at the movies, some like a dance or a show,
Some are content with an evening spent home by the radio.
Some like to live for the moment, some like to just reminisce,
But whenever I have an evening to spend, just give me one like this.
This is a lovely way to spend an evening,
Can't think of anything I'd rather do,
This is a lovely way to spend an evening,
Can't think of anyone as lovely as you.
A casual stroll through the garden, a kiss by a lazy lagoon,
Catching a breath of moonlight, humming our favourite tune.
This is a lovely way to spend an evening,
I want to save all my nights and spend them with you."

"Oh, don't stop," she sighed.

"But we're in an instrumental right now," he smiled.

"Then … hum, or something, but don't stop."

"All right," he smiled, drawing her closer, quietly humming to the melody. When the piece drew to a close, they continued to dance seamlessly into the next track, another soft jazz instrumental. By this time, their formal pose had melted into a gentle swaying embrace with dance steps a little less defined, their arms softly clasping each other, she resting her head on his shoulder while he continued to hum, his cheek brushing against her hair.

"That wasn't bad, was it?" he asked.

"Oh, no."

"Would you like to do this again sometime?"

"Yes, please," she smiled.

"Then my dear, I do believe you are cured."

"Thank you doctor, I believe I am," she chuckled, snuggling her cheek closer against his shoulder, feeling his arms wrap her a little tighter in response. "I could spend all night dancing like this." They continued to sway into the next tune, he singing along softly:

> *"We're just a kiss apart, and yet we dance on an on,*
> *We're just a kiss apart, and soon our chance will be gone,*
> *Now you're beside my heart, your eyes have started to shine,*
> *Oh but I know too well, daybreak may break the spell,*
> *So while we're just a kiss apart, kiss me and …."*

They were unable to wait for the end of the song, looking into each other's eyes, the melodic invitation was impossible to ignore. Wrapped in each other's arms and spell-bound by the close embrace, this kiss lasted longer than the last. Although her eyes were closed, she became aware of a curious flickering of soft colours, and after a bevy of muffled popping, realized fireworks really had started to fly. Interrupted by the commotion, they turned towards the window now flashing with the multicoloured sparkles and rockets lighting up the skyline.

"Oh, even that *cliché* is true!" she laughed. Now another old saying made perfect sense. "For a moment, I thought that was us," she confessed, snuggling against him.

"Believe me, it was. Every *cliché* has it's element of truth. We wouldn't keep repeating them if they didn't. In fact, I wouldn't mind repeating the *cliché* again," he noted.

"We make wonderful fireworks, don't we?" she smiled, looking up into his eyes.

"We certainly do. Happy New Year, Kathy."

"Happy New Year."

She didn't know what it was, but the way he said her name breathlessly at that moment made her legs almost give way beneath her. She held on to him a little tighter as they kissed once more, wishing it could go on forever; it was so much better than dancing. At last, they returned to simply holding each other, their foreheads resting together for a moment before pressing cheek against cheek, luxuriating in this indefinable moment.

"Oh, Gerry, I don't know what I'm feeling right now … I … ."

"Shhh," he replied, holding his forehead against hers again and placing a finger on her lips, "don't say anything, let's just enjoy the moment."

She smiled and placed her head on his shoulder, breathing a sigh of contentment. All seemed right with the world. Oblivious to everything else those few poignant minutes, they were startled when the phones throughout the apartment began to ring and bleep.

"Blast, I should have taken the thing off the hook," he groaned, "who could be calling now of all times?"

"Oh no, just let it ring," she replied, her voice muffled in his dinner jacket.

"No, I'd better see who it is," he sighed with resignation, finally releasing her from his arms, "or we may be bugged for the rest of the night. What a mood killer," he chuckled.

While he answered the phone, she looked out the window to admire the fireworks to find that the snow had reached blizzard conditions, swirling down from the inky blackness, occasionally glowing from the celebratory starbursts before gathering into soft piles and rounding the square edges of the glass with fluffy white drifts. How on earth was she going to get home in all that? While she tried to sort out the logistics of driving through the snow and ice, it was difficult not to eavesdrop on the telephone conversation. Gerry promptly cut short the call as best he could.

"… didn't anyone tell you I wasn't coming over this year? …Yeah, I know, but …yeah…no really? …Hey I can't really stay on the phone right now, I've got company…yeah…okay, Happy New Year to you too, say 'hi' to the gang for me…all right, we'll get together sometime in the New

Year…goodnight." At last, he pushed the receiver button and laid the handset on the table, ensuring they would receive no more interruptions. "Sorry about that," he apologized.

"That's all right. I couldn't help overhearing, were you expected at a New Year's party somewhere?"

"Not really, just my old buddy, Leroy, trying to drag me to his same old predictable bash. Believe me, there's nowhere else I'd rather be right now," he assured her.

"Gosh, I wish I didn't have to be such a killjoy and spoil everything, but look at the snow, I've got to get a move-on if I'm going to make it back home."

"It has thickened, hasn't it? It's my fault, I wasn't paying attention, I was enjoying your company too much. Let me check and see if the snow ploughs or sanders are rolling yet." He opened the balcony doors, sending a blast of freezing air and a flurry of snow into the room. She closed the doors, watching as he walked briskly to the balustrade and scanned the street below for a few moments before retreating to the inviting warmth.

"Nothing yet, well, I can't really see anything, it's like an avalanche out there," brushing the snow off his arms. For a moment, he looked like an antique picture of Jack Frost with the downy tufts of snow lightly laced around his hair and eyebrows. "I'd be happy to take you home," he continued, rubbing his fingers warm, "but there's no way you, me or anyone could drive through that now, not safely anyway." He was right, it would take some time for the ploughs to get going, and then there were all the partygoers, everyone would be going home wasted from all those champagne toasts … "I think it would be best if you stayed here tonight, no point taking any risks. Call your parents, I've got a comfy guest room all set up, Lottie uses it all the time when she doesn't want to be on her own, I'm sure she has a few things you can borrow," he continued, heading to the fireplace to stoke the dying embers. "There are other guest rooms, you can take your pick. The folks usually stay over when they come in to town for dinner, but forgive me, I'm rambling, go ahead and use the phone while I get this going again," he said, settling the logs into place with the hearth tongs.

"The thing is, I don't think anyone will be home yet, that means I'd have to leave a message on the machine. I have a feeling this is not going to look good," her voice trailed. She had never stayed overnight in a man's apartment before; even though Gerry's offer of a guest room did reassure her his intentions remained honourable, leaving a message for her parents under these circumstances was certainly awkward.

"Oh I see...I had no idea I may be facing a shotgun in the morning."

"Gerry, don't joke, this is serious."

"Well, try to see if you can get through to someone, if you have to leave a message, there's nothing more you can do. I'll drive you home in the morning and call a cab to take me back to town. Not only will I see you home safely, but it will give me a chance to personally assure your parents that your honour has not been compromised."

"Oh I don't think that's necessary," she replied, amused with his Victorian gallantry, but relieved by his offer nevertheless.

"I've made up my mind, so it's no use arguing."

"All right," she said shaking her head. Pressing the receiver button, she dialled home. The tone continued to blip with each ring, eventually the machine kicked in and recorded her message.

"Hi everyone, it's me. I'm just calling to let you know I won't be able to make it back tonight, not with this weather, not to mention all the tipsy drivers, well, you get the idea. Gerry suggested I stay here and has offered his guest room for the night, so I guess I'll see you all when the roads are cleared. Hope everyone's having a good time, see you in the morning, love you."

"Now, that wasn't bad?" he smiled, standing up and rubbing a few stray ashes off his knees.

"No, but I can't imagine what their expressions are going to be like when we show up tomorrow," she replied sheepishly.

"Let's not be borrowing tomorrow's worries when we have tonight's happiness to dwell on," he chuckled, giving her a reassuring hug. "Now that you don't have to rush off, you can really make yourself comfy. Look, we haven't even opened the champagne and toasted the New Year yet, and I bet you're just dying to kick off those high heels. Why not go rustle up a pair of Lottie's slippers? We can pop open the bottle, put our feet up in front of the fire and finish our dessert, the baked one left on the table of course," he clarified with a smile.

"Okay, but...where is the guestroom?"

"I'm sorry, we never finished our tour. Here, let me show you, I wouldn't mind getting into my loafers for that matter."

He offered his arm and finished where they left off, taking her into the office cum library with the expected stylish desk, armchairs and small decorative tables with lamps, all surrounded by rose mahogany shelves filled with colourful tomes. She could easily spot where he kept most of his valuable books; one section featured cases similar to the specialized climate controlled models used by the manuscript dealer he introduced her to. For an executive's workroom, it was rather inviting, maybe it was all the books, library atmospheres were always welcoming. The master bedroom was next, but she barely peeked in for a brief second before asking him to point out the guest room. Gallant as he was, she still was not about to give him any ideas.

"It's the next door," he laughed, "I'll be out in a minute, you go ahead and find the slippers."

Katherine turned on the light and looking around, found the closet. She smiled when she opened the door and looked down to see the footwear she was to borrow, fuzzy brown slippers with teddy bear heads. Well, they were comfortable, that was for sure. While she was there, she decided to examine her quarters. The bed was beautifully decked out with a quilted eiderdown with a rose pattern and an abundance of overstuffed pillows. There were soft matching armchairs, lacy doilies softening the hard look of the dressing and end tables. Lottie probably helped with this room since she used it a lot, Katherine deduced. That's probably what was missing in the other areas of his apartment, the proverbial woman's touch. Well, it was a bachelor's place after all; men obviously had their own decorating ideas. She discovered the room also had a private bathroom luxuriously decorated in Italian marble and mosaics with a profusion of plush towels. In all, one could see his guests were provided with every comfort.

They returned to the hallway at the same moment, she in her new footwear, while he had taken off his dinner jacket and exchanged it for a navy period style three-quarter length quilted house robe with velvet collar, cuffs, belt and pocket edges, his feet now clad in the comfy loafers.

"That's a fetching garment," she commented.

"You like it? Lottie gave it to me for Christmas. She says I can get away with this old-fashioned style. It feels good actually, now all I need is the pipe, a Stradivarius and the deer-stalker cap," he smiled. "You are quite … dazzling my dear," he continued, eyeing her feet with amusement. She must have looked rather funny wearing a formal evening dress and then … floppy, overstuffed bear-headed slippers. Katherine smiled, shrugged her shoulders and wiggled her toes.

"I can't say I'd make the cover of *Vogue*, but at least I'm out of those horrible heels."

"Come, Princess," he laughed, "let's go open the champagne."

They made several toasts, wishing each other all the best things they could think of for the New Year, at last taking their plates of cake and sitting together on the sofa with their feet up, the fire blazing merrily on the hearth.

"Ah, this is the life," Gerry said as he laid his empty plate aside and placed his arm around her shoulder. *"This is a lovely way to spend an evening, can't think of anything I'd rather do ..."* Katherine listened quietly, watching the flames continue their flickering dance. He definitely could give old 'Blue Eyes' a run for his money she mused as he sang along with the recordings, by now, they had already heard the croon songs a few times as the tracks made the rounds, but they didn't mind. It was such a restful feeling just being with someone who was quite content in your company, sharing a mutual understanding that a running conversation was not always necessary to enjoy their time together. Katherine closed her eyes for a moment, it was so warm by the fire and it felt inexplicably satisfying listening to him hum, tucked under his arm, she just wanted this part of the evening to last as long as it could. The warmth, the champagne and her sense of contentment became a lethal combination for drowsiness, Gerry eventually looked down to see her dozing on his shoulder. Only two glasses and she had gone out like a light.

He thought it was time to wake her, but decided to wait a little longer, she looked so peaceful, he was unable to pass up this opportunity to admire her undisturbed. The contour of her eyebrows, soft rosy cheeks, her long brown lashes, the delicate line of her nose and chin, the soft brown curls of her hair. It was a pity her eyes were closed, there were times he thought he would drown in their lacustrine limpidity. What a long year! It was almost too good to be true to think that she was finally becoming attracted to him let alone nestled by his side. Brushing aside a strand of hair from her cheek, his thoughts wandered to the time they first met. How could he forget walking into his apartment that fateful day, frustrated after a migraine-inducing meeting with a board of French executives who lacked the foresight to provide a decent translator, to find a beautiful young lady too terrified to walk around, clutching her handbag as if it were capable of exploding and inflicting severe damage to the surroundings? Then, to happily discover she was the same girl who stormed her father's office and victoriously won her cause for animal rights, how beautifully she had grown up! He wasn't sure about the poetics of love at first sight, but it was difficult not to be smitten then and there with that vision of loveliness. Perhaps that's what the poets meant. At the time, he believed the rumours she and Kraylor junior were not far from the altar rails. It was a cruel trick of fate that he would finally meet her when she was already spoken for, and then, to discover a few moments later, over coffee of all things, there was an enormous misunderstanding. Looking back on it, why he didn't ask for her number or ask to see her again right there and then was beyond him. Well, it was their first meeting, and knowing her better now, it would have unnerved her if a stranger showed even a casual interest in her company. He just had to see her again, but how? Through her he had found out the Kraylors were visiting Paris for Christmas, an accidental encounter and an informal invitation to get together was his only chance. He must have looked like a thief casing the neighbourhood with all the walks he took in the area, pretending he was out for his daily constitutional or had business to go to when he had other things on his mind. He had finally given up and had gone out to see if he could buy an English newspaper when lo and behold, he bumped into Kraylor senior and junior. Well, he didn't plan on a Christmas dinner invitation and while he politely refused at first as would be expected, was eventually persuaded to join them later that evening, much to his satisfaction. Then blast it all, to be a witness to that horrific botched proposal, it would be a long time, if ever, before she could disassociate him from that distasteful memory. Hoping that a casual acquaintance could grow into something special was too much to expect now that this opportunity had been poisoned. It would be fruitless to approach her, and with much reluctance, decided to walk away. However, fate intervened again months later, crossing their paths at the Sirrac. Had enough time passed? Maybe, maybe not, but he was not about to lose another opportunity. Bless Suzy for winning the contest; if Lottie didn't happen to like her painting, he was still bound and determined to buy it, a personal token of appreciation for bringing about this fortuitous encounter. Then, to see his archrival of the art world ready to purchase it made him see vermilion red. He could not stand by and let another chance like this be undermined. Price was not an issue, and outbidding his rival was a double bonus that evening, he certainly would be noticed. Now how to keep in contact was the challenge, until he heard about her plans to open a gallery. Perfect, they had a common interest in art; as a collector, he could always invent a legitimate reason to see her on a regular basis. Nevertheless, he couldn't wait for the premises to open and found it difficult to stay away, good thing he gave in to his growing impatience, he was only too happy to lend assistance with her exhibition space. He couldn't help but go overboard, making himself indispensable if needs be, *anything* to let her know he existed. When she finally accepted his invitation to go out with him on those few occasions, the musical, the book show, it was almost too good to be true, then, their first night out at the opera, their first kiss, she had been unprepared, in fact, he actually stole her first kiss come to think of it, which also surprised him. Many things started to make sense after that. Although she was not ignorant nor naïve, she was yet … *innocent*, somewhat of a miracle in this day and age. Content in her own world, sheltered within the family circle and absorbed with her art, she revelled in the idealized love found in a book written in a chivalric age that had long passed, perhaps too timid to discover true romance, or, in trying to protect her idealistic notion of love had unintentionally excluded romance altogether, fearing whoever she might meet would expect too much too fast. Reflecting upon the world today, he could understand her reticence, the modern liberal lifestyle with its relaxed, if non-existent moral values, would make her reluctant to get involved. Yes, he could understand; when and if she fell in love, it would be deep and lasting. She was not playing hard to get, she was aiming for perfection: intimacy would only be granted when vows had been exchanged. No wonder he could drown in her eyes, a childlike radiance danced around her like perpetual springtime. Those medieval manuscripts were the appropriate gift, oh Katherine, you are the last unicorn lost in a city of prurient mares all willingly had and used at every available opportunity. You're a brilliant diamond, the Star of Africa set amidst a world of glass and zirconia, and now, to think you're experiencing your first romantic feelings, and for *me* … . Then, their last kiss, it was so deep, he could barely keep his composure from crumbling, it was a good thing Leroy called: better to have that blockhead destroy the mood than to have her remind him of his place and ultimately rock her growing confidence in him. Looking down at her sleeping, he grew determined not to blow it like Kraylor. *Damn*, don't think of him! He wished he could shake the old doubt that her relationship with Kraylor could or would stay on a platonic level, why did he have to drag that up now? It was obvious that nothing serious had really developed between them. Jealousy? Okay, admit it. He couldn't help feeling possessive, he was aware of his feelings for her growing more intense with every tender moment they shared; her laughter, a glance here or there and their kisses bringing them ever closer together. He knew what she expected, but did she know what she truly wanted? He sighed at this thought, while he had noticed her from the start, it was only a few months for her, and any suggestion of a permanent commitment for now may be too soon for her to consider, like a frightened colt, she may bolt and run. Marriage was a big step after all, even he found it bemusing, to think that the time had come when he could envision a gold ring on his finger. Boy, if this idea was strange and new to him, she definitely would need more time; slow, delicate handling was necessary to win a woman this rare. If she needed space to sort out her feelings, if she wanted their relationship to creep like a glacier, then so be it, he was willing to let things move at that pace, after all, glaciers carved majestic mountains. He felt confident in her growing attachment for him, the time they spent together this last month had proved that … .

The recording rotated and switched to a sprightly instrumental. Katherine opened her eyes with the change of tempo, a few seconds passed before she remembered where she was. How long had she been snoozing? Now this was embarrassing … .

"I'm sorry, I warned you about what champagne does to me."

"Don't apologize, we should have gone to bed ages ago, but it was so comfortable just sitting here together. Perhaps we should head off now before it gets too late to bother going at all."

"All right," she agreed, leaning over to the side table to pick up her glass and plate.

"Don't worry about that, the dishes can wait until morning," he said, standing up and stretching before going around the room, blowing out the candles and turning off the lights, "let's rustle you up a toothbrush, Lottie suggested I keep supplies ready in case unexpected company stays over, I'm glad I followed her advice. Thing is," he said as they made their way down the hall, ducking into the den for a moment to turn off the sound system, "the housekeeper knows where everything is, and I don't. Maybe the storage closet…?" he wondered aloud. Jaunting back from the den and opening a door Katherine hadn't been through, he took a quick glance around. "Aha," he said, grabbing a new packet off a shelf laden with soaps and household cleaners, handing it to her, "a yellow toothbrush too. I think everything else you may need is already in the bathroom, but if not, it's probably in here, and if you still don't find it, don't be afraid to ask."

"Thank you Gerry. I'm sorry to be so much trouble."

"No trouble at all, Princess. Now, off to bed before the sun comes up."

"Good night, Lancelot," she replied, slipping into the guest room and closing the door. Eyeing the lock, she wondered if she should … well, I feel safe, but let's not tempt fate. *Click*, went the lock.

ଓ ✿ ଃ

"Good morning, beautiful. Thought I'd fix breakfast. What would you like? I've got eggs and bacon on, toast in the toaster, you can have some pancakes too if you like. Just name it," Gerry offered as he scrambled the eggs.

600

"Eggs and bacon are fine, thank you," Katherine replied, settling into one of the sleek swivel stools at the breakfast counter set up with linen place mats, silverware, and a small vase of roses and sunflowers. "This is funny, despite all the trouble you've gone to, I feel so overdressed for the morning."

Naturally, all she had was her outfit from the night before, no choice of wardrobe for her. He on the other looked comfortable in slacks and a thick cashmere turtleneck sweater. It was the first time she had seen him dressed in anything other than a business suit or formal evening wear, however he still cut a debonair figure when sporting casual clothes. And, what a surprise, he could make breakfast, *real* breakfast.

"You look fine to me," he replied, scooting bacon onto a couple of plates.

"Thanks. You know, just watching you, I feel spoiled … and under skilled. Where or how did you learn to cook?"

"Can't say I *really* cook, maybe if I had more practise, but breakfast isn't that hard to do. When you take off for college, there are some things you just pick up out of necessity, handy for the times the housekeeper is off or turns up late," he replied, a little distracted while dishing up the eggs.

"Here, let me help, I can serve the toast at least, I've had a lot of practise with my Pop Tarts," she offered.

"All right, the coffee machine is over there, I'm not sure how you like yours, so just help yourself. I've got sweeteners too if you use them, but after your mention of Pop Tarts, I guess you don't. Do you like strawberry jelly?"

"You bet. Can't have toast without it."

"Then you just might like to try the curds, a friend sends me boxes of the stuff from England every now and again," he said, taking the jars of deluxe seedless fruit spreads out of the refrigerator, "I like the raspberry curd myself, tastes just like the jam in the packaged Danishes, but much better."

Katherine then became aware of a machine quietly churning behind one of the under counter cupboards. Looking around at the gleaming black granite topped counters and island, the place was *too* tidy after last night's dinner.

"Gerry, did you do all the dishes from last night? I feel awful now, putting you to all that extra work. My culinary abilities may not be up to par, but I do know how to wash dishes."

"Hey, don't sweat it, the caterers did quite a bit of the cleanup as they went, and it's not a big deal to put the rest of the mess into the dishwasher. Besides, you're my guest, relax and let me handle things," he replied as they sat together at the counter.

It felt rather odd having a normal rise-and-shine breakfast together after the emotive evening they had shared, starting out with the usual greetings and chitchat, but at the same time completely aware they were sharing something special.

"Did you sleep well?" he enquired.

"Yes, thank you. I was too comfortable in fact, I could have slept on until noon."

"Why didn't you? We really don't have to rush today. Besides, I'm so glad you had to stay over, it gives us a chance to spend some extra time together."

"I'm glad I stayed too," Katherine confessed, "however, I should call home, I have to face it sometime, let everyone know I intend to show up eventually." She tried to sound nonchalant, but dreaded to think who would answer and what reception would be awaiting her.

"Of course, the phone is hanging by the pantry, but have your breakfast first while it's hot. A few extra minutes won't hurt." She was glad for the reprieve, the raspberry curd was pretty good too. However, it didn't take long to finish, the call could not be avoided. As it turned out, Steves answered the phone.

"Hi Steves, it's me. ... Well, you can see, that's not the case. Didn't anyone get my message? ... Oh that's just dandy, ... No, I'm at Gerry's ... oh grow up. ... Listen, just play back the machine and try to be diplomatic with the elders for me, okay? I'll be home as soon as it's safe to venture out. ... Okay, see you later, bye."

"Is everything fine on the home front?"

"Just great, with all the goings on, no one bothered to check the answering machine when they got home last night."

"I see, well, I don't want to make things difficult for you, perhaps we should get moving," he suggested, quickly gulping the last of his coffee.

"There's no need to rush. Gosh, I am a killjoy."

"Not at all. Just leave your plate, don't worry, I can clear all this later." Leaving the kitchen and turning into the hall, he helped her with her velvet coat. "Will you be warm enough in this? It seems pretty lightweight."

"I'll be fine, the van has heating you know."

"Still, we have to wait for the engine to warm up, I don't want you to catch a chill. You should see the park from the balcony, like a winter paradise, it's definitely freezing out there. Here, you'd better put this around you," he said, taking out the frock coat she admired and wrapping it like a protective cloak around her, velvet coat and all, before she had a chance to protest.

"I won't be able to walk now," she laughed, loving the sensation of being bundled up like a child. He pulled out a sleek steel grey wool coat and swung it around his shoulders before placing his arms inside and winding a burgundy wool scarf around his neck.

"Now, my wallet and keys," he noted, taking them from the sideboard and slipping them into his pocket, "and your keys, please."

"You really don't have to take me home."

"I insist. The roads are cleared, but there is a danger of black ice, not to mention it would be best if I reassured your parents personally that last night was unavoidable."

"Before we go, let me thank you for everything, letting me stay over and for preparing a lovely breakfast, not to mention last night. It was truly … a special way to welcome the New Year."

"The pleasure was all mine," he replied, contemplating her eyes for a moment.

"I'm sorry we … didn't meet each other sooner, I might have enjoyed going out to the débutante ball then," she confessed.

"Frankly, I would have given anything to be your escort for that night, but we're together now, aren't we?" he reminded her, gently holding her by the shoulders. "Perhaps it wasn't meant to be back then, but maybe it is now."

This still seemed all strange to her, she felt a flood of emotions she couldn't explain. She suddenly held him close, surprising him for a split second before he too instinctively wrapped his arms around her.

"Gerry, what *is* going on between us? I don't know what think. I feel so different when I'm with you, I …" her voice trailed off, unable to express the fretful yet blissful confusion she was experiencing.

"I know. You don't have to say anything. Are things moving too fast? We can slow down if you like."

"That's just it, *I don't know*," she replied with a tone of trepidation that made her feel more self-conscious than before.

"Well, that's all right," he reassured her, "it just means we're taking things slowly. There's nothing wrong with that."

"I wish I could define 'things'," she sighed.

"You still like everything in neat little boxes all ready and packaged," he noted with amusement, "there are some things, that don't come that easy, it's a mystery to be pondered."

"This certainly feels like a mystery," she agreed.

"Or … a puzzle," he realized, "my dear, you are looking for answers, perhaps I … can help you muddle through this." Katherine looked up into his eyes with anticipation. "Yes … maybe I can help define the box, and you might be able to discover what missing pieces should fit inside, or perhaps, what is already there," he said reflectively, almost half to himself, "usually the princess sets a riddle, but I suppose the knight can too."

"Couldn't you just tell me right now?"

"Not in this instance," he smiled, brushing that endearing strand of hair from her cheek, "you and I are part of this strange trick box, and therefore, part of the puzzle. This is something you must figure out, or the answer might not be as agreeable as it should be."

"Well okay, I think I understand." Curious as she was to fathom his metaphor of a riddle, it reminded her of the time his brother Pete and the Professor gave her clues to help her solve the allegorical problem with her painting, for the answer to be meaningful, she would have to discover the solution for herself. "So … how do you plan to help me 'muddle' through?" she smiled. In all, this *was* rather interesting.

"As much as I dislike keeping you in suspense, I can't tell you now," he said, shaking his head, "but you can expect your clue to arrive very soon. Keep your eyes open."

"Where … when … how? " she wondered.

"And spoil the surprise? You'll have to be patient," he laughed, stroking her cheek with the back of his finger. "We should head off, or it will be noon before we get you home."

"No extra croissants and caffeine before we go?" she shyly asked.

"Why not?" he smiled, giving her one last kiss. "That's much better than my breakfast I have to admit."

"Oh dear. Here, let me fix you, or we *will* give everyone a stroke," she joked, pulling a Kleenex from her purse and dabbing at the rose coloured lipstick around his mouth.

"You know, it's not a public disgrace to kiss someone," he whispered, taking the tissue and wiping the rest of the colour off, "I'm beginning to feel like the poor messenger from Burma in the *King and I*. '*We kiss in the shadow, we hide from the moon, our meetings are few, and over too soon.*'."

"Don't make fun," she smiled, lowering her eyes, "but … I love to hear you sing."

"I have a fan club, do I?" he replied, straightening his frock coat that by now had slipped off kilter from her shoulders.

"I guess you could say that."

"Funny girl," he said, giving her a quick peck on the forehead, "we'd better vamoose."

Closing the door behind them, they silently waited for the elevator. She couldn't help but notice the little frown that appeared on his forehead as each floor number lit up in succession.

"We could take the stairs," she suggested.

"That's all right, I'll forgo the million steps and continue to face my fear. I'm not ready to keep that classic New Year's resolution and stay fit," he laughed.

"Hey, we never mentioned any New Year's resolutions. Using the stairs at the gallery more often is a good idea," she reflected.

"You won't keep it, that's another New Year's tradition."

"Well, do you have any resolutions you plan to keep?"

"Yes, one that I *know* I'll keep: to see you as often as possible, Princess."

"Hmm, that's a good resolution too," she agreed, stepping into the elevator.

In a few minutes, they reached the garage and made their way to his parking spaces. Gerry seemed to find something very amusing as they approached the van.

"I wonder what the residents had to say about this strange vehicle in the neighbourhood." Katherine looked around and saw the funny side of parking her mercantile van in the midst of all the luxury brand cars.

"At least it's not a Winnebago," she observed.

"True," he chuckled, "it's been awhile since I've driven one of these," he remarked as they settled into the seats and buckled up, "it's great being able to sit up this high."

"I know, you can see everything from here. When did you ever drive a van?"

"Oh, all part of learning the family business from the ground up. While most kids worked in burger joints, I worked in the family warehouses, ran a forklift for a summer, then did the delivery stints with the vans, learned how to drive the articulated trucks before heading up the executive ladder."

"I can't imagine you driving a big hauler somehow," she smiled.

"I sure did, some of the jobs were pretty boring though, nothing but driving around from one drop-off and pick-up to another across several states, but it was better than the smaller deliveries, you had no idea what part of town you might end up in. On the other hand, it was one way of getting to know the city inside and out. Hey, look at the park, it's like another world after all the snow. Now would be the perfect time to enjoy a carriage ride together, but I guess that's for another day," he reflected.

"A carriage ride, you know, I've never done that."

"Neither have I," he said, "there's a first time for everything."

Katherine was glad Gerry insisted on driving the van, it was rather icy. Although he drove with caution, she could feel the vehicle slip under them at one point, but slightly turning the wheel into the direction they skid, corrected the potentially dangerous situation.

"That was close," she said, letting out a deep breath, "how did you do that?"

"It's simple. Didn't anyone teach you how to work with ice?"

"Sort of, but generally, I try not to drive out in the snow, but since I've opened the gallery, I've been on the road a lot. This would be the first winter I've really had to face."

"Well, I'll teach you the tricks. Number one, if you feel the car skid, whatever you do, *don't* turn the wheel in the opposite direction. I know, it's the instinctive thing to do, but with ice, you will skid out of control. You turn slightly *with* the skid, and don't jerk the wheel; nice, easy movements are the key with weather like this, especially as everything in a car is now automatic and reacts with the least touch."

"Okay, I'll remember that."

"Number two, never, never, *never*, slam or hit the brakes hard, in fact, don't even push the pedal as you normally would in good weather. If you break in a regular fashion as on a dry day, the car could still skid when the wheels lose motion. Drive slowly to begin with, then if you have to stop, at a red light for example, you very gently 'pump' the brake a bare tip at a time. Of course, with this pumping technique, you have to start to brake a lot earlier than you normally would to give you a chance to come to a stop."

"Gosh, that's a new thing to me, no one taught me that before," she replied.

"It takes a little practise, you might want to find an empty parking lot or a quiet block to try it out. Now, tip number three; if you find yourself in an uncontrollable skid, don't do anything, hands off the wheel and no brakes, no pedals, do nothing, or you could make it a lot worse. Let the vehicle find its own equilibrium. I know, this is the hardest thing to do: you will spin around, you may hit something, every inch of you will want to take control, but believe me, the damage will not be as bad than if you tried to correct it. Just sit tight and pretend you're stuck in one of the crazy bumper cars in a carnival. When you do come to a stop, you can sort yourself out then, not before. You get the idea?”

“Yeah, I think I do. Thanks for telling me all this.”

“No problem.”

The remainder of the drive passed without any other major incident, and Katherine couldn’t help but notice how safe she was beginning to feel when Gerry was around. How peculiar she thought, to feel protected by someone who only a sort time ago was a total stranger. Her mind wandered to their little *tête-à-tête* and his offer to provide a clue to help her figure out this … *thing* … between them. What did he mean? Just what did she have to keep her eyes open for? He really was a mystery man; never mind, she always loved a good puzzle.

Arriving safely at Oak Meadows, she was surprised to see extra cars in the driveway.

“Looks like you got company,” Gerry noted as he parked near the front door.

“That’s my aunt’s car, and that’s Charlie’s car over there. Obviously, Suzy had to stay over with him last night and he’s brought her home.”

“Could be. Well, time to face the music, I hope Papa Bear is in a good mood,” he remarked, handing her keys back. “Here, you’d better hold on to my arm, the ground is a bit slippery.” Clutching his arm, they skidded their way to the front door.

“Hi everyone, we made it back safely,” she called out as they entered the main hallway. Jasper was the first to hear them arrive, barking his greeting. Steves heard the commotion and bounded down the stairs to give her a ‘heads up’.

“Hi Kats, hi Ger. Shut up Jasper! Listen, Pops and Gramps seem to be taking it okay, but you know how hard it is to tell with them, especially when Pops goes silent. Mom’s the one who went a bit hysterical, and Aunt Martha didn’t help the situation.”

Katherine sighed.

“Thanks Steves. Where is everyone?”

“As usual, men in the den, women in the kitchen. Hey Ger, you going to stay for dinner? We have it early on New Year’s day.”

“Oh yes, of course, please do,” Katherine insisted. “I’d forgotten about that, Mom loves doing a nice big beef roast to help us get over the holiday turkey glut, you’d be welcome to join us.”

“I don’t know, I’ve dropped by unexpectedly this time around,” Gerry politely reminded, “I wouldn’t want to interrupt a family tradition. I’ll give your parents my respects though before I head off.”

"Well, I'll go get Mom anyway," Steves offered, heading to the kitchen while Katherine showed Gerry to the den.

"Looky here, the young ones are home," Gramps announced, Pops rose from his chair, but didn't say anything for the moment.

"Please, I didn't mean to disturb you," Gerry began. Katherine jumped in.

"I'm sorry, I called, but no one answered the phone, and I was sure someone would have gotten my message by now," Katherine tried to explain.

"There was no way we could have made it last night, the snow ploughs didn't get out until three AM," Gerry continued, "I had a perfectly good guestroom and promised to drive her back when it was safe."

The patriarchs seemed to reluctantly accept this explanation.

"You did the sensible thing," Gramps told him, "we didn't have as far to drive, and yet it was pretty treacherous for us to get home. Thank you for bringing our Katie home safely."

"My pleasure. Excuse me, would you mind if I use your phone?"

"Not at all," Pops replied.

"Oh Gerry, you're not calling for a cab now are you? I asked him if he would like to stay for dinner, but he's being too polite," Katherine informed them.

"I couldn't impose," Gerry said, dialling the phone. At that moment, Helen and Aunt Martha came in.

"Kathy, I'm glad you're home safe," her mother affirmed. Katherine gave her a hug.

"As you can see, Gerry saw her home," Gramps piped up, "it was kind of him to let Kathy stay in his guestroom when the bad weather hit."

"Yes it was," she had to agree, taking the hint with relief. The men could tell if something was truly amiss in these situations.

"Well, Gerard, I suppose you'll be staying for supper?" Aunt Martha sniffed, she didn't seem too pleased with the whole affair. Glad as she was that Katherine might finally be interested in someone, she could not abide the thought of her niece caught in a compromising situation.

"Please, be our guest, there's no need to hurry off, we have enough prime rib to feed an army," Helen affirmed, "that is, if you don't have something already planned with your family for the day."

"Well, not really but … ."

"Good, that's settled. Kathy, be a dear and take his coat … er … coats, and hang them up in the closet, will you?" her mother prompted.

"I'm sorry, if I knew I was staying for dinner, I would have brought something for the occasion," he admitted, unwinding his scarf. "I usually don't appear empty-handed at a get-together."

"Nonsense, m'boy, we're still making our way through the chocolates you left for Christmas," Gramps assured him.

"After the last bottle of toodle you left, perhaps it's a good thing you didn't bring anything," Aunt Martha noted wryly, recalling the silliness that prevailed at the last festive dinner table.

"Come Martha, we've got a few things to see to," Helen hinted, tugging her sister by the arm.

"Well, looks like Ger is going to stay after all," Steves noted as he came through the door, watching their guest hand Katherine his coat and scarf. "Do you play pool by any chance?"

"Sure, you want a game?"

Katherine was glad to see that Gerry and Steves seemed to be hitting it off pretty well, at least he would feel more welcome after the impromptu invitation to stay. After hanging up his coats, she ran upstairs to slip into something more comfortable for the day and was amused to find on her return that Pops and Gramps had joined the game. Gerry and Steves had teamed up and were calling themselves the 'Spring Bucks' while the opposing side were ingloriously but good-naturedly dubbed the 'Old Fogies'.

"How's it going?" Katherine inquired.

"Not too bad, I haven't lost it yet, even with my bum hip and cranky knee," Gramps affirmed, sending the eight ball directly into the corner pocket at the opposite end. "Now, beat that!" he smugly exclaimed to the whippersnappers.

"Hmm, not too bad, Gramps," Steves noted, "but watch this."

Retrieving the pool balls out of the pockets, he lined them up across the middle of the table with the exception of the eight ball, which he placed in the centre of the open space at one end, the cue ball in the corner of the other. Taking his stick, he smacked the cue ball at an odd angle, causing it to jump the line and hit the eight ball into the corner pocket.

"Hrumph! Show off," Gramps chuckled. "What about you, m' boy?" he asked, turning to Gerry, "do you have any fancy moves?"

"Let me see. May I borrow your cane?"

Gerry positioned the balls exactly as Steves had them, but using Gramp's cane for a pool stick, performed the same feat.

"Another show off. All right son, can you do anything to reclaim the honour of the Old Fogies?"

Calmly, Pops took an old trophy from a shelf and placing it at one end of the table, hit the cue ball, landing it directly into the cup.

"Way to go, Pops," Steves said in stunned admiration. Katherine laughed, she had no idea their father was that nifty with a cue stick.

"I wasn't always an 'old timer' you know," he said, lifting an eyebrow.

"I'd better go and see if I can do anything in the kitchen," Katherine returned, leaving the men to their feats of dexterity.

"Kathy, how are they getting along in there?" her mother asked, reading a recipe for Yorkshire pudding someone swapped with her at the club.

"Just great, they could give Paul Newman a run for his money," she chuckled, "they've got some pool tournament going."

"At least it's more constructive," Aunt Martha noticed, "they won't be three sheets in the breeze when dinner is ready."

"Are Uncle Tim and Aunt Barbara coming over?"

"They haven't called, so I guess not," Mom replied. Katherine hoped it was just the weather that kept them from coming and not another business disagreement between Pops and Uncle Tim. Best to leave it for now.

"You know, Charlie's car is here, obviously he brought Suzy back from town, or perhaps he stayed overnight," Katherine noticed.

"You mean Charlie stayed with Suzy?" Aunt Martha asked, a little surprised.

"Oh now Martha, almost everyone got snowbound somewhere or other last night, all under perfectly understandable circumstances," her sister reminded her, "they must have arrived after us," she continued, "we didn't see his car when we came home. You should call them over to join us Kathy, we certainly have plenty of food here to go around."

"I don't know, maybe they want to be left alone," Katherine suggested. Although Charlie and Suzy had become like two of the family after all these years, now that she and Charlie had hit a strain in their friendship, not to mention she was officially seeing Gerry, and Charlie was now with Suzy, it felt … well … complicated.

"Kathy, we can't leave them all alone when we have a veritable New Year´s feast going on over here," her mother stated.

That was true, as adopted members of the family, they could not be excluded simply because she continued to feel uncomfortable when Charlie was around, and now that Gerry's here … nuts. Buzzing the intercom, Katherine had a feeling this was going to be a long day. Five minutes later they came over to the main house, Katherine decided to go out to greet them. It was time she handled it like an adult, they had always been friends and it would be stupid to let any misunderstanding come between them now. Suzy seemed in a very good mood, bounding into the hall and wishing her a happy New Year. Charlie appeared a little reflective as he also extended his holiday greetings. Hanging up their coats, Suzy decided to head to the kitchen to see if she could do anything to help, while Charlie lingered for a moment.

"Well, all the boys are having a rip-roaring pool game in the den if you want to join them."

"Sounds like a blast all right," he agreed as a burst of boisterous laughter echoed down the hall. "Kathy, can we talk for a moment?"

"Of course. You know, I have something to say too."

"You first then."

"No, you started, you should go first," she insisted. Charlie took a deep breath.

"All right. How do I start without making this more awkward?" he said half to himself. "Ever since last Christmas, it seems we've grown … distant."

"Oh Charlie, it's my fault … ."

"No wait, let me finish. It's really my fault, assuming you felt the same way about, well, you know. I can come to terms with the whole thing that it wasn't 'meant to be', but if I had known that it would have been the end of us altogether, no matter what I felt, I wouldn't have said anything."

"Charlie, I never wanted our friendship to drift apart, it's just that … I can't promise anything, not on that level, and I was afraid if I was … I don't know, around like before, I might give you false hope or something… ."

"I never wanted to put you under that kind of pressure. What a fine kettle of fish we ended up in."

"So, what do we do now?"

"I can't believe I'm going to use that old hackneyed line," he said shaking his head, "but, can we be friends?"

"We always were Charlie."

"Then let's try and keep it that way," he smiled.

"Okay. I'm sorry for acting like a scattered rabbit."

"No apologies, we just got off on the wrong track and skidded around for a bit. I guess we have to move on sometime and not let the past derail us altogether."

"I agree, but ... Charlie, what do we do about that pricey 'gift' you gave me last Christmas?"

"You're still worrying about that? I really do want you to keep it. I understand you can't wear it as it is, but perhaps you could use the gemstones and have something done with them, maybe have a new bracelet made when you get around to it, one that you can actually put on your wrist. I know for certain you couldn't possibly wear your other one, not with the weight of all those gold charms," he joked.

"Are you sure?"

"Positive."

"Even about moving on?"

"If you haven't noticed, Suzy and I have been seeing each other quite a bit lately," he remarked with a note of humour.

"You do seem happy together, I hope it works out. Gee, that sounds awful after ... well, I didn't quite mean it like that," Katherine stammered.

"It's all right, I know what you mean. We've got to stop tiptoeing around each other," he smiled.

"You're right, I just don't want my presence to bring up any bad memories, or thoughts of 'what might have been'."

"Well, I don't want you constantly thinking 'if only he hadn't proposed' every time you see me for that matter. Of course, we can't forget what's happened, but we can't keep beating ourselves over the head either."

"I know, you're right. I really have missed our friendship, Charlie. However, I don't know if Suzy said anything, but it's only right to let you know that ... Gerry and I have been seeing more of each other too. There, I said it."

"Hmm, is it serious? I'm sorry, it's none of my business really," he replied, pursing his lips a little.

"Uh oh, I knew you might get like this," she tried to joke. "How can we 'move on' and be friends if everything we do now becomes taboo? We were always honest with each other."

"That's true," he agreed. "Well, since I put my foot in it and asked, how is everything going?"

"It's early days, we've only dated a few times."

At least that was the truth, but she wasn't about to give too many details just yet. Although they were doing their best to patch things up, trying to return to the way things used to be, she was not unperceptive either; brave face and all, it would still take Charlie some time to accept the idea she could possibly date someone else. Worse yet, how to tell him that this 'someone else' was also joining them for dinner, better just to blurt it out and get it over with.

"I know you weren't expecting this, but he's here right now."

"Oh? Well, since you *are* seeing each other, invitations are a normal occurrence after all," he noted.

"Since you seem to be taking this news relatively well, is it safe to let you in now?"

"Are you afraid I might cause a scene if I saw Gerry and you together?"

"Concerning the two of us, I honestly don't know anymore. Like you said, we've been tiptoeing around each other, worrying about making things between us more strained than before, I don't know what to expect."

"It's a pity humans don't come with 'reboot' buttons," he smiled.

"You can say that again."

"Listen, we promised to try and move on, and we will, just ... let's start the 'trying' now, shall we?"

"All right."

"And in case he ever decides not to treat you right, I'll punch him in the nose."

"Charlie!"

"What I mean is I'll always be there for you come rain, hail, sleet or shine. Isn't that what friends are supposed to be around for?"

"Of course, that goes the same for me too. Whenever you need someone for any reason, no matter what, you can always count on me. Agreed?"

"Agreed."

"Pinkie promise?" she smiled.

"All right, pinkie promise," he returned, locking his little finger around hers, "we haven't done that since ... I don't know when."

"Since summer camp, I had just figured out how to swim, but only just, and was still too afraid to jump into the lake. However, you promised that you'd never let me drown if I did."

"Hey, how could I forget? You had so many of those inflatable arm bands on, not to mention the inner tube, you looked like the Michelin Man."

"Oh yeah! And who was it that fell into that patch of poison oak? Was it you or Steves?"

"That would have been me," Charlie admitted, "I was as mad as anything, getting stuck in the medicine hut, but it's kind of funny now."

"Remember, when Steves got a group of us 'Indian braves' to join him in his midnight raids?"

"Do I ever! Raiding the kitchen cabin for midnight snacks, booby trapping the supervisor's quarters, those were some wild times. Who let the raccoon into the main office?"

"I don't remember who, but I'll never forget the look on the supervisor's face the next day: the woman really was a battle axe."

"I know, she actually frightened me."

They both started to laugh, it felt good to finally come to some amicable understanding and share a few good memories after the tension that had built up between them for well over a year. At that moment, Gerry entered the hall looking up and down, and seeing them, came over to join them.

"Princess, I need your assistance," he said quietly. "Hello Charlie, Happy New Year."

"Hello, many happy returns to you." They politely shook hands.

"I hope I'm not interrupting you two?"

"No, we're just holding up the hallway," Charlie replied. "So, I hear there's a pool game in the works."

"There is, we just called time out, and I was wondering where the 'gentleman's room' might be," Gerry noted euphemistically, "perhaps someone would care to direct me?"

"Oh, I'm sorry. I meant to show you around. It's down there, third door," Katherine directed, pointing the way.

"Thank you."

"Well, I'll go join the gang until you ladies are ready," Charlie replied.

"We have a little while to go yet, I'll call you guys."

"Okay."

Katherine returned to the kitchen, still feeling a little unsure about the situation between her and Charlie, and wondered how understanding Gerry would be, but at least she didn't feel as bad as before. She didn't know if they would ever progress to the point of going out together on a friendly 'double date', but she felt there was a marked improvement. How nice it will be not having to avoid Charlie, she thought.

"There you are, Katherine. Where were you? Never mind," her mother replied, "it's time to set the table."

"I'll help," Suzy offered, "I feel in the way, everything is done in here."

"You're a dear," Mom noted. "Nothing too fancy now girls, just the regular setting, this is a nice informal day, but do put a linen cloth out, the one in the middle drawer. I was hoping to plan something special for Gerry's first dinner here, but a roast rib fare is how it's turned out."

"Never mind, perhaps casual is better," Aunt Martha observed, "no point getting all stressed out."

"Yeah, at least he can see how we are in our relaxed mode, it's hard to get to know someone or make them feel comfortable when we get too stiff and starchy," Katherine added. She meant it; it was difficult enough trying to make the best of a sticky situation between Charlie and Gerry without the whole family acting like they were in a five star restaurant in their own home.

"That's true. Now run along, or the table won't be ready with all this chatter."

Retreating to the dining room, the girls had a chance to discuss the events of the previous night.

"So, how was Times Square?" Katherine asked, unfolding the cloth and giving it one big sweep across the large table.

"It was a bit of an anti-climax to tell the truth," Suzy replied, flattening out the cloth at her end. "First, we went out to this really fancy place at Rockefeller Plaza, that part was nice of course, then we made our way over to the Square, but it really was cold! I felt kind of silly after a while waiting for some disco ball to descend and disappear, and then sing *Auld Lang Syne*, however, at least I can say I experienced it. Did you get to see it?"

"Not this year," Katherine noted.

"Oh, right," Suzy smiled, "anyway, they did the red, white and blue lights again for the troops. You know, Charlie was really good to go along with it all just to please me. I felt guilty when we had to try and get home with all the snow, it really came down after that, not to mention the traffic and everyone else trying to leave the city."

"You guys were certainly brave," Katherine replied.

"Oh, the city officials have it all worked out, it doesn't look like it on TV, but the square is divided into sections so it doesn't get overcrowded."

"At least you made it home safely."

"We did, but Charlie couldn't make it back to his place in all the mess. So, as you can see, he stayed over. How did your evening go? You must have come home later, we didn't see the van."

"Well, I didn't," Katherine replied sheepishly, "Gerry drove me home this morning."

"Oh, I've got to hear this. Did anything happen?"

"Now Suzy, I just got snowbound like everyone else, Gerry let me use his guest room," she clarified.

"I know you, Kathy. I'm just giving you a bad time. So, how did it go?"

"We had a lovely dinner, he hired caterers, and then we danced around his sitting room practically most of the night."

"Danced? I thought you hated dancing, but how romantic! I'm dying to know, what is his pad like?"

"Well, like we suspected, he's got this fantastic art collection tucked away, he even collects forgeries and prison art."

"You're kidding. Imagine, murderers could have painted some of that stuff," Suzy remarked thoughtfully, "but it's kinda thrilling ... in a strange, creepy sort of way."

"He said they're great conversation pieces."

"He could be right. That reminds me, did you lay your penalty on him yet?"

"I did, he figured he's met his match in 'Truth or Dare'," Katherine replied, placing the knives and forks, "he found it very amusing. Then, I got curious and asked if he also had prepared a penalty for me, and so he had."

"This sounds interesting. What was he planning to foist on you?"

"Meeting his parents."

"What? That's an odd dare." Suzy was about to laugh then realized what he had done. "He wanted to make it something you couldn't refuse. He *really* wants you to meet his parents, that's a big step you know."

"Well, I don't think it's all *that* serious, he's met my family on several occasions. Thing is, I wouldn't have turned him down anyway, I'm doing his dare in the end, so much for winning the bet on D.S.'s work."

"A tie! You've certainly met your match in 'Truth or Dare', but wow, meeting his parents? That's a good sign, he truly likes you."

"I like him too ... I haven't sorted all this out yet, and I told him so. He then came up with the idea of giving me a clue to help me figure things out, he won't tell me what or when, ´just be on the lookout´."

"He's giving you a riddle of some kind. That's exciting, isn't it? You can't call him a bore, can you? Now I'm curious to know what he's got in mind ... oh, the salt and pepper shakers are running low."

"I'll go fill them in a minute," Katherine said, setting them aside. Their conversation was abruptly interrupted by Aunt Martha who came to inspect the work.

"Now girls, have you set everything out correctly? Humph, I thought so, only half done, you two should be finished by now. No doubt last night's unexpected change in accommodation is more important than today's dinner. You'll have plenty of time to dilly dally with chitter chatter later. Katherine, go get the centrepiece off the sideboard and set it out nicely, Susanna you can place the candles, and girls, be sure you fold the napkins neatly, no untidy edges please."

Nothing for it, they hopped into action. Katherine set out the floral display and after helping with the napkins, grabbed the shakers. On her way to the kitchen she could hear Gramps calling to ask if dinner was ready yet, adding that he was positively starving.

"I don't know, but it probably is, judging how Aunt Martha has just taken over the dining room," she said, poking her head in the den, "but I'll go check. It certainly smells good."

"That it does," Gramps agreed, "run along now and give us a report like a good girl."

Katherine shook her head as she entered the kitchen, Gramps was really enjoying the holidays; his diet had been relaxed, giving him a few weeks of indulgence that was much appreciated. He was not going to like it when these concessions came to an end.

"The boys are getting hungry in there Mom, is it time to call them yet?"

"Almost dear, well, I suppose you could call them now, it'll take them a few minutes to stop whatever they're doing. However, go get your father first to help carve up the roast in here while we put everything else out on the sideboard, we're doing it buffet style," Helen explained, placing the broccoli and roast potatoes in serving dishes.

"All right."

Pops obeyed the summons, and sharpening the carving knife, relayed to Helen the latest weather report. According to the news, the snow was not going away just yet, already it was coming down heavy and covering the driveway. Since the gardeners were on holiday leave, they would all have to wait until morning or sometime the next day to get the roads cleared. In the end, it looked like their guests might have to stay overnight, and he apologized for putting her to the extra work of having to prepare the guestrooms. However, this was not the first holiday season it happened, Helen had all the beds ready for any unexpected guests, so there was no need to panic. It was a good thing the men knew better than to schedule any important meeting during the first two days of the New Year, but Katherine hadn't thought about a snowbound holiday. What about the gallery?

"You might have to take an extra day off," her father advised, "just call everyone and let them know not to come in tomorrow, give them all an extended holiday."

"But not until after dinner, dear," her mother added.

Well, that was settled. Dropping the shakers off in the dining room, she called everyone to the table and informed the non-residents of Oak Meadows that they would be staying overnight.

"Great!" Gramps beamed. "We can have that game of five card stud after all."

Gramps liked company, and it had been awhile since anyone had used the poker table as most of his friends got together at the Club to play cards. Of course, Mom and Aunt Martha didn't approve of serious gambling, so any betting in the house was done using Gramp's collection of old wheat-backed pennies that had to be dutifully returned to the drawstring bank bag for another occasion.

"Okay, but I'll have to call the office later and cancel any morning appointments," Charlie noted.

"That goes for me too," Gerry added, rocketing the eight ball into the centre pocket.

"Nice one, the Spring Bucks have creamed the Old Fogies," Steves joked.

"Oh yeah? Just you wait until our poker match ... it's open hunting season on you, buck stew," Gramps returned.

Everyone began to file out of the den and met Pops as he brought out the sliced rib roast to the dining room, Mom and Aunt Martha followed with the potatoes and vegetables in hand while Jasper trotted along behind.

"A gastronomic procession!" Gramps was in his element at the sight of the large platter of meat.

"May we help with anything?" Gerry politely asked.

"Oh please do, you'll find the shrimp salad on the counter, it's too heavy for me to carry," Helen replied, "we have the rest under control. Kathy, would you go get the rolls please? The butter is already on the table. Oh, and would someone light the candles?"

"I'll do that, try and make myself useful," Charlie offered.

While they were in the kitchen, Katherine asked Gerry how he was getting along with everyone.

"I'm really enjoying myself," he said as he scooped up the salad, "I haven't played a challenging game of pool like that in ages. Your dad has been very quiet, I hope he's not upset with your staying overnight in town, but your grandfather is quite a character, and your brother? I thought *I* was a hellion in school!"

"Oh Steves, he's the mad one in the family all right. Don't worry about Pops, he's always the quiet one, it's just his nature, and Gramps keeps us all on our merry toes."

Their mission accomplished, everyone gathered around and found their seats, with the exception of Jasper who was not allowed in the dining room.

"Geeze, that's pathetic," Steves said as he eyed the excluded pooch quietly laying down at the threshold, sorrowfully gazing up at the table with his big brown eyes.

"Oops, sorry," Gramps replied, "I forgot to lock him in the den."

Katherine wondered if he had really forgotten, or if was he giving Jasper a few extra days of indulgence too.

"Well, he's seen the food, and closing the door doesn't work anymore, he's learned how to push it in. Honestly, I can't look at that puppy face while I'm eating." With that, Steves took his plate and selected a large slice of medium rare meat right from the middle. "Come on, Jasp, I'll stick this in your doggie bowel." Jasper jumped up and eagerly wagged his tail.

"Steven, the humans must come first! And grace for that matter," Aunt Martha chided.

"Okay, we'll say grace, then I'll stick this in his bowel." Jasper couldn't understand the delay and began whining impatiently.

"Gregory, will you say the blessing?" Helen directed.

"Of course. Bless us O Lord, and all thy gifts, for which we are *truly grateful*," Gramps declared with emphasis. "Amen! Everyone tuck in. Helen, a truly fine feast I must say. You too Martha." Katherine and Steves tried to keep a straight face after Gramp's deliberate, succinct invocation.

"Oh it's nothing fancy, just your basic roast. Quick now, before it all goes cold," Aunt Martha ordered.

"You don't need to tell me twice, but ladies first," he replied.

"Basic? This looks fantastic Mrs. Walsingham," Gerry commented as the men went up to fill their plates once the ladies had their turn.

"It sure does," Charlie agreed.

At first, Katherine thought that dinner might be a little uncomfortable considering that Gerry and Charlie ended up seated across the table from each other, but if there was any tension between them, they quietly kept it to themselves as everyone engaged in animated conversation.

That usually happened when politics were eventually brought up. To think that they had just finished one war in the middle east, and now this internal conflict in Yugoslavia was raging while no real effort was made to stop it.

"Oh, must everyone bring that up now, on New Year's? Harold, think of something else for us to discuss. You know how these topics get so heated, and then what good does it do in the end?" Helen complained.

"But staying silent is worse," Harold noted.

"I don't get it," Suzy said, "we end the Gulf War in weeks, and the Balkan hostilities just keep on raging, and every other conflict you can just think about. Why can't the UN just stop it all instead of standing around with their peace-keeping vehicles pretending they are doing something?"

"Oh, because nearly all the combat zones don't have oil resources, while Kuwait does," Katherine replied matter-of-factly, "Kuwait was worth our oil-greedy government's time and effort."

"Grim, but true," Gerry agreed. "Until we can develop other sources of power for transportation, the life-blood of the world economy will be dependent on affordable petroleum. You cut off major crude suppliers, or someone tries to control the supply, and costs go up for shipping, which gets passed on to the consumers. It's no secret, we have to do it in our business if we want to stay afloat during the rough times, we can absorb the costs for only so long."

"I bet the fuel crunch of '74 was tough," Charlie replied.

"I don't recall a lot of the details from back then, but it was touch and go," Gerry affirmed, "my father started a fuel stockpile for our fleet after that, buy up when the prices go down, the usual evasive manoeuvres."

"Hmm, what do you think of the candidates running?" Gramps enquired, "I don't know about them frankly, and I dread this year, all the politicking and the fundraising they will try to squeeze out of us."

"Oh, that's right," Katherine groaned, "we won't be able to watch TV, nothing but political ads and debates, especially when it gets close to November, I can't stand all the mud slinging. It's all hype about why Candidate X is not as stupid as Y, but with hardly any concrete information given about their platforms."

"Well, so far I'm not too confident with either candidate," Gerry admitted, "but I think Clinton might get in simply because everyone is fed up with the recession and the Republicans have done nothing to help get us out of it. Frankly, all the broken promises our politicians dish out to us would make one want to abstain from voting sometimes."

"Why not?" Katherine piped up, "I do."

"What? Don't you cast your vote like every good American?" Gerry asked.

"Are good Americans only those who cast a vote?"

Charlie nearly choked trying to stifle a laugh.

"Hrumph! For someone so outspoken, why don't you vote Katie?" Gramps wondered a little amused.

"Yes, I'm curious now," Pops added, "you know, they say if you don't vote, you get the government you deserve."

"And if you do, you never get the results you expected," she replied.

"Uh oh, Mighty Mouth is let loose again," Steves laughed.

"Oh Harold, you know how I dislike discussions on wars and politics, and it's hardly the appropriate conversation for New Year's Day table talk. Please let's change the subject," Helen interjected.

"What about religion, Mom?" Steves quipped.

"Now do be quiet Steven! That's not a suitable topic," Aunt Martha piped up smartly.

"Oops, we're all in the doghouse now. Sorry Helen, we were out of place," Gramps conceded apologetically.

"Do tell us about New Year's Eve and all the excitement in town last night," Helen asked, turning to Suzy.

Katherine had heard Suzy's news already and momentarily let her thoughts wander. Why were those two topics off limits at table, especially when guests were present who could offer some unique viewpoints? Of course, she realized people could often become argumentative, forgetting they are in an open discussion and end up turning the whole conversation into a competitive debate that required a winner and a loser by the time dessert was served, but on the other hand, why be forced into silence on two of the most important topics that would forever influence a person's life? Democracy was supposed to champion freedom of speech, and yet the simple rules of table decorum could clamp down on the rights their forefathers had fought and died for. Come to think of it, another right was under pressure, the right to remain silent. If it was a *right*, it could also be a *choice*, not an obligatory command. It was much like voting, that was a right too, which meant she also had the right to abstain if she did not approve of any candidate that was running. She could not give her approbation to someone via her vote if she did not agree with everything they represented, nor should she be forced to do so against her free will by a false concept of what it meant to be unpatriotic in not voting, trying to make her feel guilty for supposedly failing in her civic duty by abstaining. Everyone she spoke to about this at one point or another tried to persuade her it was best to choose the lesser of the two evils, but two negatives by any description do not make a positive she concluded. *'Ask not what your country can do for you ...'* well, there were many ways she could help her country without voting. She would wait until someone came along whom she could believe in. This would be a great topic for another Socratic painting, she thought. Hmm, I wonder what would happen if *no one* voted? What if the whole country simply ... boycotted the ballot boxes? The American people boycotted goods from another country that had a government that was against the principles of the 'Free World'. What if America exercised their right *not* to vote to show their discontent? Would the government remain at a standstill until new candidates were chosen and the election be held all over again? Would the representatives already in power just assume the people wanted them to continue and merrily keep running things following the boycotted vote? That would put the kibosh to the whole idea, but technically, the people wouldn't have voted the nincompoops back in, so they couldn't just hang on to their office. Gosh, maybe a dictator could run in and size control ... she didn't want that either. No, it may not get *that* bad, maybe there would just be a complete standstill until the officials came up with a solution, perhaps *actually* listen to the people for once. No matter what, there was one thing she could count on if this hypothetical event ever happened: the evening news would certainly be interesting to watch.

Everyone had finished their dinner by the time she had satisfied the impulse to ruminate on her notions. Noticing the empty plates, Katherine announced it was time the whippersnappers pitched in to clear the table and prepare the coffee and dessert, a suggestion the elders graciously welcomed.

"Come on everyone, you too Gerry, and Steves, don't think you can skip away this time."

"I hear and obey."

"You know Kathy, you've gone rather quiet all of a sudden. Something on your mind?" Charlie wondered as they brought out the dishes.

"You could say that, I just got busy thinking about our conversation before we changed the subject, that's all."

"Well, now that it's safe to come back to that, at least I hope so," Gerry added, laying his stack of plates by the sink, "I'd love to hear your thoughts on 'to vote or not to vote'."

"Are you sure you're ready for this? She can get a bit 'irregular' you know," Steves wryly returned, lining his handful of glasses on the counter.

"You may regret it," Charlie added, "her ideas can be quite revolutionary. We're all used to it, well, almost."

"Stop teasing you two," Suzy jumped in, "not all of Kathy's ideas are wacky."

"Gee thanks. Was that supposed to be a compliment?"

"You know what I mean, I agree with many of your observations … perhaps not with all your solutions," she admitted.

"I know, they're impractical at times, mostly idealistic or experimental," Katherine conceded.

"Still, let's hear your cogitations," Gerry prompted.

"Oh, all right." Katherine explained her reason for abstaining from the elections, they seemed to understand her point of view, until she suggested the nation could try an all-out boycott. Steves burst out laughing.

"What? Might as well do away with democracy altogether!"

Charlie and Gerry tried not to laugh, they didn't want to hurt her feelings, but barely managed to conceal their humour at the improbability of her proposal, covering their mouths with their hands.

"I did warn you," Charlie said, clearing his throat.

"Oh look," she interjected, stopping in the midst of scraping off a plate, "I'm not saying we actually go out and start a 'Non-Vote Movement' or anything like that, but since we have the right to vote, we also have the right to abstain. I was just wondering what might happen if every citizen chose to exercise that right all at the same time. That would be the greatest non-violent protest ever, it would certainly catch the attention of our lawmakers, even Ghandi would have been impressed."

"I know a better solution: boycott the Internal Revenue Service," Steves interjected, "money talks, so they say."

"Ew, Uncle Sam wouldn't like that one bit," Gerry said, shaking his head.

"No, but they can't throw the whole nation into jail, or fine everyone if we all refuse to pay anyway," Steves argued. "Then, we the people can declare the first ever fair and equal tax, something like ten percent across the board that everyone, no matter who they are, has to pay."

"Oh, I think I'd like that," Katherine replied.

"Everyone's tax bracket would be automatically adjusted," Gerry mused, "and ten percent is not a lot, but you would have to do away with deductions altogether to keep the country going."

"You know, a flat rate does seem more fair," Suzy nodded.

"It's an interesting idea Steves, but it wouldn't work because first of all, everyone would be too scared to try it," Charlie noted, "the very letters

IRS frighten most people have to death, no one would boycott their taxes to force the politicians to adopt your flat rate, and second, it would take too long to pass a bill for a flat rate, we'd have years of procrastination, so it's a non viable solution."

"Well, if everyone *did* participate in a tax boycott, with no money, you'd definitely have all the politicians on their knees," Steves continued.

"And the country too," Suzy noted.

"Yeah Steves, it's one thing to boycott a vote, and while I love tax breaks, what if the whole country collapsed economically?" Katherine observed. "If people think they can just stop paying that one time, they'll always try it even after they reach an agreement with the government. The country wouldn't have a guaranteed source of revenue, and everything would just fall apart."

"Hey, I know that. I'm not championing a Fire Sale. This was all supposed to be hypothetical," Steves reminded them.

"It *is* interesting to think about, I mean, to imagine what would happen if you could get the whole nation to do something like that *en masse*, making a sweeping change without a shot being fired," Gerry mused.

"Just, get rid of the whole government?" Steves asked rhetorically, placing the plates into the dishwasher.

"Right-o, just clear out the house," Gerry replied. "The Portuguese did it, they just ousted their former communist government armed with carnations."

"That's a bit simplistic," Steves replied, "but the people had the army on their side you know."

"Why, even if we do 'clean out' the house, we might not have a successful outcome like that. Suppose we did it peacefully using Kathy's 'boycott' with no army involved, we could still end up with total anarchy couldn't we?" Charlie pointed out.

"Exactly! Not 'anarchy' in the sense of having no government at all for the sake of chaos, but a 'clearing of the decks', " Katherine pondered, "a clean slate to start anew and get rid of anything that isn't working."

"Still, we might end up with a civil war as the new government jostled for power," Gerry noted.

"Just listen to us," Steves said, "real kitchen sink philosophers."

"Okay, what if we think out Kathy's idea. Just for fun, say no one votes and the Capitol in Washington comes to a complete standstill. How do we choose new representatives, or a president for that matter?" Suzy piped up, she was curious to know what they would come up with.

"I don't know, have a lottery?" Katherine laughed. "I have these great ideas, but then I don't know what would happen, or how to carry them through."

"A belling the cat situation," Gerry agreed.

"Hmm, how would such a lottery be set up? Would every citizen get to buy a ticket?" Suzy wondered.

"Maybe. No, we'd still have problems, lotteries can always be fixed," Katherine noted.

"And what would the price of each ticket be?" Gerry added. "You can't charge a couple of bucks for something as important as the White House, or a seat in Congress or the Senate for that matter."

"Hmm, it would be very expensive, and that would exclude your average citizen, so it would only be a government for and by the well-to-do who could afford to buy a ticket in the first place." Charlie noted.

"Well, there's nothing new there, isn't the government geared to helping the rich anyway?" Katherine shrugged.

"Oh man, listen to us, you can't just raffle off the government," Steves interjected.

"Why not? Government leaders get bought and sold every day," Katherine observed.

"Ouch!" Gerry laughed.

"Told you," Steves replied.

"We'd have to come up with some way to make it equal, put everyone's social security number into the lottery system perhaps," Katherine suggested.

"Oh great, you could get anyone in the House, from druggies to mob leaders, that wouldn't work," Steves snickered.

"Well, you could screen numbers that have a criminal record," Katherine rebuffed, "just take them out of the lottery system."

"You would still have a number of problems," Charlie noted, "you could end up selecting numbers of homeless people with no way to contact them, or people who have died and were never registered. Then you'd have to give those who can be reached the option to take the seat offered to them, they could refuse, and you have to keep picking numbers. It would take months before this was all sorted out."

"Yeah, real messy," Steves agreed, "not to mention all the people who haven't a clue how to manage their own lives let alone a whole country. Do you want them running everything?"

"I think they are already," Katherine wryly commented.

"Hey everyone, what other suggestions could we come up with to put in a whole new government after our Boycott Revolution?" Suzy enquired.

"Okay, we currently have a lottery suggestion, why not a marathon?" Steves quipped, "first one up the capitol steps and into the House or Senate gets a seat."

"And the last one in is a rotten egg?" Charlie noted humorously.

"It would certainly give the term presidential race a whole new meaning," Katherine noted, turning on the coffee machine.

"Crikey! Could you imagine watching something like that on the news? Everyone would be running all over Washington like lunatics, beating each other over the head trying to get up the stairs first," Steves replied. "Forget all diplomatic immunity on that day."

"It would definitely be a lot more entertaining than all those boring debates filled with hot air," Katherine replied.

"And since voting would literally be done away with if you had a marathon every four years, no more annoying campaigners knocking on your doors," Gerry laughed.

"Plus, it would be one way of getting people into shape, think of all the gyms that would open up getting the hopefuls ready for the big chase," Charlie added.

"Hey, Walsingham Industries could end up having a boost in vitamin sales," Steves joked, "not to mention our geriatric line."

"Gosh, a marathon like that wouldn't be funny in real life," Suzy said, shaking her head, "good grief, that would be like the Oklahoma land rush in the 1800s, settlers literally killed each other and dropped dead as they raced their way to the best plots."

"Oh I've got it! Everyone who wanted a seat would have to write an essay on why they think they are entitled to have it," Katherine laughed.

" 'Why I Should Rule America', five thousand words only please," Gerry added.

"No plagiarism either, original works must be turned in, no borrowing from the speeches of past politicians," Charlie continued.

"And who would get to judge or grade these essays? Tell me that one," Steves piped. "If there's no voting, how do you select the judges to evaluate the essays?"

"We're belling the cat again," Gerry nodded.

"Quick, we're dallying, they'll wonder what's happened to us," Katherine interjected, "and we can't have Gramps checking in on us while we get dessert ready."

"Right, is they key in the same place?" Charlie asked, "I'll go get the cake for you."

"Yeah, in the ivy plant," Suzy affirmed.

"Oh, I might as well go too, we need the ice cream," Katherine added.

"No, I'll go," Steves offered, "you serve the coffee, you're pretty good at that."

"Key?" Gerry wondered aloud.

"That's right, you don't know," Katherine realized, "everything fattening is locked in the pantry, it's for Gramp's own good, doctor's orders. He's been hunting around for the thing for months, but still hasn't figured out where it is."

"My lips are sealed," Gerry replied, running his finger across his mouth zipper fashion.

"Wow, this looks too good to eat," Charlie said as he placed the cake on the island counter. "It's huge, even with nine people, the slices are going to be enormous."

"Thank Aunt Martha, she baked it," Katherine replied. "Chocolate Strawberry 'Paradise Cake', it's one of her specialties. Okay, who wants to cut it? How about you Suzy?"

"Oh, how *do* we cut a round cake? Eight pieces is easy, one line down the middle and divide each half by four, but I can't figure out how to do it fast and equal at the same time for nine," she noted.

"Think Mercedes, piece of cake," Steves hinted. Suzy puzzled about it for a few seconds, then the light dawned.

"Oh for Heaven's sake, how simple," she said, placing the knife in the middle of the cake and drawing a three-pointed star before dividing each third into three smaller slices. "Well, it's a good thing all the problems of our country aren't up to me to solve if I couldn't figure *that* out."

"Our ideas weren't any better, it's a good thing none of us are running for office," Katherine joked.

"And they say the future of the country is up to us younger generation," Steves observed wryly, "the older generation better run and hide if that was the best we could come up with."

"We *were* only having a bit of fun. Hey look at the snow come down," Gerry noted, looking out the kitchen window. "That reminds me, may I use your phone now?"

"Sure go ahead, there's one right here by the cupboard, or you can use the one in the hallway if you like," Katherine offered as she dug out scoops of ice cream and served them with the cake.

"Good idea, I have to make a few calls too when you're done, might as well get that over with so we can enjoy dessert and that game of five card stud Mr. G.W. promised," Charlie said. At that point, Aunt Martha showed up to inspect the kitchen and find out what the delay was all about.

"Oh, you did all the dishes, now that was unexpected, we only have the dessert dishes to worry about," she noted with satisfaction. "Come now, quick, before the ice cream melts." Charlie would have to make his calls later. Katherine and Suzy quick-stepped the dessert to the table in relays while Charlie carried out the coffee pot, Aunt Martha the creamer jug.

"Aunt Martha, you outdid yourself with the cake," he complimented, "you're positively spoiling us."

"Thank you Charlie, it's nothing, I've been baking these cakes for years."

"What was going on out there?" Gramps enquired.

"You don't know the half of it," Katherine replied.

"Just solving the problems of the nation, Monty Python style," Charlie explained.

"Well, did you get anywhere?" Gramps chuckled.

"For the nation's welfare, thankfully, no," Charlie informed him.

After the family had finished their dessert, the youngsters helped once more with the last of the dishes, allowing Mom and Aunt Martha to take a quiet rest in the parlour. Katherine and Suzy decided to man the dishwasher, leaving the men to their poker game. Charlie thought it best to make his calls from the kitchen before heading into the den, and inadvertently heard part of their conversation. The girls were discussing New Year's Eve and their snowbound predicament.

"You know, it was good of Gerry to drive you back this morning, he didn't have to," Suzy noted.

Charlie looked a little surprised, this was news to him. He tried to concentrate on his call, but Katherine could tell from his expression he did not approve of her staying overnight in a man's apartment, even though nothing had happened. Nuts, just when everything seemed to be settling down! Despite Suzy's steady grounding in common sense, she could be a little slow on the uptake at times. Well Charlie, we did agree it was time to move on, don't look at me that way, you stayed over with Suzy last night, remember? The pot can't call the kettle black. Charlie must have reached the same conclusion, he never brought up the subject. Hanging up the receiver, he said smiling, "I'm off to the poker game. Wish me luck."

"Good luck," Suzy replied.

"Hope you win the pot," Katherine added as she watched him leave.

"What pot? Aren't they just playing with Mr. G.W.'s old penny collection?" Suzy asked.

"Yeah, but unknown to Mom and Aunt Martha, Gramps has devised a system that the losers have to cough up twenty bucks to whoever wins the full pot of pennies. He says it's no fun when the pennies have to be retuned; to him, it's not real poker unless a little hard cash is at stake."

"Oh no, they're going to be at it for hours trying to win their twenty bucks back from each other."

"I know. Good thing everyone is staying here tonight, isn't it? Gosh, I better let Esther know not to come in tomorrow and I'd better find out what Andre's doing."

ଓଃ❀ଃୠ

Katherine was glad to be heading back to work on Friday, as much as she enjoyed the extra day off, it was nerve-wracking sitting at home, knowing she had canvases waiting for her all the way in Dumbo. So much for rest and relaxation. Andre had arrived early and was busy getting ready for the lunch hour, but hearing the music, came out to talk to her at the front desk: he had business to discuss. After wishing her a Happy New Year, he explained several of his regulars were asking when he would start opening for dinner, they were disappointed he didn't stay open late for New Year's Eve, and since everything was going well, he could now think about operating as a full time restaurant. Katherine was delighted his business was flourishing, but of course, that would also mean new arrangements for the gallery. The open plan on the ground floor was artistic, but now commercially impractical; her major problem, how to prevent the night time restaurant patrons making their way up the staircase when the gallery was closed with only one security guard on duty. Andre had an excellent suggestion; since the elevator could be locked at closing time, why not get a fancy set of gates for the ground floor stairs? Not a bad idea actually, surely she could find something that would match the brass railing and could be folded neatly out of the way during the day. If not, she could certainly have them custom made to match the décor rather than have dreary black iron security gates that stuck out like sore thumbs. Now, what to do about the art displayed on the ground floor…well, she could roll the polies to the side and cordon them off with additional theatre ropes. If the evening diners are interested in the work on display, they can stop by during gallery business hours. Hmm, the restaurant will still bring in potential customers, this is great. Of course, she would have to hire additional security guards for the

629

place, have one man stationed at the desk for the night shift, another to walk the floors. Andre apologized for putting her to additional expense, but she told him not to worry, she knew he wanted to open for the evenings at one time or another, and since she had planned to hire additional help for the gallery anyway, might as well start the plans for expansion now. Before Andre returned to the kitchen, he checked to see if she still wanted the usual for lunch.

"Yes, my old favourite please."

"And will you try to eat it while it's hot, just this once?"

"I'll try," she promised.

Would she be able to keep it? It depended on how the day went, already things were starting to look very busy.   As soon as Suzy arrived, Katherine told her the news. She noted they would need at least two additional security guards in order to rearrange the ground floor, perhaps place additional security monitors under the counter of the main desk if required. Katherine was glad the art sales were doing so well and that the business was growing faster than she had anticipated, now all they needed was more artists. Katherine took out her notebook, so many things to plan and organize, when should they schedule another interview day, that was the question. They would have to set a date at least two months ahead to allow them to publicize the event. Two months, that seemed an age away when they needed more artists as soon as possible. Of course, a little help never goes amiss, especially if that help came from the head of the leading arts and cultural column of New York ... surely the Art Hacker was bound to know where to find real talent.

"What?   You mean you want to ask *Robert Horace* for advice? After what he said about you patronizing D.S.'s work?" Suzy exclaimed, aghast with the suggestion.

Katherine hadn't bothered to read his latest columns now that she understood his methods, he did help sell Derrick's works after all. She knew what she was doing. Katherine was about to put a call through to the paper but was distracted by a new art delivery, it completely skipped her mind that Derrick was bringing his new pieces by.

"I'm sorry guys, I should have opened the back entry for you," she said as she held the door open for Big George and Trigger T who carried in the roll. Although it was not as long as the last one, it appeared bulkier, the canvas was not as tightly wound as before and it looked liked something was sewn onto it. Curious, Katherine couldn't wait to see his new masterpiece, especially as he explained to her he had tried something different.

"I sure hope The Breeze Man likes 'em too," Derrick continued, "I can't believe he wants 'em without seeing 'em yet."

"You did more than one? I'm sure he'll approve, you've got yourself one big fan there," Katherine assured him. "Now that you're all here, perhaps you guys wouldn't mind helping to roll up the other ones for delivery. We can hang the new tapestry-murals in their place just in case Mr. Breeze stops by to see them."

Derrick apologized he only had enough new works to fill one wall for now, but Katherine said not to worry, they could fill the space with other paintings. Suzy called the guard and manned the desk while the big switch took place. Katherine was surprised with his new pieces, they were a three part series. Rather than work the mural sized roll of canvas on a horizontal plane to make one large picture, he cut the material into three smaller vertical pictures similar to medieval military standards carried by knights, complete with scalloped edges on the end, every scallop artfully held in place with the distinctive brass plumb weights. Each psychedelic-hued picture had a separate word painted vertically on them, but when placed together, made the sentence 'Give Peace a Chance' surrounded by various symbols associated with international concord; white doves, olive branches, and of course, the international sign for 'No Nukes'. That wasn't all, each letter was made from separate pieces of canvas that were sewn onto the main background and then stuffed with packing material like a pillow, making the multicoloured sentence calling for universal harmony stand out in three dimensions. Now she knew why the roll looked a little bulky. Derrick explained he got the idea watching Sheila making things for the baby, in this instance, it was a patchwork teddy bear stuffed with cotton filler.

"Never thought I'd be learnin' how to use one of them sew'n machines," Derrick said, shaking his head, "but ya got ta do what ya got ta do."

Katherine praised his ingenuity, she just knew Mr. Breeze would like his new style, however, a lot more time and work went into these three pieces, with all the sewing and packing, she figured it was definitely worth more than his first two. Derrick admitted he did spend considerable more time on it than one of his normal two-dimensional pictures.

"Is it enough to try for th' fifteen grand now?" he wondered.

"Positively, but I'll call Mr. Breeze first, make sure he's willing to go that high. Somehow, I don't think price is an issue with him," she said, thinking about the Fort Knox Deposit he left with her for security. Derrick was delighted, he said he would try more experiments with Sheila's sewing machine, however, she wasn't too happy with him at the moment since he had snapped almost all of her needles to create his latest *magnum opus*. The problem was the canvas he used was too thick for domestic equipment. Katherine remembered she still had a couple of the old industrial sewing machines abandoned by the T-shirt factory hidden away in the boiler house, there was a box of extra bits and pieces going with them, perhaps there were extra needles. If he wanted, he was welcome to take the lot, machines and all. Derrick was grateful for her offer, perhaps now Sheila might let him work in peace he laughed.

"Before I forget, ya said ya needed a paint job for a set of wheels?" Trigger enquired.

Katherine explained what she and Suzy had in mind.

"Would it be possible to paint the gallery logo and address on the white BMW parked out back?"

"Why sure, but for a nice ride like that, ya sure ya want just business stuff? I can give ya some flames down the side, make it stand out, I'll throw that in since ya've been good to our Derrick here."

While Katherine appreciated Trigger's offer, she had to refuse. Not to disappoint him, she explained people might pay too much attention to his art and ignore her address, which would be counterproductive.

"Yeah Trigger, ya got to think what the car's for, it ain't for street racing," George agreed.

"You know, you should talk to Suzy about this, it's her car now."

"All right," Trigger replied.

"Ya guys go on ahead, I've got to talk ta Miss Walsin'ham for a sec," Derrick said, sending them downstairs so he could have a private word. Was he afraid Mr. Breeze might back out? With a baby on the way, she could understand his concern. As it turned out, he had something serious to discuss concerning her father's offices in Jersey. Hmm, this was strange.

"Ya know I haven't given up on th'day job yet, just in case. Well, I've been assigned to th'team that takes care of that side of the Pike for th'last couple a months, and perhaps this is none of my business, but I thought I saw somethin' funny goin' on," he began.

"Oh? Go ahead, what did you see?"

"I think it was on the third floor, yeah, the one with the open cubicles and th' private offices around th' side. I was vacuuming out a cubicle, next ta an office, an' I saw someone searching through a desk and act'n real mad for some reason, especially when use'n the computer."

That didn't sound odd, perhaps one of the executives stayed late to try and meet a deadline. Derrick thought so too, but this wasn't the only time he had seen the same person acting like this, and what made him really suspicious, it was very obvious the man didn't want to be seen.

"Usually we don't see people dur'n the late night clean'n shifts, but if anyone is work'n overtime, they jus' ignore us, pretend we ain't there, or they watch us like we're hoods gonna take somethin', so they *want* us ta see 'em, but this guy, he always snaps the blinds down. This last time however, he looked really scared that I saw 'im, he look'd at me like he'd seen a ghost before snap'n them blinds, he then left in a hurry. It's like he's try'n ta hide somethin', an' I hardly see 'im in the same office, so I'm think'n someone's do'n a bit a snoop'n if ya ask me."

"This does sound serious, I'm glad you came to me. You say it's a man, could you describe him?"

"Yeah, kinda tall an' thin, black hair slicked back … I saw somethin' in his hand one time, coulda been his mail, it was a big envelope addressed ta a Mr. More, can't quite remember, 'Mor' somethin."

"If I showed you a picture, do you think you could pick him out?"

"Yeah, no problem, he's hard ta forget, I don't like th' look of 'im, reminds me of one of m'old dealers."

"Come with me to the office," Katherine replied, quick-stepping down the stairs with Derrick following. By now Esther had arrived for work, but Katherine was in such a rush, she could only say a fast 'hello' before diving into the office and feverishly rummaging through the drawers of her desk.   Pulling out a folder of Stephie's photos from the opening night that she still hadn't framed, she found a group picture with her parents surrounded by the board members of Walsingham Industries who attended her gala event.

"*Yes!* It's a good thing I invited him after all, or I wouldn't have a photo of him. Is this the guy?"

"Oh yeah, that's 'im," Derrick affirmed, pointing to the gaunt figure at the end of the group. Just as Katherine had suspected, Derrick had recognised 'Mr. Morgue', that is, Mr Morgan.

"Derrick, would you mind waiting while I try and alert someone?"

"Mmm, only if I ain't in any trouble, or you can promise that I'll not get inta any," he said looking a little worried.

Katherine assured him his anonymity would remain intact, just in case he could remember any more details, she wanted him to overhear her call, and to make sure she got the story straight. Her first instinct was to call Pops, but the secretary explained he wasn't there at present, he was meeting with the union leaders and making an inspection at the Williamsburg plant afterwards.

"Can I take a message?"

This was too important for that, who knows how long her message might lay around?

"No thank you, I'll try and get a hold of him at the plant. Thank you, Mrs. Davidson."

Union leaders, darn, that could take awhile, I need to contact him and fast. Wait a minute, Steves hasn't gone back to Boston yet, maybe he could do something. He had full access to the buildings and labs. *Please may he be helping out in the Williamsburg plant today…please pick up!* She heaved a sigh as she heard Steve's voice over the line.

"Hi Kats, whoa … slow down … take a breath." She tried to do as he suggested.

"I have some important news for Pops, but he's in this meeting with the union guys, and I can't get through to him. I'd try and contact Gramps, but that would take too long, and since Pops will be in Williamsburg later, I though you could tell him."

"What's going on, sis?"

"Something fishy has been going on in the Jersey offices, I'm not sure about the Manhattan branch, but I have an inside source who says he spotted Mr. Morgan skulking around late at night … where was it? Third floor?" she queried Derrick who nodded in the affirmative. "Yeah third floor, looks like he was trying to get into someone's computer files and who knows what else."

"Morgan! I should have known! If we ever did find a mole, it would be just like … are you sure?"

"Oh yeah, my source gave a positive ID from a photograph I have," she confirmed, "he also described him to a 'T' before I showed him the picture."

"Let me guess, your source is your artist who wants to stay anonymous, right?"

"How did you…?"

"Easy, you hired our maintenance crew, this source doesn't want to reveal his name, he's been in our office at night, your artist works on the same crew … yadda yadda. Okay, I get it, I won't say who blew the whistle, but I'll need to find out what 'Malignant Morgan' has been up to," Steve said half to himself, "we need some hard evidence. Anyone that high up the chain snooping around isn't up to any good."

"I agree. What do we do?"

"Well, looks like I've got some sleuthing to do, labelling Dr. Stirling's slimy slides can wait until later. Can your source tell me anything else?"

Katherine relayed the question on to Derrick.

"Well, it's th'fancy offices with th'blinds, an' it's like he's got 'em on some kinda list, not completely random like, he might backtrack at one place, but sure looks like he's working from one end ta th'other. He's kinda at the middle of the long wall, an' go'n towards the right."

"Oh, I know the reason for *that*," Steves said before talking aloud to himself again, "my program *is* working then, I wondered why there was another spike in password requests ...."

"Have you been hacking into the company computers?" Katherine asked aghast.

"Me? Absolutely not! I'm the new watch on the block. We had too many anomalies with our research and development systems all caused by viruses, outside hackers and saboteurs, so I designed a new security program for the entire internal network, with Pop's approval I might add. I installed it only a few months ago. I've stopped external hackers, they can't escape my watchdogs without their own computers getting chewed up, and internally, I've programmed each and every terminal in the company with its unique password randomly generated by computer that is sent to every employee. If they mess it up more than three times, their machine locks and they have to request an official change of password from a special office we set up. Because it's all new, everyone kept forgetting their passwords, so I didn't pay too much attention to this latest batch of requests. Pops thought the whole thing was a pain in the butt, but he'll be thanking me now."

"Hey, is that why Morgan is going from one office to another? He's trying to crack the password codes? If the same computer continually locks down, it would look suspicious."

"Exactly. Well, good thing I've prepared for this, my only problem was trying to find out which were the suspect terminals from the real password requests. Thank your source for the good work, I've got a corporate prowler to trap. Whatever you do, don't say anything to anyone, I'll tell Pops, but let's leave it at that. Complete radio silence, if you find out anything else, let's keep it between us for now, okay?"

"Er ...okay. Steves, I sure hope you know what you're doing."

"Trust me on this one, if Morgan is trying to sabotage our system, I'll get him, don't worry. No one messes around with a nerd's computer and escapes unscathed, we're going to take over the world don't you know. I've got to go."

"Okay, just … don't do anything dangerous or stupid."

"Who, *moi?* Bye sis." With that, he hung up.

How could he joke when Morgan was up to something Machiavellian in the family business? How could she not worry? Nothing for it, she would have to trust him.

"Is it all okay now?" Derrick asked a little worried.

"I think so, hopefully, my brother has got everything under control. Thank you for coming forward, you may have saved our company from a near disaster. Don't worry, your identity will remain a secret."

"I'm glad I could help, I guess I should be go'n now."

Katherine thanked him again before they went back to the lobby just in time to overhear Suzy informing Trigger that she was positive she didn't want flames painted on the car.

"Man, and they're supposed to be artists," he said, scratching his head, "no appreciation."

Katherine found it nearly impossible to concentrate on her own business for the rest of the day. She was glad when all her calls were made and she could have a quiet painting session in the studio. What was Morgan up to? Insider trading? Perhaps something worse…corporate espionage? She knew it happened, but to think that someone could be a spy and throw a monkey wrench in the works was a foreign concept to her. Gramp's favourite catchphrase was 'No quarter to the competition', but she knew that did not include hacking, inventing computer viruses, planting moles in adversaries' boardrooms, causing family feuds and destroying livelihoods. Gramps had always stressed the importance of adhering to the company mission of healing and helping, the profits would take care of themselves. They only had to be happy with what they got after everything else was taken care of. How true. Her thoughts wandered to another piece of advice he once gave.

"Remember, it was not curiosity that killed the goose who laid the golden egg, but an insatiable greed that devoured common sense."

She had seen a goose egg once, it was huge. Imagine a lump of gold that size handed to you everyday! Whoever killed that goose was certainly stupid. Can greed blind someone to that extent? It was only a fable, but pondering on fictional absurdities kept her imagination active, a practise run for deeper subjects. As she carefully painted the outline of Rome, she had to agree that Gramps was right, the key to happiness is in finding contentment. Greed, if anything, is a lack of contentment; those who are bitten by that malady are never satisfied, never at peace.

She was about to fill in Michelangelo's dome on St. Peter's when the intercom rang. Nuts, I'll never get this finished. Katherine dropped her brush with a sigh and wiped her hands.

"Hello?"

"Kathy, a package just arrived, and they won't let us sign for it, it has to be handed to you directly," Esther told her.

"Really? That's odd."

"Not only that, it has arrived with a very peculiar bouquet," Esther added, "someone must be a little colour blind if you ask me."

There was only one person she knew who would send her a motley posy.

"I'll be down in a minute!"

She hastily hooked the receiver back in its bracket and tugged off her smock. It seemed like an age before the elevator touched ground. Just as she thought, Gerry had sent, via private messenger, a lavish display of sunflowers and roses with a small package addressed to: *"Miss Katherine Walsingham, For the Princess' Eyes Only: Absolutely, Imperatively and Supremely Private and Confidential."* The sight of the bright flowers and the eccentric address cheered her up despite her worrisome day.

"Goodness, did Gerry buy a florist shop, or what?" Suzy laughed.

"If not, his custom is certainly becoming the cornerstone of their business," Esther noted, examining the bouquet over her glasses.

"Would you like to send a reply?" the messenger enquired as Katherine signed for her curious delivery.

"Oh, of course. Will he get it by tonight?"

"I'll be taking it to him right away, so yeah."

"Okay, please wait a sec while I write him a note." She grabbed one of her gallery letter sheets and penned a few lines in a deliberately scrolled handwriting:

To Sir Lancelot, Knight of Abundant Flowers,
greetings from Castle Yrellag, Obmud Quarter, Nylkroob City,
Province of Kroywen, Kingdom of Asu.

We are touched by your colourful tokens of esteem. Be assured that when we are in an Absolutely, Imperatively and Supremely Private and Confidential place, we shall, with all diligence and speed, open your parcel.

Please accept our sincere thanks and appreciation,

Katherine
Princess of Sehsurbtniap

The messenger took her envelop and hurried out the door. Katherine was impatient to open the package, but if this was the 'clue' Gerry had promised, she decided it was best to do as the address suggested and open it later in private.   For the moment, she felt the parcel, squishing it gingerly in an effort to guess what might be wrapped inside. She could discern the shape of a small rectangular box through the bubble lining, and shaking it gently, she could hear something rattle. Must be a cassette tape she thought, it fanned her curiosity. While she could simply open it in the office or in the studio, she wasn't sure what was on the tape, if that's what it was, and what might be overheard. If privacy was imperative, she didn't want to jinx Gerry's riddle. Slipping the package into her purse, she decided to open it when she got home where there would be no interruptions. Returning to her painting project, she wondered if perhaps it wasn't the 'clue' at all, it could be just a token gift that he thought she might like. No, the address to her was too precise for that: '*Absolutely, Imperatively and Supremely Private and Confidential*'. What on earth did he send her? How she wished it was closing time. When the alarm clock finally rang, she stopped all work and locked up the place with Esther and Suzy as fast as she could. She was tempted to open the parcel when she got to the van, but no, let's do this right she thought. If there was something important that required concentration, she wouldn't be able to drive safely on the slick roads.

The first thing she saw on the front hall stand when she arrived home was another beautiful bouquet for her mother sent by Gerry who wanted to thank her and the family for their hospitality. This was the second one he sent to the house, yesterday it was a lovely winter-themed spray.   Katherine shook her head, maybe Suzy was right about that florist shop. Taking off her coat, she found her mother in the sitting room writing out the plans for the next charity fundraiser.

"Hello Kathy dear, I'm so glad you're home on time. Did you see the lovely orchids Gerry sent? He's simply too generous."

"Oh I know, he also sent me a small tree today. What are we going to do with him?" Katherine said, shrugging her shoulders with a smile. "I told him to be more frugal with his gift-giving, but he insisted on reserving

638

the right to spoil me with flowers, and I guess everyone else for that matter."

"He's certainly exercising that right to the utmost of his ability. If he keeps this up, we shall all be living in a jungle. Now that you're here, would you be a good girl and call your father and grandfather into the dining room for me? Buzz Suzy too and see if she wants to join us. Mrs. Gonzales is just about ready to serve the soup."

"Sure Mom. However, Suzy is meeting Charlie in town tonight, so it's just us." Looks like Gerry's package would have to wait.

Going to the den, she stopped short of knocking on the door when she overheard Pops and Gramps animatedly discussing company business. She didn't want to be rude, but after the news Derrick and Steves had dropped on her that day, she wondered if the elders' conversation might be related in some way. Her curiosity was difficult to keep in check at times. She wished she knew more about the family industry, but the men usually kept the internal workings of the business to themselves. How was she going to learn how the world worked if everyone kept trying to protect her from it at every step? There were times she felt completely ignorant and she adamantly detested it.

"Blast it! I wish I could see what was happening, we've had a number of small companies buying up our stocks, and in certain instances, offering almost a full quarter more than they are worth. I've asked the Kraylors to look into it for me to see if they can find out who is doing the buying. That's all we need now, to face a take-over bid at the AGM."

"Hrumph! If we can trust Tim, we still have the majority holding, I've been picking up some common stock , but I admit, not all this stock buying is me, but in any case, no one can buy us out. Whoever it is, let them bid all they like."

"I know that Dad, but what if Tim is somehow behind this, increasing his percentage of the holdings? He's a wild card at the moment, he could side with anyone on the board. Even if any outside bid is neutralized by our majority vote, it still causes upheaval, projects disunity at the managerial level ....."

Katherine heard Gramps rumble something, he was obviously angry over the whole affair. Better call them for dinner she thought.

The men didn't rehash too many of their corporate troubles over dinner and the conversation remained general. She couldn't help but notice Pops didn't feel like eating too much, not from a loss of appetite, but a precautionary fear of upsetting his ulcers. No wonder Pop's stomach was always on the blink, bottling all his worries up inside couldn't be good for him. Yet, what could he do? Just sit and bear it, wait until he saw how the market played out. Tonight she understood how he felt, she was finding it difficult to act normal when she also had a tale of espionage about their company pounding within her head, screaming to get out, especially after listening to Pop's serious revelations. Gritting her teeth, she would have to trust her brother. She had noticed that Steves was not home yet for dinner and she asked Mom if he was going out.

"Oh, he said he was meeting with a few friends and not to be anxious if he comes home late."

Steves often went out with a few of his geekie buddies from high school who were now studying at different colleges, but this time, Katherine's stomach knotted. Intuitively she knew he was not cruising with his friends, but going to a secret 'office party' in Jersey. She wondered if he told Pops about her unexpected news that morning, but if he did, Pops wasn't giving any hints or letting any visual tell-tale signs slip. He was a good poker player, he did win the penny-pot a few times the other night after all. Oh, it's best to say nothing for now and wait until Steves gets home.

After dinner, Pops went to the study to catch up on some paperwork, while Gramps and Mom decided to watch TV. Katherine would usually have loved to put her feet up with them, but tonight she slipped away to her room, it was time to find out what was in that package. Perhaps it would help distract her from the disturbing events of the day since her brother made her promise not to talk to anyone for the present.

Sitting at her dressing table, she slit the puffy pack open with her letter opener. Inside was indeed a cassette tape accompanied by a thick letter written on curious writing paper sealed with period-style red sealing wax. "Read me First" was scrolled on the address side of the letter, while the cassette box, which was tied with a little red and yellow satin ribbon, had "Play me Next" written on the blank space reserved for the track listings. Her guess was correct, Gerry had personally recorded something for her, this was rather exciting. She did as instructed, gently breaking the rose-shaped seal and was surprised when a smaller letter in a pre-stamped envelop addressed to someone mysteriously named "The Messenger" at an unknown Williamsburg address slipped out. Wondering what all this could be about, she read the original letter first:

Dear Kathy,

As promised, you will find recorded on the tape the 'riddle' I spoke of, and simultaneously the 'clue' to solve it. What is not there, that is already there? That is the question! Now, you must follow the instructions below very carefully. First, since the 'clue' is enclosed, everything you need to solve the riddle is on the tape, you must not disclose to anyone what is on it or let anyone hear it, this is our little secret, nor may you ask anyone for assistance, including myself. As I said, this is something you must figure out on your own, or the answer might not be as agreeable as it should be. Second, please keep the stamped envelope in a safe place, I trust you not to open it. When you believe you have discovered the answer to the riddle, and this is imperative, you must be as sure as possible, wait a few days, then mail the envelope. You shall be promptly sent the correct answer. Please, do not mail the envelope beforehand, no matter how much you are tempted to. Will your answer be the same as mine?

Faithfully Yours,

Gerry
Riddler Extraordinaire

This was rather thrilling. She untied the ribbon and slipped the tape into her Walkman. Oh no! The batteries were dead. Not now! She high-tailed it to the kitchen and began rummaging around in the fix-it drawer that held all the odds and ends that nobody knew where else to put; screws and lost nails, a dried up paint brush or two, a roll of scotch tape, a tape measure, bits of wire, tubes of glue, picture hooks, extra Christmas tree light bulbs, a box of old birthday candles, matches, and of course, batteries. She hoped they had the right size ...*whew*. Now let's hope they are not dead too.

Returning to her room, she put the small headset on, adjusted the spongy earpieces, settled back into the pillows on her bed and turned on the tape. She wasn't quite sure what to expect. His note sounded so mysterious and secretive, she wasn't sure if he had recorded additional instructions she was supposed to accomplish. Would there be a message saying the tape would self-destruct? Quite the contrary. She started to laugh when the first thing she heard was Sinatra singing 'Getting to Know You' from the *King and I.*

Getting to know you, getting to know all about you,
Getting to like you, getting to hope you like me.
Haven't you noticed, suddenly I'm bright and breezy?
Because of all the beautiful and new,
Things I'm learning about you,
Day by day.

The songs continued, and all were sung by Sinatra:

I'll be seeing you, in all the old familiar places,
That this heart of mine embraces all day through …

It was just a selection of songs.   Were they his favourite songs? *This* was the riddle?

Click … and I forget to do,
The ordinary things that everyone ought to do.
I'm living in a kind of daydream, I'm happy as a king,
Foolish thought it may seem, to me that's everything.
…click …
You'll never know, how slow the moments go
Click …
I see your face in every flower, your eyes in the stars above,
It's just the thought of you,
The very thought of … click.

** * **

Is it an earthquake or simply a shock?
Is it the good turtle soup or merely the mock?
Is it a cocktail, this feeling of joy?
Or is what I feel the real McCoy?

Is it for all time, or simply a lark?
Is it Granada I see, or Asbury Park?
Is it a fancy not worth thinking of?
Or is it at … click.

** * **

It's all so new to me … click ,
A …click ….
It's all so new to me, I can't believe,
That this …click …enchanting and unsurpassed.
Sapphire skies of blue and nights alone with you,
The sun shines through the darkest day
And finds us happy, oh so gay.
It's all so new to me, it's such a thrill,
To know that …click … .

✳✳✳

What should I call this happy madness that I feel inside of me,
Sometime of wild October gladness that I'd never thought I'd see.
What has become of my sadness, all my endless lonely sighs?
Where are my sorrows now?
What happened to the frown,
And is that self-contented clown
Standing grinning in the mirror really me?
I'd like to run through Central Park,
… click …
Of every tree I pass for everyone to see.
I feel that I've gone back to childhood
And I'm skipping though the wildwood,
So excited that I don't know what to do.
What do I care if I'm a juvenile,
I smile my secret little smile,
Because I know the change in me … click.
What should I call this happy madness, all this unexpected joy,
That turned the world into a baby's bouncing toy,
The gods are laughing far above, one of them gives a little shove,
And I … click.

✳✳✳

Click … when there are words to say,
And …click … … …. .
Day by day, we go our thoughtless way, and only when we pray
Do we remember those …click … .

643

Too late to find a word that's warm and kind,
Is more than just a passing token.
Speak … click … to those who seek … click.
Look to your …click, your …click, will know what to say,
Look to your …click, today.

Hmm, he's not very good at making pirate tracks, that's for sure. She turned the tape, only to hear the exact same thing recorded, including all the mangled skips and jumps. She then realized Side B was an intended repetition. I suppose he wants me to keep playing it until I get the message, whatever it is. She suddenly felt like giving him a call, no, she wanted to give him a call, just to hear him. Was it possible to become addicted to the sound of someone's voice? The line rang for a moment.

"Hello?"

Yes, it was possible.

"Hi Gerry, it's me. I hope I'm not calling you at an unreasonable hour."

"Hey Princess, any time spent talking with you is never unreasonable. How fares the realm?"

"All right I suppose. Let's say it's been a long day. Thank you again for the lovely flowers, and just to let you know, I've listened to your tape, strange as it is."

He laughed at her response.

"As with all riddles, it's supposed to be bizarre. I also appreciated your reply, your Highness of Sehsurbtniap."

"Well, all in good fun. About your 'riddle', I'm not to ask for help, I understand that, but what if I get stuck?"

"I hope not! But don't worry, I know you'll get it eventually." He said the last part with such quiet, reflective emphasis that it touched her deeply, although she wasn't sure why. "So," he continued, resuming his chipper tone, "all riddles aside, it seems our plans have gone askew."

"Plans?"

"Our plans for the respective 'homestead' dinners. I appeared earlier than expected for dinner with your family, so I was wondering if we shouldn't just bump everything ahead and have you visit Long Island next."

"That would be fine with me. Okay, just name the day."

"Not this Sunday, how about next week?"

"Sounds great. Now Gerry, I know you're going to tell me I don't need to bring anything, but all the same, you know I'm going to anyway, so please help me out and tell me what your parents would actually like. I don't want to find I've brought wine they don't drink or something they're allergic to." She never had worried about making an agreeable first impression before, but now it felt very important.

"Now Princess, you don't have to worry about that, I'll bring the wine for us."

"You can't bring it all, I must contribute too."

They bantered back and forth until he laughed and finally agreed she could split the wine bill with him. With that settled, their conversation rambled to the day's trivialities, they seemed more interesting when she and Gerry discussed them. Before she realized, the wee hours of the morning had crept up on them, she had been so engrossed in their conversation she didn't hear anyone come to bed.

"Oh Gerry, I'm sorry, it's almost three in the morning, we'll never get up for work."

"Alas, reality hits again. You're right, we should call it a night. Can I drop by and have lunch with you tomorrow?"

"Sure, anytime." They said their goodnights and reluctantly hung up. Yes, his voice was very addictive. Time to get the P.J.s on, but she didn't feel like sleeping.   Reaching for her Walkman, she was about to replay the mystery tape when she heard the sound of a door close across the hall; only Steve's knob made a funny squeak like that. The sound suddenly brought back all the worries of the day. Maybe he had some news, what she wouldn't give to find out what he had been up to. She ran over to his room as quietly as possible, trying not to trip over anything in haste, and very gently tapped on his door.

"Boy am I glad to see you. Get in here, quick! You've got to see this."

Without ceremony, he pulled her inside and closed the door.

Not expecting this overexcited reception, Katherine felt abnormally privileged to be allowed into her brother's Inner Sanctum of Nerdom. Rarely did he permit anyone to enter his room, including the house cleaners, for fear something valuable might get damaged or his equipment tampered with. She had nearly forgotten what the place looked like, all the Sci-Fi and NASA posters plastered over the wall, a complete set of the first ever Star Wars and Star Trek figures, all in their original boxes, (a detail that seemed very important), an almost innumerable collection of comic books carefully stacked on bookshelves, some in special frames, a museum of old gaming consoles from the first electronic Ping Pong to the Atari and all the way through to Sega, but most important of all, the 'Big Boy' computers. He didn't have just one, but several were interconnected, all blipping, bleeping, flashing lights and humming their own electronic tune. However, there was one new metallic monstrosity stacked in one corner that she hadn't seen the last time she was a visitor to his strange chamber, it appeared to be a mass of hard drives all fused together, but they looked too sophisticated to be merely hard drives.

"What on earth is that?"

"That's my Kung Fu," he said proudly, patting the top of the futuristic-looking stack.

"Is that what you wanted to show me?"

"No, but it's impressive, isn't it?"

"If you say so."

Steves sighed and shook his head, so few people could appreciate the intellectual complexity of an almost untraceable hacking device.

"What is it then? I've been on pins and needles all day. Are you going to let me in on what's going on?"

"Oh yeah, like I said, you've got to see this."

Taking a camcorder off the bed, he hooked it up to his television. They sat on the bed and waited for the snowy static to clear, revealing a homemade video of ... .

"That's not the Jersey office, is it?"

Katherine then realized he had set up a sting operation in a cubicle facing the wall of private offices. The place was dark in the video, but she could just make out a few details from the few lights left on for security purposes.

"I knew you were busy tonight on something like this."

"Yeah. Shh, you're going to miss the fun."

At first she didn't see anything, but then a door opened and closed, the shape of a man briskly made his way along the main walkway and stopped in front of one of the private office doors before slipping inside.

"Steves, it's too dark, you didn't get anything...," Katherine noted with disappointment.

"Wait for it ... drum roll please ... ."

Before she could say another word, the man had flipped the light on by the desk, revealing who he was.

"Ta da! Yes! Got him! Malignant Morgan, what an idiot! He didn't think anyone was there and left the blinds up," Steves laughed.

Derrick was right. Katherine watched in stunned amazement as the trespasser, one of the top board members of their family company, switched on the computer and rifled through the desk like a common cat burglar.

"What is he looking for I wonder?"

"Obviously he thinks the manager who has that office might have written their password somewhere easy to find, it's a common mistake."

"Oh Steves, what if he finds it? He can't get into anything important can he?"

"If he was a good hacker, perhaps, but seeing he didn't think to lower the blinds, not a chance. He can't do anything now but twist the rope that hangs him."

"Can you explain yourself?"

"I'll try and keep it simple. I wasn't sure which computer he would try to break into, so I pre-programmed the office terminals for tonight's adventure before I hid with the camera. Any computer he tries to access in the offices on that floor will let him in on the third attempt, so he won't suspect anything. However, whatever path he takes it won't lead him where he expected. Look," Steves noted, pointing to Morgan, who at that moment, was taking some kind of device out of his briefcase and inserting it into the floppy drive, "he's had outside help. He couldn't have rigged something that sophisticated himself, not with his dearth of brain cells."

"What is it?"

"Probably a portable pre-programmed hacking and memory mechanism, a custom made 'retrieve and store' device."

"Steves! Are you sure you know what you're doing?"

"Relax, he's not going into anything important, I just made it look that way. While he or his retrieval device thinks it's found something juicy, I sent them rummaging around a 'dud' mainframe complete with difficult anti-hacker codes, yet storing nothing but fake accounts and defunct Latin formulas from useless homoeopathic remedies to Great Gramp's famous, or infamous, suppositories."

Katherine couldn't believe it.

"You didn't."

"Well, I had to make it look authentic, I bet Morgan can't read a cook book let alone any pharmaceutical recipe nearly a hundred years old. That's not the end of it," he said as he watched Morgan quickly pull the machine out of the drive slot and place it back in the briefcase, "whatever file they pull in my bogus mainframe has a special program attached to it."

"A virus?"

"Not exactly, viruses destroy computers. This is more like a Trojan horse, they have no idea they have let me enter their city gates. The minute they load their stolen information, the program will kick in and seek out a computer or terminal with a modem and send me a message with all the information about where it was activated, plus all the licensing information connected with our thief's computer and the ones connected with it, if there's an internal network. We will be able to find out where Morgan's loyalties lie."

"Steve's you're amazing!"

"I know, everyone keeps telling me," he smiled.

"Did you tell Pops yet about all of this?"

"No, not until I get that message … oops, there I go," Steves broke off, watching the screen. The picture began to jump and bounce around. "One of the guards was coming, so I had to get out of there pronto and I left the camera running. I don't want to raise any suspicions of this little spying operation or let Morgan know he was taped, not until I find out who his cronies are." Steves turned off the recording.

"But I think Pops has a right to know," Katherine protested, "which reminds me, he's got another worry on his mind. I couldn't help but overhear him speaking with Gramps tonight, it looks like various companies are buying up our company stocks big time, and they're anxious about how this will affect the overall voting power."

Steves seemed interested in this news.

"Did you hear anything else?"

"Well, they suspect Uncle Tim, if the voting percentage gets moved around, they think this might have something to do with him."

"No, I don't think so," Steves reassured her. "What else did you hear?"

"Well, nothing other than Pops said he would have the Kraylors look in to it for him, see who these companies are."

"Great," Steves grumbled half to himself, ruffling his hair.

"Is that bad?" Katherine asked with concern, "I wish I understood what's going on."

"Oh, there's nothing for you to worry about," he said, "it's a matter of timing. Judging from what you tell me, it sounds like we might have an emergency board meeting soon, and I would like to get that information from our mole before that happens."

"What if you don't?"

"It'll spoil … never mind, it's more important to nail Malicious Morgan, it's just that I'd …well, it's nothing major," Steves replied, half ruminating to himself again. She wasn't sure what he meant, but he seemed to know what he was doing.

"You will let me know if you get any news?"

"Sure Kats, in fact, when that board meeting is called, I'd love it if you were there."

"Why? I don't know much about these proceedings. Why do you need me there?" she asked a little surprised.

"Listen to you. You always complain you never get to see what goes on in the company. If anything, I just want to see the expression on your face, you did help to catch our spy after all, you should share in some of the fun."

"Catching corporate criminals and worrying about takeovers sounds too serious to be 'fun'," she replied, "but if you need me there, all right."

"Great! You're going to see Walsingham history in the making."

"Whatever. I'm off to bed, let me know if your electronic horse sends back any information."

"Okay, and please, don't say anything to Pops."

"I promise, just hurry up. I don't like keeping secrets this important from him."

"Relax, I've got it all under control."

Everyone seemed full of mysteries these days. She returned to her room and cuddled up under the covers, listening to Gerry's curious riddle before eventually falling asleep, the headphones still snugly wrapped over her head. *"Getting to know you, getting to know all about you ..."*

C3 ❀ 80

"Are you positive you can't tell me?" Suzy wheedled the next morning as they opened the gallery doors and switched on the lights.

"Sorry Suzy, I'd love to, but it's one of his conditions, he says I have to figure it out with no help, nor can anyone know what's on the tape."

"What fun! He's definitely full of surprises," Suzy smiled.

"That's for sure. Anyway, he's coming by for lunch."

"How nice. I can't say the same about Charlie today, says he's got a lot of paperwork to do, something about looking up companies, but won't give me any details," Suzy disclosed as they settled into the desk chairs.

"I think I know the reason, you can blame the family business, Pops asked the Kraylors to do some paper chasing, so I guess Charlie got assigned that job."

"That's all right, he does have to work, and so do I."

They were about to discuss their own business for the day when an eccentric figure sauntered in, it was Mr. Jim 'The Breeze' dressed in a similar

649

style as on his last appearance with the exception his fashion ensemble was a deep shade of royal purple, and he had a grizzly-looking bodyguard in tow.

"How be you ladies this be-you-ta-ful morning?" he politely asked in his lilting reggae tone of voice, tipping his purple hat, his gold tooth flashing its own glittering greeting.

"Good morning, we're fine thank you," Katherine replied, "you must be here to see D.S.'s new mural."

"That be true," Mr. Breeze nodded. "It be in the same place?"

"Yes, please, go on up and take a look."

"Thank-ee kindly," he replied, tipping his hat again before making his way to the elevator.

"That's Mr. Breeze?" Suzy asked as their colourful visitor disappeared from sight

"The one and only," Katherine nodded.

"He sure likes his gold, doesn't he?"

Their conversation was interrupted as an exclamation of surprise and admiration resounded from above.

"Oh, that be class alright! This D.S. is da *man!*"

"I guess he likes it then," Suzy noted.

"I suppose so. Looks like we're going to have our hands full trying to keep those walls filled. Derrick is going to be very busy, that's for sure," Katherine smiled.

They went into the office to check out the security monitors and watched Mr. Breeze leaning back on his ebony cane, thoroughly enjoying the new 'graff'. He eventually sauntered away from the D.S.'s work and took a tour around the floor before going up to see the exhibition space, eventually returning to the front desk to pay for the murals, including the new one.

"I hope a cheque isn't dis-a-gree-able," he enquired.

"No that's fine, we only need your cheque card."

"Sure. Oh, an' bye th' way, I don want to be diff-a-cult, but would it be possible to have them delivered today?"

"I don't know, another delivery company has to take care of it as those pieces are bigger than our van can handle, but I'll see what I can do. I'll call you if they have to be dropped off another day."

"Okay, don' worry if you can't. It woulda been great to have them up by tonight, that's all."

"I'll see what I can do, and I'll be there to personally ensure the works are handled properly. Where would you like them delivered?"

"At th' 'Breeze Club', do you have some paper? I'll give you the directions." He jotted down an address in the Lower East Side and also a few landmarks for the men to watch out for.

"Thank you, that should do it, and here is your … um … collateral," Katherine replied, handing him back his pile of luxury trinkets, "please check and make sure it's all there."

"Thank-ee, looks fine. I do app-ree-cee-ate, yo fine hos-pi-tal-i-ty. Here, I think this would look mighty fine on you," he said, searching through the pile and giving her a thick chain with a smiley face gold pendant on it the size of a silver dollar. Suzy smothered the urge to laugh.

"Oh, I couldn't take that," Katherine politely protested.

"Now don' refuse," he smiled, "this'll bring you good luck."

"Well, I guess we all could use that, thank you." What could she do? She couldn't be rude, so she slipped the large chain over her head.

"I guess I'll be see'n you later … oh, an' if anyone gives you hassle at the door, you just tell them 'Jim the Breeze lets in whom he please.'"

"Jim the Breeze lets in whom he please …okay," Katherine repeated hesitantly, a little unsure if that was a code, praying he wasn't insulted that she mimicked his manner of speech.

"Oh woman, you be funny," he laughed, "good day now." With that, he removed his hat with a flourish and bowed graciously, then turning with a swish, left the building, his bodyguard following.

"Wow, he's something else," Suzy observed.

"I know," Katherine replied, looking down at the shining smiley face. "I should have this framed to put with our lucky five dollar bill."

It was the first note of tender they earned when they opened, (for a smiley-face T-shirt no less), and according to tradition, was placed in a gold frame and hung above the desk. Katherine decided she had better call Gerry right away and find out if he could arrange the delivery.

"Sure Princess, that's no problem. I'll have a truck stop by."

"I'm sorry, but this will wreck our lunch plans, I promised I'd be there to supervise the hanging since D.S. can't do it."

Katherine was disappointed, she was looking forward to seeing Gerry again.

"Maybe the job will get done faster than you expect, we can meet in town for lunch."

"Okay, but unfortunately, I can't promise anything."

"Don't get stressed, this will sort itself out."

"Thank you, I really appreciate it. Listen, I've got to go, looks like someone is waiting to see me." A young man smartly dressed had come in and approached Suzy about 'the job' and stood patiently for her to finish her call.   Nuts, she wanted to stay on the phone a little longer with Gerry, but business beckoned.

"All right, see you later."

"Bye Gerry, have a good day."

Everything seemed to happen in spurts. Hanging up, she turned to the visitor, and noticed he was holding a card from the employment agency and a résumé folder.

"Hi, I'm here to apply for the gallery assistant's job?" he enquired. That was fast, she only placed a call to the agency yesterday. Katherine had the sneaking suspicion she had seen him before, but where?

"Oh yes, let's step into the office," she replied, shaking his hand over the counter before motioning him to join her. Closing the door, she offered him a seat. "May I see your résumé please?"

"Sure."

Handing over the folder, he was smiling as though he knew a secret she didn't. This was odd.   Opening it to his educational background, she stopped when she came to 'Master of Arts, Belvedere College'. Reading on, she found his list of academic accomplishments including being honourably mentioned in the Sirrac Contest of 1990 for his painting, *Electrovision*.

"Dennis Harrington, of course! I thought I recognised you," she noted with surprise. He had cut his long hair, that's why she couldn't place him right away. "It's been awhile. How are you?"

"I didn't know if you would remember me," he admitted, "we didn't attend the same classes. I guess I'm doing okay. As you can see, I'm looking for a job while I wait for someone to show an interest in my collection, and I was hoping to find something art-related this time. All those coffee shop and grocery clerk listings do nothing to improve my CV," he added with a smile. At least he could see the funny side of it.

"Well, you've come to the right place. We do have an opening. Looks like we really are the Belvedere Bunch," Katherine replied. "It's not very taxing work," unless Mrs. Hunt stops by she thought, but didn't voice this information, "basically we keep an eye on the customers, make sure they don't touch anything or take any photographs, give tours when needed, explain the background on the pictures when requested, well, you basically have an idea how a gallery operates." Katherine explained the general requirements of the establishment, the wages and working hour.   Of course, there was the dress code, nice and casual if he liked, but no T-shirts or jeans, which she felt was a bit ironic considering they were selling T-shirts for a while. Dennis seemed pleased with the job description.

"Now, I dislike having to ask this, but I need to know; did you quit your last job, or were you let go?"

"I understand. It was a seasonal thing, I worked as an extra waiter for the holiday rush, but then they laid me off. Honestly, I'm tired of getting these part-time jobs that don't last. Of course, I love all the free time for my art work, but you can't pay for materials without money coming in, and you can't eat paint either."

"Well, I guess since you're the first one here, the early bird gets the worm. Would you be available to start this Tuesday?"

"Sure, that would be great, but there's … no way I could start sooner?" he asked hesitantly.

"Well, we close on Sundays, and I need someone to come in to cover the latter part of the week … ," Katherine tried to explain.

"Yeah, Tuesday's fine," he agreed, he didn't want to be pushy. She then realized he must be in a tight spot and needed the money.

"Hmm, I'll tell you what. Why don't you stick around for today, consider it on-the-job training, you'll be paid of course."

"That's swell," he beamed.

"So tell me, you said you had a collection? I can't believe you're not finding anyone interested in showing it. You must have been bombarded by gallery offers after the Sirrac nomination."

Dennis actually hadn't fared as well as he would have liked. He had two gallery offers, but they only showed his work for a few months, and the few pieces he did sell, the gallery managers dragged their feet when it came time to pay. He then received a request to work on a special collection for an exhibition, and after spending all his money and time painting, the exhibition was cancelled and all the artists were left to swing. Now he had a glut of paintings and not sure where to go with them. He would have come over during her first call for artists, but as he was stuck with those two other no-good galleries, he didn't have anything to show at the time.

"That's awful. I'll tell you what. If I remember your artwork, it's a bit modernistic for this place, but I'd be happy to take a look at it. Do you have a portfolio of your work?"

"Well, just the preliminary sketches of the finished pieces, I don't really take photos of anything."

"That's all right, bring what you have on Tuesday."

Dennis looked positively relieved.

"You really have a nice place here," he commented, "old world, but very nice."

"Thank you. You can hang your coat over there in the closet. Oh, here comes Esther," Katherine noted, looking at the security monitor.

"So it's true, Mrs. Matthews does work here," he smiled.

"The Professor drops by a lot, his work is on display too, and of course, you just met Suzy again, you do remember Susanna Cooper?"

"Of course, I don't think she recognised me though," he laughed, "I did clean myself up a bit for the interview. Gosh, it's a bit like being back at Belvedere again."

"I guess I took the best of Belvedere with me," Katherine smiled. "Come on, I'll introduce you to Andre in the restaurant, then I'll take you on a tour. If you want to eat lunch here, don't worry about the prices, Andre gives us a special rate."

"Is it true you have an exclusive on D.S.'s first ever canvas paintings?"

"It's true. In fact, if you want to see one of them, it's a good thing you came today, they're sold and are going to be shipped out around lunchtime."

The morning flew as Katherine showed the new assistant around, mostly due to the conversations they had in between business. Katherine was pleased to find out that the gallery was acquiring a name for promoting new talent in addition to honouring the past history of art. In fact, many artists were now hoping that one day they might be able to attract her attention. Wow, that was good news. Since she wasn't paying too much attention to the papers the last few weeks, she was a little behind on the art grape vine. She did need to find new talent, and explained she had asked Robert Horace for advice. Dennis couldn't believe his ears: ask the *Art Hacker* for recommendations? Was she off her rocker?

"Perhaps," she laughed, enjoying his astonishment. "I'd better warn you, the Hacker comes around here to do a little critiquing, so if you want your works exhibited, you'll have to grin and bear it."

"Swell," Dennis grimaced, "I don't want him anywhere near my stuff."

"Oh yes you do. Let me put it this way, was the Hacker at your last two exhibitions?"

"No..."

"Be thankful when he *does* slash your work, you'll be a hit. There's a method to his madness, trust me."

By this time, they were in the permanent exhibition space and Dennis couldn't believe her good fortune to have so many treasures in one place, he was particularly impressed with the Matisse. Aunt Martha was definitely going to approve of the new assistant Katherine thought. Of course, he couldn't help but notice that the majority of the pieces on display came from the celebrated Reinold collection.

"Wow, how did you persuade him to loan you so many pieces?"

"I didn't persuade him, he just offered."

"He gave you these," Dennis observed, reading the brass plaque Katherine had made for the unicorn manuscripts, "methinks you have an admirer," he teased.

"All right, I confess, we're actually dating."

"Hey, I'm happy for you. If it's not too personal, especially as you're now my boss, how did you meet?"

Katherine briefly gave him a few details, trying to sound nonchalant, yet secretly indulging in reflective delight reliving those first few moments when they met. She had never felt this way about anyone before, even talking about Gerry now gave her a 'fuzzy' feeling inside. She hoped the art deliveries would be finished early, she might be able to have lunch with him today after all. No time for daydreaming, got to get back to work. Now that they were upstairs, they had better have the third mural ready for transport. After neatly rolling the new mural and spacing out the other paintings to fill the large gap, Katherine and Dennis returned to the front desk, the deliverymen should arrive shortly. They came right on time, two men and the driver dressed in their work uniforms with the Reinold corporate logo. Looking up from her agenda she was surprised to find Gerry standing before her dressed for the occasion in his company uniform and sporting a Yankees baseball cap.

"Excuse me, Miss Walsingham I presume? I believe you have several items to be picked up and delivered?"

Katherine put her hand over her open mouth, she didn't expect to see him looking quite like that.

"This *is* the Walsingham Gallery? We were given the correct address," he said, checking his clipboard and looking around.

"Oh, you've found the correct place all right," Katherine replied.

"Splendid. The instructions say you are going to accompany us, and that we are to follow your exact orders down to a 'T'. Your wish is our command. Sign here please," he said, handing her the clipboard and pointing to where he had made an 'X'. Sure enough, the instructions were formally typed out and signed by Gerard Reinold, Senior Manager of International Distribution. He then tore off her copy and handed it to her with panache.

"Why not take the whole afternoon off?" Esther suggested. "We can handle everything, now that we have a new hand on board."

"In that case, I guess I'd better get my coat," Katherine said with a smile. Gerry could be so unpredictable and …just plain funny.

After the men had loaded the murals and their iron accessories into the truck, Gerry helped her into the cabin and introduced her to his men, Leo and Dan.

"Well gents," he said as he started the engine, "meet Miss Walsingham. May I say it now?" he enquired, turning to her. "Can I finally proclaim in public you're my girlfriend?"

"Hey boss, that's swell. Pleased to meet you miss," Leo said, shaking her hand, "he's one lucky guy."

The drive to Jim's club was certainly interesting. Dan and Leo were only too happy to tell her what it was like to work as delivery men, the things they were expected to haul, the odd destinations they sometimes ended up at. Live animals were always the most difficult to handle, Dan remembered one time when a truck belonging to a circus broke down so they were hired to transport an elephant. Gerry said he would never forget that one, he was given the job to muck out the truck afterwards. Like he said, his father wanted him to have hands on experience.

"Boy, I bet you appreciate your desk job," Leo said with a smile.

Leo then reminded him of when he first worked the forklifts in the distribution centre: day one on the job, he drove right into a shipment of industrial glue. When he was finally promoted to making deliveries, he got lost five times in one day.

"Thank you for listing off all my accomplishments," Gerry wryly interjected.

"Is it safe to drive with him?" Katherine asked with a note of humour.

"Oh sure, the Boss was just starting out then," Leo noted matter-of-factly.

"That's good to know," she smiled.

Arriving at the Lower East Side, Gerry had no trouble finding the club, it was plainly marked with a stylish sign depicting a letter 'B' surrounded by purple clouds. Gerry let the truck idle in front as he jumped down and knocked on the amethyst steel door. Katherine watched as a small shutter at eye-height opened, revealing the blank stare of the bodyguard she had seen that morning escorting Mr. Breeze. At least he would recognise them and wouldn't need the password word-for-word, she could only remember the general gist that Mr. Breeze lets in whoever he wants. Now that they were given permission to use the front entrance, Gerry turned off the engine and the men went to work bringing in the rolls and the iron rails.

While they laid out the equipment, Katherine glanced around the establishment, she had never been to a dance club like this before. Other than the sign and the catching purple doors, the outside was deceptive, just a regular-looking building like many in the area, but on the inside, it was enormous, a large multi-storeyed open plan with five separate bars, a raised dance floor and various platforms with chairs, glass-topped tables and purple booths staggered at different levels around the walls for spectators to watch the dancers or simply 'hang out' in style on the various tiers with their futuristic steel railings. It was hard to form an impression of the decoration when most of the lights were off and the music wasn't playing, she suspected the place would be awash with colour and pulsating with vibration when night time arrived.

"So glad you could make it," Jim the Breeze greeted, sauntering down the stairs from his office on the topmost tier, cane in hand.

"Hello Mr. Breeze, you certainly have a very fine club," Katherine complimented.

"How can you tell when it's as dark as Hades in here, my good woman? Yo, Vee Man," he called to someone up in the office, "let there be light!"

Crackling clacks reverberated as the illuminations lit the expansive room in their various ranks and files, the final display, a series of multi-coloured laser lights began revolving around the room, making her feel quite dizzy.

"Wow, you've got yourself an electrical storm," she smiled.

"That isn't all, come on Vee Man, play her your notes, let's treat our guest to a little music."

A black teenager dressed in an oversized red gym suit with a large gold chain around his neck plus a black baseball cap modishly worn backwards bounded down from the office, did a back-flip from the third step to the ground, spun around in an artful dance turn, and jived his way to the 'DJ Command Center' overlooking the main dance floor. Katherine politely listened as Vee Man got into the 'groove', concocting the most unusual dance sounds and beats via his electronic consoles, keyboards and record tables, melding the strange soundtrack with the futuristic light display. Gerry simply stood with Leo and Dan, arms folded, enjoying her reaction.

"Do you dance, my fair lady?" Mr. Breeze asked above the din ... composition.

"Um, not this style I'm afraid," she replied, her hands over her ears. They sure liked their music loud in these places, didn't they? Finally, Vee Man came to the end of his original creation and took a bow. Katherine and the men politely clapped.

"Thanks Vee, off you go and get yor'self some fine soul food, alright?"

Vee Man waved, back flipped onto the floor, and sauntered out the main entrance.

"He don´ talk much," Mr. Breeze offered, "he likes to speak through his dance and music."

"What did he say?" Katherine asked.

"Oh, that be his way of welcomin' you."

A handshake would have been a lot easier she thought, but what could she say? Everyone was an artist in their own sphere.

Mr. Breeze motioned for one of the bodyguards to stop the light display and turn on the normal lights.

"You see those three spaces over the dance areas? That's where I want the paintings."

"Okay, any particular order?" Katherine asked.

"What would you suggest?"

"Well, dance is your main theme, so I suggest we put the dance mural in the centre section near the main floor, and the peace-related murals to the sides."

"Righteous, I like that. Kinda fitting when you think about it. If we danced and shared music, we'd be too busy en-joy-in' life to start a war."

"I suppose that's one way of promoting world peace," Katherine replied.

Looking around, she then realized she had forgotten an important detail: her gallery was prepared to display artwork, the club wasn't. She had never thought about supplying bolts or hooks large enough to support the weight of the iron rods and canvases. Of course, that would mean finding a drill and gouging holes into the club walls ... this was not going to be as simple as she thought.

"Um Mr. Breeze, can I have a word with you?"

Explaining the situation, she was afraid he might not be pleased to hear about having to bore a few holes, but he didn't seem ruffled.

"Yo, Drill Bill," he called out. A large beefy man dressed in overalls lumbered out from an 'employees only' area. "Go get your stuff, there's some work here for ya. Oh, an' a ladder too. He's our fix-it man," Mr. Breeze clarified, turning to Katherine. The guy moseyed on back and returned with one hefty-looking toolbox before making a second trip to the back room for the ladder.

"You wouldn't happen to have a second ladder?" Katherine asked. How was one person going to lift up those lengthy murals?

"Nope, sorry miss," Drill Bill replied, "not one tall enough anyway."

"Okay, we'll just have to do the best we can."

"Can we be of assistance?" Gerry asked.

"It looks like we need to take a trip to a hardware store for some bolts."

Jumping back into the truck, they combed the area and eventually found a hardware store. The guys helped her hunt through the nails and screws until Katherine discovered a bin filled with giant brass hooks that would match the mural rods and plumb weights. She also decided to invest in her own drill and a few extra ladders now that she was there; if D.S.'s murals continued to sell like this, it looked like she was going to need them. Feeling a bit constricted in her full-length puffy winter coat, she took it off and draped it over her left arm so she could examine the equipment.

"I'm sorry about all of this," Gerry smiled as he watched her dressed in an elegant skirt suit trying to lift one of the heavy professional construction-grade drills, "we don't usually carry equipment like this for regular deliveries, I would have come prepared."

"That's all right," she said, letting the drill machinery drop back onto the display with a thud. "Ow, there goes my nail," she said, shaking her hand.

"Are you sure you want a drill? I'm positive Bill at the club has one."

"I know, but Mr. Breeze will run out of space eventually, and other customers are going to want D.S.'s work, so it's a good idea to get the equipment now. Besides, it may not be a bad idea to keep one handy at the gallery. How about this one?" she asked, pointing to the machine that just decapitated her nail.

"You don't need one *that* big," he said, selecting a much smaller model. "Here, this should do it, you only need to make holes for paintings, not water pipes."

"Gosh, it's still kind of heavy."

"It's the motor, takes a lot of power to work one of those."

He couldn't stop smiling, she looked so charming all dressed up with that odd happy face pendant, completely out of her environment, awkwardly brandishing the drill in the air like an oversized Colt revolver. She then hit the button, the motor buzzed and vibrated, giving her such a shock she dropped it on the floor with an "Ahhh!"

"Whoa, careful! That's a lethal weapon!" Thank God there's no drill bit he thought.

"Hey! That thing's alive!" she stammered.

"Well, what did you expect? It's a demonstration model."

The floor manager came running to see what had caused the commotion.

"No damage done," Gerry said as he picked it up, "this is her first experience with a drill. Now that we have our machine sorted out, you'll need a long extension cable, a few extra steel bits for masonry walls, wall plugs to keep the hooks from falling out, and I don't suppose you remembered to bring a tape measure in your purse?" Katherine shook her head. "Okay, looks like we need a few more supplies," he laughed. Gerry seemed to know what he was doing, so when he offered to take over from there at the club, she didn't mind. "Just leave everything to us, you can supervise. We'll do the hard work with Bill, just direct where you want the rods put."

"Well if you insist, I'm happy to oblige."

Katherine directed the men as they held out the length of the tape measure in the desired spot with Gerry perched on a ladder at one end holding it up into place. He then began to hunt around in his pocket with his free hand looking a little perplexed; he had forgotten to bring the pen from the truck to mark the places for the hooks. Katherine rummaged around in her purse. Oh no, not her nice soft lead sketching pencil, the rough walls would tear the tip to pieces. Didn't she bring a pen? No, of course not, that would make life too easy. Time to improvise.

"Here, use this," she called out, tossing up her lipstick.

"That'll do," he nodded.

With that little snag solved, the job went much faster. Katherine made herself useful, gingerly rolling out the murals on the dance floor and snapping the brass rings into place. The men hung up the paintings and the plumb weights, mission accomplished. Mr. Breeze came down from his office to see the results while the men swept up the cement dust and hauled her new ladders back to the truck.

"They look mighty fine," he beamed, flashing his tooth. She had to agree, the wild colour schemes and the dancers fit perfectly with the surroundings. "You keep D.S. busy for me," he continued, "I got a few more places that need some artistic im-proove-ments."

"I'll be happy to give D.S. the message."

"Here, you did a fine job," he said, pulling out fifty dollar bills, handing them to Gerry, Leo and Dan.

"Thank you sir," Gerry replied, shrugging to Katherine and slipping the note into his pocket after her patron had turned back to her.

"Good bye, Mr. Breeze, I'll call you when new pieces come in."

"You can call me Jim," he laughed, as they shook hands.

"Hey Boss, not a bad shift," Leo noted as the all clambered back into the truck, "we haven't had a tip like that in awhile."

"Well, my end of the dare is complete. I know you must be starving," Gerry said, turning to Katherine, "but I must the guys back, and take the truck in for its afternoon mileage check. You don't mind if I drag you along?"

"No, not at all. In fact, I'm curious to see your base of operation."

"Okay," he smiled.

They drove to Williamsburg and pulled into an enormous bustling warehouse complex with vans, trucks and forklifts of all sizes zooming around or chugging about, a haze of diesel exhaust permeated the chilly air.

"Wow." Katherine didn't know what to say, she was glad she didn't have to manage an operation like this.

"Here we have our main distribution centre for New York," he explained, "then of course we have the dock warehouses, plus all the other centres around the world. Warehouse One," he said as he pulled up in what looked like a checkpoint area. "I've got to sign the truck in at reception, plus there's someone I would like you to meet."

"You want us to go ahead and fill the tank up for ya?" Dan enquired.

"Yeah, thanks. You guys did great. I'll see you around."

"Bye Boss. Nice to meet you Miss," Leo said as Gerry and Katherine entered the warehouse.

"If you don't mind me asking, why do you have to check the mileage?"

"Oh, we have to keep detailed records to ensure trucks aren't used for any purpose other than our registered pick-ups and drop-offs. You can get a rogue driver who tries to make a few deliveries of his own and earn a buck or two under the counter using company vehicles, and then we get stuck with the fuel and everything else that goes with it. A few extra miles of fuel doesn't sound like much, but if it happens in all our centres, plus the fees we lose, it mounts up pretty fast. If they're willing to go that far, they'll progress to selling off people's shipments, I dislike playing the taskmaster, but we do have to be vigilant."

"Gee, would people really do that?"

"They would and they do. It's a rotten world at times."

"I didn't think *you* would have to check in though," she mused.

"It's a good policy to show the master follows his own rules."

They approached a large reception desk where she noticed an excitable little old man wearing a hardhat and a florescent reflective jacket yelling out orders to the men operating the forklifts in the building. Somehow, he gave her the impression of an elf delegated the task of ensuring Santa's workshop ran on schedule.

"Hey Sammy, take a break, I have a guest to introduce," Gerry called out.

"Hi bossy boy, you're late," the little man chided as he came out from behind his command post, his accent reminding her of Jimmy Durante. "What happened?"

Katherine looked a little sheepish.

"It's my fault, I should have been better prepared for the delivery," she explained.

"Don't worry Kathy, he's a right slave driver. He still treats me likes it's my first day here. Sammy, I would like you to meet my girlfriend, Katherine Walsingham. Kathy, this is Sammy."

"Ah, it's a pleasure," he said, vigorously shaking her hand. For a moment, she felt like she was holding the live drill again.

"Sammy's been here managing the dock for as long as I can remember," Gerry continued as he handed him the clipboard and clocked in his mileage, "I don't know what we'd do without him."

"You'd all be running late around here, that's what," he laughed.

"So you're the man in charge," Katherine noted.

"That's right Toots, after Bossy Boy of course. So, are you having lunch with us today? Gracie has made one fantastic lasagne, su-*perb*," he emphasised, smooching the tips of his fingers and opening them up into the air to show his appreciation of this fine fare.

"You have a place to eat here?" Katherine wondered.

"Sure, we have a twenty-four hour cafeteria. There are guys coming in at all hours, so if they can't get home at an reasonable time, at least they are assured of finding something substantial to keep them going," Gerry explained before declining Sammy's offer. "I'm sorry, I can't join you today, I've got a place booked for Kathy and I, but I'll have that lunch with you tomorrow, there's some business we have to go over."

"Sure thing, I'll see you tomorrow then. Hey Jack-o," Sammy yelled, running after one of the guys zipping away in a forklift laden with crates, "wrong consignment! It says stack C-10, not B-10! Read your orders, will ya!"

"You can always tell the new ones," Gerry laughed. "Well, the joke is wearing thin now," he said, tugging at his workman gear. "Would you mind waiting in the car while I go get out of this?   It's just around the building to the right," pointing to the side door, "I'll only be ten minutes. Here, take the keys," he said, handing them to her, "and don't worry about your ladders, the guys have a delivery in your area and they'll drop everything off this evening before you close."

"Okay, see you in a few minutes."

She found the employee's lot around the side, his car parked in a special reserved area. Someone had painted under the 'Reserved' sign the words *for the Boss Man. The buck stops here*. It looked like one of the guys did it; Gerry obviously enjoyed a special rapport with his workers.

C3❀80

Sunday morning, Katherine's nerves were positively jittery. She had picked her outfit for this day a week in advance, a royal blue wool skirt suit with a satin blouse, and still she worried if it was appropriate. It was difficult to select something for church that would also work for an important dinner. Why did meeting his parents seem so daunting? She took extra time and care getting ready, every pat of foundation was applied with deliberation, her eyeliner finished off with a perfect slender stroke line, a new mascara was opened to ensure she didn't end up with spider leg lashes, every wavy strand of hair elegantly pinned into position. She probably didn't look any better than on other occasions, and his parents wouldn't know the difference anyway, but at least she felt good knowing she spared no effort to look her best.

On her way down to breakfast, she was sidetracked by Steves opening his bedroom door and motioning her to come in. Finally! Looks like he has some news. He had left her on tenterhooks all week without a peep of information about what was happening on his end with Mr. Morgue's corporate cloak and dagger escapades. He *would* drag her in now when they had to leave for Sunday service.

"So, what's up?"

"I've got all my info, and not a moment too soon, take a look at this," he said, indicating to one of the computer monitors. It appeared

663

several e-mails arrived from his specialized program, there was a small icon of a horse in each subject line of the inbox with the title, '*A mighty breach is made, the rooms concealed appear, and all the palace is revealed.*'

"Hmm, that's poetic for you," she commented.

"Yes, poetic justice."

"So what's in the e-mails?"

"Not yet, you'll have to wait and see," he smiled mysteriously.

"Why drag me in here then? Just spit it out."

"Pops has called an emergency board meeting for tomorrow ... ."

"Great! *Now* you tell me?" Katherine interjected with impatience, "the day when I'm meeting Gerry's parents! As if I don't have enough to worry about!"

"I'm sorry Kats, I just heard the news myself. Don't worry, there's nothing to be anxious about. You *will* be there?"

Katherine sighed. She did promise, and she wanted to see how this would be resolved.

"Of course. What time? I have to notify everyone at the gallery that I may not be in for the day."

"Nine thirty."

"Okay, a morning in Manhattan it is. Anyway, can't you at least tell me what's in the e-mails?"

"All in good time," he smiled. Katherine just shook her head.

"I'm going down for breakfast. You *will* be joining us?"

"In a minute Kats, fix me a plate, will you?"

"Sure, just hurry up."

He was so frustrating at times, but she could wait one more day. Pops and Gramps looked disgruntled as they brooded over their newspapers. They were not in the mood for food. No doubt the emergency meeting weighed on their minds. She was tempted to spill the beans about Morgan, it was hard to see them so worried, especially Gramps who always had a cheerful disposition, but come on, just *one* more day, you can do it, she pep-rallied. Steves had better have a good reason for letting them all stew like this, he probably didn't, but thankfully, it would all be over in the morning. Let's just handle today first, she would worry about tomorrow when it came.

Gerry had arranged to pick her up at her house after the service. She felt bad letting him drive up all the way to her place, but he insisted, so there was no point arguing. He would be irked enough seeing she had decided to bring along a bottle of cognac despite their agreement to split the wine bill. It just didn't feel right to arrive on his folks' doorstep empty-handed.

"Hi Princess, all set?" he asked, holding the car door open for her.

"I guess I'm as ready as I'll ever be."

"Hey, I told you no need to bring anything," he said with a hint of reproach in his voice.

"Now don't be that way," she replied, "you know how I am."

"All right, just plop it on the backseat," he chuckled. After a short time, he couldn't help but notice how quiet she was. "Is everything all right? I'm not mad at you for bringing the bottle."

"I know. It's not that, it's just I feel a bit nervous. You would think I never met anyone for the first time before."

"Don't worry, just be yourself. Anyway, you won't be meeting them alone, Lottie will be there, and so will Mrs. Hunt. Mom, invited her, she thought you might feel more comfortable if people you knew were coming. I know," he laughed when he saw her expression, "Mom had the best intentions."

"At least Mrs. Hunt won't have me unhitching paintings all day," Katherine smiled.

"No, that'll be my job, she loves Dad's collection," he explained.

Leaving the vertical monoliths of the city skyline behind, the scenery changed to a semi-rural coastline with green hills and fields dotted with mansions and elite summer holiday homes, the fumy air of the metropolis was now exchanged for the salty freshness that blew in from the Atlantic. She tried to guess which estate was the Reinold family residence, maybe that brick one by the hill, perhaps the white Georgian, or that Tudor style house by the bridge? I guess not she thought as they passed. He gave her a running commentary on who lived where if they weren't museums or heritage landmarks, a few names sounded familiar, but her parents might know more people down here than she did. Gerry eventually turned into a large gate flanked by stone pillars with the name 'Stonyvale Manor' on a forest green wrought iron arch, and drove down a curving driveway flanked by overhanging trees and shrubs. Finally, a rambling antebellum stone mansion with its slate grey mansard roofs, cupolas, turrets, delicate iron trellises and forest green shutters came into view. The immense garden, now wrapped in the silent chill of winter, looked a little dreary with its leafless trees gyrating against the sky, their limbs twisted and curled into unusual angles caused by the storms that howled in from the sea.

"Try not to let the outside of the place spook you," he smiled, "right now it looks like *Wurthering Heights* met the Adam's family, but it's a lot nicer in the summer. Mom has a thing for roses, she's cultivated a few prize winning bushes." They pulled up next to another car, an aquamarine British MG mini from the sixties. "Lottie's here already," Gerry remarked, "I keep telling her she needs to drive something safer, but she thinks it's cute and can't be persuaded to part with it."

Someone inside heard them pull up, Katherine could see from the corner of her eye the front door open as she reached in back for her gift. It was Lottie, she was glad to see a friendly face.

"Welcome Kathy! It's so good to see you! I'm sorry, I haven't had a chance to drop by the gallery since I came back from France," she apologized, giving her a big hug.

"That's all right, you must tell me all about your trip."

"Come in out of the cold first, oh, you didn't have to bring anything," Lottie protested as Katherine handed her the cognac.

"I couldn't stop her," Gerry interjected, his own offering under his arm, "come, we'll introduce you to Pater and Mater."

If the outside of the estate looked like a close second to the haunted mansion ride in Disneyland, the inside was the exact opposite; old world, yes, but completely warm and inviting, she imagined the interior of the old manor could be from a house from one of Grimm or Anderson's fairy tales, or maybe that charming scene in the Nutcracker when the family are enjoying their Christmas party just before the magic begins. The holiday decorations were all taken down by now, but the place retained a festive ambience. Perhaps it was the royal red carpeting with the sprawling gold acanthus leaf pattern, the warm coloured wood, the expansive curved staircase and the wainscoting with its unusual carving, the entrance hall looked more German than Old World English, and the brightly papered walls were laden with pictures of all descriptions enhanced with old style gilt frames. Family photographs, sketches, drawings, watercolours, icons, and of course, oil paintings. She could just get a glimpse of a large portrait up the stairway. Katherine had to control the urge to do a little exploring.

"May I take your coat, Miss?" the butler dutifully asked.

"Kathy, meet Victor," Gerry said as he took off his coat and scarf, "he's the right hand man of the house."

"Pleased to meet you."

"It's a pleasure, Miss Walsingham."

They had hardly removed their coats when another member of the family came to greet them. A steel grey object came flying madly through the air from under one of the large archways and headed straight for Gerry, landing on his right shoulder. It was an African Grey parrot with ashen coloured wings, a white fluffy chest, a short red tail, a large black beak and inquisitive pale yellow eyes brimming with intelligence.

"Ahoy maties! Gerr-eee aboard!" the feathery fellow squawked, bobbing its head up and down.

"Gerry, he heard your car," Lottie noted.

"Hey, how ya doing, squirt? Kathy, meet Captain Sinbad," Gerry said, "he likes plain Sinbad though".

"Perrrrmission to come aboard!" the little fellow bobbed.

"You've got to ask for permission," Lottie explained.

"Oh …er… okay. Permission to come aboard?" Katherine tentatively enquired, watching the feisty bird.

"Yo ho! Step aboard! Arrr, hee hoo!" Sinbad bobbed his head in affirmation. Katherine started to laugh.

"That's his way of saying 'hello'," Gerry smiled.

"He taught him that," Lottie added, nodding to her brother.

"I figured, that's amazing, he sounds exactly like you," Katherine commented.

"They mimic voices as well as they learn phrases. We love him, but he drives us all nuts, we can't figure out who's talking in the house. He calls Victor with Mom's voice all the time, keeps the poor man running."

"How long have you had him, Sinbad I mean?"

"Oh, years now. Mom's allergic to animal fur, so if we wanted a pet other than a fish, it had to be a bird, and we picked a vivacious one, that's for sure."

"Come, don't keep Kathy in the hall, Mom's waiting in the Rose Room," Lottie prodded.

"Anchors aweigh! Anchors aweigh!" Sinbad called out, clutching Gerry's shoulder as he walked towards the large oak doors to the left.

"He sings opera, and musicals too," Lottie added.

"Yeah, listen to this," Gerry affirmed, "*Oh what a beautiful …,*"

"*Morrrrr-ning! Oh what a beautiful daaaeee,*" Sinbad continued, singing at the top of his little lungs in Gerry's exact pitch and tone.

"He over emphasises the parts he likes," Lottie smiled.

After the performance, Katherine could hardly keep a straight face as Mrs. Reinold rose from her armchair to greet them. Stately and precise, dressed in a classic Chanel outfit, her light brown hair elegantly styled, she was not stuffy or overbearing, one glance told Katherine she had a bright, charming personality. She hadn't changed much from the photograph she had seen in Gerry's apartment.

"Hi Mom," Gerry greeted, giving her a kiss on the cheek.

"Kissy, kissy!" Sinbad bobbed.

"Oh, be quiet you. Mom, this is Katherine." They politely shook hands.

"Welcome to *chez* Reinold my dear. Our Gerry has told us so much about you."

"Hello! Hi! How are you?" Sinbad interjected in an unrecognisable male voice, Katherine assumed he must be mimicking Gerry's father.

"Would someone *please* do something with that bird? We won't get a word in edgeways with him today, not with company present. He wants all the attention you see," Mrs. Reinold explained to Katherine. "Lottie, be a dear and put him in his play pen, you know how Mrs. Hunt is when he's loose, she doesn't want him near her."

Handing the cognac to her mother, Lottie plucked the cheeky parrot off Gerry's shoulder and held him in her arms.

"Arrr! Avast! In the brig! No jail! No jail!" the captive pleaded.

"Be good, and we might let you out again later," Lottie said as she took him away.

"Now we might have some peace," Mrs. Reinold sighed. "Thank you, this is my husband's favourite," she noted, looking at the cognac bottle. "I do hope you had a pleasant drive down here, my dear," she enquired.

"Oh yes. It's been a long time since I've been to Long Island. I must say, you have a beautiful home, Mrs. Reinold."

"Thank you, it's been in the family for generations. After we have our luncheon, Gerry and Lottie will give you a tour."

"We'd be delighted," Gerry agreed, "here, let me take all these bottles and put them somewhere. I'll be back in a jiff."

"Come, you must be famished. I do hope you like smoked salmon?" Mrs. Reinold asked. "Gerry said he wasn't picking you up until after church, which would leave you no time for lunch, so I had a light snack prepared for the moment you arrived to help tide you over until dinner this evening, Lobster bisque with egg salad and smoked salmon croissant sandwiches"

"Thank you Mrs. Reinold, that was very kind of you, that sounds delicious."

The Morning Room had been prepared for their luncheon, so Mrs. Reinold suggested they go ahead, everyone would eventually join them.

"My husband should be with us in a minute, some busy-body on the board called him, on a Sunday of all days, and I have no idea what's keeping Mrs. Hunt, she's not usually late," she explained as they went over to the Morning Room.

Katherine was thankful for Sinbad, she felt the stress of the day melt away with his antics, making it easy for her to engage in the pleasantries now that she was alone with Mrs. Reinold. They talked about her gallery, and Katherine enquired about her roses. Of course, it didn't take long before Mrs. Reinold wanted to know all about how she and Gerry first met.

"Oh, Gerry told me of course, but men don't like details. They leave so much out," she explained.

"It's rather funny," Katherine began, "we were sitting next to each other on the plane to Paris, and yet we hardly said 'hello'." Katherine continued, explaining she probably wouldn't have met him again during that trip if she hadn't bumped into his brother first by accident. Then they met again at the Sirrac Gallery, and it all seemed to take off from there.

"Oh yes, that was the night of Yoris' new exhibition. Richard and I couldn't go, something had come up, Gerry and Lottie were very good to make an appearance for us, I remember that night now."

"Did he tell you about starting an auction to bid for my friend's painting?" Katherine smiled.

"No he didn't! Please, do tell."

"Tell what?" Lottie asked as she came into the room, Gerry following behind.

"About the bidding war your brother started over your birthday present."

"Oh that!" Lottie laughed as she sat at the table, Gerry helping her with her chair, "I thought Kevin was about to have a fainting fit from sheer elation. You should have seen the look on his face."

Katherine and Lottie didn't have a chance to tell what happened for at that moment Mr. Reinold popped his head around the door.

"Hello! There you are. We're all eating in here are we?" he smiled before coming into the room. "You must be Katherine," he said holding out his hand, "it's a pleasure to meet you at last."

Tall and robust, blue eyes, his hair now showing more grey than black as shown in Gerry's photograph, but with the same commanding presence. His tanned ruggedness suggested a man who enjoyed the great outdoors although he appeared perfectly at ease in his tailored suit. His manner of speech was short and intermittent, blustery like Gramps could be, perhaps even a little gruff, but judging from his friendly greeting, he did not give the impression he was a short tempered person.

"Pleased to meet you," Katherine replied, shaking hands.

"Please, sit down, don't let your bisque get cold. We've been hearing some wonderful things about your new gallery, apart from Horace's old trash," he clarified as he made his way to his seat. Katherine smiled.

"I've learned to ignore him by now."

"That's good. I'm sorry about your father, heard about it in the papers, and on your opening of all days. I trust he's better now?"

"Yes, much better, thank you for asking."

"You paint too I understand?"

"Kathy's a graduate from Belvedere," Gerry reminded him.

"That's right. I'm currently finishing up a gift for Gerry, it's a panorama of Rome."

"A gift? Well, that's very nice of you," Mrs. Reinold commented.

"She's promised me a picture of the Acropolis when she has a minute," Lottie nodded.

"That is mighty thoughtful," Mr. Reinold nodded. "Do you take commissions by any chance?"

"I never really thought about it," Katherine admitted. "Like portraits?"

"I was thinking more of having a picture done of my yacht," he said reflectively, "I want something appropriate to fit in the Blue Room."

"Oh, he just adores that yacht," Mrs. Reinold said, "I'm petrified every time he takes that thing out sailing. Oh, he has a professional captain and crew, but you know how bad the Atlantic can get."

"Gerry tells me you are more of a traditional artist," Mr. Reinold continued, "that's perfect. I'll gladly pay your going rate."

"Thank you, that's very kind," Katherine replied, "I don't charge anything like you would find in an auction house, I'm just starting out myself. I'm not famous enough yet," she smiled, "but I wish you would view my work before making a decision, and of course, I'd like to visit this Blue Room so I can understand your request."

"Gerry! Haven't you taken our guest on a tour yet?" Mr. Reinold asked his son incredulously.

"Not yet, Richard dear," Mrs. Reinold said, "she just arrived, and lunch was ready."

"Of course. By the way, where's Georgina? I thought she was joining us today."

"She's a little late, Dad," Lottie noted, "I wonder … oh, I hear Victor answering the door, she has just arrived."

"Here I am dearies, sorry for keeping everyone waiting, my hips are not very good today," Mrs. Hunt huffed, leaning heavily on her cane.

"Oh, I'm sorry to hear that. Come, sit down, the bisque will help warm you up."

"Thank you, Sophia. So, how is everyone getting along?" she asked.

"Just swimmingly," Lottie replied, "Dad has just commissioned Kathy to do a painting of the *Morning Glory* for him."

"Actually, they've just begun the negotiations," Gerry clarified, "Kathy hasn't seen the size of the yacht yet."

"Is it big?" Katherine wondered.

"You're going to be painting a lot of sails, let's put it that way, Kathy deary," Mrs. Hunt nodded.

"Oh, is it a *real* sailing ship?" Katherine realized. "Like in the old days?"

"Quite!" Mr. Reinold beamed, "all these modern, motorized, tin can tankers and fibre glass phonies today, no soul," he said shaking his head.

"Dad likes the old wooden beauties," Gerry agreed, "even if he does disparage our cargo fleet that keeps us running."

"Just give me a tall ship …," Mr. Reinold began.

"And a star to steer her by," Katherine smiled.

"Exactly! So, you like poetry too?"

"Some poetry, I'm more of a novel reader to tell the truth," she answered, taking a quick glance around the yellow room. While conversing with Mrs. Reinold, not to mention being side-tracked by the steady stream of arrivals, Katherine hadn't dared to take a glance around the room until now. Situated more to the south, it was bright and cheerful. Perhaps this is where they usually had breakfast she thought. Of course, the one thing she noticed first on the table was the centrepiece: a bouquet of sunflowers. She didn't know if this had been prepared intentionally or not, but Gerry gave her a knowing glance and a little smile.

With everyone's interest in the arts, there were plenty of subjects to discuss, Katherine was relieved that she didn't feel overwhelmed in their company. Mrs. Hunt insisted she drop by her estate one day to pick out works for temporary loan to her gallery, she wasn't far from Stonyvale.

"You just name the day, Kathy deary, you're welcome anytime," she affirmed.

"That's very good of you, maybe sometime at the end of this month perhaps?"

"Splendid!"

"You know, I must stop by and see your gallery," Mr. Reinold mused aloud, "I'm more of an auction buff, but I'm downright curious now."

"Oh, you'll love it," Lottie affirmed.

"Do you have any paintings of your own on display?" Mrs. Reinold wondered.

"Just my Napoléonic sarcasm," Katherine said, "right now, I've got an allegorical series on Socratic-style dialogues in progress."

"How exciting," Lottie exclaimed. "You will let us know when they're finished? I'd love to see them before they get snapped up."

"Of course, you'll be the first to see them."

"Socratic dialogues? Well, Lottie, looks like we have another Graecophile philosopher among us," Mr. Reinold smiled.

"I don't know about that," Katherine replied modestly, "I just like to think out life's anomalies and man's refusal to reason his existence, and try and paint them if I can."

"It's good to actually meet a *creative* artist, you don't find them very often these days," Mr. Reinold noted, "I'm tired of all these squiggly 'isms' that any kindergartener can do. Makes you pity the parents who spent good money on art college for all these so called *wunderkinds*, not to mention question the intelligence of their professors."

Katherine had a feeling she and the Reinolds were going to get along just fine. It wasn't long before the conversation turned to current affairs, notably, the new presidential campaign season, much to Mrs. Reinold's mortification. Her husband loved to discuss politics, and had no qualms asking Katherine what she thought, if she belonged to a particular party, or preferred to be independent in her voting preferences like Gerry. Gerry cast her a humorous glance, his eyebrows raised.

"Before I let Kathy answer, let me warn you she has some unorthodox views about our political system," he interjected, trying to stay serious.

"Oh? I'd like to hear her unorthodox ideas then."

"Well, I don't pretend to know much about politics, but it is my sincere belief that when every politician is relieved from office, they should be given a fifty year sentence without parole for all the deceit they practised throughout their term, and got paid for it too."

"Brava," Lottie agreed.

"Kathy deary, I think you will fit in just perfectly around here," Mrs. Hunt nodded matter-of-factly.

When they finished their fruit flan dessert, Mr. Reinold announced he would personally give Katherine the manor tour.

"Come my dear, you must see the Blue Room first," he said proudly. Gerry looked a little chuffed she had made a favourable impression, but grew rather quiet as he tagged along. They quickly passed through two beautifully ornate rooms, one red and the next in green, before they arrived at Mr. Reinold's pride and joy.

"My father is a bit of an old sea dog," Gerry explained, "but I guess you figured that one out."

Around the room besides the antique leather furniture were old display cabinets of various heights filled with unusual objects, brass compasses, maritime charts, a host of miniature ships in bottles and artefacts of sailing times gone by. The most numerous of the nautical curiosities were oddly shaped white and cream coloured ornaments of all sizes with strange markings on them. On closer inspection, she realized they were whale teeth or whale bone pieces with delicate line drawings carved on the surface that reminded her of old eighteenth-century black and white prints. It was the sailor's scrimshaw art developed from necessity when long voyages left them hours of free time. Using a sharp tool, they etched line drawings into polished ivory, usually taken from whales, and then coloured them with an ink wash. There were a myriad of depictions from patriotic themes with eagles, Washington, Lincoln, and the American flag to name a few, but quite a number of pictures featured whales and whaling ships. She then noticed the paintings decorating the walls, mostly antique seascapes by unknown artists featuring tall ships of every description, sea battles, port scenes, but the most numerous where whaling expeditions, a small band of intrepid sailors casting a bevy of harpoons from their small hunting boats to bring down the great leviathans lunging up from the depths. Katherine soon observed there was not only one Blue Room but three in succession, obviously the singular tense was used for convenience. The other rooms held larger objects, wooden ship wheels with their elegant spoked handle grips, brass ship lamps, a collection of globes, and in addition to the paintings of tall ships, rows of oars and harpoons and harpoon barbs, *lots* of harpoons she noticed.

"Do you like whaling?" she quietly asked.

"Hmm? Oh, that. These rooms display part of the family history as you can see, our ... museum in a manner of speaking. Didn't Gerry tell you?"

"I was hoping to spare her this place on her first visit," he sheepishly admitted, before turning to Katherine, "our family fortune began with whaling."

"Oh no...!"

She put her hand to her mouth with a mixture of surprise and dismay, but at the same time, couldn't help laughing when she saw his embarrassed expression.

"Oh no? What's the matter?" Mr. Reinold wondered.

"Kathy told me she wanted to volunteer a tour of duty on the *Rainbow Warrior*," Gerry hinted.

"I see," Mr. Reinold chuckled, "well, I do hope you won't hold what happened over a hundred years ago against us, we don't hunt whales anymore, just shipping contracts. In fact, Gerry here insists we donate to Greenpeace to make up for what he describes as our past follies."

"That's a relief," she replied with a smile. "Well, I now have an idea how you would like your painting, something classical, like this," she said, approaching one canvas depicting the old port of Manhattan bustling with ship masts.

"Exactly. Like that passage out of *Leaves of Grass*," he noted, "but something that reflects today. Could you do something with the modern Manhattan skyline in the background?"

"Sure, that shouldn't be a problem. I might be able to work one of the bridges in, though I would need to see your yacht to get the proper dimensions."

"Hmm, this will be a post-winter project then, the *Morning Glory* looks her best in vernal and summer sunlight anyhow," he reflected.

"That will give me time to finish Lottie's painting too," she noted, "how big do you want your canvas?"

"Oh … about so big," he said, indicating with his hands before giving the approximate dimensions, "maybe two meters in length, one meter in height, nothing too major, it's just that each generation adds something to these rooms, so I figured it's about time I make my contribution."

"Okay, but I really would like you to see my style before you decide."

"Very well, not this week however, maybe sometime later."

"I'm usually available at the gallery each day, just drop by."

"I'll do that. Come, since you're a literary buff, I suppose the library is the next port of call." However, they were interrupted by Victor before they could conduct her to the next place of interest.

"I'm sorry to disturb you sir, but Mr. Notherby just called. He's on the telephone, he says he must speak with you."

"Not him too? I'm sorry my dear, the board members are all up in arms about a certain shipping account. I'm afraid this may take some time, so Gerry will finish the tour, if you don't mind."

"Not at all," Katherine smiled.

"All right, see you later," he said leaving the two of them alone.

"This way, my lady," Gerry said, offering his arm.

"Gerry, I can't believe you grew up here, it's a fantastic house, you could easily get lost," she said as he led her through a series of doors through another hallway and into the library. It was so large, the upper bookshelves had rollable ladders, and separate walkways bordered with delicate iron railings that were ascended by small spiral staircases.

"I know. A film crew wanted to use Stonyvale for *The Great Gatsby*, but Mom was afraid they might destroy the place in the process, so she refused. I think they eventually gave up the idea of shooting on Long Island due to the costs involved and went somewhere else."

"Well I'm not surprised this was one of their choices, look at this," she smiled, climbing one of the spiral staircases, "I can't believe you wanted to move into the city!"

"Oh, don't get me wrong, I'm attached to the old manor all right, I don't think the city will be permanent. Like Mom said, this place gets handed down from one generation to the next. This is a rather personal revelation," he continued thoughtfully, "but I think you'll understand: a man's got to get out sometime and become independent to a point, find his own identity before he completely shoulders a time-honoured legacy. Perhaps I'm not expressing my ideas clearly … ."

"Yes, I do understand, I'm from an established legacy too," she said, coming back down the stairs.

"Listen to me prattle on, we've got a large area to cover before dinner," he smiled, offering his arm once more, "we can return to a room that catches your eye for a more detailed look later."

"Whatever you say, Lancelot."

Just how many rooms are there? With all the twists and turns, she had lost her sense of direction. They had already run out of colours, and still there was a room filled with paintings, a game room, a music room, someplace that used to be called the sewing room, although making needlepoint objects was no longer a pastime, then Gerry decided to double track again and take her down one large hallway. Opening a large set of doors, and turning on the lights, he revealed a ballroom with three large glittering chandeliers and a polished dance floor.

"I can't believe your family has one of these too."

"Of course, then there's the hothouse designed after the greenhouse in the British botanical gardens … hmm, what else? I've lost track, and this is just the downstairs," he laughed. "It's a shame, most of the place is locked up half the time. It was designed during those days when it was customary to invite lots of company, guests stayed for weeks, not just a weekend. I have to admit, the upkeep is ridiculous, it would be more practical to turn it into a hotel. I don't know what got into my great great grandfather's head when he designed the whole thing."

"Maybe he visited the Winchester Mansion at one point and wanted to copy it," she laughed.

"Probably! Once he got started, he couldn't stop adding rooms. I must admit, this was great for playing Hide and Seek when we were kids. Why of course, the dining room! How could I have missed that?" he suddenly 'remembered', snapping his fingers.

"We'll be heading there soon enough I suppose," she smiled.

"Well, now that we're *here*," he replied with a distinguished note in his voice, making a little bow and extending his hand, "may I have the honour of the next dance, m'lady?"

"Why, I'd be delighted, m'lord," she said with a low curtsey, taking his hand.

Assuming a waltz pose, he sang two words with an exaggerated pause, preparing her from an energetic sweep around the room on the third.

"*Shall, we ... dance?*"

On cue, Katherine provided the necessary instrumental accompaniment, *boom boom boom*, as they followed in Yul Brynner and Deborah Kerr's footsteps.

> *On a bright cloud of music shall we fly?*
> *(Boom, boom, boom!)*
> *Shall we dance?*
> *(Boom, boom, boom!)*
> *Shall we then say 'Goodnight' and mean 'Goodbye'?*
> *(Boom, boom, boom!)*
> *Or perchance,*
> *When the last little star has left the sky,*
> *Shall we still be together,*
> *With our arms around each other*
> *And shall you be my new romance?*
> *On the clear understanding*
> *That this kind of thing can happen,*
> *Shall we dance? Shall we dance? Shall we dance?"*

Exhausting the lyrics, Gerry continued to 'la la la' the melody, Katherine adding the accompaniment as they sprightly waltzed around the room. At last, they ran out of breath and stopped for a minute.

"You can't … tell me … anyone …can sing … and dance…at the same time," Katherine gasped before laughing herself completely breathless.

"You only … had the … boom boom booms," he wheezily pointed out.

"Gosh, that was fun," she puffed. A few seconds later, he straightened up, and holding his hand out to her like the King of Siam, declared:

"Come, we do it again! One two three, *and* one two three, *and* one …"

"So this is where you two are," Lottie noted, peeking into the ballroom.

"Hi Lottie, just one more turn," he called out.

"Okay, but Mom and Mrs. Hunt are wondering where you are, dinner is almost ready."

When they finally stopped after the second dance, Gerry had taken an extra two turns instead of one, Katherine sat on one of the gilt chairs near the wall.

"I should … call you … Sir Dancealot … from now on," she smiled.

Just before dinner was served in the formal dining room, Katherine was amused to find Gerry retrieving the sunflowers from the Morning Room and poking the cheery yellow blooms between the red roses in the centrepiece.

"Gerry, what's gotten into you? You've ruined my breakfast posy, and our dinner display," his mother protested with a puzzled frown, catching him in the act.

"I'm … just being artistic," he covered.

"If you felt artistically inclined, why couldn't you have at least taken the pink roses from the Rose Room?"

Lottie, who had never seen her brother quite like this, thought the proceedings rather funny.

"He knows I like sunflowers," Katherine shyly explained, a little mortified he had been reprimanded for trying to please her.

"Well, that's all right then," Mrs. Reinold replied. "Lottie, will you put the ships on the table? Dinner is in five minutes. Now where's you father?" she asked rhetorically, leaving the room.

"Oh, we're being *that* fancy today, are we?" Gerry observed with quiet satisfaction.

"Ships?" Katherine wondered.

Lottie practically skipped to one of the silver display cabinets and took out what Katherine thought were ornamental collectables, two sailing ships crafted in silver, but protruding from the 'hatches' were little silver spoon handles, the argent vessels were in fact salt and pepper holders.

"A good sign," Lottie revealed, "because they're so hard to keep polished, she only brings these out for holidays, special occasions, and for people she likes."

"Mom does it subconsciously, but we figured it out," Gerry smiled.

"That's good to know, but what if she doesn't like someone?" Katherine mused.

"The porcelain ones from the Morning Room are brought over, my first boyfriend got them," Lottie confessed, "she didn't like him one bit, same for his first girlfriend too," she added, nodding to Gerry. "Then there are business associates from the board she can't stand, but since she has to entertain them for Dad's sake, they get the porcelain shakers as well. Then if there's someone she hasn't made up her mind about, they get the crystal ones over there," she concluded, indicating another cabinet.

After the luncheon, Katherine didn't think she would be able to eat dinner. Funny, it was not like her to lose her appetite, but dancing with Gerry may have helped somewhat. It felt quite comfortable being with his family, getting to know them, hearing more about their colourful shipping history while she shared stories about her family with them, discussing current events, listening to Lottie's descriptions of her extended vacation to France and Mrs. Hunt's cantankerous grumbling about so-and-so from the last society get together, laughing with all the jokes and offering a few she knew in return, in all, it felt good to be … welcome. She was also discovering more about Gerry from those closest to him, including a few surprises she hadn't expected. When then finished dinner, Mrs. Reinold suggested the ladies go to the Rose Room to enjoy their coffee while the men went into the Red Room to have their brandy and cigars.

"Gerry, I didn't know you smoked *cigars*," Katherine replied incredulously as they all filed into the entrance hall, astonished to find he could indulge in a malodorous habit like that.

"Oh, not often," he reassured her, "only to please my Dad, he gets Havanas smuggled in copiously. Once in a while he likes to have company that shares his smelly vice. You don't mind if I leave you with the ladies?"

"Not at all, I'm having a wonderful time, go ahead with your father, I'll be just fine."

"Okay we'll join you shortly."

Now that the ladies were alone, Lottie had additional news that she hadn't imparted to the family yet.

"I didn't tell you everything about Paris," she smiled, "I met someone while I was there."

"What? And you're only revealing it now?" her mother exclaimed.

"It's nothing serious, we just met a few times and talked, it may not go anywhere, in all likelihood, it might just remain a casual acquaintance."

"Now don't hold us in suspense, Lottie deary," Mrs. Hunt piped. "Who is he? Not a Frenchman I hope?"

"Oh Mrs. Hunt, don't be like that. He's from Manhattan, he owns a construction firm, he's building that new skyscraper," Lottie informed them. "He was on vacation, we bumped into each other in a restaurant and we just started chatting. He had seen me around town, New York that is, but never introduced himself, so he told me."

"Well, who is he?" her mother prompted.

"David Cunningham."

"I know him," Katherine interjected, "well, not personally, but I've met him a couple of times. I haven't seen him in awhile, but he comes to our Club, especially for the golf tournaments. He seems like a very nice guy."

"Cunningham? Hmm, Cunningham," Mrs. Hunt mused, rubbing her chin, "construction firm …oh yes, the name rings a bell now. Aren't his parents members of the local historical society?"

"Why of course. Now imagine that, you had to go all the way to Paris to meet him," Mrs. Reinold smiled.

"He wanted to take me out sometime after I got back home, he gave me his number, but I haven't called him yet," Lottie admitted. "It just seems too soon after … well, you know," she finished wistfully. Poor Lottie, she was referring to her deceased fiancé.

"Oh my dear, no one could ever take Alexander's place," Mrs. Reinold consoled, "that's understood, but there is no betrayal in meeting someone else. If you do find love again, it won't diminish what you felt and continue to feel for him, you'll just experience it in a different way."

"I know, it sounds callous for everyone to keep telling you to 'move on'," Mrs. Hunt added, "but do give it a try, you may just get to like the young fellow. What do you think, Kathy deary?"

"Oh … well," Katherine wanted to help Lottie and give her encouragement, but she felt so tangled up in her own emergent feelings for Gerry, so wasn't sure if she was the best person to seek advice from at that moment, but she gave the best answer she could. "It wouldn't hurt giving him a call at least, you said it might not come to anything serious, and if it does, I agree with your mother, don't pass up an opportunity that could make you happy, I think you deserve that, Lottie."

"There now, listen to Kathy deary," Mrs. Hunt nodded.

"You think I should, Kathy?"

"Why not? One call, one lunch, you don't have to take it any further if you don't want to."

"Okay … I'll think about it. He does seem rather nice."

Katherine hoped she had given her the right advice. She only half paid attention to their conversation after that, Lottie's emotional conundrum only intensified her own feelings. Just *what* did she feel for Gerry? Was it just an intense crush or infatuation? One of those 'whirlwind romances' she heard about that fizzle out after a few months? That didn't sound good. Her thoughts meandered to the riddle he gave her, he promised that would help, but how? She listened to it every day, and still she couldn't make anything of it, she now knew the Sinatra tracks off by heart, including every skip and jump, and still it felt like the tape was some ancient hieroglyph she had no idea how to crack. The solution was probably staring her in the face, if only she could see the answer.

"We're back ladies, did we miss anything?" Mr. Reinold asked as he and Gerry entered the room, a faint whiff of cigar smoke trailing in with them.

"Only that our Lottie has met someone new," Mrs. Hunt proffered.

Of course, they had to hear all about it, so Lottie was obliged to repeat everything before she could continue with her story how she and David met. However, while Gerry said he was pleased for her, somehow, he looked a little lost in thought, his mind preoccupied elsewhere. Perhaps he was also probing his own feelings Katherine mused. He didn't have long to ruminate. Mrs. Reinold was about to suggest everyone have another cup of coffee when the clock on the mantle began to chime nine.

"As much as I hate to break up our little party, I promised I'd get Kathy home at a reasonable hour."

"Oh yes," Katherine replied regretfully, "I have to be up bright and early."

"Now that's a pity," Mrs. Hunt frowned, she was enjoying the company.

"Of course, but they do have a long drive back," Mrs Reinold replied as they all stood up.

"Well we won't press you to stay longer then, it's been a pleasure," Mr. Reinold said. "I hope you will visit us again soon."

"Thank you, I had a wonderful day, thank you for your hospitality."

"You're welcome Kathy, if you're in the area, come by anytime, our door is always be open," Mrs. Reinold nodded.

As she said her goodbyes, Gerry called Victor who promptly brought their coats. Everyone was sorry to see them leave and waved from the front door as they drove off. It was dark now, and the outside of the estate looked more intimidating than ever, but the sight of the glistening bright porch lamps with his family and Mrs. Hunt waving from the open doorway showing a glimpse of the colourful hallway behind them revealed the genuine warmth that emanated from within.

"There, that wasn't bad now, was it? So, what do you think?"

"I know this is our first introduction, but I like your family, very much."

"And they like you, I can tell, the silver ships never lie," he chuckled, "now if only I knew what you parents think about *me*."

"Well, I don't have anything like silver ships to judge by, but I do believe they like you. Knowing Pops, I would definitely have been given a rat-a-tat-tat by now if he didn't approve."

"Maybe it's the crystal shakers for me," Gerry said half to himself, "never mind, that's still good, it means there's hope, they haven't written me off as a complete scoundrel."

"Oh Gerry," she laughed, "they're not that bad, just overly protective where I'm concerned."

"I know, Princess. Oh, it's a pity it's dark now, I have half a mind to steal an extra ten minutes with you, just be by ourselves and look out on the sea, it's beautiful in the moonlight." She agreed, that sounded like a perfect idea.

"It's not too dark, we might still watch the waves come in."

A few minutes later, he pulled up at a lookout point, they could discern the outline of the waves, and rolling the windows down halfway, they breathed in the sea air while listening to the surf breaking on the shore. Instinctively they reached out and held hands, sitting quietly for a minute.

"This is nice, you like the sea like your Pops, don't you?"

"Well, not as avidly as he does, he's an all-out seafarer. I'm more of a landlubber and prefer to admire it from a safe distance, so I'm a bit of a disappointment to him in that regard, but thank goodness we have an interest in art. Pete takes more after him in the sailing department."

"I'm the same, I don't know anything about sailing, but I find listening to the ocean captivating."

They sat in silence again for a few moments before he started the engine.

"I could sit all night with you, but it's getting late," he sighed with a regretful tone that for some reason made her a little concerned.

"You sound as if we won't see each other again, are you all right?"

"I'm sorry, I didn't mean to alarm you," he said, pausing for a moment, and then turning off the engine. "It's just ... my father dropped an unexpected request on me tonight."

"It sounds serious."

"It's just business, but a rather unwelcome interruption right now. Apart from the odd executive meeting, making routine inspections at our various global hubs is part of the job. We don't rely completely on all the reports we get. It's Dad's policy we should always see things for ourselves. Like he says, no one else is going to be as concerned for the business since it's not theirs."

"He does have a point, I can't argue with that," Katherine agreed.

"But sometimes it can be a right pain, we end up missing a few holidays every now and again, these global inspections are the pits."

"Global? That sounds like forever!"

"Oh, we've split it up, we don't do the world at once. I've been given a part of Asia and Australia this time around, Dad will be taking South America and Africa. The thing is, these inspections take weeks, even months depending on the nature of the job and what we find. Blast, the Asian route always seems to run that long, but Dad says he wants me to understand the ropes over there."

"You mean you'll be gone all that time? When do you have to go?"

Katherine understood he had to travel, but to be gone for a month, maybe more? That seemed like a very long time not to have Gerry dropping around for lunch or whisking her off to some cosy dinner for two. Already she could feel the pangs of separation, and he was sitting right next to her.

"We usually end up leaving around springtime, but this time I was asked to start out early, seems like we have regional managers upsetting our clients and I have to settle a few ruffled feathers, however, I put my foot down and said you and I are not missing out on our first Valentine's Day and that's flat. At least I was able to wrangle that deal."

What was that? Valentine's Day? Her heart gave a little skip at the thought, she had never spent it in a romantic way before, usually the day meant sending and receiving cute Cupid cards and heart shaped sugar candies, but it was all in platonic celebration of friendship. This time, it would not be like that, it would be ... special.

"Valentine's Day! Yes, at least we shall have that before you have to go. What should we do? We've already spent some wonderful evenings together, this should be different."

"Is there anything you would like to do in particular, Princess?"

"On the hop, I can't think. Perhaps you have an idea prepared, you have a wonderful way of surprising me, I'll leave it all up to you, Lancelot," she smiled, giving his hand a little squeeze.

"Well, our rendition of the *King and I* today gave me the perfect idea: how about a night of music and dancing? I know just the place, and since you are now cured of your dance-a-phobia, that would certainly be a lovely way to spend the night."

"Gerry, I hadn't thought of that, I've avoided those kinds of places for so long, I never considered it, but I'd love to go dancing with you."

"That's settled then, we shall have that night, and a whole month of cappuccino, croissants and hot fudge cake before I have to don the traveller's cloak and wander to the Far East. Will you miss your poor exiled Lancelot?"

"Oh of course, a month away is so long, I hope it won't go to two. But I understand, duty calls."

"My brave Princess," he smiled, reaching up and stroking her cheek. He then leaned forward and they kissed, but she couldn't make it last, she suddenly had the urge to laugh and muffled her face on his woollen lapel.

"What is it?" he asked a little puzzled.

"That wasn't chocolate cake, more like … Cuba," she chuckled, still muffled against his shoulder. He then remembered the cigar.

"I'm so sorry! I forgot. Quick, be a dear and hand me my emergency kit, it's in the glove compartment." Curious, she rummaged around and found a new package of breath mints. "That's it," he confirmed, emptying a small mound of the concentrated flavour pastilles in his hand and popping them into his mouth in one swipe. Katherine thought she'd better have a few too. "What? That bad was it?"

"Well, a little extra help wouldn't hurt," she replied.

However, they couldn't hold a second kiss either, the mintiness was so overpowering, they had to stop and catch their breath.

"At least I spared you a second trip to Havana," he noted.

"But took me to a Clorets factory instead."

They laughed so much Gerry got a stitch in his side and the tears started to run from her eyes. At last, he started the engine, it was time to go.

"I'd better get you home Princess, but I'm determined we shall make one last attempt to get it right before we say our goodnights, mints or no mints."

"Third time's a charm, so they say."

ଓଃ❀ଃ୭

The alarm clock rang for some time before it finally broke through her dream. Darn it, not now! It felt like she had just fallen asleep, and she was in such a wonderful place. She and Gerry were walking together holding hands on a moonlit beach. He was singing the songs recorded on her mystery tape with the strange pauses included, stopping every now and again to ask if she had discovered the answer yet, but all she could do was shake her head. Trying to hold on to this image, she hit the snooze button, but it was too late, the dream faded as consciousness took over. Sitting up in bed, she realized she still had her headphones on; his music had sent her to sleep. Why did she always have nice dreams on days she had to get up early? No time to question the mechanics of the subconscious mind now, she had a board meeting to attend, and hopefully, see one mystery resolved.

Her father was a little surprised to see her make an appearance at the head office, but she explained Steves wanted her to be there that day.

"He said something about 'making family history', so I think he just wants an audience."

"I don't know what your brother has cooked up this time," he said, "but since the Kraylors refuse to tell me what they've discovered and insist he has some important news, I'm almost afraid to find out, but I'm going ahead with this impromptu meeting as they suggested."

"Why he asked for this is beyond me, but I suppose we shall have to wait," Gramps added as the other members began to arrive.

"Knowing Steven, this should be interesting," Uncle Tim noted.

At last, they were all settled around the large mahogany meeting table, Steves the last one to enter the room, bearing a briefcase. He certainly looked very official decked in a navy suit.

"I do hope you have something important to report after calling us together like this," his father stated.

"Yes, indeed I do. I apologize to everyone for the untimely summons, but Walsingham Industries has been subjected to the ravages of a corporate mole," he imperiously declared. There was a sudden flurry of murmuring around the table, Mr. Morgan began to shift uncomfortably in his seat. Wow, she had never seen Steves so business-like, a little dramatic,

684

but she was definitely impressed. She was glad to be there and decided to sit back and watch the proceedings.

"A mole? Who?" Gramps thundered. If there was one thing he could not tolerate, it was disloyalty.

"If everyone will bear with me, I shall get to that in a minute."

"Your computer program caught someone in the act," Mr. Zedder realized.

"Precisely. I apologize to everyone for the new set up, I know it was a nuisance, but I'm glad to report it's paid off. I had a tip from someone inside who I promised not to reveal," Steves said, giving Katherine a knowing glance, "but with their information, I was able to track down the computers that were targeted. In response, I set up another program that would take our hacker into a decoy mainframe with worthless but important-looking information for them to 'steal'. However, their stolen data had a third program hidden in a special file that would be activated once the information was downloaded onto our spy's computer, and any other computer for that matter."

"What was this third program suppose to do?" Mrs. Thornton wanted to know.

"It would send me back e-mails revealing the guilty computers, and therefore the guilty party, or parties. If you would all care to take a look at the booklet," he said, handing spiral ringed pads out, "you will see where my program was downloaded."

Katherine turned to the first page, Morgan's name and computer license data was the first on the list, followed by some names she didn't recognise, but were explained in a column on the right: computers registered to the head offices and labs of Snepres Biotech, one of their biggest competitors.

"Now please, is this substantial evidence?" Mr. Morgan sneered. "How can we be certain this is not a set up? For all we know," he said, turning to Harold, "your son could have hacked into my computer and those of Snepres Biotech to ensure I was ingloriously removed from the board. We all know how dexterous he is with binary code. Do you have *any* proof that I even took information from your computers?"

"I'm *so* glad you asked," Steves said. "Could someone turn off the lights please?"

Katherine reached up and hit the switch as Steves started the video on the TV set he had rolled in for the occasion. The board watched aghast as they saw Mr. Morgan rifling around the office and insert the strange device into the unsuspecting employee's computer.

"Everyone please note the date and time in the corner of the screen. Mr. Morgan, would you care to explain to the board why you were in our Jersey offices at that hour of the morning carrying a sophisticated hacking device?"

Of course, he couldn't.

When Katherine switched the lights back on, everyone had a startled look on their faces, Uncle Tim looked disgusted, while Gramps and Pops were plain grim. Mr. Morgan, however, had turned a curious shade of green.

"I think we have seen enough here," Pops replied cooly. "Are we agreed?" The board, including Uncle Tim, simply nodded. Katherine did too, even though she was not officially a member. "Mr Morgan, I expect your resignation on my desk the first thing in the morning. If you don't mind, your presence is no longer needed or welcome here."

The mole simply pushed back his chair, rose up from his seat, and after straightening his jacket, made a huffy exit. That was that. The board members erupted with a myriad of exclamations as soon as he had left the room.

"That was some fancy detective work, m'boy," Gramps beamed.

"My God, I can't believe I trusted him," Uncle Tim replied, knotting his fist.

"Well, most of us did," Mr. Riordan said, "I had the misfortune to nominate him for the position here, my apologies Gregory, Harold," he said nodding to them.

"There's no need for that," Pops said, shaking his head, "however, now that we are all here, we have two pressing matters to address," he continued.

"To find a new board member," Gramps interjected.

"Yes, and the fact that a number of our voting shares are being snapped up by a host of small companies in a way I find disturbing," he continued.

"Forgive me for interrupting," Steves stepped in, "but I can address both matters in one blow. Would someone care to nominate me to the board?"

"What? What are you going on about?" Gramps blurted.

"Is this another one of your jokes?" Uncle Tim enquired.

"As much as I appreciate this public demonstration of filial fidelity, aren't you a little inexperienced to be on the board right now? You haven't finished your graduate degree yet," his father pointed out.

"Not completely inexperienced," he smiled. "If you must know, most of those small companies you are worried about are actually my subsidiaries. Taken together, I now control seventeen percent of the voting rights."

As if they hadn't had enough to take in that morning, the board was stunned into silence.

"What? Can't I invest in a company I have complete faith in?" Steves joked.

"But where on earth did you get that kind of funding?" Pops queried, knitting his brows.

"Hrumph! Even my trust fund for you would never have covered all of that," Gramps added.

"That's why I've been carefully making my own savings grow over the years long before you gave me the fund. You didn't think I would figure the stock markets out eventually, did you?"

Gramps began to laugh, bringing his cane down with a hearty thump.

"There! I knew he could handle that little nest egg! Well, m'boy, I should have guessed!"

"Seventeen percent, that means with Dad and Har … ." Uncle Tim noted aloud, "I'm nullified. Why you sneaky rascal, to go and do that to your uncle!" Shocked by Steve's news, Katherine thought her uncle would be angry, but was surprised to see him looking a little amused with the proceedings. "I graciously yield to the majority," he smiled. "So Steven, do you think you're ready to become an executive member here?"

"Well, I have no objections having another Walsingham on the board," Mr. Conrad interrupted with a chuckle, "but if your father and uncle don't mind me butting in, my advice is to wait until you finish your stint at MIT, get your head cleared of that first before you assume anything here."

"That advice is greatly appreciated," Pops agreed. "And what about your lab work, Steven? I was planning on you to help us in our research department."

"Who says I have to give that up? Can't I do both?" Steves asked.

"In fact, I *would* like to see another qualified scientist join our team," Tim added.

"The boy has brains to burn," Gramps jumped in, "he's itching for a real challenge, that's what it is. If he says he can do it, we can at least give him a chance, when he's graduated that is," giving Steves a hint.

"I suppose the sudden 'resignation' of Mr. Morgan has given us an emergency situation," Pops noted, "and according to the company policy, we have some time to find another replacement.   You should be finished college by the time we have to formally make a decision.”

“Fine by me,” Steves beamed.

“And what should we do about Snepres BioTech?” Mr. Merrick enquired. “Do you wish to consider legal proceedings?”

“We found their mole, but we probably don’t have enough to bring them to court,” Uncle Tim noted, “well, it wouldn’t be worth the legal costs, considering they didn’t get anything.”

“Just what *did* you give them, Steves?” Gramps wondered.

To the amusement of all present, Steves proceeded to list off some strange homoeopathic remedies he discovered in medieval texts, but when he got to one item in particular … he decided to whisper it in Gramp’s ear.

“What! Not the … well, serves them right if they try and pirate generics of *that*!” Gramps chortled.

“However, I predict a backlash about to happen,” Steves continued, addressing the board again. If the saboteurs feel in any way vindictive about the little stunt I pulled on them with those quack formulas, they may try and release a mudslinging campaign reporting how we’re researching old charlatan recipes, make us look ridiculous in the news to shake investors’ confidence and slash our share price, do anything to bring us down.”

“Hmm, quick thinking Steves,” Gramps agreed.

“I don’t know if they’d go that far,” Uncle Tim mused, “but we can always counter false reports with press releases of our own.”

“Still, Steven has a point, if they set up a spy in our midst, they’re capable of anything,” Pops noted. “So for the record, let us take this as a warning: if this scenario presented to us occurs, I firmly request that you refrain from buying up depreciating shares, or we could be accused of a ruse to manipulate the markets and be charged with insider trading.”

“Very well, we won’t fall into that trap,” Mr. Zedder nodded.

“We should nip it in the bud, get Tim’s program started in advance of any problems,” Gramps proposed, “we should prepare a news release we discovered a mole and that they have been duly removed from their position.”

“Having a board member sell us out, I can just imagine the news frenzy this will create,” Uncle Tim replied.

“Father is right, a media frenzy can’t be avoided, and it’s best if we make a statement first before Snepres can start anything. I’ll have the PR department get on it right away. Now are there any other pressing matters to be attended to?”

“Didn’t we have enough?” Mr. Conrad quietly commented.

"I suppose we have. I hope there won't be any more surprises from *you*," Pops said, raising an eyebrow as he turned to Steves.

"No, that's it for now," he assured him before wryly adding, "should I ever plan to use the firm to develop biological weapons, I'll let you all know."

The board members muffled their laughter, they knew Steves and his warped sense of humour by now. In all probability, he would be the first to develop a cure for cancer, not decimate a population.

"Then this meeting is adjourned. I must say, we've had quite an eventful morning."

"You've said a mouthful there," Gramps agreed.

Although the meeting was now over, everyone lingered around the table for a few minutes, catching up on news.

"Gosh Steves, what a bombshell! You became a gazillionaire without letting us know? At least you could have shown me how to make my trust fund grow a bit faster, a little extra wouldn't go amiss to finish off the upper floor of the gallery."

"Sorry Kats, when I do take risks, I like to do it with my own cash, but if you're willing to let me suggest some trends I see coming, you can make that little bit extra in a short time. I have a feeling cell phones are really going to hit it big in the next couple of years, practically explode on a massive scale, perhaps even sooner than we think."

"Cell phones? Why? I don't think people would like being available *all* hours of the day and night, you'd have no privacy left. I can't see it becoming that popular."

"Trust me, the devices are going to be smaller and lighter like the communicators on *Star Trek*, and they won't be just phones anymore, I hear from the computer science majors in MIT that we'll have cameras in them, and perhaps be able to hook up to our e-mail."

"That sounds creepy actually, no one will talk to anyone face to face anymore, we'll all become semi-solitaires plugged into a machine. It'll be the end of society as we know it."

"Shake your head all you want, but that's what I'd invest in. Oh, and the internet is also going to explode, just watch and wait, like cell phones, it'll be a global phenomenon."

"Well, if you can show me how to invest in the market, I'll try a small investment, see how it goes."

"That's the spirit."

At last, the board members decided it was time to head off to lunch or attend to other appointments on their agendas. The family were the last to leave.

"I know this isn't official yet, but since you're about to come on board," Gramps noted to Steves, "I think we should celebrate."

Katherine knew what that meant, a grand executive lunch at the 21 Club, and as Steves was going to be the next member of the family to assume his rightful place in the firm, it was tradition that he choose an item from the company inventory to donate to the ceiling of the eccentric Bar Room.

"I was thinking of taking a box of Great Gramp's famous you-know-whatsits from our archive room, but decided to settle for a bottle of cough syrup, it was one of the first projects I helped with," Steves declared, taking a bottle with a now dated looking label out of his briefcase.

"You certainly came all prepared, didn't you?" Uncle Tim laughed.

"Well, I hope you gentleman have a nice lunch," Katherine said, "I've got to go."

"Oh no, Kats. Please join us, like I said, this is family history, you should be there."

Katherine felt torn; before, she would have jumped at the opportunity to see her brother finally grow up and take his place in the world, but now, she had another lunch arrangement.

"Well, you see, Gerry and I were suppose to meet for lunch, he'll be leaving on this semi-global tour of his company's holdings in a month, so we won't have a lot of time to get together."

"In that case, why not call him and ask if he would like to join us? We can wait for him to arrive," Steves suggested.

"Would you do that, Steves? Could I, Pops? Is that all right?"

"Sure Kathy, but you'd better call before he leaves his office," Pops replied.

"My office is closer, use my phone," Uncle Tim offered.

Katherine checked the clock, Pops was right, she hoped she hadn't missed him already. She was relieved to hear his secretary say he was just leaving, she caught him just in time.

"Hey Princess, what's up? Not a lunch cancellation I hope?"

"No, just a change of venue, if that's all right. The senior executives of Walsingham Industries are about to take a new member on the board, a.k.a. my brother, so according to our time honoured custom, it's a big lunch at the 21 Club. I was wondering, would you like to join us? Usually this is the men's day out, but my brother wants me to come, so I can't refuse, and they said it would be fine if I invited you."

"I don't want to intrude on such a momentous event, but if your family says it's all right, then I'll meet you there. Anyway, I haven't picked up my new scarf yet," he laughed, "they usually hang on to it for me until I can drop by."

"You collect them too?"

"Oh yeah," he affirmed, "it's just a bit of fun. Lottie usually ends up getting it."

What a fun tradition, all the regulars of the 21 Club received a special silk scarf at Christmas time that was uniquely numbered and featured a logo or insignia of the establishment that in time had become a trendy collector's item. She didn't know he liked to go there too, but perhaps she should have guessed.

È✻

Gerry was leaving on February the fifteenth, this news made each day seem to slip by faster than the last. Never before did she find it so difficult to concentrate on work and everything else that demanded her attention, there was no option but to carry on. Perhaps staying busy was best. Horace had recommended some artists, and that helped to keep her mind on the business. At first, she was afraid he might send a few slap-happy painters who opted to pitch house paint on a bed sheet, or use a squirt gun in lieu of paintbrushes, but she was pleasantly surprised to find their endeavours were not as outlandish as she feared, more surrealist in fact, thank goodness not overt ugliness paraded as beauty. One morning she was amused to find Horace ... Smith ... all wrapped in his dashing trench coat with two black art cases waiting patiently outside before opening hours. He decided to take her up on her offer to show some works he had laying around and brought in seven canvases.

"They may not sell, but what the heck, I had to finish them. It's worth a shot, right?"

Knowing Horace, Katherine wondered what Smith was capable of producing, but when he opened his cases and produced his work, she was amazed. At first glance she could tell he had a passion for nocturnal scenes, each painting depicting a facet of New York or Brooklyn from bustling outdoor café life, to the twinkling skyline of Manhattan, sombre back streets lit with eerie orange or stark incandescent lights, street musicians, open markets, in all, a slice of the city when the day-timers were asleep. She then noticed the signature: C.S. Turris.

"That's interesting."

"My … what did you called it? A *nome de pinceau*? I decided to keep my two initials, but needed an appellation that sounded stylish in two syllables to cover my identity. It came to my attention that most artists have last names with only two syllables. You will keep my identity a secret?"

"Of course, but preparing your bio for the customers will be difficult."

"Not really," he said, handing her a sheet with his biographical information, minus his day job, "I just wrote Christopher Smith's data, not the Hacker's; with a name like 'Turris', they won't be able to make the Smith and Horace connection, or so I hope."

Time to go he decided, he didn't want to be caught anywhere near his own work for the present. She pointed out they still needed to discuss the dollar value for his paintings. Now, this created the opportunity for him to invite her out to lunch later that day, but she had to politely decline, explaining she had a previous engagement.

"Maybe another time?" he enquired.

Nuts, business was business, it looked like she would have to drop one lunch with Gerry. She could be wrong, but she had the feeling Christopher had taken a special liking to her, if so, she had better let him down gently.

"All right, but you must understand, it will be strictly business. You see, I have a boyfriend."

"Alas! Alack! Forsooth! The stars were not aligned the day we met," he said in an overly melodramatic tone, casting his hand to his forehead in mock grief. "Who's the lucky guy, or may I ask?"

"I'm not going to tell you, you'll just blurt it out to Beatrice the Beastie," she laughed. Beatrice the Beastie, or Beatrice Brandis, the lead gossip columnist at his paper and every inch as notorious as the Hacker.

"What? Moi? Honestly, I swear I won't tell her, but if a paparazzi spots you and your mysterious boyfriend, there's nothing I can do," he mischievously smiled.

"What? You'll have your camera boys case the place? How awful! You're terrible!"

"I'm just kidding. I wouldn't do that."

"Does the 'I' refer to Smith or to Horace?"

"Ouch! Both this time. Like I said, Horace does have a conscience on occasion. Let the Beastie Bug find her own material, there's plenty available around this city."

"Still, I need some security," Katherine joked.

"Well, you know my secret identity, both of them in fact, you have my permission to use a little emotional blackmail to prevent me from blathering around the water cooler."

She laughed, he had a point, she had more sensitive information on him than he did on her.

"Considering you came clean about Robert Horace, I guess it's only fair to tell: it's Gerard Reinold."

"I should have guessed, not everyone would brave the custom officials with a mere 'Taiwan' sticker to drop a two-thousand year old vase on your front desk. Well, as much as I would like to hang around, I've got to run. We can discuss the finances some other time."

That was fine, they had to be framed first anyway. She was so glad he brought them, she now had numerous pieces to offer her patrons, and since the artists liked her rotation system, not to mention she paid on time, they kept her well stocked.

Horace was not the only one to show up with paintings that January, the Professor completed three seascapes, his promised tall ship series, and just in time for Mr. Richard Reinold's first visit to the gallery. Katherine gave him the grand tour, and of course, he couldn't pass by the Professor's new works.

"I'll take the lot," he announced as he eyed the three canvases, giving a little nod of approval, "fine work. He's got a feel for the sea." Maybe she was going to have holes in her display after all, they were barely on the wall three days. "This reminds me, where are your pictures? I'd like to take your advice and see your style before you start on the *Morning Glory*'s portrait."

Of course, all she had other than Napoléon was Gerry's picture of Rome that was now finished and in the final drying stage. He liked her close attention to detail.

"Ger's going to prize that one," Mr. Reinold commented.

"He does already, he watched as it progressed. He checked up on it everyday, I think he likes watching me work, maybe he'd like to learn how to paint. Even if he never becomes a professional, it is a very calming and satisfying hobby."

"You know, I always wanted to learn myself, I mean not just scribble, but really learn how to construct a proper picture with the right dimensions. Do you give lessons?"

"I thought about it, but haven't figured out how to fit that in just yet. Classes and seminars will probably come after I refurbish the fourth floor, the studio is actually way too big, it could easily be partitioned into a private space and a public class room sometime in the future."

"Let me know when you do decide to teach, I just might be your first pupil," he smiled.

"All right, you'll be at the top of my list."

Mr. Reinold's visit was a reminder of her promise to drop by Mrs. Hunt's estate to pick up the paintings she offered on loan. It turned out to be a whole day's excursion down to Long Island as Gerry helped her deliver his father's purchase before running through Mrs. Hunt's mansion unhitching pictures, with Mrs. Hunt directing the procedure. When Katherine finally made it back to the gallery before closing time, the van filled with new exhibits, Suzy had news that her friend from Paris had called. Justine called? That's unusual, they normally don't call long distance. Katherine returned their call to discover they had finally set the date for the wedding, but a little earlier than planned. They couldn't book the civil service, the church and the venue for the reception on the same day they changed to the first week of May, June was a very popular month. Katherine had almost forgotten about the civil ceremony, the French government didn't recognise religious ceremonies as a legally binding marriage. It was a good thing they could arrange it all on the same day, May was just fine, she had enough notice to book their flights around their schedule: she had promised tickets as a wedding present. Since she was going to be one of the bridesmaids, she would have to be there a few days in advance for the dress fittings and the rehearsals. Justine said she had the dresses all ready as everyone had given their measurements ahead of time.

"No problem, in fact, I'll come a couple of weeks early, you don't want everything rushed at the last minute, not to mention the bridesmaid should be around to help too."

"Wonderful! But that's not all," Justine continued, "I've got more to tell. You won't believe what happened. We were just sitting down to dinner a few weeks ago, Maurice and Theresa were with us, and someone knocked on the door. Just guess who it was!"

"Umm, I haven't a clue."

"Martin's father. That was an event we didn't expect."

"I'll say! I hope there wasn't an argument."

"Oh no! Quite the contrary. His father just stood there, and then finally said he had heard we were planning to get married, and would like to meet the bride to be. I don't know what happened, maybe his uncle finally gave him a piece of his mind and pounded some sense into him. They went into the hall first to have a private word. Well, you know how easy it is to overhear conversations at our place, even in the corridor. His father simply stated if art was his chosen career, there wasn't anything he could do about it, and decided he just might as well accept it. However, he concluded by saying his son may be an artist, but that didn't mean we had to live like attic snipes and could at least find a decent place to live. He offered us an apartment as a wedding gift in addition to helping with the wedding."

"Wow, that's a generous gift. Where is it?"

"In the Luxembourg Quarter, it's so beautiful, and it's very close to the gardens."

"I'm so happy for you, but I'm going to miss the old apartment on this next visit, it may have been small, but we had some fun times there."

"True, I'm going to miss living in Montmartre, but honestly, living a bohemian lifestyle is only fit for melodrama and operas, I think it's time to move on to something more comfortable. We certainly could use the space, and we don't want to give Martin's father the idea we're ungrateful. That reminds me, we have quite a number of paintings finished to bring over with us, I hope you have space in your gallery for them all."

"Oh don't worry, we'll figure something out," Katherine assured her, display options were not a problem.

"That's a relief. Before I forget, thank you for your letters, I know it's hard finding time to write, but we love receiving them, even when you can only scribble a few lines."

"I've been so busy, I'm sorry I couldn't write more often and give you all the details."

"I don't want to hold you up on the telephone, so we'll save all the news until you come. I know the wedding is going to keep us busy, but we'll still have plenty of time to catch up on everything."

"I can't wait. Please say 'hello' to everyone, and I'm so looking forward to our reunion."

"I will."

☙ ❀ ❧

As January slipped away and February rushed in, she and Gerry became inseparable as the day of his departure loomed closer. If schedules allowed, they had lunch together most days and quiet, informal dinners at night. By now, they took turns having dinner with each other's family on the weekends without the need for formal invitations. However, the one event they looked forward to, despite it being the last day before his corporate voyage, was Valentine's Day. He had promised her an evening of dancing, but every time she asked where he was taking her, he refused to tell, building up the suspense. The revelation arrived promptly on the fourteenth in a card accompanying the largest red and yellow bouquet she had yet received:

To Her Highness, the Princess of Sehsurbtniap,

Would you do me the honour of flying with me on a cloud of music at the Rainbow Room tonight? I shall arrive to escort you, eight o'clock sharp.

Your humble servant,

Sir ~~Lance~~lot. Dancelot

"Gee," Suzy remarked, noting the size of the bouquet, "aren't you getting tired of roses and sunflowers yet? He *does* realize there are other things blooming out there?"

"Not for us," Katherine quietly replied.

She knew exactly what to wear that night, even if she had worn it already; the blue formal dress she bought for the opera. She recalled his expression of admiration when he saw her in it the first time and knew it was his favourite, she couldn't think of anything else she would rather wear. For him, a dinner jacket would be a given, maybe even tails, but would he come in that dashing frock coat with the half cape? It suited him … her 'Man of Mystery'.

The limo pulled into the driveway eight o'clock sharp, the very sound of the car stopping outside made her heart miss a beat. She peeked through the slender pane of glass framing the front entryway and watched as Samuel opened the limo door for Gerry, who sprang out almost like a Jack-in-the-Box. He ducked in the vehicle for a moment to retrieve his hat, cane, and another bouquet of their signature flowers. She smiled to see he had worn the frock coat, she waited for him to come to the front door.

"Good evening, Princess," he said, removing his hat, making a sweeping bow and handing her the bouquet, "you are quite stunning tonight."

"Thank you Sir Dancelot, you look very handsome. Come in for a minute while I put these on the hall stand."

"All right, I shall wish the Lords and Lady of the house a happy Valentine's Day before we fly on that little cloud of ours."

"Oh, everyone has gone to the Club already, and Mrs. Gonzales is off tonight, so we're the only ones here right now, even Charlie has already picked Suzy up," she said, laying the flowers down.

"You mean we are truly alone at last?" he smiled, suddenly whisking into a dance pose and waltzing a few steps with her in the hall.

"So the dancing has begun already, has it?" she smiled.

"Absolutely. In fact, I shall dance you all the way to our carriage waiting out yonder."

"Wait! Let me get my coat and purse first."

He helped her with her velvet coat before waltzing her out the door, giving her a minute to lock it before resuming their circling dance. When she ducked to get into the 'carriage' she gasped in surprise, the entire cabin including the floor was filled with roses and sunflowers with just enough of their seats left available to make it a cosy ride for two. She noticed he had a covered silver tray waiting behind one of the massive posies, which he ceremoniously uncovered to reveal a plate of chocolate croissants shipped in fresh from France that day.

"Just a little something to help tide us over," he explained. He then handed each of them a travel mug filled with cappuccino. "Here's to us, may this light repast be a prelude to better things," he smiled, clinking her mug with his, "I would have included a piece of hot fudge cake, but that would have ruined our supper."

It was the first time she had been to the *Rainbow Room* since its lavish twenty five million dollar restoration and expansion. Situated on the sixty-fifth floor of the G.E. Building at Rockefeller Center, the famous dinner club with its elegant ambience, circular revolving dance floor and big band orchestra commanded a spectacular view of the Manhattan skyline. Seated by one of the windows at a table for two, it felt like they were the only ones there notwithstanding the place was filled to capacity. They never seemed to run out of things to talk about, even if the conversation veered to the mundane on occasion. Knowing that this would be their last night together for a while made everything they discussed as captivating as a Shakespearean soliloquy. The food was excellent, but being together was more important, it seemed like the dinner only got in their way. At last, he rose from the table, and extending his hand, escorted her to the dance floor under the large glittering chandelier, the ceiling lights gradually changing colour reflecting the mood of each dance number. She felt a little shy standing in front of all those people, but as he drew her close, the onlookers faded into the background of the twinkling skyline. In the beginning it was difficult to dance with the crowd, it became more of a tight shuffle than a precise step-in-time with the music. At one point, they danced too close to the orchestra, causing Katherine to wince.

"Are you all right? I didn't step on your toes did I?" he asked with concern, "I'm sorry, I didn't expect it to be this crowded tonight."

"Oh no, not you Twinkle Toes, it's just the amplifiers, they hurt my ears."

Immediately he lead away to the outer edge of the circle and gradually changed their position to the farthest point on the revolving floor whenever they were swivelled towards the offending speakers.

"Thank you, that's much better," she assured him.

"That's good, but let me know when you need a break from the maddening crowd."

The floor eventually thinned as people went back to their seats to rest, and since neither of them felt inclined to stop just yet, they continued to sway and twirl with the music.

"There, we finally have the floor almost to ourselves," he noted, "perhaps now we can enjoy the moment."

Without saying a word, they glided across the floor for several instrumentals until the orchestra faded in the last strains of *You Were Meant for Me*. At last, out of breath, they resumed their seats just in time to see a man at the next table get down on one knee and open a small box while delivering his prepared speech, asking the love of his life if she would do him the honour of becoming his bride.   After a tearful but happy acceptance with hugs, kisses and champagne toasts, the restaurant broke out into applause.

"Oh, what a beautiful moment," Katherine said, "I'm glad she was ready to accept, especially with everyone watching, it could have gone horribly wrong, I know from experience."

"At least it wasn't one of those extrovert displays with someone buying air or television time to pop the question, there would have been an audience of thousands if not millions," he noted.

"Those stunts disturb me, I don't find them romantic or considerate. I think a proposal should be offered in private; it's a romantic moment that should be kept secret until they decide to make their engagement public."

That was good to know.

Did she realize she had just revealed to him how she would like him to propose when the time arrived? He quietly studied her for a moment. How beautiful she is, he would have told her a thousand times, but he didn't want his heartfelt compliments playfully dismissed as flattery, not tonight. How correct he was when he compared her to that gleaming white creature of legend who none but the pure of heart or the most fortunate were allowed to glimpse in the silver moonlight and perhaps approach. She was a very private person, demonstrations of love and affection were not for sharing with the public, and certainly not a proposal, they were secret, sacred rites not to be paraded as common actions before the masses. Knowing her apprehensions, it was a miracle she agreed to go dancing with him tonight, and he was determined not to leave until they wore the new finish off the floor. Nothing else mattered when he held her close, gently moving to the melody. He believed he could read the same thoughts in her eyes, her wishing that the night would go on forever, but even now, she was obviously not aware what her feelings were telling her. Perhaps the riddle had only confused her further, but now that he had given it to her, he was bound to his own conditions and couldn't say the things he so ardently wanted to say, not until she found the answer. He must be patient and wait. Standing up, and with a bow:

"Shall we dance, Princess?"

How they wished this evening could last forever, so they glided in each other's arms around the dance floor as if on wings. Slowly the diners and dancers were fading away, the musicians were packing up, and still they quietly held each other and swayed to a gentle beat no one else could hear, oblivious to the clatter in the kitchens and the bustle of the waiters tidying up.

"You do realize the orchestra has left?" the *maitre d's* informed them, finally tapping Gerry on the shoulder.

"That's all right, we're making our own music," he assured him. Katherine smothered a smile, but the *maitre d's* was insistent.

"I'm sorry sir, but it's closing time."

Gerry sighed and checked his watch.

"Time to take you home, Princess."

This night's journey home to Oak Meadows was quietly poignant, both aware that in a few short hours he would be on a plane jetting to the other side of the world.

"Gerry, thank you for everything, tonight was beautiful, and all these flowers! What are we going to do with them?"

"Hmm, I honestly didn't think about that," he mused, "do you have enough room in your parlour?"

"Now Gerry, you've already turned our house into a forest with your generosity, Mom just might put her foot down this time."

"All right, but at least take a few of the ones you like."

"And the rest? We can't have them go to waste."

"I have an idea: I'll have Samuel swing by the hospital and donate them to the candy-stripers after he drops me off at the airport, they might help cheer someone up."

"Oh Gerry, are you sure you don't want me to come with you to wave a *bon voyage?*"

"I'm sure, you won't get any sleep if you see me off, and I can't stand goodbyes, especially at airports. Besides, I want to remember you just as you are right now: my beautiful Princess surrounded by a sea of red and yellow flowers, no melancholic scenes, just the perfect ending to an enchanted evening."

"Does that ending include hot fudge cake?"

"Definitely," he replied, leaning gently towards her.

It was the perfect ending, they tried to make it last. It was sad to reflect that if there was one event that was imperfect that night, it was the idea that this intimate moment signalled an 'ending' of their time together. The last month flitted away so fast, and now that their goodnight kiss was over, they had to say goodbye as well.

"I promise I'll call the minute I arrive at the hotel in Sydney, although I'm not sure what hour it will be here, I'm afraid the time zone might be an inconvenience to you."

"I don't mind about the zone, call me anytime, anywhere." She now understood what Stephie tried to explain about the irrelevance of telephone schedules. "I hope everything goes all right for you."

"Me too, it means I can come back earlier than expected. I'm really going to miss you, Kathy."

"I'm going to miss you too, it won't be the same around here without you."

"Oh dear, what was it about not having any melancholic memories … here," he finished, grabbing an armful of the bouquets and handing them to her, "there, you're covered in flowers, that's better. Let me take you in while I have this pretty picture before me." They kissed one last time on the doorstep, albeit her arms were laden with vermilion and yellow flora.

"I suppose this is good…,"

"No Princess, no goodbyes, only *au revior.*"

"*Au revior*, Sir Lancelot. Please stay safe as you venture forth to complete your quest."

"I will your highness, you take care too."

Kissing him quickly one last time, she opened the door and reluctantly slipped inside. She watched from the slender windowpane as he walked back to the limo, not with his usual sprightly step. As the long sleek vehicle drove down the driveway and out the gate into the dark, chilly morning, a vague solitude enveloped her, an emptiness that she had never felt before. There may be no goodbyes, but a *u reviors* were just as difficult, the words were different, but the emptiness experienced at parting was the same.

૭૩ ❀ ৪৩

"Wow, that's beautiful, I didn't think having a gate on the stairs would look good, but that's very stylish," Dennis noted as the workmen tidied up their tools.

"I thought so too," Katherine nodded, "now with the extra guards watching the lobby, upstairs will be secure while Andre opens up at night."

In fact, she had discovered the ornate brass gates in a most unusual place, one of the few church suppliers that continued to specialize in elaborate altar rails. It was amazing how you could find things where you least expect them. She couldn't take the credit for the idea however, she had to thank Esther for that.

"If you could call a mortuary for your statue pedestals, why not think outside the box? Where have you seen gates that attracted your attention?"

"That's easy, Gothic cathedrals."

"Then just go where cathedrals get their fancy bits and pieces," Esther nodded, matter-of-factly.

"How simple," Suzy smiled, she could never forget the day they ordered the stone stand for the Hanley piece.

It was a stroke of providence the factory had a pair of gates ready and waiting after an order had been cancelled. What an unexpected stroke of luck to find they featured a French fleur-de-ly motif that fit perfectly with the gallery's European décor. It was a pity Gerry wouldn't see the result of Esther's splendid suggestion for another few weeks. At least she had something new to tell him, it was her turn to call next morning. By now, he was on his way to Tokyo, and she couldn't wait to hear his latest chapter of 'The Corporate Traveller's Guidebook', a.k.a his descriptions of his various experiences and misadventures in the far east. He was well travelled, but still uncomfortable in non-English speaking cultures, especially in Asia where a simple misunderstanding or an innocent gesture could be read as a

701

blatant insult. Not taking any chances, he hired personal bilingual guides as chaperones whenever he ventured outside the relative safety of the international hotels.

Katherine could easily imagine the cultural tsunamis that awaited him, recalling Uncle Tim's stories of his executive excursions to Nippon when she was younger, the one vivid detail was his account of having to use chopsticks and the custom of slurping noodles, noisy eating was recommended in this instance and displayed to the host that you enjoyed the fare. She also remembered the importance of gift giving and the ceremony surrounding it. Uncle Tim went to the company PR team for help to select appropriate presents: quality food items particular to the visitor's country was deemed an acceptable gift, so he had to pack ample supplies of select See's Candies and bottles of special reserve Tennessee Whisky. Nothing sharp like a scissors or letter opener could be exchanged as it symbolised the severance of a relationship. She wasn't sure what else he had toted, but everything had to be gift wrapped at the hotel in Japan where this special service was offered to ensure the proper paper and wrapping format was used. To choose the wrong colour or add flashy Christmas style ribbons could bode disaster to a business deal: red was the colour reserved for funerals, and the innocent colour white symbolised death to the Japanese, meaning all the candies had to be taken out of their signature white boxes and repackaged in something appropriate. The quantity in a gift could not be given in odd numbers as it was considered unlucky, and the number nine also had to be avoided for the same reason, so all the candies had to be reopened and recounted, just in case. The numbers four and fourteen were also taboo as the word for 'four' was similar to 'death' in Japanese. Gifts were not opened in front of the giver, but saved until later. The fact that gifts had been brought would also be disclosed sometime during the business meeting to ensure the host was not surprised: to surprise the recipient would be considered bad form. The gift also had to be presented with both hands, and received the same way. If you received a gift, and the host happens to insist you open it, you must do so with the utmost appreciation, carefully taking your time to unwrap the item as a mark of respect, the outward demonstration of giving and receiving having more importance than the actual gift.

"Next time, *you're* going to Japan," Uncle Tim said to Pops, scratching his head as the PR team tried to coach him on all the expected protocol.

Finishing breakfast in a hurry the next morning, Katherine promptly dialled Gerry's room to see how he was faring. By now, she was adept at calculating the different time zones, in this case, a fourteen hour chasm between New York and Japan: it was amusing to think that the day was just beginning for her while he was getting ready to tuck into bed.

"Hi Princess, it's good to hear your voice."

"Oh dear, you sound a little homesick."

"That, and a little tired from hotel hopping. Vacations are one thing, but I like to stay settled when doing business: like I told you, these global inspections are murder."

"A few weeks, and it'll all be over. Take some time off, go and see the sights if you can. It might cheer you up."

"Well, now that you mention it, I had some free time after I settled in, and once I handed all the gifts to the hotel wrapping department, I thought I'd do just that, but I became one of the sights instead," he chuckled.

"Oh? What do you mean?"

"Let's just say in a tightly-packed land where the culture revolves around group harmony and the suppression of individualism, we *gaijin* stand out like sore thumbs."

"Gaijin?"

"Their word for foreigners. I really do feel like a celebrity when I go out, people come up to me and ask in English where I come from, if they can have their picture taken with me and if I wouldn't mind giving them autographs. Oh, personal questions are not personal, they want to know how big my apartment is, and how much I earn in a year."

"You're not serious."

"Very serious, foreigners are a major curiosity. I fully appreciate their saying that a nail that sticks out gets hammered."

"Wow. What else have you discovered on your explorations?"

"Well, my guide has reminded me of the etiquette expected at business meetings, particularly the importance of ...what was it? Metshi? Menshi? ... darn, I'm constantly forgetting the correct pronunciation."

Meishi she had not heard about, the all-important ceremony of the business card exchange. Gerry explained he had to have special cards printed for this trip, one side in English, the other in Japanese, and to ensure he had a good supply. After the formal greeting consisting of a bow, the card was to be graciously handed to the recipient with both hands, Japanese side up. A card was received with both hands, similar to a gift. The card must be carefully studied as a mark of respect, and it was paramount to remember who had given it to you. Writing on cards was an insult, so no quickie reminders of who-was-who could be notated on them. They could not be shoved into a pocket or wallet, or folded for that matter, it was considered defacing the card and a serious sign of disrespect. Business could not commence until the *meishi* exchange was completed.

"I've heard of deals that were suddenly called off because someone fidgeted with the host company's card during a meeting," he concluded, "personally, I think that's a bit over the top."

"I agree, that's intense, but you can understand when you consider their culture and how important showing respect and saving face is to them," she observed. "From what you just told me, a business card is not just a piece of paper with information as it is to us, it represents their career, who they are loyal to, in fact, the card is symbolic of their life. To disrespect the card is to disrespect everything they stand and work for. It's not that different than if you insulted an ambassador; you also offend the country he represents."

"I never really thought about it like that," he mused, "it's good to know there's a reason for all the pomp and ceremony. Well, enough about me. What have you been up to?"

Katherine told him about the new addition to the stairs, the two new guards were already on duty, and Andre would be opening for dinner within a few weeks, but other than that, she didn't have anything very exciting to report. She was just finishing up the sky and starting to fill in the temple on Lottie's picture of the Acropolis. While she waited for that to dry, she would work on her Socratic paintings again since his brother hadn't quite made up his mind what he wanted for a picture, that was about it.

"Maybe Pete doesn't want to take up your time, at any rate these philosophical works have me curious," he noted. Katherine had kept them a secret and hadn't shown them to anyone yet. "But an altar gate?" he continued, "talk about building temples of art."

"Oh, I know it sounds funny, but they really are beautiful, I was afraid I might get stuck with some old iron thing to block the stairs. Let's hope I haven't done something sacrilegious."

"No, you're all right," Gerry chuckled, "if they weren't used, then they weren't part of a consecrated building, so you're okay, the wrath of God won't strike you."

"Boy, that's a relief."

"Honestly, I can't wait to see them, and it's a pity I'll be missing Andre's opening night. Tell him I wish him all the best, will you?"

"Of course."

"I don't want to hold you up, I know you have to rush to work, but there's so much I want to tell you. For one thing, I've got an important meeting tomorrow, let's hope I don't do something that will end diplomatic relations between Japan and the USA, they take every little gesticulation so seriously. I can't wear anything but black, no smiling, no sudden motions, no demonstrative facial gestures, a smile could indicate displeasure if used out of context, hand movements have to be guarded, I have to be careful even when I indicate something, I must have my palm flat down and gently move my fingers. Oh, periods of silence are common during negotiations, you have to sit and wait for the speaker to reflect upon the information he gives and receives, they certainly do things differently over here."

"Don't worry, it sounds like you have everything down pat already, you'll do fine, and besides you look so dashing in black."

"Don't say that, I can't look dashing," he laughed, "or I'm a nail ready to be hammered, but thank you for the compliment."

"Well, I hope you didn't forget to slurp your noodles?"

"That's the easy part. No problem there. I do have to make sure not to sneeze or blow my nose in public, I'm so glad I don't have a cold right now. How are you supposed to hold in a sneeze anyway? That one has me bamboozled."

"Oh my gosh! We Westerners must seem like Cretans to them. Anything else you have to be careful about?"

"Let me see … oh yes, you have to be aware of what I call their 'bluffing game'. They don't like to appear difficult or uncooperative, it's their custom of maintaining collective harmony, so they won't say 'no' when they mean it. They usually say something like 'that would be difficult', circumvent an outright refusal, even a 'yes' can mean 'no'. They also have two separate words for their public opinion, what they're willing to say in public, and their own personal opinion, which they rarely reveal except to very close family and friends. If I had a better command of their language, I could tell you the terms."

"Everything sounds so precise, they couldn't be a relaxed people with all these rules, the hospitals must be filled with patients suffering from stress disorders."

"It's probably not difficult if you grow up with it. I'm glad I don't have any major meetings in Hong Kong this trip, their customs are very close, plus I still have a load of my Chinese business cards from last time, so that was one thing already taken care of, and of course, English is a recognised language, I can breath a bit easier once I get there."

"Where do you go after Hong Kong again?"

"Jakarta, then back to Sydney for a day or two, and finally, I'll be on my way home since I'm not going to India on this occasion. I can't wait to see you."

"I can't wait to see you too, take care. I don't want to hang up, but I've got to go," she said, checking the clock, "I'm running late."

"All right, don't rush, be careful on the road, Princess. I'll talk to you tomorrow."

"Okay Lancelot, I'll be waiting."

They had made a promise not to say goodbye and were determined to keep it. How difficult to put the handset down, their telephone calls had become the highlight of her day. As long as she heard his voice, several thousand miles and a fourteen hour time lapse seemed non-existent. Listening to his voice was one thing, but now, the global void took hold as she faced the day realizing the incredible distance between them. Going to work these days left her with an empty feeling knowing he wouldn't be dropping in to take her to lunch, or making plans for a magical evening together. At least she could count on the gallery keeping her busy, there was always so much to do, no time to brood when she had customers to take care of and bills to pay. However, painting was another matter, it gave her too much time to think, or rather, mope. This time of separation was difficult to assess, the first few days did not seem too bad, but then the vague emptiness she felt that night after he brought her home started to close in around her. At least it wasn't like the old days when shippers and traders were gone for years when they left for business, but trying to find ways to look on the bright side still brought little consolation. Why was she feeling like this? Pops sometimes had to go on long trips, and while she missed him, she didn't feel this inexplicable ... solitude? She wasn't *lonely*, that wasn't quite it, more like ... some piece that had just found a place in her life was now ... missing and couldn't be replaced by anything that used to make her feel happy or contented before. Curling up with a book or watching TV after work like old times made her restless. She took Charlie and Suzy up an a few invitations to join them for dinner and watch a movie. She knew they wanted to cheer her up and give her something to do rather than stay at home after work, but the nights out didn't make her feel better, especially when she didn't want to be an appendage and become an annoying example of 'three is a crowd'. Her appetite seemed to wane, and on top if that, she became more eccentric and erratic than normal for an artist. Her attention span strangely diminished, but was instantly revitalized whenever his name came up in a conversation. His mystery tape never left her Walkman, unless it was transferred to the van for her daily drive to and from the gallery. When travelling around, she was drawn to look at any truck she passed, almost playing leap frog to get to the vehicle just to see if it had the Reinold logo emblazoned on the side, and felt oddly disappointed when she didn't spot one on her commutes. She found herself taking longer routes to the gallery, just to pass by the restaurants they went to, and every so often, cruised by his apartment building. On a few occasions, she was startled when she thought she saw him walking down the street, but it was only someone who looked like him from a distance. It was almost impossible not to think about him, especially as he had made arrangements that fresh bouquets of their special flowers be delivered to her home and front desk on a regular basis during his absence. This was her first experience of feeling this obsessive single-mindedness about one person, everything else seemed to come second, or not at all. What was happening? She was always so focused, she didn't know weather to be worried or to simply enjoy this satisfying state. Just *what* was it?

A little before opening time one morning as Katherine was looking over the sales reports for the last week, she decided to turn on the local radio rather than play the usual recordings over the sound system.

"And now, for all our morning listeners, we have a request from a caller for anything by Frank Sinatra," the presenter announced. Katherine smiled, the mere mention of Sinatra also made her think about Gerry. Speaking of callers, he would be phoning any minute: he's about to leave Jakarta, Sydney next, and then he'll be home! "… here, we have a nice romantic melody for you called, '*You'll Know When It Happens*'. Enjoy, all you Sinatra fans."

She half listened to the melody as she closed the book and looked for the list of new paintings that arrived from the framers the previous day.

> *You'll now when it happens, you won't have to guess,*
> *All at once you'll find your heart is filled with happiness.*
> *You'll know when it happens, love can't be disguised,*
> *All at once the dreams you dreamed will all be realized.*
> *Your eyes will see things that aren't really there.*
> *Your lips will say things, things you would never dare.*
> *You'll know when it happens, suddenly you'll say,*
> *'Darling, I'm in love with you,' it happens just that way.*

Katherine nearly dropped the list as she listened to the reprise melodically diagnose her extraordinary behaviour. *What was that she heard?* Her mind reeled, this sudden revelation was almost too much to take in. *Could* it be love? If love could make one blind, she was definitely struck to the core, not aware of what she was feeling all this time! She reassessed everything she felt a hundred times over, checking off anything that resembled the classic symptoms experienced when a person became a happy victim of Cupid's dart, and found all her thoughts and actions matched. Her heart began to pound, she found herself holding her breath. That's what was happening: *I'm falling in love.*

How simple that sounded for this earth shattering moment!

The planet had just rocked on its axis, the sky had fallen on her, the Law of Gravity was broken: it was the most wonderful experience. In fact, a myriad of feelings bubbled to the surface. Discovering her true feelings for Gerry clarified her memories to a startling intensity, the time they spent together, the conversations they had, the romantic moments they shared, and of course, their first kiss. She suddenly had the bizarre urge to hide, it seemed as if all the world could read what was happening in her heart and mind and she needed to get away, find some private time alone to think. Why she would feel so shy and self-conscious when she should want to shout from the rooftops was an unusual reaction. Her emotional breakthrough was a mystery, but she couldn't dispel it, everything familiar now felt so new and strange. As soon as Esther and Suzy arrived, she flew to the privacy of the studio to paint and muse.

March 18th, this would be a date to remember, the day she discovered she had fallen in love. How she wanted to tell Gerry! Then, the thought of professing her love to him drew her back into the safe haven of reserved shyness. No, she couldn't say anything, not yet. For one thing, she wasn't exactly sure where he stood, he had never said anything about his feelings, it was obvious he expected his riddle to be answered first. Dropping her brush, she put on the tape and sang the muddled songs to herself, intently holding the headphones over her ears, puzzling over the missing segments. *"What is not there, that is already there? That is the question!"* Was *love* the solution? It *just* had to be, it was the only answer that seemed to make sense. Nearly every song composed or written was about love; falling in love, falling out of love, hoping to fall in love, and yet, anything that even hinted about love had been blanked out of the songs he had selected. Nevertheless, it was the reason for their composition, even when the word itself was missing. Yes, love was hidden and yet plain for all to see. The answer was so simple, how could she have not figured it out sooner? She wanted to laugh, dance and cry all at the same time.

Wait a minute, what if it *wasn't* the right answer? She froze as panic gripped her with the dismal thought: what if all this was just a bit of romantic 'fun' for him, a game with nothing serious attached to his riddle at all? Looking back, it didn't feel like that when they were together, but he had an exuberant sense of humour, it was difficult to tell when he was serious. Panic swiftly morphed into a sickening feeling of dismay. Was this the first pang that signalled the torment of unrequited love? The not knowing, then hoping, the assuming it could be, and finally realizing it might not happen at all? *Oh, poor Charlie, I had no idea.* I'm so sorry, I never meant to hurt you. Gerry made every effort to show how he cared, he just hadn't said anything yet, preferring to leave his deepest feelings unspoken for the present. She returned to her first conclusion: he was waiting for the riddle to be answered.

Katherine remembered his instructions, to wait several days before sending what she assumed was the 'sign' to let him know she had cracked his melodic code. However, the thought of posting the mysterious envelope exacerbated that paralysing feeling of bashfulness. Perhaps that's why he wanted her to wait, not only for her to be certain she had the correct answer, but to also come to terms with the flood of emotions that this self-discovery was bound to bring to the surface. He showed a wisdom in this instance, his consideration and sensitivity touched her deeply. There was so much to ponder and come to grips with, she had better wait until she came to terms with this unexpected complication in her well-ordered life. For the present, it might be best to follow his lead and say nothing until the right moment had come to send the envelope; this was all so new, she may need more than the few days he suggested.

It was going to be more difficult to talk to him on the phone, trying to stay composed, even though she longed for his call more than ever. She then realized it was well past the time he usually called. That's odd, he usually warned her when he thought he might be late, a last minute dinner invitation was the usual cause for any delay. It was probably a business commitment, he would call as soon as he could. However, the day wore on, closing time arrived, and no call came through. Maybe he would wait until she got home? No, not if he had business to take care of, it would be morning over there. Or would it? Sometimes it was hard to keep track. Well, she was resolved not to fuss, something had just come up and he couldn't get to the phone. He would tell her what happened when she called the next day. At least this delay gave her time to ponder and to be certain she had actually solved his riddle. She felt deliriously blissful, even though she wasn't sure how he felt in return. It was difficult falling asleep that night, but at last she dozed off with the cassette player tucked in beside her, the headphones nestled over her ears.

The following morning, she delayed setting out for work, calling his room the fourth time and letting the phone ring an unreasonable amount of time. No answer. By now, the family were up and bustling about, Mom was having a bran muffin while Pops was just heading out the door.

"Don't worry, Kathy," her mother consoled, "he probably had something to take care of, not to mention you've probably woken up everyone else in the hotel. Do put the phone down and have some breakfast, you haven't eaten hardly a thing these last few weeks."

"Listen to your mother now, I'll have some scrambled eggs and bacon whipped up in no time," Mrs. Gonzales added as she brought in a fresh pot of coffee.

"No thank you, I don't feel like eating. Maybe you're right Mom, it could be nothing, but this isn't like him. If he missed his time to call, I've always been able to contact him the next morning."

"Kathy, aren't you being a little paranoid?"

"I don't think so, only worried. I don't know why, but something doesn't feel right."

"Don't fret dear, he must have a good reason, and besides, the man needs his space too. Just try again later."

"All right … oh, I know! I'll call the reception desk at his hotel, find out if they saw him leave or something."

Katherine scanned the list of numbers Gerry had given her to track him down during his wanderings and carefully followed the long array of foreign codes as she dialled. After making her enquires, she discovered Mr. Reinold had not returned to the hotel the day before. They didn't know when he might be back, but that she could try again later. She asked if there were any messages for her and received a negative reply. Would she like to leave him a message? Well, she didn't want to look obsessed, a simple message that she called and would try again later would have to suffice for now, her concern surged with this unexpected news.

"Maybe he was invited to stay over somewhere, it happens," her mother pointed out when she relayed the news, "you know how easy it is to insult people with a refusal over there, perhaps he couldn't say no."

"I suppose you're right. You know how my imagination can run amok, always jumping to the wrong conclusion and panicking over something silly. Gosh, look at the time! I've got to get going. Bye Mom, see you later," she said, kissing her on the cheek and grabbing her coat and purse.

She wondered all through the day if he would try to call when he received her message, but nothing came through. She jumped whenever the phones rang only to find it was potential customers asking about opening times, or artists recommended by Horace enquiring if she would be willing to see them and schedule an interview.

"Another artist? My, I don't understand that young man," Esther said, shaking her head while tidying a stack of brochures, "he seems so helpful, sending all this promising talent to you, not to mention many established painters, and then he tears them to pieces in his columns. I can't forget what he wrote about Mr. Turris, he received one of the worst reviews I've ever read."

Katherine tried to keep a straight face, the irony was priceless, it was a pity she couldn't let anyone in on the joke. Turris may be ripped to pieces, but Christopher Smith was doing very well. In fact, Horace and his column was great for business. Andre's new night schedule was also a bonus, attracting potential art customers in the evenings even though the upper floors of the gallery were not open to the public at night. The security guard on the floor actually helped secure a sale from one of the roly polies. There were also enquires about the Hanley sculpture, but of course, she couldn't sell that. Looking back over the last few weeks, things were really looking up, not only was she able to pay all the bills and the wages, but Steves had helped to make what was left of her nest egg grow a little faster with his dexterity on the stock market, telling her when to buy and sell, which stocks she should hold on to just for dividends, and sometimes making a few deals for her when she didn't have the time to make the trade herself. In no time, she would be able to refurbish the fourth floor and move the permanent exhibition to its new home. The one disappointment she had so far was the gift corner, there were a few who showed an interest in the space, but they changed their mind and found somewhere else, or they wanted to make so many structural alterations to the corner she declined their offer. Her store section wasn't like an ordinary mall unit that could be altered with every new tenant; if they went bust, she didn't want to be stuck with their bad ideas if they had disappeared into the black hole of Chapter 11.

Thinking about the business helped her not to dwell on Gerry's strange absence from the hotel, but not for long. Aunt Martha decided to join her for lunch that day, and couldn't help comment on his floral extravagance.

"Another bouquet? There won't be a red or yellow bloom left in the city if he keeps this up. I hope he is serious and not leading you up the garden path, my dear. Has he made any intimation of his intentions?"

How could she answer that? The fact she had doubts concerning the answer to his riddle, and that he had never voiced his feelings for her other than the pleasure of her company, a situation now rendered more delicate with his unexplained telephone silence, made Aunt Martha's well-meaning questioning difficult to hear. Did she *have* to put up with this today?

"Aunt Martha, you know it's only been a few months, and he's been gone for one of them."

"Well, I only have your best interests at heart, Kathy," she replied. "You don't know who you may meet these days, someone who is too perfect is only too good to be true, so they say."

Great, my boyfriend disappears in Jakarta, and I have no idea where he's at or what has happened to him. Thanks, I really needed to hear that.

"So, any other news?" Katherine asked, trying to change the subject. Aunt Martha had plenty to tell about the latest divorce scandal at the club, but was mercifully interrupted by Gramps, who wanted to see how everything was doing and find out if Andre's lunch fare had improved, still unaware of the stealth diet that had been inflicted on him. Glad for his timely arrival, she tried to eat her lunch in peace, but Aunt Martha's comment had only caused more worry. Gerry wasn't like that, he *couldn't* be. If that was the case, he obviously would have tried to take advantage of her by now, but he was always the model of propriety.

All day long, Katherine waited for a call, and still nothing. She tried his room again when she got home after work, to heck with the time zones, but there was no answer. Now she was really beginning to worry.

"Dear, it's only a day, he'll call back," her mother reminded her after dinner.

"Almost two," Katherine replied. "I know, don't get paranoid, but we've called each other like clockwork, even if we don't have anything important to say. This is most unusual," she concluded, not knowing how else to describe it. She didn't want to become one of those insufferable clingy girlfriends that men often complained about, but the worry of what might have happened to him gnawed at the back of her mind.

"Wait a little longer, he'll get back to you," Gramps said. "Try and relax, there's a Humphrey Bogart movie on TV tonight, want to join me?"

"I have some accounts to go over … but I guess they can wait," she said, not wanting to refuse, "it's not a pressing matter. Let me get out of my monkey suit first and slip into something more comfortable."

"Okay, I'll make the popcorn. Are you two going to join us?" he asked, turning to Mom and Pops.

"Of course, getting into something comfy sounds like a good idea, doesn't it?" Pops noted.

"And remember," Helen reminded, before they went upstairs, "no butter on the popcorn for you."

"Margarine only, cross my heart," Gramps promised, making an exaggerated 'X' sign over his chest before mumbling, "the butter's locked up anyway."

Within ten minutes, everyone was cuddled up on couches and recliners in the den with a bowel of Gramp's anaemic popcorn, ready for the night's entertainment.

"Does anyone mind if I catch up on the news first before the movie starts?" Pops asked, "I haven't seen it yet today."

"Go ahead, we have plenty of time," Gramps noted, "any particular channel?"

"Anywhere we can get the international news," Pops replied.

"All righty then, let's see how the world's been turning," Gramps said, pushing the buttons on the remote and shoving the recliner back.

After the weather report, the domestic news was repeated before the international news commenced. Katherine doubted if she would be able to watch the movie with them, the humdrum of the reporter's official commentary tone was starting to put her to sleep. However, the announcement of the latest events in Jakarta instantly dispelled her drowsiness.

"According to an official statement by the local police and port authorities, a major human trafficking and smuggling operation was uncovered when illegal immigrants and over one ton of cocaine were discovered yesterday afternoon concealed inside eleven shipping containers. Several people have been brought in for questioning, but there are no reports if they have been be charged or when they may be released. We go now live to our local correspondent in Jakarta, Serena Anderson, for further details."

"Good evening. I'm standing outside the regional offices of Reinold Enterprises in Jakarta, one of the four international shipping companies whose containers were seized today by the authorities … ."

Katherine sat bolt upright, knocking her footstool out of the way, she barely heard the names of the other companies, she could hardly believe her ears.

"Jumpin' Jahoshaphat! What's all this?" Gramps rumbled, kicking the footrest down on his recliner and leaning forward. Pops stiffened in his seat, while Mom 'sushed' and motioned someone to turn the volume up.

"… in addition to the total of one ton of cocaine dispersed throughout the containers, the most tragic part of today's find was seventy-four illegal immigrants crammed into narrow spaces in the back of what can only be described as giant death traps, these things are literally steel coffins. No light or air can get in once the doors are sealed, and it's impossible to open them from the inside. Sadly, the stowaways included women and children, many of which didn't survive the terrible conditions I've just mentioned. The casualty number we have so far is forty-two. Right now, we have no concrete information on how long these people were trapped inside, where they were heading, or where they came from. So far, the police are only willing to inform us that in these situations it is usually a desperate attempt to get to America or Europe with a hope of starting a better life, and despite the dangers, people will break into the shipyards and stowaway inside the containers. In worst-case scenarios, after paying an exorbitant amount of money to traffickers, many would-be illegal immigrants are tricked with a promised passage to a developed country and end up in sweatshops working as slave labour, or may even be sold into the illegal sex industry. Considering that cocaine was also discovered in the containers, the police suspect gang-organized human trafficking is more likely in this instance …"

Katherine was unable to speak as she watched the images from the live report switch to camera shots taken earlier during what appeared to be a police raid on a cargo dock, strategically edited to magnify the full impact of this human tragedy. She felt a stomach-churning wave of panic and nausea hit as she stared in horror at the video montage of police officers in strange uniforms lining up bags of tightly bound plastic drug bundles, directing paramedics as they rushed away with survivors on stretchers, or pushing the media out of the way, the camera catching pictures of the seized containers, two with the Reinold logo clearly painted on the back doors.

This can't be happening!

"Although we have received no official confirmation, there are rumours that the son of Richard Reinold, the CEO and chairman of Reinold Enterprises, is among those detained for questioning. No one has been willing to make any public statements concerning these rumours,

although we expect an official update from the local authorities within a few hours. Back to you, Bob."

"*Thank you Serena, and now to other news making the headlines. It's official, the Duke and Duchess of York have announced they are to separate … .*"

Pops grabbed the remote from Gramp's armrest and turned down the volume, he had heard enough news for now. There was silence as they tried to process the appalling information they had just received. At last, her father spoke.

"I'm sorry Kathy," he began solemnly, "I never thought he was capable of getting involved with something like this, but under the current circumstances, I think it might be best if you didn't see him again."

"Oh Pops, surely you don't believe it?"

"Now Harold, let's not jump to conclusions," her mother interjected, "we don't know what happened, the news is not always reliable. You should know."

"Still, we can't dismiss what we've just seen," Gramps grumbled, "I thought the past would stay there, especially as he seemed like a capital young fellow, but it's obvious a family of leopards who can't change their spots."

"Gramps, what are you talking about?"

"Gregory, I'm surprised at you! Did you have to bring it up like that?" Helen remarked crossly, "Katherine has had enough of a shock for one night."

"What? Isn't it the truth?" he said, holding up his hands.

"Please! Bring what up? What's the truth?"

Her father sighed resignedly. "I'm sorry you have to find out more disturbing news, but the Reinold shipping industry had a rather … unethical beginning," he tried to explain, choosing his words carefully.

"You mean the whaling? I know about that, whaling was big business back then, they didn't know any better. I'm over it. I don't see what that has to do with … ."

"It's more than that dear, in fact, I'm surprised you don't know. I can't break this any easier: they were … involved in the slave trade. I don't remember all the details, the story was raked up some years ago and resurfaces every now and again. I suppose it's best to find out now before you hear it in the next news update."

Was there anything else that could fall on her tonight? How could she have not heard about this before now? Of course, she was not one to follow the society and scandal columns, but … the *slave trade?* If there was one thing she detested about her nation's past, apart from the invention of the atomic bomb, was this bleak chapter in the history of human oppression.

"Is … is this true Mom?"

"I'm afraid it is," she said quietly.

"I … think I need to go to my room right now… ."

"Katherine … ."

She didn't want to hear any more, she *couldn't*. She hurried up the stairs and locked her door.

"I'll go after her," Helen replied.

"Maybe she needs to be alone," Pops suggested, but Mom knew better. Getting up from the couch, and following Katherine up the stairs, knocked on the door. No answer. She tried the handle and knocked again.

"Kathy, please open up."

Silence. Shaking her head sadly, she finally turned away, but stopped when she heard the click of the lock. She entered the room to find Katherine sitting back at her dresser next to one of the bouquets now beginning to wilt, her hands filled with tissues, tears streaming from her eyes.

"There, there now. That's it, let it all out," her mother soothed, gently caressing Katherine's hair as she grasped her around the waist and wept profusely. It was a long time since she had a heartfelt cry like this with her mother holding her close, perhaps when she was actually the height of her waist. Those times of so-called unbearable sorrow seemed so childish now, a skinned knee, the untimely death of her hamster, maybe a cruel word spoken at school, the few times Pops actually yelled a bit over one of her hare-brained activist stunts: this was a thousand times more painful, acute, cutting. Several minutes passed until she could catch her breath, and then she couldn't stop, rambling her feelings and fears semi-incoherently between sobs.

"Oh Mom, I don't know what to think … I mean, Gerry couldn't be part of … he can't! … I've met his parents … they're not like that! … They couldn't be involved … in anything like … it just couldn't be true … maybe the *past* … but not *now* … I don't believe it … questioning doesn't mean anything, right? … It's just procedure … isn't it? … The whaling was bad enough! … I don't know what to believe … and he's in a strange country … with the police! … You know what they say about smoke … but it couldn't be true! … But maybe it is! … It would explain a lot … about his brother I mean … to drop the family fortune … for the priesthood?   … Make up for past wrongs … I wouldn't blame him …"

"Shh, you're just wearing yourself out, we shouldn't be jumping to any conclusions tonight. Come now, wipe your face, take a deep breath."

Katherine did as she was told, and suddenly looked up into her eyes.

"Mom, did Pops mean it? Must I … stay away? I can't believe that Gerry would …" her voice trailed. She didn't know what had happened, but the thought of having to avoid him, especially now that she at last was beginning to divine her own feelings for him, was a knife wound to the heart.

"Your father is just being overprotective as usual. You're an adult old enough to make up your own mind: what used to be orders are now … strong suggestions and recommendations."

Katherine thought about this for a moment.

"But Pops is right, isn't he? What if Gerry is implicated? Arrested? I can't see us staying together after that … this is all too much … ."

"Well, it hasn't reached that stage, and hopefully, it won't. I don't believe Gerry's involved in this, I can't see it, he's not the type."

"That's what they say about serial killers, that's what frightens me, I don't believe he's capable of something like this, but the evidence so far is overwhelming."

"Listen now, you know how the media blows everything out of proportion, making us see things in their slanted light before the true facts are revealed.   All we know is that he's being questioned, there are no charges levelled against him, and a drug gang may be responsible. For all we know, Gerry and those other shipping companies just got caught in the middle of a criminal operation and the authorities are trying to figure out what's happened."

"I hope you're right."

"I have an idea: why don't you take the day off tomorrow? Give yourself some time to get over this shock, and in the meantime, we'll wait for any news updates, see what actually develops."

"But I can't miss work, sitting at home won't help. The gallery is the one thing that will keep me going right now, I have to stay active."

"Well, if you think that's best. Lie down now and try to get some rest. I'll let you know in the morning if anything happens."

Katherine didn't feel like sleeping, but couldn't face the television right now, even for more news, afraid of what she might hear, including additional comments from Pops and Gramps about other skeletons that might be rattling in the Reinold family closet that she might still be unaware of. Slipping resignedly under the covers, her mother instinctively tucked her in, turned off the light and gently closed the door. Katherine tossed for ages, it was ironic, sleep, the one remedy often suggested after a terrible shock, now eluded her. The news report was still vivid, the tormenting images of the dock raid resurfaced and repeated like a defective tape machine stuck on a continuous play cycle. When she finally dozed off, she woke with a jolt, and the whole process of reliving the reporter's vocal drone started afresh.

At last, morning came with only a few hours of intermittent sleep. She didn't know if talking to herself was the first step towards insanity, but an audible monologue made it easier to cope, force her mind to focus on the daily routine. Never mind, no matter how tired I feel, I've got to keep busy, do something constructive, *must* blot out what I heard last night she mumbled. Accounts, right, didn't get them done yet, that will keep me occupied, April the fifteenth is less than a month away, we don't want to be overdue with that, now do we? Hmm, I can lock myself in the office while I work on the bureaucratic necessities of the gallery. As she stepped into the shower, letting the force of the water sweep away her fatigue, she realized that these annoying have-to's just might be a godsend for once. It would not be easy to face everyone today if they all had the same opinion as Pops and Gramps. She didn't want to think negative thoughts about Gerry, not when she didn't have all the facts. All she could do was worry.

After she was dressed, she went down to the kitchen to get her coffee and watch the news from the countertop television to see if there were any developments during the night. Everyone else had the same idea and hovered around the set with mugs in hand, Suzy too, even Mrs. Gonzales and Juanita were glued to the screen to see what was happening, never mind if breakfast was skipped today. They turned in her direction when they heard the door open, it was difficult to see their expressions varying between worry and pity. There was a split second of silence, saying 'good morning' just seemed … inappropriate.

"Well, there's some good news, he was released last night, our time, but the reports didn't get out until now," Mom began, knowing it was better to simply state the facts. Katherine breathed a sigh of relief, at least he wasn't charged. "You just missed it, but it looks like his father is on his way out there to see what's happening, he was mobbed by the reporters at the airport from what we could see in the background."

"Did he say anything?"

"Basically no comment, and it's unlikely he'll say anything until he finds out more."

Although she wanted to hear the commentary, Katherine was glad she didn't witness Mr. Reinold hounded by media personnel, crowding around and shoving microphones, cameras and recorders in his face when he had a problem of this magnitude to solve. It was good to know Gerry would not be alone, his father was flying to the rescue.

"Um, Kathy, are you sure you want to come in today?" Suzy asked hesitantly. "Esther, David and I can handle the gallery, I think you should take some time off."

"No, I have work to do, I'll be fine. There wasn't anything else in the news, was there?"

"Let's just say the reporters have continued to portray Reinold Enterprises in a very negative light," Pops continued, "it doesn't look good."

After what she learned last night, she was afraid to hear any more and decided she had better go to work.

"Okay, but I'm taking over the van," Suzy declared, afraid with the recent shock Katherine might be too distracted to be behind the wheel.

Katherine was glad for the company on this commute, she was afraid where her thoughts might lead her if she allowed the negative publicity influence her. Nevertheless, the recent events remained an inescapable topic of conversation for the simple reason everything else seemed trivial and unimportant in comparison.

"I didn't hear until this morning," Suzy explained, although she didn't have to, Katherine noticed Suzy and Charlie were becoming very close, spending many nights going out somewhere or other, it wasn't a surprise they missed the news. "This is just terrible. I don't believe Gerry's involved, he *can't* be, I mean, I just can't see it. He doesn't strike me as someone who would get messed up in anything hideous like that."

"I can't either, but there's more, and I don't know how to deal with it yet," Katherine sighed, disclosing to Suzy everything Pops and Gramps had revealed.

"Well, the news dragged that up all right," Suzy admitted gravely, "and ... I don't know if you should hear this yet, but there were other reports of smuggling charges that happened in the past, mostly near the Mexican border, things like that."

"Oh my God! This is a nightmare! This can't be real!" Katherine gasped, burying her face in her hands.

"I really think you should stay home, take a few days off actually. Just say the word, and I'll flip a U."

"No, like I said, I've got things to do, and work will help to keep me occupied right now."

At least, she thought it would, but today, the gallery atmosphere was anything but normal as Andre, Esther and Dennis offered their commiserations, voicing their disbelief with the situation. When she could finally escape to the seclusion of the office to catch up on her paperwork, there was a knock on the door. It was Charlie.

"Kathy, I just heard the news on my way in and I had to stop by. I know this is an asinine question, but I have to ask if you are all right."

"Let's just say I've had better days," she said, laying her pen aside. "Come in, sit down."

"Good God, I'm sorry Kathy, I wish I could say or do something to make you feel better," he began, pulling over a chair, "we promised we'd always be there for each other."

"It's the thought that counts. I am glad you stopped by."

"Do you want to talk about it?"

"I would, but … now that I'm beginning to understand what … well, I don't want to open wounds, it wouldn't be right."

Charlie was silent for a moment.

"I thought we weren't going to tiptoe around each other. What's the point of 'being there' then? I know you care for him Kathy, it's okay to talk about it with me. I only wanted the best for you, whatever makes you happy."

She took a slow intake of breath.

"There are so many things going around in my head right now, and to make it worse, Pops has strongly advised I may have to stop seeing Gerry, and by the way he said it, that also includes anyone and anything to do with him. It's like everyone has declared Gerry and the whole family guilty before they've had a chance to defend themselves, but what frightens me the most, maybe there *is* something to it after all, that what Pops pronounced is a … prediction."

"I'm so sorry all this happened, I tried not to listen to the other reports this morning, hoping for your sake it was all a trumped up smear campaign, but it looks pretty bleak."

"I know, we may have to break up, and yet, I don't *want* to, I don't *want* to believe those reports. Charlie, you know the Reinolds too, even if only on a business level. Do they seem like a family capable of a criminal action like this?"

"I wish you didn't ask me that," he said, pursing his lips.

"I'm sorry, I know you can't break lawyer-client confidentiality, but anything that would help tip the scales of justice in their favour, I would be grateful. It's terrible of me to ask you … ."

"No, it's not that, even if I could tell you all their legal history with us, what I have to say is not good, and while I want to protect you, I don't want to see you get hurt any further."

"Not good? What do you know?"

Charlie restlessly rubbed his forehead for a second.

"I could be disbarred for saying this, so please don't repeat it, but I read their files while working on their property dispute on the docks a few years back, they were constantly getting in trouble with contraband seizures. Sure, there is a huge problem with an unscrupulous element working it's way into shipping companies, corrupt drivers, shop stewards, even the police, but I can't help but be suspicious. For your sake, I didn't say anything, there was no evidence linking the actual management of their company to these illegal operations, and every charge against them was dropped, not to mention this happened a long time ago, but this is the first time they've been implicated in a human trafficking operation. In my experience, where there's smoke there's fire." Katherine's stomach tightened, Charlie's hunches were seldom wrong. "I'm sorry, I meant to help and I've only made things worse, but if this is any consolation, bitter as it may seem, maybe it's best that you find out now before your feelings for him become serious," he concluded dismally.

Katherine didn't know what to say, Pop's strong suggestion was looking more like a foreboding omen every minute.

"I think you should take some time off, go home and give yourself some space from all this right now," he added.

"I wish everyone would stop staying that!" He jumped with her sharp, frustrated tone. "I'm sorry Charlie," she sighed, "I didn't t mean to snap, but I feel like a fuse ready to short circuit."

"No it's all right, you're just stressed, it's understandable."

"I know you and everybody else means well, but this is something I can't run and hide from, hoping it will go away. It will follow me wherever I go and just make things worse. If I didn't have a routine and obligations, I'd implode with the strain of what I'm facing. Right now, work is a blessing."

"Okay, but don't overdo it and burn yourself out, you … tend to take things to extremes."

"Burn out doesn't sound bad actually, I might be able to sleep tonight," she noted mordantly.

"That bad, is it."

"Oh, don't mind me, I'll be all right. You'd better hurry or you'll be late for work, or court."

"Work today, I've got a few meetings."

"I hope they go well."

"Thanks, but I'm more worried about you."

"Don't be, things look bad, but I'll get through this. On a lighter note, are you taking Suzy out to lunch today?"

"No, maybe tomorrow. I've let a few things pile up in the office that I have to take care of. Work may be a blessing for some," he smiled.

"Oh well, I don't want to hold you up. I guess I'll see you later."

"Okay, but don't hesitate to call if you need anything," he said, giving her hand a reassuring squeeze.

"Thanks, Charlie."

Katherine gathered her scattered thoughts and tried to focus on her tax returns, another inescapable reality. Thank God for calculators, she didn't want to invent a whole new percentage bracket in her present distracted state and start any trouble with Uncle Sam. Crunching numbers and filling out forms became a mind-numbing escape, for a short while at least until the phone rang, it was Steves.

"Geeze Kats, I just heard the news. How are you holding up?"

"Give a guess," she said, "he's released from police custody, but other than that, I don't know. Given the problems his company had in the past, it doesn't look good. Pops doesn't want me to see him any more."

"Good lord. Listen, he can't order you not to, and I don't think Gerry is guilty. I thought I'd offer you my services, or rather, a friend's service who owes me a big favour."

"Oh? Who?"

"He's from South Korea, he was an exchange student here at MIT for awhile and now owns an internet service company in Seoul. He'd have no problems looking up police records in Jakarta and find out what's happening."

"Good grief! Would he do that?"

"Um, let's say his King Fu is very strong, rivals my own. I'd look up the records, if I could read Javanese."

"Oh no you don't Steves, but thank you for the offer of your … martial arts, I don't want anything to happen to you too." She knew what he meant now and was guarded over the phone, she couldn't have him hacking for her sake, although she was tempted to take him up on it.

"Okay, but if you change your mind, just buzz my communicator. This guy I know once made a … visit … to Interpol and once to the FBI with no problems, finding information in Jakarta is no sweat for him."

"I'll keep that in mind."

If Steve's proposal of criminal hacking wasn't enough, Aunt Martha heard the news and wanted to try and cheer her up at lunchtime.

"You see, what did I tell you? It's a good thing you found out now before this Gerry ruined your life completely."

Thanks, that makes me feel a lot better.

"Oh come now," Esther interjected, "you don't believe the news? We're not hearing everything yet, and I can't see Gerry involved with this trafficking business."

This media furore was hard for everyone at the gallery, they had grown used to his regular visits during the month before his departure and missed him when he left almost as much as Katherine did. He always had a joke or something pithy to say to the guards on duty, quietly watching Andre and his team making bouillabaisse hoping to discover his secret recipe, helping the girls to water the potted ferns or move pictures around the gallery, pointing out when the cleaners had missed a spot on the terrazzo, gave tours to customers when he was mistaken for one of the help, he had become a familiar face, an honorary member of the gallery gang.

Closing time came and Suzy drove her home. Katherine tried to finish her dinner to please her mother, but could only manage a few mouthfuls. It was almost impossible to settle down, it was not easy sitting, fidgeting, waiting for the evening news only to discover there were no substantial developments. Gerard Reinold was unavailable for comment, his whereabouts were unknown although it was confirmed he had not left the country. There was a quick statement released by the CEO of Reinold Enterprises declaring his son's innocence, further adding they were not involved in this shocking affair, he had every confidence in the authorities and that the true culprits would be brought to justice. Unfortunately, this was an expected assertion that didn't offer concrete evidence of Gerry's innocence, not to mention his mysterious disappearance from public view didn't inspire any confidence with Pops and Gramps. The report went on to include new information about the victims caught up in the tragedy, poor villagers from the Philippines and Cambodia who were guaranteed a passage to the United States, and did not expect to find themselves stuck in Jakarta, that was not the route the smugglers had said they were taking.

"Tim was right, this doesn't look good at all, we'll have to break our contract with them for our shipping, I don't want our cargo used to whitewash or aid and abet this tragedy," Pops grimly stated.

"I know," Gramps grumbled, "another logistical nightmare for us, but Tim can hack it. I suppose he's already investigating other shipping companies, we'll have a talk with him in the morning. Blast, we struck up a good deal with the Reinolds too."

"Oh Pops, can you at least wait until we find out if they are personally involved?" Despite what she heard during the last few days, Katherine still hung on to a thread of hope everything was not as it seemed.

"I'm sorry, but guilty or innocent, our own company may be considered guilty by association until this is cleared up. Any business seen to be a supporter may be boycotted along with theirs," Pops stated, shaking his head.

"This is unbelievable," but she knew he was right, it was easy for a business to become unjustly tarnished as he suggested. However, she wasn't prepared for his next statement:

"I know this is difficult to take in, and while it pains me to say this, you may have to return Gerard and Charlotte's loan pieces too, or this fiasco could spread to your gallery."

"What? Lottie too! What has their art collection got to do with his shipping company?"

"It's not just his company Katie, it's *anything* to do with him now," Gramps explained.

"As your father, it's my duty to warn you things may deteriorate rapidly depending on the media and the circus they create."

"Well, I'm not going to do anything just yet," she firmly resolved. "Whatever happened to innocent until *proven* guilty? We should practise what we preach. Aren't we supposed to support those we care about, not just run the minute they are in trouble? He came to the rescue and helped fill the rest of my space at a time when I needed it, the least I can do is wait and see."

"And what about that visit to Sotheby's? You haven't taken us up on our offer yet," Pops noted gently.

"I'm sorry about that," she replied sheepishly, "I do appreciate your gift, it's just that I've been so busy, and the fact nothing really interesting came up in the catalogues. If I'm going to spend *that* much, it'll be for something I like."

"That's sensible dear," Mom nodded, "there's no rush."

"I don't want to be blunt," Gramps interjected, "but we do have to rush about this shipping business. How long do you think it will take Tim to sort this out?" he asked, turning to Pops.

So much for my input.

Katherine decided to go to her room, she didn't relish having to watch the Reinolds unceremoniously dropped like this. It was bad enough

Gerry was in serious trouble; she couldn't bear to hurt Lottie too. At least she could follow her own advice, wait and see what happens before she considered packing up their collection.

ೞ❀ೞ

"How are the critics today? Any mention of us?" Katherine enquired the next morning, watching Suzy and Dennis flip through the papers. Dennis thought it might be a valuable project to archive all news related to the gallery and its featured artists, just in case they happened to make it into art history and attracted historians in future years hungry for source material. Interested in the critiques once more, it was fun watching the products of their scrap booking grow.

"Um, nothing about the gallery today," Suzy said, "not since Horace lambasted Turris."

"Of course, we don't have scheduled events, it's harder to attract publicity without a début showing or something like that to generate interest," Katherine conceded.

"But your rotation system is good, I'm not complaining there," Dennis added, still flipping through his paper. "Hmm it's odd that Horace isn't up to his usual tricks, I don't see anything written by him today at all."

"Really? That's odd I …oh no!" Suzy gasped, turning past the art section and casting a glance at one dreaded column, it was impossible to overlook the word 'Walsingham', it was too big to miss.

"What is it?"

"Oh Kathy…"

Katherine and Dennis jumped out of their seats and read the article over Suzy's shoulder:

"The New Reinold Romance: A Radiant Beginning Already in Ruins?"

> *Can love be in the air my fellow New Yorkers? Rumour has it that the city's most eligible bachelor, Gerard Reinold has finally been hooked by a charming damsel. Who do you ask? Katherine Walsingham, the most eligible, if not a little cloistered bachelorette who missed her outing at the débutante ball if you recall. They have been spotted at several locations together since December, including the Met and various exclusive restaurants …dare I mention the 'Rainbow Room' this past Valentine's Day? Of course, we should not be*

Katherine was stunned to see her private life blatantly cast into the public arena, written like a cheap soap opera for the titillation of the bored masses who had nothing better to do than to gloat on other people's heartbreaks or grow jealous of their success, and of course, all in an effort to sell more pulp at the paper kiosks. She dreaded to think what the papers printed when they reported she and Charlie were a hot item in town.

"This is typical garbage," Dennis frowned, "why can't they leave people alone?"

"Because they have a career to kick-start, bills to pay and stomachs to fill," Katherine said dejectedly. Christopher had told her all about it. Wait, did he leak this? He was the only one with whom she had discussed her relationship with Gerry: he not only worked for this particular publication, but was a senior editor for that section of the paper. Perhaps it was too tempting for Horace to pass up after all, giving the Beastie Woman the scoop if he wasn't going to write it himself. No, he said he wouldn't spill the beans, everything in the column read as though the Beastie had found all her information from outside sources like Christopher said she could. In fact, anyone who saw her and Gerry together were possible sources, and reporters had plenty of those. The strange part was, she wasn't angry. The shock of the last few days made her too weary to feel irate with this latest exposure in the press. She was more anxious about the aftermath, recalling the diverse reactions she experienced with the critique of her Napoléon.

"I'm sick of this, if it's not Horace, it's the Beastie Barbarian," Suzy said irritably, crumpling the paper and throwing it into the trash bin.

"I know, but it was bound to happen," Katherine sighed resignedly.

"Um, I think you may want to scram upstairs to the studio today," Dennis said quickly, looking up and eyeing the windows, "reporter sighted, twelve o-clock."

It was Christopher.

"Great, not him too? I suppose this story was too good to pass up," Suzy grumbled.

"Katherine, may I speak to you alone for a minute," Christopher asked. She couldn't refuse, his apologetic expression told her she should at least give him a chance to explain.

"All right," indicating towards the office. Katherine closed the door and they took a seat, sitting in silence for a moment.

"I suppose you read our paper this morning?"

"I did."

"I apologize for that. I just want you to know I never said a word about you and Mr. Reinold, and I had nothing to do with Beatrice's column. She came up with it at the last minute when we were preparing the morning edition. I pulled it, but she went over my head to the editor in chief. He decided to run it, and there wasn't anything I could do. I wanted to warn you, but I didn't have your private number."

"It's all right, I understand. I figured the Beastie found out by herself, she only mentioned all the places we went to in public, it was a matter of time before she put two and two together, and of course, now is an opportune moment to write a juicy article."

"God, some days, I really hate my job," Smith said, ruffling his hair, "I'm sorry that all I can do is offer an apology."

"I'm just glad it didn't come from you," Katherine smiled.

"Hey, Christopher Robert Horace Smith has a conscience, remember? But seriously, how are you holding up?"

"I'm fine. I'll be all right."

"I know you're just saying that for now, but it will be true eventually."

"Oh, who am I kidding? I'm a mess to tell you the truth. I can't believe Gerry could be involved in all this. I hear the reports, but … I don't know what to think anymore. Everyone keeps telling me that it's good to find out now before it's too late, that where there's smoke, etcetera."

"I don't want to rub it in, but I'm afraid I'm another one of those 'better you found out now' well-wishers."

"You don't think he's guilty, do you?"

"Well, innocent until proven otherwise, but with all the past accusations, it certainly looks fishy. Call it a reporter's pessimism if you like, but I did try and warn you about Greeks bearing gifts."

Good lord, it seemed a number of people were suspicious of the Reinolds and their operations long before now. *Was* Gerry just too good to be true?

"I'm sorry, I know this is all too much to take in right now, but I have another warning to give, just in case." Katherine looked at him with alarm.

"There's more?"

"Not like that, it's just now that Beatrice has published the first big scoop on your trysts with Mr. Reinold, it's fair game from here on out. You may get …" At that moment, the telephone rang.

"Oops, excuse me while I get this." Christopher raised his hand to try and dissuade her, but she whipped the handset up too fast. "Walsingham Gallery. Um…I'm sorry … *she's* not available right now. … No we do not have a statement at present. … No, no comment. …. I'm sorry, no interviews … goodbye." Katherine quickly clapped the receiver back down with a startled look. She was glad she had the presence of mind to pretend someone else had answered.

"Let me guess, enquiring minds want to know," he sardonically quipped.

"Not from the *Enquirer*, but close enough," she grimaced, comprehending the warning he was about to give. "This is just the beginning, isn't it?" The phone rang again.

"Don't answer it."

"I've got to, I may have customers trying to get through." This time it was the local news channel. She evaded their requests for interviews, dropped the receiver, and jumping to the door, called out in panic: "Suzy! Dennis! Fire in the hole! Damage control!"

She quickly coached them for media bombardments with the pat replies 'Katherine Walsingham is not available' and 'no comment' before returning to the office. It was difficult to talk as the phone rang, stopped, rang again, and stopped, Suzy and Dennis tackling the growing requests for interviews.

"Gee, I don't know why they are interested in me, I don't know any more than they do, in fact, probably a lot less," she noted, "gosh, Gerry and I are not movie stars."

"Well, you are high society here, and you do generate a 'Lifestyles of the Rich and Famous' type of curiosity with people."

"That sounds cheesy."

"I know, but they love peeking into your world, thinking it's like living a fairytale. They just want the girlfriend's take on the situation, hoping to capture a tear-jerker moment before anyone else. The first day or two will be rough, but it'll die down eventually. Is there anywhere you can lay low for awhile?" he suggested.

"Great, just when I thought work might help me, I have to avoid this place too."

"Either that, or lock yourself up in your studio like Howard Hughes."

"Oh for heaven's sake, I didn't do anything wrong, and I'm not about to hide away now. It couldn't be any worse than when I was active with my animal rights protests."

"Well, at least you know how to handle the situation," he nodded. "I suppose I should be heading off, but before I go, is there anything I can do to help get you over this?"

"Thanks Chris, there's nothing right now, but before I forget, I've got good news for you, two of your paintings sold and are gone, let me make out the cheque while you're here."

"Hey, that's something positive, and to be paid lickety-split is nothing to sneeze at."

"Yeah business is … was good, I don't know what's going to happen after all this."

"I don't think you have to worry about that," he observed, nodding to the security screens, "*any* publicity works."

There was a considerable number of people already browsing around, a lot more than usual for a Saturday morning. How ironic, Gerry was right; art thrived on scandal, and now it feasted on his public degradation. Instead of feeling relieved with the large turnout, she found the sight utterly distasteful.

"They've come for all the wrong reasons," she frowned, glaring at the screen. "We've been here for months, Gerry's collection too for that matter, and *now* we may have a continual packed house drawn by morbid inquisitiveness, not for a real love of art."

"I know, it gets you in the gut, doesn't it? That's why Robert Horace does so well; everyone cries 'For shame!', yet they lap his columns up like a cat with cream."

"I'd never thought I'd say this, but this is the first time I wished we had a quiet day."

"It's the public Kathy, rabble mentality. Caesar had to keep the mob happy with gladiator shows, bloody duels to the death, and you have to keep your gallery running too, just let them wander around and glut their gossipy curiosity. They may soak up a little culture along the way."

"So it's throw us to the lions for art's sake."

"That's how it is. I'm sorry to leave you like this, but I've got to head into the office. If I can be of service, just give a call. Don't worry, I can see myself out, you just hunker down in here for awhile."

"Okay, thanks."

Katherine tried to continue with other paperwork now that her taxes were finished, but the incessant blurping ring of the phone made concentration impossible. She observed the monitors for a few moments, it was a surreal situation. A large group of visitors meandered around the permanent exhibition space, paying particular attention to Gerry's loans, especially the manuscripts he had given her. A few teenage girls huddled together pointing to them, probably all infatuated with the latest romantic tragedy. Darn that Beastie woman! Until that stupid article came out this morning, nobody except her family and close acquaintances had guessed his intentions when he presented the illuminated pages; to everyone else they were simply another donation with the expected brass plaque. The feeling of repugnance surged as she watched her personal life exposed to the 'ohhing and awing' of a bunch of teeny-boppers. She didn't want to profit from this tragic situation, playing Caesar and using gladiator tactics to attract publicity. Restlessness soon followed her repugnance, an uneasiness she couldn't shake, and Katherine wondered if she should consider closing the gallery for the day, something just did not feel right. After a few minutes, she thought better of it. No, I can't close shop. Regardless of her and Gerry, the artists on display depended on her gallery and it wouldn't be fair to deprive them of this publicity, twisted as it was. It would be better if she let business run as normal until everyone grew tired of the story; the public's attention span was short and would run after a new scandal within days as Christopher said. Maybe I can just swipe the manuscripts away to the studio, the mob has enough to gaggle at for now, must take care of the lunch shifts first. Exiting the office to relieve Dennis from his post, she was surprised to see Esther had unexpectedly arrived on her day off.

"Esther! What are you doing here?"

"I saw the paper and thought you may need an extra volunteer to man the castle."

"Thank you, I appreciate that, we could certainly use the assistance, but I don't expect you to work on your free day for nothing."

"I didn't come for the overtime dear."

"No, I wouldn't hear of it."

"Let's not haggle now, I can see we're going to have a day of it," Esther said, looking around. "I saw Mr. Horace leave. I hope he wasn't pestering you."

"Oh no, he actually came to apologize for his colleague's column, said he tried to stop it from going to print, but the editor had the final call."

"Well, that's a switch for Horace," Suzy noted, "I was afraid he would be revelling in this."

"Me too. Oh, before I go to lunch," Dennis interjected, "I thought you should know, the printers got through on the phone and said they would have the shipment of brochures ready this afternoon."

"That's good, we were running low," Suzy nodded with relief.

Back to business. Katherine was glad to handle the mundane, it helped to keep her grounded amidst the ogling crowds and ringing phone lines. Stephie would be coming by later that afternoon to take pictures of D.S.'s two new murals before Dan and Leo came by that evening to pick them up for a night delivery to Jim the Breeze's other club across town currently undergoing refurbishments. It was going to be tight, she hoped Stephie would be on time. That reminded her, she wanted to take the manuscripts down, might as well do that now.

"Do you two think you can keep an eye on things while I handle something on the third floor? It shouldn't take too long, but I'll need Patrick to help."

"Sure, they're just looking around, everything's under control, no one is asking for help at the moment, go ahead," Suzy nodded.

"Okay."

Katherine retrieved the metallic case belonging to the unicorn collection in the old boiler house. She couldn't ignore the lump in her throat as she quickly glanced at the stack of similar cases in the corner. She left there fast and closed the door. Taking the elevator, she had a quick moment to catch her breath before a few visitors from the second floor got on and travelled with her to the third where she greeted Patrick and Giovanni behind the security desk.

"Hi guys, I need to remove the unicorn frame."

"Oh sure, Ma'am, no problem," Patrick replied, jumping to attention. "Is it possible to have a quiet word?"

"Um, sure. You can come up to the studio with me after we get the manuscripts."

The visitors 'awed' in disappointment as Patrick disarmed the tripwires and she quickly unhooked the popular piece, snapping the frame in the case out of sight.

"I'll take that Ma'am," he offered.

"Thank you, Patrick."

In a few minutes, they reached the sanctuary of her studio, away from the whispering crowd.

"Well, I just wanted to say I know this all looks very bad right now, but don't believe a word of it: that young man is not guilty, I can tell. It's not in him. I was on the force for many years, I can smell a rat a mile away, he's doesn't fit the profile."

"I appreciate that Patrick, but how can you be so sure?"

"I know they say intuition is not much to go on, and I may not have any of those fancy forensic psychology degrees, I got my experience first hand. Real criminals, as hard and tough as they get, know they've taken a low road, it's in their eyes, the fact they become tough shows they're trying to kill their conscience or have already succeeded. I've taken in some real rotten apples in my time, bad cops, Mafia hoods, badness exudes from them like used oil leaking from a busted motor, you know what I'm saying? Gerry is not one of them, he's got light in his eyes, you know? You can always tell, just ask Giovanni, he believes he's innocent too. Says the man's either been framed, or some hoods are using his shipping operation. We've seen all types of crimes happen in shipping, and its usually from the ground up, not the top down: mobsters hijacking trucks and selling off the goods or sneaking in drivers who do the smuggling without the owners knowing. I'll bet you anything that's what's happened. He's got one headache after another trying to run that company of his."

"I hope that's all it is. I ... goodness, what's going on?"

Their conversation was interrupted by cries of disbelief and the sound of a woman screaming above the din echoing up the stairwell from the third floor. They could hear Giovanni yelling something, but couldn't make out what was happening as Katherine raced behind Patrick down the stairs and was stunned to see Giovanni manhandling a wildly thrashing middle-aged Asian woman kicking and shrieking as he pinned her to the floor. Patrick rushed to yank the spray cans from her hands. Katherine gasped as she looked around the exhibition area, her hands flying to her mouth:

"Oh my God!"

The infuriated woman had vandalized several tapestries and two paintings donated by Gerry, spray painting huge swathes of black enamel across the wall from one exhibit to the next, inflicting atrocious damage, just missing Lottie's Rembrandt by inches before Giovanni could grab her. Visitors stumbled backed in horror, startled by the violent scene playing out before them.

"Geeze, she nearly knocked over the case with the vase too," Giovanni added, clamping a set of cuffs over the criminal's wrists. Katherine wondered why the guards bothered to carry handcuffs in a gallery, but now she knew. New York and Brooklyn were full of wackos. The irate woman continued to screech like a peacock in an unknown language, no doubt vociferating judgement on the 'slave traders' as the guards had prevented her from defacing the remainder of their art collection.

Suzy and Dennis arrived breathless at the top of the stairs, they had seen the pandemonium break out on the monitors below, but were paralysed in confusion as they watched the chaotic scene.

"Miss Kathy, I'll take this one upstairs, keep her away from any other pieces," Giovanni stated taking the still yelling woman to the elevator. "Come on lady, you *do* have the right to remain silent, you know. Geeze, what a mess," he said pushing her inside.

"Okay everyone, with the exception of those who witnessed the attack, I'll have to ask people to please clear the floor," Patrick said, assuming an official tone acquired from years of duty, directing the bewildered browsers to the stairs, "visiting hours are over for today. I'm sorry Miss Kathy," he said, taking her aside for a minute, "but it may be best to close the gallery, we have to call the police, the less confusion the better, plus, we don't want a repeat performance on the other floors. One sicko may attract another."

"All right people," she said, turning to Suzy and Dennis, "authority has spoken, let's close up."

Why didn't she follow her intuition?

If she had closed, this would not have happened. Guilt gripped her as she went to the security desk and made a broadcast over the sound system, announcing the gallery was now closing early and apologized for the inconvenience, however *Chez Garneu* would still be open for business. Now that the area had been cleared of visitors, with the exception of a few witnesses, Katherine and Patrick surveyed the damage, the sight of the saturated tapestries and the paintings besmirched with large streaks of black made her feel nauseous, her mind spinning from the vicious act of vandalism. The paintings were bad enough, but examining the tapestry, she wondered if the paint could ever be completely extracted from the delicate threads now centuries old. Rare pieces worth millions were seriously damaged, and she had no idea what do next. First things first, Patrick called the security company, they would call the appropriate authorities.

"It's amazing she didn't set off the alarms, of course she didn't pull at the pieces," he said, waiting for his call to get through, "this system wasn't designed to stop graffiti attacks."

"Is there any way they can come without making a big fuss? I've got enough publicity as it is," Katherine noted.

"Sure, I can request them to send officers in unmarked cars."

"That would be appreciated."

Everyone had to spend the rest of the afternoon giving statements to the police. Unfortunately, all they could do was take the woman to the station, the damage had now been done. However, the word had leaked somehow and reporters were flocking around the building. One of the detectives turned out to be Patrick's friend, and had no problem with his request to have a few officers remain to help keep the reporters out while allowing the restaurant to remain open, although Andre was not thrilled with this solution either, it was obvious the police presence would deter any patrons under the present circumstances.

"Reminds me of the time when that nut case broke the arm off Michelangelo's *Pieta* with a hammer, hard to believe that happened twenty years ago," Detective Shumaker sighed incredulously, flipping his notebook shut after his interrogations were over. "I'm sorry Miss Walsingham, she'll most definitely be charged for her criminal act and held over for trial, and if she doesn't end up in a psychiatric unit, she might be ordered to pay up for the restoration, but chances are she won't be able to cough up enough to fix what she wrecked. That's about it really. I hope you're covered for the damage."

"Yes, but what to do about it right now is the problem," she admitted. She hadn't heard from Gerry since the disaster broke out in Jakarta, and wondered how on earth she was going to sort this out, or break the news to him when he contacted her since according to the news he could not be located right now, he had obviously left the hotel where he had been staying. She could call Lottie, but how terrible to drop this new misfortune on her now, maybe she should wait and call her later. It wasn't going to be easy telling her that one of his Holbeins and Rubens plus several medieval tapestries were liberally spritzed with spray enamel.

"I suppose that's about it. Patrick knows where to find me, but here's my card, please call me if anything else comes up."

"I hope not, but thank you detective," she said, reading his card.

Stephie arrived just as the detectives were leaving. The police stationed at the doors prevented her from entering when they saw her hauling a camera case and tripod, but let her pass when Katherine told them it was all right.

"God! Was the article that bad you had to call for police protection?" Stephie wondered. "What's happened?"

"You won't believe it," Esther replied, quickly telling her about the destruction on the third floor. Stephie went up to check out the damage, and could be heard half-muttering exclamations when she came back down.

"I think I could do with a cup of coffee right now, and so does everyone else," Esther nodded.

"Oh well, might as well close everything down in the gallery end," Katherine decided, taking the phone off the hook. "There, that's better, it was driving me nuts. Nothing but requests for exclusives! Andre, do you think you will still be able to open tonight?"

"Yeah, the late lunch hour is shot, but my dinner reservations might still come in," Andre noted, "and we haven't had a cancellation yet."

"Will I send away the boys in blue then?" Patrick asked.

"I guess so, please thank them for keeping the reporters out," Katherine added.

"Of course."

"If they're off duty after this, tell them they don't have to leave right away, they can join us in the restaurant," Andre offered, "it's not dinner time yet, and we need some recovery food, my treat."

"They'll appreciate that," Patrick nodded.

Andre closed the curtains so they could have some peace from the lingering reporters knocking on the glass, trying to attract their attention. Considering the fact Gerry once joked he couldn't see 'bicycle red' and 'front gate black' making a splash in a formal gallery, the whole situation was quite surreal. Katherine was grateful for the coffee, tea and the large platter of pastries Andre brought out, eating seemed to take the edge off the shock, although it was a bitter irony they were all munching on croissants. Stephanie decided she had better get to work after a few bites since the deliverymen might be there soon to take down D.S.'s murals. Katherine asked if she wouldn't mind taking extra photos of the vandalism while she was upstairs, she wasn't sure whose insurance company would handle the situation, Gerry or hers, it was good to have photos just in case they were required.

"I feel bad just sitting here, I should be trying to wipe the paint off the pictures," Suzy said dejectedly, "at least Stephie can help with the insurance photos."

"I know, but we could damage the pieces further if we tried anything," Katherine replied. "The paintings can be restored, the tapestries have me worried, I don't know how they can fix those except have an expert rethread them by hand, and then it's all replaced material, not the original thread. This is terrible."

"Well, tapestries usually have threads reworked into them anyway, so it may not be as bad as you think," Esther noted, "look at the Raphael tapestries at the Vatican, it takes about three years of hand stitched replacements per tapestry to keep them in good condition."

Three years? Somehow that didn't make her feel better, but she knew Esther meant well. Soon, it came time for the restaurant staff to prepare for dinner. The night watch, Tyler and Kyle, came to relieve Patrick and Giovanni from their shift and offered their commiserations to Katherine.

"Watch those stupid reporters," Patrick warned them, "they may try to jimmy open the fire escape window to get some pictures and end up tripping the whole alarm off."

"Got it covered," Tyle nodded.

Katherine wished everyone a goodnight, she had to stay behind and wait for Dan and Leo, reminding them to tell the reporters on their way out 'no comment'. She realized as she locked the gates on the stairs she may have to come up with some statements before the two guys arrived in case the Reinold truck excited speculation on what happened in the gallery that afternoon. A sudden flurry of flashing brought her attention to the side entrance, Pops, Gramps and Uncle Tim had shown up and were rapping on the door, the reporters snapping photos as they waited like a trio of sitting ducks for someone to open up.

"Kathy, we heard the news as we left the office, are you all right?" Pops asked, concern etched on his face, "we tried calling, but couldn't get through. Your mother is worried sick."

"I think I'm fine, I'm a little light headed, must be shock, but nothing happened to me personally," she said, giving him a hug, "except for the Beastie column, but that's nothing. It's Gerry's collection, very valuable pieces have been ruined, and I don't know how to get in contact with him, and in any case, he's got enough to worry about, art is probably the last thing on his mind right now, but he must be told."

"My poor Katie, what a situation you had to face today," Gramps said, giving her a big hug after Pops. "Dare we survey the damage?"

"Sure, let me unlock the elevator."

"Hi everyone," Stephie said glumly as they gathered around while she snapped an extra photograph before packing up, "what a day."

They stared silently at the devastation for several minutes.

"I was afraid something might happen," Pops stated solemnly, finally breaking the silence, "but I didn't expect anything like this."

"If it's any consolation Kathy, it looks like the walls will be easy to repair," Uncle Tim noted, scratching at the paint on the wainscoting, "I don't know about the pieces though."

"I'm just grateful it wasn't an acid attack, that would have been a lot worse," Katherine added, "that's usually the weapon of choice for art vandals."

"Well, this is looking pretty serious," Gramps replied, leaning on his cane, "You've been publicly connected with the Reinolds now. If I were you, I'd close the gallery for the next week at least, wait until the curiosity generated by the article dies down. Andre can still open up now that you have installed the stairwell gates, just keep the gallery under wraps for a few days."

Although she disliked the idea of giving in to the pressure, she couldn't argue. Gramps was right, simply closing the exhibition area may not be enough, and now that she was loosely associated with the incidents in Jakarta, she couldn't put the work of her artists at risk, Patrick did warn her one wacko could attract more. That reminded her, she had better take all the works off the rolly-polies and lock them away in the gift corner, they were still exposed.

"You're right, better to play it safe," she sighed.

"Look, it's not all bad, you don't have to stay at home if you don't want to, they can't stop you painting, can they?" Stephie observed, trying to shine a little light on a bleak situation.

"Stephie has a point, you can catch up on some art that's been put off. Just …dodge the reporters when you come and go," Uncle Tim added.

"True, at least they can't stop my work."

"That's the spirit," Gramps agreed, "when this dies down, you'll have new items for display."

This suggestion did not make her feel better, but perhaps this was an opportunity in disguise. A little quiet time with her paintbrushes without the business pulling her attention away might be just what she needed to calm down. Suzy and Dennis could use some extra painting time too. First, there were other matters to handle.

"For now, what should I do about the press? Should I give a statement about today's incidents, get them out of the way? If the sharks have some info, they might back off."

"Or make them hungry for more, but we should try and cool this down a bit," Pops mused, rubbing his chin for a second.

"No, it's my duty to sort this out," Katherine announced resolutely, "I appreciate the support, but I've got responsibilities now, and that includes handling the nasty side since I agreed to display Gerry's collection in the first place."

"Well, I'm proud of you for that," Pops noted, "but we're not going to throw you to the wolves either. At least allow one of us to stand with you out there, just to make sure things don't get out of hand."

"Wait a minute, why not just give an exclusive to someone?" Stephie jumped in. "Let the journalist of your choice have first dibs, that might back the rest of them off, but make sure you give it to someone you know who will get the facts straight, and spell your name correctly for that matter."

"That's not a bad idea," Gramps agreed, "but you might have to release some of your pictures to show the damage, just to make sure the exclusive is thorough enough to keep the others away."

"At least you'll get some extra royalties from your photos, Stephie," Kathy said, shrugging her shoulders, "just consider it another item to add to your CV."

"I wouldn't mind that," she replied, "I hope the insurance company doesn't have anything against releasing details of the crime."

"I won't know until I get in touch with Lottie," Katherine mused.

"I'm surprised Gerard didn't give you that information," Uncle Tim noted.

"He said to call him if I ever needed it, but that was before the Jakarta fiasco. Who knew all of this was going to happen?"

"Well, I'm not familiar with the art world, but there shouldn't be a problem with a news exclusive, just as long as the scene of the crime is left untouched to allow the insurance inspectors examine the damage, that's usually how claims operate," Pops observed, "but I'd try and get through to them as soon as possible, a claim must be made within a certain period from the time of the incident in question."

"You know, maybe the news report is the only way you may be able to let the Reinolds know what happened," Stephie wryly noted.

"What a way to find out! Maybe I should just call Gerry's secretary in the morning, maybe he gave her instructions in case I had an emergency."

"You can't, not on a Sunday," Gramps reminded her.

"Nuts! I don't know what day it is anymore. I'll have to call Lottie then, I'd better do that now."

"All right, there's nothing more we can do up here," Pops noted, "might as well follow you back down."

Katherine tried calling Lottie a few times, but her number was busy. Maybe later tonight she could get through. Should she call Stonyvale? She tried the number, it too was engaged. Perhaps the manor was also hounded by reporters all day and Victor ended up having to take the phone off the hook. Modern conveniences could be terribly inconvenient at times, the minute she replaced the receiver, the bleeper went off: another request for an interview or a brief comment.

"The media have been upsetting everyone at home as well," Pops informed her as she cut the call short and laid the handset back on the desk.

"How did they get our private number? We won't be able to call anyone if they keep this up," Katherine muttered, "I'll just have to go ahead and get our reporter."

"Who're you gonna call?" Stephie wondered.

"Looks like I don't have to, he's already here," Katherine announced, nodding towards the door. A figure in a trench coat had managed to push his way through the crowd and waved to get her attention as Kyle was dutifully keeping the press out.

"Robert Horace? You're not serious," her cousin huffed in disbelief.

"Are you sure that's wise?" her father wondered, raising an eyebrow.

"In this instance, Horace will do no harm," Katherine said, motioning to Kyle to let him in.

"Aw, come on Horace, you get all the fun around here, let us have a go, will ya," one reporter called out, giving his peer a hard rap.

"Sorry Jimbo, the lady has made her choice," he replied, jumping through the door and quickly pulling over a rolly-polie with panache, blocking the other reporters from view without obstructing the entryway from the diners trying to nudge their way in through the throng.

"I thought Robert Horace was older?" Uncle Tim whispered to Katherine.

"Well young man," Gramps semi-greeted, one eyebrow raised, cane firmly planted in front of him, "you've probably heard the news, and our Kathy here has decided to give you the first scoop on the 'incident' that happened today, why, I don't rightly know, but I hope you will treat the matter with due respect and not create a bigger problem for her."

"I shall do my best to comply, as I told Miss Walsingham, I didn't approve of Beatrice's column."

"That's true, I didn't get a chance to tell you," Katherine added before turning to Christoper, "Chr … er … Robert, you said if there was anything you could do to help."

"Sure, let me see what I'm dealing with first," he said. Katherine took him upstairs, a few vulgarities escaped his lips as he ran his hands through his hair in astonishment before folding his arms in disgust, further scrutinizing the inky atrocity streaked along the wall. "I'm sorry, but that's just … man! Whatever Mr. Reinold may be implicated in, no one should take it out on poor Holbein or Rubens, not to mention the unfortunate lady who got stuck in a tower sewing those things for years," he said nodding to the tapestries.

"I thought you didn't like the old masters."

"*Horace* doesn't, Smith does."

"Of course."

Katherine explained it might be best to close for the next week and wait for the ruckus to die down. Christopher agreed.

"In the meantime, I think I can write a piece to deter any further acts of vandalism and have it out for the Sunday edition. I wish I had my cameraman with me."

"Oh, I forgot to tell you my one condition for this exclusive: you have to use my cousin Stephie's photos, she's the one who did our catalogue and all the brochure pictures."

"I've seen her around. That's an easy condition, I like her photos. In fact, I would like to have her work in my section on a permanent basis if possible. If anytime she wants a job in the paper, let me know."

"Well, she plans to open her own studio soon," Katherine informed him.

"Really? I'll give her a write-up."

"I don't think she'd appreciate your style."

"Hmm, true."

"But I really appreciate what you're doing for me, Chrisbert Horith." It was a miracle she could still joke after the last few days.

"No sweat, it's the least I can do after Beatrice went over my head, gives me one up on her, you know what I mean."

"That competitive, is it?"

"Well, in this world today, everyone is jockeying for your position, hoping to get promoted over you. I must keep my columns up too."

"Tell you what, I know you basically have a monopoly here already, but do you're best to get me through this, and you'll have an exclusive on anything else that happens in this gallery. I think I can trust you when to be sensitive with a story when necessary."

"Done. However after the Beastie column, I may not be able to stop it all, you might get a few flare ups like Horace gets on occasion for past articles, there's no avoiding it."

"Let's face it, that's the price we pay for being in the public eye. Well, let's go back to the office, we can do the interview from there."

Returning to the ground floor, Katherine asked Stephie to develop her photos as soon as possible, Horace would need them, pronto.

"Sure, let me jot down my studio address, it's not open yet, but I've got my print lab set up. I like to develop my own film," she explained.

"Great, I'll meet you after I'm done here," Smith nodded, looking over her note.

"I wish there was something we could do to help," Uncle Tim said apologetically.

"I'm glad you came by. I suppose I can take it from here, no point having everyone miss dinner. Pops, could you please tell Mom I'll be running a little later than I thought? The deliverymen haven't shown up yet for D.S.'s murals, and I have a few other things to do."

After the patriarchs and Stephie were assured she would be all right on her own, they reluctantly left her to handle business. 'Horith' took out his notebook and proceeded with his exclusive.

"No recorder?"

"No, it makes people jumpy, great for catching explosive one-liners," he winked, "but you've had enough stress today and I need some clear, hard facts. Okay, let's do this."

"Um, one more condition: if I ask you not to print a statement, like a personal comment … ."

"No problem, I'll check with you as we go along."

Katherine carefully recounted the event as clearly as she could remember. It all happened so fast, the screaming, the struggle as Giovanni apprehended the criminal, the shock when she surveyed the extent of the damage, and the detail the crazed woman nearly dashed a two thousand year old amphora to the floor.

"Bad enough to have your own Bohlmann raid minus the acid, but to think you nearly had another Portland Vase on your hands. I dread to think what the restoration costs might have been."

"Gerry's amphora is clay, not glass, it probably would not have turned out as pristine as the Portland Vase," Katherine noted, "I'm just relieved she missed it."

"Well, I suppose that's everything," he said checking his notes before sliding the small book into his breast pocket. "Um, I'm just wondering, I couldn't help but notice that the illuminated pages he gave you were gone."

"Oh, I took them away just before the attack. As you know, nobody except family and a few friends knew about Gerry and I, that the manuscripts were actually a personal gift. After the Beastie's article, everyone kept staring at them in particular. It felt like someone had found my diary and had published it, letting everyone poke his or her nose into the most intimate moments of my life. I couldn't stand it, I had to take them away. Please, you won't … ."

"I know, don't print that. That's not why I was asking," he said reflectively.

"Is something the matter?"

"No, probably not, but reporters tend to think like detectives. I don't want to invent problems that may not come up, but I hope the inspectors don't make to much of it … ," he half mused to himself. Katherine wasn't sure what he meant by that statement until she imagined herself examining the scene from a sleuth's objective point of view.

"Oh my gosh! You don't think they'll suspect *I* had anything to do with it?" she exclaimed. "I wouldn't destroy art like that just to make an insurance claim!"

"I know you wouldn't, but the inspectors will have to rule out every possibility. It just looks odd that before the attack, you happen to remove the manuscripts. They might speculate you knew it was going to happen and removed *your* piece if you didn't want it destroyed, not knowing the guard would stop the vandal from trashing the place entirely, but … ."

"But it would be Gerry who would try and make the claim then if that was the case, they are *his* pieces," she pointed out, "and he certainly doesn't need the cash. If he needed money, he could just sell them, not destroy them, and this is only one part of his collection. He has other artwork that's not on display here."

"I was just getting to that, rules out the quick profit motive," Christopher mused, "that's good, but just in case, be ready if the police come back to clear up that loose end."

"I think I need to sit down," she said, reaching for the swivel chair.

"I'm sorry to bring it up, but you never know what they're going to think. If they show up, just answer all their questions. They should know right off the bat that you had nothing to do with it, but it's good to be prepared, just in case."

"I don't know whether to thank you, or slap you after that," she half laughed.

"Thank Smith and smack Horace," he replied with a smile, "I didn't want to alarm you, just a reporter's inclination to play the schmuck and investigate all angles. Good thing Horace will play nice for your perpetual exclusives and not print any nasty rumours."

"Great. That will help," she said, "I'd stand up to see you out, but my knees won't let me."

"That's all right, don't get up. Now, I'd better go see about those photographs."

No sooner had 'Horcith' left when Dan and Leo came to pick up the murals, and after apologising for being a little late, asked if they could speak with her for a moment.

"I guess you heard the news," Leo began. Katherine just nodded, sadly looking at the Reinold logo on their uniforms. "I know it looks pretty bad, but we just wanted to tell you we've known the Boss Man for years, he wouldn't get involved in anything like this, he's a straight guy, maybe too generous, there's a lotta people who take advantage of him for that, but for sure, Miss Kathy, he's no criminal."

"Yeah, everyone's shook up at the warehouses, I mean, we've had our run ins, but this has to be the worst," Dan added.

"Run ins?"

"Oh, cargo heists, mob men using the trucks, crooked drivers making extra deliveries off the clock without the managers aware of it, loads of stuff, it's a mess trying to get all that cleared up. Sammy, Leo and I have been thinking, putting things together, you know? When the first Boss Man got the desk job, his older brother I mean, one of the first things he started was a 'tell all' policy, the Big Man at the top liked that idea, even if it got them into more trouble than they expected."

"What is this 'tell all' policy?"

"Well, if anything criminal was ever discovered, Boss Man went straight to the cops about it, or whatever authority was needed. No hushing things up, didn't care who or what was involved. Sammy said the idea was that if the management made too much of a stink about it, the mob wouldn't bother with the company no more, too much public hype, it would draw attention to their criminal organizations. Boss Man Number Two kept the policy going because it did actually work for awhile, and they didn't lose customers because they do offer good rates. However, like anyone who's a whistleblower, they eventually get connected with the problem, bad publicity, everyone assuming they're in on it all, you get the picture, even when charges are dropped."

"If they help the police, why do they get charged in the first place?"

"Usually cops gone bad making trouble, the ones in on the heists, taking their cut," Leo explained, "of course, they can't keep it up when the management comes forward to help stop the criminals, so it all gets dropped eventually."

"But the public never forgets," Katherine noted, "I just wish I knew what to believe, it's all too much to take in right now."

"Well, knowing how things get done around in the warehouses, we think the Boss Man was the first to discover the stowaways and alert the cops, explains why they held him, all routine like," Dan continued.

"I wonder where he is? He's disappeared off the radar," she remarked.

"I don't know what to make of that, except he might be in some trouble, he found some pretty serious stuff, he could be in some kinda witness protection program."

Katherine hadn't thought about that, it gave her room for hope, although with all that had happened in addition to his family history, she still didn't know what to think at this point.

"So this happens all the time?"

"Sort of, but not as bad as this," Leo admitted, "I just know the Boss Man's not involved, I'd bet my life on it. Well, I guess we'd better get to work."

"Oh, right. I'm sorry, I meant to unhook the murals, but it's been an awful day around here. Would you mind helping to pack them up?"

"Sure, be glad to Miss," Dan offered as they followed her to the stairs.

It was the last thing she had to do, supervise the delivery to Jim's other club in SoHo, and then she could go straight home. She didn't have time to lock away the art on the rolly-polies and hoped there wouldn't be any more art attacks that night. Sneaking out the back way to her van, she skipped past a few of the reporters. The delivery didn't take as long as she expected, the men were old hat at helping hang D.S.'s murals, although Jim, dressed in his customary eccentric leathers and gold, came over to talk to her for a spell.

"I heard about the graff attack, are you okay?"

"I'm all right, the exhibits aren't," she said simply.

"Yo, that ain't righteous, taking their beef out on you like that."

"I know, but there are weirdos everywhere."

"That be true, my good wo-man," he replied as he watched the murals unfurl into position, variations of the first dance tapestry with different poses and colours. "I know this is none o' my bees wax, but it be true you be go'n steady with the Reinold man?"

"Yeah, and now I don't know what to do," she admitted, why to Jim the Breeze of all things she wasn't sure, but it just escaped her.

"Hmm, there be big decisions all right, but let me give yo a piece of advice, listen to what yo head tells you, that's one thing, but don't forget the second thing," he said, lifting his sunglasses and looking her in the eye.

"Oh, what's that?"

He brought up the handle of his cane and tapped his chest.

"Listen to yo heart, my good wo-man, always get that second opinion," he winked before dropping his shades with a smile, his gold tooth glittering.

ೞ❀ೲ

The family were quiet around the breakfast table the following morning, the events of the last few days made cheerful conversation impossible, and any attempts at small talk grated on Katherine's nerves after another restless night. They scanned the papers, searching for more dreaded comments about Reinold Enterprises, already the interest in the scandal was ebbing a little, there were no further details or updates, although the Reinold stock had bobbed up and down before the weekend Pops noted. However, the gallery was now in the spotlight. Since the reporters had been barred from the premises the day before, they didn't have much to go on, there were only a few 'blurbs'. Horace and his exclusive piece in the art and culture section was the sole exception, and she had to admit, Chris was true to his word; there were no cantankerous Horace-isms, nothing personal was printed, he got the facts straight, and spelled everything correctly. She also learned a few more details, Chris must have been up all night gathering facts to put this together. Katherine read the article out loud to everyone:

Art Vandal Disaster in Dumbo

Yesterday afternoon at approximately 2.30 P.M., part of the Reinold Collection on display in the permanent exhibition space of the Walsingham Gallery was damaged when a forty-six year old woman named Kim Mayon, originally from the Philippines, spray painted a valuable Holbein, a Rubens and medieval tapestries. Visitors were stunned as the woman was wrestled to the floor by the security guard on duty before she inflicted further damage. One piece narrowly escaped the rampage, an ancient Macedonian amphora dated to approximately 150 BC.

"I'm relieved she was stopped in time," Miss Katherine Walsingham stated, owner of the gallery and resident artist, "the damage could have been a lot worse."

The woman who perpetrated the attack is currently in police custody. This is not the first time Mrs. Mayon has been arrested for vandalism, having slashed several canvases in three exclusive Chelsea galleries in '84, spray painted a Goya in the Brooklyn Museum in '89 and a statue in Central Park last year. According to our sources, she was released two weeks ago from the psychiatric ward in Bellevue after undergoing treatment for psychotic outbreaks, and had stopped taking her medication before committing this latest crime.

Detective O'Malley reports, "The woman is definitely disturbed, she hears voices telling her if she destroys or defaces a certain number of artworks within a specific timeframe, she can avert the Apocalypse. She thinks she's a specially chosen commando of Belial, or something along those lines. She needs professional help." When asked if the latest news events concerning Reinold Enterprises had anything to do with the vandalism, Detective O'Malley did not think they were.

"It's tempting to jump to the conclusion that the suspect was making a personal attack on the owner of the collection, but from her past medical history, we have every reason to believe the suspect simply saw the mention of the gallery in yesterday's paper and was more interested in preventing the end of the world. It's an unfortunate coincidence she should happen to fixate on the Reinold Collection during her latest psychotic spree."

The Walsingham Gallery will remain closed this week as the clean up commences.

"Horace's report is rather sedate," Gramps was surprised to see, "objective and to the point, coming from him. Of course, this is a report, not an art critique."

"I'm relieved your choice of reporter proved correct," Pops added, "let's hope this satisfies their curiosity."

"The poor woman," her mother *tsked*, "they should have kept her in the hospital."

"Belial, sounds familiar. A cult leader?" Katherine wondered, rereading the article to herself.

"No, I think it's some evil spirit from the Old Testament," Gramps replied, "there's a mention in Milton's poetry too, it's been years since I read it."

"That's just creepy," Katherine shuddered. To think she had some lunatic running through her place, convinced they were receiving commands from a demon. "Wait, that doesn't make sense. If she knows the evil spirit's name, why would a demon want to stop the end of the world? I thought it was the other way around."

"The woman is mentally ill, insanity is never reasonable," Pops reminded her.

Folding up the papers, it was time to go to church service. Today she dreaded the prospect, the thought of being stared at through the ceremony, and then having to politely chat with the congregation afterwards, particularly the Reverend, his wife, Aunt Martha and her gossipy friends. She didn't want to face all their commiserations and decided to make a quick getaway as soon the Reverend had pronounced the final blessing and 'Amen'. However, moping around at home was not an appealing prospect for the day, and there was nowhere she could escape to that would help blot out her whirling thoughts. She hadn't said anything, but since yesterday's episode, she felt strangely open and vulnerable as though the attack was personal, her sense of security severely shaken. It made sense when she considered that the family building had been physically violated, and right under her nose. Why she thought that going to check on it would make her feel better was inexplicable, especially since the destruction couldn't be stopped while she was there, but she felt an overwhelming compulsion to look around just to see if the place was all right. It wouldn't be a bad idea to stay and paint for awhile, she needed some quiet time alone to sort out her thoughts concerning the past few days in any case.

"Don't you want to come with us in the car?" Pops asked, seeing her reach for the van keys on the hallstand.

"I was thinking of going to the gallery afterwards."

"On a wet day like this? Are you sure you don't need a break? This is the day of rest you know," Gramps noted, "if you feel like painting, I'm sure Suzy wouldn't mind you using the apartment, just like old times."

"I'll only fidget around at home, and all my equipment is set up in the gallery."

"All right dear, just try to be home at a reasonable hour," her mother requested, "you look positively exhausted."

It was a relief to have 'emergency' business to cut the goodbyes with the congregation short, a quick 'I'm sorry, I have things to attend to,' was enough to let her slip away without much ado. Well, she *did* have things to do at the gallery, even if it was only an afternoon of therapeutic painting.

Katherine didn't expect to find anything out of place, but felt relieved to inspect the floors, checking all the paintings, verifying the alarm was on, even if it couldn't stop another graffiti rampage. It felt odd walking around the silent building. The help were off, *Chez Garneau* was closed, no visitors were present, only the security guards, and yet she was plagued with the image of the crazed woman wielding her paint cans. The poor psycho was long gone, locked up in a cell somewhere, and still Katherine found herself looking down the passageways to make sure she wasn't skulking around the next corner waiting to wreak havoc on another artwork. Katherine shook her head. *Come on, get a grip.* She took another look at the damaged pieces before trying to contact Lottie once more. Her line was still busy, and so was Stonyvale. She sighed and hung up the receiver, immediately the phone rang.

"Hello, Walsingham Gallery."

"Hi, I'm from *TeenTopics Magazine.* We were planning to do a piece on the new Reinold romance and wondered if … ."

"Sorry, no comment." She cut off the call and put the handset on the desk. At this point Katherine had stopped being polite to the intrusive media callers. This was all getting to be a little ridiculous.

"They're still bugging you?" Kyle noted.

"Yeah. So much for Horace's article, I thought it might help."

"Well, that was the first reporter for today, so it is dying down a bit," he informed her.

"That's good to know. I guess I'll head up to the studio, I have some paintings to work on."

Lottie's painting was just about dry, and while she didn't mind painting gifts, she was glad she could devote some time to her allegorical artwork. Katherine thought she could fit her first dialogue examining the nature of Freedom on one canvas, but found the concept impractical if she planned to superimpose words over images, she would end up concealing her scene under a barrage of sentences. At times, she discovered a creative artist also had to be part problem solver. The initial solution was simply not to fill in the letters but paint them in outline. The idea was appealing, she could envision the picture peeking through a delicate latticework of words. Still, she would have to devise a balanced proportion between word and picture, and if she expected to keep her canvas within a certain size, a considerable portion of her dialogue would be missing. Of course, a work of art should be mysterious, it would be amusing to keep art lovers guessing, wondering where the debate had ended, but the thought of leaving the dialogue unfinished was … frustrating. She had worked hard to make her imaginary dialogue between Socrates and Plato sound authentic. In the end, she decided she would have to break with her own rotation system and compile a collection, create a new picture when one section of conversation had filled a canvas. Talk about a running commentary she thought, but being an artist, she would be forgiven her eccentricities. However, it would not be possible to show the entire collection at once, her text had become a small essay, she might be a dottering old ninny by the time she would see the final painting completed, and that was just the first dialogue. Never mind, if Hogarth could plan and execute a multi-canvas series, so could she, even if it took twenty paintings. All right, hopefully not that many.

Her initial problem solved, Katherine turned her attention to the painting of the actual letters. She could work free hand of course, but may not paint the outline proportions correctly, although her handwriting was complimented on occasion, carefully crafted calligraphy was not her strong point, and she would be working with brushes, not quill nibs, which made the task doubly difficult. It would be disappointing if her illuminated manuscript idea turned out childish in appearance with an uneven, blocky script when she planned to achieve a precise, almost chiselled effect in Latin lettering. The base image could be corrected if something went amiss, but not the letters as they would have to be painted on after the initial picture was completely dry with the result a clumsy letter could not be scraped off or painted over without destroying the underlying illustration. Since she was dealing with ancient times, why not use Renaissance methods? Her thoughts turned to fresco painting and how artists drew bare outlines or cartoons of their figures on paper first, then poked holes along the cartoon lines and laid the paper on the plaster to be painted. The cartoon was then dusted with an opaque powder, leaving behind a fine outline of the figures on the plaster that were then coloured in. For her piece, all she needed to do was make a stencil, that is, prepare her text on a large sheet of tracing paper and cut out the letters using a fine razor or carpet blade, she could then overlay the paper on her canvas and carefully paint in a neat outline of the letters. If the interior of the letters was slightly uneven, that didn't matter, as long as the exterior lines were clear and crisp, she hoped the paper would lay flat and not ripple. Her minuscule letters would have to be at least an inch in height to make them large enough to outline and be legible, capitals would be slightly larger. Mathematical proportions of sentences would also have to be worked out to ensure she achieved an even, justified spacing from the edges of her canvas, a left-orientated text alignment would leave a ragged edge on the right side of her painting. While figuring out the logistics, she wondered if she was a painter or a typesetter. This was becoming very complicated, but she revelled in the challenge.

By now, Katherine's underlying picture was dry, the text was prepared, and it was time to begin cutting the stencil. How difficult it was, deciding upon the first picture! The original concept was to depict Socrates and Plato conversing as they worked out the philosophical intricacies of liberty and the nature of free will, perhaps have them standing before some object and quietly making some observations on it that would introduce the actual dialogue, but what could possibly symbolise Freedom? She thought about the numerous national landmarks associated with truth, justice and liberty for all. The Statue of Liberty was good, but perhaps too obvious for the first picture, she could save that for another painting along the course of the dialogue. Democracy was a good symbol, she could depict the two philosophers walking down the capitol steps as they discussed this weighty topic. That too was interesting, but not … *evocative.* Perhaps something simple would work better.

Then, an idea struck a chord: why not the Liberty Bell? There was something melancholic about that symbol of their nation's promise of freedom, a bell with a chipped mouth and cleft body. Searching through the family library, she found a pre-Bicentenary picture displaying the solitary idiophone resting silently in the background on its wooden stand in Independence Hall. Overhead, the instrument was encircled by a white colonial banister on a walkway with a tall window overlooking the buildings beyond, while on the ground, a herringbone pattern drew the eye inward from an archway in the foreground flanked by two classical-style columns. She could easily imagine the two philosophers of old standing by each pillar, looking in at the bell as they made their arguments and observations. While she disliked working from someone else's photographs, she knew she would have sketched the same view if she were there in person, so it did not feel like artistic theft, rather a respectful borrowing. In any case, the bell was no longer housed in Independence Hall, it now resided in a special glass pavilion. For her picture, it seemed more appropriate to paint the soundless instrument standing in it's old home where the Declaration of Independence was drafted and signed. She had no choice, the old photograph would have to be her guide. Of course, she had to dig a little into the history of the bell to see if she could work it into her dialogue and discovered an extensive rewrite was unavoidable. By now, her essay hardly resembled her first philosophical ramblings with Gramps and the Professor, in any case, that was just a trial run. How odd! In addition to problem solver and text setter, she was now an amateur researcher, scholar and philosopher. It was amazing how artistic projects could evolve unexpectedly beyond their original concepts.

Choosing the colours to use was the easiest task after this extensive thematic preparation. Since freedom included the process of free will in decision-making, the obvious shades to use were black and white to symbolise discernment; she would paint the bell and its surroundings in this monochromatic scheme, yet include the famous thinkers in living colour to make them stand out in contrast. However, she could not paint the words in black and white, they would wash out the picture behind, or perhaps blend into the picture, distinct colours were required. Socrates and Plato had to have their own shades to illustrate who was speaking, for instead of placing each speaker's sentence on a new paragraph line as in a book, she planned to use continuous sentences. Colours for independence? Why not good old American red and blue? That seemed apropos. In fact, almost every Western democracy adopted red, white and blue. She also wanted to ensure the bell remained a focal point, and using darker tints of red and blue on the words that overlapped the bell would prove an interesting effect. The protagonists should remain visible, best to allow the text to wrap around them instead of having them caged within her analytical ruminations.

Her tracing paper was now carefully prepared, it was time to cut out the letters, a delicate operation. Laying the large sheet flat on her worktable with a piece of thin cardboard underneath to protect the surface, she first scotch-taped the letters on both sides of the paper to make the edges stronger, then carefully began slitting along the outer lines with a carpet blade, using a ruler to keep the sharp point steady and on target for straight-edged figures. Round letters had to be done free hand and took extra care. Naturally, it was impossible not to reread the text as she painstakingly cut out each alphabetical shape, inch by inch. Eventually, a project that helped to clear her mind began to bring all the disturbing revelations of the past few days to the surface as she reflected on the nature of free choice and making informed decisions.

"There be big decisions all right … listen to what yo head tells you, that's one thing, but don't forget the second thing: listen to yo heart, my good wo-man, always get that second opinion."

Jim's lilting voice echoed in her head like a mantra, there was no escaping the situation she had to face. Although she wanted to continue, Katherine eventually had to stop work, she was unable to blot out her wildly roving thoughts. Dropping her blade, she just felt like sitting for a moment, her head in her hands.

This was all too much!

She had just discovered she had fallen in love with Gerry, and immediately her love was severely tested. She wanted to believe Dan and Leo, to place her hope in what the detective and Patrick told her, but she also respected her family's judgement, Charlie had access to their records, he seemed to know what he was talking about, and Christopher was privy to information she wasn't. Furthermore, she had seen other things that made her question her ability to give Gerry the benefit of the doubt. Her mind was drawn to little nagging incidents that at the time seemed innocent and now began to stir her suspicions. For one thing, he hadn't tried to call. That's odd, isn't it? Silence can be a sign of guilt. She tried to argue, find the positive side or some explanation. No, not really, he couldn't possibly get through the last day or so, not when they all had to take their phones off the hooks. The voice of suspicion continued to make its presence known. That may be, but surely he could have tried to contact me *somehow* by now? It's odd that he would just disappear into thin air. But how do I know? With the shock, I didn't even bother trying to call his hotel again. Yet the reporters said he could not be found, he obviously changed hotels. What if Dan and Leo are right? He could be placed under protective custody? That means he is innocent! Then again …what if he *is* guilty? Don't forget what his so-called friend said that night we went to the Met: *"What is a nice young lady like you doing with a scoundrel like this?"* Did that guy know something I didn't? I have no way of telling, that 'friend' probably believed the news reports, but were they true or false? Her thoughts meandered to his art and rare book collection, where does he get the money for all of that? Would he turn to criminal activities just to satisfy a compulsion to collect? The shipping business couldn't be *that* good, could it? Maybe it is. He could have private investments aside from the business, maybe a trust fund bigger than mine for all I know. Steves is able to make a fast fortune by astute trading, I shouldn't judge.

Katherine tried to find the positive side, but the negative suspicions kept mounting. What if money wasn't the issue? *What if he engaged in criminal activity just for the thrill of it?* She couldn't forget what Derrick told her about drug runners who craved the challenge; the ultimate 'high', to match their criminal wits against the high and mighty justice system.

"Go on, live dangerously."

Isn't that what he said on occasion? Now that seemingly light-hearted phrase became difficult to ignore. He did have a smuggler's mentality, sneaking an almost priceless vase past customs officials with a 'Taiwan' sticker, not to mention his father had a preference for illegal Cuban cigars, but was Gerry capable of trafficking men, women and children—*just for kicks?* She thought back to her visits to Stonyvale, how he reacted with his family, how close he was with Lottie and his mother, this was a significant point. She often heard that a man who respected the women in his life was a decent man. No, he couldn't possibly be involved with that debacle in Jakarta! However, she wasn't allowed to rest upon that thought, the suspicions began to swirl once more. Maybe the graffiti attack wasn't random, maybe it was a deliberate protest after all? The demented woman was from the Philippines, and some of the trafficked victims were from there. If Katherine wasn't piecing together strange deductions and observations, her mind wrestled between the two motives, criminality for the challenge or for money. No, she couldn't believe it. Gerry wouldn't do that to people, his own workers respected him too much for that, and she had to agree, he was very generous. The character of a person could also be judged by how they treat their subordinates. Dan and Leo would know if something was wrong. Didn't they say that Gerry and Pete actively sought to stop any criminal element from using their business as a front? Of course, Peter started that, there was the possibility Gerry now used this open policy if he was guilty, reporting crimes to the police to remove all suspicion. And what about his 'con-art' collection? He seemed to be fascinated with outlaws and convicts: that is not a good sign.

Stop, you're getting carried away again!

He just doesn't fit the profile of a criminal, even Patrick said so, and he had enough police experience to tell the difference. But how could she be sure? Gerry didn't need the money, she could settle on that deduction, and if Patrick was right, Gerry was not the type who would devise an elaborate smuggling and human trafficking ring for the thrill of it. He couldn't possibly excuse such actions, pretending he was doing nothing wrong, not without killing his conscience and developing that hard implacable character Patrick described. Or, perhaps he was good at hiding it? No, some clue would have come to light by now. Maybe it has: what about the vase and the illegal cigars? Perhaps she was making too much of those incidents, there was hardly a person she knew that didn't try skipping their holiday purchases past the customs officials despite the fact they could well afford the duty fees, and even Gramp's friends wouldn't pass up a box of deluxe Cuban coffin nails when they could lay their hands on them.

Her thoughts flew from one assumption, cancelled by another, only to be rebutted by a vicious, maddening whirl of doubt. Perhaps there was an innocent explanation for everything; however, there was one incident she knew she couldn't explain away, no matter how much she tried. He said the family fortune came from whaling, but her parents had told her otherwise. Did he lie or was he simply afraid to tell her? He did have difficulties admitting to the whaling. No matter, she had one last difficult question to face: if he was innocent, could she accept the fact that everything he and his family owned and worked for had been built upon the nefarious slave trade? That was the question. Of course, let bygones be bygones; whatever his ancestors did was not his fault, but that wouldn't dispel the fact everything the Reinolds owned came from a blighted beginning. You love Gerry, not his past she tried to reason, but his past was also a part of him. To accept him would mean accepting *everything* about him. Katherine then realized that also included the trouble he often found himself in with the law and the media, whether he be innocent or guilty. It would explain why Pops 'strongly advised' her not to have anything more to do with him, simply for peace and safety's sake. She sighed and looked towards the window, listening to the pigeons cooing and fluttering on the sill. Why did everything have to be so complicated? Could love conquer all?

Katherine wanted to get back to work, but she had second thoughts. With the gallery closed, she would have a whole week for artwork, and right now there were other responsibilities vying for her time, namely, to notify someone about yesterday's disaster and try to sort out the question of insurance. This was one task she did not have the luxury to let slide another day. Since telephoning was currently out of the question, there was nothing left to do but to make a visit to Stonyvale. She tided up the worktable and was about to put on her coat when the intercom rang.

"Sorry to bother you, Miss," Kyle apologized, "but you have a visitor. It's a priest, says he heard about the incident yesterday and wishes to see you. I told him we were closed and that you were busy, but he seems to think it will be all right with you." Katherine knew it was Peter.

"Oh sure, it's okay. Tell him I'll be right there."

She dropped her coat on a chair and hurried to the elevator. Although she dreaded to tell him about the damage, she was relieved to see him. Dressed as usual in his traditional black cassock and winter jacket, arms crossed as he examined the artwork on the rolly-polies much like the day she first met him at Notre Dame, his confident presence seemed to help quiet her troubled thoughts.   It felt like the cavalry had come to the rescue.

"Hello Katherine," he greeted, turning to meet her, "I read the paper and thought I'd better drop by. I saw the van out back and knew you were here. Are you all right?"

"I'm fine, but here you are asking about me when I should be asking how you are," she said. "What's happened to Gerry? Is he all right? All I've heard are the news reports and a lot of horrible rumours."

"That's another reason I had to see you, he's fine, he's been taken into witness protection. It seems he's uncovered a big drug smuggling operation that involves a break-away faction of the Tong and he's a key witness right now."

"Oh my! That's what happened, I didn't know what to think, it looked very bad on TV and in the papers. But is he all right?"

"Yes, he finally called us last night. Unfortunately, contact is minimal at the moment, he can call us, but we can't call him, so it's touch and go. He tried to phone you, but couldn't get through and he's very concerned, he asked me to check on you at the first opportunity. He didn't have an e-mail address, and would have sent a telegram, but knew that would have frightened you half to death."

"Oh, it's the stupid reporters! We've had to take all the phones off the hook," she explained.

"I thought so, in fact, I've been sent down to a friend's parish here in Brooklyn to help out for a few weeks until this all blows over, even now I still get bothered once in a while. The police have requested that Gerry stay in the country for a few more weeks, when he'll return home is difficult to say."

"That's terrible! I'll be going to Paris mid April, I may not see him before he's allowed to come back, but before you give me all the details, I'd better show you what's happened upstairs. I couldn't contact anyone, not with the reporters hogging the lines, and I was just about to drive to your parents home," she explained as they went to the elevator. He examined the damage, but didn't dwell on it for long. She expected him to be more upset that his brother's possessions had been damaged during her watch.

"It can all be repaired, I know where he keeps his insurance policies. I'll be happy to take care of that for you and let you know when the inspectors will drop by. Of course, you'll have to put the phones back on the hook."

"All right, I'll be here all week, I have work to catch up on. I feel so terrible," she began, but he calmly reassured her.

"They're only things, Gerry wants me to stress that point, and he's correct. The artwork is the least of his concerns, he'll be relieved to know you're all right."

"Still, I feel responsible, he trusted me to look after them."

"Nonsense, this is not your fault."

"I know, but now that this has happened, what should I do with the collection? The guards tell me one lunatic may attract another, and I'm afraid to expose the rest of the pieces to the public."

"First, wait for the inspectors to take a look and make an estimate for the repair work. If you would feel better taking the collection down, that's up to you. I know Gerry will understand."

"All right, I'll wait and see. You know, I'm relieved to hear Gerry is not considered a suspect, why don't they report that?"

"Sensationalism captures an audience I'm afraid. The local authorities are going to make some official statements tonight, our time, together with our father and the regional mangers from the other shipping firms, but I doubt if the public will be willing to listen, everyone prefers to remember accusations, not declarations of innocence."

Katherine was silent for a moment, but she still had many questions left unanswered. If anyone had the information, it was Fr. Peter. That quiet, soul-searching look of his told her that he of all people would give her the straight truth: no side-stepping, no false comforts, no exaggerations, no excuses.

"I hope you don't mind me asking personal questions, but all I've heard are accusations and malicious hearsay, I would like to know Gerry's side of the story."

"No, I don't mind. I know there are issues you wish to address, and I have the rest of the day free, a rarity for me considering it is a Sunday," he smiled.

"Shall we go to the restaurant? We can have some coffee, Andre lets me have free reign in the kitchen when he's not here."

"A cup of coffee sounds good."

"Are you hungry? I can rustle us up a gourmet sandwich and some pastries if you like."

Back on the ground floor, he gladly helped to put the cups and saucers on a tray as she worked the machine and prepared a plate of refreshments before settling at the head table.

"To be honest, when the news broke it was an awful shock, and everyone just assumed the worst. I hate to admit it, but I was about to fall down that slippery slope. The reports made him look guilty, and yet I knew your brother couldn't possibly be involved in anything like that."

"Well, let's start at the beginning," he said, stirring the contents of his cup. "Gerry noticed the weight records of certain cargo loads between ports didn't make any sense, small insignificant mistakes that didn't seem important, except there were too many of them. He decided to personally check the containers on the docks and to read the reports on the ground, that's when he discovered the stowaways. To cut a long story short, this new gang organization had terrorized the dockworkers that weren't in on the take, threatening to harm them or their families if they didn't do as they were told or if they tried to go to the police. They were forced to let this gang walk straight into the container areas and load up. Right now Dad and Gerry are going through all our company records with the police, trying to figure out exactly when this group began using our equipment for their seedy operations."

"This sounds like something straight out of Hollywood," Katherine said, wide eyed.

"Indeed. Now that Gerry has blown the whistle and exposed this new gang to the police, he had to be put into protective custody. Dad also has a personal police escort."

"Good lord, I just hope he'll be allowed to come home soon. Your mother and Lottie must be in a terrible state with all that's happened."

"It was a shock, but sad to say, this is nothing new."

"I ... heard about past incidents," Katherine tentatively replied. "All charges were dropped, weren't they?"

"Yes. I assure you, our family has never become involved with any drug operations or illegal immigrant rings. Unfortunately we do get infiltrations on occasion, it's difficult to find honest workers anymore, and we do have trouble with some corrupt elements in the justice system."

"That's what Leo and Dan said, but nobody wants to give your family the benefit of the doubt," she noted.

"Just being charged is enough to paint a person guilty. You said you had a personal question to ask?"

"Oh, well, I don't want to be rude, but I would like to know once and for all if what they say about how your family business got started is true or not."

"I see," he said placing his cup down and thinking for a moment. "I forget the dates. I believe it was either our triple-great grandfather or our great great grandfather who opened the shipping business, and yes, he did trade slaves. However, when the eldest son inherited the business, his two younger brothers insisted they stop slave trading and concentrate on shipping regular cargo. Apparently, he refused, so the two brothers pooled their monetary shares of the inheritance and opened up their own enterprise, eventually branching into whaling on East Long Island and Nantucket Island, ploughing the profits back into an expansion of the shipping end when they feared kerosene might one day replace the demand for whale oil. Technically, the bulk of the family fortune grew from there, the eldest brother gambled away his side of the slave-trading business, and he did not have a very glorious end I must admit. Apparently, he was shot for gambling debts. About the two brothers, whatever was made from those initial days in the slave trade that gave them their inheritance has been paid back many times over. I suppose you didn't hear that the Reinolds of old were 'stockholders' in the Underground Railroad and provided 'stations' and 'depots' in New York state." Katherine shook her head. "It's true, I think there was a 'conductor' in the family."

"How come no one knows about this?" she wondered.

"It's only our word against known historical documents," Fr. Peter explained, "you won't see a mention of 'Reinold' in William Still's work since the two brothers changed their names when they assisted with the 'Gospel Train' and pretended to be two merchants hiring the Reinold ships for their operations, just as an extra precautionary measure. Persistent slave hunters were known to follow runaways all the way to the Canadian border, and they didn't want their cover blown. We only have a few old letters and one battered diary in the library at Stonyvale as proof, the brothers were very good at undercover work and didn't leave much evidence behind. Eventually they told their story to their grandchildren, as the saying goes."

"That's amazing, but I'm sure if you got researchers on it, they would try and tell the truth, dig up some facts…"

"Maybe, but in any case, the Reinold name is forever stuck to the initial operation started by our great great grandfather, so we did commence with slavery, although the next generation rejected it. It is unfortunate that in most cases when the sins of the father fall on the son it is because unlike

God, people refuse to forgive and forget and heap past wrongs upon innocent generations."

"But Gerry was telling the truth, everything your family has came from the whaling and shipping end," Katherine replied.

"Yes, that's true," Fr. Peter said, sipping his coffee. "I must say, Gerry is not happy with how this all began, I'm not surprised he didn't tell you. It was difficult when we found out, our parents kept it quiet, waiting until we were older and could understand, but we found out the hard way when a historical documentary came out one year, school life became unbearable for awhile. One of the few times I ever got in a fist fight was when a gang of bullies called Gerry some awful name and started a brawl after school, naturally big brother came to the rescue. Fr. O'Connell gave me a good dressing down in confession that week, and then asked who won the fight after he gave me my penance," he laughed. Katherine was surprised and a little amused.

"Pete, I can't imagine you of all people getting into a fight," she said.

"Well, boys will be boys. We were young then, and while we did turn the other cheek, we were not about to be punched a third time, blame our stupid pride."

"I guess you were entitled to defend your honour," Katherine admitted, it was one thing to be caught up into a fight, another to be outnumbered and beaten up by a bunch of schoolyard hooligans. "Who did win, by the way?" Fr. Peter laughed.

"I think we did, we weren't bothered again, not in a physical sense, but the taunting was difficult to escape."

"Sitting through American history lessons must have been tough after that," Katherine noted, putting her cup down.

"It was, and it still bothers Gerry very much. Like his ancestors, he has a driving need to make restitution for past wrongs, but he doesn't like to broadcast it."

"Your father told me about his dedication to Greenpeace."

"Yes," Fr. Peter smiled, "that was his idea, not to mention contributing to various housing and job creation projects. Right now, one of his pet missions is promoting education programs for prisoners."

"That's why he collects 'con art'." He chuckled at her pun.

"Sometimes the inmates give him paintings as presents. It's an admirable charity, many convicts would not be where they are if they had access to education and a chance to improve their lives. He believes instruction and culture, not harsh justice is one way to break the vicious cycle of crime, and I agree. Of course, there are people who can't be helped, a life of tricking and dealing is all they know and they wouldn't have it any other way."

"That's true."

Katherine was silent for a moment, this was a lot to take in. Recalling the suspicions that raged through her mind only an hour or so ago made her feel guilty. She could only imagine how Gerry must have felt, finding those poor people locked away like chattel when he was working hard to correct past mistakes.

"I can't believe I gave an ear to the reports, I knew better," she admitted. "You can't imagine the horrid thoughts that crossed my mind."

"You didn't have all the information, so it's human," Fr. Peter consoled.

"Oh no, it was terrible," she continued. It felt good to talk to him, and before she knew it, Katherine had revealed all her fears and suspicions, from the Cuban cigars to her strange assumption that he gave up the business and entered the priesthood on account of their family history, concluding that was his way of making restitution for the past. Fr. Peter quietly studied her for a few moments.

"I will admit, I've reprimanded Gerry for his blockade runs with custom officials," he began. "At least he pays his taxes, but he refuses to pay more than he thinks is necessary, especially with his collectable antiquities that have already been taxed ten times over through the years. The vase is no exception in his eyes, he would probably tell you it has been taxed enough after two millennia, and after the hefty tax levied on it's initial purchase, he would refuse to pay again. About illegal contraband, Cuban cigars is as far as his brush with the law goes, and he wouldn't equate sneaking a crate of tobacco sticks on the same level as revealing US State secrets to Castro. We all have our faults," he smiled. "However," he continued, his glance becoming more reflective, "you have made an interesting observation with regards to my own vocation, something even I had missed. You are very perceptive," he noted. Katherine felt a little embarrassed having introduced her observation into the conversation.

"Well ... I'm afraid I was more presumptuous than perceptive."

"No, you have made a very good point. While I didn't enter the priesthood with that particular objective in mind, it also makes perfect sense. Gerry is combating the injustice of the world in a secular manner, I've been called to fight slavery in the spiritual world, so it is one way of correcting past mistakes."

"I hope I haven't offended you."

"On the contrary, I thank you. Sometimes it takes someone else to show us why our path in life went in the direction it did."

"I wouldn't have thought you had any doubts."

"Not doubts as much as curiosity about why I was chosen. You have given me one answer I had not thought about. Of course, a vocation is a mystery, we just have to follow the call in faith."

"Well, since I've opened my big mouth, how did you know you had a calling, especially to become an exorcist? Forgive me, I'm terribly curious."

"All priests have the power to exorcise, but we must have special permission as it is very exhausting work. Not all priests are up to the spiritual, mental, and physical challenge. We are dealing with profound evil, powerful princes and principalities who are more cunning than a million of the best geniuses put together. I know people think that exorcism is a medieval obsolete rite that has no place in the modern world, but they are wrong. The devil has not vanished simply because people refuse to believe he exists, no more than God has," Fr. Peter noted, "but to return to your initial question, one of the most influential people who helped me was Sr. Roberta, one of the nuns at our school. She had a gift for directing people to their vocation in life, be it the religious life, to be single or married. Already at grade school she told me what my path would be, and I must admit, at that age I was hesitant at first, but something happened when I was about twenty which I couldn't ignore," he stated quietly, "something out of the ordinary, and beyond what most people would experience during their period of discernment."

"If it's too personal to share, I understand."

"Well, I've never told anyone this before, not because it's embarrassing, but because few are willing to consider that the supernatural exists and that it directly or indirectly influences their lives. Considering how perceptive you are in certain areas, and the fact the supernatural had intervened the day we met, I believe you can handle what I'm about to tell you, or at least listen with an open mind."

Wow, this sounded serious. Katherine was all ears.

"One night, I had a vivid dream, more detailed than most, and let's say I was never allowed to forget it. I was walking down the street somewhere in the city, when all of a sudden many people turned into sheep and lambs and began skipping about. Other people didn't change shape and stayed human but were dressed like shepherds. This was an odd sight, and developed in a mysterious way as the dream progressed. My attention was first drawn to the sheep and lambs. Some of them ate the healthy grass around the trees planted on the sidewalks and were quite content, but others ate garbage along the side of the road that was not wholesome and they quickly grew sick or died. Then there were herds that chewed on bad newspapers, or were peaking into adult shops, some stole huge amounts of money out of cash registers from different shops and ate it; these particular sheep turned into goats and tried to pull other sheep and lambs away from the grass and join them in their evil pursuits. Some of these bad creatures were successful, others weren't, and they tormented the sheep that refused to follow them, butting them with their horns or kicking them. Eventually, nearly all the goats gambolled to what looked like a subway entrance with flames flaring up and merrily jumped into the fiery furnace and disappeared. I also saw wolves in sheep's clothing come up out of the flames and join the goats, enticing other sheep and lambs towards evil activities. I wondered why the shepherds paid no attention to the sheep, some were standing around talking to each other and completely ignoring the scene. Then I watched as others took their staffs and helped channel the wayward sheep and lambs towards the evil activities that the goats and the wolves were drawing them towards. I looked around and discovered a sheepfold with the gate wide open and realized that's where the sheep needed to be, and wondered if I could find someone to help put them back in before they were all destroyed. I then noticed that men were leaping over the wall of the fold, putting on shepherd's garments without official authority from anyone and leaving over the wall again to join the bad shepherds outside, but I ignored them, and entering by the gate, went into a cottage near the fold and discovered the true shepherds of the sheep. I could tell the difference because they had a cross over their hearts. Some were asleep and I couldn't wake them, while others were too busy making cloth from the wool of the sheep or eating the cheese and drinking the sheep's milk. There was also a group slaughtering the best of the sheep for their own use. I rushed outside to see if I could do anything, and I grabbed a shepherd's staff and a rod studded with nails to try and drive off the wolves, the goats and the self-declared shepherds. I was partially successful, and a few of the sheep followed me for awhile, but I noticed when I didn't try to help the sheep, I was left alone, but now the wolves tried to come after me and the bad shepherds tried to strike me with their staffs. While I was fending them off and trying to save the sheep at the same time, I saw something very disturbing: the disguised wolves began breathing on a few of the sheep, the goats, and also a number of the false shepherds. A black cloud entered them, making them do terrible things, like forcing them to run in front of traffic in an effort to kill them. In some cases, the wolves literally morphed into a few of the sheep, goats and evil shepherds, taking complete possession of them. That was the most disturbing part, to see animals and people assume a diabolical nature. I tried to wake some of the real shepherds, I needed help, I couldn't fight all this evil on my own, but when I turned back, instead of the fold, I saw an immense cathedral on the verge of crumbling. I ran inside and looked for the shepherds, but they weren't there, so I approached the High Altar over which hung an enormous crucifix. The crucifix seemed to speak, and yet at the same time the Voice came from the tabernacle. It was the most harmonious Voice I had ever heard in my life, yet full of sorrow."

"What did it say?"

" 'My Church continues to crucify Me and refuses to respond to My love. My sheep and lambs are scattered and left to their own devices or throw themselves into Hell. Many of My specially chosen shepherds are disinterested hirelings that do not care for the sheep, or feed themselves rather than feed the flock. Others assume the role of shepherd and take command without My authority, they do not enter by the gate. I Am the Good Shepherd, whom shall I send to help right this wrong?' Immediately I said, 'Send me, I'll go.' After a long pause, I heard 'Let it be. You believe you have chosen Me, when it is I who have chosen you.' I suddenly realized I was dressed as the one of the rightful shepherds, and somehow I could instinctively tell I had been anointed, my hands as well. It dawned on me how weak I was to carry out this enormous task, but the Voice assured me; 'Do not fear, I and my Mother will be your strength.' The altar was now completely covered with the various 'tools' and 'weapons' for me to to use, everything to say Mass, a rosary, numerous sacramentals, different allegorical objects that I knew by one glance symbolised the seven sacraments. In particular, there was a book of the Rite of Exorcism, St. Benedict's crucifix and a vial of holy water placed in front of me, so I grabbed them and ran out to face the dreadful scene once more. This time the wolves shrieked in fear and tried to goad the evil shepherds and goats to their various evil tasks, but little by little, with God's grace, I was able to free the possessed animals and people, helping to guide many of the sheep and lambs back to the fold, the cathedral had now disappeared. Some of the real shepherds woke up and came to help, and the evil shepherds and wolves were very angry. They tried to attack, but at the same time were afraid of the power granted to us. Still, it was a terrible fight. I heard the Voice once more, 'Know that you have joined a great spiritual battle that will not end until the day I call you.' I had agreed to help, so all I could say was 'So be it, it is Your Will, I shall follow.' The wolves were particularly livid and began to speak and wail in hideous voices. There's no way to describe demonic speech, each single voice sounds like several thousands put together, yet unified as one. It's filled with babble and hatred, a simultaneous jumble of wailing, moaning and roaring yet coherent at the same time, and it's neither male nor female. No human could aptly describe that soul-curdling cacophony. 'We shall stop you,' they howled. 'No you won't,' I defiantly returned, although my very soul was shaking just feeling their diabolic presence near me. It's an unearthly feeling, they literally bring hatred in a fiery rage with them, you can feel it come at you like a physical tidal wave, it's hard to describe. Sheer bitter emotions that become as tangible as this table we're sitting at," he concluded, giving it a tap that made Katherine jump.

"What happened after that?"

"I ran back to the cottage for assistance, a few shepherds stopped thinking of themselves and took up the fight while a group of the sleepy shepherds repented of their laziness in their vocation. We fought off the wolves and bad shepherds with various sacramentals and continued to help the sheep back to the fold, but the evil forces would return to fight again or lead astray new flocks of sheep and lambs that would appear. I had been warned the battle would continue for the rest of my life. However, there were times of 'ceasefire' so to speak, we could successfully drive off the enemy for a time that give us a breathing spell and a chance to rest. I sat down and began to ask myself if this was all real. Apparently, I had some autonomy and knew I was actually sleeping. Immediately, a youth dressed in a long white robe stood before me and with a grave but peaceful expression said, 'The attacks of the enemy are very real indeed.' I was suddenly ambushed without warning, a false shepherd struck me on the head with his staff and I reeled back, while the largest of the wolves leaped out of nowhere and grabbed me by the arm. I woke up to find myself on the floor."

"Wow, that's some dream," Katherine replied, "and so detailed, but how do you know it was the 'call'? I thought the Bible said we're not to read anything into dreams."

"That's true because there was a danger that the Jews might follow the pagan cults around them and practise dream divination complete with temples and priestly diviners as the Greeks did with the god Asclepius, literally making pilgrimages to sleep overnight in his shrine to see if they would receive a divine message.   I was afraid I was making too much of this, but I could not forget God also spoke to certain people in dreams and gave them the gift to interpret them. He also warned St Joseph and the three wise men through dreams, so there are times when He speaks to us in that manner. These dreams are very particular, certain signs distinguish them from ordinary subconscious ramblings. The three wise men for instance all had the same dream, which is not possible with natural dreaming. In my case, I woke up on the floor with a splitting headache, and at first I thought I hit my head on the side table when I fell, then I noticed my arm was hurting. I turned on the light, and found this," he said, unbuttoning his left cuff and rolling up his sleeve. Katherine was stunned to see a row of discernible puncture marks on either side of his arm resembling the bite from a large dog. "It was bleeding when I woke up. We didn't have a dog at that time, and it would be impossible for me to psychologically induce bleeding wounds, how could I explain the bite? Of course, I woke the house up with my yelling in the midst of my dream, and Lottie was the first one there. She only saw the blood, and I wrapped my arm fast, so she thinks I just scraped it on the table as I fell. No one has heard the full story until now," he concluded, rolling down his sleeve.

"I don't know what to say," Katherine replied after a pause. "If it was anyone else, I'd say they were reading too much into a dream, but you have the scars, it has to be real. I know you wouldn't purposely have some dog bite you to support an invented story."

"Correct. I didn't need to make up a story like that and subject myself to a dog attack plus a round of tetanus or rabies shots just to enter the priesthood. It's a fantastic story that few would be able to understand, bite marks and all, and why would I risk courting ridicule?"

"I don't know whether to feel spooked or privileged that you would reveal your story for the first time to me," Katherine admitted. "I don't mean to pry, but I heard your father wasn't happy when you decided to follow your vocation. Did you think about telling him? He might understand."

"I did think about it, but he was very angry at the time, well ... more disappointed and hurt than angry, but he was not open to hear anything of this sort, it would be a waste of time. I know he regrets losing his temper, but that stubborn Reinold pride won't let him give in. He views my leaving the family business to enter the religious life an abandonment of my duties, in fact, a betrayal, but he has yet to realize that when someone follows the path God sets before them, it is not a dishonour to their parents."

"That's food for thought," Katherine replied. "Oh, speaking of food, can I fix us another plate, perhaps another cup of coffee?"

"No thank you, I planned to run down to Stonyvale to see Mom and Lottie now that the coast is clear," he smiled. Katherine knew with his father away he could make a furtive visit. "Would you like to come? They're worried about you after reading the papers, and I know they would be very glad to see you." Katherine could not refuse.

"All right, I'll follow you in the van, give me a minute to retrieve my coat and purse from the studio."

"That reminds me, you said you wanted to paint me a picture, I apologize for not selecting a theme for you to work on sooner, but I had a feeling you were busy."

"That's all right. Now that you're here, why not come up and see Gerry and Lottie's pictures? They're finished, I just have to wait for them to pick out the frames they want."

"I'd be delighted."

They cleared up the table and went upstairs. Katherine uncovered the pictures for him and went for her coat.

"They're very beautiful. I know Gerry and Lottie will just … my, what's this?" he enquired, noticing the large vertical canvas with the two figures dressed in classical Grecian robes with the Liberty Bell in the background.

"Oh that," she smiled, "it's my new *magnum opus*, the first one in a series as a matter of fact."

"It's unusual," he replied, "this must be the Socratic artwork Lottie was telling me about."

"Yes, but I still have a lot of work to do on that." Katherine explained how Gerry's illuminated manuscripts gave her the idea to experiment with a combination of words and images. "I wanted something meaningful for the text and thought of composing something along the line of Socrates and his method of philosophical deduction. I know that's a little presumptuous since I haven't read everything attributed to Socrates past the *Apology*, the *Phaedo* and the *Crito*, and he may not have arrived at the same conclusions I have, but my main aim was to approximate his style of debate."

"It sounds very interesting. Have you written your dialogue yet?"

"Yes, I just started cutting out the first paragraphs today. Would you like to read them?"

"I'm curious, this I have to see."

"It might be easier to read from this," she said, handing him a notebook, "I thought it might be a good idea to make extra copies, just in case I spilled paint on the master draft."

He turned to the first page:

"This is a strange place which we find ourselves, Socrates. It is, Plato. We have somehow travelled to a future age and a fledgling country. It is a marvel to discover a New World across the realm ruled by Oceanus far beyond the Pillars of Hercules where some of our people once thought the kingdom of Hades began. *I agree. I would wish to know how we arrived in this new country, perhaps you have an answer.* That is a mystery, not all mysteries have answers, or at least, answers we can understand. *True, Socrates. No doubt a divine force translated us from one era to another.* Indeed. ..."

Fr. Peter looked at Katherine with amusement.
"Divine force?"
"I know that must sound ridiculous, the artist playing God, but I was trying to see how they would view this unusual situation," she laughed. He continued reading:

"... What I do know, Plato, we have been brought for a reason. It may be more productive to find out why rather than waste time wondering how we came and never find an answer. *Very true. No doubt this strange building named 'Independence Hall' and the object before us holds the key to this mystery.* I believe they do. This must be the birthplace of this new country, and the metal object, a symbol of its birth. The inscription says it is a 'Liberty Bell' and bears a passage from a sacred Hebrew text. 'Proclaim liberty throughout all the land unto all the inhabitants thereof.' *The bell bears a fissure, it is in want of repair. How strange to see a symbol of freedom damaged thus.* True, perhaps it is the key, Plato. Have you noticed on our journey how often the citizens of this new land remind each other it is a free country? *I have, and think it odd they do this.* How so, Plato? *It is like reminding a baker he is a baker, or a sculptor he is a sculptor.* You mean to say if someone is convinced of their trade, they have no need to be reminded. *That is correct.* I agree. If these citizens were convinced of their freedom, they would not need reminders. *Perhaps we are to remind them.* How do you propose we do that? *Let us take the example of the sculptor. If for some reason he does not ply his trade, he may lose his skill and forget how to be a sculptor. He needs guidance, and reminding is a form of guidance and encouragement to ensure he continues work to retain mastery of his skill. He cannot be called a sculptor if he loses his skill to carve. We would speak of him thus: he was a sculptor. If he worked, he would not need a reminder.* Then, you are implying these citizens have forgotten what freedom is, or are weak-willed in practising it and need encouragement, or perhaps have an incorrect idea and need guidance and reminding because they cannot be free if they do not act in accordance with the precepts of freedom. *That is my point, Socrates.* Then I suppose we would have to determine what perfect freedom is in order to guide them. *That is true. I propose we begin by comparing freedom with its opposite, it may be easier to define freedom by what it is not.* Very well. What is the opposite of freedom? *That is easy, slavery and tyranny.* What is slavery then? *The state of being a slave, more precisely, to be the property of a master whose commands must be obeyed without the option of choice.* And what is tyranny? *A cruel or oppressive government or rule.* Very good, before we continue, we must discover if these are in agreement. In other words, we must be certain that slavery and tyranny are united, or they both cannot be the opposite of freedom and we would be obliged to select the most appropriate opposite of freedom to continue our argument. *I agree. I would say that they are united. A tyrant controls his people no different than a master does his slaves by taking away their free will.* Yet for example, what would you say of a slave master who is not cruel like a tyrant and does not beat his slaves? Is he still a tyrant? *We would have to go further from our path and define cruelty, Socrates.* Very well, would you say that to be cruel is the same as being unkind and inflicting unnecessary pain? *Yes, most certainly.* Then, we must determine how or where pain may be felt. *That is easy, there is a pain of the body, and an invisible pain of the mind and the heart.* Are they all the same pain, or are some worse than others? *I would say the pain of the mind and heart are worse, for when the body is in pain, we may take medicines to alleviate it, but when the mind or heart are in pain, that is not easy to cure or alleviate.* Then, to inflict pain on the mind and heart is worse than inflicting pain on the body? *The argument would seem to support this.* Then how terrible is the pain of the mind and heart when the freedom of mankind is suppressed! Surely to oppress a person's option to choose, that is, the ability to use free will, is a cruelty and a terrible tyranny over the mind and heart indeed. *I agree. It would seem we have determined that slavery and tyranny are united and therefore both are exact opposites of freedom.* Yet, there is a passage in Aeschylus that reminds me of another opposition to ideal freedom: 'Praise not, O man, the life beyond control, nor that which bows unto a tyrant's sway. Know that the middle way is dearest unto God, and they thereon who wend, they shall achieve the end; but they who wander or to left or right are sinners in his sight. Take to heart this one, this soothfast word—of wantonness impiety is sire; only from calm control and sanity unstirred cometh true weal, the goal of every man's desire.' Since we have agreed that tyranny is opposed to freedom, we must determine if a life lived beyond control is also contrary to ideal freedom. To do that, we must name the conditions of living a wanton life without control as we did with slavery and tyranny. *If I may Socrates, I would begin by saying anarchy and libertinism.* We must define them also and discover if they are united in the same way as slavery and tyranny are united. *I would say anarchy is to be without rules and laws, the absence of government in a state. Libertinism is the personal anarchy of an individual and the absence of all moral laws and restrictions. I will add further these two must also be united as they both are forms of lawlessness be they public laws of state or private moral values of the individual.* Then we must see if lawlessness and the absence of moral restrictions are also opposed to ideal freedom. *First, we should examine the point there are many who say that the absence of laws, government and moral restrictions is the ideal form of freedom.* You must recall how often I have said that the opinion of the many is often not the best, but very well, it is an important point and we shall put it to the test. Let us ask why they would discard law and governments. *If they believe law and government restrict true freedom, then they are convinced law and governments are a form of slavery, or are commands and rules given by cruel tyrants. But not all rulers are cruel tyrants, and not all masters are slave owners. There are rulers who give good laws, and masters that wield authority without owning slaves. These people who say no law is the best law are in error then as not every law is evil, and therefore not every law or moral restriction is slavery or tyranny.* To clarify your argument, you are saying there are laws and governments that are good, and laws and governments that are evil. *Yes, that would be my argument.* Then you are correct in saying these people must believe that all laws are evil and cannot distinguish good laws from evil ones, or what true slavery and tyranny is from just and righteous rule. We must convince them otherwise, for I believe if people wish to do what is right and good, they would not willingly do evil if they could be shown certain actions are evil, nor would they refuse to perform good actions when cause for good is identified. In our argument, we find that to indiscriminately discard all rule of law and moral order is not good as this abolishes all good laws as well as the evil ones, and since true freedom is something good, it must be allied with what is good. To dispense with all law is to cast away good with bad, which is an evil thing, and as ideal freedom is a good thing and cannot be allied with evil, it cannot allow every law to be abolished. Again I say, as there are good laws and restrictions, true freedom must have some rules and boundaries. There cannot be laws that are cruel or slavish, nor can there be the complete absence of law and order be it state law or moral law. *That is true. It seems we have proven Aeschylus correct in the matter of a middle path, but now that we have come thus far, we must distinguish between the good laws and the bad laws so people may know which to discard and which to follow.* Rather, we must settle on the one truth that to allow mankind practise its free will is a great good, and people must be shown how to use that freedom correctly, giving it neither full rein or shackling it with tyrannical constrictions. Good laws help as guides on that middle path, bad laws drive one off course to the right or to the left. It may be more expedient to discover where good laws come from so we may find the surest guide. Good masters give good laws, evil masters evil laws. *Very true. As Aeschylus seemed correct in one point, it seems fitting we examine his observation that tyrannical and immoral wantonness comes from impiety. If this is also true, it can be argued that piety and reverence lead to correct judgement.* Very well, we shall examine this point. What is piety and reverence? *It means to be religious and respectful of all that is religious.* Then to be truly free, we must acknowledge the existence of a god in order to be religious and pious. But what of the professed atheists? *If they do not believe in a god, they cannot be pious or religious, and according to our argument they cannot be truly free if they are not pious.* Then what do you say about atheists who claim they do not need to be religious to live law-abiding and moral lives? *This takes much thought. It is true they do not need to believe in a god to follow the laws of the state or perhaps to follow an invisible law of morality accepted as good and true by the people, but we must see why atheists would follow these laws. Perhaps because it is the right thing to do, and virtue is its own reward.* Yet who imparted the ability to mankind to distinguish between right and wrong? There is an unspoken law that good must be followed and evil shunned. Is this something invented by man or does it come from something higher than man? *It may help if we examine the nature of a law though we digress from our main point.* Very well. Is not a law a decree or a command, something that is spoken, given or handed down? *Yes, certainly. Then a law of state cannot make itself, it requires statesmen and judges to make them.* Is this the same for moral laws as well as laws of state? *This is difficult, a human judge or statesman cannot declare what is moral, but make laws to abide by a Universal Law to follow good and avoiding evil for the good of the state.* But you say following good is a Universal Law, and if laws are decrees or commands that are made and cannot make themselves, who or what has declared this Universal Law? You say men of state cannot, so it must be something unseen and therefore divine that has declared this Universal Law. *Yes.* Thus in spite of themselves, atheists are following a divine command even if they do not believe in the deity that created them be they laws of state or moral laws. There may be some truth they do not need to believe in a god to be good, but then if they do not believe in a god, who do they believe gives the Universal Law of following good and shunning evil? *Obviously, mankind.* But then that is a dangerous thing, for if a man does not believe in a god capable of giving perfect laws, he is in the position of declaring all laws come from man, and as man is imperfect, he can declare that as fallible men make imperfect laws, he can pick and choose what he wishes to follow, that which, in his own mind seems good. He does not believe in divine retribution, therefore he can also declare his own morality contrary to what the divine may decree simply because he believes there is no divine decree. He may follow his every whim and passion, declaring it to be good when it may be very evil, for he like all men is imperfect, so how can he tell what is verily good? The atheist is in danger of mistaking vice for good and consequently follow another slave master and tyrant, his own physical and mental weakness. Evil would be wittingly or unwittingly perpetrated, therefore, to recognise the existence of a perfect divine being that gives perfect Universal Laws is much better than not to believe in a god, for if there is a perfect god, they will not allow their laws to be broken with impunity as in the case with many corrupt judges on earth, but will punish accordingly in due time. Therefore, to be pious and reverent is the surest path to true freedom as a perfect god will give perfect laws to prevent all manner of slavery, tyranny and moral wantonness, even if we do not understand why they are good laws at times. *That is true, even this new nation recognises the need to follow a deity, it states thus in their 'Declaration of Independence: 'We hold these truths to be self-evident, that all men are created equal, that they are endowed by their Creator with certain unalienable Rights, that among these are Life, Liberty, and the pursuit of Happiness. That to secure these rights, Governments are instituted among men, deriving their just powers from the consent of the governed ... .' See, they know the Universal Law of following Good comes from a divine source, and that it is the duty of a government to ensure the Divine Universal Law is enforced for the good of man. But which divinity? Their Declaration makes mention of the 'Laws of Nature' and 'Nature's God'. Perhaps they follow the god Liber whose name is related to the word 'liberty' as Liber is often associated with Dionysus the nature god. Liber is a god of the common plebs and protects the rights of free speech, a right this country prizes above many of their rights.* Yes, but Liber also champions ecstatic release from moral restraint, and as we have discovered, true freedom cannot be without moral restraint. *Perhaps they follow gods of their choosing as their county proclaims religious freedom or freedom not to believe if they wish.* Yes, but that is dangerous, for we have seen what atheism may lead to, and while we understand the practise of true freedom is to adhere to the laws of a deity, not all religions or deities are equal. In fact, we now know for certain Zeus and his pantheon do not exist, their temples and rites have been neglected for centuries and no retribution has occurred, these gods of old are no more, or they never existed, as gods are supposed to be immortal and will not suffer to be ignored but duly worshipped. Therefore, these deities and demigods of old were designed by men and we can see from the imperfect life of Zeus that he indeed was created by imperfect men without self control. *Then it is our duty to discover the nature of the perfect deity that we may follow the most perfect laws for our well being.* That should not be too difficult. Does a judge or lawgiver remain silent, rather does he not proclaim these laws that they might be followed? *Very true. Yet, I see a difficulty. If perfect laws come from a perfect deity, the government should imitate how that deity governs the Universe. And I have yet to see any religion that dares tell a deity what to do. A deity will not suffer to be ordered how to run the universe by mere mortals, rather the opposite occurs. If a deity will listen, it may be to grant the desire of the mortal to show their error in presuming to know better than the deity.* You question then if a government of and by the people is the perfect government. *Yes, in fact, this new country states in its Declaration that its government derives authority from the consent of the governed, thus it follows a majority rule. That may pose a difficulty in professing the true god to be followed as everyone has the right to follow what god they please and may promote their imperfect ideas of any deity, or a majority of atheists may sway the balance and the laws of the perfect deity may not be recognised or disregarded as being tyrannical.* This is indeed a difficult point, their Declaration states the need to support the laws of a deity, the Creator of Nature, which is the Creator of the Universe, yet cannot profess this perfect deity as the nation's god for their government consists of majority rule, and in order to please the majority, no single deity or religion can be followed to the exclusion of another. *Yet, we have seen not all deities are equal, the most perfect must be chosen.* Then this government works against itself and will not advance far in the promotion of the Universal Good. If it cannot follow or promote the laws of the

Perfect Deity, it cannot be truly free. *That seems to be the case, and what is more difficult to understand, the citizens declare this nation to be 'under God and indivisible, with truth and justice for all'. The citizens also declare they 'Trust in God' and state this on their currency.* Then they must choose the True Deity to follow, or this nation has built itself on a false idea of freedom. *That cannot come to pass when this nation promotes separation between Church and State, which implies their laws do not or may not follow the divine precepts of a deity.* Then they are not being true to their Declaration. *Yet, is it possible to enforce the laws of the Perfect Deity to the exclusion of all others? Rather, to enforce one set of beliefs on certain citizens who do not believe is also to impinge on their free will, and we have agreed to impinge on the free will is a terrible form of tyranny.* That is true, but if men earnestly desire truth, will they not wish to seek to discover the laws of the Perfect Deity and follow them? Truth is absolute Perfection and Good, and Perfect Laws come from Perfect Truth and Goodness. Only an evil man would wish to discard them. *Yet what of imperfect men? All men are imperfect, and it is they who write and enforce the laws that are to correspond to the Perfect Divine Law.* Yet, we know a lawgiver will not write laws that they should remain hidden, no doubt the Perfect Deity sends messengers or officers to guide mankind how to form governments according to divine precepts. We simply must discern who they are. …"

"And you say you are not perceptive? A life unexamined is a life not worth living," Fr. Peter chuckled. "I'm sorry I kept you waiting, I'd love to continue reading this, but I suppose we must be leaving. Would you mind if I borrow your notebook? I'm curious to read your conclusion."

"No, not at all. I suppose one revelation deserves another, you're the first to read it."

"I'm honoured," he smiled, slipping the notebook in his inside pocket as they walked to the elevator. "I can see why you're designing a whole collection, you would never fit all *that* in one painting. If you don't mind me asking, what gave you the idea to experiment with a philosophical discourse?"

Katherine explained how on the first day the gallery opened she was berated by an artist when she refused to show his smutty artwork.

"He was falling back on the old stop-gap of freedom of expression, and I had just started reading Plato's discourses at the time, I was just curious to see what was true freedom and misused freedom. I never thought I would like reading Socratic works, but they do make one think. However, I'm no expert, and I hope my dialogue did not go too far a field."

"Actually, it's amazing how close you've come to Plato's conclusion a democracy may not be the perfect form of government. As you hinted in your dialogue, Socrates preferred the good judgement of a few rather than an erroneous opinion of a multitude, and Plato seemed to agree with this viewpoint. Do you remember Socrates' argument that only a few people are skilled in certain matters?"

"Yes, but vaguely at this point."

"It was during his trial when Socrates asked his accuser how could every judge and Athenian be capable of improving the youth of their state, and he was supposedly the sole corrupter of their morals."

"Now I remember, he said that the opposite was more likely, and talked about horses as an example, saying that it was impossible for one man alone to harm horses and everyone else could take care of them, when in fact, not everyone is skilled in taking care of horses."

"That's it. Plato thought the same applied to leadership skills. Do the many have the skills to lead a country, or the few who are well trained and have a sense of duty to people and country? Therefore, having the multitude vote for their leaders was not a good idea according to him, his conclusion was if the leaders turn out to be terrible because of the multitude's ignorant choices, the ignorance of the nation is revealed to the world."

"What government did he think was perfect?"

"Well, he believed someone who was well trained in good philosophy and morals in order to lead people along the right path would be a good leader, and because that person would need power to enforce good laws for the good of the nation, Plato advocated a type of monarchy with a 'philosopher-king' as leader."

"That won't work here," Katherine laughed, "we threw out a tyrannical monarch, and no one in the 'Free World' is going to give up on democracy now. Wait, would Plato think of a tyrant becoming king? There's no way to ensure the heirs of a good king will not become bad."

"True, but he thought it was better to have one evil tyrant rule the people against their will and show one man to be evil than to have a whole nation display its ignorance through their bad choice of leaders."

"I don't think anyone today would like his ideas, no wonder people have no time for philosophy, but speaking of democracy, I can see Plato's point; the majority can vote in bad laws, and because the majority can make immoral and unethical actions legal, people think it's okay to have an abortion for example, just *because* it's legal."

"That's also true. Errors do not cease to be errors simply because they're ratified into law. God warned the Jews to be careful of following a crowd, 'Thou shalt not follow the multitude to do evil: neither shalt thou yield in judgement to the opinion of the most part to stray from the truth.' You know, I think you would have enjoyed Bishop Fulton Sheen's television programs, I suppose you're too young to remember them."

"I think I've heard Gramps mention him."

"He examined everything, religion to politics, philosophy and the problems of modern psychology."

"I'm surprised he was kept on the air," Katherine noted.

"He won an Emmy as a matter of fact."

"Really? Now that's something."

"He had a great sense of humour. When he received the award, he thanked his writers; Matthew, Mark, Luke and John. Those were certainly different days back then. Our culture has changed dramatically in these few short years, especially with the decline of Latin, no one cares to read the classical texts that helped shape our Western civilization."

"Not if the writers back then thought like Plato," she laughed, "but we also have a short memory, people today lose interest in yesterday's news let alone history that happened several thousand years ago."

"True, and it's a pity. We can understand the Gospels better when we look at the times and the culture that existed back then."

"How so?"

"Well, I'll give a quick example. Who would have thought it possible that John the Baptist could have used a pagan myth to teach the Jews not to be presumptuous concerning the Messiah and who would be saved?"

"You're not serious."

"Well, you won't see this in any catechism, it's just a personal observation. However, think back to the part where John rebukes the Pharisees and Sadducees, warning them not to rely on their lineage from Abraham."

"That's when he told them God could take the stones and turn them into children of Abraham."

"Exactly. John was preaching penance and a complete change of life to prepare for the coming Messiah, but they were smug in their conviction that they as descendants of Abraham were assured of the Messiah and therefore expected to receive salvation, but they had no will to amend their lives. You can't expect salvation without giving up sin and making amendment, which they thought they could. They also thought the Messiah was just for the Jewish nation, when in fact God promised all of mankind a redeemer in Genesis long before any nation came to be."

"But I don't see what this has to do with a pagan myth."

"Well, since John mentioned stones, and that God could turn them into worthy humans if He so wished, it reminded me of Deucalion and Pyrrha, the Greek myth of the Flood."

"Oh, I remember reading that. Because they were the only good people left on earth they were spared, and to repopulate the earth, they were told by a sacred oracle to throw the bones of their mother over their shoulders. Since they interpreted that to be the stones of Mother Earth, they threw stones over their shoulders, which turned into people. Still, I don't understand why John would possibly refer to that myth since the Jews were to shun all pagan things."

"He wasn't confirming the myth as truth, rather, he was using a shock tactic. The Jews were not ignorant of the Hellenic and Roman cultures around them and their various myths. By referring to a pagan account, John was literally telling them their lineage from Abraham was not enough, the Messiah would accept anyone who accepted Him and did penance for their sins, and that included the pagans, the stones who could be turned into spiritual sons of Abraham without any blood ties whatsoever."

"Now that's interesting. Are there any other references like that?"

"Christ makes mention of a proverb, 'Physician: Heal Thyself', although it's possible an early scribe invented a fable and attributed it to Aesop to fit the proverb and the Gospel passage. However, since St. Paul makes use of a famous fable by Aesop concerning the body and its members, it's possible Christ did make reference to a real fable. In any case, He gives the proverb to the people of Nazareth in the form of an ironic rebuke."

"Goodness, this I've got to hear too, but we won't make it to Stonyvale anytime soon if we continue with our philosophical academy," she smiled. By now, they had long since exited the elevator and were loitering around the lobby.

"We have time, it'll only take a few minutes. About the first proverb, you'll find it in Luke, Christ referred to it after he returned to Nazareth and read the prophesy of Isaiah concerning the mission of the Messiah to heal, forgive sin and preach the Gospel to the poor, proclaiming this had all been fulfilled in their hearing. The people of Nazareth all looked at each other and couldn't understand how or why He would dare take this authority upon Himself, saying 'Isn't he Joseph and Mary's son?' Basically,

'You come from common people, you can't do the things Isaiah wrote.' That's when He replied "No doubt you will say this proverb to me: *Physician heal thyself.* Do all the great things here in your own country that we heard were done in Capharnaum.'" He knew they expected a visual sign before they would believe Him since they wouldn't credit His divine origin despite the reports of the miracles that He already accomplished, which fulfilled the prophecy of Isaiah. The proverb He mentioned seems to be borrowed from Aesop's fable the *Quack Frog.* In that story, a frog left his marsh and went around the world proclaiming to the animals he knew how to cure all diseases. A fox then piped up and said if he had that skill, he should first cure his own lame legs and wrinkled blotchy skin to prove it. The irony is the frog didn't have proof of his skill, but Christ did have evidence of His powers from the reports of the miracles spreading throughout the land. I also find it interesting that the only person Christ ever called a fox was King Herod who insisted on seeing a miracle but had no faith, just like the people of Nazareth. 'Go and tell that fox, Behold, I cast out devils, and do cures today and tomorrow, and the third day, I am consummated.' That's also in Luke, so the link between crafty foxes who were blinded by their own conceits and who tested God must have been intentional."

"That's something you don't hear in Sunday school," Katherine admitted, "of course, I remember what St. Paul said about all members making up the body of Christ in His Church, that everyone had different gifts and each was important in it's own way."

"Yes, that's correct."

"I don't remember the fable from Aesop though, not word for word."

"The members of the Body were grumbling that the stomach didn't seem to do anything to help or work, while all the others were helping to keep it satisfied. The members of the Body decided not to slave away for the stomach and went on strike, but began to suffer when the stomach didn't receive any food. The lesson was no matter how quiet and humble a task may be, all the members of the Body had to work together, or they will all perish."

"That's interesting, but returning to the first fable, why is it wrong to ask for miracles?"

"Asking for something in faith like a miracle healing is not wrong, Christ healed people and continues to do so, not to mention miracles continue to this day. It's *how* God is asked. For instance, if you believe in God and His good works, you don't need miracles to keep you grounded in your faith. However, if you test Him by demanding signs to prove His power, it's like calling Him a liar, or that you doubt His existence. The people of Nazareth were testing Christ, refusing to believe in Him or the reports of other miracles, and God will not help people if they doubt or refuse to trust in Him. Of course, God will only grant requests if it is accordance with what is good, holy, and if it will help save souls. He won't grant anything that is harmful or will knock you off the path towards perfection."

"But not everyone is cured. I often wonder why He allows so much suffering in the world, and I'm not the only one. Since God is supposed to be all good and greater than anything, why doesn't He eliminate all misery and disease?"

"Poor God, how often He is blamed for all the suffering in the world. It's like praising Satan for allowing all the good that happens. Let's look at it this way, is pain and suffering sin?"

"Gosh, maybe it's a result that comes from sin, but sin is an action, isn't it? Pain and suffering aren't, they are more of a consequence, but then, there are other pains that don't come from evil actions at all. So not all pain and suffering is a consequence of evil."

"Very good. Sin is doing evil or refusing to do good; and as pain of and by itself is *not* evil, it is used as a warning to wake us up, or a spur to help us on to better things. If that were not the case, it would be a sin for parents to correct their children, or set punishments to teach them when they are wrong or prevent them from doing wrong. Pain and disagreeable situations tell us when something is wrong, and in certain instances, the absence of pain is very dangerous. There are times we are allowed to suffer pain for our own good, and if we do not suffer when we should, we would end up in deep trouble. For instance, when we are sick and don't feel good, we know something is wrong with our bodies, it's a sign to do something about it. Then there are those with rare conditions who cannot feel pain, and there is no way for them to know if they are falling sick. They have to be extra vigilant with regards to their health. God works the same way with spiritual matters, misery tells us when something is going wrong with the world or our personal lives and informs us we have to make improvements. Sometimes we have to suffer and work hard to earn big rewards, and the reward is often not appreciated without sweat and sacrifice. Then there is the matter of redemption, if Christ is God, He cannot sin, and if suffering was a sin in and by itself, He could not have suffered and died for us. However, since He took the most horrific death to redeem us, He showed us in fact that suffering and pain have great power. Pain, trials, sufferings are the only way now to purify us, just like gold is purified in fire. We'll have to leave it there, or we shall never see Stonyvale today," he noted.

"My, I bet you have a packed congregation on Sundays," she said, "no one explains things like this anymore. Oh, before I forget, you said you had picked out the theme you wanted for your painting?"

"Yes, but I see you have your hands full, and with very important work I might add. Your painting for me can wait until another time."

"Oh no, that's all right. I can work on it, there are various drying stages and I can do a number of canvases at the same time. Anyway, I need something different to give me a break once in awhile or I might get bored with my theme before it's finished."

"Very well. I was wondering if you could do a painting of this for me," he said, taking out a black pocketbook from his inside pocket and retrieved a few photographs inserted between the pages. They were pictures of an antique statue of the Virgin and Child wearing gold crowns, dressed in real clothes surrounded by a large halo and standing in an ornate gold altar decorated with flower vases on either side. Examining the images, Katherine noticed the statue held a shepherd's staff and keys in her right hand.

"That's beautiful, but her face is very sad," she noticed as she flipped through the pictures and came to a close-up photo. "The statue looks Spanish, 1600s maybe."

"Close, it's the shrine of the miraculous image of Our Lady of Good Success in Quito, Ecuador. The Mother of God and the three archangels Michael, Gabriel and Raphael actually finished the statue. There is also an important vision for our times connected with it." Katherine was usually sceptical of mystic visions, but for some reason this unusual statement didn't sound crazy coming from him.

"There's a connection with this picture and your dream, isn't there?"

"You could say that, it's a reminder of the responsibilities I took on. Would it be possible for you to paint the title of the statue somewhere at the bottom? There are many statues of Our Lady of Good Success around the world, and I would like this particular picture to be easily identified."

"Sure, no problem. I can design a medallion with Spanish baroque scrollwork to match the surroundings. I'll leave these at the desk for now, I'll have the whole week free for art and it will give me a chance to get the preliminary work started."

"That would be perfect," he said.

"I guess we'd better get going," she noted, quickly slipping the photos behind the front desk. "Bye Kyle, see you later."

Katherine felt much better now that Fr. Peter had explained everything to her, it seemed like a huge weight had been lifted from her. However, he had given her plenty to think about. She wondered when Gerry would be able to contact her since the lines of communication were restricted while he was working with the Jakarta police, and if he and Mr. Reinold were all right after he had stirred up a hornet's nest in the criminal world. She wondered what the news reports would reveal tonight, if her parents would watch them, not to mention if she could convince them Gerry was innocent, after Father's visit, there was so much to tell. She thought about the remarkable confidence Fr. Peter had shown her, revealing his personal story. She would keep that part of his visit to herself of course, nobody would believe it anyway.

Fr. Peter had arrived first, and Katherine was amused to find Sinbad perched on his shoulder yelling "Hi Petey! Arrr matey!" while bobbing his head before flying over to her shoulder and jabbering, 'Yo ho! Kissy kissy'.

"You don't have ask for permission to come aboard," Fr. Peter noted with a smile, "looks like you're an accepted member of the crew."

"He knows my name, it didn't take him long to learn it," she said as the bird began to playfully tug at her hair, demanding her attention.

Mrs. Reinold and Lottie were glad to see her and hoped she was all right after the vandal attack, they didn't seem too bothered about the paintings. Katherine assured them she was fine, and apologized for the damage, but they told her not to worry, everything could be repaired. They then informed her Gerry would be calling at a certain hour and hoped she would be able to stay long enough to talk with him. She wanted to, unfortunately she had to get back to Jersey, so she wondered if they could ask him to call her at home, she would make sure all the receivers were placed back on their hooks. Katherine stayed long enough to have a few cups of coffee, her philosophical academy with Fr. Peter that afternoon had taken up more time than she realized and regretfully had to leave before it got dark.

Arriving home just before dinner, she heard a heated discussion coming from the den, this time it was not difficult to overhear the topic of conversation. Uncle Tim had stopped by, and he was not in favour of changing shipping companies. Apparently, he was trying to persuade Pops and Gramps not to do anything in haste until they could see what was happening with Reinold Enterprises. Well, hurrah for Uncle Tim she thought, of course, he was more interested in keeping the good deal that Gerry had arranged for them, but at least it was something supportive rather than negative. She couldn't wait until they all sat to the table when she could have their undivided attention and clear up everything, once and for all. Everyone listened carefully as she told them the news, showing surprise when she came to the part of the Underground Railroad, and patiently waited for her to finish before saying anything.

"Well, that's something, isn't it?" Gramps began, rubbing his chin. "They've had their fair share of adventures and mishaps over the years, haven't they?"

"Are you certain this is all true?" her mother asked.

"I know it sounds fantastic, if someone else tried to tell me, I might have my doubts, but Gerry's brother wouldn't lie about something as serious as this. He's a model of sincerity."

"Maybe we were wrong to jump to conclusions," Pops said quietly, "I suppose we should have known considering what just happened to us with Morgan."

"No business is immune to skulduggery, and shipping must have its problems too," Gramps conceded.

"I'm glad we have the facts, or what can be released right now anyway," Uncle Tim added, "looks like we won't have to cancel our shipping contracts after all."

"Come everyone, let's finish dinner and watch the news," Mom prompted.

After dinner, Katherine hurried around the house, hanging phones back up before settling down with everyone in the den, Mrs. Gonzales and Juanita included. It wasn't a lengthy update, but that didn't matter. She was relieved to hear the police officially state they did not consider the Reinolds suspects and were grateful for their help with their investigations in tracking this new criminal ring that had eluded them for months. In addition, three arrests had been made that day. Gerry wasn't present for the official statement, but as his brother had said, their father and several officials from the other shipping companies came forward to offer a few comments, each affirming their innocence and that they placed all their confidence in the local justice system.

"Well, that's good news," Gramps concluded. Katherine didn't have a chance to hear any other comments as the phone began to ring. She jumped to answer it, only to be bothered by a reporter.

"Hi, I'm calling for the *New York Times* ..."

"Sorry, no comment," and she plonked the receiver down. It rang again a few seconds later. They don't waste any time, she thought. She quickly picked it up. "*No* comments, *no* interviews. Will you people ever learn?"

"Whoa! Maybe I should call back later, Princess?"

"Gerry! I'm so sorry! I thought it was another reporter," she stammered. She couldn't wait for his call, and to think she had snapped at him.

"You don't have to apologize. I'm sorry I can't stay on the line, the police are keeping my calls short, I'm one notch away from radio silence."

"Can you wait until I go to my room?"

"Sure, but please hurry, I don't want to lose any more seconds than I have to."

She quickly handed the receiver to Mom and charged up the stairs. Breathless, she picked up her phone to hear her mother was quizzing him on the information his brother passed on.

"Yes Mrs. Walsingham, it's true, Peter would not lie or exaggerate."

"But people should know! Your family should be recognised for the good they do …"

"Okay Mom, I'm on, you can hang up now."

"All right, I'll leave you two then, take care, Gerry." The faint 'click' and the absence of the droning TV in the background told her they had the line to themselves.

"I hear Pete made a visit today," he began. "I'm glad he stopped by, are you all right?"

"I'm fine, but several of your pieces are ruined, and your vase nearly hit the deck."

"Don't worry about that, I was afraid things might turn out nasty for you after the news broke. I did get your message, but there was no way I could contact you. I had to change hotels, twice in fact, as you know, I was in police protection, then the reporters would find out where I moved to, it's a bit of a mess right now."

"I can just imagine, but don't worry. Pete explained everything to me. I must admit, it looked pretty bad at first, I didn't know what to think, and everyone had only malicious rumours to pass on, not knowing anything different."

"So where do we stand now?" he asked tentatively.

"Well, let's say the silver ships are sailing, although Pops might still be stuck on the crystal shakers."

"I'm thankful for that, I bet the crystal cracked when the news broke."

"And the porcelain ones too, you can thank your big brother for coming to the rescue."

"Good old Pete. I'm sorry,Princess, for all this hassle. I suppose if I had told you about everything, it might have made the last few days easier on you, but I had no idea any of this was going to happen. I assumed I had plenty of time to fill you in on family history, well let's face it, I was hoping to put it off as long as possible. I mean, you didn't even know about our whaling background, that was hard enough to have to break to a gun-ho animal rights activist, let alone admit we descended from a slave trader."

"Gosh, that's in the past now, isn't it? From what Pete told me, your family exonerated itself with flying colours and continues to do so, in fact, he even explained your fascination with 'con art'."

"Shoot, can't keep a good deed secret anymore. Well, there goes the intrigue from *those* conversation pieces," Gerry noted with good humour, "but seriously, after we went to the book fair and you told me about the story of the cabin boy, knowing how firm you are in your principles, I thought I had better keep my family history as quiet for as long as possible. I didn't want to be scratched from your good graces before we had a chance to know each other better."

"Oh, I'm so sorry, I can't quite remember what I said, but I never meant any offence, or to rake up a painful past for that matter."

"I know you didn't, Princess. I'm just glad it's out in the open now. Blast, the cops are motioning me to finish up," he concluded, "I think they're afraid if I talk too long, I might give away my whereabouts. I can call on weekends, that's about it."

"That's all right, I'm just happy to hear you're okay. You will be coming home soon?"

"I'm afraid it's up to the cops, maybe in a few weeks. I know, you're heading to the wedding, hopefully I might get away before then. Are you sure you don't want to stay in my apartment rather than a hotel?"

"Gerry, we've gone through this," she chided, "you know I have to be where they're holding the reception, it makes it easier for me."

"All right, just checking. Okay, okay I'm finished," he said, obviously to the police on duty, "I've got to go, they're about to snatch the phone from me. Bye for now, take care, and call Pete if you need anything. I've asked him to keep an eye on you."

"I'm a big girl now," she laughed, "but thank you. You take care too."

A simple *click*, and he was gone. The call was over before she could register the fact she had just spoken to him. It was good to hear his voice, but now he was restricted to weekend calls. She understood it was for his own safety, but he was supposed to be under protective custody, not house arrest. Well, there was nothing she could do but wait and hope he would be allowed to come home earlier than expected.

☙ ❀ ❧

The next morning, bouquets arrived like clockwork to the house and the gallery; as promised, Gerry somehow managed to keep them supplied with yellow and red blooms. Everything was looking up despite the drama of the past few days. It was a breath of fresh air having a quiet week in the gallery, allowing the artists work away to their heart's content. By now, Dennis had been invited to join them as his room mate had been complaining his art was cramping their place, and with the Professor dropping by to inspect their progress, they were becoming a regular art colony at this point. Nevertheless, there were a few necessary interruptions to the creative process. Business wise, Fr. Peter had arranged for the inspectors to come and survey the damage, and if need be, transfer the pieces in question to the restorers for which she was very grateful. Mrs. Hunt made a visit oblivious to the fact the gallery was closed and was relieved to confirm her donations were safe and sound before making her usual request to have all new works on display brought to her for inspection. As for the damaged wall, Katherine had a few cans of paint and some rolls of matching wallpaper left over from the remodelling, it only took an afternoon to cover over the black splotches. She decided not to take down Gerry's collection when the repairs were completed, the police had proclaimed his innocence, and after a week, she was sure the masses would forget the whole débâcle, other tragedies in the world were vying for their attention.

April came with a bang when she received an unusual delivery, a large box of chocolates and a bouquet of red roses with a mysterious card reading '*From a Secret Admirer*'. Gerry was simply being too generous, but no sunflowers? That was odd. She opened the box and shared the unexpected treats with everyone at the desk, only to find she had started a mad race to the restaurant with a large glass of water as the coveted prize. Katherine didn't know what had happened and carefully bit into one of the tempting morsels: they were filled with hot chilli sauce. She noticed a piece of paper peeking up from the side and lifted the chocolate trays to find a note hidden underneath, '*Happy April Fools, Kats.*'

"*Steves!* I'm going to malafooster him!"

She didn't know what that actually was, but it sounded pretty painful. She flipped the note over: '*P.S. Consider this my last hurrah, time*

784

to grow up now that I'm joining the board soon. See you at Spring Break.'
Well, she could let him have one last prank, he did help rescue the family business after all.

Life seemed to jump into top gear after that, trying to run the gallery by day and prepare for her trip to Paris by night, not to mention they were approaching a major holiday, Easter. This was the first time she would see Paris in the springtime and hoped she was packing the right attire for the weather in addition to the formal functions she would be expected to attend as a bridesmaid. At least the wedding outfit was prepared for her, but she wasn't sure if the French had the same customs with regards to rehearsal dinners, or bachelorette parties for that matter. Perhaps she was bringing too many changes, but better to be prepared than caught unawares.

Although she was looking forward to the trip, she looked forward to Gerry's calls even more. She didn't know how much she was actually missing him until he was not able to call as often, and then, he had to hang up before they had a chance to talk. It wasn't his fault, he had to divide his time between his family and her, so he was doing his best to keep in contact. However, one call was disappointing: he would finally get home on Easter Sunday, the day before she was leaving for Paris.

"Oh Lancelot, we're going to miss each other by a hair's breadth."

"I know Princess, but we had a lot of records to go through for the company, I couldn't leave any earlier. What a cruel twist of fate this is."

There was nothing they could do but accept the situation. If there anything good came from it, she was discovering that another *cliché* held a grain of truth; absence made her heart grow fonder.

One day Stephie came by unexpectedly for lunch to bring her some photographs.

"What's this?" Katherine wondered as she handed her a manila envelope.

"Just something I thought you might like to have," she replied, "you two make such a cute couple."

Katherine slid the photos out to find Stephie had taken secret shots of her and Gerry around the gallery the month before he left for Asia. Using black and white film, she had given the pictures a *chic* New York pop art effect, tinting only a few objects in full colour. One picture featured them having lunch at Andre's with the floral table decoration coloured in, another image showed them walking down one of the corridors alone upstairs with one of the artworks beside them tinted in full colour. Her favourite was Gerry handing her one of his signature bouquets, which naturally Stephie had coloured in. Katherine had regretted she didn't have any photographs of him before he left, and now she had several that were taken at a very special time.

"And here we thought you were snapping pictures for the brochures. Thank you so much, Stephie. They're wonderful, you could actually use them for a Calvin Klein ad, although I'm no model."

"Don't be so modest, you're very photogenic, and so is he. You know, you're very lucky, I wish someone would look at me that way," she commented before moving on to other business she wanted to discuss.

It was difficult for Katherine to keep her mind focused for the rest of the day, the photographs brought to mind Gerry's unusual riddle and his mysterious envelope, not that they had ever escaped her thoughts. Although she had finally realized she had fallen in love with him, she still hesitated in sending his mysterious letter. He had asked her to wait for only a few days, no doubt to give her time to reflect upon her answer, but she still felt shy. For one thing, she continued to doubt the seriousness of his intentions. This could all be a mere amusement for him and was afraid to do anything in case she had set herself up for a painful disappointment. Yet, the photos didn't lie, there in black and white was an unmistakable expression of tenderness between them. Could she ask for more substantial proof? They did care for each other, that much was certain, they just hadn't revealed their feelings yet, nor would they until she sent that letter according to his instructions. Perhaps it was the fear of the unknown that prevented her from slipping that little note into the outgoing mail file, wondering what might happen afterwards. Nevertheless, the more she thought about it, the more she realized she could not leave things hanging between them like this. He had now become part of her life and not to let him know how much she cared for him was no different than when he edited Sinatra's songs, leaving empty spaces at the most important sections. It was time to take a leap of faith and fill in the blanks. Just before Easter weekend, she slid the unpretentious envelope into the post box outside the gallery, wondering if the letter would be the first thing he received upon his arrival home. Where this would lead, she wasn't sure, but she would certainly find out when she returned.

ೞ❀ೖ

"*Ladies and gentlemen, we must ask you to please return to your seats and fasten your seatbelts for landing … .*"

Katherine did as requested and looked out the window, hoping that third time was lucky and she would actually get a glimpse of the city as the plane descended. Just as before, Paris was hidden from view by endless patchwork patterns in all shades of springtime green up to the last moment when they touched ground at Charles de Gaulle.

This time she arranged a night flight out to ensure she could get a night's sleep on the plane and beat the jet lag in one blow, not to mention arriving in good time allowing her at least half a day at her destination. Retrieving her floral luggage set, a little worse for wear after a second trip, she was surprised to see the Montmartre Club had turned out to greet her, Justine waving wildly with her floral scarf to get her attention in the midst of the crowds at the arrivals gate. Martin and Justine looked so much better than on her last visit, and Maurice had brought Theresa, a tall graceful figure with dark brown eyes, her hair tied back in a ponytail. There was a joyous reunion as they all hugged, shook hands, kissed cheeks French fashion and introduced Theresa before the men began a polite argument on who should help roll the luggage to the transport van that Martin had rented for the move from the old apartment, plus whatever was necessary for the wedding.

"Oh let the men argue," Justine said, "they'll figure it out. Before I say anything, I've got more good news, go on, show her."

Theresa smiled and lifted her left hand to reveal a ring with a large sparkling diamond. In all the happy confusion, Katherine hadn't noticed it before.

"Oh, how wonderful, Theresa! Congratulations! When did this happen?"

"Three days ago," Maurice beamed, no wonder he was looking like the Cheshire cat.

"Now, all I have to do is aim right and make sure you catch the bouquet," Justine whispered to Katherine as they went out the door.

"Um … well, I wouldn't go so far as announce a wedding or anything, but I've got some news too you might say."

"Oh! You mean Paris has finally rubbed off on you? This is just splendid! Do tell us all about it," she implored, clapping her hands with glee. Even though they were supposed to be talking about the plans for her special day, Justine didn't care, she was happy when others could be happy too. It was so good to see her back to her sprightly self, it was just like their college days when their little *clique* first met.

"We should be talking about your big day first."

"Oh, okay, but let's just concentrate on today. After we get you checked into the hotel, we are going straight to the new apartment to have a nice get-together dinner with all the parents. I'm sorry, we couldn't invite you to stay with us, but my parents and my sister have the spare rooms, on top of all our art work and the wedding gifts that have taken up residence.”

“You don’t need to apologize. How did your parents all get along at their first meeting?”

“It was a little stiff and starchy to tell the truth, but I think everyone is getting along very well now. I’m so glad Martin and his father have set aside their differences. Perhaps it’s not all forgive and forget yet,” Justine whispered, “his father was really disappointed about him choosing art, but I think he’s getting used to the idea. The fact you’re showing our artwork helps, at least he can say ‘My son and future daughter in law have a collection that will be seen in New York,’.”

“I’m glad to have your paintings to tell the truth, I’ve got collectors who want to see more European artists, and you guys fit the bill,” Katherine smiled.

Driving into the city, they caught up on the latest doings, the hustle and bustle of the move, the nightmare trying to get all the venues in synch for the big day, and describing their latest pieces for her gallery, there was so much to discuss. Justine finally asked Katherine what she meant by having some news of her own, Theresa was all ears. Now that she had sent Gerry’s mysterious envelope, Katherine supposed it was all right to talk about his riddle now that she had settled on an answer.

“How romantic,” Theresa smiled.

“Hey, am I chopped liver now? Who played a Tchaikovsky serenade outside your bedroom window the other night?” Maurice laughed.

 “Oh, that means you won’t know the answer for sure until you see what this letter is supposed to do,” Justine realized. “Well, it’s definitely a start, and I’m so happy for you. You know, his brother continues to write to us.”

“That’s true,” Martin affirmed from the driver’s seat, “we really do owe him so much, we’re sorry he couldn’t come to the wedding, we sent him an invitation.”

“He told me earlier this week, and he wanted me to give you his sincerest apologies, but also his blessings and good wishes, plus he hopes to see you when you come over. He also sent a present for you, I hope the luggage handlers didn’t smash it.”

“That’s very thoughtful. Do you know what it is?” Justine asked.

“No, it’s all wrapped up, but I’ll give it to you as soon as I unpack. I also brought a little housewarming gift for you too.”

“Aw, we didn’t expect any more gifts,” Martin politely protested, “You’re generous enough as it is giving us the tickets for the honeymoon.”

"Don't worry, it's only a token really. Remember how you wanted a really good American cookbook?" she reminded Justine.

"Oh great!" she laughed. "Now, I'll have the right recipe for your style of meatloaf and corn bread." Justine appreciated old fashioned comfort food ideas.

Leaving the asphalt jungle of the freeway and modern suburbs, they entered the heart of the capital with its old-world architecture. Within a few minutes, they pulled up outside the *chic* George V, one of the classic palace hotels built during the early Avant-Garde days when the Art Deco style was introduced to the city. Justine explained in a letter they had originally chosen somewhere a little less opulent for the reception, but since she and Martin insisted on an intimate wedding dinner with only close family and friends, their parents said they would gladly contribute towards an upgrade and a deluxe suite for the night. The guys waited in the van as the girls helped Katherine unpack, which took a little longer than they expected since she had to call home first to let everyone know she had arrived safely, not to mention she needed to freshen up and change her outfit before meeting their parents. Justine and Theresa studied the cookbook in the meantime, trying to translate an ingredient into French they were unfamiliar with.

At last, they were off to the more tranquil Luxembourg Quarter made popular by its beautiful garden park. Pulling up outside their new home, she could see their sandstone coloured building with its classic architecture was certainly a major improvement from their former compact garret accommodations accessed by the narrow twisting staircase in the Montmartre district. They now had their own parking space and storage facilities in the converted cellar, plus an elevator to reach their third floor apartment.

"Wow, this building is lovely," Katherine commented.

"Oh, wait until you see inside, this is just the hallway. We have decorating to do, and we are minimalist in the way of furniture right now," Martin smiled sheepishly.

"Hey, you're just starting out with your own place. You don't have to explain. Rome wasn't built in a day."

"True enough. Anyway, we'll take you on the tour after we introduce you to everyone. They can't wait to meet you."

"The mothers were fussing about what to prepare for supper, but I told them you like French home cooking, and I have to warn you, my sister is going to plague you with questions about America. I begged her not to be a pest, but I can't promise anything," Justine said as they entered the elevator.

Opening the door, they were immediately greeted by Lucille, Justine's younger sibling. Katherine was surprised to see she was much taller than Justine with light brown hair and hazel eyes. Excited to meet Katherine, it wasn't long before she indulged in her insatiable curiosity, barraging her with a hundred well-meaning questions about what it was like living in New York, hardly giving her time to answer one question before firing another. Mr. Ambroise felt obliged to come to the rescue. A short, jolly man with bright blue eyes, greying hair and a bushy moustache, he vigorously shook her hand and heartily welcomed her back to France before greeting her French fashion with a double kiss. She could see immediately where Justine inherited her stature and cheerful disposition. Martin's father wasn't there yet, he was still at work, but as Justine had announced, her mother and her soon-to-be mother-in-law were in the kitchen preparing dinner. On entering the apartment, the aromas evidenced that dinner would be a mouth-watering adventure. It was not difficult to recognise Justine's mother for she looked very much like Lucille and tended to be a bit excitable. Martin's mother in contrast had blue eyes and was quite calm and collected. Their personalities were like night and day, but Katherine knew that was the reason they could work so well together in the same kitchen. She hardly had time to greet them before Justine whisked her away for the tour.

The space they now enjoyed was a big improvement; in addition to gleaming wood floors, they now had a decent sitting room with a dining area, three bedrooms, and an additional room that would probably have been a den, but had been turned into their studio. The only new furniture they had at present was a dining table with six chairs and a bedroom suite courtesy of Martin's aunts and uncles who wanted to contribute towards something practical. There was one piece in the master bedroom that caught Katherine's eye in particular, an elaborate wooden chest with brass handles and a lock. Justine proudly explained her father also had an artistic gift and wanted to preserve the provincial tradition of carving a unique hope chest for his daughter's *trousseau*, the special gift of household linens to help the bride establish her new home. Martin also received something special for the occasion, his mother gave him a precious heirloom, the family *coupe de marriage*, a two-handled silver goblet from which the bride and groom drink a toast to their health and their new life together. Everything else came from the old apartment and looked a little out of place, the faded sofa, a few chairs, the dated television set, and of course, their record player and collection of antique records. Somehow, it was good seeing these old faithfuls dotted around the place, they brought back some pleasant memories.   Katherine suddenly remembered Fr. Peter's present and wondered if they would like to save it for the special day or open it there. They decided to go ahead and open the flat package to find he had managed to secure a papal blessing complete with formal scroll bearing the pope's image and his blessing in Italian sealed with the Vatican seal.   Everyone seemed impressed with the gift and admired the colourful scrollwork on the nuptial document as Martin hung up the frame.

Without further ado, they showed her the paintings they had completed, and hoped their collection would do well in New York, it would help them towards the purchase of decent furnishings and maybe give them a little extra to put aside for a rainy day. Perhaps painting for the sidewalk market was all in the past. Martin had continued his *pasticcio* idea, melding various montages of famous self-portraits of artists into a complete collection, it was difficult to stop at one painting he explained. He also experimented with his own style of abstract expression, which was bound to be popular with the modern art connoisseurs. Justine's paintings turned out to be a delightful surprise, usually she enjoyed painting in the abstract like Martin, but this time she had given a whole new meaning to the phrase 'urban jungle', becoming fixated with fusing flowers and Parisian street scenes into whimsical illusions *ala* the proto-surrealist style of Giuseppe Arcimboldo. White buildings blossomed from a mass of white flowers, lilies and daisies, sandstone structures teamed with cream blossoms, red doors or cars were shaped from red roses or tulips, hydrangeas supplied blue hues, bushy leaves for green objects, buttercups for yellow, green vines and slender tendrils for drain pipes and rain chutes, lampposts were spindly poppy stems with buds ready to open, the sky a wash of blue corn flowers with snow drops for clouds. Asphalt black for the roads was substituted with purple-black callas. To Katherine's chagrin, they had the pictures already pre-framed, it must have cost them a mint when they could have had the job done cheaper from her framer in Brooklyn, but they explained they wanted to see their new works in her gallery and it would take too long to have them all done. Of course, they were thinking ahead, so the least she could do was remind them to set decent prices on their work to cover the additional expense. The next problem, they would never get them on the flight back to New York as she had hoped, for instance, how to explain to the custom officials all these paintings were not bought in Paris. There was nothing for it but to have them shipped via a professional company, and, she had the perfect one in mind. They didn't want her to go to all that trouble, but she explained she had come early to help, so it was useless to argue. This was a project she could arrange for them, and the paintings would be all ready and waiting across the Atlantic when they left for the honeymoon. Unable to refuse, they thanked her profusely before they returned to the sitting room to chat with everyone, eventually setting the table when dinner was about ready.

Martin's father arrived and apologized for being late, the traffic was abysmal. No wonder Martin was at odds with his father, serious, solemn and strong-willed, they were very much alike. They each had their own way of doing things and that was bound to create sparks when one didn't agree with the other. However, he did not seem like an angry man, just … exacting in his expectations. He had only one son and wanted the best for him, it must have been difficult to accept his sole heir was a creative spirit and refused to wear the shackles of convention in what was considered a 'proper career'. True to decorum, he greeted Katherine by shaking hands, reserving the familiar double kiss until he knew her a little better, but he was still polite and sincere in his welcome.

Dinner was a compact yet enjoyable experience as ten people were snugly arranged around the table with the help of a few extra chairs. The parents wanted to hear in Katherine's words how she met their children and they listened with interest as she told them how Martin became the hero of the day, stopping a purse-snatcher dead in his tracks with Justine and Maurice helping her to overcome the shock. If they hadn't been there, she would have lost everything, in particular, her wallet with her passport and all her identification, it would have been an harrowing time trying to sort out the catastrophe at the embassy had the thief been successful. They hoped she didn't find Paris distasteful after that terrible experience: to think she was robbed in their country in broad daylight! One thing was certain, the French were fiercely patriotic and cringed when something happened that would cast a blight on their proud nation. On the contrary, she wasn't afraid to visit Paris again, it was an unfortunate incident that could have happened anywhere, and in any case, she never would have met such wonderful friends if the crook hadn't picked her bag as a target. Their parents were grateful she was showing Martin and Justine's work in New York, and were very curious about her gallery, Katherine had brought some photos that were eagerly passed around. There was so much to discuss, they had read reviews in the English papers, including Horace's brash witticisms, and wondered how she was taking his rude approach. Never better she smiled, he kept things interesting. They found it almost impossible to believe she gave him *carte blanche* to come and go, wielding his acidic pen, or rather, his recorder. Of course, the recent events did not escape the conversation, and Katherine was obliged to tell all, but assured them she didn't expect any more graffiti attacks and promised their works would be safe.

Eventually, the conversation turned to the parents and their occupations, and of course, the wedding plans. Katherine wasn't sure what to expect with French nuptials, so they filled her in on the itinerary for the big day. First, there would be the civil ceremony at the Hôtel de Ville, the city hall located in the Place de Grève, a detail that provoked a few tongue in cheek jokes around the table with everyone reminding Martin and Justine they still had a few days of freedom left before the knot was tied. At least they all had a good sense of humour, even sombre Martin found it funny, saying love was worth dying for and reminding Maurice his time to tie the knot would come soon enough. Katherine didn't understand what was so amusing until she remembered reading in Victor Hugo's work that the Place de Grève once hosted the municipal gallows. After the civil proceedings, it would be a mad dash to the church in Montmartre for the religious ceremony and they hoped no one would get lost on the way. Next, there would be the first reception in the famous café at the Place du Tertre where Martin had worked. Since they were artists, they couldn't have it in a better place Justine concluded. Katherine didn't know what they meant by the 'first reception' so they explained it was customary to prepare for guests who were invited to the wedding but not the formal dinner so they too could toast the bride and groom and share in the celebration. Their former classmates from college and casual acquaintances had been invited to this event. Then, it was time for the formal reception at the George V, and of course the wedding breakfast the next morning for the last goodbyes before they left on their honeymoon. Maurice had gathered fellow string musicians from the *conservatoire* and was providing the quartet for the wedding services and the receptions, plus he found a decent band for those who wanted to dance the night through. Justine's father was going to prepare the wedding cake with the help of a friend who owned a bakery not far from the apartment and who graciously offered his facilities.

After the general plans had been discussed, dinner was over and the table was cleared. As the men went to the sitting room for their coffee, the women naturally brought up the subject of the bridesmaids' dresses. Justine's mother and sister were excellent seamstresses and decided to make them all by hand. There was no time like the present to do a quick fitting as Katherine's dress was the last to be checked, so the ladies sequestered themselves in the main bedroom to see if the measurements she sent were correct. She was a little afraid wondering what style was about to be foisted upon her as Justine loved wearing pre-war bohemian fashions, but she was surprised the eccentric bride was reserved on this occasion and had chosen a springtime peach for the bridesmaids' dresses in an airy chiffon material with a three quarter length skirt and delicate sleeves to the wrist, on the day, they would have floral hairpieces to complete the ensemble. The ladies were pleased to find the dress fit Katherine perfectly and only needed a tuck in the shoulders, sparing them from having to make major alterations when there was so much to do. With that settled, they had one last round of coffee with the men before it was time for Martin and his parents to go home as his father had to be up early for work next morning. Justine explained his parents would not hear of him sleeping on the couch when he had a perfectly good bedroom with them, so Martin was back under the parental roof until the wedding day. Since they were now saying goodnight, Katherine decided it was time she return to the hotel, she needed to get a good night's sleep. Tomorrow she would arrange shipping their artwork to ensure it was sent to the States in plenty of time and not left hanging over their heads when the last minute preparations began to accumulate. Justine gave her an extra set of keys to their apartment just in case she needed them, and checked for the hundredth time to see if she had their new telephone number. Maurice's pager began to bleep, calling him to duty at the hospital, so he and Theresa said hasty goodbyes, and they were off, prompting everyone else to call it a night. This time Mr. Dubois let down his crusty reserve and gave Katherine the familiar double kiss as he wished her a pleasant evening.

03 ❀ 80

Katherine woke next morning feeling refreshed, but slightly melancholic at the same time. Here she was, spending the last weeks of 'April in Paris', the most romantic city in the world and her friends happily caught in the throes of love, yet her own Lancelot was thousands of miles away, the Atlantic ocean between them. She missed Gerry so much she felt lost and strangely out of place. It was a peculiar sensation, to feel emotions that were blissful and yet could simultaneously inflict sensible pain without any perceptible wound or bruise. Although she longed to see him, a simple call would have been a welcome palliative to assuage the ache his absence was generating. She wished Gerry had left her a message by now, but maybe it was still too soon to expect him to call. Possibly, his flight from the Far East was delayed and he didn't arrive home until yesterday morning, deciding he didn't want to disturb her on the last day she had to prepare for her trip, or after his long ordeal, he simply crashed and was currently

794

sleeping off the last two months of stress and jet lag. Perhaps his lack of communication had something to do with the mysterious envelope. Never mind, she would try and get through to him tonight, and in two weeks they would see each other again she finally reminded herself. At least she had errands to keep her busy, the ironic part was she would be calling the Paris branch of Reinold Enterprises later that morning to arrange the art shipment, another blissful albeit painful reminder of his absence. His logo seemed to follow her everywhere, and yet the man it represented was half a world away.

The concierge wished her a pleasant good morning as she was about to enter the breakfast area, presenting the unexpected news that a package had just arrived for her. The odd looking box piqued her curiosity. Wrapped in brown parcel paper, it was covered with a legion of stamps as though someone couldn't be bothered taking it to the post office to have it weighed properly. Was this another of Steve's practical jokes? Impossible, for she discovered the return address: it simply read 'The Messenger'. Katherine thought she had better sit down and open the package in the lounge, the concierge politely allowing her to borrow the desk scissors. Settling in a corner by a window overlooking the courtyard, she was grateful the lounge was unusually quiet this morning with only one misanthropic gentleman in the corner across the room completely engrossed with the morning edition of the *Le Monde*, blocking out his surroundings with his paper as though it was a shield. There were a few people in the courtyard having their coffee, they too were busy talking or reading the morning news. She carefully studied the motley stamped parcel before opening it, and realized it was in pretty good condition: there were no post marks except for an unusual ink stamp with the date, today's date. How on earth did it arrive on the same morning? The postage stamps clearly displayed it had come from America, and while the Federal post office was always reliable, it was never *this* good, even Fed Ex couldn't pull something like this off. That envelope she sent was truly beginning to wield some strange magic indeed. Carefully slitting the paper, she found a gift box with a red and yellow ribbon tied with a bow. Opening the box, she discovered a brand new Walkman with a note: *'Play Me'*. Here we go again she smiled, more melodic riddles brimming with blanks to be filled in? She slipped on the headphones, whatever happened to be on the tape, she wouldn't disturb the few people that were around. Pausing for a moment and taking a breath, she turned on the machine:

Should I reveal exactly how I feel?

Should I confess I love you?
Should I recite beneath the pale moonlight,
And swear by the stars above you?
Could I repeat the sweetest story ever told?
Could I entreat, would it be too bold?
Should I reveal exactly how I feel?
Should I confess I love you?

...

Let someone start believing in you,
Let him hold out his hand,
Let him touch you and watch what happens.
One someone who can look in your eyes and see into your heart,
Let him find you and watch what happens.
Cold, no I won't believe your heart is cold,
Maybe afraid to be broken again.
Let someone with a deep love to give
Give that deep love to you, and what magic you'll see.
Let someone give his heart, someone who cares like me,
Let someone give his heart who cares like me.

As if the confirmation of her answer wasn't enough to make her eyes fill with tears, she was stunned to hear *Gerry* singing to the lilting orchestral music, not Sinatra like she expected, revealing his true feelings for her in song and sealing it for posterity on a recording. She wanted to laugh and cry, this was all too much to take in. Pushing the rewind button, she was about to play the tape again when the waiter approached her with a tray.

"Excuse me, Mademoiselle, forgive me for disturbing you, but the gentleman over there sends this with his compliments."

Katherine was unable to see the drink that was offered, not with her teary eyes and the way he was holding the tray over her head, but she could just discern the tall contour of a champagne flute. Oh great, that's all she needed right now, some obsequious stranger trying to catch her attention at this hour of the morning, with liquor no less. Well, she would have to deal with this as politely as possible. She was about to tell him to thank the gentleman on her behalf but to inform him she didn't drink at that hour, that is, until she finally noticed as the waiter lowered the tray that the libation offered was not champagne, it was a bottle of ginger ale. Through the glass pedestal of the champagne flute she could see someone had written a message on the cocktail doily: *"Is your answer the same as mine?"* Startled, she looked over at the avid *Le Monde* reader who suddenly dropped his screen.

"Hello, Princess," he called out softly, folding the newspaper with panache.

"Gerry!"

Within seconds they were standing in the middle of the room, clasping each other tight. Dumbfounded with his surprise appearance, she couldn't say anything. It was a good thing he spoke first.

"May I assume from this happy reunion that our answers match?" he said quietly, searching her eyes. She nodded her head and finally confessed:

"I love you so much, I didn't think it possible to be able to feel like this."

"Oh my dear Katherine, you have no idea how long I've waited to hear you say that," he sighed. They were unable to say anything more until they kissed, and even then, they didn't want to let each other go. At last, they sat down in her quiet corner, there was so much they wanted to say and to ask each other.

"Gerry, I can't believe you're here, and after your long flight from Jakarta, you must be exhausted."

"Are you kidding? I never felt more alive. When I got the news the riddle note had arrived, I booked the first Concorde out of New York, and I've been on cloud nine ever since. After what happened this last month, I was afraid that note might never come," he admitted quietly before asking when she discovered the answer to his romantic enigma.

"March eighteenth," she replied with a smile.

"Down to the precise date?"

"I realize now I was falling for you a long time before then, I just didn't know it until that day when I heard Sinatra's *You'll know When It Happens* on the radio."

"Good old Blue Eyes, he came to the rescue."

"Gerry, you put so much time and thought into your riddle, when did you know? I mean … ."

"The day you saved me from getting scalded by the steam jet."

"Steam jet?"

"When I made our first cup of coffee," he clarified with a smile, "I've been falling more in love with you every day since."

"All that time! I'm sorry it took so long for my heart to catch up."

"It was worth the wait," he replied, taking her hands in his. "And I did have fun setting up that riddle."

He explained the Messenger's address was Sammy's office in the main distribution centre, he could trust him to keep a secret and secure the envelope when it arrived. Katherine had guessed correctly the note was to signal she had discovered the answer, but wondered what was actually in the envelope.

"What if I was too curious and opened it?"

"You would have found a card reading 'Naughty Naughty, you must wait until the Messenger sends his answer. Now seal me back up and send me along my way.'"

How simple! Gerry was really good at creating mysteries. He then explained he paid one of the professional studios to make his second recording for a very special member of the Reinold Fan Club. He didn't tell her, but one of the managers happened to be in the studio that day and was adamant about setting up an audition for their label to which he politely declined. The final touch, that is, wrapping the answer up in patchwork of American stamps was a stroke of genius that hit him before he left for Paris. He wanted the suspense to last as long as possible and not give away he was actually in the same room.

"Well, what a way to find out! Surprising me like this."

"If only you could have seen the look on your face. Well, I know you have responsibilities on this trip, is it possible to take the day off? I mean, we should do something to celebrate this happy occasion, just you and me."

"I think I can take today off," she replied, adding he wouldn't believe the first job she had originally planned to do. He laughed when he heard she was going to call Reinold shipping.

"Well, it helps having the Senior Manager of International Distribution at your service. We can certainly prepare your shipment tomorrow. Any other plans for today?"

"Not really, at least they haven't told me if they want anything else done yet. I guess I can call Justine and tell her before she leaves for work."

"That's settled. Now, what should we do, Princess? Something different would be nice, let's really make this day a memorable one."

"It's already memorable," Katherine smiled. "Let me see. We've gone to restaurants, we've been to the opera twice already ... hmm, what can we do on an April day in Paris?" Suddenly, an idea came to mind. Gerry had his chance to give her a riddle, it was time she devised something mysterious too. Watching her eyes brighten, he wondered what she had come up with. "Uh uh, I'm not telling you, it's nothing stupendous, but you said something to make the day memorable, and I have just the thing."

"You aren't going to tell me?" he asked as he helped her with her coat.

"No, I'm taking you on a mystery tour."

"This certainly sounds interesting," he noted, swinging his camel hair coat onto his shoulders. "I guess since the knight has had his riddle, the princess now gets to set her own, am I right?"

"You just read my mind, Lancelot."

After calling Justine and telling her 'something just came up', Katherine returned the scissors to the concierge and asked if he wouldn't mind keeping her gift box in a safe place, she didn't want to waste any time running up to her room, every second without Gerry was a second lost.

The intrepid knight had no idea what his ladylove had planned, and sitting in the taxi he was still left in the dark when she asked the driver something in French. Apparently, it was something odd, for the driver looked puzzled for a second, but he shrugged his shoulders and off they went. Gerry playfully wheedled her, asking what she was up to, but she refused to give in. After a short drive they arrived at the destination, it looked like a small family-run hardware shop.

"You stay here, Lancelot, that's an order," she said, before turning to the driver and asking him to wait.

"I hear and obey, your highness."

Gerry watched as she lightly skipped into the store with a beaming smile. Suddenly, the driver turned to him and spoke in English.

"Monsieur, I don't know what your secret is, but if you would tell me so I could get *my* wife into a hardware store looking like that, I'll gladly waive your fare."

"Honestly my good man, I wish I knew," Gerry replied, shaking his head. In fifteen minutes, she skipped back out with a brown bag in her hand. When he tried to feel what was contained inside, she snatched it away.

"Not yet, you must be patient."

"Gosh, I don't want you spending your money, let me at least contribute something towards … whatever it is."

"Shush, this is my surprise, I get to pay for it. You're always spoiling me, so it's my turn to do something." He didn't want to argue and let it go. She then gave the driver their next destination. This time they pulled up outside a jeweller's shop, and when Gerry tried to get out, she gave him the same command to wait.

"This part may take awhile," she added, before leaving him to his thoughts. This was peculiar, and he wondered what on earth could be happening inside. After almost an hour, she finally emerged, the brown bag gone, replaced with an exclusive bag from the *chic* shop.

"Princess, I hope you didn't spend a fortune."

"Shush, not another word, this is my treat."

"Monsieur, I really must know your secret," the driver added before asking where they would like to go next. Katherine had a quick conversation with him in French, apparently, she was asking him for directions or advice, Gerry wasn't sure, but he heard Notre Dame come up in their discussion, a detail that seemed to please her, and so they were off.

"Well, now I know what the secret is," the driver smiled.

"Hey, how come he knows and I don't?" Gerry chided her in good humour.

"Just wait and see." It wasn't too long, a few minutes drive, and they stopped once more. "Okay, you can get out now," she laughed, paying the driver who thanked them and wished them the best of luck.

The third and final stop happened to be the picturesque Square du Jean XXIII behind the iconic cathedral, its elegant flying buttresses arched in the background. At first he thought she planned a quiet moment that they could share in the small park, it was a beautiful setting with the spring flowers in bloom, the new mint green leaves of the trees gently swaying in the breeze. He grew curious when she by-passed the verdant square and the venerable old building, leading him in the opposite direction towards a bridge, a quaint narrow structure with the grand appellation, Pont de l'Archevêché.

"You can look inside now," she declared as they walked up to the bridge. Taking the little bag, he was amused to find a large brass lock inside. Holding it up, he discovered she had '*Gerard & Katherine*' engraved on the side complete with a large heart encircling their names. He then noticed the rows of padlocks lining the metal railings of the bridge.

"A lover's lock, that's something different," he smiled, "much better than carving our initials on a tree. Shall we go to the middle?"

"The perfect place."

Facing the cathedral, they chose a space near the top railing.

"Do you wish to do the honours, or shall I?" he enquired.

"Let's lock it together, I just hope we don't drop it," she laughed.

"I'll hold it, you clamp it shut," he decided. Locking it into place, he held her close for a moment. "Now what do we do, Princess? Seal it with a kiss?"

"We're not quite done yet," she announced as she reached into her handbag and took out a black velvet box. Inside were two long gold neck chains with the keys on the ends. Handing him one chain, he observed she had his initial engraved on the key, her initial on the other.

"We're suppose to throw them over the bridge so the lock can never be opened again, but I think giving each other the 'key' to our hearts is a better idea," she explained quietly, holding the chain up. "On the count of three?"

"Okay, one … two … three."

The bells of the cathedral began to peal midday as they slipped the chains over each other's heads.

Immediately, something inexplicable had occurred as they gazed at the keys hanging over their hearts, the chains glinting in the spring sunshine. Looking into his eyes and watching him reflectively hold the key in his hand, she knew something had happened between them that was difficult to describe, and then suddenly, a myriad of revelations coalesced into a single thought and fell upon her like an invisible bolt that nearly took her breath away: with love, there was no turning back—*this was the man with whom she would spend the rest of her life.*

Holding her close, he sensed her feelings had made a quantum leap, but was almost too afraid to say anything. After what seemed like an age, he finally spoke.

"Kathy, I don't mean to alarm you, but do you know what that just felt like?" he tentatively asked.

"I … I know," she stammered, "this is more than just a steady relationship now. We've gone past the stage of just planning a nice day together and having a few dinners out, although that has all been wonderful, it's just that I understand now why couples say it's time to take it to the next step, but I'm …. not the kind of girl who just moves right on in with the boyfriend," she tried to explain, "I … I have traditional expectations you see …."

He held his breath: *is she trying to say what I think she's trying to say?*

"Katherine, is this … a proposal?"

She bashfully looked into his eyes, wondering what on earth he must be thinking. This was not how she imagined a proposal would be: how in heaven's name did she bring it up? This was a bombshell for him too, but the opportunity he had been waiting for had suddenly arrived and he was not about to let it go.

"It is leap year, and of course, ladies have the honour of springing the question."

"Oh! I had forgotten about that! It's not like I planned this."

"I admit, this unexpected moment has caught me unawares, but I shall not keep you waiting for my reply … with all my heart, I accept your proposal, Princess."

"You what?"

"I accept your proposal," he repeated calmly.

"Gerry, you really do mean it."

"Of course I do."

"We're … engaged now," she said, hugging him tight. "This all so strange! Are we doing the wrong thing?"

" 'Wrong?' I don't think so, we've just announced to each other that there is no one else in the world for us, we just locked our hearts together."

"Oh, 'wrong' is not the right word, I mean, are we rushing into this?"

"My dear, marriages are not to be rushed into, but an engagement is a different matter. We can stay engaged for ten years if you like before we ever have to discuss a date," he reminded her quietly.

"I never really thought of it like that," she reflected, "oh, aren't we a funny pair, you and I?"

"I know. I never expected it to happen this fast, not on the day we first professed our love to each other," he admitted. "Knowing you wanted it to be a private occasion, I was going to wait until I had everything planned to perfection, and to think, here we are on a public bridge in the middle of Paris with all the traffic and passers-by in attendance."

"Gerry, you were going to ask me," she repeated quietly, realizing he had already been prepared for quite some time. "I'm sorry, I hope my impetuosity hasn't ruined the occasion for you, but it couldn't have happened in a more appropriate place. Did you ever notice when you fly into Paris, you never really see the city before you land? You have to wait until you reach its heart before you can see all the treasures it hides. It reminds me of what you once said about love, that like everything else in life, it should be a discovery, and like most adventures, you don't know you're having one until you right in the middle of it. Don't you see? It was all meant to happen here, right in the heart of the city of light and love."

"Activist, artist, philosopher, poetic soul … you continue to amaze me," he said quietly, brushing a strand of hair from her face, "and no, you didn't ruin anything for me. You have just made me the happiest man on earth, and I hope to make you the happiest women that ever lived. Kathy, I want to spoil you senseless," he smiled.

"I don't need things Gerry, and you don't have to spoil me, all I want is you to be with me always."

"Well, I'll be darned if I'm letting this happy day go by without at least presenting you with a lavish engagement ring, and now you have the opportunity to choose the one you want."

"I guess that's the rest of our day sorted out."

"Not quite yet, first, there should be dancing in the streets."

Taking her hand, he led back to the corner in a gentle dance singing 'What are you doing the rest of your life'. On any other occasion, she would have been mortified, but this was Paris after all: if you couldn't dance down the avenues and boulevards with your fiancée here, you couldn't dance anywhere. She started to laugh and he wondered what she thought was so amusing.

"While you're singing something romantic, I can't get the lyrics to 'Love and Marriage' out of my head, and that tune always reminds me of the jingle from Jeopardy."

"They do sound alike don't they? Come to think of it, G.K. Chesterton once wrote marriage is a duel to the death that a man of honour and courage should not decline, and I'm always saying we should live dangerously."

"Well Mr. Danger, what do we do next now that our dance is done?"

"Find someplace for lunch, you didn't get any breakfast this morning, not even a cup of coffee."

"Gerry, your surprise appearance was better than any breakfast," she laughed.

"That may be, but despite the cliché, no one can live on love alone."

"I guess another cliché will have to do."

"Which one is that?"

"The way to a man's heart is through his stomach."

"Touché, Princess," he laughed. "Come, you must be starving, I know a fantastic bistro that's not too far from where we need to go. Problem is, I don't see where we can flag down a cab."

"Looks like we'll just have to dance our way to the next Metro station."

Checking his watch, dancing was not an option if they wanted to get a table before the lunch rush, but a walk together to the Metro was just as pleasant. She had never been to the Benoît before, a charming establishment that had retained it's original 1912 décor and was famed as the epitome of bistro dining.

"Well my dear," he said after they had placed their order. "Are you deliriously happy?"

"You know I am, it's just," her voice trailed off for a moment, "this is a serious step we're about to take. I don't know how I'm going to break the news to Mom and Pops when we go back home."

"Reality dawns so soon, we have barely been engaged for an hour and already we are all business," he sighed, "but all joking aside, I'm in a quandary myself. I had every intention of following the proper protocol and formally asking your father for his approval before I proposed. I know, it's old fashioned, and legally you're of age to make up your own mind, but I'm a stickler for certain formalities … ."

"Which I just threw to the wind," she sheepishly interjected. "Well, now that the deed is done, could we speak to them together? Pops approves of formalities, and I should confess it was my fault the proposal came first."

"If you think it would be best. In fact, I would like to be there when you tell them, I don't want you to have to do that on your own."

"What about your parents? Have you told them yet?"

"No, but I suspect Mom is hoping I pop the question, I caught her looking through her wedding album before I left for Asia. They're just waiting for me to break the news."

"It might be best if we tell them together." Katherine suddenly held her breath. "You know what this means; our parents will have to be introduced to each other…."

"Battle of the In Laws," he jumped in, impersonating the suave tone of a film narrator, "It was a dark day on the windswept fields of Long Island when the enemy approached the Stonyvale bunker …."

"Oh Gerry, it's not really funny you know," but she couldn't help smiling.

"I'm sorry, I do know how you feel, I'm still waiting for my silver ships to come in where your Pops is concerned."

"Don't worry, he'll come around. After all the terrible rumours connected with your family over the years, he was worried about what I might be getting into, but since I told him everything, he may not be so frosty when you next see him. You know, I think I've discovered what's truly bothering him, and it's not you as much as reality."

"Oh? How so?"

"When I was a toddler, he used to call me his 'Little Princess', and when he hears you call me that, I think the full realization has finally hit that

I've grown up, that maybe some day he will literally be giving me away to someone. I always thought Mom was the overprotective one, but in his own quiet way, he's just as concerned."

"I can understand that," he replied thoughtfully. "Well, I suppose the main thing is we actually like our in-laws, that's half the battle won, which is a rare thing."

"That's true," she smiled. "I really do love your family."

"I know they've taken to you right away, but what about me and the Walsingham clan?"

"I think you've earned Mom and Gramp's approval, and Steves thinks you're a blast, just give Pops some time."

"I will." He then stopped for a moment with a slight pensive expression. "I can understand his concern in the sense that ... how should I say this? I want to do everything I can to make you happy, but as you have just discovered first hand, I can't promise everything will be perfect. It's only fair to remind you I have responsibilities that take me away for long stretches, not to mention the trouble we Reinolds seem to find ourselves in with the media. If we are not society column celebrities, we end up front page scandals. News seems to get twisted out of all proportion, and I won't be able to protect you from all of that. The only recourse we have is to ignore it, or sue if any allegations are libellous, but that doesn't do much to avoid the problems. I don't mean to alarm you, but I want to make sure you know what you're getting into and to think it over carefully."

"Gerry, what a stupid reason to turn you down! Who cares what they write when I know the truth? Isn't that what matters?"

"Of course, I think I could put up with anything that's thrown at me now that you understand it isn't true, but the business trips?"

"It'll be difficult, but I think I can deal with that. I love you so much, and if all I can have is a month with you a year, I'd rather have that than not to have you at all."

"I sure hope I'll never be away for eleven months. That certainly wouldn't be a marriage, I'd have to bring you with me," he concluded.

"Well, I was exaggerating, I'd never be able to get away that long from the gallery. Oh ..." she stopped.

"Something the matter?" There was a pause before she continued.

"Gerry, how old fashioned are you? I mean, how traditional are *your* expectations?"

"I'm not following," he said, a little puzzled.

"The gallery: you don't mind having a wife who has a career, do you?"

"Why, of course not. I don't expect you to give up something you love," he said a little surprised. "I know how much the gallery means to you, not to mention the building is part of your family's heritage. You know, I'm glad we're actually settling a few things and getting them out of the way, even though I wanted this to be a romantic day," he added with a smile. "While I'm thinking about it, I don't expect you to change your maiden name on the building or on your artwork for that matter."

"My, that will be something to get used to," she said half to herself, there was so much to consider, the inevitable name change to Mrs. Gerard Reinold had yet to be pondered upon let alone sink in.

"What's so funny?"

"I'm sorry, it looks like I'll be progressing from a crow to an automobile."

"Excuse me?"

"My initials," she said before heaving a sigh. "My middle name is Amelia, I generally keep that to myself because…."

"K.A.W.," he noted in amusement, "but I do like Amelia, that's beautiful."

"That was my Grandma's name, my father's mother. I can't believe we haven't told each other our middle names. What's yours?"

"Wait for it … Johannes. I have no idea where they came up with this. It would have been simpler if they just called me John."

"That is a mouthful. Gerard Johannes Reinold. It sounds like 'Your Highness, Reinold.'"

"Looks like I'll be promoted too, the knight becomes your prince in shining armour."

"That's what happens when you marry a princess," she joked. "Let me see," she mumbled, retrieving her notebook from her purse.

"What are you writing?"

"My name to be, I want to see how it looks. Hmm … Mrs. Katherine Reinold, Mrs. Gerard Johannes Reinold! That will take some time to get used to, 'Mrs.' makes me sound so old." As she was writing, a few flower petals fell out. She had dried a rose bud and a small sunflower from his first bouquet to always have them with her.

"You know," he said, studying the petals, "it was difficult keeping to our agreement send you nothing but bouquets and chocolates, and after today, you will have something special that will last longer than flowers. I can't wait to see the ring you choose."

After lunch, they took their time as they made their way arm in arm to the Place Vendôme, address of the best jewellers in the city.

"Now Princess, here's Boucheron, Mauboussin is over there, and if you still don't see anything you like, Cartier is just down that street. Where would you like to start?"

Boucheron was the closest, therefore, the first on the list. Katherine was not in the habit of buying jewellery for herself, most of her pieces were gifts. It was difficult choosing when there were so many velvet trays and satin lined boxes bearing a myriad of scintillating jewels, rings with brilliant white solitaries, rings with rows of diamonds and baguettes, rings with diamonds and gemstones of every hue.

"What about this one?" he said, indicating a ring with one mammoth solitaire.

"Gerry," she whispered, looking around the stiff and starchy showroom, a little shy with the shop attendant watching the proceedings, "you'd have to get me a footman to hold my arm up," she smiled, "maybe something smaller than an ice cube would be better."

"Funny girl. Okay, but I do want you to choose something truly beautiful, one of a kind, don't be afraid to pick the best." He watched her slowly make a second tour from case to case before joining her.

"They're all so beautiful, perhaps you should have left me outside and just chosen one for me," she said, shaking her head.

"I would have ended up with the ice cube. I know, how about something unique, maybe have one custom made?" he finally suggested. "Hmm, anyone can get white diamonds. I would love to give you a ring no one else in the world has."

"Maybe something in our colours, something with rubies and topazes?" she smiled, no one else would think of wearing *that*.

"Rubies? Topazes? Don't be absurd, it's diamonds or nothing," he said, amused, "it certainly would be an odd ring, but ... it's not a bad idea. Would you like a red diamond with yellow baguettes like petals on the side? Of course, we would have to wait for it to be made," he said nonchalantly, "it'll take them some time to acquire a three carat red, I won't get you anything smaller."

The attendant grew a little pale.

"Gerry, I was just teasing. Think about it: red and yellow for a ring?"

"You're right, maybe we'll just settle for red."

"I wish I could see one first before we decide anything."

"Very well. Sir, do you happen to have any reds in your inventory?"

"I regret to say, not at the present time," the gentleman replied, "due to their rarity, they usually are special orders."

"Are they really that hard to find?" Katherine wondered. She knew red diamonds existed, but didn't know anything else about them other than that.

"Oui Mademoiselle, they are the most rare."

"I'd be afraid to ask the price," she noted, looking at a three carat white solitaire wondering what the difference would be simply because of the colour.

"Don't worry about it," Gerry smiled, "if I'm willing to go high for old bits of canvas and paint to hang on the walls, I am quite happy to buy you a ring."

"Gerry, those old bits of canvas cost millions. Just how much are we talking about here?" she said, suddenly turning to the attendant.

"Take pity on me my good sir and don't answer that," Gerry said putting his hand up, "you can see I'm having enough trouble trying to get her to pick a plain old brilliant."

"Please Gerry, if it's that rare, I know I wont be able to wear it."

"Why not, Princess?"

"Think about it," she said gently, "we wouldn't be able to keep something like this quiet, I wouldn't be safe to go out in the street with it. It would be too dangerous, and in the end, it would have to be locked away somewhere. What's the point of an engagement ring that never sees the light of day? I want something I can wear and always have with me."

"You're right Kathy, I didn't think about that," he said quietly, his eyebrows furrowed. He wanted to give her the best, never realizing he might be putting her in harm's way. Her observation brought terrible images of her being mugged, and what could happen if the would-be thieves couldn't pull the ring off in time to make a fast getaway.

"Don't look so serious, I didn't mean to burst your bubble, and I do appreciate your generosity," she said, giving his hands a squeeze, "not many woman get offered a gem fit for an empress. If it's any consolation, I do keep returning to a particular ring."

"Aha, now she confesses," he said, his eyes brightening, "show me." She pointed to an eye-catching vintage style cluster, the diamonds arranged in the shape of a flower around a solitaire, the gems set upon a raised platinum ring, the sides hand carved in a delicate acanthus pattern.

"I know, it's not as big as some of the others, but I think it would suit my hand better, not to mention we have to leave some room for the wedding band," she smiled.

"Let's take a look." The attendant retrieved the ring, a little disappointed the prospect of ordering a red diamond came to naught. Gerry took the shimmering flower off its cushion and slipped it on her finger. "Actually, this does look nice, it suits you," he said as he gently turned her hand, "you can't beat the old classic designs. Now, are you sure you want this one?"

"Um hmm," she nodded.

"Does it fit?"

"Perfect."

"Consider it yours Princess, however," he said, sliding it off her finger and putting it back into its box, "leap year or not, I insist on presenting this to you properly later tonight, so no wearing it until then."

"Ah, we're painting the town tonight, are we?"

"Of course, my dear."

The big purchase complete, they returned to the bustling street, arm in arm.

"Now, are you sure you're happy? Honestly, I was expecting to look around a bit," he admitted. "If you happen to see something else, we can always take this one back," he added, patting the small lump in his breast pocket.

"No Gerry, I'm very happy with it."

"In fact, if you see anything else other than a ring you would like, we don't have to stop," he said with a twinkle in his eye. "How would you like a shopping spree?"

"The first day of our engagement, and already you're trying to spoil me," she remarked, nestling close to him. "You're very kind and generous, but I told you I don't want things. Why would I want anything else when all that matters is right here?" she said, giving him his arm a gentle squeeze.

He knew she spoke from her heart. This simple statement meant so much to him, he wanted to tell her, but could only remain silent and return the comforting pressure. She was so unlike the other girlfriends he dated, he could never be sure with any of them if they truly cared, or if they waited for the next occasion when his cheque book or credit card appeared. He always felt stealthily led towards a store or could sense when they expected something big on holidays. Now that he had really found the love of his life, try as he might, he wasn't allowed to give her anything when he ardently wished to shower her with gifts. It frustrated him, and yet, it made him love her even more. There was no mistaking the look in her eyes: Katherine loved him for who he was. She enjoyed his collections, not for their value as much as visual revelations of his artistic preferences and passions. She may appreciate his wealth, but had no desire to possess it. Not that today was a deliberate test, but if turning down red diamonds and colossal knuckle-dusters didn't prove her affections, nothing would. In fact, the way she asked what he thought of her running the gallery once they were married displayed she was not above making further sacrifices if he asked. Unexpectedly, the unicorn had chosen him and was prepared to leave the sanctuary of her enchanted forest to follow wherever he led. What did he ever do to deserve her?

"Gerry, are you all right? I didn't mean to hurt your feelings by refusing a bigger ring," she said, a little concerned by his silence.

"I'm not hurt, far from it," he replied, stopping for a moment, taking a measured breath. Rarely did he let his deeper emotions show, but this day was filled with too many agreeable shocks and poignant surprises to maintain his measured composure. "Kathy, I love you. I just wish I could show you how much, that's all."

"You don't have to buy me the Hope Diamond or the Star of Africa," she assured him with a thoughtful expression.

"There's nothing I can get for you?"

"Well, a cup of coffee would be nice. I just want to spend time together, you've been gone for so long, and there's so much to get caught up on. Of course, if you don't feel like talking, we can just sit and watch the world go by Parisian style at a café somewhere. There are times when silence is golden."

Selecting a table at a quaint sidewalk café, they sat quietly and enjoyed the moment holding hands, watching the locals dash about or observed the tourists meandering around with their guidebooks in hand, either looking a little lost or enjoying the experience of visiting a new city.

"I can't believe you're here," she finally said after some time had passed, "it feels like a dream."

"I know," he replied, "if this is a dream, it's the best I've ever had."

"So much has happened today, I can't take it all in, this is all such a surprise."

"No regrets already I hope?" he asked with good humour.

"No," she said quietly, "I just haven't gotten used to the idea we're engaged." She studied the key hanging around his neck with a little smile.

"If it's not too personal a question, what happened on the bridge today?"

She thought for a moment.

"It's not easy to put into words. The way you held the key in your hand, I suddenly knew you wished it to be more than a mere gesture, I could feel your longing that someday my heart would be promised to you forever. That's when I realized I wanted that too, wishing that your key next to my heart would someday be more than a symbol. When we exchanged our keys, it was a moment of truth. I understood that these gold chains were in anticipation of wedding rings to come. I wasn't completely sure how you felt until you confessed you experienced something that moment too and were already making plans to propose."

"You were inspired," he replied gently, "and bless the angel, saint or muse that gave you a gentle shove. This chain will never be taken off from this day forward."

"Neither will mine; with this key, I do engage thee," she continued.

"After today, I realized something else," he said, leaning on his elbow.

"What's that?"

"Life with you will never be dull, but tell me, if you don't mind, you've never really thought about marriage until now?"

"Well, yes, I've *thought* about it, in a general sense, but it all seems to be happening the other way around for me."

"I don't understand."

"Take Suzy for instance. She always wanted to have children, and many women seem to feel that way, dreaming about starting their own family and then finding the man of their dreams to fulfil it. I was quite content seeing my plans come true, the gallery, my artwork ... I guess you could say my paintings were my children, they're just as hard to let go. What I'm trying to say is I thought my life was complete. I didn't know anything was missing, that there could be much more, not until we met, and especially after today. Now that I've found the man of my dreams ... ."

"Starting a life together is the next happy step," he concluded.

"Oh Gerry, the funny thing is, I wasn't even trying, I mean, I wasn't on the lookout to find 'Mr. Right', then you came along and turned my world upside down."

"So, I'm the icing on the cake?" he chuckled.

"My favourite part."

"Well, if I'm going to add any coloured sugar sprinkles *vis* a night out on the town, it's time I take you back to the hotel to let you have a quick rest and freshen up."

"You have something special planned, I gather?"

"As special as I can make it on such short notice."

Returning to the hotel, he gallantly kissed her hand before she stepped into the elevator, it was difficult letting him go, but he would be returning in a few hours. Suddenly, she felt a wave of panic now that she was alone. What had she done? Was she rushing into things? No, the more she thought about Gerry, she knew there was no other person she would rather be with, and as he observed, an engagement didn't necessarily mean they were heading down the aisle tomorrow. It was a welcome relief knowing he was prepared to give her as much time as she needed to allow the realization sink in that they were engaged before they made any life-changing plans. Just take it one bridge at a time she smiled to herself, wondering what he could possibly do to make the day more special than it already was.

Early that evening he arrived dressed to the nines in a black coat with white scarf, dinner jacket and bow tie. In one arm, he held a bouquet of red and yellow roses.

"Hello tall, dark and handsome."

"Good evening, slender, bright and beautiful. I'm sorry Princess, the florist I found didn't have sunflowers. Can you believe it?"

"Don't worry, it's an evening for roses, isn't it?"

"You are absolutely stunning, you take my breath away," he complimented. He could blame Aunt Martha, Katherine thought. Her aunt had insisted she buy some new outfits before she left for Paris, and now she was glad she did. Tonight she had chosen a full length deep rose silk crepe evening dress with a matching jacket hand worked with pink bugle beads and satin trim, her hair pinned up with a matching beaded hair piece.

"Shall we?" He bowed slightly and offered his arm. Stationed outside was a black vintage Rolls Royce, a chauffeur patiently waiting to take them to their destination. Katherine wondered where that could be until she noted they were heading in the direction of the Champ-de-Mars: he was taking her to the Eiffel Tower.

"Are we dining at the *Jules Verne*?" she asked.

"Yes, but first, I want to take you dancing at the highest point in Paris," he announced, leading her to the ticket line. She felt funny and a little overdressed amidst the sightseers as though they were going to the opera, it was then she heard a small café orchestra with the traditional accordion playing in the background. Gerry took her in his arms and began dancing with her while holding their place in the queue. She thought the musicians were performing for the tourists, until Gerry motioned them to come forward.

"Yes, you're playing for us, come on, let's get your tickets."

Katherine started to laugh. He literally intended to take her dancing complete with musical accompaniment at the top of the tower. The ticket man looked curiously at the romantic ensemble, but didn't refuse to let the café orchestra through, instruments and all: far be it from a Frenchman to interfere with love. Katherine suddenly wondered how Gerry would hack the cable car elevators.

"Lancelot, have you ever gone to the top before?"

"No, and don't talk me out of it, I'm prepared to do this," he replied resolutely, already growing a little pale with the thought. She knew from experience the tower looked small from a distance, it was only when the visitor stood underneath the gargantuan quadruped legs of the iron sentinel did the full scale of its size come into focus. It was also an unhurried ride to the top as Monsieur Eiffel did not want to compromise safety for the sake of speed: reaching the first two levels was not bad, but the last car to the top would be the ultimate test. Crammed in with the tourists and musicians, she noticed Gerry's fists clench on the bar behind, his knuckles turning white.

"Princess, this thing's moving ... ."

"It's supposed to, it's an elevator," she whispered back.

"But *sideways?*" he returned through clenched teeth. She gently squeezed his arm to reassure him while he quietly mumbled something to himself, obviously to keep his nerves welded together. He told her not to talk him out of it, so she couldn't warn him the structure was capable of swaying on a windy day, especially at that height. It was also a good thing Gerry didn't know that the original hydraulic lifting system from the 1880s was still in operation on the lower levels, he might have to be sedated and carried off the tower in a stretcher. Reaching the top, some of his colour returned on the observation deck and he eventually resumed the dance, a hundred onlookers smiling at the sight of a young couple dancing above the twinkling Paris lights to *La vie en rose*.

"I can't believe you braved the elevators for me," she whispered.

"Anything for you, Princess, I'm just glad my knees are still working after that, or we would have to settle for a serenade."

"You poor thing, we have to ride down again."

"We shall overcome," he said, not sounding as positive as his words proclaimed.

"Oh Gerry, what a pair we will make. I never liked dancing in public before I met you, and you wouldn't even think of coming up here because of the elevators, not until you met me. Look at what we were missing."

"Imagine, we're already surmounting our difficulties and bringing out the best in each other. We have so much to look forward to."

They danced for some time, waltzing around half aware of the tourists who were observing them almost as much as the city skyline.

Although they didn't want to stop, the time arrived to go back down to the second level where their table overlooking the east side of the capital awaited. Paying the musicians an extra hefty tip, Gerry once more ran the gauntlet and travelled on the elevators, although this time he was better prepared for the tower's own swaying dance. The *maitre d's* greeted them with a smile and escorted them in; apparently, the news of their mini-ball had travelled ahead and was creating a little sensation with the staff and diners. Settling at their cosy table for two near the window, she glanced around. While she usually didn't care for sombre colours for a dining environment, the *Jules Verne* was one exception.   The sleek, black décor was perfectly suited for the iron monument with its delicate trellis pattern and distinctive rivets, it almost felt like they were aboard the *Nautilus* although they were towering in the sky and not gliding under the waves. After placing their orders, Gerry quietly looked around before making a little space in the centre of their table without attracting attention. He then laid his linen napkin across the table.

"All right Princess, place your hand under there please." Curious and trying not to laugh at his strange behaviour, she did as she was told and he slipped the ring onto her finger, removed the napkin and arranged the table settings. "I know you didn't want me to make too much of a scene," he explained, "let's keep our engagement just between the two of us for now."

"Thank you, Gerry."

She realized he probably wanted to get down on one knee, but he knew how she felt, putting a lock on a bridge and dancing in the midst of a crowd was one thing, this was another. She was touched he had managed to make it wildly romantic while keeping the one important detail a secret just for them. It was a pity she could only wear it tonight.

"What's the matter?"

"Nothing, I just remembered I can't wear my ring in public for the moment. I don't want to overshadow Justine's special day. Maurice and Theresa have recently announced their engagement, and another one might eclipse the attention that should be given to the bride, she's more important than the bridesmaid you know."

"Oh, that's right. We won't say anything," he replied, relieved nothing major was wrong, "it means we get to keep our secret a little longer."

"Of course, it would be best to keep our engagement quiet until we talk to our parents first."

"Even better, they're going to get enough of a surprise as it is, and it'll give us time to get used to the idea ourselves."

"True," she smiled.

The most beautiful moments always seemed to accelerate and slip beyond one's grasp just when you want to hold onto them for as long as possible. Eventually, they had to face the rigours of time when the restaurant looked like it was closing for the night. Riding the private elevator back down to earth, Katherine suddenly remembered she wanted to ask what he was muttering on the way to the top.

"Oh that," he smiled, "a poem I made up in history class once. It's not anything as grandiose as Lazarus' poem for Lady Liberty, but it was something I could remember."

"What is it?"

Clearing his throat, he began to recite:

"When Hitler marched
across the Rhine
To take the land of France,
La dame de fer decided,
'Let's make the tyrant dance.'
Let him take the land and city,
The hills and every flower,
One thing he will never have,
The elegant Eiffel Tower.
The French cut the cables,
The elevators stood still,
'If he wants to reach the top,
Let him walk it, if he will.'
The invaders hung a swastika
The largest ever seen.
But a fresh breeze blew
And away it flew,
Never more to be seen.
They hung up a second mark,
Smaller than the first,
But a patriot climbed
With a thought in mind:
'Never your duty shirk.'
Up the iron lady
He stealthily made his way,

815

Hanging the bright tricolour,
He heroically saved the day.
Then, for some strange reason,
A mystery to this day,
Hitler never climbed the tower,
On the ground he had to stay.
At last he ordered she be razed
Down to a twisted pile.
A futile attack, for still she stands
Beaming her metallic smile."

"It looks like I'm not the only poetic soul," Katherine smiled, "is that all true?"

"I'm pretty sure, it has been said Hitler took France, but could never take the tower."

"Well, I must say we did a good job storming it tonight," she laughed.

"I guess we did," he smiled, looking over his shoulder at the tower as he slowly escorted her back to the car.

Nestled together, she didn't want the evening to end. Apparently, he had the same wish and asked the driver to take them on a night time tour around the city. It felt good just sitting together, driving down the Seine more than once, watching the lights and the famous monuments go by. At last, the inevitable could not be avoided, he took her back to the hotel.

"Katherine, I will never forget this day," he said as they sat in the car a few minutes.

"Let's give it the perfect ending," she said, drawing him close. The kiss didn't last as long as they wanted, not with the chauffeur sitting in front, but it was beautiful nonetheless. The chauffeur looked in the mirror but turned away with a smile as he sensed their reserve; they needn't have worried, he was a professional. What happened in the car, stayed in the car. *L'amour*, he always felt a littler younger when that passenger was on board.

CB❀BO

Katherine didn't get much rest, she didn't mind. She had lain awake thinking about their day together and admiring the ring, watching it sparkle in the golden light of the bedside lamp until she finally dropped off. Sadly, she took off the glittering promise of a new life to come and looped it onto the golden chain with the key before going downstairs, at least it was hanging close to her heart.

Wishing the concierge good morning, she was puzzled when he returned the greeting with a congratulatory remark, adding the chef had prepared a special breakfast of crepes and strawberries. Not paying too much attention, she made her way to the breakfast room and noticed the staff were all smiles this morning, a few people were turned in her direction for a few seconds, but she tried not to notice. Maybe the emotional reunion she had with her Lancelot yesterday was making it's rounds in the hotel. Thinking of him, she looked at her watch; he was a little late meeting her for breakfast and finally decided she had better start without him, the crepes it is then. Gerry came rushing through the door looking flustered as the waiter brought her breakfast.

"I'm sorry I'm late, and for the terrible fishy smell," he said, skipping the expected hug and sitting across from her, "but I had to sneak in the back way through the kitchens, with the fish delivery no less," explaining he had picked up a crate with the men for additional cover.

"Smell? I didn't notice anything. Sneak in? Cover? What are you talking about," she blurted, trying to figure out why all the cloak and dagger manoeuvres.

"There are a few paparazzi hunkered down across the street, the doormen won't let them close to the building, but I still had to avoid them. That's not all," he said, looking perturbed, "I heard our names on the news this morning and 'Eiffel Tower'… it seems we were spotted."

"Oh no," she gasped, her crepes forgotten, "we'd better check the morning papers."

She now understood the change of atmosphere in the hotel. He retrieved a stack of complimentary papers provided for the guests and they began searching. It wasn't long before they found the society pages with pictures of them leaving the jewellers, sitting at the café, dancing around the third level of the tower and shots of them heading back to the car complete with close ups of her ring. Apparently, they weren't followed to the bridge, at least that moment was not reported, but everything else was now fodder for the masses.

"It's my fault," he muttered, "after Jakarta, I'm going to be a potential target for awhile. I'm sorry," he said looking downcast, upset his warning uttered the previous day about the press was already happening. However, he was surprised to see her laugh.

"Fire in the hole: we need damage control!"

"Well, we're certainly in the soup, that's for sure," he commented, at least she could see the funny side of things.

"To think you had to sneak in with the shrimp and the salmon."

"But Katherine, this is serious, think about our parents … ."

She quickly sobered up with a gasp.

"You're right! Oh Gerry, surely this won't get into the American papers?"

"Are you kidding? They're probably printing the morning editions as we speak. One thing is for certain, we'll have to call them before they see the news over breakfast."

"Martin and Justine, what are they going to say? This is terrible, I'll have to call them too," Katherine added, crestfallen.

"Well, first thing's first: we can't call anyone from the hotel, not through their switchboards, and you can't stay here, that much is certain. We have to get you moved somewhere else, you won't have a moment's peace after this, and the only place I can think of on the hop is my apartment. I'm sure they don't know where it is, at least I've never been bothered there. After we get you settled in Lottie's room, we can call everyone then. Be a good girl now and go pack your bags while I see if the concierge can arrange some way for us to escape out the back way. What's your room number?"

"210," she said simply, trying to fathom this strange turn of events. Hearing him spell out his plan of action, it sounded like they were on a mission that was a matter of life and death.

"All right. Oh, be sure to change into something more casual if you have it. I'll help you with your bags when you're ready. We must hurry before more paparazzi come on the scene."

In shock wondering what her parents might read, she was in no condition to argue and did as she was told, tearing around the room packing her clothes and clearing out the bathroom. Twenty minutes later, there was a knock on her door.

"It's me," he called. She opened the door to see Gerry wearing a long white deliveryman's working coat with the name 'Jacques' machine embroidered in blue on the front. He came prepared, wheeling in a large laundry bin. She would have laughed if he didn't have such a concerned expression.

"We're in luck. The linen delivery is here, the concierge has arranged for us to sneak away on their truck. We can put your cases in here," he explained, nodding down to the wheelie bin. "Are you ready? May I help you with anything?"

"I just have to empty the drawers, but you can't help me with that," she said, lowering her eyes.

"Okay, I'll wait outside, but don't lift your cases, I'll put them in the bin for you. Hurry now, Katherine."

She continued her mad dash, and in her scattered frame of mind nearly packed the complimentary sightseeing material provided by the hotel. After a few minutes, she let him in to assist with the bags, concealing them under a large tablecloth. He then tried to cover her hair with a large white linen napkin and she wondered why.

"Is there anyway you can pin this? We have to make you look like housekeeping staff," he clarified.

"Oh," she smiled, taking a hair clip and settling the makeshift kerchief into place. "Thank you, *Jacques*."

At last, he began to smile as they wheeled the bin to the elevator, eyeing her casual wear and new headgear. They made their way unnoticed through the working area of the building and exited the service doors where the truck was waiting. Loading the bin into the back and settling on a bundle of clean bed sheets intended for another hotel, they were off.

"Gerry, the hotel bill!" she suddenly realized.

"Relax, I took care of it, and we can argue about paying me back later," he added, pre-empting her protestations, "we had to make a clean getaway, please forgive the pun," he concluded, eyeing the pristine laundry before cautiously raising his head and peeking out the small rear windows. "We're all clear, I don't think we're being followed."

"What a mess, I didn't notice any photographers yesterday. Well, I saw flashes, but I thought it was just tourists taking pictures."

"I didn't notice either, my mind was somewhere else," he replied.

She sighed resignedly, taking stock of their situation: imagine, bumping around Paris in the back of a linen truck!

"I wonder, is this a preview of our future life together?" she queried wryly, raising an eyebrow. He suddenly burst out laughing.

"Well, I did say life with you would never be dull," he noted, settling beside her on a linen stack. The journey didn't take long and they soon arrived outside his building, scanning the street, they decided the coast was clear. Gerry gave the coat and 'kerchief' back to the deliverymen, paying them handsomely for their assistance in the Great Escape before carrying her bags in.

"Uck, let me change my jacket. It's probably in my head, but I still smell of fish," he grimaced, heading to his bedroom. Katherine simply stood in the middle of his sitting room, looking around. So much had happened since she was here last. Who would have guessed then what the future held?

"Are you all right?" he asked, straightening his sleeves as he walked in.

"Oh, I'm just thinking, we're back to where it all began," she smiled. His expression softened and he held her for a moment.

"I know. Now Princess, since we'll be tying the knot soon enough, I want you to consider this place already yours, don't be afraid to make yourself feel at home."

"Thank you, Gerry," she said quietly.

She held him close, the fact they would soon be sharing everything together was a little too much to take in right then. How strange, that something beautiful and exciting could also be tinged with trepidation. It wouldn't be happening tomorrow or the day after that, but a time would come when she would be packing her things and leaving the familiar surroundings of Oak Meadows to begin a new life with the man she loved.

"What's this? My Princess shedding tears?"

"I'm sorry, don't mind me. I'm so happy, and yet … I'll be leaving home."

"Oh, I see," he said, "come, let's sit for a minute. This is what the engagement is for, to let *everything* sink in," he smiled, handing her his handkerchief. "I understand, this is going to be a big change for you, but don't worry. It's not like I'm going to lock you away from your parents, they're only going to be a drive up the road, and one day, trust me, it will get to the point you wish they would give us some space. I can just hear it now: 'Gerry, I love her, but your mother is driving me nuts, tell her I have my own way of arranging the spoon drawer.'."

"Spoon drawer?" Katherine laughed, daubing her eyes.

"Well, you know what I mean. There we go, there's that smile."

Feeling better that he understood, the mention of 'parents' reminded her they should begin making their calls. Clearing her throat and waiting a few seconds to regain her composure, she called Justine first.

"Well, now we know what that 'something' was that kept you away yesterday," her friend laughed. "Paris didn't rub off on you—it hit you over the head."

"You've seen the papers. Oh, I'm so sorry about all of this, I feel terrible, but I don't think I'll be able to attend the wedding, not with all the photographers following me around."

"Don't be silly! Tell me what happened first, then we'll discuss what to do."

Katherine relayed in quick synopsis how Gerry surprised her yesterday morning with everything rocketing towards a proposal after that, and was surprised Justine seemed to be taking it all very matter of fact. She thought it was positively romantic. After all, it was Paris.

"Aren't you upset all of this might take away from your own big day?" Katherine wondered.

"Oh *au contraire*," Martin interjected. With only one phone, apparently they were trying to share the handset so they could both join in her call, "it would be fun to have celebrities invited to our wedding."

"Celebrities? I don't know about *that*," she said, then realizing he spoke in the plural and asked him to elaborate on that point.

"Why, you must bring your *fiancée*," Martin explained, "as it happens we can fit more guests with no problem, two have backed out at the last minute."

"My grand aunt and uncle," Justine jumped in, "she's not feeling good so he has to stay home too. We would be delighted if your Gerry came."

"Umm, hold on a sec," she said, holding the mouthpiece and motioning for Gerry. "They want to invite you to the wedding."

"Oh my, I couldn't crash their party," he said, "it wouldn't be right, I've caused enough trouble as it is." Katherine relayed his message, but Martin and Justine wouldn't hear of a refusal and insisted he come.

"They say it would be an honour having one of their first collectors and admirers attend."

"All right, let me speak to them for a moment. Hello…yes, of course I remember you Justine. Why thank you … she says we make a charming couple," he whispered to Katherine, naturally, they had seen their picture in the papers. "Thank you for inviting me, but I will attend on two conditions. First, I shall arrange to have your artwork sent to New York since I distracted your bridesmaid from her duties, so please don't worry about deducting the shipping from your commission. Two, I must contribute towards your happy day. Have you arranged transportation for your honeymoon? … Taxis and subway, uh huh, I think we can do better than that. How would you and Martin like a limousine at your disposal for the entire week? … No, I'm positive … I rarely use it, except for the odd business meeting," he said, winking at Katherine, who started to laugh. "I'm glad that's settled, when shall I arrange for the men to pack your artwork? … Yes, they can do it tonight, I'll have everything sent by our air freight service. … All right, I can't wait to meet Martin, see you soon. Bye for now, let me hand you back to Kathy."

"This is just wonderful," Justine exclaimed, "now that we have that settled, please tell me all the details. I have a half day and won't be going into work until this afternoon." Katherine was obliged to tell everything again, this time including her wild ride that morning in the linen truck and the necessity to change her lodgings. "I don't believe it! This will make it difficult for you and Gerry to get around the city. Tell you what, if you need a lift anywhere, no one will recognise you in Martin's van." Katherine thanked her for her offer, but it looked like they were going to be housebound for the time being. "Just as well, take some days off with Gerry, you have a lot of catching up to do, and we really don't need you here right now. The few days before the ceremony is going to be when it all hits."

"Are you sure?"

"Positive. Oh Kathy, I'm delighted for you, and what an ending to his riddle." No kidding, Katherine thought. "Okay, I'll leave you go so you can call home, this is not going to be easy to explain, I hope it goes all right."

"Me too, thanks for being understanding about this. We'll see you later."

"*Au revoir.*"

Hanging up, Katherine checked the time; too soon to call home yet with the hour difference. In the meantime, Gerry showed her to Lottie's room and she began unpacking, after which he surprised her with a large, thin flat box wrapped in sedate gift paper when she returned to the sitting room.

"What's all this?"

"Something I picked up in Japan, I thought you might like it," he said, presenting it with a formal bow, Japanese style.

"More gifts?"

"Go on, open it," he smiled. She remembered what he told her about gift giving in the Far East and carefully examined the box, admiring the wrapping before carefully opening it, slow and precise, without ripping the paper. Lifting the lid, she discovered a silk kimono with a classic scene of a Japanese garden in bloom.

"Oh, it's beautiful. Thank you, it's almost too pretty to wear," she noted, slipping it around her shoulders.

"Pretty as a picture," he smiled, "well, I suppose we can't delay the dreadful task any longer, we have to call home. Now, we should do this together, so when your call goes through, tell me so I can get on the other set."

Katherine took a few deep breaths as Gerry went to the den cum office where the second phone was located.

"Hello, Good morning Mrs. Gonzales, yes I'm fine. Oh, yes Paris is beautiful this time of year …umm, …no … I need to speak with Pops first….thank you. Gerry, you can pick up now," she called. *Oh dear*, this was not going to be easy, Pops was not much of a morning person.

"Hi Kathy, good morning, or rather, good afternoon. Are you having a good time?"

"I guess you could say that Pops. Umm, I need to talk with you about something. You haven't read the morning papers yet by any chance?"

"No, I just sat down with my coffee. Why, is something wrong?"

"Oh no, well …I have very good news, which is going to be a surprise. Gerry arrived in Paris yesterday … in fact, he's on the phone with me right now."

"Good morning sir, I'm sorry to bother you at breakfast … ."

"Good morning," Harold replied perplexed, "what is happening over there?"

"I'd better just say it: Pops, we're engaged."

Silence.

"Pops, are you still there?"

"*You're what?*"

"We're engaged, sir," Gerry said, "forgive me, I had every intention of coming to you first, but things happened much faster than I expected."

"I think you two had better explain yourselves," he noted quietly and with much deliberation. Katherine gritted her teeth, she could just see him reaching for his ulcer medication.

"Now Pops, don't blame Gerry … I was the one who proposed."

"*You* proposed? Oh Katherine, you're so impulsive."

"Well, it is leap year."

They proceeded to explain everything from the beginning and how they were caught unawares by the paparazzi, not knowing they were being watched.

"Aren't you two rushing into this?" he enquired.

"Maybe the engagement, but we're not going set dates until we're ready," she assured him. "Pops, we love each other."

"I wonder what your mother is going to say about all of this," he noted frostily, "Helen, you'd better get on another phone, you won't believe what your daughter has done now," he called out. The repentant lovers explained everything a second time for Helen, who took the news better than Papa Bear.

"Now Harold, this is wonderful news, a little premature maybe, but we don't want to spoil this happy occasion for them."

"We had every intention of keeping this quiet until we spoke with you," Gerry explained, "but the media caught up with us. It may hit the gossip columns this morning on your side of the pond. We wanted to warn you in advance. I'm sorry the way it all turned out." They then had to break the news Katherine was no longer at the hotel because the reporters were camped across the street hungry for photos. Leaving out the detail of the linen van, too much news was not a good idea right now, he concluded the only alternative was to move Katherine in his apartment so she wouldn't be hounded by the paparazzi, and he felt confident that the media was not aware of this location. He assured her parents they would maintain proper protocol, and she would be staying in his sister's room.

"You see you behave yourself young man," Pops warned, "and I hold you responsible for the welfare of my daughter."

"Oh Pops, don't be angry with Gerry, he is the perfect gentleman at all times, you can be assured of that."

"Now Harold, I'm sure they will conduct themselves with all propriety. I have every confidence in them. I don't believe we have anything to worry about. Katherine, I'm so happy for you both, we'll talk more about this when you come home."

"Okay, and we'll keep our heads down and try not to attract any more attention than we already have."

"See that you do, young lady," Pops replied. They gave her parents the address and the telephone number before they said their goodbyes.

"Whew, glad that's done," Gerry said, letting his breath out slowly. "Your Pops is intense, looks like my silver ships won't be coming into port anytime soon."

"Oh, he gets impatient with me at times, but he always comes around, you'll see."

"I can understand why he's upset, we haven't handled things properly, Kathy."

"It's the media's fault," she observed a little nettled, "they just ruined everything, and things were so perfect."

"Well, since we're on a roll, we'd better call Stonyvale next." As Gerry suspected, his parents were not surprised by their news and heartily congratulated them.

"It was only a matter of time, and we partly guessed what might happen, you hardly said 'hello' to Lottie and I before you were off to Paris," his mother pointed out.

Glad that the disclosures were finally out of the way, Gerry called in to arrange the art shipment, the last duty to be taken care of. He then noted they should really get something to eat, especially as this was the second time he had interrupted her breakfast. Unfortunately, there wasn't anything decent in the apartment since he had just arrived two nights ago and had been out most of the time. Of course, his cooking skills were not the best, nothing past breakfast anyway, neither was hers she reminded him. Thinking for a moment, he told her they couldn't stay cooped up inside for the next two weeks, not with their terrible culinary skills, and he decided on a plan. They would go to a large department store and shop for a few things to help them travel around incognito, they could then skip off the beaten track to find somewhere to eat away from the main thoroughfares and tourist traps where they might be recognised. Katherine laughed, that sounded like fun.

"We're really having an adventure, aren't we? Okay, Agent Double-O-Seven, let's go pick out our disguises, I know just the place."

Calling a taxi, she gave the directions for the Galeries Lafayette, a large store where she felt certain they could find what they needed. Gerry walked around and picked out a few hats. Katherine had decided on a couple of wigs and a pair of dark glasses. He almost didn't recognise her in the new get-up.

"Hey, you're just as beautiful as a blonde," he smiled, eyeing her golden locks.

"Wait until you see me as a red-head. You don't look too bad yourself, hot stuff," she smiled, glancing at the hat he selected.

"Still, this is not exactly what I had in mind for a shopping spree," he said, shaking his head. After paying for their new identities, they decided to take a test run with their disguises and walked up the Rue La Fayette, eventually turning down one of the side streets that looked interesting where they discovered a restaurant that seemed like somewhere the locals would frequent.

"*Le Papillion*, 'Butterfly', looks quaint, we can hide away in here," she suggested.

"Let's give it a try," he said, admiring the deep honey wood décor, the petite bar and the house whippet curled up fast asleep in the wicker basket in the corner, paws up in the air. It was a unique experience dining in the Parisian bistros where pets were just as welcome as their owners.

"You know, we may be wearing disguises, but there's one good thing you don't have to hide anymore," he whispered after they sat down.

Katherine smiled and took the ring off her chain, which he placed on her finger.

☘❀☙

It was fun playing tourist in Paris like two undercover agents, but April showers slipped quickly into May flowers and the newly engaged couple had to set their romantic idyll aside for Martin and Justine's big day. At least they could finally be themselves and discard their store-bought alter egos. It was a mad dash as they all arrived at the Hôtel de Ville for the civil ceremony, they had to be on time for they didn't want to miss their slot and throw everything askew. If you had to have a secular ceremony, at least the setting was certainly grand Katherine noted, admiring the town hall with its French Renaissance decorations encrusted with niches and elegant statuary. It looked more like the châteaux of the Loire Valley than a municipal building. Gerry joked the mayor must really enjoy his job.

Everyone assembled in one of the special chambers reserved for the civil weddings with Maurice and his quartet playing in the background. Martin was certainly handsome in his new suit with his peach coloured boutonnière, although he looked slightly nervous as he escorted his mother in first according to tradition. Justine was simply beautiful that day, dressed in an oyster coloured chiffon dress with peach roses and orange blossoms in her hair, holding a matching bouquet. They didn't know who would officiate, and it turned out the deputy mayor did the honours looking very impressive in his tricolour sash. After a small reception, the couple collected their official *livret de famille*, the booklet that would legally document their life together starting with a copy of the marriage certificate, and eventually, the birth of their children. Exiting the building, they were showered with the usual rice, wheat and *dragees* by their friends and family. Finally, they made they way to the church for the religious ceremony, the exchange of vows and blessings.

The venue was a strange choice compared with the regal town hall and the host of historic churches in the city, but her friends decided on a church that reflected their modernist appreciation of art. Katherine smiled as the guests looked at the austere brick exterior of St. Jean l'Evangéliste de Montmartre with quizzical expressions. The first church in Paris to have been built with reinforced concrete, they could be forgiven for mistaking the ecclesial building to be a mosque with its Arabic style interlocking arches and colourful abstract mosaics decorating the entrance. The interior of the building was adorned with Art Nouveau floral motifs. Once more, Martin escorted his mother down the aisle, then the bride entered with her father. The couple exchanged vows, which was followed by Mass, and received a final blessing with a white silk canopy, or *carre*, held over their heads that the newlyweds would save for the baptism of their first child. Katherine was profoundly moved by the quiet, poignant reverence of the ceremony. Not a whisper was heard, a hushed silence prevailed as if everyone held their breath, denoting the solemn reverence of the proceedings. The civil rite was to satisfy the secular authorities, but here, the vows exchanged were recognised by God and man and truly blessed.

Leaving the church, again showered with rice and *dragées*, the wedding party made its way to the Place du Tertre for the semi-formal reception. Katherine remembered many of the former art students she met during her exchange term and enjoyed the happy if noisy meeting and greeting together with all the news and exchange of views and trends in the art world. Of course, business could not be turned off for the day as they eagerly asked for her card and hoped she didn't mind if they sent her photos of their artwork. At least she didn't have to look far for new European talent Gerry laughed. Eventually, the wedding party filtered over to the George V for the formal reception. By now, the paparazzi had left their post and the lovebirds could enter the establishment unhindered by reporters. The concierge recognised them and came to offer his sincere apologies for the trouble they experienced, giving an explanation on how they were discovered: they had no idea the breakfast room was a popular hangout with many members of the media. To make amends for their disagreeable experience, he would gladly arrange to have a private car meet them in the back exit to take them anywhere they wanted to go after the party, and they thanked him for his thoughtful concern.

In keeping with traditional wedding receptions around the world, there was the formal toasts and dinner, but with national customs that made the day a truly French experience. In addition to the tradition of the silver toasting goblet, Martin's father went 'all out' and hired a guard of the Napoléonic Order of Champagne. Dressed in the long established military uniform the guard deftly opened bottles of bubbly with his sabre, lifting the wire and cork without spilling a drop. It was said the emperor could also accomplish the same feat for the amusement of his soldiers. The cake was also unique, a golden mountain of profiteroles filled with cream and encrusted in a hard caramel glaze topped with spun sugar earning it the nick-name *croquembouche*, or 'mouth-cruncher'. Dinner was delicious, and Katherine and Gerry were delighted when the music started and the dancing commenced. They were inseparable until the moment arrived for the bride and groom to say goodnight, signalling the tossing of the bouquet, which Justine saved for the last tradition, the *chiverie*, where they would be prevented from leaving by a boisterous but good-natured 'interruption' by the guests until they had one last drink with them. The bouquet became the decoy that finally allowed the newly-weds to slip away from the party. Due to her short stature, Justine tossed it high in the air to make sure everyone had an equal chance to catch it, perhaps a little too exuberantly; it bounced off Katherine's head and landed in Lucille's waiting arms. While the guests looked like they had no intention of leaving, especially the cousins of the newly-weds who wanted to keep the party going, Gerry and Katherine took their leave since they had to finish packing for their flight home the next day.

On the way to the apartment, they talked about the day's events, commenting on the various traditions, and how exhausted they were after it all.

"I didn't know a French wedding had so many receptions, it was fun, but I'm positively all in," he said, shaking his head.

"My head hurts from all the translating," she smiled, not everyone spoke English and she didn't want Gerry excluded from the conversations.

"I'm sorry, I've been a nuisance for you today."

"Oh no, it's just a shame you couldn't understand everything, Martin's uncle had some very funny stories, I'm glad I could keep you in the loop for most of them."

"Thanks, I didn't feel like I was out in left field. Gosh, did you see how that officer just topped all the bottles?" he laughed. "That's what I call doing things in style."

"Poor Justine, I thought she was going to pass out when he made her hold a bottle over her head for him to open."

"You'd be nervous too if a man came that close to you with a sword, you'd pray he had a steady hand."

"I don't think I could do what Justine did. You know Lancelot, the whole day was really nice, the main reception wasn't too big and it didn't get out of hand. Martin and Justine were right to keep the day as intimate as possible. When we decide to set our day, I think we should plan something along those lines."

"I agree, I've been to some pretty big receptions and it just ruins the whole experience. I mean, who wants hundreds of people that you don't even know suffocating your one big day? Endless congratulations while they party to the hilt, and you never see them again."

"You're absolutely right," she nodded resolutely, "do they really care or mean it? I'd just like to have our family and real friends with us that day."

"Well, here we are," he noted as the car pulled up outside his building, "home sweet home."

They decided to finish packing right away rather than leave it all to the last minute, after which they settled down on the sofa together with their feet up on the coffee table.

"Our last night," he noted with a sigh, "I've enjoyed our few weeks together, it went so fast, just us two with no work to worry about and no one bothering us."

"I know, this has been wonderful, I'm glad we had this time together to get to know each other better."

"Well, we've had a chance to see what living under the same roof is going to be like," he whispered with a smile.

"Not yet, you haven't seen me in my rollers. Oh Gerry," she then sighed, "no one's going to believe nothing happened between us, this is going to be embarrassing when we go home."

"Who cares what they think? Try not to worry about it."

That was easy for him to say, some people had spiteful thoughts when the bride walked down the aisle, she had been to a few weddings too and overheard the gossipers, even today she heard people comment about Justine's choice of an off-white dress. Backstabbers, she was glad Justine didn't hear it. Sitting silently for a moment, she realized Gerry was right. They knew the truth, and so would their parents; if people wanted to think otherwise, then it was their rotting minds. Good old Socrates had a point, the opinions of a few good men were better than the bad judgement of the many. She turned her thoughts to the ceremony at the church and began comparing the different customs, the white canopy was a nice touch.

"Gerry, I was thinking about the ceremony, do they do that in your church back home, or is it a French idea? The canopy I mean."

"We don't do that in the States, Catholics in different countries have their own customs, but the Jews do the canopy thing, don't they? Hmm, Pete would know what that part means. Some countries have a tradition where the priest binds or wrap the couple's hands together before the final blessing to symbolise their union."

"That's nice too." They sat in silence, until he asked what she was thinking right then. "I was just curious, I can understand why I couldn't go for the communion part of the service, but you didn't go up either, and you're Catholic."

"Oh … well, not everyone goes. There were others who stayed behind. Some people probably didn't watch the time and broke their fast at the reception in the town hall, so they couldn't go up. We have to fast at least an hour before we go to communion as a mark of respect."

"Huh, some people in our church do that too. That's interesting. What if you go up after breaking the fast?"

"Well, it would be a sin, we'd have to confess it."

"You *have* to? Hmm, you have a lot of 'have to's' in your church. I mean, it sounds tough to follow."

"Look at it this way: communion is not a symbol for us, it's literally Christ, and dropping the Son of God on a full stomach is not a nice thing to do."

"Gee, when you put it *that* way," she said, "it does sound bad." She sat for a moment, thinking about what he told her and noticed he said 'some people' broke the fast. "Did you break the fast?" she wondered.

"Well I…what is this? My Princess conducting her own Inquisition?" he said, a little bemused. It was like Sister Roberta's catechism class all over again.

"I'm sorry, I was just wondering. Other than Justine, I had no experience with your church, I'm curious, and I'd rather find out from someone who actually goes than from someone who doesn't have an idea of what they're talking about."

He relented a little, she wasn't judgemental, just interested, but it didn't make discussing sticky subjects any easier.

"Who 'actually goes'? You should really be asking Pete then," he said.

"Oh," she realized, he wasn't a regular attendee. After a pause, "are you … excommunicated?" she whispered. She hoped not, for she knew that was pretty bad, and she didn't want Gerry to be in trouble with anyone, certainly not his church.

"Excom … what gave you that idea?" He didn't know whether to laugh or be annoyed with her, but looking into her eyes he could see her concern, there was no self-righteous prying. He sighed, wondering how he could explain his shortcomings without going into too much detail. Heck, she was perceptive without realizing it, he might as well be excommunicated. "Well, I haven't attended in a long time, not that I don't believe, but when you stop going, it's … hard to come back."

"Do they make it difficult for you?"

"Well no…it's just … look: one of our precepts is to attend church on all Sundays and holy days of obligation like Christmas Day and Easter, that sort of thing. If we don't go, it's considered breaking the commandment to keep the Sabbath holy, that's pretty serious, so I just can't pop back in and go to communion as if nothing has happened."

"I get it, it's a confession thing, we have confessions in our church too you know," she said, suddenly yawning. "Oh, excuse me, I'm tired after today. Why don't you just go, confession I mean? Might make you feel better."

"It's not that simple." Blast, Sister Roberta taught him too well, he couldn't dull his conscience completely, and his Princess wasn't helping. "I don't know about your church, but with ours, you can't just confess, you have to have the will to change what you're doing wrong, not to mention you have to believe what you've done is wrong and be sorry for it, or it's not a valid confession, and … I'm fuzzy on certain points myself in that department. There, I said it."

"You believe, and yet disagree on certain things. Well, with all those rules you have, I'd be fuzzy too. Maybe you should ask Pete, I'm sure he'd help you out," she yawned again, nestling under his arm, "everything he says makes sense."

He studied her calm features as she dozed off, she made things sound so simple, and what made it more uncomfortable, she was right. He should talk things over with his brother, in fact, he would have to eventually with the wedding and all, but that's what made matters worse, giving his saintly big brother the satisfaction of seeing the stray lamb return to the fold when the stray lamb was quite comfortable where he was right now. He hadn't been to church in years, it felt liberating skirting the 'have-tos' as she put it, and yet … blast it! In her innocence, she had a way of raking up things that he preferred to ignore, and he certainly didn't want to face his inner demons on their last night in Paris. Well, looks like there wouldn't be anymore discussions that night he noticed with relief.

"Whoops, can't leave you sleep here, Princess, upsy-daisy, off to bed with you," he said, patting her on the shoulder. She stretched and gave him a kiss before heading to her room.

"Good night, Lancelot, pleasant dreams."

"Sweet dreams, and remember to set the alarm."

☜❀☞

The flight back was rather awkward with Katherine up in first class with Martin and Justine, while the only seat Gerry could find on short notice was back in coach, crammed right into the tail end. He couldn't wait

831

for the seatbelt sign to be turned off so he could go up to join her, but the air hostess hooshed him from the exclusive area and swished the curtain closed. Katherine could not help laughing when she saw this performance and went to meet him in the aisle.

"I'll offer the guy next to you my seat up front, then we can sit together."

"In the canned sardine section? No, you hang on to your seat, Princess, it's more comfortable."

"Poot! I'm coming back with you, we can hang around the hostesses' station, they have some space there." They weren't allowed to 'hang' for long as they began serving the refreshments almost immediately.

"Please, you'll have to take your seat," they reminded Katherine.

The couple tried again when the trolleys were stowed, but one of the hostesses was getting annoyed with them until a fellow passenger whispered in her ear and showed her a newspaper; apparently, another article about the lovebirds had been printed. Now recognising them, the hostess decided to let Romeo and Juliet have their space, although it was invaded once in a while by some passengers who wanted autographs, excited at meeting someone famous for the first time. They laughed and humoured them with a quick scrawl on a cocktail napkin or a defunct boarding pass before resuming their conversation, that is, until they were forced back to their seats because of turbulence, mealtimes, and eventually, the landing. Touchdown was a little bumpy, a reminder of what faced them when they were reunited with their families.

"Well, looks like the honeymoon is over for us," Gerry joked as they went to retrieve their bags.

"Isn't this exciting," Justine exclaimed, looking around. "Imagine, we're in America!"

"Wow, and this is only the baggage reclaim," Martin laughed, turning to Gerry, "I'm afraid to take her outside, she's been looking forward to this for such a long time she might pass out with excitement when she actually sees the city."

Katherine dreaded to find out who had come to greet her, and her hunch was correct, nearly everyone had come. Pops was not looking too happy, but he seemed resigned to the situation, or was bottling his temper. Mom and Aunt Martha were very eager to see the ring right away, while Gramps pat Gerry on the back.

"Well m'boy, welcome to the family."

"Oh, imagine! We finally have a wedding to plan," Aunt Martha beamed.

"Speaking of weddings, let me introduce my friends to you first," Katherine interjected, seeing Martin and Justine patiently waiting.

"Our Katherine has told us so much about you," Helen greeted, "we hope you will have dinner with us some evening."

"Oh yes, of course, we would love that," Justine replied.

"Do you need a ride into town?" Pops politely enquired.

"Oh, Gerry kindly took care of that for us," Martin explained, telling about his generous offer of his limousine for the entire week.

"Speaking of which, let me go find Samuel, I don't know how we missed him, he's never late," Gerry said, heading over to the arrivals door. It didn't take long to track him down, Gerry helped with Martin's luggage cart while they talked with the Walsinghams for a moment, explaining that for the first night they would just stay around the hotel area and settle in, but tomorrow they planned to go straight to the gallery, they couldn't wait to see it and regretted they couldn't come to the opening.

"You're here now, and that's what counts. Everyone is dying to meet you, and it will be fun choosing where you want your work to be displayed," Katherine added.

"Well, we won't hold you up. I hope you enjoy you stay, and if you need anything, don't hesitate to call us," Helen added. Martin and Justine said their goodbyes, waving to everyone as they followed Samuel out the door. Now it was just the family, and Gerry.

"How about you, young man? We can drop you off at your apartment," Pops offered.

"Thank you sir, but I don't want to put you out, I can take a cab."

"Nonsense, I can at least offer my future son-in-law a ride into town."

"All right, thank you sir."

Katherine's sympathies went out to Gerry as she saw him follow Pops to the car.

"Gramps," she whispered before he followed them, "nothing happened, you know what I mean. Please don't let him get out of hand."

"Well pet, your Pops has to get a few things off his chest first, but don't worry, I'll referee the situation."

Aunt Martha had brought her car, so the ladies ended up driving home together, which was fine, because they could discuss everything with the men out of the way. She just hoped Pops wouldn't be too hard on Gerry without her there to jump in and explain things, but she would have to trust Gramps in that department.

For the umpteenth time she told the engagement story, the linen van still excised from the account. Aunt Martha was in her element and wondered what date they had in mind for the festivities.

"Oh we haven't gone that far yet, we're going to wait until we're absolutely ready, considering this has surprised us too," she explained.

"You're very sensible," her mother agreed. "There are many things you have to think about, not just the celebrations."

"I know Mom. I'm glad I had these few weeks with Gerry, when it does come time to move, it won't be such a shock. Now, nothing happened," she clarified, eyeing the look on her aunt's face, "he's been very good. I haven't said anything, but he seems to know I want to do everything just right, and he's respected my wishes."

"Looks like he wants to do the right thing too, I'm glad for that much. Mutual respect is a good sign," her mother noted half to herself.

"True," Aunt Martha agreed.

"You know, he doesn't expect me to stop working at the gallery, and he says I can keep my maiden name for my art. I wasn't sure if he wanted a stay-at-home wife, considering he is old-fashioned in some respects and doesn't like me paying for anything."

"That's considerate," Aunt Martha added, "but I'm rather disappointed in the ring, I expected something bigger and grander, he can afford it after all."

"Now Martha," Helen chided.

"Don't misjudge him, he wanted to get me a big one, but it was so big it was embarrassing. I mean, it was like a walnut. I had to refuse it. Then he asked if I would like something custom made in our colours in the shape of a flower, but I had to refuse that too, I couldn't wear a red diamond, it would be stuck in a safe the whole time. So I chose this one, I think it's beautiful."

"Of course it is," her mother agreed, "and I'm glad to see how sensible you are."

"But goodness, a *red* diamond? He is serious," Martha gasped.

"He doesn't know what to do to please me, and I keep telling him he doesn't have to conquer the world. Gee, you should have seen the two of us sneaking around Paris in our disguises," she laughed, "we had so much fun."

"You know, we'll have to meet his parents," Mom observed, "that will be the proper thing to do next."

"Oh Mom, I know you will like them, I do, and as Gerry says, liking your in-laws is half the battle."

"And how does Gerry feel about us?"

"He likes our family, but he's worried about Pops, and I don't blame him. I sure hope he's not roasting my fiancée on the way home."

Katherine's intuition was correct, as the men made their way to Gerry's apartment, Harold did keep the heat at a steady, even temperature as he probed the situation, the electricity spiking every now and then.

"Well, I must say, this was not handled very well. Could you not have waited until she retuned home?"

"Cut him some slack son, they hadn't seen each other in months," Gramps reminded him.

"I apologize sir, I should have, but … I wanted to surprise her. I didn't expect *her* to propose, on the same day no less."

"Well, our Katherine can be impetuous, but you said you had already planned to propose. I must ask, how long have you been thinking about this? Marriage is a big step and not to be taken lightly," he reminded him, casting a patriarchal glance through the rear view mirror.

"I know that sir. Almost from the start, when we began seeing each other."

"That soon?"

"Well, I've been attracted to her a long time before then," he confessed, explaining the day they first met in his apartment. "Thing is, she may be impetuous in certain ways, but as I have discovered, she doesn't give her affections easily, they must be earned, and since we had just told each other about our feelings the day I arrived, I didn't expect her to be thinking about marriage until some time had passed. I assure you sir, I did wish to speak with you first."

"I see," Harold mused, thinking this over. "I suppose it's a consolation to know you had planned to make your intentions known to us before you asked her."

"Well, now that we're together, might as well discuss things," Gramps added. Katie was his girl too and he was not going to be left out of something this important.

"All right, how about my apartment? We'll be there soon."

"You've been away for months, maybe after you've had time to settle," Harold was magnanimous to offer.

"No, that's all right, I'd like to talk now if you don't mind," Gerry replied.

"Give him the benefit of speaking on his own turf," Gramps interjected, "as I recall, it wasn't that long ago when you faced Helen's parents."

"Dad," Harold replied, slightly nettled.

Getting to his apartment and tucking his luggage away in the bedroom, Gerry offered his future in-laws a drink. "It may be early afternoon, but I need one," he replied. Harold relented while Gramps wouldn't refuse.

"Well, I suppose I don't need to verify one thing," Harold noted, as they sat down in the living room, "I have no doubts you will be able to keep my daughter in the manner to which she is accustomed." Gerry hoped that was a joke.

"Actually, that's going to be difficult," he replied, but realized his mistake right away; Papa Bear was not too much for engaging in a repartee and he quickly had to explain himself. "She won't let me give her anything, trying to give her a decent engagement ring was sheer agony. Do you know she turned down a red diamond? I thought women liked big engagement rings." Gramps started to chuckle.

"Our Katie can be an odd cookie at times, but this is how it is: you've earned her affections now, she probably doesn't want you to feel you have to keep doing something crazy," Gramps observed.

"Oh, I'm not trying to *buy* her if that's what she's afraid of, but I do want to show her I care, and it's not easy."

"I can understand that," Harold noted, "but she's very selective in what makes her happy. She's always lived in a sheltered, quiet world of her own."

"I see that," Gerry agreed thoughtfully, "she doesn't seem a part of …out there," he said, indicating towards the city, not sure how to explain it, "and it's one of the things I love about her, the fact she's willing to let me in is nothing short of a miracle."

"How do you feel about her, m'boy?" Gramps asked quietly. "It might help us determine that she shall be in safe hands." There was silence for a moment.

"How do I describe the indescribable? I thought I knew what love was or could be until I met her, she is the centre of gravity in the weightless mass of my existence, she is everything worth living for. I am no longer myself …." All he could see was the bridge thousands of miles away and the golden chain he wore as a remembrance, a testament to their love, two keys, one lock. "I am her, and she is me," he stated simply. They wouldn't understand, but if they insisted on words to plumb the sacred recesses of the soul, he could not reveal the depths with any other phrase.

Harold studied him for a moment, he didn't know what had happened over there, but there was no denying they had set their hearts on each other. His statement was not calculated, this was not an attempt to win them over or try and earn their approval, although he knew that would be appreciated. Nevertheless, he had acted recklessly, and in his enthusiasm, wanted to spend uncontrollably. Harold needed to be certain he truly knew what he was doing and would not leave him off the hook just yet. For heaven's sake, the world knew about their engagement before the family did!

"All right, since you insist you're ready for marriage, I would like to know, what *have* you discussed so far?"

"Well it's early days yet, not too much at this point," he began, explaining how she asked what he felt about the gallery. "I want to make it clear I have no intention of interfering in her business or painting, or force her to stop doing the things she loves."

"That will be difficult when you both start a family, she will have some decisions to make when it comes time to prepare a nursery," Harold pointed out.

"I know, and I don't want all the changes and adjustments to fall on her, I do intend to pull my weight, but we haven't gotten that far yet, I'm not sure if she's even thought about it, which is why I want her to take as long as she needs before settling on a date. We need to discuss many things."

"That's obvious. Well, you have thought what the responsibilities of marriage and family are all about, I presume. Katherine firmly believes in the traditional precepts of marriage, now is the time to learn if you have any disagreements in your ideals and expectations. People forget that's what the engagement period is really for."

"I understand," Gerry replied. *Whew*, there was nothing like getting hit with some hard realities smack between the eyes. In truth, he was ready for that, his Princess did aim for perfection all right, he knew for certain what to expect. Perhaps this period of waiting was a good thing, he liked the idea of having kids and wanted to start a family, but was intimidated b the thought of becoming a father. Who wasn't? He took a quick gulp from his glass.

"So m'boy," Gramps jumped in, "I suppose you haven't discussed where you two might live, none of the practical things yet?"

"No. I'll have to ask her, maybe she just expects to move right on in here, thinking I won't give her an opportunity to have her say. Honestly, if she doesn't like the apartment, that's fine by me. I'll keep it as an investment property and let people use it when they want, my family likes to stay here when they come to the city," he explained. "Maybe she has her own ideas since she's used to a house with a garden. Of course, there is the matter of Stoneyvale Manor. My brother would have been the one to inherit the property, but as it turns out, it could be me or Lottie now, whatever my parents decide, but usually it goes to a son in the family. That will be years down the road I hope. I guess what I'm trying to say is, Katherine is aware of our family legacy and that the manor may eventually become her home."

"A big responsibility, I agree, but as she proposed to you, she must be willing to assume them with you."

"It's daunting, but she seems to love the old place. However, if it's too much for us, we can always figure something out."

"Well, I'm glad you're upfront about all of this," Harold noted, "now, about your trouble with the press, have you discussed this?"

"Yes, that we did discuss, right on the first day. I have fully warned her I cannot protect her from the ravages of the media, but she said it was a stupid reason to split up."

"Well, it's not like we haven't had our fair share of it too," Gramps said, "you can't let news and the reporters stop you from living your life."

"That's pretty much what she said."

"Now, there is one other matter I must bring up that will be distasteful, but in these times, I wish everything to be out in the open. Have you thought about making arrangements in case the unthinkable happens and the worse comes to the worst?"

"You mean wills? Life insurance policies?"

"A pre-nup. I would like to know that if things should ever deteriorate between you, what is already hers is secured."

"Now Har," Gramps butted in.

"I pray nothing like that will happen, but as I said, I have no wish to take anything from her. If it will make you feel easier, I will sign a pre-nup," Gerry offered, "with a respectable settlement fee to ensure she is taken care of."

"Our Katie's not going to be happy with you, Har," Gramps rumbled, "so much for love and trust."

"I'm not upset, honestly," Gerry jumped in, "you want what's best for her and cushion her from the hard knocks when and if they happen, I understand that. Whatever it takes to make her happy, but be assured, I plan to live out my days with her, whatever we get hit with, we'll get through it. She is the love of my life."

"Right now, but if you do anything to break her heart and make her miserable ... ."

"I won't sir. This is not some passing whim, she'll always be the love of my life."

"Anything else you'd like to throw at him, son?" Gramps added.

"Yes, something important: you do know she was raised Episcopalian, to be precise, the Anglican Communion, and according to your Church, you must have special permission to marry with the agreement your children are raised Catholic. I assume you haven't told her this."

"Umm, correct, sir. She knows I'm Catholic, but where that leaves us with marriage and raising a family, we haven't spoken about it yet."

"I see."

"Now Har, this is for them to discuss, if Katherine already knows he's Catholic, she's willing to … make some adjustments."

"But does she know what's expected? The thing is," Harold said, turning back to Gerry, "would you be willing to marry outside your church if she refuses the rules of yours?"

"I … I don't know, this is something we would have to discuss."

"Don't push it Har, this is their decision, and Katherine can just go over your head now if you place any obstacles in her way. You know how she is," Gramps reminded him. "The important thing is we're all Christian, even if we have disagreements on what authority we follow, let's leave it at that for now, shall we? We only want to see our Katie happy."

Harold wasn't happy, but his father was right, he couldn't forbid the union when Katherine was now an adult and could make up her own mind. He would end up precipitating the situation faster by a refusal. What could he do anyway? He had always supported whatever his children wanted in life, as long as they thought long and hard about the possible consequences and made an informed decision.

"One last thing, no moving in together until after the wedding."

"I've already been warned, she told me she has traditional expectations, sir."

"Well, I think we've covered the important topics," Harold slowly concluded, "of course, we shall have to meet your parents, but we shall leave that for the women to plan."

"That reminds me, our Katie is not much of a cook, we won't get her back in a week will we?" Gramps interjected.

"I am aware of her skills in the kitchen, or the lack thereof," Gerry said, clearing his throat, trying not to laugh but grateful for a little comic relief, "not everyone can be a Julia Child, I do have a housekeeper and a cook, and if Katherine needs additional help around the home since she has the gallery, that's no problem. Anything she wants, she can have."

"Good, there's something else settled," Gramps noted, "it'll be up to you and Katie to discuss everything else."

"I guess this means … welcome to the family," Harold finally said, offering his hand.

"Thank you, sir."

"And we'll have to do something about this 'sir' business," Harold said, finally lowering his paternal wariness, "only my workers and strangers call me 'sir'."

"Umm, 'Pops'?" Gerry tentatively suggested.

"Maybe just 'Harold' will do for now," he returned, a glint of humour showing through.

"Well, you can just go ahead and call me 'Gramps.' I think that calls for a top-up," he beamed, rattling the ice cubes, "a toast to new beginnings."

"Of course," Gerry said, topping up their glasses.

"So tell me, how is Paris this time of year?" Harold asked.

"Wonderful, the best time ever," Gerry smiled, relieved the oven had been turned down. There may be many things to think about yet, but it was good to know his silver ships were allowed to approach the harbour at last.

Katherine grew worried when she noticed Pops and Gramps had been gone for hours. Poor Gerry, he's not just getting roasted, they're slowly turning him on a spit. At last, the masters of the house arrived home and it was her turn to do a little grilling, pouncing on them with Jasper the minute they came through the door.

"Pops, you were gone for ages. What did you do to Gerry? You didn't say anything embarrassing to him I hope?"

"Now pet, don't fuss," Gramps replied, putting his arm around her and giving a comforting squeeze, "your Pops had a few things to sort out, that's all. It's a father's job. You do want a peaceful life, don't you?"

"Well yes … ."

"Then the worst part is over, best to let him get it off his chest now before you two say 'I do'."

"So, what's the prognosis?" she asked hesitantly looking at Pops, who was listening to this conversation with amusement as he took off his coat.

"Looks like I'm gaining another son," he replied. Katherine gave him a big hug. "Let's have another look at the ring," he continued.

"I see everything is straightened out?" Helen noted with a smile, observing the happy reunion in the hallway.

"You could say that," Gramps smiled, "whew, I'm beat. I think I'll go up and take a nap before dinner, c'mon Jasp."

Katherine couldn't wait to call Gerry despite having spent two weeks and another Atlantic crossing together, skipping past Gramps and running up to her room for a little privacy.

"Hi Lancelot, are you all right? My overprotective guardians just came home."

"Let's say your knight in shining armour has braved the fire-breathing dragon and lived to tell the tale," he chuckled.

"That bad?"

"Well, your Pops likes his meat well done and crispy on the outside, but we're okay now."

Down in the den, her parents were engaged in their own discussion.

"I hope you weren't too hard on him, Harold dear," Helen said sitting next to him on the sofa.

"Hard enough, what makes it worse, I actually like the young man. I feel like an ogre, but I had to make sure she would be taken care of. We knew it was coming, but to think she's going to be making her own home, raising a family … my Little Princess has grown up," he said finally.

"Hmm, imagine, you'll be called 'Gramps' soon, and I'll be 'Grandma'."

"Makes you feel old, doesn't it?" he sighed.

"At least you don't have to face 'Grand Gramps' like your father," she smiled. "I think it's wonderful having a romance blossom in the family, makes me feel young again."

ର ❀ ଓ

Exhausted as she felt after the trip, Katherine still couldn't wait to get to the gallery the next day to see how Suzy, Esther and Dennis had fared while she was gone. Since the news broke about her engagement, the place had been hopping the last few weeks, and they were glad Martin and Justine's work had arrived to fill the resulting gaps on the walls, although they dutifully refrained from unpacking it all until she arrived.

"We thought business would be quiet while you were gone, but so much for that," Esther smiled.

"Man, what publicity!" Andre beamed, "I'm booked for yonkers."

"Great for our artwork too, you should get engaged more often," Dennis laughed.

"I wonder what the wedding will do," Suzy noted.

841

"I don't know," Esther replied, "but my hubby is pleased all his works are sold, he plans to take me on that Mediterranean cruise he's been promising for years."

The first visitor Katherine received as the doors opened was good old Christopher Robert Horace Smith with his boyish smile, who wanted to be the first to offer his congratulations on the happy news.

"I didn't know where you were staying," he then added, "I would have warned you that the George V is a ...."

"Favourite hangout for the press. Talk about finding out the hard way," Katherine noted. "So, I guess I've given you plenty of ammunition for your columns."

"You could say that, and I can't wait to meet the French artists whose work you'll be showing. In fact, I'd love to do a whole write-up, their wedding with you as bridesmaid, then the engagement if I may. You did promise an exclusive on everything that happens at the gallery, and that includes you, owner and resident artist," he grinned.

"I guess you're also branching into the society column?"

"An eclectic mix is good, and besides, it might teach Beatrice not to go over my head again. Sad to say, she's had a field day with all of this, heralding you and Mr. Reinold as the most romantic couple in town, gushing about how love has finally conquered all obstacles, and predicting your wedding will be the society event of the year."

"Two weeks, and it's already a circus," she sighed, "but if it helps the gallery and my artists, all right. I did promise you exclusives, didn't I?"

"You're darn toot'n. Umm, any chance your cousin might be willing to do the photos?"

"Yeah sure. I think she might drop by this afternoon."

"Great." He then leaned closer over the desk. "She's not seeing anyone by any chance?"

"No one special that I can think of," Katherine smiled.

"Do you think she'd turn me down if I ask her out?"

"You won't know unless you try."

"So, when's the big unveiling of the new pieces?"

"You mean Martin and Justine's work? They'll be here soon to supervise the proceedings. They may not like being interviewed by Horace the Horrible, they're afraid of being torn to shreds by your critiques, so if you want them to cooperate, be nice, okay?"

"Got it, I shall win them with my wit and charm," he bowed. "I'll see you later then, there's another gallery I have to terrorize first," he declared, waving goodbye and heading out the door.

It was pandemonium after that, everyone she knew was calling or dropping by to extend their congratulations and wish her well while she was trying to show Martin and Justine around and help them display their work. The hardest well-wisher to face was Charlie who came by at lunchtime. He too had learned from the papers just like her parents, and it would happen in Paris of all places. She hardly had time to think about Charlie's reaction during those two happy weeks, but she must face the awkward situation now.

"Um, I guess we'll leave you two for a minute," Martin noted after he and Justine greeted Charlie, "we have more paintings to unpack in the boiler house."

"All right, I can't wait to see your new masterpieces. Hi Kathy, I heard the good news. Congratulations." He wasn't angry or bitter, just obviously resigned. "I hope you will be very happy, and I do mean that."

"Thank you Charlie, this must have been a surprise."

"You know, not really, maybe hearing it on the news this soon," he said with a smile and a slight shrug, "I was afraid how your parents might take it."

"Pops wasn't too pleased, but he's read Gerry the Riot Act, so things might settle down now."

"Nevertheless, my offer still stands: if he ever steps out of line, I'll punch him in the nose." He was actually smiling when he said that, maybe the engagement had helped to give him closure at last.

"Charlie, behave now."

"Okay. Do I get an invitation?"

"Oh, of course, as long as it won't upset you … ."

"Why? Are you afraid I might do something stupid when the reverend gets to 'if anyone here is aware of any reason why these two should not be joined in holy matrimony….'?" he joked.

"No, I'm afraid of Steves actually. I can just hear him yell, 'Run while you still have a chance!'"

"Oh yeah, that would be his cue," he laughed. "Honestly, I'm very happy for you, and I wouldn't want to miss your big day."

"I do want all my nearest and dearest to be there." Awkward as the situation was, he would always be one of her best friends. "That's settled then."

"Okay, I'd better go find Suzy, or we'll miss our lunch hour together."

"All right, I'll see you guys later."

After ten minutes, Justine poked her head through the elevator door.

"Is it safe to come back up now?" she checked.

"Sure. Don't worry, there was no big scene, Charlie's coming to the wedding."

"That's splendid," she said, carrying over two of her floral pictures, Martin followed with two more, the last to go on display.

"Well, they really look good in a gallery like this," he said approvingly.

"I know you tried to tell us, but I didn't think the gallery would be this big," Justine smiled.

"Neither did I," Katherine laughed. "Oh, I'd better warn you guys, Robert Horace is coming later to do an article on your new work, the wedding, and everything."

"We'll be ruined," Justine exclaimed, "so much for our big showing."

"Don't worry, he's only mean on paper, and you won't be ruined, you'll be made for life. I'll have trouble trying to keep you loyal to my gallery with all the offers you'll get."

"You can always count on us," Martin assured her. "You gave us our big break, remember?" Before they could say another word, Lottie came bounding up the stairs.

"There you are, Kathy! Isn't this wonderful? We're going to be sisters!" With that, she grabbed her in a bear hug.

"It's good to see you too. Guys, this is Gerry's sister, Charlotte, but we call her Lottie. Lottie, meet my friends from Paris, you bought a few of their works at the grand opening."

"Of course, I'm very pleased to meet you at last," she said, shaking hands before quietly whispering, "Gerry's going to be here soon, and I hate to cast a cloud, but Mrs. Hunt came with me today. She wanted to congratulate you too, and see the new artwork."

"Oh dear, we nearly got them all hanging too!"

It was a busy afternoon, unhitching the paintings for Mrs Hunt's viewing pleasure, but the newly-weds took the eccentric American lady very well and thought the proceedings were rather funny as she sat in the centre of the lobby, ordering them around and creating colourful havoc as the circle of paintings grew around her in the swivel chair.

"Well Mrs. Hunt, you've beaten me here today," Gerry smiled, making his way through the mass of easels.

"There you are, now don't you dare take anything until I've had my pick, you and your sister are always getting the best pieces before I've had a look-see," Mrs. Hunt had no qualms informing him.

"Fair enough, ladies first. I can see you've had a busy morning," he noted with humour, giving his Kathy a quick kiss on the cheek. "Any chance you and your friends can escape for lunch?"

"Not a chance," she sighed, nodding to Mrs. Hunt who was busy eyeing one of Martin's portrait collages of famous painters and figures from history. "Charlie has taken Suzy out, so we're a little short-handed now, and I must leave Esther and Dennis off after she comes back. I hope you don't mind, but I've given Robert Horace an exclusive on our engagement news, he wants to do a full piece on Martin and Justine's visit, and everything that happened in Paris."

"Urrr, we're not finished with the press yet," he groaned, "that's okay, I suppose we'll have to give him official photos too."

"Yes, he wants Stephie to do them."

"Okay, but I've got to get back to work after lunch, I've been gone for well over two months you know."

"Oh that's right, and I don't know when Stephie … never mind, everything seems to be sorting itself out," she smiled, watching Stephie and Christopher enter at the same time, they must have bumped into each other on the way to the gallery.

Katherine introduced her friends to the art critic and family photographer, and was amused when Justine whispered in French that Robert wasn't exactly how she pictured him. Their lunch hour was busy giving interviews and posing for official photos, Mrs. Hunt ignoring the activities, demanded to see more pictures in the middle of the hubbub, throwing incredulous comments at the unnecessary presence of the press.

"Kathy deary, I don't know why you allow him in here," nodding to Horace, "his recorder seems to play back nothing but tripe."

"Hmm, my readers seem to relish a little every now and then," he replied waggishly before whispering to Martin and Justine, "don't worry, nothing I write is personal, but if anyone asks you, I'll deny I said that," he winked. Stephie smiled as she snapped a few more photos of the new artwork. She then posed her cousin and Gerry by the new brass gates on the stairs, the ring in full view.

"Already at the altar rails are we?" Gerry joked, looking at the ornate security feature originally intended for a church. She had forgotten he hadn't seen the flamboyant gates.

"Shh, don't make me laugh, or I'll mess up the picture. Stephie already gets mad at me for blinking with the flash. That reminds me, I've something to show you when we're done here."

The photos taken, she slipped with him into the office where they could greet each other in private, then showed him the black and white pictures with the coloured tints taken of them before he left on his travels.

"My, look at us," he said quietly, "our first pictures together."

"I know," she said, watching him browse through the emotive images. There was always something evocative, majestic about black and white photographs, perhaps it was the way the film caught the reflective nuances of light and darkness, details were clearer, reflections brighter, emotions unmistakable.

"These are beautiful, I had no idea she was following us around, your cousin did a wonderful job. We should have these framed," he noted, slipping his arm around her. "May I have one for my desk?"

"You can have as many as you like, they're yours too."

"Hmm, moments in time caught forever when we were young and carefree … ."

"Carefree? Not exactly my Prince, I've got a handful out there today," she smiled, nodding towards the door, Mrs. Hunt's voice just audible through the wooden barrier.

"True enough. Tell me, will you still love your Lancelot when he's old, grey and saggy in the middle?"

"Gerry," she chuckled, "question is, will you still love me when I'm old, grey and baggy."

"Of course, my Princess will always be beautiful."

"Just listen to us, already worried about hitting our mid-life crises, and we haven't started our life together yet. Is this what an engagement does to you?"

"I guess so," he laughed.

"You know, we shouldn't worry about such things, I think love always makes a person age gracefully, and since we have plenty of that to last us into eternity, we should be quite distinguished when we reach seventy."

"You think so? Hmm, just like a couple of old Stradivariuses and Rembrandts, we shall get better with age. Speaking of ageing treasures: when were you planning to have your official museum floor ready? The fourth floor I mean."

"Umm, well, I was thinking it would be time to start that soon, maybe in a few months. The plans are done and the wiring for the security system is already waiting, it's just a matter of building the partition walls and planning the decorating. Why do you ask?"

"I've been doing some thinking. Remember when we went to choose your ring you told me you didn't want something you had to lock away?"

"Of course, how can I forget it?"

"Well, I've been looking around my apartment and realized you are right, and not just about the diamond. What's the point of having a priceless collection tucked away that no one sees? I mean, paintings stashed in security closets, *objets d'art* hidden in safes, pieces thousands of miles away in a holiday apartment. How useless! These things should be seen and enjoyed, I've always said art should not be tip-toed around, and it's time I put my words into action. How would you like to have the Walsingham Gallery be the sole, permanent venue to display my, or rather, our, entire collection?"

"*What?*"

"Well, it'll be yours too, I just thought it made sense to have it here instead of at the Met or the Brooklyn Museum … ."

"You mean the *entire* collection?"

"Sure, why not? I think you have enough space. This will be fun, I have lots of things you haven't seen yet, and I can call back the pieces I've loaned at the Met. Of course, getting the stuff out of my Paris apartment is not going to be easy, export licenses are going to be needed, there's only so much I can do with souvenir stickers," he chuckled.

"Oh Gerry, I don't know what to say … but are you sure you want to do this? After the graffiti attack and everything?"

"That was a once-off, and it could have happened anywhere, in any museum. Chances are we'll not face trouble like that again."

"But to strip your apartments … ," she observed.

"Well, naturally there may be a few pieces we'll want to keep just for ourselves, but as you say, this will be months down the road yet, and when we *do* begin making plans to build a life together, you want a clear canvas for your home decorating, right? I can live with a few bare walls in the meantime."

"Gerry," she sighed, holding him close, "this is generosity bordering on madness. You're too good to me. Why do you want to spoil me like this?"

"Because you don't want things, you don't want to be spoiled, and you mean it." She looked into his eyes, now she understood. Never before had he been certain he was loved for his own sake, and how she wished she could let him know how much she loved him, words never seemed adequate. "There! When you look at me like that, I know it's real. You are the one in ten million who cherishes the man more than his fortune."

"Oh it's more than real, so much more. I'm so glad you can see what I feel because I can't say it often enough."

Although she could not see her own eyes, she understood what captivated him, certain her expression was a mirror image of how he looked at her: that same deep searching gaze he had when they walked out of the jeweller's in Paris, an instant when all barriers slipped away and she alone was allowed to peer into his soul. It was not the first time, it happened many times, occurred more frequently, and on each occasion, it was as if that enchanted moment they shared on the bridge was rekindled with a deeper intensity.

"You know what's ironic? Falling in love is very real, but I used to shake my head when people talked about soul mates, poor deluded individuals grasping at some supernatural ideal not intended for mortals but sounded pretty in a poetry book. Then, we met, and everything changed, the cynic has become the converted, the sceptic, an ardent zealot." To hear him speak like this moved her deeply, that she could evoke a confession like this was almost unfathomable were it not for the fact she knew how he felt.

"Do you think this happens to everyone who falls in love?"

"I'm not sure, but this is not like anything I've ever felt before. I suppose you think it strange to hear a man reveal his true feelings? Just letting them spring forth with no reserve?" he asked, feeling vulnerable to her response as though she had the power to strike a fatal blow with her words and he quietly awaited his fate.

"No, it would be tragic if you couldn't share your thoughts and feelings with me, especially as we're going to spend the rest of our lives together. Love is supposed to be based on trust, and trust on love, it's something rare and beautiful when people can confide in each other without fearing what the other person will think."

"But you understand, don't you?" he asked tentatively.

"Yes, we aren't ourselves anymore, are we? Not our solitary, individual selves like before, I feel an invisible transformation taking place, and I begin to wonder; is it possible we are melding into a single awareness? Whatever is happening, love, it's deep, and there are no words for it, perhaps it dares go beyond love."

"Katherine, would you like to know what I told your father and grandfather when they asked how I felt about you? All I could say was, 'I am her, and she is me'."

"Oh, that's it! That's it exactly," she exclaimed, clasping him tight.

A knock on the door broke their quiet moment, reminding them there was another world outside demanding their attention. It might just as well have been the land-cracking rumble of an earthquake.

"Sorry, but Mrs. Hunt's wondering when you guys are coming out," Suzy informed them.

"In a minute," Katherine called, "oh, I miss our weeks in Paris already."

"We must be brave, chin up, we can't hide away in here forever," he said, brushing his finger under her chin. "Think of all the fun you're going to have refurbishing the fourth floor and putting all that artwork on display. If you need help fixing it up, I'll be happy to foot the expense."

"Oh thank you so much, but I've saved for this project, and besides, the gallery must be able to support itself. I do appreciate your help, but you'll be giving enough as it is with the collections, and while I want you to be a part of everything, this is … how do I say it?"

"Your trailblazing, independent enterprise. I know exactly how you feel."

"But there is something you can help me with, for instance, I wouldn't know where to find proper cases for some of your display pieces, like your Roman coins. I had your vase in a regular gift display, and it nearly bit the dust. We will need some museum grade cases for public viewing."

"Of course, that's no problem. I can help you pick them out."

"Oh dear, I just realized, I can't tell my parents about this, not right away. I haven't been to Sotheby's yet, and their feelings might get hurt."

"That's right, we'll have to sign you up for their catalogue and get you searching for something you want."

"It's complicated, I mean, I'd feel bad taking them up on their offer now that we'll have weddings plans not too far in the future."

"Hmm, maybe you should talk it over with them, see what they say."

"All right."

A second knock on the door.

"We're coming," Katherine called once more. "Well, back to the whirlwind."

Mrs. Hunt swivelled around as they emerged from the office.

"Well dearies, thought you two love birds were never coming out. When's the big day? No one seems to know yet."

"That hasn't been decided, but you'll be one of the first to know," Gerry smiled.

"Hey, I hope some members of the press are on your invitation list too," Horace Smith called out.

"We might have *one* reporter on there somewhere," Katherine laughed, "just as long as he promises to behave and won't terrorize the guests for any juicy gossip."

"No sweat, Horace shall be a perfect angel."

Katherine couldn't help but feel amused with a tinge of chagrin, already the invitation list was making itself, she wondered what might happen when the planning actually went into full swing.

With Suzy back from lunch, it was time to let Esther off. Gerry didn't want to leave Katherine without lunch and decided to join her for some of Andre's special 'take out' that was promptly delivered to them at the front desk, although Katherine could only get a few mouthfuls in with all the conversations and the art première in the lobby. There was so much to get caught up on, and with all her friends present, plus Lottie bantering with Mrs. Hunt for who-gets-what painting, it was almost like a party. Of course, everyone wondered when they would have the engagement bash, but Katherine didn't know, soon enough though, there was so much to sort out, and besides, their parents hadn't met yet. They could only cross one bridge at a time.

03 ❀ 80

As expected, the matriarchs of the families did not waste time planning the initial meeting of the clans for that Sunday. It was a big decision wondering where they would all gather for the first time, Oak Meadows or Stoneyvale, and the latter was finally decided upon, since they would in all probability have a second get-together and visit the other parents' home in due time. It was exciting and yet nerve-wracking, wondering how they would get along.

Good thing they had Martin and Justine to help keep them sane that week. Katherine had promised to show them around New York, although it was difficult getting away from the gallery. Why was it they could fit everything in when they attended college? Another one of life's mysteries she noted. She was glad nobody minded her taking a few days off, and when she couldn't go around with them, Gerry was happy to step in one day, the Professor another.

850

"Kathy, your Professor knows so much about the city, not to mention the art," Martin told her one day when they came back from their visit to the Metropolitan, "I think twenty years of college courses got crammed into my head today."

"I know, he's something else, isn't he?"

"I have so many notes and sketches, it's not funny," Justine said, showing her books, "I can't wait to see what New York will look like in a sea of flowers."

"Oh that will be spectacular," Suzy replied, she and Justine both liked experimenting with optical illusions and had become close over the past few days.

"It's hard to believe our week here is almost over," Martin sighed, "we had such a wonderful time, it's a shame we couldn't stay longer."

"But you will come to the wedding I hope?"

"Oh of course! We should have more paintings ready by then," Justine smiled, clapping her hands in her ebullient way.

"But you don't have to wait if you don't want to, just send what you have anyway." Katherine was going to have a time keeping the gallery filled once the museum space moved to the fourth floor.

"All right, but speaking of weddings, I hope the Meeting of the Parents goes all right for you tomorrow," Justine noted, "the worst will be over when that hurdle is passed."

Katherine and Gerry were glad her family would see the Stoneyvale estate in May when the trees lost their twisted, witching look and the garden sprang back into life. Sophia met them at the door and cordially invited them in, forgetful of another family member who also wanted to offer his greetings.

"Arrr! New crew! New crew! Perrrmission to come aboard!" Sinbad bobbed, after he landed on Harold's shoulder. Harold simply stared at the feathered creature whose large beak was too close to his nose for comfort, while Helen turned white and held her breath.

"Hey! I always wanted one of those," Gramps beamed, oblivious to Helen's near marble complexion.

"Oops, be good now, Sinbad," Katherine replied, plucking him off her Pop's shoulder, "I'm sorry Mom, I forgot to warn you he might be loose," she said apologetically, afraid this might jeopardize the introductions with the in-laws to be.

"Oh my, are you all right?" Sophia asked with concern, "He can be a terrible nuisance, I hope he didn't frighten you, he doesn't bite."

"He's hand reared," Gerry added.

"I …I'm all right," Helen finally whispered, "it's not biting, it's feathers … I can't be near feathers…"

"Mom has a phobia about that," Katherine explained, noticing Sinbad had learned a new phrase in Gerry's voice, 'Katie, Katie, she's my matie'. She would have found that funny if the boisterous feather ball hadn't created a scene. "Gerry, you'd better put him in his playpen."

"Okay, come on you scallywag, in the lock-up you go," Gerry said, carefully clutching the struggling bird who detested the mention of 'lock-up'.

"Arrr! No brig! No brig!"

"Can I come with you?" Gramps asked, "I heard these grey ones are great talkers."

"Sure, he's got his own room in the back, we don't like putting him in a cage," Gerry replied as he led the way.

Hearing the commotion, Richard came out to greet the guests.

"Sorry about Sinbad, Mrs. Walsingham, he loves to meet people," he explained, shaking hands. "Are we missing a guest?"

"Oh, my Gramps has gone with Gerry, he's fascinated with parrots, but he can't have one," Katherine informed him after introducing him to her parents.

"My wife suffers from pteronophobia," Harold explained.

"Sounds serious," Richard noted. Sophia explained it was Sinbad's feathers that caused the panic.

"I know how you feel, Mrs. Walsingham," Lottie replied, "he used to bother me too until I started holding him, he's quite cuddly really."

"I'm all right dear," Helen smiled, relieved the grey mass of pinions was removed from view, "he seems friendly, but I'll refrain from cuddling him for the present."

"Well, let's go on in and have a drink before dinner, shall we?" Richard offered. "Stupid bird, we love him, but certainly not a nice introduction, giving everyone a shock at the door."

Sinbad may have given them a shock, but he was a great ice-breaker even if he caused Helen to freeze up momentarily, helping to ease everyone over the formalities and engage them in polite conversation. The topic foremost on everyone's mind was the unexpected engagement and the wonderful expectations of the wedding sometime in the future, eventually extending to more general topics. Of course, the Grand Tour of the manor was not to be missed, so Sophia did the honours before supper. By that time, everyone was more relaxed and both parties had realized the other was likeable indeed, wondering how they had not managed to meet before, considering all the social functions they attended over the years in the city.

While everyone was heading back towards the dining room, Katherine, Gerry and Lottie conveniently lagged behind in the library to discuss how the evening was going so far.

"They all seem to be getting along very well, and just for the record, I saw Mom put out the silver ships," Lottie smiled, "and that's not all, we're having the heavy armoury cutlery tonight."

"Fantastic! It seems our house has signed an eternal peace treaty with your house," Gerry laughed, turning to Katherine, "it's been a long time since that set came out, we're made for life. Of course, our parents already approved of the engagement, so Mom is doing her best to show her approval."

"She needn't worry, my parents have given their blessing too. In fact, I have a feeling our in-laws are going to be good friends, especially our mothers, which will be a relief."

"I think you're right," Lottie nodded, "and I'm so glad. It would be unbearable if there was antagonism, the holidays would be just dreadful, wouldn't they? I just wish we knew what to do about Pete, Dad can be so stubborn, but perhaps he may come around," she noted with a sigh. Gerry didn't say anything, but pursed his lips with regret, this would be one difficulty to resolve. With his father still at odds with his brother, he didn't know what to do, to think one or the other would be compelled to stay away from his wedding was hard to swallow.

Katherine didn't have to read his thoughts to sense the pain and disappointment this estrangement between Richard and his eldest son was having on the youngest brother who loved them both and refused to take sides. No doubt Gerry wanted Pete to marry them, but had said nothing to her, not yet anyway, considering how everything was happening so fast. He probably didn't want to burden her with too much to think about at one time, but she had been doing her own thinking too these past weeks. It was impossible not to muse about the service they might have once they had become engaged, it reminded her of *Love and Marriage*; you couldn't have one without the other, and so it was with an engagement and wedding plans, they naturally followed the big announcement. Already she knew she wanted an intimate celebration and was glad he felt the same way, but had not told him she wanted Pete to marry them.

To think his brother might officiate was a wonderful thing; not many people had a family member who could do the honours and really become an integral part of their big day, it was his spirituality that helped to make up her mind. Before she knew about Peter's dream, she had always felt the unseen had somehow put its mark on him, and it didn't matter what church he was in, God must be with him, and believed without a doubt that whatever vows he witnessed and blessed were indeed sealed for eternity. She hadn't told Gerry yet because she needed to be certain this is what she wanted, but try as she might, she couldn't see anyone else standing with them at the altar. Would her parents be upset? Knowing Pops, probably, but she knew this was how it was to be.   Her heart went to Gerry just then, already feeling like a member of his family, loving each member more every time she visited or met them, and now had to face the prospect of one member being forced to keep their distance. She would talk about this with Gerry when the time was right, and for the moment, gave his arm a reassuring squeeze to let him know they would find a solution, which he understood and appreciated, patting her hand gently. It was strangely comforting to realize how fast they could communicate with a mere gesture or look, they had no need to exchange words.

After dinner, the men went off to have their customary chat, and cigar for those who smoked, the woman went to the Rose Room for coffee and chocolates. Katherine and Gerry slipped away to be alone. At Stoneyvale it was not difficult to find a room where they could be by themselves. The library had quickly become their private retreat and they seemed to gravitate in that general direction whenever they had the opportunity.

"Well, everything is going well tonight, Dad and your Gramps are having a great time swapping stories, and our mothers seem to be as thick as thieves," Gerry noted, settling into the leather sofa made comfortable by much use over the years, wishing it was winter so he could have a cheery fire blazing

"I know Pops is quiet, but I can tell he's enjoying himself too, it's the way he leans back in his chair relaxed, gone is that look like he's on point duty."

"I figured that," Gerry laughed, "he had the same expression when he got through roasting me last week."

"Was it really bad?"

"Well, it's what I expected from a father who cares, basically questions on if we had discussed things in detail yet, but at that stage we hadn't, so he didn't have too much to whip me with."

"I see. When should we discuss 'things'? We should not be rushed, but with everyone already asking for invitations, mothers who can't wait to pick out table settings, leaving things unsaid makes it feel like its all hanging over us.”

“Now is just as good a time as any, I suppose. Have you thought about where you want to live for instance? Would you like to have a house with a garden, something like Oak Meadows?”

“I’ve thought about it, but I don’t think it would work for us, we’d be too far from the city and away from everyone, plus a house seems like so much to handle when we’re just starting out. I wouldn’t mind moving into your apartment.”

“Now Kathy, I don’t want you feel you have to move there just to please me.”

“Oh no, Paris gave me a lot to think about, I liked being with you at the apartment there, I don’t think it would be much different here. Besides, it’s a very practical location, we’re close to our parents and work, and I love the view. It seems the right place.”

“All right, but you know we may be facing the old homestead one day,” he said, looking around the room. “How do you feel about that? Just impressions for now, no decisions.”

“I think we’ll be comfortable,” she said, nestling with him on the couch, “I understand there will be a lot to manage, but it’s nothing to panic over, is it? Your parents seem happy here, and I know you love the place deep down, I don’t see why we couldn’t be happy here too.”

“I think we’ll be happy wherever we are, although I was wondering how you might feel if something happened to one of my parents, God forbid, and we had to move in to take care of one of them. You don’t mind living with an in-law or two?”

“Hey, you’re talking to girl whose Gramps lives with her father and mother, I’m all for taking care of family, and I really do love your family, they don’t feel like ‘in-laws’.   What about you? Something could happen the other way around, I wouldn’t want one of my parents left alone, however, there is Steves, it stands to reason he’ll take over Oak Meadows one day, but just in case … .”

“Why Kathy, they could move on in, perhaps they won’t want to leave Oak Meadows, but we certainly have plenty of room in Stoneyvale, we’d be one big family puttering around the manor, and still have our privacy. Well, I don’t know what’s going to happen in the future, but I want you to know I’m not going to be one of those skulking husbands who resents having the in-laws around, or I hope not anyway,” he laughed.

“Only if they tell us how to organize our spoon drawer,” she smiled.

"Maybe then. In the meantime, we'll have the apartment, and I want you to decorate it anyway you like. It was fine for a bachelor, and I didn't spend too much time there. Too much of the interior designer stamped on it I think, it could certainly use whatever you ladies do to make a place a home. Well, decision number one, that wasn't difficult, it looks like we've been doing some thinking already," he noted. "Now, do you want to decorate first before we have the wedding, or after?"

"I don't know … I suppose it would be nice to have it ready, but I won't know what to do with the place until I'm actually living there and get a feel for it."

"Well, we can wait and fix it then, no big deal, and besides, you'll be too busy with wedding plans, not to mention the fourth floor at the gallery will be a big project, you'll have enough on your plate without having to worry about the apartment."

"Don't forget, I have to start painting the *Morning Glory* for your Dad, I really will be busy."

"That's right, I almost forgot. You poor struggling artist, no financial troubles, but no time for your art," he noted whimsically.

"I know, if it's not one, it's the other. I'll never get to my painting at this rate. I've got to paint to be an artist, or I'm just a gallery owner."

"I may be to blame, I've been distracting you from your work, adding more remodelling projects when I was the one who warned you when we first met not to let the business kill your artistic spirit. I don't want to do that either."

"*You* kill my artistic spirit? Gerry, don't think like that, since when did love ever kill artistic creativity? But, you *are* a most welcome distraction," she noted with amusement. "This is funny: we know we want to be married, we've pretty much planned where we want to live, it seems like things are falling into place very fast."

"I know, but there are many things to think about yet."

"True." They sat quietly for a moment, listening to the clock on the mantelpiece ticking. Strange how the 'right moments' to discuss deeper matters also came faster than expected. "Gerry, I've also been thinking about the wedding ceremony, I really would like Pete to marry us."

"Do you mean that, Kathy?" he asked with quiet surprise.

"Yes I do, I know how much it would mean to you."

"Don't make a decision like that just for my sake," he noted. "Do you know what that would involve? What would be asked of you?"

"Not really, but I do know he has the authority to marry us, of course, we really marry each other, but I know with Pete officiating, the ceremony won't be a mouthful of words like some generic formula."

"I understand how you feel, I'm not one for civil ceremonies, but Kathy, that means marrying in the Catholic Church. We'd have to have special permission to marry, of course, it's rarely denied, but for you, it would mean more than just staying away from communion … our children would have to be raised Catholic, it's part of the agreement."

"Oh … I see." She was quiet for a moment, mulling this over. Now she really did have something to think about.

"Of course," he eventually continued, "you're right when you say we marry each other, I could get married in your church … ."

"You could," she noted, then shaking her head slowly, "you believe in your church even if you do have doubts in certain areas, I couldn't ask you to that. Would you feel right being married in a church you *completely* doubted?"

"Well, I … suppose not. God help us, we really are caught in the middle."

They sat in silence again, musing upon the situation they now had to face.

"I would like Pete to marry us," she stated quietly.

"But don't you have questions about our church too? If you couldn't ask me to go to your church, I can't very well ask that of you. Let's face it," he continued, a little discomfited, "I'd be a hypocrite to ask you. I haven't been to church in years, and I can't very well turn around and expect you to agree to Catholic conditions when I, a supposed member, haven't exactly lived up to par."

She could sense his difficulty talking about this subject.

"Gerry, I know it takes a lot for you to admit that," she said, holding his arm a little tighter, "and I appreciate your frankness. I'm not judging. If it's any comfort, I'm no great shakes with my church either."

"You? I bet you've never missed a Sunday service," he noted with surprise.

"I used to go because Pops insisted, but now, I just feel guilty if I don't go. It's better than nothing, but it would be better to go because we want to. I'm not a religious person, I believe in God and the Bible all right, but … I know the balance is wanting."

"That's some declaration for a girl with traditional expectations," he observed with astonishment. "The balance is wanting? Far from it."

"Don't put me on some pedestal Gerry, I'm not perfect, that's what I'm saying."

"No one is perfect, but you want to be, you want to do what's right, that's half the battle. You know, for the first time, I wish we were atheists, we could just have a civil ceremony, and that would be it," he sighed.

"But we're not, and since we believe the unseen joins a couple, a secular rite performed by a government isn't good enough. The state can't *bless* a union, only God can."

"You're a deep thinker, aren't you?"

"Socrates has corrupted me," she joked, "but I do know, I want Pete to marry us."

"Can you tell me why? Apart from being my brother I mean, it might help us." She thought for a moment.

"I know that God is everywhere, sees everything, that He works through everyone, but for the first time I sense and feel it in a more tangible way with Pete, and of all people I know, he's the one who would really help us when we are married, not that our families wouldn't be there, but there's more to a marriage that we can't see now, and he has the answers. You don't know this, and I can't tell you very much, but you've met my friends from Paris. Well, they hit a terrible rough patch a couple of years ago, and it nearly ruined everything for them: if I hadn't met Pete, they wouldn't be married right now, and I'm full sure their lives would be in absolute chaos. He still keeps in contact with them, and I've seen the difference his counselling has made. I'm not saying we'd ever have the same problems, but I know God is really working through your brother, and … I'd just like him to be there for us like that. If only there was … ."

Suddenly, she fell silent. If she really felt that way, didn't it make sense that God just might be with the Church that Peter belonged to?

"Are you all right?"

"I'm just thinking," she said quietly. He left her to her thoughts. At last he spoke:

"Oh Katherine, to think we love each other, our families seem to accept each other, and in the end, it might be our religions that may keep us apart."

"No, Gerry. We're meant to be together," she said calmly but emphatically, "if God is in religion, and since He blesses a marriage, then our religions can't and won't keep us apart. 'Let no man put asunder', right? Our churches will even grant us permission, it's just a matter of…what we want our children to learn, isn't that it?"

"I suppose that's it when you boil it down."

"Then I suppose I'd better find out what your church teaches, I won't be able to make any decision until then."

"Just like that, huh? What if you don't like what it teaches?"

"I won't know until I find out."

"Kathy, I don't want you to feel forced into accepting what my church demands … ."

"No, to be honest … this is not the first time I've thought about it … you're not the only one with doubts about their religion, I've got a few questions of my own, and since our marriage depends on sorting this out somehow, I'll look into your church first. You really don't believe in mine anyway, do you?"

"Will you be offended if I tell you why?"

"No, please, you can tell me anything," she assured him.

"Basically, I don't believe the monarchy of England had the right to break away from the church in Rome. If you think about it, it broke away and became its own institution tied to one nation, and if it really belongs to the one universal church as it preaches, it wouldn't be setting up *Anglican* churches in other countries but only run the churches on its own soil and within its own jurisdiction under the rule of the king or queen. Then, when you look at later history, things became worse over here with the American Revolution, Anglicans didn't want to stay under the religious leadership of the King, so Episcopalian churches came to be, yet continued to stay with the Anglican communion. It's a paradox isn't it? Protestants don't know who they really belong to."

"There's something to that when you think of it," she mused, "and I don't disagree with you, the universal church is suppose to be united, and Christ founded the church, not the British monarchy, right? I always thought looking at the beginning of things would shed light, and I keep coming back to one conclusion."

"What's that?"

"The pride and lust of a king are bad foundation stones for a church."

"Whew! That's a mouthful. You really are serious about this, aren't you?"

"Whatever concerns God is a serious matter, it's just … I'm still not sure if your church is the right one either, that is … not until I'm with Peter," her voice trailed.

"I think I know what you mean, sometimes my brother frightens me, often I think he can see and read my very soul, and I haven't got a secret left in the world, and yet … ."

"He's strangely comforting at the same time, like you don't mind him seeing through you."

"Yeah, I guess that's it."

"Gerry, before we get stressed out, we should really talk to him. He would help us, I know it."

He sighed deeply, decisions he didn't want to face right then were thrust upon him.

"There's more I should tell you: I have to be a practising member of the Church for six months at least before I, and therefore, we, can receive the sacrament of marriage."

"I see, well, all the more reason to speak with Pete then," she sagely observed.

"Aren't you worried about what might be my deepest, darkest scruples?" he asked, suddenly curious.

"Yes and no," she said after a thoughtful pause, " 'yes' because I want to help, I wonder what could be so terrible or difficult you won't go to a church you believe in, and 'no' because I should mind my own business. I don't think I'm knowledgeable enough or qualified to help, and so I shouldn't pry, I might only make matters worse. I don't think we're supposed to meddle with someone's conscience."

He didn't quite know what to say to that and kept silent, the ticking clock continuing its quiet rhythm. Already she was moving him in ways she could hardly imagine. For years, his mother and sister worried about him, and it now took his Princess to finally make him consider talking to his brother. Did he want to, that was the question. Katherine was right, the purity of intention was everything, wanting to do things right because you wanted to, not because you felt you had to. He was in a quandary, but if he was really serious about spending his life with her, and he was, very much so, the least he could do was see his brother as she advised, especially as she was willing to investigate the teachings of his church.

"Well, when should we talk to Pete?" he asked at last. "Should we do this together, or would you like to speak to him on your own?"

"Umm, I don't know how this works," she admitted, "maybe together first, then he can advise what to do."

"All right. Oh," he then realized, his worries resurfacing, "let's say you agree to all of this, what do we do about my Dad? I'm afraid he might not be willing to come to the wedding if … ."

"I know, but one thing at a time. Let's not worry about it now. I don't think he'll want to miss his son's wedding. Gerry, can we keep this to ourselves for now until we decide?"

"Sure. Are you afraid what your family might say?"

"Oh, I know what they'll say, they won't be very happy, but it's not just that. We're going to need time and space to figure this out. It really concerns no one else, so we need to do this on our own."

"I understand. It'll be enough just facing Pete with his x-ray vision," he half joked. "I'll call him, see when he can meet with us."

A gentle knock on the door brought them back to the present, it was Lottie.

"There you are, everyone is wondering where you've disappeared to."

"Oh dear, we've been very rude, leaving everyone for this long," Katherine noticed, checking the clock on the mantle.

"We'd better go make our apologies," Gerry noted. It was amazing how time no longer seemed to exist when they were in their own little world, oblivious to the larger world around them. Reluctantly, they left their comfortable retreat, notwithstanding they were discussing a serious matter. At least they had resolved to do something about it.

☘

The next day Katherine was busy in the office catching up on paperwork when she was interrupted by another visitor who came to offer his congratulations, Fr. Peter.

"Hi Kathy, do you mind if I come in?"

"Oh no, please take me away from my bills," she laughed, "it's good to see you, Pete."

"I know I congratulated you on the phone, but it's about time I do it in person," he said, dropping his large briefcase and giving her a brotherly hug, "and I wanted to see your friends before they head back home Wednesday."

"That's great, they hoped they might get to see you, they're meeting me for lunch today, and the Professor is taking them out on another tour of the city since I can't get away from here."

"Wonderful, would you mind if I joined you?"

"Oh please do. In fact, I need to speak with you now that you're here," she added quietly.

"I heard, Gerry called me last night, I had the feeling he wanted to book me right away before he lost the nerve to call. I believe you had a very serious discussion yesterday," he noted.

"Yes, we would like you to marry us, but there are a few things that might pose a problem, especially where I'm concerned with your Church, it frowns on mixed marriages, and permission would be required in our case."

"That's true, but I understand you want to learn what we believe first before making any decision."

"That's right, especially as I would have to agree to raise our children Catholic."

"Very well, but there are other conditions for you to be married: you must allow him to practise his faith, and he is required to share our faith with you, but I don't think that will be a problem as you wish to learn by your own volition," he smiled. "The irony is he doesn't go to church, and there cannot be a sanctified marriage without that, which is why I need you to do something for me, or rather, for him."

"Me?"

"Yes, I've arranged the joint meeting you both requested for this Wednesday evening at his apartment, but he has no idea I'm here today, and I need you to keep that a secret."

"Um, okay."

"I also need you not to show up that night," he added, "don't call him, and don't answer the phone if he happens to call to see where you are or what might be holding you up."

"What? That's weird, but …okay, you're the boss."

"At the same time, I'm not ignoring you, we should get the ball rolling as they say."

"All right. What do I need to do? Enrol in one of your Sunday school classes?" she wondered.   She figured he might send her to lessons like most converts would be expected to attend.

"No."

"No?"

"No. Now I want to make one thing clear," he continued gently, "I'm not here to proselytise you, force your will in any way. I will help inform you on what we believe, and you just ponder upon it. A classroom environment and leaning answers by rote is one way to be introduced to our beliefs in God and the Church, but it's sometimes a soulless operation. There must be time for discovery, reflection, meditation and discussion, especially as you are a soul that likes to search for answers *ala* Socrates," he smiled. "After reading your little dissertation on Freedom, you are quite capable of deep reflection. So, while our church teaches via preaching, I'm going to make an exception in your case and try some books first. In them you will find all our teachings of the faith," he said, opening his briefcase.

"This is everything in a nutshell," he declared, handing her a copy of the old Baltimore Catechism from the mid 1800s. "Now, its questions and answers are in a rather dry form, but if you want information with no fluffing or vague rambling, this is it. Second, this little beauty has everything that's in the Baltimore book, but with detailed explanations," he declared, taking out an old tome from the 1920s. "I find it the easiest to read and it's the best we have to offer until we get the new book the church is preparing for publication." Katherine gasped.

"Oh dear, that's very big," she noted, reading the title silently, *'The Catechism Explained: An Exhaustive Exposition of the Catholic Religion'*. "Gee, it's almost eight hundred pages," she said, flipping through the book.

"I know, but I don't expect you to read these overnight. What I want you to do is find a quiet place where you can concentrate, say a prayer to help you get started, it doesn't have to be long, it can be in your own words. Then read a portion each day starting from the beginning, and just think about what you've read. If you find something you want to drill me about, then write it down and have your questions and disputations ready," he smiled, a twinkle in his eye. "I'll stop by every few days and we can have it out over Andre's excellent French roast."

"That's it?"

"Yep. That's about it for now. Of course, there are some church rules in these old books that are obsolete, for instance, a number of the fasting regulations have been lessened, and I must warn you if you are a feminist, there are explanations and terms that will appear insulting, so don't be afraid to have it out with me there too. Discuss everything with me, all right?"

"Okay. You mean like 'Man' being used as a collective term for the human race?"

"Yes, plus there are other issues, like the obedience a wife shows to her husband, I get pounded with that all the time, so I will explain what is meant there."

"Well, I'm not a die-hard feminist in the sense I have to trample all over men, and I'm not pushed out about those so-called politically incorrect words, but I have always wondered about the obedience thing, I mean, God didn't want women to be treated as slaves or servants."

"No, He didn't. Are we slaves when we obey authority placed over us?"

"Well no, not if the authority is good," she reasoned.

"It's the same with marriage, God declared the husband has authority over the family, like all units in society that require government, but he must not misuse his authority and become a tyrant. As his wife will become one with him, he must consider her wishes too, but the wife must follow her husband's decisions for the family unit providing they are not sinful."

"The Bible describes this authority as 'dominion', and it's given as a punishment," Katherine observed.

"True, there's no denying that, but the husband must not make it more so. Would you like to know why that was declared?"

"Well, I know it's because she tempted Adam and he ate the forbidden apple."

"Yes, she tempted Adam and he disobeyed God, but there's more, God doesn't give punishments without due cause, the Bible tells us we are punished according to the nature of our sins, obviously to help us realize what we did wrong. If you read Genesis carefully, you will notice that God gave the commandment not to eat from the Tree of Knowledge to Adam before he ever created Eve. When God made her and brought her to Adam, it was Adam who declared the institution of marriage as God intended. Therefore, he already had authority from God to pass on His commandants to Eve, and if you've noticed, you don't see God speaking directly to Eve in the beginning, except for the blessing to increase and multiply, Adam was given the honour of teaching her. She must have learned about the command not to eat from the tree from Adam, so when she listened to the serpent and believed it over her husband, she not only disbelieved God, she mistrusted Adam and put her faith in the words of a lesser creature. In punishment, she would now be compelled by divine decree to acknowledge the authority of her husband."

"Wow, I guess I can't really argue with that," she mused quietly.

"Kathy, are you afraid Gerry might be harsh or will mistreat you?"

"No, I've never seen him lose his temper or get really angry, and from how we've been able discuss and decide certain things already, I know he wants my input in everything, he's not demanding. He's very considerate. Actually, I'm beginning to wonder what I'll be expected to obey."

"I see. It's true, he's not the type who blows his top, he sulks a bit and bottles things up until he can think things through. When he's troubled, he doesn't like to talk until he's ready, but I'm glad to see he already confides in you. In fact, it's a good sign you are already working as partners, it's a good start. Basically, the idea of yielding to his authority as husband means not to do anything that would affect or involve him and the children you will have without discussing it first and hearing his decision.

He told me he wants you to continue running the gallery, so I know he won't be overbearing and cut off your freedom to do what's necessary for your business for one thing, but having said that, being married means you just can't decide things on your own and only for yourself, and that goes for him too. Don't worry, I'll be sure to tell him that," he laughed. Sometimes she didn't know what to make of Peter, very serious with a dash of good humour thrown in.

"I understand," she smiled, "it's all common sense, isn't it?"

"Yes, pretty much. Of course, we'll discuss this in more detail during the marriage counselling sessions when we get to them. It's required in our church now to ensure that a couple aren't rushing into things without having all the consequences of this state of life explained to them. I know, people often complain to me how could we priests know what marriage is all about when we don't have wives and children of our own, but mostly, we concentrate on the spiritual aspects and what God expects."

"Hmm, well, these sessions are a good idea actually. Will you be taking care of that?"

"I plan to. I'll ask permission from my superiors to do that personally with you two, it's better to go over these things face-to-face with someone who knows you. Oh, before I forget, I also want you to have this," he said, reaching into his case once more and pulling out a Douay-Rheims edition of the Bible, "I promise, this is the last," he laughed, seeing her pained expression. "The King James version doesn't have all the books that our Church declares necessary for the formation of doctrine, so I thought you might want to have this handy to read through and to check the references the other two books will list. If you recall, this is the same edition I advised you use for your Babylonian research."

"Oh, I noticed there were more books in it, I found them interesting. I wonder why our church decided to omit them," she mused aloud.

"Why do most people edit books, even secular books?"

"Well, generally they eliminate what they consider useless filler, something that they feel takes up space, or they don't understand it's content and toss it away, but you know? Editors can be stupid at times. They just ignore that author's intention. I always try to read unabridged editions, so much is lost with cut versions of classic literature, even movies don't make sense when they are edited too much. I love the *longueurs* of a book even if they seem pointless because you can get a peek into the author's mind, a glimpse of their creative soul. I mean, how would people like it if editors came along and said to an artist, 'Whoops, you left just a tad too much space around that lily pad there, lets crop that a bit, shall we?'. Monet would be ripping his hair out."

"Excellent point; even in music, we find Beethoven's deliberate pauses and seemingly pointless *da capo* repetitions are just as important to the overall structure of a piece as much as the musical notes, but I'm meandering," he smiled. "Indeed, with the Bible, certain mysteries revealed by God were tossed away because they could not understand them, or they became a thorn in their side and it was easier to get rid of them. What always puzzled me, why anyone would ever cut the book of Tobias out where one of the most powerful archangels explains what makes a marriage holy, not to mention giving a few tips to us exorcists warning how the devil and his minions can gain a foothold over people, but I am digressing, we shall go over the book of Tobias during the marriage counselling sessions," he concluded, "you're going to have enough on your plate with these books as it is."

"No kidding," she joked, eyeing the weighty volumes placed before her.

"Well, forgive me, I have one more book," he said, reaching inside his jacket.

"Oh no," she interjected before she could stop herself, only to see he was taking out the copy of her artistic dispute he had borrowed. They both laughed.

"Pete! You had me going there. Speaking of exorcisms, tell me, how is your new order coming? I keep meaning to ask you, but we never get to it."

"Sadly, it's not, or rather, it's set aside for something else. Instead of an order, we now have an International Organization of Exorcists."

"Still, that's a good thing, isn't it?"

"I guess so, it's hard enough trying to find priests willing to do exorcisms, let alone try and discern a vocation to join a particular order devoted to that work of mercy. At least an organization is a start, it might lead to an order."

"What's the difference? An organization sounds like the same thing."

"Well, the organization has diocesan priests who also have parish obligations, they're spread too thin. With an order, the entire prayer and working life of the community would be concentrated on binding the devil, and provide the support needed for exorcisms. Although I'm not a medical expert, it's the difference between having a general surgeon or a specialist in a particular field."

"Wow, you would think they would appreciate specialists working in this area. Is it really tough? I mean, how can you tell if anyone's possessed?"

"Well, if someone comes running up to me saying they think they are possessed, they usually aren't," he smiled. "Maybe they are suffering from spiritual obsession or oppression, but they are not personally possessed."

"What's the difference?"

"It's when the assaults of the enemy are made manifest, mostly in external ways, like violent temptations against faith and purity that fall hot and heavy and refuse to relent at times. Sometimes the devil is allowed to torment the senses, physically strike people, disturb surroundings and houses much like a haunting, often he can send sickness and bodily pain that must be patiently borne. However, the free will of the person is not touched, so he cannot do permanent harm as he cannot make them sin. Basically, he tries to frighten us into giving up following God. This doesn't happen all the time, these are special cases, and usually to purify those who are afflicted much like a hero who receives high honours from a king because of the intensity of the battle he overcomes. Oppression is pretty much the same."

Katherine could feel the goose bumps rise on her arms.

"That is so creepy," she shuddered, "how do you get possessed then?"

"Through sin, it depends on how far free will has succumbed to evil as opposed to general human weakness. Then of course, there are extreme cases of people who are possessed not by their own fault, but because someone else has cursed them, even children who are innocent can be possessed through curses or evil wishes directed against them. Sometimes it can occur through curiosity of tarots cards, ouija boards, plus consulting horoscopes and mediums, which gives evil an open door. However, it depends on how open the person is to evil around them, and these days are particularly dangerous: people are living their lives in an environment that parades sin as natural and good. If you are what you eat, you are what you see and hear. Evil influence is like a nicotine patch, you cannot help but absorb what sticks to you. Just look at our so called entertainment today, violence, immodesty ... people start accepting that, and the devil gains a foothold."

"But obviously, not everyone is possessed? How can you tell who is?" Katherine wondered.

"The most obvious are extreme cases, like when the person changes character and seem to assume characteristics akin to mental illness or split personality disorder, but with supernatural qualities that can't be explained by medical science such as levitation, objects flying around the room, the victim speaking in languages unknown to them, usually ancient languages, at times, delivering these languages backwards. Sometimes the body will contort in ways that would kill or seriously injure a person under normal circumstances, but do not inflict the least damage while under the influence of possession. On other occasions, they will display hidden awareness about subjects they had no knowledge of before. You see, the devil is so filled with pride he forgets himself and ends up showing his hand like any braggart. Unfortunately, not all the time, which makes these cases of absolute possession seem rare. We have to contend with his ability to mask possessions with mental illness so we can't tell the difference who is suffering medically, and who is really under attack from the devil, unless we literally begin the rite of exorcism, and then it's only with special permission, which we can't obtain until the supernatural signs become manifest and there is visible cause to begin the rite. The devil knows how to use the virtue of obedience against us," he sighed. "However, he's becoming more blatant. Already, requests for exorcisms and prayers to relieve oppression are rising in our office, and it's going to get much worse, I fear. It's the sign of our times, and it's one of the reasons I hoped the church would permit the founding of an order to combat the problem."

"Perhaps they plan to wait and see what will happen with this new organization," Katherine suggested, unsettled yet intrigued by his account.

"Maybe, God arranges things in His own good time, we shall see."

At that moment, Esther knocked on the door.

"I'm sorry to disturb you, but your friends have arrived."

"Okay, thank you. I'm so glad you get to see them Pete, they are doing so much better since you first met them."

"That's good, two less people out of the enemy's grasp," he noted half to himself. "Shall I come back next week to see how you are doing with your studies?"

"All right."

"And remember, not a word to Gerry about my visit."

"Okay, whatever you think best."

It was difficult to follow Pete's instructions when Gerry called that night to inform her about the meeting, knowing she was not going to show up. All she could say was "All right," when he gave her the time, and left it at that. Obviously, Pete wished to have a discussion with his brother alone, and considering how he explained Gerry had difficulty talking at times, he must have a plan in mind. She was curious to know how Wednesday would turn out, but she had other things to handle and thought it best to leave them at it.

Tuesday was Martin and Justine's last day in New York, and they decided on a simple day, no sightseeing, no rushing, just a quiet day with Katherine at home followed by a dinner with her family, before it was time to pack up that night for the flight back to Paris. Katherine was amused by their split honeymoon; part business trip and part vacation as they showed her more sketches they made the previous afternoon. They also sold a few paintings that week and were delighted to be going home with some cash rather than returning broke after a few shopping sprees since Justine insisted on visiting the famous department stores. Martin tried to tell her they basically had the same items in Paris, but it was not the same as buying them in New York now, was it?

It was a sad farewell the next morning at the airport, but they promised to have a new collection ready for the gallery when they returned for her wedding. Now, all she and Gerry needed to do was set a date, and they would know when the next happy reunion would take place, but that was something that could not be rushed they reminded her. After one last round of hugs and double kisses, she watched them pass though the gates and out of sight, their destination reminding her about the madcap weeks she spent there with Gerry, then realized she hadn't heard from him since Monday evening. Although she didn't want to intrude if Pete had a plan in operation, he didn't say she couldn't speak with his brother. She tried to call Gerry on Tuesday, but couldn't reach him, and, he didn't return her call. Well, he did have to work too, not to mention he probably didn't want to bother her on the last day she had with her friends, but not to leave a message? That was odd. After the long months they were not able to communicate properly during his misadventure in Jakarta, they hadn't lost touch a single day since they returned from Paris. Oh, it is only one day after all. Was she already becoming clingy? She hoped not, she didn't want to push him away. No, people in love keep in contact, that's all you think about doing when you're in love with someone. Katherine then wondered if Pete had advised his brother to give her space to begin her reading … that couldn't be it, not if Pete was keeping his visit with her confidential for now. Whatever was happening, she would have to be patient, Pete must know what he's doing.

However, Pete didn't have anything to do with Gerry not calling on Tuesday, at least, not directly. The very thought of him made Gerry restless.

After he had called Peter to set up the appointment that Sunday, he felt strangely unsettled, finding it almost impossible to concentrate on work and needed some time to think things through, knowing the big Saint versus Sinner showdown would commence sometime in the near future. Perhaps not until after the first meeting to discuss what to do about wedding plans he thought, but it was coming, and he dreaded it, imagining his brother's expression as he finally heard all the prodigal's wilful misdemeanours and his reluctant attempt at contrition. The problem was, he knew what the church considered a mortal transgression, but in his exuberant rush to live life to the fullest, he wondered why very pleasurable activities were 'sinful', considering they felt good, and yet, he knew full well he was indulging in his human weaknesses. After all, who could declare what was evil and what wasn't? Yet, despite all his questions and doubts concerning this matter, he was not about to commit sacrilege, thanks to Sr. Roberta and her catechism classes that still stuck with him. At first, he stopped receiving communion, but later decided it was better he just stay away. What was the point of going if he wasn't about to go to communion anyway? Might as well not go at all. Besides, you just have to be a good person to make it to the pearly gates, isn't that it? Yet, if Katherine was planning on a church wedding, and as he actually wanted Peter to marry them too, which was ironic, that meant changes were afoot and the time had come to straighten himself out. The problem was, he would have to feel sorry for everything he did, and it was difficult feeling sorry for anything that felt good. That was until he met Katherine. When he realized he wanted to marry her, his life was slowly filled with regret that began to grow more intense as he made a serious effort to comply with her conservative expectations and checked his growing devotion, keeping it within dignified bounds. At last, in her presence, he began to understand he had failed somewhere. This was still difficult to think about let alone voice it to a confessor, and he had slipped so far, it seemed near impossible to do anything about it. Go back to church? I'm comfortable where I'm at! But, losing Katherine because of his own obstinacy was out of the question. "Talk to Peter, you'll feel better." She was right, but still, he doubted, wavered, willed and willed not.

Wednesday evening arrived with a vengeance as time raced by, his thoughts in a restless turmoil. He almost wished he was back in Japan with all those black-clad stony-faced businessmen and their business card rituals, it was easier to deal with that tight-laced culture than navigate the minefield of his conscience. He found himself pacing around the sofa, eventually staring out the window, fixating on the skyline, anything to calm him before meeting Peter's knowing gaze. He jumped when the doorbell rang and hoped Katherine had arrived first.   Although he needed some time alone, he missed being with her these last couple of days. However, it was Peter.

"Hey Pete, just on time as always, come on in. Can I get you a drink?" he offered, trying to sound nonchalant, but feeling strangely unsure of himself.

"Water please, and if you don't mind, I'm going to sit down. I've been on the run all day. Fr. Jenkins was unable to make his rounds at the hospital, so I was summoned."

"Well go on in, put your feet up. So, I guess you're surprised your little brother has finally decided to settle down," he began, pouring him a glass of bottled spring water. Might as well cut to the chase he thought, forget the small talk.

"No, not really. You weren't destined to live the life of priest, nor a bachelor for that matter."

Crikey! This was far out. He did know him too well.

"Hmm. Maybe not, but it seems I've landed myself in a real pickle, falling in love with an Episcopalian, right?" he tried to joke.

"Pickle? Far from it, Katherine puts many Catholic girls to shame," Peter noted quietly before turning to more general topics. "So tell me, how did the first meeting with the parents go on Sunday? You didn't give me any details when you called," he noted with amusement.

"A lot better than I expected," Gerry was glad to report, "the heavy cutlery was brought out for the occasion."

It felt good telling him how well the dinner went, Katherine's Gramps and their Dad seemed to get on very well, although he still had reservations about her Pops. Somehow, the conversation rolled around to his two weeks in Paris with Katherine, and then realized she hadn't arrived.

"Gosh, it's been half an hour, she's not here yet," Gerry noted. "Is she stuck in traffic I wonder? She's not usually late."

Peter didn't say anything, but asked how things were at the firm. Gerry distractedly told him the latest doing at their offices, the latest plans that were in operation, the new services they were thinking of launching to compete with UPS, but it was difficult to engage in casual conversation when he worried why his Princess was late. If only she had a car phone or a cell phone with her, but she didn't like too many gadgets.

"Gee, maybe she hasn't left the gallery yet."

He tried phoning, but only reached the answering machine, obviously the place was closed and she was stuck somewhere in traffic. He tried talking with Pete again to pass the time, just in case it was only a bottleneck that delayed her, but grew restless when the clock ticked another agonizing fifteen minutes, then twenty ... thirty.

"Something's not right," he finally said, "I'd better call her at home." The lines were busy. "Geeze, perhaps she's been in an accident."

"Don't worry, everything will be fine. Sit down, wait a few more minutes," Peter said calmly, seemingly oblivious to his brother's growing anxiety. This time they sat in silence for awhile, Gerry resumed his pacing, then sat down again.

"This just isn't like her," he muttered, ruffling his hair. "I hope she's not in an accident or something."

"No, she's fine."

Gerry didn't listen and tried Oak Meadows again, but the line was still busy.

"I wonder what's happened," he mumbled, beginning to imagine the worst.

"You really do care for her."

"Yes, of course I do! I wouldn't be marrying her if I didn't," he snapped worriedly, not in anger, but he couldn't talk while he was anxious, prodding made it worse. He sat down and tried to reason things out in his mind. Did she forget? Was it traffic? Maybe she's...*oh no*. He abruptly jumped to a stark possibility:

"Heck, who knows? Maybe she's having second thoughts ... decided not to come at all ... I wouldn't blame her ... ."

"Now why would you say that?" Peter asked quietly.

"Because I would if I were her," he blurted out before he realized it. He looked up to find himself facing that calm, searching gaze that used to unnerve him, but now had disarmed him completely. He was not looking at his brother, although it was still Peter, but was staring at a compelling yet simultaneously frightening mirror in the shape of a familiar person that reflected back past thoughts, actions and omissions he did not want to face and had tried to submerge for so long. He began to quake as he felt the fibre of his being lose its sense of fleshy corporeality, become transparent and grow strangely visible to the Unseen, completely exposed to the heavens, not stripped ingloriously, but respectfully laid bare by a skilful Physician of the soul. To his utter amazement, it wasn't Peter who was doing the examining, he was scrutinizing himself in his deep, prolonged glance, seeing the true decrepit being he had let himself become by his own inaction. He was judging himself. The misery became like so much garbage that he suddenly felt he had to jettison in order to reach the pure, exalted spheres he once enjoyed without being aware of it. He couldn't bear the filth sticking to him like pitch any longer. He knew what sin and evil was.

"B…because she deserves Sir Galahad, not Lancelot," he continued. He wanted to pour everything out at once but could only babble that curiously apropos metaphor. He couldn't help himself back then, but *he didn't want to be like this anymore! Do you understand?* He must make him understand. It was hard to speak coherently when he continued to feel this strange translucency, forcing his mouth to work when everything internal had been transformed into pure thought and seemed to flow like light between them, yet he was compelled to speak, he had to in order to free himself from this terrible burden, and by his own will power with great effort, everything came out in an anxious cascade that simultaneously felt laborious and languid: "She deserves someone who waited … I now know what Sr. Roberta meant when she said I was meant to share my life with someone, but to wait until I had 'found my princess across the sea'. Sometimes she spoke in riddles, we hardly knew what she meant at times, but now I know! I didn't find the love of my life until I left my country for a run-of-the-mill business trip and found her standing right in my own apartment! And then, as you say, she puts many girls to shame, and men too I might add. Since I've met her, I see things differently. I *understand* why I should have waited: the first time should be saved, given to the one who vows to love and honour you until death, and to no one else, and I've robbed her of that, given it to another, many others … robbed myself of it too, which rightfully belonged to her from the beginning," his voice trailed.

"You found out the hard way," Peter sighed.

"Yes, the church never condemned it, just proclaimed … certain conditions … and with good reason."

"True, it's part of the sacrament: a marriage is not fully consummated until the couple join together in the physical bond of wedlock, which is good as it leads to life and the creation of a new immortal soul. The giving of self to each other is a lifelong gift that cannot and should not be given to anyone else but to whom you have vowed it to."

"I didn't understand when I was younger … ."

"No, and yet, your conscience bothered you. It was still alive. A dead conscience is the sign of a dead soul, so Gerry, don't condemn yourself. You did not sin in malice, but through human weakness. You have just made the first step to save yourself from becoming another Herod."

"Who killed the innocents?" Gerry wondered aghast with the thought.

"No, the other Herod who beheaded John the Baptist. He enjoyed giving in to his weaknesses, but at the same time, loved to listen to John because truth attracts people, even when it is hard to bear. John became Herod's conscience, the problem was he didn't put knowledge of the truth into action and change his life; in the end, his own vices outsmarted him despite himself, making him kill the one voice of reason still left to him. Gerry, as you say Katherine deserves someone worthy of her, why not at least get your spiritual life back in order? Do you wish to build your new life with her on the putrid wreckage of the past?" Gerry shook his head. "Would you like to get rid of it?" This time he nodded. "Then you know what's needed to restore your baptismal innocence, it's not that difficult, you've already made a start."

"But I've been away for so long … ."

"That may be, but it's not difficult to resume your obligations, Mass, a morning and evening prayer for starters, the will and an honest effort not to commit the same sins again … ."

"Oh, that part will be easy, there won't be anyone but Katherine, I've never felt this way about anyone before."

"Yes, she is a great gift. Because you are open-hearted and generous, God had preordained that you should meet her from the very beginning before the world ever came to be. Isn't that a consoling thought? God knows you better than you know yourself, and He doesn't want to lose you."

"I'm not much of a gift to her … . " Gerry returned.

"Yes you are, your guilt is just getting the better of you. Now, would you like to get rid of those burdens you've been carrying for so long?"

"I'm going to need help with the rest … ."

"That's all right, I can walk you through the examination of conscience as we go," Peter assured him. Slowly, Gerry got down on his knees as he was taught so long ago and made the sign of the cross.

"Bless me … Father … for I have sinned, it's been almost twelve years since my last confession … ."

This time, he was sorry, truly sorry for everything that he had messed up, failed to do, it all came rushing out, how many girlfriends he had in the past, and how often he had known them in the Biblical sense. Then, everything else bubbled to the surface, things he did way back in grade school and back again to the present. One slight prod from Peter, and he could suddenly remember incidents he had long forgotten, although it was not difficult remembering in many instances when he still felt strangely transparent, exposed to the surgeon's skilful scalpel. How Peter knew certain things he thought were deep secrets known to him alone was alarming, but he suddenly realized, it wasn't Peter, rather, whoever was using him, and it wasn't long before he had finally laid bare every fault and failing he had committed, despite the number of years he had been away. Confession was never this thorough, not anything like he remembered it at all, but then, Peter was not an ordinary priest he realized by the time they had reached the moment for the penance to be declared. Suddenly, he dreaded what might be given to him as the penance due his sins, maybe something long and lengthy to make up for everything he did and didn't do, but Peter only requested one thing: to offer his next communion in reparation for his past transgressions. That wasn't too hard, that meant going to Mass and offer communion received at that service, nothing earth-shattering or beyond his reach. Peter then helped him to recall the act of contrition, and absolution was given. After years of wandering, only an hour or so, and he had finally come home. Was it really that simple? Shouldn't he be made to suffer or something? At last, he looked at his brother, and felt he was no longer open to his calm scrutiny, the house had been swept clean. It now required due vigilance to keep it that way, and after the hell he had been through, he was now determined to make an earnest effort.

"Well, I wonder what you could possibly think after hearing all of *that*," Gerry said, shaking slightly from the shock of this revealing experience as he felt backwards for the couch, slowly getting off his knees to resume his seat. He thought he would see his brother smugly smile in triumphant victory having finally brought the stray sheep back, but it was a quiet, joyous sense of relief he saw. He suddenly realized how relieved he felt too, so light in spirit he wondered if he was actually sitting on the couch or hovering over it.

"All I can say is what St. Francis de Sales once said: 'I think you must be a holy person indeed, for only a saint would make such a good confession as that.' Now, let's do something about you receiving communion. Your soul is starving after nearly twelve years of famine." Dumbstruck, Gerry watched as Peter picked up the phone and dialled, letting the receiving end ring for a few seconds and then replace the handset. "Fr. O'Conner is on his way up," Peter stated simply, watching his brother with a gleeful expression.

"What? You mean Fr. O'Conner has been waiting all this time? Why, you planned all of this didn't you? Katherine isn't coming tonight at all, is she?"

"Nope," Peter said, still smiling. "You've wanted to have a chat with me for some time, but hadn't the courage to do it. While Kathy has been the catalyst to your recovery, tonight she might have been a distraction, so I just changed the nature of the distraction. Concentrating on one problem sometimes helps to deal with another. How do you feel after that? Better?"

For the first time in years, he no longer felt uncomfortable around Peter, he had seen every way he had failed, and yet, there was no judgement in his eyes, just … peace. It seemed to flow over to him. While he was no longer open to the heavens, nevertheless, that strange communication had not been switched off completely. They seemed to share a connection concerning the unseen he had never felt before. He knew from that point on, he would never be hesitant again to open his soul to him whenever it needed help. "Yes, a little shaky to tell you the truth, but …strangely elated. I don't know how else to put it," Gerry replied,

"You have good reason to feel elated, God doesn't remember what is confessed, neither does the devil for that matter, he is not permitted to hold any of your transgressions against you anymore. Now, let's recollect our thoughts, Fr. O'Conner has the Blessed Sacrament with him," he announced as the doorbell rang, getting up to let him in.

It was a long time since he had seen Fr. O'Conner, the auburn hair was now silver, his face older and creased, but those youthful pale blue eyes were still the same. He could only nod a greeting right then as he entered the room, keeping a respectful silence while carrying his precious treasure over his heart, the stole around his shoulders to show he had come as an official messenger travelling with the most import Visitor Gerry would ever receive. Instinctively, Gerry remembered to get back down on his knees again, Peter kneeling beside him. Fr. O'Conner's presence helped him to recall the formal protocol for extraordinary visits like this, a tough wiry Irishman who taught his boys well, made sure they stuck to the straight and narrow, often telling hilarious slapstick jokes now and then, all of Gerry's childhood memories came flooding back. He was always one of his favourite priests, arranging football or baseball games on weekends to keep them occupied and out of trouble, checking up to see how they were doing with their schoolwork, a man fully dedicated to his vocation and had a way with kids. He then remembered he had to collect his thoughts, prepare for communion, remember the intention of reparation he was to offer up… . Fr. O'Conner patiently waited a few minutes, then opened the pyx.

"Behold the Lamb of God, who takes away the sins of the world, happy are those who are called to His supper."

"Lord, I am not worthy to receive Thee, but only say the word, and my soul shall be healed," they both replied. Fr. O'Conner was a stickler for tradition and said the more formal response as Gerry received, "May the Body of Christ preserve thy soul unto life everlasting." Fifteen minutes of reflection and silent prayer with his brother and his old mentor beside him, all felt right with the world.

At last, Fr. O'Conner could finally speak, giving him a hearty handshake as they stood up.

"Well lad, it's good to see you again. Your first general confession I take it?"

"Yeah," Gerry replied simply, this was all too much right now.

"Ah, they're tough to be sure, but there's nothing like a good spring cleaning, is there now, m'boy?" he laughed. "We should celebrate, which reminds me, I believe congratulations are in order, you have just proposed."

"Um, you could say that," he smiled, "rather I planned to, but she proposed first."

"Oh laddie, this I have to hear," Fr. O'Conner noted settling back into the sofa. "Be good now and begin at the beginning, how did you two meet?" Gerry told him everything, even the comic ride in the linen van, he couldn't hold it in any longer. He thought Fr. O'Conner would split his sides laughing. "And I thought we Irish got ourselves into some crazy situations. Well, your Kathy seems to have done you the world of good, I'm happy for ye, she sounds like a grand girl, I hope I get to meet the lovely lady soon."

"The thing is Father, we were *supposed* to meet Pete tonight to discuss what to do about the wedding," he replied, shooting a glance at his brother, "she isn't Catholic."

"Yes, yes, technicalities ..." Father sighed, but a little concerned. "You know you can't marry in her church."

"I know, it would be considered invalid in ours, and no civil ceremonies, but she doesn't want that either."

"In fact," Peter added, "she asked me to do the honours, and has agreed to learn all about our church and beliefs."

"Is that so? What does her family think about this?" Father O'Conner wondered.

"I have a feeling her father has an issue with it, but at the same time, he seems to be resigned to the possibility of a ceremony in our church," Gerry explained, telling him about his meeting with the Walsingham patriarchs.

"I hope this won't cause problems between the families, yet, I can see you two were destined to meet, despite the obstacles. Just leave it all in the hands of the Almighty."

When in doubt, throw doubt out and have a little faith; that was Fr. O'Conner's best advice. However, it seemed to Gerry the Almighty had left the ball in Katherine's court, it was up to her now.

☙❖☘

Gerry showed up at the gallery quieter and more thoughtful than usual the next morning. Katherine had seen that look before, Fr. Peter had caught another fish in the net, obviously the fish had been taken off guard, however, he still had that special smile reserved just for her.

"Feel better?" she asked with a perceptive glance.

"Much better," he said, giving her a hug. "So, you were in on the loop I take it."

"Enough to know Peter had something up his sleeve, and when that happens, it usually ends with a confession session."

"Funny girl, but honestly, I do feel better," he admitted.

"That's good. You should see what he landed *me* with," she added, leading him to the office and opening the bottom desk drawer to reveal the small library his brother had loaned.

"Uh oh, looks like we won't be married anytime soon," he began to chuckle.

"Well, you did say to take my time."

"True enough. Anyway, don't get stressed out about it. How fares the realm? Started planning the fourth floor yet?"

"Whoa, what's the rush?" she laughed, "I've got lots of things to think about first. I have to find more artists, *again*, because I'll have a whole display floor that needs to be filled. That doesn't happen overnight you know. Plus I still have to ask my parents about Sotheby's or if I should set that project aside for now with the wedding to consider, I haven't told them about your offer yet."

"Hmm, looks like you'd better get started, doesn't it?" he smiled. "I can't wait to see everything on display. Hey, where is everybody?"

"Oh, Suzy is off getting the morning papers for our scrapbook on the gallery, and Esther is at the framers helping the Professor pick out something for his latest painting. He enjoys creating, but couldn't be bothered picking out frames once the creative process is finished, he just

878

wants to get started on the next picture. She says he'll never find anything unless she's there to push him. Dennis will be here a little later."

"So, it's just the two of us," he said, "at least for the moment."

"Moments, that's all we seem to have together since we came back," she sighed, "work is getting the better of us, and this summer is going to be particularly busy. Steve's graduation is coming up, so is Stephie's, how I'm going to fit all this in, I don't know."

"Hmm, and here I was going to take you out tonight, but you have your artwork."

"Gosh, I have a lot to catch up on in that department now that you mention it. Wait, why not have a working date? You could join me in the studio after hours, have a picnic with me. Suzy and Dennis have other plans tonight, so we have the place all to ourselves."

"Mix a little pleasure with business, huh? All right, I like watching you paint," he said, giving her a quick kiss. "Does Chinese takeout sound good?"

"Very good. Shall I order?"

"Nope, I'll surprise you."

"You always manage to do that, just … make sure it's something I can recognise, okay?"

"Ugh, thanks a lot, maybe I should get pizza instead," he laughed. "Hello, who's this?" he noticed, looking at the security monitors, noticing a smartly dressed lady in a red pant suit standing politely at the front desk, looking around for someone to assist her.

"Customer or new artist I guess, must get back to work, my Prince," she replied, giving him another quick kiss on the cheek before they left the office to face the work day. She hated to see him go.

"Hello, may I help you?" To her surprise, the lady at the desk was a prospective tenant for her vacant shop space.

"Yes please. My name is Olivia Conti, I was wondering if it would be possible to see your space for rent over there? I've been looking for the perfect place to open a new business, and this is certainly a wonderful location, very classy."

"Of course," Katherine replied, introducing herself and hunting for the keys. "May I ask about your new venture?"

"A gift shop to be precise," Olivia replied as they made their way over to the corner.

"In that case, you might be glad to know T-shirts seem to sell very well here," Katherine informed her, relieved someone was actually interested in the corner for the purpose she originally intended.

"T-Shirts? Not a souvenir shop, a proper gift shop," Olivia replied, a little disgruntled with the thought of selling something that ... *common* ... in an exclusive gallery. "Special collector's imports," she clarified, "Hummels, Lladro, Venetian glassware, Irish Dresden, Anri from Italy ..." she trailed as Katherine opened the shop door. Olivia looked around the space, admiring the cases already provided, eyeing the dimensions and turning back to the gallery, possibly gauging the headcount of walk-through traffic and potential customers.

"Great, my aunt loves Hummels. Well, may I get you something to drink? Coffee? Cappuccino? Tea?" Katherine offered.

"As you wish. Are the lights on their own switches?" she asked, all business like, no beverage specified.

"Yes, the lights are separate, this is an independent unit, although you will be interested to know our security company handles the alarm system, that comes with the rent."

"Excellent. These collector's pieces are quite valuable and security would be required. Oh, I don't see a private storage area," Olivia noted with undisguised disappointment. "Collectors like to save the original boxes, I would need somewhere to put them all, plus any back stock I would need to keep on hand."

"Hmm, well, we do have the old boiler house, it's also wired to the security system."

"May I see it?" she asked briskly.

"Of course." Katherine brought her to the large area, which she still didn't know what to do with, considering the old and new heating systems, plus Gerry's art cases, there was plenty of space still available.

"Hmm, no shelving. Can anyone just walk through here?" Olivia enquired.

"Well, anyone who works here, plus the deliverymen, but I can have a proper private storage area prepared if you require it," Katherine quickly replied, seeing the dissatisfaction on her prospective renter's face. The gift corner had been left vacant for seven months, and she didn't want to lose this perfect opportunity. At least she now knew what to do with the extra space in the old building, maybe Olivia and her practical eye was a godsend.

"Hmm, how do you propose to do that, if you don't mind me asking," she replied.

"Well, I have a new construction project about to go into operation on the fourth floor, and while the workmen are here, it wouldn't be that much trouble to build up a storeroom. In fact, I have to thank you for pointing out what was lacking."

"No thanks necessary. Let me see," she said, thinking to herself for a few moments. "I suppose I could bring in minimum stock, just keep empty boxes back here until then," she muttered. "Thing is, I wouldn't want to put you to extra expense."

"Don't worry, it's obvious the unit needs storage, an oversight on my part, it would explain why I couldn't rent it for all this time," Katherine replied. "A few extra building materials in the project won't cost much, it's trying to get those men to finish…" Katherine said, shaking her head.

"Oh, I know, honey," Olivia said, suddenly displaying a softer side, sounding less official. "You know, I do like your space, and the display cases too, I won't need to do anything, just place the merchandise. May we go over the rent and contract details?"

"Sure, I'll order us a cup of coffee and we can discuss everything in the office."

Olivia seemed pleased with the rent, the fact she could name the shop, and the lack of storage could be straightened out, although she would take a copy of the contract just to read the details before making anything official. Katherine promised to hold the space until she decided. Olivia then quizzed her about the security guards and if they watched the gift unit, Katherine replied in the affirmative and that was also included in the rent.

"Well, this is a choice spot and the rent is a good deal I must admit," Olivia noted, "reading the contract will just be a formality."

"I will be happy to welcome you to the gallery. Tell me, is this your first business venture?"

"Yes, I just needed something to do. I've just divorced that no good, cheating, son-of-a-b…witch husband of mine, and while I made sure to take him for everything he's worth, I can't just sit around the penthouse. At least I'm not slaving for his no good friends and all his business dinners anymore. I can do something for myself for a change. My advice: don't get married honey…whoops," she added, just noticing Katherine's left hand. "That's right, I saw it in the papers, you just got engaged, well, congratulations. Don't listen to a sceptic like me, shooting my mouth off, maybe your shot at marriage will be different," she concluded. *I sure hope so*, Katherine thought.

"Do you have any children?"

"Yes, and thankfully they're older and can handle this better. I've one son, George, he works for a PR firm and just got transferred to LA, and two daughters, Francis and Rose," Olivia said, hunting in her purse for her wallet to show her the family pictures, "Francis tells me she's going to become a writer, and Rose is a reporter for NBC." There were no grandchildren yet, but her children all had their own lives, so she figured since she knew a lot about collectables, having spent a good deal of money collecting them herself, she might as well put that expertise to good use as a working hobby. What the hey? As a registered dealer, she could also add to her collections at the wholesale price.

"Well, I would love to stay and chat, but I've got an appointment at the salon."

"I understand. Let me introduce you to the gallery gang before you go," Katherine said as they stood up. She could see in the monitors that Esther and Suzy had returned and were busy cutting out the latest articles for their archives with the Professor looking on. After a quick 'hello', she was off for her manicure and the latest gossip in the city. Katherine didn't know what to make of Olivia, business-minded, efficient, but certainly a character.

"Finally," Esther said as they resumed their clipping, "we can take down the Christmas paper from the shop windows. It looked like we were already getting geared up for the holiday shopping season."

"Nothing like beating everyone to the punch," the Professor chuckled.

"Well, how is retirement so far?" Katherine enquired.

"Not too bad, a nice party by the faculty, the expected gold watch and fountain pen, plus a few graduation ceremonies coming up, and that's it. A rather quiet end for thirty years of service," he replied. "I was hoping I could move my stuff in right away before I atrophy."

"Sure, whenever you like, Professor."

"I hope today isn't too soon, he's got most of it in the back of the car," Esther warned.

"That's all right, there's lot's of storage and cupboard space. You go ahead and pick a place to work in and we'll dub it the Professor's Corner. That reminds me, it's time to get the fourth floor ready, so be prepared for a lot of noise this summer."

"Wow, that's good news," Suzy noted, "but that means … ."

"Yeah, I know, more art interviews, but we're better prepared this time," Katherine said, "we know what to expect."

She decided to strike while the iron was hot and called Mr. Hendricks to enquire when he might be free for a consultation on the museum project, and had no sooner put the phone down when she heard Andre bang the kitchen door in the back service hallway. He was not in a very good mood. Katherine thought she had better check on him.

"Of all the … one of my chefs hasn't shown up, and he's one of my best. He must have fallen off the wagon again, he's off on a toot somewhere, *and*, I have no idea where to find him, not that he could do anything if I did find him, he's probably cross-eyed."

Unfortunately, she couldn't make him feel any better when he and the kitchen crew now had to pick up the slack. She would have offered her services if she wasn't such a dismal cook herself, and just had to hope he could hang in there until the soused chef made an appearance. By this time, Dennis had arrived and could help the Professor with his equipment, stopping to leave Esther and Katherine off for lunch. Katherine wanted to do some painting while she had that free hour, but Mr. Hendrick's would arrive earlier than expected to discuss the next course of action and she had to wave her creative time goodbye. If that wasn't enough, the field trip that was scheduled for a tour the next day actually showed up that afternoon. She didn't know what happened, maybe the teacher changed the day and forgot to notify them at the gallery, or they managed to mark the tour on the wrong day in the books. In any case, it was a trying few hours showing a bunch of moody high schoolers around the gallery who rarely showed an interest in art and who usually took art classes for an easy ride. Katherine preferred the grade schoolers, they still liked to draw and were curious about the exhibits. Finally, it was time to close the place and she wished everyone a good night, deciding to take her required reading upstairs to the studio to peruse for the few minutes while she waited for Gerry. When he arrived he found her dozing at the worktable, face down nose in the Bible, having succumbed to the temptation to lay her head on the pages for a moment to enjoy the peace and quiet.

"A reprise of Sleeping Beauty I see," he smiled, laying out his takeout repast of Chinese and pizza, not knowing which she would prefer.

"Oh, I just closed my eyes for a moment. What a day! Who would have thought a gallery would be this tiring? Mental fatigue has to be worse than physical exhaustion."

"You poor thing, I wouldn't worry about doing any artwork tonight, tomorrow's another day. Take a break and have some hot and spicy bamboo shrimp, or a piece of Four Seasons with a double dose of mozzarella if you'd prefer," he said, opening up the cartons, releasing enticing aromas of the Far East and the Mediterranean. "I've also got Mu Pu Pork, plus cashew chicken, and spring rolls. You know, I had to sneak up here, I couldn't let Andre see me with culinary fare from his competition," he laughed.

"Especially not after today, he's ready to spit fire," she said, relating everything that had happened after he had left that morning while he handed out a choice between chopsticks and plastic cutlery with paper napkins.

"Well, how far did you get in your reading?" he asked.

"Not far past 'In the beginning God created heaven and earth,'" she noted.

"You really do need a break, even God took a rest. Here, grab a box and tuck in." He then told her about his day, catching up on paperwork, and making a spot inspection around the warehouses.

"Sammy says 'hello' too," he finished before dropping his shrimp the third time. "Darn it, even after two trips to China, I never will master these things," he said flipping a chopstick over the side of the carton onto the table. "Thankfully, I didn't do *that* over there, I might have insulted someone's ancestor and lost a huge contract," he joked, his brows knit with amused annoyance as he finally surrendered to the familiar grip of the bendy fork.

"Here, you hold the bottom chopstick tight and against your thumb and you move only the top one, like this," she said, manoeuvring the slender utensils in the air.

"Huh," a little intrigued, "how did you figure it out?"

"Oh, must be the paint brushes, it comes with the territory."

"They write with brushes over there, don't they? Hmm, there must be something to that," he noted, pleased he could now hold his dinner without sending it flying.

"I still have problems eating rice with them though," she admitted.

"That's when you pick up your dish, it's okay to have your chin in it."   "Chin," she laughed, nearly choking on a hot pepper, the pun was hard to ignore.

"Glasshoppel must rern not to raph when eating flied chirri peppels," he sagely advised.

"We're cruel," she chided, but unable to stop laughing, the tears rolling down her cheeks.

Of course, after dinner came dessert, flied pineapple and banana flitters now gone cold, followed by a steaming cappuccino Gerry brought up for them from the restaurant. They didn't want to go home just yet and enjoyed the May evening sitting out on the fire escape, listening to the sounds of the city and the ruckus in the kitchens five stories below, lazily watching the diners coming and going from the back parking lot like a pair of eagles perched on their high wrought iron eyrie overlooking the world.

"Are you chilly?" he asked, his arm around her.

"No, it's lovely tonight. You know, I'm having such a good time, just sitting here with you."

"Even with just plain old takeout?" he smiled.

"Even with plain old takeout."

They sat quietly for a moment, listening to the night time bustle. Katherine then realized something.

"You know, you've spent so much time with me these last few months, not that I'm complaining," she said, giving his hand a little squeeze, "but you must have had some social life before you met me. I mean, I haven't met any of your friends yet. Um, you do have friends?"

"Oh sure, well, mostly acquaintances, but Leroy would be my closest, oldest buddy," Gerry said. "That's right, you haven't met him yet, and it's my fault. I like having our time to ourselves."

"Hmm, that's nice too, but you shouldn't drop your friends for my sake," she chided.

"Okay, I might as well warn you now, being a friend and all, he could be a bad influence at times. For one thing, he's going to insist on hosting a wild bachelor party, and I'm not really into that stuff. Party, yes; floor show, no."

"Uh huh, the guy who throws the big New Year bashes," she recalled, remembering the telephone call at Gerry's apartment that interrupted their romantic evening for two.

"That's the one. He may be wild, but honestly, he's a good bloke, when Pete wasn't there to watch my back, Leroy was."

"Well, he couldn't be worse than Steves. We should get together sometime, I'm going to meet him eventually, right?"

"That's for sure. If I can track him down, maybe next week or the following we'll set something up."

"Oh, Steve's graduation … gosh, my agenda is getting more cram-packed by the day, Leroy may have to wait a little longer, I'll be going to Boston with my parents soon."

"Then, let's just enjoy tonight, no agendas, no have-to's. We can worry about plans tomorrow."

That was the best idea she heard all day. Leaning her head against his shoulder, she softy hummed *La vie en rose* and then started to laugh.

"Gerry, look, an iron tower with a view of the rooftops right next to an art gallery with a French restaurant down below. Isn't this splendid? We have our own little Paris right here."

"Hey, you're right. We'll have Paris every day," he replied, giving her a hug.

As she predicted, the next few weeks were hectic, running the gallery by day with the added complication of workmen lumbering up and down to the fourth floor in their mucky boots, hauling their menacing, grimy equipment through the finished sections of the building. At least they weren't hanging off scaffolding and hooting at her like a pack of ill mannered baboons, that seemed to be an outdoor activity; thankfully, all the external work was completed already. Gerry didn't want to distract her at lunchtime, thinking he would give her more time for her artwork, but her mother and her aunt were busy taking up the slack, dropping by with wedding magazines and invitation samplers, trying to give Katherine ideas and tips. It was never too early to start planning, even if the day had not been set. Gerry came by after work with a different takeout or a special dinner sent up by Andre, sitting with her out on their Eiffel Tower with a glass of wine for half an hour or so before Katherine went back to the brushes, Gerry quietly watching her apply the paints. One night, she asked if he would like to try his hand at painting a picture, but he humbly declined with the excuse he lacked the talent, and he could only appreciate the masterpieces of others.

"Don't be silly, you have a wonderful eye for art, so the talent must be latent in there somewhere, we just need to bring it out. It's not that difficult. Here, we'll start with a few drawing lessons," she announced, dropping her brush into the jar of white spirits. "I've finished this section and need a break before moving to the next painting."

"Um, all right, guess it couldn't hurt."

She sat him at the large worktable with a pencil, a sharpener, an eraser and a piece of paper as though he were back at school.

"We'll start with something simple, lay your left hand out, palm on the table, you can draw that … no, not flat, let your fingers curve a little, you want your first sketch to have some curved features to it to make it interesting. Now, I'm not going to *teach* anything per se for your first attempt, but I'm going to give you the Master Rule for drawing and let you carry on: '*Draw what you see, not what you know is there*'."

"Hmm, a riddle, that doesn't sound simple to me."

"But it is, just give it a try."

He followed her instructions, a little sceptical how it might turn out. Katherine went back to her work, taking out Pete's picture in order to give her new student some space. A few minutes later:

"I'm done, but it ain't a Degas, that's for sure," he joked.

She went over to take a look and tried to keep a straight face as she examined the blob with alien projectiles for fingers, trying to find something good to say in an effort to give him encouragement. That was not an easy task, but of course, she didn't expect him to get it right the first time, this was intended to be a 'before and after' session.

"I told you," he said with a grin, eyeing her expression. "My third grade hand-turkey pictures were better."

"Well, you did what I told you *not* to do, you didn't draw what you were looking at, but what you knew was there."

"Okay, can you demystify the riddle for me?"

"You were looking at your hand and thinking of it in its entirety, knowing that a hand has fingers, you just plonked them down. What you are to 'see' are lines and curves, and one at a time. When you work on one line, forget the rest of the lines until you get to them, you just use them for judging your dimensions. It's like playing connect the dots, but your mind sees the lines, and you have to put the dots in and draw the lines. Art is all about imitation."

"The answer sounds worse than the riddle," he laughed, "show me."

"Okay, we'll start with a central part of your hand so the dimensions stay in the middle of your paper to a certain degree. Now, you see where the line on the top of your middle finger ends at your knuckle right here?" she asked, standing behind him and looking over his shoulder, trying to see his field of vision. "Follow that point, or invisible 'dot' with your eye along the line to the next point, the top of your central knuckle right here," she said, tracing the line on his hand with a pencil. "You then *copy the line exactly*, or as close as possible with its slight curvature. If you make it bigger than the actual line on your finger, that's okay, you scale up the next line to match the dimension you just drew."

"Umm, which next line?"

"Well, to keep your proportions intact, I'd finish the top of your middle finger, following the 'dot' on your central knuckle to ... ." she trailed,

"That point on the nail where the line ends," he replied.

"Right. Then, I'd do the top of your index finger, imagining the dots between the main line on the index finger, but you must also match the distance between the line you plan to draw with the line you already finished with your middle finger, and you keep picking out your most important lines and drawing them in step by step. Don't look at the hand as a whole until you've connected your dots and added your shading, because it'll look weird until it's finished."

"Oh, I get it. It's because we can envision the whole thing already finished we try to do it in one go, not take it in minute sections and copy what we see."

"Exactly. Now, shading is easy, you just imitate the varying degrees of darkness, the more you pass the pencil over when filling in your shades, the darker it gets, plus, the harder you push the pencil, the darker it gets too. You must experiment with a blend of pressure and strokes to get it right, and that will come with the feel of the pencil," she explained, making a few shade doodles on his paper. "You can also smudge the lead with your finger to blend it. Plus, watch the direction of the strokes, make the shading follow the general direction of your sketch lines, the lines create movement, and you don't want your hand looking like it's moving contrary to its natural muscle position, unless you're going to go surrealist," she laughed. "It's up to your own style really."

"Hmm lines also equal movement, even in shading, like Van Gogh's cypresses and *Starry Night*, huh?"

"You've got it," she cheered, hugging him around the middle and kissing him on the cheek from over his shoulder. "Now, I'm taking this paper and giving you a fresh one to try it again, don't be afraid to use the eraser either."

She went back to her palette, squeezing out fresh colours, glancing over her shoulder to see how he was faring. He was very intense as he copied his lines, finger, by finger to finger, biting his bottom lip, erasing lines that didn't make the grade and trying again. Michelangelo couldn't have looked more serious when he worked out the artistic intricacies of God's hand raising Adam from the earth than Gerry did that half hour. Eventually he came over with his sheet of paper.

"Wow, that's a lot better," she beamed, "now, compare it with the first one, and just see the progress you've made."

"Holy smokes, and that was just the first lesson," he remarked. "It *is* simple. Why didn't they teach us that in high school? What they taught us was mostly arts and crafts, not practical drawing lessons."

"Oh, they did that to us too, just kept telling us what to draw without showing us *how* until a good substitute teacher came in for a few months and gave us the basics. Now, go try drawing your hand in different positions. When you get used to eyeing the lines between the different visual points and sketching them, you can do it a little faster and you'll be relying less on the eraser. The best part is once you've acquired the knack for drawing, you never really lose it unlike most skills. It feels good to make something, doesn't it?"

"Sure does."

"The next lesson will be the vanishing point and how to master the illusion of three dimensional distance, the breakthrough of the Renaissance."

"I can't wait," he said, returning to the desk.

"The thing is, don't tell your Dad; I promised him that if I ever gave art lessons, he would be my first pupil."

"Your secret is my secret," he laughed.

They spent most nights during those couple of weeks dining at the worktable or sitting out on the fire escape before turning to their art projects, giving her a chance to catch up on the work she had left waiting while she was in Paris. After he had mastered drawing his hand, a few nights later she set up different still life objects for additional practise, and then taught him the secret of the greatest 'line' and 'dot' of all: the horizon and vanishing point.

"Amazing to think it took centuries before artists discovered something so simple," he mused, "the literal dividing line between Medieval and Renaissance styles of artistic expression."

It was one thing to study the artwork, but to learn how to construct a picture yourself was an uplifting experience. It was quite therapeutic too, working on the satisfying symmetry between line and shading after a day of haggling with the port authorities in LA on the phone. Katherine was glad they now had another shared interest, and they were quite happy spending time together in the studio chatting away as they sketched and painted rather than going out to a restaurant or a show.

Of course, Katherine couldn't spend every night with Gerry and had to pack for the weekend in Boston, Steves was finally coming back home. This was a special trip, and as the whole family were going, Pops arranged for the flight aboard the corporate jet. They were all proud of Steves as he went up to receive his degree, especially Katherine considering his confession to her on how annoying he found it to stick it out and get that piece of parchment. Funny enough, the cap and gown didn't quite suit him, the dangling tassel looked a bit silly, especially after witnessing him address the board members of Walsingham Industries with as much professional aplomb as Gramps and Pops. Maybe he had grown up after all. On the flight back home, he made an unexpected announcement; once he had a few days rest, he was going to start looking for his own apartment. The men seemed to understand, Katherine did too after Gerry had explained a man's need to assert his independence first before assuming family legacies, but her mother didn't seem to take it very well.

"Oh, so soon? The house is already feeling empty with Kathy busy about her work, and she'll be marrying and moving out before we know it, and now Steven won't be staying...". She was so happy seeing all the deliveries of Steve's belongings arriving from Boston the last month, shipped by Reinold Shipping of course, and now she had to face the prospect of those boxes heading straight back out the door unopened.

"Now Helen, it's his decision, and it's not like he's moving to another state again, is it?" Harold tried to reason with her. "You do plan to visit us once in a while, right son?" he asked.

"Oh sure Pops, I just need a place of my own, that's all. To be honest, I've gotten kind of used to my own space at college."

"That's understandable," Gramps replied.

"I was wondering," Steves then added. "Jennifer has just graduated too, top of her class, and plans to move to either New York or New Jersey for a job. I told her we'd look at her qualifications first before she got picked up by the other research labs. Is that all right?"

"Why sure," Gramps, jumped in, "no quarter to the competition! I'd hate to have a top notch scientist swooped up by Miffter over in Williamsburg," he rumbled, mentioning the *nom de satire* they had dubbed a rival who operated labs and a chemical factory in the same location.

"Especially as she's my girlfriend," Steves added, "I'd have to break up with her if Miffter nabbed her, or anyone else for that matter."

"I wish you had discussed this with me first," Pops added, a little disgruntled, but since they probably would have hired her anyway via the college recruitment process as they did with all the best students, he couldn't really argue. "However, have her qualifications sent straight to me, I'll go over them with Tim. I'm sure we have a suitable opening available."

"Thanks, Pops."

"However, no special favours. If we accept her, she has to pull her weight in the labs like everyone else."

"No problem, but you won't be disappointed, she's one of the brightest bulbs in the graduate chandelier this year, top tier," Steves assured him.

"And while you'll be joining the board, remember, we still need your help in the labs too," he added.

"Naturally," Steves agreed.

It was another busy week, and then it was Stephie's turn to graduate, everything seemed to happen at once. Like Steves, she was glad to be leaving college.

"Oh, it was fine in the beginning, but man, it becomes a pain when your career starts taking off before you get your degree," she admitted to

Katherine after the graduation. Since Gramps had helped her to set up her own studio, not to mention all the work she did for the gallery and Horace's columns, she was already in demand. Several of the new graduates from various modelling schools were booking her to compile their fashion portfolios, making it difficult to fulfil her gallery obligations to Katherine.

"I hope you don't mind if I arrive in the evenings from now on, do you?" she asked.

"No, not at all, I'm so glad you've got your foot already in the door. It's great, isn't it?"

"Thanks for spreading the word, Kathy, you gave me my big start, I'll never forget that, plus, you introduced me to Horace. Those newspaper freelance gigs were a godsend. You know, I never knew he was such a nice guy, and good looking too. You never would have guessed it from his crotchety columns. Guess what? He asked me out."

"No! Really?"

"Yes really," Stephie beamed.

"What did you say?"

"I said I'd think about it."

"Oh Stephie, don't be mean. If you like him, give him a chance. Don't make him suffer."

"That's rich coming from you," she laughed, "Gerry practically had to find the golden fleece before you went out with him."

"Yeah, and it's a shame I hesitated, I didn't know what I was missing," she smiled, "but I certainly made up for it when I did the proposing."

"Talk about proposing, I know you haven't set the day for the wedding yet, but what about the engagement party? I'm surprised the mothers and Aunt Martha haven't suggested something yet."

"Um, they have, but I think Mom and Aunt Martha want to get to know the Reinolds a little better before they arrange a party. Oh dear, I've got so much to do on top of it, who can think of a party? There'll be plenty of parties when the wedding happens anyway."

"Oh lighten up and enjoy yourself. Have you thought about an engagement gift for Gerry?"

"What to get the man who has everything! I thought about it for ages, I was even tempted to check out Hammacher Schlemmer for something different, but it should be something personal that he can have with him everyday, like an engagement ring."

"Yeah, I'm afraid you may have to go more traditional in the way of a gift."

"I thought so, I hope he won't think it boring."

"Nothing is boring when someone you love gives it to you. Speaking of gifts, when is your new shop tenant opening up? I'll do some photos for your next batch of brochures."

"Oh, not for a month anyway, she has to get the business license and sign up for exclusive dealerships with her gift distributors, then ship the stuff in, I'm a little fuzzy how it works, but Olivia will certainly fit in with our crazy bunch, that's for sure."

ᴄꙅ ❀ ᴇᴐ

By the end of July, the major work in the gallery had been completed minus the decorating. Mr. Hendricks was true to his word and hurried the men this time, but he probably had his own agenda, inside work was not as desirable as a major construction job and he needed his men elsewhere during the summer months while the weather was good. It was a relief to get most of the men out of there after weeks of listening to saws, drills and hammers resounding upstairs in addition to the men yelling out commands and directions to each other. The worst was watching them trail bags of plaster and cement through her building, the cleaners had a terrible time maintaining the stairs and elevator. Eventually, Katherine requested the construction crew to use the fire escape whenever possible, unfortunately, 'whenever possible' was almost never.

That wasn't the only mess, Olivia had her problems unpacking and stocking her shelves, trying to manage all the empty boxes and leftover packing *vis* a mountain of Styrofoam peanuts, tissue and bubble paper until the storage cum office space in the boiler house was completed. Her greatest frustration was waiting for shipments to arrive and then to find a number of expensive limited edition collector's pieces broken, which had to be returned. To overcome her annoyance, she would sit with the Gallery Gang at the front desk during her coffee break popping bubble paper as she told them all about the latest gossip she heard while having her hair coiffured.

"It's a lot cheaper than therapy," she explained, puncturing another helpless pocket of air, "when you listen to other people's problems, mine don't sound quite as bad, but you know how it is, misery loves company."

Katherine wondered if she imagined her ex-husband's face every time she popped the bubbles.

"Surely, listening to everyone's problems must have a depressing effect? Maybe it would be better to dwell on the positive and enjoy the

892

good things each day."

"Like alimony, I enjoy that. I can see him squirm every time he has to write me a cheque," she replied, snapping another air pocket, "and wait until I sell his pride and joy; *his* house, he didn't live there most of the time anyway. Whoops, here comes UPS, I've gotta go girls, another shipment of goodies. I must say, I'm really enjoying the idea of my own gift shop. I should have gotten out of the house and done this years ago," and with a wave, she was off to greet the deliveryman.

"The poor thing, she must have gotten stuck with a right louse," Suzy commented, shaking her head.

"It happens," Esther replied, filling in another line of her favourite crossword puzzle. "Not all men are like that, thank heavens ..." with that, the Professor poked his head out of the elevator, a hint of his spattered smock showing around the sliding door.

"Dear, you haven't seen my spectacles anywhere, have you?" he called.

"Try your breast pocket," Esther replied without raising her head. He patted his chest, gave her the thumbs-up sign and pushed the button for the studio floor. "However, they can be quite worrisome at times," she sighed, finishing her thought once he was out of sight.

When Katherine wasn't handling construction work, there was the infamous art interviews to fill the third floor. Already she received a number of portfolios from the graduate students in Paris that she had given her card to during Martin and Justine's wedding, which helped to get the ball rolling. Horace was also a great help, and while he couldn't make a public call for artists for her without getting in trouble with the editor since the paper made it's money from selling advertising space, he managed to give her recruiting efforts a plug by a scathing critique of her allowing accredited artists drop by anytime rather than scouting for talent herself. As a result, she was politely accosted at all hours during the day with people dragging in large cases and samples of their artwork. It was difficult to get her own paintings finished, but she now had all the artists lined up to fill the former museum level when the new floor was finally operational in addition to the artists already on her books.

Decorating was the easy and enjoyable part. Considering the flamboyant Louvre effect on the second floor and the light golds and cream colours on the third, she envisioned this floor with more introspective surroundings that would bring out the colours of Gerry's masterpieces similar to a professional museum setting with deep navies, charcoal greys, wine reds and velvet forest greens for the various walls with a deep mahogany wainscoting. Since the other levels were bright and varied, she was certain she could incorporate this conservative environment without boring the visitors. For a bit of fun, Gerry suggested she decorate a few of the sections intended to house the con art in the style of a jail cell, but that might be taking artistic creativity too far she told him.

Glancing through Sotheby's catalogue one day, she found an entry that looked promising; a private collector had passed away and in accordance with his last wishes, his treasures were being auctioned for charity. According to the catalogue, there was an eclectic mix of German, Italian and French masters from the eighteenth and nineteenth centuries, and when she voiced an interest, her parents decided to make a day of it. Helen was eager to see what was on offer for Katherine's first art auction, and Gerry came along as he didn't want to miss the fun, not to mention he too was interested in scouting out the valuable collection that had be sequestered from the public eye for years. The atmosphere was exhilarating as they went through the pre-auction viewing, slowly examining the paintings on display and talking with the specialists on hand.   Of course, the experts were very friendly when Gerry arrived, rarely did he leave an auction without buying something. They had heard about his engagement and were delighted to meet his fiancé and her parents, and visibly displayed a keen interest in her when he disclosed she was in the process of enlarging her own collection. Katherine was spoiled for choice, Pops advised her to pick several paintings just in case an eager bidder went over his offer. After a few more rounds of the exhibits, Katherine told him there were a few paintings she kept coming back to, four *vedute* scenes of Venice by the artists Canaletto and Guardi, her favourite was a spectacular scene by Canaletto showing the famous sea-festival of the canalled city with the Doge's regal red and gold ship as the pivotal focus. Katherine loved French artists, but she was attracted to the vibrant boat scenes in the elegant Venetian setting. It had been some time since Harold had attended an auction now that Helen had found enough antiques to fill the house, but he knew what to do, register to bid and collect the bidding paddle. Gerry followed suit and collected a paddle, offering her very important instructions to remember as they entered the auction room: don't blink, try not to sneeze, and no head or hand movements of any kind when the bidding starts. It was a good thing she left that job to Pops, she was petrified to move in case she got landed with items they didn't want. Helen tried to tell her not to pay any attention to him, but Katherine immediately turned to stone when she sat down, Gerry laughing quietly as they took their seats. He couldn't leave her like that indefinitely through the proceedings and told her he was only joking, the auctioneers knew what they were dong and wouldn't mistake a nod for a bid, but she was not taking any chances and barely flicked an eyelash when the auctioneer took up his gavel. It was a packed house, and the atmosphere was electrifying as the bidding started, one piece after another was displayed to the eager collectors, each item destined for a new home after the *thump* of the hammer. By now, Katherine could see Gerry had pulled the wool over her eyes, but it still wasn't easy to relax, not with the thrilling drama of the incessant price wars being waged around her. Several bidders had cast their eye on the Canalettos to Katherine's dismay and the adrenaline really began pumping as Pops continued to bid over one lady in particular who was not going to give up the Doge's ship without a fight. Pops doggedly hung in there and secured the prize receiving a bear hug from Katherine as a reward for his gallant efforts, while Gerry started bidding on the next Canaletto, he also emerged victorious from the battle.

"That will look nice beside yours I think," he smiled.

"Oh Gerry, you didn't buy it just for that, did you?"

"Don't worry, I like it too," he assured her, "remember, from now on, everything I collect goes to your gallery anyway, so why shouldn't I pick pieces that will compliment yours?"

It was hard to argue with him when he set his mind on something, she was discovering he had a stubborn streak, but she was getting used to that.

They arranged for both paintings to be delivered the following day at the gallery, Gerry insisted on sharing his new acquisition right away, and so Gramps and Aunt Martha were the first on the scene waiting for the new arrivals to be unveiled in their temporary home on the third floor. Gramps rambled off to check the decorating for the umpteenth time on the fourth, reporting he was pleased with the progress so far, while Aunt Martha was distraught when she discovered Gerry's plan to make a permanent loan of his collection.

"Oh dear, and what will happen to my donation?" she sniffed, thinking her pieces were going to be relegated to a back corner somewhere.

"Don't worry, the first donation gets the main wall, it will remain so, brass plaque and all," Katherine assured her.

Aunt Martha brightened up after that and turned her attention to wedding plans, this time, pestering her about table linen colours for the reception and what to avoid since so-and-so already did it last year for their wedding reception.

Steves also stopped by that afternoon to catch his breath and grab a bite to eat with Katherine after a tiring real estate hunt. He had good news, he had found an apartment he liked and planned to visit the bank the next morning to apply for a mortgage, not that he needed it, but just in case he wanted to get rid of the pad at any time, it would be easier to unload if not completely paid off. Katherine was proud how he had become so efficient and businesslike, but maybe it was always there, just submerged during his madcap years. She realized he had been letting off steam before he assumed the heavy responsibility of the family's expectations. She asked how he was faring with the board members, especially since the shareholders at the latest AGM voiced concerns about his age and lack of experience to join the board, but not to worry he told her;

"You just have to learn to speak their lingo and in the correct accent."

"Lingo?"

"Yeah: if you can learn a language do it. Speak French to the French, Spanish to the Spanish, and mumbo-jumbo to a jumbo mumbo. However, with board members there are basically four dialects."

"What are they?" she started to laugh, wondering if there really was a Jumbo Mumbo.

"Hard Board, when you have to do some boot licking; Blackboard, when you try to teach the board something; Bored Stiff, when endless small talk is called for, and Chipboard, when you have a grievance to air that's as big as a redwood on your shoulder. Of course, there's the rare fifth dialect; Overboard, when you have to convince members to expel an unwanted piece of baggage or get them to resign, like Malignant Morgan."

"Steves, you *are* terrible. Don't ever let them know you've put them in those boxes."

The last wall had been painted in the museum section before Katherine realized she had forgotten something: benches. She needed to order more seating arrangements. This time she would settle for whatever the furniture stores had in stock that would match her décor, she was not going to wait six to eight weeks for the benches to be shipped in again. Of course, Suzy wondered if she planned a Grand Opening for the new collection.

"Gosh, should we?" Katherine wondered.

"Well, it's been almost a year since the official opening of the gallery, a nice function would be good to put in the papers," Suzy observed.

"Hmm, that means another party, already the parents are clamouring for an engagement bash, I won't be up to the wedding reception when it comes around," Katherine sighed.

"Why not put them together?" Dennis suggested. "Just make your engagement party coincide with the unveiling of the new museum, your bash is going to make it to the society columns anyway, might as well throw the gallery in for good measure."

"Talk about mixing business with pleasure," Esther drolly commented.

"I'd have to ask Gerry of course," Katherine mused aloud, "but he might think it's a fun idea."

"Good morning, beautiful. What would you like to ask me?" he enquired jovially as he entered from the back door, a fresh bouquet tucked in the crook of his arm. A quick kiss, and she told him about Dennis' practical brainwave.

"Hey, we should have thought of that," Gerry smiled, "I kinda like it."

"Really? Are you sure?"

"Sure. Why not combine the two? Everyone had such a good time at the grand opening, we should do it again, not to mention Andre would do an excellent job catering for the event."

"Or, book the restaurant for the night. We'd have to book a date when he doesn't have reservations, but we could manage it ... problem is, it would be a working party, we'd have to be ready to attend to the gallery as if it was open for business."

"Get paid to attend a party? No sweat, I could use some overtime," Dennis chuckled.

"I wonder if our parents will go for it," Katherine thought aloud.

"I don't see why not," Gerry shrugged.

Their families thought it a bit odd, but couldn't see any objection to the gallery as a venue for the happy celebration. Now, it was a matter of finishing off the museum floor. Katherine rushed around in the mornings trying to find the necessary benches while Gerry began packing his artwork to be delivered to its new home. He had to make a special trip to Paris to make arrangements for his collection currently housed in the apartment there, but it was just a matter of paperwork and the duty. However, before he left, Katherine warned there was one item she would prefer not pass through her doors:

"Gerry, I don't mean to sound ungrateful, but you can keep the Canopic vase, I don't care how valuable it is, I'm not having King Tut's liver sitting on a shelf upstairs."

"That's not King Tut," Gerry corrected, amused by her squeamishness.

"Whoever it is, I don't want their bits and pieces on display, it's like sticking a cremated relative on the mantelpiece."

Laughing, Gerry conceded, "Okay, no kibbles and bits," promising to bestow the jar to a museum with an ancient antiquities section. "I'll consider it my organ donation to society, and it'll be a good tax deduction. I suppose this means you don't want Obi the mummy I've got stashed in my closet, my mother wouldn't have him at Stonyvale."

"Gerry! Don't speak like that of the dead, it's so irreverent," she gasped, wide-eyed.

Esther looked over her glasses at Suzy, "You know, these two were just made for each other," before turning to Katherine, "he's only winding you up, dear. Gerry, you're a rascal."

"So I've been told many times."

In addition to the hectic schedule of finishing the decorating work and the plans to move in Gerry's collection, she had to gradually return the other temporary exhibits and replace them with the saleable work of her new artists. Mrs. Hunt was not happy Gerry was having all the fun as usual and insisted she keep a few of her pieces on loan just a bit longer. Katherine didn't want to upset her and gave in although she was not sure were she was going to squish the extra pieces after reading Gerry's inventory; not only did he have pieces in Manhattan, Paris, and a few exhibits currently on loan at the Brooklyn Museum, he had 'one or two' items hidden in a secured warehouse, and then he said there were a few *objets d'art* in a number of safety deposit boxes.

"Gerry, where am I going to put it all?"

"Where there's a will there's a way," he laughed as he helped her decide on the number of museum grade cases she was going to need.

As if she didn't have enough on her plate, she also had to squeeze in her required religious reading and the only time she had left was in bed just before she fell asleep. Nevertheless, she gradually made her way through the books. Pete kept his promise and stopped by every so often to see how she was getting along. She actually didn't have many questions she admitted, if the small book seemed harsh and dry as he already warned her, the larger book had interesting explanations that made the doctrine easy to understand. When he started her on this program, she expected major debates and scathing arguments considering the turbulent history their two religions shared, but all they did was discuss what she had read. Eventually she offered her overall observation:

"You know, I don't have any objection to your explanations of the commandments, and everything your church teaches about ethics and morals I can't find anything to disagree with, but your church really has a problem with mixed marriages, even though it permits them."

"Yes, for the simple reason the family is the nursery of Christianity, the building block of Christ's Eternal Kingdom. To have children brought up in a house with conflicting beliefs instils confusion with the result they will end up dropping God or search for Him where He is not to be found."

"Between two parents the children will fall," Katherine finished, "there must be unity as well as harmony in a marriage, that's why you prefer a one religion agreement."

"That's true. If a man cannot serve two masters, neither can Christianity, or several thousand of them as the case may be," he noted. Whenever they got together for their catechetic coffee hour, he always managed to leave her with a weighty observation that was impossible to ignore.

Notwithstanding all her projects, there were other obligations that continued to pop up now and again. Mr. Reinold was wondering when she would make time to visit to the *Morning Glory* and perhaps, go for a sail. The summer was fading fast and she would miss seeing it at its best he explained. Mrs. Reinold tried to get him to wait until next year, he commissioned that painting before Katherine and Gerry became engaged, the young couple had enough to do right now without adding any more to their busy schedule.   However, Katherine didn't want to disappoint him and agreed to do a sketching session and photo shoot of his majestic vessel one Sunday before the party, although she warned him it would be some time before she could begin work on the actual canvas. That was all right by him, just as long as she could catch the summer light before it disappeared. He invited her family out for the day, but looking at the windy conditions, everyone decided to stay at the yacht club, leaving Gerry and Katherine to brave the high sea with the captain. Aware of his guarded respect for the open ocean, Katherine assured Gerry he didn't have to come, but he didn't want her going off on her own either, just in case. He could still swim after all.

"Katie, when are you going to give art lessons?" Mr. Reinold called out loudly as the masted yacht lunged with the waves, thinking she was also fixing the studio for classes, "I hear your old Professor from Belvedere is already installed on the premises."

"Umm, not this year, maybe the next, I can barely get my work done as it is," she shouted back over the wind, darting Gerry a guilty glance as she thought about the drawing tutorials she was giving him. Already he had made leaps and bounds, and just received his first lesson on how to mix oil paints to achieve his desired colour effects. "Whoops! How am I to make sketches in a choppy sea like this?" she thought aloud as the boat rolled and lunged from side to side, rocking her in the deck chair and sending her pencil off its course.

"With much determination, me hearty," Gerry called out, decked in a florescent orange life vest and hanging onto a rope for dear life, his face turning a pallid green from a bout of thalassophobia. "Will it take much longer?"

"No, I'll take photographs instead," she smiled, putting her notebook in her art case and taking out her camera. One more lunge, and his hue turned a tad darker, a shade she was positive she had never seen before, a rare sight for any artist who could name all forty shades of green by their proper names. "Are you okay Gerry?"

"Yeah, I shouldn't have had anything to eat before we braved the waves," he shouted back, clutching the rope tighter.

"He's fine, he just never found his sea legs," Richard chortled loudly before giving commands to the crew to turn around and set a course back to port, much to Gerry's relief.

Near the end of August, everything began to fall into place, the gallery would be ready by the date set for the engagement party, Saturday September the 12th, almost a year to the day when the gallery officially opened, and just two years two days when she first met Gerry on that flight to Paris, although they didn't really have a conversation until weeks after the event. He was amused with the proximity of the dates and wished they could have celebrated their party on the 10th.

"Everything seems to happen in September," he noted. "Would you believe I still have the boarding pass? To think we hardly said a word to each other on that flight," he mused while sitting with her on the fire escape one evening, enjoying some quiet quality time after a chaotic day at work. Of late, they had decked up the top platform of their Eiffel Tower with a cosy wicker loveseat for their evening *rendezvous*.

"I had a terrible flight a few years before that, the lady next to me wouldn't stop yakking, so I was determined to keep my nose buried in a book for some peace and quiet," she confessed.

"And I had a tedious meeting to prepare for. I guess we just oozed antagonism and knew better than to bother each other."

"Imagine, we could have enjoyed a nice flight instead of being so antisocial," she reflected, "it's amazing how we met afterwards. Pete was right."

"About what?"

"That there is no such thing as a coincidence. We were just destined to be together."

They didn't say anything for a few minutes, quietly listening to the motorized hum and swishing slipstream of the traffic in the distance. Finally, she broke the silence;

"Oh, I can't wait, I have to give it to you now," jumping up and leaving him for a few minutes wondering what on earth she was up to. When she returned she held a long thin box wrapped in gold paper and a blue bow with a petite card, handing it to him as she settled back beside him.

"I should wait until the party, but I want to give it to you now while we're by ourselves."

He read the card first and laughed that deep musical laugh of his:

"*Roses are red, sunflowers are yellow, I'm in love, with a handsome fellow. Happy Engagement, from Your Princess.*"

"I hope you like it," she smiled.

Taking off the paper, he revealed a black velvet jewellery box, inside lay a gentleman's gold wrist bracelet with his name studded in diamonds.

"Wow, I didn't expect anything like this, thank you, I love it, and the poem too," he said, giving her a kiss. "Would you do the honours please?"

"Of course. Umm, which wrist?"

"Since it's an engagement gift, it should be on the left, but with my watch, maybe you'd better put it on my right hand." She slipped the bracelet from the box and clasped it on. "It looks majestic," he noted, chuffed with the gift. "I can't wait for the party, it means we can dance all night again."

"That's right," she said, giving his hand a squeeze, "I'm so glad I could book the same jazz group, they were a big hit the last time."

"Yeah, they were good."

"You know, they have a few more members, so now the *Hazy Crazy Trio* is called the *Hazy Crazy Band*. To think I didn't want to dance that night, remember?" she giggled, recalling the complete metamorphosis Gerry had accomplished with her regarding her former aversion to dancing in public.

"You danced with me under sufferance, did you?" he humorously enquired.

"You know how I felt, but now, I only have twinkle toes for you."

"A satisfactory proclamation, I must say. Oh, I can't believe I almost forgot, I finally got in touch with Leroy, he says he can make it to the party. He'll be flying back from the advertising convention in Las Vegas tomorrow."

"That's good news, I didn't think I would get to meet him."

"It wasn't intentional," Gerry smiled, "he travels a lot, and since his career took off, it's almost impossible to see him except for the holidays."

"That's a shame, especially since he's your best friend," she noted.

"Well, I have to say, we had great fun growing up together, but we don't seem to have that much in common anymore."

"It looks like your lives have just taken different directions, that's all. It happens," she said, trying to console him.

"Yeah. Well, I guess we should let you do some more painting," he said, standing up and holding out his hand.

"And you too, my Prince. You're artwork is coming along quite nicely, the Professor likes your still life," she reported as they went back inside.

"Really? That's great, although I don't know if I'll ever develop a unique style, everyone seems to have invented it all by now."

"Don't worry, style also depends on what message you want to express, it'll come eventually," she explained as she uncovered the canvas she was currently working on, Number Two of her Socratic dialogues to be precise with the philosophers continuing their conversation sitting down on a park bench outside Independence Hall.

"Hmm, I wonder what the critics will call *your* style," he wryly mused, glancing through her notebook. "Dissentism? Is my Princess being irregular again?"

"Only if you call freedom of speech irregular," she returned, slightly peeved with his teasing, "people have lost the ability to think for themselves, that's what's wrong with the world today. I'm displaying some hard truths. They don't have to like it."

"Still, that's some horizon line you've got there, you're going to have a hard time selling your point of view," he observed with a smile, "that's going to be on the wall for an age."

"Maybe not, people are attracted to what makes them uncomfortable. At least I'm giving them a beautiful painting, even if some of my reflections are hard to swallow."

"If you say so, I think I'll stick with my fruit bowel and leave everybody in their comfort zone," he announced, nodding towards his still life study.

03❀80

902

Everything seemed to be going so well, the family didn't expect an uproar only a few days before the party. After spending a long vacation with her parents for the summer, Jennifer had given her credentials to Steves to pass on to his father, but had one difficulty to sort out: what to fill in for her address. There was no escaping it, might as well put the address she was now living at he told her—his apartment. It didn't take long before he received a visit from Pops and Gramps.

"Now we know the rush to find your own place," he glowered.

Gramps was also disgruntled, but there was nothing they could do, Steves was old enough to make his own decisions be they good, bad or improper.

"You did tell us that when we had homes of our own, we could live as we pleased," Steves pointed out.

"Yes, but I expected you to take the good example you learned at home with you," Harold returned. "What is your mother going to think about this? Wait, don't answer that. Ask an obvious question, you get an obvious answer. It'll break her heart, that's what," Harold said bitterly.

"Well, do you plan on doing the honourable thing, eventually?" Gramps rumbled.

"Umm, marriage? Maybe, I dunno," Steves replied, "I don't think we're ready for that yet."

" 'Yet', you have at least thought about it then," Harold continued.

"Well, yeah … ." Steves returned, more than a little uncomfortable.

"I dunno, this is a right kettle of fish," Gramps said, scratching his head, "all the young ones moving in with each other these days, then expecting a big marriage and honeymoon afterwards. What for? Everyone's already been together and missed the point of it all." The problem was, they couldn't really say anything now that it had tumbled upon them that Steves and Jennifer were probably living together in Boston.

Pops and Gramps then deliberated on whether or not they should keep this quiet until after the party, and decided in the affirmative, until Helen noticed Harold was unusually sullen that night and asked what was wrong, while Steves went to see Katherine at the gallery to bewail his woes, although he didn't get too much sympathy.

"Steves, what did you expect? A pat on the back with an 'It's all right, we don't mind'? You know how they are."

"Yeah, but they're so … behind the times," he griped.

"Gee, thanks. That includes me too," she returned, "since when did doing the right thing become obsolete?"

"Kats, that's not what I meant ... ."

"It is, in a roundabout way. Steves, you know it's not right."

"Geeze, Pops, Gramps, and now you. I don't need this right now," and with that, he left the studio in a huff. A few minutes later, she heard the DeLorean rev up and screech out of the parking lot followed by a few blaring horns. Katherine sighed, she loved her brother, but that didn't mean she could accept or agree with everything he did. True love meant telling him when he was on the wrong path. The elevator door opened, it was Gerry bringing up some takeout for their nightly *soirée* since they had eaten at Andre's the day before.

"Hey, what's up with your brother? He nearly side-swiped me on the way out."

"Jennifer's moved in with him, our parents are up in arms, and he came to me to solicit support, although I couldn't help him there," she admitted. "I feel bad, but I can't tell him he's doing the right thing if he's not."

"Uh oh, family squabble. I guess you wont feel like having any curry tonight," he replied gently, putting down the boxes on the worktable. "Come here," he said, giving her a hug.

"Gosh, I didn't even yell at him, and he went all narky," she sighed.

"You've just twisted the thorn in his side," Gerry noted, "he'll get over it."

"I hope this won't wreck the party, but it will be worse if he won't come. Why do things always go wrong at the last minute? Everything is going just fine, and them something comes along to make it all uncomfortable."

"It happens, it's just life. It has a way of throwing the unexpected at you."

"Well, I should have seen this coming, I mean, Steves has never stayed with anyone this long before, and then Jennifer applies for a job with the company and plans to move to New York, then Steves gets his own place ... I didn't connect the dots."

"Don't let it upset you too much, it's his messed up dots, isn't it? If he wants the landscape of his life to come out a jumbled mess, it's his choice. You can't do anything about it."

"I suppose not," she conceded.

"Come, let's eat something, you might feel better," he said, unfolding the tablecloth she had brought for their dining pleasure while she lit the candles and turned off the bright studio lights. By now, she had also equipped the studio with a mini-kitchen counter complete with a microwave and compact refrigerator for the resident artists who wanted to paint through their lunch hour and brought their own lunches rather than waste time ordering out somewhere. Gerry popped their dinner into the microwave and opened a bottle of wine. It wasn't fancy, but they now looked forward to their informal studio dates, a satisfying yet romantic routine they enjoyed sharing; a quiet candlelit dinner, a half hour or so out on their loveseat when the weather permitted, and then a few hours of painting before they reluctantly went home for the night. They had also developed their own little tradition of reciting his valedictory ballad of *La Dame de Fer* before they stepped out onto the iron platform; "*When Hitler marched across the Rhine to take the land of France ...*". It felt good to say it somehow, as if it had become their personal anthem.

"I hope everything goes all right on Saturday," she remarked, settling beside him.

"Don't worry, everything will be fine, even if we have a few snags with family hiccups," he noted, "we can survive it."

"I want to enjoy it, not just survive it."

"I know, but it'll be all right, you'll see."

Well, he was used to it, she wasn't. It was difficult enough knowing Gerry's father might not be pleased to know Pete was coming. Now, Steves had a bug up his nose, and she wasn't sure what to do about him. Maybe he'll cool down before Saturday.

By the time Saturday came, she couldn't worry about it, there was too much to do. Talking it over with the mothers, they agreed with her that having a private late-afternoon showing of the new museum section for the guests with *hors d'ourves* and champagne followed by the formal sit-down dinner in the restaurant that evening with the music and dancing afterwards was the best way to arrange the art première cum engagement party. On this occasion, there were fewer guests than the original grand opening, and as they were just family and friends, Katherine decided to trust them with their nibbles and drinks on the upper floors as they viewed the exhibits as expected with a typical gallery showing. The worst they could do was spill their refreshments on the corridor carpets, at least the cleaning crew had provided her with a special spray that would work in a pinch if any accidents occurred before they arrived for their usual cleaning shifts. She just prayed Mrs. Hunt would not expect her and the girls to unhook all the new paintings and clutter up the lobby while she was trying to meet and entertain their guests.

Of course, the mothers and Aunt Martha arrived that morning to see if they could help, but there was not much for them to do, Katherine, Suzy and Dennis had the rolly-polies arranged for the makeshift bandstand and dance floor, and since Andre took care of the restaurant, they just spent the morning talking with Esther and Olivia. Aunt Martha was duly impressed with the new gift shop and was in awe of the large selection of Hummels on offer. She then noticed that most of the pieces were all on the open displays that Katherine had provided, anyone could pick up the figurines and perhaps break them. Olivia told her not to worry, she had that eventuality sorted out, pointing to all the various signs she had posted around: 'Butterfingers Handle At Your Own Risk' and 'It's pretty to look at and nice to hold, but if you drop it, darn, consider it sold.'

"They break 'em, they bought 'em, I can't help if people are accident prone, it's one way of covering the light bill," she shrugged.

Pops and Gramps were the next to arrive, Jasper following right behind them. Uncle Tim and Aunt Barbara came next, unfortunately, William couldn't come; he caught a stomach bug that was going around, so Katherine called to see how he was doing. He told her he would live and was sorry to miss her party, but would drop by the gallery to see her whenever he could get up off the couch. Jon was away volunteering a few months of medical service to the Red Cross in Haiti, so he would be missing the event as well, although he did send them his best wishes and a colourful painting by a local Haitian artist as an engagement gift. Stephie of course made it, she was the official photographer, the funny part was she arrived with Horace, arm in arm. They decided to make a working date out of it since he had the exclusive to cover the gallery event as a member of the press and was invited to the party as a friend.

"We're all working tonight," he laughed, "it's nice to walk in the front door on this occasion without crashing the joint. Can I go up and see the new additions?"

"Sure, go on up," Katherine told him.

"You know, he really is a nice guy," Stephie said, "how he can write those articles is beyond me, it's like he has a split personality or something." With a smile, she followed him up with her camera. Obviously, he hadn't told her the secret to his writing success yet. Mr. Reinold then arrived and nearly suffocated her with a big bear hug, Lottie following him.

"This is so exciting, I can't wait to see the entire collection in one go, Gerry only showed it to us in fits and starts, it really needed a proper place to be displayed," Lottie noted. "By the way, where is he?"

"Here I am," he beamed, arriving through the side door with another bouquet for his Princess, "fashionably late as always, even for my own engagement party."

"Don't worry, you're not that late, you made it before most of the guests arrived," his mother observed.

The Professor was already there, he was upstairs changing out of his paint gear in the studio, Suzy was handing out the brochures about their new artists as everyone came through the door, and Dennis checked off the guest list. Mrs. Hunt hobbled in with her cane, her hips were not too good, so Esther introduced Olivia to her and together with Mrs. Reinold kept the feisty lady company on one of the benches whenever possible after she had greeted the young couple.

"I'm sorry dearies, I won't be able to walk around to see the new museum."

"Would you like me to roll you around in the big chair, like I usually do?" Katherine offered.

"Thank you, Kathy deary, but no, you have enough to do tonight, I'm just glad I could come and be part of the festivities."

Of course, Charlie would not miss the big event, it was an awkward moment as he greeted their parents and then shook hands with Gerry, wishing him and Katherine all the best. Aunt Martha didn't help when she decided to come over and share her enthusiasm with them all;

"I must admit I had my doubts, but this really was a good idea, having the engagement party at the gallery. Since they both love art, it just suits the bill, doesn't it?"

"Speaking of art, anyone want to go see the new pictures with me?" Gramps jumped in, doing his best to clear up a sticky situation made worse by her well-meaning observation.

"Okay, I'll come," Uncle Tim piped up, Pops decided to go along, while Katherine offered to give them a tour. They met the Professor on the way out of the elevator, and he also joined the group. They went to see Katherine's work first on the second floor before she brought them to the new exhibits on the third. She had decided to show the two finished Socratic paintings and not wait to build up the collection, they might think it remiss if she had nothing new on display. The Professor chuckled as he saw the small sign next to picture Number Two: 'To be Continued'.

"Uh oh, she's at it again Har," Uncle Tim laughed. "I wonder where this series is leading."

"It's anyone's guess," he said quietly, his eyes glued to the colourful text.

"You know Har, this could put us all on the CIA watch list," Uncle Tim added.

"Oh come on you two, she has the right to free expression, and at least she's expressing herself with a little more panache than you did in your day. Oh how quickly you forget your own follies of youth, but I live to tell the tale," Gramps reminded them.

"So my paintings are follies, Gramps?" she asked, a little peeved.

"Er, well, youth has it's own viewpoint, and things may not seem quite the same when you're forty, take my word for it," he replied.

"What about you, Professor? Don't be shy," Uncle Tim smiled.

"I rather like it, she has followed the advice I gave a few years back, quite admirably I must say."

"Oh? What was that?" Gramps wondered.

"To paint the unpredictable and the unexpected."

"Ah, to boldly paint what no one dared before, or after," Uncle Tim smiled.

"She certainly has that down to a fine science," Pops noted wryly. Gramps was now finding it hard not to chuckle.

"Okay everyone, back to our tour," she sighed, better get them away from there before they thought up any more wisecracks.

They continued their tour, and turning a corner, came across Stephie and Horace bantering about C.S. Turris' new series of New York night scenes.

"Oh come *on*! How can you write such terrible reviews about him? His stuff is so cool," she said, defending the artist.

"I really don't know what you see in his style," he said, looking askance at them with that irksome Horace eye.

"If you speak one nasty thing about these paintings, I'll smash that recorder… ." Stephie warned.

"Don't worry, I've got more," he returned, trying not to laugh when he saw Katherine leading the group, overhearing their good-natured quarrel. She decided not to intervene and led everyone on her tour to the third floor. As they made the rounds, they noticed she was now selling quite a number of abstract artworks.

"I thought you didn't like the stuff, Katie," Gramps observed.

"I don't, but there are collectors who do, so I had to lower my high expectations down a notch or two if I wanted to stay profitable," she admitted. "I don't like it, and I feel rather guilty selling it to people when it's not very attractive, but art is in the eye of the beholder. I'm so glad Dennis is here, he appreciates it, so he does a better job presenting it to our customers. Just as long as it's not anything indecent, I'll turn a blind eye."

"Don't worry, we know how you feel. I'd love to find a cure for Alzheimer's and every other major disease, but it's the vitamins and cough syrups that keep us going," Uncle Tim consoled her, "we all get the corners knocked off us eventually."

They heard the elevator bell ding, and out stepped Steves and Jennifer.

"Hey, did we miss the tour?" he called out.

"Some of it," Katherine replied, giving him a hug and shaking hands with Jennifer, she was afraid he might skip the event, knowing the family would all be there. Pops was a little grim, but at least Katherine knew he wouldn't make a scene, while Tim asked jovially if he had seen his sister's work.

"No, not yet. Why? What has she painted now?"

"Go see for yourself."

"In a minute, I'll see what's up here first."

At that moment, Gerry came up.

"Oh good, just in time to help," Katherine said, "I'm not familiar with the details of your collection yet, and you know all the history," she added as they went to the elevator.

"Of course, I'm here to oblige," he smiled.

For those who had not seen the museum, it was a pleasant surprise. Expecting the typical hushed atmosphere with pieces placed at a considerable distance from each other giving the sensation of Spartan creativity with the dark colours she had chosen, there was an eclectic gathering of paintings and objects in impressive display cases from almost every notable culture and age nestled together lit up by soft golden lighting, making the various walkways resemble a curious chain of period drawing rooms of an eccentric collector rather than a tedious bevy of starchy museum corridors.

"Interesting," Pops noted with satisfaction.

"Talk about Ye Olde Curiositie Shoppe," Tim laughed, "but I must give family its due first, sorry Gerry. Where's the new Canaletto?"

"Over there, in the Eighteenth Century section," Katherine indicated, "generally, we put items together by age or cultural period so people could see how art developed over the years, the only thing, Aunt Martha insisted on keeping the first wall that faces the visitors as they enter, so if you find some modern art looking a little lost among the Ancient Babylonian, Grecian and Egyptian exhibits you'll understand."

"Hey, where's the con art? I've got to see that," Steves piped up.

"Oh you would," Jennifer noted before turning to Gerry and Katherine, "I heard you had some Renoirs, I'd love to take a look at them."

"Why sure."

Instead of giving the tour, it seemed all she and Gerry had to do was point people to their desired cultural periods and let them off, but it proved one thing, the museum section would be a hit and helped her to accept the necessity of having to sell abstract nonsense. She held Gerry's arm a little tighter as they watched everyone browse.

"I've said it a thousand times already, but I'm going to say it again; thank you so much."

"You're very welcome, my love. I'm glad to see your brother decided to come," he said, looking at Steves as he minutely examined a copy of a Van Gogh.

"Me too. Now, if only Pete was here ... ."

"Yeah, the only thing, Dad may avoid him for the night," Gerry said wistfully. They hoped the evening would be the opportunity for his Dad to mend fences with his brother, but that might be too much to expect just yet. The elevator bell dinged and out stepped Pete with Lottie.

"Look who I found," she smiled. Katherine and Gerry went to greet them.

"Well, you made it. You didn't bump into Captain Contention, did you?" Gerry wondered, giving him a brotherly embrace and a friendly pat on the back.

"No, not yet," Peter smiled, "although I saw him slip behind one of the mobile displays as I came in," he added.

"Never mind, Petie," Lottie consoled, "that icy crust will melt eventually. Come, let's take a look at the collection, it's the first time it's all been assembled in one place, isn't it wonderful?" With that, she gently nudged Peter by the arm.

"All right, have fun," Gerry called after them. "I suppose one of us had better head down and greet the guests, I'll go," he offered, turning to Katherine. She stayed with everyone for a few more minutes before she decided it was best to follow him, she couldn't have him meeting and greeting everyone on his own. Exiting the elevator, she arrived just in time to witness a strange sight; a tall man with a shock of curly, flaming red hair slapping Gerry on the back, grinning from ear to ear:

"So Ger, it's true! You decided to tie the knot! But if you change your mind, never fear, McFadden's here."

"Honey bun, are you going to introduce us?" his lady companion prodded.

Leroy had brought an unexpected date.

"Yes, who is this ... charming creature?" Gerry enquired, his question curiously apropos as he shook hands. This vision of Hollywood stunned everyone as she stood teetering on needlepoint stiletto heels, wearing large glittering rhinestone earrings, mesmerizing them with her gleaming blonde hair, an obvious product of a bottle. Her slender, model form with its artificially enhanced bosoms was clad in a tight, strapless, siren red satin slinky outfit that obviously cost a small fortune but had little material to show for it, above or below, while the side slits of the skirt made it appear more like a loin cloth than an evening dress. She could see why Gerry had declared his friend could be a bad influence.

"Sorry snookums. Ger, meet Sandy, we met on the flight back from Las Vegas last night and we just hit it off. It's like we were made for each other."

"Pleased to meet you," she giggled as she shook hands, her long nails studded with rhinestone accessories making the custom a little awkward.

"If I may ask, what brings you to New York?"

"Oh, I've done quite a few gigs on the Strip and thought I'd try out for this new musical off Broadway, a friend I know has a few connections and said they could help get my foot in the door."

"That sounds interesting, I wish you the best of luck."

By now, Miss Sandy's presence was causing quite a few heads to turn. Pops looked like he might be ready for another angina attack, and Aunt Martha might be in for a seizure any moment as she tugged at Helen's arm and nudged in Leroy's direction, Katherine could almost hear the sharp intake of her mother's breath from across the lobby. Mr. and Mrs. Reinold glanced at each other with a look that said 'here we go again', while Esther looked to heaven and shook her head, obviously wondering what the world was coming to these days as she took the Professor by the arm and led him away from the scene. Mrs Hunt scowled from her seat, making no effort to hide her disapproval of the new additions to their exclusive party.

"Where's your rib?" Leroy asked jovially.

"My what?" Gerry wondered.

"Why, your rib! Your Eve! Your blushing bride to be!" Leroy clarified with enthusiasm and another slap on the back. "I can't wait to meet your darling damsel, she must be a beauty to make you skip my New Year's bash."

Oh dear, time to come forward and get this introduction over with Katherine thought.

"Here she is, Katherine, meet my friend, Leroy, and his new friend, Sandy."

"Ah, so this is the party wrecker, Ger, you're forgiven. *Enchanté*," he said, taking Katherine's hand and kissing it with a bow, "Leroy's the name, advert's my game."

"Pleased to meet you," Sandy replied, shaking hands.

"I'm so glad you could come," Katherine replied. Why did that feel like a fib?

"You have a fantastic get up here," Leroy said looking around. "Have you considered launching a full marketing campaign? With a place like this combined with *my* expertise, you could bury the Sirrac so deep they'll think they've relocated their gallery to the earth's core, and appreciate the new location."

"Now Leroy, no shoptalk, you promised," Gerry warned humorously.

"Just testing to see if you remembered my promise," he grinned. "Here, have my card, you never know," he winked.

"I'd like to look around," Sandy said, turning to Leroy.

"Sure, be my guest," Katherine replied. "Oh, could you excuse me for a minute?" Katherine said as she spotted Horace Smith who had finished his tour with Stephie and was motioning her to come over for a quick parley.

"What's up?"

"I just thought I'd warn you, Kathy, that's Leroy McFadden, he's fun to be with, but whatever you do, don't buy his spiel. He's notorious for using every slick trick and sales pitch in the book to land a contract."

"How bad is he?"

"Let's say he's not above selling you a grave a hundred times over the market price and blame the increase on the cost of living."

"Thanks, warning taken," she chuckled.

By this time, everyone had arrived and were browsing through the gallery after offering their congratulations to the newly engaged couple, returning downstairs when the jazz band started up, it felt like the grand opening all over again. Gerry didn't waste time asking Katherine for the first dance, the second, then the third, everyone admiring and whispering what a handsome couple they made before joining them on the dance floor. Horace and Stephie were busy recording the comments and snapping photos, while the Professor, Dennis and Esther took turns giving tours and keeping poor chair-bound Mrs. Hunt company along with Sophia. Olivia was in her element, meeting all these new people, running back and forth to the shop to see if anyone needed assistance between dance numbers. The band then took a well-deserved break when the dinner hour arrived as everyone filed into the restaurant.

Sadly, the family contentions at the head table couldn't be completely ignored as displayed by the seating arrangements for Peter who had to be kept at a safe distance from his Dad, Mrs. Reinold looked over at him, apparently trying to bridge the gap between father and son by sheer will power. Of course, Leroy took the cake by bringing his latest squeeze who then had to be squeezed in somewhere at the table. Mrs. Hunt was extremely ruffled by this inconvenience: imagine this riff-raff assigned an honoured position in this company! Pops still looked disapproving at Steves and Jennifer, Mom was obviously worried, and Aunt Martha kept nagging her sister under her breath, enquiring what had gotten into her and Harold. Under the circumstances, they had decided not to divulge the news about Steven, they didn't want her adding any melodramatic fuel to the fire on Kathy and Gerry's special evening. Eventually, Aunt Martha gave up on Helen and turned her attention to the unsuspecting Sophia, pumping her for the latest gossip on Long Island. And of all things, Charlie *would* end up seated right across from Gerry, yet despite the awkward situations, dinner did proceed smoothly, especially as Andre spared no effort to make sure the dinner and wines were positively delectable. Mr. Reinold eventually cajoled Harold into proposing a toast.

"It's Katie's gallery after all. Please, would you do the honours?" he said, clinking his glass with his spoon.

"The newly-weds to-be specifically requested that there be no long winded toasts or embarrassing speeches tonight, and we all agreed, so we'll save them for the wedding reception," quiet laughter followed Pop's observation, "but I will ask everyone to raise their glass for one short but special toast … may the engaged couple make it to the church on time, live a long and happy life together, may sorrow never darken their threshold, and may blessings always be near. To Gerard and Katherine."

"To Gerard and Katherine," everyone called out, raising their glasses.

When the dessert dishes had been cleared, the jazz musicians resumed their posts. This time, Mr. Reinold invited Katherine to dance, then Pops, Gramps and Uncle Tim before she was whisked away by Gerry who refused to share her with anyone else, and, he had to protect her from Leroy. He was right, they could survive their family foibles, when they were together, everything disagreeable seemed to fade away. When they couldn't dance any longer, they withdrew to the studio for a few minutes of private time, sitting out on their lover's balcony.

"You don't think anyone will miss us?" Katherine worried, she didn't want to be rude to her guests.

"Not right away, fifteen minutes without us won't kill them," he said, putting his arm around her. "Are you enjoying tonight?"

"Yes, I am. This really makes our engagement official, doesn't it? Hmm, K.A.R., Mrs. Katherine Reinold … ."

"Still trying to get used to it, huh?" he laughed.

"It's sinking in."

"Still no regrets?"

"Maybe meeting Leroy and his lady friend," she said. Gerry laughed again. "But seriously, I have no regrets," she continued, holding his hands, "just … silly thoughts that keep trying to unsettle me."

"Like what?" he asked gently, wondering what would make her anxious.

"Umm, like we've never had an argument since we've met. You know how people joke about the perfect engagement followed by a nightmare marriage? I just hope we can keep always stay this happy and not start bickering after we say 'I do'."

"I see," he said, relaxing a little, relieved it was the common anxieties, he had them too. It felt good to hear them voiced out loud. "I have an idea, let's come up with a solution while everything is perfect, just in case we do have a heated moment."

"How do we do that?" she wondered with amusement. "You can't find a solution to an argument until you have one."

"Well, how about deflating all future arguments right now? We could devise a sacred treaty, invent a sign to show that if ever things got out of hand, no matter what, we give the signal that automatically declares a ceasefire and give us a chance to make peace. No more bickering."

"Never let the sun go down on your anger, hmm, I like that. What should we use? The 'time-out' sign doesn't seem good enough."

"Neither does waving a white flag or handkerchief for that matter," he added.

"It must be something that grabs our attention and makes us stop to think," she continued. Katherine then realized they already had a special sign, the keys over their hearts. "Whenever I look at my key with your initial, I always think about that day on the bridge, I could never stay angry when reminded of that day."

"Of course, that's perfect," he agreed, feeling for the chain around his neck. "Should we ever have a problem, we shall hold up the keys, that will be our sign for sanctuary."

"Agreed, but I still hope we'll never have an argument, that would be better."

"It would, but I have a feeling I'm going to need this key when Leroy wants to plan the bachelor party," he said with humour. Just then, Leroy yelled from the street below, shattering their quiet moment.

"Oy! There you are! The lovebirds are perched in a nest no less. You're missing you're own party!"

"We're coming," Gerry yelled back before turning to Katherine, "speak of the devil. I guess we'd better go in before he climbs up here and disturbs the tranquillity of our private hideaway."

℀ ❀ ℅

After a quiet Sunday, it was back to the usual routine. The party was declared a success, despite the family tensions and the unexpected guest. Gerry decided Katherine needed to get away from the gallery for a spell, a change was as good as a rest, so they decided to go out for dinner and a show once in awhile. These were quiet romantic breaks away from their busy days, one night a restaurant, other times he invited her to his apartment. Glancing around, she felt uncomfortable, he really had stripped the walls for her, leaving the bare essentials to keep the place from looking completely forlorn, notably, her picture of Rome above the mantelpiece.

"Don't feel bad," he smiled, "use this opportunity to envision how you want the place decorated."

After dinner, they just put their feet up and talked, or watched a movie with his arm around her, just like Paris. There was more than the decorating to think about, it was impossible not to imagine what life would be like with him, sharing breakfast together, rushing to get ready for work, running around searching for the car keys, gathering the laundry, actually managing the house and all the little things that no one paid much attention to. She would then be struck by an anxious thought or two, wondering if the dreaded Curse of Banality would descend upon them, dulling the sparkle of romance they now shared when the irksome, mundane incidents of everyday life set in. Perhaps that's where most arguments found their source.

"Gerry, we won't ever lose this, will we?"

"Our home together?" he asked, not quite understanding her concern.

"No, I mean ... *us*, what we have now ... ."

"Oh, the perfect engagement," he replied gently. "Never, my love. We won't allow anything come between us."

He could always reassure her whenever she felt anxious. Laying her

915

head on his shoulder, she closed her eyes for a moment, eternally grateful for having someone who once was a complete stranger love her to this extent, and to experience this deep love for him in return. Soon, it would be time to go home again, and she felt strangely torn in two. It was growing stronger every time they were together, the deep, intuitive awareness that her place was no longer where it had been from the time she was born. Often she would look at Mom and Pops as they sat together watching TV, or getting ready to go out for an evening, sharing all their problems and joys, or fuss over the daily routine. Despite her anxieties, that's what she wanted too, to start a new life with her first and only love, to actually share everything and not have to leave him when the day was over. Katherine then realized she was finally accepting the fact her wings were growing a little too big for home and it was time to learn how to fly. Perhaps that's how people knew when it was time to set their wedding date.

She didn't say anything yet to Gerry, she still had one serious decision to face, the religious obligations. Reading and pondering many times over the books Pete had given her, she could find no real objection to the moral and ethical teachings. If she agreed to allow her children become Catholic, she now knew they wouldn't learn anything contrary to Christianity, but she still had that one wavering doubt: if it was all right for her children, why wouldn't it be for her? Unless you become as little children, you cannot enter the Kingdom of Heaven. Pete was correct, there would be nothing but confusion if Gerry and the children went to one church, she going to another. A couple had to be united in everything, or they would be building on a shaky foundation that could lead to ruin. Unless God builds the city, the guardians watch it in vain. Man cannot serve two masters, neither can Christianity: one Christ, one church. Finally, she laid out this one last doubt to Peter when he stopped by during lunch hour one quiet Thursday.

"Pete, I once came to the conclusion that a tree is known by its fruit, and a long line of pure fruit comes from a long line of pure trees. There can be only one church, but how can I be certain it's the Roman one? Sure, we can trace the popes all the way back to Peter, and therefore to Christ, but is there any additional evidence in the Bible? I know about the passage '*Upon this rock I will build my church*,' but is that all? I really could use some help here."

"No problem. The scriptural proof weaves like a golden thread through the Old Testament all the way to the Book of the Apocalypse and back again. You just have to follow the mystical clues, God doesn't give the answer straight away because since the time of the Fall, we have lost the right to have all good things handed to us without work, we must work for the spiritual bread as well as the earthly one. It makes us appreciate it more."

"Well, I'm having a tough time following the thread. Could you please show me?" she asked, handing him the Bible.

"Sure, finding the passages will take longer than the explanations. Let's begin with 'Upon this rock'," he smiled. "The first problem many people have with the pope proclaimed as the appointed vicar of the one church is they are not convinced Christ gave the popes that authority. Well, if hell is never to prevail against the church, it must have a government that continues to this day exactly as it was set up with one visible leader in union with the other apostles, whose offices have been passed down to this day to all the bishops. Now, Christ said he would give to Peter the keys to the kingdom of heaven, giving him the power to shut and loose, and that what he bound and loosed on earth would be bound and loosed in heaven."

"Yeah, I understand that passage. Christ didn't just step out of the picture, though, did He?"

"No, this is when we turn to the other books in the Bible to back your observation. First to the Apocalypse, chapter three, verse seven: *"And to the angel of the Church of Philadelphia, write: "These things sayeth the Holy One and the true one, he that hath the key of David; he that openeth, and no man shutteth; shutteth and no man openeth."* Christ, as the Alpha and the Omega speaks this, so He has confirmed to St. John that Peter and his successors cannot declare any doctrine contrary to faith or morals as Christ reigns supreme over the Church, He is the true Head. Of course, a pope is human and can still sin, even Our Lord called Peter a Satan at one time, but Christ will never allow an untruthful dogma be declared as a kingdom built on lies and falsehood cannot stand forever, and He promised the church would prevail for all time against the attacks of hell."

"Okay, I get that. Do we hear more about this 'opening and shutting', just to make sure?"

"Yes, first we have to go to Isaiah, hang on, let me search for it," Peter said, flipping through the pages, "I really should memorize the Bible complete with the verse numbers, that's one thing I wish … ah, here we go, chapter twenty-two, verse twenty-two; *'And I will lay the key of the house of David upon his shoulder: and he shall open, and none shall shut: and he shall shut, and none shall open.'* If you recall, Christ opened the eternal kingdom for us by carrying our sins on His shoulder symbolised by the cross. After His death He declared, 'All power in Heaven and on Earth has been given to Me," and rightly so, for He not only opened the kingdom to us, but had also taken on our punishment and earned the Kingdom for Himself as admitted in so many words to the two disciples on their way to Emmaus, explaining how the Son of Man had to suffer in order to enter into His glory. To put it simply, we must watch for the word-clues of 'key', 'house of David' and 'upon his shoulder'. The next passage in Isaiah contains these references with the promise of a Redeemer and an everlasting kingdom: "*For a child is born to us, and a son is given to us, and the government upon his shoulder: and his name shall be called Wonderful, Counsellor, God the Mighty, the Father of the world to come, the Prince of Peace. His empire shall be multiplied, and there shall be no end of peace: he shall sit upon the throne of David, and upon his kingdom; to establish it and strengthen it with judgement and with justice, from henceforth and for ever: the zeal of the Lord of hosts will perform this.*" There is also an important passage in Job referring to God's power and authority: '*With him is wisdom and strength, he hath counsel and understanding. If he pull down, there is no man that can build up: if he shut up a man, there is none that can open.*' Then, there is one passage in Sophonias, also called Zephaniah, foretelling the one church where all people will come to praise God: '*Because then I will restore to the people a chosen lip, that all may call upon the name of the Lord, and may serve him with one shoulder.*'"

"My, there are many references about this 'opening and shutting'," she replied, it all made sense when he pointed it out to her. She then realized something, "Is that why we are also directed to pick up our crosses and follow Him? Not just for atonement, put to accept the one Church He established and pull together with the 'one shoulder' like the prophet talked about?"

"An interesting observation," Pete smiled.

"This is deep, and I thought Socrates was an eye-opener," she remarked, taking down the verse numbers to think about in her own time. "Okay, so this establishes the papal authority, but you also used the phrase 'the first problem people have with the pope', what's the other problem?"

"The dogma of Apostolic Succession, that is, how papal authority extends to the bishops as the successors of the Apostles. Now, finding the passages that support this will take us on a wild ride through the Bible in a mystical sense, there are new clues we have to follow that seem difficult, it's all about following the allegorical symbols."

"Hmm, it can't be that difficult, I don't think God intended to confuse people, and I couldn't be called an artist if I couldn't understand symbols. We just connect the dots, right?"

"I guess you could say that," Pete laughed. "Okay, let's start with dot number one, back to the Book of the Apocalypse we go, chapter one. You notice how John is instructed to send messages to the seven churches in Asia? John then sees seven stars representing the 'angels' of the seven churches, while the churches are represented by seven candlesticks."

"I'm with you so far," Katherine replied.

"Now, the following chapters show John receiving the instruction to send his letters to the 'angels' of these seven churches, that would represent the heads of those churches, which is understood by scholars and theologians to be the bishops governing them."

"But I thought angels were different. They're spirits in heaven, aren't they?" Katherine wondered.

"Yes, but here Christ is using word-symbols. The spirits in heaven are called 'angels' because they are His messengers. The word 'angel' means messenger. They are also his servants and minister unto Him. In one word, Christ has shown the bishops hold a similar office of ministry similar to the angels in that they spread His Gospel and commandments, they are His messengers on earth. Through the bishops, and the believers they instruct, the Light of Christ is shown to the world represented by the symbol of the candlesticks. Remember how Christ told the Apostles they were to show their light before men and not hide it under a bushel, and that's a command that includes all Christians. Now, as the angels stand before the throne of God, the apostles also receive their commands from the throne, and as Christ holds the throne of David, you can see the apostles are taking their commands from the King whose kingdom will never end. The symbolism is further strengthened by the connection of the seven 'angelic bishops' in the seven churches, which corresponds to the special guard of seven angels that stand before the throne of God."

"Okay, that's a lot to take in, but I get that part now," she said, jotting down some notes, "but what about the symbol of the seven stars?"

"Ah, this is where it gets interesting. I hope you can stay with me on this one."

"I'll do my best."

"To the next dot then," he smiled, "the stars further strengthen apostolic authority through the bishops. Let us start with Matthew, nineteen verse twenty-eight when Peter asks Christ on behalf of the apostles what shall be their reward for leaving everything and following Him: '*Amen, I say to you, that you, who have followed me, to the regeneration, when the Son of Man shall sit on the seat of his majesty, you also shall sit on twelve seats judging the twelve tribes of Israel.*' Now, from the very beginning, the twelve tribes have been referred to by the symbol of stars, notice Joseph's dream in the Old Testament where his brothers, the fathers of each tribe, were referred to as stars."

"I'm with you so far."

"Okay. Now, we must turn to the mystic visions of Ezechiel who saw the glory of the Lord and how His Spirit moved with the four living creatures with the four faces and wings. The creatures had the face of a man, a lion, an ox, and an eagle and moved upon fiery wheels wherever the Spirit led. The wings automatically suggest angels, and as the footnote in the Bible explains, this was an allegorical vision of the cherubim that surround and support the Throne of God. So, we have the angels and the throne again, but this is where the stars come back in. From the earliest times, the Jews recognised the four creatures were also represented in the constellations Aquarius, Leo, Taurus, and Scorpio. Scorpio used to be recognised as an eagle, not a scorpion."

"Wow, constellations? Talk about connecting the dots," Katherine said with surprise, "but isn't that following horoscopes?"

"No, the stars were given as signs and for seasons, the enemy has twisted the signs in the sky into something diabolical to divert mankind from their true meanings. Of interest, the Jews represent the twelve tribes by the signs of the Zodiac, you'll see in ancient mosaics the names of the tribes or the Zodiac surrounding the throne of God as they equated the never ending movement of the Zodiac with the burning wheels that continually revolve around the throne. Today, you will still find the signs of the Zodiac in synagogues."

"Okay, so we have 'angels' and 'stars' representing the twelve tribes, which also point towards the twelve apostles and their heavenly thrones with Christ."

"Exactly. On to the next set of dots then, back to the Apocalypse."

"Gosh, that's right. The strange creatures are mentioned there too, and the seven angels before the throne," she remembered.

"Yes, this time we look at the vision of the Woman clothed with the sun and crowned with twelve stars, this not only represents the Mother of God, but also Mother Church, *"And the dragon was angry against the woman, and went to make war with the rest of her seed, who keep the commandments of God, and have the testimony of Jesus Christ."*

"Yes, twelve stars, and the word 'testimony', that means those who witness for Him and are his followers via the bishops."

"Correct, but there is more. In the Old Testament, the high priest wore a breastplate with twelve different coloured stones that represented the twelve tribes. Now let us turn to chapter twenty-one of the Apocalypse where the walls of the Heavenly Kingdom have twelve foundation layers of coloured stones, and twelve gates of pearl. When you think of it, does Heaven need a wall and gates? It's not like an earthly city that can be attacked, Heaven by its nature cannot have anything impure or dangerous enter it. Therefore the walls and the gates are allegorical, a sign to show how one may enter the Heavenly Kingdom."

"I get it, 'upon this rock', the coloured 'foundation' stones refers to the authority of the apostles, and therefore the bishops," she noted, "but the gates of pearl?"

"In jokes you always hear about St. Peter manning one set of gates, but as you can see there are twelve, obviously representing the Apostles and their Twelve Thrones. As Christ gave Peter the keys to the kingdom, these gates also shut and open on His authority through Peter, so Peter's authority extends to the bishops. Pearls represent wisdom, like the pearl of great price in the parable."

"Oh, it really is all here, isn't it?"

"There's one last thing to consider: could St. Peter, and therefore his successors, appoint bishops? Yes, for remember in the Acts of the Apostles Peter replaced the traitor Judas with Matthias in order to fulfil the prophecy spoken of Judas' betrayal, '*And his bishopric let another take.*' If you noticed, the Apostles prayed to the Lord first to see which of the two men selected were actually chosen by Him for the ministry. Therefore, the popes have the authority to appoint successors to the Apostles, the Pope is the chief bishop after all. The bishops also have the power to ordain priests and deacons, as seen in Acts six verse six, with the laying on of hands."

"We've really connected some dots today," Katherine replied, her writing becoming a scrawl as she tried to take all this new information down before she lost the thread. "After all of that, I'm curious now about the rest of the Book of the Apocalypse. You wouldn't happen to know what that stuff about the Beast and what the Number means, would you?" she asked, intrigued with the answers he provided so far.

"Well, there is much to discover in the Apocalypse, and I don't pretend to have all the answers. God sometimes gives enlightenment on a need-to-know basis."

"But you do know *something*," she wheedled.

"If I do, that's for another time, you've got a lot to think about already. Mysticism can only be taken in small doses, or you might end up with a headache."

"All right, I won't pressure you," she said putting her pencil down, wishing she could hear more. "Well, now that we've had our big discussion, how was your week?"

"Pretty good, I was asked to say Mass for one of the parish grade schools, then visit the classes. Of course, they wanted to show me how well their junior catechism class was doing, and one little chap was so nervous, he gave me an unusual definition for matrimony by forgetting an 'L'."

"An 'L'?" Katherine wondered, flipping through the small book he had given her, then started to laugh as she figured out the erroneous answer: *'Matrimony is the sacrament which unites a Christian man and women in awful marriage'.*

"See what happens when you leave out one letter of the law?" Peter joked. "How was your week?"

"Busy to put it mildly. Ever since Gerry's collection arrived, we've had a non-stop stream of visitors. Andre just won another award for the restaurant, the plaque goes up tomorrow, and Olivia is faring pretty well too, the extra buzz created by the museum has kept her hopping, she's really enjoying her new gift shop."

"I'm glad to hear that. Not to pry, but how have your Socratic paintings been received? I'm a bit curious," he admitted.

"Um, Horace did a good job on them, so they've attracted their fair share of criticism, but that's better than being ignored. Right now, I'm taking a break from my philosophical pictures and I started work on your Dad's ship."

"Ah yes, the new addition for the Blue Room, he practically idolises that boat."

"Gerry said you like to sail too."

"Yes, I love the sea."

"Poor Gerry, you should have seen him the day your Dad took us out for a sail, he prefers to look at the sea from the safety of the beach."

"I know," Peter laughed, "no sea legs, but I'm pretty sure I've lost mine too by now. Dad would not be happy if he heard that."

Katherine suddenly felt sorry for him, and more for Mr. Reinold. She felt she had to say something about the strained relationship with his father.

"I have to confess, Gerry and I thought the party last month would help bridge the gap between you two, but it's obvious your Dad is still not budging. We didn't mean to make it uncomfortable for you or for him … ."

"Don't apologize, I do thank you for the opportunity, but like I said, it's that stubborn Reinold pride that won't let him give in and say he's made a mistake."

"You think he realizes that now?"

"Yes, because he's avoiding me, not outright confronting me, but pride makes things difficult, it's one of the last stumbling blocks. It's not easy for people to admit they were wrong."

"Oh Pete, this will make the wedding sticky, won't it? Gerry's afraid your Dad might not come if … ."

"No, don't worry, he'll come. He won't make the situation any more difficult, it just means he may not speak to me for the day, that's all."

"It doesn't make it any easier for you either," Katherine sighed, "and Gerry feels caught in the middle, I know it. I hate to see your family split like this, especially as I feel part of it already. If only I could help, but that's not all, my family isn't fairing any better at the moment. Steve's girlfriend, Jennifer, has moved in with him and everyone at Oak Meadows is shell-shocked. Mom is heartbroken, Pops is fire and ice, Aunt Martha's comments cannot be repeated, and poor Gramps is silent. How the wedding is going to turn out with all the family side-shows is anyone's guess."

"You have the heart of a peacemaker," he said, smiling, "but sometimes all you can do is pray and then do your best not to worry over the things you cannot mend. We cannot force people against their will to do the right thing. The only advice I can offer right now is to pray for your family and try not to feel anxious, look forward to everything else about the wedding. I know, it's easier said than done," he added, "life is not easy."

"Oh life is fine, it's people that make it difficult," Katherine replied ironically.

"Misanthropy does not a cheerful person make," Pete noted sagely in a humorous tone.

"No, I guess not."

At that moment, Peter's cell phone rang.

"Well, they need me back at the rectory," he announced, "I'm afraid I must head off. I'll try and drop by the same time next week if that's all right."

"Sure, anytime Pete. See you later."

Katherine wished he didn't have to go, she looked forward to his visits, she couldn't quite put her finger on it, but he always seemed to bring a feeling of tranquillity as if he were a symbolic eye in the midst of life's tumultuous hurricane. She felt recharged and ready to face the daily grind for the rest of the week after their engrossing conversations. However, this day he had given her much to think about, almost too much, but he was true to his word; he never forced anything on her, only when she asked a question did he give a straight answer or an interpretation of the scriptures, and he never treated anything they discussed with a dogmatic take-it-or-leave-it arrogance. His own quiet conviction was impressive enough. One day when they were discussing the courage of the early martyrs, Katherine wondered how many could be so brave, particularly St. Lawrence who was roasted over an open fire on an iron griddle and joked to his executioners to turn him over for he was now well done on that side. Peter agreed the *pain* of death is fearsome, but not the passage of death itself, not when you are dying for the truth.

"In fact, if someone were to point a gun directly at your head and told you they would spare your life if you denied your faith, and you were perfectly aware what you believe is the truth, you would have no qualms in saying 'pull the trigger', no matter how frightening it is to stare death in the face."

She was about to ask him if he was truly ready should martyrdom knock on his door, but she didn't need to, that penetrating glance was sufficient.

The ultimate sacrifice, that dividing line discerning truth from error. She thought about the latest biblical study he had given her for the rest of that week, she couldn't ignore her own conclusions or conveniently push them aside. If she was ever truly faced with that one, harrowing decision, she could not die for a belief where the foundation was built on shaky ground, its beginnings unsure, however, she could for the King of kings and for the Kingdom He established. Well, unless it actually happened, she wasn't sure if she could be brave enough if the ultimate became expected of her, but it certainly was one way of determining where one should place their loyalties. She wasn't ready to make any decisions and continued to read over the books, this time with the latest interpretations Pete provided, pondering it all minutely. The decision to convert to another religion was a serious matter, far more important than worrying what dress style she wanted for the big day. However, she knew she had to come to a decision before speaking to Gerry about setting a date. Concentrating on work was almost impossible and her distraction was beginning to show. It was hard to listen to Mom and Aunt Martha when they brought in another armful of the latest editions of the glossy wedding magazines to hunt for ideas, or rather, to avoid their suggestions, as every other bride-to-be would be using them as Aunt Martha smartly pointed out.

"Kathy, you're not *looking*," her aunt reproached, finally shaking the magazine under her nose with impatience.

"I'm sorry, I've got so much on my mind lately," she said apologetically. "What were you saying?"

"Never mind, dear," her mother jumped in, "we have enough time to decide what to wear. Martha, don't make things difficult."

"But we'll never be prepared for a wedding this spring if you don't get the ball rolling soon," she noted.

"Now Martha, since when did you get to decide the season? Perhaps Kathy and Gerry would like a summer wedding, perhaps an autumn celebration, there's no rush, we have plenty of time."

"That may be, but they haven't said anything, what's up with you two lovebirds?"

"We're just not in a hurry, that's all," Katherine replied a little nettled. In truth, she would like a summer wedding next year, but was not about to let her aunt frog-march her up the aisle. After all, it was her and Gerry's decision. She had enough to think about right now as it was.

"You're perfectly right dear," Mom agreed, "we just want to help with ideas, nothing is set in stone."

No, but something else would have to be, and soon, talk about 'upon this rock' Katherine thought.

Peter couldn't make it that week, duty called, another round of sick calls and a number of house blessings. That was all right, it gave her some extra time to ponder over the decisions facing her, but the more she thought about it, she realized there really was no decision left to be made, it was time to move ahead on faith, literally. Nevertheless, she felt strangely paralysed, not knowing who she should talk to first and break the news. Her parents? Peter? Gerry? She felt strangely uneasy, especially not knowing how her parents would react.

Gerry noticed she was unusually quiet when the parents got together at the weekend, or when they went out for evenings on their own. By this time, it was past mid October, and it was either raining or too chilly at night to sit out on their iron balcony, so the loveseat had been brought inside and set by the window with a small coffee table for the times they wanted to paint together after business hours. One night he noticed she was lost in thought as they dined together at Andre's before heading up to the studio. Later, they sat together in the candlelight, feet up on the small table, not saying anything, until he couldn't bear to see her looking so concerned and asked if everything was all right.

"Yes ... well, I've been doing a lot of thinking lately," she began.

"That's obvious," he replied, giving her hand a gentle press, "something's on your mind. Don't be afraid to say it. What's up?"

"Gerry, how do you feel about setting a date?" she asked quietly, returning the gesture.

"So that's why you've been so withdrawn," he beamed. "Feel? Over the moon to tell you the truth. Don't you know, this is great, I was beginning to think you were going to wait a couple of years," he admitted, giving her hug. "Well, I did say take your time, but it's not easy to be patient. Hey, listen to me babble on, looks like we have some talking to do. You still feel the same about Pete marrying us?"

"Yes, and I have no problems agreeing with the conditions," she replied, "I've been doing quite a lot of studying, and I understand what's expected."

"You poor dear, I can see why you're worried, wondering what everyone's going to think with us having a Catholic ceremony, not to mention the conditions expected as you say. Kathy, don't worry. I don't think your parents would turn their backs on you."

"I'm not worried about that, they wouldn't have given their blessing if that were the case, knowing I would be faced with this decision and may agree to it, but I've got more to say—I want to join your church."

"What?"

"I want to join your church," she repeated with calm deliberation.

"Kathy, I hope you haven't decided this just for my sake, or that anyone has forced you in this direction. Pete didn't …?"

"Oh no, I have to say right now he didn't force me in any way, he pretty much left me to study at my own speed, and then helped me if I had any questions, that's it. Honestly, I couldn't find anything to argue against in his answers and I can see the truth in everything he told me, he didn't make excuses when I asked him about the times when the Church went wrong. I admit, I had some questions about papal infallibility, but Pete made it clear the *man* is not infallible, but only those times when he formally declares doctrine on faith or morals as dogma, or canonises a saint, for instance. Putting it in a nutshell, Pete noted that the Church is made up of imperfect people and will always have its share of problems, but that the faith itself is perfect. It's hard to explain but I can see the truth in that. Basically, the onus is on us to follow the teachings because they are good and true, and not to follow the bad example put forward by others, no matter who they may be. Jesus even said so in the Bible as Pete pointed out."

"I forget that passage," Gerry admitted.

"I'm paraphrasing, but He told the people to follow the doctrine of the scribes and Pharisees if it is good, especially as they had been given the authority to teach the commandments, but not to follow their bad example for their teachers preached but didn't practise. If you boil it down, just because someone else does the wrong thing we are not exempt from doing what's right."

"Wow, you've been doing your studies, they say converts make better Catholics," he smiled.

"Gerry, please don't tease."

"I'm not, it's common knowledge. We grow up with our religion and take it for granted, while you have to leave everything you grew up believing in order to follow it, you basically fight for it."

"Well, there's something to that," she said, "I have no idea how I'm going to break the news to my parents, a Catholic ceremony they may accept, but to see me enter the Church might be the breaking point. I just don't know."

"Man, I *would* put my foot in it," Gerry said apologetically, realizing if her parents went from supportive to non-speaking terms, she might literally be giving up the people she loved for this decision. "Katherine, are you sure about this?"

"Oh Gerry, don't worry. Like I said, no one forced me to make this decision, and I've had niggling doubts about my religion for some time now. I'm pretty certain I would have taken this road eventually, I'm too curious not to investigate things, although I don't think anyone would have explained everything as clearly as Peter, it might have taken me a long time to come to this point without him."

"Well, are you absolutely certain?"

"Oh yes. Not only do I agree with the Church, but I also want to be fully part of it. You see, Pete told me with a mixed marriage, we may not get permission to have a nuptial Mass in church, although we would be permitted to exchange vows, which still is a valid marriage. But, I have to confess, it felt like something vital would be missing, especially after reading how important the Mass really is and talking it over with Pete. It felt like we still wouldn't be completely united, unity is everything, so, in order to really see how I felt, I decided to attend some of his early services the last few mornings, and I'm convinced he's right about everything … ."

"You went to Mass?"

"Uh huh. It's not the first time, I went with my friend Justine to the Madeleine in Paris long before their wedding. These last few mornings, I don't know if Pete saw me, I just stayed near the back, but I'm more certain now than ever I'm doing the right thing."

Gerry understood what she meant. He had been keeping up with his obligations now that Peter had finally got him back to church and went to Brooklyn to attend some of his services, but if he thought going to confession to his brother was an experience, Mass was more soul stirring. He could finally begin to grasp its importance when Peter ascended the steps to the altar, the congregation almost held its breath. The reverence he showed was precise, humbling even, his sermons clear and to the point, very informative and never insipid, never filled with vague generalities that made everyone feel good but leave as empty headed as before. He also had no quibbles about preaching on Hell and Purgatory. Gerry was surprised when he heard a few people afterwards whisper they couldn't wait for the next sermon. Pete may not have been given the grace to work visible miracles, but he accomplished the ordinary to an extraordinary degree that elicited an earnest desire in those around him to want to do better. Gerry wished he could have attended a few of Katherine's meetings with Pete to hear what weighty matters they discussed.

"Okay, if you're positive about this, I'm not quite sure what to do first, in order to be married in the church, you have to be a participating member, but admittance for converts generally doesn't happen until Easter. If we want a spring or summer wedding, we'd have to ask Pete if it's possible to get special permission to marry shortly after that. Maybe if you attend regularly before then, they might make an exception, I'm not sure how this works."

"If that's the case, I'd better ask Pete what's expected before I break the news to Mom and Pops, we can't really plan a date until this is figured out."

"All right, but when you tell your parents, would you like me to be there with you?"

Katherine thought about it for a moment, then shook her head.

"No, they might think you pressured me into it, it's best if I tell them in my own way."

"Okay, I just wish you didn't have to do this by yourself."

"Especially after Steves and his new living arrangements has everyone in a tizzy, but it must be done. I'll wait until I talk with Pete, he said he'd stop by tomorrow."

"All right, that sounds like a good start. You know what? We should look at the positive side and not talk ourselves into a stressful situation unless we're forced to face it. We should discuss where you would like to go for the honeymoon," he suggested.

"You're right, that would have to be decided in advance too, but it's not just my decision, is there somewhere you would like to go?"

"I guess we've done Paris," he laughed, "we really should travel somewhere that's new to both of us, but that's going to be difficult where

I'm concerned," he pointed out, a little amused.

"That's a challenge, where to go for the man who's trekked everywhere from Timbuktu to the Himalayan foothills."

"Well, the location doesn't have to be new to me, there are so many places I'd love to show you, especially Italy. It's certainly romantic there, Rome, Florence, and Venice, Venice is definitely an experience, and all the art museums? You'd be in your element."

"Gerry, that sounds wonderful, I'd love to visit Italy with you, I bet you know all the sites."

"That I do, and what about London? You haven't been there either, we could stop off for a week there too."

"Um, how long did you have in mind for the whole thing?"

"Oh, we must have a decent honeymoon, anything less than a month simply will not do," he affirmed.

"It sounds wonderful, but let's stick to one country at a time. Wow, to think we're going to Italy! That reminds me, you never said how your villa turned out. Did you buy it?"

"No, I didn't. I wouldn't be there often enough, it's easier to rent a place for extended visits and let the owners worry about the upkeep. The apartment in Paris keeps me busy enough as it is."

"That's sensible. You can only live in one place at a time."

"Yeah, I'm wiseing up. So, would you like a Grand Tour of Italia, or stick to one city?"

"Oh dear, that's a tough decision," she admitted, "I know I'll regret it if we miss something."

"A tour it is then, from the alps to the boot heel. Imagine, in a matter of months, we won't be sitting on a couch, but floating along the Grand Canal in a gondola. That's certainly something to look forward to."

If only telling her parents what she was planning to do was as easy as deciding the honeymoon itinerary. However, first things first, when Pete arrived the next day, she disclosed her wish to enter the Church, telling him everything she told Gerry the night before.

"Are you sure this is what you want to do?" he asked.

"Positive," she assured him, "the only real questions I had concerned recognising the true church, and after your explanations, I know I don't have to look any farther than Rome," she smiled. "Sure, there are many mysteries I don't quite get, but if you need answers and signs all the time, where does faith come in? All I know is God can do anything, and I don't need to know how He does it. A boss isn't going to tell his employees how he runs the company or give away his trade secrets."

"That's one way of putting it," Peter noted with amusement. "All right, if you are determined to go ahead with this, I'll tell you what's next. You'll participate in the RCIA, the Rite of Christian Initiation for Adults. It's aim is to prepare you for entrance into the Church. The good news is, you are already baptised, the Anglican church uses the Trinitarian Rite of baptism, which is valid in our church, so you will be spared the longer process the unbaptised are expected to follow. First, there's the Period of Inquiry where you attend meetings and the faith is explained to assess if converting is truly what you want to do, but as you have had several months of study with me, you may be skipped through this part, the meetings are not obligatory and there is no strict time limit set for this period. Having said that, attendance during a full liturgical year is the norm, so I'd advise you to follow the RCIA program in the church you plan to attend with Gerry as soon as possible, it's important to demonstrate an earnest commitment to be incorporated into the life of the Catholic community."

"That makes sense, I'd have to show I was participating some way in the parish before we married anyway, like Gerry has to, right?"

"Yes."

"All right, it means there really can't be any delay. I'm going to have to break the news to my parents sooner than expected," she sighed.

"I understand this is difficult for you. Are you afraid they will object?"

"Yes, to tell the truth, but it's really up to me anyway, so I'll just have to face the music, won't I?"

"It will be a shock to them, but don't worry, I think they will support your decision eventually. They'll always love you, remember that."

"Thanks Pete," it felt good to hear him say that. "Is there anything else I should know?"

"Yes, a few things. You'll also need practising Catholic sponsors to stand by you as guides along your spiritual journey in the RCIA. They'll also stand at your side for your Confirmation at Easter. I'm sure Gerry and Lottie would be honoured if you asked them, so you don't have to worry about scouting strangers out for the duty," he assured her. "The stages for adults to join the Church sounds very official, but don't let it bother you, you don't have to memorize them now. During the Period of Inquiry when you're examining the call to conversion, you'll be known as an Inquirer. There are joint rites if the parish decides to combine the initiation of the unbaptised, or Catechumens, with baptised Christians of other denominations, but for the sake of clarity, I'll concentrate on the rites for your situation. When the Period of Inquiry is over and Lent arrives, you'll be received as a Candidate during the Rite of Welcoming the Candidates. On the first Sunday of Lent, you'll take part in another ceremony, the Rite of Calling the Candidates to Continuing Conversion. When the Second Sunday of Lent approaches, the Candidates are prepared for their first confession."

"Oh dear, that's when all must out, right?" she joked sheepishly.

"I'm afraid so, but don't worry. The confessor won't hit you over the head with a baseball bat."

"Still, I'll probably wish I was one of the unbaptised when the time comes, because when the are baptised, they don't need to go to confession."

"True, but confession's good for you, it helps to keep you humble, and even the newly baptised must go to confession eventually."

"I'm worried I might get it wrong, forget something," she admitted, "Catholic confession is a little more thorough."

"That's also true, but it's not an impossible ordeal. Of course, it all seems a bit much right now, so much to take in at one time. Hmm, it's a good practise to have a spiritual director, a regular confessor that you go to so they can help you keep track of your progress."

"That's not what the Sponsors are for?"

"No, they guide you in Catholic teaching as practising members, but a spiritual director monitors the health of your soul when you go to him regularly for confession and advice, but one should not go to any one for a director, it can take years to find the right priest who can understand the intricacies of a person's soul and spiritual development. No two souls are the same, each one is like a distinctive universe. The saints had to pray that they receive a good director."

"Wow, umm, Pete? Will you be my confessor for my first confession?"

"It depends, usually you go to a priest of your parish where you're attending the RCIA process, but the Church won't force you to go to any particular priest or stay confined to any one parish, you can choose. Would you like me to be your confessor?"

"If you wouldn't mind, you know me much better by now, and I think I'd be able to confess anything to you at this point, going to a stranger for something so personal seems … odd."

"All right, usually people like going to someone unknown to them for their confessions in case they bump into them again," he smiled.

"Well, there's something to that," she noted, "but we're going to be family, and I'd rather open up to a family member than with a stranger, no matter how embarrassing. Besides, you've been with me this far along my journey." She didn't say it, but with Pete to help, somehow she knew she wouldn't mess up her first confession session from nerves.

"Okay, I'll see what I can do, but you're not to worry, it's not that painful, I promise. Just in case I can't officiate, the minute you tell the confessor he is hearing your first confession, he knows you will be completely new to this and will help you through. Now, where were we? Right, Second Sunday of Lent, as you've already been baptized, you'll be prepared for your first confession after that, then you'll be received into the Church on the Easter Vigil where you'll receive your First Communion and Confirmation."

"Will I be a full member then?"

"Yes, but you will have one final stage, the Mystagogy, which occurs for the fifty days after Easter until Pentecost."

"This whole process sounds very involved," Katherine noted with alarm.

"Don't worry, this last part basically helps you to settle in to the complete sacramental life of the Church, everything will be so new to you, this a period were you can reflect upon everything you have experienced."

"Okay, I get that, like orientation days at school," she reflected.

"You could say that. It also gives the community a chance to welcome and get to know the new members."

"So, basically I go to classes, then Lent comes around and that's when I go through all the rites and confession, then Easter means Communion and Confirmation, then orientation up to Pentecost, okay, I think I got it. That doesn't sound so bad."

"Of course, you'll have the added marriage counselling sessions with Gerry before your wedding," he noted.

"We'll never get to say 'I do' at this rate," she sighed.

"This can't be your first experience with faith and perseverance, hang in there," Pete smiled.

"Do I have to wait six months after I'm a full member before we can get married?"

"I'll have to see about that, I may be able to request special permission from the Archbishop to shorten the time, but like I said, you have to participate in the RCIA as soon as possible."

"All right, a-converting we will go," she replied, trying to sound chipper, but dreading the showdown with her parents. "Should I attend Mass right away too?" she then wondered.

"Yes, but continue to attend without receiving Communion."

"Oh, you saw me then," she realized.

"Of course, I was glad to see you. However, I must say something," he trailed, growing a little solemn, "this means you cannot sit on two stools. Once you begin to plough, you mustn't look back. You must be positive about your decision and not have any regrets nor hesitate because of fear."

"I understand, although I don't know how I'm going to explain to the Reverend why I'm not coming to his services anymore. He's been our pastor for as long as I can remember. Gee, it was easier protesting for animal rights and braving Pops with my placards than having to come out with this," she admitted.

"This calls for a special kind of bravery, the type the saints and martyrs displayed."

"Well, I don't know if I can be that brave, but I have an idea how St. Lawrence felt, my Pop's favourite method of torturing us kids and everybody else is a slow, steady roast."

"Now you understand the importance of praying to the saints, they've been there before us and are always ready to intercede for us, love for our neighbours does not die the minute we enter heaven, it intensifies."

"I'll remember that, I have a feeling I'm going to be bugging St. Lawrence a lot."

Her hunch was correct, the next day was Saturday, and if she planned to follow Peter's advice and attend Sunday Mass, she would have to tell her parents soon, very soon. St. Lawrence received a number of 'I hope you're listening to me' reminders as she tried to pluck up the courage to tell Mom and Pops, wondering what time would be best. The morning? The afternoon? After dinner? No, the sooner before Sunday rolled around would be better, perhaps at breakfast the next morning, Gramps would be there too, and everyone would be told in one swoop.

"Kathy, aren't you hungry?" Mom asked, noticing she wasn't eating much, just sipping her coffee, "It's not healthy to start out just on coffee, and you're looking positively tired this morning."

"I'm not tired, just … I don't know how to say this gently without upsetting everyone, but I've got something serious to discuss … ."

Everyone stopped eating and reading the papers, wondering what could be the matter.

"What's wrong, Katie?" Gramps asked.

"Kathy, you're not thinking of breaking off the engagement with Gerry, are you?" Mom said with concern. "If it's a case of cold feet … ."

"No, nothing like that, I'll never break up with Gerry," Katherine clarified.

"What could be so serious that it would upset us?" Pops asked.

While Katherine was trying to find the right words, her mother jumped to another probable cause more drastic than the first.

"Oh dear, Kathy, you're not … *expecting* … are you?" she moaned. Gramps started coughing, while Pops looked very grim and troubled as this suggestion sank in. "First Steven and now … no, we won't get upset. It's hard not to crumble when under temptation, especially when you love someone, we're glad you came to tell us," she continued, "we'll … just have to plan a date a little sooner than expected, that's all." Despite the shock of this scenario, Mom was surprisingly level headed. Mothers seemed to have instinctive damage control skills.

"Mom! That's not what I was trying to say," Katherine gasped, finally getting a word in and turning a little red. "Nothing like that has happened, Gerry has been very good. We're going to do the right thing," she hinted.

"Thank heavens," her mothers sighed, "you've been out at night so much lately, I just thought … ."

"Oh Mom, it's all been very innocent, most nights we're at the studio. I've been teaching him to draw and paint. He's getting very good at it already, but you're sidetracking me…" she noted.

"Go ahead, spit it out Katie. You aren't sick are you? Is that it?" Gramps prodded.

"No, I'm not sick either." Perhaps it was best to let them down by degrees. "Gerry and I want to set a date."

"Well, what's so serious about that? You were looking all doom and gloom there, I thought we had a real disaster on our hands," Pops smiled, relief now showing.

"Oh Kathy, this is wonderful! What date have you decided on?" Mom wanted to know, "Spring? Summer?"

"This is the thing," Katherine said, taking a deep breath, "we both want a Catholic ceremony."

There was silence for a few minutes.

"All right," Pops said slowly, "we figured this might happen. Are you sure you want to do this? Have you discussed all the requirements attached to such a ceremony?"

"Yes, the children must be raised Catholic, things like that. I've been doing some studying, and I can't find anything objectionable in their teachings. For the record, no one has pushed me in this direction, this is my own decision."

Another long pause.

"Hmm, well, if this is what you want, I'll support you Katie,"

Gramps finally came in, "all that's important is we do what's in the Good Book."

"Pops? Mom? You're not disappointed, are you?" she asked tentatively.

"No Kathy, I'm not disappointed in you, I've always been proud of you, standing up for what you believe in, even if it throws me through a loop at times," Pops replied quietly.

"Me too," Mom affirmed, "we'll always love you dear, no matter what."

"Um, before you go any further, I've got another loop," she said sheepishly. *St. Lawrence, I hope you're watching over me.* "I don't want a mixed marriage."

This time there was a deafening silence.

"You don't want a … oh Katherine, you're not saying you …" her mother trailed.

"Yes, I want to become a Catholic."

"Are you sure no one has forced you into this?" Pops asked steadily, assuming his usual stoic pose whenever he had something momentous to grapple with, his fingertips pressed together in a quasi-meditative lock.

"Absolutely."

"Well, how did this come about?" Gramps wondered, not upset, just a little flabbergasted.

"Perhaps I should begin at the beginning," she said.

This was one of the most difficult things she had to do so far, telling them about her own interior journey, knowing they probably wouldn't understand because they could not see or feel what led her in this direction, but ploughed ahead with her narrative nevertheless. To show this was not some mere whim, she truly began at the beginning, telling them about how she attended a Catholic service with Justine in Paris a few years ago and how she began to doubt the origins of her religion, not the Christian faith. The doubts continued to remain until she was obliged to learn about Catholicism to figure out what she wanted to do about the wedding, and finally came to the conclusion she no longer had any doubts about who was given the authority to lead the church. She also tried her best to repeat the latest biblical explanations she had received from Peter, taking her notebook out and showing the different 'dots' as she called the significant verses. Although she may not have been as clear as Pete, at least she made a thorough effort to explain and hoped they could understand. When she eventually finished, silence continued as everyone mulled this over, reeling from the initial shock and trying their best to recover. The silence seemed like an eternity, she began to wonder if they would rather she was eating for two that morning than hear news of her impending conversion. At last, the silence was too much, she couldn't stand it any longer and had to say something to try and dispel the heavy atmosphere, even if she made it worse.

"I'm sorry, I know this is hard on everyone, but you always said one of the main rules of this house was to attend church on Sunday, but you never laid down in stone which one."

Another long pause, and finally a reaction: Gramps began to laugh.

"She's got you there, son. Maybe you should have become a lawyer before you set the house rules."

"My children use my words against me," Pops noted mordantly with an ambivalent mixture of disquiet and resignation. "And what about example? You *have* noted the church we've been attending all this time?" he continued, folding his arms.

"Of course she did, she's not blind, Harold," Mom noted.

"Well Katie, after what you told us, it's clear you've thought about this long and hard," Gramps observed, "and everyone does have the right to make their own decisions. At least you will still be going to a church rather than none at all. I suppose this means you won't be coming with us to service this Sunday."

"That's right, I'll be going with Gerry to his church."

"Oh, how are we going to tell the Reverend and Elena? This will become the gossip of the parish," her mother suddenly realized.

"I'll tell them. It's my decision, my duty, and I'm sorry if I cause a scandal in the Episcopal community," Katherine said dejectedly, "I've made up my mind."

"Now Katie, don't be like that," Gramps noted gently before looking at Mom and Pops with an authoritative eye. "What was that about always being proud of her? It took some courage for her to come forward and tell you, she could have gone off and done her own thing without so much as a by-your-leave. I must say she's handling this bravely, and without that streak of impulsiveness that usually has us in a flap. At least she's not heading off to join some New Age yippee hippies and their crazy ideas, howling at the moon, or whatever they do."

"But I can't say I agree with her decision," Pops noted.

"You won't object to it either," Gramps butted in, "do you plan to throw her out of the house?"

Katherine looked up in alarm, hoping Pops wouldn't go so far as to exile her from the family.

"Of course not, but … ."

"But nothing then! You cannot hinder someone's free will, that's the first law of the Universe, no matter what the decision. Katie, you do what you feel is right, if your conscience is guiding you this way, I'll go for it, you've always been a good girl and I know you wouldn't purposely do anything wrong."

"Thank you, Gramps."

There was nothing left for her parents to say, they pushed their plates aside, unable to finish. Who could eat anything after that?

Katherine hoped the worst was over, she had told her parents and survived the trial by fire. She had arranged to take the day off, so time had come to drop by the rectory and break the news to Reverend Dobbson, who after hearing her news, looked like he had suffered a tragic death in the family. At one point, he appeared to be on the verge of tears, perhaps now she had to face a trial by water. He tried to reason with her, reminding her how she would be upsetting her parents, and on a more drastic note, pointed out that to leave her faith could lead to her eternal perdition, quoting scripture to display her error, "How shall we sing the song of the Lord in a strange land? If I forget thee, O Jerusalem, let my right hand be forgotten. Let my tongue cleave to my jaws, if I do not remember thee," but to no avail. Her parents would always love her, she was certain of that, and she didn't believe the Lord would send her to Hell now that she was convinced her decision was the right one, and anyway, it wasn't like she was abandoning the Christian faith. She wasn't leaving the Heavenly Jerusalem, she had found it. At length, when the Reverend realized he couldn't say anything to dissuade her, he asked if she would at least take some more time to think it over, but she had thought about it enough already. Resignedly, he asked if he could participate in the ceremony since he wouldn't be officiating. Katherine readily agreed, it was possible he could work something out with Peter, they still believed in the same God after all. After an hour or so of this heart-wrenching experience, she said goodbye, the Reverend watching her sadly from the door as she returned to the van. In some ways, breaking the news to Reverend Dobbson was worse than telling her parents, but at least she had overcome another hurdle. Katherine still didn't feel very brave, even if the worst was behind her, she felt shaky, perhaps she too was suffering a slight shock. She didn't want to go home right away, but couldn't face everyone at the gallery, not yet. Gerry said he would call her later to see how she had survived the ordeal and hoped he wouldn't mind if she dropped by to see him instead, deciding to drive straight to the apartment.

"Kathy, are you all right? Come in," he said with visible concern as he opened the door. "They didn't kick you out did they? I was afraid of that, I've set up the guestroom just in case."

"Oh no, it didn't come to that, but telling them was certainly difficult. My knees won't work, I don't know how I drove here," she explained, laughing and shaking at the same time, caught between a state of relief and shock, and incredibly glad to see him. He held her until he was certain she wouldn't collapse right there in the hallway.

"Come in, let's sit you down and get you something to calm your nerves. I wish I could have been there for you," he said wistfully, "especially after seeing you like this."

"No, it's all right, I had to do this in my own way. I went and told the Reverend today too."

"Good Lord, no wonder you're in such a state. Talk about getting it all done in one go. Slow, deep breaths now while I go and make some tea, coffee won't be good right now, maybe you need a shot of something stronger," he then noted, looking towards the liquor cabinet.

"No, tea is fine, thank you. I hope you don't mind me dropping in on you like this."

"Of course not, now don't you worry, love, you relax while I get you your tea." He didn't know what to do for her and brought out all the herbal infusions Lottie left behind after her visits. "I don't know what you would like, Lottie says camomile is calming, linden blossom is supposed to be good too, I'm not really up on all of this."

"We'll mix them then," Katherine decided.

"Okay, the stronger the better, heck, I might as well try a cup myself." Returning with their herbal concoction, he sat down next to her and waited for her to tell him how it went. When she finished, he sat quietly for a moment thinking, then, found he couldn't ignore the funny side.

"You mean they actually thought you were in the family way?" he said, a little amused.

"Mom tends to jump to the wrong conclusions, she never knows what to expect from Steves and I."

"So much for trusting us," he smiled, "but what a day you had. Well, let's think happy thoughts, this means we're getting closer to the wedding now that you've broken the news."

"True, but we still have to see if Peter can verify the time period I have to be a member of the Church before we can set the date."

"That's right, but I wouldn't worry, tomorrow we go to Mass, we'll visit the parish office on Monday and get the ball rolling."

That sounded like a good plan, just keep ploughing away she told herself, although it wasn't easy the next morning, her parents silently eating breakfast, casting a glance in each other's direction once in awhile, or burying their nose in the Sunday papers. Eventually, they asked Katherine again if she was sure about her decision, and when she replied in the affirmative, they didn't force the issue any further, there was not point in arguing. Making their way to the car, she to the van, it was hard watching them and Gramps drive off in a different direction, but another milestone had been reached and there was no turning back.

She had arranged to meet Gerry at the apartment first so they could arrive at the cathedral together, while there were churches close by, he said he liked attending St. Patrick's when he wasn't at Pete's services, and she agreed. She used to go there to make sketches of the neo-medieval carvings and always appreciated the regal atmosphere, and now, to think she would be entering the Church there! She still had a number of those sketches too. On their way, they had an important discussion: Katherine didn't want to sit up front because she couldn't go to Communion and was shy of sticking out like a sore thumb in the seat, while Gerry wanted to sit up as far as possible, heading up the aisle from the back for Communion with a crowd always felt awkward, as if the whole church was staring at him. At last, they decided on a middle pew to halve the quandary. Quietly sitting in the majestic surroundings before the service began, she tried to take it all in. Their first Mass together since the wedding in Paris: it was a comforting, unifying moment, already it felt like they were becoming a family. After the service, a number of the congregation approached Gerry wanting to chat, and he happily introduced them to his fiancée, notably, his Reverence, Archbishop Foley, who officiated at the High Mass.

"Gerard, good morning, no, let me guess, your charming fiancée," his Reverence said, shaking Gerry's hand.

"Yes, this is Katherine Walsingham, Kathy, meet His Excellency, Archbishop Foley."

"Pleased to meet you," she said, feeling a little shy as the Archbishop dressed in Mass vestments with mitre and crosier held out his hand towards her. She wasn't sure if they continued the custom of kissing the ecclesial ring, but since no one else was doing it, decided to do as the Romans did and politely shook hands.

"It's a pleasure, my dear. Well Ger, your brother has been calling me a lot lately," he smiled with a knowing look. "Would you both mind waiting until I finish my meet and greet? I would like to speak with you for a moment, perhaps in the sacristy?"

"Of course," Gerry said, glancing towards Katherine, who also nodded. Wow she thought, Pete certainly did not believe in wasting time. Obediently, they went back to the sacristy and waited as the priests and altar servers busied themselves, putting things back in order after the service. A few people seemed to be waiting for his Excellency, obviously to do with diocesan work, the poor man looked like he rarely got a chance to stop and take a breath. Eventually, his Excellency had finished greeting his parishioners and arrived in the sacristy, ducking into a room for a few moments and emerging without his Mass vestments, dressed in a black cassock with red sash, red zucchetto and gold pectoral cross. Asking to be excused, he first attended to the people who were waiting before them and at last called them into another room where he could speak to them in private.

"I'm sorry to keep you waiting," he apologized, motioning them to take a seat.

"That's all right, you're a busy man," Gerry replied.

"You've said it. Well, first let me congratulate you on your engagement. When did you propose again? I saw it in the papers, but I've so much news to keep track of."

"April twenty-first to be exact," Gerry replied, "but I can't lie, she beat me to the punch." His Reverend looked a little puzzled. "It's leap year." Gerry clarified. Katherine thought that might scandalise his Excellency, but she was surprised when he broke out laughing.

"You mean the ladies *actually* propose? That's the funniest thing I ever heard, but there's nothing against a lady proposing," he continued to chuckle. "I'm sorry my dear, I don't mean to make merry at your expense," he said, turning to Katherine.

"It's all right," she smiled, "it is rather funny, I surprised myself when it happened."

"Well, I certainly wish you all the best. Now, I hear you not only want a Catholic ceremony, but you wish to enter the Church. Is that correct?"

"Yes, from the beginning I wanted Pete to marry us, and decided I had better study your faith to see if I could agree to the condition to have our children raised in the Church. I didn't want to say 'yes' without meaning it, or else that would be making vows in your Church under a false pretence, and I couldn't do something like that."

"That's true my dear, you've considered this prudently. Please continue."

"Well, Pete has been helping me the last few months, letting me study at my own pace." She continued to explain her journey, just as she did with her parents, adding she wasn't forced in this direction, or was making this decision just to marry Gerry. Gerry listened intently as she explained the few observations that she couldn't ignore, One Church, One Master, and the intriguing scriptural hunt. "So, Your Excellency, I can't run away from this now. I've already told my parents and my pastor, I'm determined to go ahead."

He studied her thoughtfully for a moment, hand on his chin.

"I can see this is an earnest desire," he then noted, "and with Peter instructing you, well I have a feeling the Period of Inquiry has already been taken care of single handed. He's a stickler for tradition, and I know he's instructed you well. He did tell you about the RCIA process?"

"Yes, the general steps," she confirmed, repeating to him what she knew about the rite.

"Yes, yes, of course Peter would, very thorough he is," the archbishop noted half to himself, "I wish I had a hundred more like him. All right, just sign on up at the earliest opportunity and we'll get you started. This reminds me, I have some news for you two, I was thinking of bringing Peter back here to St. Patrick's, the Brooklyn parish he was hiding out in requested to keep him a little longer, and so I left him there since he was reviving their lagging spirits, but I could use another hand here. Since he left, fewer people have been coming to the weekday Masses."

"Does that mean he'll be here when Kathy joins?" Gerry asked, happy with the news.

"Of course, it makes sense as he's to marry you, it makes things simpler, doesn't it?"

"I guess so, and you're the boss," Gerry smiled.

"Since he's seen you through this far, I'll make sure he's specially involved with your progress in the RCIA," his Reverence continued, turning to Katherine, "you also wanted him for your first Confession, right?"

"Yes, that's true."

"That's settled too then. There's one more thing I'm forgetting, oh yes, permission about the wedding date. Well, if you continue to attend Church as a regular member and fulfil the Holyday obligations, without Communion until you are fully admitted you understand … ."

"Of course, I understand," she nodded.

"All right, in that case, I grant permission for you to have a date anytime after the Mystagogy period. Just check with the parish register and grab a date before they get filled up, and if they give you any problems because of lack of Catholic certifications, Confirmation documents, etcetera, just tell them I've given you permission and that they can call me to confirm it."

"Thank you, your Excellency," Gerry smiled.

"Of course, depending on the date you pick, I just might be able to concelebrate with Peter, if that's all right … ."

"Why of course, we'd be delighted," Gerry continued. Katherine was surprised, an Archbishop to marry them too? Was this usual? She wasn't sure, but she certainly wasn't about to turn down an honour like that, especially after Peter explained the bishops were the successors to the Apostles.

"Splendid. So, now that we have the official topics discussed, how's the family, Ger? I haven't seen your father for an age."

"He's all right, ship-shape as always, well, almost … ." Gerry trailed.

"Ah yes, he's still angry over that is he? It's a pity, 'anything you want, but not my son'. We lose quite a number of good vocations because of a parent's disapproval."

"We were hoping the wedding might bring about a reconciliation, but it looks like it's a long way off yet," Gerry continued.

"He will come to the wedding though?" his Reverence wondered.

"I hope so."

"Hmm, I'll keep this in my prayers, hopefully something will work out."

They then discussed other happier subjects, how he and Katherine met, and her art career and the gallery.

"If my memory serves me right, I read in the paper you painted a rather strange allegory featuring a pope…?" his Reverence noted with curiosity.

"Oh dear, that distortion keeps popping up like a imp," she replied, a little mortified, hoping this wouldn't somehow cause him to think twice and revoke his permission for an early wedding. Noticing her expression, Gerry looked a little amused as she tried to explain her Napoléonic allegory, again, even the Archbishop was smiling when she had finished.

"Don't worry my dear, after meeting you today, something told me your work had been rakishly twisted out of context. Besides, you wouldn't be entering the Church if you held a grievance as that critic reported, and if you did, it's obvious you've changed your mind."

"In other words, you're absolved, you're not going to Hell," Gerry added with a note of humour.

"In fact, I'd love to see your work someday," his Excellency continued, apparently familiar with Gerry's mischievous quirks, "when I have some time, I'll drop by, I'm curious to see this legendary painting, and the new museum of course."

"Please do, you're more than welcome," Katherine smiled.

Regretfully, the Archbishop told them he wished he could stay and talk a little longer, but he had to rush off, All Saints and All Souls were now upon them, and there was always a lot to do when feast days approached. Naturally, they understood and said goodbye, leaving his Reverence attend to his duties.

Leaving the sacristy, they went to a nearby restaurant for lunch, by this time, they were famished. Glad they had permission to plan an early date, they immediately commenced the important discussion on what month they would like. Easter would fall on April the nineteenth that year, and figuring out the fifty days to Pentecost for the Mystagogy period, they calculated a June or July wedding was possible. Gerry thought it might be too hot to travel through Italy in August and suggested they have the wedding in June. As much as Gerry wanted to tell her about Italy right then and plan which city to visit first, Katherine suggested they should really start pinning down the fine points of the ceremony before they plotted out the stops on their honeymoon. Well, it was obvious they were getting married in the cathedral, Katherine hoped it would work out.

"If we have a big venue, we're going to end up with a huge guest list. What about the small ceremony we wanted?" she observed.

"True, we could tell his Reverence we've changed our minds and would prefer a smaller church to restrict the seating, it would be one way of ensuring our mothers don't get out of hand," he joked.

"Well, I *do* like the cathedral," she admitted, "I never did care for modern buildings, and we can't have anything *too* small."

"All right, love, St. Patrick's in June it is. What next? Better take out your little notebook."

"I'm not sure," she confessed, "I'm probably the only woman clueless about wedding plans. Do I pick bridesmaids next?"

"Gee, I dunno, I'm just as bad. Aren't the women in the family supposed to help you with that?"

"I guess … ."

"Oh wait, I think you have to pick a Matron of Honour who will also be your witness to the marriage, but I'm not sure. If so, that means … ."

"Nuts, do they have to be Catholic?"

"I don't know, I don't think they have to be any more, but if Pete's handling the ceremony, he may be the one calling the shots. You heard his Reverence say Pete is a stickler for tradition, so big brother may just request a Catholic matron and a best man.”

“Darn, Stephie is not going to like this, I should have kept my mouth shut until we sorted everything out. I promised she could be my Matron of Honour, I think she was expecting it, and she is my cousin after all. The only person I know who could do it is Lottie. I’d ask Justine, but with the distance, I’d hate to put her under the obligation to come, even though she said she would … .”

“Slow down Miss Locomotive, we’ll figure it all out. If Pete sticks to his guns, at least you have Lottie,” Gerry said. “I’ve got a right problem, who to ask to be my best man, and let’s face it, Leroy is not exactly a moral pillar of society, my folks might be in shock if he stood waiting with me at the altar.”

“Oh no,” Katherine gasped, but then started to laugh as she pictured the scene. “Actually, I’m more afraid of who he might bring to the reception.”

“There’s that, and of course, he’d be the one to forget the rings and use soda can pull-loops for a substitute.”

“We can’t have that,” she laughed. “Don’t you have anyone else?”

“I’d ask Pete, but he’s marrying us,” Gerry replied, “and I would like someone I know to do the honours.”

“Gosh, and everyone I know is non-Catholic. I hope Pete relents in this one instance … but wait. What about Andre? I think he’s Catholic, he’s always asking Pete to bless things when he comes for lunch.”

“Well, that’s an idea,” Gerry said thoughtfully, “but we have months ahead of us yet, we don’t have to decide every detail in one day, this is just suggestion time.”

Be that as it may, there were many suggestions to consider, where to have the reception for instance, and what colour she would like for her bridal theme. She wondered what would be picture perfect for a June wedding, and then mysteriously smiled to herself as she shook her head.

“No, that won’t work … .”

“What’s up?”

“Everyone will think this is crazy, but I would love a red rose and sunflower theme, for the floral decorations, although I haven’t the foggiest idea how to match everything else around that without making the event look like a McDonalds birthday party.”

“Now that would be something, with his shock of red hair and a sunflower boutonnière, Leroy could be the perfect Ronald McDonald.”

"Oh Gerry! I needed a good laugh, particularly when I think of the music that's facing me when I get home. More than likely, it's Mozart's *Requiem* for dinner, and of course, Aunt Martha will be there, adding her two-cents worth to the dirge. I wish I was going with you to Stonyvale."

"Would like me to skip Stonyvale tonight and come with you for support?"

"No, I'll be all right, thank you for offering. You go ahead and have dinner with your parents while I brave the sombre notes, I'll give you a call when I can escape to my room."

As soon as she crossed the threshold of Oak Meadows that evening, her Aunt wasted no time hurrying to meet her at the front door.

"Katherine Walsingham! What possessed you to consider abandoning our faith? Whatever got into you to *think* of doing such a thing? Isn't it bad enough you're marrying a Catholic? And now, you're joining their denomination? Upon my word, I never heard of such a thing!"

"Oh Martha, give over," Helen said, coming down the hall and conducting them into the den, "you're being melodramatic as usual."

Gramps and Pops looked up from their papers as they entered, a resigned look on their faces, they were well used to Martha's tirades.

"Come, sit down and try not to get all upset," Harold suggested.

"Upset? Of course I'm upset! After all the care and solicitude we invested in raising Katherine and Steven in a traditional, conservative home and creed, to think they can throw it all to the wind and abandon everything they were raised to consider sacred. Where did we go wrong? We failed somewhere! It was bad enough hearing Steven was leaving home and getting his own apartment and attending a church in the city, but now Katherine is leaving home, and leaving her church! I don't know if Reverend Dobbson and Elena will ever get over the shock," she wailed. "This is all too tragic! To think you won't be attending our church anymore! If only you had married Charlie, everything could stay perfect, with that nice house down the street on the corner for sale, you would still be here with us, and we'd all be attending church together as we always do."

"Please Martha, do be quiet, don't make things any worse than they are," Harold interrupted.

"Make things worse? How could they possibly get any worse than they are right now," she returned.

"Oh dear, shall I tell her?" Helen said, looking to Harold for permission to raise the topic.

"Might as well, better she hear it from us than the gossips at the Club," he conceded.

"Hear what first?"

"Jennifer is now sharing the apartment with Steven," Helen began, but couldn't get any further.

"What! You mean they're ... *cohabiting*? What's the world coming to? Our Katherine leaving our church, Steven living in sin... I *knew* I should have taken more Valium today, not that they can help much under these circumstances, I think I'm becoming immune ... ."

"Oh boy, Katie, looks like we're going to have a rough night of it," Gramps said under his breath, soon wishing he had stayed quiet.

"And you're no help, Gregory," she said flatly.

"Me? What did I do?"

"I hear you're backing Katherine in her latest stunt, surely you want her to remain with the creed she was born and raised in?"

"I dunno. You'd better pray nothing happens to the Reverend, we might end up with a lady pastor the way things are going. Now *there's* a scandal for you. If that should come to pass, I might be tempted to take a leaf out of Katie's book and head to ancient Rome," he said, giving Katherine a wink. Like Steves, he couldn't resist the opportunity to wind her up.

"Oh, you're hopeless," she huffed, disgruntled with his flippant attitude in the midst of this family crisis. Eventually, she calmed down a bit, having heaved all her frustration off her chest onto everyone else before they went into dinner, although a few quick quips would escape her on occasion, as when Katherine wanted to tell everyone about her day and explained Archbishop Foley might concelebrate the nuptial Mass with Peter:

"Well, if it's archbishops you want, I'm sure we had a few in *our* church that would have been happy to oblige."

Katherine decided it was best to stay quiet for the rest of the evening while Aunt Martha was present, anything she said could and would be used against her, no matter how innocent. Only speak when you are spoken to she thought, and perhaps you might get away to your room soon. Aunt Martha then offered a final blow to Helen over dessert:

"Just how do you propose we plan a wedding now? We really don't have much to say or do at this point, not with Katherine doffing her religion, I suppose *his* family are going to take over," she sniffed.

"Martha, what are you talking about? Of course not, they would have helped anyway, and Sophia is an absolute dear, she won't railroad the bride's family from the happy occasion," Helen said.

" '*Happy*?' You think it will be a joyous occasion? Will anyone come? They might all stay away when the news spreads, we'll be the only ones there in a sea of strange Catholics."

"Don't be ridiculous," her sister returned, "we and everyone we know has attended mixed marriages, no one is going to boycott our Kathy's day."

"That's what you think, those mixed marriages took place on our territory, remember? Now it'll be the other way around and there's no telling what may happen. Well, do you have anything to say?" she turned, looking straight at Katherine.

"You can still help me plan, it's not going to be that much different than all the other weddings, the reception will be the same, even the service will be similar … ."

"Then why change to *their* persuasion? Oh, do be reasonable Kathy dear, I think you're making a big mistake," she wheedled, trying to change her mind by heart-twisting anxiety if she couldn't budge her by brute verbal force.

"*I* don't, and surely we're entitled to change our persuasion," Katherine replied, dropping her napkin on the table and politely asking to be excused. Pops nodded and she left the table, she just had to escape, and headed straight to the quiet sanctuary of her room.

She flopped on the bed, burying her face in the eiderdown. Since she announced her intention to convert, the tension in the household was oppressive, and on top of it all, Aunt Martha's lecture questioning her decision to marry Gerry made it more unbearable, everyone was acting like she was betraying the family. It was all getting too difficult to handle, Katherine's mind was whirling in confusion. Can everyone else be right, and I'm wrong? Am I doing the right thing, or is it too late to change my mind? A tidal wave of uncertainties surfaced and threatened to submerge her. I don't feel like I'm betraying my family just because I'm adjusting my faith, I'll always love them, and I never wanted to disappoint them, but that's the problem; they are disappointed, questioning my choices and regretting how everything is turning out contrary to all their hopes and dreams. I'm not only turning my back on their religious convictions, I've turned down the man they thought I would marry. I wish I could please them, but I know I can't, not this time. Oh yes, I could have married Charlie and move into the house down the block and attend the same church, but if I did, everything may not end up as perfect as they expected. There are many factors to consider, the most important one, I didn't fall in love with Charlie, not in that way, and that makes all the difference. You can't choose the person you will love, and I know for certain if I had married Charlie trying to make everyone else happy, I would have ended up miserable. People-pleasing is a weak foundation upon which to build a life with someone, and all those you try to please are not the ones getting married, I would end up living with the consequences, not everyone else. I'm positive if I continued to attend the family church, I would have eventually questioned my faith as I explained to Gerry. Perhaps I wouldn't be converting as soon as this, but it would have come. Let's not turn back now, I know I've discovered what I was looking for, an answer to all my spiritual uncertainties. The Good Book said to seek, and I've found my answers, or rather, I've confirmed what I've suspected all along. I will always love my parents, and I hope they can eventually accept the path I've chosen, this is one of those times when I have to make my own decisions.

This sense of division at home promptly made her heart freeze with anxiety as her thoughts jumped to her impressions at church that morning, how she already felt she and Gerry were becoming a family. While that was encouraging and exciting then, she now felt troubled and unsure, especially after Aunt Martha's caustic remarks. Everyone dismissed the feelings of pre-marriage anxieties with the sedate description of 'cold feet', but there was good cause for second thoughts. Looking back, she could see that when she drove off in a different direction to meet Gerry, a change was already taking place, not only with her new faith, but within her family. She would be leaving the security of her childhood home to step out into the unknown with someone new in her life who she hoped would always love her and would not betray her trust. He would come to the fore as her husband while all her family must quietly step back into a secondary role to allow her form this new union. Once she was married, life would never be the same again, there was no going back. Katherine loved Gerry with all her heart, but the thought of this irrevocable change and an unpredictable future still filled her with apprehension. She didn't want this paralysing fear to grip her, and she held the key in her hand for a moment, closing her eyes and imagining his face, the special way he looked at her, just being with him and hoping what he predicted about arranging the spoon drawer would come true. She felt better thinking about him, especially all the times they shared together, she truly did love him, but strangely, it did not make this emotional transition any easier, one love now taking over another and changing her life to this extent, it almost felt like a bereavement, moving ahead on faith away from her parents and practically everything else she had known. So it's true, when all is said and done, grief is the price we pay for love.

Katherine wondered how this could be, that something as beautiful as love could be tinged with sorrow, but she loved Gerry, she knew she would not change her mind, they were meant to be. Still, the upheaval of the last couple of days left her feeling vulnerable and she dialled his number, longing to hear his reassuring voice.

"Hello my love, I've been worrying about you. How did it go?"

"To begin with, my Aunt is treating me like a heathen, I just slipped away before she tried to reconvert me."

"At least they all know, hang in there, just give them time."

"I still have to tell everyone at the gallery, but that won't be as bad as breaking the news to the family and the pastor. I have to say, Gramps has been a trooper to stand by me, but I think the only ones in the house who are happy about the whole thing are Mrs. Gonzales and Juanita, after breakfast yesterday, they gave me a load of rosaries and medals to start me off, it's all a bit overwhelming to tell the truth."

"I'd better warn you then," he started to laugh, "since Mom and Lottie have heard the news, they've gathered a few things for you too, so expect a few welcome wagons to roll your way, everyone means well."

"I suppose they do, and they are being kind."

"I noticed you said 'to begin with', what else happened?"

"Well, I hope you don't take this the wrong way, but Aunt Martha pretty much hinted that you and your family may be to blame for my apostate ways, but it's not true. I already had my doubts, but I know she doesn't see it that way.   It makes me wonder if everyone else is thinking the same thing, no one has said anything, but I hope this won't cause a rift eventually."

To her surprise, he started to sing a ballad in a thick, exaggerated Irish brogue:

"My father he was Orange and me mother she was Green ..."

"What?" She wanted to laugh.

"I know it's not exactly the same situation, but you just reminded me of a song about a boy in Northern Ireland whose father is Protestant and his mother is Catholic. He ends up attending two churches, has two first names, William and Pat, and has to join the Orange Order to please his father and celebrate St. Patrick's Day with his mother. Can you just imagine that?"

"At least we won't have a mixed marriage, so hopefully our kids aren't going to get confused. I feel like we're in a Romeo and Juliet situation, one pair of lovers, two divided households."

"What an analogy, one lover dies by poison, the other by a knife-thrust to the heart. We're not *that* bad off I hope, we do have our parent's blessings after all."

"You're right, they'll get used to it, it's just … ."

"I know, your house feels strangely divided, already you're hearing remarks about 'his' family and 'ours', not to mention leaving everything is a major shock to the system. As they say, moving house is the closest thing to suffering a death in the family, so I can't even imagine what the thought of moving in with me, on top of the inevitable wedding jitters, and changing your religion is doing to you right now."

"Oh Gerry, you've said it, not that I don't want to marry you, I do, but you've hit the nail on the head. It'll be a big change, and unlike most of my adventures, this will be permanent.   Perhaps I'm not making sense … ."

"I understand, a new home, a new life, but don't forget what I said about the spoon drawer."

She could almost picture him with that encouraging smile and felt her insecurities abate. It was a comfort to know he was aware of what she was going through without having to spell it out, and that he still remembered his odd analogy of the spoon drawer, it drew her back to their weeks in Paris and how happy she was, also recalling their romantic nights out and the feeling of incompleteness she experienced when they parted.

"I won't forget," she replied. "I love you Gerry, I'm so happy when we're together, I just know it will all work out."

"I love you too. Don't be afraid, whatever the ups and downs, we're going to have a wonderful life, you and I against the world. Right now, I wish we weren't on the phone, I'd almost drive up there right now and whisk you away to our Artist's Corner just to talk into the wee hours until the last star fades.   Doesn't that sound like a good idea?"

"It does, and I wish I could, but we have work in the morning."

"Must we have practicalities now? Why can't we just live on love?" he wheedled.

"Because we can't live without sleep," she returned.

"Ouch, love gets shot down by logic."

"Not shot down, only persuaded to return to earth for now. I'd love to fly and meet you, but you can join me in the Artist's Corner tomorrow."

"All right, fair enough. I suppose that's my cue to let you get a good night's rest, and after the evening you've had, you need it. I'll see you tomorrow, my darling, and remember, I love you, that's all that matters."

"I love you too. Goodnight dearest, sleep tight."

Sweetheart, darling, dearest, it was funny to think that these endearments, which used to sound exceedingly sentimental in movies and books, now held great importance, simple but true verbal affirmations of how they felt for each other.   They were words only the heart could hear and understand, words that could impart entire pentameter sonnets in their few, short syllables. She undressed for bed and snuggled under the covers, drifting off to the sound of his voice, *"we're going to have a wonderful life, you and I against the world … I love you, that's all that matters …"*. The future did not seem daunting now, they would face one day at a time, together and always.

❦

The next morning, Suzy wondered why the atmosphere at the main house was so uptight, having missed the latest events the last few days, deciding to fix breakfast at the apartment on Saturday and sleeping in on Sunday. She asked Katherine what had happened on their way out to their respective vehicles, and received the reply if she was ready to hear a long story, she might want to ride with her in the van today. After she revealed to Suzy her latest decisions, her friend did not seem that surprised.

"Judging by the way Fr. Peter was dropping by all the time and the involved discussions you two were engrossed in, I figured something like this might happen. I see it was a shock to your folks though, but don't worry, I know they'll understand. So, what do you have to do now?"

"Just attend church and classes, then get officially initiated at Easter. Of course, they insist on marriage counselling sessions before we marry, I don't know how long they will take."

"It sounds involved, you'll have to paint during the daytime on the nights you have to go to classes. Imagine, it's almost like going back to school."

"Yeah, night classes, and I thought I was all finished with those," Katherine noted.

"Maybe these will be different."

"Perhaps, but enough about me, how are you and Charlie doing? You two have been pretty scarce lately, I hardly see you guys after work, and you don't drop by for dinner that often, not like you used to, of course, I've been out most of the nights too come to think of it."

"We're growing more inseparable since I took your advice."

"Gosh, what did I say? I can't remember what I told you."

"About hinting to him it was all right if he wanted to kiss me. Like you said, Charlie has difficulties expressing his feelings, he just needed a nudge. Maybe he's afraid to because of all these harassment claims, not knowing where displaying how you feel and crossing the line comes in."

"That could be true, but that was a long time ago when I offered

951

you my two cents. Oh, I do hope this means you're both madly in love with each other."

"It is, I love him, but we haven't quite said anything to each other … ."

"What? How could you two not say you love each other if you're inseparable, and having the most romantic kisses of your life I might assume?"

"Like we discovered, he can't voice his feelings, not comfortably anyway. He hasn't said anything, and if I do, I'm afraid to push him away, just in case it hasn't gone that far for him yet … ."

"Oh dear, you two are spinning wheels again. I don't mean to drag this up, but I didn't know until he literally brought out the ring box. You'd better say something first, tell him how you feel, it would be a lot better than waiting around for him to say it."

"Honestly, if his first declaration of love came with a ring, I wouldn't mind, I'd gladly accept both," Suzy confessed.

"Well, go ahead and spill the beans, the ring might come a little faster if you do. Just look what happened with me and Gerry, love proclamation and engagement all in the one day," Katherine reminded her.

"I wish I was as brave as you to do the proposing," Suzy laughed, "but your advice has worked so far, I'll tell him how I feel, tonight, no delays."

"That's the spirit. Love, like Fortune, favours the bold."

The morning started out quiet enough, Dennis wasn't there as it was his day off, the kitchen sounded tame today, no missing chefs, no meat that needed to be pounded. Esther had a stack of morning papers under her arm for their customary article hunt for the gallery archives, Olivia was filing and polishing her nails to pass the time during the morning lull, while the Professor decided to sit and have cup of coffee with them before heading up to the studio, everything seemed like a routine morning. Deciding not to delay breaking the news, she told the Gallery Gang about her religious conversion, and had to repeat herself when Mrs. Hunt arrived just in time to hear the tail end of her story and wanted her to start all over again with all the details.

"Well, Kathy deary, I wish you well. At least your family is still on speaking terms with you, you're practically still in the same faith after all. As you know, I'm Jewish, and when I married my Christian hubby, it didn't go down well at all, especially with the Orthodox members of my clan, they held a funeral and wouldn't speak to me again."

"Are you kidding?" Olivia gasped, nearly dropping her bottle of nail varnish.

"Do they still do that?" The Professor wondered, "I thought that died out ages ago."

"My dear, that's just terrible," Esther consoled.

"You mean they *literally* held a funeral?" Katherine asked, astounded that people could be so cruel.

"Yep, *in absentia*, they threw a reception, the whole shebang, but I got over it, I loved my hubby, and that's what counted."

"Gee, but I can't imagine family doing that to you," Suzy said, shaking her head in disbelief.

"Well, it's the ignominy of a mixed marriage, the children may grow up without the faith, and so the person marrying the gentile is pretty much considered as lost and dead to everyone as they have endangered their children," the Professor explained.

"That's it in a nutshell," Mrs. Hunt affirmed, "but what nonsense, Christians follow the Ten Commandments, so there's hope for you all, that's what I figure. Now, any new pictures, girls? I have a birthday party to attend, and the person is an art collector, I want to get them something unique. After that, I want to see your new figurines, Olivia deary."

"Sure, got a new shipment on Friday," Olivia replied as she resumed her careful nail polishing.

"Dennis and Turris have painted some unusual images, they just went up last Friday," Katherine told her, gearing up for the unhitch-and-fetch routine expected by their feisty regular to the gallery. Mrs. Hunt kept them hopping as usual, creating havoc in the lobby with her chaotic browsing habits, at least she had come early this time before the place became crowded with visitors. Katherine was glad when Gerry called, it gave her a break from the running for a moment. He forgot to tell her last night she might have to leave early for the day to make it to the parish office before it closed in order to sign up for the RCIA program, and wondered if she would like to go out for dinner afterwards. Of course, she would have to leave everyone else close up the place that night, but he observed that's what she was paying them for and added that an early night out of the gallery wouldn't kill her. He would pick her up and that was that. Mrs. Hunt was still hanging around for some company after adding a few new figurines to her collections in addition to the birthday gift when he stopped by at four to pick up Katherine.

"Looks like I've come in the nick of time, you need to get away from a day of that," he noted.

"Don't worry, we're used to it now," Katherine assured him, "poor thing, she's really had it rough, she just told me about the funeral her family held for her."

"What? Say that again?" After she told him, his eyebrows furrowed for a moment, his usual reaction when he disapproved of something or was worried. "That's tough," he continued, "she never told us about that, or if my parents knew, they didn't say anything. Makes me regret the times I've been impatient with her."

"Poor thing, another reason she craves company, it must be hard when you've been cut off like that."

"I feel like a right heel, I'd nearly bring her with us for dinner, but we have to go to the parish office today."

"We'll have to pay more attention to her, she must be very lonely," Katherine thought aloud.

"Okay, we'll take her out some night, but right now, it's just us two again," he smiled, "how about Thai cuisine? There's a new place that's been wowing all the food critics, and afterwards, we can snuggle up in the apartment with our feet up in front of the fire for awhile."

"That sounds delightful."

While they were in the office, they took down a list of dates that were free in the last two weeks of June for the wedding, hopefully the mothers might agree on one of them before they were snapped up as the archbishop warned. Katherine didn't mind what day, it was exciting to think they were taking one step closer to becoming officially inseparable. At last, the thrill of planning the day began to sink in as they left the office, the style of dress she wanted to wear, maybe have something unique designed, what colours would be chosen for the bridesmaids, the linens, the invitations, the cake, then there was the gift registry, that would take some time to set up.

"You've gone quiet all of a sudden," he noted as they drove to the restaurant.

"I've been thinking about all the plans that have to be made, it's rather exciting. I'm going to try and enjoy it and not let it stress me out and ruin the big day when it arrives, but it doesn't seem fair the bride gets to choose practically everything, you're getting married too. Do you have any ideas you'd like to add?"

"I don't mind really, you ladies do a good job planning colours and linens and all of that, it's your natural gift, and as long as the food is good, everyone else will be happy. Tell you what, you plan the celebration any way you like it, while I plan a working itinerary for the honeymoon and bring it to you for your approval. How's that?"

"That sounds fair, you know Italy, and you always manage to surprise me."

"All right, my love, just leave it to me. I'll make it so special, you'll think you've arrived in the Elysian Fields."

It was wonderful to plan and dream, but putting those plans into action was another matter, everything depended on timing and co-ordination. Mom and Aunt Martha eventually surmounted the shock of the weekend and began the wedding preparations in earnest the next day, immediately chiding Katherine for not using her head, she should have grabbed a Saturday for the date and not worry about asking their opinion, but perhaps there was still time. Saturday was good her mother pointed out because she could close the gallery plus they had Sunday off, not to mention allow time for the guests to travel if needs be. Get that date first they told her, and they could settle a rehearsal date later. Katherine immediately obeyed and rushed to the parish office after lunch, there were only two Saturdays near the end of June, and to her relief, the last one on the 27th was still free. Once she had secured the day, it finally felt like things were happening, they had an official date to look forward to, which also meant they now had a deadline. Katherine reminded herself she was not going to worry about the plans, they still had plenty of time. Next, the ladies had to book somewhere for the reception, Sophia was invited for this important parley the first week of November.

"Now, Gerry and I would like a small to medium celebration, nothing too big. We were hoping we could have somewhere intimate and personal, hotels seem too … plastic," Katherine said.

"You're quite right dear, hotels are impersonal at times, aren't they?" Sophia agreed.

"Yes, a prefabricated ambience," Aunt Martha chipped in.

"Did you have somewhere in mind?" Mom asked.

"Well, I was thinking about our country club, but then, when I told Gerry, he wondered about the security issues, we can't keep it a private celebration there, someone from the press might sneak in, you know how it is."

"There's that to consider," her mother nodded, "but dear, we should tell you, we can't promise a small guest list, not with your father and grandfather's obligations, and I don't think we could have the reception at home. There will be a number of people that will expect an invitation, including business associates, and I'm sure Richard and Sophia have similar commitments."

"Yes, there are courtesies we have to consider," Aunt Martha added.

"Are you serious?" Katherine replied, wide-eyed.

"I'm sorry Kathy, it's true," Sophia confirmed, "In addition to family and friends, Richard has a number of people who cannot be excluded, and I think he mentioned something about business associates from Hong Kong, Japan, I forget where else."

"Oh that's right, Harold said he'd check with the PR department to see if we have to print special invitations in Chinese, Javanese and Japanese for the occasion similar to the business card custom, you know how that is," Helen continued.

"I know, I'm glad the men handle that part of their trips," Sophia observed.

While the mothers and Aunt Martha thought a large celebration was all just dandy, Katherine couldn't believe it, the wedding reception was starting to sound like the World Expo. She poured out her consternation to Gerry that evening as they drove to her first RCIA meeting.

"I'm sorry pet, but it's true, Dad reminded me of my duties too," he replied apologetically, "I've got to invite quite a few Asian associates, they might not come, but it's a courtesy to send an invitation. It depends how close you are in business relations."

"Oh no, this really will become a circus, they could all show up. We won't be able to pick somewhere small and special if the guest list gets as large as Santa's."

"Don't worry, just wait until we have kids and you can take over their big day, maybe then you can have the wedding you always wanted."

"Gerry, don't tease," she replied, "but how are we going to find somewhere large enough to handle what I fear the matriarchs are planning and still keep it private, not to mention a venue that means something to us? It'll be difficult enough having all those strangers attend. It looks like we're going to end up in a hotel."

"You know, we already have the perfect place. Why not Stonyvale? We have the large formal dining room and the ball room, we've got plenty of space for a marquee in the gardens that overlook the sea, there would be plenty of room, the house always looks its best in June, and it's secure and private. What more could we ask for? That is, if you don't mind having it there … ."

"Oh, that would be perfect! It's your family home after all, when you think of it, we couldn't have the reception in a better place, but will your parents be all right with this idea?"

"Are you kidding? Mom would be in seventh heaven, and Dad would love to see the place crowded like the old days when the grandparents threw parties, it's a shame to have it all locked up. They probably haven't come forward to suggest it because they didn't want to look like they were pushing us, but I know it's got to be on their minds."

"Better check with them just to make sure. It's all happening so fast, I hope we're not rushing things … ."

"Aw Princess, don't worry. It's what we both want, isn't it? And we'll let the folks have their way, let them invite the United Nations if they feel they must. We have each other, everyone else is just surplus to requirements."

"You're right, I'm not going to let any of it bother me from here on out. Let them all manage it anyway they like, our preferences are filed in the trash can anyway, they completely ignore us.

"Or," Gerry continued, "they ask us what we want and then proceed to explain why we can't have it."

"Gerry, you should have been there the other day when all the women were together, my Mom, your Mom, Lottie, Aunt Martha, Aunt Barbara, even Stephie, all planning up a storm. They talked over me and around me, you and I are only an incidental."

"See? Don't let anything stress you, let them at it. They're in their element, so let them enjoy it, as I said before, we have each other."

From then on, they decided to let the parents have their way and not worry about it, handing in their list of guests they wanted to invite to be added to the growing multitude. Before the end of November, the number was over three hundred people, and that was a modest number her mother informed her. Gerry advised Katherine not to look it over if she wanted to stay sane, it was enough the elders did not cross anyone off their list, but she just had to see who was coming. Half the people she didn't know, Gerry pointed out the guests who were from his family, others were business associates, while she showed all her distant relatives who had been added, although she didn't know most of Pop and Gramp's friends, so it looked like they were having a few surprise attendees. Katherine was then mortified when she saw Mr. and Mrs. Kraylor marked down and asked her mother if that was a good idea, considering the way everything had turned out.

"Well, just because we haven't seen them in awhile, they still are friends of the family, and it would be in poor taste not to invite them, especially since you've invited Charlie and Suzy. Besides, the Reinolds also included them, they are their lawyers too, you know."

Katherine couldn't argue, but now began to fret how the day would turn out.

"I know darling, it's a sticky predicament, but we'll just have to grin and bear it," Gerry consoled her, "it's only one day."

Katherine had one consolation other than marrying Gerry, she was allowed to pick the bridesmaids colours, and since a red and yellow combination were out, decided a soft pink would be appropriate for a June wedding complete with pink and white roses for the floral arrangements.

"What? Pink? Every bride is going to pick pink," Aunt Martha exclaimed, "you can't have that. You'd better choose something else."

"Oh, leave her alone, there's not much else other than lavender, and that's more for Spring, and the darker colours are for fall and winter, not to mention her friend in Paris chose peach, so we can't repeat that. We can work with pink," her mother decided.

"If you like Kathy, you can have some roses from my prize-winning bushes for your bouquet," Sophia offered, "I've never released them into the market, you'd be the only bride to have roses like them."

"Thank you so much, that's very kind," Katherine replied, "but I wouldn't like to strip your rare bushes. I saw them this past summer, they were beautiful."

"All the more reason to give them to you rather than watch them die. They cut well and won't wither before the day."

"Thank you so much, I'd be delighted to have them."

"That's settled then, the men can have the white Firepearl Glories to offset the pink, I'm happy with the way those blooms turned out, took me a couple of years to get the strain just right," Sophia beamed, "now let's hope we have enough buds for the day."

"Don't worry, we can always augment from the floral arrangers," Helen noted.

Aunt Martha suggested they had better take a few days in the city with Katherine to register for her crystal, china and silver, and get that out of the way as the holidays were fast approaching. This felt like an unnecessary extravagance to Katherine, it seemed to her Gerry had plenty of everything at the apartment. They almost had palpitations trying to explain to her the importance of the bride selecting her own special pattern.

"You *must* have your own table settings! Whatever is getting into you, Katherine? You can't present your guests with other people's cast-offs. I've never heard the like," Aunt Martha breathlessly exclaimed. "Helen, what are we going to do with her? She displays no interest in the finer accoutrements of establishing a proper household."

"Well, it's not like I'm going to be cooking and entertaining, everyone knows I can't cook. Who would I entertain?" Katherine sheepishly pointed out.

"But dear, you will have special occasions, and holidays, and who knows, maybe business entertaining for Gerry, and don't forget the gallery, you may have people over too," her mother explained.

"I thought I would be coming home for the holidays, or going to Gerry's parents," Katherine reflected, "I'm not leaving home altogether."

"Yes, but a wife needs to create a proper home for her husband to be proud of," her mother continued.

"Well, okay, if you think it's necessary. I don't know where we'll put it all in the apartment, the kitchen and dining room are overflowing as it is."

"You'll figure it out dear, don't make a fuss, we have enough to do, and you will make it easier for the guests to select gifts. Now, let's get on with things, we have Thanksgiving and the holidays to organize, and don't forget the charity event after New Year's," Mom concluded. This year would be different, it was Katherine's first experience of deciding who she would spend the festive seasons with, her family, or the in-laws. Let's not make waves she thought. She didn't want to start a rivalry over who-would-have-who over first, especially as everyone was getting along so well right now.

"I have an idea; why don't Gerry and I take turns by alternating the holidays like we do going to Uncle Tim and Aunt Barbara's? We could go to Stonyvale for Thanksgiving, then my family for Christmas depending who is hosting it, then switch it next year. That way no one is left out, and we know what's happening, at least until I can find my feet and learn how to cook a holiday dinner."

"All right dear, that should work," Sophia agreed.

"For many years to come, I'm afraid," Aunt Martha added with a sigh, thinking of her niece's paltry culinary accomplishments, "she's not exactly domesticated. I'm so glad Gerry has a cook and a housekeeper, you know how artistic types can be."

The holiday preparations began, most of the wedding plans had to be set aside until after New Year's. Most of the details would not be worked out until six months before the day in any case, so there was no need to panic just yet.

However, Pete decided to take the opportunity during this period to begin their private pre-Cana marriage counselling sessions to ensure they were still calm and collected while he imparted to them the responsibilities of the married state. He had learned from experience that trying to fit in the sessions close to the wedding date was not a good idea when the bride and groom were trying to get everything else to fall into place. While it was difficult trying to worry about Thanksgiving and Christmas, she had to agree with his idea, it was better than waiting until the last moment, and rather than dreading it, she began to look forward to their Monday evening meetings in Gerry's apartment. Pete had a gift for explaining the spiritual beauties attached to the sacrament as well as the practical advice for daily life as a couple. He explained the importance of love and trust much as Justine had explained the advice he gave to her and Martin, but hearing him face-to-face made a much stronger impression, especially when he arrived with an unusual exercise:

"Tonight we're going to read 'Jo Meets Apollyon'," he announced, handing them each a book. Katherine knew that sounded familiar and almost laughed when she saw the cover.

"From *Little Women*?" Gerry replied in amusement. "You're going to prepare us for the weighty duties of marriage with a children's book?"

"Unless you become as little children," Peter smiled with a knowing look. "Remember, a married couple must help each other not only in the earthly life, but on the road to heaven. Now, who wants to read aloud for us?"

When Katherine got home that night, she couldn't help but think about the division between Peter and his father. By now, she fully understood leaving his family was part of the sacrifice of entering the priesthood, but to have a parent disapprove of his choice to the point of estrangement was a terrible state of affairs. She had an inkling of what he must be going through, having braved telling her parents about her conversion, and of course, she could not forget Mrs. Hunt's story about her family declaring her dead when she married outside her faith. This was unacceptable; life was too short to make it unbearable for people. Katherine wished she could do something for Peter and Mr. R., especially as in her estimation, Mr. R. was suffering more from the rupture than he was aware, he was missing so much, losing the time he could be spending with Peter when permitted. She was certain he would be proud of his son if he knew the good he was doing and that he had found where he belonged. She must speak with him, at least try to heal the breach in the family she loved just as much as her own.

Thanksgiving seemed to be the perfect opportunity, she would be spending the night at Stonyvale as Sophia did not want them out late on the roads, not to mention a night over would give them more time to enjoy the holiday with the family. Through that whole evening, she tried to find the perfect moment to implement Operation Mend Fences, it was difficult with everyone milling around. Mrs. Hunt was invited as on all holidays, and Lottie had invited David Cunningham, the construction magnate whom she met in Paris. Lottie finally accepted his invitations to go out with him and Katherine was glad to see they seemed to be enjoying each other's company, although Mrs. R was not too sure of him yet and continued to hand him the crystal shakers when he asked for the salt or paper. However, she needed to speak with Mr. R. alone, preferably a quiet moment without the threat of interruptions. She hoped no one would notice how distracted she was as she bided her time, watching and waiting. At last, her chance came when everyone decided they would head off to bed, Mr. R. said he would stay up a bit and enjoy one last smoke and a swig of brandy before turning in. After Gerry escorted her to her guestroom and kissed her goodnight, she waited a minute or two before opening the door, turned the antique knob very slowly to ensure it wouldn't squeak, scouted the cavernous hallway to see if anyone was still up and about, tiptoed back down to the Red Room and tapped gently on the ornate wood door, her heart in her mouth, praying she would say the right thing.

"Two more puffs, and I'll be up, Sophie."

Katherine gently opened the door.

"It's me, Mr. R."

"Katie? Come in. What brings you to this den of iniquity?" he joked, sitting back in his favourite arm chair by the fire, holding the stub of his ill-gotten Cuban cigar in one hand, the last sip of brandy in the other. Katherine entered the room turned hazy from smoke and sat in the armchair next to him, her eyes beginning to water from the stinging smog. "Oh, here, let me put this out," he said, reaching for the ashtray, attempting to wave away the smoke and downing the last drop in his glass.

"No, you don't have to do that … ."

"It's all right, I know how you ladies detest these stogies. Come to keep me company have you? I know, this old house is a bit spooky at night."

"The house doesn't frighten me, and I didn't see any ghosts on my way down."

"That's good to know," he chuckled, "come, tell me what's on your mind."

"Well …" she began, but wasn't sure how to proceed.

"Come come, you're not usually lost for words. Something's troubling you, I could see it tonight, and I don't like to see my girls upset. Just spit it out, dear." He may be a tough old sea dog, but had a soft spot for Katherine, already he considered her part of the family and hoped Gerry realized how blessed he was. She thought for a moment before deciding to ask him outright:

"Mr. R., you'll come to the wedding, won't you?"

"Huh? Er, of course dear, whatever made you think I wouldn't?" he quietly asked, caught off guard by her simple, unexpected question, his eyebrows furrowing for a moment.

"That's good to know. It's just that Pete will be officiating and … are you *very* angry with Pete?"

"Well I … ," he hesitated.

"I know, he's special, isn't he? There's something about him that draws everyone."

Mr. Reinold, studied her for a moment, his eyebrows still slightly furrowed, not irritated, just interested. He continued to let her speak, waiting to see what she had to say. Why he would listen to her when he had tuned every one else out was difficult to explain, but he had better let her speak her mind.

"I can see why it was not an easy thing to do, watching him go when he had such a wonderful family legacy waiting for him. I didn't understand it myself until I met Gerry and realized when we have a family of our own, we have so much to give our children, perhaps one of them will be artistic and would be glad to have the gallery someday. It's true, you're more inclined to do better and work harder for someone else than just by doing something for yourself, but I wouldn't be happy if I thought I had forced one of my children into something that they weren't called to do. I'm finding out a lot lately that the plans we've cherished for a long time don't always work out as you thought they would, and it's best not to let it bother you but work with what you've got."

"Huh," he grunted, but continued to remain silent. After a few moments watching the fire, Katherine plucked up the courage to continue.

"I wish you could see Pete in action. I know he would have made a great CEO of Reinold Enterprises judging from the way Sammy and the deliverymen speak of him, but he's doing so much good for people, he's much better as a priest, even his morning services are filling up. I've started going, and you'd be amazed at all the people that show up at that early hour. I haven't told anyone this, so please, don't say anything, but I'm positive he saved my friend from contemplating suicide, now she's happily married, and I just received a note two days ago saying they're expecting a baby. Honestly, Pete is where he's needed most. It's like this," she trailed, trying to think of an appropriate analogy, "I don't know much about boats, but let's say you're a captain of this tip-top ship, and you have this marine who is excellent, you're proud to have him on your crew and want to hang on to him, hoping perhaps one day he'll be captain and run the ship exactly as you wanted it to run when your time comes to retire, but the Commander in Chief recognises the natural skills this marine has and puts him on a different ship where he can do more to serve his country, perhaps more than if he stayed on your ship. The marine hasn't deserted, just obeyed the commands of a higher authority, and the captain can't be angry with the marine for obeying orders, nor give out to the Commander in Chief, whom he had also sworn to obey. Pete … just followed orders from the Supreme Commander, you can't help but admire him for that. Well, I guess I'd better go to bed, goodnight Mr. R." Having said her piece, she scurried from the room before she said too much, and possibly make him angry.

"Er, goodnight Katie," he called after her, finally finding his tongue before she closed the door behind her. "Huh," he grunted to himself, taken aback yet curiously amused with the parable. He couldn't go to bed after that and took out another cigar, puffing on a stogie helped him to think, and he had to admit, his Katie had certainly given him a lot to think about. After all the years of pleading from his Sophie and Lottie, to which he had stubbornly turned a deaf ear, there was something in her quiet attempt to share her observations that he could not dispel, no hysterics he couldn't abide, just a simple, honest-to-goodness logical explanation for one of life's major disappointments—and all this from a young one who had not yet been tried by the sorrows that life could throw at her. He puffed away, mulling it over. Sure, he would have gladly seen Pete head of Reinold Enterprises some day, he was an excellent businessman, a hard worker, good to the crew and treated everyone fairly. He would have made their forefathers proud, but perhaps he placed too much of his expectations on him, which was not difficult to do; first born, similar interests, heck, they looked so much alike, it was almost like seeing himself young again, starting out with everything to look forward to, it was like a window into immortality. If truth were to be told, he wanted his son to be happy, and if that meant letting him obey some mysterious call he could not fathom, there wasn't much he could do about it. Shucks, if he was really helping people that much, it's certainly more important than shipping junk around the world. Maybe his Katie had something there, Pete wasn't abandoning them, he left to join a different ship, that's all, and it wasn't like the family name was dying with him. Gerry was turning out to be a model executive, and now, would become a good husband and loving father, he was always good with kids. Having Katie join the family, everything was going to be left in safe hands; impetuous, but with a sound head on her shoulders, conservative with an appreciation for tradition, plus beauty to boot, he could see why Ger was smitten with her from day one. Come to think of it, he hadn't been terribly fair to Gerry, not that he loved him less, but he did not give him the credit he fully deserved. He had proven himself repeatedly when he was unexpectedly called upon to assume additional company duties where Peter left off, and yet he had not fully commended him for all the hard work he was doing, letting his disappointment over Peter cloud the praise Gerry deserved to hear. At last, he gave himself a hard dressing down, which was long overdue. So what if things didn't turn out the way you planned? Are you a captain or a cabin boy? Pull yourself together man, stop skulking, look how everyone's been torn up over this, you have two sons who could do with a little encouragement, your family needs to be put back on kilter.

The next morning, very early to be precise, Mr. Reinold was all dressed in his best suit before the house was awake and went to the kitchen for a cup of coffee, but was startled to find Gerry up and about in his bathrobe, nursing a glass of Alka-Seltzer.

"Ho, someone doesn't look so good, what's wrong, son?"

"I ate too much, the heartburn woke me up, you know how I love Mom's cooking, I had a third helping of her famous turkey stuffing and blew it this time."

"Well, your mother is a fine cook, can't argue there. Well, now that you're here, there's … something I want you to know."

"Aw Dad, if it's about the Finley contract again, tell him I … ."

"Hang Finley, that's not what I wanted to say. I …well, you've done a fine job this past year, heck, every year, I'm just real proud of you son, and I just wanted you to know that. Couldn't run the company without you."

"Dad, I … ."

"Don't interrupt. I also know how you paid for the medical bills and found jobs for all those people they found stowed in the containers, though you tried to hide it, and don't think I don't know about you building a new house for Lenny when it burnt down two years ago when he had no insurance and couldn't rebuild, the shop stewards told me. Yes, you've made us proud, real proud." With that, he grabbed him in a hearty embrace, then quickly straightened himself out and left, leaving Gerry speechless holding his glass of plink-plink-fizz in mid-air. He was still in the kitchen with his half-glass of physic now gone flat when his mother came through the doorway.

"Gerry love, what are you doing up so early? Oh," she said, as she noticed the glass and antacid packet, "the third helping, was it?" However,

Gerry no longer felt any heartburn.

"Mom, is everything all right with Dad?"

"As far as I know dear. Why do you ask?"

"Hell froze over and pigs are flying, he just went … all fatherly, which I haven't seen in a long time. I wonder what's gotten into him?"

"I don't know, maybe he was concerned to see your stomach upset. I do know he was up awfully late last night, I'm surprised to see he's left already, but I don't think he's sick or anything, you know how he is about work."

Richard was heading to Manhattan, but his first stop wasn't the offices as Sophia assumed. He pulled up outside St. Patrick's and just sat there, letting the car idle as he watched a surprisingly large group file though the cathedral doors. He knew he should follow them, but somehow couldn't bring himself to do it and pulled away. Two whole weeks went like that, pulling up, trying to talk himself into going in, but then drove on, convinced he had let the rift develop into a chasm from which he could find no way to cross. He watched as everyone else went in, some days driving around the block until the service was over and then observe the worshippers leave. He spotted his Katie going in some days, once or twice with Gerry. They looked so happy together, and to see his Ger return to church was nothing short of a miracle, Sophie wasn't looking as worried since she discovered this news and was more like her old self, knowing her boy was treading the right path again. Something peculiar was happening, and his curiosity got the better of him, so one morning, he too joined the congregation, finding a pew near the back just before Mass began. One thing really struck him, the reaction of the congregation, he knew he shouldn't eavesdrop, but it wasn't difficult to overhear a few excitable ladies in the vestibule before and after the service, or when they sat near the back, the acoustics of the building amplifying their hushed voices, echoing to his place behind the pillar.

"What a holy priest, his parents must be very proud of him, oh, and when he says Mass…!"

"I know, just like Mass should be said. He's every Irish mother's dream, imagine to have a blessing like that in the family."

"Have you been to confession to him?"

"No, not yet, not that I don't want to. I can't get in, the queue is almost as long as a procession some days. He's a saintly man."

"Ach, you've said it. Did you hear about Maire's son?"

"No, do tell."

"Well, you know he hadn't been to church in years, fallen away he had, was in all kind of trouble. Somehow, she managed to have Fr. Reinold drop by to meet him, and whatever happened, Sean went to confession and started going back to church.”

“You don’t say!”

“Sean told her he knew everything, could read him right down to his boot-soles, was sobbing by the end of it and knew he had to change his life.”

“Sakes alive, I wish I could get my daughter to see him … .”

He listened to commentaries like that for over a week, stories of conversions and extraordinary confessions. There were startling accounts of Fr. Reinold ordering certain men out of the church instead of hearing their confessions, people who had not come to confess but die-hard atheists who had swaggered in to test him.

“Do not steal time from those who truly desire to be saved,” he thundered after them, “crush your hard hearts before it’s too late!”

According to another story, as told by the penitent, he gave her absolution, but as her penance she had to ask forgiveness of the person she had wronged, and she didn’t have too much time left to do it. The woman, terrified he meant she didn’t have much time to live, went and did as he requested, only to find the man she had wronged was dying of cancer, and didn’t wish to see her at first. Eventually, he relented, and she humbly asked him for forgiveness, they were reconciled before he passed away. She could not explain how Fr. Reinold knew she had little time to make amends.

Richard could see why the ladies were in awe of Peter’s Masses as he observed the dignified respect, the calm, collected, exacting and deliberate way Peter conducted the service, the Mass was no mere rite to him, the congregation was fully aware they were attending the Heavenly court. In that entire week, Richard never saw him rush as in the case with some priests who appeared jaded with their religious obligation and celebrated in a distracted manner like any humdrum routine. Richard was curious when he heard the ladies say they loved to hear his simple no-nonsense homilies, and wished he too could hear what Pete had to say, unfortunately, homilies were not given during the weekday Masses, and he patiently waited for Sunday. This service was earlier than the others, and yet, there was a sizeable crowd; Peter had secured permission to offer a Latin Mass at this time every week and the word had spread like wildfire. This particular Sunday had a special significance for the congregation, Rose Sunday had almost slipped Richard’s mind, a feast of hope that happened only twice in the liturgical year, on this occasion, the third Sunday of Advent. He could hear them all whispering about the distinctive rose-coloured vestments worn on that day.

At last, Peter came forward to read the gospel aloud in English, then, prepared to give his homily. He placed his hands on either side of the lectern and carefully looked out into the congregation. Everyone sat still as he calmly gazed in their direction, however, Richard received the distinct impression he was not really looking at the people, rather, something above their heads seemed to have his full attention. Without warning, he quickly cut this reverie short and addressed the sea of faces, looking them directly in the eye:

"Who is afraid of Judgement Day?"

Dead silence, then people began to look around, whispers were heard.

"Come, let's see a show of hands, don't be shy."

Everyone continued to timidly survey their surroundings and slowly put up their hands, eventually raising their arms higher when they saw they weren't the only ones.

"This won't do," he continued. "Christ said we are to hold our heads up and be glad when that time comes, and Rose Sunday reminds us to rejoice for the Lord is coming, but it looks like no one is ready to rejoice today. We must find the reason. We can begin by asking why the Church continually reminds us to prepare for Christ's birthday during Advent when He was born almost two millennia ago and continues to come down upon on our altars and resides in our tabernacles. The answer: as a reminder He will come again on the Last Day, but we must not be afraid. We must be able to rejoice at his Second Coming as much as we should during His birthday. What are you afraid of? The wars that will precede Him? The famines? The Antichrist? Our Lord said we should fear only what causes death to our souls. Ah, is it *death* you fear?   All right, that's understandable, it's one of the greatest sorrows Satan brought into the world, but we know Christ was born in a stable, died a cruel death, and rose from the dead to conquer that sorrow. If we truly loved and followed Our Lord as He directed, we would have no fear of death, hell's onslaughts, nor the appearance of the Antichrist when the end comes near.   Perhaps you are anxious about the end because your house is not in order, and by that, I mean your soul. We must also be prepared for the end of our lives, for we will be judged then too. If your conscience is free from sin, you would have every reason in the world to rejoice, particularly on this day of hope, Rose Sunday. I know many of you have a particular attachment for these rosy-pink vestments. Did you ever stop to think that your soul may be trying to tell you something? Pink is a blend of red and white. Red stands for charity and sacrifice, white for purity, and that red and white also represents the

Divine Mercy of God. Let's take to heart the readings today: '*The Lord is near. Nothing must make you anxious.*' … '*Straighten out the way of the Lord.*' Therefore, prepare the way of the Lord by straightening out your lives, wash your robes in the Blood of the Lamb and remove all reasons to fear God's justice. Only those who are men of good will are given the peace of heaven as the angelic choirs declared on Christmas. Have you broken the commandments? Have you committed the most heinous crimes imaginable? Then amend your lives, earnestly ask for forgiveness and repair the evil you perpetrated. Do as Christ commanded, He loves you more than you will ever be able to fathom. Seek to do His will, then fear nothing except committing sin that kills the soul. Rejoice and be glad, for He is coming, perhaps not today or tomorrow, but soon enough. After Mass, I will be hearing confessions for one hour. May God bless you all with peace this holy season."

With that, he stepped down from the lectern and continued with the service, after which there was a rush to line up beside his designated confessional. Richard watched as he returned from the sacristy area dressed in his black cassock and was besieged by parishioners begging him to remember their intentions in his prayers, wanted special Masses offered, holding out religious articles or shoving them into his hands for his blessing before he slipped into the dark recess of the penitential chamber to cleanse their souls.

Katie was right, Peter belonged here.   How blind he had been! Regret gnawed at Richard as he thought back to his ferocious outbursts when Pete came to tell the family he was entering the priesthood, and now wished he had been present with Sophie and Lottie for his ordination in Rome. He had stolen a few furtive glances at the photographs when they came home, and continued to do so on occasion when he thought they wouldn't know, but it was not like being there. He could never make up for his absence. This week had opened his eyes, he *was* proud of his son, he had to tell him, and, to seek his forgiveness.

He waited for Peter to emerge from the confessional an hour later, watching the orderly crush resume as he came out, for people continued to seek his blessings and give him their petitions. Eventually, he had to break away from them and retreated to the sacristy to allow the next Mass commence without disturbance. Richard quickly left his pew and made his way past the parishioners, following him into the sacristy. Sensing someone behind him, Peter turned, and seeing his father, met him with a smile. Richard wasn't expecting that, by rights Pete should be angry, hurt, perhaps even bitter after the harsh reprove he had lashed at him, but certainly not

"Hello Peter … I'm sorry … ."

"All water under the bridge."

"No, I was way out of line … I hope you can … ."

"If you need forgiveness, you're forgiven. I'm free for an hour or so before duty calls me. Would like to come for coffee, maybe grab something to eat with me? It's a pity you didn't come in right away instead of driving around the church for weeks, we might have sorted this out sooner," he continued with a smile.

How did he know? Did someone see him sitting in the car? No, if people spotted him, they would have come up to say hello to him at church, and Richard had made sure he sat in an inconspicuous spot so he wouldn't be noticed. In any case, it didn't matter, a bite to eat with his son sounded like the best idea he had heard, they had much to catch up on.

"Well, I'm here now, and I could use a good breakfast. Since we're on the subject of food, are you free later tonight? For dinner I mean … ."

Stonyvale was turned upside down as Richard and Peter entered the front door together that evening, talking and laughing just like the old days. Sophia nearly fainted, Gerry was struck speechless, Lottie laughed and cried at the same time after giving them a suffocating hug, while Sinbad heartily welcomed Petie home with a barrage of 'Ahoy Maties' and head-bobbing. Victor seemed the most composed of them all as he calmly carried out his duty, taking their coats and neatly hanging them in the hall closet, but he too could not contain his excitement when the help in the kitchen asked him what was causing all the commotion upstairs. Katherine, who had also come for dinner, watched the happy homecoming shocked and elated, unaware up to that point Mr. R. actually listened to her bold speech all those weeks ago and had taken it to heart. As they went into dinner, he took her aside for a moment:

"I hope you're satisfied, Miss Philanthropy," he huffed, adding a playful wink.

"Very," she returned with a smile.

For the first time in years, the Reinhold family were together for midnight Mass on Christmas Eve with Peter concelebrating the service with the archbishop. Mr. R. proudly marched them all up to the front pew, including Katherine, determined to make up for his years of absence and lack of support. Judging from the looks of it, Katherine was convinced Pete had managed to get him into a confession session too. She was glad to see everyone so happy, even Gerry had brightened up more than usual.

However, a disappointment soon loomed on the horizon when

Gerry announced a few days after Christmas that he had another company tour ahead of him.

"I'm sorry Kathy, I know I should have told you sooner, but I hate breaking news like this to you, and everyone was in such high spirits this holiday season, I didn't want to throw a wet blanket on us."

"Not another globe trot?" she moaned in dismay.

"No, at least not an international one this time, it's a short domestic tour, Chicago, Denver, Seattle, San Francisco and LA, some ports, some trucking hubs. I don't have too many stops, thank goodness. It should only take a month."

"Only a month, that seems so long, but I knew this was coming, it's been almost a year since you were in Asia," she reflected. "When do you have to leave?"

"Well, I want to get it over and done with long before the wedding, so the second week of January, I also had to give myself time in case anything unexpected comes up."

"I hope not! Let's pray nothing like what happened in Jakarta."

"No, that was a major deal, I don't think that will happen again, we're staying on top of things. The bad news is, I won't be back in time for Valentine's Day."

"Oh Gerry, it'll be sad being on my own that day, well, you know what I mean."

"I know love, I'm sorry, but we'll have New Year's and the week after that. At least we won't have a huge difference in time zones when I'm gone, it should be easier to keep in touch."

"I guess that's something. Still, I'm depressed, just great," she said dejectedly, folding her arms and watching the fire flicker. "Maybe I should go ahead and start decorating this place when you're gone, anything to keep me busy and stop me from moping."

"Anything you want dearest, go ahead, rip the place apart and put it on my tab. I *am* getting tired of white walls, I never was one for austerity," he joked.

"Well, I may not be able to, I know the mothers will start up the wedding plans once New Year and the charity event is over, so you'll just have to wait until we're married." She sighed, "it's not going to be fun planning when you're gone."

"Aw don't be upset, I'll be back before you know it."

"I'm going to miss you terribly."

"I'm going to miss you too, I wish I could bring you with me." He then sat up on the sofa. "Kathy, would you consider doing something completely irregular and globe trot with me? I might still have time to book your own rooms," he added.

"You know I can't," she sighed, "Please, be good now and don't tempt my impulsiveness, didn't you hear me talk about wedding plans? And I've got the gallery, remember?"

"You're right," he replied resignedly.

"Never mind dearest, we will be going on a long honeymoon soon enough."

He then brightened up. "Speaking of honeymoons, I have something to cheer you up. I've planned out our Italian itinerary, well, mostly the cities and accommodations, if you would care to see," he said as he got off the couch, going to retrieve a large folder from his office.

"Oh, do show me." That did help to cheer her.

"I thought we should pretty much stick to the major cities we named for your first trip," he began.

"First trip?"

"Believe me, after your first visit, you'll want to see the rest of Italy, we'll have to plan a second honeymoon for our anniversary."

"Talk about thinking ahead, please proceed, I'm all ears."

"How about we start in Venice, head down to Florence and Pisa, you can't miss the tower, then finish up in Rome? I've drawn up a list of the must-see spots in each place in addition to the obvious tourist haunts, not to mention the art museums you'll want to visit, you can pick out the daily agendas for us if you like."

"You'll have to help me decide, this all sounds wonderful to me." He then showed her the accommodations he had selected, majestic private manors and palazzos with enclosed gardens that once belonged to royalty. "Oh Gerry, these places look like they cost a mint, and we'll be gone most of the day sightseeing."

"Let me worry about the cost, we'd only be renting them for a week or so, we're not buying them, and besides, my Princess deserves a few palaces. Would you *please* let me spoil you? It is our honeymoon after all."

"Oh, okay," she smiled. He wanted to go all out, and she didn't want to upset him. In any case, she couldn't argue with the itinerary or his choice in accommodations, he had excellent taste as always.

"I had to find places that offered security, we don't want another paparazzi fiasco like Paris."

"Good thinking, how could I have forgotten that?" They burst out laughing as they recalled their crazy escape from the hotel and the disguises they wore. Turning to look at the painting of Rome hanging over the mantelpiece, practically the only picture left in his apartment, she now had most of his collection in her gallery, they were determined not to sneak through Italy with the daily fish deliveries or in linen trucks, especially on their honeymoon.

"Would you like to drive through Italy, or take the planes and trains? I'm up for a helicopter ride between cities if you want something different."

She thought about what might be best and wasn't sure what to do until he noted that while driving might take longer, there would be no gaping crowds or stations and airports to battle. It would just be the two of them cruising though the Italian countryside. That sounded so romantic and she nodded her approval. He pulled out brochures of classic two-seater roadsters available to rent and asked which one she liked.

"Gerry, where are we going to fit a month's supply of luggage in that?" she said, looking at the trendy but compact vintage cars.

"We don't: we ship it forward using Reinold Express Shipping Service, no marked vans of course, we don't want our honeymoon becoming a publicity stunt. All we need to bring is an extra change of clothes and some personal items just in case the van arrives a little late, but I don't think it will, not when the Boss Man and his beautiful bride are the customers."

"You've really thought this all out, haven't you?"

"I must admit, my ingenuity surprises me at times," he replied, his eyes twinkling with merriment. "Would you like me to rent us a convertible?"

"Oh yes, that would be fun. You'd better go ahead and book everything now before they all get snapped up."

It was pleasant just the two of them sitting on the couch, listening to his descriptions of Italy and all the places he wanted to show her while they were there, imagining them driving along the autostradas with the top down without a care in the world. It helped her to bear the thought of him leaving on his business trip in just a matter of weeks.

CB ❀ BO

New Year's did not turn out quite as they expected when Leroy would not take 'no' for an answer this time and insisted Gerry bring his 'rib' to his New Year's bash. Gerry wasn't happy about the prospect and was going to skip without telling Leroy, but Katherine said that would not be a nice thing to do to a friend.

"Kathy, you've never been to one of his parties, you remember his last lady friend, he drags people in from wherever he finds them just to make his dos interesting, and you have no idea where it's all going to end up."

"It won't hurt to make an appearance for an hour or so, then sneak away. If he has a lot of people, no one will miss us. I don't want to cut you off from your friends."

"You may change your mind later," he noted wryly, "but okay, especially since he may end up being my best man. I told him you don't drink much, but he said he'd look after you."

On their way to Leroy's bachelor pad, Gerry gave her a worrying piece of advice to mind her glass and not to leave it unattended, someone might try and slip her something thinking it was funny.

"Leroy wouldn't do it, but some wisecracks he invites every year do."

"They have a twisted way of having fun, I must say."

"Okay, here we go," Gerry said as he rang the bell, the door opening to reveal Leroy in a loud Hawaiian shirt, Bermuda shorts, multiple plastic *leis* draped around his neck, and a lampshade on his head.

"Ger! Kathy! You missed the Conga line, but you're just in time for a nice game of Limbo. Don't stand there, my castaways, come in and meet the crew of our Technicolor extravaganza."

"Limbo, hmm, I'll think we'll pass on that one," Gerry noted.

"Ah, I'm sorry, I forgot to tell you we were having an outdoor indoor beach party, but never mind, you both look grand, no on will notice," Leroy said, slipping a few synthetic *leis* around their necks.

"Well earthling, welcome to Mars," Gerry said as they went in.

Katherine timidly followed Gerry eyeing the trappings of Leroy's bash and feeling terribly overdressed as she observed a number of people clad in flowery muumuus, others dressed in straw hats and swimming trunks, while a few scantily clad girls ran around in bikini's and grass skirts. Then there were the plastic palm trees, fake parrots with motley feathers glued on them, coconuts and Tiki masks, not to mention flashing rainbow-hued disco lights abounded while the open bar was housed in a beach hut. Outside, the balcony was lit up, copiously covered in sand and sporting a large inflatable paddling pool with beach balls and pink toy flamingos, however, no one ventured outside, it was too cold, already the water had frozen in the bottom, trapping the plastic flamingos in a sheet of ice. Leroy took them around, introducing them to his guests, half of whom he didn't know even though he was the host. Quite oblivious to the tropical setting and large Calypso band were a small trio playing Irish traditional music, one musician pumping out reels on his *uillean* pipes, another played the tin whistle while the third kept time on a pair of spoons which he clacked on his knee as deftly as if they were Spanish castanets.

"They're my friends from Galway," Leroy explained, "they always have to start a set when they're together, they tell great jokes, but they're in a world of their own. I'll introduce you later, hey guys, Guinness is flowing, I'll send you another pint," he said, turning to them.

"Ta mate, send over a couple'a Paddys while you're at it," was the appreciative response from the piper.

"Hey Leroy, whatever happened to Sandy?" Gerry asked, not seeing her in the crowd.

"Who?"

"You know, the girl you met in Las Vegas?"

"Ah sure, it was too good to last," Leroy said with mock sorrow, "she found someone else after her off-Broadway début as an extra. But you learn to love and let go."

Eventually, they made it through the large open plan penthouse and Leroy offered Katherine a glass of fruit punch while Gerry took a glass of champagne, not anything too strong that would dull his senses as he kept watch on her in this dubious environment. After engaging in polite conversation with a few people, Katherine quickly got bored, she didn't have too much in common with them as they all liked bands and rock music she didn't listen to, or discussed the names of artists whom she was not familiar with, not to mention the fashion designers who she couldn't take seriously as they seemed to make their reputations off trashy catwalk stunts rather than design elegant, wearable clothes. Gerry then asked her to dance, trying to stay as far away from the band as possible, but her head started to swim, and the loud music gave her a thumping headache, it was impossible to escape it.

"I think I need to sit down for a bit," she said, indicating a sofa.

"Okay, I'll see if I can find some aspirin and a glass of water. Will you be all right on your own for a minute? You didn't drink anything strong, not that I could tell anyway."

"It must be the music and all these spinning lights, it's making me dizzy."

"Well, perhaps it's time for us to sneak away, I'll try and find our coats. Sit still 'till I get back."

Poking around the bedrooms looking for their coats amidst the mounds of furs and wraps of all descriptions piled up on the beds, he eventually found what he was looking for and returned to see Katherine fast asleep where he left her.

"What's happened to her?" Leroy asked, "it's not even twelve yet."

"Clearly you gave her more than fruit juice," Gerry turned, not impressed.

"All right, who spiked the Maui punch?" Leroy called out, looking around, the tassels on his lampshade swinging.

"Probably you," Gerry noted sarcastically.

"Moi? When we have enough libations flowing? It has to be Harry, I caught him the last time, not that I minded, but I did warn him we had teetotallers joining us tonight."

"Great, that's like waving a red flag to a bull, you moron. Thanks a lot Leroy, that puts paid to our Happy New year, and I wish you the same. I have to get Sleeping Beauty home now."

"Aw, don't get sore, no harm done, she'll get over it. Poor thing," he *tsked*, the tassels still swinging, "she can't hold her happy juice, can she? Got to learn sometime, Ger. Besides, you don't have to go, let her sleep it off, you can still have some fun. One of your old girlfriends just arrived, what's her name? The one over there with Harry?" looking at a couple in the corner laughing raucously.

"You invited Sherry? She stuck to me for a whole year like a burr, that women can't take a hint. I'm going, goodnight Leroy," he said quickly heading to the sofa where Katherine lay purring. He escaped from the mayhem and brought her back to the apartment to help her sober up, he couldn't bring her home to Oak Meadows in her inebriated state.

"Here sleepy," he said, handing her a strong cup of black coffee, "I'm sorry about that."

"First time I ever had spiked punch," she said, rubbing her head, "what a party, it was like *Gilligan's Island* on acid."

"I'm glad we left before twelve. You should have been there the time he threw the toga party and then came up with the bright idea we should all go skating at Rockefeller plaza, at two in the morning no less. Of course, not that you could call what we did *skating*, a few were passed out on the ice, it's a wonder they didn't get frostbite. Then Leroy got lost on the way home and the police found him next morning conked out on a subway bench with the laurel wreath dangling over one eye, blue with the cold. There was nothing for it but to send him home in a taxi. I heard when they asked how he got there, he said he couldn't remember, he must have taken a wrong turn somewhere, he was heading for the coliseum."

"Oh Gerry," she wanted to be shocked, but started to laugh, picturing Leroy with his flaming hair dressed like Caesar, spending the night hobo style in that condition.

"Then there was my 21ˢᵗ birthday at Stonyvale, he told everyone it was a splendid evening to get in touch with Nature and convinced most of my guests to jump in the Atlantic, then started up a massive bonfire and had everyone dancing like a tribe of natives on the warpath. Lottie barricaded herself in her room, while Mom went frantic and called an ambulance to stand by in case of an accident, or if anyone got hypothermia. It was like the grand finale from *Lord of the Flies*."

"I sure hope you didn't join him that time."

"No way, Pete and I were busy hauling people out of the ocean, clothes and all, trying to sober them up. By then it was painfully obvious Leroy and I were no longer on the same wavelength, we parted frequencies somewhere."

"You left FM for AM," she noted, "Foolish Mentality for Adult Maturity."

"Yeah, that's one way of putting it. Some people like Leroy never grow up."

"I can see why you like him though, he's a loveable imp. You don't think he'll pull a stunt like that at our wedding, do you?" she asked in alarm.

"No, don't worry, he knows when to behave, and one dirty look from my Dad will pull him back in line if he dares to try. Well, Happy New Year," he said, as the fireworks began to glow through the windows.

"Happy New Year, love. Where's the aspirin?"

ෆ❀ౠ

They made up for their disappointing New Year's celebration at the country club a week later as Helen and several of the society ladies had decided to hold their annual charity ball for the Heart Foundation there. The family were all in attendance, and the Reinolds were invited to join their party.   For the first time Katherine actually enjoyed one of the Club's big dos, Gerry was always good fun, he had a knack for lightening up a formal gathering and getting everyone in a good mood. Katherine thought *she* was critical when she toured the charity auction donations, but he was just as bad, for he too had offered his share of donating and bidding at various events. By now she was used to these items as they had all been delivered to Oak Meadows before Helen had them brought to the Club, but they were new to Gerry, well, almost.

"So much for being a very 'desirable' one-of-a-kind piece, I could have sworn that got auctioned for the Autism Research Fund a couple of

976

years ago," he remarked, comically looking askance at the descriptive label set in front of a monochromatic painting that looked more like an accidental ketchup splurt than artwork. "Would you like it for your museum, my dear? All in a good cause."

"Don't you dare," she warned, trying not to laugh.

"Aw, have a heart and help save a heart," he wheedled.

"Not on your life. If you must, try and find something worth bidding for."

"Okay, the fondue set it is then."

Steven and Jennifer joined them, and could not help laughing at their running commentary, Steves naturally adding his two-cents worth to the jokes.

"Fondue set? Not a very cholesterol conscious item to pick, Ger. At least you have to admit the painting fits the event, it looks like someone's aorta exploded."

"Maybe both items were donated by the same person as a warning to all," Gerry added.

"You two are hopeless when you get together," Katherine said, shaking her head, eventually, they got back to milling with the guests.

While the dinner was excellent, the part they looked forward to the most was the dancing. The music started, and as usual, he was very considerate of her aversion to loudspeakers, dancing her away and out into the adjacent room when the noise became too much for her sensitive hearing.

"The music sounds just as good from here, sometimes these amplifiers just ruin it all," he said, which was in exact accord with her sentiments on electrical sound systems. "Anyway, speakers or no speakers, this is a major improvement from Leroy's jamboree," he smiled. "I love the old-time big bands. Have you ever felt like you were born in the wrong decade, or came just a bit too late and missed out on all the good stuff when it was in its heyday? Maybe it comes from growing up in that old house and listening to Dad's records," he continued to muse.

"I know how you feel, Oak Meadows is not that different, growing up surrounded by Mom's antique collection. Sometimes I feel completely out of synch with my own generation."

"We'll just have to create our own little world, won't we?"

"We're off to a very good start," she noted, nestling her head on his shoulder, the slow pieces were her favourite. When the music stopped, they stole away and settled into one of the leather sofas by the fire in the reading room, but weren't allowed to remain there for long.

"There you are, we've been looking all over for you," Aunt Martha puffed as she burst in upon them, "your mother is about to start the auction, and you both said you would help display the donations onstage. Come on, hurry up now."

"There's the end of our little world," he sighed, as he escorted Katherine back to the ballroom.

"We *did* volunteer," she reminded him, "no good deed goes unpunished."

"Well, let's see if we can shift that heart attack they call artwork."

"I wonder where it will turn up next year?"

After the charity event, she and Gerry had precious few days left before he took off on his trip, the last few nights they didn't do anything exciting, they just sat and talked in the loveseat up in the studio. Knowing he hated goodbyes at the airport, she promised not to see him off, although she gave him a quick call the morning of his departure to wish him a safe and pleasant flight to Chicago. Now that the matriarchs had her undivided attention, the wedding plans were resumed. The first thing on the agenda— to comb the wedding salons for the perfect dress.

"Katherine, would you *please* stand still?

"I'm trying, my hair is caught on a hook somewhere. Ow! Please Mom, tell her not to yank too hard."

"Sorry dear," Aunt Martha replied as she rustled through the layers of material, trying to find where she had been snagged. At last, they straightened her out only to hear Aunt Martha pronounce that the gown was nice, but declared they could do better and proceeded to pull it off again. "I just *know* we'll find the right one here," she continued, searching through the racks. This was the fourth day beating the pavements in their endeavour to visit every bridal shop, and by now, her feet were burning and she felt blinded after gazing at a never-ending sea of white brocades, laces and satins.

"Oh no, I see her ogling after another leg-a-mutton sleeve dress after I telling her they don't look good on me."

"Martha, why not try that display over there?" Helen hinted, indicating the wall furthest from them.

"You're right, they must have a few beauties hiding we haven't seen … ." she said as she went to scout, leaving mother and daughter a chance to catch their breath.

"You know, I could have made this simpler for everyone and just wear my coming out dress, I never got to the débutante ball," she joked.

"Don't let your aunt hear you say that, or you wont hear the end of it for a month," her mother warned her, but understood how Katherine was feeling. "Tell me dear, have you seen a dress you would like?"

"Remember the one with the baby roses and the beautiful long train? We saw it in the first shop we tried, it was the best place we went to."

"Yes I do remember, and I agree, that's a beautiful dress, understated elegance, it was perfect on you. You know your aunt only wants to make sure you have the chance to see everything first before you decide."

"I know, she means well, but we're never going to get anything else done if she keeps dragging us around like this. We still have to choose the going away outfit and prepare my trousseau, not to mention get the bridesmaids ready … ."

"You're absolutely right, come Martha, I think we've done enough damage here for one day," Helen called.

"What? She hasn't tried this one on yet," she called in dismay, holding up a dress that looked a little too puffy. Katherine was glad to be making an exit, while she appreciated the luxuriant weight created by plentiful material in a gown, she did not want to look like an oversized baby doll.

At night, she would report to Gerry by phone how her days went, while he told her how his tour was going. To ensure she did not fall behind in her work, she rigged up a hands-free device by taping a cordless headset to a pair of earmuffs minus one muff so she could paint and talk at the same time, but was chagrined when Gerry suggested she get a speaker phone.

"Oh, never mind, I've fixed it up now, so I'm not letting my invention go to waste. How are you doing over there?"

"Oh, stuck in a Seattle hotel, just finished my day of drudgery and missing you like crazy. What are you working on now?"

"The fourth Socratic scene, I've got my two philosophers standing next to the famous picture of the Continental Congress drafting the Declaration of Independence. You know the picture on the back of the two-dollar bill? My dynamic duo are offering their critique on the proceedings."

"I can't wait to see it," he laughed. "Let me guess, everything is in black and white, while the two problem-solvers and their fine speech are all in colour."

"Yep, with the letters slightly darker when they run over the Congress in session. I made it look as though the famous picture is hanging in the gallery on the second floor, complete with the French wallpaper. I thought it would be kind of funny pretending the scene was happening right here."

"That's quirky. You know, I've been keeping up with my sketching and brought my notebook around, I don't know if any of it will make great material for a painting, but I don't want to get rusty while I'm gone."

"Hey, I'm proud of you. You'll have to show me when you get back. Oh, your Dad found out about your lessons and marched in here yesterday declaring he wanted to learn too. I'm starting him on his first lesson on Saturday."

"Looks like your art academy has really taken off now."

"I've got so much to do, but I did promise, and you know I don't want to disappoint him. That reminds me, you won't believe what happened today. This woman came in and asked if our resident artists did portrait commissions, I said we might consider it. I thought she wanted a family portrait at first but then told me she wanted a picture of her rabbit, DeeDee, her google-eyed pug, Bozo, and her rat, Squeek, I think that's what it was called. A rat! Can you believe it? And, she wanted a group image. We're not that bad off we have to be landed with pet portraits with rodents, so I politely told her we're not set up to work with live animals and gave her the name of an artist who specialized in that particular work."

"You had a name ready?"

"Yeah, I had a call from a rancher in Texas who offered to fly me out all expenses paid to paint his prize winning steer, I can't believe I forgot to tell you that. I prepared in case something similar happened again."

"At least they heard about you in Texas, that has to count for something," Gerry noted, "you're art is becoming famous."

"In what way, I wonder."

No matter what the day threw at them, they managed to burn the phone lines without fail every evening, wishing the month of business trekking would end. Katherine hoped she wasn't a bore, but she wanted to be sure to update him on the planning process and how the mothers and aunts were faring with the approaching nuptials. By this time, they had hired a wedding planner and were discussing the caterers. Andre had been chosen to do the honours, but he admitted he was not set up to cater for so many. He recommended a friend who specialized in large receptions and said they would have no problem working together, so discussing the menu would be the next thing to look forward to. It looked like the cake was taken care of as Andre said he wanted to contribute to the event, no 'buts'. There was a big deliberation on where the dinner would be served; the ballroom, or the marquee. Considering the number of guests, Sophia was not certain if they could fit everyone in the ballroom for dinner and allow space around the tables, so Helen and the planner decided to go with

Sophia's advice to have the dinner in the marquee. That way the ballroom could be set up to receive the guests with a light course of *hors d'œuvres* and champagne, and could be cleared for the dancing while everyone sat down to dinner in the marquee. Of course, they now had to choose table settings, decorations, floral arrangements, and naturally, the colour scheme was of paramount importance to Aunt Martha, who tried to tell the planner his job and took control of all the minor details such as the wedding favours, place cards, and appropriate confetti, marching around with her etiquette book on weddings, advising all and sundry on proper protocol. Steves was the recipient of many sermons on his behaviour as he was volunteered as an usher, she would tolerate no mischief on the big day, no tricks or games of any kind. Apart from the wedding plans, her RCIA program was going well, Lottie was attending with her since he left, and one night the archbishop made a visit to meet all the new candidates, later telling her he was free to concelebrate on the day they had picked and gave permission for Reverend Dobbson to do one of the readings. Katherine laughed, the ceremony was growing bigger by the day; an archbishop, two priests and a minister to officiate? By this time, they had invited Fr. O'Connor to take part as she knew he and Pete would want him included.

Gerry said he wished he had as much news to tell, some afternoons he did a little sightseeing when he had a few hours off, but it was no fun going around by himself. She was sorry he was having a ho-hum time, however, Katherine was glad to hear when he didn't have much to report about work, it meant nothing serious was transpiring at the docks or warehouses and she could breathe a sigh of relief, for she dreaded a reprise of the human trafficking and smuggling scandal that had everyone in an uproar last year. She was on tenterhooks every day, wondering if he was all right until she heard nothing unusual had happened, just tons of reports to wade through and warehouses to inspect. Yet, just when it was going well, her heart gave a flutter on the last few days before his return when he noted something odd about the truck shipments in LA, and to be on the safe side, decided to bring in the narcotic squad to inspect the premises.

"Don't worry, this happens all the time, we have problems in LA and San Diego, it's one of our big trucking routes to and from Mexico, so we get smuggling of all kinds. The cops know that and appreciate a tip-off. We just let them at it and move on, I'll be home on time, don't worry, love."

ଔ ❀ ଓ

Katherine watched Gerry walk through the arrivals door, her heart skipped a beat and a half. He looked tired after the long flight, but wore a big smile and waved when he could pick her out from the crowd ready to greet the travellers. Not waiting to go around, he abandoned his cart, dropped his carry-on case and hugged her over the barrier.

"Hello beautiful, you're a sight for sore eyes. Give me a kiss."

"I'm so glad you're home! When you called the last couple of days, I was so afraid you were going to say something came up."

"Knock on wood," he said, rapping his head, "nothing happened. I told you not to fret. Come on, let's get out of this place, I'm sick of airports."

Samuel drove them to the apartment, Gerry was unable to wait and opened his case with pomp and ceremony, handing her a number of gifts that made her laugh: a T-shirt from Chicago, a key chain from Seattle, a snow globe with the Golden Gate bridge, a souvenir coffee mug from LA, and … a small box wrapped in gift paper. "A belated Valentine's Day gift," he explained. Inside was an unusual heart-shaped gold brooch the size of a silver dollar with scrolled engravings surrounding a heart-cut diamond and a curved gold bar on top making it look like a lock. Examining it closely, she discovered it had tiny hinges on the side—it was a real locket. Opening it carefully, she found their picture on one side, an inscription in tiny lettering on the other: "*Two hearts made one, never to be undone.*"

"I thought you might like it, but it was hard coming up with a poem that would fit inside and still be legible."

"It's absolutely beautiful, I love it. Thank you so much, you're always spoiling me, how do you manage to find such pretty things? Please, would you pin it on?"

"Of course, dear. You really like it?"

"Yes, it's gorgeous," she replied as he pinned it to her lapel, giving him another hug and a kiss before adding, "I got something for you too."

"Darling, you didn't have to get me anything."

"Yes I did, I couldn't leave it. It's not fancy like this, but I thought you might like to have it, it's waiting for you in the apartment."

Dropping his suitcases off in the bedroom after they arrived, he wondered what she had discovered. She handed him a small rectangular box and he opened it with unconcealed curiosity.

"Hey! A first edition of *Call of the Wild.*"

"The first printing too."

"So I can see," he said, looking like a kid on Christmas morning as he examined the inside cover. "Wow, I love it. It's in excellent condition, no inside marks or *ex libris* plates, thank you so much, that's one book missing from my collection I planned to get someday." He then looked up with concern, "Kathy, I truly appreciate your gift, but I hope they didn't take you on it."

"Don't worry, I was taught by a master and did my homework, and if they did overcharge me, you're definitely worth the extra."

"On top of all the work and the running you had to do this month, I can't believe you took the time to scout around for this. Come here you," he said, giving her a big hug and another long kiss. "I love you so much, Kathy."

"I love you too, welcome home."

Although they had talked every night on the phone, there were other things they had to catch up on, like his sketchbook for one thing. Instead of staying glued to pay-per-view to pass the evenings he couldn't sleep, he worked on skylines as seen from his hotel windows.

"And you say you don't have material for painting projects? You could give Turris a run for his money," Katherine declared, not a little proud to see how fast her pupil had progressed in his art.

"You like them?"

"Goodness, yes. In fact, I'd start turning them into paintings right away."

"And would I receive a début showing in your gallery?"

"Need you ask?"

"I'm only joking, your customers want accredited artists, I'm still only an amateur."

"Hey, you can't call yourself an amateur, especially after the Professor has helped you, and besides, to be an 'amateur' means to literally be a lover of something, that word is so misused in our vocabulary. Trust me, people can tell when they see a work painted by someone who loves what they do, they won't care if you've been to art school or not."

"I suppose there's something to that. Anyway, enough about me, how are the wedding preparations going?"

Katherine entertained Gerry with descriptions of Aunt Martha pestering the wedding planner to distraction, on two occasions they ended in a war of words. Everyone was convinced he would walk off the job, but he showed up on time at every meeting and deserved a medal for perseverance.

"Right now, we're all busy getting the invitations ready for the mail, they're stacked all over our library, we've done nothing but address envelopes for two weeks, and we don't dare make any more mistakes, or we'll run short of envelopes. Aunt Martha continually berates our handwriting when we're in a hurry, and she almost measures to see the stamp is applied exactly on the right spot. She's driving us all crazy. I've come to the conclusion wedding plans can be made easier, it's the people that make them difficult, and who cares if everything isn't exactly perfect? *We're* not perfect."

"It sounds like you need a break, you're worn to a frazzle."

"No time for that, we only have four months left until the wedding, and there is so much left to do."

He could have been mistaken, but he thought he detected the first hints of panic in her voice.

"Just so you know, I did some thinking while I was gone about who would be my groomsmen."

"Oh good, the mothers were wondering about that."

"After choosing Leroy, I bet they were, but don't worry, the rest of my choices are sane. I thought first of all, since Justine will be a bridesmaid, I'd like to ask Martin, he's a really nice guy, and it's the least I can do for crashing their wedding."

"I don't think he'd expect that."

"I know, but I like him, and I can tell he's very steady, Leroy won't be able to talk him into any of his stunts when the bachelor party rolls around. I hope that won't make fitting him out difficult since your friends won't be here until a day or two before the wedding."

"I don't think so, if you like, I can ask Justine to take his measurements. Who else do you have in mind?"

"There's Thomas, he's been with us for years and we work pretty close at the office. He manages everything under Dad's supervision when I'm off on my inspections, I couldn't run the place without him. Dad calls him the last of the great dependables and he's right. You haven't had a chance to meet Thomas yet, but I know you'll like him, and I have another friend, Nathan, who works at Christies. We used to get together a lot, but with work and all, it's not as easy as it used to be, especially as he does a lot of field work valuing clients' estates. He has a great sense of humour and is a rock of sense." Katherine was relieved he actually had people he could count on.

"This sounds great, and I *knew* you had more friends, I can't wait to meet them. Well, that has us nicely balanced, Pete says the Church isn't as stringent about who the witnesses are, which means my plans are unchanged. Since Stephie is my Matron of Honour, she'll help to keep Leroy in check, she's a tough cookie and is up to the challenge. Of course, she won't be able to do all the photographs, so she's recommended someone else to do that when we're at the altar, but she said not to worry, she's still bringing her camera, so we can expect some gorgeous pictures. Justine will have Martin, and Lottie and Suzy will be accompanied by your friends, I'm so glad that's all settled," she concluded with a sigh of relief.

"Never fear, we'll get it all sorted out."

"But there's still so much to do!"

Gerry was beginning to understand her panic, from that moment on, he was no longer left on the sidelines. First, he was commandeered for various missions to help with the preparations such as picking up or returning items from the planner's boutique before and after work, then, he was requested to attend the various meetings with the mothers and aunts as they made their final selections for the marquee and ballroom decorations, Katherine didn't want him to feel he was being left out of his own wedding plans, time permitting of course, he still had to work. There were a myriad of details to consider, table settings, the linens they would use, the colours of the linens, the glassware, the floral arrangements, musicians to hire, the list seemed endless. He thought most of this had all been decided already, then realized that was just the shortlist they had prepared: now they had to choose for real. He had told Katherine she could arrange the reception any way she wanted, and the women seemed to know what they were doing, so it was easier just to nod and say, "that's looks great, I'd go with that one," or "I like it, dear," whenever a sample of something was brought forward for his inspection. At least he did not feel like he was being flippant, they had excellent taste and he could safely agree with whatever they had chosen. He also had a secret to confess when Katherine hoped he did not mind having a soft rose theme.

"For your ears only, I like other colours besides blue and red, but I'm too macho to admit it, have to protect my manly image you know."

Half the time Katherine was not sure if he was being serious or trying to help her see the funny side of things in the midst of the pressure, he always managed to cheer her up.

"You mean that?"

"I do, the pinks you've selected are beautiful, I have no complaints. I can't wait to see my darling bride walk down the aisle surrounded by a sea of pink roses."

"This is all really happening now, isn't it?"

"Don't panic. All will be well," he said, gently jingling the key around his neck. Although this was their sign to thwart an argument, it had become a lover's amulet, reminding them what was important when the world threatened to close in on them and disturb their serenity.

If the wedding wasn't enough, Lent had now come upon them, and he wanted to support Katherine every step of the way as she made her final preparations to enter the Church. One night instead of painting, they delved through tomes on saints she checked out of the public library to help her find an appropriate patron saint to choose for her Confirmation name. Peter had instructed she pick a saint she would like as a role model to emulate, but that was difficult when many seemed to have horrific deaths. Eventually she become so confused with all the lists, she closed her eyes, opened a book at random and let her finger drop on the page. Gerry looked closer to view the result:

"Monegundis, I think you should give it another shot."

"I guess so, plus, it says she became a hermit. While I like my privacy, I don't think I'm up for that either."

"Okay, no martyrs and no hermits, but you don't have to follow your saint's life down to a 'T', mostly it's their virtues you're supposed to follow."

"Who did you pick then?" she asked, suddenly curious.

"Thomas."

"The Apostle?"

"No, but God knows, 'Doubting Thomas' did seem like my patron saint for awhile," he smiled. "Thomas More, I had just read about him and I remember being very impressed with his life, how cultured and ahead of his time he was, educating his daughters and teaching them Latin when it was unheard of, not to mention how steadfast he was, never taking a bribe and sticking up for what he knew was right. Perhaps I was too ambitious, he's not easy to live up to."

"I don't know how any of us could live up to these people, but I'd like someone like him too," she said, flipping through the book again before handing it to him. "Do you have any suggestions? For names, I mean." He went back to the beginning, stopping at the B section.

"What about Bernadette?"

"You mean, like in the old movie?"

"Yes, she has a pretty name, and you remind me of her in a way; gentle, yet not to be pushed around. Bernadette stuck to her guns no matter what the city officials and the townspeople threw at her."

"She sounds like the saint for me."

Katherine confided to Gerry she was a little anxious about her first confession, and while she knew Pete would help her through, she was convinced she would do something stupid to mess everything up.

"My poor Kathy, this is all getting to you, you really need a break.

Tell you what, Leroy is throwing a party on St. Patrick's Day, would you like to risk making an appearance?"

"No thank you, I'll pass," she replied.

"Okay, just kidding. How about Monday night I whisk you off for a show and a romantic dinner for two after work? We need to do something away from the gallery, the plans and the have-to's."

"The fifteenth, all right, I'm free that night, I really need to escape from all of this, and a show sounds like fun. We haven't done that in awhile."

"Shall we see a comedy, or attend a musical?"

"Just surprise me, I love it when you do that."

"Your wish is my command."

℃✿ℂ

"Like clockwork, your bouquet's arrived," Esther noted as the deliveryman entered the lobby. Gerry never failed to send Katherine a fresh posy for the front desk, always crimson roses and cheery sunflowers. By now, some of their regular customers thought the unusual display was an intentional artistic signature piece of the gallery.

"You two are like ketchup and mustard, a perfect combination," Olivia added, straightening out lumps of tissue paper that came in the latest shipment, she hated waste. "What show is he taking you to tonight?"

"He hasn't told me yet, it's a surprise, I won't know until I see the theatre marquee."

"Maybe it won't be a play or musical at all, but the opera, maybe the ballet. He could have suggested those ideas to throw you off," Suzy noted, "he's good at hiding his surprises."

"I must say, he's got a romantic streak, your Gerry," Olivia noted, "I definitely missed out somewhere."

"Do you at least know where he's taking you to dinner?" Suzy asked.

"No," Katherine admitted, "he's been completely secretive about the whole thing, he likes to keep me guessing. What about you, Esther? When are you going to start planning your cruise with the Professor?"

"Probably never, it seems the closest I'll get him to the sea is his seascapes, and here I thought he would break his neck to go on a tour with me to the Greek islands."

"I'm sorry Esther, I shouldn't have let him establish himself in the studio, it looks like he's moved in for good."

"That's all right dear, I do have a contingency plan: I'll hide his paintbrushes and leave travel brochures around until he gets the idea."

"I don't think that solution will do anymore, you'll have to hide our brushes too so he can't borrow them," Suzy observed.

"That's okay, we can lock them up for a good cause," Katherine added.

"But," Olivia piped up, "he's the 'full immersion' type, he might miss the message and bring in his toothbrush. Men usually don't let anything interfere with work, especially the artistic ones."

"Good point, I'll hide that too, or, just book us in at the travel agent. The woman of the house must do everything or nothing gets done, as usual."

"You said it," Olivia nodded, smashing down the growing pile of paper.

"You two are scaring me," Katherine said, lifting an eyebrow, "I'll never walk down the aisle if I keep listening to you. How about you, Suzy? Do you and Charlie have anything planned?"

"Nothing exciting, we're going to rent movies and stay in for the night, we've gone out the last few times and decided to do something quiet."

"That's a …oops, here we go," Esther stopped short, looking up at the door, "the interviews begin. It's a pity Dennis is off today, he's going to miss the fun."

Katherine decided they needed additional help on the floor before she left on her honeymoon and started scheduling everyone's vacation time when she came back. In any case, it was high time she hired more attendants to cover the expanded exhibition area, she had let that issue slide considering all the other plans she had to worry about. On this occasion, Katherine decided to dispense with ceremony when it came to interviews, she held them right there and then at the front desk with the rest of the Gallery Gang in attendance, allowing everyone to pose questions and look over the applicants' *résumés*. A little unorthodox perhaps, but she figured throwing the prospective employee straight into the deep end with this public examination had several advantages; she could see how they got along with the team, how they coped with unexpected situations, (an important skill considering the artistic types and eccentric collectors they would be working with), and, to observe the Gang's reaction as many heads were better than one. They had to work together, and they could detect situations or offer advice about a candidate she would not have thought of on her own.

This morning there were several candidates to interview, most of them were newly graduated art students. While she would like to help them all, she was looking for someone with selling experience this time around who was *not* an artist, they had enough people wishing they could paint instead of mind the gallery floors, the studio was just too tempting. They needed help who could take up the slack and allow everyone else to paint when needed. Thankfully, the interviewees weren't all students, a few people had gallery experience, and there was one lady who graduated from Sotheby's art management course who seemed like she would fit right in with everyone. Esther and Suzy liked her, and Katherine trusted Esther's judgement, however, she did not expect one gentleman to be sitting on the bench, looking around and patiently waiting to be interviewed, his hair neatly styled, his suit pristine, pants perfectly pressed to a sharp pleat, shoes shined to a high gloss that rivalled the gleam on the terrazzo floor.

"*Mr. Alcott?*"

"Yes?" he replied, looking over, then approached the desk. Suzy nearly dropped her coffee in astonishment.

"What a surprise. Surely, you haven't come for the interview session?"

"It's a pleasure to see you again, Miss Walsingham, Miss Cooper," he said holding out his hand with a slight bow. "Yes, I am afraid there has been a distressing new development at the Sirrac establishment. It is my sincere regret Mr. Sirrac was wont to retire a month ago, the gallery has been sold to a new company, and as with all new management, they had their own expert staff, my services were no longer required and I was unceremoniously relieved of my position. You can imagine my devastation."

"Mr. Alcott, I'm so sorry to hear that. Mr. Sirrac seemed like a nice gentleman, and I didn't expect him to retire so soon," Katherine replied.

"Oh, I felt quite dejected by the whole affair, and his retirement was unavoidable due to unfortunate circumstances quite beyond our control. Imagine my elation when I heard you have an opening for experienced personnel. I can hardly contain my hopeful aspiration to fulfil the requirements of this position. I present to you my extensive *curriculum vitae* for your consideration, and of course, it would be my pleasure to answer any questions you wish to propose."

"Cecil will be so sorry to hear this news. What happened to Mr. Sirrac? Is he ill or something?" Esther enquired.

"Well … yes and no, you might put it that way … you see, it was the small matter of his memory that posed the difficulty. Oh dear … how may I put this delicately? For some time Mr. Sirrac was displaying a mild form of forgetfulness, it was under extreme duress we endeavoured to carry on the gallery with the same formality as was customary. One never knew from day to day what was required, or indeed, what Mr. Sirrac would request from the staff. Sad to say, he took a trip to London to visit an exhibition at the Tate Gallery. Mrs. Sirrac asked me to keep in contact and check to make sure that his trip proceeded according to plan. Of course, we all understood at the gallery he should never have been allowed to travel alone, much to our dismay, he failed to show up at the Tate, or indeed his hotel that night. Next morning we informed the London police of his disappearance and a search immediately commenced. To our utter amazement, Scotland Yard informed us he had followed the Salvation Army band from Hyde Park to their building, was safely in their charitable custody, and would someone kindly come to London to collect him. The dubious honour of this errand was delegated to me, and with great difficulty I extracted him from the guardianship of the Salvation Army. It appeared Mr. Sirrac was struck with an amorous fascination for a very buxom blonde lady in the band, and was quite persistent in demanding a uniform and a position in their ranks. I administered the sedatives supplied by his doctor for the occasion, and without further ado, whisked him to Heathrow. Mr. Sirrac is now under professional supervision, and by all accounts, he is doing very well. Subsequent to this tragic event, I could see the handwriting on the wall and was fully aware the Sirrac's days were numbered. So you see, due to this unfortunate state of affairs, I stand before you, hat in hand, so to speak, to request your kind consideration."

"That's a very sad story, Gerry told me something was happening over there, but I hadn't heard all the details."

"Oh yes, you mean Mr. Reinold, that reminds me, I have been absolutely remiss, please allow me to congratulate you on your upcoming nuptials," Mr. Alcott continued, "and on the exquisite refurbishment of your building. You have captured the elegant ambience of days gone by and the grandeur of the Parisian salon exhibitions of old. I wanted so much to come and visit your new gallery, but of course, under the circumstances, that was out of the question. Mr. Sirrac would have considered that disloyalty to him, and nobody wished to upset him in his delicate condition."

"Thank you. I quite understand, and I'd be happy to give you the grand tour," Katherine offered, trying to stifle a smile. "Would you like to join me for coffee first at Andre's?"

"It would be my pleasure, Miss Walsingham. How absolutely marvellous of you to think of incorporating a gourmet restaurant to complete the refined elegance that so represented the art and music world of the nineteenth century."

"Well, it seemed to suit the building, you have to work with what you got."

Katherine could tell by Esther and Suzy's expressions that like her, they were amused with Mr. Alcott's surprise appearance, but approved of the new candidate. With his expertise and gracious rapport with people, he could fill the position perfectly, it would be foolish of her to turn him down. Making their way to the restaurant, Katherine asked if he also liked to paint.

"No, but I appreciate other people's talents, I neither have the skill nor the inclination to follow the masters, which reminds me, if you will forgive me for rudely changing the subject, do you still have your magnificent Napoléon, or did you decide to sell it?"

"I couldn't part with it, it's upstairs in the museum section. Mr. Alcott, if you don't mind my curiosity, do you happen to know who wanted it after it was nominated in your contest?"

"I do apologize Miss Walsingham, we were never privy to that information, and after Mr. Sirrac's unfortunate misadventure in London, it appears we may never find out."

"I suppose not, poor Mr. Sirrac, I'm surprised it hasn't shown up in the papers."

"Well, that horrible Horace hadn't been terrorizing the premises for some time, not since he has chosen you as his latest victim," Mr. Alcott noted apologetically, "so it was not too difficult to keep it hush-hush, but the change of management will be announced shortly."

"That explains it, but I'd better warn you about Horace, he has exclusives here, so if any other critic asks for comments, mum's the word."

Mr. Alcott looked aghast at the thought.

"Surely you are not serious! *Exclusives?* Why, that's nothing short of artistic suicide! Mr. Sirrac would *never* permit him to darken the door of his establishment."

"Neither would I, until art sales doubled after his scathing visitations."

"Oh dear, sales or no sales, this is a predicament. Upon my word, I don't know if I am capable of working where such an odious person is allowed the freedom to traverse the exhibition halls, at will no less, to the detriment of all that we hold sacred in our cultured circles."

"Well, let me show you around, before you decide if you're unable to tolerate Horace," she noted with an incredulous smile.

"Does this mean I'm no longer unemployed?"

"It's up to you."

After they finished coffee, Katherine conducted him on the promised tour, introducing him to the guards and explaining his duties as they went through the corridors. He really was an expert art advisor, could recognise a few of the artists on show by their style, could tell which part of the corridors received more foot traffic, was satisfied with the security systems after eyeing the tripwire mechanism, and seemed in his element when he was shown around the museum section. Naturally, he knew the famous paintings on sight, but could also date many of the antiquities and was knowledgeable about their historical background without looking at the labels. He was somewhat taken aback with D.S.'s street art, and Gerry's odd con art collection, but overall, she could see the gallery had won him over and working in this grand setting was more than enough compensation for having to face the Art Hacker should he appear. In fact, he seemed very emotional, was he tearing up?

"I have reached my Shangri La," he sniffed. "When would you like me to start, Miss Walsingham?"

"Well, anytime you like, and please, the ambience may be formal, but we are rather semi-informal around here, you can call me Kathy."

"As you wish, and I would be pleased if you call me Kevin."

"Great. Well, if you don't have anything else to do, you can stick around, consider it an open house day and have some fun."

"Oh no, I must make myself useful, is there a task I may do for you?" he asked, instantly pulling himself together.

"Not that I can think of off hand, but perhaps you would like to become familiar with our new artists' work and their bios?"

"Of course, right away Miss Kathy. You are quite correct, I can see there are some new names and trends emerging that I do need to become familiar with, and let me take this opportunity to say, I find your philosophical discourses very refreshing, art for the mind as well as the eye and the heart. If I may impose upon your creative muse, whatever gave you the suggestion?"

"Well, it's a long story. Let me show you the studio first, you haven't seen that yet, and you have to meet the Professor, he's up there right now engrossed with his latest masterpiece."

"Professor Cecil Matthews is here right now? Oh, what an honour!"

Kevin was an excitable character, a colourful personality that would fit right in with the eclectic personnel that had drawn together at the gallery. Enormously impressed with their private studio, "A capital idea," he called it, he watched the Professor at work, praising his mastery of the brush. Returning to the front desk, he dutifully set himself to studiously memorize all their brochures.

"Now that's what I call dedication," Suzy whispered to Katherine.

"Don't forget to take a lunch break," Esther reminded him.

Eventually, he did as she suggested and took a break, having almost completed his first task. For the rest of the day he entertained them with gossip from the other galleries that he had heard until Katherine almost forgot the time.

"Oh no! I have to go get ready, Gerry's picking me up early today."

"How delightful, I haven't seen Mr. Reinold in a long time, although I can understand why," Kevin smiled, "but forgive me, we mustn't delay you any longer."

Katherine locked the door behind her when she went to the office to change into the rose dress and matching jacket with bugle beads she wore the night of their engagement in Paris, then ran to the bathroom to pin her hair up and touch up her make-up. When she emerged, everyone agreed she looked absolutely beautiful, although there was one detail that looked strangely out of place.

"Forgive me for saying, but … that is an unusual neck ornament you are wearing tonight, Miss Kathy," Kevin observed.

She quickly looked down and laughed, no one had ever seen the gold chain with the key before, she was able to conceal it under her shirt or blouse, but with her formal dress and its becoming neckline, the amulet could not remain hidden.

"It may be an ordinary key, but to me, it's more precious than all the diamonds in the world."

"Somehow, I think your brooch is a clue," Esther said, indicating the heart-shaped locket pinned on her jacket. Katherine wore it almost everyday.

"May I?" Kevin asked.

"Of course," Katherine replied, opening the brooch for him.

"My, how exquisite," he noted, "Gerard always had an eye for the beautiful and the rare."

"That's true. One of these days I'll tell you all about the key."

"Ah, don't leave us on pins and needles," Suzy replied, "I'm mush when it comes to a romantic story."

"Gerry will be here any moment, you don't want me to rush it, do you?"

"No I guess not, you'll leave us on a cliff-hanger then," Suzy laughed. The telephone began to ring, and Katherine picked up the receiver since she was the closest.

“Good evening, Walsingham Gallery, how may I help you?”

“Just love me, that’s all I ask.”

“Gerry?”

“Yours truly. Are you all set?”

“Yes, Cinderella has tossed her work garb, she’s all dressed up and ready to go.”

“All right, I just called to let you know I had to stop and pick up a few files at the main warehouse first, but I’m on my way. I’ll be there in a few minutes.”

“Okay. I’ve got so much to tell you, you won’t believe who’s joined the Gallery Gang.”

“Someone I know?”

“Definitely, you’ll find out when you get here.”

“It seems we’re both full of surprises. Now you have me curious, I can’t wait.”

“See you in a few minutes, I love you.”

“I love you too, bye Princess.”

“He’s running late I bet,” Esther noted after she hung up.

“He just had to pick up some files, he’s on his way.”

“Maybe now that you have a few minutes, you’ll tell us your story,” Suzy wheedled.

“Oh … all right.” Katherine gave in and told them all about the wild drive around Paris they took when she repaid Gerry’s riddle recording with her lover’s lock mystery tour that culminated with the Lock Ceremony on the bridge and the promise they made to always wear the keys. “Now, nobody better breathe a word about this, it’s one of the few things that didn’t hit the gossip columns, and I would like to keep it that way.”

“We shall be models of discretion, won’t we ladies?” Kevin affirmed.

“Okay, I’m officially ‘mushed’, I’m a sucker for romance, and that has to be the most romantic escapade I’ve heard in a long time,” Suzy sighed.

“Ah, young love,” Esther smiled, “don’t worry, your secret is safe.”

“It’s a shame Dennis isn’t here, he just missed a real good story,” Suzy noted.

“Dennis?” Kevin wondered.

“That’s right, you haven’t met Dennis yet, it’s his day off. You might remember him, the same Dennis Harrington who received a nomination the same year I did,” Katherine clarified.

“Yes, I do remember, his painting was entitled *Electrovision* if memory serves,” Kevin thought aloud.

"Wow, good memory," Katherine replied, "Dennis will be pleased his work made a lasting impression."

"With all the colours he used, how could it not?" Kevin drolly returned.

"True," Katherine laughed. "Hey, Gerry should be here by now," she realized, she had lost track of the time in the midst of their conversation.

"Don't worry, it's probably traffic as usual," Esther reminded her.

"Maybe, but I don't know when the show is, I hope we don't miss the first act. We've never done that before."

"Don't worry, he'll be here," Suzy returned.

"But it's almost closing time, I hope something else didn't come up at the last minute, but he would have called … hi Charlie, rough day at court?" He looked a little tired as he joined the group at the desk.

"Hi everyone, no court today, endless depositions, I'm beat," he reported. "Hey, someone looks nice. Gerry taking you out? Special occasion?"

"A mystery show and dinner, but he's running late, he likes to be fashionably late, but never for a show. I hear you're taking it easy tonight with Suzy."

"Yeah, I've rented an armful of movies on our 'to see' list," he replied. "It's a night for feet on the coffee table and relaxation."

"I have a feeling he won't get past the credits, he'll be asleep before the movie starts," Suzy added.

"No I won't, I promise to forgo the wine at dinner so I won't get dozy."

"Where have I heard that before?" Suzy said with a wink at Katherine.

"Well, it looks like Andre is getting ready for his evening patrons," Esther said, looking over at the restaurant, "would you like us to start closing?"

"Yes, I suppose so, it's been a long day, time to shut up shop." Katherine made the closing announcement over the sound system, before resuming her instructions. "I'll help Suzy with the upstairs and remind the stragglers. Kevin, you can follow Esther and see how to check the alarm system and arrange the lights. Gerry might be here by the time we get done. Is the Professor still upstairs?"

"No, I think I saw him leave an hour ago, muttered something about a new tube of Burnt Umber, he says he's been using that up like shaving cream," Esther informed them, "I hope he remembers to pick me up. Last time he stayed talking with the manager at the art supply for hours. I can always join Olivia at Andre's and just wait it out as usual."

"That might be a good idea, Suzy," Charlie piped up, "we could have dinner at Andre's, we don't want to cook tonight or get a dinner to go, do we?"

"I guess not, anything you like," Suzy agreed as she turned off the main computers at the desk.

"Well, that's settled then, afterwards we can have our film festival, let's make life easy when we can."

Katherine looked up when the main door opened, it was just the change of security detail. She sighed and followed Suzy on the rounds. While they walked the fourth floor, an announcement interrupted the music on the sound system.

"*Katherine, please come to the front desk. There's a call on hold for you,*" Esther calmly relayed.

"Oh no, looks like the show is off," Katherine said, shaking her head as she turned towards the elevator.

"I'll come with you," Suzy said, "everything seems all right up here, and the security can manage the rest."

Approaching the desk, Katherine could tell from Esther's expression it was no ordinary call or 'I'm running late' message.

"It's from someone named Sammy, he says it's urgent," Esther informed her, handing over the receiver.

"Sammy?"

"Miss Kathy, I don't know how to tell you this, but something's happened in the warehouse depot … ."

"An emergency? What's wrong? Not another drug haul?"

"No Miss, worse than that, I wish I wasn't the one telling you … the Boss Man's been in an accident and it don't look good."

"Sammy! What's happened?"

"I'm not sure Miss, he was in a hurry to leave, he was all dressed up so I know where he was heading, but I didn't see it happen. I can't say much right now, the police are here and they want me to round up the workers who were in the yard for questioning."

"Oh God, I'm on my way … ."

"No Miss, you don't want to come here, and anyway, they'll be taking him to the hospital as soon as … well, I'll call you again when I know where."

"What do you mean 'as soon as'? Sammy, please tell me what's happened!"

"Miss, I hope you're sitting. From what I can tell, it was a freakish thing; one of the articulated trucks ploughed into his car at high speed as he was leaving and just kept going until it crashed him into another truck coming up behind. The firemen are still trying to cut him out of the car, and the ambulance crew are on standby."

"Oh my God, he's not … ."

"He's unconscious, but like I said, it don't look good. I've called the Big Boss, and I … oh, I've got to go, the boys in blue are getting impatient, I'll call when I have more news."

"I'll be right here, thank you, Sammy."

By now, all eyes were on her as they guessed from her side of the conversation that something terrible had happened.

"Kathy, what's wrong?" Suzy enquired.

"It's Gerry, he's been in an accident at the warehouse yard…." There was silence as she relayed the details Sammy had given her. She felt ill and incredibly weak, Esther immediately took her by the shoulders and sat her down.

"Miss Kathy, is there anything we can do for you?" Kevin asked, looking pale after this news.

"No, they're cutting him out of the car as we speak, Sammy said he'd call as soon as he knows what hospital they're taking him to."

"We'll take you," Charlie jumped in, his eyes grave, "you're had a shock, you're in no condition to drive."

"Yes, we can't let you go alone," Suzy agreed.

"We'll stay with you until the call comes, then don't worry about here, we'll take care of the gallery, you take the time you need," Esther assured her, "if necessary, Cecil will also step in, he's dependable in an emergency."

"Thank you, oh I've got to call my parents," she realized, not sure what to do first. Calling Oak Meadows, her mother answered and she repeated what little news she had from Sammy. This was the second time she had to tell this tragedy, and still it felt strangely unreal, like she was watching some television show or telling a story.

This couldn't be happening, not now, not to Gerry. This is all just a bad dream.

The sick feeling in her stomach gave way to shock, and quickly to an icy fear as she realized the possibility that when Sammy called her back, it may not be to the emergency room they were taking him, but the morgue. The tears were flowing by the time she had told her mother everything while everyone searched for tissues around the desk or in their purses and handed her a fistful, trying to be helpful and feeling useless.

"I don't know where they're taking him … ."

"I'll call your father, he's at the office late tonight, do as Sammy says and wait until he calls, then tell us where to meet you. Dear, listen to me now, don't drive, take a taxi if you have to."

"Don't … worry … Charlie and Suzy … are taking me … they're right here," she explained between sobs.

"All right, I'm going to call everyone, I wish I was there with you dear, but hold on, wait for Sammy's call."

"I'm all right," she cried, although the opposite was true, "okay … I'm … going to hang up now," Katherine didn't know what to say, shock had dispelled her ability to give appropriate replies, not that anyone expected her to be coherent at a time like this.

"Suzy, run over to Andre and get some tea," Esther ordered as she put her arm around Katherine. Suzy immediately jumped up and obeyed the command, eager for something to do to relieve the tension. "I know you don't feel like drinking it, but you'll need something to hold you together," she concluded, turning to Katherine.

"Thank … you," she replied, the tears refusing to stop.

Charlie and Kevin didn't know what to say and waited silently by her side at the desk. They couldn't promise Gerry would be all right, not after hearing the details about the articulated trucks; whenever the Jaws of Life were required at a rescue, it was usually a life-and-death situation. Every second weighed heavily, Katherine watching the phone as if her vigilance could make the news travel faster. Suzy returned a few minutes later with a large tray, Olivia right beside her.

"I thought I'd better get us all something," she explained.

"Good girl," Esther replied.

"Suzy told me what happened, it's unbelievable," Olivia exclaimed. Andre came out the back door dressed in his chef's uniform, looking as pale as everyone else.

"One of the waiters just told me, please tell me it isn't true."

"I'm afraid it is," Esther replied, "we're waiting for a call to say where they're taking him."

"Oh God, if there's anything I can do … ."

"I'm afraid there's nothing any of us can do but wait," Charlie said, pursing his lips.

"I … oh, I have to head back to the kitchen," Andre noted, looking at the customers arriving for dinner, "but really, if there's anything you need Kathy, let me know."

"I will, thank you Andre."

"Come, I think we'd better take the tea and go to the office, we're creating curiosity," Esther noticed. Katherine had forgotten people were still arriving for dinner, everything around her seemed unreal. The Professor sauntered in behind another group of diners, clutching his bag of paint tubes.

"Heavens, what's happened here?" he enquired, looking at the pensive expressions on everyone's face at the front desk, Esther conducting a sobbing Katherine into the office with Kevin bearing the tray behind them.

"Oh Professor, there's been an accident, Gerry's been hit by a truck, and we have no idea how he's doing yet. We're all waiting for a phone call. Katherine is in bits, you had better join us for tea," Suzy blurted out, her eyes filling with tears.

The office was cramped as everyone tried to find a place to settle and wait for the phone, while Suzy doled out the teacups and Esther poured the tea. Katherine sat motionless at her desk, staring at the phone, silent tears flowing, dropping on her rose jacket as she had used up her handful of Kleenex.

"Here, Miss Kathy, a box of tissues, we must keep hoping for the best," Kevin consoled, although he too was on the verge of tears. Charlie suggested to Suzy she put extra sugar in Katherine's tea.

"It's supposed to help after a shock," he explained.

"Maybe it's a glass of brandy she needs," Suzy whispered back.

"I heard that, I … don't need brandy … I need to stay awake," Katherine replied in a choked voice.

Charlie glanced at the clock and noticed it was almost an hour since Sammy had called, he pursed his lips again. One by one, everyone succumbed to the urge to follow suit and glanced at the clock, fearing the worst. The phone suddenly blipped, causing everyone to jump, but not as fast as Katherine who snatched the receiver with a lightning reflex. Everyone held their breath and waited attentively for the news.

"Hello?"

"Miss Kathy? It's Sammy here, I'm sorry, the police held me up, and I had to call the Big Boss again … ."

"That's all right, what's happened? Is Gerry…?"

"He's knocked out bad, but he's a fighter, they got him out about five, maybe ten minutes ago and they're taking him to the hospital now."

"Oh thank God," she replied. There was a palpable intake of breath as everyone started breathing again, surmising from her reply he was all right. She listened carefully to the hospital details and asked if there were any more developments.

"Yeah, the driver who smashed into him has disappeared, the police are on the hunt for him now. A real hit a run this was. Thing is, it's still touch and go, the paramedics said he's in a critical condition. You'd better go to the hospital right now, Miss Kathy."

"I'm on my way, thank you Sammy, I'll call you later when I get news from the hospital."

"Thank you Miss, I'd appreciate that, we're all pretty shook up around here, especially Leo, he saw it happen. After he gave his statement, he went with him in the ambulance, he felt someone had to go with the Boss Man."

"Poor Leo, I'm glad he went, I'm glad Gerry isn't alone. Thank you again, Sammy. I'd better go."

"Right Miss, you hang in there now, ya hear?"

"I'm trying, bye Sammy."

She replaced the receiver and quickly relayed the latest update before calling her mother, then anxiously looked for her bag and keys, but was at loss wondering where she had put them.

"Here's your coat and purse, Kathy," Suzy said, holding her coat and helping her to put it on.

"Thank you, will you all … ?"

"Yes, we'll be all right, now go, we'll take care of everything here," the Professor replied, "don't worry about us."

"I'll call when I know anything," she promised.

"All right dear, don't worry, you just get to the hospital," Esther said, patting her arm.

Charlie and Suzy quietly escorted her to the parking lot and decided it was better to take his car. It was a solemn, pensive drive to the hospital. Everything still felt uncanny, surreal, as if a strange wormhole had opened up and sucked them into a parallel universe that faintly resembled their world yet looked completely alien. Sitting silently in the front seat, Katherine could not focus properly, her mind envisioning what last terrifying image Gerry saw as she stared blankly at the dim lights on the dashboard glowing in the darkness, the speedometer, clock, the heater symbols, the radio station display, anything to keep her from looking out the windscreen, paranoid she might see a pair of lights veer from the opposite side of the road and head straight for them. Her companions kept silent, they knew instinctively it was a time to be quiet, although they wished they could say something to comfort her. It seemed like they would never get to the hospital, that the end of the world would come first before they found a place to park, but at last, they made it to the emergency waiting area. Charlie jumped to the fore and made Katherine sit with Suzy while he went to the desk and asked for information; if there was bad news, he wanted to hear it first and break it to her gently if he could. As they waited for Charlie, a man in a workman's outfit hanging around looking glumly at the floor, lifted his head and immediately came over. When he approached, she saw it was one of the deliverymen's uniforms, the Reinold logo unmistakable. However, what frightened her the most was the reddish streaks on Leo's cuffs and arms, he obviously was the first on the scene and had tried to help Gerry. He covered his arms as he sat beside her.

"I'm so glad you stayed with him! Sammy said you saw what happened."

"I did, God it was awful, I was coming out of Warehouse Two in the forklift heading across the yard, it happened before I could do anything to warn him. The driver barrelled at him from the open area, you know as you face out the main entrance? Well, Sammy must have told you the rest."

"Didn't he see it coming? Couldn't he have gotten out of the way?"

"He stopped for a moment, he wasn't moving, I think he was rummaging in the papers that he came for, making sure he hadn't forgotten something. He often stops to double check stuff before he leaves, it's a habit. It looked like he had the papers on the passenger's seat and probably didn't see anything. His car wasn't in the way or anything, you know the warehouse depot, it's got plenty of space, I mean, you wouldn't expect one of the trucks just to plough straight at you. I've never seen anything like it after all my years working there."

"Sammy said the driver ran off, there's no sign of him."

"You serious? I thought maybe something had happened to the truck, but that sounds suspicious to me. God, I tried to get him out of the car, but no good."

"Leo, you did your best, you stayed with him until help arrived, that's the important thing."

"There's something else; when the paramedics were placing him on the gurney, this slipped out of his jacket pocket," Leo said, handing her a long, slender velvet box. "He also had flowers on the front seat, so I know this was meant for you."

Katherine slowly opened the box to find a gold bracelet with a miniature heart-shaped padlock ornament in the centre of the delicate links bearing a heart-shaped diamond to match her brooch.

"He's always spoiling me," she said quietly, the tears starting to flow again. Suzy hunted in her purse for more tissues.

"They're not giving much news," Charlie noted grimly as he came back to join the mournful group, "asked if anyone could fill in some forms, but I don't know his medical history."

"They asked me too," Leo noted, "but I said his folks or his sister might be able to do that when they come."

"How's he doing?" Suzy asked, Katherine still wiping her eyes.

"He's being prepped for surgery, they didn't tell me more than that, I'm not family. We'll have to wait."

"The Big Boss is here," Leo said, standing up, "I'd better go meet him."

Katherine had never seen Mr. Reinold look so ashen. He remained stoic, but was certainly grief struck. Leo told him his side of the story while Katherine quickly left her seat and went to meet him, he grabbing her in his customary bear hugs, this time refusing to let go. They didn't speak, what words could they utter? None. Katherine quietly cried into his lapel, she wanted to be brave for him, but could not help express her sorrow when she at last found her voice.

"How could this happen to us? We were so happy, why would God do something like this to us?" she sobbed.

"I don't know why He allows things at times, and we can't really question Him, but, if it's any consolation, I don't think this was God's doing," he replied quietly, holding her tight.

"Pete said pain gives us power that we're not aware of, but I feel so weak and helpless right now! What will we do if we lose him? What will we do without our Gerry?"

"Shhh, Katie, we won't lose him. We Reinolds are stubborn, we don't give in that easy. Your father and brother are here," he noted.

"Oh Pops," she said, hugging him as he shook hands with Mr. Reinold, while Steves quietly stood to one side.

"I'm here now Kathy, your mother is on her way, and your Gramps is coming with her. I'm so sorry, Richard. When Helen called, we couldn't believe the news. How is he?"

"We don't know yet, I'll go see if they can tell us anything."

They retreated to the waiting room while Mr. Reinold went back to the main desk. Everyone let Katherine sit with her father for a moment, trying to give them some space, which was almost impossible in the bustle of the emergency area. She told him all the news after which she wiped his lapel with a fresh tissue, apologising for drenching it.

"I'm wrecking everyone's coats tonight," she sniffed.

"Don't worry about that, what have you got there?" he asked quietly, noticing the slender box she still clutched in her other hand.

"He was going to give it to me tonight, Leo found it in his jacket when he …," her voice faltered as she opened the box. Harold sighed and held her close as the tears continued. A few minutes later, Sophia and Lottie arrived, their eyes red from tears and looking worried sick. Harold and Katherine went to meet them, explaining Richard had gone to scout for anyone who could give him any information before telling them everything they knew. While they were in the midst of their news report, Helen and Gramps arrived, and they had to start all over. After all the repetition, Katherine could still not comprehend what had happened, the accident was not sinking in, that Gerry was fighting for his life somewhere in this building was bizarre. *It simply couldn't be happening!* No one could believe it, they sat in the waiting room dazed, waiting for Mr. Reinold to come back. They didn't have to wait for long, he retuned a little paler than before, and noticed Sophia and Lottie waiting anxiously for him. He had received grave news:

"One of the doctors spoke to me for a moment or two, Gerry's gone for surgery. I'm not up on all the medical jargon, so he broke it down for me. The one piece of good news is it's a miracle his neck or back isn't broken, however, he was hit pretty bad. There's no point hiding it, and there's no way I can make this easier to hear."

"Please, don't hide anything, I'm his mother, I have a right to know," Sophia replied quietly but with a firm resolve to bear whatever catastrophe he had to report.

Mr. Reinold took a deep breath.

"He's in a critical condition, he's got concussion, a punctured lung, a ruptured spleen that will have to be removed, cracked ribs, but the worst part is his legs, the truck seems to have crushed the car on him in such a way his legs and hips are completely shattered. They've called in a team of specialists from all over the city and they're doing their best, but this is major, he'll be in there for hours. They have no way of knowing how long at present."

"Oh my God! Will he … will he…?"

"Sophie, he may not have a broken spine, but the doctor said the way it looks, they don't know if he'll … be able to walk again."

Sophia sank into the nearest chair while everyone sat in stunned silence after hearing this litany of injuries and the final blow that Gerry could possibly be confined to a wheelchair for the rest of his life, that is, if he pulled through the arduous operation to repair all the damage. They didn't have time to let it sink in, two men in overcoats looking officious came, quickly introducing themselves, flashing their IDs, and asked if Mr.

Reinold was present. Mr. Reinold went to speak with them, it was obvious from the moment they walked through the door they were detectives coming to ask questions. They had already questioned everyone at the warehouse yard and he was the last on their list.

"It's all right Detective Davenport, you can speak in front of everyone here," he assured him.

"Mr. Reinold, we're sorry to trouble you, we know this is very a bad time, but we have to act fast you know."

"It's all right. Go ahead."

"We need to know if you were in the warehouse yard recently, perhaps noticed anything suspicious?"

"No, I haven't been to that centre in a month, I trust Gerard to handle the main warehouse depot here in New York, and when I dropped by, everything seemed business as usual."

"Okay. Was there anyone you know who would bear him a grudge? Someone who got laid off, maybe? Perhaps he had an enemy with some personal vendetta? Any detail, no matter how insignificant, would be of help."

"Enemies? Take your pick, we're probably on every cartel's hit list since we've cracked down on the smuggling rings shanghaiing our trucks and warehouses. Have you found the driver yet?"

"No," the second detective replied, "he's completely disappeared. The bad news is, we're going to have a hard time tracing him: it seems your company hired a man who's been dead six years."

"What?"

"Yeah, stolen ID and social security number, this guy's a ghost."

"I don't believe it," Mr. Reinold rumbled, "our background checks are rigorous. How could someone like that slip through?"

"Whoever he is, he managed to do it," Detective Davenport replied, "this could all be a freak accident with an inexperienced driver who skipped past your background checks, but we're still looking at other angles, especially after all the trouble you've had. We've put out an APB and a description of the man, with any luck, someone will spot him. Well, we won't take up any more of your time for now, sir. We hope your son will be all right."

"Thank you, Detectives."

How much more bad news would they receive tonight?

"Oh, did anyone think to contact Peter?" Sophia asked suddenly, sitting up in her chair, "I'm in such a state, I didn't think … ."

"I did Mom," Lottie replied, "well, the parish office, they said they'd contact him, he should be here soon."

"We should go up and wait in the main waiting area," Mr. Reinold stated, "we shouldn't hold up the emergency area."

"Mr. R., I said I'd call Sammy if there was any news," Katherine said, her voice shaking, "oh, and the gallery … the gallery … they might still be there …."

"Don't you worry Miss Kathy, I'll tell Sammy, I have to head back to the yard now anyway," Leo said quietly.

"No you don't," Mr. Reinold answered, "go home to your family Leo, take a few days off, you've seen enough for one night, you can't go back to work after … I'll call Sammy. Do you have anyone to drive you home?"

"I can call a cab, sir."

"Don't do that, I'll take you," Steves offered, glad he could do something practical to help than sitting around. Katherine had whispered to him Leo was the first on the scene and didn't leave Gerry alone. Helping Gerry and making his sister feel a little better earned Leo an A-plus rating in Steve's good books.

"Thanks, I'd appreciate it," Leo replied.

"Leo, thank you," Sophia said, standing up to see him off, "our Gerry mentions you and Dan quite a bit, I'm so glad you were with him."

"I wish I could have done more, ma'am," he replied quietly before leaving with Steves.

"Kathy, I'll call everyone at the gallery, or tell the guards at least," Suzy offered.

"I guess we should move to the main waiting area," Harold said as another family arrived to wait for news about a loved one.

"I know we don't feel like it, but this is only a suggestion. I'm sure no one has had a bite to eat yet, I know Kathy hasn't, Harold and I haven't …" Helen noted as they all stood up. Somehow, mothers always remembered mealtimes and ensured everyone got fed, even in the midst of a disaster.

"That's right, I know we should all eat something, but … I don't think I can face anything right now," Sophia replied.

"Oh Mom, I just couldn't eat anything," Katherine agreed.

"I don't feel like eating myself, but I thought I should suggest it, it's going to be a long night, and we might feel hungry later."

Dinner now discarded, everyone decided to move to the general waiting area in the admittance section, it was quieter and less distressing than the ER with its continual stream of injured and worried people. The attendant at the desk said they would send Peter to the main area when he arrived. Suzy came back and reported that everyone had gone home except Andre and the guards, they would have to wait until tomorrow to tell everyone else at the gallery.   Helen thanked Charlie and Suzy for coming, but that they really should go home too, however, they insisted on staying until they had more news.

Sitting on the edge of their seats or pacing the floor, the vigil of waiting and watching continued. Gramps, who had been unable to say anything since he arrived, simply sat with his Katie, patting her arm every now and then. He had taken a liking to Gerry right from the beginning, practically adopted him, and received the news as if it had been one of his own sons in the accident. Helen sat in the other chair by Katherine, Sophia sat with her, Lottie sat next to her mother, while Suzy sat in the row of chairs across from Katherine, the ladies forming a quiet support group. Charlie decided to sit across from Gramps while Harold talked with Richard, sat for a moment, then paced the floor with him. Eventually, the two fathers stood out in the hall together for a change of scenery, although the hall was just as clinical as the waiting area.

"Looks like the wedding will have to be postponed," Richard quietly remarked, simply stating fact. They knew that … if … Gerry came out, there would be a long recovery period that would take months if not weeks.

"I know, I don't dare mention that to Kathy yet, although she may have thought as much already. God, I'm sorry I was so hard on him." Richard looked at Harold questioningly. "The 'you-had-better-take-care-of-my-daughter' speech when they became engaged. I needn't have worried, since I've gotten to know him better, I can see he idolises Kathy, worships the ground she walks on."

"Don't be hard on yourself, I understand, especially after the stunt he pulled running over to Paris. You should've heard how I grilled Lottie's fiancé, I have my regrets as well," Richard replied, "it's our job, had to be done. We have to watch out for our girls."

"Still," Harold replied.

"Still nothing. I'm glad you gave him something to think about, make Ger appreciate his responsibilities. If Katie was mine, I'd do the same thing. You and Helen have done a mighty fine job raising her. She's the best thing that happened to our family, not just to Ger. I have to confess, she was the only one who could knock some sense into me," Richard admitted, looking down the hall to see Peter carrying a black briefcase.

"And you've raised a fine family," Harold replied, "not an easy feat in this day and age."

"You've said it, and now *this* to happen … a *wheelchair,*" Richard replied bitterly.

"I'm sorry, I would have been here sooner, but I got detained," Peter apologized, dropping his briefcase and giving his father an embrace, then shook hands with Harold. "How bad is it?"

Richard relayed the news they had received so far, Peter simply lowered his head and exhaled slowly as the preliminary prognosis was disclosed.

"Your mother, sister and Katie are in there waiting," Richard said quietly.

Peter quickly went in and held his mother and sister while everyone else tried to avert their gaze as they vented their grief to him, a sorrowful meeting that was difficult to watch. When they calmed down, he held Katherine as she too could not hold back her tears, it felt good to see him and cry on his shoulder, still a rock of strength even in the midst of his own anguish. She could see it in his eyes, pain and heartache, but an unquenchable desire to help others and forget himself. When her tears subsided at last, he gently sat her down, and holding her hands still clutching the velvet box, crouched down to meet her at eye level.

"Now Kathy, you must listen to me, Gerry needs you to listen," he began gently, but firmly. "I know this is difficult, but Gerry needs you to be strong, very strong, not just now, for a long time."

"Peter, I don't feel strong, I don't feel it," she whispered, her voice quavering.

"You're stronger than you know, and he's going to need that strength. Yes, he has a father, mother, brother and sister who love him, but he's going to need *you* most of all," he impressed upon her, gently squeezing her hands.

Looking into his eyes, she understood. She loved Gerry so much, that at times, the mere thought of him made it feel like her body was not big enough to hold her heart. Silently tapping into the love she felt for him, the pain abated a little. She understood what Peter meant by a hidden strength, and a quiet resolve took hold.

I'll always be with you Gerry, no matter what happens.

Peter pressed her hands again with a little smile.

"That's it. Love makes us all strong."

He continued to hold her hands a few more moments. Their last few months of religious discourses and philosophical ruminations had blossomed into one of the deepest, purest friendships. Katherine had no idea a platonic relationship could reach such a high spiritual plane, it was difficult to let each other go as they silently comforted each other in their shared tragedy.

"I'm sorry to bother you, Father," a nurse interrupted apologetically, "but I saw you come in, and there's a family in the ER who's asking to see a priest. Are you a Catholic priest?"

"Yes, I'm coming."

"Must you go?" Sophia asked quietly.

"People are in need, I'll be right back," he promised, pressing Katherine's hands one last time before getting up, retrieving his briefcase and quickly following the nurse.

"That's just like him," Lottie noted, "he's always helping everyone, even when he's barely able to keep going at times."

"I'd better go and call Tim and Martha," Helen remembered, getting up from her seat. She had promised to give reports on Gerry's condition, but seeing Katherine so upset had put it out of her head. She no sooner left the waiting room when Steves returned, looking nettled.

"Well, it's all over the radio, and the local news vans are starting to pull up outside," he announced, going to the window and lifting one of the blinds a fraction, "we can't even be left alone at a time like this."

Richard grabbed the remote and turned on the television provided for the visitors. Katherine was still too dazed to listen to the report and just stared at the images of the reporters standing outside the hospital busily relaying the scanty details they had so far and a picture of the missing driver. However, one segment showed the chaos at the warehouse yard just after the accident had occurred, trucks still trying to carry on with shipments amidst a sea of police and fire vehicles with their lights flashing, the ambulance as it sped off, and worst yet, video shots taken of the crashed vehicles before the cops could stop the reporters. While it was only a few seconds, each detail seemed to loom in front of her eyes as though the picture was shown in slow motion. Katherine watched in dismay at Gerry's Jaguar being towed from the scene, completely crushed together at both ends like a flimsy soda can, the windscreen cracked into a glassy web and caved inward, the door missing where the firemen had eventually pulled it off. The driver's seat was barely visible as the front end, flattened as well as shoved forward, had been pushed almost on top of it. It was a miracle Gerry made it out alive. She could just see the bouquet Leo told her about, the red and yellow flowers smashed in the passenger's seat.

"Please, Richard, turn it off," Sophia begged, unable to watch any longer. Pursing his lips, he swiftly hit the 'off' button and sat down, while Steves closed down the blinds to prevent any curious media reporters peeking in. By now, Helen had returned from her calls and joined Sophia, everyone sat silently for several minutes, watching the clock and waiting for Peter to return. They did not expect Leroy to dash through the door, a very different man from the one Katherine had met, his bright eyes now sombre with shock and disbelief as he quietly greeted everyone.

"I was on my way home from a late night at work when I heard the news. How's Ger?"

"It's not good," Richard said, quietly filling him in on the details.

"Ah geeze, not *Ger*," he said running his hands through his hair. "Why all the *good* people…? It's *always* the good people … now if it were *me*, that would be another matter … when will he come out?"

"We don't know, this is going to be a long operation," Mr. Reinold admitted, "it may last until morning."

"Ah geeze … is there anything I can do?"

"We can do nothing at the moment, but thank you. All we can do is wait," Sophia replied, touched that Gerry's friend, as wild as he was, would drop everything and rush to be with him. Peter arrived, Leroy immediately jumped and shook hands with him, offering his support and assistance once again.

"Thank you Leroy, but I think the best thing we can all do right now is pray," he advised and began the Our Father, everyone solemnly joining in, even Leroy, who had not uttered a formal prayer for as long as he could remember, but had not forgotten what the nuns had taught him. Not stopping there, Peter took out his black beaded rosary, Sophia and Lottie doing the same, searching for their pearly sets in their purses. Gramps watched quietly as Katherine finally laid the velvet box down and took out her new beads, a white mother of pearl set with golden links and crucifix, a gift from Lottie.

"Should we … go?" Helen tentatively asked, not sure if Episcopalians were permitted to join a solemn prayer meeting like this, yet wishing to stay with Katherine.

"No, please stay," Peter replied, "we're praying the Gospel, and you don't have to be a Catholic to do that."

"You think about the Gospel passages assigned to each section as you pray," Katherine explained, showing her and Gramps the beaded decades. No one wanted to be disrespectful, so they decided to stay as the Reinolds, Katherine and Leroy said the rosary and contemplated the Sorrowful Mysteries of the crucifixion, joining in at the Our Father when it was said. When the devotion ended, Leroy asked if he could get anyone a cup of coffee or something from the vending machines. Despite the fact everyone politely refused, he decided to go anyway, and snatching a clipboard from one of the nurse's stations to use as a tray, came back laden with steaming styro-cups and a pile of packaged portions on offer from the coin operated snack machines.

"Come on, don't refuse, I know you're all famished," he said, carefully setting his makeshift tray down and handing out cups of coffee. "You wouldn't tell me what you liked, so I just pushed sugar and milk for everyone. Come love, have a sup. If it's an all-nighter we have to do, this'll put hair on your chest and help keep you up till doomsday, might as well have a sticky bun while we're at it," he said, trying to sound chipper while handing Katherine a cup and a packaged Danish, then turning to hand everyone else a cup. At last, they gave in and decided to eat something to pass the time, thanking Leroy for bringing it for them. "Ah sure, this is nothing," he replied, pulling out more snacks from his pockets that he could not fit on the clipboard, "if Ger needed a kidney, I'd be glad to give it." Gerry was right, despite his antics, Leroy was a 'good bloke' deep down. At that moment, a cross-looking nurse came in, placing both hands on her hips.

"I'll have my patient reports for room 157 back please," she wryly demanded, eyeing her clipboard.

"In a minute, don't get your petticoats in a twist, I'm on a mission of mercy here," he calmly replied, removing the last cup with slow deliberation and taking a sip, a little of his mischievousness returning.

"I'll 'mercy you' if you don't give me that clipboard, pronto."

However, he just flipped through the reports on the board.

"Liver infection? Poor blighter, hospitalised for that, is he? Why, all he needs is a swig of cranberry juice and a dose of liver salts, and he'll be as right as rain in the morning. Here you are then, if you insist," he concluded, handing it to her with a flourish, then watched her huff off. "That's some bedside manner! Ladies and gentlemen, Nightingale´s imposter has left the building," he commented with a side-nod of his head. While this was no time to laugh, for a moment, Katherine thought she saw the corner of Steve's mouth flicker into a smile, while Lottie just looked up to heaven. Gramps could not stifle a chuckle, that Leroy McFadden was a loveable scamp, but he knew what he was about, and who could not appreciate his effort?

"Leroy, behave yourself now," Richard reminded him, he was glad for this spirited interruption to the sombre vigil. His son had a sense of humour, and he knew Ger would not have wanted to see them all miserable, even at a time like this. God sometimes did send strange angels of mercy when they were least expected. Leroy continued to do his best to keep everyone's spirits up, quietly spinning yarns about his and Gerry's room mate years at college, the few episodes he could relate in front of the ladies.

"Did I ever tell you about the time I jellied Gerry's loo?"

Steves could not hide his curiosity on that opener.

"Jellied? You mean, cover it in jam?"

"No, not jam, ah right, I keep forgetting it's Jell-O here," Leroy remembered.

"Go on, spill the beans," Steves egged, sitting next to Leroy.

"First, you melt your Jell-O, but leave it real thick like … ."

"Now Leroy, don't give my brother any ideas, he's got enough of his own," Katherine replied quietly, it was difficult to find anything funny right now, but she could not help but think how Gerry would have been amused to see these two put their heads together, an explosive combination. She listened to their conversation, learning a little more about her Gerry from his friend's point of view, the practical jokes they got up to, and Leroy's confession Gerry often pulled him out of scrapes and saved his neck.

"Gerry said you did the same for him," she replied.

"Well, he did a lot more for me, I have to say. That's a pretty piece," he then noticed, coming over to look at her locket. Katherine opened it for him. His eyes grew wistful as he looked at the picture and the inscription. He then patted her hand.

"Don't worry, love, if I know Gerry, he'll pull through, he's got so much to live for sitting right here." He then quietly sat back in his seat next to Steves and looked at the clock, wondering when the doctors would come to give them any news.

Finally, someone dressed in what she assumed was surgeon's garb came in and asked for the Reinold family. Richard quickly acknowledged he had found them and asked what was happening. The operation was proceeding as well as could be expected considering the injuries, they were currently mending his legs and pelvis area with steel pins and supports, it would many hours before they finished. Richard thanked him for the update, but looking more weary after hearing this news, so did everyone else. The idea of Gerry literally being pieced back together with metal bits and pieces was disturbing, it sounded alien, inhuman, as if the surgeons were transforming him into a robot.

Katherine's heart ached when she imagined what they might be doing in the operating room, and she instinctively reached for the little velvet box that slipped beside her, clutching it tightly. How she wanted to hold him right now! To feel his arms around her, and never let go, or just to sit holding hands at their special place on the fire escape, that was all she wanted right now. He was always gentle with her, yet his arms, his hands always felt so strong and powerful, it was difficult to think of him lying unconscious on a table somewhere, helpless, his life now in the hands of others. She could not think of anything else, just desperately wanting to be with Gerry. *When Hitler marched across the Rhine to take the land of France ... .* She was unable to stop herself from interiorly reciting their poem repeatedly, turning it into a mantra, a soldier's song to keep her spirits up. *Gerry needs me to stay strong.* Noticing her distraction, her mother decided she should take over matters that needed to be handled, motioning Charlie and Suzy to come out with her to the hall.

"Suzy, Kathy's not going to be capable of running the gallery for the next few days at least, she's going to need your help to keep everything ticking smoothly. Would you do that for her?"

"Of course, Mrs. W.," she eagerly nodded.

"Good girl, while I know you would like to stay with her, you need to go home and get some rest to face the morning."

"I understand," she replied, "although I'm not going to feel like sleeping, but I'll be glad to do what I can for Kathy."

"Thank you for staying as long as you have, you too Charlie, this has been a difficult evening, and you also have work in the morning. Could you please take Suzy home?"

"Of course Mrs. W.," he replied, "if you or the Reinolds need anything, please, let me know."

"I will, thank you, and mind the reporters on your way out, take another exit."

"All right, we'd better go in and say goodnight and explain why we're going," Suzy said, feeling guilty to be leaving everyone yet knowing Helen was correct, Katherine would need her at the gallery, not standing around.

"Suzy, you don't mind do you? Running it all?" Katherine asked when they reminded her of the gallery, she just could not think of the place right now other than the fire escape.

"Hey, what else are you paying me for?" she tried to joke. "Your place is here right now, don't worry about the gallery, the gang will take care of it."

"Thank you, I really appreciate it, and thank you for driving me."

"Don't mention it," Charlie replied, he didn't like leaving Katherine in this state, but Helen was right, there was nothing else he could do, and Suzy did need to get home.

The most difficult hours of waiting had arrived, the early hours of the morning when it seemed as if nothing would ever happen, like the doctors had completely forgotten about them. Leroy and Steves continued to bring in cups of coffee when required, or replenished their stock of vending machine fare when they all needed something else to do other than watching the clock or staring at the walls. Peter sat quietly in the corner all this time, breviary and rosary in hand, his head bent over the book, he continued to pray. Occasionally the men would go out to the hall to talk and stretch their legs, especially Gramps, his knee was bothering him tonight. Although Katherine did not feel like moving from her seat, Helen eventually suggested the ladies take a few turns down the hall, wishing they could also go out for a breath of fresh air, but the reporters had made that impossible. Walking helped to keep everyone awake. Time seemed to creep, they eagerly watched as doctors and nurses passed through the area, wondering if they were coming to give them an update, only to walk by them briskly and enter into a room down the hall, come out a few minutes later and turn down a corner, vanishing from sight.

At last, the dark hours gave way to the first glimmer of dawn, the blinds slowly brightening with the rising sun, the hospital starting to sound busy with the morning activities as doctors and nurses changed shifts, an audible bustle as the breakfast carts were being wheeled through the corridors. Finally, they saw a doctor approach looking exhausted, but relieved.

"He's out of surgery and on his way to the ICU," he reported, "he's pulled through the worst part, and so far, everything is looking good. However, he's still critical, and we have no way of telling how long he will remain on the critical list. The next forty-eight hours should tell us a lot."

"May we see him?" Sophia asked.

"He's still unconscious, but yes, you may see him, only for a few minutes, and please be very quiet, and not too many people. Immediate family only for the moment. How many family members are present?"

"Well, four," Richard replied.

"That will be more than enough for the present, you understand I'm sure. And now, I must be going, and I'll see you all again later, but sooner if there is anything new to report."

"Thank you doctor," Sophia whispered, then turned to Katherine, "I'm sorry, I wish you could see him with us. We'll find out if it's possible for you to see him when we come back. It looks like we won't be gone long dear, as he said, we're only allowed a few minutes. I ... I don't know what to expect."

"It'll be all right, go to him," Helen said, "we'll wait."

"In case I can't come up, tell him I love him and I'm here too, will you?" Katherine pleaded, wishing she could follow them.

"Of course dear," Sophia replied.

Peter picked up his briefcase and the Reinolds left. It was difficult to watch her spiritual confidante leave with that item, Leroy also warily eyed the black case. One day during their talks Katherine asked Peter if he had anything special in there and he opened it to reveal a small travel chalice and paten for when he was asked to say Mass somewhere outside of church, and also, the items necessary for the Last Rites. Although Peter had carefully explained it was not always the 'Last' sacrament, that the Anointing of the Sick could help give strength and grace to the ill and injured, it was still a visible reminder of mortality. Katherine's heart wrenched as she imagined what would take place, Peter solemnly anointing his own brother, either helping him to recover, or preparing him for the end with their father and mother attending, depending on how many were permitted to be by his bedside.

Half an hour or so passed before Lottie came back, looking shaken, but motioning for Katherine to come with her.

"The doctor upstairs said you can see him, we're only allowed a moment or two."

"That's all right," Katherine said, jumping up, grateful for whatever few seconds she might have with him. Gramps patted her arm, and she quickly followed Lottie.

"Now Kathy, be prepared for a shock," she told her quietly as they went to the elevators.

"How ... bad is it?"

"You know those steel frames when people fracture their necks? It's like that, but a lot of it, all over his legs," she whispered.

Exiting on the ICU floor, they met the rest of the family in one of the waiting areas, disbelief etched in their faces, although they looked like they were taking it bravely.

"I told her, Mom," Lottie explained.

"He's down here," Peter said gently. "Would you like me to come with you? Two are allowed in."

"Yes please," Katherine replied. Escorting her with his arm around her shoulder, they stopped outside the window facing into his room. Katherine could only gasp, she involuntarily stiffened, she could literally feel the colour drain from her face. The sight of him lying amidst an array of machines, intravenous tubes, his head bandaged, half his face badly bruised, was almost too painful to look at. A large sheet discretely covered the lower half of his body, but the unwieldy, bizarre shape immediately suggested an intricate system of steel, screws and wires underneath, holding him together. He looked so fragile, shattered, she could hardly believe this was her carefree, confident Gerry. Could this be the same man that she loved? But it was, and he needed her. *He needed her.* Peter gave her shoulder a comforting squeeze and they silently entered the room. Peter stood at one side of the bed, while Katherine sat on the other.

"Hey Ger," Pete quietly whispered in his ear, "you've got one more visitor." Ignoring the ominous machines and the slow, steady bleeping of the monitors, a strong desire to care and watch over him took hold, and she gently held his hand, tubes and all. She did not have much time, and there was so much she wanted to say, even silly things. Who cares if the doctors thought he could not hear? In her heart, she knew he was aware of her presence.

"Gerry, it's Kathy, I was so afraid they wouldn't let me see you, but I'm here. So is everyone else, but they can't come up, Pops, Mom and Gamps, Steves too, and even Leroy, he was driving the nurses mad a few hours ago, it's a shame he can't come up to tell you a few jokes. However, he's behaving pretty good. You're right, he's a good guy underneath all the blarney. Do you know he said he would give you a kidney? Look Gerry, Leo found the bracelet," she then told him, taking the box and putting it into his hand for a moment as though the sensation of its soft velvet might break through his medicated slumber. "Thank you dearest, it's beautiful, but you didn't have to, you're always spoiling me. I told you, I don't need things, I just want you, so you must get better, you hear? I'm not going to wear it until you give it to me yourself, like you planned to," she resolved, taking the box and putting it in her purse, then held his hand again, gently caressing his fingers. Nearly everything she wanted to say suddenly evaporated, it was more important to be with him right now. "I love you Gerry, I love you so much, please hang in there."

A nurse came in and politely asked that they leave so the patient could rest. Katherine was about to give Gerry a kiss on his unbruised cheek, but stopped and looked enquiringly at the nurse, wondering if it was all right. Pete nodded.

"Mom gave him one too."

Giving him a goodbye kiss, she quickly brushed his cheek with her hand and whispered she would see him as soon as she could before leaving with Peter, looking over her shoulder, reluctant to leave him alone in that place.

"Don't worry, someone will stay with him, out here," he assured her, giving her shoulders another squeeze. "You need to go home and get some rest now."

"Oh Pete, I can't go, I have to stay with him too, even out here."

"Listen to me, you won't do him any good if you fall apart from lack of sleep, and your family needs to go home too, they've had a rough night You can come back later."

"What about you? You've been up all night."

"Don't worry, his Excellency has given me a few days leave, and my parents and I will work out a watch schedule, Gerry will always have someone here."

"All right, but as soon as I've had a few hours, I'll be back."

They rejoined Mr. and Mrs Reinold, and Lottie in the waiting area down the hall, Peter explaining he told Katherine she should go home.

"Yes dear, you should, there's nothing more you can do right now, and you look positively exhausted," Sophia said, brushing Katherine's cheek. "We'll come down with you and see your parents."

"Excuse me," another nurse interrupted, bearing a plastic bag, "forgive me for bothering you, but I've collected your son's personal items, I thought you might want to hold on to them."

"Thank you," Sophia replied, taking the bag.

"Oh! Forgive me for asking, is there a key on a gold chain, and a bracelet?" Katherine exclaimed, afraid that these precious items might have been lost in the confusion.

"I don't know what's here, sit down with us for a moment," she said, settling into a seat and emptying the bag on the coffee table. A wallet, an envelope, and Katherine's engagement gifts to Gerry slid out.

"May I mind these two for him?"

"They're important to you, aren't they?" Sophia said gently, looking at the other key around Katherine's neck. Katherine smiled wistfully as she showed the initials on the two keys and explained their significance. Lottie began to tear up. "Of course you can mind them, when he wakes up he'll be happy to know that you have them and be the one to give them back to him," Sophia noted. Katherine took the chain and slipped it over her neck where it jingled against the other chain, then placed his bracelet next to the new one in the velvet box. Richard took the envelope and opened it up.

"Tickets, for *Sleeping Beauty*," he noted.

"Oh Gerry, *that's* the surprise show you were taking me to," Katherine sighed, covering her face with her hands, not knowing whether to laugh or cry. "I warned him when we first met I couldn't drink too much, champagne goes straight to my head, I'm always falling asleep when we go out, he calls me Sleeping Beauty," she explained.

"Well, I think Sleeping Beauty better live up to her namesake and go home to bed," Richard hinted quietly.

Peter stayed in the ICU ward while the rest of the family went with Katherine to speak with her parents, Steves and Leroy, thanking them for coming and offering their support.

"As soon as we can, we'll come back," Helen assured them. "Is there anything we can do?"

"No, you've done so much just being here," Sophia said, "you should go home, get some rest, we'll be all right."

They said their goodbyes, hugging and shaking hands. Leroy was about to shake hands with Katherine but she surprised him, giving him a hug, thanking him once again for being there.

"Well, I should give you sticky buns more often," he said, patting her back. "Let me give you my private number, if you need anything, be sure to give me a ring, okay?" taking out another card, writing his number on the back.

"Thank you, I will."

"Blast, what do we do about the press?" Steves wondered, peeking through the blinds again.

"Those eejits, I'll take care of them," Leroy said, jumping to attention, "you take another exit, and I'll hold them off."

While the Reinolds went back to the ICU ward, 'Operation Leroy the Decoy' went into effect, the smooth-talker keeping the reporters busy with his wit and charm, telling them everything yet saying nothing as Katherine and her family scooted out another doorway. Steves drove back to his apartment to get a few hours sleep before heading into the office, Pops and Gramps drove home together, while Katherine went with her mother. After the bleak, dark night of waiting, it was almost impossible to believe a new day had started, the sun seemed out of place, the typical bustle of the city seemed disrespectful of their pain for nothing felt normal to them. Katherine told her mother how Gerry was, then fell silent, the image of him in the ICU was distressing, she could not shake the sight of the steel braces hidden under the bed coverings from her mind.

Then, it struck her—he would never dance again.

With this stark revelation, everything began to hit like the pummelling blow of an avalanche, why it did not until now she could not explain, the mind had a strange way of dealing with tragedy in piecemeal.

"Oh Mom, the wedding...the wedding...!"

"I know dear, I know."

The wedding would be postponed, how long, there was no way to tell.

Arriving home, with Pops and Gramps just pulling up behind them, Katherine could smell an aroma of baked goods wafting through the house. As usual, Mrs. Gonzales had taken to the kitchen to work off her worry, piling up plates of bread rolls, cupcakes and biscuits as though she were feeding an army. Jasper ran to the door and barked his usual greeting, glad to see everyone, especially after Gramps left him at the house all night. However, Jasper soon quit barking when he sensed in his canine way something was wrong, seeing Katherine just sit in the first available chair in the parlour, sitting there not sure what to do, or where she should be. He wagged his tail and put his muzzle in her lap, whining his commiserations while Helen went to give Mrs. Gonzales the latest news, returning with a glass of water and a pill.

"Katherine, it's a light sedative, I know you don't feel like sleeping but you must. Take this now like a good girl, and go to bed, if only to please me."

"Go on Katie, do as your mother says," Gramps coaxed.

Katherine did not argue, she obediently swallowed the tablet, then dragged herself up the stairs.

"She just thought about the wedding," Helen whispered to Harold and Gramps as soon as they were alone.

"Poor Katherine, and there's no way we can comfort her through this," Harold said.

"All we can do is be there," Gramps replied.

"Yes, that's all. It pains me to see her now all grown up, and the adult crosses of the world start taking their toll," Helen sighed bitterly, "we can't spare anyone from them."

ଓଷ୍ଠ୦

Katherine woke up to a dark room, the sun now gone, only the digital numbers from her clock giving any light. She immediately sat up.

I must go to Gerry.

Turning on the lamp, she stood up and began to tremble, chills rippled over her skin, she was barely able to keep her balance. She wondered what Mom had given her, but then realized she was suffering from shock, that had to be it, not to mention she did not have anything substantial to eat since yesterday afternoon. She was not hungry, but it was not good to leave off eating any longer. Slipping out of her nightclothes she took a quick shower and dressed in something simple, anything to hurry, get down to eat and out to the hospital.

"Thank heavens you're up, I was getting worried," Aunt Martha replied who had come over for dinner. Uncle Tim, Aunt Barbara, Stephie and William had come too, wanting to see Katherine and hoping she was all right.

"You look positively wrecked. Are you sure you don't want to stay home?" Suzy asked, she too had joined them that evening.

"I'll be all right, I'm not leaving Gerry any longer, and I got a day's sleep," she said sitting down.

"A little more than that, you slept through yesterday, last night and today," her mother informed her.

Katherine stared blankly in disbelief. That could not be right, she remembered waking up and seeing the sun still peeping through the curtains where she had not draw them fully, then closed her eyes for a moment ... did she really lose a whole day?

"Did anyone go to the hospital yesterday?" she asked.

"Your mother and I did," Gramps said, but not offering anything further.

"Any change?"

"Well, I wish we didn't have more bad news, but ... Gerry hasn't come around after the surgery, the doctors say he's slipped into a coma ..." her mother said, trying to break it gently.

"What? What does this mean?" Katherine blurted, feeling frightened for Gerry.

"It just means he hasn't woken up, and they don't know how long it will last, a day, maybe a few, they don't know," Helen continued.

"Maybe it's a good thing," Aunt Martha added, "he won't be in any pain, it'll give him a chance to heal."

Katherine forced herself to eat a few mouthfuls, her appetite completely gone. She quietly listened to everyone's news as she poked the food around her plate. They had to take the phones off the hook for awhile since the accident. Every time the phone went, it was either reporters seeking news, or friends calling to ask how Gerry was and how she was holding up. While it was good to hear from the well-wishers, they needed some peace. It was bad enough the details of Gerry's condition had been leaked and were plastered all over the evening news and the main pages of the local papers. They ended up getting new cell phone numbers yesterday, which they gave to the Reinolds, their business contacts and the gallery. Suzy said reporters were also prowling around the gallery, and advised

Katherine not to go back for her van yet, she would be glad to drive her where she needed to go for now. Stephie agreed, and said she would also give her a lift whenever she needed it. Everyone at the gallery were asking about her and Gerry, and wanted her to know not to worry, they were handling everything. Kevin had stepped in and handled everything professionally for his first days on the job, politely telling the reports in his suave manner where to get off, but in accordance with Katherine's wishes, suffered Horace to pass through to ask how she was doing. Derrick came by after work yesterday, even Jim the Breeze made an appearance. It was touching to see so many bouquets of flowers arriving at the hospital and the gallery. Helen told how they could not have any bouquets cluttering the ICU, so Sophia asked the candy-stripers to give them to patients in the hospital who didn't have any. Katherine was glad to hear that, Gerry would have liked to see the goodwill spread around. The amazing thing, the bouquets were not sent just by family and acquaintances, absolute strangers were wishing them well. Some people started lighting candles and leaving bouquets on the sidewalk outside the main entrance of the hospital, and then many more joined in the vigil, the entrance was starting to look like a shrine. Suzy put it down to the Beastie woman's gossip column; since the accident hit the news, Beatrice had let her pen flow about the latest tragedy to hit New York's most romantic couple and speculations about postponing the wedding. To top if off, they republished pictures of their romantic night at the Eiffel tower, then juxtaposed them to the totalled Jaguar for maximum impact, and the story caught the public's imagination. Horace tried to stop her, but the editor had the final say and let it go to print.

Katherine excused herself from the table for a moment and looked at the pictures in the papers lying on the sideboard; there was the hospital, people leaving get-well messages, flowers, and candles by the gateway. Some people were praying. Katherine thought things like this only occurred when an accident was fatal, but obviously, people wanted to show their support, and this was their way to express it. Through her pain, she could not help but feel touched by the outpouring of their well wishes, from people she probably never met, and may never meet. When the chips are down, people come together and in solidarity, pour out their feelings and concern for others in their time of need, displaying the goodness that exists in the world, a goodness that you are not made aware of everyday.

"That's something, isn't it?" Uncle Tim remarked.

"It is, I don't know what to say, or to think," Katherine replied quietly, reading the captions. In another paper, there were pictures showing a gathering of truck drivers and their wives laying flowers and candles by the entrance.

'It's the least we could do,' says Jim Harper, trucker for seven years at Reinold Enterprises. 'None of us believed the reports spread about him the last few years. He's a great boss, he sticks up for us workers. We've never gotten a raw deal from him. We're all praying for him and his family. We all hope he gets well soon.'

"I guess you're finished dinner," her mother noted.

"Come dear, we'll drive you, they're only allowing family and you to visit him for now," Pops added.

"Thank you for coming," Katherine said to everyone else, "you don't mind if I …?"

"No dear, you go ahead, don't worry about us," Aunt Barbara replied.

As they were leaving the house to go to the garage, Katherine thought she heard a commotion outside the main gates.

"I'm sorry, I forgot to warn you," Pops replied, "there are a few reporters on standby here, we'll have to rush past them."

Katherine slid down in the back seat and covered her face with her purse as they sped out the gates, hoping none of the photographers or cameramen caught her at this miserable time. She realized after seeing all those photographs that eventually she might have to give a statement, thank the public for their kind support, but she was not about to give the paparazzi piranhas any satisfaction right now. In any case, she had promised Horace all her exclusives and she could trust him with anything she would release to the press. What a strange twist, that the city's most despised art critic would become the most dependable and sympathetic reporter she knew!

Driving up outside the hospital, the photographs did not do justice to the scene, flowers piled by the pier, candles flickering in the darkness, news vans with their bright lights waiting for any titbit of information, it was humbling to watch. Speaking with one of the guards, Pops was waved in and permitted to park in a secure section away from the more public area of the lot.

This time, Mom and Pops were allowed to come up and sit in the waiting area of the ICU. Katherine paused for a moment outside the interior window of Gerry's room, watching a tired Sophia talk to him, stroking his cheek, holding his hand, carefully straightening his bedclothes, anything to let him know she was there. She looked up and smiled, motioning for her to come in.

"Hello Kathy," she whispered giving her a hug, "I'm glad we sent you home, you *were* exhausted, your mother told me you were asleep for ages. Gerry, Kathy's here," she said taking his hand. Katherine took his other hand, it felt so good to hold it again.

"Oh Gerry, I wish you could see all the flowers, they're everywhere, the nurses got posies too since you're not allowed to have anything in here just yet. I wish I had more news, but Mom gave me something to help me sleep, and it must have worked, because I was out for the whole day yesterday, well, you know what champagne does to me, pills are determent to my system. Mom and Pops are down the hall, they wish they could see you too, I don't know if that's permitted yet."

"Are they dear? Come with me for a moment, I think we can bend the rules now, he's almost past the forty-eight hours, and if I ask, the doctors may not refuse."

"All right. Gerry, I'll be back in a minute, you don't mind, do you?"

Sophia took her by the arm and they left the room.

"Mrs. R., how long will he be out? Mom told me it could be days," Katherine whispered.

"We don't know, the doctors say with this type of coma, it could be even longer, and when he does wake up, the recovery period will take time, he'll need physiotherapy and everything."

Katherine just hung her head, she didn't know what to say. 'Longer' could be anything from weeks, to even months; she may not be a medical expert, but she knew that comas were notoriously unpredictable. Her heart froze, months could mean years. Gerry might be transferred to a coma ward —and never come out. Sophia guessed what had crossed her mind and held her arm tightly before greeting her parents.

"Any news?" Harold asked, shaking her hand, while Helen gave her a hug.

"No change, but please, go visit him. If anyone asks you, say you're family. It's not a lie, you're Father and Mother Number Two."

Katherine and Sophia watched as they went down the hall and into the room before sitting down. Katherine asked if she had been there all day.

"No, Peter and Lottie were here, then he took her home when I arrived, Richard will be coming shortly. We're allowed to visit a little longer since we can't really disturb him while he's ... well, you know, and of course, they let us stay out here all the time, the nurses and doctors have been very kind."

They quietly waited for Katherine's parents to come out, which eventually happened when a nurse arrived to take blood tests. As could be expected, Gerry's condition had a marked effect on them, pensive and solemn, they sat in the waiting area.

"At least he looks as comfortable as they can make him," Harold replied, "I hope he comes out of this soon."

"Yes, but at least he is getting complete rest in this state," Helen agreed. There was not much they could say, Gerry's injuries were horrific, and until he started to show signs of recovery, it would not be easy to say much more than that.

Richard arrived and they all shook hands, Harold explaining they were allowed in for a few minutes, which he was glad to hear. Richard then went back in with Sophia, leaving Katherine with her parents. Staring at her shoes, she heaved a sigh;

"Mrs. R. let me know how bad the coma is, I guess it's a good thing the invitations weren't sent yet, we're going to have to postpone the wedding."

"I know dear, but don't worry, it won't be indefinitely," Helen said, putting her arm around her, "it just means we have to wait a little while, that's all. I discussed it with Sophia yesterday, and she agreed that Aunt Martha, Aunt Barbara and I will take care of cancelling the few things we have to for now. We can set everything back up again."

Although her mother tried to make her feel better, the thought of all their plans cancelled, she would not begin a new life with Gerry, that he lay half alive in a room down the hall was more then she could take, but there was nothing she could do, she could feel her heart ache with every breath, every beat. Ten minutes later, Richard and Sophia returned, he was allowed one more visitor to his room, so Katherine quickly went to his side. Already, the machines surrounding him were familiar pieces of furniture, and the shock of his condition did not deter her from talking to him like normal, she had so much she wanted to say. If he was reminded of life around him, surely he would wake up to be part of it again with her?

"Hello dearest, I'm back," she said, taking his hand, holding it to her cheek for a moment before sitting next to him and gently caressing his fingers once more. "I'm so glad Mom and Pops got to visit this time, they're very strict on the visiting schedule here, they might relax it if you wake up. I wish I could spend more then five or ten minutes with you, maybe they just don't like us getting in the way with all their check ups and fancy machines. I forgot to tell you, Kevin Alcott is working at the gallery now, I hired him. Can you believe it? He doesn't like the idea I let Horace have exclusives, but wait until I tell you about poor Mr. Sirrac, you wondered what had happened over there, well, Kevin gave me the low down, it's pretty pathetic actually… ."

She told all the news, thanked him for the *Sleeping Beauty* tickets, told him they could see the ballet next season when he felt better, anything that popped into her head that she would normally talk about when they were in their favourite spot on the fire escape. Her ten minutes went by so fast, and there was so much more she wanted to say, but all she could do was kiss his cheek, straighten out the lock of hair peeking under his bandage and kiss him again before saying goodnight as the nurse patiently looked on, reminding her it was time to go.

Saying good night to the Reinolds, Katherine and her family retuned home. Although she had slept most of the day, she still felt very weak and decided to go back to bed. Perhaps she was still in shock, she needed to get over this: Gerry needed her. Tomorrow was another day, another visiting time. She was about to turn into her room when she stopped and slowly made her way to the guest room that had been set aside to hang out her wedding gown and all the bridesmaids' dresses, her going away outfit had already been bought and was left waiting with all the rest. Sitting on the bed, she sadly glanced from one thing to another, dwelling on the details; her bridal shoes, the little beaded purses, the laces, the shimmering, rich materials, the floral patterns, the little rosettes on her dress, the way the white material from her dress and train cascaded to the floor from where they had hung it on the closet door to prevent them from getting creased. Then, imagining her and her bridesmaids walking down the aisle in this regal attire with a smiling Gerry waiting for her, dressed to the nines for this auspicious day, perhaps in an elegant morning suit as they wore in Europe with his best man and groomsmen in attendance, and of course, with Peter, the Archbishop, and Fr. O'Connor waiting to receive them at the altar, Reverend Dobbson also waiting to take part with one of the readings. It was such a beautiful thought, that after an exchange of vows they would belong to each other for life. The words 'husband' and 'wife' sounded august, almost royal as if they too were no different from the titles of 'prince' and 'princess, 'duke' or 'duchess', for royal blood does not dissolve even if a kingdom disappears, neither do the ties between husband and wife until death came between them, and even then, they would be forever known as husband and wife. With this exchange of sacred vows similar to a noble coronation, the world all around them would legally proclaim what was now so private and special between them. They would be king and queen of each other's hearts, and that was what so loved most of all: no matter what happened, no man would have a legal or rightful claim over her, and no woman but her could ever claim him as hers no more than an usurper to a royal throne had the right to hold it. Marriage was a beautiful possession of love, trust and respect that would bind them forever, not a servile mastery. She had fallen in love with a good man who truly loved her in return, to think of Gerry as her husband and that she would be his wife would make her heart soar, and now, she wondered when that time would come to pass.

"Kathy, I thought you went to bed an hour ago," her mother asked, noticing the light and entering the room.

"I just had to come in," she replied, almost inaudible, hanging her head. By now, she thought the tears were gone, but again they began to flow.

"My poor dear," her mother said, sitting on the bed and holding her.

"Do you think we'll ever get married now?"

"Of course, maybe you might have a fall or winter wedding instead of a summer one," her mother tired to console her, stroking her hair.

"He may never wake up Mom, I have to face it."

"But then again, maybe he will, we just have to pray and hope. This is one of the testing times: do you love him enough to wait for him to recover? Even if he is in a wheelchair?"

"Oh, of course!" she said, looking up. "There never will be anyone else. No matter what happens, I won't leave him."

"Then your love will keep you strong. Peter, was right, Gerry needs you, he needs to feel your love, if anything, that will help bring him back. Come now, you need to go to bed."

Obediently, she followed her mother, took one last look around the room, and turned off the light.

੦੩ ❀ ੮੦

The next day, Pops dropped her off at the hospital were she found Peter on visitor's duty, sitting next to Gerry's bedside and telling him his news.

"Leroy's been asking when he'll be allowed in to see you ... hello Kathy, look Ger, Kathy's here too," he said, getting up and giving her a hug.

"Hi Gerry, it's me darling," she said giving him a good morning kiss. "Is it just you today, Pete?"

1025

"Yes, until you came. Lottie had some things to do for Mom while she rests up after last night, she stayed the night you know. Mom insisted Dad go home to get some rest because he had to head back into work. We had a big family pow-wow over breakfast, I'll tell you about it in the hall," he said, "we'll be back in a minute Ger."

"What's up, Pete?" she asked when they were out.

"Dad realizes he's going to need someone to take Gerry's place at the firm for his recovery period, and just in case things don't improve for awhile, I think you know what I mean … Dad wants someone from the family to help run the business, so the burden has fallen to Lottie. If anything happens to Gerry, the business would all go to her anyway."

"Lottie! Oh the poor girl, she's a classical Greek literature buff, her heart is in books and ancient drama, how on earth is she going to step in? Does she know anything about shipping and distribution?"

"No, which is where I come in—Dad has made a special emergency request that I come back and help train her with Thomas at the offices, for a month or so at least."

"But what about your ministry? Are you allowed to do something like this?"

"If I receive express permission from the archbishop, but Dad will have to ask him himself, I cannot do anything that would try and get me snared back into the world away from my calling," Peter noted.

"Did Mr. R. agree to that?"

"He understood, and said he'd call his Excellency, I said if the archbishop approved, I would help out, but with an important condition; that I stay in my collar and cassock. He had no problems with that."

"Gee, this is news, I bet Sammy and the guys would be glad to see you again. I don't know what to make of this, poor Lottie, I hope she'll figure it out."

"She's been a bit aimless since her fiancé passed away, and she's not sure if she's ready to make a new commitment, even with David. This will help give her some direction and reveal some talents she didn't know she had. She would make quite the businesswoman actually."

"Hey, what about you? Do you think you can get back into big business like this?"

"I may have been away for a few years, but it's just like riding a bike, Ger was pretty good at telling me all about his new business deals and contacts, I should get back into it with no problems, only, I could do with some prayers to keep me from temptation's way," he said with a smile, "my place is with the church, as with an earthly bride, I must leave father and mother and begin a new life."

"I get it, and you're always in my prayers." She then fell silent for a moment, thinking about the tragedy that had befallen them.

"Come Kathy, let's sit down for a moment, I see you need to talk," he noted, walking towards the waiting area. Sitting together, he patiently waited for her to collect her thoughts. At last, she spoke:

"You know what is special about today? For Gerry and I? It's the eighteenth, one full year to the day I found out once and for all I was in love with him. When I found out, that terrible fiasco broke out in Jakarta, and even I thought Gerry might be guilty of all those terrible accusations, everyone advising me I may have to break everything off with him and keep my distance. Now, it's happening all over again, he's in a coma, we don't know if he'll ever be able to walk again or even wake up, the wedding will have to be called off for now, and everything is just falling apart. I can't help but wonder if God is punishing us, that we just love each other too much and it's wrong somehow … ."

"Listen to me Kathy, God never punishes love, when the commandment says we are to love God with all our hearts and strength, we must not put anything above Him. Let's say Gerry wanted you to do something wrong that you knew for certain God would not approve of, would you do it?"

"No, I'd like to think I wouldn't," she replied.

"Then you are not putting your love for Gerry above that for God, love for God is the desire to do His will in all things and an earnest attempt to do it, no matter what anyone else says. If you've noticed, loving ourselves and our neighbour equally is also part of the greatest commandment, so don't let the Enemy of all that is good try and drive you and Gerry apart. God sanctions marriage and the love between husband and wife, it was the first sacrament He created before mankind ever fell. God wishes you to love Gerry, so you may put your mind to rest about that."

"Still Pete, why would God allow something like this to happen to us? We were so happy, I can't help but feel like we're being punished."

"Why God allows this is not easy to understand at times. Yes, we know we must all carry our crosses, and it seems unfair that some people appear to have been given larger crosses than others, sometimes we forget how many blessings and graces God gives the world. Let's say God came right now and said He would change time, prevent you from meeting Gerry so you would never have to experience this pain. Would you agree?"

"Not to meet Gerry? I probably wouldn't know the difference if time was changed, but knowing and loving Gerry like I do right now, I don't think I could go back. I love him too much."

"You see? Life and existence is a great gift, we have the opportunity to love, feel loved, and do good in return, even if it means shouldering our crosses, whatever they are, in order to make our way back to the Kingdom. No one escapes pain, but don't forget pain equals power, Christ opened heaven through the cross. Through His agony, He showed how much He loves us, and this pain you feel right now tells you how deep love is, how selfless it makes us. You would be willing to stand by Gerry for the rest of his life if he needed it, am I correct?"

"Oh yes, I won't leave him."

"Then you see what I mean. Yes, this is difficult, there is no escaping the hardships in life, but love is there, and that's the important thing." At that moment, Peter seemed very tired and drained, like he was carrying a ton weight on his back.

"Are you all right, Peter?"

"As much as can be expected, I too blame myself," he admitted.

"How? You didn't do anything," she replied in surprise.

"Not directly, the powers below are not at all pleased with my vocation, they will stop at nothing to make me leave the priesthood, or to make everyone I care about suffer in retaliation: they're putting up a ferocious front in both strategies."

"Pete, don't blame yourself, there's nothing any of us could do, if we can't protect ourselves, how can we protect anyone around us?"

"Regardless, to see Ger like this weighs heavily on me. However, this is all part of God's will, He has permitted it for some hidden reason we may not understand until we reach eternity, but at least I have the consolation of knowing He only allows that from which He can bring forth a greater good, perhaps not in our lifetime, but in the lives of those who will come after us. This is where faith comes in, and it's faith that creates miracles."

"Well, if there is any good coming from this suffering, seeing all the well wishes people have sent to Gerry and your family, and to me too, from complete strangers in a city noted for its aggression and indifference, you can see there is decency in humanity, it just needs to be brought out. It's a shame there has to be a tragedy before the best in people will finally shine."

"That's why God gives us a good pruning once in awhile so we bear good fruit. Speaking of faith, will you feel up to returning to your RCIA classes? You're almost through it now, and Easter is almost upon us in just a few more weeks. You still wish to go through with this?"

"Oh, yes, I haven't changed my mind, it's just that everything has gone out of my head. You're right, I don't want to fall behind now. It's just … Gerry was going with me, it won't be the same without him."

"I know, but we'll all be with you, Lottie will be happy to be your sponsor on Easter, and the Archbishop said I may prepare you privately for your first confession to give you some time to recover after the initial shock of the accident."

"That's very kind of him, honestly, I had everything all ready, but after this, I don't know what I've done wrong or what to say. I was afraid I would mess up, but now I'm really in the soup."

"Don't worry Kathy, I'll help you through."

"Thank you Pete. Imagine, I now have a big-brother-to-be who can absolve all my sins," she sheepishly smiled, "at least I know you won't blabbermouth my transgressions to my parents like Steves used to when we were kids."

Pete laughed quietly.

"My lips are hermetically sealed.   Come, let's go see Gerry."

After a week of only minimal visits permitted with Katherine and the Reinolds ducking in and out of his room and spending the rest of the time in the halls, Gerry was finally taken off the critical list although he was still in a coma. Transferred to a private room, he was allowed visits from friends and acquaintances, and visiting times were lengthened. The first to make an appearance was good old Leroy. While he was aghast at the strange contraptions holding his friend's legs together, he still kept up his spirits, yakking away with jokes and yarns as if his buddy was wide awake and laughing at his crazy nonsense.

"Like you, I don't believe this 'they-can't-hear-you' malarkey," turning to Katherine before asking Gerry if he would like him to exchange one of his intravenous drip pouches for a bottle of Paddy.

"Oh Leroy, be good, you know you can't do that," Katherine chided.

"Now Katie, you never know, a good drip-drop of whiskey may be just the thing he needs. Don't look so serious, I'm only joking, you should know me by now," he said with a wink and a nod.

"Not exactly, you're a mystery."

Everyone else now had an opportunity to visit, Aunt Martha, Steves, Aunt Barbara, Uncle Tim, Stephie, Suzy and Charlie, the Professor and Esther, Dennis, Mrs. Hunt, who was terribly upset and unable to speak, Thomas from the Reinold head office, Gerry's friend Nathan who worked at Christies, and everyone they knew at the gallery eventually made their way to the hospital, time and work permitting. Andre dropped by when he could, bringing in pastries for the nurses and the visitors, and Olivia also paid several visits, for although she did not know Gerry as well as everyone else, she could not help but like him the moment they met. Sammy, Leo and Dan came in a trio, telling him the latest goings-on at the yards and the mishaps the new drivers got into. The nice thing was Gerry could have bouquets to decorate the room and his surroundings did not look as dismal as before, although they still had to send any extras around to other patients.

However, after one week with Gerry in the ICU, and now half a week in his new room with the visitor's rules relaxed, Katherine decided it was time to pick up the van and try to resume a daily schedule at the gallery, although she did not feel like it and would have gladly spent her days waiting by Gerry's side. A rota was worked out where she would visit with him every night during regular visiting hours, visit the entire day on Sunday after church, and alternate staying with him whole nights with Sophia, each taking their turn for the graveyard shifts so they had a chance to catch up on sleep. Richard was busy most days at work and could only stay during the regular visiting hours, the same with Lottie who was under the tutelage of Peter and Thomas at the office, trying to learn the complicated ropes of the international shipping business, and her first days were not going as smoothly as she would have liked.

"Oh Kathy," she said near to tears one night as they sipped their abysmal vending machine coffee in the hall, waiting for the nurses to finish their rounds in Gerry's room, "just when I think I'm getting somewhere, Peter or Thomas tell me something else, and it's all a muddle. I'll never understand a company this large!"

Katherine wished she knew how to comfort her.

"Gosh, this is your first week, you won't get it all at once. The problem is, Pete and Gerry learned from the ground up, working the forklifts and the trucks, learning the rhythm of the warehouses, things like that. You haven't."

"I know, but I don't have time to spend acquiring ground experience like that. Can you imagine me driving one of those big things? I don't think I could go near one of them after what happened to our Gerry. What will I do?"

Katherine thought for a moment.

"Please dear, for Gerry's sake, you must be brave, he needs you to help run things for him. About business advice, I don't know what to say, except spend at least a week or two with Sammy in Warehouse One, he'll help give you the basics, and if you want to know how the trucks are managed from the driver's end, ask Leo and Dan, you met Leo already, I know Gerry trusts them and they would be more than happy to help you out.”

“Thank you, Kathy. Imagine, you thought of that and I didn’t, you really belong more in our family than I do at times.”

“Oh, don’t say that, you’ve just never been around all the workings before, Pete has every confidence in you, he says you’ll make quite the businesswoman.”

“Really?”

“Positively, you know Pete doesn’t lie.”

“That’s true,” she said, wiping her eyes. “Thank you, I needed to hear that. You know, every time I think of it, I can’t help but admire you, how you’ve taken on that huge gallery and manage it beautifully, I don’t think I could have done it, and now, I’ve got an international juggernaut to come to grips with.”

“Oh shoot, I didn’t have too much to do with the gallery to tell the truth. I just wanted a small boutique-type place, and look what happened! I got landed with this monstrous building just like you did with the business, and I had a lot of help to get me through, I never would have managed without Gramps and everyone making their contributions and working along with me. Honestly, when I got the place, it frightened me at first, all the work that had to be done and the fact I had no idea how to run a gallery let alone a business, but if you just take it one day at a time, you’ll find your feet, just don’t let the size scare you off.”

“All right, I won’t, I’ll try and do better.”

“That-a girl, and don’t forget to see Sammy.”

“I won’t.”

Poor Lottie, Katherine found it difficult to imagine her in the midst of that preserve of macho masculinity, the warehouse and dock yards humming with large machines and working men roaring out orders and commands to each other. She remembered feeling strangely out of place the one time she visited, and she hoped everything would turn out all right for Lottie, but from what she saw, the guys were pretty good and respected the Boss Man and his family. They might be protective over her once she arrived and actually started to run the place. Would they change the sign on the parking space for her benefit Katherine wondered? She smiled as she imagined the sign ‘*Reserved for the Boss Man: the buck stops here,*’ replaced with ‘*Reserved for the Boss Lady, the dear stops here.*’

For a few days, similar scenes occurred with friends and family arriving to visit Gerry and give each other support during this trying time. Katherine and the Reinolds could expect anyone appearing in the hospital halls to pay their respects. Horace dropped by one day, wrapped in his signature trench coat with the collar rakishly ruffled up, bearing a floating bouquet of multi-coloured helium balloons. She could not help smiling as she saw him approach with the shiny blimps and globes bopping off the ceiling.

"Horace, those are a brilliant idea, Gerry's going to love them."

"I hate to be a cad, I should think of the injured man, but these are actually for you," he replied, handing her his fistful of strings.

"For me?"

"Yeah, I knew you would need some cheering up."

"Aw, thanks Chris, you're not a cad," she said giving him a hug. "How's your grandma doing?"

"So-so, the last few days she thinks I'm my Dad, not so bad. Other days, she thought I was the handyman, that's when she's really out of it."

"Gee, I'm sorry," Katherine replied.

"Ah, don't get all upset, I've adjusted to my many personalities," he smiled. "Thanks for asking about her, at least she's comfortable at home, I don't want to see her in a place like this," he concluded, looking around slightly revolted with the medical surroundings.

"I don't blame you, there's no place like home. By the way, how are you and Stephie doing? She hasn't told me much about her news lately, I think she's afraid to look happy in front of me right now."

"Just great, that cousin of yours has some spunk, I like that, we're having a great time together, at least I am, I hope she is too."

"Well, she hasn't dumped you yet, that's a good sign, definitely means she likes you."

"That's good to know, I think we hit it off pretty well."

"Oh, here, I've got to share these with Gerry," Katherine said, looking up to the balloons, "let me tie these on his bed, he can't see them, but I'll tell him they're there. Come on in, try not to mind the creepy beepies," she said, referring to the battery of machines. Opening the door for her, Christopher's face went a little pale, he hated hospitals, but gallantly gabbed with Gerry and Katherine, ignoring the reality that Gerry was still unconscious. Eventually, Katherine asked Gerry if they could be excused a moment, and taking Chris out into the hall, wondered if he would not mind doing something for her.

"I'm glad you stopped by, for a lot of reasons. You see, you're my exclusive reporter, and it's time I thank the public for all their prayers and generosity, it's been almost two weeks, and I have to say something, give an interview… ."

"Are you sure you want to do this? Now?" he asked, his eyes growing concerned, his brows slightly knitted. "Honestly, I didn't come to profit from your sorrow. Can't it wait until you've had some real time to get used to all of this?"

"No, I'm all right, and yes, I have to do this, reporters are still trying to wring an interview from me, and you would save me a lot if you could do this right now, get them off my back and perhaps away from the house and the gallery. I've been hiding up in the studio the last couple of days, on top of the fact I really don't feel like painting." Of course, there were other items in the studio that made the place unbearable at present, the empty loveseat by the window, the canvases Gerry had left unfinished, not knowing if he would ever wake to complete them, but she kept these sorrows to herself, not mentioning them to Chris right then.

"All right, if you're sure you want to do this," he said with uncertainty, taking out his notepad and pen while they went to the sitting area. The interview did not take long, the session finishing with a hug as Christopher had to return to work.

"Hey 'Robert', before you go, you don't mind if I ask you if you've disclosed your double-identity to Stephie?"

"Not yet," he smiled, "let's say I feel like Bruce Wane, wanting to have a relationship, yet wondering how on earth to tell the women in his life he's Batman. Let's hope the tangle between Christopher and Horace doesn't doom me to the life of a bachelor."

"Or, Stephie may turn out to be the special woman in your life with a unique understanding."

"You never know," he replied with a smile before giving her a goodbye nod and heading towards the elevators.

One night, Charlie came alone to see how she was doing, and to check on Gerry. After a bedside visit, Charlie motioned for Katherine to come out to the hall.

"I'm hanging in there," Katherine sighed when he asked how she was, keeping a loving vigil close to three weeks in a hospital was difficult, but she was determined to brave it out. "Suzy didn't come with you?"

"No, I told her a fib actually, said I had some work to catch up on in the office, but I just needed to see you alone, if that's all right."

"Oh, sure. I wish you didn't have to fib though, I was hoping you'd be a model lawyer like Honest Abe and stick to the truth at all times," she smiled, trying to cheer him up, she did not want him feeling upset on her account.

"Well, I wanted to see how you were, but, I'm ashamed to say, I also needed to talk to you.   I feel like kicking myself, this is not a good time to say these things I know, but I would like to get them out in the open.”

“All right,” she said, taking her friend by the arm, wondering what could be bothering him, leading him to the waiting area that had become a regular meeting centre for their little support groups.

“What’s on your mind, Charlie?” she asked as they sat down.

“You know how bad I am at opening up,” he began, wondering how best to express what he wanted to tell her. “I like talking about good hard facts, and bottle up my feelings, but sometimes you have to speak about feelings, or they’ll drive you mad at times while you try to figure them out. Well, I’ve been a right emotional mix up to tell the truth, and I know I shouldn’t drag anything up, but after I fell headlong for you, I never thought I would feel anything for anyone else … .”

“Charlie I. … .”

“No, let me speak now that I’ve started. Well, I’ve fallen for Suzy, I must admit, not quite the same way, I love her as much, but different, it’s hard to explain. However, at first I felt terrible about it, wondering that if feelings could be so fickle, am I *really* in love with her? Is this just a passing fancy? Then of course, I realized, no, I really am falling in love again, it *is* possible, perhaps not the same way, it’s just that I was not really letting go of you either, and I realized I can’t move on until I learn how to let you go.”

“Oh Charlie … .”

“Wait, hear me out,” he continued quietly, mortified by his confession, but at the same time relieved that he could at last clear the air. “Let’s face it, we said we’d get over what happened between us and not tip-toe around each other, but we must have known I was still stuck on you, just a part of me at least, we still have been shying away from each other because of it, but now I’m able to finally love and let go.” She sat quietly waiting for him to explain if he could. “It was the way Fr. Peter held your hands the night of the accident and kept telling you how much Gerry needs you, he needs your strength. You do have a quiet, hidden strength that’s unshakable, it’s one of the many hundred things I love about you, but I realize, *that strength was not meant for me.* I don’t know why knowing your strength was meant for Gerry made the difference, but it did. I may love you, but you were never meant to be mine, Gerry really does need you, he’ll need your love, and you need his, you were truly made for each other. I told you to come and tell me if he ever treated you badly, but he’s truly head over heels for you, so I don’t have to worry about that anymore. In fact, if your love wasn’t for me, I’m so glad you have him, he is a decent guy and will keep you on a pedestal, and, I can see Suzy and I were destined to meet, we really do have a chance to be happy together. ”

“But, you still have feelings for me, Charlie. Is it really possible for you to love Suzy?”

“How can I explain it? What I feel for you Kathy is first love, that’s something you can never forget simply because it’s the first experience, it’s blissful, but there can be a deeper love that follows even if perchance you are not destined to be with the one you first set your heart on, it seems I’m there. With you, your first love is also your deepest, your one and only, so perhaps you may not understand what I’m trying to say, but it *is* possible to fall in love again.”

“You really do love Suzy then?”

“Yes, in fact, I’ve bought the ring, been waiting for the right time,” he said, looking a little shy, “but didn’t feel free to make the proposal until now, not until I had sorted out exactly what I was feeling, it wouldn’t have been fair to Suzy. I just wanted you to know I’m finally okay about what happened between us, truly. I don’t want you to feel uncomfortable or worried anymore that you turned my proposal down, I shall be happy just to be your friend as always.”

This time, Katherine could see he was not just trying to make her feel better, there was a peaceful acceptance in his eyes without false hopes or regret. She could also sense a giddiness in him, but then, a second attempt at a proposal was an anxious yet exciting occasion, especially as he had been turned down once before, and it looked like he was wondering what to do about it.

“I’m sorry, I did hurt you, not intentionally, but I’m so glad you’ve fallen in love with Suzy. You have the ring! When did you plan to propose?”

“Well, she’s pretty tired helping to run the gallery for the time you were here, so I really should wait until she feels rested up, and, after the accident, I don’t think the mood would be right to try and pop the question. I can’t believe I’m asking you, but you know her better than I do in some ways, what would you advise?”

“Oh, don’t wait too long! I know any time will be right for you and Suzy. I shouldn’t say anything, but she’s been in love with you for years, long before your proposal to me.”

“What?” he said with surprise, thunderstruck with this revelation, “she told me she loved me, but I can’t believe she never told me *that*.”

“It’s true, she never said anything at the time because she thought that we were …well, you know. I didn’t find out how she felt about you until after we came home from Paris that time. She probably hasn’t said anything because like you said, you don't open up easily, and maybe she's a little timid to let everything gush out just yet. Oh, do propose! I'm so glad you have someone now who can give you the love you want and deserve."

"So, you're happy for me then?" he smiled quietly, that giddy look coming back into his eyes with the news she had given him.

"Yes, now we can really be friends again with no fears or regrets. Just, don't be afraid to open up to her."

"I thought women liked the strong silent type," he noted with amusement.

"Yes, but not so much that you end up a marble Hercules; all magnificence, but cold stone. We like to know what's going on in those masculine heads and hearts of yours once in awhile."

"Okay, point taken, I shall unburden my heart and mind more often."

"If you really want my advice on your proposal, take her somewhere really romantic, make it so wonderful she has a feeling something special is about to happen. She's a quiet one, but she's the type who likes the public yet decorous proposal."

"All right, I'll do that. I've got the ring with me, would you like to see it?"

"No! Suzy must see it first you dunderhead! You and I may be best friends, but you can't share *everything* with me," she laughed. "That's Suzy's honour, let her show it off."

"Gee, you're right! How are we going to manage as a couple since I nearly botched *that*?"

"I'll leave that for you two to figure out, but if you or Suzy ever need anything, I'll come to the rescue if needs be, like you would for me," she smiled, giving him a hug and feeling better that his heart was not so tangled with her as much. Charlie would never forget how he felt about her, Katherine knew he would still care deeply for her, but the love that belonged rightfully to a fiancé had been transferred to Suzy, and she was happy for them.

Watching Charlie leave, she returned to Gerry's room and sat by his bedside, taking his hand as she always did. Tonight it was just her and Gerry, despite the long nights, she looked forward to when it was her turn to keep the midnight oil burning, when she could just be with him all alone.

"Gerry, have I got news for you. If you were ever jealous about Charlie and his friendship with me, you don't have to worry any more, he's about to propose to Suzy. He told me so just now, isn't it wonderful? I hope they'll be happy, it's a blessed thing to love and feel loved in return."

Sadly, she watched the bedclothes rise and fall gently with each slow, regulated breath, his eyes closed, wondering if she would ever see them open and sparkle at her, shine with merriment, or glance at her with that tender look they only shared with each other. Looking at the bedside table, she noticed the red rose and sunflower bouquet she had brought him was wilting.

"I'm sorry dear, I thought it would last longer, it's the heat in this place, they keep it like an oven and won't let in any fresh air. I promise, I'll get you a fresh one tomorrow." He had always brought her the bouquets, it was her turn now. No matter how many floral arrangements arrived at the hospital, nothing could ever hold a candle to their special blooms.

"What shall we do first tonight, Gerry dearest? Literature, or good old Blue Eyes? I think we'll have some of Jack London first. You'd like that, wouldn't you?"

Before she fell asleep on the nights she was at home, she always played the tape he gave her in Paris, it was the only way she could hear his voice now. She then realized she did not want Gerry left without the beautiful things in life he enjoyed. The last few nights on her watch, she brought in a small CD player with several of Sinatra's re-releases featuring all their special songs and one of his favourite books, quietly reading it aloud to him, then turning to the music when her eyes become too tired to continue, and back to the book again before falling asleep in the chair beside him.

After she had read a chapter from the *Call of the Wild*, a nurse came in and sadly shook her head.

"You know dear, he can't hear anything, don't tire yourself out."

"I'm not tired Deborah, not very, and he can hear me, I know it," she said simply, unshakable in her conviction that her Gerry still retained one last subconscious thread connecting him to the outside world, and she was determined to keep tugging at it gently until he woke up. The nurse sadly shook her head again and left.

Katherine read a few more sentences, then sighed and put the book back down, turning on the music low but leaving it audible.

> *"Let someone start believing in you, let him hold out his hand,*
> *Let him touch you and watch what happens ..."*

"Oh Gerry, look how you have touched me, I never knew what real love was like until I met you," she said, stroking his hand.

She would never leave him, love was not only a blissful emotion, it was something worth fighting for, and love certainly brings its own battles. Although they were not married, the fact they were engaged was awe-inspiring, a promise that they *would* marry each other, an unspoken understanding they would accept vows that would bind them, and that acceptance in itself was a deep bond. Was there really a difference from the few months she would proclaim those vows formally in public and now when they were betrothed? Even Peter told her once she and Gerry were affianced they could never become engaged with anyone else unless they mutually broke the agreement. She had already promised her heart, everything to Gerry simply by their engagement, and he to her, for better or worse, she knew she would never desert him. Socrates declared he could never abandon the mission given to him from heaven to try the Athenians in their knowledge of truth, only a coward would desert the orders of his commander, and if she was destined to love and honour Gerry all the days of their lives, if her love was being put the test, she would not forsake him in his hour of need. But like all wars, battles, and protracted sieges, this pensive watching was difficult, seeing him in this helpless state, reliant on everyone for his basic life-sustaining requirements, she felt just as helpless at times, but love was strength, and she did tell him once they had plenty of love to see them through the rest of their lives.

"Oh Gerry, I miss you, I miss your flashing brown eyes, I miss talking with you, your funny sayings, the surprises you pull, I miss our coffee, croissants, hot fudge cake," she said, the tears trickling. "I'm trying to be brave, but I miss you so much, and you're right here!" She took his hand and kissed it gently over and over before holding his palm against her cheek wet with tears. "Gerry, please come back to me," she whispered. "Don't worry, I'll wait, but please, do come back to me … ," she repeated while the music continued to play softly in the background.

> *"…Let someone give his heart, someone who cares like me,*
> *Let someone give his heart who cares like me …"*

ଔ✿ଓ